JAMES A. MICHENER

JAMES·A
MICHENER

JAMES·A MICHENER

THE SOURCE
·
THE BRIDGES AT TOKO-RI
·
CARAVANS
·
SAYONARA

Secker & Warburg/Octopus

The Source first published in Great Britain in 1965
The Bridges at Toko-Ri first published in Great Britain in 1953
Caravans first published in Great Britain in 1964
Sayonara first published in Great Britain in 1954

This edition first published in 1976 by
Secker & Warburg Limited
14 Carlisle Street, Soho Square, London W1
in association with
Octopus Books Limited
59 Grosvenor Street, London W1

ISBN 0 905712 13 7

Printed in Great Britain by
Jarrold & Sons Ltd., Norwich.

·CONTENTS·

·THE SOURCE·

JAMES·A·MICHENER

ACKNOWLEDGMENTS

The translations of Psalm 6 on page 225 and of Proverbs 31 on pages 341–342 are from Samuel Sandmel, *The Hebrew Scriptures, An Introduction to Their Literature and Religious Ideas* (New York, Alfred A. Knopf, 1963). Psalm 33 on page 224 was specially translated by Dr Sandmel. The Psalms of Ascent on page 236 were translated for this book by scholars in Israel.

Other Biblical quotations are from the King James Version, except the words of St Paul, which are taken from II Timothy 4:7–8 in the Revised Standard Version, and those passages from Deuteronomy specifically noted on page 136, which are from *The Torah, the Five Books of Moses. A new translation of The Holy Scriptures according to the Masoretic Text* (Philadelphia, The Jewish Publication Society of America, 1962).

The response which appears on page 667 has been adapted with permission from Rabbi Ephraim Oshry, *Responsa from the Depths* (Brooklyn, 1959).

Archaeological drawings used throughout the book are the work of Ruth Ovadia, research scholar in the Department of Archaeology, Hebrew University, Jerusalem. Four of these drawings were adapted from illustrations in *The Guide to Israel*, by Zev Vilnay (Jerusalem, 1963).

Certain Jewish documents are cited from C. K. Barrett, *The New Testament Background: Selected Documents* (New York, Harper and Brothers, 1961).

Direct quotations from the sayings of Rabbi Akiba have been adapted either from the tractate Pirke Abot of the Mishna or from the excellent life by Louis Finkelstein, *Akiba, Saint, Scholar and Martyr* (reprinted by arrangement with World Publishing Co., New York—A Meridian Book).

Quotations from and references to the Pirke Abot tractate of the Mishna are taken principally from Judah Goldin, *The Living Talmud* (New York, The New American Library, 1957).

Quotations from and references to the Babylonian Talmud are taken principally from Leo Auerbach, *The Babylonian Talmud* (New York, Philosophical Library, 1944).

Quotations from and references to the Jerusalem Talmud are taken principally from Dagobert Runes, *The Talmud of Jerusalem* (New York, Philosophical Library, 1956).

Quotations from Maimonides have been for the most part adapted from Leon Roth, *The Guide for the Perplexed: Moses Maimonides* (London, Hutchinson's University Library, 1947).

For the list which opens the second section of Level III, I am indebted to Professor Cecil Roth of Jerusalem, who drew my attention to the fact that a list like this originally appeared in a little-known work, *Wolf's Jews in the Canary Islands.* Roth's version of this list appears in his *History of the Marranos*, by Cecil Roth (reprinted by arrangement with World Publishing Co., New York—A Meridian Book).

Details of Judenstrasse life appearing in the third part of Level III are verified principally by Marvin Lowenthal, *The Jews of Germany* (New York, Longmans, Green, 1936). By permission of David McKay Co., Inc.

Maps and drawings by Jean-Paul Tremblay.

This is a novel. Its characters and scenes are imaginary except as noted. The hero, Rabbi Akiba, was a real man who died as described in 137 C.E. All quotations ascribed to him can be verified. King David and Abishag, Herod the Great and his family, General Petronius, Emperor Vespasian, General Josephus and Dr Maimonides were also real persons and quotations ascribed to the last are also verifiable.

Akko, Zefat and Tiberias are existing places in the Galilee and descriptions of these towns are accurate, but Makor, its site, its history and its excavation are wholly imaginary.

The Tell

The tell of Makor at site 17072584 in western Galilee as seen by archaeologists on Sunday morning, May 3, 1964, while standing in the olive grove to the south. From the visual appearance of the tell nothing could be deduced as to its genesis, construction or history, except that the uniformly smooth surface of the slope would suggest that at some time around the year 1700 B.C.E. it could have been paved with heavy stone blocks by Hyksos invaders moving against Egypt from the north; and the slight rise toward the eastern side of the tell might indicate that there had once been a building of some size standing at that point.

On Tuesday the freighter steamed through the Straits of Gibraltar and for five days plowed eastward through the Mediterranean, past islands and peninsulas rich in history, so that on Saturday night the steward advised Dr Cullinane, 'If you wish an early sight of the Holy Land you must be up at dawn.' The steward was Italian and was reluctant to use the name Israel. For him, good Catholic that he was, it would always be the Holy Land.

Some time before dawn Cullinane heard a rapping on his door and went on deck while the stars were still bright, but as the moon fell away toward areas he had left, the sun began to rise over the land he was seeking, and the crown of stars that hung over Israel glimmered fitfully and faded. The shoreline became visible, mauve hills in the gray dawn, and he saw three things he knew: to the left the white Muslim mosque of Akko, in the center the golden dome of the Bahai temple, and to the right, high on a hill, the brown battlements of the Catholic Carmelites.

'Just like the Jews,' he said. 'Denied religious liberty by all, they extend it to everyone.' He thought that might be a good motto for the new state, but as the freighter approached land he added, 'I'd feel more like a traveler to Israel if they'd let me see one good synagogue.' But the Jewish religion was an internal thing, a system for organizing life rather than building edifices, and no Jewish religious structures were visible.

Even at the dockside his introduction to the Jewish state was postponed, for the first man who recognized him was a genial, good-looking Arab in his late thirties, dressed nattily in western clothes, who called from the shore in English, 'Welcome! Welcome! Everything's ready.' Two generations of British and American archaeologists had been greeted with this heartening call, either by the present Jemail Tabari or by his famous uncle, Mahmoud, who had worked on most of the historic digs in the area. Dr Cullinane, from the Biblical Museum in Chicago, was reassured.

For many years he had dreamed of excavating one of the silent mounds in the Holy Land, perhaps even to uncover additional clues to the history of man and his gods as they interacted in this ancient land; and as he waited for the freighter to tie up he looked across the bay to Akko, that jewel of a seaport, where so much of the history he was about to probe had started. Phoenicians, Greeks, Romans, Arabs, and finally Richard the Lion Heart and his Crusaders had all come to that harbor in glorious panoply, and to follow in their footsteps was for an archaeologist like Cullinane a privilege. 'I hope I do a good job,' he whispered.

As soon as he cleared the papers for the ponderous amount of equipment stored in the freighter – the books, the chemicals, the photographic equipment, the little Diesel locomotive, the thousand things a layman would not think of – he ran down the gangplank and embraced Tabari, and the Arab

reported, 'Things couldn't be going better. Dr Bar-El will be here shortly. The
other Americans are already dug in, and the photographer is flying down from
London this afternoon.'

'Weather been good?' Cullinane asked. He was a lean, tall man just entering
his forties, an Irish Catholic educated at Harvard and Grenoble, with
excavation experience in Arizona, Egypt and the area south of Jerusalem.
Under normal circumstances it would have been unlikely for a Catholic to head
such a dig, for the earlier field directors of the Biblical Museum had usually
been Protestant clergymen, but the bulk of the money for this particular dig
had come from a Chicago Jew who had said, 'Isn't it about time we had a
professional doing the work?' and Cullinane had been agreed upon, particularly
since he spoke Hebrew, a little Arabic and French. He was the crop-headed
type of new scholar, solidly trained and not given to nonsense. On his departure
from Chicago, loaded with gear, he had been asked by a newspaperman if he
expected to dig up any records which would prove that the Bible was true.
Cullinane replied, 'No, we're not out to help God steady the ark.' The
impudent reply had been widely quoted, but when the businessman who had
put up the quarter of a million dollars for the dig saw the wisecrack he felt
reassured that his money was in sober hands.

'Weather's flawless,' the Arab replied, speaking with the fluent ease of a man
whose father had been Sir Tewfik Tabari, O.B.E., K.B.E., one of the Arab
leaders whom the British had trusted. Sir Tewfik had sent his son to Oxford,
hoping that he would want to follow him in the civil service, but the boy had
from the first been enchanted by his Uncle Mahmoud's work in digging up
history, and his professors at Oxford had turned him into a first-rate scientific
archaeologist. In the winter of 1948, when the Jews threatened to capture
Palestine from the Arabs, young Jemail, then twenty-two, had debated a long
time as to what he should do. He ended by making a typical Tabari choice: he
stayed in Akko and fought the Jews vigorously. Then, when his haphazard
army was crushed, he announced that he would not seek asylum in Egypt or
Syria. He would stay in Israel, where he had always lived, and would work with
the Jews to rebuild the war-torn land. As a result of this bold decision he found
himself popular and almost the only trained Arab available for the many
archaeological excavations that were proliferating throughout the country. His
presence at any site meant that the highest scientific standards would be
enforced and that good spirits would be preserved among the workmen, who
said of him, 'Jemail once dug twenty feet straight down using only a camel's-
hair brush.'

As the two friends talked a jeep squealed its brakes outside the customs area,
and the driver, a petite young woman in her mid-thirties, jumped out and ran
past the protesting guard to give Cullinane a leaping kiss. 'Shalom, John! It's so
wonderful to have you back.' She was Dr Vered Bar-El, Israel's top expert in
dating pottery sherds, and without her assistance Dr Cullinane's dig could not
succeed; for she had the unusual capacity to memorize the scores of scientific
reports issued during the twentieth century, so that whenever someone like
Cullinane or Tabari handed her a fragment of pottery, a sherd left by some
household accident that had occurred seven thousand years ago, she could
usually look at the piece, then summon from her extraordinary memory pieces
of similar construction found in Egypt or Jericho or Beit Mirsim.
Archaeologists of five countries called her 'our walking calendar,' and the
commendable thing about her work was that when she did not know she said so.

She was a small woman, beautiful, bright-eyed, a pleasure to have at any dig. She was also one of the first major experts who had been trained wholly in Israel: when the state came into being in 1948 she was but seventeen, and had later attended Hebrew University in Jerusalem.

'Leave the gear where it is,' she said with a musical Hebrew accent. 'I've brought along two of the crew, and they'll stand guard till it's unloaded. Right now let's head for the dig. I'm hungry to get started.' She led Cullinane to the jeep and with deft turns of the wheel soon had him on the ancient road that led from Akko to Zefat, and beyond that to Damascus, the capital of Syria.

As they entered this classic road—for some five thousand years a major east-west artery through which had flowed the contributions of Asia on their way to Venice and Genoa—Cullinane took pains to orient himself. 'Could you stop the jeep for a moment?' he asked Mrs Bar-El. 'I'm sorry, but if I get mixed up at the start I never get straightened out later.' He got out of the jeep, studied his field map, turned firmly towards the direction from which they had come, and said, 'Straight ahead to the west is Akko and the Mediterranean. To my right, the Crusader castle of Starkenberg. To my left, Jerusalem. Behind me, to the east, the Sea of Galilee. And if you continue in the direction the car's headed you reach Zefat and, far beyond it, Damascus. Right?'

'Roger over,' Tabari said, but he thought it strange that in the Holy Land a man should orient himself by facing away from Jerusalem.

For some miles the riders discussed the coming dig and the allocations of work that had been agreed upon. 'The photographer coming down from London is excellent,' Cullinane assured his colleagues. 'Chap who did such good work at Jericho. And our architect is top-notch. University of Pennsylvania. I haven't seen any drawings done by the girl you've chosen for draftsman. Is she capable?'

'She was good enough for Yigael Yadin at Hazor,' Dr Bar-El explained.

'Oh, that the girl? How'd you get her?'

'We're training some great artists in this country,' the little pottery expert said, and Cullinane thought: I must remember to titillate their national pride. I must. Aloud he said, 'If we've got the girl who did the art work for Hazor, we're lucky.'

'We are lucky,' Dr Bar-El said, almost defensively.

Now all grew quiet as they neared the point from which the mound to be excavated would first be seen. Cullinane leaned forward, tense with excitement. To the north substantial hills appeared, and from time unremembered they had protected this road from the marauders of Lebanon. To the south matching hills were beginning to rise, offering security in that direction. A small valley was thus being formed, and along its northern edge short, sharp fingers of rock jutted out like opened hands, warding off anyone who might want to attack the ancient lifeline along which so much wealth had traveled. Dr Bar-El turned a corner, straightened out the jeep, and drove for a few minutes. Then it loomed ahead—the mysterious target.

It was Makor, a barren elliptical mound standing at the foot of one of the projecting spurs and rising high in the air. It was difficult to believe that it was real, for it had two strange characteristics: its top plateau was quite flat, as if some giant hand had smoothed it down; and the visible flanks of the mound were perfect earthen slopes, each a glacis forty-five degrees in angle, as if the same monstrous hand had stuck out a finger to round off the edges. It looked unnatural, like a fortress without walls, and this impression was augmented by the harsh rocky spur that rose to the rear, by the hills that rose behind that, and by the rugged mountains which backed up everything. The mound was thus the terminal point of a chain of fortifications, the lowest of four descending steps, and it was perfectly placed both for its own protection and for guarding the important road that passed its feet.

Its full name was Tell Makor, which signified that the local citizens knew it was not a natural mound, laid down by tectonic forces, but the patiently accumulated residue of one abandoned settlement after another, each resting upon the ruins of its predecessor, reaching endlessly back into history. From the bare rock on which the first community of Makor had been built, to the grassy top, was seventy-one feet, made up of fallen bricks, ruptured stone walls, broken turrets, bits of prehistoric flint, and, most valuable of all, the fragments of pottery that would, when washed and inspected by Dr Bar-El, tell the story of this solemn, yet exciting spot.

'We've picked the best tell in the country,' Dr Cullinane assured his team, and he took from his briefcase the preliminary maps made from aerial photographs in which a grid of rectangular squares, ten meters to the side, had been superimposed upon the tell; and at that moment the three archaeologists in the jeep could feel that their will was being imposed upon the mound and would finally squeeze from its secret inner places the remnants of the once vital existence. Yesterday Tell Makor had been a beautiful elliptical mound sleeping on the road from Akko to Damascus; today it was a carefully plotted target where not one pick-axe would be applied aimlessly.

'Let's check with the 1/100,000 Palestine map,' Cullinane suggested, and Tabari unfolded a section of that beautiful map, drafted years ago by British engineers. On it the two men made calculations which zeroed in the location of Tell Makor so that other archaeologists around the world could accurately identify it: henceforth the site of their labors would be 17072584, in which the first four numbers indicated the east-west orientation and the last four the north-south. In Israel, in Asia, in the world, there could be no other spot like this, and when the super-imposed layers of earth had been penetrated, one by one, the world would be able to say with some exactitude what had happened at 17072584. It was the meticulous re-creation of that history which would occupy John Cullinane and his skilled crew for the ensuing years.

He put aside the maps and jumped from the jeep. With long strides he climbed the steep glacis and finally swung onto the plateau, some two hundred yards long by one hundred and thirty wide. Somewhere in this mound he would start his men digging, and to a disagreeable extent the success or failure of the first years would depend upon how cannily he had chosen; for archaeologists had been known to select their spots without luck and to dig through fruitless levels, while others coming later to the same tell, but with superior insight, had quickly found rewarding layers, one after another. He hoped that he would be one of the lucky ones.

'Deciding where to start?' Tabari asked as he reached the plateau.

The Irishman waited for Dr Bar-El, then said, 'I'm like Sir Flinders Petrie. He organized his digs on the principle that if you command one hundred different communities to build towns on one hundred different mounds, more than ninety will place their major buildings in the northwest area. Why, nobody knows. Possibly because of the sunsets. So naturally I'm inclined toward the northwest, and we can dump our rubble over here.' He pointed to the northern edge of the plateau from which the archaeologists could look down into something not visible from the road: a precipitous gully, called throughout the east a *wadi*, whose cliff-like sides had always protected Makor from armies seeking to establish a siege from the north. The wadi was deep enough to absorb rubble from the entire tell, should any millionaire have enough money to pay for such a total excavation.

The dig at Makor, as planned by Cullinane, would require ten years at a cost of $50,000 a year, and since he had in hand funds only for the first five years, it was essential that he quickly uncover areas of interest; for he had found that people who finance archaeological digs can be depended upon for additional funds if their interest is sustained through the first year, whereas they quickly close their checkbooks if no finds are forthcoming. It was therefore crucial that he locate his trial trenches in the right spots, for even after he had spent ten years uncovering selected levels his team would still have excavated less than fifteen per cent of the site. As he had explained to his board in Chicago, 'Our educated guess is that in this tell we may have the remains of about twenty different layers of civilizations. You must understand that for me to peel these off, one by one in proper scientific style until nothing is left but the original perimeter, would require about fifty years. What we'll do is sink two short exploratory trenches down through all the layers. That'll take a year, but when we're through we'll know in general what's at hand. Then, in subsequent years, if we get the funds, we'll go back and dig more deeply in selected areas that promise returns. But bear with me if I repeat that we cannot possibly uncover the entire tell. What we can uncover is a picture of what happened there, and it's that we're after.'

'Isn't it pretty important where you locate those first trenches?' a member had asked.

'That's what I'll sweat about for the next six months,' he had replied, and now the moment was at hand when he must make the critical decision.

As he stood that morning on top of the tell whose secrets he must probe, he was no ordinary man, come to the Holy Land with enthusiasm and a shovel; he had won the title archaeologist only at the end of a long period of subtle training. At Harvard he had learned to read Aramaic, Arabic and ancient Hebrew scripts. During graduate work with Professor Albright at Johns Hopkins he had mastered Mesopotamian cuneiform and Egyptian hieroglyphs until he could read them as an average man reads a newspaper. He had taken off a year to attend Carnegie Tech for advanced work in metallurgy, so that he would be able to identify with some certainty the provenience and smelting processes of local metals and their alloys. Later he had spent three winter terms at Ohio State University, taking advanced ceramics, precisely as if he intended making cups and saucers for the rest of his life, and from this experience had trained himself to guess within a hundred degrees centigrade the furnace heat at which any given piece of ancient pottery had been fired; he knew less of the historical relationships of ceramics than a real specialist like Dr Bar-El, but in technical analysis he excelled her. Following these scientific courses he had lived for a year in New York, studying costume and armor at the Metropolitan Museum, and for another year–one of the best of his life–in the little French university town of Grenoble, specializing in prehistory and the cave art of France. Coincident with his work among the Indians of Arizona he had attended summer sessions at the state university, working on problems of dendrochronology, whereby time sequences in desert areas could be established by comparing the wide rings left in wood by growing seasons which had enjoyed heavy rainfall and the narrow ones left by years of drought. This was followed by a full year at Princeton, enrolled in the Presbyterian Seminary, where he worked with experts on problems of Bible research; but as often happens, one of his most valuable skills he had picked up by himself. As a boy he had found pleasure in collecting stamps; perhaps he was now an archaeologist because of this accident of his childhood, but his Irish father used to growl, 'What are you doin' with them stamps?' He did not know, but when he became a man he vaguely sensed that he ought not to be fooling around with bits of paper and in some fortunate way he shifted to coins, which seemed more respectable, and this field of specialization was to prove of great value in Biblical research. He had written one of the papers which had helped prove that there had been two issues of Jewish shekels: one used in the initial Jewish revolt led by Judah the Maccabee, 166 years before Christ; and a second minted during the final revolt of Bar Kochba, 135 years after Christ. As a result of this paper he was known as a numismatic expert. All these skills, plus others like ancient architecture and the conduct of war in Biblical times, which he had acquired pragmatically during his various digs, he was now ready to apply to Tell Makor, but the location of his two trenches was so important that he intuitively postponed the decision. When the others left the tell, he remained alone, walking aimlessly across the mound, kicking idly at the topsoil to determine its construction.

A plateau only two hundred yards by a hundred and thirty wide doesn't sound like much, he mused. Two ordinary football fields. But when you stand looking at it with a teaspoon in your hand and somebody says, 'Dig!' the damned thing looks immense. He prayed to himself: So much depends on this. God help me to pick the right spot; but his attention was diverted from this problem when he noticed protruding from the earth a small object which did not look like a pebble. Bending over to inspect it, he found a small piece of lead, slightly flattened on one side. It was a spent bullet and he started to throw it away, but reconsidered.

'*Voilà!* Our first find on Tell Makor,' he said to himself. Spitting on his fingers, he cleaned the bullet until it lay dully, heavy in his hand. Holding it between thumb and forefinger, he asked himself, 'Level? Age? Provenience?' thus using the bullet as an excuse for postponing his decision on the trenches. Taking from his briefcase an excavation card, he sat on the edge of the mound and filled it in with that exquisite, almost feminine, care he had always used in such work. The bullet had probably been fired from a British rifle, since they were the most common in these parts. Any recent date would be acceptable, but around 1950 A.D. was logical, since the bullet showed signs of aging, and he wrote that down; but he had no sooner done so than he erased the A.D. in some embarrassment and substituted C.E. He was working in a Jewish country which had formerly been a Muslim country, and here the use of Anno Domini was frowned upon; yet the world-wide system of dating had to be respected, and that required a Before Christ and an After Christ whether Muslims and Jews liked it or not, just as all longitude was measured from an English observatory near London, whether Anglophobes liked that or not. So Cullinane wrote his date 1950 C.E., which had originally signified Christian Era but which was now universally read as Common Era. Dates before Jesus were written B.C.E., Before the Common Era, and this satisfied everyone.

With precise pen marks he sketched the bullet and indicated its scale, 2:1, which meant that the drawing was two times as large as the original. Had the reverse been true he would have labeled it 1:2. Reviewing his playful entry, his Item One of the excavation, he was pleased to find his pen still accurate and added a neat J.C.

LEVEL I
ABOUT 1950 C.E.

SCALE 2:1

BULLET FROM A BRITISH RIFLE

As Cullinane finished the final dot, he looked up to see that the most important member of his staff had arrived from Jerusalem and had climbed the tell to greet his colleagues. He was a tall, slender Jew, two years older than Cullinane, with deep-set eyes peering from beneath dark eyebrows. He had sunken cheeks but full lips that were eager to smile. His dark hair came well down onto his forehead and he moved with the grace of a man who had been both a soldier and a scholar. At present he worked in one of the government ministries in Jerusalem and was pleased with the invitation that would keep him at Makor from mid-May through mid-October, for he was a trained archaeologist whose political skills had been found so valuable to the government that he was rarely allowed out in the field. His position at Makor was ambiguous. Ostensibly he was to serve as chief administrator of the project, determining salaries, working hours and living arrangements. If he were not efficient, the complex personalities involved in the dig could waste their time in petty squabbles, if not outright feuds. He was hired to be the dictator, but no one at Makor would recognize this fact, for Ilan Eliav was a master administrator, a man who rarely lost his temper. He was probably the best-educated scholar in the expedition, speaking numerous languages, but his greatest asset was that he smoked a pipe, which he had a habit of rubbing in the palms of his hands until the complainant before him reached some kind of sensible decision without depending upon the intervention of Eliav. Workmen at previous digs had said, 'I'm going in to see if the pipe will approve a raise.' And the kindly Jew with the deep-set eyes would listen as if his heart were breaking, and the bowl of his pipe would revolve slowly in his palms until the workman realized for himself how preposterous a raise would be at that time.

Actually Dr Eliav was the official watchdog of the dig; the tells of Israel were far too valuable to allow just anyone to come in with a team of amateurs to butcher them. The nation contained more than a hundred unexcavated sites like Makor, and during the next two or three centuries teams from universities in Peking and Tokyo, or from learned societies in Calcutta or Cairo, would accumulate the necessary funds to dig out these long-forgotten cities, and it would be a disservice to humanity present and future if the sites were now abused. The problem was especially acute when archaeologists like Dr Cullinane proposed to excavate by the trench method, for many crimes against history had been perpetrated in Israel by enthusiastic men with shovels who dug hasty trenches through improperly recorded levels. Normally the Israeli government would have rejected a trench proposal like Cullinane's, but the Irish scholar had established such a good reputation, and he was known to be so well trained in archaeological matters, that in his case permission was granted; nevertheless, Dr Eliav had been detached from his important desk job to be sure that the valuable tell was not mutilated.

He now strode across the top of the mound, extended a long arm to a man he instinctively liked, and offered an apology: 'I am most sorry not to have been here when you arrived.'

'We're fortunate to have you on any terms,' Cullinane said, for he knew why a scholar as important as Eliav had been released to work with him. If he had to accept a watchdog, he was pleased that it was to be Eliav; it was much easier to explain problems to a man who knew more than you did.

'I tried to break away last week,' Eliav explained. 'I had three good days up here getting things organized, but they called me back. I want you to see the camp.' He led Cullinane to the western end of the plateau, where an ancient footpath led zigzag down the glacis toward an old rectangular stone building whose southern face was composed of three graceful Arab arches forming an arcade which led to four cool white rooms. The largest would be Cullinane's office and the library; the others would house photography, ceramics and drafting.

'This looks better than I expected,' Cullinane said. 'What was the building originally?'

Eliav pointed with his pipe stem to Tabari, who volunteered, 'Probably the home of some Arab olive grower. Two or three hundred years ago.' Cullinane was impressed with the easy manner in which Tabari and Eliav worked together, showing none of the area's traditional antagonism between Arab and Jew. They had co-operated on several previous digs and each respected the competence of the other.

'Out here are the sleeping tents, four of them,' Eliav continued, 'and along this path lies Kibbutz Makor, where we'll take our meals.' As he led the way to the communal agricultural settlement, Cullinane noticed the bronzed young men and women engaged in the work of the kibbutz. They were unusually attractive, and Cullinane thought: It took only a few years to change the hunched-up Jew of the ghetto into a lively farmer. Looking at the muscular young people, especially the free-moving women, he could not detect that they were Jews. There were blonds with blue eyes, and these looked like Swedes; there were blonds with square heads shorn flat, and these looked like Germans; there were redheads who looked like Americans; studious types who looked like Englishmen: and others who were sunburned to a near-black and who looked like Arabs. An average man, put amongst the lithe young people of Kibbutz Makor, would have been able to isolate only about ten per cent who looked like his preconception of a Jew, and one of them would have been Jemail Tabari, the Arab.

'We've reached three major decisions about the kibbutz,' Eliav explained as the group approached a large dining hall. 'We won't sleep here. We will eat here. And up till harvesting begins we'll be allowed to employ the kibbutzniks on the dig.'

'Is that good or bad?' Cullinane asked.

'Rest easy,' Eliav said. 'We brought this tell to your attention only because the kibbutzniks kept pestering us with samples. 'See what we dug out of our tell!' These kids love archaeology the way American kids love baseball.'

The archaeologists were seating themselves in the large mess hall when a lean crew-cut young man of thirty-five, wearing sandals, shorts and T-shirt, approached to introduce himself as 'Schwartz ... secretary of this kibbutz. Glad to have you eat with us.'

Cullinane launched a formal and somewhat academic reply, beginning, 'We want you to know how much we appreciate . . .' but Schwartz cut him off.

'We appreciate your dollars,' he said, leaving abruptly to signal a girl who was serving coffee.

'Genial fellow,' Cullinane mumbled as Schwartz deserted him.

'In him you see the new Jew,' Eliav half-apologized. 'He's what makes Israel strong.'

'Where's he from? He spoke like an American.'

'No one knows, really. He's probably called Schwartz because he's dark. He survived, God knows how, both Dachau and Auschwitz. He has no family, no history, only raw drive. Look at his arm when he comes back.'

A good-looking, husky girl in tight shorts strode to the table, dealt out some cups and saucers and began pouring coffee as if she were a laborer pouring cement. Slamming the pot down, in case anyone wanted seconds, she went off to fetch some sugar, but Schwartz had anticipated her and slapped down a sugar bowl before Cullinane.

'Americans want everything sweet,' he said, but Cullinane ignored the remark, for he was staring at Schwartz's left arm where in blue indelible ink was tattooed a concentration-camp number: S-13741.

'Birthmark,' Schwartz said.

'You speak like an American.'

'After the war I tried living in Boston. But I came here to join the fighting.'

'Did you get your name in Boston?' Cullinane asked.

Schwartz stopped. 'How'd you guess that? They were the family I lived with. Nice people but they didn't know from nothin'. I wanted to be where the war was.'

The husky girl now returned with a second bowl of sugar, started to slam it onto the table, saw that Schwartz had got there first, and retreated with the bowl to another table. As she left, Cullinane said, 'It's refreshing to see a girl who doesn't wear lipstick.'

'She does it for the defense of Israel,' Schwartz said belligerently.

'How's that?'

'No lipstick. No salon dancing.'

'For the defense of Israel,' Cullinane repeated.

'Yes!' Schwartz half-snarled. 'Ask her yourself. Come here, Aviva.'

The stocky girl sauntered back and said contemptuously, 'I'm not one of those salonim.'

'Salonim,' Schwartz interpreted. 'Those of the salon.'

'I pledged with all my friends. Never dance salon style.' She looked insolently at Cullinane and left with the awkward rhythm of a girl who excels in folk dancing, and Schwartz followed her.

'I hope Aviva's not on the pottery crew,' Cullinane said quietly.

'Wait a minute!' Dr Bar-El flashed. 'When I was seventeen I took that same pledge. We felt then as Aviva feels now. Israel needed women who were ready to bear arms . . . to die at the battlefront if necessary. Lipstick and salon dancing were for the effete women of France and America.' Primly, she put down her coffee cup and said, 'I'm glad the spirit still exists.'

'But you wear lipstick now,' Cullinane pointed out.

It was an odd statement, which Cullinane preferred not to explore at the moment. 'I think we should get back for the meeting,' he suggested, and the four scholars wound their way along the pleasant path toward the arched stone house serving as their headquarters, but as Cullinane reached the building he happened to look south across the road and noticed for the first time the olive trees of Makor: they were incredibly old. Their existence was not measured in years or decades but in centuries and millennia. Their trunks were gnarled, their branches broken. Many retained no center wood at all, for the years had rotted away their cores, leaving only fragments standing, but these were sufficient to provide the twisted arms of the tree with life, and in the late spring the olives were covered with those gray-green leaves that made the trees so attractive. Each wind that came down the ancient road rustled these leaves, turning the aspect of the grove from green to gray to some intermediate, shimmering color. Cullinane had seen olives before, but never a grove like this, and as he was about to enter the building from which the dig would be directed, he felt himself pulled across the road to inspect one notable tree–a veritable patriarch whose gnarled trunk was merely a shell through which one could see in many directions. The tree bore only a few branches, but these were thick with maturing olives, and as the archaeologist stood inquiringly beside this stubborn relic he was as close to the mystery of Makor as he would ever be, and in the presence of this august tree John Cullinane felt humbled. It was a proper preparation for a dig and he walked in silence to the room where his paid staff and their nineteen helpers had assembled from various parts of the world in response to an advertisement he had run in various British and Continental newspapers: 'An archaeological dig is proposed in western Galilee for the summer campaign of 1964 and succeeding years. Qualified experts are welcomed if they can pay their own transportation to Israel. Food, lodging, medical care provided, but no salaries.' More than a hundred and thirty experienced men and women had applied and from the list he had selected the team who now sat before him. They were dedicated scholars, eager to work at their own expense if only they could help probe the secrets that lay buried in the tell, and each was prepared to use his mind and imagination as skillfully as he used his pick and hoe.

On the blackboard Dr Eliav had printed the exacting schedule that would govern work for the next five months:

5:00 A.M.	Reveille
5:30 A.M.	Breakfast
6:00 A.M. to 2:00 P.M.	Work at dig
2:00 P.M.	Lunch
3:00 P.M. to 4:00 P.M.	Siesta
4:00 P.M. to 7:00 P.M.	Work in offices
7:30 P.M.	Dinner
8:30 P.M. to 10:00 P.M.	Consultations

'Any questions?' Eliav asked.

In a high, petulant voice the English photographer whispered, 'I don't find any break for afternoon tea.' Those who knew how tough he could be laughed, and he was assured by Eliav that he, at least, would be provided for. 'I shall resume breathing,' the English scholar said.

Eliav then turned the board around to display five lines of data summarizing former digs to remind the archaeologists of the high standards facing them. The lines read:

CAMPAIGNS	ARCHAEOLOGIST	SITE	DIMENSIONS	AVAILABLE AREA
1902–08	Macalister	Gezer	800 x 175	140,000
1926–32	Albright	Beit Mirsim	300 x 140	40,000
1929–34	Garrod	Mount Carmel	Small Caves	1,800
1952–58	Kenyon	Jericho	400 x 200	70,000
1955–57	Yadin	Hazor	1,250 x 730	900,000
1965–74	Us	Makor	200 x 133	20,000

Now Cullinane took a pointer and said, 'Gentlemen, and you very able ladies, I've asked Dr Eliav to list these five earlier digs because we must remember them as we work. The dimensions are in yards and the last figure gives in square yards a rough estimate of the site actually available for digging. You'll notice that one of the greatest was very small in size, but the results Dorothy Garrod achieved in the Carmel caves were incomparable. She seemed to be digging through deposits of pure gold. I think we could also remember profitably what Kathleen Kenyon accomplished at Jericho, because she didn't get to that tell till it had been worked over by many predecessors. It took Miss Kenyon to dig down and find the answers. Two other digs are my favorites. Gezer was excavated by one man, Macalister, a church organist from Dublin, with the help of one man, Jemail Tabari's uncle. But the excavation and reporting done by these two men remain a masterpiece. We're ten times as many and we must accomplish ten times as much. But our ideal shall be Albright. We give his figures for the last campaign only. He found nothing spectacular at Beit Mirsim, but he taught archaeologists how to work scientifically. When we're done, I want it said, "They worked as honestly as Albright."'

He paused, then pointed to the last line. 'As you can see, we're a small tell, so we can afford to go slowly. We'll sketch each item exactly as we find it and photograph it from several angles. Our plateau contains only four acres, but remember that in the days of King David, Jerusalem wasn't much larger. In point of fact, this year we shall attack no more than two per cent of our total area.' He asked for maps of the tell to be distributed, and as the scholars studied the contour lines, Jemail Tabari started his briefing.

'All we know of Makor's history appears in six tantalizing passages. Ancient Hebrew sources mention it once. When the twelve tribes were receiving their apportionments. It's listed as a town of no significance on the border between the portion of Asher along the sea and of Naphtali inland. It was never a major city like Hazor nor a district capital like Megiddo. In the Amarna letters found in Egypt and dating back to about 1400 B.C.E. one reference: "Crawling on my belly, my head covered with ashes of shame, my eyes averted from your divine countenance, I humble myself seven times seven and report to the King of Heaven and the Nile. Makor was burned." A commentary on Flavius Josephus provides a cryptic passage: "Jewish tradition claims that Josephus escaped by night from Makor." In a famous commentary on the Talmud we find a series of delightful quotations from Rabbi Asher the Groats Maker describing day-to-day life in our countryside. In the next seven hundred years silence, except for one brief sentence in the report of an Arab trader out of Damascus: "And from the olives of Makor, much profit." The groves we see on the other side of the road could be several thousand years old. In the Crusader period, however, we come to substantial written records, and I hope all of you will read *Wenzel of Trier's Chronicle*. You'll find three photographic copies in the library, Briefly, Wenzel tells us that Makor was captured by the Crusaders in 1099 and for two hundred years was the seat of the various Counts Volkmar of Gretz. We're convinced that at this level we've got to find something of substance. After 1291, when Makor fell to the Mamelukes, the site vanishes from history. Not even traders mention it, and we must assume that human occupation ended there. But from the bedrock of the tell, insofar as we can identify it, to the top, is a distance of seventy-one feet, and we have a right to suppose that many good things lie buried in that vast accumulation. John will explain what we're going to do.'

'Before he does,' the English photographer interrupted, 'what's Makor mean?'

'Sorry,' Tabari said. 'Old Hebrew word. Makor. Source.'

'Any significance?' the Englishman asked.

'We've always supposed it referred to a water supply,' Tabari replied. 'But there's no record of where the water was. If any of you have bright ideas, we'd be pleased to hear them.'

'Isn't it hidden under the tell?' the photographer said.

'We've often wondered. Go ahead, John.'

Cullinane fastened a large-scale map of the tell to the blackboard and studied it. 'Where to begin?' he asked. 'We shall dig two trenches, but where to locate them?' He surveyed the map for several moments, then turned away to face his team. 'Each dig has its special problems, but we have one I've not encountered before. As you know, for some years I've been trying to gather the funds for this dig without luck, until one night at a dinner party I chanced to mention the fact that the tell I had in mind contained a Crusader's castle. This man to my right repeated, "A castle?" When I nodded, he said, "That would be a great thing to dig up, a castle!" I carefully explained that when I said castle I meant a ruined castle, but this captivated him even more. "Can you imagine," he asked his wife, "digging up a ruined castle?" Before the week ended he had put up the money. Three times I explained to him that although he was interested in the castle, I was concerned with what lay below. I'm sure he didn't hear. So at Makor . . .'

'We'd better find a castle,' Tabari suggested.

'And if we do, I'm sure we can jolly the gentleman along regarding the real work that you and I wish to accomplish. Now"—he returned to the map—'where do you find a castle?' He allowed the question to sink in, then said slowly. 'My whole intuition warns me to start at least one trench in the northwest quadrant, but I'm deterred by two factors. The tell has a slight rise from west to east, from which I conclude that the Crusader fortress must have defied tradition and stood in the northeastern quadrant. Second, we haven't determined where the main gate to the tell stood, and both Eliav and Tabari believe it to have been at the southwest. I've argued that it must be dead south in the middle of this wall. But now I'm willing to concede that the others are right. If they are, we'd have to dig in the southwest for the gate and in the northwest for the castle, and that's putting all our eggs in the western basket. So late this afternoon I made the final choices. Here in the southwest our major trench,' and he drew a bold straight line into the tell, 'and here in the northeast a trench into the castle,' and he marked a short north-south cut. The scientists relaxed. The decision had been made and it was obvious what Cullinane was doing: he would dig quickly for the Crusader castle in order to find something that would satisfy the man putting up the money; but he would dig quietly at the presumed gate area in hopes of finding those significant layers, those sherds of broken pottery, those stone fragments of wall and home, that would reveal the greater history of the tell.

When the meeting ended and the others had gone, Tabari lingered, looking dissatisfied, and Cullinane thought: Damn, he's one of those who listens, says nothing, then comes around to warn you that he can't approve your decision. But almost immediately Cullinane dismissed the thought as unworthy. Jemail Tabari was not like that. If he was perplexed it was for substantial reasons. 'What is it, Jemail?'

'You're right in every detail,' Tabari began.

'Except one?'

'Correct.' The Arab pointed to the big map. 'Trench A is where it should be. Trench B is bound to hit the castle. What I don't like, John, is your plan to dump the rubble in the wadi.' He pointed to the deep gully to the north of the tell and ran his long fingers lovingly back and forth across the area that Cullinane proposed to fill.

'Why not?' Cullinane asked. 'It's a natural spot for the rubble.'

'Correct,' Tabari agreed. He pronounced the word koe-rect, giving it a humorous twist. 'But for that very reason it's also a natural spot in which other things might have happened. Burials, dumps, caves. John, we're gambling on some very big ideas here. We're not just excavating a Crusader castle to gratify . . .'

'Correct!' Cullinane interrupted, using Tabari's word against him.

'In my research one thing perplexes me . . . always has. Mind if we go out to the tell?' He led Cullinane up the footpath until they reached the plateau, where to their surprise they saw the figure of Dr Eliav, kneeling on one knee at the eastern end, where Trench B was to run, and when he heard their approach he slipped quietly down the eastern slope and disappeared. 'Wasn't that Eliav?' Tabari asked.

'I doubt it,' Cullinane replied, but he knew it was.

Tabari led the way to the northern edge of the tell, from which they could look down the very steep flank and into the bottom of the wadi. It was an ugly, sharp fall, broken by one area halfway down where level land appeared for a hundred yards, before the sheer fall continued to the bottom of the gully. 'The missing factor in all I've read,' Tabari said, 'stems from the word Makor itself—source. That from which another thing springs. The life factor. Why did generation after generation of people settle here? It could only have been because there was water . . . and plenty of it. But we've no idea where it was located.'

'Where does the kibbutz get its water?'

'Modern artesian wells.'

This provided no clue, so Cullinane asked, 'You think the original well may have been outside the town walls? Like Megiddo?'

'I don't know what I think,' Tabari said cautiously. 'But I don't want you to fill up that wadi, because in a couple of years we may want to dig. Right down there.'

'Your Uncle Mahmoud is famous in the reports because he followed hunches. You want me to follow this one?'

'Koe-rect', Tabari replied, and the dump was relocated.

Next morning Tabari distributed the small picks and hoes used by modern archaeologists—no shovel would be permitted at a respectable dig—and proceedings got off to a favourable start, principally because he followed another hunch. At Trench B in the northeastern sector he happened to see one of the kibbutzniks inspect an object and start to call a supervisor. On second thought the young man hesitated, as if he were going to place a small object in his pocket, keeping it for later sale. 'Did you want me?' Tabari asked nonchalantly, walking up and holding out his hand.

'Yes,' the kibbutznik said. 'I think I've found something,' and he handed Tabari a coin, which later occasioned much debate at the mess.

LEVEL II
ABOUT 1875 C.E.

J.C.

SCALE 2:1

TURKISH GOLD COIN

It had obviously been issued by some Arabic-speaking nation, but what it was doing on Makor was not so easy to determine. Cullinane argued, 'It was found within a few inches of the top. It can't signify the presence of an Arab town nobody ever heard of. Yet it looks quite old. Can you decipher it, Jemail?'

Tabari had read some of the Arabic script and was trying to untangle the rest when the photographer appeared with two books from the library showing the coins of Palestine, and after much checking back and forth proved that the coin had been issued some time around the year 1000 C.E.

'That's hard to accept,' Cullinane protested. 'That's a hundred years before the Crusaders, and if what you say is right . . .' He hesitated, then used the classic complaint of the archaeologist: 'That coin has no right to be there!' Later he told Tabari, 'Everything would have been a lot simpler if you'd let that kibbutznik keep his damned coin and maybe sell it to some tourist in Akko. Warn your men not to dig up any facts that confuse the issue.'

But four days later the men at Trench B found something that was indeed bizarre, and when Cullinane finished his card he joked, 'Tabari, somebody's salting our dig.' This was a constant danger at an archaeological site:

enthusiastic workmen, seeking to gain bonuses and also to please the foreigners whom in general they liked, were accustomed to hide things in the soil and then to come upon them triumphantly with their hoes; but cursory inspection of the new find satisfied even Cullinane that no workman could have procured this particular item for salting: it was made of gold.

LEVEL III
ABOUT 1550 C.E.

GOLDEN MENORAH

SCALE 1 : 4

The menorah, because it was so exclusively Jewish, occasioned much excitement both at the dig and at the kibbutz, but it was impossible to date, for the seven-branched candelabrum had been used by Jews at least since the days of Exodus, when God handed down detailed instructions as to how they should be made: 'And six branches shall come out of the sides of it; three branches of the candlestick out of the one side, and three branches of the candlestick out of the other side.' The Lord had gone on and on, for apparently the menorah was an object of personal importance to Him.

'It's a work of art,' Cullinane admitted grudgingly, 'but of no archaeological value.' He pushed it away, unaware that it was to become the most notorious single object that would be found at the dig. 'Damn,' he growled. 'A bullet, a gold coin nearly a thousand years too old and a menorah. All in the wrong levels at the wrong times. What kind of dig is this?'

Three mornings later an event occurred which at the time he did not consider important: a journalist from Australia, a likable, breezy fellow, stopped by the dig and after asking many irrelevant questions happened to see the gold menorah. 'What's that?' he asked.

'It's called a menorah,' Cullinane explained somewhat impatiently.

'This mean you're going to find a lot of gold . . .'

'It's much too recent to be of any archaeological value.'

'I understand, but even so, could I have a photograph of it?'

'I think we'd better not.'

'By the way, what is it?'

'A seven-branched candlestick,' Cullinane explained, and some days later, when time came to review what had gone wrong, he was able to recall two things that had happened at this point. The Australian had carefully counted each of the arms—'five, six, seven'—while a look of almost boyish pleasure came into his frank and appealing face.

'Dr Cullinane, if I were careful to explain that this menorah, as you call it, had no historical significance, couldn't I please have just one photograph?' And against his reasoned judgment, Cullinane gave permission. Quickly the Australian whipped out a Japanese camera and called for one of the older kibbutzniks to pose holding the candelabrum. 'Look at it,' he ordered the man, and after a few whirlwind operations he thanked Cullinane and hurried back to the airport at Tel Aviv.

'I wish I had such energy,' Cullinane laughed, but he was diverted from further comment by Tabari, who came running from Trench B with a coin that had been dislodged from a crevice among some buried stones. It was so large that it must originally have been of considerable value, but when cleaned it turned out to be not a coin at all but a bronze seal.

LEVEL IV
ABOUT 1290 C.E.

SCALE 1:1

SEAL OF THE CRUSADER VOLKMAR VIII

It was a striking find, an authentic Crusader piece, and while it did not prove that Trench B was going to intercept the castle it did prove that at least one of the Volkmars had been on the tell. 'I think we're close to the castle,' Tabari said with quiet enthusiasm, and Cullinane sent Paul J. Zodman, his Chicago millionaire, a cable stating that positive identification of the ruins seemed near at hand.

Before Zodman could reply, a copy of a London paper reached Makor with news that shook the dig, and it was followed by papers from Rome, Paris and New York, repeating a lurid story about goings-on at the Makor dig. For the Australian had released with photographs an exciting yarn under the title, 'The Candlestick of Death,' relating how in Bible times an evil king had identified his seven principal enemies and of how he had lighted seven candles, instructing his general, 'By the time the seventh candle burns out, my seven enemies are to be dead.' The first candle guttered down and the first enemy was beheaded. The sixth flickered away and the sixth enemy was gone. 'But as the seventh candle trembled in the central cup, the general turned unexpectedly and lopped off the head of the king, for he was his own worst enemy. And then the general buried the hateful seven-branched candelabrum beneath the wall, where Dr John Cullinane has so brilliantly found it, for it was a thing accursed.'

The main photograph showed a distinguished-looking elderly scholar recoiling from the menorah in horror. The caption read: 'Dr Gheorghe Moscowitz, renowned archaeologist, says, "This evil piece may well doom all who possess it, for it bears the curse of death."'

Cullinane groaned and did something he rarely did. He swore. 'Who in hell is Dr Gheorghe Moscowitz?'

Tabari said, 'He's that nice old Rumanian who sweeps up.'

'Get him in here,' Cullinane snapped, but when the kibbutznik appeared, soft-spoken and apprehensive, Tabari took over.

'This you in the picture?'

'Dr Cullinane was standing there when the man took it.'

Cullinane studied the picture and said, 'I don't remember you looking that way.'

'Just before the man took the picture he made a face at me,' the Rumanian explained. 'I jumped back.'

'But surely you didn't say anything about a "curse of death"?'

'No. But as the man was going to his car he called me over and asked if I thought a candlestick could carry a curse, and to get rid of him I said, "Maybe."'

That afternoon the first excursionists stopped at the tell, asking to see the Candlestick of Death, and the next morning a tour bus arrived. Cullinane was distressed and sought out Eliav, to whom he said, 'I've worked hard to protect the good name of this dig. Six of the applicants who volunteered to help us were publicity hounds, and I kept them off. Like Stikkler of Geneva.'

'We saw your sensible interview when the Chicago reporter wanted you to say that you were expecting to dig up new revelations about the Bible.' Eliav lit his pipe.

'And yet we are digging among the foundations of three great religions. We've got to keep it clean.'

'Do you expect to find materials relating to Christianity?' Eliav asked.

'Materials? You mean manuscripts . . . proofs? No. But insights? Yes.' The two men fell silent, and after a while Cullinane asked, 'As a Jew, don't you hope to find something that will illuminate . . .'

'Why do you suppose I work on these digs?' Eliav asked. 'Each time I sink a pick into the earth, I hope, in a vague sort of way, to turn up something that will tell me more about Judaism.' He hesitated. 'No, that's wrong. Not tell me. Tell the world. Because the world needs to know.'

The responsibility of the task on which the two men were engaged caused them to look with disgust on the newspaper stories, for although neither expected to uncover specific new materials relating to Judaism or Christianity or Islam, each hoped that Makor might provide some serious information which would advance understanding of the societies in which these religions arose. 'From now on we keep newspapermen and tourists out of here,' Cullinane concluded, but even as he spoke, Tabari appeared with a cable from Chicago:

CULLINANE STOP REGARDLESS OF WHAT OTHER FINDS THE ISRAELI GOVERNMENT MAY DEMAND FOR ITSELF IT IS IMPERATIVE THAT YOU SECURE CANDLESTICK OF DEATH FOR CHICAGO PAUL J. ZODMAN

Cullinane shook his head and gave Tabari the job of reassuring Zodman that it would be arranged. Chicago would get the treasure.

On the next day such trivia were forgotten, for Eliav reported that workmen in Trench B had uncovered positive proof that they were digging in Crusader ruins. 'An inscription which can be dated 1105 C.E. John, it looks as if we've hit the castle!'

As word of the discovery sped through the kibbutz, a strange thing happened: clerks counting eggs, cooks at work in the kitchen, boys in school and the volunteers from the various countries stopped what they were doing and hurried silently to the tell, where they stood in expectant groups, watching as the archaeologists tapped gingerly at pebbles while girls with brushes cleared away the debris. From thousands of miles away men had come to probe into the secrets of the tell and at this hour they had struck a significant thing. It was a magnificent moment.

But so many spectators crowded the edges of Trench B that Tabari had to move them back, lest the sides collapse; and as the crowd withdrew, ten of the stronger workmen jumped down to haul away the last of the rubble. But the rock bearing the inscription they did not touch, for it would first have to be photographed in situ and then sketched by the camp draftsman in the precise position in which it was found, because from such photogaphs and drawings some imaginative theorist who had never seen Makor might construct an explanation which would illuminate a whole period of history. When the pictures were taken, Tabari called his workmen out of the trench and spectators were allowed to file in and see for themselves the first major find at Makor. Cullinane waited his turn, and when he saw the beautiful old stone, carved so carefully by some medieval guildsman, he experienced a rush of joy. The castle existed! The first stage of the dig was a success, and in succeeding years the beautiful ruins could be leisurely explored. In the meantime he filled out the provisional card.

HEADSTONE OF THE CRUSADER VOLKMAR I

When Tabari saw the date he objected, pointing out that in this instance the stone could be ascribed with finality to the year 1105 C.E. because there was documentary evidence in *Wenzel of Trier's Chronicle* that Count Volkmar of Gretz had died that year, but Cullinane observed dryly, 'We know when he died, but we don't know when the stone was carved and let into the wall. More likely around the date I suggest.'

An unfortunate atmosphere now developed at the dig, the kind of thing an experienced administrator tries to forestall; nothing of even minor importance had been uncovered at A, so that the team working at that site began to lose spirit, while the gang at B greeted each morning eagerly, wondering what evidence they would lay bare that day: perhaps Crusader dining plates decorated with fish, pieces of chain armor, carved fragments from a chapel, dozens of stones which could impart a very real sense of a castle in which knights had lived and from which they had gone out to fight. During one period of three weeks in June, the diggers found stones that were heavily charred—even cracked apart by some forgotten heat—and they speculated on what accident could have built up a blaze so great as to scar a whole section of castle. Digging at Trench B in those days was an exciting experience, and if one wanted a good example of the manner in which archaeology could uncover lost secrets it was there.

At the same time Trench A showed how a dig could go wrong, for it had obviously missed the main gate. After weeks of disappointing excavation Cullinane assembled his crew at the barren trench and asked, 'What's to do?' Eliav now admitted that the gate must stand well to the east, where Cullinane had suggested in the first place, and he advised abandoning the disappointing trench and transferring operations seventy yards eastward, but Cullinane said no: 'At Trench B we've found the castle, and if the rest of the tell is unproductive we need to know that too.' To the disappointment of the Trench A kibbutzniks he ordered them to go ahead as planned, trying to convince them that 'what you're doing here is just as important as what they're doing over there.' He found this a difficult thesis to defend.

So the gang at Trench A plodded through the unrewarding rubble until by brute strength they had thrown out enough soil to lay bare the three concentric walls that had guarded Makor. Sometime around 3500 B.C.E. men not yet identified had built the thick outer wall by throwing together huge stones in haphazard piles. Two thousand years later, well before the age of Saul and Solomon, some other unidentified group had built the sturdy middle wall. And two thousand five hundred years after that, at the time of the Crusaders, the inner wall had been erected, and it was a European masterpiece. How it had been penetrated and what part the castle fire had played in its destruction Cullinane, as a scientist, refused to guess. He supposed that after the completion of this final wall the sloping flanks had been repaved with rock, the most recent construction on the tell, a mere eight hundred years old. Attacking Makor could never have been a simple undertaking. Cullinane, visualizing the plateau crouched within the triple walls—they did not stand, of course, in three separated rings; all were crumbled and each grew out of its predecessor, but each also existed in its own unique construction—told the others, 'All we're looking for occurred within this little stone cocoon. We've laid bare the pattern but not the significance.'

And then in quick succession, some distance inside the inner wall, the diggers at Trench A came up with three finds, none so spectacular as the remnants of the castle but all of a nature that sent the history of Makor rocketing backwards, so that after these items were appraised by the scholars the balance between the trenches was restored, and the hidden secrets of the mound began to unfold in an orderly pattern. The first find was merely a piece of limestone intricately carved in a manner no Jew or Christian would adopt; it was obviously of Muslim origin, a poetic decoration for a mosque—but on its face some later Christian hand had imposed a panel with five crosses.

LEVEL VI
ABOUT 640 C.E.

SCALE 1:20

MUSLIM TRACERY WITH SUPERIMPOSED CHRISTIAN PANEL

The experts now focused on Trench A, where a picture of chronological confusion developed, indicated by interrupted building lines and broken foundations. The Muslim stone proved that either a mosque or part of a building used as a mosque had once stood in this area, but that later Christians had converted it into a church. However, as the diggers probed deeper, it became clear that the significant building had been a great Byzantine basilica with a mosaic floor, and Cullinane dug with increasing excitement, hoping to uncover some kind of substantial proof that Makor had owned one of the early Christian churches of the Galilee; but it was Tabari who finally brushed away a pile of dust to reveal a handsome stone on which had been carved a set of three crosses in bas-relief.

When he climbed out of the trench, Eliav went down with the photographer for a series of shots of the stone in situ, for it was essential to record where it had stood and how it had fitted into the wall, especially since the stone was lodged in a section which seemed to have been built and rebuilt several times: whether it had formed part of the mosque could not now be determined; only later excavations would establish the relationships. But as Eliav brushed away some earth so that the camera could catch a shadow showing how the rock abutted onto those above and below, some irregularity on the upper surface of the stone caught his practiced eye and he asked for a small pick and a brush. With these implements he dislodged the dust, sixteen hundred years old, that had sifted in between stones, and he satisfied himself that he had come upon something of great moment. Without speaking, he made way for the photographer, and walked slowly over to where Cullinane was showing his sketch to Vered Bar-El and Tabari. Taking the card, Eliav said quietly, 'I'm afraid you've some more work to do on this one, John.'

'What do you mean?'

Eliav looked soberly at his colleagues. 'The kind of thing we dream about,' he said.

The other three experts lined up behind him as he led the way back to the trench. No one spoke, but at the newly found stone Cullinane asked the photographer to retire, then fell on his hands and knees to peer into the dusty space a quarter of an inch high. When he rose his eyes were alight, and Dr Bar-

El and Tabari, when they saw what Eliav had partially uncovered, reacted in the same way.

'I want the draftsman down here right away,' Cullinane called. There were only a few hours of good light left, and he directed her to sketch from all angles the Christian rock with its stalwart crosses. At the same time the photographer was directed to shoot the rock lavishly, after which they would pull out the stone to inspect the hidden face; but in spite of the urgency that communicated itself throughout the dig, it became apparent that the remaining hours of that day would have to be spent in drawing. Any further work on the rock must wait till next morning.

'We could do it under lights,' Tabari suggested, but this Eliav quickly vetoed, and as darkness fell a sense of deep excitement settled over Makor.

At dinner the older kibbutzniks were as pleased as the youngsters who worked at the dig, partly because every family in Israel had at least one amateur archaeologist–rare was the house that had no flints, no pottery, no echoes of the past–and partly because everyone in the kibbutz thought of the work as 'his dig'. 'I hear we hit something big today,' one of the serving men said to Cullinane. The Irishman's eyes were too bright for him to deny his excitement.

'We found the cornerstone of a Christian church,' Cullinane replied. 'Great day for the Irish.'

'But that running around at the end?' the man asked. 'What was it about?' He propped his tray on the table, leaning on it as if he were the owner of a restaurant.

'We don't know,' Cullinane said.

'Can't you guess?' the kibbutznik demanded.

'We'll guess tomorrow,' Cullinane replied. He was becoming irritated with this man.

But the young fellow said, 'Could we come up and watch?' and Cullinane became aware that eight or nine of the kitchen staff had crowded about his chair, eager to know what was happening on their tell.

'All right,' Cullinane said. 'Be there at six.' And as day started, more than a hundred persons lined the trench, watching silently as the four senior archaeologists descended to work on the Christian stone. 'You have enough photographs?' Cullinane asked the English cameraman.

'Developed them last night. All okay.'

'You have enough sketches?' The young woman nodded, so Tabari began working cautiously along the edges of the rock, but it could not be moved.

'We'll have to take out those layers on top,' Eliav suggested, and to do this required the better part of an hour. None of the watchers left.

The important stone now stood with only one large rock bearing down upon it, and Cullinane called the photographer in for a final series of shots, after which he and Eliav began to lift the obstructing stone with crowbars. Slowly they raised the ancient burden until Tabari, peering into the dusty darkness, could see the surface about to be exposed. 'It's there!' he shouted, and Dr Bar-El, looking over his shoulder, whispered, 'My God! It's perfect.'

They took away the cover stone, then brushed the dust from the long-hidden surface to display the carving of a little flat wagon with funny flat-sided wheels bearing a house with a curved roof, guarded by palm trees. The archaeologists stood back so that the kibbutzniks could see the treasure, but no one spoke.

Finally Eliav said, 'It's a great day for the Jews,' for this was a folklore representation of the flat wagon bearing the wooden Ark of the Covenant in which the tablets of the Ten Commandments were supposed to have been carried from Mount Sinai to the Promised Land. Originally this stone must have enjoyed a place of honor in the synagogue of Makor, but when that structure was torn down by the victorious Christians, some workman had carved his three crosses on a different face, while the vanquished Jewish side was cemented into the darkness of the basilica. To have the Jewish symbols exposed now, before Jews who had returned from exile to build their kibbutz near the ancient site, constituted a luminous moment; and Dr Cullinane,

LEVEL VII
ABOUT 350 C.E.

SCALE 1:25

STONE FROM A SYNAGOGUE REUSED IN A CHURCH

happening to look up from the trench, saw that some of the older kibbutzniks had tears in their eyes. With deep pleasure he modified his earlier drawing and filed it.

Almost before he was finished, a workman found a coin that completed the violent sequence of that period: Roman temple, synagogue, basilica, mosque, church . . . all equally collapsed into a shared destruction.

Cullinane allowed the stone and the coin to be exhibited at the kibbutz for some days, and grave-faced Jews stood before them looking first at their long-buried ark but staring mostly at the hard face of Vespasian, whose armies had destroyed their temple, and at the figure of Judaea Capta as she mourned in humiliation under the palm tree. It was one of the most beautiful coins ever issued, this flawless union of imperial force and tribute sorrow, and it fascinated the modern Jews whose history it summarized. Cullinane, himself deeply affected by the three emotionally related finds, cabled Paul Zodman:

THINGS HAPPENING VERY FAST STOP BETTER COME ON OVER

The relationship between the two trenches was now reversed, as often occurred at a dig. Trench B wallowed about in the foundations of the Crusader fort, whose walls cut deep through many levels of occupation, obliterating them all and rendering them largely useless for contemporary study; the diggers in this trench now seemed mainly occupied with shifting heavy stones. But in Trench A, which transected the multiple religious structures, intellectual and archaeological activity was keen, and the reason for bringing along an architect from the University of Pennsylvania became clear. At the top

LEVEL VIII
ABOUT 70 C.E.

SCALE 1:2

ROMAN COIN

of the trench was only thirty feet wide and it had sloping sides, so the amount of wall exposed was never great, but by pecking away at the earth and guessing at what had stood on what, the architect could sometimes come up with clever deductions as to how the various jigsaw pieces had fitted together. He was a patient man who allowed the sweating kibbutzniks to stalk past him as if he did not count, but when they were through lifting and tugging he was there, on his knees, often with a whisk broom, trying to catch signs of how the stones had been dressed and whether they bore fragments of earlier cement, indicating a prior use in some other wall. The quality of this man's imagination would determine what course the excavations would follow in future years, and the amount of information he could deduce from what to another man would be merely one line of rocks crossing another line, was surprising. Not one of the four top archaeologists at Makor could approach his proficiency in this specialized field.

Only one thing interfered with his work, and he complained about this to Cullinane: 'Really, John, you've got to tell those girls to wear more clothes. I find them a very disturbing element.'

'I've wondered about this myself,' Cullinane said. The dig at Makor was witnessing a phenomenon of the age, common to all countries: for protection from the near-tropic sun young men wore hats, long-sleeved shirts, shoes and socks to protect their ankles, while girls got along with little: sleeveless blouses, shorts, no stockings and tennis shoes. After a few days of sunburn the kibbutz girls became bronzed goddesses, rounded and beautiful. They were modest and well behaved, but they were also alluring, and there could have been few men working at the dig who were not at one time or another tempted to reach out and pinch these lovely Jewish maidens. Of course, such temptation was one of the unexpected pleasures of archaeology in Israel, but Cullinane agreed with his architect: 'It was a lot easier digging in Egypt. There the women had to wear clothes!'

But when the architect protested a second time–'John, I was truly worried. If she had lifted that rock she'd have popped out all over'–he decided that something must be done. He therefore summoned Dr Bar-El and said, in his best administrative manner, 'Mrs Bar-El, I think you'd better speak to the girls. They really must wear more clothes.'

'What do you mean?' she asked innocently.

'The men . . . they've begun to complain.'

'You mean the shorts?' She began to laugh at his embarrassment. 'Really, John, no sensible man's complaining about shorts, I hope.'

'Not exactly,' he stammered.

'Aren't the girls doing a good job?' she asked defensively.

'Yes! Yes! In fact they're superior to any others I've worked with. But won't you please speak to them . . .'

'I wonder if I'm the proper one to do it,' she said shyly.

'Well, you're a woman.'

'But you haven't seen the shorts I propose to wear,' she said quietly, and he was left alone, fumbling with a pencil.

That afternoon she wore them, and although her outfit was not immodest it was tantalizingly arranged, and when Cullinane first saw her heading for Trench A he stopped what he was doing to watch. Then he smiled as he saw the architect follow her approvingly down the trench, and he made no further effort to discipline the kibbutz girls. They were, as he had told Dr Bar-El, the most energetic and intelligent workers he had ever employed, and if they wished to provide a daily beauty parade, that would have to be one of the extra features at Makor; but when Vered Bar-El went past, holding a piece of broken pottery, he asked himself: What would Macalister and Albright think if they could see a dig like this?

She was a delightful person, Vered Bar-El, thirty-three years old, a widow from the War of Independence and a fine scholar who had been offered university posts in several countries. That she had not remarried since 1956, when her young husband was killed during the Sinai Campaign, surprised Dr Cullinane. He asked her about it once as they were going across the tell, and she had said frankly, 'I have been married to Israel, and one of these days I must get a divorce.' He had asked her what she meant by the first part of this sentence, and she explained, 'An outsider cannot imagine how hard we fought to gain a state here. It absorbed all our energies. At Zefat, for example. . . .'

'The town in the hills?'

She stopped, and it was obvious that she felt herself assailed by memories too difficult to discuss. 'You ask Eliav some day,' she said, and she had run down off the tell.

As for the second part of her sentence, Cullinane understood this only too well. As the son of an impoverished Irish day laborer on the Chicago and Northwestern Railroad, he had devoted himself so single-mindedly to an education, acquiring a polished accent and a Ph.D. at the same time, that he had not married, and his devout mother had fairly well given up parading before him the daughters of her Irish friends. Yet he knew that for a man to be forty without a wife was patently absurd–and open to suspicion as well–and since the fortunate offer by Paul Zodman to finance the Makor dig had settled his economic and professional problems for the next decade, there was no reasonable excuse for delaying marriage any longer; but like the meticulous man he was, the man who signed each card so precisely J.C., he was studying the problem with scientific detachment. He had, one might say, excavated his way through Levels I to XIII of Chicago's Irish society, and he had come upon some interesting pieces, but he had so far found nothing in the human field to compare with the Christian-Jewish cornerstone that he had found at Makor's Level VII.

Then there was Mrs Bar-El, working beside him each day, wearing her shorts and smiling at him with her flashing eyes and white teeth. She was an easy girl to remember when one was at the other side of the tell, or sleeping in the next tent. He responded to her in two interesting ways which had little to do with her personality: when considering marriage he remembered how men his age often made asses of themselves, and he had sworn never to become involved with any girl more than twelve years his junior–Vered was only seven years younger; also, he had an affinity for girls who were shorter than he was, and Vered was positively petite. That she was also an archaeologist neither added to nor detracted from her general appeal, and as for the fact that she was Jewish and he Catholic, he dismissed this as a problem of little consequence. In fact, he chuckled as he recalled the joke that had been popular during his navy service in the Korean war: 'Soldier calls his Irish mother in Boston and says, "Mom! This Xavier in Korea. Just wanted to warn you that I've married a Korean girl." To his surprise his mother makes no objection. In fact she seems pleased. "Bring the girl home, Xave. You can stay with us." "But where can we stay in your house, Mom, it's so small?" "You can use my room, Xave, because the minute that Korean bitch puts her foot through the door I'm gonna cut my throat."' It seemed to John Cullinane that more than half his friends were married to what their parents thought were the wrong mates–Catholics with Baptists, Jews with Armenians, and Xavier with his Korean wife–and he gave the problem no more thought.

His present liberal views in these matters marked a sharp change from his youth in Gary, Indiana, where he had grown up in a Catholic neighborhood whose popular sport had been the seeking out of Jewish schoolchildren during the tedious afternoons. He and his friends would lurk behind fences, rock in fist, waiting for the occasional Jew in the district to come furtively home. With yells they would spring upon him, pummeling him harshly and shouting:

> 'Jew boy! Jew boy!
> Gonna crucify a goy.'

Once the truant officer had come to the Cullinane home with a warning: 'Mike, your boy has got to quit picking on the Ginsberg kids.'

'A fine thing,' his father had stormed. 'An officer of the law wastin' his time over such a matter.'

'Mike, it's gotta stop. The Jews is makin' protests to the mayor.'

'Over what? They crucified Jesus, di'n they?'

Why did we do it? Cullinane sometimes asked himself in later years, and he found no difficulty in determining the answer. As each Easter season approached, the priest in his parish launched a series of sermons recounting the crucifixion of our Saviour, and his Irish brogue would hang almost longingly upon the terrible mystery of our Lord's passion. Young Cullinane and his friends would listen in growing anger as they heard of the manner in which the Jews betrayed Jesus, forced a crown of thorns upon His brow, nailed Him to the cross, pierced His side, mocked Him in His agony and even bargained in selling His clothes. It was almost more than the boys could bear, and it infuriated them to think that descendants of those same Jews were roaming the streets of Gary that day.

It was not till Cullinane reached college that he discovered that it had not been the Jews who had done these things to Jesus; it had been Roman soldiers. He also discovered that no Catholic dignitary who had advanced beyond the stage of parish priest any longer proclaimed such views, but by then it did not matter. On his own recognizance he had discovered that an instinctive hatred of the Jew made no sense, and that a rational dislike could be supported by no evidence whatever. And he had changed so completely that now he could even contemplate marrying a Jew.

He found himself thinking about Vered a good deal, and one of the thoughts that recurred most often was a warning delivered years earlier by a French archaeologist in Egypt: 'Many digs in the Near East have come to grief because God made little-girl archaeologists and little-boy archaeologists, and when you put them together in tents at the edge of a desert . . . the strangest things can happen. Now this is particularly true of digs organized by Englishmen, because somehow the Englishwoman, so proper at home, seems to go to pieces as soon as she sees a pickaxe plopped in the earth . . . in a nice way, that is.' In furtherance of this theory the English photographer was romancing with the kibbutz girls, and Cullinane didn't blame him a bit.

In spite of the strenuous schedule laid out by Eliav, there was a good deal of social life at the kibbutz, and in the long summer evenings the group used to gather for folk dancing. Word had gone out that Big Boss was a bachelor, and some very pretty girls hauled him onto the floor while the accordion beat out folk music and partners swept through beautiful old dances, some from Russia, others from the steep hills of Yemen. Cullinane found the kibbutz girls too young for serious attention, but he did confess to one change of opinion, which he shared with Tabari: 'In America I always thought that folk dancing was for girls too ugly and too fat for modern dancing. I stand corrected.'

In July he became uncomfortably aware of the fact that at the kibbutz dances Vered Bar-El usually preferred to dance with Dr Eliav, and they made an attractive pair. His lank frame moved with masculine charm through the peasant steps, while her petite body had a lively grace, especially in those dances where girls were required to pirouette, their petticoats flying out parallel to the floor. Tabari also arranged evening excursions to historic sites like Tiberias on the Sea of Galilee or the poetic ruins of Caesarea, King Herod's ancient capital, where Cullinane saw Vered standing in the moonlight beside a marble column that had once graced the king's gardens, and she seemed to be the spirit of Israel, a dark-haired, lovely Jewess from Bible times, and he had wanted to run to her and tell her so, but before he did, Dr Eliav moved beside her; he had been standing behind the pillar, holding her hand, and Cullinane felt like an ass.

And then one night in mid-July as he inspected the dig in moonlight he was alerted by someone moving along the northern edge of the plateau, and he suspected it might be a worker out to steal a Crusader relic; but it was Vered Bar-El, and he ran to her with a kind of release and caught her in his arms, kissing her with a vigor that astonished both of them. Slowly she pushed him away, holding on to the lapels of his field jacket and looking up at him with her dark, saucy eyes.

'John,' she laughed warmly, 'don't you know I'm engaged to Dr Eliav?'

'You are?' He brushed her hands away as if he were afraid of them.

'Of course. That's why I came on this dig . . . rather than Massada.'

He'd wondered about that in Chicago: Why would Bar-El pass up a sure thing like Massada to work with me? He became angry. 'Damn it all, Vered. If he's engaged to you, why doesn't he do something about it?'

For just a moment she looked as if she had been asking herself the same question, but quickly recovered and said lightly, 'Sometimes these things . . .'

He kissed her again and said most seriously, 'Vered, if he's held back this long, why not marry a man who means business?'

She hesitated, as if inviting him to kiss her again, then pushed him away. 'You mean too much business,' she said softly.

'How long have you been engaged?'

Standing apart from him, she said, 'We were in the war together. I roomed with his wife before she was killed. He fought beside my husband. These are things that bind people . . .'

'You make it sound like patriotic incest.'

She slapped his face, with all her force and all her anger. 'These are serious matters. Never, never . . .' Then she threw herself into his arms and sobbed. After a while she whispered, 'You're a man I could love, John. But I fought desperately for this Jewish land and I'd never marry anyone but a Jew.'

He dropped his arms. Her statement was archaic and somehow offensive. It was inappropriate for this moment when two people were groping for love. If the Jews of Europe had gone through what they did in order to build a state in which an attractive widow of thirty-three could talk like that . . . 'You're no farther along than the Irish Catholics I used to know in Gary, Indiana. "You bring a Polack husband into this house and I'll horsewhip the both of you." That was my father speaking to my sister.'

'I didn't ask you to kiss me,' Vered pointed out.

'I'm sorry I did,' Cullinane snapped.

She took his angry hands and held them to her cheeks. 'That's an unworthy remark and you know it. I've watched you working in the trenches, John. You want to know every fact there is and no prejudice diverts you. All right, you've been digging in this trench and you've uncovered something you don't like . . . a Jewish girl who has seen so much terror that there's only one thing in the world she wants to be. A Jewish girl.'

The force of her words made Cullinane respect what she said, but he could not rationally accept it: if he understood anything about human relations, he knew that Vered Bar-El was not going to marry Dr Eliav. She gave no impression of being in love with him and he no sense of being hungry for her. Like the Israel of which she was a part she was caught in historical cross-currents, rather than in the emotion of love, and she betrayed her awareness of this unsatisfactory situation. With compassion Cullinane observed her uncertainty, then said, 'Vered, I've spent the last twenty years looking for a wife. I wanted someone who was intelligent, not afraid of big ideas, and . . . well, feminine. Such girls aren't easy to find, and I won't let you go. You'll never marry Eliav. Of that I'm convinced. But you will marry me.'

'Let's go back,' she said, and when they entered the main room of the Arab house the others began to giggle, and Cullinane gained reassurance for his theory when Dr Eliav said lightly, not as an outraged lover but as a boy in college might have spoken to his roommate, 'Looks to me, Cullinane, as if you've been kissing my fiancée.'

The Irishman wiped his lips, looked at his fingertips and said, 'I thought Israeli girls had forsworn salonim and lipstick.'

'They sometimes do,' Eliav said, 'but later they reconsider.'

Cullinane decided to play along with the make-believe and extended his hand. 'In later years, Eliav, your wife can truthfully taunt you: "If I hadn't married you I could have gone to Chicago with a real man!"'

'I'm sure I'll hear about it,' the tall Jew said, and the two archaeologists shook hands.

'If it's a formal engagement,' the English photographer cried, 'we'll celebrate all night,' and somebody jumped into a jeep to dash into Akko for some bottles of arrack; but for John Cullinane the songs and dances were tedious, for watching Vered and her man he knew that this was a spurious engagement party. More important, he had admitted to her and to himself how much he needed her and he wondered what their relationship could be during the remainder of the dig.

Next morning, as Cullinane was sketching the first object so far uncovered which might date from before the Christian Era, Dr Eliav received a phone call from the prime minister's office in Jerusalem advising him that Paul J. Zodman, of Chicago, was arriving at the airport that afternoon and was to be extended every courtesy becoming a man who had contributed generously to the establishment of Israel. A few minutes later a cablegram reached Cullinane advising him of Zodman's arrival, and a few minutes after that the Tel Aviv agent of the United Jewish Appeal called to say, 'Is this the Zodman dig? I want

LEVEL   IX
ABOUT   5   B.C.E.

GLASS PHIAL   SCALE 1:3

the director. Zodman's arriving this afternoon, and for God's sake keep him happy.' Cullinane finished his sketch and called in to the other room, 'Now we can all begin to sweat.'

Two cars drove down from Makor, Tabari and Eliav in one, Mrs Bar-El and Cullinane in the other. It was Eliav who had insisted upon this arrangement, sensing that the potential unpleasantness of the night before must be thoroughly dispersed if the dig was to function properly. 'Furthermore,' he added, 'I've found that it never hurts when you're meeting a millionaire to have a good-looking girl around. Makes him feel the operation is first-class.'

'This girl's not good-looking,' Cullinane said. 'She's beautiful.' Vered kissed him lightly before the others, and any tension that might have persisted was relaxed.

On the long trip to the airport Vered said, 'We've heard a lot about Paul

Zodman. What kind of man is he?'

Cullinane reflected. 'He's three times more intelligent than you're going to think. And three times more stupid.'

'Has he ever been to Israel?'

'No.'

'I've read about his gifts. Fifty thousand for planting trees. Half a million for the school of business administration. How much for the dig? Third of a million?'

'He's not altogether ungenerous, as the British might say.'

'Why has he done it? If he's never been here?'

'He's typical of many American Jews. One day he said, "In Germany I'd be dead. In America I own seven stores. If I didn't give to Israel I'd be a jerk."'

'Strictly charity?' Vered asked. 'He has no particular sense of partnership with us?'

Cullinane laughed. 'When he sees how successful this country is . . . roads, hospitals . . . he's going to feel let down. He thinks he's been feeding outcasts in a ghetto.'

'What does he look like?'

'What do you think?'

'How old is he?'

'That I'll tell you. He's forty-four.'

'Married?'

'Yes.'

'He get his money from his father?'

'Four of his stores he inherited. The rest he's done himself.'

'I see him as a big man,' Vered said, 'aggressive, never read a book but respects college professors like you. He must be liberal or he wouldn't have hired a Catholic for your job.'

'Did you mean it when you said you'd never marry a non-Jew?' Cullinane asked abruptly.

'I certainly did. Our family has a story which sums it all up. When we moved from Russia to Germany my aunt wanted to marry an Aryan.'

'Whatever that means.'

'In her case it meant a blond-haired, blue-eyed Prussian with a good university education. Our family raised hell, but it was Grandmother who delivered the telling blow. She said, "For any man being married is difficult, and no man should be tempted later in life to get rid of his wife merely because she's a Jewess. He'll have enough other reasons." My father said that everyone laughed at the old woman's reasoning, and my aunt wept, "Why would Otto be tempted to get rid of me because I'm a Jewess?" and the old woman explained, "The day may come when Germany will make its men give up their Jewish wives," and my aunt cried a good deal, but she didn't marry Otto. He married another Jewish girl, and in 1938 he was forced to get rid of her, and the poor girl was sent to an extermination camp. Of course, my aunt went to the same camp, but she went with her husband.'

'You think the time could come in America when I would be commanded to get rid of you because you are Jewish?'

'I don't bother about specific cases,' Vered replied. 'I only know that the wise old grandmothers were right.'

When the jet landed, there could be no mistake as to who Paul Zodman was.

The first passengers to alight were ordinary French and American businessmen, bearing no marks of distinction. The next were some elderly men weighed down with cameras, and one could not think of Zodman as bothering to collect visual records of where he had been, for he was mostly concerned with where he would go next. Two powerfully built men descended, but they lacked any intellectual quality, and they were followed by three or four who might have been Zodman except that they were sloppily dressed and careless in manner. Then came a man about five-feet-eight, underweight, dressed in a dark blue English suit conservatively tailored, sunburned not from the sun but from a barber's quartz lamp, eager, bouncy, liking all that he saw and running down the stairs to greet Cullinane.

'John! You didn't need to drive all the way down to meet me'–but God help John if as an employee he hadn't been there!

'This is Dr Bar-El, our pottery expert,' Cullinane said. He knew how impressed businessmen were with the title 'doctor'; they cursed professors but they wanted their help to have doctorates. 'This is Dr Ilan Eliav. And this is the top expert of them all, Jemail Tabari, Oxford University.' Businessmen felt the same way about Oxford.

Paul Zodman stepped back, surveyed his team–three goodlooking sunburned men and a beautiful woman–and said, 'You've got yourself a fine-looking group. I hope they know something.'

'You cross-question them while I get your bags.'

'One bag,' Zodman explained, throwing Cullinane the ticket. 'A small overnighter.' That also proved that he was Paul Zodman; he had learned that most travelers load themselves with preposterous amounts of luggage. When Cullinane got to the bag he found it to be one of those super-expensive fiberglass-and-magnesium jobs that weighed practically nothing. As a matter of interest he asked the El-Al man to put it on the scales, and fully loaded it hit just under nineteen pounds. Two Jews from New York struggled by with seven bags weighing nearly two hundred pounds.

On the trip back to the dig Zodman suggested that he ride with Tabari and Eliav for the first half and that he then change to Cullinane and Bar-El, and as the cars left the airport Cullinane asked Vered, 'Well?'

'I'm impressed. He's younger and smarter than I thought.'

'Wait till you see how smart he is,' Cullinane replied.

They were permitted to do so at the halfway mark, when Zodman jumped out of Eliav's car and came to Cullinane's. 'Two excellent men,' he said as he climbed in. 'I'd hire either of them for my stores right now. That Tabari's a shameless charmer. Tried to snow me with flattery. Eliav's the powerhouse. You paying them decent wages, John?'

'Starvation,' Vered replied.

'Well, if they're as good as they look, after six or seven years raise them five dollars. That goes for you too, Miss Bar-El.'

'Mrs Bar-El.'

'This matter of wages on an archaeological dig is most perplexing,' Zodman said. 'Since you've gone, John, I've had Miss Kramer get me the reports of all the important digs in this area–Macalister, Kenyon, Yadin, Albright . . .' He rattled off some dozen names.

'You've read those reports?' Vered asked. 'The big folio volumes?'

'The big expensive volumes. I've spent almost as much on the books as I have on you, and John . . .' He stopped, and there began that series of events which was to prove how stupid he could be. 'Do you suppose I could see the trees?'

'What trees?' Cullinane asked.

'I gave eighty-one thousand dollars to plant trees in this country.'

'Well . . .' Cullinane mumbled.

Vered rescued him. 'The forests are over there,' she said, waving generally toward the right, and to distract Zodman she began asking specific questions about the archaeological reports, discovering that he had not skimmed the books but was well versed in details.

'They never tell you what the expeditions cost,' he complained. 'Correction—Macalister did say that to continue at Gezer would take about . . .' He took out his wallet and with no fumbling produced a slip of paper from which he read: '". . . at least £350 *per mensem* would be requisite; and this does not allow any margin for extra expenses." That was in 1909. And what was the pound worth in 1909? About five dollars? That's $1,750 a month eleven thousand dollars for a season. Now Makor's a lot smaller than Gezer was, yet you're charging me about fifty thousand dollars a season. How come?'

'Macalister had only himself and Tabari's uncle and they hired their diggers for twenty-one cents a day. On our payroll . . .'

The car had turned in the direction that Vered had indicated, and Zodman asked, 'Is this where the trees are?'

'Down that way,' Vered replied, seeking to sidetrack him, but soon the road turned 'that way' and Zodman asked, 'Now do I see the trees?' Vered assured them that they were somewhere ahead, and in this way they reached the tell, but when Cullinane started to describe the Crusader castle, Zodman said quietly, 'You're going to think it silly of me, but I'd like to see my trees. That castle died a thousand years ago. The trees are living.'

Tabari took Eliav aside and warned him, 'Here we go again. You produce some trees, or we're in trouble.'

Temporary relief was provided when Cullinane brought forth the gold menorah. 'This is your Candlestick of Death,' he said, and for some minutes Zodman was lost in contemplation of that fateful object.

'Which was the candle where they cut off the king's head?' he asked.

'The middle one,' Tabari assured him.

Eliav did not smile, for he was in trouble. Often before he had encountered this problem of the trees, for skilled Israeli collectors, criss-crossing America for the Jewish Agency, cajoled many wealthy American Jews into contributing dollars for reforesting the Holy Land. 'Imagine!' the collectors wheedled. 'Your trees. Growing on land where King David lived.' So when these donors reached Israel, the first thing they wanted to see was their trees. Paul Zodman had given half a million dollars for buildings, but he had no desire to see them, for he knew that plaster and stone look pretty much the same around the world, but a living tree growing from the soil of Israel was something which commanded his imagination.

Unfortunately, Eliav had found, a newly planted tree looked exactly like what it was: a wisp of potential growth with less than a fifty per cent chance of living, and amicable relations between the new state of Israel and her Jewish friends in America had been damaged by this inability to show men like Zodman where their contributions had gone. Eliav had several times tried taking such donors to mountainsides where millions of fingerlings had been planted, but from a distance of even twenty feet no living tree was visible. Some visitors never recovered from the shock.

'What we need is a ready-built forest,' he whispered to Tabari, whereupon the Arab snapped his fingers.

'We've got one! Relax. Our problem is solved.'

'What are you going to do?' Eliav whispered.

'Mr Zodman,' Tabari announced expansively, 'tomorrow morning you are going to see one of the finest forests . . .'

'You're to call me Paul. You too, Mrs Bar-El.'

'Tomorrow morning, Paul, I'm driving you to see your trees.'

'Could we possibly go now?'

'No,' Tabari said with firmness, and he was surprised at how easily Zodman accepted decisiveness. The Arab then took Cullinane aside and asked, 'You got any quick-dry paint?'

'A little . . . that cost a good deal.'

'It could never be used for a finer purpose.'

'What purpose?' Eliav asked.

'I am going to convert, here and now, the Orde Wingate Forest . . .'

'Wait a minute! Those big trees?'

'Paul Zodman will never know the difference,' Tabari said, and that evening he painted an impressive sign:

THE

PAUL J. ZODMAN

MEMORIAL FOREST

After the paint had dried, the sign looked rather garish, so Tabari took it out to the tell and scuffed it about in the dig, after which he disappeared for the rest of that day.

That evening, through a chain of misunderstandings, the Makor dig almost collapsed. Trouble started when Paul Zodman, strolling away from headquarters at sunset, asked a kibbutznik, 'Where's the synagogue, young man?'

'Are you kidding?' the farmer laughed as he went off to milk his cows.

Zodman returned to the office and complained to Eliav, 'I arranged my flight so I would arrive in Israel on Friday. To attend prayers my first night. Now they tell me the kibbutz doesn't have a synagogue.'

'This kibbutz, no. But others do,' Eliav temporized.

Vered asked, 'Do you attend synagogue at home?'

'No, but Jews who support Israel . . . well, we sort of expect . . .'

Vered was contemptuous of this reasoning and met it head-on. 'You expect us Israeli Jews to be more religious than you American Jews?'

'Frankly, yes. You live in Israel. You have certain obligations. I live in America. I have other obligations.'

'Like making money?' Vered asked.

Zodman realized that he was being foolish and lowered his voice. 'I'm sorry if I raised embarrassing questions. But, Mrs Bar-El, your people do come pestering me every year for funds . . . to keep Israel a Jewish state.'

'And each year you send us a few dollars so that we can be holy on your behalf?'

Zodman refused to lose his temper. 'I'm afraid you've put it rather bluntly, but isn't that what we Jews have been doing for centuries? When my ancestors lived in Germany, men from the Holy Land came round each winter begging funds which would support religious Jews living in Tiberias and Zefat . . .'

'Days of charity are over,' Vered snapped. 'A new kind of Jew lives in Israel.'

And Paul Zodman was about to meet one of them. As he sat down to dinner he saw before him a tureen of soup, some chunky meat, some butter . . . He looked aghast at the combination of meat and butter and called for a waiter. He happened to get Schwartz, the kibbutz secretary.

'Is this butter?' Zodman asked.

With a bold forefinger Schwartz took a dab of butter, tasted it, wiped his finger on his T-shirt, and asked, 'What else?'

'Isn't this kibbutz kosher?'

Schwartz looked at Zodman, then at Cullinane. In an American accent he asked, 'He some kind of a nut or something?' He stopped a waiter and took from him a pitcher of cream. 'Cream for your coffee,' he said contemptuously.

Zodman ignored the gesture, but when Schwartz had moved along to another table he said quietly, 'Don't you find it extraordinary that this place is not kosher?'

'Are you kosher at home?' Vered asked unsympathetically.

'No, but I . . .'

'Expect Israel to be,' she finished sardonically.

Still Zodman refused to grow angry. 'I should think that a kibbutz, where young people are growing up . . .' He shrugged his shoulders.

Eliav offered concessions. 'Our ships, airplanes, hotels . . . they're all kosher. Doesn't that reassure you?'

Zodman did not reply, for he was truly disturbed by his discovery of a kibbutz that had no synagogue and a mess hall that was not kosher; it was Tabari, an Arab Muslim, who brought him consolation.

'Paul, when you see your forest tomorrow!'

'His what?' Vered asked.

'His forest. I checked it this afternoon and it looks fine. After we see it, why don't we go on to Zefat? It'll be Shabbat and we can attend the Vodzher Rebbe's synagogue.'

'Good idea,' Eliav agreed. 'Mr Zodman, there you'll see the Israel you're searching for.'

But Zodman did not respond to the offer and that night the group went to bed irritated and apprehensive. Zodman felt that he was wasting his money on a Jewish state that ignored synagogues and ritual; Cullinane suspected that he might have lost his chief financial supporter; Eliav felt that as an agent of the Israeli government he should have been able to keep Zodman happy; and Vered remembered the American as an irritating fool, condescending in his attitude toward her country. She wished that he would leave so that the experts could get back to their jobs. Only Tabari was satisfied with that first day and at midnight he came to Cullinane's tent, wakened the American and Eliav, and offered them bottles of cold beer.

'We're in real trouble,' he said blithely. 'But there's a way out. My Uncle Mahmoud knew more about digs than any man in Palestine, and he had one basic rule. The man who is putting up the money has got to be kept happy. Mahmoud always kept one major find buried under sand so that when a visitor of importance arrived . . .' He leaned back. 'By tomorrow night we are going to have in Paul J. Zodman one of the world's happiest millionaires, because you should see what my boys dug up this morning! It's hiding out there now, with two guards watching it. Lie down! Lie down!' He rose and barred the exit. 'Tomorrow morning, just as we drive off to the forest, Raanan from Budapest is going to come running up to my car, shouting "Effendi! Effendi!"'

'Effendi?' Eliav growled. 'He doesn't even know the word.'

'And at the Paul J. Zodman Memorial Forest, I have a surprise for all of you, and when we get back from the Vodzher Rebbe's we'll have the biggest surprise of all . . . Let me say this, John, if you want more money from Zodman ask for it tomorrow night. You'll get it.'

As Tabari had predicted, early next morning when the cars were about to drive off, bowlegged Raanan hurried up, crying 'Effendi! Effendi! At Trench A!' and all piled out to see what the picks had uncovered.

Cullinane gasped. It was a fragment of Greek statuary, a rhythmic marble hand so delicately poised as to make the heart pause in admiration. The hand grasped a strigil, the blade now broken but perfect in its relationship to the hand, and the two items–barely a fiftieth part of a complete statue–indicated what the whole must have been, just as the statue, if it were ever found, would epitomize the long struggle which stubborn Jews had conducted to protect their austere monotheism against the allurements of Greece. The statue of the Greek athlete had no doubt once adorned a gymnasium at Makor, the pagan center from which Greek officials had tried to impress their will on subject Jews, and as Cullinane sketched the find he could hear the sophisticated philosophers from Athens arguing with the awkward Jews; he could hear the tempting rationalizations of those who followed Zeus and Aphrodite as they clashed against the immovable monotheism of the Jews; and he could visualize the struggle in which Hellenism, one of the most spontaneous civilizations in history, had tried to smother Judaism, one of the most rigid. How provocative it was to discover that the contest had reached even to Makor and had finally died away to the symbol of one athlete's hand grasping one broken strigil.

'You go on to Zefat,' Cullinane called up from the trench. 'I'll work here.'

'John,' Tabari shouted, 'you're needed!' And Cullinane was brought back to the present. He was needed, and the rest of the statue, if it lay buried in the tell, could wait.

On one of the hills between Akko and Zefat, grateful Jews in 1949 had

LEVEL X
ABOUT 165 B.C.E.

SCALE 1:4

STRIGIL

planted a small forest in memory of Orde Wingate, the understanding Englishman who had once served in Palestine and died in Burma. The trees had flourished and now showed substantial trunks and broad-spreading crowns. As the two cars pulled to a halt, the sign that proved this to be the Orde Wingate Forest was hidden, and a newer one—well scuffed—was in its place. The four archaeologists, somewhat ashamed of themselves, climbed down and tried to control their smiles as Zodman descended to inspect his forest. He stood for some minutes in the roadway, looking; then without speaking he moved in among the trees, feeling their stout trunks and looking up at their piney needles. Some resin attached to his fingers and he tasted it. He kicked at the earth and saw how a humus had begun to form, a mulch that would hold water and prevent the floods that used to ravage this area. He turned to look back at the people he was employing to dig at Makor, but his throat was too choked with emotion for him to speak, so he resumed his contemplation of the trees.

At this point Tabari had arranged for a troupe of children to come running through the forest—none had been there for months and their childish voices began to echo among the trees. Zodman turned with surprise as they ran past, and he caught a little girl, red-cheeked and pudgy. She knew no English and he no Hebrew, but they looked at each other for a moment; then she struggled to pull away, but Tabari had coached her and now, over Zodman's shoulder, the Arab made a sign and the child kissed the American. Zodman drew the little girl to him and bowed his head. He let her go and she ran after the others to where a car would return them to their village. After a prolonged and painful interval he came back to the cars and said haltingly, 'My relatives in Germany included many children ...' He wiped his eyes. 'It's a good thing to have children running free in a forest.' He sat in the car and for the rest of the trip said nothing, but Eliav found Tabari and whispered, 'You take that damned sign down!' The Arab refused, pointing out, 'He'll go back to it again and again.'

They drove to Zefat, an exquisite town hanging in the hills, and as time for morning worship approached, Eliav explained, 'At the Vodzher synagogue no place is provided for women, so it would be best for Vered to wait in the car. Cullinane and Tabari aren't Jews, but I've brought yarmulkes for them, and they'll be welcomed. I've a cap for you, too, Mr Zodman.'

He led the three worshipers away from the main street and down a series of steep winding alleys that clustered along the sides of a hill, and sometimes these alleys were so narrow that Zodman could reach out and touch the houses on either side. Occasionally the buildings joined in their second stories and the men walked through tunnels, winding back and forth through the maze of history, until Eliav pushed open a small door that led into a cramped room not more than twenty-five feet square. Along the sides stood stone benches, hundreds of years old, and on them sat a collection of men who seemed even older: they were bearded, rheumy-eyed and stooped; they wore long black coats and caps trimmed with fur; some had prayer shawls of white wool striped with black. But they were primarily conspicuous because long and sometimes beautiful curls dangled beside their ears, and as they sat they prayed, moving their bodies back and forth in a series of compulsive jerks.

They were Hasidic Jews who gathered about the Rebbe of Vodzh, a holy man who had emigrated from the Russian town of Vodzh many years before, bringing with him these old men and others who were now dead. The famous little man sat huddled by himself, wrapped in a prayer shawl, only his piercing

blue eyes visible through a white beard and side curls. He was known as the
Vodzher Rebbe and this was his synagogue; but even more memorable was his
beadle, a tall, cadaverous man with no teeth and a filthy robe with a hem so stiff
with dirt that it scraped the floor. He wore cracked shoes that squeaked as he
made his way from one routine job to the next, and his fur cap was moth-eaten
and bedraggled. As he led Eliav and his three guests to the benches, Eliav
whispered, 'When he asks you, "Cohen or Levi?" you reply "Israel."' And as
soon as the four were seated the pitiful beadle shuffled up to ask, 'Cohen or
Levi?' and the men replied, 'Israel.'

It would not be accurate to say that formal worship started. There were
seventeen men in the synagogue that morning, and each conducted his own
service, coming together now and then as some special prayer was reached; but
even then they recited at seventeen different speeds, so that the result was a
mad jangle. During the service the beadle shuffled back and forth, talking,
cajoling, suggesting, while two old Jews sat in a corner conducting a business
discussion. Two others prayed in loud voices on a line of their own, while the
old rebbe, incredibly ancient, Cullinane thought, mumbled prayers that no one
else could have heard. 'I've been in some synagogues, but nothing like this,'
Cullinane whispered to Eliav, who said, 'Don't whisper. Speak up.' And
Cullinane said above the rumble of voices, 'Catholics aren't supposed to enter
other churches,' and Zodman said, 'This isn't a church. It's a synagogue.'

In the middle of the service the old beadle went to the niche where the Torah
was kept–those first five books of the Bible ascribed to Moses–and as the
silver-tasseled scroll was brought forth, old men kissed it reverently. The
beadle carried it to a kind of pulpit where a reader began chanting the holy
words. No one listened, except that from time to time the beadle summoned
different members of the congregation to stand beside the chanter, honorary
readers as it were. 'He takes first a Cohen, then a Levi, then an Israel,' Eliav said
above the noise. 'What're they?' Cullinane asked. 'I'll explain later,' he replied.

And then the beadle was at Cullinane's elbow, tugging at Paul Zodman's
sleeve, and it was apparent that the Chicagoan was being asked to assist at the
reading of the Torah, and suddenly the whole significance of the day was
altered. Tears came into the millionaire's eyes. He looked in bewilderment at
Cullinane and Eliav, who pushed him forward. He went to the rickety pulpit,
where the reader, using a silver wand, pointed out the words on the scroll, and
over the man's shoulder Zodman looked at the ancient Hebrew characters.
Recollections of his grandfather reciting these words came to him, recollections
of the little German town at Gretz, from which he had sprung. The drone of
voices in the Vodzher synagogue was like an orchestration of his ancestral
memories, and when, at the end of the reading, the beadle asked in Yiddish how
much Zodman would contribute to the synagogue, the latter said in a low voice,
'Two hundred dollars.'

'Six hundred lira!' the beadle shouted to the worshippers, and all stopped to
look at Zodman, even the rebbe himself, and the American returned to his seat,
sitting very quietly throughout the rest of the service.

Cullinane, used to the rigid formalism of Catholic worship, with its
masterful alternation of priestly chant and group participation, was unable to
assess the Jewish ritual. Here there was no organization, no systematic division
and no apparent beauty. The voices of women were absent. The beadle shuffled
up and down, the old rebbe prayed on his own, and each man was his separate
synagogue. He looked at the two men in the corner, still arguing their business

problem, and he concluded that while Judaism might be meaningful for Paul Zodman it could never substitute for the controlled beauty of Catholicism.

Then just as he was dismissing the religion, a moment arrived that he would never forget, one of the supreme religious experiences of his life. In later years, as he dug through the layers of Jewish history at Makor, it would return at unexpected times to illuminate his understanding. It started simply. The beadle shuffled up to an old man sitting beside Zodman and indicated that he must take off his shoes. The old Jew did so and the beadle banged his way to a little closet under the niche, and while the others prayed he rattled a chain of keys, finally selecting one that unlocked the closet doors, behind which hung a copper pot. This he handed to the man, who went to a spigot outside the door as the beadle threw down a narrow rug. Three other men took off their shoes, and when the first returned with water, washed their hands. Four white prayer shawls were then procured and these the four shoeless men threw over their heads–not their shoulders, their heads–and took their places on the rug, where they prayed in silence, facing the wall.

Now the Vodzher Rebbe began a different kind of chant, composed of short phrases, whereupon the four beshrouded Jews turned to face the congregation and, bowing from the waist, extended their arms to form a kind of cloth tent which hid their faces but allowed their voices to sound forth, and from this strange position they uttered a series of moving cries, meaningless but profound. Cullinane stared at the ghostly figures–these headless Jews lost in their shrouds–and wondered what their performance could signify. It was archaic, passionate, a group of voices shouting some message from the most ancient history of man, and finally the shawls were dropped back over the heads and the voices ceased. The ceremony, whatever it was, had ended, and seventeen different men moaned and grumbled and argued their way to the conclusion of seventeen different services. The rebbe mumbled a prayer and the synagogue service ended.

'What was it?' Cullinane asked, deeply shaken by the last segment of the service.

'The shawl thing?' Eliav asked. 'All Jews are divided among Cohens, Levis and Israels. Cohens are priests, Levis are the temple attendants and Israels are the majority that's left over. At each Saturday service the Cohens in attendance–they don't have to be named Cohen, though many are–rise, put on their shawls and bless the congregation.'

'Zodman looks as if he has taken it seriously.'

'So do you,' Eliav said.

Zodman left the Vodzher synagogue in a state of euphoria, relieved to know that Israel had some persons, at least, who sustained Jewish ritual–and when the men returned to the cars where Vered waited, he stunned them by stating solemnly, 'I don't think it's right to drive on Shabbat,' and he would not allow the cars to move until the holy day ended.

'Has he ever done such a thing in Chicago?' Vered whispered.

'No. He loves college football. Drives to Urbana every Saturday.'

'I believe,' Zodman pronounced gravely, 'that with enough saintly men like the Vodzher Rebbe, Israel is in good hands.'

'Enough men like the rebbe,' Vered whispered, 'and this country is doomed.'

Since the cars could not be used, Cullinane walked his group to a hotel that had old olive trees in the court, and there over a cold lunch, since no fires were allowed in Zefat on Shabbat, the archaeologists explained to their patron what they were accomplishing at Makor. 'Let's climb up on the hill,' Cullinane suggested. 'I can show you there.'

'We won't have to use the cars?' Zodman asked suspiciously.

'Walking is allowed,' Eliav assured him, 'for two thousand paces in each direction,' and the five climbed to the top of the hill crowning Zefat, where they found the ruins of a Crusader castle. Zodman was delighted to see the great rocks and asked, 'Will ours look as good as this?'

'Better,' Cullinane assured him, 'because Makor was a better castle to begin with, and I think we're going to uncover more of it. But you understand, Paul, that when we do uncover it we'll have to remove many of the stones and go on down to the levels beneath.'

'What happens to the castle?' Zodman asked.

'Some of it vanishes . . . stone by stone.'

'But I gave the money to find a castle.'

'You will, but the important finds will be the ones underneath, the ones going far back into history.'

Zodman frowned. 'I sort of fancied that when we were through we'd have a castle, so that when my friends came over from Chicago I could send them up to . . . well, see my castle.'

Cullinane took the next step cautiously: 'In Israel we have half a dozen good Crusader castles. Here . . . the one at Starkenberg. But what we're digging for may be nowhere else. The ultimate secrets of Jewish history.' This was a preposterous statement, but it sounded good.

Tabari added, 'The sort of thing you saw at the Vodzher Rebbe's.' This was completely nonsensical, but as Tabari had guessed, it caught Zodman's imagination.

'You think there's something worthwhile down there? Beneath the castle?'

'Where we're standing, here at Zefat, history goes back to the time of Flavius Josephus . . . about the time of Christ. But at Makor it may go back an additional seven or eight thousand years.'

'Like Gezer?' Zodman asked. 'Jericho?'

'Like them,' Cullinane said.

'Maybe not as far,' Eliav said with professional caution.

'But there's a chance?' Zodman asked.

'Koe-rect,' Tabari said. 'A treasure-house of Jewish history.'

'Then we should dig for it,' Zodman said, 'even if I must lose some of my castle.'

'We'd better get in the cars now,' Tabari insinuated, 'because I have something quite special arranged for tonight.'

Zodman consulted his watch and his conscience and said, 'I think it's now all right to travel,' but when the cars reached his memorial forest and Tabari asked, 'Do you want to stop and see your trees again?' he replied, 'I think we can let the trees go back to their rightful owner. You see, when I was playing with those phoney little children I saw the other Orde Wingate sign which somebody overlooked.'

For a moment no one knew what to say, but Tabari broke the silence with the breezy observation: 'Tonight, Paul, you're going to see something you'll never forget.'

'I'll never forget the forest,' Zodman replied, and they could not tell whether he was joking or not.

In Israel the festive night of the week is Saturday, for 'when three stars can be seen in the heavens at one glance' Shabbat ends and the orthodox, who have observed its restrictions, are free to travel and to celebrate. On this Saturday night Kibbutz Makor was playing host to the Galilee finals of the biennial Bible Quiz, in which participants were subjected to the most penetrating questions regarding Old Testament history. Winners of tonight's contest would move on to Jerusalem to qualify for the world finals in which many countries would participate, so excitement was high as buses arrived in the kibbutz from Akko, Zefat and Tiberias.

Before the contest began Tabari asked permission to address the crowd, and said, 'Tonight our contestants will compete not only for the right to go to Jerusalem, but for cash prizes which our distinguished guest from America, Mr Paul Zodman, has agreed to award.' Zodman, knowing nothing of this plan, fidgeted uneasily as the shameless Arab stared at him and said, 'First prize, one hundred American dollars?' Zodman nodded and the crowd cheered. 'Second prize, fifty dollars. Third prize, twenty-five.' He smiled blandly at Zodman and sat down.

The Chicagoan had expected the evening to be a perfunctory affair, but he was soon disabused. Twelve Israelis, mostly under the age of thirty, lined up while a group of experts from Jerusalem began firing questions at them: 'Name seven birds mentioned in the Bible, citing your authority for each.' That gave no difficulty, nor did the call for seven animals. 'Name three princesses from outside Israel who caused trouble.' A young man from Tiberias answered that one. 'Differentiate between the three Isaiahs and distribute the Book of Isaiah among them.' That knocked out one girl, who knew the difference between the First Isaiah, who was purely Jewish in his theology, and the Second, who seemed to foretell the Christian faith, but not the Third Isaiah, a shadowy figure who returned to Hebraic thoughts. The next woman, a Yemenite from Zefat, was able to answer the question and to specify the chapters and verses at which the Isaiahs were separated. At the end of the second hour three contestants still remained, two men and an attractive girl from Kibbutz Makor, and the questions became minute. 'Differentiate between Jedaiah, Jedidah and Jeduthun, citing your authority for each.' That took care of one man, but the girl was able to rattle off the answers, and in the end she defeated the other man as well, to the joy of her kibbutzniks.

'Young lady,' Zodman said with respect, 'I have never seen a person win a prize more deservedly than you have just done. That goes for you, too, gentlemen. But I would like to ask one additional question. Was this a hand-picked group? Do the other young people know the Bible as well as you did?'

'Excuse me,' Schwartz interrupted, collecting the girl's hundred dollars, for the kibbutz was run on a basis of pure socialism, 'in Israel we all study the Bible. From our kibbutz alone we could have offered a team which would have done just as well.'

'Amazing,' Zodman said, and that night before he went to bed he intended to tell Cullinane that he was thinking more kindly about Israel, even if the kibbutz didn't have a synagogue; but he found his director sitting silent before the Greek hand with the strigil, so he did not interrupt, but when Vered Bar-El appeared he walked with her beneath the olive trees, confessing, 'I'm afraid I was fairly stupid about your Israel.'

'I was sure you couldn't have been as ill-informed as you sounded yesterday,' she said.

Next morning there was much energy at the dig, for Tabari had promised an extra ten pounds to any worker who turned up a significant find while Paul

Zodman was on the premises, and before noon a girl at Trench B started crying, 'I win! I win!'

'Shut up!' Tabari cried, quieting the cries lest Zodman hear, but when he saw what the girl had unearthed–a Babylonian helmet and a spear point, bespeaking the days when Nebuchadrezzar had enslaved Makor and taken into captivity much of its population–he himself became excited and started shouting, 'Hey! Everyone!' And in the confusion Zodman came running up to see the mysterious armor which must have struck terror into ancient Makor when its owner stalked into town. Cullinane sketched the find, then turned the trench over to the recorders.

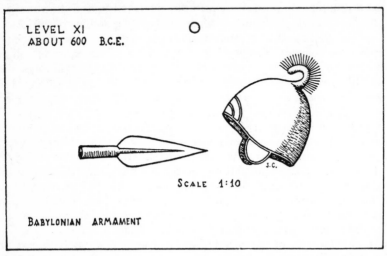

LEVEL XI
ABOUT 600 B.C.E.

SCALE 1:10

BABYLONIAN ARMAMENT

On his way back to the office he saw with apprehension that the team at Trench A was gouging out the earth with unscientific haste and no doubt destroying minor objects. He protested to Tabari, but the Arab said, 'We've got ten years to impress scholars, and one morning to impress Paul J. Zodman. If I had a steam shovel right now, I'd use it.' And this scheme proved profitable when a boy from Trench A turned up one of the real finds at the tell:

LEVEL XII
ABOUT 1000 B.C.E.

HORNED ALTAR

SCALE 1:8

'What is it?' Zodman asked.

'The most Hebrew thing we've found yet,' Cullinane explained. 'The kind of horned altar they speak of in the Bible. This could date back to the time of King David. He may even have worshiped at it, although I doubt that he was ever here.' Zodman bent in the dust to study the old stone altar, so strange and barbaric, yet the foundation of so much of Jewish religion, the kind of altar at which the first sacrifices were made to the one god. Tenderly he patted the antique piece, then said, 'I'm flying out tonight. To Rome.'

'But you've been here only two days!' Cullinane protested.

'Can't give you any more time,' the busy man said, and on the way to the airport he observed to Vered and Cullinane, 'These two days were worth two years of my life. I saw something I'll never forget.'

'The Vodzher Rebbe?' Vered asked, with just a touch of malice.

'No. An Israeli soldier.' Silence. Deep silence. Then Zodman's quiet voice: 'For two thousand years whenever we Jews saw a soldier, it could only mean bad news. Because the soldier couldn't be Jewish. He had to be an enemy. It's no small thing to see a Jewish soldier, standing on his own soil, protecting Jews . . . not persecuting them.' More silence.

At the airport Zodman assembled his staff and said, 'You're doing a wonderful job. Last night after I talked with Mrs Bar-El I surrendered my sentimental interest in the castle. Go on down to bedrock. You're a great team and you can do it.' He hesitated, then pointed at Tabari. 'But this one, John, I think you should fire.'

Vered gasped, but Zodman, without changing his austere expression, said, 'Lacks the scientific attitude. Doesn't pay attention to details.'

'His Uncle Mahmoud . . .' Cullinane stammered.

'Not only did the Orde Wingate Forest have two signs,' Zodman said, 'but that first night, while you men were plotting in the tent, I took a walk on the tell and a guard cried, 'You can't go there,' and when I asked why not, he said, "Because Mr Tabari is keeping a piece of Greek statue buried in the sand so that tomorrow he can please some jerk from Chicago."' And he was gone.

As the plane roared off, its jet engines so reminiscent of the passenger they were bearing aloft, Vered Bar-El sighed, 'In Israel there's bitter discussion about why American Jews refuse to emigrate here. At last I understand. We couldn't find room for more than one or two like him.'

She looked at Cullinane quizzically, and he said, 'America's a big place. We can absorb all sorts of energy.' And on the long ride back to Makor he again asked Vered why she and Eliav were not married, and she replied cautiously, 'Life in Israel's not altogether simple. Being a Jew is not always easy.' On that subject she obviously preferred to say no more.

Cullinane remarked, 'You didn't see the Vodzher Rebbe and his team, but you can imagine.'

'I used to know the rebbe,' she said cryptically. 'Side curls, fur hat, long cloak, frenzy, frenzy. That's part of the burden we carry.'

'Why do Jews make things so difficult for themselves . . . and others?' Cullinane asked. 'What I mean is this. We Catholics are holding ecumenical conferences to minimize the archaic structure of our religion, while you Israelis seem to be doing everything to make yours more archaic. What's the reason?'

'You're looking at the old Jews in the Vodzher synagogue. Why not look at the young Jews at the kibbutz? They refuse to fool around with archaic forms, but they know the Bible better than any Catholic you've ever met. They study it not to find religious forms but to discover the organic bases of Judaism. I think, John, that it's in our young people we'll find our answers ... not in the old rebbes.'

'I wish I were as sure as you are,' he said.

Then, unexpectedly, he gained a series of rapid insights into kibbutz life and discovered for himself reasons that supported Vered's belief that the salvation of Israel probably rested in the idealism and dedication generated by the kibbutz. It was a Friday night and he had returned to the dig after participating in the evening service at the synagogue in Akko, and as he sat at his table in the mess hall he saw coming out of the kitchen, working as a waiter, a man whose face he recognized. It was the strong, vital face of a man in his mid-forties. His steel-gray hair was cropped short in the German fashion and he had no left arm, his shirt sleeve having been pinned up tight with a safety pin. He was General Teddy Reich, one of the heroes of Israel's War of Independence and now a cabinet minister. For two years he had been the Israeli ambassador to the United States and was well known in America, where he had proved himself a witty and successful diplomat.

But more than soldier, diplomat or statesman, Teddy Reich was a member of Kibbutz Makor and from it he derived his strength. He had helped establish this communal settlement and had organized its economy and its rules of living; he owned not a penny's worth of property in the world, only his share in the kibbutz, and frequently throughout the year he came back from Jerusalem to attend the policy-making Friday-night sessions. Whenever he did so, he worked in the kitchen, with one arm, to show the younger members what he had discovered in the long years when Jews had no homeland: that work, productive work, is the salvation of man, and especially of the Jew.

He brought a platter of meat to the archaeologists' table and said to Eliav: 'Could I see you in the kitchen?' Cullinane noticed that Vered watched Eliav go as if she were an apprehensive mother hen, but when she caught Cullinane observing her she laughed nervously: 'They say Teddy Reich's backing Eliav for some important job.'

'In the government?' the Irishman asked.

'Ben-Gurion considered him one of our brightest young men,' she said, and Cullinane thought: She speaks of him as if he were her neighbor's boy, unattached to her in any way.

In the kitchen Eliav and Reich spent some hours talking politics while the general washed dishes, but when the kibbutz meeting convened, Reich absented himself and came to the headquarters building seeking Cullinane. 'Could we talk for a moment?' the one-armed cabinet member asked. Cullinane was pleased at the opportunity, and Reich said, 'Mind if we walk back to the kibbutz? I want you to meet someone.'

And for the first time, in summery moonlight, Cullinane actually visited the kibbutz at which he had been impersonally taking his meals. He saw the buildings which men like Reich had wrenched from the soil, the small homes for nearly fifteen hundred people, the wealth accumulated through years of communal work, the schools, the nurseries, the hospital. To walk past these living buildings occupying land that had lain barren for nearly seven hundred and fifty years was an experience that made the state of Israel come alive, and Cullinane listened attentively as Reich explained the rationale for this move or that, but finally the former general said, 'What I really wanted to talk with you about is the possibility of getting my daughter into the University of Chicago.'

'Can be done. If she's a good student.'

'I think she is. But I want you to judge.'

'She live here in the kibbutz?'

'Where else? Reich led the way to a series of dormitory buildings, where he knocked on one of the doors, waiting for a girl's voice that advised him in Hebrew to come on it. When the door was pushed open Cullinane saw a beautiful young girl of seventeen or eighteen, and like a schoolboy he pointed at her: 'You won the Bible Quiz!'

'Yes.' She nodded gracefully and indicated four iron beds where they could sit.

Cullinane sat on one and told Reich, 'You don't need to worry about her getting into the university. In Bible she knows more than the professors.'

'But does she know enough English?'

Cullinane began speaking with the charming young woman, and after several exchanges, said, 'Heavy accent, but she certainly knows enough to get by.'

'I hope so,' Reich said. 'I could have sent her to the Reali in Haifa. They offered a scholarship, but I thought it more important for her to know kibbutz life. Even if the school here isn't first-class.'

'It's an excellent school,' the girl protested.

'In academic subjects it's rotten,' Reich said, and before his daughter could object he held up his right hand. 'Rotten, but she's found herself a good education, nevertheless.'

He was about to discuss entrance requirements when the door burst open, admitting a rugged young fellow of about eighteen dressed only in shorts and with a face full of shaving lather. He seemed to belong in the room, for after apologizing to General Reich and nodding brusquely to Cullinane, he went to the bed next to the girl's and fumbled about in a locker, looking for his razor. When he finally found it he handled it gravely, like a young man who has not yet shaved regularly, and after further apologies, backed out.

'Your son?' Cullinane asked.

'No,' Reich said.

Cullinane was left hanging. Obviously the young man lived in this room. Obviously Reich's daughter lived in it, too. He looked at her fingers, finding no wedding ring, and he must have blushed, for suddenly Reich burst into laughter. 'Oh, the young man!' His daughter laughed, too, and Cullinane felt embarrassed at a joke which he failed to understand.

'Here at Kibbutz Makor,' Reich explained, 'we decided from the first that our children would be brought up outside the home. So while they're still babies we take two boys from two different families and two girls from two other families and we put them together in one room. And they stay together till they're eighteen.'

'You mean . . .'

'Yes,' the general said. 'In this bed my daughter. In that one the young man you just saw. Where you're sitting another girl. And over there another boy.'

Cullinane gulped. 'Till eighteen?'

'That's a natural stopping age,' Reich said. 'At eighteen everyone goes off to the army. There the boys and girls meet other people their own age and they get married quite normally.'

'They don't . . .' Cullinane could scarcely frame his questions.

'What you mean,' the girl said easily, 'is that we almost never marry boys from our own kibbutz. We know them far too well.'

Cullinane looked at the proximity of the beds and said, 'I suppose so.'

'As for the other problem that worries you,' the lovely girl went on, 'I've lived here at Makor for eighteen years and in that time we've had only two pregnancies and one abortion. In our grammar school when I was in Washington we had ten times that many in one year. And the girls there were only fourteen.'

Suddenly, in the small room, Cullinane could see his sister in suburban Chicago. The silly woman had three daughters and at thirteen each had become, under her tutelage, a premature Cleopatra, with lipstick, permanent and some pimply-faced teen-age boy as her steady date. The youth of his nieces had been a fleeting thing, and at sixteen each had begun carrying in her purse a flat tin box of contraceptives, in case her escort had forgotten. It was difficult for him to comprehend what Teddy Reich and his daughter were saying–that there was a different way of rearing children, one that worked at least as well as the preposterous system now being followed in America. His reflections were halted when the young man returned to his room, clean-shaven but still in his shorts. With some awkwardness he dressed and ran off to a meeting being held in the schoolhouse.

'Tell them I'll be along in a minute,' Reich's daughter cried. Then she turned to Cullinane and asked, 'Do you think I'm ready for Chicago?'

'More than ready,' he assured her.

'And you'll help with my application?'

'I'd be proud to sponsor you.'

The girl left and the two men sat alone in the room. 'Do you find it so incredible?' Reich asked. Not waiting for an answer from the stunned archaeologist, he said, 'The results of our system are striking. No juvenile delinquency. None. A minimum of sexual aberration. Of course we have our share of adultery and backbiting, but our success in marriage? Far above normal. And when they become adults they have the sturdy drive we need in Israel.'

'But living together . . . till eighteen?'

Reich laughed and said, 'I knew a lot of psychotics in America who'd have been much better off if they'd lived that way in their youth. Saved them from a hell of a lot of mental disturbances.' Cullinane wondered if Reich was alluding to him, a man in his forties and not yet married; perhaps things would have worked out differently if he had shared a room with girls in this normal way until he was eighteen. But these speculations were ended when Reich said, 'We kibbutzniks represent only about four per cent of the total population of Israel. But we have supplied about fifty per cent of the national leadership. In all fields. Because we grew up with honest ideals. Solid underpinning.' He rattled off the names of Israel's notable leaders, and all were old kibbutzniks.

'And none of those men own anything?' Cullinane asked.

'What do you own? Really?' Reich countered. 'Your education. Your force of character. Your family. Do you really own the other things? Or do they own you?' But as they walked back to the archaeological headquarters Reich confessed, 'Each year the kibbutz' percentage of the total population diminishes. Today people are no longer interested in our ideals. Only in making a fast buck.' He shook his head sadly. 'So much the worse for Israel.' And in a gloomy frame of mind he walked back through the buildings he had created with one arm.

September came and the dig settled down to the great, serious work before it.

The distractions of the Crusader castle were past; the wars between religions were silenced; Romans and Greeks had known their day in the dust; the Jews had built their horned altars; and now the archaeologists had come in those shadowy, those fruitful centuries when remembered history was only just beginning. At last the two trenches operated at the same level, substantiating each other and turning up fragments of clay vessels broken by women not yet accustomed to kitchen utensils, while beds of flint called across the centuries their messages of men who knew no iron for hunting, but only the sharpened edges of stones and lengths of wood in which to fasten them.

Now Vered Bar-El became the most important member of the team, for she alone could look at pottery and assure the men that they had dug through one civilization and were entering another; it was uncanny how she could identify the pieces, some no larger than a shilling, by their glaze, their decoration, the manner in which they were baked, their constituent clays, or whether they had been smoothed down by hand, a wad of grass or a comb. Her pert little figure, clad in a playsuit, could be seen darting into the trench each morning and huddled over her work-benches the rest of the day. Tabari and Cullinane ratified Vered's findings by inspecting the thin layers of rubble in which the sherds were found; the tell contained seventy-one feet of accumulation laid down during eleven thousand years, and that meant less than eight inches added per century. But recent levels like the Crusader castle had accounted for much of the deposit, so that in the pre-Christian periods whole groups of centuries might be represented by only two inches of silt, but these two inches could contain records as easy to read as if they had been reported in the morning newspaper. It was hard to believe, unless one saw a thin band of soot extending uniformly from Trench A across to B, how the burning of the town—either by enemies or accident—could have left a record that was unmistakable; and when good samples of soot were found, say, a charred deer's horn or a seashell brought to Makor by some ancient trader from Akko, they could be airmailed to Chicago or Stockholm, where scientists could analyze the carbon of the charring and wire back the date when the fire had taken place.

For example, when Tabari found the two pieces of pottery marking Level XIII, he also came up with a good deposit of burned ram's horn near them, laid down as part of a general conflagration which must have destroyed Makor at that time. Cullinane, listened to the deduction of Vered Bar-El, made his sketch and put down his estimate of the probable date. But at the same time he airmailed carbon samples to the laboratories in America and Sweden and awaited confirmation or alteration of his guess.

Throughout the history of life on earth, two kinds of carbon have been available to all living things. Carbon-12 is the normal, stable substance familiar to anyone who has cleaned a stove or burned dead leaves in autumn, and each living object contains substantial amounts of this carbon. Plants get it through photosynthesis, animals through the plants they eat. Carbon-14, on the other hand, is an unstable, radioactive substance heavier than normal carbon. It is formed in the earth's upper atmosphere and finally mixes itself into our atmosphere in the almost imperceptible ratio of one-trillionth of a part of Carbon-14 to one part of Carbon-12. But even such a slight trace of the heavier carbon is detectable in all things that live or have ever lived; as long as they continue to live they absorb Carbon-14, but at the moment of death they absorb no more.

Carbon-14 would be of no significance to archaeologists except for a peculiarity which makes it invaluable. At the death of a living organism, its Carbon-14 content, which is non-stable, begins to disintegrate, losing half its remaining total every 5,500 years. For example, if the ram's horn that Jemail Tabari dug out of the fire-level at Makor were found to retain only half its Carbon-14, it could be dated roughly 3535 B.C.E., plus or minus 330 years, so that the ram which grew the horn must have died sometime between the years 3205 B.C.E. and 3865 B.C.E.

LEVEL XIII
ABOUT 1400 B.C.E.

SCALE 1:6

CLAY POTS

Laboratories determine the Carbon-14 content in a sample by counting the number of Carbon-14 disintegrations per minute per gram of ordinary carbon. Living samples give off 15.3 such disintegrations a minute; those that died in 3535 B.C.E. give off half that number, or 7.65; and those that died in 9035 B.C.E. yield 3.83 disintegrations per minute. Unfortunately, material that died more than 50,000 years ago yields such a diminished rate that present instruments cannot accurately measure the disintegrations, so that dates earlier than 70,000 are largely guesswork, although a similar substance, potassium argon, promises to yield reliable dates back to two million years. Cullinane had submitted his carbon samples to two different laboratories—he had more than forty to choose from, in countries from Australia to Switzerland—so that one result could be checked against the other.

While the archaeologists waited for reports to confirm their guess of 1400 B.C.E. for Level XIII, the harvest season approached and the kibbutz works committee began to recall their people for that job, so that one by one the rugged diggers were taken from the tell. They hated to go, and General Reich's daughter protested at being forced to leave the dig just as the intellectually challenging sequences were being brought to the surface, but the girls were needed and Dr Cullinane assured them that next spring they could have their jobs back, and for many years into the future. He watched with regret as their lovely bare legs tramped out of his office to head for the gleaning as Jewish maidens had done at Makor thousands of years before. 'They're wonderful kids,' he sighed, and the dig stumbled into inaction because of no help.

Dr Eliav solved the work problem one morning by announcing that he had made contact with the Jewish Agency and they had agreed to allocate from the next immigrant ship twenty-four Moroccans to Kibbutz Makor for work at the dig. 'They'll be pretty rough diamonds,' Eliav warned. 'No English. No education.'

'If they speak Arabic I can handle them' Tabari assured the leaders, and two nights later the team went to greet the large ship that plied monotonously back and forth across the Mediterranean hauling Jewish immigrants to Israel.

'Before we go aboard,' Eliav summarized, 'I've got to warn you again that these aren't the handsome young immigrants that you accept in America, Cullinane. These are the dregs of the world, but in two years we'll make first-class citizens of them.' Cullinane said he knew, but if he had realized how intellectually unprepared he was for the cargo of this ship, he would have stayed at the tell and allowed Tabari to choose the new hands.

For the ship that came to Israel that night brought with it not the kind of people that a nation would consciously select, not the clean nor the healthy nor the educated. From Tunisia came a pitiful family of four, stricken with glaucoma and the effects of malnutrition. From Bulgaria came three old women so broken they were no longer of use to anyone; the communists had allowed them to escape, for they had no money to buy bread nor skills to earn it nor teeth to eat it with. From France came not high school graduates with productive years ahead of them, but two tragic couples, old and abandoned by their children, with only the empty days to look forward to, not hope. And from the shores of Morocco, outcast by towns in which they had lived for countless generations, came frightened, dirty, pathetic Jews, illiterate, often crippled with disease and vacant-eyed.

'Jesus Christ!' Cullinane whispered. 'Are these the newcomers?' He was decent enough not to worry about himself first—although he was appalled at the prospect of trying to dig with such assistance—but he did worry about Israel. How can a nation build itself strong with such material? he asked himself. It was a shocking experience, one that cut to the heart of his sensibilities: My great-grandfather must have looked like this when he came half-starved from Ireland. He thought of the scrawny Italians that had come to New York and the Chinese to San Francisco, and he began to develop that sense of companionship with Israel that comes very slowly to a Gentile: it was building itself of the same human material that America was developed upon; and suddenly he felt a little weak. Why were these people seeking a new home coming to Israel and not to America? Where had the American dream faltered? And he saw that Israel was right; it was taking people—any people—as America had once done; so that in fifty years the bright new ideas of the world would come probably from Israel and no longer from a tired America.

Nevertheless, he was startled to find that exactly half the twenty-four people promised him were comprised of Yusuf Ohana and his family from Morocco. Yusuf looked to be seventy, but he had three wives, one apparently his age, one forty and one twenty. The latter was pregnant, and the others had eight children between them. When Yusuf moved—a tall, thin man in dirty robes and turban—it was as if a perpetual dust storm moved with him, for he was obeyed. A Jew who came from a small town near the Atlas Mountains, he had lived as if he were still in Old Testament times, and his word was patriarchal law. Tabari greeted him in a mixture of French and Arabic, explaining that he and his family would be working for Dr Cullinane until the kibbitz found permanent homes and work for them. Yusuf nodded, and with a grand gesture of his hands over the members of his brood, said that he would see that they worked well, but Cullinane noticed that he and his first wife were nearly blind. What can they do? he thought.

The other twelve newcomers were from various nations, and when they were all in the special bus that would carry them to Makor, the man from the Jewish Agency passed among them, handing them parcels of food, Israeli citizenship papers, unemployment insurance for a year, rent money, health insurance, and cellophane bags of candy for the children. In Arabic he shouted, 'You are now citizens of Israel, and you are free to vote and criticize the government.' At the door he bowed and left.

Cullinane sat up late that night. Eliav said, 'We'll accept any Jew from any part of the world in whatever condition he finds himself.'

'We did it,' Cullinane said, 'and we built a great nation.'

'Critics complain that the old people, like Yusuf and his first wife, or the three Bulgarian women ... They say they'll never be productive. But I've always maintained ...'

'Eliav was instrumental in helping form the policy,' Vered explained proudly.

'I look at productivity from an entirely different point of view,' Eliav said slowly, polishing his pipe with his palms. 'I say that it takes four thousand people to make a town. You've got to have four thousand human beings to fill the places, as it were. They don't all have to be in their middle working years. It's easy to see that some have to be children to keep the town going in the future. But some should also be old people to fill the places where wisdom is needed, or to act as baby-sitters, or just to sit around as human beings.' He looked intently at Cullinane and said, 'How much better the world would be tonight if that boat had been landing at New York. Symphonies and cathedrals are not built by the children of upper-middle-class families. They're built by the units we saw tonight. You need these people very much, Cullinane, but we can't spare them and you're too frightened to take them.'

The next few days at the dig were historic, in a horrible sort of way. Yusuf and his family of twelve were not only illiterate; they were also il-sociate—if there were such a word: they knew nothing of organized life. They had never seen a privy or a public shower or an organized dining hall, or an archaeologist's pick or a hoe, and life would have degenerated both at the kibbutz and at the dig had not Jemail Tabari stepped forth as the sponsor of the newcomers. He planted six pieces of pottery in the dust and showed Yusuf how they were to be dug out; but this was an error, because Yusuf himself intended doing no work. He showed his three wives how to do the digging and then yelled at his eight children. Patiently Tabari explained that unless Yusuf dug and dug right, he would damned well not eat, and the old patriarch went to work. By luck, it was he who dug out from Trench A the first substantial find, a laughing, lovely little clay goddess, a divinity sacred to pregnant women and farmers who brooded about fertility. It was Astarte, the Canaanite goddess, and she reminded Cullinane of a little statue of Vered Bar-El.

'Congratulations!' He called to Yusuf in Arabic, and on the spot he authorized Tabari to pay the old man a bonus; and that night Yusuf was allowed to carry the goddess to the kibbutz dining hall, where he showed it proudly to the young people who had been working on the tell, and one of the boys shouted, 'It looks like Dr Bar-El!' The naked little goddess with circular breasts was brought to Vered's table, and she said quietly, 'I'm sure I don't know how he could tell!' So the boy tore his handkerchief and made an improvised bikini and halter for the clay goddess, and the antique little girl did look amazingly like the archaeologist, and probably for the same reason: that each represented the ultimate female quality, the sexual desire, the urge toward creation that can sometimes become so tangible in a bikini or in the work of a long-forgotten artist in clay. Then came the cable from Stockholm:

CULLINANE STOP YOUR LEVEL III STOP 1380 B.C.E. PLUS-OR-MINUS 105 ROYAL INSTITUT

Within a few days the laboratory in Chicago reported '1420 B.C.E. plus-or-minus 110,' and Cullinane felt that if that was the date for the two clay pots, he probably ought to date his Astarte at about 2200 B.C.E.

LEVEL XIV
ABOUT 2000 B.C.E.

SCALE 1:3

CLAY FIGURE OF THE
GODDESS ASTARTE

J. C.

He permitted the make-believe bikini to remain on the little goddess, and each day as he looked at her, standing impudently on his desk, urging him to fertilize his land and have children, he thought more hungrily of Vered Bar-El. It was a serious mistake that she was making, not marrying him, for it was becoming quite clear that she ought not to marry Dr Eliav. Between those two there was a lack of passion, an obvious lack of commitment, and he felt a desire to restate his proposal. He was stopped from doing so by a cable from Zodman in Chicago asking him to fly immediately to that city, bringing with him if humanly possible the Candlestick of Death. A meeting of the sponsors of the Biblical Museum was being held, etc., etc.

'I'm damned if I'll go.' he growled, and he summoned a staff meeting to support him.

'As a matter of fact,' Eliav said, 'I don't think you should. Zodman's just looking for some cheap publicity.'

'I'll cable that I can't do it,' the Irishman snapped.

'Wait a minute!' Tabari interrupted. 'Remember Uncle Mahmoud's first rule: "The man that pays the bills, keep him happy."'

'If it were anything but that damned candlestick. No!'

'John,' the Arab repeated persuasively, 'you certainly shouldn't prostitute yourself. But I've never seen Chicago. I could take that menorah and in my sheikh's costume I could give such a lecture . . .'

Vered began to laugh at the prospect of Jamail Tabari's knocking the women of Chicago dead.

'I can't spare you either,' Cullinane said. 'Next year, all right, because you might do something for Chicago. But with these Moroccans . . .'

'You haven't heard my other suggestion,' Jemail volunteered. 'Send Vered.'

'Would you go?' Cullinane asked.

'I'd like to see what America's like,' she said.

'She wouldn't have the same effect that I'd have,' Tabari said. 'A Jew never does, compared to an Arab. But she is . . .' He blew at the bikini on the little clay goddess.

'We're just getting into the pottery phase . . .' Cullinane objected.

'Keep Paul Zodman happy,' Tabari warned, and he drafted a cable which said that in Cullinane's absence in Jerusalem he was making bold to point out that the director could not possibly leave, but that if all expenses were paid, Dr Vered Bar-El and the Candlestick of Death . . .

The next morning one of Yusuf's wives found in Trench B two small stones; she took them to Dr Eliav, suggesting that they might be of interest, and they were of such construction that the tall archaeologist halted all work and got the professionals down into the trench. The two stones were flints, not more than an inch long and sharpened to a glistening sheen on one serrated edge. The opposite edge was quite thick, so that the flint could not have been used either as a spearhead or as a hand knife; yet the two unimpressive flints caused as much excitement as anything so far found on the tell, and the team dug through the dust for some minutes before Vered cried, 'I've another! It matches!' And when placed beside the first two, it did. The hunt was intensified, but an hour passed before Yusuf himself turned up a fourth flint, after which no more were found.

The archaeologists placed the flints in approximately the positions in which they had fallen, and the records were made. They were then hurried to the washing room, where Vered herself polished them and laid them out on Dr Cullinane's desk, where he sketched them.

They had once formed the cutting edge of a sickle, these four bits of flint, and they went back in history to the first mornings when men and women, like the

LEVEL XV
ABOUT 10,000 B.C.E.

SCALE 1:8

SCALE 1:2

FLINT SICKLE

young Jews of Kibbutz Makor, started forth to harvest their grain. This instrument, saved from the dust, had been one of the earliest agricultural devices ever used by man; it was older than bronze, much older than iron; it came before the creatures of the farmyard or the taming of the camel. It was so old, so incredibly old, an invention of such wonder–much greater than a Frigidaire or an Opel automobile–and its flanks were so polished and luminous from the stalks of grain that had passed over it, that it had been cherished as one of the differences between the man who owned it and the animals he hunted. For the man who had made this instrument, this marvelous, soaring invention, was no longer required to move from place to place in search of food. In some mysterious way he had made grain grow where he wanted it, and with this sickle to aid him, had been able to settle down and start a village that had become in time the site of a Roman city, of a fine Byzantine church and a towering Crusader's castle. With reverence the archaeologists looked at the four matching stones, and three mornings later, at both Trench A and Trench B, the Moroccans came down to the bedrock of the tell. Beneath it there was nothing; the long dig ended.

That night Vered Bar-El packed her grips for Chicago, but when she had done so she was inspired to go onto the tell for a last sight of the mound and the living rock which the picks and hoes had uncovered. She was scraping the latter with the heel of her shoe when she became aware that someone had followed her from the main building, and she called, 'Eliav?' but it was Cullinane, and with what could only be called a sense of relief she said, 'Oh, it's you, John.' As he walked down the trench she added, 'It's a little disappointing . . . coming to the bedrock.'

'In a way,' he agreed. 'I'd sort of hoped it would go on down . . . maybe to caves like the Carmel. A hundred thousand years of something like that.'

'What we have is perfect . . . in its way,' she said in a consoling voice.

'We can make it so,' he said. 'In the next nine years we'll convert this tell into a little jewel. We'll excavate the three walls, all around. Leave them standing and go for the best that's inside.' He stopped. 'Will you and Eliav be with me for those nine years?'

'Of course.'

'I've had a premonition recently that you might not be.'

'How silly,' she said in Hebrew. The unexpected shift of language caught Cullinane off guard, as if she had winked at him or blown a kiss.

'Because if you weren't to be here . . .' he began.

To her own surprise she reached up and put her small hands about his face. 'John,' she whispered, 'you've become very dear to me,' She spoke in English, then raised her face until it was close to his. 'Very dear,' she said in Hebrew.

He kissed her passionately, as if he knew that this was the last time he would ever stand with her in the Galilean night, and for one brief moment she did not resist but remained close to him, like a little Astarte whose responsibility it was to remind men of love. Then, as if she were pushing away part of her life which had become too precious to be carried carelessly, she forced her hands against his chest and slowly the Catholic and the Jew parted, like comets which had been drawn to each other momentarily but which now must seek their separate orbits.

'I told you the truth when I said I could never marry you.'

'But every day I watch you, I'm more convinced that you'll never marry Eliav.' He paused, then asked, 'What's wrong between you.'

'We're caught in forces . . .'

'Has it something to do with Teddy Reich?'

She gasped, then asked, 'Why do you ask that?'

'Because that night when Reich talked with Eliav . . . you watched them as if you were a jealous schoolgirl.'

She started to speak, stopped, then said in Hebrew, 'Don't worry about me, John. I need to visit America . . . for time . . . to think things out.'

'While you're in Chicago you will think of what it would be like . . . living with me there?'

She was tempted to kiss him then, to throw her life completely into his, for she had come to know him as a sensitive man, honest in everything and capable of deep affection; but she would allow herself no gesture of submission. Slowly she turned away from him and left the bedrock of Israel to pack the gold menorah for the flight to America.

LEVEL XV

The Bee Eater

Found at Makor–four from a set of five sharpened flints
intended for fitting into a bone handle to form a sickle for
reaping grain. The fifth flint was pointed on the end for use in
the first position in the sickle. Original flint cores were found in
limestone deposits at seaside cliffs in 9831 B.C.E. Shaped in that
year and deposited at Makor during the summer of 9811 B.C.E.

There was a well and there was a rock. At the well men had been drinking sweet
water since that first remote day, about a million years ago, when an apelike
man had wandered up from Africa. The watering place had always been known
in memory if not in speech as Makor, the source.

The rock was a huge, flat expanse of granite with a high place in the middle
from which gentle slopes fell away on all sides. The rock was barren; it
contained absolutely nothing, not even a carving or a pile of stones to mark
some deity, for in those infinitely distant ages gods had not yet been called forth
by the hunger of men. It was simply a rock, large enough to form in the future
the foundation of a Canaanite town or the footing for a Crusaders' fort.

The rock stood higher than the well, but halfway down the slope that
separated it from the well appeared the entrance to a deep and commodious
cave and one spring morning nearly twelve thousand years ago a husky, bandy-
legged old man in a straggly beard and bearskin stood at the entrance to this cave
in the twilight of his life and laughed with gaiety as children ran at him with
roly-poly legs, leaping into his arms and squealing with animal joy. The old
man embraced the children, even though they were not his own, and roughed
them about when they tugged at his beard.

'Honey, honey!' they teased.

'You run away when bees fly past,' he chided, but when they repeated their
pleadings he promised, 'If I can find where the bees hide it I'll bring you some.'

He left the cave and walked down to the well, an old man at ease with the
forces that ruled his world. With his uncanny sense of land he knew the paths
through the forest and the choice spots where fawn deer came to graze. His
mind was still active and he could track the wild boar. He was as happy as a man
could be, more productive than most in his generation, a hunter who loved
animals and who consciously endeavored to bring pleasure to men. Anyone
looking at his witty eyes and bandy legs experienced a sense of merriment.

Three years later, when all that he had attempted had prospered, when his
old wife had found strange peace and understanding, when his son was well
begun in life and his daughter happily pregnant, he would stand alone in a
thicket of thorn and pistachio, trembling with a mighty terror that he could not
even describe. It is with this man's experiences in these three culminating years
that the remembered history of Makor begins.

When he reached the well Ur bent down and splashed cool water onto his face. Taking a wooden cup which had been laboriously carved by flints, he drank the water and was about to put the cup aside when he saw his face looming up from the well. It was hairy, surrounded by a circle formed of hunched shoulders, small tight ears and drooping brow, but it was marked by two blue eyes that shone like little stars.

The light reflecting from his eyes fascinated Ur and he began to laugh, but as he did so a tiny pebble, scarce bigger than a bee's wing, tumbled into the well and set up ripples which distorted the image of his face, and something in the way the water moved, taking his eyes and ears and mouth with it, frightened Ur and he drew back. But as quickly as the ripples had passed, the water restored his features to their proper place and he was once more Ur. He shivered to think that some unknown power could alter the essential *he* and smear it into a distorted form. Then he smiled at himself but he was not so free and happy as before.

Above his head he heard a soft whisper. It was surely a bee, and he dropped the wooden cup, staring here and there at the sky, and like the hunter he was he spotted the insect and saw its direction down the wadi in which, when rains accumulated, a muddy river roared briefly on its way to the sea. There were dead trees in the wadi where bees kept their homes, and Ur sprang to his feet, chasing after the insect, for if he could keep pace with it he might find his next cache of honey. With long-practiced eyes he followed the elusive bee until he was certain he had spotted the hidden tree. Motionless he sat on the ground, and after a while he saw where bees were flying in and out with whatever it was they stole from flowers to make their honey.

Ur's lips began to drool. Slapping his face, to prepare it for the pain ahead, he pawed his powerful feet in the sand like an animal about to fight, and with a sudden rush he sprang at the dead tree, climbed far up its side before any bees detected him, and with strong hands he began tearing away rotted portions of the trunk. The passionate sound of bees springing into action assured him that there was honey to be found, so before the bees could swarm to drive him from their treasure, he tore down into the heart of the tree until he felt the honeycomb.

Then the bees struck! Fifty, a hundred flew at his face, covered his hands, tried to find his soft parts. They stung him and died with their bodies distended. But his numb hands kept tearing at the comb, bringing out luscious chunks which he threw to the ground below. Finally, when he could scarcely see, he slid down from the tree, killing hundreds of bees as he fell. Only then did he start brushing the fiery creatures from his face, and when this was accomplished he took off the animal skin he was wearing and piled the chunks of honeycomb into it. Then, as quickly as his bandy legs would carry him, he ran from the wadi, smarting throughout his body with an exquisite pain.

When he reached the well his face had swelled like a mid-month moon and his eyes could hardly see, but a child from the cave spotted him coming and shouted, 'Ur found honey!' And he was besieged by children, who led him up from the well to the cave, pointing at his distorted face and screaming with joy. With brave hands they touched his sack of honey and their mouths watered. But when Ur reached the safety of the cave and opened his sack to show the luscious hoard he had stolen from the bees, he found trapped in the honeycomb more than a dozen insects, and with his thick, hard fingers he picked them out and set them free.

'Make us more honey,' he told each one. 'And do it in the same tree.'

The cave into which Ur retreated had only a narrow opening, perhaps twice the height of a man, but inside it developed into a dark, capacious room with space for many people. At the far end it narrowed into a tunnel which penetrated the earth beneath the rock, and in the ceiling there was a small opening which permitted smoke to escape, while from somewhere deep within the tunnel other fresh air entered, so that the cave was comfortable. In the center a smoldering fire was maintained, which women could feed with extra wood when a flame for cooking was required, and along the smoke-stained walls hung spears and clubs, animal skins drying for later use and baskets containing grain. It was a warm and comfortable refuge, a tight cocoon made of rock, and for more than two hundred thousand years it had provided shelter for the manlike creatures who had from time to time crept into it.

In Ur's day six associated families lived there permanently, brothers of one group who had married sisters from another, strangers who had wandered in to marry extra daughters, all members of a common stock and all working together at the gathering of food and the maintenance of the community fire. The men were hunters, and they ranged far in search of animals, killing them with arrows and spears of high efficiency. They were no longer dumb brutes plodding after primordial beasts and stoning them to death; they were skilled huntsmen who took no unnecessary risks. Their women tanned the hides of the dead animals, making an excellent leather, and spent long hours garnering the wild grain that grew haphazardly in many fields. Holding a skin beneath the brown and ripened stalks, they would beat the heads with sticks and thus collect the precious grains which they ground in stone hand mills, making a flour that would keep throughout the winter. As for the children, they played upon the flat rock, tumbling and grunting like a pack of bear cubs delighted with the sun. And at night all gathered in the great cave, beside the flickering fire, as men recounted what they had done that day and women sewed.

When Ur appeared with his honey normal activity in the cave stopped and the inhabitants fell like a pack of animals upon the rare treasure, for honey was the only sweet the cave men knew, and for a few moments the smoke-stained room was filled with grunts and growls as each hand grabbed for its chance share of the sweet, waxy stuff. Children had a hard time getting their portion, but Ur helped them wedge their way among the elders, and their squeals of pleasure proved that their small hands were reaching the board. Two lesser hunters were absent trying to find deer, but no one thought to save them a share of the honey; and before long Ur's bearskin was picked clean and people were spitting the wax into a bowl, where it would be melted down to treat the sinews used in sewing. And now that the honey was gone Ur could sit on a large stone while his wife put cold water on his puffed face and combed dead bees from his beard.

The Family of Ur formed a closer group than some. It was led by the bandy-legged old man who, having lived for thirty-two seasons, was now approaching the time when he must die. His elderly wife had survived thirty; she looked after the children, a son whose distaste for hunting worried Ur, and a lively daughter who, having lived through eleven seasons, was almost old enough to have a man for herself, except that she favoured none in the cave and no stranger had yet come by in search of her. It was her mother's hope that when one did, he would want to live with the family and in time take Ur's place.

Old Ur was a man whom the cave people respected. He was five feet, four inches tall and weighed about a hundred and seventy pounds, a stocky figure with the huge shoulders that characterized his species. Above his beard gleamed his bright blue eyes and the ruddy cheeks that liked to wrinkle upward in a grin. He laughed a lot, and now that his own children were grown, played with the offspring of his neighbors as the little round ones scrambled across the rock in sunlight. Unlike the brutish creatures who had originally wandered to the well from Africa, Ur walked erect, lacked heavy bones over his eyes, and had a smooth skin that produced no great amount of body hair. He had acquired full dexterity in the use of his relatively small hands, although he never understood why his right hand remained more agile than his left and did most of the work and all of the throwing. His skin had a peculiarity which surprised him: under his bearskin it remained a pinkish white, but where the sun touched, the coloring became dark brown, so that from a distance Ur and his partners looked like black men. In the last forty thousand years his throat, his tongue and lower jaw had been much modulated and were now flexible instruments adapted to the articulation of language; he had a vocabulary of more than six hundred words, some of which comprised three syllables and a few four or five. Every hundred years or so new experiences would accumulate, requiring the invention of new words; but this was a slow process, for Ur and his neighbors were extremely cautious and the utterance of a new word might upset the balance of nature and call into being strange forces that were better left at rest, so words tended to be restricted to the same sounds that time had made familiar. There was one other use to which the flexible voice of man could now be put, although not many used it in this capacity: men could sing–their women in particular–and sometimes in the early morning Ur would hear his wife and daughter making pleasant noises, using no words or made-up ones like 'traaaaaaa' or 'sehhhhhhhhh.'

That night, when the two hunters returned with no deer and the fires were banked, when the roly-poly children slept like bear cubs and a cool breeze issued from the tunnel, the community sat in shadows as Ur with his puffed eyes explained how he had found the honey: 'From the well Makor, from the depths of the water a single bee rose and called to me, "Follow, follow!" I ran through the wadi till the sun was tired. Over rocks and trees where the deer feed and where the wild boar comes at night I ran. You would have fallen with cracked lungs, but I ran on, for the bee kept calling, "Follow, follow!" And so I came to the hidden tree, which all have searched for but none found.' He told how he had climbed the dead trunk and, fearless of the attacking bees, had torn into the heart of their treasure, and as he spoke of the sweet burden that had filled his bearskin he threw back his head and cried in the ecstasy of the hunter who shares the spirit of the animals he tracks:

> 'Burning with pain, I brought the honey home.
> My eyes closed with pain, I followed the voice.
> For the bee flew before me singing, "Ur found our honey.
> Ur, the great hunter, was not afraid.
> I will lead him home, back to his cave.
> Back to the well I will lead the brave hunter.'

No sound came from the cave except the quiet sleeping of the children, and all could hear the voice of the bee leading the hunter home.

Ur would probably have lived out his life hunting animals and bees and telling about it at the fire if he had married an ordinary woman, but his wife did not come from the cave. Years ago, when Ur was just beginning to run with the hunters, his father had led an expedition into lands east of the Whispering Sea and had there come upon a strange people with whom he had naturally engaged in battle. The cave men were triumphant, but after the slaughter they found that one twelve-year-old girl was living and Ur's father had brought her home.

She knew nothing of caves; the dark interior frightened her and she supposed when she was dragged inside, that it was to her death. Later, when she learned to speak the language of the cave, she explained to Ur that in her land families did not live underground; but he could not imagine how they did live, for her explanation of how men could use stones and walls of wood to build their own caves above the ground made no sense to him. 'It's a better way to live,' she assured him, but he could not understand.

Nor did he understand, when this strange girl became his wife, her preoccupation with gathering wild grain; but she knew that unlike raw meat it could be stored throughout the winter, and she would wander considerable distances to find the best stands of cereal. One day in an open field east of the great rock she found an accidental accumulation of wild grain, and she brought Ur to the spot showing him how much easier it was to reap a concentration of stalks instead of searching far and wide, and she asked her husband, 'Why don't we make the grain grow where we can watch it? For if we do, when autumn comes it will ripen in fields that we remember.' Ur, knowing that if the wild grain had wanted to grow at man's command it would have done so, ridiculed his wife and refused to help her dig out the grass and move it closer to the well. His wife, bending over the stalks, looked up and said, 'My father made the grain grow where he wanted it to grow,' but Ur rejected the concept: 'He also built caves on top of the ground.' And with amused tolerance he went off to hunt.

Nevertheless, for the first fifteen years of their married life, Ur's wife went out of the cave in all seasons trying fruitlessly to tame the wild wheat, but each year it was killed either by drought or flood or too much winter or by wild boars rampaging through the field and rooting up all things with their tusks; and it seemed evident to Ur that the wild grass did not intend to grow where his stubborn woman dictated. In the meantime, the other families who shared the cave went about their business of tracking down the wild wheat where it chanced to grow; and they ate well. But two years ago Ur's wife had found along the far banks of the wadi some young shoots of a vigorous emmer wheat and these she chanced to place in proper soil along one edge of the great sloping rock, so that throughout the dry season enough moisture drained off the rock to keep the grain alive; and although its yield in edible wheat was disappointing, the grain lived as she had directed, and in the spring it reappeared where it was wanted. Ur's wife told her family, 'We'll see if we can make the wheat grow along the edges of the rock, because I think that in those places the soil helps us.' And as the determined woman had foreseen, here her wild grain prospered.

When her daughter had reached her eleventh year, Ur's wife satisfied herself that she could make the emmer wheat grow where she wished and she felt it necessary to reopen another problem which she had been pondering for some time, hesitant about discussing it with her husband. Now, without warning, she told him, 'We ought to leave the cave and live by the well. There we can watch our grain.' The bandy-legged hunter looked at her as if she were a child trying to steal his honey.

'Men should live together,' he said. 'Around the fire at night. Telling stories when the hunt has ended.'

'Why are you always so sure that your way is better?' she asked, and Ur was about to mock the question when he saw her lively face. She was a delicate woman with long black hair and whenever Ur looked at her small, determined chin he could remember the joy he had known with her when they used to lie in moonlight on the rock, staring upwards at the stars. As a wife she had been hard-working and as a mother, tender and responsive. But she had always possessed strong ideas—it had taken Ur's father a hard fight to kill her family—so he did not laugh when she repeated her question, 'Why is your way better?'

'Where would we live . . . if we did leave the cave?' he asked defensively.

'In a house,' she said. 'With its own roof and walls.'

'The first storm would blow it down,' he predicted.

'Storms didn't blow down my father's house.'

'You don't have storms over there the way we have over here,' he said, and that ended the discussion. He was therefore surprised some mornings later, as he was leading his hunters forth to track gray deer, to see his wife and son working at the flat area near the well.

'What are you doing with those rocks?' he asked.

'Building a house,' his wife replied, and he saw that she had laid out a circle of rocks some fourteen feet across. Shrugging his shoulders at her obstinacy, he went off to the swamp with his hunters, but at dusk when he returned to the cave he could see at the well a substantial pile of rocks and the beginnings of a solid structure. Four days later he came back from a hunting trip to find his son erecting upon the wall of rocks a palisade of tree trunks cut from the wadi.

'Now what are you doing?' Ur asked.

And his son replied, with words that put him into formal opposition to his father, 'If the trees give us walls, we should use them.' And Ur saw that his wife was bringing rushes from the wadi and reeds to be woven into a tightly matted roof, under which the family would find protection from the sun. And what he saw Ur did not like.

At nightfall he led his family back to the cave, where he recounted in vivid phrases the story of his hunt, but he ended the narration much sooner than usual, for he was worried about what his wife and son were doing. He loved this cave, so cool and convenient to the well. It bred lice, to be sure, and it smelled, but the fire was warm and the companionship a thing to be cherished. For the past seventy thousand years the cave had been continuously occupied by Ur's ancestors, one generation after the other, leaving behind them brief mementos of their short and ugly lives. Ur could remember as a boy, in that far corner over there, finding a long-forgotten skeleton encased in hard rock which had formed when rainwater seeped down over the limestone, and later, back in the narrow part of the tunnel, he had come upon a hand axe, adroitly chipped from a core of flint by some brutish, stooped figure more than two hundred thousand years ago. On fleeting occasions in his life Ur had caught the inner spirit of the cave, that closed community which embraced its members and excluded all others. The cave lent strength to those who lived within it and the preposterous idea of his wife and son, to build a separate house for one small family by the well, was instinctively repugnant to him. Men should live together, smelling each other and bringing honey home to all.

He especially liked the moment when a dozen men surged out of the cave bent on hunting, twelve men guided by a single will, and that will most often his. He could remember how, as a boy, he had surprised the older hunters with his unusual feeling for the land and his ability to predict where animals would take cover. 'Come along and show us where the lion is hiding,' they had often called, and he had led them westward as far as the Roaring Sea, clinging to the lion's spoor until he could point to a thicket, saying, 'He's in there.' In the opposite direction he had scouted paths leading to the Whispering Sea and had taken his men along these paths in search of deer, who grew panicky when Ur and his team followed their trail, smelling them out with a canniness that was frightening. It was no uncommon thing, when the men of Ur's cave spotted the track of a lion, for them to maintain the chase for three days or even four, driving the beast at last to cover where they could assault him with their spears and arrows.

But the finest part of any hunt came when they struck the spoor of a wild boar and tracked it to the vast wilderness south of the wadi, for then the cave men were required to plunge into the mysterious swampy area where sharp-thorned vines clutched at them and sucking mud tried to grasp their ankles. For several days the team of hunters would move cautiously through the swamps, marking their way as they went, until at last, in moments of blazing excitement, they would rout out the monstrous beast, the wild boar weighing as much as six hundred pounds, with flashing tusks and cruel visage, and they would harry it to death, minding always those scimitar-like weapons which could cut down a man or impale him and send him shrieking into the air. For men like Ur the final moments of a boar hunt were the ultimate experience, and he was proud that in the middle years of his life, from twenty to twenty-four, he had often served as captain of his hunters, directing them to move thus and so in the last stages of the fight.

But now, as the house by the well grew to completion, Ur became aware that when it was finished he would be expected to move from the cave and live in the separated house, subject to storms and loneliness and wind. It was not a commodious house his wife and son were building, nor was it completely rainproof. It was susceptible to fire, and winds easily penetrated the walls; but it had enormous advantages over a cave; it was better ventilated and was therefore healthful; it could be moved or added to as occasion necessitated; and it could be placed so that its owner might watch his fields and stay close to his well. But the greatest advantage came in an area which the old man could not have foreseen: In the cave Ur's ancestors had lived much like animals. They had been forced to live where the cave was and within the space it provided; they were its prisoners both in acting and thinking, and in their older years they were apt to be killed or starved to death because younger families required the cave. But with the building of the self-contained house Ur would become the master and the house would be his servant. He would be forced to engage in new ways of thinking, whether he wanted to or not.

When the house was finished Ur reluctantly assembled his family in the cave, where many were inclined to laugh at him for his fatuous venture but refrained from doing so because of his reputation as a hunter. He grabbed his four spears, his two animal skins, a bowl and a stone hammer and started for the narrow exit, but sensing that this was his farewell to a way of life, he stopped to look once more at the grimy walls that had protected him from birth, and on the opposite side of the cave he could see the dark tunnel reaching far back into darkness. Turning his face toward the light, he passed through the exit and moved rapidly down the path to the well. There he threw his spears against the wall and sat for a long time looking at the clean white trunks of the trees that formed the wall. To him they looked most alien and uninviting.

The family had not been in the house long when Ur's son discovered that the springtime planting of wheat need not be left to the chance scatter of autumn grains. By holding back some of the harvest and keeping it dry in a pouch of deerskin, the grains could be planted purposefully in the spring and the wheat could be made to grow exactly where and when it was needed, and with this discovery the Family of Ur moved close to the beginnings of a self-sufficient society. They did not know it, but if a food supply could be insured, the speed of change would be unbelievable: within a few thousand years cities would be feasible and civilizations too. Men would be able to plan ahead and allocate specialized jobs to each other. They would find it profitable to construct roads to speed the movement of food and to devise a money system for convenient payments. The whole intricate structure of an interlocking society became practical the moment Ur's son mastered his wild grains.

It was Ur's wife who first appreciated the change immanent in her son's discovery. It was an autumn day, a glowing time of gold and falling leaves, and she stood on the rock watching her husband return from the swamps, helping to lug a great boar to the rock where it would be divided, and she heard the chanting of the men:

> 'Ur led us to the swamps where the soft sand bites
> He took us to the darkness where the birds hide.
> Ur caught the gleaming eyes of the boar in darkness.
> It was he who shouted, "Now! Now!"'

It was a pleasing chant, gratifying to the wife whose husband it memorialized, but as she watched the hunters approach the rock she saw them outlined for a moment against the ripened wheat and realized for the first time that in the future, men like Ur would not go venturing into the swamp like excited boys but would stay closer to home, guarding the wheat; and a sense of sadness possessed her, so that she wanted to leave the triumphant men and weep for their lost simplicity. She saw their whole way of life modified by the taming of a thin stalk of wild grass. She saw them leaving the oak forests where the deer roamed, and going no more to the dark swamp where the wild boars hid. She had loved her brave young mate in the days when he led the hunters, and she felt for him the pain which he had not yet discovered for himself.

And barely had she recognized this change than she became aware of an even more disturbing problem evoked by the grain, one too powerful for her to formulate in words. As her development of the wild wheat had proved, she was both courageous and perceptive and now she began to wonder about the unseen forces that influence men, and just as she had been quick to sense the impact of cultivation upon men like Ur, so she was the first to perceive, no matter how incompletely, its relation to forces greater even than the hunters.

Through ten thousand centuries the animal-like people living near this well had worked out a plodding but viable relationship with the forces that surrounded them. Throughout the alternating ages of ice and great heat they had learned to live with these forces. They did not understand them, nor their interrelationships; they did not even give them names, but they knew them intimately as the source of supreme power. The proper balance between life and death had been painfully ascertained and all were anxious that it not be disturbed. At night, when towering storms thundered over the Carmel mountains to the south, it was apparent that the spirit of the storm was angry with man and wished to destroy him. How else could one explain the blinding flash of lightning that tore a tree in half and set fire to forests? How else describe to a neighbor the unexpected cloudburst that struck the wadi, washing away all things before it? How otherwise could an immovable boulder, many times larger than a man, suddenly run with the flood and strike that man? Obviously the spirit of storm was angered by something men had done and was personally seeking revenge.

The same behavior could be noticed regarding water. Sometimes it loved men and served them with life; at other times it grew angry and stayed away until men nearly perished. Even the water in the well behaved this way, retreating in petulance deep to some unknown cave until men came close to dying, then surging back with joy and kisses for the gasping children. The air, the spirit of death, the burning wind from the south, the spirit that opened the body of a woman so that new men could be born, the tree that gave fruit or withheld it–everything of importance in nature had a will of its own that operated in favor of man or against him.

No ritual had yet been established for placating these conflicting forces. In those years no precious children were sacrificed to the god of the storm in order to win his favor, nor was the hideous wild boar given human blood in order to assuage his enmity. There were no altars to the rain, nor temples to the god of day who regularly conquered night. Men had not yet discovered that the forces of the world could be propitiated by conscious acts of subservience; many times in the preceding two hundred thousand years the cave had been deserted when food supplies in the region diminished, but when the animals returned the apelike men came back too. They were attentive to the commands of nature, and they watched for omens, but they were not slaves either to the spirit of the storm or to its warning omens. It was known that the wild boar was malevolent, both in appearance and conduct, but it had not yet been dicovered that this malevolence could be counteracted by some conscious act of man. In other words, the embryonic beginnings of religion had not yet been conceived. The closest approach, perhaps, to a ritualized behavior came at the moment of death, when it was acknowledged that the dead man would require some food and protection in the unknown days ahead. He was therefore buried in a specified position, his head on a pillow of rock, accompanied by a few pots of food, a spear and some ornament he had loved, perhaps a carved shell or a necklace of beads.

Up to now the attitude of Ur's wife toward these matters had been clear-cut: the storm had a living spirit, as did water and wind and sky and each tree and every animal. Ur's wife was constantly aware of these spirits and she treated them with awe. Had she ever seen the spirits openly? She thought so: once when lightning struck close and she heard an extraordinary voice speaking in a hiss of sulphur. Prayer had not yet been invented, but she spoke confidently to that voice and it did not harm her. The great rock had a spirit, broad and generous, as did the fish in rivers, the flint that threw sparks, and the swamp and the trees therein. What her relation to these myriad spirits was she did not rightly know, but as a rough rule she said, 'They must not be offended.' Therefore she did not boast about having survived the storm, and told no one of her conversation with the spirit of lightning. She did not throw stones at animals or waste water, and when Ur's father died she buried him with her best carved bowls, Ur's good spear and a small string of stone beads.

But with the advent of cultivated wheat, the balance of nature was disturbed and she knew it. Before the first season ended it was obvious that success in planting depended upon sufficient rain and the faithful performance of the sun–not so much heat as to wither the young plants but enough to ripen the maturing heads–and she began to watch with apprehension any shift in the attitude of either the spirit of water or the spirit of sun. In the second and third seasons, when the area planted was considerable, she became actually terrified when rains were postponed, and she began speculating on what tangible things she might do to encourage the spirit of rain to send the coveted water. Finally she cried to the open sky, 'May the rain come!' and she begged for mercy; but even in doing so she assumed the I-It relationship which had always been maintained in the cave, for she conceived of the rain as an impersonal spirit, powerful but inanimate.

When she spoke of these growing fears to Ur, he laughed at her apprehension and said, 'If a man tracks the wild boar right, he finds him. If he fights him right, he wins.'

'Is it the same with grain?' she asked.

'Plant it right. Guard it from your new house, and it will bring food,' he promised her. But even as he spoke he remembered the day at the well when his image had been moved about and altered by some unknown force, and in this moment of recollection his new life began. His arrogance faded, and when his wife left him he wondered if killing a wild boar was as simple a thing as he had said. Once or twice in the past he had suspected that his hunters would not of themselves be able to subdue the formidable beast; there must be some mysterious force of nature assisting them, as if it too were afraid and allied itself with man to conquer the ugly beast. But the men from the cave called, 'We're ready,' and he left his fields to lead them toward the dark swamp.

So his wife turned with her questions to her son, and before she had finished formulating the problem she found that he had anticipated her. Sitting on a rock beside the grain field, the boy watched the hunters depart, then shared with his mother certain speculations that had troubled him: 'In the wadi we have many birds. The black-headed birds that sing in the evening, and those beautiful things with long bills and blue wings that nest in river banks to catch fish. And the crested larks walking about the field out there, searching for grains. And that swift bird, faster than all the rest . . .' He hesitated. 'The one that eats bees.' He pointed to where a bird somewhat larger than his hand, with long sharp beak, blue body and a profusion of bright colours on its wings and head, darted in and out among the trees. It was a magnificent bird, swooping in lovely arches through the sky, but what concerned Ur's son was not its beauty. 'See! He catches a bee in mid-flight. He takes it to a dead branch. And there he eats it. But watch! He spits out the wings. And this he does all day.'

Now the Family of Ur knew, better than most, that bees were an asset to the wadi, and one of the boy's first memories was of his father coming home, near-blinded with stings, swearing and slapping at his beard, with a hoard of honey which the children of the cave had fought for. The flowers of the area were so diverse in flavor that honey from four different combs might taste like four quite different things. For their sting, bees were respected; but for their song and their honey, they were loved. And to think that a bird as alluring as the bee eater existed solely to feed upon bees raised in the boy's mind a whole new range of questions: How could two things, each so excellent, be in such mortal conflict? How could two desirable aspects of nature be so incompatible?

He asked his mother, 'If a bee does so much good in the wadi and is tormented by an enemy as fatal as the bird . . .' He followed the flight of the dazzling predator and watched as it swooped down upon a bee returning from the flowers and then spit out the wings. It was an ugly incident and he said, 'Is it possible that we also have enemies somewhere in the sky, waiting to pounce on us?' Again he paused, and then put into exact words the problem that had begun to torment his mother: 'Suppose the rain has a spirit of its own? Or the sun? What then with our wheat?'

A second aspect of nature led the boy to an even more difficult question. The cypress, that tall and stately tree which marched along the edges of open fields serving as a dark pointer to the sky, was a splendid tree in whose narrow body birds loved to nest, and it produced each season a crop of small cones about the size of a thumb-tip, remarkable for the fact that each contained nine faces cleverly fitted together to hide the seeds inside. There were never eight faces and never ten, but always nine, ingeniously matched in a manner that could not have happened by accident. Some spirit within the cypress had consciously willed its cone to appear as it did, and if this were true of the tree, why was it not also true of the field in which wheat grew? And of the wheat itself?

The boy sat with his mother in the sunlight pondering these matters when a bee eater flew past, creating brilliance in the sky, then disappearing among the cypress trees which stood like warning sentinels. A tantalizing thought played across the boy's mind, a thought not easy to formulate but one that he could not throw aside. A trio of crested larks marched past, pecking for fallen grains, and after they had disappeared he stared at the cypresses and asked, 'Suppose the spirit that forms the beautiful cone is not within the cypress? Suppose the rain comes or stays away not because of what the rain wants to do . . .' His thoughts were leading him into areas too vague and shadowy for him to explore, and for the moment he dropped the matter, but the fear he had aroused would not go away.

It would not be correct to say that with the discovery of cultivated wheat fear was also discovered for ordinary fear the Family of Ur had long known. When Ur came upon a cornered boar or a lion from the north he knew fear. And when a woman in the cave was about to give birth Ur's wife knew fear, for she had seen women die at such moments. And one mournful night when Ur had lost a hunter in the swamps, killed by a boar, his daughter had heard the messenger's cry from afar, 'He is dead!' and she had thought it was Ur himself. Even she knew fear. But the fear which the family was now discovering was of another kind: it sprang from the slow-maturing apprehension regarding the relationship of man to his world, the gnawing suspicion that perhaps things were not so simple as they seemed on this average autumn day when ripening grain hid in the stalks and a rumor of deer echoed in the forest. Again and again the glorious bee eater flashed through the wadi, driving the mother and son to wonder whether it had been dispatched by some outside power as an exquisite messenger to warn men that the same force which endangered the bees was ready to swoop down on fields and houses.

And then one morning, as the grain approached its harvesting, Ur cried suddenly, 'That's it!'

'What?' his wife asked, looking at him suspiciously.

'We've been trapped into putting all our energy into wheat.'

'What do you mean, trapped?' she asked, caught by an ugly suspicion that Ur had discovered her own source of fear.

'When we have all the grain in one place, it can easily be destroyed.'

'You mean the sun? The fire?'

'Those, or the wild boar rooting up the fields.'

She looked at her husband with unashamed fear, for Ur was an authority, a sensible hunter and a man whom others respected. Therefore he must be listened to. What was more, he had dared to express in words the growing fear that she and her son had experienced, for it was a rule of life that the Family of Ur was discovering: the more committed a family becomes to a given project, the more vulnerable it also becomes. Having partially conquered nature, they were now a prey to it. 'What can we do?' she asked quietly.

Ur's son was at this moment watching the iridescent bee catcher dart among the cypresses for his prey, and he observed, 'If we knew some way to make the rain and sun appreciate our problem.' But the family could think of no way to accomplish this and late that afternoon they discovered that their enemy might lie in other directions than the ones they feared, for a towering storm brewed over the Carmel and moved north accompanied by flashes of lightning and the roar of thunder. Drops of rain fell in the dust and splattered like broken bowls of broth across the flat rock. Others followed, and soon a slanting wall of water was dropping from the sky, filling the wadi and sending a yellow flood swirling among the trees.

'It's reaching for the house!' Ur shouted, and he saw that if the deluge continued, his wife's fields must be swept away.

'The storm fights us for having stolen the wild wheat,' his wife wailed as the turbulent flood sent its fingers into her fields.

Ur was no more willing to surrender to the flood than he would have been to flee a lion. Running to the house he grabbed his best spear and with it rushed to the edge of the wadi, a bandy-legged old man ready to fight the elements. 'Go back!' he roared at the raging storm, not knowing exactly where to throw his spear. Always before, when floods came, he had retired to the cave to wait out their subsidence, but now that his home was in the middle of the storm he was involved and there was no retreat, no refuge. 'Go back!' he roared again.

But his son saw that if the rain stopped falling in time, say, within the next few moments, he might by building a dike hold back the wadi and prevent it from washing away the fields. Accordingly, he began running about placing rocks and sticks and mud along the lower portions of his land, diverting the water. Summoning his family he showed them what to do. And when Ur finally saw what might be accomplished, he laid aside his spear, stopped bellowing and speeded the construction of the dike. The girl called others from the cave, and as the thunder crashed about the trees above them, all worked to build a wall to hold back the muddy water, and it was obvious that the fields would be saved if only the storm would halt.

In these critical moments, when the fall of rain was greatest, obscuring even the mouth of the cave, Ur saw his wife standing in the storm, her tired face uplifted, crying, 'Storm, go back! Go back and leave our fields!' And whether the spirit of the storm heard or not, no one could later say, but it abated and the waters receded.

When the storm was gone Ur sat bewildered on a rock, marvelling at how close the flood had come to destroying his home and at his son's dexterity in building the dike. Then, out of the corner of his eye, he saw his wife doing a most perplexing thing. 'Wife,' he shouted, 'what are you doing?' And as she threw handfuls of wheat into the swirling waters she explained in a low voice,

'If the storm has left us our wheat, the least we can do is offer him some in thanks.'

It was an epochal event, this utterance of the word *him*. For the first time a human being at the well of Makor had spoken of an immanent spirit as 'he', a personified being who could be approached directly on a woman-to-deity basis. This was the inchoate beginning of the concept that a human-like deity could be propitiated and argued with on a personal basis. Throwing her arms wide she tossed her last grains on the water and cried, 'We are thankful you went away,' and the storm sighed as it roamed overhead, whispering to her in reply. This was the first fumbling effort to evoke the I-You relationship–'I am begging You, my partner, for mercy'–under which society would henceforth live, until the multitude of gods would become more real than sentient human beings.

When Ur saw how the planned fields could be protected from floods, and how they could be depended upon to provide an abundance of grain for all, he was gradually lured away from hunting, as his wife had foreseen he must be. He began to speak of 'my fields' and of 'my house', and his feelings toward each were different from those he had entertained about the cave. That reassuring hole beneath the great rock had not been owned by him nor by anybody; no one had built it nor improved it; he merely shared a portion of it for as long as he could bring in more food than he ate. With the new house it was different. It was his house, not his brothers' who lived in the cave. The fields were his, too, for he had cleared them. And at the height of the storm he had been ready to fight the wadi and the sky to retain them. In his new apotheosis as owner Ur began to bring new fields into cultivation, but the word *fields* could be misleading. For Ur a field was an area no larger than a table, at its maximum as large as several tables placed together. Men of the Family of Ur had always possessed an intuitive sense of the land, and now it was the reluctant farmer who discovered one of the essential mysteries of earth on which all subsequent agriculture would depend: he found that if he continued to plant his wheat in one field near the edge of the sloping rock it would grow better because the grains would be assured drainage from the rock, but soon the earth would tire of nurturing the seed and after a time would halt maliciously and send forth only sickly wheat; but if he planted his grains in some spot lower down on the sides of the wadi, where the rain was free to wash down, bringing with it each year bits of new earth to add to the old, the soil would be replenished and such a field could be used season after season. So in an age when fertilizer was unknown Ur had stumbled upon the flooding-principle that would later operate along the Nile and the Euphrates: allow the rivers to overflow and bring fresh soil to rebuild the old. Ur could not formulate his theory in words, but his inherited sense of earth assured him that somehow the soil was pleased with this replenishment, so he hacked out his little fields, keeping to the lower levels where fresh silt could filter down cycle after cycle. Fortified with this secret of how to keep his land fertile, Ur was tied ever more strongly to that land.

As Ur was thus tricked into neglecting hunting in favour of tending fields, he experienced a vague displeasure over the fact that his son showed no desire to take his place in the woods. 'A boy like you ought to know how to kill a lion.' Ur said sharply one day. 'Otherwise how can you expect to find a woman?' Once or twice, lately, Ur had suspected that his son might lack courage, for the boy inclined toward working the fields or chipping flints into new patterns. Yet Ur did remember that at the height of the storm it had been the boy who had fought the flood, and the old man admitted grudgingly, 'He's neither stupid nor lazy.'

Ur did not know it, but his malaise stemmed not from any disappointment in his son, but from the crushing impact of a new way of life that seemed to bear down on him alone: he was a hunter required to tend grain, a man instinctively of the cave forced to live in a house; he was a man who had developed a pragmatic adjustment to nature but who was now being lured into the first steps toward polytheism; but most of all he was a man who had been a happy, indistinct member of a group living in a cave, and now he was asked to be Ur, one man standing by himself, who knew how to track lions in an age when lions were beginning to move inland.

One morning, in the third year of this metamorphosis, he burst out of his new house as if the atmosphere were crushing down on him. He ran up the path, past the entrance to the cave and on up to the great rock, where he went to the highest point and stood breathing rapidly as if it was air he needed. When his lungs were full and he found that he had gained no relief, he sat down in a kind of terror. 'What's happening?' he asked, and in this moment when the possibility of death first became a reality he happened to see his daughter working in the fields, and he began to find in her the solace he did not find in his son.

At fourteen she was an attractive woman with long brown legs and a graceful neck which she adorned with jewelry made of shells and stone beads. She was ripe for motherhood and the responsibilities of a home, but she also retained the lively interests of her childhood and thus occupied a hesitant, uncertain place by the well. As a near-adult she worked with her mother, learning what she could of tanning leather and sewing, and like her family was in close contact with the manifestations of nature. She, too, felt that there must be ways to appease the unseen spirits. Ur, watching her, felt pride in her attainments and knew her to be the kind of woman who would make a round hut a warm and pleasant place, while her vital body promised many children. But it was primarily as a child that the girl impressed her elders most.

In one of the trees near the well a family of singing birds had its nest, and the Family of Ur used to take much pleasure in watching the parent birds hustling back and forth to feed their young. The adults had black heads, gray bodies and a smart dash of yellow under the tail, so that they were easy to see as they foraged for insects along the edges of the wheat fields. They sang beautifully and were charming birds to have at one's door, except that when their four babies were partly grown they detected that one had a defective leg, and in the manner of birds they put their two bills under the weakling and with an upward toss threw him from the nest. He half flew, half fell to the ground, where he would shortly have died had not Ur's daughter seen him fall and run to rescue him. In the following weeks she nursed the foundling to health, and although he continued to have one weak leg he became a robust little creature, hopping about the well and across the large flat rock where the girl sometimes lay watching the sky. In time he began to sing and would often fly far to catch insects, but always he came back to the round hut, perching on the shoulder of his mistress, biting at her beads and chirping in her ear. Ur was pleased with the bird, for he properly sensed that it had been sent as some kind of assurance that the birds of the forest were not angry with the people at the well for having left the cave to start a new form of life; and the girl loved the delightful bird as the last symbol of her childhood and a premonition of the more serious years ahead.

Once as Ur watched the two and saw the warm affection the bird had for his daughter, hopping after her on his one good leg and using the other as a balance, he threw his arms about the girl and cried for no apparent reason, 'Soon you'll have real babies of your own. I'll find a man.' Shortly after he said this a flight of the black-headed birds came up the wadi, and among them was a female, dark and lively, and never again did the Family of Ur see their friend.

At the far end of the wadi there lived a family of wild dogs–pariah dogs they would be called later–smaller than hyenas but larger than coyotes, and they lived by killing weakened deer or foraging at the edges of human settlements. They were powerful animals, real beasts of the forest, and occasionally an old man left aside to die would be attacked by them. When they first surged at the useless man he might think they were wolves come down from the north, but if he were brave he could drive them off and live a little longer, for they were not wolves, nor even of that breed. They were dogs; and although in their wild state they did not know it, they were capable of great friendship for the men they fought; and the men, equally blind, could not foresee that they required the dogs in order to initiate any kind of herding process, for without intelligent dogs no man could keep his more stupid animals like cows and goats under control. But all this was thousands of years in the future; for the present the two creatures–man and dog–shared the same wadi without anticipating the rewarding partnership that lay in store for them.

It was the daughter of Ur, hungry over the loss of her singing bird, inchoately hungry for the babies she had not yet had, who first noticed the great dog, largest of his pack, who volunteered to come away from the depths of the wadi and to approach the plantation in search of scraps. When Ur shied a rock at him he snarled and withdrew like the other dogs, but he did not stay away. And then one day as Ur's daughter lay on the high place of the rock looking at the flying clouds, she became aware that the large dog was watching her, unprotected by any tree but simply standing at the far edge of the rock. The two were about a hundred yards apart, each staring at the other, when Ur, working below, looked up to see the wild animal menacing his child, and he threw a well-aimed rock which struck the beast in the right flank and drove it howling into the woods. Ur scrambled up the side of the wadi and ran to rescue his daughter. 'Are you hurt?' he shouted, but when he came to her side she was crying.

It was some days before the large dog ventured back to the rock, but when he did so he found waiting for him a chunk of boar meat, which he ate cautiously, keeping his eye on the girl. Gnawing at the bone to which the meat was attached, he watched the girl for some minutes, then retreated quietly into the woods. That night the girl told her father that he must never again throw stones at the dog, because she intended feeding him regularly at the edge of the rock; and after she had done so for some months, moving always closer to the spot where he ate, he allowed her to sit less than forty feet from where he took the meat, and she could see his powerful jaws. She could also see the dancing lights in his eyes and the manner in which he held his tail when he assumed that she would not attack him, and she was tempted to move closer and perhaps to touch him, but whenever she showed an inclination to do so, the dog moved cautiously away. In these tentative years of introduction, forty feet was the minimum distance of safety between dog and man, and so long as this was maintained, the girl and the wild dog cultivated their friendship. That the relationship was significant to the dog, even when the girl failed to feed him, was proved one morning when, during the time that the girl sat watching the animal, she was called back down to the well. As she left abruptly, the dog seemed disappointed that she was leaving and followed her, at his distance of forty feet, until she reached the house. He then sat for a long time waiting for her to reappear. As soon as he was satisfied that she was there he left the unfamiliar terrain and ran back to the woods.

Perhaps Ur's daughter could in time have diminished the distance between the two, for she was patient and the dog was inquisitive, but one day as she worked in the wheat fields, unmindful of the beast yet aware that he was watching her, she heard a human voice utter a cry of victory which was drowned by the piercing wail of a dog, and she dashed with passion to the rock to find that her animal—her proud, wild dog of the forest—had been slain by a spear which had passed through the chest. The dog lay inert, his brown eyes still open in sad surprise, but at the far edge of the rock stood a tall young man shouting exultantly, 'I've killed the wild dog!' And she leaped at him with an anguish which only the bereaved can know, and began beating on him and driving him from the rock.

THE TELL

With Vered Bar-El absent in Chicago, Cullinane was free to direct his whole attention to the job of drafting a preliminary report on the year's campaign, but in doing so he found that any sentence he wished to use in describing how early society came into being was apt to be vague unless each word was carefully explained. The simplest phrase required qualification plus a warning that it could not have meant in the year 9000 B.C.E. what it meant today. For example, once when he was trying to describe how his imaginary family dressed, he wrote of the father, 'He wore skins,' but as soon as the three words appeared before him on the paper he realized that each, to be intelligible, required special definition.

He, the pronoun used to identify one man from among many—the singular human differentiated from all others, with a will of his own, a personal destiny and a unique personality—was a concept which must have come late in human development, and when Cullinane used it as he did, it raised various philosophical problems. Originally there had been men and women dwelling in a mass in caves, and of course there had been a distinction between male and female, but within those two categories there could not have been much individualization. A child was born and manifested no special characteristics. At fourteen or fifteen he was strong enough to muscle his way into full participation. At thirty he was an old man. And when his first tooth fell he could feel the claw of death at his throat, for the day could not be far off when he would no longer be able to fight for his food or rip it from the bone with his fangs. If he survived till forty he was a white-haired sage who existed only because some tender-hearted woman foraged his food for him. He lived and died within a blurred, undifferentiated destiny, and for nearly a million years in Israel his going was not even marked with a burial of any kind. The identification of *he,* the unique human being, probably resulted from an expanding social order in which categories became more clearly defined. A man began to perform a certain job or to live in a specified portion of the communal cave. He thus existed in relationship to known verities and in time began to partake of recognizable characteristics, even to develop them in order to fulfill the requirements of a burgeoning social order. As a result, he developed a personal space that moved with him and was his, a function that was his, and a manner of behavior that distinguished him. Most important of all, he painfully and with some terror, Cullinane supposed, began to develop, say, twenty thousand years ago, a way of thinking that was characteristically his, and in group meetings in the cave he began to defend the results of that thinking. There was an additional implication in the word *he*: it signified that the bearer of the pronoun existed in some kind of relationship to the forces of nature that surrounded him; he knew his place, as it were, and developed a strong sense of private property, and this discovery must have come very late indeed–within the last ten or twelve thousand years, Cullinane guessed–in what might be termed the age of speculation. Prior to that, men had known that an atmosphere of power existed around them, but they had also known that they were impotent to affect it. Man and storm coexisted in a kind of armed truce; with animals there was open warfare. So far as Cullinane knew, the dog on whom so much of man's early pastoral life depended had been domesticated in other parts of the world as early as 12,000 B.C.E., but at Makor not until sometime around 7000 B.C.E., while the cow and the goat, which the dog was to tend and upon which civilization so strongly relied, were to come much later. It was doubtful, Cullinane thought, if man had appreciated his capacity to influence the future and his animals' incapacity to do so until quite late. It was instructive and accurate to imagine earliest man as living for most of his first two million years within an insulation of stupidity, not fully differentiating himself from the physical world, the spiritual world, or the world of the other sentient animals. 'So when I use the word *he* to specify one man living in one house by one well, I am speaking of an intellectual revolution so enormous in magnitude that I have not the words to describe it,' Cullinane wrote. He put his pen aside and mused: How I should like to see the eyes of that man who first brought wheat into cultivation. The first man to tame a wild dog. Or to arrange for the giving of his daughter in a formalized kind of marriage. Or to discover that in the high places a god was standing.

Wore, as Cullinane used the word, implied a whole scale of social judgments and was the end result of many moral decisions. Why did men decide to wear anything? How much of that decision sprang from cold or from a desire to inherit the power of animals by wearing their skins; how much from a need for sexual propriety, as suggested in Genesis? When some men began to *wear* something, what kind of pressure did they apply against others to make them do the same? At what point did women discover that they were more functional as women if they wore some ornament to differentiate themselves from men? This last was more significant than the layman would like to think, for beads had been found in Israel dating as far back as 40,000 B.C.E. and evidences of intentionally prepared perfume were common before the invention of writing. The businessman in Chicago who objects to his wife's expenditures on jewelry should visit a prehistoric cave, he thought. There he'd find that his wife is in the grand tradition. A woman requires jewelry as a man requires food. Still, he thought, it was remarkable and a mystery not yet explained why contemporary men, who could watch the birds and animals and see that it was the male who was gaudy in decoration, had decided that among human beings this fundamental law should be reversed. He supposed that this could be one of the essential differences between man and animals: the former beautify their females. As to the components of utility, ritual and taboo that went into the formulation of a concept like *wear*, he preferred not to speculate. When enough sites had been excavated and enough research completed, some scholar would be able to specify how those concepts had developed; meanwhile he didn't know, but almost every word symbolizing a value judgment had a unique history dating back some hundred thousand years before the age when man first learned to speak. To be specific, he still pondered what force had given the categorical imperative, 'Wear clothes,' its social effectiveness. Vaguely he remembered that as an officer in the hottest and most humid parts of the Solomon Islands he had commented on the fact that all men and women had worn some kind of clothing, 'and it certainly wasn't because they needed to keep warm!'

Skins, the last word in the exacting sentence, pitched the reader into the imprecise origins of technology. At what age of man's development did some technician discover that the skin of an animal could be scraped clean of fleshy particles, dried in the sun, rubbed with fat and the juice of oak galls, and crudely tanned into a pliable substance adaptable to the human form? Really, Cullinane reflected, so many problems are raised in that sentence that only a super-mechanic like Thomas Edison could find a place to begin. It probably took about fifty thousand years of step-by-step accumulation of experience until the complicated process was mastered. He repeated the phrase: fifty thousand years. It was an incomprehensible amount of time, ten times as long as man's entire written history, and it was but a fragment of the total time that men had grappled with the problem *skins*. All Cullinane knew for sure was that sometime around 40,000 C.B.E. the men of the Mount Carmel caves had produced flint stones with serrated edges that could be used for scraping skins, so it was likely that they had at least begun the tanning process. But the word *skins* conjured up related technical problems that were even more fascinating. It's probable, Cullinane reasoned, that our people at Makor in 9000 B.C.E. wore skins that fitted the body. Sewn together, if you like. Now where did they get the needles? The thread? And most important of all, the concept? It was the latter that was crucial, for once a group of people had the intelligence to say, 'Let's sew our skins,' ways would surely be found to do the sewing. But who had first proposed, 'Let's sew'? He guessed that it had been some woman watching a bird build its nest, sewing the strands of straw back and forth and tucking the ends in place with her sharp bill. Once this process was understood it was relatively simple–Say it took fifty thousand years, Cullinane mused–for the woman's husband to cut a flint so that it could be used as an awl. Or some man had found a deer's bone that could be sharpened, or a fragment of human shin that would serve nicely as a needle. In any case, over a period of time staggering to imagine, men had acquired their trial-and-error technology, and if today one could visualize the persistent will required to bring such a thing as a *skin* to the point of utility he would be made humble by the years, the toil of awkward fingers, the blockades of mind, and the yearning for accomplishment that underlay even the simplest process.

He wore skins. 'What an infinity of comprehension is required,' Cullinane wrote in his report, 'to appreciate this simple sentence in which I have compressed so much.' The first word implied a philosophical system, the second a social order, and the third an attitude toward technology; and he concluded that in each category his reader must grasp three fundamental developments. In philosophy: speech, the idea of self, the idea of god. In the social order: the domestication of grains and animals, group observance of accepted norms, the concept of a community. In technology: fire, flint tools, the principle of the fulcrum. He looked at his four pieces of flint, each a minute work of art, and wondered how a man's hand, eleven thousand years ago, could have created these simple, lovely tools, and he found himself back where he had started: 'How can I convey the thousands of centuries it took to bring man to the place where he could control flint so precisely?' And then the larger question: 'How was he able to conceive of a sickle in the first place?'

When the young hunter retreated from the rock, the enraged girl followed him, still clubbing at him with her fists, and she would have used stones could she have got them, but in time her father and her brother managed to bring her under control. With anguish she broke away from them and ran to the fallen dog and threw herself on his bold, dead form, embracing the head that had sought her friendship. He was dead, this wonderful wild creature, and she sensed that she would never be able to find another like him. In later millennia at Makor other girls with her sensitivity would find other dogs willing to risk the tremendous step from forest to house, but she would not then be living. 'Oh! Oh!' she sobbed, beating the rock with her fists, for she knew that something superior had been stolen from her.

The hunter was bewildered by the girl's behavior. He was from the lands north of the well and loved to roam the deep wadis and the forested hills. As the accuracy of his spear had shown, he was a skilled hunter and at seventeen a rugged young man with visibly powerful legs for the chase. Ur, looking at him, was reminded of his own youth, and as the hunter stood at the edge of the rock, perplexed as to what he had done to arouse this grief, Ur said, 'Stay with us for a while,' and the men left the rock where the girl lay burdened with sorrow.

Later the young hunter discovered that in killing the dog he had broken the point of his spear and he asked Ur if there were any sharpened flints that he might tie to the shaft. But Ur merely pointed toward his son, saying with some condescension, 'He works the flint.' After the hunter had shown the boy what was required, the latter went to work on a nodule of flint which he had found imbedded in a white stone. There was nothing then in existence hard enough to cut flint, and most of the metals to be discovered later would not suffice; the artisan had to visualize the inner structure of the flint or he could accomplish nothing, so Ur's son carefully chipped away the whitish outer coating of limestone until he could see the brown hidden core. He worked patiently on the fat end of the core, chipping it down until he had a level platform from which he could inspect the flint and decide how best to attack it. After some moments of study, during which he seemed to penetrate the secrets of the stone, he placed the small end of the core against a piece of wood, holding it with his left fingers so that he could feel the ridges and the lines of strain. He then took a pointed rock and held it exactly so against the platform, and with a smaller stone in his right hand delivered a slight tap, barely strong enough to kill a wasp. A large segment of the flint broke away exactly as he had intended, exposing a clear and shimmering face that narrowed to a point. Deftly he turned the core, tapped lightly again to strike off another face. For some time he continued this process, chipping away one fragment after another until at last he had a long, slender-point powerful enough to penetrate any hide. The watching hunter was impressed, but then the boy did something not known in areas where the hunter came from. He laid the finished spearhead flat, and with a saw that he had made of flint he cut two deep notches in the flank, flint etching flint, and these would provide a means of securing the head to the shaft.

'He's the best flint worker I've seen,' the hunter said admiringly.

'He's not much of a hunter,' Ur replied.

'Could you make two or three more points?'

'In this wadi there isn't much flint,' the boy explained.

'You need flint?' the hunter cried, and this was the beginning of the deep friendship that developed between Ur and the young stranger, for he told the family of a white cliff rising out of the Roaring Sea two days' journey to the west where flints were so numerous that in a few hours a man could gather enough for a lifetime.

'Do you know how to get there?' Ur asked.

'Of course! I'm a hunter!' And he led Ur and his son through the dark glades to the west, and on the second day they came to the Roaring Sea, which the boy had not known before, and it glistened in the sun. The hunter took them to the white cliffs of which he had foretold, and there the boy found something he could scarcely believe: towering walls of chalk from which, at intervals laid down millions of years ago, layers of flint nodules protruded. With one hand Ur's son could reach fifty, a hundred, a thousand perfect flint cores, waiting to be knocked loose from the easily broken chalk. The boy's eyes gleamed, and he directed his father and the hunter as to what kind of flints he wanted: 'The ones that are longer than they are wide through the middle.' And in a few hours the three men had all that they could carry.

They had come upon one of the surprises of nature, a bed of flint, whose nodules if properly worked could provide tools that would not be surpassed until other men along this great sea discovered copper-bronze. Ages upon ages ago, when the shores of this sea were being formed by the deposits of tiny animal skeletons that would later be transmuted into chalk, enormous colonies of alien sea animals congregated in special currents and died. Their bodies contained peculiar chemicals, and when billions of the little creatures deposited their corpses in one spot a kind of pocket was formed in the future chalk, so that later, when great pressures were applied from above, these dead bodies coagulated into knots which formed nodules of flint scattered through the more ordinary substance. Man had discovered the nodules, how long ago?—at least a million years, surely—and from them had fashioned the instruments whereby he lived, for flint could be worked into axes, arrowheads, spears, needles, saws or almost any tool that man could envisage; of equal importance, two pieces of flint when struck together produced fire. And now the son of Ur had unlimited quantities of this vital substance.

He made the hunter his extra spearheads, and for his sister he shaped three needles with which she consoled herself by sewing skins for the family; and one day Ur suggested to her, 'You ought to sew a new skin for the hunter,' and somewhat against her will–for her lamentation for the dead dog had not ceased–she did so, and in time the hunter built a round house for her and she was pregnant with her first child; but the wild dog, that trusting beast who had sat with her on the rock, was never forgotten.

Ur's son worked on his flints and one day asked the hunter, who was now his brother-in-law, to find him a curved bone of a certain dimension; and when this was provided, the boy went into seclusion for some time, after which he handed his mother an implement of new design. It was a sickle, a curved knife whose flints were wedged into the bone and tied with tiny thongs and secured with a substance made of resin from the cypress trees and honey. The beauty of this new device was that its curved tip sought out the stalks of wheat and brought them to the cutting edge, as if a man's arm had been extended enormously. Entire families from the cave came to stand and watch enviously as the boy's mother swung her arm in extensive circles, gathering the wheat to her and cutting it with an unbroken motion. It was miraculous.

Then came the great days at the well, the kind of days that men in all societies know occasionally, the few days that make the many years endurable. Ur's wife and son worked the fields and found new ways to make the earth produce; the sun shone upon them approvingly and enough rain came, but no more. The others in the cave thought it significant that these two were growing enough grain to feed almost the entire cave, and husbands began to ask difficult questions of their wives: 'Why can't you do what his wife did?' Ur's daughter cared for her first-born and wished that another bird would fall to her care, but none did; the lovely bee eaters flashed through the wadi and crested larks followed the reapers gathering grains. Sometimes a deer would dart across the fields beyond the rock and owls would call from the cypresses. How good the days were.

For Ur and his son-in-law these golden days were a continuous dream. Inspired by the young man, Ur returned to the hunt, setting forth each morning to probe the far ends of the wadi or the edges of the swamp. It was amusing to watch them go, the young man striding ahead with stocky Ur chugging along behind, pumping his bandy legs and calling instructions, trying to teach the hunter all the secrets of the land. Sometimes, when they got on to the track of a boar, the young man would leave Ur to mark the spot while he loped easily back to summon others from the cave, and often there would be a mass chase. But usually it was Ur and the young man going it alone in the companionship of the hunt that was so treasured by the old man.

At intervals Ur felt the intimations of death. Some of his teeth had broken off, and after running uphill for two or three hours he felt a shortness of breath. He sensed that he must be going, and although he felt a kind of animal fear of death, he found much joy in the fact that his son-in-law was such a stalwart hunter. The boy was swift and daring, as brave as Ur had hoped his own son would be. He could use a spear better than Ur himself, and when Ur had time to teach him the tricks of fighting close to the tusks of the wild boar he might possibly excel the old warrior. 'He's a great hunter,' Ur reported proudly as the men sat about the fire. 'I think he's better than my father was.' The young men of the cave nodded but the old ones said nothing, for they remembered Ur's father.

Then, as so often happens when the seasons have been too cooperative and the sun too gentle, the forces that surrounded the well and the wadi struck back to remind the men of the kind of world they lived in. Out of a cloudless sky, on a day when babies could play in the sun, lightning struck the wadi and set the grain on fire. By concerted effort the people of the cave were able to subdue the flames, but half the crop was burned away, and suddenly the food situation facing the people of the well was radically changed. Instead of an abundance, there was now only just enough, and the Family of Ur began to speculate on what might have caused the lightning to strike at that time; and no matter what rationalizations Ur offered, his wife became convinced that the aggrandizement of the family, its disregard for the immanent rights of nature, had brought this rebuke. 'The hunter killed the dog,' she pointed out, 'and we rejoiced that his first child was a boy, and we gave none of the grain to the waters of the wadi ...' She went on and on, reviewing the arrogant actions of her family. She concluded that the forces which shared the wadi with her people were properly angry, and she felt that she must erect some sign of contrition to let them know that neither she nor her husband intended ever again to usurp their rights. In this reasoning her son supported her, but old Ur said he didn't know.

The monolith was her idea. She said, 'If we erect on the highest part of the rock a tall stone, the storm and the wind and the wild boar will see it and will know that we wish them well.' Ur asked how they would know any such thing, but his son assured him, 'They will know.' And so all the men of the cave went with Ur's son to a part of the wadi where stones grew, and there, with flint cutters and wedges and heavy stones dropped as hammers, they broke away a monolith much taller than a man and rounded on one end. They shoved and hauled it onto the highest point of the rock, where after two months of sweating and building of earthen ramps, they upended it into a socket that the boy had hacked into the solid rock. Securing it with stones wedged under the corners they left it standing upright, a thing without a name, but a thing from which they nevertheless took much consolation. It was their spokesman to the storm.

On the third night after its institution as guardian of the well, a wild boar–the symbol of implacable hatred–came rampaging out of the wadi and tore up a good two thirds of the remaining wheat field. When dawn broke and the cave people saw the devastation, and realized how much food they had lost–crested larks were already feasting on the fallen grain–they became panicky and tried to push over the monolith, but Ur's wife and son prevented this, reasoning, 'If they have come at us even though they can see our sign, what might they have done otherwise?' Ur and his son-in-law followed a simpler reasoning. The wild boar had ravaged their fields. They would kill him. So they gathered their spears and set upon the chase that would long be recounted in that wadi.

In the dawn they went down to the swamps, where his trail lay, and among the waters and the flying birds they probed until they found his ugly foot marks leading deeper into the areas where the biting bugs hid. For a day they splashed their way through green water up to their knees, and at night they slept among the dreadful bugs. They could hear the great boar and knew that he was beginning to feel panic, and in the morning they were after him. He led them on a long chase away from the swamp and through the glades of lovely forests thick with oak and pine. He hurried up hills and towards caves, breathing harder as the persistent hunters clung to his muddy trail. The huge beast gathered strength and ran far down the valleys until the men could see before them the bright Whispering Sea which Ur had known of old but which his new son had not encountered. They followed the boar to the southern end of the sea, where hot waters bubbled from the ground, and there in a thicket of pistachio and thorn they finally cornered him.

'Remember what I said,' Ur called as they prepared to move in from opposite sides. His heart pounded with unprecedented speed, and when he was alone he whispered, 'I must not die now. Not till the boar is killed. The young man doesn't know how . . .'

With a scream the young hunter flew into the air, for the wily boar had lured him into range of his flashing tusks.

'Fall away!' Ur shouted, rushing into the thicket, but the young man could not control his fall, for there was nothing to grasp, and he fell onto the tusks again and was slashed to death. Before old Ur could penetrate the tangle the triumphant beast was galloping to the north, leaving the young hunter destroyed behind him.

It was then that the immensity of life, the awesome, aching mystery of man in conflict with the things about him, overwhelmed the old man. He looked at his dead son and visualized the man's wife and little boy. 'I was the one ready for death!' Ur cried. 'Why was he chosen?'

From the north came echoes of the distant beast crashing about in victory. 'Why should a thing so evil have triumphed?' Ur protested, rending his garment in anguish.

He thought of the futile monolith his family has raised to ward off just such contradictions and he wondered what extra thing he might have done to save this bravest of hunters. What had he left undone? Standing in grief over a man he had loved more than his own wife, more than well or cave, he began to formulate words which expressed his spiritual bewilderment:

> Why is the young hunter dead, why do I live?
> Why has the mad boar triumphed, why does he growl?
> Where is the path home, why is it hidden?
> Why does the sun hide its face, why does it mock?

And as he felt the tragedy of these recent days he again entertained those mysterious thoughts which had begun that day when he saw his broken reflection in the well: was it the boar which had willed this dreadful day or was it a force far greater than either the boar or the lightning or the storm—some entity outside them all? Deep in the thicket he stood over the body of his son and wondered.

And the anguish that Ur knew that night—the mystery of death, the triumph of evil, the terrible loneliness of being alone, the discovery that self of itself is insufficient—is the anxiety that torments the world to this day.

LEVEL XIV

Of Death and Life

Found at Makor–clay figurine of the Canaanite goddess of fertility, Astarte or Ashtart. Known to the Hebrews as Ashtoreth (plural Ashtaroth), to the Babylonians as Ishtar and to the Greeks as Aphrodite, this goddess appears repeatedly throughout the Old Testament as a permanent temptation to the Hebrews. Struck from a two-part mold in the seaport of Akka, 2204 B.C.E. Fired at 750° Centigrade. Purposely buried beside the wall of Makor sometime after dark on an autumn evening in 2202 B.C.E.

High in the heavens over the desert a vulture wheeled, its glinting eye fastened to an object almost invisible in a clump of brush that grew where the drifting sand met fertile earth. Its wings flat against the rising currents, the powerful bird drifted aimlessly in huge circles, but kept its sharp eye focused on the tiny object below, which seemed to be hesitating between death and life. The vulture showed no impatience, nor did it change its elevation. If the decision were to be death, the rapacious bird could drop quickly enough, and in the meantime its steady, waiting flight continued.

Then a change occurred. It appeared that death had come, and quickly the hovering bird ceased its drifting and inclined its wings into a steep dive. From the warm rising current which had sustained it, the vulture entered into the cold outer layers, descending in a great arching curve, its sharp eye fixed on the object that had just died. Speed and determination were necessary, for before long other birds would spot the lifeless target and would come swooping in to claim it, but on this day the solitary vulture was to be the angel of death and it sped down on silent wings.

On the ground a small donkey lay trapped with its hind leg pinched into the fork of a desert shrub, and its efforts to extricate itself had brought exhaustion. Vainly it had cried and twisted and pulled and now it could do no more. Death was very close, for from the desert came a torrid wind that intensified the little creature's thirst, and in its last extremity the donkey ceased struggling; it was this surrender that the soaring vulture had interpreted as death, and now through dimmed eyes the little beast could see the final bird approaching. Both were prepared for death.

At that moment, pushing his way through the bushes that marked the edge of the desert, appeared a nomad wearing sandals whose thongs came upward about his ankles; across his right shoulder was fastened a cloak of yellow marked with red crescent moons. He wore a beard and carried a crooked stave which he used to knock aside the impeding brush, and from time to time he stopped to listen for a donkey that had disappeared from his caravan. He heard no sound but his eye did mark the descending flight of the vulture, and by a calculation which he had learned from his father, who had also been a nomad, he deduced from the actions of the scavenger where his donkey might be. He was afraid, from the appearance of the vulture, that the little creature was already dead, but nevertheless he hurried on, and in a moment his shepherd's crook pushed aside the last brush—and at its base he saw his donkey very close to death, but now restored to life.

The vulture, robbed of this promised meal, uttered a croaking cry of anger, then sought an ascending current, on which it rose in great circles to a height from which it was almost invisible to the herdsman in the brush at the edge of the desert, and then remembering past good fortune, it drifted effortlessly to the west, over green lands from which it had often feasted in earlier days, until it came to the mound of Makor, in whose town another contest between death and life was about to occur, involving more important characters than a stray donkey, and more complicated forces than a hungry bird and a nomad dressed in a yellow cloak with crescent moons.

It was in the early summer of 2202 B.C.E., and in the more than seven thousand years that had elapsed from that day on which the Family of Ur had erected its monolith on the rock a sequence of changes had transformed the area. One unrecorded civilization after another had flourished briefly—successful ones had lasted a thousand years; the unsuccessful, only two or three hundred—but each had left behind an accumulation of rubble as its buildings were demolished and its inhabitants led away to slavery. Ruins had grown upon ruins until some twenty feet of debris obscured the original rock, obliterating even its memory, except that from its secure footing in the high place the ancient monolith still pushed its head through rubble to protrude a few feet into sunlight. It was the holiest object in this part of the land and was believed to have been placed in its exalted position by the gods themselves.

The rest had vanished. The roof of the cave was collapsed and the mouth, which had seen so much traffic in its numberless millennia, was filled in, so that not even goats could creep into the cool retreat that had served them for so many years. At the well, which still explained the concentration of life in the area, earth had built up until ropes thirty feet long were required to reach water, and the rocks that formed the upper lip of the well were worn with deep grooves showing where the girls of Makor had guided their ropes while hauling up the water.

The mound now housed a town of a hundred mud-brick houses located along winding streets, and contained a population of some seven hundred people who engaged in trade, kept animals and grew agricultural produce in the fields south of town. The most conspicuous change, however, was the great wall which surrounded the settlement and which kept off all but the most determined invaders. It had been erected sometime around the year 3500 B.C.E., when a people whose tribal name was no longer remembered decided in desperation that they must protect themselves or perish. Accordingly, they had built a massive wall nine feet high and four feet thick, using no mortar but only large chunks of unworked rock piled loosely atop one another. From a distance the wall looked as if at any given point it might easily be breached, but when the attackers moved close they found that against the inner face of the stone the defenders had jammed a second wall of beaten earth, eight feet thick, and had faced it with two additional feet of rock, so that anyone seeking to pierce the defences had to hack his way through fourteen feet of rock, then earth, then rock, and this was difficult to do.

In the thirteen hundred years that the wall had stood, it had been assaulted sixty-eight times—once every nineteen years on the average—by Hittites and

Amorites from the north, by Sumerians and Akkadians from the Land of the Two Rivers, later known as Mesopotamia, and by Egyptians from the Nile. Even the predecessors of the Sea People, making preliminary forays on the port of Akka, had tried to capture Makor, too, but of the numerous sieges only nine had succeeded. In recent centuries the town had been totally destroyed—that is, burned to the ground and desolated—only twice, and was thus more fortunate than some of its larger neighbors like Hazor and Megiddo.

Primarily Makor was an agricultural center whose rich fields produced a surplus which could be traded for manufactured goods. During recent centuries caravans had begun moving past Makor on their way from Akka to the inland city of Damascus, and exotic goods were becoming known: obsidian knives from Egypt, dried fish from Crete and Cyprus, stacks of lumber from Tyre and fabrics from the looms east of Damascus. The wealth of Makor was controlled mostly by the king, but this word could be misleading. The size of the town and its importance in world affairs were best illustrated by what happened in 2280 B.C.E., when the neighboring city of Hazor was in trouble and called for help. The king of Makor responded, sending to the imperiled city an army of nine men.

It was strange, perhaps, that there should even be a king of Makor ruling over a town of only seven hundred persons, but in those days this was no mean assembly, and if one took into consideration the surrounding fields and undefended hamlets protected by the king, one had an area just large enough to constitute an economic unit. It never belonged permanently to any one national system; from one century to the next it had been subject to Egypt for a while, then to empires having their home in Mesopotamia. For the most part it enjoyed the same status as larger communities like Hazor, Akka and Damascus, a subject town floating this way and that as the tides of history swept in or receded.

In an age of violent change, when the super-empires were trying to establish themselves, Makor was allowed to exist only because it was a minor settlement off to one side of the major thoroughfare connecting Egypt, which had long ago built its pyramids, to Mesopotamia, which had already built its ziggurats. It was never an important military target and could be safely by-passed, as it usually was, but after the significant battles had been decided elsewhere, victorious generals usually dispatched a few troops to let Makor know what new hegemony it now belonged to.

On the occasions when Makor had to be destroyed, its population was dealt with severely: all men who could be caught were massacred; their wives were raped and dragged off to harems, and their children led away to slavery. Later, when peace came, other groups would move in to take their places and to rebuild the town, and this accounted for the varied types one saw in Makor. There were tall, slim Canaanites with sunburned complexions, blue eyes, small noses and well-defined chins, while those who came from Africa were dark. Hittites wandering down from the north were swarthy, squat men with powerful bodies and large hooked noses, but those from the southern desert were lean and hawk-faced. They were the Horites. Even some of the Sea People had decided to live ashore—robust, thick-chested men. They were the forerunners of the Phoenicians. And all lived together in a kind of indifferent amalgam, finding for themselves about as good a life as was then available in the area.

In this age of uncertainty, only one thing was certain: the confusion about religion had been permanently settled. It was now known that the world was governed by three benevolent gods–storm, water, sun–and each was represented by a special monolith rising from the high place in the center of town. There was, of course, a fourth stone in the solemn line facing the temple, sacred beyond all others, rounded on top by erosion and almost submerged in earth that had accumulated through the years. Because it looked something like a human penis, it was revered as the father of all gods and was known as El, but in appearance it was trivial, rising only a few feet from the soil, whereas the others were impressive monuments. It was as if the god to whom the rock-penis belong was old and worn out; he was still revered by his subjects as a potent force, the source of all power, the god El.

After these major gods came the multitude of others for whom no monoliths were raised at the high place but to whom prayers were said daily: gods of the trees, the rivers, the wadi, the birds, the ripening grain, and particularly gods for any feature of the landscape that stood out prominently. Thus the hill behind Makor had its god, as did the mountain that stood behind it. Baals, they were called, little baals and greater baals, and each was worshiped in a separate way, but there was one special god whom all the citizens of Makor kept close to their hearts, and this was Astarte, the tempting, rich-breasted goddess of fertility. It was she who brought the grain to ripening and the cow to calving, the wife to the birthing stool and chickens to the nest. In an agricultural society, smiling little Astarte was the most immediately significant of all the gods, for without her nothing that concerned the cycle of life could come to pass.

By and large the baals had been generous to Makor, for even though the town had been twice destroyed, it had been revived and under Astarte its fields prospered, but few were the families who could say, 'We have lived in Makor for many generations.' Most were newcomers, but in one rambling mud-brick house to the west of the main gate, its back tucked snugly against the wall, lived a man whose ancestors through one trick or another had managed to survive both war and occupation. When bravery was called for, the men of this resilient family voluntarily leaped with their spears to the ramparts, but when defeat became inevitable they were the first to scramble into some hiding place, covering themselves until massacre and fire were over. And with the coming of each peaceful cycle they returned to their expanding olive groves and wheat fields.

The present scion of this resourceful clan was the farmer Urbaal, thirty-six years old, lineal descendant of the great Ur whose family had started farming at Makor and who had erected in the high place the monolith which was to become the god El. Urbaal was a husky man, stout and strong as becomes a farmer, with big teeth that flashed when he smiled. Unlike others of his age, he was not bald nor was he inclined to fatness. In war he had proved himself a good soldier and in peace a productive farmer. He was gentle with his wives, boisterous with his children and kind to his slaves; and if he had wanted to be king or high priest, he could have been either, but his love was farming and women and the growth of things. But now he had a consuming worry, and as he hurried from his house to the high place where the monoliths stood facing the temple, his forehead was wrinkled and he thought: My well-being for the whole year depends on what I do right now.

The street which led from Urbaal's house did not march impressively from the main gate to the temple area; to do that would have required planning. Instead, it dodged and twisted in unforeseen ways like the hit-or-miss village

footpath it had once been, and as the farmer passed along its inconvenient
cobbles, citizens of the town nodded pleasantly; but he did not acknowledge
them. His mind was preoccupied with serious matters, and when he reached
the high place he proceeded gravely to the farthest monolith, the remnant that
barely pushed its head through the earth, and bowed before it, kissing it many
times and mumbling, 'This year, great El, let it be me.' He then moved to each
of the other three and uttered similar prayers: 'Baal-of-the-Storm, this year let
it be me. Baal-of-the-Waters, Baal-of-the-Sun, I have asked you for little.'

He crossed the square and entered the cluttered shop of Heth, a Hittite who
dealt in goods imported from many areas, and there he said to the bearded man
who stood beside lengths of cloth, 'This year I must be chosen. What shall I
do?'

'Why not consult the priests?' Heth evaded.

'From them I've learned all I can,' Urbaal replied, pretending to inspect a
large pottery jar brought down from Tyre.

'All I can tell you,' Heth replied, 'is to tend your groves.' He looked at the
troubled man, then added slowly, 'And buy for yourself the best Astarte you
can find.'

This was the kind of counsel Urbaal had sought. Turning from the pottery,
he brought his face close to Heth's and asked the bearded merchant, 'Would
that help?'

'It's how Amalek won last year,' the merchant assured him.

'I already have three statues,' Urbaal protested.

'With your trees? Is three enough? Really?' The wily trader stroked his beard
and stared at the rich farmer.

'I've wondered myself,' Urbaal confessed. He turned away from Heth and
walked about the small shop mumbling to himself. Then, like a child pleading,
he grasped Heth's hand and asked, 'Do you truthfully think it would help?'

Heth said nothing, but from a corner he produced a small clay figure of a
goddess. She was six inches high, nude, very feminine, with wide hips and
hands cupped below circular breasts. She was erotic and plump, delightful to
study and reassuring to have in one's presence. The merchant was obviously
proud of her and was bound to ask a good price.

Urbaal looked at the statue with special concern. To him this was not a piece
of cleverly molded clay, no abstract theological symbol. It was the veritable
goddess Astarte who determined the fertility of land, of women, of olive trees.
Without her help he was powerless. He could pray to Baal-of-the-Waters and
to Baal-of-the-Sun, and they could send the right amounts of rain and warmth,
but if Astarte frowned olives would not produce oil; and unless she smiled he
could not win this year.

He adored Astarte. Others feared her capriciousness–famine one year,
abundance the next–but he had adapted himself to her arbitrary behavior. He
worshiped her faithfully and in return she had been good to him, as she had
been to his fathers before him. If the fields and the beehives of Urbaal
prospered, even when others failed, it was because he and Astarte had reached
an understanding.

'The statue you sold me last year worked,' the farmer rationalized as he
looked at the new goddess.

'For three years you couldn't get Timna pregnant,' Heth pointed out. 'Then,
with the proper statue . . .'

'I'll take it!' the farmer decided. 'How much?'

'Seven gurs of barley, seven of wheat,' Heth replied.

Urbaal had known that the price would be steep, but now he did some calculations. 'That's more than fourteen gin of silver,' he said. 'Last year it was only eight.'

'It is fourteen,' Heth agreed, 'but this Astarte is special. She wasn't made by hand, like your others. They've found a new way in Akka, and it costs.'

'I'll take her,' Urbaal said, and he picked up the little goddess, put her to his lips, and went back across the plaza to where the monoliths stood.

The secret of Urbaal's success in farming lay in what he was now about to do. He knew that if Astarte was the goddess of fecundity, she must cherish the sexual act as the source of her power, so he never left his goddesses alone but saw to it that they were generously provided with male gods. Bearing his new goddess to the ancient monolith of El, he introduced her to the half-hidden one and whispered, 'Tonight, great El, you can come to the house of Urbaal, where the goddess will be waiting.' He then took her to the other baals, holding her seductively against them, rubbing her body against theirs and whispering, 'Tonight, when the moon goes down, come to the house of Urbaal, where Astarte will be waiting.'

Holding the little goddess tenderly in his cupped hands, he bowed to the four monoliths and started homeward, but as he did so, along the porch of the temple there passed a tall girl of sixteen wearing rough-spun robes and golden sandals. She was slender, and with each step her long bare legs broke through the garments; her black hair, which fell below her shoulders, moved in the sunlight. Her face had an extraordinary beauty: dark, widely placed eyes, long straight nose, high cheekbones and silken skin. She walked with conscious grace and was aware of the effect she created on men, for that was her purpose.

Ever since her arrival in Makor, a slave captured during a raid to the north, Urbaal had been fascinated by her. He saw her striding through his dreams. She was in his olive groves when he inspected them, and when the girls of Makor trampled his grapes she was among them, the red juice staining her long legs. Even when the farmer's second wife, Timna, had had her child, Urbaal could think only of the tall slave, and it was she who had driven him to purchase his fourth Astarte. Clutching the goddess closer to his heart, he watched the girl until she disappeared into another part of the temple, a man wholly captive to urges that seemed about to consume him. Bringing the clay goddess to his lips, he kissed her and whispered, 'Astarte! My fields must produce. Help me Help me!'

He waited in the shadows for some time, hoping that the tall slave might return, but when she did not he wandered disconsolately back to the main gate, a complicated zigzag affair with towers from which archers looked down into a maze of twists and turns. Long ago the town of Makor had learned that if its gate were wide and forthright, opening directly into the heart of the town, any enemy who succeeded in rushing that gate found himself comfortably inside the town, which he could then despoil. The entrance to Makor provided no such opportunity; as soon as a would-be invader passed through the main gate he had to make a sharp turn to the left, and before he could gain speed an equally sharp turn to the right, all in such tight compass that he stood exposed to the spears and arrows of the defenders who crouched above him. It was in the tangle of wall thus produced that Urbaal had his home, and it was almost as convoluted as the gate.

In the center stood an odd-shaped courtyard which served as the heart of the house, with wings radiating out in various directions. In the arm nearest the gate lived his two wives and their five children: four from his first wife, a recent boy from his second. In the opposite wing clustered the granaries, the wine pots, kitchens and rooms for his slaves, including two attractive girls who had already given him a series of children in whom he found delight. Some twenty people lived in the house of Urbaal, a center of vitality and love, and they kept it a noisy place. Peasants preferred working for this gusty man to serving in fields belonging to the temple, because although they had to work harder for Urbaal than they did for the priests, they loved him as a peasant like themselves. He ate in gulps, guzzled wine and loved to stand with them in the fields, sweat rolling down from his jug-shaped chest.

He now entered this sprawling house, passing through the courtyard, and proceeded at once to the richly adorned god-room where he kept his three Astartes on a small shelf, each accompanied by a length of stone representing one of the monoliths in the high place. His fourth Astarte he placed in position, adjusting her carefully to her new surroundings, then taking from a hidden place a piece of basalt stone which he had been saving for this purpose. It was obviously phallic, a mighty manly symbol, and he tucked it close to his goddess, whispering, 'Tonight when the moon goes down, Baal-of-the-Storm will come to lie with you.' He had found that if he kept his goddesses happy they would reciprocate, but now his need was both urgent and specific, and he wished his new patroness to understand the proposed bargain: 'Enjoy yourself tonight and every night. All I ask is that when the measuring comes, let it be me.'

He was interrupted by the arrival of his second wife, Timna, who normally would not enter his god-room, but who now appeared in some distress. She was the stately kind of wife that men for the past eight thousand years have represented in their statues—motherly, considerate and understanding. Her dark eyes were distended with fright and before she spoke Urbaal could guess what had happened. Some years before he had seen this same terrified look in his first wife's eyes, when she, too, had been unable to face reality. It was the weakness of women to look so, and Urbaal prepared himself for tears. 'What is it?' he asked gently.

Timna was an unusual girl who had come from Akka with her father on a trading visit, and she had won Urbaal's respect for the congenial manner in which she had adjusted to Matred, his domineering first wife. Instead of fighting, Timna had insisted upon a house of love—which was the more credit to her in that for the first three years of her life with Urbaal she had been childless and the target of contempt from Matred, but with the recent arrival of her first son a more harmonious balance had been achieved. As a mother she could demand respect from Matred, but now, her composure fled she told her husband, 'The priest of Melak was here.'

This was what Urbaal had expected. It was bound to come and he wished he knew something that would console his gentle wife, but he had learned that in these matters nothing could be done. 'We'll have other children,' he promised. She started to weep and a clever lie sprang to his mind. 'Timna,' he whispered seductively, 'look at what I've just bought you. A new Astarte.' She looked at the smiling goddess, so bursting with fertility, and covered her face.

'Could we run away?' she pleaded.

'Timna!' The idea was blasphemous, for Urbaal was definitely a part of the land . . . this land . . . these olive trees by the well.

'I will not surrender my son,' she persisted.

'We all do,' he reasoned gently, and he pulled her to his couch, from which she could see the reassuring Astartes who promised her fertility for years to come. Placing his arm about her he tried to add his personal reassurance, telling her of how Matred had found courage to face the same problem. 'At first she nearly perished with grief,' he confided, and Timna wondered how that austere woman had found a way to show grief. 'But later she had four other children, and one night she confessed to me, "We did the right thing." You'll have others playing about your knees, and you'll feel the same way.'

She listened attentively, but in the end whimpered, 'I cannot.'

He was tempted to show his irritation, but she was so gentle that he did not. Instead he reasoned, 'It is to Melak that we look for protection. Great El is necessary, and we cherish him, but in war only Melak is our protector.'

'Why must he be so cruel?' Timna pleaded.

'He does much for us,' Urbaal explained, 'and all he asks in return . . . our first-born sons.' To the farmer this was persuasive logic, and he started to leave for his olive fields, but Timna held his hands, pleading, until he felt that he must shock her into reality. 'As long as Makor has existed,' he said harshly, 'we have delivered to Melak our first-born sons. Matred did so. The slave girls did so. And you shall, too.' He left the room, but as he passed the courtyard he saw his latest son, six months old, gurgling in the shadows of the courtyard, and he experienced a paralyzing regret which he had been afraid to share with Timna, but she had followed him from the room and from the doorway saw his involuntary gesture of grief. She thought: Three times he has surrendered his first-born sons—Matred's and the slave girls'. His pain is greater than mine but he dares not show it.

Timna was right. Her simple-minded husband was enmeshed in the contradictions that perplexed the men of that age, the conflict between death and life—Melak demanding death while Astarte bestowed life—and he fled from the house of gaiety where his slave girls were singing with the children, and stamped through the gate, seeking solace in his olive grove. As he walked among those lovely gray-green trees whose leaves swirled upward in varied patterns, turning new faces to the sun and shimmering like jewels, he tried to counteract death by conjuring a vision of the seductive slave girl he had watched at the temple; and he recalled the first day he had seen her. The warriors of Makor had marched out on a minor raid of no consequence, one little town pestering another, and he had not bothered to go along, but when the troops returned he had come out of his house to greet them. They had come singing through the zigzag gate and among their prisoners was this enchanting girl, then only fifteen and not a resident of the town the troops had fought against, but a slave who had been captured by that town from some site farther north. Since no specific soldier had captured her, she was claimed by the priests, who saw in her a symbol which they could manipulate for profit in the town. They had sequestered her, allowing her to be seen only infrequently, and had let it be known that she was reserved for a solemn purpose. Their plan had worked. The men of Makor were excited by her presence and were tending their fields and olive presses as never before. Now her tantalizing vision moved with Urbaal as he inspected his trees.

By habit he went first to the center of his grove, where a rounded stone, scarcely six inches higher than the earth, served as the home of the baal who commanded the olive trees. Paying his obeisance to the god, Urbaal summoned his foreman, who ran up sweating. 'Still a good crop?' the farmer asked.

'Look,' the foreman said. He led Urbaal to an area of sloping rock where an ancient machine produced much of Makor's wealth. At the highest level a deep square pit some ten feet on the side had been hacked into the solid rock. It had required both tools and patience to dig so deep a hole, but the use to which it was put required inventive genius. Rising from the middle of this first pit stood a wooden table with a high rim inside which the oily fruit of pitted olives was piled; fastened into a hole in the northern face of the pit was the butt end of a stout pole, free to move up and down with considerable leverage. Over the rimmed table fitted a heavy square of wood which pressed down to squeeze the olives and extract the oil, and it was against this pressing board that the pole was brought down with considerable force. Then, because men were scarce at Makor and could not stand hour after hour merely pulling down a pole, huge stones were provided to be hung by slings on the far end of the pole so as to keep the pressure constant day and night. It was one of the world's first complicated machines, and it worked.

But part of its ingenuity lay in the fact that below the first pit lay a second, and below it a third. Through the solid rock connecting the various levels, some skilled workman had driven a small hole, so that by gravity the olive oil from the pressing pit could filter down into the second and then into the third, losing its sediment and impurities on the way. The entire process represented a sophisticated system that would hardly be improved upon in the next four thousand years. Urbaal, dipping his finger into the bottom pit, tasted the results and told his foreman, 'Good.'

'This time you're sure to win,' the foreman winked.

Then Urbaal exposed the fear that disturbed him. 'How's Amalek doing with his cows?'

'They say very good,' the foreman replied.

'He always does,' Urbaal said, not trying to hide his worry.

The foreman moved closer. 'We could turn some dogs loose among his calves.'

Urbaal shook his head. 'We don't need such tricks, but in case he's thinking the same way, I hope you're guarding the pits.'

The foreman pointed to a booth which he had recently constructed, four poles stuck in earth supporting a platform two feet off the ground, roofed over with a canopy of branches. 'From now till the end of harvest I'm sleeping in the booth.' the foreman said, and after praying to the baal of the oil pits Urbaal left the grove with a feeling of confidence; but as he returned through the zigzag gate he passed the one man who could destroy that feeling, the herdsman Amalek, a strong, wiry man taller and younger than himself, with huge muscles on the back of his legs and a confident, sunburned grin marking his amiable face. He was no mean opponent, for once before he had won and apparently intended doing so again. He greeted Urbaal with a friendly wave and left the town with long swinging strides.

When Urbaal reached home he received the ugly news that Timna had feared. The priests of Melak had returned to deliver their decision: 'The stars indicate that we shall be attacked from the north. By a host larger than before. It is therefore essential to take steps and we shall have a burning of first sons tomorrow.' With a red dye obtained from the seashore they stained the wrists of Urbaal's son and then directed the farmer to halt the screaming of his wife. Proving by their implacable detachment that there could be no appeal from their decision, they stalked from the house and proceeded to seven others, where they similarly stained the wrists of children from the leading families of Makor.

It was a moment when Urbaal wished to hear no lament from Timna, so he left the house and in the street encountered Amalek hurrying back to town, and when Urbaal saw the look of anguish on the herdsman's face he knew that Amalek's son had been selected, too. The two men did not speak, for if either had betrayed any dissatisfaction with the priests' decision he could have brought disaster upon his household.

The priests of Makor were implacable but they were not cruel. They sponsored no unnecessary barbarity and ordered only what was required to protect the community. They were the only ones who could read, and to Mesopotamia they sent their clay tablets inscribed in cuneiform, while to Egypt they sent messages in hieroglyphic. They knew figuring and astronomy and how to manage the year so that crops flourished. Without their intelligence life in Makor would have been impossible, for they served also as doctors and judges. They supervised the king's extensive lands, controlled his slaves and managed the warehouses in which food was stored against the day of famine. Only the priests understood the mystery of El rising silently from the earth and of Melak with the fiery throat, and if they now decided that the threat of war could be forestalled only by another burning, their judgment must be accepted. For they were judicious men, and when Makor was last destroyed a surviving priest had explained to the stragglers, 'Disaster came because for the past years you have sacrificed to Melak only the sons of poor families, or boys defective.' They blamed the burning of the town on this slackening of dedication and reasoned, 'If the respectable families of Makor refused Melak their first-born, why should he bother to protect them?' The logic was self-evident, so in the reconstructed town only the sons of leading families were offered to the god, and from the moment that Timna had borne her child, Urbaal had known that it must go to the fire.

Urbaal spent that night by himself in the room of the four Astartes, and there he entered upon the full conflict of death and life, for in a cradle in a corner slept his son with red-marked wrists, unaware of the ritual which he would sanctify next morning; and death was very close. But above the child stood the new Astarte smiling benevolently, and with her arrival the oil pits in the olive grove had produced their most copious run. Already she was bringing new life to the house, new fecundity, and it was possible that she would bring the tall slave girl, too. In that strange mixture of death and eroticism which marked so much of the thinking in that age, Urbaal lay on his couch listening first to his son's even breathing, then dreaming of the slave girl whom he yearned for with such passion. Death and life pervaded his thinking, as they did the room and all of Makor.

Shortly after dawn a group of priests in red capes passed through the streets banging drums and sounding trumpets, and it was a mark of Urbaal's confusion that in spite of the grief he felt over the impending loss of his son, he nevertheless hurried to the door to see if the tall slave girl was marching with the priests. She was not.

When the procession had made several circuits of the town, the drumming ceased, the priests separated, and mothers began to feel the ultimate terror. Finally a knock came on Urbaal's door, and a priest appeared to claim Timna's first-born son. Timna began to scream, but her husband placed his hand over her mouth and the priest nodded his approval, carrying the child from the house. After a while the drumming resumed and cymbals clashed. A trumpet blew and excited mutterings were heard in the town. 'We must go,' Urbaal said, taking Timna's hand, for if the mothers were not present it might be judged that they offered their sons with a grudging spirit.

But Timna, who was not of Makor, could not bring herself to attend the terrible rites. 'Let me at least stay hidden,' she begged.

Patiently Urbaal took her to the room of the gods and showed her his smiling Astarte. 'Last night,' he assured her, 'Baal-of-the-Storm came and made sport with the goddess. I watched them. She's pregnant now, and you shall be too, I promise you.' He dragged her to the door, pulled her hands away and she tried to hold herself to an entrance pillar. Then he lost his patience and slapped her sharply.

'What are sons for?' he asked. 'Stop crying.' But when they were in the street he felt sorry for her and wiped away her tears. Matred, his first wife, who had known this day, said nothing but watched from behind. 'Let her know sorrow,' she mumbled to herself.

With an aching pain in his chest Urbaal led his two wives along the twisting street to the temple square, but before he entered that sacred place he took a deep breath, set his shoulders, and did his best to quell the panic in his guts. 'Let us all be brave,' he whispered, 'for many will be watching.' But as luck would have it, the first man he saw in the holy area was the herdsman Amalek, who was also trying to control his anguish, and the two men whose sons were to go that day stared at each other in mute pain. Neither betrayed his fears, and they marched together to the monoliths, lending strength and dignity to the ritual.

Between the palace and the four menhirs dedicated to the gentler gods had been erected a platform of movable stones, under which a huge fire already raged. On the platform stood a stone god of unusual construction: it had two extended arms raised so that from the stone fingertips to the body they formed a wide inclined plane; but above the spot where they joined the torso there was a huge gaping mouth, so that whatever was placed upon the arms was free to roll swiftly downward and plunge into the fire. This was the god Melak, the new protector of Makor.

Slaves heaped fresh fagots under the statue, and when the flames leaped from the god's mouth two priests grabbed one of the eight boys—a roly-poly infant of nine months—and raised him high in the air. Muttering incantations they approached the outstretched arms, dashed the child upon them and gave him a dreadful shove downward, so that he scraped along the stony arms and plunged into the fire. As the god accepted him with a belch of fire there was a faint cry, then an anguished scream as the child's mother protested. Urbaal looked quickly to see that the cry had come from one of the wives of Amalek, and with bitter satisfaction he smiled. The priests had noticed this breach of religious solemnity, and Urbaal thought: They will remember that Amalek couldn't control his wife. This year they will choose me.

Seeking to prevent a similar disgrace in his family, which would bring him into disfavor with the priests and lose him whatever advantage he had gained from Amalek's misfortune, he gripped Timna's arm and whispered, 'Silence.' But four other boys were consigned to the flames before Timna's son was raised whimpering into the air and crushed down upon the voracious arms. With tumbling turns, as if he were a little ball, the infant dropped into the flames. Rancid smoke hissed from the red mouth and a cry started from Timna's throat, but with his free hand Urbaal caught her by the neck and preserved the dignity of sacrifice. He saw that the priests had noticed his action and had smiled approval. More than ever he felt the omens were good that he would be declared the year's winner.

The last child was a boy of nearly three–his parents had prayed that the years had passed when he might be taken–and he was old enough to understand what was happening, so with frightened eyes he drew back from the priests, and when they lifted him to the god he screamed, trying to hold on to the stone fingers and save himself, but the priests pulled away his small, clutching hands, and with a violent push sent him tumbling into the flaming mouth.

As soon as the boy had disappeared, wailing in fiery smoke, the mood of the temple changed. The god Melak was forgotten; his fires were allowed to die down and his priests turned to other important matters. Drums resumed their beat–this time in livelier rhythms–and trumpets sounded. The people of Makor, satisfied that their new god would protect them, left him smoking by the monoliths and gathered about the steps of the temple itself, where a sense of excitement replaced the terror that had recently held sway. Even the mothers of the eight boys, numb with pain, were moved into new positions, and although they must have longed to flee that place and grieve in silence, they were required as patronesses who had pleased the god with their first-born to remain in locations of honor. They were permitted neither to comment nor to look away, for this was the tradition of their society and would be forever.

When a community like Makor dedicated itself to a god of death like Melak and to a goddess of life like Astarte, the believers entered unknowingly upon a pair of spirals which spun them upward or downward–as one judged the matter–to rites that were bound to become ever more bizarre. For example, during the long centuries when the town confined itself to worshiping the original monolith El, the priests were satisfied if the town praised its god with libations of oil or food set out on wooden trays, for the inherent nature of El was such that he demanded only modest honors. And, when the three additional monoliths were added, their natures required no extraordinary honors; as for the humble baals of the olive grove and oil press, they were satisfied with simple rites: a kiss, a wreath of flowers draped over the pillar, or a genuflection.

But when the god Melak was imported from the coastal cities of the north, a new problem arose. The citizens of Makor were eager to adopt him, partly because his demands upon them were severe, as if this proved his power, and partly because they had grown somewhat contemptuous of their local gods precisely because they were not demanding. Melak, with his fiery celebrations, had not been forced upon the town; the town had sought him out as the fulfillment of a felt need, and the more demanding he became, the more they respected him. No recent logic in Makor was so persuasive as that of the priests after the destruction of the town: 'You were content to give damaged sons to Melak and in return he gave you damaged protection.' Equally acceptable was the progression whereby Melak's appetite had expanded from the blood of a pigeon to the burning of a dead sheep to the immolation of living children, for with each extension of his appetite he became more powerful and therefore more pleasing to the people he tyrannized. What he might next require in way of sacrifice no one could predict, least of all the priests, for when the new demands were announced they would not be something forced down upon the people by the priests: they would be rites insisted upon by the people, who within limits received the kinds of gods they were able to imagine.

Furthermore, the cult of human sacrifice was of itself not abominable, nor did it lead to the brutalization of society: lives were lost which could have been otherwise utilized, but the matter ended in death and excessive numbers were not killed, nor did the rites in which they died contaminate the mind. In fact, there was something grave and stately in the picture of a father willing to sacrifice his first-born son as his ultimate gift for the salvation of a community; and in later years, not far from Makor, one of the world's great religions would be founded upon the spiritual idealization of such a sacrifice as the central, culminating act of faith. At Makor it was not death that corrupted, but life.

For in the case of Astarte things were different. To begin with, she was a much older deity than fiery Melak and perhaps even older then El himself, for when the first farmer planted wheat intentionally he bound himself like a slave to the concept of fertility. Without the aid of some god to fructify the earth the farmer was powerless. It was not what he did that insured prosperity, but what the god chose to do; and it required only a moment's reflection to convince men that the force behind fertility must be feminine. Even the crudest representation of the female form could be recognized as a symbol of fertility: her feet were planted in the soil; her legs carried the receptacle into which the seed must be placed; her swelling womb reflected the growth that occurred in the dark earth; her breasts were the rains that nurtured the fields; her bright smile was the sun that warmed the world; and her flowing hair was the cool breeze that kept the land from parching. Once men took the cultivation of their fields seriously the worship of such a goddess was inevitable. In principle it was a gentle religion, paralleling man's most profound experience, regeneration through the mystery of sex. The concept of man and goddess working hand in hand in the population of the world and in the feeding of it was one of the notable philosophical discoveries, both ennobling and productive; of only a few religious patterns could this be said.

But ingrained in this enchanting concept was a spiral more swift and sickening than any which operated in the case of Melak, the god of death. The homage that Astarte demanded was so persuasive, so gentle in its simplicity, that all were eager to participate. Once a goddess guaranteed a town's fertility, certain rites became inevitable: flowers rich with pollen were placed before her, white pigeons were released and then lambs which had finished weaning. Beautiful women who wanted children but were denied them came to seek her intervention, and maidens who were to be wed gathered to dance seductively before her. Her rites were especially attractive because they were conducted by the fairest citizens of the town and the strongest farmers. A spell of beauty encased the goddess: she saw only the largest bunches of grapes, the most golden barley, and when the drums beat for her their rhythms were not martial. The spiral of Astarte was a succession of the loveliest things man knows, except that any sensible man could see where it must end, for once Makor gave itself over to worshipping the principle of fertility it became inevitable that the rites must finally be celebrated in the only logical way. And sooner or later the citizens would insist that this be done publicly. It was neither the priests nor the girls nor the men involved who demanded these demoralizing public rites: it was the people, and the inevitability of sickening spin was about to be demonstrated anew in the person of Urbaal the farmer, who had just offered his first-born to the flames and who would, in any normal society, have been burdened with grief, as his wife was at that moment.

But in Makor, Urbaal switched easily, almost with joy, from death to life, waiting for the next celebration which had been cunningly arranged by the priests for that purpose. With mounting excitement he listened as the drums beat joyously, accompanied by a flurry of trumpets which brought the music to a vivid crescendo. It was halted by a priest who came from the temple, raising his arms above his head and crying, 'After death comes life. After mourning, joy.'

A group of singers, including both old men and young girls, began chanting happily of the seasons through which the year passes. Their words spoke of growth and the fertility of animals which abided in the fields. It was a song as pristine in thought as one could have devised and it summarized in ideal form the basic elements of the fertility rites: man was able to live because the earth and things thereon increased, and anything that spurred this increase was automatically good.

The priest now spoke directly to the parents whose sons had died to protect the town: 'It does not matter at what age a male dies to defend his community. The infant of months'—and here he looked at Urbaal and his wife—'is as notable a hero as the general of forty. Men are born to die gloriously and those who do so as children achieve greatness earlier than we who grow older. For them we do not grieve. They have fulfilled the destiny of males and their mothers shall feel pride.' It was an inspiring theory, and to some it brought inspiration, but not to stubborn Timna, who knew instinctively that an evil thing had been done: her son of six months had had before him the great years, and to cut him off for the good of the town was reprehensible. 'But in the hour of death, even the death of a hero,' said the priest, 'it is obligatory to remember life. To those whose children died to save this town Astarte, goddess of fertility and life, offers new life, new children, new fields and new animals grazing upon those fields. Now, in the hour of death, life is born again!'

The drums exploded and the songs of the singers rose to heaven as two priests from the interior of the temple led forth a priestess clothed in white. It was the moment that Urbaal had been awaiting—for this was the slave girl, tall and most radiantly beautiful. Standing at the edge of the temple steps, she kept her hands folded and her eyes downcast while the priest signaled for the music to cease, whereupon priestly hands began taking away her garments, one by one, allowing them to fall like petals until she stood naked for the approval of the town.

She was an exquisite human being, a perfection of the goddess Astarte, for no man could look at her provocative form without seeing in her the sublime representation of fertility. She was a girl whose purpose was to be loved, to be taken away and made fertile so that she could reproduce her grandeur and bless the earth. Urbaal stared with unbelieving eyes as the naked girl submitted herself to the crowd's inspection. She was much more beautiful than he had imagined, much more desirable than he had guessed when he watched with such hungry eyes her infrequent appearances. The priests had been right in predicting that if they exhibited their new slave sparingly they could build up to the excitement that now throbbed in the crowd.

'She is Libamah,' the priest in charge announced, 'servant of Astarte, and soon in the month of harvest she will go to the man who has this year produced the best, whether it be barley or olives or cattle or any growth of the soil.'

'Let it be me,' Urbaal whispered hoarsely. Clenching his fists he prayed to all his Astartes, 'Let it be me.' But his rational-minded second wife, Timna, seeing this extraordinary thing—that a man who had just lost a son could be lusting so quickly after a slave girl—thought that he must be out of his mind. She saw his lips forming the prayer, 'Let it be me,' and she felt sorry for him that his sense of life should have been so corrupted.

The priest raised his arms in blessing over the naked girl, then lowered them slowly to indicate that singing was wanted, and the musicians began a hushed chant to which the tall girl started quietly to dance. Keeping her head lowered she moved her arms and knees in seductive rhythms, increasing the tempo of her movements as the drums grew more prominent. Soon her feet were apart, and she was gyrating in taunting patterns until the men of the audience were biting their lips in hunger. Urbaal, watching like a fascinated boy, observed that never did the girl open her eyes. She danced like a remote goddess, being no part of the ceremony herself, but the passion of her virgin body summarized all the earth for him, and he wanted to leap onto the porch now and take her, to open her eyes, to bring her down to this world.

'In the month of harvest,' the priest shouted to the crowd, 'she will belong to one of you.' Quickly his assistants covered her tall form with the discarded clothes and whisked her from sight. The crowd groaned, even the women, for they had hoped to see a more complete ceremony; but the steps were not empty for long: four well-known priestesses were led forth—many men had known these four—and they too were stripped naked, revealing far less inviting bodies than Libamah's, but symbols of fertility nevertheless. With no delay the priests nominated four townsmen to join the priestesses, and the citizens—lucky or unlucky as the case might be—left their wives and leaped up the steps. Each grabbed for the woman designated for him, leading her to the chambers set aside for this periodic rite.

'Through them life will be born again!' the chorus chanted, and the drums echoed quietly, continuing until some time later when the men reappeared. In the days following the formal announcement that Libamah would be given ritually to the man who produced the finest crop, Urbaal spent most of his hours working at the oil press, often reaching the spot before his foreman had climbed down out of the booth in which he slept. Before he spoke to the man or looked at the results of the previous days' pressing, Urbaal went to the rock into which the vats had been cut and there, at a knob in the rock, he paid obeisance to the baal of the oil press, thanking him for what he had accomplished yesterday and begging his help for today. He then prayed to the baal of the vats and the baal of the jugs in which the oil was stored, that it be kept sweet. Only then did he consult with the foreman, after which he went to the baal of the grove itself and to the small stone pillar representing the god of the highway along which his jugs would be transported, and to each of these baals he spoke as if the god were a living entity, for in the world that Urbaal knew, he was surrounded by an infinity of gods.

In his present preoccupation Urbaal found much assurance in the existence of these baals, for if he hoped to win the ravishing Libamah he required their assistance. It pleased him to know that he shared the earth with such puissant creatures—a god of the olive press, for example, who could produce a wonderful substance like olive oil: good for eating with bread, good to cook in, for spreading hot on one's limbs or cool on one's head, an oil appropriate for anointing gods or for burning at night in clay lamps. It was obvious that only a god could have called forth such a commodity, and the one who had done so should be cherished; such reliance created a psychological assurance that men of a later age would not know. The gods were immediately at hand and could be bargained with; they were friends as long as life lasted, and if perchance they turned against a man it was only because he had done some wrong which he could rectify:

'Place the burdens on me, great El, that the gods may be free.
Let my back bend, that theirs may be straight.'

Thus was the song of Urbaal as he sweated at his press, striving to squeeze out the last drops of oil.

The priests, watching the diligence of the free farmers, were satisfied with the stratagem their predecessors had devised thousands of years earlier: by giving the owners of free land an incentive to work hard the temple could establish standards for judging what its slaves should be expected to accomplish. But at the same time the priests were canny men, and although they held up to their slaves the examples set by men like Urbaal and Amalek, they knew that they could not enforce such quotas, nor did they try; for on the one hand the temple slaves did not own their land, and on the other they had not the powerful attraction of a living goddess like Libamah luring them on. It was remarkable, the priests reflected as they observed the sweating Urbaal, what men could accomplish under proper enticement, and it was reassuring to see that his example permeated the community, even though few could match it.

In these midsummer days, when the quality of Makor's harvest was being determined, Timna was led to review the principles by which she lived. She was now twenty-four years old and had come a stranger to Makor, so that some of its customs she could not comprehend, but she had never believed that life would have been much better in her home city of Akka. True, in Akka the god Melak would not have grabbed her first-born in his fiery arms, but other gods would have exacted other tribute, so she had few illusions; on balance, life in Makor was as good as it could have been in any of the neighbouring communities. From time to time, however, she heard rumours in merchant circles of a much different manner of life in distant areas like Egypt and Mesopotamia. One year an Egyptian general, much harried and suspicious of everyone, had stopped in Makor, spending three days with the king, and he seemed a man who saw enormous distances beyond the confining walls of one town. On passing Urbaal's house he had stopped out of natural curiosity to inspect the place, asking through his interpreter a series of intelligent questions. It was from this experience that Timna had first entertained the concept that beyond Makor there was another world and beyond it another, and she wondered what authority cruel Melak enjoyed in those worlds, or to what extent half-buried El could dominate those communities. Watching her husband report to the baals of his fields, one after the other—olive grove, olive press, oil vats, oil jugs, highway, beehives, wheat, barley—she deduced that these must be very puny gods indeed, no better really than extended men, and that if one god went down or were lost it could not matter much. Now, as she found herself pregnant again, she was delighted to think that her lost son would be replaced. But when she went in to give thanks to the new clay Astarte and saw that seductive body and the enticing smile, she felt a most serious contradiction: her pregnancy had coincided with the arrival of this winsome little goddess, and perhaps Astarte had been directly responsible; but on the other hand why should anyone assume that Astarte was any more powerful or extensive in her realm than the pitiful little baals that her husband worshiped were in theirs? It was a perplexing question, but on the day she told her husband that she was pregnant again Urbaal was so delighted that when he carried her into the god-room and placed her gently on his bed, crying, 'I knew that Astarte would bring us children,' she stifled her skepticism and concurred, 'Astarte did it.'

But as soon as she had made this surrender she had to look at her foolish husband and say to herself: He's happy that I'm pregnant, but not because of me. And not because of my future son. But only because it proves his new Astarte is powerful. He thinks that she will give him the right to stay with Libamah. And thus was born the contempt that she could never thereafter stifle.

As the month of harvest approached, it was obvious that Astarte had blessed not only Urbaal and his wife, but the town as a whole. Herdsmen reported record growth amongst their cattle, weavers piled bolts of cloth on their shelves, and the wheat crop was plentiful. Urbaal, at the olive grove, had riches unmatched and was already supplying oil and honey to donkey caravans from Akka, where boats were putting in from Egypt and Tyre for the surpluses. The military threats from the north had subsided, as the god Melak had predicted, and there was bounty in the air.

In the regions around Makor there had developed a tradition that would later be observed in many nations: thanksgiving for such a year of fruitfulness; and as the harvest ended, music began to sound and people prepared themselves for the forthcoming celebrations. The men who might logically aspire to winning Libamah grew nervous as the priests came to review their year's operations, and Urbaal heard with some dismay that Amalek had done wonders with his cattle. At home Urbaal grew irritable and Timna, satisfied with her pregnancy, looked at him with a gentle condescension. It seemed ridiculous to her that a man with two wives and adequate slaves should drive himself to nervous distraction over the prospect of spending some time with a girl who, after some months of serving as the chief attraction at the temple, would gradually subside into being one of the ordinary prostitutes who were served out in batches of three and four at the conclusion of celebrations, ending at last as an unwanted old woman given to slaves in hopes that an extra child or two might be lured from her womb. In no way did she resent Libamah; the girl was pretty and Timna could understand why a man might want her, but that Urbaal should take the matter seriously was disgusting. Furthermore, the wise wife could guess at the other apprehensions that must be tormenting her husband as the time for choosing Libamah's mate approached: there had been a year when the man chosen had been so excited and nervous that he had made a pitiful spectacle of himself, throwing the whole ritual into confusion and bringing disgrace upon Makor, so that Astarte was annoyed and refused to make the ensuing crops bountiful. One night as Timna sat brooding in the courtyard, she heard her husband praying to Astarte that he might be the chosen one, then praying a second time that if he were chosen he might be equal to the task—for it would be ridiculous to celebrate a fertility rite in which fertility was obviously impossible.

All these matters the priests took into consideration as they approached the day on which to make their final selection of the year's representative. Amalek and Urbaal were each strong men and each had proved himself by having numerous children. The fact that Timna was pregnant again aided Urbaal's claims, but the unusual fecundity of Amalek's cattle was equally impressive and the priests wavered between the two.

The climax of thanksgiving began with three days of feasting in which enormous banquets were provided by the temple priests, drawing upon stores of food accumulated by their slaves in the preceding year. Cattle were slaughtered and wine from temple jugs was liberally distributed. There was dancing and tumbling and juggling. Musicians played long into the night, and passing traders were encouraged to lay up their caravans and share in the celebration.

Then, on the fourth day, the entire town and its surroundings—something over a thousand people—congregated at the temple, where appetites were whetted by having one of the prettiest of the older temple prostitutes dance nude, after which she allowed herself to be led off into one of the chambers by a youth of sixteen who had been fortified with wine to prepare him for the ritual. There was other dancing of an erotic nature, adoration of both the male and female figure, and finally the presentation of the young priestess, Libamah, who was again ceremonially undressed by the priests. A hush fell over the crowd, and the men who might be chosen leaned forward as the enchanting girl began her final dance of the year. It went far beyond what she had done before, and as she drew to a conclusion, any man in the audience would have been a capable partner; but the priests assembled and their leader cried, 'Urbaal is the man!'

The farmer leaped onto the steps and stood with his feet apart, staring at Libamah, who turned to accept him while the priests quickly stripped away his clothing. He stood forth as a powerful man and the crowd cheered as he strode forward, gathered the young priestess in his arms and carried her into the hall of Astarte, where he would lie with her for seven days.

Timna, still grieving for her son, watched the performance dispassionately and muttered, 'What folly! The fertility is in the soil. It is in me.' And while others celebrated she walked slowly homeward, seeing life in a new and painful clarity: with different gods her husband Urbaal would have been a different man; and she went into his god-room, looked with abhorrence at the four Astartes, and methodically smashed the first three along with their phallic companions. She then lifted the fourth goddess and would have smashed it, too, except that in the moment of doing so she was struck by the atavistic suspicion that perhaps this Astarte had indeed caused her present pregnancy and if destroyed might end it. She couldn't be sure, so she took the figurine and the fragments to an empty spot along the wall, where she buried them deep in earth, ridiculing as she did so both the goddess and the man who had so disgustingly committed his life to her.

THE TELL

The archaeologists had rigged a shower in back of the administration building, and when anyone used it he must afterward hurry along a footpath to return to his tent for dressing. One evening as Cullinane was returning, he came upon Dr Eliav headed toward the shower, and the Irishman said, 'When you're finished, would you clear something up for me?'

The Jew nodded, and after Cullinane had rubbed down and slipped into his shorts and sports shirt he waited on the edge of his bed until Eliav appeared. 'The other day,' Cullinane reminded him, 'we were speaking at lunch and I described Israel as part of "the fertile crescent." You started to make some observation but we were interrupted. What did you have in mind?'

Eliav leaned against the tent pole and remarked. 'To me the phrase sounds old-fashioned.'

'I picked it up in Chicago. Breasted used it for the land between Mesopotamia and the Nile.'

'It was a useful cliché,' Eliav granted, 'but no longer.'

'The land's still fertile,' Cullinane argued.

'But if you conceive of Israel as being merely passive, the arable fields over which people walked on their way to other arable fields, your thought remains passive. You miss the dynamism of our history.'

'How do you think of the land?'

Eliav took three of Cullinane's books and laid them casually on the bed, their corners touching and with an empty space in the middle. 'Asia, Africa, Europe, and this empty area—the Mediterranean. Leakey's discoveries in Kenya last year pretty well prove that man originated in Africa at least two million years ago, plus or minus. He wandered into Israel rather late, possibly from Asia, more likely from Africa.'

'I don't see how this relates to the fertile-crescent concept.'

'Since the area's a natural highway, it's always been a focus of forces. Even in geology. We're a fracture point where continents meet and twist. Many earthquakes and violent storms. You remember what Stekelis found along the River Jordan?'

Cullinane recalled the discovery that had startled the archaeological world some years before: an area where rocks that had once been horizontal was torn apart and tilted vertically in the air. Such fractures were common throughout the world, but imbedded in his tilted areas Stekelis found parts of a skeleton and unmistakable tools of men who had been living before the upper soil had been laid down or the area tilted . . . say, a million years ago. 'Imagine the earthquake those characters went through,' he said.

'Point I'm trying to make,' Eliav insisted, 'is that even the first men in this area were caught up in violence. Ever since, it's been the same way. Down here mighty Egypt. Up here the Mesopotamian powers. As these great forces pressed against each other, the point where they usually met was Israel. When we stand out on the tell, John, we shouldn't visualize fertile fields but dusty Egyptians thrusting up from the south with mighty armies, and the Mesopotamians swinging down from the north with equal strength. It was in this cauldron, this violent marching of many feet, that Israel was born.'

'You think this has been the permanent characteristic?'

'Yes. Because after the Egypt-Mesopotamia struggle came the Sea Peoples arriving from the west'—with a broad sweep of his hand across the Mediterranean he indicated the coming of the Phoenicians and the Philistines with their chariots and weapons of iron—'opposing the Syrians moving in from the east. More fractures, more violence, then the Greeks from the west locked in mortal combat with the Persians from the east. Then Romans on their way to fight Parthians. And Byzantines thundering against the Arabs. Most dramatic, I suppose, were the Crusades, when Christians from Europe smashed against Muslims from Asia. This was always the battleground, the focus of forces. In recent times we've had Napoleon here battling the Turks in Acre, and lately the Germans of Rommel trying to capture Jerusalem and Damascus.'

'You think the focus-of-forces concept more meaningful than the old fertile-crescent idea?'

'Yes, because it reminds us of the conflict and the intellectual confrontation we've witnessed.'

The manner in which Cullinane sat on his bed caused his left hand to represent the armies of the west and his right the east. Bringing them together with a bang over Israel, he recalled the struggles Eliav had summarized: Egypt versus Babylonia; Greece crashing against Persia; Rome vanquishing the east; Crusader fighting infidel; and finally Jew battling Arab. 'All right,' he conceded, 'this is where violence met violence. What am I supposed to conclude?'

'I don't rightly know,' Eliav confessed. Then tentatively he added, 'But I do know that if you visualize Israel merely as a stopping place along a fertile crescent where placid farmers rested on their way to Egypt, you miss the whole point. It wasn't like that at all. It was a meeting place of dynamisms. And because we Jews were at the focus of forces we became the most dynamic of all. We had to. To stay alive. We were spun in a terrible vortex, but because we were Jews we loved it. On the faces of our kids at the kibbutz, don't you sense a kind of radiance? We stand where the fires are hottest. We're at the focus of forces. John, don't you sometimes see it on their faces?'

He stopped, embarrassed by his unusual display of vehemence, and replaced the books, but as he did so he saw Schwartz climbing down from the tell, where he had been inspecting the day's dig. 'Eh, Schwartz!' he called, and when the dark-skinned secretary entered the tent, Eliav asked, 'From here, how far north to the enemy border?'

'Ten miles.'

'East to the Syrians?'

'Twenty-three.'

'West to where Egypt tried to invade us?'

'Eight.'

'With the enemy so close? The threats you hear them make over the radio? Aren't you scared?'

The tough Israeli snorted. 'Since I'm living in Israel no week passes without at least one story in the newspaper how Egypt is going to wipe us out with rockets made by the German scientists. Or Syria massacre us. Or some Arab army push us into the sea.' He thrust his jaw at Cullinane and said dispassionately, 'If I scared easy I wouldn't be here. I feel a lot more relaxed right now than I ever did in Germany.'

The customary procedure when a man had lain for seven days and seven nights with one of the ritual prostitutes—for that is what Libamah was, no matter how often she was termed a priestess—was for him to go back to his regular wives and forget the girl, who often became pregnant with a child which was upon birth sacrificed to the fires of Melak; but this year the outcome was to be different, for Urbaal left the temple at the end of his performance inflamed with a permanent infatuation for the priestess. He had found her an enchanting, ingenuous girl who enjoyed telling in broken accents of her life in the north and of the manner in which her crafty father had defrauded the men of his region. She had a gift of mimicry and pantomimed the soldiers who had captured her in the various battles leading to her slavery, and with intriguing insight summarized their attempts to seduce her while others were not looking. She was especially amusing when she described in a husky voice, which Urbaal relished, how the local priests had coached her to look shy: 'Keep your fingertips close to your knees and your eyes lowered. When you look sideways try to press your chin into your shoulder.' She also demonstrated how they had taught the erotic dances, and Urbaal found her capable both in her evaluations and in her love-making. It was not surprising that he became infatuated with her.

For her part, she recognized the sturdy farmer merely as an average man, more tender than most who had tried to make love with her, and certainly more honest than her father. One morning she said casually, 'I admire you because you are not vain of yourself, nor too exalted in your opinions, nor overly bothered with mean thoughts.' The words excited him and he began wondering; he laughed noisily at her stories and was not offended when she pulled gray hairs from his head or mimicked the manner in which he had leaped onto the steps to take her; at the moments when she made believe she was Urbaal she became an awkward, likable farmer, and he conceived the idea that she was acting so because she desired him, an impression that was fortified by her ardent passion in love-making. Could the priests have spied into the sacred room during the hours that Libamah and Urbaal occupied it, they would have been distressed, for here there was no lofty sense of ritual, no male principle fructifying the handmaiden of Astarte; here were merely two uncomplicated human beings who enjoyed each other and who laughed a good deal while doing so. When the day of parting came, it was understandable that Urbaal could not accept it as final, for under the auspices of the goddess of love he had fallen in love, and when he kissed the enchanting girl good-bye he surprised her by making a dramatic promise, delivered in quivering voice, 'You are to be mine.'

More from amusement than from passion she asked, 'How?' and he did not understand that she was mocking him.

'I don't know,' he said gravely. 'But I'll think of something.'

At the exit from the love-room the priests handed back his clothes, and as he put on his linen breeches, woolen shirt tied at the waist, and sandals, he scarcely knew what he was doing, for tall Libamah stood naked in his imagination and he could not dismiss her, nor could he reply when townsmen in the square asked with envy, 'Did you get her with child?'

Refusing to share in the ribaldry customary at such times, he walked in a kind of daze through the streets until a loud-mouthed shepherd cried, 'Five months from now at the new year I'll be sleeping between those long brown legs.' Urbaal whipped about and would have struck the man for his insolence except that the stupid, lascivious face made striking inappropriate. Urbaal managed a sickly laugh, but as he approached his house he met his frend Amalek, tall and bronzed from his life with the cattle, and it was then that he began to conceive his powerful jealousy.

What if this one should want to lie with her? he thought to himself. And unfortunately Amalek said half-jokingly, 'We haven't seen you for seven days.' There was no clever reply that Urbaal could think of. He couldn't joke; he couldn't show how deeply the week had affected him; and he dared not show his newly born jealousy. Dumbly he looked at the sunburned herdsman and passed on.

At home he paused in the courtyard to greet his wives and to play with his many children. A slave girl brought a jug of freshly pressed pomegranate juice and a set of clay cups made in Akka, so that in spite of his agitation he experienced a moment of quiet satisfaction in being home again with his noisy family. Tomorrow he would go down to the fields and report to the baal of his olive grove, to the deities of the honeycomb, the olive press and the wheat fields his gratification for the boon they had delivered to him. In that relaxed moment he would have been judged the leading citizen of Makor, at peace with his gods, respected by his neighbours and loved by his wives, his slaves and his children. But when he passed into his god-room to drink wine before Astarte in thanks for the crucial aid she had given him in his sexual triumph, he was gripped with cold fear. His goddesses had vanished. Rushing back to the courtyard he cried, 'What happened?'

'To what?' Timna asked quietly, masking the fact that she had been awaiting this critical moment.

'The goddesses. They've gone.'

'No!' Matred cried. Followed by Timna she hurried to the room and promptly returned, anxiety showing in her dark face.

Urbaal fell onto the hard-earth bench that ran along two sides of the courtyard, showing a degree of fear Timna had not anticipated. 'What could have happened?' he asked. In bewilderment he pushed away the food offered by the slaves.

'Even the four stones are gone,' Matred whispered.

Urbaal drew back from his women, and asked, 'Has anyone been here who might want to hurt me?'

'No,' Matred said.

His face tensed. He had hoped that the goddesses had been stolen, for this would mean that they had left against their will; if they had fled of their own accord it could mean only that Astarte was displeased over something; his olive trees would wither and the press would yield no oil. He was so frightened at this prospect that Timna realized she should explain that she had destroyed the statues and there was no mystery. But intending to help her husband she temporized: 'On the day of the burning we returned to find the door ajar.' She knew this was true, because she had left it so when running out to bury the Astartes.

'Yes!' Matred remembered. 'When you took the priestess into the love-room, Urbaal, we stayed to hear the music. Later I found Timna and when we reached home the gate stood open.'

Eagerly Urbaal interrogated the slaves, and they also recollected. 'We discussed it at the time,' one of them said. But who could the thief have been? Urbaal drew farther away and sat with his arms clasping his knees against his body, suspiciously reviewing a list of his enemies, until his nascent jealousy proposed one, 'Amalek!' he cried. 'When I met him today he was very shifty.' It had been the other way around; he had been the shifty one, not Amalek.

Then Timna, deploring the fear that had captured her silly husband, tried to comfort him by adding a lie that she would often regret: 'I believe it must have been Amalek. He was jealous that you won the tall girl.'

Eagerly Urbaal accepted the solution: 'That thief!' And since he could now believe that an ordinary enemy had stolen his goddesses instead of their having deserted him, he felt a burden of fear dissolve. It was with actual relief that he ran from the house and went to the shop of bearded Heth, where he refused to answer the Hittite's questions about Libamah but did buy three new Astartes, which he installed on the shelf of his god-room. He then went out into the fields to find for his goddesses the phallic rocks they merited.

Through his olive grove he wandered, inspecting stones and pausing to worship his comforting baals, but when at the oil press he whispered, 'Thank you for winning me Libamah,' the mention of her name reminded him how vulnerable he had become; for as he walked among the trees he saw her moving ahead of him, her sinuous form emerging from their twisted trunks. Through the shimmering leaves her voice called to him, joyously and with a promise of sex. When bees hummed in the autumn grass he heard her chuckling laughter and was reminded of how permanent his hunger for her had become.

Then, as he crossed the road in search of a third stone in the shape that goddesses preferred, he happened to come upon Amalek tending his cattle, and the tall herdsman had the bad fortune–in view of its consequences it might almost be termed fatal–to ask casually, 'What are you doing, Urbaal? Finding stones for your new goddesses?'

How could Amalek have known that Urbaal had new goddesses? The olive grower looked at his recent competitor suspiciously, placed his hands behind his back and asked, 'How do you know what I'm doing?

'If I'd won the tall one,' Amalek said generously, 'I'd buy some new Astartes.'

Urbaal interpreted this devious reply as meaning that Amalek now had the four stolen goddesses working for him. 'I suppose you know how to keep Astarte happy?' Urbaal asked in clumsy strategy.

'I wish I did. Then at new year maybe I'd win the tall one.'

To Urbaal the words were infuriating, and he tried to think of something effective to reply, but he was muted. He turned, still with his hands behind his back, and stalked off. 'I see you found the stones,' Amalek said as he led his cattle away.

For Urbaal the day was ruined, and on his way back to the zigzag gate he launched the series of tragic dislocations that were to mark the last months of that year: he forgot to salute the baal of his olive grove. All he could visualize was the herdsman Amalek, who had stolen the Astartes. The man's own words condemned him, and what was especially infuriating, he was bold enough to joke about the matter, as if he knew that Urbaal had lost his power. Gloomily he carried the stones to his god-room, but his three new Astartes gave no sign that they appreciated his thoughtfulness. His mouth had an ashen taste, proving that things had gone savagely wrong, and his mood was not improved when he walked to the temple area, lounging idly in hopes of seeing Libamah. She did not appear, but toward dusk Heth the Hittite closed his shop and came to speak with Urbaal. With his natural shrewdness the merchant could easily guess why Urbaal lingered there, and said, 'Forget her, Urbaal. In the months ahead we'll all enjoy that one.'

The farmer was outraged, morally shocked, and he would have struck Heth were he not forced to acknowledge that what the Hittite said was true: once

Libamah had been used to sanctify the harvest, her uniqueness was spent and she would be quickly offered at the lesser feasts. When the new year came at the beginning of the planting season she would be brought forth again, and by the next autumn she would be available at monthly festivals while some new girl occupied premier place at the harvest 'A year from now you can have her any time you want,' Heth said. 'Just knock on the temple door.' The Hittite's insinuating laugh agitated Urbaal and in growing darkness he left the holy place but did not go home. By a narrow alley he made his way to the house of Amalek, where he stood in shadows trying to guess where his stolen goddesses might be. What galled him was the vision of Amalek's using the stolen Astartes against him, and he constructed several ways whereby he might break into the enemy house and recover them. At the moment none of the plans seemed feasible, so he went home, mean in spirit and hungry for Libamah.

It was more than a week before he saw her again, but when he did the effect was more powerful than before: with stately grace she walked across the temple steps and when she saw him ogling her from the monoliths she gave him a casual glance which cut him like a copper arrow-point, for he convinced himself that she had tried to send him the signal: 'How will you rescue me?' He wanted to cry, 'I'll save you, Libamah.' But all he could do was stare at her as she disappeared.

The following days speeded his deterioration. He began to lose his sense of continuity; ignoring the fact that now his olive trees required attention, he stopped going down to the grove. He searched no more for the dead trees in which fall honey rested, and his wheat fields by the white oaks could wait. He spent his time alternately brooding over the wrong Amalek had done him and longing for the slave girl, and inescapably the two preoccupations began to blend, so that he could not keep his mind focused on either. One night when there was no moon he found a dark cloth and tied it over his face, slipping out of his house with the intention of harming Amalek—how, he did not know. He stayed all night in the street waiting for a practical idea but none came, and with the dawn he stuffed the cloth inside his shirt and went to the temple to study ways whereby he might break through its portals and rescue Libamah. Again he could devise nothing.

A minor festival for Baal-of-the-Storm arrived, and Libamah was brought forth to dance, keeping her eyes downcast as she had been coached, but twice she happened to look in the general direction of Urbaal and again he was satisfied that she was signaling him. At the conclusion of her erotic performance, when Urbaal was burning with desire for her, she retired and the priests threw out the four old prostitutes, nominating him for one of them. The idea was repugnant and he refused to move forward, but Timna, who appreciated what was happening, whispered, 'If you misbehave they will kill you,' and he simulated eagerness in going to the steps. But when he was alone with his substitute priestess he could do nothing, not even visualize her as a woman, though she stood naked before him, and this behaviour the disappointed prostitute reported to the priests, who became suspicious; they compared this performance with his earlier reaction to Libamah and shrewdly guessed what was in his mind.

Now, lost in a hopeless mania, he devised a clever trick for killing Amalek. He would meet him on the street and drive a spear through his chest. Escape afterward? He had no time to bother about such details. Punishment if caught? All he could see was the laughing face of Amalek and the sudden fear that would take possession when Urbaal leaped at him. In his god-room he practiced the fatal leap many times, then heard Timna standing beside him in her nightclothes: 'Husband, evil days have overtaken you. Can I help?'

Unable to determine exactly who she was, he looked at her stately form and half remembered the joy they had shared when she had first become pregnant with the son who had been burned. He saw those fires of death and drew back. Then he recalled that he had loved Timna in those placid days as now he loved Libamah, but in a deeper, more mature manner. He saw Timna as the smiling Astarte of life and his brain became confused. She was in the way and he pushed her from his room.

Knowing that she was needed, she stubbornly returned and said, 'Urbaal, if you continue in this madness your groves will diminish. Forget the prostitute. Forget Amalek.'

Gripping her by the arm he asked fiercely, 'How do you know my fears?'

'The night you were planning to kill Amalek . . .''

'How do you know that?'

'Urbaal,' she confessed gently, 'I stayed near you in the street, watching for hours to help you.'

He pushed her away as if she were a spy. 'Who has told you these things?'

Patiently she explained, 'It's you who tell everyone. Don't you suppose the priests already know? At the festival if I hadn't urged you . . .''

He felt a strangling rage. On the one hand he wanted to rush out and kill Amalek wherever he stood, and on the other he wanted to surrender to Timna's quiet consolation. He wanted to rescue Libamah–no matter how many priests protected her–and yet he wanted to recapture the simplicity he had known with Timna. In the darkness, broken only by the flickering light that came from a clay lamp burning oil from his olives, he looked with surrender toward the dignified woman who had come to him from the strangeness of Akka. He knew her now as his loving wife, quiet and understanding, with more wisdom than the ordinary woman, and he was not surprised that she had been the one to fathom his secrets. He allowed her to sit on his bed and the strangling insanity subsided. For the first time in many weeks he prayed to Astarte, but as he did so, Timna said, 'Forget the goddesses, Urbaal. They have no power over a man like you.'

He did not argue. The idea was strange and repugnant, but on this weary night he did not wish to debate, so she continued unhindered. 'Forget your hatred of Amalek. He didn't steal your goddesses. It was an ordinary thief, of that I'm sure.' He leaned forward, wanting to believe her words, for he had long known Amalek to be an honest husbandman.

'You think he was not to blame?' he asked hopefully.

'I know he wasn't. And you must also forget . . .''

'Don't tell me to forget the priestess,' he begged.

Timna smiled. It was preposterous, and she knew it, for a wife to be consoling her husband over a temple prostitute, but she stifled her repugnance and reasoned, 'Urbaal, if you love her so much, perhaps later on you'll be chosen again to lie with her . . .''

'No! She will be brought to this house and she will be my wife.' He took Timna's hands and insisted, 'You'll teach her to weave and sew cloth.'

'I will,' Timna promised. 'But truly, husband, what chance is there?'

Vaguely he remembered that he had worked out a plan whereby it would be simple for him to fetch the girl, but he could not recall it now.

'What must I do?' he asked like a child.

'You must forget the Astartes and remember your trees. Work in the fields, and before long our new son will be born and you can teach him to find the honeycombs.' He acknowledged the reason in her words and surrendered. 'Let us go right now,' she whispered, 'to the one god who matters – El – and pray to him that the fires in your heart may subside.'

Urbaal left his bed and she called two slaves to light the way with lamps, and when suspicious Matred cried out, 'Who is opening the door?' she answered, 'I, Timna, going to speak with the god El.' So saying, she led her husband into the starry night where the heavens dropped close upon the whitewashed roofs of Makor. As they passed the gate, guards came out to inspect the flickering lights and told her to pass on. Along the winding street, past the low houses in which the townsmen slept, she led her befuddled husband to the line of monoliths standing solemn in the night. Ignoring the three prominent menhirs she knelt before the ancient one, and Urbaal stood beside her as she prayed for his release from the angers that consumed him. Dimly he perceived what his wife was trying to do for him, and he caught a fleeting sense of El, standing alone without the encrustations of fiery pits and smiling Astartes and naked priestesses. A healing peace crept over his tormented mind.

Unfortunately, at this moment someone inside the temple moved with a lamp, and he cried, 'It's Libamah! Signaling to me.' His attention was drawn away from the god El and he was seized with an uncontrollable hunger for this priestess of love. He fled from his wife, who still knelt beside the monolith, and rushed to the temple, leaping over the steps where Libamah had danced and throwing himself against the doors until the priests, barely dressed, came out to summon Timna: 'Take your crazy husband home.' And so she led him back to the rambling house by the gate and took him into his god-room, where he stared at the three grinning Astartes and huddled in a corner till dawn.

Timna went to her room and wondered what to do. She was convinced that she had done right in destroying the false Astartes, for obviously there must be one god, El, who controlled human affairs, and the others must be only interlopers trying to make man feel a little more secure. Real power they could not have, and she felt no remorse in having discarded four of them. But as she rubbed her tired face with a sweet oil which she kept in a small phial, she had to admit that she had not anticipated the derangement their loss would create in Urbaal, nor his obsessive hatred of Amalek as a result. For his present sickness she accepted responsibility, and it grieved her to think that if she had confessed her guilt at the beginning, none of this would have happened and Urbaal might have been able to forgive her. But she also realized that if she said anything now it might result in more harm than good.

Before she fell asleep she decided what to do. On the one hand she would watch over her husband through this difficult period, diverting him from his determination to hurt Amalek; and on the other she would begin bringing some order into his collapsing estate. After a short rest she rose and went down to the olive grove to see what work required doing, and found that the foreman had abandoned his booth by the oil press, leaving no one to attend either the press or the trees. She returned to town and spent some time rounding up Urbaal's workmen, warning them that she was in command now and would halt their wages if they betrayed her sick husband; but as she finished instructing the last one she heard a riot in the streets and with apprehension ran toward Amalek's house, where she found that Urbaal had broken into the herdsman's home, demanding that his Astartes be returned to him.

Soldiers were required to bring him under control, and he would have been treated roughly had not Amalek, bewildered by the attack, protected his neighbor by saying, 'He did no harm.' The soldiers hesitated, and Timna made their decision for them by saying, 'I've come to take him home.' But when the soldiers were gone, Amalek shook Urbaal and said, 'Old friend, come back to this world,' and under the patient ministrations of those who loved him the stupefied farmer lost his madness and began to know himself. He found it difficult to believe that he had tried to injure his neighbor Amalek and felt ashamed when it was explained that only the herdsman's good nature had saved him. He studied Timna, pregnant and beautiful, and was able to recall the patience she had shown in trying to win him back to sanity. When the time came to go home Timna chose a path that would avoid the temple, but he guessed her strategy and remarked, 'We can go past the temple now. I've forgotten her.' He insisted upon walking even to the monolith of El, where he gave thanks for his deliverance, and as he prayed Timna again reflected that if this town had not had its profusion of deities, its shocking rites that pulled the human mind this way and that, Urbaal would have remained the laughing, simple-hearted man who had begun as such an understanding husband. She was reluctant to think that the moral structure of a town could determine the kind of people who lived therein, but that appeared to be the case.

The days that followed were a kind of benediction to the faith Timna had shown. Urbaal returned to the winter prunings of his trees, and in the late afternoons when work was done, took his accustomed place in the rambling courtyard and talked with his children. He kept a set of dice with which he played a kind of backgammon with his slave girls, and he ordered some jars of good wine from the vintners, where great clay pots were sunk in earth to keep the liquid cool. He no longer worried about the big monoliths before the temple, but each day he walked among his fields, paying his respects to the petty baals who supervised his interests.

His strangest satisfaction, however, came from a quarter that he could not have foreseen: when word of his incompetence with the ritual prostitute had first spread through town it had caused him much embarrassment, but now he was able to look at himself as he was, and he laughed at the humiliating experience. He was a man of thirty-six, approaching old age, and he recognized that the wild excitement Libamah had caused was merely an attempt on his part to revitalize his memories. 'Now I can leave her to Amalek,' he confided to Timna. 'He's six years younger than me.' He laughed at himself and in doing so paved the way for a return to the gaiety he had once known with his slave girls. His greatest love, however, was saved for Timna, who, as her child grew near her heart, became even lovelier than she had been on that first hot afternoon when she climbed the ramp leading to the zig-zag gate. There she had met Urbaal, playing dice with the guards, and her happiness had begun. Now, when she saw her restored husband actually seek out Amalek to joke with him over the misunderstanding, she was reassured that she had behaved correctly throughout this difficult time.

Then came the end of the year, the end of winter, a time marked by apprehension as to how the gods would treat Makor in the growing season ahead. The various rituals of an agricultural community were observed, and as an act of faith in every kitchen all bread and wheat left over from the passing year was burned. In Urbaal's house the children scurried in and out, looking for little caches of cereal left by Timna for them to find, and these they brought triumphantly to the fire, where Urbaal burned them in an ancient ceremony, praying, 'We trust the gods that this year our harvest will be good.' He then produced fresh wheat from the winter fields, and this was hastily ground and made into bread without even stopping for the leaven so that there should be no empty space of time when bread was not in the house. All women able to walk then assembled with jars and paraded to the great well of Makor outside the wall, where instead of drawing water from the well they gave back samples taken from their homes, praying that in return the well would sustain them through the coming year.

On the last day of the dying year the town fasted, and before dawn, assembled at the western end of the temple, where doors not used at any other time were thrown open. At the eastern end similar doors were opened, so that the townsmen could look straight through the empty hall, from west to east, and as the sun approached on this day when day and night were of equal length, all grew reverent and whispered prayers imploring Baal-of-the-Sun to protect this town for another year. The sun rose, and the astronomy of the priests was so exact that the rays shone straight through the temple without touching any wall. The year would be a good one.

As the crowd chanted praises, the ritual gates were swung shut for another year and people left the west portal, moving to the monoliths where the priests had trundled out the war god Melak, under whose hungry maw large fires were lit. The crowd cheered and drums were beaten with frenzy as one perfect boy of three, fair-haired and lovely as a yellow bird darting after bees through an olive grove, was crushed down upon the stone arms and tumbled into the gaping pit.

The sacrifice had a startling effect upon Urbaal and the apparent cure of the preceding months was placed in jeopardy. He began to tremble, and Timna understood why. At the harvest-time burning he had been so preoccupied with the impending dance of Libamah that he had not truly accepted the fact that his own son had been burned alive. It was something that had occurred at the periphery of consciousness, and later the seven days of ritual sex had obliterated all memories, following which his derangement had prevented him from missing the boy at home. Now he awakened to the meaning of these terrifying facts and trembled.

Timna, anticipating disaster, knew that at this moment she should take him home, but when she started to do so, Matred commanded her to leave him where he was. 'The priests would punish you severely,' the first wife warned, so against her sure judgment Timna allowed Urbaal to stay, and when he showed signs of weeping for his son, she placed his hand upon her swelling belly and consoled him. His trembling diminished, for as Timna knew, it was never death that corrupted.

The priests ordered music, whereupon a door opened and Libamah came forth, now an ordinary prostitute but dressed in a spun cloth that looked handsome on her slim body. Slowly and with ritual grace the priests took away her clothing, and she stood alone with that provocative power that had filled the seven days and nights that Urbaal had known her. She was more exciting than he had remembered, lovelier than the concept of Astarte, a mirthful, lively young woman who could make a man experience joys he could not forget.

Her effect upon Urbaal not even Timna had expected. The dark trembling now ceased entirely and a sense of irresponsible, youthful excitement took its place. He could see only Libamah, as if she were dancing for him alone, and he jerked his hand away from Timna's and began preening himself as if there were a chance that again today the priests might choose him to lie with Libamah and insure fertility for the coming year. Edging himself into a prominent position, he pulled in his stomach and tried to look like a younger man. He held his head back to attract attention and smiled handsomely, but most of all he followed the girl on the steps, living again with her the surging ecstasy they had known in their service to Astarte.

'That poor, silly man,' Timna whispered as she maneuvered to be near him in order to console him when the priests nominated another for the spring rites, but as she drew closer to her grinning husband Libamah began a portion of her dance that was appallingly sensual, and Urbaal moved nearer to the steps, dragged on by the hope that he would be called. He could not control himself, and Timna saw his lips forming the pathetic prayer, 'Astarte, let it be me.'

The drums stopped. Libamah ended her dance with her feet apart, her eyes waiting to welcome her next lover. The priests cried, 'The man is Amalek!' and the tall herdsman leaped onto the steps and allowed his clothes to be torn away.

'No!' Urbaal protested, stumbling toward the temple. On the way he grabbed a spear held by a guard, and as Amalek stepped forward to claim the priestess, Urbaal drove the spear into his back.

Amalek staggered to the right, seeking to control his legs and failing. Libamah, watching as the foolish-faced Urbaal came at her with trembling hands, screamed, and this act of rejection stunned the farmer. Before anyone could stop him, he stumbled down the temple steps and dashed wild-eyed through the zigzag gate.

Almost as if they had anticipated tragedy, the priests moved swiftly into command. 'Be silent,' they ordered as the high priest satisfied himself that Amalek was dead. But Libamah stood waiting, and since she was the earthly personification of Astarte, the rites centering on her must continue or Makor would face famine. Not even death could be allowed to interrupt the rites of life, and a priest cried, 'The man is Heth.' Eagerly the bearded Hittite leaped to the steps, disrobed, and in a condition of astonishing virility, considering the preceding events, stepped past the dead man and carried Libamah to the love-room. Drums rolled, the sacred door was closed, and the symbolic ritual of homage to Astarte was continued.

Urbaal, when he fled through the gates, ran blindly toward his olive grove, where he stumbled about for some minutes trying to comprehend what had happened, but all he knew, and this only vaguely, was that he had murdered someone. Confused, he left his olive trees to seek the road to Damascus, and along it he staggered eastward. He had gone only a little way when he saw approaching him a kind of man he had not met before: the newcomer was shorter than he but leaner from hard years in the desert; he had blue eyes and a dark beard, an air of competence and bravery, but he walked as one seeking no trouble; he was accompanied by sheep and goats and many children and by numerous wives and younger men who had attached themselves to his leadership; he wore heavy sandals secured by thongs which wound about his ankles, plus a wool robe which fastened at one shoulder, leaving the other free; the robe was yellow, marked with red crescent moons; and he led a caravan of donkeys.

He was Joktan, a nomad from the desert who had elected to try life inland, and he was the first Habiru to see Makor, at a time when the great empires of Mesopotamia and Egypt were already crumbling. In later millennia experts would argue as to whether he had been the forerunner of the people known as Hebrews, but with such matters he was not concerned. He came late to the well of Makor, some two thousand years after the first formal town had been established on the rock, but he arrived with a reverberating force, not physical nor seeking war, but a spiritual force that would not be denied. His sudden appearance–looming up out of the east with many donkeys–startled Urbaal, who halted in the middle of the road. For some moments the two men stood silent and it was apparent that neither feared the other. Urbaal, now under control though still unaware of whom he had killed, was prepared to fight if necessary, but the stranger did not wish to do so, and it was Urbaal who spoke first. 'From where do you come?'

'The desert.'

'Where do you go?'

'That field near the white oaks. To pitch my tents.'

Urbaal became the canny farmer, and although he sensed that with murder he had forfeited his ownership of land, he behaved as he would have done under normal circumstances. 'That field belongs to me.' He was about to drive the stranger away when he remembered the precariousness of his condition and the fact that he needed a place to hide. 'You may stay near the oak trees,' he said.

When the tents were pitched, there came a moment of uncertainty when the Habiru realized that Urbaal did not intend leaving their camp. Joktan dispatched his sons to care for the donkeys and waited. Finally Urbaal came to him hesitantly to say, 'I have no home.'

'But this is your field . . .'

'And this is my town.' Urbaal led Joktan to the edge of the field and there the Habiru first saw the walls of Makor rising from the mound and protected by hills on the north, its white roofs glistening with promise. The town was so compelling after the empty spaces of the desert that Joktan could say nothing. He summoned his children and they stood with him, staring at their new land, and the shadow of Makor seemed to reach far across the fields and fall upon them. But Joktan was a clever man and he asked, 'If that fine place is your town but is no longer your home, and if you were running down the road alone . . . Have you killed a man?'

'Yes.'

Joktan said nothing. He stood in the sunlight and took counsel with himself, a man consciously trying to decide what course to follow. Still holding his silence he left his sons and walked to an area beneath a large oak tree where his men had already erected a simple altar consisting of stones gathered from the field, and before this altar he stood alone, praying. The words he used Urbaal could not hear, but when the prayer was finished Joktan returned and said, 'You cannot stay with us, but I shall give you a donkey so that you can escape eastward.'

Urbaal rejected the offer. 'This is my land and I have decided not to run away.'

This Joktan understood, and the two men discussed the matter for some time, at the end of which the Habiru told the murderer that he could have sanctuary at the altar. Joktan then assembled his wives and his sons and the husbands of his daughters and warned them that soon an army would march out from Makor seeking this murderer, and the first crisis in their new land would be reached. The men took counsel together but did not divulge their decision to Urbaal, who moved to the altar under the oak tree trying to understand the tragedy that had overtaken him.

That day no army marched out of Makor, but a woman did, hurrying among the olive trees, looking here and there for her husband. When she did not find him she walked along the caravan way leading to Damascus and in time reached a spot from which she could see the unfamiliar tents pitched in her husband's field, and she ran across the wheat stubble, crying, 'Urbaal! Urbaal!' When she found him crouched by the altar she ran up to him and fell upon the ground, kissing his feet. She explained that the priests would not send the army after him till morning, trusting that he would be far to the east where his crime need not be known. She wanted to start immediately—a pregnant woman with one pair of sandals—but he said stubbornly, 'This is my field,' and neither she nor Joktan could make him leave.

The sun went down and a strange night followed. Urbaal, suddenly an old, bewildered man, huddled by the sanctuary while Timna spoke with the strangers, telling them that her husband was an honest farmer and explaining the inconsequential steps whereby he had destroyed himself. 'You take much of the blame on yourself,' Joktan said.

'We are all to blame,' she replied.

'But surely the fault was finally his,' Joktan reasoned.

'He was bewitched,' she said, and in the light of the campfire she looked toward her husband with great pity and said, 'In another town, at another time, he would have died a happy man.' And she wept for the inconsiderate fate that had overtaken him.

At dawn Joktan went to the altar to pray alone, and when he returned Timna asked, 'To what gods do you pray?' and he replied, 'To the one god,' and she looked at him.

When the sun was up the army of Makor, eighteen men and a captain, marched out, hoping that the insane farmer had made his escape and that they could avoid further action, but when they saw the tents of the strangers they had to investigate, and under the oak tree they found Urbaal cowering beside the altar. 'We have come for the murderer,' the captain announced.

Joktan stepped forward, and without raising his voice, replied, 'He has taken sanctuary at my altar.'

'He is not inside a temple,' the captain declared, 'and he must come with us.' But Joktan stood firm and his sons gathered about him. The captain withdrew to consult with his men, and they saw that whereas they could surely overwhelm the strangers, many lives would be lost in doing so, and they fell back.

They sent for their priests, and when these came in regalia the captain explained, 'Urbaal is here, but this stranger refuses to deliver him.'

'He has taken refuge at my altar,' the Habiru said. The priests were inclined to order the troops to drag the murderer away, but the apparent willingness of the strangers to fight deterred them.

Finally the priests said, 'We shall respect the sanctuary.'

The high priest then went to Urbaal and told him, 'Amalek is dead, and your life has come to an end. You must walk with us as forfeit.'

The addled farmer did not fully comprehend what they were demanding, but at last he understood that it was Amalek, who had been his friend in this and many fields, whom he had killed, and he began to weep. The priests went to Timna and said, 'Go and fetch him from the altar, for we must take him with us,' but Joktan insisted, 'If he is determined to stay by the altar he shall stay here,' and the priests respected this honourable decision and stood apart.

It was Timna who made the decision. Going to the oak tree she knelt beside her husband and said quietly, 'The end of days has come, Urbaal. We have done all the wrong things and I shall die with you.' He looked at her helplessly, then placed his hands in hers, a gentle, tender man who had loved his fields and the sound of bees humming in the flowers. She pulled him to his feet and led him to the priests, who directed the soldiers to place a halter about his neck.

'I shall die with him,' Timna said, 'for the fault was mine.'

'You shall wander along the roads,' the priests replied, but as far as the gates of the city she clung to Urbaal till she was pushed away, falling into the dust. She looked up to see her uncomprehending husband, the little king of the olive grove, walk for the last time up the ramp and through the zigzag gate.

'No, no,' she wept as he disappeared. 'The terrible thing I did to him.' The god of death he had been able to withstand, but the goddess of life had destroyed him. It was not mean-spirited Matred, who had never loved him, who had betrayed him, but Timna, who had tried to be a dutiful wife. Now she heard a rumble of drums, then silence.

She had lain in the dust for some time when Joktan said to his sons, 'Go fetch the woman, for she was a loyal wife.' And in this manner the widow Timna became part of the Habiru encampment.

In the days that followed there took place those interchanges of curiosity which marked the arrival of any new family in the fields outside a walled town. The Habiru women walked sedately to the well, using a path that did not intrude upon the town. On their heads they bore large jugs to be filled with the good water, and the women of Makor studied them in silence. Priests left the town to inspect the nomad tents, where they discovered that all the newcomers were members of one extensive family–the people of Joktan, who had been willing to die rather than betray the sanctuary of his gods. The exact nature of his deities he seemed unwilling or unable to communicate, but the priests explained that if he intended sharing water from the well at Makor he must acknowledge the god El, the major baals, plus Melak and Astarte; and although Timna tried to dissuade him from making such a promise, he said that he did not object but made it clear that he would at the same time maintain his own altar under the oak tree, and to this the priests consented.

It was not surprising that Makor so easily accepted the strangers, the forerunners of a mass immigration that would come centuries later, for in the past thousand years many isolated families had drifted into the outlying fields and then into the town itself, accommodating themselves to Makor, its customs and its gods. The Habiru, even upon careful inspection, gave no evidence of being different from the others, and the priests had a right to assume that within a relatively short period the newcomers would be absorbed as their altar under the oak tree became incorporated into the worship of the monoliths in front of the temple. Such assimilation had always occurred in the past and there was no reason to suppose that it would not happen again. They were impressed with Joktan as a powerful man with sturdy sons, and they were pleased to welcome him as part of their town.

Having been accepted by the community, Joktan was now free to visit inside the walls, where the luxury of Makor astonished him. He had never lived in a house nor had he seen many, but here were more than a hundred jammed together and their effect upon him was startling. The shops were crowded with goods that excited his envy: wine and oil, crockery and cloth. Especially compelling was the temple area, where the four monoliths bespoke authority. When the priests introduced him to the ancient statue of El he said quietly, 'The god I worship is also El,' and the priests nodded in satisfaction.

Timna, in the tents of the Habiru, learned what a robust race they were, fond of eating and singing, quarrelsome when drunk and close-knit to face all strangers. Boy babies were marked by the rite of circumcision, and girls were married young–frequently to their cousins. To the Habiru the rude altar of El was not so important as the temple was to the town of Makor, but it was treated with a greater reverence, and Timna went there often, finding votive flowers or the feathers of a pigeon. The god who inhabited this holy place did not require first-born sons nor did he desire to see naked girls lying with farmers. Timna was especially impressed when Joktan, who had moved her in with his wives and who was accepting her unborn child into his camp, went to the altar alone to pray in silence, with no drums beating, no trumpets and few words.

'Who is your god?' she asked one day.

'The one god,' he replied.

'Then why did you accept the baals, as the priest required?'

'In any land I enter, I worship the local gods.'

'I believe that among the many gods there is one who counts, and the others do not merit worshiping. What is your god named?'

'El.'

'The one who lives in the little stone in front of our temple?'

'El has no home, for he is everywhere.'

This simple idea reached Timna's inquisitive mind like sunshine after storm, like a rainbow after a fall of cold rain. She recognized Joktan's explanation as the concept she had been groping for: a solitary god of no form, residing in no monolith, with no specific voice. With Joktan's permission she began placing each day upon the altar of this transcendent god a few spring flowers–yellow tulips, white anemones or red poppies.

It was Timna who showed the Habiru the road to Akka, where Joktan took his donkeys on a trading expedition, for Habiru meant *donkey driver* or one who was *dusty from the roads*, and when the caravan returned, laden with goods from the seaport, Joktan sent his sons to the olive field while he went through the zigzag gate to consult with the priests: 'In Akka I found much trading to be done. I should like to live within your walls and I shall bring Urbaal's wife with me, for she is now my wife,' and the priests assented. But when Timna walked nervously past the house of mirth which she had done so much to destroy, she remembered that day when she had first stepped over its threshold as Urbaal's wife. On the stones Amalek had broken a ripe pomegranate, crying, 'May you have as many sons as this fruit has seeds.' Now Joktan led her to a mean shed which the priests had assigned him along the eastern wall, but soon Timna transformed it into a place of dignity with an altar to the one god, and she found consolation when a son was born whom she insisted upon naming Urbaal, that his line might continue. But her joy in this son was tarnished when priests came to the shed, saying to one of Joktan's slave girls, 'Your baby is a first-born of Joktan, and his wrists we shall mark with red.'

In the anguish of this bereft slave girl Timna relived her own grief, which gnawed at her heart as rats gnaw wheat, and she felt more sorrow for this poor girl than she had for herself, for now she was able to see infant sacrifice as the incomprehensible cruelty it was. Leaving the shed with its red-marked infant, she fled disconsolately into the streets, past the house of Amalek, where she had stood guard one night, past the house of mirth, where Matred now ruled in bitterness, up past the monoliths who would never again have power over her, and down along the western wall till she reached the street spot where the four Astartes lay buried with their ridiculous phallic stones. Over their heads she stamped her feet, crying, 'You sleeping down there, you contain no life. You are corruption. Life lies in the womb of the slave girl.' And she wept for Urbaal, for the slave and for the red-marked infant lying in its crib; in this deep humility of spirit she leaned against the wall and became the first citizen of Makor to pray of herself, with no altar and no priest, to that formless god whom the Habiru had introduced to this vicinity.

In the morning, when drums called worshipers to the place of sacrifice, Joktan was bedazzled by the power of these new gods. Fiery Melak fascinated him, a deity of immense potential, and when his child was lifted into the air and thrust down upon the stone arms, he experienced a sense of religious awe unknown before, and when the festive part of the celebration began, with music and soft singing, Joktan guessed that something exciting was about to happen.

Leaving Timna and the slave girl mourning at the altar of the fiery god, he moved into a front position among the crowd and saw for the first time the tall priestess Libamah appear through the temple doors, a living goddess moving with more than human grace. In her spun robes she was lovelier than any woman he had encountered in the desert, and when the priest finished undressing her so that she stood fully revealed, he gasped with a delight he had not imagined possible.

Timna left the weeping slave girl and moved into the crowd just as her husband realized that some man in the audience was about to be nominated to lie with the dazzling priestess, and she watched with incredulity as Joktan leaned forward, his mouth agape, staring like a small boy as the lithe prostitute completed her dance. With her feet apart Libamah waited for the priests to indicate her mate for that day, and in that moment of hesitation Timna saw with horror that Joktan's lips were moving and he was praying, 'El, let it be me!' And when a pottery maker from the town leaped onto the steps to fulfill the demands of the rite, Joktan stared at the proceedings with such intensity that Timna, who had seen that look before, could guess what heated imaginings were racing through his mind. And the solitary altar under the oak tree was remembered no more.

LEVEL XIII

An Old Man and His God

Found at Makor–two clay pots thrown on a potter's wheel and
fired at 880° centigrade at Makor, 1427 B.C.E. Bodies light red in
color. Left pot decorated on inside with dark red and yellow
stripes in slip. Right pot on outside with slip in same colors. All
colors darkened by absorption of ash laid down during a
conflagration in midsummer, 1419 B.C.E. (See chapter 1 for
drawing.)

The sun-swept desert was as silent as the heavens on a night when there are no
falling stars. The only sound was a soft rustle on the sand as a serpent, reacting
to some unspecified fear, left the sun to seek the protection of a tall rock. A few
goats grazed silently among the scattered boulders, finding shreds of grass
where none seemed to exist, and two gray dogs from the encampment moved
silently to keep the goats from roaming far. Like the snake, they were
apprehensive and kept looking not at the goats but at some mysterious thing
that moved they knew not where.

Then came a rustling sound from a bush–a tumbleweed kind of bush, half
as big as a man, which ran and twisted across the desert when it dried–and the
two dogs looked sharply, as if a hyena had come creeping in to snatch a goat, but
still they did not bark, for they knew that the trembling in the bush was caused
by no animal.

A light began to glow in the branches but no smoke came, nor flame either,
and the bush shook as if it were determined to tear itself loose now, this hot
afternoon, and go tumbling across the desert, even though no wind was
blowing. As both the light and the trembling increased, a voice came, speaking
gently and with persuasion.

'Zadok?' All was silent. 'Zadok?' The dogs leaned forward. 'Zadok?'

From behind the rock to which the serpent had fled an old man
appeared–bareheaded, lean and leathery from his more than sixty years in the
sun. He had an untrimmed beard that reached his chest, and wore a coarse robe
of knotted wool and heavy sandals; he carried a shepherd's stave but did not
lean upon it. Cautiously he moved out from the rock and like a reluctant child
took his place before the burning bush.

'El-Shaddai, I am here.'

'Three times have I called you, Zadok,' the voice said.

'I was afraid. Have you come to punish me?'

'I should,' the voice said gently. 'For you have disobeyed me.'

'I was afraid to leave the desert.'

'This time you must go.'

'To the west?'

'Yes. The fields are waiting.'

'How will I know where?'

'Tomorrow at dusk your son Epher and his brother Ibsha will return from spying out the land. They will show you.'

'Are we to occupy the land?'

'Fields that you did not cultivate shall be yours and olive presses that you did not build. The walls of the town shall open to receive you and the gods of the place you shall respect.'

'These things I will do.'

'But remember the curse that shall be upon you if you worship those other gods. Or fail to observe my instructions. I am El-Shaddai.'

'I shall remember, I and my sons, and the sons of my sons.'

The trembling of the bush ceased and the light began to fade, whereupon he prostrated himself and cried, 'El-Shaddai, El-Shaddai! Forgive me for not having obeyed you.' And as the light retreated the voice said, 'Sleep in the shade, Zadok. You are a tired old man.'

'Will I live to see the fields of promise?'

'You shall see them and you shall occupy them and on the eve of victory I shall speak with you for the last time.'

There was silence, and that day the hyena did not come.

As in all times, these were years when El-Shaddai had power to command and men had free will to accept or reject his commands as their consciences dictated; therefore Zadok carefully considered the fact that his god had ordered him to sleep but decided that he might better spend his time on tasks which he must complete if his clan was to cross enemy territory. Finding a place in the shade of the tall rock, he chipped away at the big end of a flint nodule, building a smoothed platform from which he could later knock off a series of sharp knife blades to be fitted into wooden hafts which some of his sons were carving, and as he huddled over his flint, like a young apprentice taking care not to ruin the nodule, he epitomized his history. For the past three thousand years copper tools had been known in these regions, and at least two thousand years ago smithies in the towns had discovered that if they mixed one part of tin to nine parts of copper they could produce bronze, which was harder than either of the original component metals used alone. With this bronze the townsmen were now making tools of subtle precision and weapons of power. In the towns, life had been revolutionized; but this old man still clung to his flints, making from them whatever tools and weapons his people required. He used flint not only because he could get it for nothing—whereas bronze tools cost dearly in hides—but also because he knew that if his god had intended his Hebrews to use bronze he would have put it in the world for them and not have asked them to mix metals, which was a suspicious occupation and an evidence of human arrogance.

To all problems the old man reacted in the same way: there was an ancient truth that had been proved by long years of usage and there was innovation which might lead men into unknown regions, and he was determined to keep his people secure in the old ways. He preferred the practical thing done in the practical manner. His people worked harder than most, so their flock prospered. His women spent long hours making cloth, so his men dressed better than other nomads. He taught diligence in all things and reverence, too, so the families about him multiplied. And since his people were content to live within the protection of El-Shaddai, they were happy and creative.

For if the old man who led them was practical, sitting on his ankles and working his flint to that richly satisfying moment when he could begin tapping with his small stone hammer, flaking off one sharp knife blade after another–the reward for having done one's preliminary work carefully–he was also a spiritual man whose tired eyes could see beyond the desert to those invisible summits of the imagination where cool air existed and where the one god, El-Shaddai, lived. In later generations people who spoke other languages would translate this old Semitic name, which actually meant he of the mountain, as God Almighty, for through devious changes El-Shaddai was destined to mature into that god whom much of the world would worship. But in these fateful days, when the little group of Hebrews camped waiting for the signal to march westward, El-Shaddai was the god of no one but themselves; they were not even certain that he had continued as the god of those other Hebrews who had moved on to distant areas like Egypt. But of one thing Zadok was sure. El-Shaddai personally determined the destiny of this group, for of all the peoples available to him in the teeming area between the Euphrates and the Nile, he had chosen these Hebrews as his predilected people, and they lived within his embrace, enjoying security that others did not know.

He was a most difficult god to understand. He was incorporeal, yet he spoke. He was invisible, yet he could move as a pillar of fire. He was all-powerful, yet he tolerated the lesser gods of the Canaanites. He controlled the lives of men, yet he encouraged them to exercise their own judgment. He was benevolent, yet he could command the extinction of an entire town–as he had done with the town of Timri when Zadok had been a child of seven. He lived in all places, yet he was peculiarly the god of this one group of Hebrews. He was a jealous god, yet he allowed non-Hebrews to worship whatever lesser gods they pleased.

As Zadok chipped away at his flint, he knew that the mountain in which El-Shaddai was supposed to live did not exist in any ordinary sense of the word, for it would be offensive to imagine so powerful a god as limited to one specific place, with a tent, a couch and a concubine; no sensible man would commit himself to a god so restricted. El-Shaddai was a deity of such all-pervasive power that he must not be tied down to one mountain, unless that mountain were like the god himself–distant and everywhere, above and below, not seen, not touched, never dying and never living, a one god towering over all others, who existed in a mountain of the imagination so vast that it encompassed the entire earth and the starry heavens beyond.

It was his possession of this god that had caused Zadok his recent fear, for the old man sensed that such a deity could never have been conceived by men who lived in a town, nor by settled farmers who occupied river valleys where growing seasons had to be protected by propitiating seen gods who lived in known places over which they exercised a limited jurisdiction. Such settled people required seen gods to whom they could return; they needed statues and temples. But nomads who lived at the mercy of the desert, who set forth on a journey from one water hole to the unseen next, taking with them as an act of faith all they owned and everyone they loved, trusting blindly that the path had been ordained for them and that after many days of near-death they would find the appointed well where it was supposed to be . . . such nomads had to trust a god who saw the entire desert and the hills beyond. Reliance upon El-Shaddai, the unseen, the unknown, was a religion requiring the most exquisite faith, for at no point in their lives could these lonely travelers be sure; men often came to water holes that were dry. They could only trust that if they treated El-Shaddai with respect, if they attuned their whistling harps to his, he would bring them home safely through the bleak and empty spaces.

Looking up from his flints, Zadok turned his face toward the silent bush and said, as if reporting to a trusted advisor from his camp, 'El-Shaddai, I am at last prepared to take my people to the west.' The bush said nothing.

For fifty-seven years, beginning as a child, Zadok son of Zebul had been speaking with El-Shaddai, and in accordance with instructions from the solitary god, had kept his clan in the desert while others had left for the south on adventures that would be long remembered. Centuries earlier the patriarch of all, Abraham, and his son Isaac had moved down into Egypt, where now their descendants languished in slavery. The clan of Lot had settled the country of Moab, while the sons of Esau had conquered Edom. Lately the clan of Naphtali had swung off to occupy the hill country of the west, but Zadok had kept his group in the northern desert, listening for the clear word of El-Shaddai that would take him out of the lonely desert and into the land of promise.

The desert in which the Hebrews had lived for so many generations consisted of three parts. There were sandy wastes where nothing grew, and these the nomads avoided, for no man dependent upon donkeys could traverse them; in later years, when camels had been tamed, it would be possible to travel these wastes, but not now. There were also vast expanses of rock and arid land with occasional oases of reliable water, and here men with donkeys could just barely live; 'the wilderness,' this desert was called. And, finally, there were long stretches of semi-arid land lying next to settled farms, with not enough water for the regular planting of wheat or olive trees but enough to nourish sheep and goats, and it was in these lands that Zadok and his clan had been living for the past forty years. The wiser Hebrews felt certain that sooner or later El-Shaddai would command them to move on, but what they did not know was that three times the god had ordered Zadok to do just this, but the patriarch had been afraid and had temporized.

El-Shaddai, having at last become impatient, had delivered his latest command not to old Zadok but to the red-headed Epher. As a result of this message Epher had come to Zadok some weeks ago, saying, 'Father, we ought to move into the good lands of the west.'

'El-Shaddai will instruct us when to move.'

'But he did instruct us. Last night. He came to me and said, "Go to the west and spy out the land."'

Zadok had taken Epher by the shoulders and had asked directly, 'Did El-Shaddai himself speak to you?' And Epher, a hot-headed young man of twenty-two, had insisted that the god had come to him. 'What kind of voice did he use?' Zadok had probed, but his son could not explain, and that night Epher and Ibsha had run off to spy out the west. During their absence Zadok had worried as to whether Epher had spoken the truth. Why would El-Shaddai deliver a message of such importance to a youth? It seemed most unlikely, but now the god had indirectly confirmed Epher's story, saying that tomorrow the young men would return with instructions for the move west; and when Zadok reflected on the matter he had to admit that it was not so strange if El-Shaddai had spoken to Epher directly, for Zadok himself had been only seven when the mysterious god had first spoken to him, saying, 'In the rocks on which your father Zebul sits, there lurks a serpent.' He had stood transfixed, for the voice came from nowhere and he could not believe it. 'Go,' the voice continued, 'and warn your father, lest he be bitten by that serpent.' And he had run to the rocks and caused his father to leave just as the snake unwound itself from an inner crevice. From that day he was a child apart.

His name, Zadok, meant *righteous*, and he had continued to serve as the agency whereby El-Shaddai kept his chosen people informed. They were never many, the Hebrews of the desert. When Lot and Esau journeyed south they took with them less than a thousand people each. The clan of Zadok, as it waited for its culminating drive to the west, contained only seven hundred persons, for the great Hebrew tribes had not yet been formed. Zadok's group of nomads could not be called a family, because it comprised much more than a single unit; for example, Zadok's four wives and thirty children, many of whom had families of their own, did not add up to even a quarter of the total. But all in the group were related in some way to the old man, so although they were not a family they were a clan, and in the centuries ahead when several of these clans coalesced, the tribes known to history would emerge.

The clan of Zadok was one of the better-organized units, thanks principally to the righteous character of the man who led it. In all things he relied upon El-Shaddai. In war he was not overzealous, for he loved peace and sought it whenever possible—even at the displeasure of his sons, who were willing fighters. In trading he was honest and in charity generous. Among his wives he kept peace and among his children gentleness. He loved animals and initiated the practice of never slaughtering one member of a family in the presence of others, of never killing a kid and a dam on the same day, lest the creatures be offended by injustice as well as by death. In his clan women who had borne children could not work until five months had passed, except for kitchen duties that were not onerous. Yet he was a stern judge who had sentenced numerous persons to death, because infractions of divine law, such as adultery, filial insubordination, any profanation of El-Shaddai, were punishable by death. But when sentence was passed, with the old man warning that no appeal was possible, he usually allowed the victim a chance to escape, and it was understood that any condemned man might take with him one donkey and three water bags. But return to the clan of Zadok was forbidden.

The most intimate details of life were regulated by the old man. It was he who instituted the rule that unmarried men might not tend sheep alone: 'lest it lead to an abomination.' Two young unmarried men were not to occupy a booth alone when they hired themselves out to settled farmers at the harvest: 'lest there be an abomination.' Nor could men dress as women or women as men: 'lest it lead to an abomination.' From centuries of experience in the desert the Hebrews had built up a body of sensible law which Zadok had memorized and which he transmitted to his older sons, who would serve as judges when he was gone: 'A man may not marry two sisters, lest there be an abomination, nor may he marry a mother and daughter, lest it lead to an abomination.'

And because it was essential that the great life of the family and of the clan continue uninterrupted, he enforced the ancient law that if a husband died before his wife had children, it was obligatory for one of the dead man's brothers to take the widow immediately and get her with child so that the life of the clan could go forward with children to replenish it. If the surviving brothers were already married, no matter; if they despised their sister-in-law, no matter; so long as she had no children it was their responsibility to lie with her until she conceived—in the name of her dead husband, that his name might continue.

If Zadok was insistent upon carefully organized sexual behavior, this did not mean that he was contemptuous of this function of life: two years ago, at sixty-two, with his children grown and his wives occupied with many matters, he had looked one day upon a group of slaves which his sons had captured in a minor skirmish with a settled village and had seen one girl of sixteen who was particularly appealing. Claiming her for himself, he had found much joy in having her in his tent in the long nights. She was a Canaanite who worshiped Baal the omnipotent, but as Zadok lay with her, feeling her warmth against his tired body, he spoke with her against the Canaanite god and convinced himself that he was winning her away from Baal and to an acceptance of the true god.

His principal joy, however, was his thirty children. His oldest offspring were now the secondary heads of the clan, men and women with children of their own and several with grandchildren, so that Zadok could boast, 'A hunter is happy when he has a quiver full of arrows to shoot into the future.' But it was his younger children—the offspring of his fourth wife—who interested him most: Epher the daring one, who had organized the scouting expedition to the west and who was always eager to engage an enemy; Ibsha, younger and quieter, but perhaps more seriously dedicated to understanding the world; and above all Leah, a girl of seventeen, not yet married but studying with alert eyes the various men her father suggested as possible husbands. If a man had produced only these three children he could feel proud, and to have them arrive in his later days was a serene pleasure.

For many years it had been Zadok's custom to spend his late afternoons sitting with Leah and any other children who cared to join him, recalling the traditions of the Hebrews. Recently the young slave girl had begun to appear each day, sitting at the right hand of her master and listening with delight as he told of his ancestor Noah, who had escaped the great flood, or of Nimrod the hunter, whose exploits were renowned, or of Jubal, who invented the harp. For hours he would speak of these men, telling this story and that, but each day he came to some episode in the life of Abraham, who had been the first to travel in this desert—'He passed by these very rocks on which we sit this day'—and it was his pleasure to expatiate on the matter of Abraham and his son Isaac, contending that on the day that El-Shaddai outlawed human sacrifice he proved himself to be a god of mercy, a god so superior to all others that comparison was meaningless. 'There are other gods, of course, and Baal is not one to laugh at,' he said approvingly to the slave girl, 'and in the lands my fathers passed through, it was always our custom to respect the gods we met. El-Shaddai demands this of us, but there can be no question as to which god is superior, reigning above all others.'

On this last afternoon during which Zadok awaited the return of his sons from their scouting trip, he did not appear for his restful conversation with the children, so Leah and the slave girl went about their tasks, and from her tent the latter could see the old man standing apart from the camp, looking at it critically, like a judge. At last we are ready, he said to himself. Our cattle were never more numerous and our donkeys are fat. We have nearly two hundred warriors and our tents are mended. We are like a mighty bow drawn taut, ready to shoot arrows westward with force, and if it is the will of El-Shaddai that we move, he has brought us to superb condition. Approving what he saw of the equipment, the old man next studied his clan. It was well organized, faithful to one unifying god, disciplined, vigorous. It was as cohesive a unit as could then have been found in the desert regions—less educated, perhaps, since no member was able to read or write or cast bronze—but unified as no other similar group could be, for it had been Zadok's stern command that no strangers be allowed to enter his clan without a period of indoctrination so rigorous as to repel most applicants. A Canaanite man could live beside the Hebrews for years without their trying to convert him away from his belief in Baal, but once he asked permission to marry one of the Hebrew women–and they were beautiful women who attracted men–he had to present himself to Zadok, forswear his former gods, undergo circumcision if that rite had not already been performed, abandon his former associates, and then spend eleven days with Zadok, trying to penetrate the mystery of El-Shaddai. Afterward, allegiance to any other god meant death, and few men were willing to submit themselves to such treatment merely to wed a Hebrew girl, no matter how attractive, so where men were concerned Zadok had kept his clan homogeneous.

The Hebrews insisted upon the circumcision of their men for a logical reason: it not only formed a covenant between the man and El-Shaddai, an unbreakable allegiance whose mark remained forever, but it also had the practical value of indicating without question or quibble the fact that the man so marked was a Hebrew. In war against the uncircumcised the coward might want to run away and later on deny that he had been a Hebrew. His captors had only to inspect him to prove he was a liar, so the circumcised man had better fight to the death because for him there was no masking his identity. The Hebrews were therefore strong warriors who were sometimes defeated but rarely demoralized, and for much of this cohesive spirit the desert rite of circumcision was responsible.

With women the problems were different. In their constant wars with settled tribes Zadok's men often took prisoners and they were apt to be enticing creatures. Not even Zadok could keep his sons from lying with the strangers, and he was smart enough to realize his impotence in this matter. But he did insist upon precautions. When a slave girl was captured she was put into sackcloth of the meanest sort, her head was shaved and she was allowed nothing with which to clean or cut her fingernails, no oil for her face and little water for washing. After one month of such treatment she was led forth to stand beside the man who had captured her, while Zadok asked, 'Do you still want this woman?' If the man said yes, she was tested as to her willingness to accept El-Shaddai; she was not required to surrender her old gods completely, for she was a woman, but she must acknowledge that El-Shaddai was superior, and if she did this she was delivered by Zadok to her captor, with the admonition, 'Have many children.' With his own slave girl Zadok had followed this regimen and was gratified to see that she was becoming a true child of El-Shaddai.

Next day, as El-Shaddai had said, the young men Epher and Ibsha returned from the west with exhilarating news. 'It's a land of oil and honey,' Ibsha reported.

'It's a land with armies,' his red-headed brother added, 'but not too great to conquer.'

'It's a land with fields covered with grass,' Ibsha continued.

'It has cities surrounded by walls,' Epher reported, 'but they can be scaled.'

'It's a land with more trees than I have ever seen before,' Ibsha said. 'Mountains and valleys to delight the eye.'

'It has roads that we can march along,' Epher told those around him, 'and rocks behind which we can take cover.'

'It's a land which I cannot describe to satisfaction,' Ibsha said. 'Where that bush grows over there, a dozen olive trees are standing. When you shake the limbs the fruit comes down like dark rain.'

'They have metal spears,' Epher went on, 'and we have stone.' He showed his brothers some metal weapons he had acquired along the way.

Then Zadok spoke to the clan, on the last evening that they would reside in the desert. 'El-Shaddai has spoken. We are to occupy the land. The olive trees are to be ours and the walls of the city will open for us.'

The Hebrews began to cheer but Zadok silenced them, for he comprehended the gravity of the step they were about to take, and as dusk fell upon their tents he commanded them to gather, a lean and sinewy group dressed in skins and woven cloth and leather sandals. They formed an intense congregation, kneeling while Zadok prayed: 'Mighty El-Shaddai, whom no man has seen face-to-face, into your hands we deliver ourselves. It is your desire that we leave our ancient home for the valleys and the towns. Protect us, protect us from the dangers we cannot foresee.' With their faces upraised, the Hebrews praised their god, each man and woman committing himself to the deity that brooded over the desert, and finally they separated and by the light of flickering rushes packed their tents.

As they worked, Zadok the Righteous went alone into the womb of the desert, for only he appreciated what a terrible thing his children were attempting, this leap from the ancient ways into the modern. He had never been inside a town–not in sixty-four years of life; he had helped besiege several and had sent his sons trading inside their walls, and of course his little slave girl had lived in a Canaanite town to the north, which she delighted in describing as they lay together. But he himself did not fully understand what a town was, except that it was a place so crowded that El-Shaddai seemed not to frequent its narrow alleys. Other gods flourished in towns, but not El-Shaddai. Yet it was apparent to the old man that the moment had come in the life of his people when it was appropriate for them to try the town, uncertain and ominous though it was. El-Shaddai himself had ordained the move, and the eyes of his older sons had glittered with expectation as they listened to Epher and Ibsha describing the towns they had seen; but he looked back to the desert.

How far the horizons were this starry night, how sweeping the rocks as they fell sculptured by the hand of El-Shaddai. How sweet the waters were when they were found, how cruel the scorpions in the midday sun. It was the desert that tested a man, that issued the dreadful challenge, 'Come upon me and see if you have courage.' It was this desert of illimitable magnitude that encouraged a man to consider the ultimate questions: not the matter of food tomorrow, nor the child to be born next week, nor the battle in the offing, but the questions beyond that and then far, far beyond that, too. Why, in the infinity of the desert, does this small speck called man have the confidence to move from this unknown point to that, finding his water and his food as he goes along? What divine assistance guides him and how is that assistance governed? Above all, how can man ascertain the divine will and then live in harmony with it?

The old man walked across the sand until he could look back and see his entire encampment, all the flickering lights and the shepherds guarding their flocks, and he remembered that night so very long ago when his people had been lost far east of Damascus in the worst desert they had ever traveled, and all were at the point where they must perish, but his father, Zebul, had said, 'In the cool of the night we must push on.' The stricken Hebrews had protested, 'We can go no farther,' but he had struck the tents and they had moved on till the next dawn, finding nothing. Through that day they had rested, parched and dying, and at night Zebul again said, 'In the cool of the night we must march on,' and again they had protested that they were perishing, but they marched and they did this for three nights–wholly incapable of moving another step yet moving nevertheless–and on that last night when they refused to march, saying that they were finished, he went through the tents lashing out at them and shouting in rage, 'Do you think, men of faltering faith, that El-Shaddai has brought us to this spot to perish without purpose? Does he not have an enemy waiting at the well to kill us in battle? Or a king to carry us off in slavery? Have we come so far to die inconsequentially? Up! Up! Let us see what terrible thing El-Shaddai has waiting for us.' And he drove his Hebrews, dying as they had threatened, but dying on the way to the well, not in some surrendered heap. And as the last sun rose–the one that none could have survived–Zebul found the well, and there they rested for three years.

Tonight Zadok did not intend to pray. No further communication between him and El-Shaddai was needed, but he did look with an aching hunger at the desert which he had known for all but seven years of his life, and he wondered if he would ever again find the peace, the consolation he had known amidst its sweep and challenge. He sensed that henceforth his vision would be diminished and his nearness to the stars removed. A way of life was being lost beyond the point of recovery and he was apprehensive about the future, but he felt certain that wherever his Hebrews went they would carry with them memorials of these desert years when they had lived close to their god.

Now he turned from his study of the tents, as if he wished to stand where none of his people could see him, and when he was hidden he wept, for he alone was conscious of the sin he had committed. 'Almighty one, forgive me,' he said, and he spoke to El-Shaddai as if he were a little boy communicating with his father at the end of a day of naughtiness. 'Six years ago, when the last of the clans moved south, you came to me in the desert and said, "Zadok, it is time for you to leave the desert and occupy the walled town." But I was afraid of battle. I was afraid of the town. I wanted to hold on to the security of the desert, and here I procrastinated, offering you this excuse and that. My sons came to me, asking that we move our flocks into the green valleys, but them too I ignored, and for the past six years I have stood against god and man, afraid to move. You were patient with me, El-Shaddai, but last month you spoke to Epher and sent him exploring by himself. Now he has turned with your commands and we shall move, as you ordered me to do six years ago.' He humbled himself in the dust and prayed, 'El-Shaddai, forgive me. I was afraid.'

There was a rustling sound across the sand, as if a fox were running, and the voice of El-Shaddai said to Zadok the Righteous, 'As long as you live, old man, you will be free to ignore my commands. But in time I will grow impatient and will speak to others, as I have spoken to Epher.'

'My home is the desert,' Zadok said in self-justification, 'and I was afraid to leave.'

'I waited,' El-Shaddai said, 'because I knew that if you did not love your home in the desert you would not love me either. I am glad that you are now ready.'

'El-Shaddai!' the patriarch cried in anguish, laying bare the real fear that had held him immobilized. 'In the town will we know you as we have known you in the desert?'

'Inside the walls it will not be easy for me to speak with you,' the deity answered, 'but I shall be there.'

With this eternal promise to his Hebrews, El-Shaddai departed, and when dawn came Zadok was at last prepared to order the small red tent to be dismantled.

In those centuries when the Hebrews dwelt in the desert, each clan maintained a sacred tent constructed of three layers of skin: upon a wooden frame so small that two men could not have crawled inside, goatskins were stretched and upon them were laid skins of rams dyed red with expensive colors brought from Damascus, and over the whole were thrown strips of soft badger fur, so that the tent was clearly a thing apart. Whenever Zadok indicated that his clan was to halt in a given place, the small red tent was erected first, signifying that this was their home, and on days like this, when the Hebrews were permanently abandoning an area, the last tent to be struck was always the red one, and it came down as the elders stood in prayer.

'We have lived in the desert as you commanded,' Zadok prayed, 'and if we are now to occupy green fields, it is because you wish it so.'

When the tent was dismantled only a carefully chosen few were allowed to see what it contained. Zadok's tabernacle held a curiously shaped piece of wood with which Zebul had killed a coward who had tried to convince the Hebrews to die in the desert rather than attempt the three-day march to the oasis east of Damascus. There was a string of beads whose history no one knew and a ram's horn which had been used nearly a thousand years ago to usher in a memorable new year. There was a piece of cloth from Persia, and that was all. Most particularly El-Shaddai was not in the tent, nor was there anything representing El-Shaddai. He lived elsewhere, on the mountain that did not exist.

'Our god is not in these shreds of leather,' Zadok reminded his Hebrews 'He does not live in this tabernacle. He is not a god held prisoner in our tents, but we are held prisoner in his.' As the assistants packed the tabernacle prior to the march inland, the old man added a fifth item which would henceforth ride with the clan of Zadok wherever it went, in memory of the beneficence El-Shaddai had showered upon them in the desert. From the arid waste he picked a rock of no significant shape; it was just a rock from the desert which they would see no more but which they would remember whenever they saw the stone of Zadok.

At the head of the seven hundred Hebrews as they started forth walked a little donkey bearing the red tent, and behind the beast came old Zadok, sandals on his feet, coarse woolen breeches tied at his waist, a light woolen robe slung over his shoulders, and a long staff in his left hand to steady himself on the rocky path. Sometimes his beard flowed back over his left shoulder and his age-dimmed eyes were squinted as he tried to pick out the way ahead, but in this task his sons helped him. At his side walked the young slave girl bearing a waterskin, and behind him came his wives, his eighteen sons, his dozen daughters, their husbands and wives, their cousins, grandchildren, uncles and all who had attached themselves to this sprawling unit. The goats, the sheep, the few cattle and the dogs came along, but mostly the donkeys did the work, for on their backs rode the tents, the food and the babies. At a rise atop the first hill many of the Hebrews stopped to look back with longing at the great desert which had held them safely for so many generations; but Zadok did not. He had said his farewell in his heart, where the anxiety of this day would live forever.

Decisions on the westward trip were made by Epher, the red-headed youth who had often waged war against walled towns, and on the nineteenth day this stocky warrior brought his clan and its wandering flocks to the crest of a hill—in later years it would be remembered as a mountain—from which the Hebrews looked down for the first time into the land of Canaan, lying to the west of a beautiful river called even then the Jordan, and it was seen to be a land of extraordinary richness. Never before had the people of Zadok seen so many trees.

'We shall cross the river there,' Epher explained. 'To the right lies a small lake and to the left a large sea shaped like a harp and called Kinnereth.'

'When we cross the river, which way do we turn?' his father asked.

'Neither right nor left. We march through those hills ahead and come at last to the road leading west.'

As the Hebrews gathered about their patriarch some argued that if the land flanking the river was so rich it would be folly to move past it in search of better, but Epher for once preached caution, warning his brothers, 'Not far to the north lies Hazor, a mighty city, and we shall be fortunate if its army allows us to cross the river, much less occupy lands which they call their own.' The men who would have to do the fighting if the Canaanites attacked while they were fording the river looked with apprehension toward the unseen city, but old Zadok looked not at the potential enemy but at the centuries ahead, and El-Shaddai allowed him to foresee men like Joshua and Gideon, and he prophesied: 'In some future day Hazor will be humbled and the sons of El-Shaddai will occupy all Canaan, as we now move forward to occupy our small portion.' And he gave thanks that this fair land was to be the heritage of the Hebrews. But it was young Epher who led the clan noiselessly to the banks of the Jordan, where the families crossed the river without being detected and headed westward, eluding the armies of Hazor.

As the Hebrews skirted the hills that lay between the Jordan and Akka they were free to inspect at first hand the rich valleys of Canaan and were fascinated by the numerous rivers that carried water to vineyards, the slopes where more grass grew than sheep could eat, the olive trees, the fruit orchards, the bees humming by laden with pollen, and the flight of innumerable pigeons waiting to be trapped. As the desert had reached to the horizon in barrenness, so these valleys reached to the hills in fruitfulness, and the Hebrews resolved that if they must fight for this inviting land they were ready to do so. As they drew close to Makor, Epher began forming his people into a more compact unit; the donkey with the red tent continued in front but cattle were moved near the center of the slowly moving mass and children were stopped from ranging too far from their mothers. A sense of excitement pervaded the clan, for all sensed that the moment of trial was at hand. Finally, as the time approached when day and night were of equal length, the first day of spring when the new year began, Epher and Ibsha moved ahead to scout the exact location of the target town, and in the afternoon they ran back to advise their father that early next morning he would reach the town called Makor. That night the timorous old man pitched his camp some miles east of the town and assembled his sons and the leaders of the subsidiary families.

'We have been marching toward a battle,' he told them, 'and tomorrow we shall see the walls you want to assail. But there shall be no battle.' His sons murmured among themselves. 'We shall exist in peace among the Canaanites,' Zadok continued, 'they with their fields and we with ours, they with their gods and we with ours.'

The more daring men of the clan opposed this idea, but Zadok was firm. 'El-

Shaddai has promised us this land, and it will be ours. But not through bloodshed.'

The idea of a negotiated occupancy disappointed the Hebrews. Was it for this that they had made their flint weapons? And traded with traveling smithies for bronze axe heads and arrow tips? They remonstrated with the patriarch and demanded that in the morning they march in battle array to the walls and assault them.

'The walls of Makor we shall overcome without the use of force,' he argued.

'You haven't seen them,' his younger sons protested.

'But El-Shaddai has seen them,' he insisted, 'and to him all walls are alike. They are captured only when he gives the command.' He warned his sons and the other eager warriors that it was the will of their god that occupation of the fields be peaceful, and his sons said, 'Ask him again what we must do,' for they could not visualize obtaining fields without bloodshed; but they trusted their father as a man who spoke directly to his god, and when he walked alone down the Damascus road, coming at last to a valley of red rock, they did not try to follow him, for they knew that the old man was with his god.

'What are we to do?' the indecisive patriarch asked the face of the rock.

'As I explained in the desert,' came the patient voice, 'you are to occupy the land apportioned to you.'

'But in the desert you did not tell me whether I should bring war or peace. My impatient sons are eager for war and the death of many people.'

'Are you still afraid of war, Zadok?'

'Yes. When I was a boy and we were besieging Timri . . .'

'I remember Timri.'

'You ordered my father Zebul to destroy the town for its abominations, and he forced me to stand beside him as he slaughtered men and women and children. And my ankles were red with blood. And I got sick and wanted never to see a spear again. And I hated you, El-Shaddai, for you were cruel.'

'I remember that night,' the god said. 'You were seven years old, and you cursed me, and was it not then that I spoke to you for the first time? On the morrow of Timri when your father was sleeping near the serpent that would have bitten him?'

Zadok recalled that remote midday, fifty-seven years ago, when he had first spoken with his god, and not once in the intervening years had it occurred to him that El-Shaddai had chosen him that day precisely because of his opposition the night before to the massacre of Timri. El-Shaddai could have elected older men and wiser as his voice, but he had chosen the child Zadok because even as a boy of seven he had been willing to judge the questions of mercy and humanity with his own conscience.

'I have not spoken to you of war or peace,' the deity continued, 'because these are matters which I alone determine. To you they are of no concern. Occupy the lands, and whether there shall be war or peace I shall decide–according to how the children of Canaan receive me.'

'Then I must approach the town without knowing?'

'You man of little faith? Did you not live in the desert on those terms? Who can be certain that when he approaches a town the walls will open to his command? Yet I have promised you that the walls of Makor shall do so, and you ask–in war or in peace? Remember your grandmother Rachel, who went to the well of Zaber eight hundred days without event and on the next day she went and was killed by a scorpion. Could she have prevented this by taking precaution? Remember your son Zattu, who passed through the pit where a hundred men had died of serpent stings, and he came out alive. Could he have arranged this by taking thought? I am El-Shaddai, and I have promised you that the walls of Makor shall open to your command. Can you, by taking thought, increase that promise?'

The old man humbled himself before his god, but when he returned to his sons he interpreted El-Shaddai's words to his own liking: 'Tomorrow there shall be no war.' The Hebrews, content that this was the will of their god, slept that night without fires and in the morning girded themselves for the final march to the walled town.

THE TELL

On one unhappy day three different groups of tourists came demanding to see the Candlestick of Death, and after Cullinane had explained three times that it was on display in Chicago he felt depressed. He locked his office door and sat inside brooding about the problems of the dig. It happens every time, he reflected. You start what looks like a simple dig. Historical fragments hiding in earth. And before you've filled the first basket you find yourself digging into your own understanding of the civilization involved. He leaned back and recalled his days in Arizona. He had begun that excavation knowing as much as most experts about the American Indian, but had ended by spending two years of concentrated research into their mental processes, reviewing everything written on the subject and venturing far afield for collateral suggestions from the Ainu in Japan or the Eskimo in Alaska. Now he spent his days digging physically into the earth of Makor and his nights probing the spirit of the Judaism that had been responsible for building so much of the tell.

When he was satisfied that the last tourists had gone, he unlocked his door and wandered into Eliav's office. 'Have you any new material that I could read about the Jews?'

'You catch me off guard,' Eliav replied.

'The nonsense I've been hearing today. I'm disgusted. I'd like to bite into something solid.'

'You've read De Vaux, Kaufmann, Albright?'

Cullinane nodded.

'Maimonides?'

'He's the best.'

'There's one better.'

'What?'

'Read Deuteronomy five times.'

'Are you kidding?'

'No. Deuteronomy. Five times.'

'What's your thought?'

'It's the great central book of the Jews and if you master it you'll understand us.'

'But is it worth five readings?'

'Yes, because most Gentiles think of the ancient Hebrews as curious relics who reached Israel ten thousand years ago in some kind of archaic mystery.'

'How do you think it happened?' Cullinane asked.

'Deuteronomy is so real to me that I feel as if my immediate ancestors–say, my great-grandfather with desert dust still on his clothes–came down that valley with goats and donkeys and stumbled onto this spot.'

'Will reading Deuteronomy give me such a feeling?'

'Read it five times and see,' Eliav countered.

It was in this way that Cullinane renewed his acquaintance with the old Jewish masterpiece which he had first seriously studied at Princeton. Deuteronomy purports to be the farewell address of General Moses to his Jews as they are about to leave the wilderness and enter into the land of Canaan, and at the opening line, 'These be the words which Moses spake unto all Israel on this side Jordan,' Cullinane had the feeling that Deuteronomy resembled General Washington's farewell address to his colonial soldiers; and the analogy was apt.

At Makor there was no Douay Version of the Bible, so Cullinane could not use that Catholic translation; but this didn't bother him. At Princeton he had become familiar with the Protestant King James Version of 1611, and now as his eyes ran down the columns they caught phrases and sentences which he had once vaguely supposed to be from the New Testament: 'Man doth not live by bread only,' and 'From the hewer of thy wood unto the drawer of thy water,' and 'Thou shalt love the Lord thy God with all thine heart, and with all thy soul, and with all thy might.' He discovered concepts that lay at the core of his New Testament Catholicism: 'But the word is very nigh unto thee, in thy mouth, and in thy heart, that thou mayest do it.' And he came upon other phrases that jolted him regarding the story of Jesus; these made him go back for a second reading: 'If there arise among you a prophet, or a dreamer of dreams, and giveth thee a sign or a wonder . . . thou shalt not hearken unto the words of that prophet, or that dreamer of dreams: for the Lord your God proveth you, to know whether ye love the Lord your God with all your heart and with all your soul.'

When Cullinane finished his first reading he was inclined to tell Eliav that he was now refreshed and could face the next busload of tourists, but he had found the tall Jew to be canny in these matters, and so, to indulge him, he began again at the beginning of Deuteronomy. This time he gained a sense of the enormous historicity of the book: the unknown author, who had used the literary device of speaking as Moses, had been a scholar immersed in Jewish history and spoke of it as if it had happened yesterday–as Eliav had said, in the life of his great-grandfather–and this involvement began to communicate itself to Cullinane. He now read the Ten Commandments as if he were among the tribes listening to Moses. It was he who was coming out of Egypt, dying of thirst in the Sinai, retreating in petulant fear from the first invasion of the Promised Land. He put the Bible down with a distinct sense of having read the history of a real people . . . not the real history, perhaps, but a distillation of hundreds of old traditions and national memories. Eliav had guessed right: Cullinane was beginning to feel that a band of living Hebrews had one day come down these gullies to find Makor. He wondered what new thing he would uncover on the remaining three readings.

At this point Eliav appeared with a book under his arm and took away the King James Version. 'John, I wish you'd do your next two readings from this new English translation done by a group of Jewish scholars in Philadelphia.'

'Why Jewish?'

Eliav hesitated, then said, 'It's a ticklish point. But Deuteronomy is particularly Jewish in nature. It's our holy book and it means double to us what it could possibly mean to a Catholic or a Baptist. Yet everybody reads it in Protestant or Catholic translations . . .'

'To me a translation's a translation,' Cullinane protested.

'Not so,' Eliav retorted. 'Even when the King James Version was made, it was purposefully old-fashioned. Something beautiful and poetic. Today it's positively archaic, and for young people to study their religion from it can only mean they'll think of that religion as archaic–clothed in dust and not to be taken as contemporary.'

'Perhaps, but why a Jewish translation?'

'The other thing that's wrong with the King James Version is that it's purely Protestant in its choice of words. You Catholics discovered that early, so you held to your Douay Version, which was just as lopsided on the Catholic side. And all the time, the book you're wrestling over is a Jewish book, written by Jews for the instruction of Jews in a very Jewish religion. We can be forgiven if we feel that we ought to have a translation which takes these things into account . . . especially with Deuteronomy.'

'So now you've slanted everything into a Jewish bias.'

'We didn't, but that's not the point. Do you know Isaiah 7:14?' Cullinane was always impressed with the way Jews could cite the Bible, and now Eliav repeated the Old Testament words that lay at the heart of New Testament Christianity: '"Therefore the Lord himself shall give you a sign; Behold, a virgin shall conceive, and bear a son, and shall call his name Immanuel."'

Cullinane consulted his Protestant Bible and satisfied himself that Eliav had quoted accurately. But then the Jew said, 'Now look it up in the Jewish translation,' and there Cullinane found the word *virgin* translated as *young woman.*

'On what authority did they make that change?' he asked in some surprise.

'Look at the original Hebrew,' Eliav suggested, handing him a third version, and in the original language of the Bible the word *virgin* was not mentioned. It had been introduced by Christian scholars as a device for proving that the Old Testament prophesied the New and that the New should therefore supersede the Old. 'Throughout the centuries,' Eliav explained, 'hundreds of thousands of Jews were burned to death or massacred because their own Bible was misused against them. I think we're entitled to an accurate Jewish version.'

When Eliav left, Cullinane began what was to be a startling experience. The new Jewish translation, by divesting Deuteronomy of its Shakespearean poetry, offered the reader a blunt and often awkward statement. The old and the new compared in this manner:

Hear, O Israel, the statutes and judgments which I speak in your ears this day, that ye may learn them, and keep, and do them.
Hear, O Israel, the laws and norms that I proclaim to you this day! Study them and observe them faithfully!

He checked the modern translation against the original Hebrew and discovered the Jewish translation to be literal and the King James Version not. He tested half a dozen additional passages and satisfied himself that the Jewish translators had at least tried to render their version faithfully if not poetically.

But gradually his critical judgment receded and he found himself reading for the pure pleasure of contemporaneous expression; and on his second run he came upon that verse which has always had such a powerful hold upon the Jewish reader: 'It was not with our fathers that the Lord made this covenant, but with us, the living, every one of us who is here today.' And the point Eliav had been trying to get across was burned into Cullinane's consciousness: Deuteronomy was a living book and to the living Jew it had contemporary force. When he came to the scene in which the Jews, having received the Ten Commandments, urged Moses to go back to God for further instructions, the simple idiom of the new translation gave him the sensation of being actually with the Jews at Horeb as the commandments were being delivered: 'You go closer and hear all that the Lord our God says; then you tell us everything that the Lord our God tells you, and we will willingly do it.'

When he was finished with his fourth reading he told Eliav, 'I see what you mean. It has a sense of actuality. You can almost touch the Jews.'

'Now for the last one, this time in Hebrew. Just as it was written down.'

'My Hebrew's too rusty, Cullinane protested. 'I'll take your word that it's a fair translation.'

'I want to prove quite a different point,' Eliav said. 'And for it your Hebrew's adequate. Skip the words you don't know.'

It took Cullinane about a day to make his way through the Hebrew text, and it was one of the best days he was to spend at Makor, for as he dug his way into the powerful Hebrew, in almost the same way as he had to dig through the soil hiding Makor, he came upon that quiet yet singing declaration of faith that is the core of Judaism, the passage which expresses the essence of Jewish history: 'My father was a fugitive Aramaean. He went down to Egypt with meager numbers and sojourned there; but there he became a great and very populous nation. The Egyptians dealt harshly with us and oppressed us: they imposed heavy labor upon us. We cried to the Lord, the God of our fathers, and the Lord heard our plea and saw our plight, our misery, and our oppression. The Lord freed us from Egypt by a mighty hand, by an outstretched arm and awesome power, and by signs and portents. He brought us to this place and gave us this land, a land flowing with milk and honey.'

At dinner Eliav said, 'The point I wanted to make is this. The Hebrew used in writing Deuteronomy sometime in the seventh century B.C.E. is the same Hebrew that we've revived in Israel after it had been a dead language for a thousand years. Call over one of the kibbutzniks. Son!' A youth of fifteen ambled over, sloppy, happy, his sleeves rolled up for the job of cleaning the dining hall. Eliav asked, 'Can you find me someone who speaks English,' and the boy said that he did, so Eliav handed him the Hebrew Torah, pointed to a passage in Deuteronomy and asked, 'Can you read this?'

'Sure.'

'Go ahead.' The boy studied the words, some of the oldest written in Hebrew, and said tentatively, '"My father was an Aramaean with no home. He went to Egypt. Not many. There he became a nation."'

'Good,' Eliav said, and the pleased kibbutznik returned to his work.

Cullinane was impressed. 'You mean . . . any educated Israeli today can read the Bible exactly as it was written?'

'Of course. For us this is a living book. Not necessarily a religious book, you understand. That boy, for example. Son!' The youth came back, smiling. 'You ever go to synagogue?'

'No!'

'Your parents religious?'

'No!'

'But you know the Torah? The Prophets?'

'Sure,' and he left.

'That's what you must remember, Cullinane. Every Jew you see on this dig can read the original Bible better than you can read Chaucer.'

'You've proved your point,' the Irishman admitted.

'I haven't got to the point yet,' Eliav corrected. 'We Jews persisted in history ... where are the Babylonians, the Edomites, the Moabites with their multitudes of gods? They're all gone, but our tenacious little group of Jews lives on. And we do so because what you've been reading in Deuteronomy is to us a real thing. One crucial passage you must have noticed. It has an historic actuality, whether you Gentiles and we Jews like it or not.'

'Which one?'

Without consulting the Torah, Eliav quoted, '"For you are a people consecrated to the Lord your God: of all the peoples on earth the Lord your God chose you to be His treasured people."'

'I wish I could believe it,' Cullinane said.

'He does,' Eliav said, pointing to the kibbutznik, 'and the fascinating thing is that he believes it exactly as I do, in a non-racial sense. I suppose you'd call me a free thinker except that I believe in the spirit of Deuteronomy.'

This was too finely drawn for Cullinane, and he pushed aside the Hebrew Bible, but Eliav picked it up. 'The key to the Jew,' he said jokingly, 'is my favorite passage in the Torah. Moses is being eulogized as the greatest man who ever lived, knew God face-to-face and all that. But what is the very last thing said of him as a man ... as a living man? It seems to me that this is a profound insight ... It's the reason why I love Deuteronomy. I'm going to quote it from the King James Version first: "And Moses was an hundred and twenty years old when he died: his eye was not dim, nor his natural force abated."' Eliav repeated the last phrase, '"nor his natural force abated." But in our Hebrew original this last eulogy on a great man ends, "His moisture was not fled."' Eliav closed the book and placed his hands over it. 'A man who had known God, who had created a nation, who had laid down the law that all of us still follow. And when he dies you say of him, "He could still function in bed." Ours is a very gutsy religion, Cullinane.'

In the town of Makor eight hundred years had passed since that memorable day when five of its citizens had been involved in tragedy, and because of poetic dirges composed at that time the men and women of the tragedy had been transformed into gods who had added spiritual richness to the religion of the area.

Joktan the Habiru was now remembered as a heavenly stranger arriving from the east with many donkeys to give protection to the murderer, and the legend left no uncertainty as to the welcome Makor had given him. He had been quickly absorbed into the town, primarily because he had been willing to recognize the gods of Makor as superior to his own.

> Welcome the stranger, Astarte,
> Welcome the one who comes from afar,
> Who comes to worship you on donkeys.

Later verses made it clear that Astarte had smiled upon him, making of him a principal citizen who had inherited the house of mirth once occupied by the man he aided.

Urbaal the farmer enjoyed a more spectacular transformation, for when the local poets reviewed his tragic history they saw a great man, the owner of fields and the father of many children, caught in the grip of passions he could not master, and it became obvious that he could not have been a man. He was the god Ur-Baal, sent to Makor for a divine purpose, and through the centuries the poets had shortened his name and made him the principal god of Makor, known simply as Baal the omnipotent.

Amalek the farmer suffered a curious fate, for although he had been in many ways the most decent actor in the tragedy, he was always remembered as the enemy whom Ur-Baal had to kill, and thus he was gradually changed into the villain Malek, and then into Melak, the god of war. When this was accomplished, what had happened on that new year's day of 2201 B.C.E. was made clear: Ur-Baal had slain Melak in order to protect Astarte, and only Ur-Baal's courage, his willingness even to travel abroad among the donkeys, had saved Makor:

> Ride on the clouds, Ur-Baal,
> Ride on the clouds of storm.
> Behold, you shall ride the storm!

Libamah the enticing slave girl was now seen as a manifestation of the lovelier aspects of Astarte, and her capacity to inflame Ur-Baal had come to represent the creative processes of nature.

Timna the faithful wife also contributed to the concept of Astarte, and it was recalled that although she had loved Ur-Baal she had also been directly responsible for his death; but it was Timna's willingness to follow her husband barefoot and pregnant into his exile that had provided Astarte with one of the most beautiful adventures in Canaanite mythology:

> The year closed and the rains came,
> Even to Makor came the rains,
> And Ur-Baal fled to the olive grove,
> Fled to the night, to the realm of Melak,
> Down to the realm of Melak, god of the night.

There Ur-Baal would have remained in banishment, depriving Makor of its spring growing season and causing it to perish of starvation, had not Astarte gone seeking him to lure him back to earth and his assigned functions:

> Pregnant she left the zigzag gate,
> Pregnant with children of tomorrow,
> Seeking tomorrow and her lover Ur-Baal.

She had found the greatest of the gods imprisoned at the altar of Melak, and in a terrible hand-to-hand fight she had slain Melak, chopping him into small pieces and scattering his fragmented body over the fields like seeds of grain. This had brought the wheat to germination and the olive trees to blossom, and each winter since then the voyage of Astarte to the nether world had been repeated.

So now Makor was governed by a benign trinity: El, the unseen father of the gods whose characteristics grew ever more vague as the centuries passed; Baal the omnipotent; and Astarte his wife, who was both forever virgin and forever pregnant as the mother of all. The trinity had one additional peculiarity: Astarte both loved and hated Baal, and it was this conflict that explained the world's confusion, the contest between female and male, the warfare between night and day, between winter and summer, between death and life.

El, Baal, Astarte. In a tightly knit and beautiful partnership they watched over Makor, guiding it through the turbulence of that unsettled age. In the last eight hundred years Mesopotamia and Egypt had often contested the great valleys to the east; strange armies belonging to neither of those powers had also swept through Canaan, gutting and burning, but the little town on its slowly rising mound had managed to survive. It had been occupied by many victors and had been burned twice, but it had always recovered, thanks to the manifest interest taken in it by the trinity.

The town looked different. The mound had grown fifteen feet higher and now stood thirty-five feet above the surrounding plain. This meant that the original wall had long been submerged in rubble, but the wall itself still stood, locked in earth and providing the solid base from which subsequent walls had risen, as strong and as wide as before. Also, when the savage Hyksos had appeared out of the north to conquer the area, they had adopted Makor as a fortress city and had imported slaves to surface the slope with smooth stones, thus forming a glacis which protected the approaches to the wall. Makor was now practically unassailable.

Inside the walls other changes had occurred. The rising level of the town had quite obliterated the four monoliths, over whose heads rested a small temple consecrated to Astarte. No longer was there a Baal-of-the-Storm or of the water or of the sun; these attributes were now concentrated in Baal himself. The big temple was no more, for Baal resided on top of the mountain in the back of town, but there were homes for his priests, whose principal job was to guard the underground silos where grain was stored and the water cisterns where emergency supplies were kept in case of siege. Makor now contained more than one hundred and eighty houses and the greatest internal population it would know—nearly fourteen hundred persons. Another five hundred farmers lived outside the walls, which were broken by two large gates built of oak imported from Tyre. The first, preserving the original approach from the south, was much wider than before and was marked by four square towers, two abutting the outside wall and two inside. In the various times that Makor had fallen to enemy troops the main gate had yet to be forced.

It was the second gate, a postern in the north wall, that accounted for the most noticeable change. In several sieges of Makor the enemy had triumphed by capturing the well outside the wall and mounting siege until the internal cisterns were empty. Then, faced by thirst, the town had been forced to surrender, so in 1440 B.C.E. the town fathers, led by a strong-minded young man named Uriel, had decided to build a pair of stout walls leading out from the postern gate and surrounding the vital well. The walls were built and then roofed over, which had the effect of bringing the source of water inside the town, so that in time of siege the women of Makor could walk in darkness and safety from town to well and thus keep the cisterns full. As a result of this extension to the north, Makor now looked like a symbolic representation of the male reproductive organs; and perhaps for this reason the waterwall had proved its effectiveness during several would-be sieges from which the attackers had withdrawn after discovering that they could not capture the water supply.

The great Family of Ur was now represented by this builder Uriel, who had persuaded his elders to construct the waterwall. Incontestably he was the leading citizen of Makor, the man who owned the olive groves south of town and the oak forests to the east. He was forty-one years old, taller than the average Canaanite and more thoughtful. The priests of Baal looked to him for guidance; at first they had opposed the building of the waterwall, arguing that if Baal had intended his well to be protected he would have cared for the matter himself, but when Uriel's strategy proved right they changed their criticism to support. There was now no king of Makor, the Hyksos invaders having exterminated the royal family, but Uriel served so many of the ancient functions that he enjoyed a quasi-kingship. In the official records kept in Egypt, which now ruled the area, he was known as governor, a role which he filled rather better than most of the Egyptian appointees in neighboring towns like Hazor, Megiddo and Akka.

Uriel wore a black beard, trimmed square below his chin, and he was unusual in that age in that he had but one wife, Rahab, by whom he had one child, his son Zibeon. Concubines were not important in his life; he had several, as befitted a man of his dignity, but their children he did not bother about and as he grew older he no longer found it necessary to surround himself with younger women. He loved his one wife and found her both a congenial companion and a wise counselor.

He was a man devoted to Makor. When younger he had served as general of the army in days when a force of four hundred well-armed men could be put into the field. Twice the Egyptians had chosen him to serve as their field commander of contingents requisitioned in the area, and he had roamed as far afield as Carchemish and Damascus, but always he returned happily to Makor. It was he who initiated the practice of having the governor live adjacent to the main gate so that any merchant entering or leaving town might find him easily to consult on matters involving taxation. His home was a large fortified building wedged into the western wall of the gate, with two entrances, one for his family leading into the town and the other an official door that led from his office directly into the zigzag passage. He was so concerned with the administration of Makor that he often perched himself on a three legged stool inside the gate, chatting with anyone who passed and gossiping about the government of the town. Under Uriel's leadership Makor had prospered. Outside the walls many farmers produced food surpluses that were sent by caravan to Akka, while inside the town other men operated a sophisticated economic system based upon the manufacture of pottery from clay found in the wadi, the weaving and dyeing of cloth, and the casting of bronze implements of a high quality: the copper required was brought north by donkey caravan from mines south of the Red Sea; the tin came to Akka by ship from ports in Asia

Minor and the finished ware went out to many towns and cities. In Makor no one used flints.

The primary producers of pottery, cloth and bronze were supported by middlemen who provided funds for bringing raw materials in and who undertook the risk of shipping the goods out. They also supplied local shops, which sold not only things manufactured in the town but also objects imported from specialized centers as far away as Cyprus, Greece and Crete to the west, and Damascus and India to the east. The people of Makor ate well, dressed well, prayed to an organized trinity of gods who protected them efficiently, and enjoyed as secure a form of government as any known in the region between Mesopotamia and Egypt.

If on the one hand they had not yet discovered the concept of coinage, they did have a well-tested system of money-by-weight, whereby gold and silver could be sent long distances to pay bills; and if they did not have an organized system of posts they had messengers who moved regularly back and forth between the rivers. Uriel could write in three languages: the Akkadian cuneiform of Mesopotamia, which was the principal language for all diplomatic or business transactions; the hieroglyphs of Egypt for governmental reports; and the new form of writing used in northern Canaan, from which the alphabet would ultimately develop. On his desk he kept a set of scarabs carved in Egypt which he used to sign his clay tablets or to stamp the handles of jugs used to measure wine and grain. He had no books, but he did have collections of clay tablets on which important ideas were codified, and he knew by memory many rhymed legends from Mesopotamia and Canaan, especially the local epic dealing with Baal and Astarte in the nether world. He did not realize that this poem was a recapitulation of adventures in which his ancestors had been involved, and if someone had informed him of that fact he would have been embarrassed, for he was a man devoid of vanity or any desire to compete with the gods.

At forty-one Uriel was a judicious administrator who found personal pleasure when his fields produced more wheat or his olives a better press of oil. The only point on which he could be considered vain was his son Zibeon, twenty-one years old, dark-haired and handsome. For a while it had looked as if the young man might get into trouble by trying to force his attentions upon girls whose parents did not wish their daughters to marry at fourteen, even though peasant families permitted this; but as a result of pressure from Uriel, his son had taken a Hyksos mistress and that crisis had passed. In the meantime, the governor had been reviewing the families of his friends and it seemed probable that soon his son would marry.

On the spring day in 1419 B.C.E. when Zadok and his Hebrews were approaching Makor from the east, Governor Uriel perched on his three-legged stool, so situated that he could inspect anyone coming up the ramp and at the same time look into town to see what was occurring there. In the latter direction he could view a complex society consisting of Hyksos soldiers who had left the battlefield, Egyptian settlers, a few Africans, a handful of Hebrews who had straggled down from the north, and half a dozen other kinds of people from the sea and the desert. Even those who were properly called Canaanites were of a grandly confused background, but all lived together in a kind of tolerant amalgam. A short, swarthy young man with a sharply hooked nose detached himself from the crowd and walked toward Uriel.

'Would the governor care to inspect?' the young Hittite asked. His parents had reached Makor during a raid by mercenaries from the north.

'Are things prepared?' Uriel asked. The young man nodded, whereupon the governor directed a guard to take the stool back into the office while he joined the Hittite and walked along the broad main street that cut directly across the mound from the main gate to the postern. As he went he inspected the shops that lined the thoroughfare: the pottery shop that sold beautiful ware from the Greek islands; the cloth shop that had more than two dozen kinds of fabric; and the metal shop that had swords and daggers and jewelry highly burnished. As always, he checked the grain silos and the water cisterns to see that they were in good order, then proceeded to the area east of the postern gate where the potters threw clay upon their wheels and shaped the vessels that would be sold next month. Here kilns burned slowly, baking the better clay until it rang like glass, while at the bronze forge teams of young apprentices blew through long pipes bringing small furnaces to a blaze, or worked bellows to achieve the same effect in the larger furnaces.

Today, however, Governor Uriel was not inspecting his craftsmen. His guide led him to the section west of the watergate to the point where the wall of Makor bulged northward, and there, in a series of low wooden buildings, the young Hittite showed Uriel the ultimate weapon on which the defense of Makor rested, a device so terrifying that it would probably make future sieges unprofitable.

'Is everything in order?' the governor asked.

'Yes,' the young man said, calling to attention a group of Hittites assigned to the low buildings.

'Are these men able to act quickly?'

'At your command,' the Hittite assured him.

Satisfied that the defenses of Makor were secure, Uriel returned to the postern gate, where he went some distance into the dark waterwall until he reached the first guardhouse, from which he looked ahead to the well where women were gathered. Then he returned to the town, where he walked back along the line of shops, nodding to his townsmen, until he came to the gate and there he called again for his three-legged stool. Before it could be brought, his son Zibeon ran up the ramp accompanied by a young farmer. They bore exciting news.

'An army is marching down the road.'

Instantly Governor Uriel thrust out his hands, one toward Akka, one towards Damascus, as if he were once more in command of troops. 'From where?'

'There,' Zibeon indicated, and Uriel turned his whole attention to the east.

His first thought was of the cisterns, and he had just satisfied himself that they were filled. Grain was also plentiful and he had seen that the waterwall was in good repair. He next thought of the five hundred peasants who lived outside the walls, and his first inclination was to sound the bronze trumpets used to summon them to the town, but as he was about to give the order he visualized the rich fields awaiting their spring planting and the vines about to mature and he was reluctant to interfere with the normal processes of the land. It was in that moment of indecision that he determined the fate of Makor.

He was certain that some kind of truce could be arranged with whoever was marching down the road, so he took his son by the shoulders and asked, 'Zibeon, why did you say it was an army?'

'It's not a handful. There are hundreds of men.'

'But did they have sheep?'

'Yes.'

Uriel was relieved. Nomads had been straggling through Canaan for centuries and nine times out of ten the walled cities had experienced no trouble–that is, if no trouble was initiated by the townsmen. The strangers usually took one look at the walls and the protecting glacis and were quite happy to wander on, unless they decided to settle outside the walls, where they formed little villages which in time helped to enrich the cities. Uriel was satisfied that once more the traditional pattern would be repeated.

He therefore did not cause the trumpets to be sounded, but he did alert his soldiers to man their positions and he sent guards into the waterwall. He ordered the gates to be closed, then climbed one of the towers in order to study the approaching horde. At first he saw only the empty road, resting in spring sunshine and obscured some distance to the east by the flank of the mountain on which stood the altar to Baal. The road looked as it had for centuries–a narrow, rocky, dusty path winding through the countryside, silent and waiting for the next footfall, indifferent as to who might be approaching. Now Uriel saw a flurry of dust as if a breeze incorporeal and unreal had swept across the road, foretelling events of great moment. It was an ominous passage and Uriel drew back, but then a donkey appeared, followed by two children, small and brown and almost naked, who came running ahead to see which could first detect the waiting town. When Uriel saw them he broke into a relaxed laugh.

'Behold the army!' he cried, and the children, seeing the mighty walls and towers, stopped in the middle of the road, stared at the town, then rushed back to tell their elders.

Governor Uriel was still laughing when the first Hebrew appeared. He was a tall old man, covered with dust and clothed in rough-spun garments, bearing a staff and nothing more. He was bearded, and his white hair fell to his shoulders. He wore a rope about his waist and heavy sandals and walked with a determination that was not going to be interrupted until he reached the main gates of the town. If this old man shared any of the surprise shown by his children at seeing the stout walls of Makor, he did not betray it. On the other hand, Governor Uriel observed, neither the old man nor the men following him paid any attention to the peasants whose fields lined the road, and this was a good sign. Had the newcomers been set upon ravaging the countryside they would have started by now.

Nevertheless, Uriel was unprepared for the number of nomads who kept appearing from the east. This was not the ordinary Hebrew family he had met with in the past; Makor had often absorbed such units and had easily inducted them into Canaanite cults. Some families had arrived with as many as twenty children, but this group was different. It was, Uriel saw, a congregation of families, a veritable clan, and its conspicuous feature was not children but grown men of military age. The governor was not afraid, for he saw that the newcomers had few metal weapons, but the order in which they marched made it impossible for him to disregard his son's earlier report. This was indeed an army, whether bent on military objectives or not, and Uriel climbed down from the tower a much-sobered man.

Custom of that age required the ruler of a city to stay within his walls when a stranger approached awaiting a formal visit from messengers who would advise him of the intentions of the men gathered outside, but in this instance the nomads were apparently unfamiliar with diplomatic procedure, for no messengers were forthcoming. Instead, the stalwart old man who led the group stalked up to the gates alone, beat on them with his staff and shouted, 'Gates of Makor, open for Zadok, right arm of El-Shaddai.'

It was a strange command, unlike any the town had previously heard, for it assumed that the gates were going to open without the application of military force. People on the wall began to laugh, but Governor Uriel went to the gates, peered out through a slit and reassured himself that the men around Zadok were not armed. 'Open,' he told the guard, and when a small door in the gate was only slightly ajar the old man thrust his staff through the opening, pushed the door aside and stepped boldly in to confront the governor.

Of the two men who thus met for the first time, the Hebrew was the taller and the elder. He was the more thoughtful, the more dedicated in his spiritual life, and the one better adjusted to nature. The Canaanite was by far the more civilized and the better educated. His service with the Egyptians had also given him a better understanding of contemporary society. As judges of their people, the two men were equal in their appreciation of justice, and as practical heads of their religions, equal in their respect for the sanctity of gods. Neither man was intemperate, nor boastful, nor cruel. Their principal difference lay in the fact that Uriel accepted his trinity of gods as useful but not essential, whereas Zadok lived personally within the bosom of El-Shaddai and could visualize no existence outside that all-encompassing deity. But the opposing leaders were alike in two remarkable characteristics: neither wished to impose his gods on the other, and each was dedicated to the idea that two people as different as Canaanite and Hebrew could live together in harmony. Zadok was repelled by war, and Uriel, who had been an imaginative general for the Egyptians, had no desire to sacrifice his own people in battle. If trouble were to develop from this fateful meeting of nineteen hundred Canaanites and seven hundred Hebrews, it would not come because of anything Uriel and Zadok initiated, for they were men of peace.

When Zadok entered the gate he was awed by the maze in which he found himself and by the gray-green towers which seemed to press down upon him. He was confused by the quick turn to the left which brought him up against a blank wall and then by the turn to the right, where guard rooms were joined together by chains of hammered bronze. No man could easily storm his way through this gate, but it was not this military foresight that impressed Zadok most. Beyond the chains the patriarch saw for the first time a Canaanite town, with its crowded streets, its tempting shops, its people of many faces and varied derivations. He was bedazzled by the wonder of this place, yet instinctively suspicious of it, for he could feel the oppressive weight of the walls and the confusing manner in which one house crowded in upon the other, so that no man or house had much space to itself. In his first moment of looking into the mysterious town he longed for the freedom of the desert and wondered again if his clan was making an error in coming to such a settlement.

Governor Uriel, flanked by guards in leather armor, moved forward to greet the old man. 'I am Uriel, governor of Makor,' the Canaanite said.

'I am Zadok ben Zebel, right arm of El-Shaddai, seeking a place for my people.'

'Are you prepared to pay taxes?' Zadok nodded, and the Canaanite said, 'Along the roads the fields are taken. But beyond them lie rich pasturelands and areas where vines will grow.' His words were more conciliatory than he had intended, but the old man had spoken with such simplicity that the governor intuitively liked him, and judged on the spot that Makor would prosper with such a man as part of its complement.

'Which fields do you speak of?' the Hebrew asked.

'Beyond the olive grove. Beyond the field of oaks. All the area leading down to the swamp.' Then he turned from the empty fields and pointed to the mountain. 'But on this land you may not dwell, for it belongs to Baal.' The old man nodded, for wherever he had taken his people during the past forty years certain places had been sacred to certain gods, and although he did not worship such gods himself he understood when others did so.

'We respect the gods of all high places,' he said. He, too, felt that the meeting was going well, and the apprehensions reported by his sons found no echo in him. Obviously Makor was a town of wealth but its distant fields were lying waste, and it was only sensible for the town rulers to welcome strangers. One point however had to be clarified: 'We worship El-Shaddai, he of the mountain.'

Uriel frowned and drew back, for this was a matter on which he could not compromise. 'The mountain belongs to Baal,' he repeated.

'Of course!' Zadok agreed, and the Canaanite breathed more easily. 'The mountain will be sacred to Baal, for the mountain that El-Shaddai occupies is not that pile of rocks nor the one beyond, but the other mountain that no man ever sees.'

'Then there is no conflict?' Uriel asked with relief.

'None,' the patriarch said honestly, but Uriel noticed that the old man's eyes glowed with an intense fire such as he had never seen before–the passionate fire of zealotry–and at first the Canaanite was inclined to draw back from the Hebrew, as one might from a thing unknown, but then the fires subsided and he saw only Zadok, a reasonable petitioner.

'I will go with you to the fields,' he said. Summoning his Hittite guards Uriel led the way from the town and walked among the Hebrews, who had clustered near the walls awaiting the outcome of the meeting. The Canaanite noticed with respect their manly bearing, the tall, straight sons of the leader and the others who waited easily, ready for either peace or war, but hoping for the former. He saw clear-eyed women and their children, silent and wondering. It was a much better group than the usual rabble which came down that road, and he treated them with appropriate respect.

'The olive grove is mine,' he explained, 'but according to our custom you are free to pick the fallen ones and any left on the trees after the harvest.' The Hebrews nodded, for such was the law of all lands. 'No one must tamper with the oil press,' Uriel said. In a thousand years of warfare no one, not even the Hyksos, had destroyed the three stone pits; in the lever socket of the press, nearly two hundred different poles had been worn out during that time, one replacing the other, but no invader had ever harmed the press or cut down an olive tree, for whoever occupied Makor required the trees and their press. In fact, without the olives and the well . . .

'Water?' Zadok inquired.

And here the fundamental problem of Canaanite and Hebrew sharing the same land came to focus. In the swamp the water was brackish, as women who had run ahead were already discovering, and it could not be used; while the waterwell constructed by Uriel allowed no outside contact with the well of Makor. If the Hebrews wanted water their women would have to climb the ramp, pass through the zigzag gate, walk down the main street, exit by the postern gate and walk along the dark corridor to the well. Daily they would pass to and fro, and Hebrew would become intimate with Canaanite and each would come to know how the other lived, and how he prayed, and in time there would have to be marriages–it simply couldn't be avoided when beautiful Hebrew girls passed handsome Canaanite men day after day–and before long the superior culture of the town must inevitably conquer the rude vitality of the desert. The Hebrew must succumb, not in defeat or humiliation, but in a kind of quiet surrender as he allowed himself to be lifted to a higher standard of civilization and a new system of values. It was this battle that would engage the Hebrews and local residents for a hundred generations, with the outcome never clear and with victory favoring now the townsmen, now the Hebrews. It would involve people like Delilah and Samson, Jezebel and Elijah, Sanballat and Nehemiah, and long after they were dead similar perplexities would confuse men in such places as Moscow, Witwatersrand and Quebec. The problem of how Canaanite and Hebrew should share the same land but not the same religion would never be wholly settled.

'Then our women must go through the town?' Zadok asked.

'There is no other way,' Uriel said.

'Couldn't we open a gate, at the well?'

'No.' In no respect would Uriel breach the walls of safety which he had so carefully planned.

The two men studied each other for some moments, and each appreciated what disturbed the other, but since both were sensible men, eager to devise some system of mutual co-operation, they weighed the situation–and after a while Zadok said, 'We will accept these fields and pay taxes on them.' And Uriel returned to the walls, satisfied that he had done right in not using military power to oppose the strangers. 'In the past,' he said to his Hittite lieutenant, 'Makor has absorbed many kinds of people, always to its benefit. Our only problem here is that the Hebrews are more numerous.'

'We'll keep the weapons cleaned,' the warrior replied, and when the young man had a chance to meet with Uriel's son he said, 'Today your father has made a great mistake. We should have driven the strangers off.' Zibeon thereupon went out to inspect the Hebrews and returned with the same opinion. He discussed the matter with his mother, Rahab, and together they went to see Uriel.

'You've done a wrong thing,' Rahab said quietly.

Uriel had learned to listen to his perceptive wife, and they rarely quarreled. 'Perhaps I have,' he admitted, 'but in Makor we have scarcely enough people to do the work.'

'But you're bringing in the wrong ones,' Rahab argued.

'You haven't seen them.'

'Zibeon has. So has the Hittite. They saw desert people. Who do not respect walls and towns and proper houses.'

'They respect fields and cattle,' Uriel countered. 'And high places and gods. We need them.'

That afternoon he admitted that just possibly Rahab was right, and that the strangers might give trouble, but he had already rented them the unused fields and he was not unhappy in his decision.

Zadok was also satisfied. As day ended he assembled his people before the small red tent which his sons had erected beneath an oak tree, and there he reported to his dusty hundreds, 'El-Shaddai has brought us to this spot, as he promised. These fields and these hills shall be our habitation, but it is not we who have won this dwelling place. It is El-Shaddai who has done this thing for us, and it is to him that we now give thanks.'

He indicated to his sons that they should bring forth the white ram, the perfect beast of the flocks, and the struggling animal was dragged before the tabernacle, where with a sharp stone knife the old man offered sacrifice to the glory of the one god. The horns, half-twisted and strong, would form the trumpets that would henceforth summon the Hebrew to prayer on this spot. The wool of the ram would be woven into a black and white prayer shawl that would finally go into the tabernacle in memory of this day, and from the blood which now dripped from the altar would spring the bond that would unite this group of Hebrews permanently to the god who had chosen them to inhabit this fair land. It was a moment of intense dedication, which Zadok heightened by crying, 'El-Shaddai, you of the mountains, you of the storm, we place ourselves in your hands, advise and direct us in the paths we should follow.' And he fell before the tabernacle, waiting for instructions. But none came.

Trouble started in a quarter that neither Uriel nor Zadok could have foreseen. For many generations the wiser men of Zadok's clan had worshiped El-Shaddai with the understanding that whereas Canaanites and Egyptians could see their gods directly, El-Shaddai was invisible and inhabited no specific place. Unequivocally the Hebrew patriarchs had preached this concept and the sager men of the clans accepted it, but to the average Hebrew who was not a philospher the theory of a god who lived nowhere, who did not even exist in corporeal form, was not easy to comprehend. Such people were willing to agree with Zadok that their god did not live on this mountain–the one directly ahead–but they suspected that he did live on some mountain nearby, and when they said this they pictured an elderly man with a white beard who lived in a proper tent and whom they might one day see and touch. If questioned, they would have said that they expected El-Shaddai to look much like their father Zadok, but with a longer beard, a stronger voice and more penetrating eyes.

Now, as these simpler-minded Hebrews settled down outside the walls of Makor, they began to see Canaanite processions leave the main gate and climb the mountain to the north, seeking the high place where Baal lived, and they witnessed the joy which men experienced when visiting their god, and the Hebrews began in subtle ways and easy steps to evolve the idea that Baal, who obviously lived in a mountain, and El-Shaddai, who was reported to do so, must have much in common. Furtively at first, and then openly, they began to climb the footpath to the place of Baal, where they found a monolith rising from the highest point of rock. Here was a tangible thing they could comprehend, and after much searching along the face of the mountain, a group of Hebrew men found a straight rock of size equal to the one accorded Baal, and with much effort they dragged it one starless night to the mountaintop, where they installed it not far from the home of Baal.

Before either Uriel or Zadok heard of this unauthorized development–and it would be of equal concern to each–a more immediate problem erupted. Three Hebrew maidens were walking through Makor bearing water jars when they heard a commotion and were drawn off the main street to a small temple which rose above the spot where the four monoliths had once stood. It was sacred to Astarte, before whose gates danced a nude young man in a manner which the Hebrew girls had not seen before, and at the end of his erotic performance a woman from the audience ran up and dropping her clothes embraced him passionately, whereupon he led her into the small temple while the crowd applauded. The girls did not report these things to Zadok, but around the Hebrew campfires there was much whispered discussion, so on the next day Zadok's sons, Epher and Ibsha, strolled into town to see a similar performance—except that this time the dancer was a woman who finally accepted a male partner from the lascivious crowd. Epher asked, 'What's happening?' and a Canaanite explained, 'Sacred worship to insure the growth of our seeds.'

'Can anyone . . .'

'If you're a farmer.' The Canaanite led the two Hebrews to the temple door, banged on it and said to the pleasing young girl who opened it, 'These two are farmers. They wish to pray,' and she led Epher to an experience which would help determine the events of that summer.

That night there was new speculation in the Hebrew camp and on succeeding days several men left their work and slipped into town, but the scandal that finally reached Zadok's attention was the behavior of a young married woman named Jael, who went out of turn with her water jar, then slipped aside to the little temple, where she waited for the nude young man to perform his dance, at the end of which she hurried forward, leaving her water jar beside the door.

When Zadok heard of her offense he struck his forehead. He caused the ram's horn to be sounded, and when its mournful echoes reverberated along the valleys the Hebrews knew that evil was abroad and they gathered in contrition, many men and one woman realizing why El-Shaddai was angry. They were prepared to offer retribution, but when Zadok stormed that the woman Jael had forfeited all respect and must be stoned to death as ancient law required, three men of equal guilt spirited her away and found refuge for her inside the walls.

That night Zadok heard of the rock dedicated to El-Shaddai, and in the morning he took his staff and climbed up the hilly paths to the summit, where for the first time he saw the monolith to Baal, before which he bowed in proper respect. But alongside the ancient stone he saw one recently implanted—a rock to the unknown god of the Hebrews—and it was decorated with flowers and the head of a slaughtered lamb. 'Abomination!' he cried, and with his staff he knocked away the lamb's head. Then he leaned against the stone, seeking to unbalance it and roll it down the mountainside, but he could accomplish nothing and the stone mocked him.

Confused and worried, the old man strode down the hill and for the first time since the day of agreement he entered Makor, where he stalked through the town to see the temple for himself. There was then no dancing but he could visualize the abominable rites, and with disgust departed to seek out Governor Uriel, whom he hammered with direct questions: 'Have you given refuge to the whore Jael?'

'A woman joined us.'

'In your temple are there male and female whores?'

'From time out of mind we have worshiped Astarte.'

'Did you give approval for the erection of a rock to El-Shaddai? In the high place of your own god?'

At this Uriel frowned. No one had told him of the monolith, and if one had been erected it could cause trouble. Of the visits by Hebrew men and women to the sacred prostitutes he had been aware and had approved, for this kind of intimacy represented a wholesome interchange; it was in the interests of Makor to see that the Hebrew farmers produced maximum crops, and through the ages it had been proved that only worship of Astarte could insure this. He had also known of Jael's arrival and had personally found her a home with a Canaanite widower, for inter-marriage between the two groups would also speed assimilation; he expected to see quite a few additional Hebrews taking up residence inside the walls, and he would approve the day when Canaanites began to move outside to marry with the Hebrews. From what he could see of their women they were attractive and he imagined that his townsmen must think so, too. This interchange of women was the traditional way in which newcomers fitted into a town, and he hoped the process would accelerate.

But the erection of a monument to an alien god, and in the high place of Baal, was an infraction which he could not tolerate. Summoning his guard he went forth with Zadok to inspect the heresy, and when the two leaders had climbed the spiral path to the sacred place, they viewed with equal disgust the new monolith dedicated to El-Shaddai. Uriel was appalled because he had to trust in the supremacy of Baal, whom he knew to be a jealous god. Zadok was outraged because the supposition that El-Shaddai was no more than another Canaanite god to be represented with a stone was a degradation of the Hebrew god. To Uriel's surprise, the old patriarch was as eager as he to thrown down the intruding rock, so after men of the guard had used their spears to loosen the earth about the new monolith, they toppled the offensive stone and sent it clattering down the side of the mountain.

The soldiers withdrew, leaving Uriel and Zadok alone on the high place to discuss the matter, and as the thoughtful old Hebrew talked with the tough-minded younger man, the fundamental differences between them were for the first time openly exhibited.

ZADOK: You must never again permit my Hebrews to visit your sacred prostitutes.

URIEL: One day we shall be one people, living together in harmony, worshiping the same gods.

ZADOK: I will oppose such integration.

URIEL: Do you believe that our two peoples can exist side by side with no give and take?

ZADOK: I believe that you must follow your gods, and we must follow El-Shaddai.

URIEL: But you just helped me destroy the monument to your god.

ZADOK: Why do you think I did it?

URIEL: Out of respect for Baal, who rules this town.

ZADOK: I am amazed. Did you not understand that I threw down the lifeless rock because it was an insult to the one god who requires no earthly home?

URIEL: Are you suggesting that your god is greater than Baal?

ZADOK: I respect Baal . . . out of the respect I feel for you. I respect him as I do an old woman with nineteen grandsons. But no more. Baal must one day perish, for he is only a thing. El-Shaddai will live forever because he is not a thing?

URIEL: Then you believe that your god must triumph?

ZADOK: Of course!

URIEL: And you expect to live in those fields over there . . . for endless generations. With your god at enmity with mine?

ZADOK: The enmity will not continue long. Your people will soon join mine in acknowledging the one god. And we shall live in peace.

URIEL: In the meantime, you refuse to permit your people to worship Baal and

Astarte? You refuse to let them mix with us in all common ways?

ZADOK: I refuse to countenance abominations.

URIEL: You dare to call Baal and Astarte . . .

ZADOK: For your people they are righteous gods. You are entitled to worship them as you have in the past. But for my people their rites are an abomination.

URIEL: That is a harsh word.

ZADOK: Abomination.

The two men remained in the high place in the shadow of Baal, each trying so desperately to understand and to convert the other to logic, and there was fear between them, for absolute differences had been identified; but below them stretched some of the finest fields in Canaan and one of the best-governed towns. Surely, with good will these two virile peoples could make of this enclave a small paradise, and each man recognized that fact. Zadok spoke first. 'The fields are very rich,' he said quietly. 'In the fields we passed no olive trees bore fruit like yours.'

'Your people are industrious,' Uriel said, eager to draw back from the ugly confrontation that had developed.

'Of all the land we saw,' Zadok continued, 'this is the best. We hope to stay here for many generations.'

It was a gesture of true conciliation, and Uriel responded with the classic words of compromise: 'I am sure that between us something can be worked out.'

On the surface he was right. Canaanites and Hebrews had started their national histories sharing the same god, El, who represented an unseen power, but even in the first moments of sharing they had treated El in contrasting ways, for the Canaanites had consistently diminished his universal qualities. Being townspeople, they captured El and made him a prisoner inside their walls; they fragmented him into Baal and Astarte and a host of lesser gods. They seemed determined to drag him down to their level, where they could know him personally and give him specific jobs to do until he dissipated his force. The Hebrews, on the other hand, beginning with the same god having the same attributes, had freed him of limiting characteristics, launching a process that would ultimately transform him into an infinite god of infinite power. Each modification the Hebrews introduced in the desert years intensified the abstract powers of El. They called him Elohim, all the gods; or Elyon, the most high; or El-Shaddai, the god almighty. And soon they would end by dropping the El altogether and calling him by no name at all, representing him only by the mysterious, unpronounceable letters YHWH, whereupon his transformation would be complete. But later generations would back away from the austere Hebrew apotheosis and would once more give him a name: God.

Thus it was the tragedy of Canaan that it encountered the Hebrews when the two peoples were at a mighty crossroads: the Canaanites were degrading the concept of god while the Hebrews were elevating it. The conflict between these two philosophies would continue for more than a thousand years and there would be many times when it would seem that Baal of the Canaanites had triumphed.

Zadok accepted Governor Uriel's gesture of compromise. 'We will respect Baal,' he agreed, 'but you must warn your temple prostitutes not to welcome our people again.'

'I will tell them,' Uriel promised, 'but you must remember that this is a custom which has produced the prosperity you see down there. When your men understand farming a little better they'll appreciate the priestesses and insist upon worshiping with them.'

There was the serpent! There was the wound that would not heal–this constant encroachment of the town upon the ways of the desert. Since Uriel the Canaanite was a man devoted to the town, when he looked down at Makor he saw clearly that most of man's progress up to now had come when he lived in towns and worshiped gods that had developed from towns. Only inside a wall would men dare to build a temple, only within that safety could a library accumulate texts written on clay. In a thousand years men who roamed deserts had accomplished nothing: they built no roads, invented no new method of erecting homes; they had discovered neither pottery wheels nor silos for conserving grain. Only in a town like Makor could men prosper and make those material advances which when added together would be termed civilization. The history of this mound below us, Governor Uriel thought, is the history of men learning to live together in a town, faithful to the gods of town life, and this is the only history in the world that matters.

Zadok the Hebrew looked down upon the town and weighed it in different scales. As a free man of the desert he could not escape viewing Makor as the breeding place of contamination. In the desert a lusty man might rape a nubile woman and this was understandable. Zadok himself had taken his second wife in this manner, but when the rape was completed a strict code required the pair to marry and lend dignity to the process. In the desert a system of sacred prostitution would be impossible. The cleanliness of the rocks would fight against it, for prostitution of this sort could only be a product of the town. In open country a woman like Jael might prove unfaithful to her husband, but to this there was a sudden, blinding solution–death; it took the town to recognize such a woman as a heroine and to offer her sanctuary. The town was filled with men who had never worked in open areas tending sheep and discovering for themselves the actuality of their god; these men sat cramped before a wheel making pottery. They wrote on clay which they did not dig and sold wine they had not pressed. Their values were warped and their gods were of a trivial dimension. As Zadok looked at the frightening town he remembered the instructive history of two former members of his clan and he could hear his father Zebul telling their story: 'Your ancestor Cain was a man of the town and when he brought his gift to El-Shaddai, the god despised it, but your ancestor Abel lived in the open as we do, and when he brought his gift El-Shaddai was pleased, for our god has always preferred honest people who live outdoors above crafty ones who live in towns. This rejection angered Cain and he slew Abel, and from that time there has been enmity between town and desert.' But to Zadok the critical matter was still the uncertainty that had kept him in the desert for six full years after El-Shaddai himself had told the Hebrews to move into the town: he still wondered if men could live in a contaminating place like Makor and yet know their god as his Hebrews had known him in the desert. But as he drew back, afraid of the days ahead, he remembered the reassuring words of El-Shaddai: 'Inside the walls it will not be easy for me to speak with you, but I shall be there.' He looked at the townsman who stood beside him and thought: If we can co-operate with any Canaanite it must be with Governor Uriel, for he is a man of integrity.

So the two leaders started their descent from the high place, sharing a clear understanding and honest intentions. They would go down to the plains, one to his town, the other to his open fields, and each would do his best to keep the diverse peoples at peace. Each was certain that the task could be accomplished, for each was dedicated to conciliation. That evening the first test came, for Jael's Hebrew husband lingered inside the walls when the gates were closed and when night came he rushed to the house where his wife was living and murdered her. Before he could escape over the wall, the guard was aroused and killed him.

It was nearly midnight when Governor Uriel and Zadok met, but it was easy for them to prove to their people that the two deaths had canceled each other: an adultress had been slain, which ought to satisfy the Hebrews; and an invader had been killed by guards in uniform, which ought to pacify the Canaanites. The populace recognized the wisdom of this judgment, and an incident that could have led to inflammation was disposed of. The two leaders hoped that this was an augury for the future.

But then began the pressures upon Uriel and Zadok that would never diminish. When the governor returned home from the parley his wife Rahab asked why he had permitted the Hebrews to insult the town. 'A stranger hides himself inside our walls and kills a woman to whom you yourself offered sanctuary. Don't words mean anything these days?' She kept hammering, reminding Uriel of how her father when he was governor had reacted to similar insults. Uriel asked what he ought to do, and his wife replied, 'What my father did when the Hittites attacked the farmers outside the walls. He captured the lot and made them slaves, and today their sons are the best soldiers you have.' Uriel asked if she thought he ought to march out and destroy the Hebrews, and she said, 'You should have yesterday. You blind yourself to how serious their threat is. Go forth and kill half of them and you'll settle the matter now, while you can. Wait, and you'll face terrible consequences.'

That night Governor Uriel walked for long hours through his town, inspecting the richness he had brought to Makor: the industry, the silos filled with grain, the sixty additional houses tucked in here and there. It was a town of affluence and peace, one that must not be imperiled because of vacillation on his part. He argued with himself: I suppose I ought to march out and destroy the Hebrews, but then he remembered the conciliation offered by Zadok and concluded: To attack such people would be criminal. At the secret place along the north wall he asked his Hittites, 'Could we defeat the Hebrews tomorrow?'

'Easily,' they assured him. At home he asked Zibeon if he thought the Hebrews could be defeated, and the young man said, 'Easily, but each day they watch our ways and grow stronger.'

When dawn came Uriel temporized. He went to the secret building and ordered his Hittites to mount the horses kept inside and to deploy along the Damascus road, presenting a show of force to the Hebrews, who were unaccustomed to these powerful beasts; and not long after sunrise the gates opened and the horsemen rode forth, galloping some miles east of town, brandishing their bronze spears and then returning to the town.

The lesson was not lost on Zadok's sons. Epher and Ibsha, from a vantage point among the olive trees, watched the horses sweep down the road and studied them carefully on their return. The beasts were impressive, and the ease with which the mounted soldiers handled their long spears spoke one clear message. As soon as the dusty horses had disappeared, the young men ran to

Zadok and said, 'The Canaanites mean to destroy us. Since there is bound to be war, we think you should give the signal now.' They sat with the old man and explained with diagrams in the dust how they had scouted the town, using women who went to the well, and had devised a complex strategy for puncturing the waterwall and taking possession of the well. 'We can subdue them with thirst.'

'They surely have cisterns,' Zadok said.

'We can wait,' the boys replied, but he forbade them to discuss such matters and they said no more to him. However, they borrowed dresses from their sister Leah, and going as women to the well they accumulated the solid intelligence that they would need if war came. And they spoke to all the younger men, warning them of Canaanite intentions.

In the middle of this summer of uneasiness Leah went often into the town for water, passing through the main gate and along the crowded street whose shops were so enticing. Like other girls of good breeding she stayed away from the temple of the prostitutes and each day kept her eyes lowered as she went through the postern gate and into the long, gloomy waterwall leading to the well. She was a beautiful girl, seventeen years old, with the supple loveliness of one who had walked to many a well carrying her water jar on her head. Many Canaanite men had noticed her with approval, stopping their work to smile as she went past.

It was Zadok's intention to marry Leah to a young man who had already shown promise of becoming a leader, perhaps even a judge, but as she walked each day through the town she began to see, lounging in the corner of the gate or sitting on the governor's three-legged stool, the handsome young man Zibeon, and although she did not smile at him, both became aware that their meetings came oftener than chance would dictate. Zibeon was at the gate. He was at the postern. He rode along the olive groves on a horse. And once he met her at the door of the shop where clay goddesses were sold. He had an ingratiating smile and a generous manner, which Leah appreciated after the rough customs she had known in the desert.

One morning as Leah entered the town, hoping to see Zibeon, he disappointed her, and it was with regret that she left the sunlight and entered the long, dark waterwall, but as she reached the first guardhouse, empty that summer, for men were at work in the fields, she was seized so forcibly that her water jar toppled from her head and crashed to the ground, while she was whisked into the guardhouse and kissed many times. At first she was terrified, for no man had touched her so before, but when she discovered that the man was Zibeon she lost her fear, for he was gentle with her and that day they did no more than kiss passionately, and after a long time she was still loath to leave. He whispered that she would need a new water jar, and he left her in the guardhouse while he ran back to purchase a replacement, warning her that if anyone asked about the strange jar she should say, 'I must have picked the wrong one at the well.' That day the substitution was not detected, and during the hot days of summer Leah went often to the well, always hoping that Zibeon would reach for her as she passed the guardhouse. And they went far beyond kissing.

One day Epher chanced to notice that her water jar was unlike those carried by the other girls and he asked her how she had come by it, and she blushed deeply, saying, 'I must have picked the wrong one at the well,' but this he did not believe. He asked an older woman who carried water to watch his sister and in due course the spy reported that Leah and the governor's son were meeting in the guardhouse.

'The guardhouse!' Epher repeated, for those two projections from the waterwall formed focal points in his plan for assaulting Makor. He was both fascinated by the knowledge that the guardhouses were unattended and repelled by the thought that his sister should be spending time there with a Canaanite, for his experience had been with the temple prostitute. He thought first of advising his father, but decided not to do so because the old man was busy establishing the routines required in settled life. Epher consulted with his brother Ibsha and these two began keeping watch upon their sister.

Before long they were convinced that she was behaving strangely, and one afternoon they lingered near the main gate to overhear her saying good-bye to her lover, and as soon as she was outside the range of the guards they grabbed her and started running with her to Zadok's tent. But the governor's son had gone up to the tower to watch her cross the fields; without summoning assistance he ran after the three, catching up with them inside the Hebrew camp.

'She's been whoring with the Canaanites!' Epher shouted to his father.

Zibeon, running up from behind, struck Leah's brother across the lips. Stone knives flashed and the Hebrews would have killed the young man had not old Zadok intervened. 'What have you done?' he asked his daughter.

'Hiding in the dark with a Canaanite,' Epher broke in.

Again Zibeon leaped for the young Hebrew, but Zadok intervened and waited for Leah's reply. She said that she loved the governor's son and that if their fathers could arrange it, they wished to marry.

'They have married already,' Epher warned, and Leah flushed as the men of her family felt her body and satisfied themselves that she was pregnant.

'Let us stone them now!' Epher demanded, but Zadok sent his hot-headed son away and interrogated young Zibeon for some time. Like many of the Canaanites he was circumcised. He was willing to accept El-Shaddai as the one god. He would not force Leah to worship either Baal or Astarte. And he seemed an attractive, honest young man whom Leah obviously cherished.

Satisfied on these points, Zadok handed Zibeon over to the protection of his older sons and withdrew to the tabernacle before which he had prayed for so many years. 'El-Shaddai, what is your intention in this matter? Are we to accept a Canaanite into our family? Are we to submerge their gods in you?' No answer came, but at least the great god of the clan of Zadok did not object to the union, so the patriarch returned to his sons, saying, 'If Governor Uriel approves, your sister will marry his son.' Further argument he would not permit, and in silence he led a delegation back to the zigzag gate, where an excited crowd lined the walls and where the Hebrews confronted Uriel and his wife Rahab.

'Our children wish to marry,' the patriarch announced, and the good will that marked the two leaders was put to the test. Uriel signified his acceptance of the marriage, for this was the kind of development he had hoped for. He was surprised that his own son was involved, but it was a merging of the two groups that should be encouraged.

His wife took a different view. 'Zibeon should marry inside the walls,' she said. 'One day he will be governor . . .'

'This is a good marriage,' her temporizing husband said.

'Baal will not approve,' Rahab warned. 'Astarte will not bless our fields.'

'Your son will not marry under Baal and Astarte,' Zadok pointed out.

'Have you agreed to join their god?' Rahab asked her son. When he nodded, Governor Uriel was startled, but he remained hopeful that peace of some kind could be maintained.

'It's possible to worship Baal and El-Shaddai both,' the governor said.

It was a difficult moment, one which could destroy the Canaanite-Hebrew relationship, and Zadok made a generous concession: 'Governor Uriel is right. His son can worship both gods.'

Uriel sighed. He appreciated Zadok's desire to avoid trouble and he knew how close the two groups had been to an open rupture. He started to discuss ceremonies, hoping that contentious problems were past, but his clear-seeing wife said bluntly, 'Such a union of gods will not work. This marriage must not take place.'

Red-headed Epher elbowed his way forward and said sternly, 'Leah is with child.'

Rahab tried not to speak harshly. 'I am sorry,' she said, 'but my son is to rule this town one day, and he must have a proper wife.'

'Your son has contaminated my sister,' Epher cried, and there would have been fighting if Uriel and Zadok had not pacified their adherents. The governor went to Leah and asked if she was pregnant, and when she nodded, the black-bearded Canaanite said, 'They shall marry.' But Rahab and Epher, appreciating the dangers of such a union, maintained their opposition.

With great force of character Uriel and Zadok worked to evolve a plan whereby the marriage could go forward, and thanks to their determination, Canaanite and Hebrew began to show signs of being able to live together in some kind of harmony. Zadok's only demand was that the couple be married under the auspices of El-Shaddai, and this was granted. Uriel insisted that in all other respects Leah must become a Canaanite, must live within the walls and must rear her forthcoming child as a Canaanite. To these demands Zadok surprisingly agreed, reminding his rebellious sons, 'The wife should follow the husband.' He furthermore astonished both the Canaanites and the Hebrews by volunteering to send with his daughter six fat sheep.

So the marriage was solemnized before the small red tent of the Hebrews, and a kind of peace, engineered solely by the good will of the leaders, settled over Makor. But Leah had lived in the town only two weeks when one of the Hebrew women reported that they had seen her and her husband in the public square praying openly to Astarte. There was protest in the Hebrew camp, but Zadok silenced it by reminding his people that he himself had given the young man permission to continue worshiping his old gods so long as he acknowledged that El-Shaddai was superior. But two days later other Hebrew water carriers saw Zibeon patronizing the temple prostitutes and word of this also reached Zadok. Again he explained to his people that the young man was entitled to worship his gods in the accustomed manner, but he was apprehensive about what might happen next.

And then his attention was taken away from his daughter, for Epher and Ibsha asked him to go with them to the top of the mountain, and as he reached the high place of Baal he saw that stubborn Hebrews had rescued their monolith to El-Shaddai and had hauled it back to the crest of the mountain, where once more it stood close to Baal. Father and sons tried to dislodge the evil thing, but they could not, and Epher spat upon it many times, crying, 'Father, your laxity has encouraged this,' and a bitterness grew up between them.

Now Zadok was alone. His daughter was surrounded by gods of the basest sort. His Hebrews were worshiping stone idols. His brilliant son, Epher, was drifting away from him, and he felt contamination oozing out of the town, but he did not know what to do. At the foot of the mountain he walked alone for many hours, calling upon El-Shaddai for guidance.

'What shall I do with my stiff-necked people?' he pleaded. 'I have told them of you. I have instructed them in your ways and I have thrown down their heathen altars, but they have gone whoring after false gods. What can I do?'

In the rocky fields he found no answer, and in the plowed fields near the oak trees there was no reply. At the tabernacle there was no voice, and among the tents no echo. 'What shall I do?' the old man begged. He muttered, 'I'll lead my clan to some other spot,' but he knew that if this was required El-Shaddai would have advised him. Furthermore, would not the next location contain the same kinds of temptation? Was it, perhaps, intended that the Hebrews be submerged into the corruption of Makor? 'El-Shaddai, what shall I do?'

For several days no answer came. Then, as the critical period of the growing season approached, when the collaboration of the gods was essential–and this even Zadok acknowledged, for in the portentous days he prayed repeatedly to El-Shaddai for good crops–three of his waterwomen came running into camp, their eyes wide in wonder and horror, to tell him of the other god that Makor worshiped. 'He is fiery,' they gasped, 'and has a mouth of flame into which little children are thrown while men and women dance naked.'

'Children?' Zadok asked, his hands trembling. Once when his people were traveling to the north he had heard of this god.

'And at the end of the dance women like us run to embrace the male prostitutes while their husbands go into darkened rooms with the female whores.'

Zadok staggered back, and the water-women concluded, 'Many of the Hebrews are there now, sacrificing to the strange gods.'

'Abomination!' Zadok cried, uttering again the fearful word that condemned, the ultimate charge that could not be withdrawn once it had been invoked. He left his tent and wandered for many hours till night fell, and from the town walls he heard the sounds of revelry and the beat of drums. He saw the smoky fires. But after midnight, as he stumbled exhausted through the olive grove, he became aware of a presence speaking to him from behind an olive tree, and softly an admonishing voice said, 'It was you who uttered the word, Zadok. That town is an abomination.'

'What shall I do?'

'It was your word. It is your responsibility.'

'But what must I do?'

'The abominations must perish.'

'The town, the walls?'

'The abominations must be destroyed.'

Zadok fell on his knees before the voice, bowing to the olive tree that hid the terrible countenance, and from this position of surrender the old man expressed his trembling pity for the condemned ones inside the wall. 'If I can make the abominations cease,' he pleaded with his god, 'may the town be saved?'

'It shall be saved,' the compassionate god replied, 'and not a single rock will be unseated.'

'Praise be to El-Shaddai,' the old man sighed, and the presence was gone.

Without consulting anyone the patriarch threw his robe about him, took up his staff and walked through the night, his heart ablaze with love for the people he had been permitted to save. At the town gate he pounded with his staff, shouting, 'Awake and be saved!' but the guards would not permit him to enter. He hammered again, crying, 'I must see the governor now!' and Uriel was routed from his sleep; and when he looked through an arrow slit to see that the messenger was his colleague Zadok, he said to the guards, 'Let him enter.'

Like a bridegroom rushing to greet his bride the old man swept into the governor's room and shouted, 'Uriel, Makor can be saved.'

The sleepy Canaanite scratched his beard and asked, 'Old man, what are you talking about?'

'You have only to halt the abominations.'

'What is this?'

Joyously the old man explained, 'You must destroy the temple to Astarte and the fire god.' Then generously he added, 'Worship of Baal you may continue, but you must accept El-Shaddai as the one god above all.' His eyes were ablaze with the fire of zealotry that Uriel had seen that first day.

Uriel sat down. 'You never demanded this before.'

The Hebrew, seeming not to hear the governor's logic, ranted, 'Divert this sinful city into the ways of the true god.'

Rahab was awakened by the noise and entered the room, wearing a nightrobe. 'What is the old nomad saying?' she asked.

Zadok ran to greet her as if she were a beloved daughter. 'Tell your husband to accept El-Shaddai's will.'

'What frenzy is this?' Rahab asked her bewildered husband.

'Makor can be saved,' Zadok explained ecstatically, 'if you halt the sacred prostitution and stop feeding babies to the fire god.'

Rahab laughed. 'It is not prostitution,' she said. 'Those girls are priestesses. And your own daughter Leah sent Zibeon to lie with them, the way I sent Uriel when I was pregnant. To insure an easy delivery. Old man, these rites are necessary, and your daughter has more sense than you do.'

Zadok did not hear what Rahab was saying. He was so ecstatic over El-Shaddai's offer to save Makor that he expected others to react as he had done, and when they did not he became confused, but before he could react to the introduction of his daughter's name, Zibeon joined the meeting, bringing Leah with him. When the girl saw her father, bewildered and looking very old with his unkempt beard, she ran to him with compassion and would have kissed him, but when he saw her the words of Rahab took meaning and with his staff he fended her off, asking, 'Did you send your husband to the prostitutes?'

Zibeon answered, 'I went to the temple to protect your daughter in childbirth.'

The patriarch looked at his son-in-law with pity and said, 'You have committed an abomination.'

'But you agreed that I was free to worship Astarte,' the young man protested.

Then Leah interrupted: 'I asked him to go, for my sake.'

Leah's voice, uttering such words, startled the old man and he leaned forward to study her face, while a hideous fear took possession of his mind. 'Leah' he asked, 'did you also take yourself to the male prostitutes, consorting with them in the same manner?'

'Yes,' his daughter replied with no shame. 'It is how the women of Makor worship.'

'And if you have a son, will you give him to the fire god?'

'Yes. It is the custom of this town.'

Zadok drew back from the four Canaanites, for after this confession his daughter could no longer be a Hebrew, and he was struck by a dizziness that almost felled him. But he managed to focus his weary eyes upon the four doomed faces, and when he saw them clearly, uncomprehending and obstinate in their sin, he realized that El-Shaddai had arranged this night to exhibit the true abomination of the town. Yet even in that moment of discovery he remembered the god's promise that if the Canaanites should repent they could still be saved. Raising his right arm he pointed a long body finger at Uriel and asked, 'For the last time, will you order these abominations to cease?' No one spoke. Directing his finger at Leah and her husband he asked, 'Will you abandon this doomed town, now?' Neither spoke, so he fell to his knees and knocked his head three times upon the tiles, and from this position looked up at the governor, pleading, 'As the humblest of your slaves, can I beg you to save yourself?' The Canaanite made no reply, so the old man pulled himself back to his feet.

At the door he turned back and pointed to each of the four in turn and then to the town. 'This shall all be destroyed.' And he was gone.

It was too late to go to bed, so Rahab called for some food and said, 'Your father sounds like an old fool.'

'In the desert he often talked to himself,' Leah explained.

'I warned the governor to destroy him at the beginning,' Rahab muttered. 'Now it is he who speaks of destroying us.'

'We may have to turn the Hittites upon him,' Uriel said, and when Leah was gone Rahab directed her son not to let her wander from the walls. 'For she is a Hebrew and cannot be trusted.'

'You think there may be war?' the young man asked.

'He talked like a madman,' Uriel replied, 'and madmen bring war.' In the early dawn he went to the north wall to consult his Hittites.

Zadok, as soon as he reached his tent, summoned his sons to ask what plans they had devised for the capture of Makor, and they asked, 'Is it to be war?'

'Last night El-Shaddai commanded us to destroy that town,' he replied.

To his surprise Epher and Ibsha laid before him a detailed plan for investing the powerful town and forcing its surrender. 'It will cost us many lives,' they warned, but in his growing fury the old man refused to consider losses. Taking his sons with him to the tabernacle he dedicated them to the work of El-Shaddai, and the three prayed in silence.

That morning, as soon as the gates were opened, four Hebrew women went to the well while a detachment of men crept through the wadis until they were close to the waterwall. Of the four women, two walked with an awkwardness that should have been detected, but they were allowed to slip through the postern gate and into the dark passageway, where they hurried to the unoccupied guardhouses. There the two awkward ones slipped quietly into the retreats, throwing off their women's clothing and unleashing long bronze knives. The two real women walked quietly forward, found two Canaanite women at the well and killed them. With rocks they signaled to their Hebrew brothers on the outside, and these troops started breaching the wall that surrounded the well. Canaanite soldiers from inside the town, belatedly aware of the danger, rushed through the postern gate and into the tunnel, where they were intercepted by Epher and Ibsha, who had constructed from pots and benches a kind of barricade. The way was narrow and the two Hebrews were courageous, so that the Canaanites were held back, and after a quarter of an hour the Hebrews on the outside had broken through the wall and taken possession of the well. They ran forward to relieve the two sons of Zadok, but when they reached the barricade they found Ibsha dead and Epher sorely wounded.

The Hebrews had won the first encounter. They controlled the well and would try to strangle the town with thirst. Governor Uriel appreciated the significance of this move, but in spite of the fact that five of his soldiers had been killed in the waterwall he still hoped that any honest grievances the Hebrews might have could be adjudicated, and to this end he sent messengers to Zadok asking what might be done. But the patriarch refused to meet with the Canaanites, and they returned knowing that complete war was upon them.

When Governor Uriel heard their report he decided to recapture the well at once and summoned his Hittite captain from the stables. Together they climbed a tower from which they studied with satisfaction the unmilitary manner in which the Hebrews were gathering before the town walls. 'We can massacre them,' the Hittite boasted, rubbing his hands with pleasure.

'Ride back and forth and kill as many as possible,' Governor Uriel directed. 'We'll end this war quickly.'

The Hittite ran to the stables and ordered his men to harness their horses, two by two, to the war chariots which up to this time Governor Uriel had kept hidden. Few citizens of the town were aware that these ultimate weapons had been smuggled in at night from the seaport of Akka, and none of Zadok's Hebrews had encountered such machines of war. Into each driver's bucket stepped a Hittite whose left hand would control the horses while his right was free to swing a chain to which was attached a huge bronze ball studded with spikes. One swipe of this weapon would break a man's back. Behind each driver stood two soldiers lashed to the chariot so that their hands were free to wield swords and heavy maces. And from the wheels of the chariot projected scythes that revolved as the wheels spun, cutting down anyone the chariot brushed against. They were horrible instruments, calculated to terrorize and kill, and Governor Uriel now moved them to the main gate.

When they were in position, and when the maximum number of Hebrews were milling aimlessly about the walls, he directed trumpets to sound and foot soldiers to rush forth as if this were to be an ordinary sortie. The Hebrews, surprised by the daring of the Canaanites, began massing at the exact spots Uriel had anticipated, and when they were most vulnerable he ordered the gates to swing open and the chariots to gallop down the ramp and into the midst of the stunned Hebrews. The Canaanite soldiers, instructed as to what was coming, slipped deftly aside, leaving a clear path for the terrible chariots, whose drivers lashed their horses directly at the milling Hebrews while the mounted riders ripped and cut at them.

It was slaughter, for if the Hebrews stood to fight, the horses trampled them; if they sought retreat, armed riders chopped them down from the rear with maces that broke their necks; and if they merely stood, the whirling scythes on the wheels cut them to death. Zadok, seeing the carnage, cried aloud, 'El-Shaddai, god of hosts! What have you brought down upon us?' But Epher broke away from the women binding his wounds and leaped onto the neck of one of the Hittite horses, cutting its throat and toppling the chariot onto the rocks. The red-headed warrior thus proved that the vehicle was not invincible nor the horses immortal, and his Hebrews rallied, driving the Hittites back with stones and flint-headed arrows.

Judged numerically, the first day's battle represented a clear defeat for the Hebrews. They had captured the well, but when Zadok mustered his forces before the tabernacle he could count thirty-four dead, and as he moved among the fallen he recited their names: 'Naaman, my son. Joktan, my son. Aaron, my son. Zattu, my son. Ibsha, my son.' Not many generals could walk a battlefield at dusk and count as one day's loss five sons and twenty-nine relatives, and when he reached the last corpse, 'Simon, son of Naaman, son of my loins, son of Zebul who brought us from the desert,' he was possessed by a consuming rage and he stood before the tabernacle, swearing, 'This town shall be destroyed. Not one roof shall rest upon its beams, not one man committed to the prostitutes shall live.' In this manner the peace-loving old man finally surrendered himself to the accomplishment of El-Shaddai's will, but at the moment he could not know that his submission had come too late.

In his determination to crush Makor he became like a young warrior; in moral ardor he was again the primitive man of the desert facing the corruption of the town. But gradually he had to see that the effective decisions regarding the war were now being made by Epher, who, in spite of his wounds, led his father and his brothers to the mountaintop, where this time they succeeded in throwing down the offensive monolith which their Hebrews had erected to El-Shaddai. As the group was about to leave the high place Epher cried, 'Let us throw down Baal as well.' The old man tried to stop his sons as they rushed toward the remaining rock, warning them, 'No! It is only the abominations we fight. Baal rules here and El-Shaddai approves.' But Epher was headstrong and shouted, 'Our war is against Baal, too,' and he brushed his father aside. Leaping at the monolith he called for his brothers to join him, and they toppled it down the mountainside.

It was a revolutionary moment. For it would be more than a hundred and fifty years before El-Shaddai, in his later manifestation as Yahweh, would deliver to the Hebrews in Sinai a commandment requiring them to abandon all other gods. It was this evolution that Epher was anticipating when he acted upon the principle that El-Shaddai was not only the supreme god of Zadok's clan but of other peoples as well. When Epher made this arrogant extension of definitions Zadok knew that the boy was wrong.

'That was not the will of El-Shaddai,' the old man thundered, but Epher ignored him, as if through a vision he had foreseen the direction in which El-Shaddai must grow. And that night when the wounded young leader laid before the others his final plan for capturing Makor, Zadok realized that he had had no part in the building of this plan. It is the daring of a young man, he told himself, one bold enough to throw down the rock of Baal. And at that moment he was forced to acknowiedge that the grandeur of leadership had slipped from him.

While others planned the forthcoming battle he walked alone through the olive grove, seeking to talk with his god, from whom he needed guidance. It would be difficult to penetrate the meaning of the words *he talked with his god*. Certainly El-Shaddai was no lackey to be summoned at will, as oracles were summoned by the witches of nearby En-dor; many times Zadok had needed advice from El-Shaddai when none was forthcoming. On the other hand, Zadok was certainly not an insane man, as his daughter had suggested, who heard demonic voices; he was never more clearly in control of his faculties than when he conversed with El-Shaddai. Perhaps the explanation was that when the Hebrews faced moments of decisive crisis, especially those involving moral impasses where decision could not be deferred, they found guidance coming to them from the lonely places. A voice cried out from unexpected quarters, the voice of accumulated reason; it could not be conjured up, for El-Shaddai appeared only when he was ready. But the voice could be relied upon, for the god delivered a consistent message; and now as the patriarch sought him among the trees, El-Shaddai did not take refuge in burning bushes or flaming rocks. Like a father he walked beside Zadok, conducting the last great conversion he would offer the old man.

'The abominations shall be destroyed,' El-Shaddai assured him.

'And the walls, will we penetrate them?'

'Did I not promise you in the desert, "The walls shall open to receive you"?'

'According to the plan of Epher?'

'Have I not said, "The sons are wiser than the fathers"? Even according to the plan of Epher.'

'Then my headstrong son was correct in destroying Baal?'

'He was hasty, for the time has not yet come when I shall command people to have no other god before me.'

'Will you forgive my son his arrogance?'

'He is to lead my people in battle, and such men require arrogance.'

'And me? Always I have sought peace, El-Shaddai. When the town has surrendered, what must I do?'

'Destroy the abominations.'

'And the Canaanites?'

'The men you shall kill, every man of the town. The children you shall take as your own. And the women you shall divide among you, each man according to his losses.'

This terrible judgment, not delivered as a parable permitting choice of interpretation but as a firm, hard command from the god himself, appalled the patriarch. He was being ordered to repeat the massacre of Timri, and this he could not do. It was an act too grisly for him to perform, even though El-Shaddai himself commanded it.

'All the men of this town I cannot slay.' Again he had opposed the word of his god and was willing to accept the consequences.

El-Shaddai was in a position to carry out the executions himself but he always preferred to reason with his Hebrews, and now he said to Zadok, 'Do you think it is from cruelty that I order you to slay the Canaanites? Is it not because you Hebrews are a foolish and a stubborn people, apt to fall captive to other gods and other laws? I do not command this thing because I hate the Canaanites, but because I love you.'

'But among the men of Canaan must be many willing to worship you. If these accept circumcision may I spare them?'

From the olive trees no voice replied. Zadok had posed a difficult question, even for omniscient El-Shaddai. He had raised the question of salvation, and even a god required time to weigh the proposal. Great risk was involved in what the patriarch proposed: surely some Canaanites would swear falsely and accept circumcision while in their hearts they were determined to resume worship of Astarte. But the relationship between El-Shaddai and his Hebrews was not an absolute thing; not even a god could order Zadok to obey blindly a dictate that was wholly repugnant to him or one that contradicted his moral judgment. El-Shaddai understood why the old man was wrong in his estimate of the Canaanites and the error would entangle El-Shaddai in many future difficulties, but apparently he could not make Zadok understand. So for the moment it was the god who surrendered.

'If among the Canaanites you find just men,' he agreed, 'they may be spared.'

'What sign will you give me that they are just?'

'In the moment of victory you must rely upon your own signs.'

The old man was reluctant to bring up the next point, but he could not avoid it. 'El-Shaddai, today I have lost five sons. I need the help of wise men. When we capture the town, may I spare the lives of Governor Uriel, who is a man of wisdom, and of my daughter and her husband?'

To this question El-Shaddai did not reply, for he knew that when the battle was over, Zadok would no longer be the leader of his clan and the decisions which tormented him tonight would not be his to make. But more important, there were some matters which a man must decide for himself, outside the reference to any external agency, even his god; and the killing of one's own daughter and her husband was such a matter. In this hallowed silence El-Shaddai departed, never again to speak to his trusted, his timorous, his obstinate servant, Zadok son of Zebul.

Captain Epher's plan of battle required daring from all the Hebrews and soul-testing courage from a few. Men and women alike were divided into four groups—mob, gate, waterwell, stables—and success required a day when the wind swept down from the north. For such a day they waited, and in the interval each morning the mob-group massed in apparent stupidity before the walls so that Governor Uriel would grow accustomed to unleashing his chariots at them. On each calm day one or two Hebrews were killed and all feigned terror as the scythe-wheeled engines of the Hittites coursed among them. But in an unseen part of the olive grove the other three groups practiced their plan of battle and waited for the wind.

Late in the month of vintage the days of desert heat arrived—those searing days when there was no wind but only a superheated air from the southern desert hanging over the land and suffocating even the beasts. These days were called 'the fifty,' for fifty were expected each year, and in later centuries it would be a law that any husband who murdered his wife after three days of 'the fifty' could go free, for under such circumstances no man should be held accountable for his behaviour toward a nagging woman. In the stifling heat Epher sent his mob-group before the wall once or twice, but Governor Uriel was wise enough not to dispatch his chariots; the horses could not have galloped long. So a kind of truce settled over the town, a blazing desuetude, while all waited for 'the fifty' to pass.

At dusk on the eighth day a Hebrew watchman came sweating into camp to tell Zadok, 'A slight breeze is moving down the wadi.' Zadok called for Epher and the two circled the town and found the watchman to be correct. A tantalizing breeze had begun to move from the north, not yet strong enough to stir the branches but enough to make leaves quiver on the olive trees. The strategists returned to camp and prayed.

By the next day there were clear signs that 'the fifty' was passing. Birds that had lain dormant began chasing bees through the olive grove and donkeys grew restive where before they had been content to hide in shade, not caring whether they ate or not. On the Damascus road a spiral of dust formed, hurrying along like an old woman with a basket of eggs, and from the town came sounds of

activity. 'Tomorrow morning,' Epher predicted, 'the Canaanites will be
willing to use their chariots again.' At sunset Zadok predicted, 'Tomorrow, a
strong wind.'

That night Epher's four groups of Hebrews gathered before the tabernacle,
where the patriarch blessed them: 'Our fate is in the hands of El-Shaddai, the
god of hosts, and from old he has led us into battle. You men of unusual courage
who go to the gate, El-Shaddai goes with you. When you run to the battle, he
runs with you, clearing the way.' The god of the Hebrews was not an
indifferent deity who remained above the contest; he sweated with his warriors,
determined to bring them victory. 'As you go to sleep this night,' Zadok added,
'remember that in the past we have known worse days. When we struggled
through the desert east of Damascus, perishing of thirst, El-Shaddai saved us.
Tonight let us think upon those days and take courage.' And at the command of
El-Shaddai the wind rose, and inside the walls of Makor the Canaanites felt
refreshed and grew eager to throw their chariots once more against the stupid
Hebrews, who did not understand that they must not gather in masses before
the gate.

In the long history of the Hebrews there would come many crises when only
a miracle could save them, times when the ordinary courage of men would not
suffice, and the unprejudiced observer, looking back upon a series of such
moments culled from three dozen centuries, would find it difficult to explain
what had supported these miracles. Was it destiny or accident or the
intervention of a god like El-Shaddai? No event would be more difficult to
explain than the one which took place on a windy morning during the summer
of 1419 B.C.E. Inside a town that had withstood mighty sieges, protected by a
wall and a glacis that had thrown back even Egyptians and Amorites, waited
fourteen hundred well-fed, well-armed Canaanites fortified by five hundred
farmers called in from the surrounding countryside. At their disposal they had
metal instruments of war, horses and chariots against which the Hebrews were
practically powerless. Opposed to them were less than seven hundred ill-armed
Hebrews led by a long-bearded old man who was afraid of war, and who on his
arrival had signified his willingness to accept peace on almost any terms.

When the wind was strong the four groups of Hebrews moved into action.
The largest mass of people gathered in front of the city walls, making futile
attempts to scale the glacis, but among them were hidden the second group,
forty determined young men prepared to die, knowing that if only five of their
number broke into the town their sacrifice would have been justified. In the
segment of the waterwall controlled by the Hebrews waited the third group,
twenty men aware that they faced heavy odds when they tried to force the
postern gate. And crouched in the steep wadi north of the town hid the fourth
group, composed of Epher and thirty hypnotized young men prepared to scale
the glacis and climb the wall while bearing lighted fire pots. The plan was
insane, and only a miracle could bring it success.

Governor Uriel, looking down upon the part that he was intended to see,
realized that the Hebrews were doing precisely what he had wanted. 'They still
mass before the gate,' he commented in disbelief. 'Summon the Hittites!' The
chariots were wheeled into position and armed men climbed aboard bearing
swords and maces. The gates were swung open and the dreadful chariots
thundered down the ramp, the Hittites flailing at the disorganized enemy, but
as the last chariot left the gate the second group of Hebrews leaped onto the
ramp and dashed into the zigzag gateway, where they were trapped by the

chains and subjected to arrows from the towers.

'To the main gate!' the Canaanite captains shouted through the streets, as they saw the trapped Hebrews start to throw lighted brands into the town. The fighting was desperate. From the doorway leading to the governor's house young Zibeon appeared, slashing with a sword and killing a brother of his wife. From the towers other Canaanites put new arrows into their bows and fired with shuddering force. It looked as if this second part of the operation would fail, for no Hebrew had yet broken into the town and many fell at the gate to be consumed by their own burning torches.

However, their diversion accomplished its main purpose, for guards were drawn away from other parts of town, so that when the third Hebrew unit started forcing its way through the tunnel it met a weaker opposition than expected, and these Hebrews edged forward, two abreast, with others crawling over them as they fell, and in the end nine men reached the postern gate, which they tore from its hinges, placing four men with ropes inside the town before the startled Canaanites could summon helpers from the fight at the main gate. By this time three additional Hebrews were dashing from the postern to the stables, where horses too old for chariots began to whinny.

From the walls the invaders signaled to Epher, waiting in the wadi, and the red-headed captain was first to climb up the ropes, lugging a fire pot with him. He was joined by others, and at this moment three heroic Hebrews who had survived the spears at the main gate forced their way into the town, also bearing fire, which they spread upon the rush roofs in that part of town. Into the stables filled with hay Epher advanced, killing a one-legged Hittite guard and setting fire to the horses' bedding. Other Hebrews threw their pots along the stable walls, and soon the wind whipped them into a tall blaze that fanned out over the town into which Governor Uriel had crowded as many horses as possible. Old horses left in the stalls whinnied pitifully, and townsmen ran to the cisterns, prepared to throw drinking water on the soaring flames.

Within moments the wind of El-Shaddai drove the various fires across the doomed town, producing a conflagration so powerful that it turned mud bricks to an angry red, as if a mightier Melak were consuming the whole city. Limestone lintels were transformed into powder and unfinished pottery was baked into those blistering shapes that would be recognized twenty-six hundred years later as the products of a holocaust. As the flames raced across the dried roofs of the town they formed at first a giant suction which absorbed all breathing air, and women perished unscarred as they ran to lift babies from their cradles. They died without anguish and with a certain beauty, as if some gentle god had halted them in a timeless moment, but soon fire followed and the dry empty space exploded into flame, and the beautiful women vanished. Cloth, water, stores of grain, food for that day's hunger and all human life were burned away.

Some Canaanites managed to escape through the ruptured postern gate, their faces black and swollen, and a few fought their way past the pile of dead Hebrew bodies blocking the main gate, but as they stumbled chokingly from the flames they ran into the spears of Captain Epher's men, who butchered them before they could rub their eyes clear of the smoke. By midday, when the wind-streaked sun stood over the ruins, the town of Makor and its people no longer existed. The wall remained and the towers at the gate. The tunnel to the well still stood, its roof burned away, its walls naked and humiliated, and the well itself continued to send forth sweet water to the conquerors. But over the silent mound rested a thick deposit of blackened ash, which as long as the earth existed men would be able to read as the death mark of Canaanite Makor.

One group survived intact. The Hittite charioteers had been ranging far outside the town when the fire started, and now they wheeled their horses homeward, returning in triumph to a town that no longer existed. They studied the desolation for a moment, made sharp calculations, and then like practical mercenaries turned their chariots around and galloped off to the east, down the Damascus road, their bloody scythes revolving in the sunlight. And they were seen no more.

For Zadok the Righteous, who had wanted peace, the hours of triumph brought only pain. His thinking life had started with the sack of Timri, fifty-seven years before, and it was ending in a repetition, with the hands of his clan smeared in blood. Those few Canaanites who escaped the holocaust by climbing over the wall were dragged before him, their faces half-burned away, and in vain he tried to save their lives. 'This one says he will accept El-Shaddai,' he pleaded, but Epher had seen too many of his brothers killed that day, and now he commanded the clan. On this day of burning, his thirst for revenge was strong. His spear would flash past his father's eyes and the charred prisoner would die.

'Stop this killing!' Zadok ordered. 'El-Shaddai commands you.' Epher looked at his father with contempt, for he knew that El-Shaddai had ordered the Canaanites to be slain, so he killed them, man after man who might have helped rebuild the town.

Finally his brothers dragged forth Governor Uriel and his son Zibeon, who were forced to crawl on their knees to Zadok. 'These must be saved,' the patriarch ordered, but Epher prepared to kill them. The patriarch threw himself across their bodies, crying, 'These two El-Shaddai gave to me.'

For a moment Epher interpreted this to mean that his father wished the two prisoners set aside for special tortures, and he released the Canaanites, whereupon the old man in an act of humility kissed Governor Uriel's hands and said, 'I plead with you, accept El-Shaddai.'

The governor, whose indecision had brought this smoldering ruin upon the town, looked at Zadok and at last understood the fires he had seen in the old man's eyes. 'I live with Baal and Astarte,' he said, and Epher slew him.

Zadok, stunned by his son's insolence, cried, 'El-Shaddai wanted the life of that man!'

In the heat of the killing Epher dropped his tired arm, stared at his father and uttered the fearful, forbidden words: 'You are a liar.' The old man gasped, and Epher said, 'Last night when you were asleep El-Shaddai came to me. I know the truth.' And in accordance with El-Shaddai's will he prepared to kill his brother-in-law, but Zadok protected the young man with his own body. 'Do you accept El-Shaddai?' the patriarch asked.

'I accept the one god,' Zibeon declared.

'Where is Leah?'

'Slain.' And the old man's grief was so pitiful that Epher allowed him the life of Zibeon, through whose later children the great Family of Ur would survive.

Of the nearly nineteen hundred Canaanites only nine men escaped the slaughter, plus fifty women and some two dozen children. To each, old Zadok went as if he were still leader of the clan, exacting promises that they would worship El-Shaddai, and after the women had been distributed among the Hebrew farmers he gathered the Canaanite males and personally circumcised all who had not undergone the rite. At the end of his labors he sat before the tabernacle and wept, a tired old man from whose eyes the fires of zealotry were fled; but he was not missed, for Epher was giving commands.

Unnoticed, Zadok betook his age-bent shoulders, his untrimmed beard and his staff up to the high place where the monoliths had stood, and there he looked back upon the town that his people had been forced to destroy, and he lamented:

> 'Gone are the granaries of yellow corn,
> Emptied are the reservoirs.
> The streets are ashes
> And the homes are black with soot.'

He was ashamed of his part in this day's sorrow and cried, 'El-Shaddai, why was I chosen to author this destruction?' That day he had lost nine more of his cherished sons; his slave girl had been cut down by the chariots, and his daughter by her brothers; but at dusk he thought principally of the Canaanites slain needlessly, and since he could not accept what his people had done he openly defied his god: 'You are without mercy, to kill so many.' And El-Shaddai grew impatient with his patriarch, and after enveloping the mountain in a cloud of light, appeared before him face-to-face. And the old man was dead.

It was night before his wives found him, fallen across the spot where Baal had once reigned, and his sons came to bear him down from the mountain, chanting that he was the hero who had destroyed Makor, the patriarch who had triumphed over Baal. And as they placed his almost weightless body before the altar and closed his wonder-struck eyes, they speculated among themselves as to which of them El-Shaddai would talk with now, delivering his commandments for them to follow. There was extended discussion, for of the old man's four surviving sons three were more than forty years old and each was devout, and it puzzled the Hebrews as to which El-Shaddai would choose as his servant for rebuilding the town. But that night as the Hebrews celebrated victory and mourned the death of their patriarch, their god spoke directly to red-headed Epher, and all saw the young captain tremble and draw back from the nomination. But the older sons acknowledged the principality of their brother, whereupon El-Shaddai said to Epher: 'Zadok the Righteous have I taken this day because he disobeyed me, but he was a great man on whom I relied for many years. He was a man with whom I walked and now you shall serve me in the same way, for this is the promised land that I have brought you to inherit.'

But as the years passed, with old Zadok long buried under the oak trees, Epher heard rumors which disturbed him and he climbed to the high place. There he found that his people, aided by Canaanite survivors, had once more set up the monolith to Baal and the accompanying monument to El-Shaddai, and he wrestled with the stones and would have thrown them down, but he was alone and was not powerful enough to do so.

LEVEL XII

Psalm of the Hoopoe Bird

Found at Makor–horned altar cut from one piece of basalt rock using iron tools. 1116 B.C.E. Bull's head carved in low relief. Aperture for blood of animal sacrifices. Religious significance of the four corners known as 'horns' not clear, but on consecrating a new altar the blood of animal victims was rubbed on each of the horns, according to the directions given by Yahweh to Moses in Exodus 29:12. 'And thou shalt take of the blood of the bullock, and put it upon the horns of the altar with thy finger, and pour all the blood beside the bottom of the altar.' Fugitives seeking sanctuary, even from the king, were secure so long as they grasped the horns of the altar, as explained in I Kings 1:50: 'And Adonijah feared because of Solomon, and arose, and went, and caught hold on the horns of the altar.' Deposited at Makor in late spring, 963 B.C.E.

It was morning in Makor. Birds chattered on rooftops and children played noisily in the crowded streets below. As the little town nestled securely within its girdle of newly built stone walls, the door of the governor's quarters opened for the departure of a chubby man who wore a dark scowl on his fat bearded face and a host of freckles on his bald head. Obviously disappointed over some adverse decision handed down by the governor, he entered upon the curving main street of the town and walked disconsolately homeward, but he had gone only a short distance when he was joined by a group of children who began chanting, 'Hoopoe, Hoopoe, Hoopoe!'

He stopped. His worried face lost its scowl and he began to smile until his features formed a great half-moon, reaching from the back of his bald head to his chin, all wrinkled in laughter. Catching up a little girl, he tossed her in the air and caught her with a kiss as she fell back to his arms. 'Sweets, sweets!' she squealed, so he put her down and began gravely searching his pockets as if he did not know where the treats were hidden. Other children ran up and danced on nervous toes as he continued feeling his robe, from which he finally produced a cloth bag filled with sweetmeats. Distributing them to the children, he continued homeward as the crowd at his heels cried happily, 'Hoopoe, Hoopoe!'

For as long as men had existed upon the land of Israel they had been accompanied by a curious bird, the hoopoe, who had given them more amusement than any other living thing. He was a stubby creature, about eight inches long, with a black and white body and a pinkish head, and was remarkable in that he walked more than he flew. He was always busy, hurrying from one spot on the ground to another, like a messenger responsible for an important mission whose details he had forgotten. The laughable bird seemed to go around in circles, trying to recall what he was supposed to be doing.

His appearance added to his grotesqueness, for he had a head shaped like a slim, delicate hammer, which he tripped up and down with surprising speed. One end of the hammer-head was obvious, a yellow bill nearly two inches long, but the balancing end was amazing, a tuft of feathers also about two inches long which could be either compressed into a single projection that matched in size and color the beak or flashed out into a spreading crest, so that the bird seemed to be wearing a jeweled crown.

As he hurried about the ground he probed into worm holes until a grub was located or insects were caught hiding, whereupon the hammer-head would thrash up and down until the long beak grabbed the meal. Then the happy bird would strut away to some rock where he would throw the captive onto a hard surface through which it could not escape back to earth, and the hammer-head would flash up and down as the bird tore the grub or insect apart and ate it, after which he would go waddling back to the hunting ground, poking his inquisitive head here and there.

As long as man remembered, this comical bird had been called the hoopoe because of its ugly, short, sharp call. It could not sing like the lark, neither could it mourn like the dove, and to the men of Israel it evoked no poetry summarizing the earth on which they lived. To the Egyptians the hoopoe was sacred; to the Canaanites it was clever, for Baal had given the bird an evil smell and then hidden rare jewels in its nest, and the smell kept thieves away. To the Hebrews the hoopoe epitomized family loyalty, for young birds tended their parents with care, covering them on cool nights and plucking dead feathers from their wings in the moulting season. But to all, the funny little bird that could fly and didn't was an object of amusement, and even seemingly important men like the governor often stopped their work to watch these busy little excavators.

During the last years of the reign of King David in Jerusalem, the town of Makor had an engineer whom its citizens called Hoopoe because he, too, hurried about most of the day, peering into holes. Like the bird for which he was named, this short, dumpy fellow was regarded with affection, partly because he made the citizens laugh and partly because he was known to be a man without a single malicious intent. He was so amiable and generous that the governor, in a rare moment of clarity, said of him, 'Hoopoe is the happiest man in this town, because he loves his work, his wife and his gods, in that order.'

Hoopoe's work was the building of the new defense wall around the town of Makor, a task on which he had been engaged for some years. His wife was the inquisitive young woman Kerith, whose father had been a priest and who had once taken her to Jerusalem, where she had actually seen King David in his grandeur. And his gods were the traditional ones of Makor. There was Baal, the old familiar watchman of the Canaanites, who stilled lived in the same monolith on the same high place, watching over mundane activities like water supplies and the building of walls; and there was Yahweh, the god of Moses, a new Hebrew deity who had developed step by step from El-Shaddai, a god now so mighty that he controlled both the high heavens and the deep heart of man. In Makor there were a few Canaanites who worshiped only Baal, a few Hebrews like Kerith's father who worshiped only Yahweh, and the great mass of people like Hoopoe who had accepted Yahweh as the awesome deity of the outer heavens while continuing to worship Baal as the local deity for day-to-day problems.

Hoopoe was thirty-nine years old, the father of two lively children by his attractive wife, and of several others by his slave girls. In spite of his humorous appearance he was a man who had conducted himself with courage in his younger years while fighting for King David, and it was because of this loyal service that he had been given the job of rebuilding the wall of Makor.

He was a short, stocky man with broad shoulders, big muscles and an oversized bottom which wiggled when he walked. His bald head was overlarge and on it he wore no covering. He had a pointed nose for probing into corners to detect where builders had tried to substitute crumbling earth in place of solid rock, and he wore a square-cut black beard which quivered when he laughed, and he had blue eyes. In fact, he looked much like a chubby version of his well-remembered ancestor, Governor Uriel, who had perished four hundred and fifty years ago while trying to keep Makor from being burned by the Hebrews, as related in a group of clay tablets stored at Ekhet-Aton in Egypt. In the decades following that disaster the great Family of Ur, like many Canaanites, had accommodated itself easily to Hebrew rule, becoming nominal Hebrews. Hoopoe's parents, hoping that their son might win the confidence of the ruling group, had given him the chauvinistic Hebrew name of Jabaal, which meant 'Yahweh is Baal,' trusting that this would imply that he was more Hebrew than the Hebrews, and this mild deception had worked, for Jabaal was accepted not only as an honest Hebrew, but also as the son-in-law of a priestly family.

These were the exciting years when Hebrews controlled for a few brief decades a well-knit empire which King David had put together from fragments left scattered around by Egypt and Mesopotamia when their vast holdings fell apart. David's kingdom reached from the Red Sea on the south to Damascus on the north and provided the Hebrews with unexpected wealth, since it sat athwart most of the major caravan routes and derived much profit from them. Even Accho, that constant thorn in the flank of the Hebrews, had been captured from the Phoenicians, although it was not held long; and this rapid growth of empire meant that Makor, key to a fluid frontier, was now of more significance than before, and the judges and kings were interested in keeping it a Hebrew bastion if it could be maintained without too much cost to the central government. King David and his generals had therefore been pleased when they heard that in the little town there was an engineer who acted as if he were in charge of the empire's main city: he worked ten and twelve hours of hard labor each day and spent additional time in planning the schedule for others. As a user of slaves he was unusual, for he treated his men well and few had died under his custodianship. Moabites, Jebusites, Aramaeans, Philistines and Amalekites all found it tolerable to work for Hoopoe, for on the job he fed them well and allowed them to rest when they became sick. In fact, they enjoyed seeing him come paddling along the ramparts, sticking his sharp nose into this area or that and joking with them as he encouraged them to speed the construction.

In the evenings he came to their miserable camp outside the walls, bringing them scraps of food or dregs of wine, and often he raised the subject of their accepting the Hebrew god Yahweh, always on the reasonable ground that if they did so they could become Hebrews and thus regain their freedom. He carefully explained that they were free to maintain their former gods, as his own name proved, and he was an effective missionary, for he spoke in the language that practical men could understand. 'My god Yahweh is like your god Dagon,' he assured the captured Philistines, 'only greater.' And he made it both easy and honorable for his slaves to become Hebrews. In this way his corps was constantly diminished, but from it went converts of good character to serve in other parts of the Hebrew empire, and it was one of these former slaves who finally carried the good name of Jabaal the Hoopoe to Jerusalem, where General Amram, in charge of fortifications in the empire, heard of the master builder in the north.

'One of these days I must see what the man has accomplished,' the general said, marking the name of Makor in his memory.

The new wall which Hoopoe and his slaves had finished was made necessary by the gradual submersion of the old Canaanite wall. Alternate burnings and rebuildings had piled an additional eight feet of rubble on the mound, bringing it level with the top of the walls, so that something had to be done; but as the mound grew in height its crown of usable land contracted in size, which meant that the new walls could only be built inside the old ones, and when Hoopoe did this, the area available for the town was sharply diminished. In Governor Uriel's day fourteen hundred Canaanites had lived inside the walls, but now only eight hundred could do so; however, the tranquillity brought to the area by King David's good government permitted nine hundred farmers to live outside the walls, the largest number who had ever done so. This was the golden morning of Makor, the glorious apex of the town; it was also the period when Hebrews were demonstrating their ability to govern a kingdom, and if Makor were to be taken as the criterion, they governed well.

Hoopoe, for example, lived in a comfortable house in the west portion of the town, and now as he walked homeward along the curving street he could see a visual summary of Makor's affluence. The governor's quarters were substantial and from them he dispensed an impartial justice which protected men in their ownership of fields and property. According to the ancient laws of the Hebrews the weak had rights, the pauper had a claim upon the charity of his neighbors, taxes were allocated fairly and punishment could not be capricious. The shops that lined the first part of the curving road were filled with materials imported from many parts of the world: faïence from Egypt, brocades from India, silk from Persia, delicate bronzeware from Cyprus, beautiful pottery from Greek islands and marvelous ironware from the nearby Phoenician city of Accho, plus the ordinary trade goods brought by regular caravans from Tyre, Sidon and Damascus. In back of the shops stood the spacious houses, built of stone for the first two or three feet, then finished in wood and lime plaster, with strong wooden ceilings and lovely courtyards. To the left as Hoopoe started home stood the ancient temple of Epher, now an inconspicuous building where men worshiped Yahweh, and across from it the little shops that sold the day's necessities: wine and olives, bread and wool, meat and fish brought inland from the sea.

Two characteristics marked Makor in these days. Almost none of the shops were run by Hebrews, for they had originally been a desert people, unused to commercial ways, and they instinctively avoided occupations like shopkeeping or moneylending, partly because they had no aptitude for such ventures and partly because they had leapfrogged from nomad life to farming, and their love was for the land and the seasons. 'Let the Phoenicians and the Canaanites run the shops and deal in gold,' they said. 'We will tend the flocks, and in the end we will be the better off, for we shall stand closer to Yahweh.' The second distinguishing mark was that culturally Makor remained pretty much a Canaanite town. For example, it held to the ancient calendar of Canaan, which was divided into two seasons, the hot and the cold, and in Makor the new year began in ancient style at the end of the cold, but certain other parts of the Hebrew empire had begun to favor a year beginning at the end of the hot. The temple building and its rituals were of Canaanite origin, for on that spot El and Baal and Astarte had long been worshiped, and it was only logical that when the grandson of Epher introduced Yahweh to the town, the new god's temple should have consisted merely of a refurbishing of a building dedicated to the old. In fact, when the average citizen of Makor prostrated himself before Yahweh he could scarcely have explained which god he was worshiping, for El had passed into Baal and he into El-Shaddai and all into Yahweh, the god of Moses our Teacher.

These were the great formative years of the Hebrew ritual, for from Jerusalem, King David and his priests were endeavoring to impress upon Israel one clearly defined religion, but these reforms were slow to be adopted in Makor; its little temple continued to function as the focus of an ancient community ritual rather than as a surrogate of the unified national religion.

Near the end of the street stood the house of Hoopoe, built many years before by his ancestors and occupied by a succession of decent men who had tried to live decent lives. As Canaanites they had often had to dissemble regarding their allegiance to Baal, but that was about as far as their duplicity went; in recent generations they had become outright converts to Yahweh, circumcising their sons and marrying their daughters into the best Hebrew families. This process of assimilation had reached its climax when Hoopoe had become betrothed to the only daughter of Shmuel ben Zadok ben Epher, the Hebrew priest, and now this couple had taken over the family residence.

It was built mostly of stone, plastered on the inside to a cool white finish. Two of the rooms bore murals in red and blue paint, not showing particular scenes but indicating the desert from which the Hebrews had come and the hills which had been the homes of the Canaanites; but the principal adornment was Kerith, Hoopoe's lovely wife of twenty-seven. She was slightly taller than Hoopoe and much slimmer. Her face was better proportioned, too, with a shapely nose, blue Hebrew eyes, ivory skin and dark hair. Her husband loved her to the point of foolishness, and since he knew that she cherished jewelry, not acquisitively but as works of art, he often bought her bits of glazed ware made in Egypt or enamel from Cyprus; but these minor treasures she kept in small rosewood boxes and wore only a large pendant made of silver from Persia into which had been set a rough oval of amber brought down from the northern countries. Against the gossamer woolen gowns which she preferred, this golden amber shone with a radiance matched by the wide bands of yellow cloth with which she often hemmed her robes. She was a tensely perceptive woman, intelligent, devoted to her children and an adornment to her fat little husband. Between them there was a genial relationship, for if in Makor there were more handsome men—and Kerith could see many in a ten-minute stroll through the streets—there were none who would have adored her so. Only one significant difference existed between them, and this was vital: Kerith was the daughter of an austere religious man who had almost known Yahweh face-to-face and from whom she had inherited her commitment to that deity; Hoopoe as a builder who had to work with the earth was willing to acknowledge Yahweh, but he also knew from hard experience that Baal ruled the soil and it would be folly for an engineer to ignore or denigrate the permanent deity of the earth in which he had to work. In many Makor families this dualism existed, but usually it was the man who inclined toward the Hebrew god while his wife held superstitiously to the old familiar deities; in Hoopoe's case it was the Family of Ur's timeless preoccupation with the land that had reversed the process, but he and his wife lived in harmony, for each was tolerant of the other's spiritual attachments.

Now, in the month of Abib in the spring of the year 966 B.C.E., when spring rains marked the day and floods filled the wadi, when barley was ripening in the fields and anemones and cyclamen were reappearing along the swamp, nodding to that strange flower which people of another religion would later call jack-in-the-pulpit, in this month of Abib when the rebuilding of the walls had ended, Hoopoe walked home along the curving street in some dismay, and when his wife greeted him at the door of their home he fell heavily onto the earth-and-tile bench.

'I'm worried, Kerith,' he said.

'I saw your new walls and they seem very solid.' She brought him some barley cakes and a drink of hot wine mixed with honey, and he relaxed.

'When I was inspecting them today I looked down upon the richness of this town. In back of this street, the best dye vats in the north. Outside the walls, the resting places for the camel caravans. And these good houses. Kerith, this town is a temptation to all our enemies to the west. It's the gateway to Jerusalem.'

'But isn't that why you built the wall?' she asked.

'The wall will hold them off. Of that I'm sure. But do you know how we'll lose this town?'

She knew. Like all the young women of Makor she had often placed her water jug upon her head and walked through the postern gate and down the dark waterwall to the well. One day during the siege four years ago, when she was pregnant with her youngest son, she had made the dangerous journey and had heard Phoenician warriors trying to pierce the fragile protecting walls, and the people of Makor knew then that if the Phoenicians had brought their siege engines against the well instead of trying to reduce the old town walls they would have captured Makor. It was illogical to suppose that in the next invasion, when the new town walls would appear so formidable, the invaders would again fail to hit upon the obvious strategy of knocking down the waterwall. Kerith well knew that whenever the Phoenicians really wanted to capture Makor they could, and she acknowledged that her husband's new wall represented not security but an additional hazard; but in the tentative discussions that would recur in the weeks ahead she would refuse to admit these facts because of the complex reasons which now kept her silent. She loved her dumpy little engineer and supported him against men like the governor who viewed him with amusement, but she also knew that if Hoopoe launched some extensive new building project in Makor she would be held prisoner in the town and thus her dream of the future would be destroyed.

Therefore it was with apprehension that she heard him say, 'I've made up my mind. The Moabite and I have a plan that will save this town. Today the governor wouldn't listen, but tomorrow he must.'

Convinced that she was doing right, Kerith placed her hand on Hoopoe's arm and said quietly, 'Don't make a fool of yourself, Jabaal. If the governor doesn't agree with you, don't argue. You can find work elsewhere.'

Her words soft and reasonable, her voice low and comforting had an almost frightening effect on Hoopoe, for he understood exactly what they meant, and for a fleeting moment he was prepared to sit down with her now and to speak frankly of all problems confronting them; but so many significant ideas were involved that he shied away. He loved Kerith too much to disturb her before his plans were formulated, so he finished his sweet wine and carried a roll of scraped leather into another room, where he stayed up late drawing rough sketches of his scheme to save Makor, and in the morning, after he had started his slaves upon their work, he reported to the governor's office, where he told that official, 'Sir, now that the wall is completed I grow more worried about our water supply.'

'I asked you to mend the waterwall,' the governor said. 'I inspected it the other day and your Moabite did an excellent job on the repairs.'

'Sir! It fools no one. Fifty Phoenicians could knock it down.'

'Last time they overlooked it.'

'Next time they won't.'

'What do you want to do?' the governor asked. 'Have your slaves build a new set of walls?'

'I have a much different plan,' Hoopoe said.

The governor laughed. Placing his hand on the shoulder of the fat builder he said condescendingly, 'I understand your problem, Hoopoe. You've finished the town walls and you're afraid that if you don't start something right now Jerusalem will take away your slaves. Isn't that it?'

'I'm concerned not about slaves but about the safety of my town.' He corrected himself. 'Your town.'

The little man had spoken with such gravity that the governor had to listen. 'Well, what is it?'

Hoopoe gulped from nervousness and made the first formal presentation of his daring scheme. Using his hands as great shovels he said, 'Here in the center of town, inside the walls, we must dig a shaft almost as big as this room straight down through rubble and solid rock for ninety cubits.' The governor gasped. 'At the bottom we begin to dig a tunnel that will take us far under the town walls and out to the well.'

'How long a tunnel?'

'Nearly two hundred cubits, and high enough for women to walk in. Then we bury the well under mound after mound of rock, and we are secure from any besieger.' He moved his right hand back and forth to indicate women walking in safety through the subterranean passageway.

To the governor the concept was so fantastic that he could only laugh. He was unable to visualize a hole almost as big as his room, sinking so far into the earth; and as for the idea of a tunnel burrowing through solid rock and somehow striking the well, he knew this to be folly. 'Hoopoe, we need no more digging around here,' he told his engineer. 'Get yourself a farm outside the wall and dig for worms.' His joke appealed to him, so he bobbed his head up and down like a hoopoe bird and added, 'For worms! You understand?'

Hoopoe hid his resentment. 'On one point you're right, sir. We should start this before they take away our slaves.'

'See! I knew that's what worried you.'

'It does. We have a trained team now. The Moabite is the best foreman we've ever had in Makor, and the others make a fine unit.'

'I'm sure Jerusalem will take the slaves,' the governor said. Showing his engineer to the door he bobbed his head up and down several times. 'You go dig worms.' And he closed the door on the preposterous idea of digging a hole through the heart of the town.

Hoopoe did not go to the workings but wandered home, where he laid before Kerith his intricate plan: shaft, tunnel, burial of the well; and she irritated him by saying that she was sure the plan wouldn't work. 'How could anyone start from the bottom of a shaft, dig a sloping tunnel, and hope to find a thing as small as a well?'

'That's my job.'

She laughed. 'How will you see underground? Like a mole?'

He was weary from trying to explain ideas to people who could not visualize them, so he kissed his wife good-bye and climbed onto the ramparts back of his home; and the mound on which Makor stood had now grown so high that from the walls Hoopoe could look westward and see Accho, where Phoenician ships from many ports brought the men and the riches which would one day be thrown against Makor. How far away the tempting city looked to one who had seen it only as a boy; how close it seemed to a man who understood the power and cupidity of the Phoenicians.

In deepening gloom he walked along the ramparts to the north edge of town, where he studied the doomed waterwall as it left the postern gate and ran to the well, but he did not spend much time worrying about that obsolete system which had rarely impeded a determined adversary. He looked instead down into the wadi and up the opposite slopes until he reached a point on the mountainside above which stood the monolith to Baal. He satisfied himself that on the mountain he could reach the point he sought. 'I know it's possible,' he growled. And then he looked again at the waterwall, and in its place he visualized the combination of shaft and tunnel that would comprise his system. Imagining it to be already in operation, he looked westward at Accho and thought: When the Phoenicians do strike at us again they will find no well to attack.

But for some weeks it looked as if there would be no system of tunnels, for when Hoopoe returned to the governor's office, fortified with new enthusiasm, he accomplished nothing. The governor had won Jerusalem's respect by sending surplus income to the capital rather than asking for assistance, and he had no intention of reversing this process. He would not divert Makor's wealth into a bunch of hoopoe holes struck here and there in the ground. 'If I took this plan to Jerusalem,' he predicted, 'they'd hoot me out of the capital.'

Hoopoe became angry. 'How could you take the plan to Jerusalem? You don't know what it is.'

'I can recognize waste without seeing plans,' the governor replied, and a servant showed the engineer to the door.

In order not to lose his well-co-ordinated team of slaves, Hoopoe put them to work resurfacing the temple square. When this was done he started them on two additional silos for wheat storage, and as the slaves dug deep into the earth of Makor, waterproofing the sides with lime plaster to keep out insects and seepage, he often climbed inside to inspect the work; and when his round face and black beard appeared at the openings as he came back out, townspeople would cry, 'What you looking for, Hoopoe? Worms?'

But in the evenings, when his slaves were dismissed, Hoopoe used to go to the northern wall and continue the calculations that would form the basis of his work if the water system were ever authorized. Judging from the relative terrains he deduced that he would have to sink his main shaft from a point inside the postern gate through some forty feet of rubble that comprised the mound, then ninety feet below that through solid rock, at which level he would begin his sloping tunnel, which would run for a distance of about two hundred and eighty feet to the well. The finished system would thus require about four hundred and ten feet of boring, mostly through solid rock. 'But in the end we'd have a system that no enemy could touch.' He could see women walking down the stairs of the shaft, bearing empty water jars on their heads, then reaching the tunnel and walking along an easy slope to the buried well, impervious to enemies that might rage above. Even to the imagination Hoopoe's system imparted a sense of security, so one evening toward the end of Abib he finished his master drawing on the leather and began scratching working details onto a set of small clay tablets.

It was frustrating to have no one at hand with whom he could discuss his revolutionary plan—the governor could not imagine what abstract lines meant and Kerith was hampered by her initial visualization of Hoopoe as a mole digging blindly in the earth—so late that night he rolled up his leather and left the town, heading for the slave camp outside the walls. It was a ghastly place, the last way station of futility, where prisoners from many nations were herded in foul pens and fed on slops. Hebrew guards ringed the encampment, ready to kill those who tried to escape, and the slaves dragged out their lives in the misery of forced labor until after a few cruel years they died. Only two justifications could be found for the ugly system: when Hebrews were captured by Egyptians or Amalekites they were treated the same way; and from these particular slave pits there was a steady flow of men into positions of responsibility or even freedom, because Hoopoe despised the system and did what he could to liberate men from it. Many of the present citizens of Makor had started their local lives in this foul camp and in response to the engineer's pleading had converted to Yahweh and had won a new life.

On this night the engineer ignored the ordinary pens festering with rats and sought the worst part of the slave area, the walls within the walls where dangerous prisoners were kept, and there, lying on a rush mat, he found a tall, clean-shaven, rugged man some years older than himself. He was well known in the town as Meshab the Moabite, a man of extraordinary fortitude, captured by King David in one of his wars against Moab, and he was the most resourceful and intelligent of the slaves. For the building of the wall he had served as Hoopoe's foreman, and from his rotting bed he now raised himself, half insolently, on one elbow to greet his superior. The faltering old lamp that Hoopoe carried showed the man's strong face against the filth, and the engineer said, 'Meshab, the time has come to build the water system.'

'It can be done,' the big slave grunted, 'if you solve one problem.'

'We face many. Which one?'

'The shaft we can dig. The tunnel we can dig.'

'Then you're not afraid of the rock?' Hoopoe asked.

'You get us iron tools from the Phoenicians,' he growled, 'we'll cut the rock. But when we stand hidden at the foot of the shaft, how will we know where to start our digging to reach the well?'

Hoopoe laughed nervously. 'My wife asked the same question.'

'What did you tell her?'

'I said, "That's my job."'

'You have a plan?' the slave asked, sitting upright among his foul rushes.

'When I was a boy we used to recite an old Canaanite proverb: "There be three things which are too wonderful for me, yea, four which I know not: The way of an eagle in the air; the way of a serpent upon a rock; the way of a ship in the midst of the sea; and the way of a man with a maid.'" The flickering light threw deep shadows across the bald head and composed features of the engineer, disclosing the face of one who even as a child had wondered about the natural world. '"The way of a ship in the midst of the sea,"' he repeated softly.

'What have we to do with ships?' Meshab asked, for he had never seen the sea nor the ships that go upon it.

'One day years ago when I was in Accho with my father, we walked along the sea front and watched as a small ship . . . Meshab, it was so small it had no right to be upon the waves. Rocks lurked everywhere and there were shoals, but somehow this little ship from Cyprus picked its way exactly into harbor. How?'

'Magic?'

'I thought so, but when I asked the captain he laughed and pointed to three flags rising from the tops of buildings far inland. "What are they?" I asked. "The range," he said, and he explained that a sailor lost at sea, if he watches those flags and keeps them in line, will be on a secure course to his anchorage.'

The two men sat silent while bugs, attracted by the lamp, whirred in the night and snores came from filthy mattings where exhausted slaves were sleeping. Then Hoopoe said, 'The other day . . .' He stopped, considered his words and started over. 'I stood on the north wall by the postern gate. I could see where the well was. And looking up the mountainside I could see a spot at which we could put a flag . . .' He paused. 'No, we'd need two flags.'

He had scarcely spoken the word *two* when Meshab caught his wrist. 'We'd have a range. We could see the flags from inside the walls and they'd control our direction.'

Excitedly Hoopoe placed his clay lamp on the ground and tried to clear away a small area on which to spread his leather, but even the earth was contaminated, so Meshab, with a bold swipe of his right arm laid bare an area, and in flickering light Hoopoe showed his slave the well, and the mountain behind. Poking his finger at a spot halfway up the slope he said, 'If we put our first flag here, and our second here . . .'

'Our third, our fourth . . .' With great jabs of his finger Meshab indicated the fifth and sixth flags, placing the last on the roof of the governor's quarters. 'It would work! We'd have a range!'

'You have seen into my mind,' Hoopoe said in a solemn whisper, and the two men were so tantalized with the project that they could not wait till morning and wanted to climb the mountain that night to check their theory, but at the gate leading from the camp, guards stopped them, warning Hoopoe that Meshab was a dangerous prisoner who must not leave the compound.

'He is my foreman, and I need him,' Hoopoe replied.

'He has killed many men,' the guard said, but Hoopoe took him through the gates on his own recognizance and they entered the moonless night.

They crossed the road to the walls of Makor but did not enter the zigzag gate. Instead, they circled to the north where the waterwall made a small circle, indicating that the well lay beneath. Climbing to the roof they stuck there a small cloth which would be visible from a distance. They then left the well and started to climb the mountain of Baal, halting now and then to look behind them, and when they reached a spot which put them well above the level of the town they stopped to review their position, and the Moabite said, 'Here we put our first flag. Let's wait a little and the moon will rise.'

They sat in darkness and studied as much of the town as they could see in the flickering lights which burned in some areas like distant stars on a murky night.

The slave was much larger than Hoopoe, more powerful, and he could easily have killed the engineer and fled westward to Phoenicia; instead, he sat beside his friend and said, 'Now that we've seen the town from here I'm convinced we can do it.'

When the three-quarter moon rose over the Galilean hills, the waterwall stood out clearly, a sharp, straight line leading from the postern gate to the well, and the two planners maneuvered themselves until they stood in a direct line with that wall. Hoopoe said, 'See how the line projects itself across the town till it intersects the roof of the governor's house.'

'That's where we'll put the sixth flag,' Meshab said, and he could visualize that unfaltering range which the engineers would use to maintain their orientation when digging the first deep shaft, but he could also visualize himself at the bottom of that shaft, about to start the tunnel toward the unseen, unknown well. 'There's the hard part,' he growled. 'From the bottom of the shaft, how can we see the range?'

'That's my job,' Hoopoe said and he was about to lead the way back to the slave camp when he saw, coming down the mountain, a chain of people bearing torches. They had spent the night on the high place, worshiping Baal in the old manner, and since this god had been so generous to the engineers that night, Meshab suggested, 'Perhaps I too should go to the high place to worship Baal?' And Jabaal said, 'I shall go with you,' and the two men crossed the mountainside until they came to the footpath which the pilgrims had descended, and this they climbed to the sanctuary which had been the site of worship for more than a thousand years.

At the crest of the mountain they found the monolith, long sacred to Baal, at whose feet lay the familiar signs of a placid nature worship: some flowers, a dead pigeon. Makor no longer worshiped a fiery god who consumed children; there were no public prostitutes administering to Astarte, for such practices the Hebrews suppressed. But the quiet worship of Baal they had been powerless to eliminate because it was the Hebrew farmer as well as the Canaanite merchant who felt the need of this vital deity; even King Saul had paid his homage to Baal by naming his sons after the kindly god. Occasionally the Hebrew rulers of Makor discussed outlawing the Canaanite god, but pressures from the people kept the deity alive. Now in King David's reign directives had come from Jerusalem suggesting that the time had come when the worship of Baal must be forbidden, but governors of the recently conquered northern regions, with large Canaanite minorities, had always cautioned against precipitate action which might later be regretted. In this way Makor kept its ancient deity, and citizens climbed regularly to the mountain seeking assistance from the one god they knew personally—the god who had always insured the prosperity of their fields.

Meshab the Moabite knelt before the monolith, repeated prayers he had learned in the southern desert, then rose prepared to accept once more the stinking slave camp to which Baal had temporarily assigned him, but before he could start his march down the path, Hoopoe asked, 'Why aren't you sensible? Why not accept Yahweh and become a freedman?'

Then Meshab voiced the difference between himself and Hoopoe. 'I live and die with Baal,' he said quietly, and it had been this intransigent answer thrown at King David after his capture in Moab that had prevented him from now being a Hebrew general.

'Wait,' Hoopoe said, drawing the big man onto a rock from which they could see both Accho and Makor in the moonlight. 'My family used to be like you, contemptuous of the Hebrew god. For centuries out of mind we worshiped Baal. But gradually we came to see that the Hebrews . . .'

'Aren't you a Hebrew?'

'I am now. But not long ago my people were Canaanites.'

'How could that be?' Meshab's own family had died rather than surrender their god.

'We lived in Makor side by side with the Hebrews in an easy friendship,' Hoopoe explained. 'One of my ancestors named Zibeon made believe he was a Hebrew, and once or twice he fell into trouble. But in the end the Hebrews discovered that they needed Baal and we found that we needed Yahweh. And we've all prospered ever since.'

'How could you be false to your god?' Meshab asked suspiciously.

Hoopoe looked down at the walled town of his ancestors, the scene of the struggle between the two great deities, and it was difficult for him to explain the power that Yahweh had come to exercise upon the minds of Canaanites who had sought the truth. 'All I can tell you, Meshab, is the legend I learned as a boy. Our people lived in the town with Baal, and from the desert came the Hebrews on donkeys bearing their god El-Shaddai. They camped outside the walls and a great battle developed between the two gods for the possession of the mountaintop. Baal triumphed of course, so in revenge El-Shaddai burned the town and gave the ruins to the Hebrews. For many years El-Shaddai ruled down in the valleys and Baal ruled up here. But after some centuries an agreement was reached, and the Canaanites accepted the new god Yahweh and the Hebrews accepted the old god Baal, and we have lived in contentment ever since.'

'You say that Yahweh is a new god?'

'Yes. Another group of Hebrews went down into Egypt, where they were treated rather badly, and the god they had taken with them developed into a most powerful deity, capable to striking his enemies with terror. This new god, Yahweh, brought forth the man Moses, who led the Hebrews out of Egypt and guided them for forty years in the desert, where Yahweh became more and more powerful . . . unlike any god ever known before. Under Yahweh and Moses the Hebrews became a driving force . . .'

'We knew Moses,' the Moabite interrupted. 'He tried to enter our land, but we drove him off.'

'We Canaanites were not able to do so,' Hoopoe said. 'So now Yahweh rules us all.'

With some accuracy Hoopoe's legend reflected history. Centuries before old Zadok had brought his clan to Makor, other patriarchs had wandered into Egypt bearing with them an ordinary desert god little different from El-Shaddai, but during the vicissitudes suffered in Egypt and Sinai this god had matured into a supreme concept, notably superior to any deity developed by lesser groups of Hebrews who had stayed behind, so that when the tribes which had coalesced around Moses returned to Canaan, the superiority of their god Yahweh was manifest to all. This maturing of Yahweh was another instance in which a challenge had produced an illumination which an easy acceptance could not have. The complaisant town of Makor with its amiable gods could never have produced Yahweh; that transformation required the captivity in Egypt, the conflict with the Pharaohs, the exodus, the years of hunger and thirst in the desert, the longing for a settled home and the spiritual yearning for a known god . . . these were the things required for the forging of Yahweh.

Yet even in his hour of triumph over the lesser gods of the Hebrew tribes, Yahweh remained only the god of those Hebrews. The time had not yet come, in these years of Saul and Solomon, when the people of Israel would openly propose that their god should rule universally; such extension would not take place for several centuries. But now in the time of David, Yahweh was acknowledged as the god of all the Hebrews, from north to south, and the various covenants which he had concluded with his chosen people from the time of Abraham were recognized as binding even in remote spots like Makor. The various Els–the Elohims, the Elyons and the El-Shaddais–were now happily merged into the great successor.

But as Yahweh grew more powerful he also grew more remote, so that it was no longer possible to walk with him in the olive grove; it had been four hundred and fifty years since the last Hebrew of Makor had spoken with his god directly. That last conversation had involved General Epher after the destruction of Canaanite Makor. When the temptation to worship Baal had become too alluring, the red-headed general decided to move his Hebrews to some cleaner spot, but on the eve of departure El-Shaddai had appeared for the last time, saying, 'Have I not brought you to this town and delivered it to you after manifold difficulties? Is it not your responsibility to accept it as it is and to make of it something good?' So Epher had built a new town upon the ruins of the old and it had prospered and influenced the countryside. Thus, in later years, when the unified Hebrews of Moses had come across the Jordan from the east, they had found in many obscure corners of Canaan little settlements like Makor prepared to accept Yahweh.

But the remoteness of Yahweh, his stern invisibility, made it inevitable that many Hebrews would cling to lesser deities who provided them with the personal warmth that Yahweh no longer did. Baal still flourished throughout most of King David's empire. Astarte was worshiped in many places and fire gods who consumed children were being revived; it sometimes seemed that across the land there were local altars under every verdant tree.

As Hoopoe and the Moabite talked of these things, they saw in the moonlight two Hebrew women climbing the hill. They were coming to worship Baal and they did not see the men sitting off to one side, for the women were concerned with domestic worries which only Baal could solve. Climbing, out of breath, to the high point, the women prostrated themselves before the monolith and after a while Hoopoe heard one praying, in short gasps, 'Baal . . . let my husband Jerubbaal come safely home from the sea . . . let the Phoenicians not molest him . . . in Accho protect him . . . great Baal . . . bring my man home safely.'

The two women prayed for some minutes, re-establishing their friendly relationship with the ancient god, and as they rose to place their frugal offerings before the monolith, one happened to see Meshab in the moonlight, and she screamed. Hoopoe ran to her, and when she recognized who he was she laughed nervously. 'I saw that one,' she said, 'and I thought the slave had come to kill me.'

'He kills no one,' Hoopoe assured her.

He recognized the women as Leah and Miriam, two housewives who depended upon Yahweh to guide them on essential matters but who also needed Baal to reassure them on family affairs.

'Why are you praying, Miriam?' Hoopoe asked the second woman.

'My son is going to Jerusalem, and I pray that King David will look upon him favorably and find a place for him in the army.'

'He will,' Hoopoe promised, and she sighed, but when the women were gone back down the hill Hoopoe said to Meshab, 'You shall sit here while I pray,' and he went alone to the ancient monolith and prostrated himself before Baal, bringing before that god the domestic problem from which he had retreated: 'Dear Baal, my wife Kerith yearns to live in Jerusalem, there with the god of her father. My home is Makor, here with you. But let it be that I shall build my tunnel well and that King David shall see it and call me to Jerusalem to build the things he needs for the glory of Yahweh.' He pressed his face into his hands and with powerful fingertips tried to crush his own skull in a gesture of humility before his god. When the pain in his temples became acute he relaxed his fingers and ended: 'Baal, it is not for myself that I ask this thing, for I am content to live with you. But my wife Kerith must go to Jerusalem. Her god is there. Her heart is there. Great Baal, send us to Jerusalem.'

Never before had he dared to voice this confession, either to himself or to his wife, but now he shared it with Baal, and saw nothing contradictory in what he was doing: praying to Baal that he might be summoned to Jerusalem, where he would build temples in honor of Yahweh. Meshab, the stern Moabite, could he have heard the contradictory prayer, would have been filled with disdain; a man should cling to his own god.

For the next two weeks Hoopoe accomplished nothing in his scheme for digging a water system, and he was taxed to find other work for his slaves: the wall was done, the temple court was paved, and soon the silos would be dug. Unless he could think of something soon, his efficient team would be scattered through the kingdom, so he tried anew to enlist the governor's interest in his shaft-and-tunnel idea, but that official remained unable to comprehend the possibilities and Hoopoe was overcome by gloom, which was not relieved when his wife chanced to question him about their future.

It was a warm spring day, the kind that made the Galilee seem one vast flower garden, and she had gone into the olive grove to pick bouquets with which she adorned the house. Then, because she was tired from the work, she bathed and chose for her dress, by whim and not by design, the costume which her husband loved best: her gray woolen robe with yellow borders at hem and cuff, plus the amber pendant shining like the late afternoon sun. At the door she kissed Hoopoe and cried, 'Look at the flowers!' And as he looked she said, for no apparent reason, 'I'll miss the Galilee when we're gone.'

He tensed, then asked, 'Where are we going?' And before she spoke he knew the answer.

'Your work's done here. We'll go where they need builders. Jerusalem.'

He took her hands and drew her to him, kissing her again. 'Desperately I want to take you there, Kerith. But I wonder . . .'

'If they'd have you?' She laughed gaily at his fears and told him, 'Jabaal, you're the best builder in the empire. They know.' And for a moment they stood in silent hesitation at the threshold of a discussion which could have brought them understanding; but the stolid engineer was afraid to speak about his fears regarding Jerusalem, and Kerith had not yet formulated those profound moral and philosophical problems which had begun to haunt her. So the golden moment when the pollen of ideas was in the air vanished and she said prosaically, 'Something will happen.' And that was all they said that day about Jerusalem.

But in the middle of the month of Ziv, when wheat was in the grain and barley in the bag, Kerith was visiting the governor's wife when she heard news that seemed to have been created especially for her. 'General Amraam is coming north to inspect Megiddo,' the governor said, 'and he's promised to visit Makor. Wants to see our new fortifications.'

'Who is General Amram?' Kerith asked.

'He's in charge of fortifications for King David.'

Kerith clenched her hands to keep from crying out with excitement, but through her being hammered a mighty drum thundering one word, 'Jerusalem, Jerusalem!' Finally, when she had gained control, she asked the governor, 'May I be excused?'

'You want to tell Hoopoe? More holes for him to dig?' He flashed his head up and down, and Kerith knew she was supposed to smile.

'If I may. Please.' And at the gate she asked the guards, 'Have you seen Jabaal?'

'Who?'

'The Hoopoe.' She said this without showing her distaste for the name.

'He's at the slave camp.'

And she crossed over to the olive grove from which she had recently picked flowers, but this time she passed through it and came to the walled compound where the slaves were kept, and even before she entered that noisome place she was revolted by the smell. She asked the guards, 'Where is Jabaal?' and when they did not know she had to explain with some embarrassment, 'The one you call Hoopoe.'

'Follow me,' and without noticing what he was leading Kerith into, the guard walked nonchalantly through the filthy outer circle of hovels: rats ran in the road and sunlight fell on piles of straw so rancid that each had its colonies of bugs and lice. The water standing in clay jars was covered with scum, and in the few spots where some slave had tried to beautify the place where he would die, the neatness looked obscene. 'Almighty Yahweh!' Kerith whispered. 'You let men live here?'

But when the guard opened the inner gate and led her to the walled section where dangerous prisoners were kept, and here not even the sun was allowed: dismal huts with floors still muddy from the rains of spring were marked with piles of rotting straw and shreds of cloth. Broken bowls and food pots gray with filth stood in corners, while the section reserved for the privy was unspeakable. A slave captured on some desert raid, now too old to work, shuffled by unable to stand erect, while young men who would have been tall in their homeland orchards north of Tyre moved glassy-eyed to their death.

'Yahweh, Yahweh!' she whispered, and the thought that this hell existed in the same land with Jerusalem was almost more than she could bear and she felt faint. And then she passed into the meanest hovel of all, and there she saw her husband talking with a man she had not noticed before, the slave Meshab, and something in his controlled, resourceful manner as he bent over the hide filled with drawings gave the place a dignity she could not have believed.

After nodding to the slave she said, 'Husband, General Amram is coming to inspect your walls.'

The effect of this information upon the two men was striking. Hoopoe leaped to his feet, not afraid to show his pleasure. 'At last we'll have a man who understands.' But Meshab drew back toward a corner, not through fear, Kerith thought, but in response to some instinctive prudence; and it was obvious that he had known General Amram before, perhaps on a battlefield, for to the

Moabites the Hebrew generals had brought much destruction and Kerith could see that Meshab had no desire to meet this particular general again.

However, when Hoopoe in his enthusiasm turned to the slave for confirmation of his feelings, Meshab said, 'Amram is one who will understand.'

Kerith now suggested that Hoopoe come home with her to discuss other aspects of this exciting news, so with some reluctance the builder accompanied his wife back through the filth, after which they climbed the ramp to Makor. But at the gate Kerith turned to look at the slave camp and asked, 'How can you allow men, humans like yourself, to live down there?'

'They live as long as they do only because of what I'm able to do for them.'

Inside the gates Kerith said softly, 'Oh, Jabaal, General Amram is bringing us our freedom.'

'I hope he likes the walls.'

'And if he does,' she suggested shyly, 'don't be afraid to let him know that you were the one who made the decisions.'

As if they did not want to reach home, where the basic reasons for their excitement might have to be explored, they loitered before the wine shop opposite the temple, and there Kerith said hesitantly, 'Above all, Jabaal, you must mention Jerusalem.' The little engineer said nothing. 'You must ask him to take you to Jerusalem. Now.'

In the spring sunlight Hoopoe swallowed, shifted his feet and said, 'No, Kerith. What I must do is explain to him my water system.'

Kerith gave a little cry, as if she had been wounded, then looked about to see if any loungers at the wine shop had heard her. 'Dear Jabaal,' she whispered. 'Have you lost all reason?' Then seeking to be fair she asked, 'If he did approve your tunnel? How long would it take?'

'About three years.'

She bit her knuckles. Three years! Three years more in exile from Jerusalem! Then, giving her husband a smile of love and compassion, she said, 'All right. If that's your dream, I'll wait three years.' But the prospect, stated in her own words, was frightening and she caught his hands. 'What if your tunnel fails?'

'It's my job to see it doesn't fail,' he said.

And then she said a word of great significance, not ushered forth by her own will but by her longing: 'You're being a fool.' Never before had she used this word, for she loved her husband and appreciated the tenderness he showed her; but gradually she had been forced to admit that the substantial men of the town, like the governor, had come to look upon her husband as merely an amusing person, running about the streets and poking his sharp nose into cisterns and silos like a true hoopoe bird. Indeed, he was a foolish man. But this sense of disappointment she could have tolerated, like any average woman approaching thirty who saw her husband as he was destined to be for the remainder of their lives together, except that in her case a special dimension had intruded: the holy city of Jerusalem. It had been as a girl in mourning that she had first seen the hilltop fortress recently captured by King David from the Jebusites and her emotions that day were so entangled as to have produced an everlasting effect. It was in the winter that her mother died, and her father had gone up to Jerusalem to pray, and as they climbed out of the flat lands they saw upon a crest of hills a city covered with snow, as pure and white as a stork in spring, and involuntarily she had cried, 'Oh, the City of David!' By that name it was known to Hebrews, but in Makor the old Canaanite name of Jerusalem persisted, which was proper, since the city had been Hebrew for only a few years. As

Kerith and her father stood looking up through the cold air she had intuitively known that Jerusalem would become famous not for its growth or its fortress walls, but because of the fact that here Yahweh would take his spiritual residence; and from the first moment she saw Jerusalem she longed to be a part of it, to grow with it into its new functions and to share the radiance which was certain to envelop it. From this city the nature of Hebrew life would be determined.

Her father had sensed this when he said, as they continued to stare at the snowy battlements, 'Before I die we shall see the temple at Makor abandoned, for in Jerusalem will stand the everlasting temple of Yahweh.' She asked him if he would feel regret at the passing of their little temple, and he replied without hesitation, 'Just as our bodies must climb to reach Jerusalem, so will our souls have to climb their spiritual hills to reach Yahweh. It's time we started.' But he had died before he could lead his people to the new understanding of religion as symbolized by Jerusalem, and the Makor priests who had succeeded him had lacked his vision and had clung jealously to their trivial prerogatives. It was therefore partly in furtherance of her father's vision that Kerith longed to make her permanent ascent to Jerusalem; but if she had been asked for one simple reason why she yearned for the royal city she would have said honestly, 'Because there Yahweh will make himself known.'

Her longing placed her in sharp contrast to her husband. He would go to Jerusalem, but only because it was a city where building was to be done. Because he loved Kerith he was willing to help her gain something she so keenly desired, but her preoccupation with Yahweh he only half comprehended; as a man of Ur he knew that Baal governed the earth of Makor and he was content to build here on the old familiar site. Where he worked and on what was of little importance, for like a good engineer he accepted whatever commissions reached his hands and he never inquired too closely as to their origins. He would have been as happy to build a new slave camp as he would have been to reconstruct the small temple of Makor, for he would have seen in the former job a chance to keep the slaves alive for a longer time, which was a sensible ambition.

So Jabaal the engineer committed to Baal, and Kerith the mystic dedicated to Yahweh came to their home at the end of the street and to that confrontation which would often be repeated within the walls of Makor during its long history: the conscious choice between gods. Like many people faced with this ultimate decision of which god they will worship and in what way, they shied away from direct dialogue, hoping that time would solve the problem and make the decision for them. Kerith started to point out that when General Amram arrived . . . but Hoopoe did not hear her, for he was already constructing imaginary plans. He rolled up his sheet of leather, collected his drawing materials and returned to the slave camp, where he directed a group of his men to build a rough table at which he and the Moabite could work in the critical days ahead.

On the roll of leather, made from a calf's skin whose hairy side had been scraped smooth, and using a reed pen and an ink made from soot, vinegar and olive oil, Hoopoe finished the details of the master plan for his water system, and Meshab noticed that he took much care to insure that the diagonal of the shaft followed the range established by the six flags, and he asked why. Pointing to the diagonal, Hoopoe said, 'It's this that will make the tunnel possible.'

Saying no more, he began to impress into soft clay tablets sectional drawings of the various kinds of work that would have to be done, some forty-five tablets in all, and when these were finished Meshab hauled them off to a kiln for baking into permanent form, so that on the evening before General Amram's arrival the two men had their data complete: a large roll of leather which the general could use for explanations in Jerusalem and the series of indestructible tablets to govern the work in Makor.

Next morning, on a bright day at the end of the month of Ziv, when flowering trees made the Galilee a land of singing beauty, when pistachio bushes sent forth red budlets and pomegranate leaves were a tender green, General Amram and his company rode in from Megiddo upon horses, which were rarely seen in Makor. Children ran along the road to greet the visitors, while at the gates of the city the governor waited with clay pitchers of wine and lavers filled with cold water, which the soldiers sloshed over themselves, drying their heads with cloths supplied by women of the town, among whom was Kerith, who had volunteered to serve the general.

Amram was the typical military leader of the Hebrew empire, nearing fifty, hard and spare, with a close-clipped beard and stubby red hair. He had blue eyes, deep wrinkles across his brow and a short scar along his left cheek; he was relaxed and thoughtful, attentive to the life about him and able to judge it with a detached shrewdness. In these first minutes he saw that Kerith was a beautiful woman of the age he preferred, not entirely happy in Makor, who wanted to impress him with her husband's accomplishments, and he suspected that if he responded he might have an enjoyable time in this provincial town. So when Kerith handed him a cloth he took it slowly and smiled, showing between his hairy lips white teeth that were widely spaced.

'Your name is?'

'Kerith,' she replied, adding hastily, 'wife of Jabaal, who built these fortifications.'

'From the approaches they looked strong.'

Before she could assure him that they were, the governor interrupted to announce that the visitors were invited to his quarters for the speeches of welcome, but after two were offered General Amram said, 'I've come to inspect the new walls and I wish to do so.' Brusquely he left the ceremony and entered upon the walls, pleased to see that Kerith was staying at his side.

'These are strong walls that we have built,' the governor said unctuously, and Hoopoe, following at the rear, thought: For a whole year I had to fight him for permission to build them, and now they're his walls. Condescendingly the governor added, 'They were built by this man, whom we call Hoopoe,' and he bobbed his head up and down like a hoopoe bird. General Amram's men laughed, but the general thought: They call him Hoopoe, which infuriates his pretty wife, but he does look fairly stupid.

In his various inspection tours General Amram had often been involved in similar situations and he now saw what he must do in this one: Flatter the husband before his superiors, get him out of the way, and then see what his lovely wife wished to do. Accordingly, he said, 'Jabaal, since you're the one who built the walls, let's climb that hill in back of town and see how good they are.'

'I'll bring the wine,' the governor volunteered, but Amram cut him off.

'We'll go alone,' he snapped, striding off with such vigor that Hoopoe's fat legs had difficulty keeping up.

For more than an hour the two men circled the town, checking various points, then climbed halfway up the mountain to study the fortifications methodically. 'Those slopes of earth leading to the wall,' Amram asked. 'Have you thought of protecting them in some way?'

'We've considered two possibilities. We could pave the present slopes, which would take much rock. Or we could cut away two cubits of earth all around, which would lay bare the old Hyksos glacis which is paved and in good condition. Which would the general suggest?'

'Neither,' Amram said. 'Take too many slaves. And in the end you wouldn't be a lot better off than you are now. But one thing I would do.' He pointed to a section of wall where private houses were encroaching upon the battlements, using the town wall for one side of the house and continuing it upward, with windows cut into the upper wall. 'I'd get rid of those windows right away. Remember how Rahab let down the ropes for our spies at Jericho?'

'What would the general suggest?'

'Brick them up, today. While you still have some slaves.'

Twice General Amram had referred to Hoopoe's slaves. 'Are you going to take away my slaves?' the little man asked.

'When the work's finished here we can use trained builders in Jerusalem. And it looks as if you were about finished.' He was a gruff man, long in the field, and although he had begun by feeling contempt for Hoopoe, an inspection of the man's work forced him to recognize it as a superior job. Placing his arm about the little engineer he said, 'And I shall tell the king that it was work well done.'

Hoopoe mumbled his thanks, then muttered a silent prayer to Baal and tackled the bigger problem. 'General Amram, the new fortifications mean nothing so long as the water supply is vulnerable.'

'From here that waterwall looks strong.'

'It's been patched. It's stronger than it was. But we both know that even one of your lesser armies could knock it down.'

The general had to like this honest builder. In Amram's first minutes on the mountainside he had spotted the fatal weakness of Makor, but he had said nothing, realizing that the town was a frontier settlement which might have to be sacrificed. If the Phoenicians ever decided to assault it, he knew they could puncture the waterwall and strangle the town, but the loss need not be crucial to the empire. Nevertheless, he was impressed that Hoopoe understood the tactical situation.

'But there is a way that Makor could be made so strong that no enemy could capture it,' Hoopoe said, trying to make himself sound convincing.

'How?'

In a few crisp sentences Hoopoe explained that a shaft could be dug in the middle of town and connected by a tunnel to the wall. Glancing nervously, he was pleased to see that General Amram understood. 'Then we tear down the waterwall, erase all marks that it had ever been there, roof over the well with large stones and bury it in thirty feet of earth. No one would ever see our well again except from the inside of the tunnel.' He became inspired by the concept, and suddenly words spouted from his mouth. He was a poet, a general, compelling in his logic and command of detail. He spoke of the security that Makor would know, a security which the empire would share for centuries to come. 'Against this town,' he cried, 'the Phoenicians could thunder for fifteen months on end, while your garrison, General, would rest secure inside. Jerusalem would be safe.'

Against his will–for he was not a man prone to enthusiam–Amram became infected by Hoopoe's excitement and he was seduced into visualizing Makor as a permanent bulwark of the western frontier. As Hoopoe continued, the little town began to look different: the ramparts became stronger, the fatal waterwall vanished and he saw Phoenicians mercenaries beating against the town in futility. Hoopoe stopped speaking and waited.

'What would it require?' Amram asked bluntly.

'The slaves I have. Plus fifty more.'

'Have you plans?' He was sure the enthusiastic little man did.

'Come to my house,' Hoopoe said quietly, afraid lest he appear too eager, and as they re-entered the main gate he called to one of the guards, 'Fetch me Meshab the Moabite.'

'Who?' Amram asked.

'My foreman. He has the clay tablets.'

Waiting in the governor's house Kerith heard that General Amram and her husband had gone directly to her home, and she ran through minor alleys hoping to reach there first so as to receive them properly, but when she ran up, out of breath, the men were already there, lying flat on the floor, studying Jabaal's leather roll of the water system. 'Oh no!' she whispered to herself. 'My foolish husband is bothering that great man with such nonsense.' She brought them cool drinks, but they took no notice of her, so she sat where she could watch the general and where finally he found time to watch her while Hoopoe continued to draw imaginary tunnels with his finger.

The three remained thus for some time, when the big Moabite appeared, led by one of the guards. The tall southerner had barely entered the room with his clay tablets when General Amram saw him, leaped to his feet and cried, 'What is this one doing here?'

'He is Meshab, my foreman,' Hoopoe explained. 'Show General Amram . . .'

But before the Moabite could lay out the detailed drawings Amram turned his back and said, 'Take him away.'

'Sir,' Hoopoe protested, 'he's our best workman.'

'I know who he is,' Amram snapped. 'He killed my brother.'

'He was sent to us some years ago.'

'I know when he was sent. I sent him.'

Meshab remained silent as General Amram recalled King David's struggle against the Moabites. In strict fact, the Hebrews had never really defeated the desert kingdom, for Meshab and a few like him had conducted a brilliant strike-and-run defense, but in the end Moab had been reduced to a kind of vassaldom: 'As peace was being discussed, this one struck at our camp and slew my brother. When he was captured I wanted to kill him with my own hands.'

He turned away and silence in the room became embarrassing, but Kerith said, 'Place the tablets here, slave, and return to camp.' Her command reminded everyone that Meshab was now only a slave and the tension eased. General Amram thought: That woman's clever.

At the feasts prepared by the governor, the general had additional opportunity to observe the superiority of this woman, and she, guessing at some of the ideas going through his mind, took pains to present herself appealingly: when he wished dates or honey he received them from her, and by the end of the second day it was apparent to General Amram that Hoopoe's wife wished to be alone with him.

Hoopoe, preoccupied with the chance of gaining authorization for his water system, overlooked his wife but continued to press upon Amram arguments in favor of the tunnel, so on the third day Amram said, 'Hoopoe, why don't you take your Moabite slave and go up the mountain and see if you can lay out the line of flags you've been talking about?'

'We've already tried,' Hoopoe said. 'We're sure the plan will work.'

General Amram was irritated. 'I'll tell you what to do. You go up on the hill while he stays here, and you can actually erect the flags.'

A flush of joy came over the bearded face of the fat builder. 'Does this mean that you are going to authorize the tunnel?'

'Well . . .' General Amram had about decided not to waste the effort on Makor, but he could now see, standing behind the builder, his lovely waiting wife and something must be done to get rid of the foolish fellow. 'Go ahead,' he said on the spur of the moment. 'Dig the tunnel.'

'I'll bring the governor!' Hoopoe cried, and before either Kerith or General Amram could halt him he appeared with the governor, and the authorization for the tunnel was made official. 'Now I'll go on the mountain and locate the flags,' he cried, and with the joy of a child he ran through the streets, calling for the guards to send him Meshab from the slave camp.

When he was safely gone, when the pompous governor had returned in bewilderment to his quarters, wondering how Hoopoe had persuaded General Amram to authorize the water system, the general suggested to Kerith, 'Perhaps the slave girls would like to take the children for a walk,' and when the servants were gone he relaxed easily in Hoopoe's wooden chair and speculated upon what was to happen next.

General Amram was a man with much experience and three wives, two of whom he had taken from other men, and he fancied this lovely Makor woman. Certainly she had given him cause to arrange this meeting and he could guess the reason why: She's annoyed with her fat little husband who can do nothing but dig holes in the ground. She thinks of anyone from Jerusalem as a man bringing adventure. He had other clever explanations in which he figured large, but none came close to the problem that Kerith now placed before him.

'I wanted to talk to you so much,' she said, sitting primly on a three-legged stool some distance away.

'About what?' he asked with grand condescension.

'I must get to Jerusalem,' she said in a burst of words. 'My husband can build so much there. You've seen his work. And I . . .'

'What about you?' the general asked, leaning forward and showing his wide-spaced teeth.

'I want to be where the worship of Yahweh is pure,' she said softly.

'You what?'

'My father was priest here in Makor, and his father before him as far back as we can remember.'

'What's that got to do with going to Jerusalem?'

And she told him. For the first time in his life General Amram heard the complaint that was going to echo throughout Israel for many centuries: 'In Makor we are far from the sources of Yahweh, but in Jerusalem we could live near the sanctuaries of his holiness. In Makor we share the world with Baal; but in Jerusalem, Yahweh alone reigns. In our little town the great kings are not; but in Jerusalem, David lives, and to be near him is to be near the sun.'

'There are many ways you could get to Jerusalem,' the general said, starting to come toward her, but in innocence she misunderstood his purpose and rose to greet him as if he were a travel-weary member of her family.

'You must be very tired,' she said, leading him to a room where tubs of cool water stood. 'May I pour the buckets over your head, and then you can sleep.' She made him take off his upper tunic and bend over a drain, while she washed his head as she would have done her father's. Then she roughened his hair and chest with a heavy cloth and gave him a robe to throw about his shoulders. She led him to a bed and promised to call him if he slept too long, and as she closed the curtains she happened to see her husband on the mountainside. 'He's still up there,' she said, 'waving his arms and making silly signals.'

'I intended him to be there . . . for some time.'

Kerith looked down at the relaxed general, so close to sleep and in such unexpected circumstances, and asked, 'How shall we get to Jerusalem, General Amram?'

The warrior looked up at the enticing woman and smiled. 'Help him to build his tunnel. When it's finished the king will surely hear of it.' And before he fell asleep he pictured Hoopoe on the hill, waving his arms.

Hoopoe's plan was simple. On a spot above the town, but in line with the waterwall, he had planted the first red flag which for the next three years would serve as the standard marker for the job, since it was visible from all parts of the town. Next he had climbed higher and planted a second flag, establishing a range which passed through the first flag, the well and the middle of the waterwall. Whenever the slaves had these two flags in line they could be sure they were properly oriented for digging the tunnel. This completed, he had begun doing what his wife had described to General Amram as 'making silly signals.'

On four different roofs in Makor, Hoopoe had stationed slaves with poles to which red flags had been tied, and by means of prearranged signals he was now moving his slaves back and forth until all were in line with the range he had already staked out on the mountainside. When each man was in position he waved a white cloth, and the slaves began fixing their flags in the permanent line that would be used for digging the main shaft.

Meshab the Moabite had been assigned the roof of the governor's house, for this rose higher than the others and thus formed a prominent landmark; but as the slave walked back and forth among drying seeds to position the important sixth flag which would anchor the range, he annoyed the governor, who left his quarters to cry, 'Who is on my roof?'

A crowd collected as the official began ranting at the slave and there might have been trouble, for the Moabite was loath to take down his needed flag, but just as the governor was becoming ugly, General Amram appeared, washed and relazed, and he could see the desirability of keeping the flag in its present position. He joined Meshab on the roof to study the range of flags, then summoned everyone including Hoopoe to a council below. 'The governor is right,' he announced. 'The last flag should not be on his roof.' Hoopoe started to protest, but before he could do so the general added, 'But since the flag is essential, why not place it on the wall?'

The crowd murmured its approval of this wise decision, but Hoopoe said, 'From the wall the stick will be too short for the flag to be seen.'

'I've thought about that,' General Amram said, 'and what you must do tomorrow is go into the forest and find a young tree that will be tall enough.'

So the naïve little engineer disappeared into the forest while General Amram returned to the house by the west wall, where he spent the afternoon with

Kerith. Meshab the Moabite, working on the wall, saw the trick that the clever general was playing and was incensed. When on successive afternoons Amram devised new ways to keep the fat engineer occupied, the big slave felt a growing bitterness; but his suspicions of what transpired in Hoopoe's house were not justified. General Amram, at ease in the engineer's chair, was finding Kerith even more complicated than he had taken her to be on their first afternoon together. She tended her famous visitor as if he were her father, bringing him cold drinks and comforts like a slave, yet rebuffing with charming innocence his attempts to seduce her. Had he been younger he might have wrestled with her; as a man nearing fifty he was amused by the faithful wife and tried to penetrate her reasoning, discovering that she really believed that if she were kind to him he might take her husband to Jerusalem.

'Why are you so dissatisfied with this pretty town?' he asked one afternoon, clutching at the hem of her gray robe as she went past.

Like a dancer from the desert she twisted and her skirt flew out in rhythmic swirls, passing over his hand and leaving an enticing fragrance in the air. He laughed, then listened as she said, 'I feel corrupted, living in a town like Makor, where Yahweh and Baal are both worshiped.'

'I've found Makor attractive,' he said. 'Not as much so as I had hoped.'

She ignored his response and asked, 'When you waken in the morning in Jerusalem, doesn't it thrill you to be at the center of the earth? Where Yahweh dwells?'

General Amram coughed. Kerith was being either naïve or taunting, and in either case he was growing bored. Seeing no reason to prolong evasions he said frankly, 'To tell you the truth, I'm loyal to Dagon.'

'Dagon!' Kerith cried, appalled at the idea.

'Yes. I served with King David when he was hired by the Philistines, and I grew to like them. They're good warriors and Dagon is a powerful god. Oh, I suppose Yahweh is satisfactory too. I know the king worships him, but I'm a fighting man and I keep to simple tastes.'

Kerith stepped back. This man, this famous general, saying without fear that he was loyal to a god made of stone like Dagon. 'I'm surprised Yahweh doesn't . . .'

'Strike me dead?' Amram laughed. 'Oh, I pay homage to Yahweh, too. As a soldier you mustn't overlook anything that may help your side. But my personal loyalty . . .'

'Is to Dagon?'

'Yes.' He rubbed his stubbled head, pulled himself out of Hoopoe's chair, and to Kerith's surprise caught her by the waist and embraced her with chuckling good humor. 'You're a dear wife, Kerith.' He kissed her. 'And some day you'll reach Jerusalem.' He kissed her again, holding her arms to prevent her struggling. 'And Yahweh will be waiting.' He kissed her farewell and left the house, laughing to himself. She stood alone in the room, defiled, not by his kisses—which she understood—but by his blasphemy. Slowly she knelt beside her husband's chair and prayed.

'Yahweh, let me ascend to your city. Let me come singing to your gates, Jerusalem.'

That night at the final dinner General Amram was astonished when Hoopoe announced, 'Governor, I'm leaving my house by the west wall.'

Kerith gave a cry of joy. 'Jerusalem?'

'No,' Hoopoe said. 'Tomorrow we start digging the main shaft, and I'm going to build myself a new house along the edge.' The guests reacted noisily, and he added, 'The work is so important that I'll need to be on hand.'

'Good idea!' Amram said. 'We'll start tonight.' And with a spurious gaiety he led the party out of the governor's house and along the curving street, past the silent shops and to a spot near the postern gate where Hoopoe showed him the location of the shaft. Pouring a glass of red wine onto the ground, the general made a short, sardonic speech: 'It has been a long time since I have visited so charming a country town and met such charming country people.' He bowed toward the governor and Kerith. 'In my travels I have seen no fortifications superior to these built by the man you call Hoopoe.' The crowd began to cheer this gracious compliment, but Amram spoiled the effect by bobbing his head up and down like a hoopoe bird, and there were giggles. 'I feel sure,' he concluded, 'that the new water system, if it is ever completed, will be the marvel of the north.' Kerith realized that he was mocking both Hoopoe and Makor, and that sense of disillusionment set in which would lead to her final judgment of the general: she felt pity for him, that he should live in Jerusalem so close to Yahweh and King David without having discovered the inner significance of either the city, the god or the king.

When the mock ceremony ended he smiled at Kerith condescendingly and said, 'Go home now and help your little man build his little tunnel, and maybe some day you'll both get to Jerusalem.' She was humiliated, yet in the morning she stood in the crowd that lined the town walls to cheer the general on his way back to Megiddo, and as he disappeared toward the swamp she thought how strange it was that he who appreciated Jerusalem so little should be allowed to reside in that city, while she who longed so desperately for Yahweh should be denied this boon. She resented the basic unfairness of life, and tears came to her eyes, but as she climbed down from the wall she caught Meshab staring at her with undisguised contempt, and she wondered what had occasioned this reaction.

She went home with Hoopoe, who now became so absorbed in launching both the water system and his new house that she was increasingly left alone in the old, to which the general had brought a fragrance of Jerusalem, and staying there with her two children she was able to see with unemotional accuracy what she must do: as carefully as her husband planned his punctures of the earth, she planned how she would reach Jerusalem, that citadel of the one true god. The next three years would be tedious, and she knew it, but she suspected that General Amram's cynical advice was accurate: 'Rely on your husband's completion of the tunnel.' This she would do and with the compassion and love she had formerly felt for him, for she could not ignore the respect General Amram had shown for Jabaal the engineer, even while laughing at Hoopoe the man.

She therefore dedicated herself to helping him attain his ambition, trusting that if she did so she would gain access to Jerusalem. She helped him transfer his headquarters into the new house, then listened with understanding as he discussed the various difficulties he was encountering. In all outward respects she became a woman content with her life in Makor, attentive to her husband's problems and respectful of the local gods; but never for one moment of one day did she submerge her longing for the presence of Yahweh and the reality of Jerusalem. When some months later word reached Makor that King David's general of the eastern forces, Amram, had been slain in an expedition against the rebellious Moabites, she felt a personal involvement and went back to the old house and stood alone in the room where the robust general had sat. She remembered him now principally as the conniving, self-opinionated man who had spoken arrogantly of Yahweh and King David, and she was amazed that so insensitive a person had progressed so far in a spiritual city like Jerusalem, and when at table Hoopoe eulogized him she remained silent. 'He was the author of our good fortune,' the little builder said, 'and what is more important, when he promised me fifty new slaves he sent them.' He was deeply moved by the general's death, for he had imagined that when the water system was finished and he went to Jerusalem, Amram would adopt him as a kind of protégé, but now the first man to have championed the tunnel was dead, and Hoopoe felt abandoned.

The excavation of the various holes that would unite to form the water system, required, as Hoopoe had predicted, a full three years. The first seventeen months were spent sinking the square main shaft, whose diagonal, twenty-nine feet across, Hoopoe took pains to keep aligned with the flags. In the beginning the great hole had to pass through the accumulated rubble of the mound, and the diggers uncovered relics first of the bronze age when the Hebrews were bringing El-Shaddai to the site, then of the earlier copper age when Canaanites were erecting monoliths to Baal, and finally of the stone age when the Family of Ur was first erecting its menhir to El. In the digging Hoopoe occasionaly found some article of interest which he took to his wife, so that the main room of their home became lined with small shelves on which he placed old statues and bits of metal. It was his opinion–not shared by others–that down along the sides of the hole one could detect signs of many towns that had vanished, and he was particularly impressed with one solid band of black soot that reached across the entire area some eight feet under the surface. 'I think that at this point Makor must have been burned away,' he told Meshab, and he recalled the poems and legends kept alive in his family regarding the fight between Baal and El-Shaddai which had ended in a general fire, but others were sure that if a town had burned so long ago its ashes would have washed away in the rain. They proved their argument by lighting a fire, making ash, and then washing it completely away with a bowl of water. Long after the experiment Hoopoe found the answer: 'Of course you can wash away a little ash. It goes from here to there. But suppose everything is ash? Both here and there? Where then does it go?' But by that time the slaves were digging into solid rock.

It was here that Meshab the Moabite became so valuable. The rock of this area was a semi-soft limestone which when soaked with water could be worked like a hard clay. Iron-edged tools could be driven into it and huge chunks broken away, square-edged to be used in building houses later. It was Meshab who discovered the proper sequence for working the limestone: slant the floor of the hole in one direction so that water could seep into stony crevices, then excavate the portions over which the water had been standing, tilting the floor in the opposite direction. He also rigged the thick ropes that hauled out the quarried stone and built the two circular inclines that would take one set of women down to the well on one set of stairs while their sisters climbed up another flight that did not interfere with the first. Meshab became more than a foreman; in every respect he was Hoopoe's second in command, and it was Hoopoe who finally suggested that he leave the slave camp and move into a small room at the rear of the new house so that he could be available throughout the night in case of emergency. At first Kerith did not like the idea of having a murderous slave so near at hand, but when she remembered the hovel in which he had been living she consented. The governor objected, but Hoopoe insisted that the project was too big and too important to go unguarded by the man who knew it best, so the tall Moabite took up his residence in the rear of the house. One night, as the two builders studied the gaping hole they had chopped into the earth, Hoopoe said, 'Next week we start the tunnel. You go in from here. I'll go in from the well and somewhere down there we'll meet. At that moment, Meshab, I shall embrace you as a freedman.' The slave said nothing, for he was wondering how he could keep his tunnel headed straight through the darkness, through the concentrations of solid rock. How could two men, starting from opposite directions, find each other in the bowels of the earth?

When the shaft was completed Hoopoe and Meshab stood at the bottom and looked upward at the small square of sky which showed its blue impartially by yielding no hint of direction, and Meshab said, 'From here no range is visible. The well might lie in any direction,' and Hoopoe replied, 'Would I have brought you so far if I did not have a secret?' And he led Meshab out of the well and out of the town to a spot far in the hills where tall trees grew, and he asked the slave, 'How high is that one?' and Meshab judged the tall tree to be at least thirty cubits. 'It will do,' Hoopoe said confidently and he sat down to wait while Meshab returned to Makor for a gang of slaves to chop down the tree; but when the Moabite was gone Hoopoe lost his sense of assurance and humbled himself before the tree, clutching its trunk with his hands and praying, 'Baal-of-this-Tree, I depend on you to help us find our way.' And for the better part of an hour he prayed, an engineer seeking guidance from the tool he was about to use.

When the tree was felled and its branches trimmed away, the slaves began hauling it back to town, and when it was brought through the postern gate Hoopoe said, 'Take it to the square shaft at once'; and there he placed it diagonally across the gaping square so that its direction duplicated the range established by the six flags; and since the range now passed directly along the tree, any tunnel that followed the line of the tree would have to intersect the well.

'Your job is to follow the tree,' Hoopoe told the Moabite.

'And how will I do that after the first day, when I can no longer see the tree above me?'

Then the genius of Hoopoe manifested itself, for he disclosed the secret he had been perfecting over the last two years. He asked for a ball of strong white cord, to one end of which he fastened a heavy stone. Then, going to the point where the tree formed the southern end of the diagonal, he tied the free end of the cord about the trunk and slowly allowed the rock to fall till it just touched the bottom of the shaft. Next he went to the northern end of the diagonal and repeated the process, so that now he had at the bottom of the shaft two rocks holding taught two perpendicular strings so placed that a line between them would exactly reproduce the line of the tree and therefore the range of the six flags. And now Hoopoe's care in orienting his diagonal so precisely bore fruit, for by this device he had insured that the two strings would be as far apart as possible and thus give maximum protection against error. If Meshab could keep these two strings in line as he dug, he must find the well.

The Moabite, with a shout of joy—such as a hunter utters when he sees a deer, or a sea captain when he sees the harbor—cried, 'It can be done!' And when he hurried down to the bottom of the shaft and saw what a clean, hard line the two taut strings provided, he said, 'At night we can place two lamps at the foot of the strings, and we can see our way into the heart of the earth, no matter how dark it gets.' And he looked at the engineer, so like the hoopoe bird when he walked, and felt an inexpressible admiration for the intelligence of this man.

And so on a bright sunny morning in Ethanim of the second year–when summer had ended and only the major rivers found enough water to stay live and when men waited for rain so they could plow their fields and sow their winter's wheat–Meshab the Moabite hammered the first iron wedge into the limestone barrier separating the bottom of the shaft from the well, and for twelve months thereafter he would keep his men working away at the rock, digging a tunnel that slanted downward. At the first sledge blow Hoopoe prayed, 'Baal, lead us through this darkness,' and aloft at the edge of the pit Kerith prayed, 'Yahweh, bring him success that he may take me up to Jerusalem.'

Now Hoopoe moved to the well end, and there his problem was more difficult. Originally Makor had obtained its water from a spring which bubbled freely from the earth, but as the millennia passed two changes occurred: the earth about the lip of the spring grew upward year by year because of accumulated rubble; and during each century the chopping down of trees in the area–not many yet, but each year more and more–caused the actual water level to be drawn downward. These two agencies working in contrary directions meant that the surface of the spring sank lower and lower into the earth, so that by the time the first walls were built about the mound the spring had already become a well whose sides had to be dug constantly deeper and walled with stone.

Since it was essential that his workmen see the range flags, Hoopoe ripped away the roof of the waterwall. He also demolished the circular wall around the well, and when the area was cleared he began sinking a narrow shaft straight down to water level. But when he approached the surface of the well he found an old cave that had been inhabited by men more than two hundred thousand years before. In the days when his forefather Ur had been worried about the cultivation of wheat, this earlier cave was already two thousand centuries old, buried and forgotten. Now Hoopoe walled it up again and continued his way down to the water level, and when he reached the desired spot he ordered his slaves to dig out a considerable hollow, providing a floor space from which his men could work and on which women seeking water in future years could rest their jars. Then across the upper opening of the shaft he placed a tree in line with the range of flags, and again he dropped two weighted lines to the well, and these showed the intended direction; but since the diameter of this temporary shaft was so much less than the diagonal of Meshab's main shaft, the strings could not be far apart nor the accuracy of his range so precise, and the reason he had chosen to work from the well was because there the responsibility was greater. Eight and nine times a day he would lie on his stomach to check the range, satisfy himself that he must be headed right, then study the clay tablets to determine the upward pitch his slaves must follow. After that he had to trust that sooner or later his men digging on their upward slant would meet Meshab's as they worked downward.

When these problems of direction and slant were solved there remained another of even greater difficulty. Hoopoe had always intended his water system to accommodate many women passing to and fro with jugs on their heads, and this required the tunnel to be about ten feet high and six feet across, and no matter how skillfully Meshab dug downward from the shaft and

Hoopoe upward from the well, if they dug massive full-sized tunnels it would be a miracle if they met exactly. 'I'd never find you down there,' Hoopoe confessed. 'You might be digging on that level, I on this, and we'd go right past one another. We'd waste years.'

Meshab agreed: 'If we did happen to meet it would be pure luck.'

'But what we can do,' Hoopoe reasoned, 'is to start with very small holes. Just big enough for the diggers to work in. We'll penetrate until we can hear each other through the rock. Then we'll join the small holes. Yours may be above mine or off to one side, but that won't matter. Because we can go back and dig our tunnels the proper size, making whatever corrections are necessary.' Meshab had agreed to the plan, and now in the month of Abib, at the beginning of the third year, when in the fields above the spring rain came down and brewers sought the new barley, the two men drove at each other through little tunnels barely four feet high and only two feet wide. For hours at a time a skilled slave would work in cramped position, hardly able to swing his hammer. When he had finished chopping away the rock, other slaves would crawl in to pass along the debris until it reached the well, and then a day fresh cutter would move to the face of the rock; twenty-four hours a day the work continued, since the presence of daylight was of no consequence. But each evening, when sunset colored the town a shimmering bronze, came the most exciting moment of the excavation. The slaves would withdraw from their little tunnels and Meshab the Moabite would descend the main shaft and crawl with a sledge to the end of his tunnel, while Hoopoe would climb down into the well and lug his sledge to the face of his. On the town wall between the two entrances a slave would stand holding a long pole bearing a white flag. When other slaves at the two openings signaled that the men with the sledges were in place, the slave on the wall would wave his flag ceremoniously, then dip it sharply toward the town. Slaves stationed in the main shaft would shout down the echoing deep, 'Meshab, Meshab! It is your turn.' At the entrance to the downward tunnel other slaves would cry, 'Meshab, Meshab! It is your turn.' And at the face of his tunnel Meshab the Moabite would hammer the solid rock nine times in slow, steady rhythm, hoping that somewhere in the earth his partner Hoopoe might hear.

At the end of the ninth blow Meshab would call back that he had finished, and the signal would pass to the shaft and up to the slave on the wall. With a flourish he would drop his flag toward the well outside the walls, and there other slaves would echo, 'Hoopoe, Hopoe! It is your turn,' and in the darkness of his tunnel the master engineer would strike his wall nine times in stately rhythm while Meshab listened; but always the mass of rock between the two men absorbed the sound.

Each dusk the men sent nine signals nine times, then crawled out of their holes and met to discuss what was happening. Since they could measure with cords how far each had penetrated into the earth, and since they could lay off those measurements along the line of the waterwall, they could see from the ground approximately where the ends of the tunnels must be, and as night came they would stand on the surface where the cords lay and deduce how far apart they were.

They were now separated by some sixty feet and were reaching the point at which it ought to be possible for sounds to be carried through limestone, and they began to hope that at the next sunset they would hear each other, but even when they didn't they felt a growing sense of assurance that they must be on the right headings. Their work was an act of faith so intense that of itself it had sustained them during the first two years, and they went each morning to the tunnels refreshed. Perhaps this would be the day when the first sound would be heard. But when the month of Abib passed and Ziv came again, when men coming out of the dark tunnels looked with whatever joy slaves can know at the new flowers, the two leaders began to lose courage because of the failure of their signals to penetrate the rock. Could something be wrong? Could they be so wide of each other, or so ill-placed vertically, that they were missing by a large margin?

Patiently they reconstructed the operation, confronting each possible source of error honestly like men well trained. 'You go to the mountain this time,' Hoopoe suggested, 'and check the range I laid out.' The Moabite left the town while Hoopoe climbed the walls and the various houses, making signals with a flag, and Meshab satisfied himself that all was in order. He came back to report, 'The range is right.' They then checked to see if the poles across the two openings conformed to the range, and they did. Next came the critical part of the work. Did the lines dropping down into the holes accurately reproduce the range established above? At the main shaft this was relatively easy to check, for the diagonal was adequate, permitting the two cords to stand relatively far apart, and this insured a secure heading. 'This end has got to be right,' Hoopoe said, but when they went to the well, where the opening was small and where the critical cords could not be far apart, it was apparent that error might have crept in.

With the greatest care the two men checked and rechecked the orientation at the well and they had to conclude that it was impossible to be sure. 'It could be a little more to the north,' Meshab said honestly, and even a small error at the beginning would yield a tragic error when the length of the tunnel was so great. It was at this moment that Jabaal spoke like a true engineer. He was lying prone near the well while Meshab stood by the strings, and from this position he said, 'This tunnel has got to be right. There can be no error and we must meet. But if we do not, it is because I have failed. My eye has erred and the fault is on me.'

Disconsolate, he left the slaves and climbed out of the well, a tired, perplexed man. Turning his back on the tunnels, on the flags that hung limp in the humid heat, he climbed the mountain seeking the high place where Baal lived, and there alone he lay face downward before the god of this earth, these rocks, these dark burrowings in the ground that seemed to have gone wrong. 'Baal, show me the way,' he pleaded humbly. 'I am lost in the deep earth like a pitiful mole and my eyes are blinded. Great Baal, guide me through the darkness.'

He stayed for many hours talking with the ancient god from whom his ancestors had derived much consolation, and as the night progressed on the high place, the stars moving across the heavens as Baal had long ago appointed them to move, Jabaal the Hoopoe felt his confidence returning, and he intensified his prayers; and as dawn came it seemed to him that Baal was giving his blessing. Then, as he started down the mountain, morning broke out of the eastern hills and its radiance filled the valleys of Galilee, showing the olive trees gray and beautiful, the birds winging from the tall oaks and the little town snug within its walls, with red flags fluttering slightly in the morning breeze, and the glory of that day was so profound that Jabaal fell to his knees and cried, 'Yahweh, Yahweh! I am your child, your instrument. Use me as you will. Drive my head through the earth like a battering ram to accomplish your purposes, great Yahweh, who has given me this day.'

And he left the high place where he had talked with his gods, and he went to the cave of the well and once more laid himself flat in the tunnel to study the critical strings on which so much depended; and again he cried, 'It has got to be right! It can be no other!' And he drove his slaves all day, working often at the rock face himself, and that evening when the slave on the wall signaled and the slaves in the well cried, 'Hoopoe, Hoopoe! It is your turn,' he slammed his sledge against the rock nine times, but before he had finished there came from the other side, through feet upon feet of primeval rock, the unplanned hammering of another sledge, and the two captains beat upon the rocks, ignoring signals and hearing each other through the solid darkness. Men began to cheer, first in the well and then from the shaft and then all across the town, and flags were waved from the walls and after a while Meshab and Hoopoe met in the open field where the cords were approaching each other, and they knew where they were, and it was exactly as they planned so long ago.

That night Hoopoe walked with the Moabite to their house by the edge of the shaft, and he bade the southern slave good night. He entered his portion of the house, where he bathed; he came into the room where Kerith had a fine meal waiting, but he was not hungry. 'We have done it!' he told her with quiet exultation. 'In a few weeks we shall meet.'

'I heard the shouting and ran to the shaft. Even the governor came and we were very proud.' And as she kissed him she whispered, 'Today Jerusalem is closer,' and she begged him to eat. But he could not eat that night, and after a while he took his fair wife to bed, where he was soon the happiest man in Makor.

By sound testings Hoopoe and Meshab corrected their headings and set their teams to work on the final push that would unite the two test tunnels, but work was slowed by the fact that the iron tools required for chopping out the rock had been overused and were no longer effective. The two men decided that new tools were required, and to obtain them it was necessary that someone go into the Phoenician seaport of Accho, which was the only source for iron tools in the area. Because bargaining for a just price was important, Hoopoe felt that he must go, and at first it was his intention to take Meshab along—as an earned reward for having dug his end of the tunnel properly—but the governor dissuaded him from this by pointing out that now more than ever it was essential to have skilled help on hand to supervise what seemed to him the critical stages of the work. Hoopoe was tempted to point out that the true critical stages had occurred seven months ago when he and the Moabite had studied their strings and had oriented their tunnels properly. 'Anyone who can listen to sounds can finish the work now,' he said to his wife, but she supported the governor, and so when he started out for Accho he was forced to go alone.

To have seen Hoopoe set forth on his exciting journey one would have thought that he was heading for some distant territory: even though the hot season was approaching he dressed in a long robe, wore a dagger, climbed on a donkey and waited while the caravan of two groats merchants formed up around him. He waved goodbye to Kerith as if he did not expect to see her for some years, called instructions to the Moabite, who stood on the wall, and saluted the governor. He kicked his donkey, gathered his robes about his knees and was off.

Accho lay eight miles west of Makor, along an easy road that caravans had been traveling for thousands of years, but it was a mark of this land that throughout history Accho and Makor were rarely held by the same nation. In most ages Makor marked the westward terminal of some inland people; in all conditions of the land strangers usually occupied the seaport. This year after long negotiation it happened to be Hebrew in Makor, Phoenician in Accho; in other years it would be other combinations, for control of the sea was so vital that tribes and nations would fight to retain Accho, whereas they usually lost heart when called upon to besiege Makor for even ten or eleven months; so that over a period of several thousand years, to go from Makor to Accho was usually a trip of magnitude, an exploration into unknown ways and alien tongues.

Two miles west of Makor the caravan of the groats merchants came to a border guard, where Phoenician soldiers wearing iron shields inspected them, took away Hoopoe's dagger, gave him a clay tablet receipt and grudgingly allowed him to pass. After a few more miles customs officials checked his possessions, noted the amount of gold he was carrying and gave him another clay tablet, which when presented on his return trip would insure his right to depart. The Phoenicians were polite but they seemed like powerful men who would tolerate no nonsense from strangers, and Hoopoe treated them with deference.

Soon he saw on the horizon the walled city of Accho, rising from the plains at the point where the River Belus entered the sea. It was even then, in the years before it was moved westward to the hooded promontory where it would become famous in history, an enticing city, for ships from many parts of the Mediterranean came to its harbour and its shops contained a variety of goods matched only in the bazaars of Tyre and Ashkelon. It was through this port that the iron smelted in distant forges reached the Hebrews, and in the shops of Accho, Hoopoe expected to find the tools his slaves needed.

At the gate to the city he was stopped for the third time, and the receipts given him by the outlying inspectors were filed against the day of his departure. He was warned that he must not get drunk; for the Phoenicians had found that whereas their men could drink copious amounts of beer with little damaging effect, visiting Hebrews after a few jugfuls were apt to become riotous. Hoopoe promised to behave and was allowed to enter the exciting world of Accho.

He went first to the waterfront, which had charmed him as a child, and there he stayed for some time fascinated as before by the concept of a floating house that was able to drift across an open sea yet put into port whenever its sailors directed. He still could not understand the principle of the sail and wondered how sailors could slow the craft down when it approached land; he was delighted with the ships and the multitude of strange faces that looked down at him from the decks, and he was pleased to see that one of the boats was unloading a cargo of iron.

How varied were the men who climbed half naked up the gangways leading from the dock! He could recognize the Egyptians, the Africans, the Canaanites and the Phoenicians, but there were half a dozen other types, stalwart men with enormous shoulders whom he had not seen before. They must have come from Cyprus and the distant islands, and they spoke languages which he did not understand. In those years Accho was an international seaport, and it took a rural Hebrew from Makor to appreciate the wonder of the place.

He left the docks and wandered along the main thoroughfares, looking into shops whose richness was strange to him: one jeweler who dispatched camels to various parts of the east had turquoise from Arabia, alabaster from Crete, amethyst and carnelian from Greek traders and chalcedony from Punt. He had faïence and enamel from Egypt and from the workshops of Accho one of the loveliest things Hoopoe had ever seen: a short length of glass rope braided from eighteen strands of different-colored glass. Across the face it had been cut on a diagonal, which was then polished, so that from any angle the intricate interweavings were resplendent. 'I would like that for my wife,' he said hesitantly to the shopkeeper, not knowing whether he would be understood or not, but the jeweler could speak in half a dozen languages–poorly but enough for trade–and the bargaining began. Hoopoe feared that the cost might be prohibitive, for the glass rope was more appealing to him than turquoise, and he was surprised at how little it cost. 'We make it here,' the jeweler said, and he showed Hoopoe his courtyard where slaves were blowing the colored glass, spinning it out like cobwebs.

Finally he came to the ironmonger's, where he entered with reverence, for it had been with iron that the Phoenicians and their southern neighbors had conquered the land of Israel. King David, in his years as mercenary for the Philistines, had learned the use of iron and in the end had accumulated enough of the metal to turn it against them and win back much of the land; but dark iron, in many ways more mysterious than gold, remained a monopoly of cities like Accho and it still accounted for Phoenician superiority along the seacoast.

The ironmonger stared at Hoopoe with suspicion, for the Hebrew was obviously a wanderer and it was forbidden to sell iron carelessly, but Hoopoe was able to present a signed clay tablet granting him permission to purchase iron tools 'providing none be weapons such as soldiers use.' The Phoenician shopkeeper could not read, but he understood the restrictions and indicated the portion of the shop from which the stranger was free to choose. With his arms akimbo he stood protecting the other area where spearheads, sword blades and pikes were stacked along with other weapons whose use Hoopoe could not fathom. The Phoenicians wanted their visitors to see this arsenal, so that when they returned to the hinterland they would repeat its awesome character; and Hoopoe, properly impressed, muttered a small prayer to Baal: 'Help us finish the water system before these men of iron decide to attack again.'

From among the permitted items Hoopoe identified the chisels, hammers and wedges he needed for finishing the tunnel, but when the time came for him to place them in a pile, an amusing impasse took place which the Phoenician had anticipated by inviting several of his neighboring shopkeepers in to watch. Iron was so precious that as soon as any was cast and sharpened, it was covered with animal fat to prevent rusting, and now Hoopoe grasped the first of his implements. The fat stuck to his fingers and he drew his hand away, staring at the greasy substance.

'That's right,' the ironmonger said. 'It's pork.'

Even in those days the Hebrews were forbidden to eat pork, which they had learned from sorrowful experience could cause death if improperly cooked, and to them the entire body of the hog was repugnant. Phoenicians, of course, and the other sea-coast peoples who knew how to prepare the meat, liked the tasty food and enjoyed laying little traps to embarrass the Hebrews–which the ironmonger was now doing.

'It's pork fat,' he repeated, and Hoopoe backed away, but when he saw the precious tools he could not refrain from grasping them and placing them in his pile. His hands became covered with pork fat, which at the end he smeared back onto the implements lest they suffer. At the end the Phoenicians laughed and helped the little engineer, providing him with a cloth for cleaning his hands.

'Pork fat never hurt a man who likes iron,' the storekeeper said. 'I'll watch the tools till you bring your donkeys around.'

Hoopoe left the ironmonger's to inspect the interior of the city and was met by a guard from his caravan, who advised him where they would be sleeping, for he was not concerned about hurrying home; a sensible man could have left Makor that morning, been in Accho before noon, completed his business and been home again by nightfall, but the opportunity to visit a Phoenician city came so seldom to any Hebrew that Hoopoe intended to stretch it out as long as possible. Beside the waterfront he found an inn, where he sat at ease eating strange fish and looking with increasing thirst at an Egyptian merchant who was attended by two attractive girls who served him jugs of beer. Some of the brown liquid spilled along the corners of the man's mouth and as it wasted itself on the pavement Hoopoe became increasingly fascinated by the bubbles it formed. They seemed like the essence of liquid, water intensified and wine improved upon.

Remembering the warning that Hebrews must not drink beer in Accho, he turned away from the Egyptian and attended to his fried fish, but it had been so richly salted that his thirst increased. Bad luck brought an Aramaean to the eating place, and he ordered beer, which he drank in four huge draughts, throwing the last inch of liquid onto the pavement in front of Hoopoe.

'They don't strain the husks out,' the Aramaean said, ordering a second jug.

'No, they don't,' Hoopoe echoed, professionally. He picked up one of the barley husks and tasted it.

'You like to have a beer?' the Aramaean asked.

'I think I would,' Hoopoe said, and the Phoenician beer man brought him a large jug of the cool beverage.

'Tastes good with fish?' the Aramaean asked. When Hoopoe nodded without taking the jug from his lips, the man said, 'You know, in these places they put extra salt on the fish to make you want their beer.'

At midnight Hoopoe was still at the inn, drinking beer and singing Egyptian songs with some sailors. He was loud but not boisterous, and the Phoenician guards did not molest him, even though they knew that he was not supposed to be there at that hour. It would have been difficult for them to explain why they did not arrest him, but primarily it was because he was a happy-looking man, visibly free of mean intentions. They supposed he had been working hard on some farm and was enjoying himself. At the one-o'clock watch he was singing noisily but stopped to explain to bystanders. 'I do love a song. Listen to how that Cypriot sings. I tell you, a man who can sing like that is very close to Yahweh.' No sooner had he mentioned his god's name among the unbelieving Phoenicians than he clamped his hand over his mouth in apology, but when he did so he began to giggle. 'You mustn't mind me,' he told the guards. 'At home they call me Hoopoe.' And he left the table and walked unsteadily up and down, bobbing his head this way and that as his fat bottom weaved in the moonlight. 'I'm a hoopoe bird,' he said.

'Would you like to visit the girls?' the Cypriot singer asked.

'Me? I'm married,' and he began to describe his wife while the innkeeper and the guards listened. 'She is about this tall and more gentle than a breeze blowing in from the sea. All things that are beautiful she cherishes, so today I bought her this.' With fumbling fingers he unwrapped the length of braided glass and in the flickering light the eighteen multicolored strands were as beautiful as the woman for whom they were intended.

'I have the best wife in the world,' he said with maudlin sentiment, 'and the best friend, too, even though he is a Moabite. And let me tell you this! A lot of you people say unkind things about Moabites. They fight. They're hard to govern. They attack you when you're not . . . But let me tell you this. I trust my Moabite so much that on the day . . .'

The two groats merchants from Makor came looking for him, and the Phoenicians said, 'Better take the little fellow home.' And the Hebrews steadied him while he tried to straighten his legs.

As the merchants walked him along the waterfront where ships rode at anchor in the bay, Hoopoe looked with poorly focusing eyes and knew only that the night was beautiful. 'I was digging in that tunnel a long time,' he mumbled to the merchants, and he began to resent the fact that Meshab the Moabite had not been allowed to visit Accho with him. 'He should be here,' he began to shout. 'He did more than half the work.' He was willing to defend the merit of all Moabites, but his knees crumpled and he spoke no more.

During the week that Hoopoe lingered in Accho work in the tunnels progressed, and in some ways, Meshab thought, it was providential that the fat little builder was absent, for Meshab could now go first to his own rock face and listen for sounds from the well end, then around to the well, where he was free to enter Hoopoe's tunnel and listen to echoes coming from the shaft, and because the sounds grew stronger he was able to determine his location exactly and to modify slightly the direction of Hoopoe's tunnel so that the two would meet as planned. Had Hoopoe been present it might have been embarrassing when it was discovered that his tunnel was definitely off target. However, when the Moabite saw again the short distance between the guide strings at Hoopoe's end, he marveled that the Hebrew had been able to orient his tunnel at all. 'The man's a little genius,' Meshab told the crew. 'He must be able to smell his way through rock.' And each day the sounds from one tunnel to the other became more distinct and the sense of excitement in the dark spaces increased.

It had been Meshab's custom, when his day's work was done, to climb out of the shaft, check the tree to be sure it was still in line, flick the two strings to see that they hung freely, then climb the parapets to inspect the waterwall, which would soon be torn down when the silent tunnel that lay beneath was functioning. Then he would wipe his face and go to the house of Jabaal the Hoopoe that stood beside the shaft. There, in a rear room separated from the rest of the building, he would wash away the dirt and put on a robe which he had salvaged from the disaster in Moab. In heavy sandals he would sit for a while, contemplating the day when the tunnel would be finished and he would leave it a freedman. The years of his captivity had been tedious, but he had discharged them with dignity, remaining loyal to his god and dedicated to the future of his people. Often, when night was upon the town, he would walk in his Moabite robe slowly through the streets, out the gate and across the road to the slave camp, where he shared the noisome scraps served his men, trying by his example to keep the slaves inspirited; but on the morning Hoopoe had left for Accho, the little engineer had said, 'Meshab, I want you to take your evening meals with Kerith,' but this the slave was unwilling to do, lest it bring Hoopoe in ridicule, and on the first evening he ate in the slave camp.

On the second evening a slave girl came knocking on Meshab's door, with the message: 'The mistress has more food than she can consume and wonders if you would care for some.' Putting on his Moabite robe he went forward to the main part of the house, where Kerith greeted him kindly and they shared the evening meal.

In Moab he had been a man of some importance, owning fields and wine presses. 'In not too many months I shall be back with my own people,' he told Kerith.

'How much more digging is there to do?' she asked.

'The little tunnels should meet . . . this month perhaps. We'll see how they match up and then enlarge them into the real tunnel'—he showed her how their system would permit adjustments in any necessary direction, up, down or sideways—'unless we're too far apart in some direction, and I don't think we are.'

'It's very clever,' she said.

'Your husband is the clever one,' Meshab informed her. 'I could go elsewhere now and dig another tunnel like this one, but I could never have foreseen the many little problems . . .' He laughed. 'I'm telling you things you don't need to know,' he added.

'When you go back to Moab, will your family . . .' She hesitated.

'My wife and children were killed during a Hebrew raid. That's why I fought so desperately. In a way, I'm surprised that your people let me live. Do you remember when General Amram saw me . . .' He noticed that she blushed shyly at the name of the Hebrew general and he recalled the contempt he had felt when he thought her involved in some way with the visitor, but he said nothing. He was forty-eight years old now and had seen much of life. He had learned that among the hot-blooded Hebrews it was a rare family that did not in the course of years experience some violent cascade of emotion; the stories men told at night of how their ancestors had lived, or of what King Saul or King David had done in his youth summarized the Hebrews. They were a mercurial people, running through a man's hand like quicksilver, never fully to be grasped, and if Hoopoe's pretty wife had been somehow engaged with General Amram, that was her problem. Hoopoe and Kerith were contented now, and he liked them both.

'Do you think that when the tunnel is finished . . .' Kerith interrupted herself. 'Well, you'll be a free man then and you can go back to Moab. But Hoopoe . . . Do you think he might be invited to Jerusalem?'

So that was it! Now Meshab understood what had happened. Kerith had longed to go to the capital. Why? Was it because Jerusalem was where decisions were made and where men and women of importance gathered? She had ingratiated herself with General Amram in hopes that he would further her wish, and the man had been killed in battle, ending that approach. The big Moabite smiled. It was nothing very serious when a woman wanted to be where she wasn't, nor was it permanently reprehensible if she tried to further her own and her husband's ambitions in the one practical way she had at her disposal. He had always liked this good-looking Hebrew woman, and now he appreciated her even more—but with a touch of amused condescension.

'Why are you smiling?' she asked.

'You remind me so much of myself,' he said.

'I?'

'As a boy I longed to see other lands. The deserts of Moab were quite dull and I used to dream about Egypt or the sea of Jerusalem, the Jebusite capital. Finally I got to see Jerusalem.'

'You did?' Kerith asked eagerly, bending forward across the low table.

'Yes. On a rainy day I was marched up a steep hill with a yoke about my neck, and if the king had recognized who I was, I would have been killed. I saw

Jerusalem. Kerith, be careful you don't see it at the same expense.'

'Are you saying that I ought not to long for such things?'

'I'm saying that after I had seen Jerusalem with a yoke about my neck I realized that if the second part of my dream had come true, my wish to be on the sea, it would have come only if I were a slave chained to some Phoenician ship. A man can see Jerusalem any time he wishes. It depends upon the kind of yoke he's willing to accept.'

'I will see it. On my terms,' she said.

On the third night Meshab was again invited to have his supper in the front part of the house, and on each succeeding night. He and Kerith discussed many things and he awakened to the fact that she was an exceedingly intelligent woman. Some of her chance remarks about General Amram–his arrogance, his vanity regarding victories over tribes that had owned few weapons–led him to believe that she was now able to assess her former actions, whatever they had been, rather honestly. But he also discovered that if any stranger were now to enter Makor with a more visionary attitude toward life, he could surely win this woman, for in a sad and passive kind of way she was weary of Makor and he guessed that she was weary of her good-natured husband, too.

'If Bathsheba succeeds in making Solomon your next king,' he told her on the fourth night, 'it's supposed that he'll try to build Jerusalem into a rival of Tyre and Nineveh. I'm sure that if that's the case, a builder as diligent as Hoopoe will find a welcome.'

'Are you?' she pleaded, and after a while she turned the conversation to Moab, asking Meshab if life there was similar to Makor's, and he described the beautiful upland valleys that lay to the east and the Dead Sea.

'We always fought with the Hebrews,' he explained, 'and I'm sure we always will.' He told her the enchanting story of his countrywoman Ruth, who had left Moab to become the wife of a Hebrew. 'This made her the great-grandmother of your King David,' he added.

'I didn't know that!' Kerith said, leaning her head back as she tried to visualize this unlikely story.

'So David's really a Moabite,' Meshab said, 'and at the same time our most cruel enemy.'

'David? Cruel?' A slave had spoken disparagingly of her king and she felt insulted.

'Have you not heard? When he first conquered the Moabites he caused all prisoners to kneel before him on the battlefield and we were numbered One, Two, Three, each man with one of those numbers.'

'Then what?'

'Then David sent his soldiers among us, unarmed as we were, and all prisoners numbered One and Two were slain.'

In the silence Kerith asked in a kind of fascinated horror, 'And you were Three?'

'No, I was Two, but as the soldiers were about to slay me David stopped them and asked, "Is this not Meshab the leader of the Moabites?" And when he found that I was, he said, "He shall not be slain. He is brave and shall become my general," and he asked me, "Will you accept Yaweh and become a freedman?" and I said, "I live and die with Baal." His face grew dark with rage and I thought he would kill me then, but he ground his teeth and cried, "No matter. He's a brave man. Set him free." And with my freedom I rallied my defeated people and during an honorable foray I tried to overwhelm the tents of

the Hebrew generals. It was then I killed the brother of Amram.'
'That first day Amram said he had wanted to destroy you with his own hands.
Why didn't he?'
'Because David had once offered me sanctuary. Instead of death, Amram
gave me slavery.'
She sighed and turned to other matters. 'The other day the governor said
that David might come north to see the water system. Tell me, is there a chance
he would take Hoopoe south with him?'
'Possibly.' The Moabite wished he could say something that would calm this
impatient woman, but all he could think of was, 'Jerusalem with a yoke around
your neck is nothing to yearn for.'
'I shall not be going with such a yoke,' she said firmly.
'You're burdened with it already,' he said. 'A far heavier one than I wore that
day.'
On the fifth and sixth nights they met again, talking till the middle watch,
and the big Moabite again felt a desire to remove the hunger that was
endangering Hoopoe's wife, and on the last night he said, 'Kerith, is it possible
that you fail to see what a great man your husband is, no matter whether he
stays or goes to Jerusalem?'
'No one thinks of Hoopoe as a great man,' she replied.
'I do. When it looked as if our tunnels were not going to meet, he took the
blame upon himself. Even though he was the master and I the slave.'
'He's honest,' she granted. 'But his name Hoopoe tells the story.' She
laughed pleasantly, and not in derision. 'He's a dear man, and we all love him. I,
too,' she added. 'But in the past three years I have discovered that he is not the
kind of man kings call to Jerusalem. And I am afraid.'
'Remember the story of what your god Yahweh said not far from here?
"Look not on his countenance, or on the height of his stature. Yahweh seeth not
as man seeth, for man looketh on the outward appearance, but Yahweh looketh
on the heart."'
Kerith accepted the rebuke but did not respond to it, for the slave's mention
of Yahweh diverted her attention and caused her to ask, 'Meshab, why not
accept Yahweh now and become a freedman?'
'I will not turn my back on Baal of the Moabites,' the slave said, and this
reiteration of faith, evoking in Kerith's mind the misery of the slave camp, had
a profound effect upon her and she asked in a hushed voice, 'You would endure
that camp?' She shivered at her recollection of it. 'For how many years?'
'Seven.'
She bowed her head in recognition of a man who would accept such
humiliation and filth rather than deny his god, but next evening toward
sundown her thoughts were brought back to Hoopoe, for he came stumbling
home at the end of a six-day drunk. He had walked the distance from Accho and
was unkempt, dusty and chuckling to himself. He had walked because the
Phoenician officials had become so attached to him that when he left Accho
they gave him not only all the iron tools he had paid for but another portion as
well, and he had deemed it preferable that the donkey haul these tools rather
than himself. At the guard post he had forgotten to reclaim his dagger, for there
he and the guards had finished his last jug of beer and had sung songs from
Sidon, but in its place he had a beautiful Cypriot sword, given him by the
governor of Accho, and two iron spearheads. He was relaxed and happy, and
when he pushed his donkey through the gate he dumped off the cargo in front

of the governor's quarters, bowed to that official and staggered home to his wife. But as soon as he had washed up and cleared his head he called for Meshab, and the two men climbed down the shaft, where Hoopoe scrambled into the face of the rock to hear with startling clarity the night crew at the other facing, and he looked back at the Moabite with joy showing across his bearded face.

'You were on the exact heading!' he said with generous approval, and when they climbed down into the well and started into that tunnel he saw at once the sharp correction Meshab had made in his absence. He crawled to the facing rock, listened to the hammers in the other tunnel and realized how far off course he had been and how Meshab's intervention had protected him from what would have been a conspicuous error. He embraced the Moabite and said, 'As we broaden the tunnel we can smooth out the bump and no one will ever know,' and when they had retreated back to the well he pledged his gratitude: 'When your chisel penetrates that last rock, you're a free man.' And he scrambled out of the well and ran home to tell Kerith, pointing to one of the baked tablets and saying, 'What we scratched on clay three years ago we've dug in solid rock.' Pushing the tablet aside he hugged Kerith and cried with sheer joy, 'Jerusalem is yours.' He kissed her many times and whispered, 'It was for you I dug the tunnel' He was about to lead her to their bedroom when he thought of an important responsibility, and he banged on the wall to attract Meshab's attention.

'Let's take the new tools down to the men right now. That's why I went to Accho,' and before he went to bed he saw to it that his slaves got the sharp new tools for cutting away the last of the intervening rock.

Late in the month of Ethanim, at the end of the hot season in the third year, when early rains began and plowing and sowing were possible, it became obvious that within a few days the two teams would meet, but the relative positions of the approaching tunnels could not yet be determined; almost certainly one would be higher than the other, or off to one side, but there seemed little doubt that at least part of the two openings would coincide and that subsequent corrections could be easily made. Excitement grew and even the governor got into old sandals and crawled along the little tunnel, gaining for himself a sense of the wonder that had been accomplished: each man had dug for nearly a hundred and forty feet through solid rock, relying upon the most primitive surveying equipment, and were about to meet as planned, within a tolerance of two feet in any direction.

On what would be the last day Hoopoe tried to mask his excitement, and he refused to be the man at the facing when the puncture was made. He chose an ordinary slave who had done good work and sent him crawling in with his sledge while he remained in the well cave, looking at the sweet water which would bubble quietly to the surface for the next two thousand years as women came along with their water jars. His work had made the future existence of Makor possible; and since he was deep in the earth, working with the earth, he prayed to the god who controlled that earth: 'Sweet Baal, you have brought me face to face with my friend Meshab. Hidden from the eyes of others, you have brought us together, and the triumph is yours.'

'Hoopoe!' the men in the tunnel began calling. Shouts of joy echoed through the cave and reverberated across the surface of the water. 'Hoopoe!' The voices became confused and men backed out of the tunnel, their eyes filled with tears.

'You must go in!' the slaves shouted, and they pushed their master into the tunnel. On his knees he crawled through those difficult first cuttings which had determined the success of the venture, past the bulge that Meshab had corrected for him, and to the longed-for spot where he saw a lamp shining through the rock. The men on the other side were waiting for him and he heard a slave saying, 'When he puts his hand through, shout!' And when he reached the small opening he could see Meshab the Maobite and he said, 'You are my brother. This moment you are free to leave.'

'I'll finish the tunnel with you,' the Moabite promised; and at that glowing instant when they met in the darkness of the earth, a slim, exhausted man with a black beard was painfully climbing the ramp to enter the town, and when the guards at the gate stopped him he said that he was Gershom, seeking sanctuary, and he carried with him a small kinnor, called a lyre.

THE TELL

Vered Bar-El had been in Chicago only a short time giving her lectures on the Candlestick of Death when a withering example of the 'fifty days' drifted in with searing winds from the desert, making work at the dig almost impossible. These days were now called khamsin, from the Arabic word for *fifty*, but they were as enervating as they had always been. During khamsin only the Moroccans made any attempt to keep digging, and even they preferred the bottom of the trenches, where they could hide in shadows and pick at the rubble with their fingers.

In this impossible weather John Cullinane often sat on the back porch of the headquarters building, watching the amusing little hoopoe birds as they hurried about, probing into sandy holes, and he remembered Vered's lilting voice as she once said, 'The hoopoe bird ought to be the world symbol for archaeologists. We also go furiously about, poking our noses into the earth.' He missed Vered even more than he had expected, and hoped she would soon return; at his desk he sometimes blew at the skirted figurine of Astarte and convinced himself that he was going to take both the clay goddess and the living back to Chicago. In fact, he was pleased that she was having a chance to see the city which was to be her future home.

When the lingering khamsin continued to make digging impractical, he resumed work on his progress report, but even here Vered's lovely figure haunted him, for when he wrote of ceramics he could see her darting back and forth to her washing troughs with basketfuls of fragments, and he recalled with affection the phrases that so often appeared in the prefaces to archaeological reports: 'I am especially indebted to Miss Pamela Mockridge (later Mrs Peter Hanbury)' and a few lines farther on one would discover that Mr Peter Hanbury had been the expedition's architect. Few presentable girls could survive two seasons of digging in the Holy Land without getting married, and Cullinane thought how saucy it would be to include in his preface: 'We are all indebted to our brilliant ceramicist, Mrs Vered Bar-El (later Mrs John Cullinane).' He chuckled. 'Let me figure out what happened on *that* dig.'

But when he submitted his provisional draft to Eliav and Tabari he ran into trouble, for they feared that in his section covering Level XII at Makor he had been too much influenced by what had happened at collateral sites elsewhere. Eliav warned, 'Your guesses are too derivative.'

'What he means,' Tabari interpreted. 'You'd be a lot smarter if you were a lot dumber.'

'Forget what happened at Megiddo and Gezer,' Eliav advised. 'Trust your own eyes.'

'We don't work in a vacuum,' Cullinane said defensively. 'Don't you suppose the men at Gezer an Megiddo faced the same problems our fellows did?'

Tabari evaded the question. 'We want you to take a little trip with us, John,' and as the three men climbed into the jeep the Arab said, 'It's the year 3000 C.E. and we're archaeologists coming to excavate four sites, all of which perished in some great cataclysm in 1964.'

'Let's just use our eyes,' Eliav said, 'and decide what kind of report we'd write.'

They drove to a bright new suburb of Akko, where Tabari stopped at the home of a friend to show Cullinane and Eliav a modern house, whose components he ticked off: 'Age of electricity, refrigerator, stove, air-conditioning, wiring in all rooms. Accessible to a lively foreign trade, because the rug's from Britain, the radio from Germany. Where'd you get the chair, Otto?'

'Italy.'

Eliav continued the analysis: 'And if we found fragments of these books we could state that the family had attained a high culture with works in German, French, English, Hebrew, Arabic and something I don't recognize.'

'Hungarian,' Otto explained.

'We could go on through the rest of the house,' Eliav said, 'with eyeglasses as proof of medical skill, the wine bottle linked with France. So let's agree that this is the norm for Level XLV.'

'And a very high norm it is,' Cullinane said amiably to the owner.

'We've worked since we got out of Hungary,' he replied.

They drove to a village not far away, where Tabari sought permission to enter a house, which was granted by a group of recent oriental immigrants who as yet spoke no Hebrew. 'Look at the contents here,' he said. 'No electricity. Practically no objects dating since 1920. Very few signs of cultural attainment. Different cooking methods, different mode of life altogether.' He gave the owners some cigarettes and thanked them for their kindness.

'But the real jolt to our archaeologists in 3000 C.E. will be when they dig up this next house,' and he led the way to an Arab village north of Makor, where he shouted to a man standing in the unpaved road, asking him if they could visit his house. The villager nodded, and standing amid chickens, Tabari pointed out, 'Completely different architecture. No electricity, no stove. Clay pots such as were used two thousand years ago. No books, one picture with Arabic writing, a manner of dress centuries old. But what I want you to see especially is this mill for grinding wheat. It's all wood, but tell me—what are those little things sticking out to grind the grain?'

Cullinane got on his hands and knees to inspect the ancient grinding system from whose upper section small points projected. 'Are they what I think they are?' he asked.

'They're not metal,' Tabari said.

'They're flints,' Cullinane said. 'Where'd they get flints in this age?'

'Where the people of Makor got them ten thousand years ago,' Tabari replied. In Arabic he checked with the owner of the mill. 'That's right. Nodules from the wadi bed.'

The three scientists returned to the jeep, where Tabari said, 'Now before you tell me how you're going to date that Arab hut when we dig it up, let's look at item four.' He drove to a ravine up whose sides they climbed on foot until they came to the mouth of a cave, at whose entrance they called. From the dark depths came a petulant voice, and they crept in to find an old man who lived alone with his goats. Eliav whispered, 'This cave's been occupied like this for at least thirty thousand years, and the only thing that I can see that would tell us it's the twentieth century is the plastic buttons on the old man's shirt.'

'You're wrong,' Cullinane said as he probed into the area where the goats slept. 'Here's a Danish beer bottle.'

'Suppose you dug that up,' Tabari continued. 'You'd swear it was an inappropriate intrusion.' He gave the old man three pounds and said, 'Get yourself some more beer.'

As they descended to the jeep Eliav said, 'This is what we meant about your report, John. Within a few miles in modern Israel we find a 1964 house, a 1920, a 1300, and a cave dating back to who knows when? Yet side by side they exist, and it takes all four to represent our civilization. Don't you think that in King David's time Makor must have been equally varied?'

'I'm not sure your reasoning's good,' Cullinane said cautiously. 'Today we have so many more levels that might be held over from the past. After all, King David could have seen houses from only four or five different levels at most.'

'Granted. But the homogeneity you write about probably didn't exist.'

'Point's made,' Cullinane admitted. Standing in the road he tried to summarize the trip. 'In Akko, the new house . . .'

Tabari interrupted. 'On our first day you oriented yourself by pointing west to Akko. Do you always start that way?'

The Irishman considered this for a moment, then said, 'In Israel, yes.'

'Why?' Tabari asked.

'I don't know,' Cullinane replied. After a moment he offered tentatively, 'As a child I'd heard a good deal about Jesus,' and he pointed back over his shoulder to Galilee. 'But the Holy Land never became real for me until I read about the Crusades. For weeks I went around making believe I was in the boat that brought Richard the Lion Heart to Acre.'

'Interesting,' Tabari said. 'You visualized yourself coming ashore to save the Holy Land, so you've always moved from west to east.'

'For me, that's the way Israel is.'

'Most curious,' Eliav said with restrained enthusiasm. 'I've always seen it lying north to south. I'm Abraham wandering out of the north and seeing this marvelous land for the first time. Or I'm a Jew of King Solomon's age, stationed up here and looking south towards Jerusalem.' He hesitated, then added, 'I first saw Israel from the north, and its wonderful hills invited me southward as they must have done Abraham. It never occurred to me until just now that you could visualize it any other way.'

Tabari said, 'During the War of 1948 I met an Arab from across the Jordan and he told me how excited he was when his unit invaded Palestine. Coming out of the desert and seeing our explosive richness . . . the greenness. His company had merely to march westward to the ocean and the land was theirs.'

'How do you see it?' Cullinane asked.

'Me?' Tabari asked in surprise. He had never considered the question before. Cautiously he continued, 'I see it as if it had always been here, with me standing on it. No west, no east, no south. Just the land as far back as my family can remember. I could probably live in any of the four spots we've been in today and be reasonably happy.'

'Even in the cave?' Cullinane asked.

'I'd get rid of the goats.'

And the three scientists, each with such a different view of the land they were excavating, returned to Makor.

Gershom was a singer of the hills, a man who had tended his father-in-law's sheep in the upland valleys where he had killed a man and had fled, leaving his family and his wife behind. He wore the plain sheepskin garment of a countryman and he arrived in Makor with no trade, no spare clothing, no tools and no money. He carried a small seven-stringed lyre made of fir wood trimmed with antique bronze and strung with twisted sheep's gut, which now hung slack across the sounding board. He came seeking sanctuary from the brothers of the man he had slain and it had been his hope to reach the anonymity of Accho, but his strength had given out and his pursuers were bearing down upon him, for they rode donkeys while he had to make his way on foot.

He stumbled past the guards, gasping merely, 'Sanctuary.' They pointed toward where the temple lay, then ran to inform the governor, who appeared in time to see the shepherd hurrying down the main street. As he disappeared to the left three dusty men on donkeys rode up the ramp and demanded entrance. 'If you're looking for the other one,' the governor said, 'he reached the temple.'

The men were disgusted, and their sense of urgency vanished. Stiffly they dismounted, kicked their donkeys free to find their own shade, and followed the governor as he showed them the way to the temple. The building was intentionally kept small to avoid giving the priestly leadership of Jerusalem competition; it was built of a reddish uncut field stone and was quite plain, lacking even columns or imposing steps. Its two doors were of olive wood–thin strips nailed together with little art–and when the governor pushed them aside their stone hinges groaned. Inside was darkness, for the temple held no blazing windows or perpetual fires, but a few simple oil lamps did show the built-up levels, one after the other, terminating in a raised section upon which stood an altar of black basalt, well carved and decorated with the head of a bull which represented the sacrifices that were traditionally associated with such altars, though no animals had been offered in Makor for many years, that function being reserved for Jerusalem. The outstanding feature of the altar was a series of four horns which projected upward from each corner; through the centuries these had undergone such modification that except for their name, few in Makor would have known they represented horns, for they had become merely rounded corners of rock, but they had always held a special significance, and now as the murderer knelt on the topmost platform, his sheepskin falling carelessly about him and his kinnor thrown to one side, he clutched two of these horns.

'He's taken sanctuary,' the governor said, pointing to the altar.

'We'll wait,' the brothers said.

'We're obligated to feed him,' the governor warned. 'As long as he stays by the altar.'

'We'll wait,' the brothers repeated.

'Not here,' the governor ordered.

'We'll go outside.'

'Not within fifty cubits. King David established the law, not me.'

The three brothers said they understood and left the temple without speaking to the man who had murdered their brother. When they were gone the governor asked the fugitive what crime had been committed, and the man with the lyre replied casually, 'Angry words . . . over nothing.'

'For that you killed a man?'

The kneeling man dropped one hand from the altar and pointed to a scar across his neck, a long, livid welt that had not yet healed. 'For that I killed a man,' he repeated.

'What will you do?' the governor asked, indicating the three watchers outside. They had retired the stipulated fifty cubits and were asking townspeople for water.

'They're hot-tempered,' the murderer said. 'If they could catch me now, they'd kill me. In three days they'll see how foolish this is and go home.'

'How can you be so sure?'

'They saw their brother cut me. I think they may even be pleased that I found sanctuary. Gives them the excuse they need.'

The governor was surprised at the cynical realism of the exhausted man, and with some doubts stationed four guards at the temple, charging them with the preservation of the fugitive's life so long as he could grasp even one horn of the altar. This was a custom which the Hebrews of the desert had had to adopt when they moved into settled land, for blood feuds had ravaged the tribes, continuing through generations and causing the loss of many men who were needed as herdsmen and husbands. Moses himself had proposed a system whereby cities of refuge would be established to which accidental murderers could flee, achieving sanctuary merely by entering the city gates, but nothing had so far been accomplished in this respect. In the meantime, in any town, refuge was assured those who succeeded in grasping the horns of the altar, as Gershom now did.

'Feed him,' the governor directed the guards, and he was about to consult with the brothers concerning the fugitive's story when shouts came from the northern wall of the town, and excited figures started running toward the governmental quarters. 'What's happened?' the governor called, and the messengers turned in their running to cry, 'The tunnels have met!'

He hurried to the main shaft, at whose base he heard the shouting of the slaves, and excited hands wanted to lead him down the steep stairs so that he might see the penetration, but he was satisfied with their report. After a while Meshab the Moabite climbed out, exulting, and the governor greeted him as an equal. 'Hoopoe told me that when this happened you would be a freedman,' the governor said.

'I am.'

'Are you returning to Moab?'

'I promised Hoopoe I'd help round out the tunnel.'

'That will please him. How did the two ends meet?'

Using his forefingers Meshab started with his elbows wide apart and slowly brought the fingertips toward each other. Even without words the gesture was dramatic, and the governor could sense the blind probing that had been involved. 'At this point we could each hear the other side, and Hoopoe's tunnel was slightly off line, but right in elevation. Mine was a little high.' He brought his fingertips together, not perfectly but showing his tunnel a little high and Hoopoe's skewed to the north. Only a quarter of the two faces had met, and the nearness of the miss demonstrated what a miracle had occurred.

'We were fortunate,' the governor said, appreciating the drama.

'Hoopoe did it,' the Moabite replied, and the governor realized that this was not flattery.

'What do we do next?' he asked. During the months when it looked as if the project might fail he had shown no interest in the slaves burrowing under his town, but now that success was assured he was clever enough to see that it could be used to bring him to the attention of Jerusalem. Henceforth it would be 'our tunnel.'

'The rest is easy,' the Moabite said, but before he could explain, Hoopoe came through the postern gate, dirty and happy, and Meshab deserted the governor, running to Hoopoe and embracing him as a brother, after which the governor called in to Hoopoe's house. 'Kerith, come and greet the victor!' She appeared in a shimmering blue robe which her husband had brought her from Accho, which it had reached by boat from Greece, and as a pendant she wore the braided glass rope. She understood the happiness of the two men and kissed her husband warmly, whereupon he directed her, 'You must also kiss my brother Meshab, who is today a freedman.' Gravely Kerith kissed the former slave, and he had to bite his lip to keep his face from trembling, or perhaps even from showing tears. He grasped the hands of his two good friends and said, 'You are indeed of my family.'

To Hoopoe the governor said, 'Tomorrow we start paying him a salary,' but to Meshab he said, 'Why not accept circumcision and become one of us?' As the governor spoke he gestured toward the temple with his right hand, and to those who were watching, the movement was a subtle invitation, for his hand indicated the many different peoples who had come to make up the Hebrew population of Makor: the men from Cyprus, who had accepted circumcision in order to marry local girls; the Hittites, who had made a secure place for themselves after years of slavery; the Babylonian refugees; the clever Egyptians, who had stayed behind with local families when their empire crumbled; the dark-skinned Africans and the red-headed Edomites. All were now legally Hebrews and there was no reason why a Moabite should not join them.

Affected by the moment, Meshab took the governor's hand and kissed it. 'I have seen the greatness of Yahweh, but I am a man of Baal.'

'You could be both,' the governor reminded him, pointing out that foreign wives of the royal family were not only permitted to retain their ancient gods but were encouraged to do so. 'Jerusalem contains many private temples to Egyptian and Philistine gods, and you could have the same here.' He indicated the mountain and concluded, 'Baal will remain there for you.'

Meshab bowed his head and looked at the ground. 'I belong to Baal of the

Moabites,' he insisted, and the governor tried no more to contest his dedication. As Kerith watched with admiration he congratulated Meshab on his freedom and departed, pausing to look again at the three grim-faced men who stood guard at the temple, waiting till the murderer tried to escape. It was not necessary, the governor thought, to post his soldiers to protect the temple where the man had taken sanctuary, for this sacred privilege had not been violated in hundreds of years; there was little likelihood that the brothers would want to set an ugly precedent and the governor was satisfied that after a few days of waiting, which blood-feuds required, they would, as the murdered man had predicted, climb on their donkeys and go home.

In the days that followed, the presence of the fugitive in the temple became a matter of general interest, for it had been a generation since a murderer had sought sanctuary in this town, and children begged their mothers to be allowed to take him his food. Of course, the Levites, those assigned to tend the temple, were required to provide him with water and privy accommodations, which they did by means of clay pots, but townspeople were responsible for the feeding, and so a stream of children filed in and out bearing gifts. And when the prisoner had eaten, the children stayed to hear him tune his lyre and lean against a wall and sing old songs of the mountains and new ones that he had composed while tending sheep in the valleys:

> 'I shall sing a new song to Yahweh,
> A song of the hills,
> From whence comes my redemption,
> From whence comes my salvation
> And my sustenance.'

The children were surprised that from his slight body could come so strong a voice and they brought their parents to hear him, and the older people noticed what the children had not: that no matter how impassioned the man's songs became, he always kept himself in position to grasp the altar horns should the watchers suddenly burst into the temple to catch him unawares. He was wise to take this precaution, for often one of the brothers would push open the door with his sword to ascertain where Gershom might be at that moment.

On the third day it fell on the house of Hoopoe to feed the murderer, and since Hoopoe was occupied at the tunnel Kerith gathered together some food and took the pots herself to the temple, where she heard for the first time the sweet singer of the hills. He was seated in the shadows, his dirty, sand-stained sheepskin about him and his matted beard hiding his thin face. His lyre was tuned and he was strumming it for some children, so that when she entered he did not see her but continued singing idly, and she remained by the door waiting both with food and the exciting news that would set him free. And as he sang she listened:

> 'Yahweh is my abode forever,
> His palace is the firmament,
> The pathway of the heavens.
> He is the joy of morning
> And the consolation of the rising moon.
> Him I worship with song
> And the cry of seven strings,
> For he is my salvation and the song of my heart.'

When he finished with the latter phrase he drifted his fingers across the strings and smiled at the children crowding in upon him, but as he did so he saw Kerith standing by the door, and as they stared at each other he plucked the strings with one finger. He did not stop playing but he did stop singing so that he might watch her as she came across the temple to bring him her gift of food, and as she approached him she said, 'They have gone away.'

'The three?' he asked.

'They have gone,' she assured him, and he played a joyous song.

This was the month of Bul–when wheat was harvested for sale to the groats maker and grapes were hauled to the vintner–and Hoopoe and Meshab spent many hours in the earth, spurring the slaves to complete the routing out of the little tunnels into one large one ten feet high by six feet across. The original joining had produced a common hole less than two feet high by one across, and at the meeting point the planners had put their men to work excavating the first full-size cross section, calculating in the abstract how the enlarged hole must stand so as to provide when extended an even rate of fall from the bottom of the shaft to the level of the well, and they had done their calculations so neatly that when the dimensions of the first ten-by-six cut were extended in each direction the finished tunnel would be uniform, of predetermined incline and with no marks remaining to show where the join had been made or where Hoopoe had lost his bearings for a while. Only the two friends could appreciate what a marvel of accuracy the Makor water tunnel was.

As the two men worked, during the last part of the third year, Hoopoe's wife Kerith had many occasions to hear the stranger Gershom sing his plaintive songs of the shepherd's country and his exultant accounts of Yahweh's triumphs. When the necessity for his staying close to the horns of the altar passed, he found a job with a man who kept a shop across from the temple, where surplus wool was bought for shipment to Accho, and he became a popular figure with younger people, sitting in the wintry sunlight before the temple and singing to them. There was a wine shop next door where olive oil was also sold, and it was frequently filled with yellow-stained workers from the dye vats, men who enjoyed hearing Gershom sing of ways of life they had not known:

> 'Yahweh is my protector when the serpent strikes,
> Yea, my shield in time of anguish.
>> He saves the lamb in the thorn,
>> Yea, the bullock struck with pain,
> Yahweh is my food, my wine, my meat in the desert,
> Yea, my sustenance in the lonely places,
>> My joy when I am alone in the night.
>> He is my song, my cry of thanks,
> My exultation at the rising of the sun.'

Gershom himself could not have known that this ancient song had originally been sung by Canaanites more than a thousand years before, when they accorded their baals the same attributes that he now gave Yahweh, but the song as Gershom had modified it was a true hymn of praise to whatever god guided the movement of the heavens and the sure return of the seasons, bringing with them the blessings that men require.

Often, as Gershom sang outside the wine shop, Kerith came for wine or olive oil–a task which she had formerly assigned her slave girls–and she listened with increasing pleasure to the singing of the fugitive. His name, she learned, meant 'a stranger among us,' and the brothers of the slain man had told the people of Makor that the story of the murder was not quite so simple as Gershom had represented it. They explained that he had arrived in their village without a genealogy but had talked himself into marriage with the daughter of a man whose sheep he had subsequently stolen. The wound across his neck had not come from their murdered brother; his father-in-law had slashed him while trying to regain his stolen sheep. As for the murder, without reason Gershom had ambushed their brother at dusk. 'How did he become an outcast in the first place?' the people of Makor asked, and the brothers replied, 'Of his past we know nothing.'

'He told us he was of the family of Levi,' a boy said. But the brothers shrugged their shoulders. 'Maybe,' they said.

At first Kerith wondered what the truth might be, but when the people of Makor began to accept him, she ignored his shadowy antecedents and began listening to his songs, and one day when she heard him outside the wine shop singing to a group of children, his song was such a devout cry of thanksgiving that she was held captive, as if the stranger were grasping not the horn of the altar but the hem of her gown:

'Thorns clutched at my ankles,
Yea, rocks bruised my heel,
But Yahweh watched my progress from on high.
He guided my steps and I came to cool waters.
Men pursued me through the night,
Yea, on donkeys and camels they pursued me
And I was afraid.
But Yahweh saw me dying in the dark places,
In the lonely place he saw me
And with his love he led me to his altar.'

It was a song which assumed a personal relationship with Yahweh, who stood forth as the culmination of all preceding gods. Its words had a special effect upon Kerith, for they constituted a logical extension of the ideals her father had taught her as a child. In Gershom's songs Yahweh not only controlled the heavens of heaven, he also had time to watch with pity a man whose ankle was pierced by thorns; and this dual capacity was critical, for although Kerith had never felt the need of Baal, she did realize that Yahweh had not brought her the close personal consolation that her neighbors had found in Baal. Now Gershom was stating that Yahweh was the kind of god she had longed for: he was at hand and could be known. It was this lyric rapture that had up to now been missing in the religion of the Hebrews, as practiced in Makor, and it was the revelation of this new Yahweh, disclosed through the agency of an uncertain stranger, that struck her with disrupting force.

Her visits to the wine shop grew more frequent, until it became apparent even to the loungers from the dye vats that she was buying more olive oil than the demands of her simple kitchen would have dictated. She lingered by the entrance to the shop, staring at the man with the seven-stringed lyre, and many in Makor began to speculate that she had fallen in love with the stranger, and before long Meshab the Moabite heard the gossip.

He went straight to Hoopoe, finding him in a section of the tunnel where the diggers were striking hard rock. It was in the month of Abib, when men were harvesting barley for shipment to Accho, where it would be brewed into beer, that Meshab said, 'Hoopoe, your wife is running like a lamb toward a cliff.'

The fat little engineer sat down. 'What's happened?' he asked.

'She's fallen in love with Gershom.'

'Is he the man who plays the kinnor?'

Meshab looked with pity at his friend. 'You must be the only man in Makor who doesn't know who he is. And Kerith is in love with him.'

Hoopoe swallowed, then licked his lips. 'Where . . .'

The noise in the tunnel was too great for conversation, so the Moabite led Hoopoe back to the bottom of the main shaft, where in the coolness of the shadows he said, 'When you were in Accho buying the iron I had a chance to know Kerith. She's a good woman, like my wife before she was killed. But she's hungry . . . the uncertainties . . .'

Hoopoe became excited. 'I know exactly what you mean,' he said reassuringly, as if it were Meshab who should be worried. 'Kerith's always dreamed of going to Jerusalem. She says she'd be happier there. And I have the most exciting news.' He was nervous with pleasure and cautioned, 'You mustn't tell anyone. I haven't even told Kerith, because I didn't want her to become overhopeful.' He dropped his voice to a happy whisper. 'But King David is going to visit the tunnel. He's heard about it even in Jerusalem.' The little engineer looked about and confided, 'Of course he'll ask me to go up to Jerusalem with him.'

The Moabite shook his head in pity. 'You're placing all your hopes in that?' he asked.

'Oh yes! And then Kerith will be contented. In Jerusalem, that is.'

'Dear friend, her trouble is now. In the wine shop . . . now.'

'I'm sure it's exaggerated,' Hoopoe replied.

Meshab felt that he must stun his friend into reality, so he said bluntly, 'Three years ago, when General Amram came here . . .'

'Now, now! Don't say anything against General Amram,' Hoopoe warned. 'After all, it was thanks to him that you're now a freedman.'

Meshab was about to speak further when it occurred to him, for some reason he could not have explained, that Hoopoe had known about General Amram's dalliance with his wife, and that the little engineer had been so determined to keep working at some new job after the walls were finished that he didn't really care what yoke he would have to bear to win the next authorization. If Kerith could obtain his permission only by being congenial with the general, if that was the way it had to be achieved, there was nothing Hoopoe could do to alter the facts. Meshab looked at his friend and wondered if Hoopoe had gone willingly on those afternoon excursions which the general had invented.

To his surprise, Hoopoe volunteered the answer. 'Did you think that I didn't know that General Amram was trying to make a fool of me? "Go here, Hoopoe. Go there, Hoopoe." And did you think that when I went on his meaningless missions my wife was giving herself to him? Have you known Kerith so long without discovering that she is a woman of great purity?' Sorely wounded by Meshab's conversation, he turned away but immediately came back to grab Meshab's arm, saying with disdain, 'On the day Amram reached Makor he had one thing I wanted, this tunnel, and I got it. I had one thing he wanted, but he never came close to winning her. That year who was the foolish man?' And Meshab said no more.

At that moment Kerith was leaving the wine shop, for the third time that day, and she was impelled to do something she had not done before: she stopped

boldly in front of the place where Gershom sat and for the first time spoke to
him in the open street. 'Where did you learn your songs?' she asked.

'Some I wrote,' he replied.

'And the others?'

'The old songs of my people.'

'Who were your people?'

'Levite wanderers.'

'The story you told about the scar? It wasn't true, was it?'

'I have the scar,' he replied, and at that moment she wished more than
anything else to be alone with this singer and with a laver of cool water to bathe
his scar. But Meshab was entirely wrong when he guessed that she was in love
in any physical sense with this stranger; she was not bedazzled by the lyrist, but
she was captivated by the concept of a man expressing the religious longings of
all men in song, and she responded to his music as if he had composed it for her
alone.

'Could I ask how you got the scar?' she said.

'You could ask,' he replied.

'Would you care to sing in my home?' she suggested. 'My husband will be
arriving soon.'

'I would like to,' he replied, and although she was inclined to take the singer's
hand and lead him through the streets, she refrained from doing so, but he
followed her casually and when she reached the shaft she asked one of the
slaves, 'See if Jabaal can join us,' and the man answered, 'He's down there now,
talking with Meshab,' and she went to the rim and called into the deep hole,
where her voice reverberated softly against the perpendicular rocks: 'Hoopoe!
Hoopoe! Hoopoe!' and on to a muted silence. It was the first time she had used
his name in public.

In the weeks that followed, Gershom was frequently in the home of the
engineer, most often when Hoopoe was there, but occasionally when only
Kerith was free to listen to the singing. He showed himself an intense but gentle
man, not forthright about his own history but unequivocal where his testimony
concerning Yahweh was concerned. On the hills he had undergone some deep
personal experience with his god and this took precedence over any personal
problems. He had pretty well forgotten his wife and the man he had murdered.
These were incidents that no longer concerned him, as were the conditions of
his parents and his brothers. His songs of faith encompassed all these matters
and in a sense explained them away; even Hoopoe and Meshab grew to enjoy
the stranger's singing, sitting for long spells in the evening as he told them,
accompanied by his lyre, of the actuality of Yahweh:

> 'He is in the whimper of the lamb I seek at night,
> Lo, he is in the stamping of the wild bull'

And after Gershom had sung for some weeks, while the tunnel was being
finished, all in the house of Hoopoe were willing to accept him for what he had
offered himself to be: a man who had run away from everything but the
pursuing power of Yahweh.

At Hoopoe's his listeners heard the songs from three different levels of
comprehension. The Moabite listened to statements about Yahweh as he
would have listened to a Philistine chanting about Dagon or a Babylonian
singing of Tammuz. Since Baal was not involved, he was not involved; he
respected Yahweh as the Hebrew god—no better, no worse than the others—and

that was all. Hoopoe, on the other hand, was confused. Even his name Jabaal bore testimony to the fact that Yahweh took precedence over Baal, and Hoopoe was therefore inclined to accept the message of Gershom's songs. But he also knew, as a practical engineer, that Baal continued to be far more real than this stranger cared to admit. 'Let him dig a tunnel through rock,' Hoopoe whispered to Meshab, 'and he won't dismiss Baal so easily.'

Kerith exhibited a more complex reaction, evoked partly by the songs themselves but mostly by her maturing personal experiences. As for the songs, she was still gratified to hear in them a definition of Yahweh that included both austerity and lyric joy. As for herself, even before Gershom's arrival she had been groping toward a more purified spiritual experience, as many in Israel would do in the centuries ahead, for the disappointments and contradictions of her life had proved that men and women required some central force to cling to. She had almost decided that for no man could this force operate effectively if it were shared between two different kinds of god: there could not be Yahweh and Baal. Reason told her that the time had come to accept one unifying entity who would absorb all lesser deities and she longed for identification with that all-embracing god. Personally she had long since abandoned Baal, but she was now prepared to condemn those who refused to do likewise, and these ideas she had nurtured by herself. To a minor degree they were an outgrowth of her longing for Jerusalem, but to a major degree they had generated that longing. She saw that Makor was merely a frontier settlement concerned with things that could be felt and touched, such as walls, olive presses and dye vats, and it was only logical that the town should insist upon holding on to its practical gods like Baal; but she had faith that in Jerusalem ideas were more important than things—the relationship of god to man, justice, the nature of worship—and she was convinced that in Jerusalem there must be many who thought as she did.

Then Gershom had arrived, empty-handed and without a history except for the charge of murder, and in simple words that soared through the dimly lit white-walled rooms and through the narrow alleys of the town itself he had stated that all she had been dreaming of was true. There was one god of unlimited power who could evoke joy in the human heart and security among nations. She had spent more than six years preparing herself for the seven strings of this chance lyre, and its music reverberated in her heart as if she were an echoing cave constructed for just such melodies. In the long days that she talked with the outcast she never allowed him to touch her, nor when he was gone did she wish he had done so. He had brought her a message from the mountains, and one does not embrace messengers; one listens to them. For his part, he had understood Kerith in those first few months when she had brought him the food in the temple: she was a woman hungry for the higher world, for the more complete song, and in Makor she was miserable, tied down to its uninspiring syncretism of ritual for Yahweh and worship of Baal. He respected her and found joy in singing for her, since she grasped what he was saying.

As for his personal life, he kept one small, dirty room at the rear of the wool merchant's. He worked as little as he could and still earn his pay. He ate wherever there was free food and drank what he could beg or steal in the wine shop. Among the slave girls of the town there were several who were pleased to entertain him, and he became expert in climbing walls. Whenever possible he picked up bits of silver which he passed along to the guards at the gate, so that they might warn him if the brothers of the dead man tried to creep back unexpectedly and murder him before he could reach the horns of the altar; in fact, wherever he was in Makor he marked the shortest way back to the temple, against that day when he might have to flee once more to its sanctuary.

In the month of Ziv in the fourth year of the digging– when thistles bloomed in the valleys and yellow tulips along the edges of the marsh, when storks had flown to the north and bee eaters were seen darting above red poppies–Hoopoe and Meshab went to the quarry on the other side of the mountain and selected six great lengths of stone, cut in eighteen-foot sections and squared on the ends like timbers for use in building some gigantic temple. They sent slaves in great numbers to drag these huge monoliths to the well, and during the days when the stones were being transported they directed other slaves to clean out all rubbish from the tunnel and haul it for the last time up through the opening at the well. The water system was now complete except for the final precaution which Hoopoe was about to take, the hiding of the well itself under such depth of rock that no invader could find it or uncover it if he did.

When the rocks reached the well on sledges that ran on saplings thrown under the wooden runners. Hoopoe directed his slaves to dig three pairs of slots running north and south above the well, and when these cuts were straight and deep, three of the large stones were lowered into position, forming a grid over the well. When this was completed, big rocks from the waterwall were thrown in, followed by smaller stones, pebbles and earth, until it was covered. Then three more cuts were made running from east to west, and when these were dug the remaining three long stones were dropped into position, forming a second grid running crisscross to the first, and this too was covered until the surface of the earth was reached.

'Now tear down the old waterwall,' Hoopoe commanded, and the slaves attacked the Canaanite wall with pleasure, knocking it to pieces. The stones were taken inside the town for the building of new houses, and on a bright day when daisies covered the hills back of town, Hoopoe and Meshab climbed to their observation point to see if anything remained that might betray the existence of the well to a besieging army.

'The lines of the old waterwall stand out too clearly,' Hoopoe said apprehensively.

'Grass and weeds will take care of that,' Meshab said, 'but there's something else that would tell me the secret. Do you see it?'

Hoopoe studied the town and saw the flags. 'We'll take them down tonight.'

'I don't mean the flags. I mean that line of mortar along the wall. It says in a clear voice that some construction used to be attached there.'

'Of course!' Hoopoe agreed. It stood out like a signal, darker rocks that had been protected from sunlight by the waterwall, standing beside lighter ones that had weathered in the sun. The men considered what might be done to obliterate this telltale line and it was the Moabite who found the solution.

'We could build a small tower. As if it were protecting the postern gate.'

'That would do it,' Hoopoe agreed and he asked Meshab to remain the short time required for such a task.

'No, I must go home,' the former slave replied.

But when Kerith heard that Meshab was determined to leave she wept and kissed him as Gershom watched. 'Stay with us a little longer,' she pleaded, and to Hoopoe and Gershom she said, 'In a dark period of my life this man was greater than a brother.' So against his better judgment Meshab consented to build the tower at the postern gate.

One morning as work progressed Hoopoe came from the governor's quarters with the news that his wife had been anticipating for three years: King David was at last coming north from Shunem to inspect the water system and to dedicate it as the David Tunnel. When Kerith heard the report she retired to her room and prayed, 'Yahweh, you alone brought him to these walls. You alone shall take us to your city Jerusalem.'

At the end of the month of Ziv squadrons of riders appeared at the gate to inform the governor that King David was approaching along the Damascus road, and trumpets were blown, while priests in the temple blew rams' horns in flurries of provocative sound. All the citizens of Makor lined the walls or stood upon housetops looking eastward, as they did when siege was threatened, and after some time they saw men on donkeys and then a few on horses and finally a palanquin carried by slaves, and this was treated with such deference that all knew the king must be therein.

The procession came to the great gate, where the men on donkeys sounded their trumpets, which were answered from the wall, and the king's palanquin was borne inside and set carefully before the governor's house where all the trumpets sounded many times, after which the curtains parted, showing not King David, but one of the most beautiful young women in Israel. 'It's Abishag,' the women of Makor whispered, and all watched in wonder as she stepped forth to greet the governor.

She was the marvel of these last years of King David's reign, a peasant girl found in the remote village of Shunem after a nation-wide search for some gentle child to live with the old king in his declining years, 'a girl to sleep with him on cold nights,' the counselors had explained when they were searching for her, and unlikely as it had seemed at the time, they had found the perfect maiden for the task, an almost flawless girl who served the king with compassion and made his terminal years endurable. A brief time from now, when David was dead, his sons would quarrel more over this radiant concubine than they would over his kingdom, and Adonijah, fleeing the rage of his half-brother Solomon, would be slain because of her, the most desirable woman in Israel.

Now she reached into the palanquin and gave her hand to a frail old man nearing seventy, with white beard and half-trembling hands, and when she brought him before his subjects as if he were a child, Kerith whispered, 'Can that be David?' But then the old man heard the adoring cry of the multitude, 'David! David!' and he seemed to straighten; sunlight fell across his beard, showing a few strands which still retained the red coloring of his youth. He put Abishag aside and slowly turned his head, nodding his acceptance of the people's homage, and there could be no question as to who in that assembly was king. His luminous eyes, set deep in their sockets, gleamed as the cheers continued, and his shoulders threw off their weight of age. His body moved with regal grace, and when twoscore trumpets sounded and drums rolled, he became once more the great king, the slayer of Goliath, the extender of boundaries, the builder of empire, the sweet singer of Israel, the sage, the judge, the generous David of the Hebrews, in all the world the king nonpareil.

Kerith, staring at him as if he were more than king, saw that his beard was trimmed and his garments carefully arranged, for he was vain of his appearance. He wore heavy sandals with golden thongs clasping his ankles, a garment shot through with gold and emerald, and a brocaded cap protecting his white hair. He walked through the crowd with such noble grace that none could have envisaged the emotional wars he had known with Michal, daughter of

Saul, and Bathsheba, wife of Uriah. His passionate friendship for Jonathan, son of Saul, was now only an aching memory, and he gave the impression of a man who had finally subdued the violent impulses of his young manhood. Then suddenly the posture ended, and he replaced his hand in Abishag's. The last trumpet echoed on the wall. The drums beat no more. And he allowed her to lead him quietly on, hearing nothing, seeing nothing, a man aloof from the world he had created. 'He's turning the kingdom over to Solomon,' a Phoenician whispered. 'He no longer cares about the principalities of this world.' For Kerith it was a moment of exquisite pain, seeing the old king thus, and she knelt in the path that he must cross and grasped his hand and cried, 'In Jerusalem you danced in the streets for us when you rescued the ark.' He looked at her and for a moment the fires returned to his eyes; then he smiled and said, 'That was a long time ago.'

Kerith, looking up at the tired, white face as it passed on, was tempted to think that the great man's vitality had fled, but later in the governor's quarters she realized her error when he divested himself of his outer robes and sat at ease in a large chair, holding Abishag by his side. Then Kerith saw that his body was still strong and free of lazy fat and she heard him utter words that made her heart leap: 'The walls of the city are excellent. Fetch me the builder.'

'Here is the man,' the governor volunteered, and he pushed Hoopoe forward. But the little engineer stopped to reach for Kerith and together they bowed before the king.

'Are you also the builder of the water tunnel?' David asked.

'I am he,' Hoopoe said with another bow.

'I should like to see it,' the king announced.

'When you are rested,' the governor suggested, but the king said that he would go now to the tunnel, and with hammering excitement Kerith joined the procession to the shaft, where the governor surprised everyone by making a secretly rehearsed speech which ended flamboyantly: 'And we of Makor, who have worked so hard to dig this tunnel, hereby dedicate it to be the David Tunnel.' The crowd cheered, but Kerith noticed that the king paid no attention, while Hoopoe saw that the one man who should have shared in the celebration was not there: Meshab had no intention of paying homage to King David.

A cordon of special ropes, festooned with flowers, had been strung down the stairs; but when David reached the opening he refused to descend and merely looked down into the gaping hole.

'And where does the tunnel run?' he asked.

'You'll see when you reach the bottom,' Hoopoe explained, but the king said that he did not wish to see the bottom.

'Which direction?' he asked impatiently.

Hoopoe was too stunned to respond. It was inconceivable that a king would come so far to see a tunnel and then not explore it. The governor nudged Hoopoe, who still could not reply, so the governor said, 'It runs over there, Your Majesty,' and he led David to the top of the northern wall to show him where the well lay; but with the removal of the waterwall and the clever masking of the former lines, the fumbling governor could not discern where the well lay hidden, and there was a moment of embarrassment, after which he called for Meshab, but the big Moabite had hidden himself and was not available.

'Where's the well?' the governor snapped at Hoopoe.

Kerith nudged her husband and finally he came to the wall, pointing in a confused manner toward a slope which looked like any other. He might have said, 'Your Majesty, we have hidden the well so cleverly that not even the townspeople remember where it is. How could an enemy find it?' Instead he mumbled, 'It's down there.'

'I see,' said David, seeing nothing. In some irritation he left the wall and asked, 'The slaves? What will they be doing now?'

The governor looked at Hoopoe, who had nothing to say, so Kerith volunteered, 'They can be sent to Jerusalem.'

'We need them there,' the king grunted. At this point Abishag indicated that David must return for his rest, but he was in a difficult mood and refused to comply. 'I have been told that you have in Makor a singer who plays on the lyre.'

The governor looked about to see who this might be, and Kerith said to the king, 'There is a fine singer. Shall I fetch him to my house?'

'I'll go to his,' David said, and not one of the officials knew where Gershom lived, but Kerith did, and she led the king to the temple, then to the wine shop, then to the wool merchant's, and finally to the small room in back where Gershom lay sleeping beside a jug of wine. The place was dark and smelled of rancid sheepskins, and the governor started to drag the king away, but David insisted upon entering the room, where he stood with Abishag on one side and Kerith on the other, looking down at the sleeping man.

'It's the king,' Kerith whispered, shaking him.

Gershom looked up, thinking that children had come upon him as they often did, and he saw that the king had lifted his lyre and was trying the seven strings, which were slack upon the pegs. Gershom brushed his hair back, adjusted his dirty garment and pulled himself to his feet. 'It's a good lyre,' the young man said.

'And I've been told that you're a good singer,' the king replied. He handed the young man the instrument and waited. Gershom reached down, took a swig of wine, washed it about his mouth and spat it into the street. He indicated a broken chair, which Abishag brought for the king, but he paid no attention to Kerith or the king's beautiful attendant. He sat on a pile of wool which had not yet been combed and spent some time adjusting himself and tuning the strings. It was a quiet moment, with men in the alleyway pressing against the door as the governor warned them to be silent. It was an apprehensive moment when no one should speak, but Kerith said quietly, 'Sing of the lamb and the bull.'

Gershom looked at her in surprise, as if she were an intruder, but the king asked, 'Is that a fine song?'

'It is one you would like,' Kerith said, and the king nodded.

Gershom was now finished with tuning his lyre, and he played random music until, unexpectedly, he struck a series of harsh, commanding chords which seemed to please the king. Then, in a powerful cry, he called:

'Oh, who among us can speak of Yahweh?
Who knows his mysterious ways?
He is in the whimper of the lamb I seek at night,
Lo, he is in the stamping of the wild bull.'

And the manner in which he changed from the initial cry of longing to the simplicity of the night scene, then to the vigor of the bull's actions pleased the king, and he sat back in the solitary chair, listening to the artistry of the young man, and after more than an hour of songs the old king took the lyre himself and let his fingers fall across the strings, but he did not try to sing. Tears came to his eyes and he sat for some time with the lyre, until Abishag said quietly, 'Now we must retire,' and he followed her like an obedient child.

That night there was singing in the governor's house, which marked the first time that Gershom had been invited into that august center, and on succeeding days the king repeatedly asked the young man to sing for him; and the time came when David was prepared to take the lyre himself and to sing some of the glorious compositions which he had offered Yahweh in the young years when he was loved as the sweet singer of Israel, and the two psalmists sang together for many hours. On the fourth day, when the king had not yet seen more of the tunnel than the mouth of the square shaft, he concluded a singing session by stating firmly, 'When I return to Jerusalem this young man shall accompany me,' and he put his arm about Gershom as though the latter were his son.

When King David uttered this command Kerith was sitting beside him and the words reached her with climactic force. The visit of the king had been like a series of hammer blows, coming at the end of six years of metaphysical turmoil: she had witnessed the humiliation of her husband and had seen the low regard in which a man like King David held the mere digging of a tunnel; she had also seen the clarity of judgment with which he had selected Gershom as the one talent in Makor worth taking to the capital. All that King David did placed the abstract wisdom of Jerusalem athwart the pragmatic values of Makor, for without knowing it the king had acted as if he wished to prove her tentative conclusions correct. For a brief spell following the departure of General Amram she had allowed Jabaal and Meshab to divert her attention from Jerusalem and she had begun to doubt her own conclusions; but now King David and Gershom fortified them and she would never again be deterred from doing what she had long ago decided was right. She was ready to take the decisive steps that would lead her to the City of David.

When the singing ended she walked boldly with Gershom to his hovel, and at the doorway she said quietly, 'When you go with the king to Jerusalem, I shall go with you.'

He was in the act of throwing his lyre onto a pile of wool and he did not bother even to break the rhythm of his arm. 'I want you to,' he said, without looking at her.

'Tonight I will stay here,' she said, but even with those words they were afraid to embrace.

Slowly she walked home, considering what she must tell Hoopoe, but when she entered the house by the shaft that had accomplished so little she said simply, 'I am going to Jerusalem. With Gershom. I shall live with him the rest of my life.'

Later she recalled that as she said these words her fat little husband looked just like a hoopoe bird, twisting his neck this way and that, as if he were seeking a hole in which to sink his foolish, his lovable, his laughable head. 'You mustn't,' he pleaded, following her from room to room as she packed a few belongings. When they reached the room where they had spent their passionate nights he said, 'You can take the rope of glass,' but she left it behind, not willing to hurt him by saying that it was gaudy Phoenician ware; but the chunk of amber set in Persian silver she took.

At the door of the house, standing by the great empty shaft that had mocked her plans, she said good-bye to the pathetic little engineer, and when he tried in trembling voice to ask why this wrong thing was happening, she said at last, 'Stay with Makor and the old gods, I cannot.' And she was gone.

In his desolation, alone with two children that his wife had deserted and the tunnel that the king did not want, Hoopoe sought the one man who could give him counsel. In the gray and somber twilight he went to the postern gate where Meshab was finishing the tower that would hide the telltale marks and there in his perplexity he asked the Moabite to reason with Kerith, but to his surprise Meshab refused to leave the tower. 'I shall keep hidden until King David leaves,' he explained.

'But why?' Hoopoe asked. All that was happening confused him.

'King David bears deep hatred for my people.'

'But he's part Moabite himself,' Hoopoe protested, and his need for help was so obvious that Meshab, in spite of what he knew might happen, laid down his trowel, washed his hands and consented to talk with Kerith; but as the two men left the wall, one of King David's captains spotted the Moabite and ran crying through the streets, 'The assassin of Moab is among us.' At first Meshab tried to run back to the wall, but gleaming spears cut off that escape, so he did what he had long planned to do if trapped as he now was. He ran past the shaft, along the curving street that led from the postern gate and into the temple, where he threw himself upon the altar, clutching the stone horns.

Hoopoe had scarcely reached him in the sanctuary when soldiers appeared at the door, only to draw back when they saw what action the Moabite had taken, but shortly King David himself, unattended by Abishag, alone and old and white with fury, strode to the altar. 'Are you the Meshab whose life I spared in Moab?'

'The same. I seek your sanctuary.'

'Did you not kill Jerebash, the brother of Amram?'

'In battle, yes.'

'And throw down the temple to Yahweh?'

'In siege, yes.'

'You have no sanctuary.'

'I plead the sanctuary you ordained.'

'I refuse it!' David thundered. 'I saved you once and you warred against me. Guards! Seize him!'

A shocking fight marred the silence of the temple, for Meshab had no intention of being taken alive, and the struggle became more violent when Hoopoe sprang to the defense of his friend and shouted at the king, 'He is a freedman claiming sanctuary.'

'He defied Yahweh!' David cried, half insane.

Spurred on by the king the guards knocked Hoopoe aside, but even as he fell to the floor he shouted once more, 'David! Don't defile your own sanctuary.' Then a guard kicked him in the mouth, bringing blood that choked him.

The guards were now free to concentrate on the Moabite, but he defended himself with mighty strength until ten dragged him from the altar, causing it to crash to the floor, where it broke into two pieces, and the sight of this shattered altar infuriated David even more: he was a man capable of nursing terrible enmities and he cried, 'Slay him!' And seven came at the former slave with spears, and his powerful arms gathered them to his chest as flint sickles once gathered wheat, and he fell at the feet of the king, where he was stabbed many times until his blood flowed across the temple floor to where Hoopoe lay. A priest, reveling in the horror, chanted, 'Yahweh is revenged. Thus Yahweh strikes those who oppose him.'

Finally the young girl Abishag found her king in the bloodstained temple and took him by the hand and led him to his couch. Then he had time to reflect upon the vengeful thing he had done, and he beat his forehead with his fist and repented this latest in a long chain of sudden passions that had scarred his life. He found that he could not banish from his mind the figure of the Moabite freedman clutching at the altar, nor from hearing the pleas for sanctuary. The execution had been an impulsive, ugly outburst and already David was haunted by regret.

In deepening repentance he asked for the young lyrist, whose consolation he needed, and messengers went to the small room at the back of the wool store, where they found not only Gershom but Kerith, kneeling over a small bundle of clothes which she had brought from her husband's house; and when the messenger told Gershom that he must bring his kinnor to comfort the king, the psalmist said, 'I must bring Kerith, too. I cannot leave her here.' And when he passed through the streets to serve his king, Kerith walked behind, wearing a gold-colored robe and an amber amulet.

They found King David huddled in a corner of the governor's quarters, Abishag at his side and holding his left hand. He was ashen with remorse, an old man tormented by ghosts—the latest less than an hour old. 'I have betrayed my own law,' he mumbled and he would have confessed more, but Gershom took a stool by the door and as Kerith sat on the floor beside his feet he began playing some of his songs, and he kept to those the king had already heard. And as he plucked the seven-stringed lyre, bringing from it sounds like the wind and the movement of lambs across the fields in spring, the old king lost his bitterness and he closed his eyes as if he were asleep, but the fear of loneliness with which he clutched the hand of Abishag proved that he was well awake and listening with great longing to the words of the young singer.

After Gershom had reviewed songs which the king knew, he was inspired, for some reason that he could never thereafter explain, to launch into a song which he had composed some years before on a day in the mountains when he had been wondering what things the ideal king would do; and his words echoed across that white room as the conversation between the people of Israel and their king:

> 'Rejoice in Yahweh, you righteous men,
>   For praise becomes the upright.
> Give thanks to Yahweh with the lyre,
> Sing praises with a psaltery of ten strings.
> Sing to him a new song.
> Play skillfully with shouts of joy.
>
> For the word of Yahweh is upright.
> His works are established in truth,
> And he loveth righteousness and justice.'

The last three lines of the poem were but the preface to ideas of the kingly state, but they struck the guilty king with such vigor that without opening his eyes he signaled with his right hand that the music was to stop. He rose, and still self-blinded groped his way a few steps across the room, then fell on the floor, on his knees and elbows, from which position he beat his head several times on the floor until Abishag rescued him and forced him to open his eyes and make his way back to his chair.

'I have betrayed Yahweh,' the old man wept. 'All my life I have done those things that Yahweh has condemned. At whose hand was the Moabite slain but mine? At whose altar but mine?' He shivered with the memory of the profanation and pleaded, 'Tell me of the Moabite.'

And Kerith, still seated on the floor, said, 'He was a just man. In darkness he built the David Tunnel to save your town. When my husband was absent it was the Moabite who protected me. When he was freed from slavery he remained with us to finish the king's tunnel. Meshab was a man that I shall remember with tears the rest of my life.'

The simple words were exactly those that King David wished to hear, the eulogy for a brave warrior and a good man. 'Sit on my right hand,' he said to Kerith, and she took the position that she would often know in the king's dying years; and to her David said, 'The Moabite was valiant in battle, and I slew him. He was a vigorous defender of his gods, and I caused him to be slain. What have I done this day?'

The white-haired old man rocked back and forth between the two women who guarded him, and at last he said to Abishag, 'Fetch me the kinnor,' but when he took the instrument which long ago he had played before King Saul he did not play it in the ordinary sense, as Gershom had been doing; he allowed his tired hands to fall across the strings in aimless fashion, building chords of no pattern and with no rhythm, and when the music had taken for him a form that the others could not hear, he chanted a psalm which he had composed many years before and which he often remembered in these late years:

> 'Oh Yahweh, do not rebuke me in your anger,
> And do not chastise me in your wrath.
>> Have mercy upon me, for I am weak,
>> Heal me, for my bones tremble.
>> I tremble very much.
>> But you, O Yahweh, how long?
>
>> Return, O Yahweh, save me.
> Deliver me in accord with your reliability.
>> If I die I cannot sing to you,
>> For who in the grave can give you praises?
>> I am weary of my groaning.'

He continued his lament for human weakness, referring to the anguish he had known so often throughout his turbulent life, and those four who sat in that room, those misfit four who had gathered to converse with Yahweh—the white-haired king who had committed both adultery and murder, the exquisite child who had been cynically chosen to be an old man's comfort and his last bedfellow, the loyal wife who was about to betray one of the truly good men of Israel, and the stranger whose crimes were not spelled out—that night those four seekers after Yahweh represented the future generations of the world who would respond to the cry of grief as they now did. The Judaism that King David had inherited was often a cold religion, rigorous and even forbidding, but it was saved by this outcry of human passion which David was now uttering and which Gershom had uttered on the hills. Remote and removed, there was Yahweh; here in the actuality of the white room there was a human heart approaching the end of its allotted seventy years; and between the two there was a passionate dialogue expressed in song:

'Each night I make my bed swim.
I drench my couch with my tears.
My eye has wasted away from grief . . .
O evildoers, go away from me,
For Yahweh has heard the sound of my weeping.'

Thus David lamented, and the listeners in the night accepted the heartbreak of
the vengeful old king as part of their own experience. Fully as much as the
rigorous laws, his cry would become a part of Judaism.

Kerith saw Hoopoe no more. She spent that night in the hovel at the wool
merchant's, and in the morning when the royal procession turned southward to
Megiddo and thence to Jerusalem she was lost somewhere in the motley,
marching to the city she had been so determined to see. It was the
transformation of Gershom the outcast that was the more spectacular, for he
became in Jerusalem the keeper of the king's music, directing the scribes as
they collected on clay tablets many of the poems written by the king, and in the
compilation appeared not a few written by Gershom himself. In time they
passed into the liturgy of Judaism; they were sung in plain chant throughout
the Presbyterian churches of Scotland; they became the hymns of Australia and
the church music of South Africa; they were sung to many different tunes in
many different religions, for wherever the words were read they were
recognized as part of the authentic cry of man seeking his god, for Gershom was
a singer, a man who could formulate words into patterns, and his words would
live forever.

Hoopoe experienced a different transformation. When King David departed
for Jerusalem, having ignored the tunnel, the heartbroken engineer climbed to
the town walls like a farmer from the countryside or a yellow-stained
Phoenician from the dye vats, and there he joined the mob as it shouted farewell
to the great king. Hoopoe tried vainly to see where Kerith was, but she kept
herself hidden. Nor was the king visible, nor Abishag nor Gershom; the four
vanished from his life like ghosts that had come to wreak horror during a windy
night and had fled with the dawn.

For some time he could not believe either that they had come or that they had
gone. The governor, remembering that Hoopoe had abused the king at the
death of the Moabite, thereafter refused to speak with the little man. With his
slaves gone to Jerusalem, no further commissions of any importance were
found for him. Townspeople, recounting the story of how his wife had run
away with Gershom, made ballads of the affair to which they added the earlier
escapade with General Amram, so that one of the most contradictory women
who had ever lived in Makor was debased into a simple slut, and sometimes
even Hoopoe heard men at the wine shop singing of her.

'They don't understand,' he muttered to himself. In the house by the shaft
he was left with two children who were destined to preserve the Family of Ur
for future generations, but they took no interest in the shaft where women
walked up and down, year after year, bringing into the city the sweet water
from the hidden well. In Hoopoe's lifetime the defenses of Makor–all due to
his building genius–were not put to the test, so the townspeople could not
appreciate what a brilliant thing he had accomplished; they began to take the
well and the walls for granted, and as Hoopoe grew older they remembered him
only as a queer little man who ran about the town poking his head into this hole
or another, finding nothing.

'No man in Makor has a more appropriate name than Hoopoe,' they said, and the older he grew the more pathetic he became in their eyes: a chubby little man with no wife, no job, few friends. When Solomon became king and there was much building in Jerusalem, with boats shuttling back and forth between Accho and Tyre, Hoopoe developed the illusion that he would soon be called to the capital to help the resplendent king, but in the beautiful city his name was unknown, and he was not sent for.

When he was an old man he disappeared for some time, and his unloving children suspected, or perhaps even hoped, that he was dead; but he was in the depths of the tunnel, that flawless piece of engineering which he alone had conceived, and he had brought with him a hammer and chisel and a small wooden scaffold from which he worked on the ceiling for several days. Young women passing beneath brought him a little food and speculated upon what he was doing.

'Is the roof going to fall?' they enquired.

'Have rats gnawed a hole downwards from the fields?' they teased not even knowing that it was he who had built the David Tunnel.

Hoopoe said nothing but kept chipping away, holding a blanket on the scaffold lest bits of stone fall on the heads of the patient women who walked back and forth. Finally he finished, and although he could not be aware of the fact, walked for the last time through his beautiful construction. At the well the great crisscross tiers of rock protected the roof from any trespass and would remain in position–a part of the earth–for three thousand years. The deep caves of antiquity were sealed and hidden. The well itself was cold and sweet and secure, sending forth as much water as the people needed, and the clean, fair tunnel climbed at its preordained pace to the foot of the shaft, which rose with its two lovely, twisting pairs of stairways into the sunlight.

As he climbed out of the shaft for the last time he went through the postern gate to the cemetery beside which, years ago, he had buried Meshab the Moabite when no others would touch him, and there he sat on the grave recalling their good days of friendship and shared work, perhaps the only thing an engineer remembers. It was a spring day and he was inspired to climb the mountain where Baal resided, for he would like to be with his old god once more; but it was a steep path and as he rose from the Moabite's grave a sudden dizziness overtook him, and he sensed that death was at hand, and he sat down again.

'Almighty Yahweh,' he prayed, 'accept me at the end of my days.' And he was dead.

Of Gershom the Psalmist, his words echoed to the end of the world. Of Hoopoe the Builder, his great square shaft was ultimately filled with rubble, and his tunnel forgotten. For the poet, regardless of the expense in human lives, had glimpsed the true face of Yahweh and had dedicated himself to the one god. But the builder had early found himself trapped between Baal, whom he knew to exist in the earth, and Yahweh, whom he was willing to accept as the unseen deity; and it is impossible for any man to vacillate between two gods: if he tries, he is slowly eroded. On the afternoon of his death Hoopoe recognized these facts and wished that he had had the clear understanding of King David and Gershom and his beloved wife Kerith. But their understanding had been denied him and he died a useless old man, trapped by his gods.

But in the autumn of 1964, in the month of Bul–when rain clouds make their first tentative appearance over the Carmel and farmers gather wood for winter fires–a descendant of the great Family of Ur stumbled upon the long-forgotten tunnel, and shortly it was excavated, with photographs of the notable work becoming common throughout the world. Engineers hailed it as a masterpiece of construction, 'one of the first great surveying feats,' and in an age that appreciated science many words were written on the timeless message which the unknown engineer of Makor had sent the world; a French philosopher claimed that 'this mute genius of the Makor water system speaks to modern man more cogently than those who wrote the Psalms, for he exemplified in work that portion of the divine spirit which has always prized acts as much as words. His tunnel is a psalm in fact, the song of those who accomplish God's work.'

And then one day the American archaeologist John Cullinane would discover the real psalm of Tell Makor. Each part of the tunnel would by then have been investigated by experts, who would cleverly deduce how the unknown builder must have operated: they would reason that he had punched two small tunnels through the rock, joining them somewhere near the middle, then broadening them out to absorb the error, but they would not be able to guess how he had established his pitch and headings underground, for age and lichen had dimmed the ceiling so that carvings which existed there were long overlooked. But on this day Cullinane would be walking through the tunnel guided by a cheap flashlight and his wondering eye would catch a kind of shadow on the rocks above. Calling for a ladder he would examine the damp roof, then summon his assistants. With infrared photography, with talcum powder and camel's-hair brushes, the archaeologists would lay bare a dedication whose effect upon scholarship would be pronounced for several reasons. It would provide one of the earliest samples of Hebrew writing; establish an anchor for a sure chronology; and evoke from the past the figure of a real human being wrestling with problems. The same French philosopher would title this inscription 'The Psalm of the Tunnel Builder,' under which title it would serve to summarize the age:

Jabaal of Makor built this David Tunnel. Using six flags he found the secret. Using white cords he probed the earth. Using iron from Accho he cut the rock. But without Meshab the Moabite nothing. Jabaal worked from the well and wandered. Meshab from the shaft and true. For Meshab was his brother and is now dead, slain by King David. From the heavens Yahweh directed. From the earth Baal. Praise to the gods who sustain us.

LEVEL XI

The Voice of Gomer

Found at Makor–Babylonian armament (see chapter 1). First
piece: Iron spearhead cast in the city of Urartu (Ararat) on the
northern shore of Lake Van in Asia Minor, 684 B.C.E., and
traded southward to Babylonia in exchange for woven fabrics.
Originally fitted to the end of a four-foot cedar stave imported
from Tyre. Second piece: Helmet in the Assyrian style, made of
hammered bronze fitted with bronze rivets, made in 653 B.C.E.
in the city of Shushan (Susa), capital of Elam on the border
between Babylonia and Persia and traditionally antagonistic to
the former. Deposited at Makor in late summer, 605 B.C.E.

These were the generations when Yahweh smote his Hebrews, for still he
found them a stiff-necked people.

To punish them he used the Assyrians. In 733 B.C.E. he unleashed Tiglath-
pileser III from Nineveh, and of his depredations the Bible says; 'In the days of
Pekah king of Israel came Tiglath-pileser king of Assyria . . . and took Hazor,
and Gilead, and Galilee, all the land of Naphtali, and carried them captive to
Assyria.' In this onslaught 185,000 people were slain and 591 towns were
ravaged, but not Makor, for the defenses erected by Jabaal the Hoopoe held off
the invaders through a formidable siege until an agreement of suzerainty was
worked out. But in 701 B.C.E. Sennacherib came out of the north, and of him the
Bible says: 'Now in the fourteenth year of king Hezekia did Sennacherib king of
Assyria come up against all the fenced cities of Judah, and took them.' Even
against this scourge Makor defended itself, protected by its David Tunnel,
until at last the Assyrians appealed for negotiation, whereupon the community
opened its zigzag gate voluntarily. At dawn Sennacherib entered the town; by
noon he had assembled the tribute; and at dusk there was not a single house
standing. Makor, gutted and burned, its walls thrown down in many places,
had ceased to exist, and its Hebrew inhabitants were led way in slavery to join
those Ten Tribes of the north who would henceforth be lost to history if not to
legend: fanciful writers would try to prove that these lost Jews found new
existence as Britons, Etruscans, Hindus, Japanese or Eskimos.

To castigate his Hebrews, Yahweh also used the Babylonians. In the year
612 B.C.E. this rising power humbled Nineveh, driving the Assyrians from the
two rivers, and in 605 the mighty Nebuchadrezzar led his troops into one of the
significant battles of history at Carchemish along the banks of the Euphrates.
Of him the Bible says: 'For thus saith the Lord God; Behold, I will bring upon
Tyrus Nebuchadrezzar king of Babylon, a king of kings, from the north, with
horses, and with chariots, and with horsemen, and companies, and much
people. He shall slay with the sword thy daughters in the field: and he shall
make a fort against thee, and cast a mount against thee, and lift up the buckler
against thee. And he shall set engines of war against thy walls, and with his axes
he shall break down thy towers.' And these things Nebuchadrezzar did.

And invariably Yahweh used the Egyptians to accomplish his purposes, throwing them sometimes against Assyria, sometimes against Babylonia, but always against the Hebrews, so that during these dynastic struggles the armies of Egypt were much seen in the Galilee; regardless of who the enemy was, the battles were apt to be fought here. For example, in 609 B.C.E. Josiah, one of the wisest kings the Hebrews were to produce, must have suffered a temporary derangement, for he entered a pact of mutual support on the side of upstart Babylon against established Egypt and Assyria. Of the pitiful battle that resulted the Bible says: 'Necho king of Egypt came up to fight against Carchemish by Euphrates: and Judah went out against him.' The confrontation between Egyptian and Hebrew took place at Megiddo, that recurring site of Armageddon, and the good king Josiah was slain. Always the Egyptians were a threat.

During these turbulent years the stubborn Family of Ur managed to maintain Makor as a minor outpost in no way comparable to its predecessors. Even the town wall, built by Jabaal the Hoopoe in the reign of King David, existed only in fragments, while the principal street, if it could be called such, ran from the main gate to the postern past a miserable collection of buildings. Where a score of enticing shops had once flourished, offering wares from all parts of the Mediterranean, two now offered little. Citizens eked out a frugal existence, for the luxury that had characterized the days of David and Solomon was no more.

At opposite ends of the Water Street stood two houses which summarized the new Makor. By the main gate, in a low, poorly built establishment that rambled over a considerable area and was kept to one floor because Makor could no longer afford timber, lived Jeremoth, scion of the Family of Ur and willing to serve as governor for whatever empire ruled the valleys. He was fifty-two years old, a resolute and crafty man whose ancestors, by one trick or another, had kept the town intact through the civil war that had destroyed the empire of King Solomon and through two hundred years of unremitting Phoenician, Aramaean, Assyrian and Egyptian pressures. In the mournful chaos of those years the Family of Ur had trimmed its banners to each new conqueror marching up to the battered walls. In siege, in pestilence and in terror the determined men of Ur had somehow managed to hold on to their olive trees south of the town and to some kind of governmental residence near the main gate.

Jeremoth, black-bearded, wiry and courageous beyond most of the men in his town, was governed by one fixed idea: this continuity of occupation must be preserved. If the erupting power of Babylon made war against Egypt inevitable, there would have to be war, and Makor would again be trapped between the armies; but if guile and persuasion could preserve the little town, then he was prepared to temporize with anyone. He had five daughters, four of them married to leading merchants and farmers, and he also had a group of brothers who were just as tough as he. Like many families in Makor they had relapsed into being Canaanites who worshipped Baal on the mountain back of the town, and as a well-disciplined unit they relied on the hope there would always be some trick whereby they could keep their holdings intact, diminished though they might be.

At the other end of the Water Street, cramped into a corner near the ruins of the postern gate, stood a small one-room house made of unbaked clay bricks. It had an earthen floor, no furniture, only one window, and the clinging smell of meanness and poverty. It was the home of Gomer the widow, a tall, gaunt woman of fifty-eight who had known a difficult life. An ugly girl, she had married late as the third wife of a miserable man who had derided her in public for being childless and who used her as a slave. After many years, and as the result of a scene she had tried to erase from her memory—Egyptian soldiers rioting inside the walls—she had become pregnant, and the wretched old man had suspected that the child was not his. In public he was afraid to challenge her lest he himself look foolish, but in the privacy of their mean home he had abused her; yet when he died it was she and not his earlier wives who tended to his burial.

She had only his one child, a son whom she had named Rimmon, after the pomegranate, hoping that like the seeds of that fruit he might have many children to send her line forward, and Rimmon had grown into a handsome young man of twenty-two whom the young girls of the town admired and who now held the job of supervising Governor Jeremoth's olive grove. He and his mother were staunch supporters of Yahweh, the Hebrew god, but as a man who worked in the fields for a Canaanite, Rimmon found it prudent to worship Baal as well—a fact which he did not discuss with his mother.

Gomer was a gawky, forbidding woman. Her hair was not even a clean gray, which would have brought her respect; it was a muddy gray. Her eyes were not clear nor was her skin attractive. She had worked so hard that she walked with a stoop which made her seem older than she was, and the only thing about her that was appealing was her soft, quiet voice, hushed through half a century of obeying first her father, then her abusive husband, and finally her handsome son. She spoke quietly, as if she were still in the fields, living in the harvest booth with her father as he guarded the barley and the vines. In her long life those were the only days she remembered with affection, the happy days of harvest time when men built booths so as to be near the produce of their lands.

Now, in the year 606 B.C.E., in the days before Ethanim, the month of feasts—when heat from the desert spread over the land, when late grapes were ripening for the wine presses, and when great Egypt and Babylonia were getting ready to tear at each other while Greece gathered strength in the west—Gomer left her mean house by the postern gate, balanced a clay jug on her head, and descended the gaping shaft that cut into the earth not far from her home. By a considerable margin she was the oldest woman lugging water, and her long spare figure in tattered sackcloth looked out of place as she patiently went down the familiar steps in the company of young wives and slave girls. But since she had no slave or daughter-in-law to help her she was forced to fetch the water for herself.

She had descended to the well, had filled her jug and started her return journey, when she came to a section of the David Tunnel where the oil lamp that hung over the water could no longer be seen, yet where the daylight coming down the shaft brought little illumination, and in this dark passage she heard a voice saying to her, 'Gomer, widow of Israel! Take your son up to Jerusalem, that he may cast his eyes upon my city.' She looked around to find who had spoken, but there was only darkness, and she thought that one of the younger women had hidden to taunt her, for often they made fun of her; but again the voice surrounded her, and this time she was certain that it could not belong to any woman. It said, 'Gomer, let your son see Jerusalem.'

Not in fear but in bewilderment she left the tunnel and climbed the shaft, ignoring the calls of younger women who were descending by the other stairs, and in a kind of trance she sought for her son, but he had already gone to the olive press, so she put her jug down, went to the main gate and crossed the Damascus road, entering the olive grove belonging to Governor Jeremoth. After a few moments she saw her son working at the press, that ancient system of square stone pits cut into the solid rock and connected by lead pipes so that the settled oil could fall and filter of its own weight. Fortunately, she stopped before coming upon her son, for he was kneeling by the press and she realized that he was saying his morning prayers to Baal, pleading for a good run of oil. She waited until he was finished, disturbed that he should be trafficking with Baal on this particular morning, then went to him.

As always, when she came upon him suddenly, she was impressed anew with what she could only call his radiance: like many of the Hebrews he was bold and freckle-faced, tall and with a quick intelligence. As the son of a widow who was almost a pauper, he had worked in the fields all his life and could neither read nor write, but he had learned from his mother the cherished stories of his people, particularly the steps whereby Yahweh had revealed himself to the Hebrews. At twenty-two he was a young laborer in charge of the one operation which brought surplus money into Makor, so he prayed to Yahweh for moral guidance in the conduct of his life and to Baal for success in his daily work.

Under the fruitful trees Gomer asked, 'Rimmon, have you made any plans for going up to Jerusalem?'

'No.'

'Have you ever wanted to go?'

'No.'

She said no more. Returning home she went about her business of trying to borrow some scraps of meat to make a lentil soup for the evening meal of her hungry son, but there was scarcely any food, so at midday she walked along the Water Street until she came to the rambling house in which Governor Jeremoth lived, and there she appealed to the various women living in the house for any sewing or mending jobs which they might have. None could be found, but the governor's wife took pity on her and said, 'My daughter Mikal has been asking for a new white robe in case she accompanies her father to Jerusalem for the feasts.' And she summoned Mikal, a small, dark girl of eighteen, about whom there was much speculation since she was not yet married. She was a lively girl, appreciated by men and women alike, for she had a merry laughter and a birdlike way of tilting her head to smile at whoever addressed her.

Mikal was pleased that the making of her new dress was to be turned over to Gomer, for she had found the older woman pleasant to work with: Gomer was never late, never unpleasant, never delinquent in getting the dress of the undergarment finished as planned. In addition, she had a peasant's dignity, talking quietly of interesting matters as she worked, and on this fateful afternoon Mikal and Gomer renewed their pleasant friendship.

But next morning as the widow came back through the David Tunnel, her jug filled with water, she was halted as if a mighty hand were obstructing the passageway and a voice said to her, 'For the salvation of the world it is essential that Rimmon see Jerusalem.'

Gomer tried to pass the barrier but could not; her feet were nailed to the tunnel floor. 'Are you Yahweh?' she asked.

'I am that I am,' the voice replied, echoing from all sides. 'And I command you: Take your son up to Jerusalem!'

The invisible barrier was removed, and after a few hesitant steps Gomer could see daylight coming from the shaft. She ran home and forced all thoughts of the tunnel from her mind. She worked upon Mikal's white dress as if it were the sole undertaking in the world, and her preoccupation was so complete that she was able to bury all thought of Yahweh and Rimmon and Jerusalem. But in the evening, when the voice of cattle came to the gate, and when she could no longer see to thread the needle, she again asked her returning son if he wished to visit Jerusalem.

'No. That's for priests.'

'You have no desire to see the City of David?'

'You've never seen it. Why should I?'

'I've always wanted to,' she said in the darkness.

'Why didn't you go?'

'Can a widow go to Jerusalem? At the Feast of Tabernacles? Who would build her a booth?'

He could not see her face, but it had become transfused with yearning. Like many Hebrews of her generation she longed for Jerusalem as bees long for spring to open the flowers or as lions trapped in the valley hunger for the hills. It was the golden city, the site of the temple, the focus of worship, the target of longing. No other city in the world until the advent of Rome would have the profound effect upon its adherents that Jerusalem had upon the Hebrews, and this in spite of the evil days that had befallen the land. After the death of Solomon the vast empire of King David had degenerated into civil war, splitting into two separate nations, Israel on the north, with its capital at Samaria, and Judah in the south, with its capital at Jerusalem. But with the conquests of Sennacherib the northern kingdom was practically exterminated, as the Bible says: 'Then the king of Assyria came up throughout all the land, and went up to Samaria, and besieged it three years. In the ninth year of Hoshea the king of Assyria took Samaria, and carried Israel away into Assyria, and placed them in Halah and in Habor by the river of Gozan, and in the cities of the Medes.' However, a remnant of Hebrews continued to exist in towns like Makor, subservient to alien rulers and forbidden to make pilgrimages to Jerusalem. Even so, faithful northerners like Gomer still maintained the City of David as their earthly goal.

'For more than fifty years Jerusalem has been before my eyes,' Gomer said.

'I'm afraid you won't see it now,' her son replied, not mockingly.

'Suppose I said tonight, "In the morning we shall go up to Jerusalem"?'

Rimmon laughed. 'We have no money. I must watch the olive press and you must finish the garment.'

Those were Gomer's ideas, too, and she sadly dismissed from her mind any plans for going to Jerusalem; but next morning in the David Tunnel she was stopped for the third time, and the voice said like the roar of a lion, 'Gomer, widow of Israel, for the third time, take your son and go up to Jerusalem, or the penalty will rest upon your children's children till the end of days.'

In the darkness she answered obediently, 'I will take my son to Jerusalem, but may I halt here until the white dress is finished?'

There was a silence, as if the presence were spending his time in judging this humble request, and after a while the voice said, 'You are a woman who earns her bread by sewing. For you it is proper first to finish the work and then to leave for Jerusalem.' And Yahweh bided his time.

It took Gomer two days of concentrated work to complete the dress, and

when she fitted it on the governor's daughter that young woman seemed more
beautiful than ever. 'I shall wear it at the dancing,' she said with excitement.

'Then you're going to Jerusalem?' Gomer asked.

'Father has decided. It's been four years, and as governor . . .' The girl grew
grave, with shadows across her youthful face. 'Do you think the Egyptians will
call us to war again?'

'The Assyrians and the Babylonians and the Egyptians and the Phoenicians
and the Aramaeans,' Gomer recited as she cut the last threads, 'they call us to
war perpetually. Your father has protected us well and I'm glad that he's going
to Jerusalem to talk with the leaders of Judah.' She hesitated. 'Would you
please ask him if he could pay me today?'

'Of course!' the young woman said, and she ran to find her father, but when
he heard of the widow's unusual request he came into the sewing room,
showing displeasure.

'Have the people of Jeremoth's house ever failed to pay?' he demanded.
Ordinarily a widow like Gomer would have been overawed by the governor, for
he could be a frightening man, with unsympathetic eyes that had gazed with
equal courage upon disaster and triumph. He had governed Makor under seven
different rulers and in doing so had developed a hardness that almost glittered.

But this was not an ordinary day nor was Gomer any longer an ordinary
woman: she had been commanded by Yahweh to perform an act upon which
the salvation of the world depended, and Governor Jeremoth did not cow her.
In her soft voice she said, 'You have always paid, sir. But in the morning my son
and I must leave for Jerusalem . . .'

'What?'

'This year we shall build our booth in the holy city.'

'You?' the governor sputtered, then he asked, 'Does Rimmon know of this?'

'Not yet, but . . .'

In amused contempt the governor turned away from Gomer and directed
one of his guards to summon Rimmon from the olive press, and when the
young foreman stood before him Jeremoth said, 'Rimmon, your mother tells
me that you're going up to Jerusalem tomorrow morning. Leaving my groves
without permission.'

'Jerusalem?' the young man repeated in surprise. 'I have no plans . . .'

Then came the moment of decision, that fragile moment which was to
determine so much of Makor's history in the months ahead. Gomer, seeing the
contempt of the governor and her son's unwillingness to oppose him, was
briefly tempted to abandon her plans, but when she tried to withdraw her
statement she found herself incapable of doing so. The words of retreat simply
would not come from her throat. Instead, she looked directly at the governor
and said in a low, soft voice marked by an intensity she had never shown before,
'It is commanded that I take my son to Jerusalem tomorrow.'

As soon as she said the words, she knew that she had evaded the one central
problem of this day: it had not been intended for her to say, 'It is commanded';
she should have said, 'Yahweh commands.' But as a poor widow of humble
origins she had neither the courage nor the arrogance to use that dreadful
sentence. This day she avoided the issue and placed the responsibility upon an
anonymous force. 'It is commanded,' she said.

But even that evasion was sufficient, for something transpired in the room
that Governor Jeremoth could not have explained. Somehow he knew who had
done the commanding; with the Hebrews these mysteries occasionally

happened and he avoided a confrontation in which he did not consider himself involved. A Canaanite rather than a Hebrew, a man of Baal rather than of Yahweh, he was nevertheless eager, as a practical politician, to avoid antagonizing any god at a time when the shadows of Egypt and Babylon loomed so large across the Galilee, and it was this that kept him from challenging Gomer. To his daughter's surprise and to Rimmon's, too, he announced, 'Very well, Gomer. Here's your bag of money. Build the best booth in Jerusalem.'

Rimmon tried to apologize, 'Sir, I had nothing to do . . .' but the governor was gone, glad to have escaped the onus of decision. Thus the first of the critical challenges that would mark this pivotal age had occurred, although at the time neither Gomer nor Jeremoth recognized it. And Gomer of the soft voice had prevailed.

The journey up to Jerusalem in that hot month of Ethanim was, as Yahweh had intended, an experience that Rimmon would never forget, although while undergoing it he perceived it as a physical adventure rather than as a spiritual ascent. It was a distance of more than ninety miles over difficult and wearing terrain, to be finished in the hot time of autumn, so that the journey occupied eight days. Mother and son left the zigzag gate at dawn, a tall pair dressed in the cheapest clothes, shod in heavy sandals and carrying staves. On their backs they carried a little food, in their purses a few pieces of silver, but Rimmon had with him an additional item that would prove of considerable value: lengths of cord with which to build his booth on the slopes leading up to Jerusalem's walls.

Leading his gaunt mother, who had no idea as to where the city lay, Rimmon started south through the olive grove, where he was minded to ask Baal to tend the trees during his absence; but when he started to kneel by the olive press his mother took him by the arm, saying, 'There is no Baal, forevermore,' and her grip was like the clutch of iron upon his muscles and turned him away. He led her through the dark swamp, where insects tormented them, across the Kishon River and up to the fortress city of Megiddo, where they wept for the good king who had recently been slain in his futile war against the Egyptians.

From this mournful spot they dropped down to Samaria, the capital city of the former kingdom of Israel, a strange place occupied by aliens forcibly settled there by the father of Sennacherib, and through the years these strangers had perfected a unique religion, borrowed from the Hebrews but a faith apart. Samaria both fascinated and repelled the travellers, and they gladly left it to climb to Bethel, where a problem of serious proportion confronted them, for this town had always marked the southern outpost of Israel and had served as a kind of watchdog to keep northerners from crossing the border in their attempts to visit Jerusalem. Even now many in Bethel considered it disloyal for a man of fighting age like Rimmon to leave the north, and certain fanatics tried to prevent him from doing so. But soft-spoken Gomer countered their arguments, saying, 'I am an old woman who must see Jerusalem before I die,' and she led her son through the taunting Bethelites until she reached the village of Anathoth, where prophets lived, and from there she and her son began the steep ascent to Jerusalem.

In the first hours they climbed without actually seeing the noble city, but they were assured that they were on the right path by the hundreds of other pilgrims streaming in from outlying regions to celebrate in Jerusalem the high holy days which marked the beginning of each new year.

There were young priests from Dan and date farmers from the shores of Galilee come down to pray for a bountiful harvest. There were Hebrew dyers who kept their vats in the seaport city of Accho, nestled among Aramaean and Cypriot merchants. There were Hebrews from Samaria who had doggedly held to their own religion amidst the enemy, and there were poor villagers from Shunem, where King David had found his last and greatest concubine, the sweet child Abishag. Those who could afford to do so led animals for sacrifice at the temple altars, and one could hear the lowing of cattle and the cry of sheep. Others carried chickens intended for their own consumption and some women had white doves captured in cages made of reeds; these were for the temple. A few farmers rode donkeys, but most came on foot to worship at the central shrine of the Hebrews, to see with their own eyes the everlasting glory of Jerusalem.

Gomer and her son were struggling up the last steep, rocky path, surrounded by barren hills and deep wadis, when they heard ahead of them the joyful chant of people singing the traditional songs of the ascent:

> 'I rejoiced when they said unto me:
> "Let us go unto the house of Yahweh."
> Our feet are standing
> Within your gates, O Jerusalem . . .
> Whither the tribes go up, even the tribes of Yahweh.'

All joined in this song of delight, but never for long did this mood prevail, for always some tormented voice, unable to believe that it was on the threshold of Jerusalem, would cry in humble supplication:

> 'Out of the depths have I call upon you, Yahweh.
> Yahweh, hear my voice.
> Let your ears be attentive to the voice of my supplications.'

Most endeavored to suppress their own desires and to submit themselves to the will of Yahweh, trusting as Gomer did that his guidance would sustain them:

> 'Yahweh, my heart is not haughty nor my eyes lofty;
> Neither do I exercise myself in things too great,
> Or in things too wonderful for me.'

And when they entered upon the last league they made a solemn promise that they would march uninterruptedly to the holy city regardless of what impediments they might encounter:

> 'Yahweh, let me remember David and his afflictions,
> How he swore unto Yahweh
> And vowed unto the god of Jacob.
> Surely I will not come into the tent of my own house
> Nor go up into the bed that is spread for me;
> I will not give sleep to my eyes
> Nor slumber to my eyelids
> Until I find out a place for Yahweh,
> A dwelling place for the mighty one.'

And then, when the day was very hot upon them, Gomer and Rimmon heard the singers ahead suddenly cease, and everywhere there was silence as those behind pushed forward, and at last the multitude looked south across bare hills and saw rising before them a stout, high wall, a most massive thing built of enormous stones that shone pink and gray and purple in the noonday sun; and from the walls rose towers marking a gate, and beyond it the majestic outlines of a temple, heavy and monumental and brooding. Many fell to their knees, to think that they had lived to see this city, but Gomer noticed that Rimmon stood apart, staring at the extraordinary walls and the ineffable grace that invested the stones of this sacred place. Watching her son absorb the wonder of Jerusalem she tried to guess what divine need had brought him to this spot, but she knew not, and then she found herself pulled to his side and her soft voice began whispering words and ideas that she herself could not have conjured up: 'Look not to the walls, Rimmon son of Gomer. Look rather to the west to those slopes by the fullers' field. A hundred years ago did not Sennacherib, having crushed Makor, camp in that spot, his army as thick as locusts in the seventh year? And did he not make preparations to destroy Jerusalem'—of these matters Gomer knew nothing—'so that the holy City of David lay powerless before him? The terrible Assyrian needed only to press against those pink-grey walls, and Jerusalem was his that he might crush the temple and destroy the sons of Judah forever. But at the middle of the night I moved among the tents of the Assyrians. More powerful than chariots was I that night, more deadly than arrows tipped with iron, and in the morning death was upon the host and it melted away.'

Rimmon noticed the peculiar use of the word *I*, and he realized that his mother could not be the one who was speaking; she, regaining consciousness, experienced for the first time the mystery of knowing that words had come from her mouth which she had not uttered. Both were aware that an incident of tremendous significance had occurred, but each was loath to investigate. Rimmon did not want to believe that Yahweh was speaking to him, for he could not consider himself worthy of such elevation, while Gomer knew that she was an ignorant woman who could neither read nor write, with no more possessions than she could gather into a large bag. In her life no man had loved her, and her son owned a father whose name no scroll recorded. It was not to such persons that Yahweh spoke; he did not choose people from the postern gate to represent him, and Gomer and her son drew away from any assumption of prophecy.

Trying to be matter-of-fact Rimmon asked, 'Didn't Sennacherib destroy Jerusalem? Like Makor?'

'I don't think so,' his mother said in her own voice. Vaguely she remembered an old fable of how the city had been saved. 'The cohorts were ready to strike, but they vanished.' And as two ordinary pilgrims they entered the city.

They came upon a scene that could not have been duplicated anywhere in the contemporary world, neither in young Greece, where mysteries were practiced, nor in old Egypt, where celebrations along the Nile were sumptuous. In Babylonia, of course, there was grandeur and in Persia an awakening power, but only in Jerusalem could one see the solemn passion of an entire people, coming to focus on one splendid temple constructed centuries earlier by Solomon. It was to this apex of Hebrew faith that Gomer had brought her son for a purpose which she could never have comprehended, and before the temple they bowed.

Then Rimmon led his mother outside the walls to a mount of olives at whose foot ran the Brook Kidron, rich with gardens and pomegranate trees and beds of many vegetables. From the trees the young farmer cut boughs and four corner poles, and with his cords built of them a booth in which he and Gomer would sleep for eight nights: on the mount as far as one could see were these booths, each with its branches so interlaced that a sleeping man could waken in the middle of the night and see the stars. Thus the Hebrews remembered the lonely decades in the desert when they were coming to know Yahweh in their ragged tents: each year all men of Israel and Judah took to their booths as Gomer and Rimmon did now.

In the morning they rose early and left the mount of olives, returning inside the city, where they worshiped at the temple, Gomer standing outside with the women while her son went into the sacred place to gaze at the holy of holies, to which only a few priests were admitted. Later he joined his mother to observe the animal sacrifices during which perfect bulls were led lowing to the altar, and here as the solemn rite was concluded, with incense penetrating the brain, Rimmon caught an understanding of man's eternal submission to Yahweh; and as the sacrificial fires twisted upward the significance of his faith was burned into his consciousness. This city he would remember forever, and on the sixth day Gomer heard him whispering, 'O Jerusalem, if I forget you let my eyes be blind, let my right hand lose its cunning.'

But it was not only for these solemn moments that pilgrims made the long trek to Jerusalem; for after the days of worship had ended, after the fields were gleaned and the grapes were pressed, lyric celebrations occurred in which festivities as old as the land of Canaan were re-enacted, and none was more compelling than the night on which the unmarried maidens of Israel dressed themselves in white gowns, newly made, to go out into the vineyards on the way to Bethlehem where ceremonial grapes had been held in reserve, and there to nominate one of their number to enter the wine press with her new dress clutched about her knees, where she would dance upon these final grapes while her sisters sang in the most ravishing tones the unharmonized plain chant of longing:

> 'Young men, young men of Jerusalem!
> Lift up your eyes and see whom,
> See whom, see whom,
> You shall marry.
>
> Look not for beauty,
> Look not for smiles,
> But look for a girl of good family,
> A family that worships Yahweh.'

And as the girls danced about the wine press Rimmon watched with growing wonder the freshness of the faces and the desirability of these laughing eyes as they flashed past him in the torchlight, begging him to sample them, to see whom he would marry.

But after a while the girl whose ankles were deep among the grapes grew weary, and she signaled for a replacement, and by chance the girls of Jerusalem picked as her successor a beautiful stranger from the north, Mikal the daughter of the governor of Makor, and men swung her into the wine press. As she clutched her new dress to keep it from being stained, Rimmon experienced the curious sensation that the dress was in a sense his dress—it had come from his kitchen and he had known it before even Mikal had known it—and it danced of itself, a swirling, beautiful white robe; and he reached for his mother's hand, congratulating her upon having made such a garment.

Then his heart exploded with the love that would never leave it, for it was not the dress that was dancing, but a girl twisting her head to the music, laughing, trying vainly to keep the juices of the grapes from staining her new dress, and finally, when she saw that she could no longer protect it, dropping it and throwing her hands in the air as the tempo of the music increased and she became stained even to her face with the purple that in the end dripped from her chin as she tried to taste it with her red tongue. It was a primitive moment that recalled the entire history of the Hebrews from before the days when they knew Yahweh or the Pharaohs, and Rimmon stood entranced, but when the music ended and it became some other girl's turn to press the symbolic grapes, it was he who lifted Mikal from the vat, and she hung for a moment in the air, looking down at him.

'Rimmon!' she cried, and she allowed him to set her upon the ground and to brush away the grape juice, and when his rough hand reached her face she did not draw back, but kept her stained chin raised towards his, and he kissed her.

On the way home from Jerusalem he informed his mother that he was going to marry Mikal, and she objected on the grounds that a Hebrew boy should not marry a girl whose family was more Canaanite than Hebrew. Rimmon would not listen to this argument, and his mother found in him the same kind of hardness that she had had to develop over the preceding decades. This pleased her insofar as her son's character was concerned, but it frightened her when applied to the matter of selecting a wife, and she wondered what she could do to present a hasty decision. As they were picking their way through the swamp north of Megiddo she asked casually, 'Are you aware of what Governor Jeremoth's name means?'

To Hebrews a man's name carried a significance unknown in other nations, and Rimmon, anticipating his mother's purpose, said, 'It means high places, and he worships in the high places.'

'His whole family does, and for him to go to Jerusalem, or for his daughter to dance at the festival, is offensive.'

'Are you warning me against Mikal?' he asked abruptly.

'Yes. Our town has many excellent Hebrew girls, loyal to Yahweh.' She was strongly impelled to advise him that he had been chosen by Yahweh for some austere purpose, that it was imperative for him to make his peace in all ways with Yahweh, but she could not do this, for she had no conception of what mission he had been called upon to serve. She therefore gave the limpest of all arguments: 'Have you considered marrying Geula? She comes from an old priestly family.'

At that moment they were heading through the worst part of the swamp, and at the mention of Geula's name Rimmon made an ugly face, which angered his mother and she berated him: 'Geula may not be beautiful, but she knows virtue, and it is not proper to make faces at a girl of marked devotion.' Rimmon stopped this argument by saying, 'I was making faces at the water snake that slipped from the rock,' and his mother grew silent and moved closer to him, for the nearness of a poisonous snake was frightening when she knew that her son had been singled out for some austere purpose.

When they cleared the swamp and climbed to higher ground they saw ahead of them the broken walls of Makor, and each compared that poor town with the grandeur of Jerusalem, and they saw for themselves what a miserable place it was; the invading armies had destroyed so much. Where eight hundred people had lived inside the walls in comfortable houses during King David's time, fewer than five hundred now lived in near-poverty. The rich fields outside, which had supported nine hundred farmers, had now only a hundred peasants who never knew when the next marauder would burn their crops and carry them off to slavery. These were dreadful years in Galilee, during which Makor sustained the smallest population of its long history, but Gomer suspected that evil of greater magnitude lay ahead. It must have been for this reason that Yahweh had spoken to her in the tunnel, charging her with the task of preparing her son for the trials that faced the Hebrews, and now, as she returned to the town which had brought her such little happiness, she clutched his hand and headed for the main gate, unaware that the test would fall not upon him but on her.

Against his mother's wishes Rimmon married Mikal, and against Gomer's own wishes she soon had to confess what a pleasing girl the governor's daughter was: laughing and beautiful, Mikal quickly proved that she was going to make Rimmon an excellent wife; she brought him a dowry larger than he could have expected and she prevailed upon her father to let him run the olive grove, not as foreman but as co-owner. She moved into the bleak house by the postern gate, sewed the necessary clothes, and then gave testimony of her love for Rimmon that no governor's daughter was required to give. One morning as Gomer lifted the water jug onto her head preparatory to the long descent and longer walk through the dark tunnel, Mikal took down the jug and said, 'From now on I shall fetch the water.'

The tired old woman looked down at the bright face, so hopeful in the morning light and so satisfied with the child that was growing near her heart, and Gomer said, 'Today you have brought me rubies,' and she bent down and for the first time kissed her daughter and continued, 'The only remaining thing I can do for my son is going to the well.' She carried the jug herself, but each morning young Mikal would watch for the moment when her mother started for the well, and she would lift the jug and say, 'Now I shall fetch the water,' and each morning old Gomer would refuse the offer, but her heart was overcome that her daughter had again volunteered.

Then came the days of terror. Out of the south, eastward of Megiddo, appeared the great army of the Pharaoh Necho, with men by the thousands and chariots whose dust obscured the sun, with generals in pleated tunics and foot soldiers burdened with spears. Fanning out swiftly in all directions the army occupied crossroads and villages and even walled towns.

'We are going north to crush Babylon forever,' the armed emissaries told Governor Jeremoth, 'and from Makor we require two hundred men and their supplies. By sunset tonight.'

A cry of protest went up from the town, and when Jeremoth was reluctant to identify which men must go, the Egyptians did the job for him. Throwing a cordon about the town they first marched off everyone living outside the walls. When Jeremoth protested that these were the farmers who fed the town, the Egyptian general shouted up at him, 'When you begin to starve, your women will find the fields. You have five daughters. You'll eat.'

They then searched the houses and picked every man who looked as if he could walk a hundred miles. At Gomer's they grabbed Rimmon as a prize soldier and told him on the spot that he was to be a captain of the Hebrews, and before he could say good-bye to his mother or his wife they had him outside the walls, where they began immediately to give him orders. He started to protest that he would not lead his Hebrews against the Babylonians, but he did not finish. An Egyptian soldier—not even an officer—struck him across the neck with a war mace and he fell unconscious to the ground.

From the wall his mother saw her son fall and she thought he was killed. Like an ordinary woman struck with terror she wanted to wimper softly, but an outside power took possession of her throat and from the walls she pointed with a long right arm and an extended forefinger. Her hair blew in the evening wind and her figure seemed to increase in its gaunt height, losing its stoop, and from her throat came for the first time a voice of extraordinary power, echoing across the town and into the hearts of the Egyptian invaders:

'O men of Egypt! Too long have you tormented the children of Yahweh, too long. You march north to battle which hyenas and vultures will long celebrate as they tear at your bones. You proud generals in pleated tunics, at the great battle your eyes will be put out and you will spend your years in darkness, toiling for the Babylonians. You insolent charioteers in armor, your horses shall drag you through cinders, and rocks of the field will clutch at your brains. You priests who accompany the mighty force to give it sanction, how you will dream of Thebes and Memphis'—if Gomer could have heard her words she would have been perplexed, for she knew nothing of Thebes or Memphis— 'how you will dream of Egypt when you toil in the slave pits of Babylon. And you, Pharaoh Necho, ride north with your banners flying and the wheels of your chariot churning dust. But you ride in vain, for Egypt is lost.'

Her words shattered in the air like spears striking rock, and an Egyptian captain, seeing their effect on his troops, shouted, 'Silence that foolish woman,' so that Governor Jeremoth himself ran to her and shook her; and when she regained her senses she saw that Rimmon was not dead but had risen and was doing as the Egyptians wished, and thus the army moved northward, picking up whole towns and nations as it went, preparing itself for the day when it must face the Babylonians. As an ordinary woman Gomer watched her son disappear, then sought the consolation of her daughter Mikal, and they joined the other bereft women along the wall, looking eastward to where eddies of dust marked the latest desolation to visit Makor.

THE TELL

In the kibbutz mess hall Cullinane was always amused, when the subject of women arose, to see how vigorously his Jewish friends argued that in their religion women were treated as equals. One night before Vered left for Chicago she had said, 'No religion in the world treats women with more regard than Judaism,' and Eliav added, 'Our religion reveres them.'

'If there ever was a case of protesting too much,' Cullinane said, 'this is it.'

'What do you mean?' Vered snapped.

'I can only judge by four things,' the Irishman said defensively. 'What the Torah says. What the Talmud says. What I see. And what I hear.'

'What have you seen?' Vered asked.

'I've been going to synagogues a good deal,' Cullinane replied, 'and in the new ones, if women want to attend they have to sit in a balcony behind a curtain. At older ones, like the Vodzher Rebbe's, there's no place for them at all.'

'Women prefer it that way,' Eliav insisted.

'Not from what I overhear from the tourists at the dig,' Cullinane said. 'American Jewish women tell me, "I'd refuse to be tucked away in a balcony behind lattices," And even the men say, "When I go to worship I want to sit with my family."'

On this matter the testimony of the Torah was clear. Women under Judaism were treated no worse than Near Eastern women in general: deplored at birth, endured in adolescence, married off as soon as possible, discriminated against in law and subjected to misery if they became unwanted widows. Numerous were the Biblical texts in which some Old Testament hero rejoiced at the news he was the father of a son, and one of the morning prayers recited by men included the passage: 'Blessed art Thou, O Lord our God, King of the universe, who hast not made me a woman.'

The sixty-three tractates of the Talmud developed each of these themes: 'Happy is he whose children are male and woe to him whose children are female.' In passage after passage this massive body of Jewish teaching admonished against the dangers of the female. 'Talk not overmuch with women, even with one's own wife,' read one passage, to which Maimonides himself added the gloss: 'It is known that for the most part conversation with women has to do with sexual matters, and by such talk a man brings evil upon himself.' The Talmud specifically directed that women must not be taught to read religious works, and often during the dig Israeli religious newspapers carried reports of resolutions drawn up by one group of fanatics or another: 'It is the function of Jewish girls to marry at seventeen and have children as quickly as possible.'

One night the English photographer appeared at dinner with a passage from the Talmud which summarized the ideal Jewish wife. 'She was married to the famous Rabbi Akiba. She found him when he was forty years old, an illiterate peasant. She married him and sent him to the yeshiva, where he lived apart and studied while she worked to earn their living. At the end of twelve years he returned home one night to tell her that he must do more studying, so she sent him back for another twelve years and kept her job. After twenty-four years he finally came home, but she was so old and decrepit that his followers tried to throw her aside as a beggar and, I quote, "the great Rabbi Akiba allowed her to come forward and kiss his feet, saying to his followers, 'All that is mine or yours comes from her.'"'

Vered was angry. 'Don't forget that when the judges were weak, Deborah rallied the Jewish people in battle against General Sisera.'

'When was that?' the Englishman asked.

'1125 B.C.E.'

Eliav said with more restraint, 'And there was Huldah the Prophetess, who was of critical significance in getting Deuteronomy accepted as the core of Jewish faith.'

'When did she live?' the photographer asked.

'621 B.C.E.'

'Isn't it strange,' Cullinane asked, 'that whenever we get on this topic you cite two women who lived more than twenty-five hundred years ago . . . '

'What about Beruriah?' Vered cried. None of the Gentiles had heard of her. 'Or Golda Meir?'

'My point,' Cullinane said, 'is that the Catholic church showed real capacity in finding places for women like Saint Theresa and Catherine of Siena. A sect of Protestants did the same with Mary Baker Eddy. In Judaism this doesn't happen.'

Vered was eager to reply. 'As little girls we play a game in which we ask, "Why were women made from Adam's rib?"' And she could still recite the answer: 'God deliberated from which part of man to create woman. He said, "I must not create her from the head that she should not carry herself haughtily; nor from the eye that she should not be too inquisitive; nor from the ear that she should not be an eavesdropper; nor from the mouth that she should not be too talkative; nor from the heart that she should not be too jealous; nor from the hand that she should not be too acquisitive; nor from the foot that she should not be a gadabout; but from a hidden part of the body that she should be modest."'

'I am impressed,' Eliav said, 'that in religions which do as Cullinane wants, female unhappiness is so great, whereas we Jews go pleasantly along with little divorce, little prostitution and neuroticism.'

'Everyone knows that a Jew makes the best husband in the world,' Vered said.

'You have no feeling of being left out?'

'We Jewish girls get what we want,' she insisted. 'A home, a family, a secure haven. Public praying in the synagogue? That's for men.'

The more Cullinane heard on this matter—and it came up at many dinners—the more correct he found Vered to be, in a thirteenth-century sense. In primitive societies it was man's job to placate the gods and woman's to keep the home, but this was dangerously close to the Germanic ideal of Kaiser, Kinder, Küche. He was willing to concede Eliav's point, that one of the reasons why Judaism had been so strong internally was its subtle relationship between the sexes, but he could not forget that Christianity overwhelmed Judaism partly because of its emotional appeal to women. Judaism was a religion for men, Cullinane sad to himself. Christianity for women.

Now, with Vered gone, he thought increasingly about women and it was often he who raised the question in the dining hall. Tabari held that Arabs had the best attitude: 'My father once said he never wore a new shoe until he had limbered it up three times over the head of his fourth wife. You Americans have ruined the relationship between the sexes, and Israel would be ill-advised to follow your example.'

'Actually,' Eliav added, 'Israel has an excellent approach. You've seen our bright young girls in the army.'

'I've also seen the statements of the religious groups. "Every honest girl is married by seventeen."'

'The nutty fringe,' Eliav commented.

'Do you also dismiss the desire of American Jews for their women to join them in synagogue?'

Tabari interrupted. 'It's the same in Islam. Women are free to enter the mosque if they sit apart and shut up. I think they prefer it that way.'

'Wait till some kind of reform Judaism hits this land,' Cullinane forecast. 'You'll find one million Israeli women behaving just like Russian women and American women.'

'You forget two points,' Eliav said. 'Have you read any recent studies on circumcision? How it eliminates some kinds of female cancer? How it insures better sexual relations in that it decreases man's sexuality somewhat but increases his ability to perform well when he does?'

'I never found that circumcision slowed me down,' Tabari reported.

'Are Muslims circumcised?' Cullinane asked.

'Of course. Besides, we Arabs are Semitic.'

'My second point,' Eliav continued, 'is an ugly one to bring up. But throughout two thousand years the religious loyalty of Jewish women has been tested many times, in the most horrible ways men can devise. They've been burned alive, thrown into ovens, torn apart . . . Invariably the most faithful Jews have been our women. They like their religion as it is.'

'And they'll continue, until a reform movement hits the land,' Cullinane said.

'Don't you believe it,' Eliav replied. 'Judaism has always provided a special place for women. You take Deborah . . .'

'Please! Not somebody three thousand years old.'

'All right, Golda Meir.'

'Making her Foreign Minister was one of the smartest things Israel has done,' Cullinane granted. 'Gives the men an example to point to for the next three thousand years.'

In the long months of the dry season when the Egyptians were moving into position to crush the Babylonians permanently, so that the land between the rivers might know peace, Gomer and her daughter Mikal managed to construct a life for themselves which, if not pleasant, was at least endurable. As the Egyptian general had predicted, with the farm families gone and all men of working age conscripted, it did not take long for the women of Makor to find their way into the fields, where they worked like animals to gather what little food had been left by the marauders. Mikal, as the daughter of the governor, could have escaped this drudgery–her four sisters did–but even though she was pregnant she felt that she must work with Gomer.

Each morning she volunteered to fetch the water, and each morning Gomer refused her offer, for two reasons. She knew that if she were ever to hear the voice again it would come to her within the depths of the tunnel; she therefore climbed down the dizzy spiral, along the damp passageway to the well, where a small clay lamp reflected its light from the surface of the water, and then back up the slope, waiting for the voice. But the more important reason was that she wished to protect Mikal. This fetching of water was not easy, for the stone steps which the slaves of Jabaal the Hoopoe had dug three hundred and sixty-one years before had been used each day by at least a hundred women–which meant that more than thirteen million trips had been made so far–and these had worn pockets in the stones so that every step had to be taken with care lest the woman slip sideways, lose her balance and pitch headlong down the shaft. Old women and pregnant ones ofttimes lost their lives in this way, and Gomer felt that she, as one who had trod the tunnel for fifty years, could better protect herself than a pregnant young girl whose father had never required her to draw water. So each day Gomer went to the well, praising Yahweh that he had sent her absent son such a wife.

Only one thing disturbed her about Mikal: the girl followed the traditions of Canaan and often climbed to the high place where she worshiped Baal. And as the time approached when her child must be delivered, she stopped working the fields and consulted with the priestesses of Astarte, asking them what she must do. In the little temple which stood over the site of the original monolith to El, three sacred prostitutes lived, their services rarely needed in these mournful days when men were gone. They were pleasant girls and they knew the sacred rites for delivering babies, so that when the days of Mikal were completed she went not to Gomer and the Hebrew midwives but to the priestesses, who delivered her of a fine boy whom she named Ishbaal, signifying that he was a man of Baal.

When Mikal brought the boy home from the temple Gomer could not hide her displeasure, and when she heard the boy's name she spat in the dust; but when she observed the love that Mikal lavished on the child and when she saw how much he resembled Rimmon she had to accept him, and she went into the fields for sixteen and seventeen hours a day, grubbing food to keep her little family alive. As soon as Mikal was strong enough to help in the work she placed her son with an old Canaanite woman and joined Gomer at the slave's work; and the two women working side by side developed a love such as mothers and daughters know. It was the love of women striving to their utmost so that a family might be preserved.

Each morning and night they prayed to Yahweh that Rimmon might return from the solemn battle that was forming in the north, and if at other times Mikal climbed the mountain to ask for Baal's intercession, too, Gomer chose not to know, for these were days of tragedy and if Mikal could do anything to bring her husband home alive she was free to try it. In the tunnel there was no voice; the people of Makor had forgotten Gomer's strange prophecies to the Egyptians, and she herself did not remember that she had once shouted with the voice of Yahweh.

Then messengers began arriving from the fields of Carchemish, far to the north on the Euphrates. They ran gasping up the ramps to the gates of Makor and fell exhausted with dust in their mouths and terror in their eyes. 'Great Egypt is destroyed! The chariots of Babylon were like seeds of the cypress tree blowing across the fields in winter. Woe, woe! Egypt is no more!' They rested, with gloom upon their foreheads, then resumed their running toward the Nile, where the court would cause them to be strangled because of the calamity they were reporting.

Other fugitives followed. 'The Babylonians captured our generals and blinded them on the battlefield, leading them off with yokes about their necks. Our charioteers had their tongues and ears cut away and they were led to slavery.'

'The men of Makor?' Governor Jeremoth asked. 'What happened?'

'Those who lived were blinded on the battlefield, then taken away to tread water pumps for the rest of their lives.'

'How many?' the governor asked, his knees trembling with anguish for his town.

'Not many,' the messengers said, and they too ran on.

Finally a man whom the Egyptians had conscripted from Accho wandered through the gates. He had lost his arm in the battle and had been released by the Babylonians to report the battle properly. 'We marched north with overwhelming power,' he said as if he were a ghost reporting to the ancient gods of Phoenicia in some afterworld, 'but Nebuchadrezzar of Babylon was waiting for us with an army that was ten to our one. At Carchemish he led us cleverly into a trap where his chariots destroyed us as if we were wheat at the harvest. He was so powerful that Egypt had no chance. Her generals were like children and her lieutenants like sucklings. But you had better prepare. For soon Nebuchadrezzar will march down the wadis. Makor and Accho are no more. The little kingdoms that we played with are no more.'

Gomer and the other women besieged the man to see if he remembered their men. 'They are all dead,' he said indifferently. Then he looked at the pathetic walls, broken by Sennacherib, and he began to laugh hysterically.

'What is it?' Governor Jeremoth demanded.

'These pitiful walls! Manned by pitiful women! You remember Sennacherib as a fearful man. But can you imagine what Nebuchadrezzar is like?' He stopped laughing at the helplessness of Makor, and his silence, the look of terror that came over his face, told the citizens all they needed to know.

The next months represented one of the most despairing times in the history of Makor. When Sennacherib had destroyed the town it was a swift, terrible vengeance that eliminated almost two thousand people in a few hours; but when it was ended the town was permitted to rebuild as an outpost of an Assyrian province. The months following Carchemish were more hideous because of the near-starvation, the captivity of the men and the uncertainty as to when Nebuchadrezzar would strike in revenge because the Hebrews had sided with the Egyptians.

'We didn't want to fight with them,' Mikal pointed out, but her father said that the Babylonians would not take such subtleties into account.

'We must gird ourselves to withstand the first shock,' he warned, and rarely in the long history of the Family of Ur was one of their members to behave with such voluntary courage as Governor Jeremoth now displayed. Assembling his people he announced, 'We are a poor group with few men. But we have found in the past that if we can hide behind these walls for three or four months the besieger grows weary and goes away.'

'We have no walls,' an old man pointed out.

'When Nebuchadrezzar arrives, we shall have,' Jeremoth replied, 'and you will have blisters on your hands from building them.'

He drove his starving people at a pitch that they would not have believed possible. He became the builder, the hortator, the priest, the general. Wherever he went he inspired his people to additional work, and when a committee of the faint-hearted approached him with the idea that perhaps it would be better in the long run if the town surrendered to Nebuchadrezzar, trusting to his benevolence, he dismissed them scornfully: 'Our fathers surrendered. They trusted Sennacherib. And four hours after he took the booty the town was demolished. This time if we perish we perish on the walls and at the gates.'

One morning, when the fortifications were beginning to regain their former strength, he climbed down into the tunnel to inspect the water system, and on the way back he stopped in the darkness to mutter a prayer to Baal for the miracle that the god had permitted Jeremoth's ancestors to accomplish. 'With this water in our hands, great Baal, we can hold off the Babylonians.' As he rose he saw Gomer coming toward him with her water jug balanced on her head, and she stopped to greet him.

'You're a brave man, Jeremoth,' she said. 'Yahweh will bless you.'

Governor Jeremoth thanked her, and she added, 'For all the fine men we lost, for our sons, we shall be avenged.' She took the governor's hand and kissed it.

'Thank you, Gomer,' he said. 'When the day for fighting comes you shall stand beside me on the wall.'

'For the memory of my son I shall kill fifty Babylonians.' And they passed on.

But after the governor had climbed the stairs, and after Gomer had gone to the well and filled her jug, she was returning alone through the tunnel when an extraordinary thing happened. She was walking toward the shaft, brooding upon the revenge she would take on the Babylonians, when she was suddenly knocked to the stone floor, where her clay jug was broken, sending water upon her face, while from the bottom of the shaft shone a light more powerful than the sun.

From her prone position Gomer had one curious thought: Our shaft is so located that the sun never shines to the bottom. It had never done so and she knew it never could, but there it was.

A voice said, 'Gomer, widow of Jathan, in the days ahead I shall speak through your lips.'

'Is my son alive?' she asked.

'Through your lips will I save Israel.'

'Is my son Rimmon alive?'

'The walls must not be finished, Gomer, widow of Israel.'

'But we must destroy the Babylonians,' she cried, still prone on the wet stones.

'In chains and yokes shall you march to Babylon. It is the destiny of Israel to perish from the land it has known, that it may find its god once more.'

'I cannot understand your words,' Gomer muttered.

'Gomer, widow of Israel, the walls must not be finished.' The light diminished and the voice was gone.

She picked herself up and looked at the broken water jug, and the sight of its fragments brought her back to reality and she began to weep, For she did not have enough money to purchase a new jug and did not know what to do.

Climbing the shaft she placed her feet carefully so as not to slip into the deep holes, and all she could think of was that the voice had refused to speak of her son, so when she reached her home and saw her grandson Ishbaal playing in the sun and her cherished daughter-in-law Mikal working at the noon meal, she wept again, moaning, 'Now I am sure that Rimmon is dead, and I have broken our water jug.'

The two tragedies were of equal weight to the unfortunate women, and they wept together, for the loss of the jug was so unexpected and so costly that they could not comprehend what had happened to them; and in this lamenting Gomer ignored the wall, and it was finished.

Then came the day that made the long months endurable. A child was playing on the new wall and to the east he saw a flurry of dust rising along the Damascus road, and he cried, 'Some men are coming home!' No one attended his foolish words, but after a while he saw real men and shouted, 'Our men are coming home!' And again no one bothered to listen to him, but finally he saw a man whose face he knew and he screamed, 'Gomer! Gomer! Rimmon is coming home.'

The cry spread out across the town, and Gomer and her daughter hurried to the walls and saw below them Captain Rimmon, tall and blond and very thin. He had with him thirty or forty men of Makor, neither blinded nor mutilated, and no one spoke, neither the men in the road nor the women who saw them through tears that were beyond pain, but the child kept calling off the names: 'There's Rimmon and Shobal and Azareel and Hadad the Edomite and Mattan the Phoenician . . .' One by one he called them from the dead and they climbed the ramp to their poor town.

The released prisoners clutched at their women, embraced their children and uttered little animal cries of joy. At the temple of Astarte the three young prostitutes danced naked and took all men, one after the other, into their booths for celebration, after which a procession headed by the priestesses and two old priests marched to the mountain, where sacrifices were offered before the monolith of Baal. Food that had been hoarded for months was brought out, and there was dancing and crying and love-making and men and women alike getting drunk without the help of wine. The men were home! Once again Baal had saved the little town.

It was dawn before Rimmon and his friends had finished telling of Carchemish and the wonders of Babylon. Of the battle they said only that Egypt was so crushed that it would never rise again. No more would Makor know the tramp of Egyptian armies; the scarabs of the officials could be thrown away, for they would no longer be needed to sign official documents. At this news there was little mourning, for Egypt had been a careless and a cruel administrator, and perhaps the first weakness was worse than the second, for under her dominion the land had deteriorated, the forests had diminished and security had changed to anarchy. Egypt was dead, and Hebrews who had suffered under the Pharaohs felt no grief.

'But Babylon!' Rimmon cried. 'A city of magnificence beyond imagination! At the Gate of Ishtar . . .' He wondered how he could explain. 'Mikal,' he called to his wife, 'fetch me your jewel,' and his happy wife ran to their home and brought back a piece of glazed ware from Greece shaped in the form of a bird. 'This is precious,' Rimmon said, holding the brooch so that it shone in the night flares, 'but at the Ishtar Gate there are walls three times as high as Makor, all studded with glaze finer than this fragment.' Above his head rose the imaginary gates of Babylon.

'They have canals that bring the river from a greater distance than Accho, gardens that float in the air, temples as big as all of Makor, and at the edge of the city a tower so big and so tall that words cannot describe it.'

'Why did they let you go free?' an old man asked.

'So that we could tell Israel of Babylon,' Rimmon said.

From the shadows Governor Jeremoth stepped forward, a stubby, hard man of demonstrated courage, to say, 'They sent you back to frighten us. But we are going to defend this town with our courage and with our blood. Rimmon, tell us no more of Babylon's might. Let us tell you that here we shall defend ourselves.'

To the surprise of the townspeople the governor's harsh words did not offend Rimmon, for with a broad smile he grasped Jeremoth's hand and said, 'Azareel, tell him what we've been talking about.' And a battle-tough man with a bandaged head explained, 'All the way home we've been deciding what to do. We're going to defend this town. Because we found that when a town resists, it wins a more favorable treaty. We pledged, "When we get home, we'll rebuild the walls." ' Through the night shadows he peered at the battlements and asked, 'Who had the courage to do that?'

A toothless old man pointed to Governor Jeremoth and said, 'He did.' And the soldiers embraced the governor and assured him that he had done right, and at the height of the celebration Jeremoth stood under a flare and announced, 'Old men and women built the walls. Young men shall defend them.'

Most of the soldiers, like Rimmon, went home with their wives, and some, like Azareel, wandered to the temple of Astarte, where they enjoyed themselves with the priestesses, and some like Mattan the Phoenician, who had never expected to see Makor again, climbed the mountain to offer sacrifice to Baal, and a few were so lost in a mixture of joy and sorrow that they went from house to house to comfort the widows whose men would not return and to assure them that their husbands had died bravely.

And when the sun was up, old Gomer descended the shaft with a new water jug and went to the well, but as she was about to lower the bucket the water fell away many cubits until the well was dry: at the bottom a fire burned and incense filled the air and a voice thundered from the depths and terrified her so that she dropped her new jug and broke it: 'Gomer, widow of Israel, for the last time I command you. Speak the words I send you. Israel has gone whoring after false gods and must be destroyed. Makor has built walls of vanity upon foundations of sand and they shall be thrown down. Your people worship Baal and lust after naked goddesses and in captivity they shall suffer. Tell your son to remember not Babylon but Jerusalem. Gomer, speak these things.'

'Thank you, Yahweh, for returning my son.'

'He shall stay but a little while,' the voice said, and as the fire died down the water returned. And there was silence.

This time Gomer showed no petty concern over her broken water jug, for at last she understood that it was Israel that was broken and that only the tremendous fires of defeat and exile could recast the shattered pieces. Like a moon-mad woman she climbed the upward stairs, not caring where she placed her feet, but because she had been assigned a providential purpose her life was preserved. Walking past her house she heard Mikal calling, 'Mother! Mother! Did you break the water jug again?' and she replied in a voice that was hardly her own, 'It is Israel that is shattered. Israel is no more.'

Like a disembodied spirit she continued to the wall where Governor Jeremoth was directing refinements to the fortifications, and pointing to them as she had at the doomed Egyptians, she cried in a harsh and penetrating wail, 'O men of vanity, throw down these useless walls. For it is written that Babylon shall capture Israel. And you shall see the hills and valleys of Galilee no more.'

Her words were clearly demonic and Governor Jeremoth did not feel it necessary to reply. He merely stared at her, but his men stopped their work and stepped aside as she strode along the walls and came to face him, staring down at him as if she were his mentor. In this unexpected manner they started the confrontation that would mark these last days of Makor, and it was a most uneven conflict upon which they were engaged. At fifty-three Governor Jeremoth was a tested man, a toughened warrior. He was clever and was supported by the principal family in town. He was determined to save Makor, and both the women who had rebuilt the walls and the soldiers who had returned to man them trusted him, for his personal courage gave him a power of leadership that words alone could not have done. She was fifty-nine, a confused old woman at the end of her life, with barely enough to live on and no capacity for either leadership or logic. Even to her neighbors she was a woman of no importance, yet Yahweh had chosen her as his spokesman during these critical months, and as such she would determine what transpired in Makor.

Now she cried, 'Tear down the walls and open the gates, for it is the fate of Israel to be dragged into captivity.' There was silence. The woman was speaking treason but Governor Jeremoth refrained from arresting her, for she was the mother of the captain upon whom the defenses rested.

'Did I not tell you that the Egyptians would be humbled?' she wailed. 'And their generals led away as slaves? Do I not speak the truth as you know it to be in your hearts?' Still Governor Jeremoth made no response.

Now Gomer went into a kind of spasm; her right shoulder hitched upward and her elbow trembled as she intoned, 'On that mountain the statue of Baal must be torn down. In that temple the priests and priestesses must be driven out. In all of this town the abominations must cease.' There was silence, and in a powerful wail of lamentation she cried, 'Today these things must be done.'

Guided by a force outside herself she did three symbolic things: she went to the wall and threw down one stone; she went to Governor Jeremoth, grabbed a staff he was carrying and broke it, and she went to the temple of Astarte where with curses she drove one of the prostitutes out of her booth. She then went home, where her son and daughter were ignorant of her performance, for they had gone into the tunnel to satisfy themselves that she had again broken her water jug—'She is too old to carry such a burden,' they had decided—and when she faced Mikal, Yahweh directed her to deliver a fourth symbol of her new identity; but when she looked at her daughter-in-law, that generous young woman who had saved her life during the time of starvation, what Yahweh required her to do was too horrible to perform, and she ran from the house sobbing in her human voice, 'Almighty Yahweh, I cannot!'

That day her children could not find her. She had fled to a stable near the wall, where she huddled in the straw, fleeing the intolerable duty that had been placed upon her. She prayed, seeking release, but found none. She remained hidden in the stable, unable to muster strength for the final obligation that Yahweh had put upon her; when evening came she felt stronger and started to rise, but when she did so she saw ahead the task that awaited her, and in fear she collapsed in the straw, weeping in agony and praying, 'This last command, Almighty Yahweh, take from me.'

All that night she remained hidden under the straw, as if in this way she could escape her god, and in the morning she went to a neighbor's house and borrowed a water jug, saying, 'I will fetch your water for you,' and she went into the tunnel and on the way back from the well she prayed, 'Merciful Yahweh, do not break this jug, for it is Rachel's and she is a needy woman. But let me speak with you.' And she was not thrown to the ground, but the light shone and for the last time the voice addressed her, using tones of deep compassion.

'Gomer, faithful widow of Jathan, I have heard your plea but there is no escape.'

She sobbed. 'The monolith, the temple, the wall, these things I can tear down. But the final thing, Yahweh, I cannot do.'

'I am striving for the salvation of a people,' the voice said. 'Do you suppose I find joy in ordering these things?'

She spoke not as a prophet, but as a woman pleading with her god: 'When I was dying Mikal saved me. Like a slave she worked in the fields. She is my blood, the eyes of my face, the tongue of my heart, and her I refuse to hurt.'

'It is required.'

'No!' In fury Gomer dashed the water jug to the floor, breaking it into many pieces in the presence of Yahweh. 'I will not.'

There was silence. Then patiently the voice said, 'Gomer, that was the jug of a poor woman and it is needed,' and at her feet the water jug was made whole again and filled itself with sweet water. 'If I consider the jug of this needful woman to make it whole again, do I not consider the people of Israel, to make them whole again? You shall do the things I command and you shall speak of Jerusalem to your son, that he may remember. For in every generation we seek that remnant who know Jerusalem, and in Makor it is to you and your son that remembrance is given.' The light failed and never again did the voice speak to Gomer, but through her it would accomplish the fearful tasks that had to be completed if in this generation Israel were to be saved.

In a trance Gomer picked up the water jug and lugged it back to Rachel, where she set it down without speaking. She then crossed the street and presented herself before Rimmon and Mikal. There was straw in her hair, betraying where she had spent the night, and deep lines in her face. When she saw that Mikal was wearing the white dress, she tried to run from the house, but ·she could not. Her finger pointed. Her voice grew harsh, and facing her daughter-in-law as she nursed the boy Ishbaal, she cried, 'All the daughters of Canaan shall be cast out. Yea, all the sons of Israel who have whored after the daughters of Canaan shall cast them away.'

Mikal fell back with a painful gasp. Hiding her bosom as if she were defiled she whispered, 'Gomer? What have you done?'

'Out!' the old woman shrieked. 'You are no more! You and the child. Out!' Like a fury hounding the condemned she pressed down upon the stricken girl, screaming at her, 'Whore! Corrupt! Daughter of Baal!' And she forced the gentle girl from the house and into the street. For a moment Rimmon tried to intervene, but his mother interposed herself between husband and wife and in the end Mikal had to run sobbing down the Water Street to her father's house, taking her son with her.

When she was gone Gomer imprisoned Rimmon in their little home and said, in words that of herself she could not have invoked, 'Remember Jerusalem, how it lay nestling in the mists, with the temple of Yahweh within its arms, and you climbed through the slanting sunbeams, whispering praises to the noble city. O let Jerusalem live in your heart, let it be the breath of your life, the kiss of your beloved.'

Rimmon was appalled at what was happening. His mother had become insane, and he could do nothing to help her. She had humiliated his wife and banished his child, and he was disgusted with himself for even having stayed behind to reason with her, and he made as if to leave, but what she said next transfixed him, and when he heard, he was able for the first time in his life to see the years stretching out before him; even when he had been working in the slave pits of Babylon he had supposed that it would prove temporary, and it had. But now his mother spoke in apocalyptic tones: 'You shall suffer in Babylon, O Israel. In Babylon shall you groan in the sweat of slavery. You shall be tempted, yea, you shall be tempted sorely and your strength will fail. You shall curse me, and other gods will offer promises that must seem sweet to you. But among you there will be those who remember Jerusalem, who heard the fall of my foot along the sacred ways, who knew the temple, who saw the fair girls dancing in the moonlight, who saw the pillars Jachin and Boaz, who sang the sweet psalms of David and Gershom. Remember Jerusalem, you who have forgotten so much, and redemption will be upon you.'

Gomer fell back. Neither she nor her son spoke, and after a while she left the house without him and went into the market place, where she cried in a loud voice, 'You children of Israel who wish to prepare yourselves for the long captivity ahead, come with me to the mountain that we may destroy the god Baal, forever and ever-from this day forth.' And she led a small group of men and women devoted to Yahweh toward the sacred place. But Governor Jeremoth, knowing that he must not start the defense of Makor with Baal destroyed, dispatched guards to halt the fanatics, and there was struggling, and only Gomer and one old man named Zadok reached the top of the hill, and they were clearly quite inadequate for the knocking down of so great a monolith, deeply rooted in the earth, but when they put their shoulders against the stone, their loose hair flowing in the wind, they toppled it and sent it crashing down the mountainside, where it broke into many pieces. And Baal would not go into captivity with them.

With the loss of the local god a sense of gloom began to settle over Makor, and those who revered Baal began to mumble against Gomer, and Jeremoth fell into a rage and ordered the old woman to be arrested. She was put into a jail, but people of the town, wherever they were within the walls, heard her piercing voice as she warned them, 'Israel will be destroyed, for you have abandoned Yahweh. You, all of you who hear me this day will die in Babylon, using the salt of your tears to savor your food. You are doomed. Surrender to Nebuchadrezzar before he storms your gates. Go out and bend your necks before him, because he serves as the scourge of Yahweh, who commands this servitude upon you. Miserable men of Makor, you who have whored after Astarte, you are lost forever. Your town, your pretensions are no more.'

Her dreadful wailing disturbed the night, and when Governor Jeremoth, beset by many problems relating to the defenses, summoned Rimmon and asked him what to do about his mother, the young captain was outside the spell of her incantation and he said, 'Her misery has driven her mad and she is speaking treason. We had better silence her.'

Governor Jeremoth sighed with relief and said, 'I'm glad you see it as I do. I was afraid you might . . . '

'About Mikal. What my mother did was horrible, and I'll explain to your daughter.' He volunteered to accompany the governor home, but as he started to do so Gomer, who could not possibly have seen him, screamed from the jail, 'Sons of Israel! Do not go back to the evil women of Canaan! Take no foreign women with you to Babylon. Take only the daughters of Israel! If you fail to heed these words, Yahweh will strike you with boils, with plagues, with leprosy. My son Rimmon! Do not slide back to the whore of Canaan!'

The words hung in the night like a brazen curse, etched from metal and burning into the consciousness of the Hebrews. They had found the daughters of Canaan attractive, and they had married them and many had slipped into the way of Baal. They were perplexed about the future, and here came this dire voice reminding them that they had done evil in turning their backs on Yahweh and neglecting the daughters of Israel.

Rimmon was especially struck by the malediction, for of all the Canaanite girls he had picked the fairest, a wife so good that she brought dignity to the term, a girl who was more faithful to the precepts of Yahweh than many of the Hebrew girls he had known. Now he was told to abandon her in preparation for the exile ahead, and he could make no sense of such instruction. But he and Governor Jeremoth were not to worry about this problem tonight, for they had scarcely reached the governor's home, where Mikal waited, when they were called to the temple area, where a fire was blazing. As if she had the power of Samson, Gomer had broken out of jail and had led a group of her followers to the Astarte temple, and there she had driven away the prostitutes and set fire to the holy place. A small wind kept the flames roaring, and before long the temple lay in ashes.

This was more than Governor Jeremoth could tolerate, and he caused the insane woman to be chained and led to the bottom of the shaft, where bolts were hammered into the wall and where she was kept prisoner during the critical period required for finishing the defenses. But from the well she cried her message to those who passed and to those who gathered at the lip: 'Gird your hearts for the tragedy ahead. Say farewell to the olive groves, to the sweet wine presses, to the children of your neighbors, to the well where you drew the sweet waters. All is desolation. Israel is condemned to wander across the face of the earth. You have been faithless. You have been evil. You have been obstinate and unfaithful to our covenant. O Israel, who will have mercy upon your afflictions? How terrible are the scenes you shall witness with blinded eyes. How you shall choke upon food that is denied you. Desolation, desolation. You shall wander across the earth because you have betrayed me.'

In his mean quarters by the town gate, Governor Jeremoth finished his plans for the defense of Makor, and as he was doing so a messenger appeared to confirm the anticipated news that Nebuchadrezzar himself was descending upon all the territories formerly held by Egypt. 'Riblah has fallen and mighty Damascus. Sidon is raised and Tyre is under siege. He will be upon you within three days.' And the haggard man had staggered on to Megiddo and Ashkelon, which were also doomed.

Now Jeremoth displayed his fortitude. Placing scouts upon the walls he went personally to every man in Makor and swore him to defend the town till death crashed down upon him. He called the women together and said, 'Your men have seen the slave pits of Babylon. They know. In this town we shall fight together, and if need be, die supporting our brothers. This is the honourable way to behave. May Baal protect us.'

Each day he walked upon the walls, in knee-length battledress and bearing a shield of hides, assuring his men that the town was safe. He pointed often to the water system, reminding them, 'In three hundred and fifty years no enemy has forced these walls. Nebuchadrezzar cannot do it either, and when he discovers that fact we shall make a peace with him that will protect us for years.' He assembled his own family—uncles, brothers, five daughters and their husbands—and gave each a task which kept him visible to the ordinary people. To Mikal he said, 'Forget what the crazy old woman shouted. Rimmon is a good husband, and when this is over you'll have many children.'

'I shall have another soon,' she revealed.

'Does Rimmon know?'

'Yes.'

Then the iron-hearted warrior went to his own command position atop that part of the wall that was most often attacked in the first days of a siege, and here he tested his sword and looked down the fateful road that had brought so many armies from Damascus, and he saw to the south the olive trees that his family had owned for thousands of years. 'How sweet this town is,' he muttered to himself. 'How worthy it is of our defense.' Then he looked with apprehension at the mountaintop from which Baal had been tumbled, and he wished that the mad old woman had not done that thing, and over the murmurs of the town he heard the cry from the bottom of the shaft, 'A few days, a few more hours, O Israel! Then the long torment begins. It is the will of Yahweh that you march forth with yokes upon your necks. Surrender now to Babylon. Go to your destiny and work as slaves through the years of your agony . . . '

'Gag her!' Jeremoth ordered, pressing his head in regret that he should have to do such a thing to a poor old woman, but when men started down the steps Rimmon took away the cloths and said, 'I will silence my mother,' and when he stood before her in the shadows she looked at him as if she were again his mother–as if she were merely an aging pauper who had lost her head for a while–and she said, 'In a few hours the testing will begin. But the battle is unimportant. Yahweh asks only that you remember Jerusalem. It was in there,' and she indicated the place within the tunnel where the theophanies had occurred, 'that he told me to take you to Jerusalem. He wanted you to see and to remember.'

'But why?'

'So that when you are in slavery and others forget, there will be one who remembers Jerusalem. You are the chosen of the chosen.'

'And Mikal?'

'She cannot go with you.'

'But she's having another child.'

The old woman bowed her head, both as the servant of Yahweh and as a mother. Hot tears ran down her wrinkled face and she could not speak. She could only remember the days when Mikal had helped keep the family together by working like a slave in the fields, the long talks they had had, and the child Ishbaal. She would rather had died than say what was required next, but she said, 'When you leave for captivity in Babylon it is the will of Yahweh that you take Geula with you as your wife.'

Rimmon's shoulders dropped as if the great stones of the olive press had been thrown upon them. He did not look at his mother, but made preparations to gag her. She stopped him by saying, 'I am silenced.'

'You will let us fight?'

'I am silenced,' she repeated, and he stuffed the offensive cloth in his pocket and climbed out.

'My mother is gagged,' he reported. 'Now we can fight.'

Nebuchadrezzar had found that since he had almost unlimited manpower it was best to attack a fortified town like Makor with a series of stupendous rushes, and when dawn broke on the day of battle there was no orderly march down the Damascus road. Instead, from every side except the steep north where the wadi lay, thousands of shielded warriors shouting and hurling rocks leaped upon the town as if they were a band of locusts and it a doomed bush.

But Governor Jeremoth was not terrified by this tactic, daring though it was. He waited until the Babylonians were struggling up the steep flanks that guarded the walls, and then he unloosed a shower of jagged rocks that caused many deaths. The Babylonians were forced to retire without having effected a breach, but before Jeremoth's men could completely rearm themselves, a fresh wave of Babylonians struck the walls, and then another and another; but

Jeremoth cooly directed his men where to run to shore up weak spots, and repeatedly the attackers were thrown back.

At dusk that day it became aparent that Makor could not be taken by frontal assault, so Nebuchadrezzar ordered his men to mount a siege, even from the wadi, and he demanded to know where the little town got its water. When prisoners from Accho exclaimed, 'From a deep well inside the town,' he growled, 'Bring up the rams,' and through the night the ponderous engines of war were shoved into position, but when they were ready to strike, Governor Jeremoth found them out and sent expeditions which set them afire, and in the morning Makor was still secure.

'Who is that one commanding on the walls?' Nebuchadrezzar inquired, and when he was told that it was a Canaanite he said, 'Him I want taken alive, for he is a mighty general and we could send him against the Cilicians.'

These were the days when Jeremoth added luster to the name of Ur, for by his moral determination he held off the armies of Babylon, but on the eighth day a miracle was directed against him, one that he did not witness: in the depth of the shaft a stroke of light shattered the chains which held the widow Gomer, and with a radiance about her head she climbed the stone steps and when she crawled out of the shaft she watched as the light moved on to the postern gate, where with a mighty blow Yahweh knocked down the defenses, and nine Babylonian soldiers who had been pressing against that spot rushed into the breach to be followed by tens and hundreds. Makor was lost, but Jeremoth continued defending along the southern wall, unaware that Yahweh had already defeated him at the northern. Finally the defiant Canaanite turned to defend himself against the Babylonians surrounding him from the rear, and with only a wooden staff tried to hold them off, but he was borne to earth and his arms were pinioned. When he saw what had overtaken him and beheld the light hovering above the head of Gomer he asked in a stricken voice, 'Woman, what have you done to us this day?' And in a terrible voice came the answer, 'No woman, but Yahweh.'

In those historic generations when Yahweh was wrestling for the soul of his Hebrews, and using the prophets to summon them away from Baal and back to their appointed tents, he often spoke and acted with a harshness that seemed incredible. Because the Hebrews were an obstinate people, loving Astarte, consorting with her sacred prostitutes and throwing live children into the fiery jaws of Melak, he had to visit them with terrible punishments. Why did he not destroy them outright? Because they were truly his chosen people and he loved them. And to prove this, when his discipline fell upon them and they submitted, he gave them assurances of the utmost gentleness to succor them during the years of darkness; for although he had to be cruel he had also to be merciful. And it was for this reason that the voice of Gomer now broke upon the wounded town of Makor in a gentleness hitherto unknown, uttering words of consolation that would often be recalled by the slaves in Babylon: 'O my beloved children of Israel, I bring you hope. No matter how deep the dungeons where you tread the waterwheels, I shall be with you. My love will protect you forever, and after the slave pits you shall know green fields once more. The world shall be yours and the sweetness thereof, for when you accept my punishment you also accept my divine compassion. I am Yahweh, and I am beside you forever.'

Now the Babylonians began to muster the Hebrews for the long march to slavery, and it became Gomer's duty to visit each group of prisoners, reassuring them, 'In your distress remember Yahweh, for I am a well of cool water. Will I forget you now, when your need is greatest?' And when the Hebrews expressed their amazement at this contradictory message of love arriving at the moment of punishment, Gomer said in tones as gentle as those of a mother singing to her child at night when the father must work in the fields, 'The Canaanites and the Babylonians shall perish, but you shall remain, for in the bitterness of my punishment you shall grow strong.'

And she came to the group where her son stood in chains and to him she said, 'Remember Jerusalem, O remember the city on the hill. Speak of it in the tents and sing its praises in the darkness. Remember Jerusalem, for you are a people commanded to remember. When your breath grows weak and your heart fails and death comes to you in a strange land, remember Jerusalem, the city of your inheritance.'

Mikal saw her husband waiting with the prisoners, and with their son Ishbaal she ran to him, volunteering out of love to follow him into slavery, and other Canaanite girls offered to do the same for their husbands, but to these latter Gomer came and sent them away, shouting, 'The whores of Canaan are not required in Babylon. False wives shall be left behind.' But when she came to Mikal, standing in the white dress that she herself had made, she could not utter the words, for her tongue clave to the roof of her mouth, and with tears of love she looked at the faithful girl who had worked beside her in the fields and she would have moved away in silence; but she was forced to stand and cry, 'The scarlet woman of Canaan who gives birth in the temple of Astarte, who names her son Ishbaal, she shall be cast aside.' Mikal hesitated, and her mother-in-law shrieked, 'Go! Stay not with him for he is no longer your husband. Begone.' And with a powerful thrust she threw the weeping girl away, so that her uncle had to lift her from the ground and lead her to a place among the watching Canaanites.

When Rimmon picked up his chains and tried to follow he was intercepted by his mother, who said not in her own voice, 'These things I do not in hatred but in love. Other nations shall vanish but Israel shall survive. For in captivity shall you cling together and each shall be loyal to the other, and all shall remember Jerusalem.'

Then Gomer left her son and strode among the prisoners till she found the girl Geula, standing in chains, and with great force she broke those chains apart and led Geula to her son. Joining their hands she announced, 'Rimmon, son of Gomer, you are divorced. This day you are divorced. And in the presence of three you are married to Geula. You are children of Israel, and your former children of Canaan are forgotten, those born and those unborn. For only you are the people that I have chosen.'

It was a phrase that brought smiles to Babylonian lips. These slaves in chains, this remnant of a once proud town! The chosen! Soldiers began to laugh outright and soon gusts of ridicule came from Babylonian and Canaanite alike. But Gomer, in her rage, turned her matted head toward Nebuchadrezzar in his hour of triumph and pointed her long finger at him, crying in tones of lamentation, 'How brief will be your triumph, Imperial One, how brief your pause at the apex! Already the Persians are gathering along your frontiers, impatient to invade your dazzling city with its intricate canals. Even now have I composed the decree that the Persian Cyrus will pronounce, sending my chosen people home. O King, how very brief is this day's triumph.'

And she turned to the Hebrew captives, whispering those words of timeless consolation, 'I am Yahweh who walks with you in darkness and shall lead you back to light if you but remember Jerusalem.'

Nebuchadrezzar would hear no more and with his right arm made an impatient gesture, commanding, like the Egyptian before him, 'Silence that dreadful woman!' in obedience to which a Babylonian soldier stabbed her through the chest. Then, seeing the deep shaft that yawned behind her, he whistled for two friends and with little difficulty they pitched her head-first down the opening, so that her gaunt body struck the pock-marked steps and plunged to those dark depths where once she had talked with Yahweh.

LEVEL X

In the Gymnasium

Found at Makor–Hellenistic carving of the hand of an athlete
holding a strigil used for scraping sweat and dirt from the body
after competition in the gymnasium. Carved in Antioch, 184
B.C.E., from white marble imported from Cerrara, north of
Rome. Work complete in its present form, having been
intended to suggest a fragment of a classical statue. Original
bronze blade cast of Macedonian metal, now corroded away.
Deposited at Makor during the Antiochene riots which
occurred in the autumn of 167 B.C.E.

Many times in their long history the Jews would be threatened with extinction
because of planned religious persecutions, but none of the later holocausts
would start so gently and with such persuasiveness as the first in the series,
launched in the year 171 B.C.E. by Antiochus IV, tyrant of the Seleucid empire.

In 605 B.C.E. the Hebrews of Makor had been hauled off to their Babylonian
captivity, but some fifty years later, as the voice of Gomer had predicted, Cyrus
of Persia had crushed Babylon in a war that lasted less than a week and the Jews
of Makor were not only permitted but encouraged to return home, so long as
they remained obedient to Persian rule. In 336, at the age of twenty, Alexander
the Great ascended his throne and began his conquests, so that for the next
seven hundred years everyone from Sparta to India experienced Greek culture
and most spoke the Koine, a Greek dialect common to all countries; but the
distances in the new empire were so vast, and so few citizens could have direct
contact with Greece, that a kind of substitute Greek culture developed, the
Hellenism born of men who loved the Greek ideals of beauty but who
interpreted them in Egyptian or Persian or Syrian terms. It was this Hellenism
that was to rule the known world for many centuries; but the empire was not
destined to remain unified, for in the confusion following Alexander's death,
the eastern portion was finally divided between two of his Macedonian
generals. Ptolemy took Egypt, including Makor, as his northernmost outpost,
while Seleucus took enormous holdings from Thrace to India, later to be
known as the Seleucid empire, with its resplendent capital at Antioch, some
two hundred and thirty miles north of Makor.

In 198, after a century of border warfare between the two Hellenistic
empires, the Seleucids under Antiochus III finally humiliated the Egyptians,
taking from them Israel as a prize of war, and Makor switched from being the
northern outpost of Egypt to being a southern outpost of Seleucia. One of the
first things the new ruler did was to promulgate a decree which gave much
encouragement to the Jews of Makor: 'Be it known that our majestic emperor
advises his new Jewish subjects that they are now free to worship their god as
they wish. They may build synagogues. Their priests may offer sacrifices—the
only requirement being that they must in no way offend Zeus, whom all accept
as the supreme deity of the Seleucids.' Not only was the pronouncement
generous; its enforcement was sympathetic. In the center of Makor, above the

ancient site where the monolith of El lay buried in rubble, a beautiful little temple was built, with six small Doric columns and a pediment showing goddesses at rest. It contained one small head of Zeus carved from Parian marble, and neither the temple nor the god was obtrusive. In another part of town, tucked in against the eastern wall, stood a synagogue equally unobtrusive but not equally beautiful. In fact, it was ugly–having been built of muddy-colored clay bricks and rough timbers–but for the first twenty-seven years of Seleucid rule those Jews who remained loyal to their synagogue lived easily with the bulk of the citizenry who adhered to Zeus and his temple. Each group followed Greek customs, used coins with Greek inscriptions and in their public life spoke the Koine. Though they had never seen Greece they referred to themselves as Greeks, so that in all respects Makor was a typical Hellenistic town.

In 171 Antiochus IV announced a small change in the religious life of his dominions, and if the Jews of Makor had enjoyed first-rate leadership they might have foreseen at that moment that trouble of great magnitude was upon them; but they were poorly led and the fact escaped them. The new rule was clear-cut: 'Henceforth all citizens must acknowledge that the god Zeus has come to earth in the person of our divine emperor, Antiochus Epiphanes.' At first the idea seemed startling to the Jews, but they were assured by the town officials that the new ruling would affect them in no way. Some time later a gigantic head of the emperor was moved into the temple, the small head of Zeus having been placed to one side, and when the new god was at rest, all citizens were assembled in the square facing the temple, where an official read the law: 'Those who enter the temple of Zeus must pay homage to our imperial leader, Antiochus Epiphanes, and accept him as Olympian Zeus appearing among us in mortal form.' The citizens, straining their necks to see the massive head, agreed that Antiochus looked like Zeus, with godlike curls and benign visage. 'Jews who prefer to worship in their synagogue are not affected by this law,' the reader continued, 'for our great emperor has no wish to offend any man so long as his deity is acknowledged.' As a matter of fact, when the Jews heard that they did not have to worship Antiochus a good many through natural curiosity wandered into the temple, where they stood bewildered before the heroic head, genuflecting before Antiochus the emperor and smiling to themselves at Antiochus the would-be god. They found the name Epiphanes to be especially arrogant–'God-Made-Manifest'–and they wondered how their Greek masters could delude themselves into believing such folly. They saw only an ordinary stone statue of an ordinary man, and they could not visualize him as a god. They bowed, bit their lips to hide their contempt, and returned happily to their synagogue, where they were free to worship the true god YHWH without fear.

In 170 a law was announced requiring all citizens to present themselves four times a year to pay formal homage to Antiochus Epiphanes as the senior god of the Seleucids, and this did entail hardship on the Jews–but in an area that they could not have anticipated. The day chosen for these periodic submissions was Shabbat, when Jews preferred not to leave their homes, this being their day of prayer. They therefore directed their leaders to protest the law, but the Greek officials explained, 'Our choice of Shabbat was in no way intended to offend the Jews. This day was chosen for the whole empire because it was acceptable to the most people.' When the Jews pointed out that it was certainly not acceptable to them, the Greeks replied, 'Our empire contains only a few Jews, and it would be unreasonable for us to make our laws conform to their wishes. However, Antiochus himself has commissioned us to say that so long as he is emperor, nothing will be done to offend you in any way.' The Jews tried to protest that the Shabbat genuflection did just that, but the local Greeks made a notable concession: 'Let us, for the sake of peace, agree upon this compromise. We Greeks will bow before Antiochus during the daylight hours, and on Shabbat evening, when your prayers have ended, you shall do likewise.' And in this honorable truce the Jews marched each quarter to the temple to pay proper homage to Antiochus the emperor; but in their hearts they ignored Epiphanes the presumptuous god.

In 169 the Jews were summoned to hear the next edict: 'In order to halt the perpetuation of differences among the peoples of his great empire, Antiochus Epiphanes has decided that Jews shall no longer circumcise their male children.' This caused an immediate outcry from some Jews, but its force was lost because others saw the reasonableness of the Seleucid request. They argued, 'The Greeks hold that the human body is a temple which must never be profaned or altered, so this is only a minor request which our emperor makes.' They were supported by others who argued, 'Antiochus is right. Circumcision is an old-fashioned, barbaric rite whose only function is to make us look different from the Greeks.' But there were others who knew that the covenant which Abraham had made with YHWH regarding circumcision was binding through eternity, and these continued to circumcise their sons, but their protest was lost because of the indecision of the Jewish community; however, word of their obstinacy reached the ears of Antiochus, the God-Made-Manifest, and he remembered.

In 168 the Greeks of Makor were required to promulgate an edict which was bound to cause trouble, and they put an extra force of men into military uniform before they announced it. Then, summoning all citizens to the temple of Zeus, onto whose portico the giant head of Antiochus had been moved, they directed the herald to read: 'throughout the empire it is ordered that from this day the worship of Antiochus Epiphanes shall be the one and official religion of all people.' This disturbing news was greeted with an angry murmur–and not only from Jews–so that the herald quickly added, 'But after a man has paid proper homage to Antiochus he shall be free to worship his old gods as his second and private religion. Thus Phoenicians may worship Melkart, Canaanites may worship Baal, and loyal Jews may go to their synagogue to worship . . .' The herald hesitated, and Jews leaned forward to see if he was going to profane their deity, for following their return from Babylon they had adopted the convention that the god who had saved them was so powerful that his name must never be pronounced, nor did they write it, nor refer to it in talk among themselves. Their god was known simply by the sacred tetragrammation YHWH, unpronounceable and unknowable. Now, in granting exception to the Jews, the herald avoided offending them. He did not announce that they were free to worship YHWH; he added simply, 'Our loyal Jews are free to worship their peculiar god.' But then he prepared to read that portion of the law which was certain to cause trouble, and he was gratified when he saw armed men moving into position to quell any riot. 'Sacrifice to the new god Antiochus Epiphanes shall be made four times each year, both at the altar of Zeus here in the main temple, and in any other such temple or holy place as may exist within the town.' Here he nodded gravely to the Phoenicians and the Jews. Then he swallowed and tensed his shoulders as if preparing for a blow.

'And this sacrifice, which is to be repeated four times a year, shall consist of a perfect animal, brought alive to the altar, and this animal shall be a swine.'

In 167 came the inevitable climax to any religious persecution. The instructions from the outrageous emperor were so brutal that the Greek officials of Makor were loath to read them, and the edict was handed to a common soldier, who caused the Jews to be marched to the public square, where they stood sullenly to hear what their punishment was to be. In harsh, guttural tones the soldier shouted, 'Jews of Makor, approach in single file and kiss the god of Asia,' and the recalcitrant ones were moved inside the temple to the monstrous head of Antiochus, where they were made to stand on their toes to kiss the great stone neck below the protruding Adam's apple. Then, in the awesome silence of the holy place, the soldier rasped, 'You Jews of Makor, having disobeyed the law of our emperor by continuing to circumcise your sons, and having offended our god by refusing to sacrifice swine in your synagogue, have surrendered any claim to mercy. Hear and obey! From this moment on, any Jew who refuses to accept Antiochus Epiphanes as the sole god, supplanting all others, including your god known as Yahweh'–the Jews shuddered–'any Jew who persists in following the law of your prophet called Moses, any Jew who circumcises his son, or any Jew who refuses to place his hand upon the sacrificial pig, shall be arrested and dragged before the temple of Zeus. There he shall be scourged with fifty blows, after which he shall be placed upon the ground so that his skin may be pulled away while he still lives. Thereafter he shall be slain, his body cut apart and thrown to the dogs. Hear these penalties and obey.' The astonished Jews were then herded back into the square where a large pig had been brought for sacrifice, and as it squealed and twisted in the sunlight they filed past and each placed his hand firmly on the forbidden beast. But there was one old Jew who had had enough of spineless leadership, and of his own will he refused to honor the emperor's pig. The Greek soldier started to manhandle him, but the captain of the guard intervened gently and said, 'Old man, you have not obeyed our god Antiochus.' The old Jew, his beard testifying to the years he had studied Moses, drew back in disgust, but again the captain warned him in a low persuasive voice, 'Dear friend, it will go hard with you if you do not obey the law'; but again the old man refused, whereupon the captain had one of his men produce the lash–a club containing several dozen leather thongs. 'They are tipped with lead,' the captain explained, rustling the dreadful pieces. 'Do you think you could stand up against such punishment?' The old man spat on the sanctified pig, and the soldiers quickly proceeded as they had been instructed, should such an emergency occur. They stripped the old man till he stood naked; they then tied him to a pillar, where ten swift blows of the lash tore at him terribly. The speeding lead tips caught at his face and ripped out one of his eyes. They tore away a corner of his mouth and laid bare the muscles of his neck. 'Will you now acknowledge the pig?' asked the captain, and when the old man refused, the man with the lash directed his blows lower on the body, where the lead tips tore away the old man's testicles and laid open his loins; and at the fortieth blow the humane intention of the captain became apparent: he hoped that the scourging alone would kill the old man that he might be spared the agony of being flayed, but the old Jew had within him some profound source of resistance and he survived the hail-storm of pellets, so that he was finally thrown to the ground, where he lay quivering as men with sharp knives came to cut away the mutilated skin. And when it seemed that he must surely be dead, he raised his head and called the permanent prayer of all Jews: 'Hear, O Israel, the Lord our God, the Lord is one.' And on the long, wailing pronunciation of the last word he died.

Among those who watched with anger this first of the afflictions were two men of dissimilar inheritance who were partly to blame for the tragedy. They had been born in Makor of families with ancient antecedents, and their friendship explained why the Jews had accepted one after another of the preliminary restrictions without comprehending what was occurring or what the end must be. The more important of these men was Governor Tarphon, the thirty-five-year-old gymnasiarch, a clean-shaven, handsome, red-haired athlete who affected the short dress of a Greek army officer. He was an attractive man, forthright and generous in his impulses and doubly appreciated as a public official because he had a beautiful wife who had been born in Greece and who added dignity to his public appearances and intelligence to his private entertainments. Tarphon had come from a middle-class Canaanite family, but he had enjoyed a spectacular leap to prominence with the arrival of the Seleucids, for they had recognized him as a child with potential and had sent him to Athens for his education. Upon his return he was made assistant to the governors of Ptolemais, as the ancient seaport of Accho was now called, and it had been he who had persuaded the governors to build a summer palace along the northwest wall of Makor, where cool breezes came from the wadis and where the afternoon sunsets were so entrancing. Tarphon had also shown his governors how to invest in olive groves, and as they prospered he prospered. Only a few Seleucid officials had seen Athens, and although all could speak the Koine, not many could speak the classical Attic which Tarphon had learned and in which he had read the principal authors. His Greek education, his Greek wife and his athletic prowess were bound to make him conspicuous, and when Antiochus Epiphanes came to dedicate the little temple to Zeus he said of Tarphon, 'It is amazing to find in this small town a young man who is not only Greek in speech and Greek in manner, but also Greek in spirit.' Encouraged by these words Tarphon had proceeded with a venture which had brought him increased praise from the emperor: he organized a group of local citizens to put up the money for building along the southern wall of the town an impressive gymnasium with hot baths, statues, a small arena for games and stone seats for spectators. At the dedication Tarphon gave all credit to the local businessmen, pointing out, 'It must be admitted that a small frontier town like Makor, only recently taken over from the Egyptians, can lay no claim to an outdoor stadium. Not even Ptolemais has one. But we do have a right to our own gymnasium. How could we be a Greek community without one? And you men are to be thanked.' No one in Makor was surprised when Antiochus Epiphanes selected young Tarphon to be his next district governor, and although his duties took him to Ptolemais much of the time, he spent as many days as possible in Makor, the comfortable little town which his ancestors had helped to build. Each afternoon when he was in residence he would report to the gymnasium for exercise, a hot bath and some cool drinks with friends who enjoyed watching the younger men of Makor prepare for the regional games that were held in larger cities like Damascus and Antioch. Tarphon remained a fine athlete; in his student days at Athens he had represented the Seleucid empire in both running and wrestling, and in the latter sport he could still defeat most of the younger men in his district, while as a runner he was locally famous. Each year he donned athletic sandals, placed a small cloth about his loins and raced the eight miles from the main gate of Makor to the assembly in Ptolemais, inviting runners in the area to compete against him; and if he could no longer outrace the swiftest, he never finished poorly. It was partly due to the misguided efforts of this good man that the Jews of Makor had stumbled into the trap as they did, for he had in his heart a special fondness for them. For many centuries his family had worked with them, and some of his ancestors had actually followed the Hebrew religion, so when the first of the repressive laws arrived in Makor it was Tarphon who reasoned with the Jews, proposing the concessions that made the laws endurable. By force of his generous personality he diminished the initial impact of the restrictions and thus prevented them from having the effect they should have had. He and his wife Melissa were always ready to entertain Jews, to listen to the grievances, to help if papers or certificates were required. They liked to talk with young Jewish boys and to get them started in their studies. They gave money to build a roof over the synagogue, and it had been Tarphon who contrived the evasion whereby Jews made their customary obeisance after sundown so as to avoid breaking Shabbat. Thus, unwittingly, he helped pull the teeth of Judaism, leaving it defenseless when the persecutions began in earnest. Then Tarphon could no longer protect his friends, and the tortures had to proceed. Unable to believe what was happening in his peaceful world, Tarphon had watched the first hideous flaying while hidden behind a pillar on the temple porch.

Now the inadequacy of the Jewish leadership began to exact its toll. Someone among them should have sounded a rallying cry, but no one did. Gone were the days when a patriarch like Zadok was willing to fight even with his god over matters of policy, risking his life and that of his clan in the process; now men avoided such dialogue. Nor was there among the Jews a Gershom with a seven-stringed lyre, speaking directly from his heart to the heart of his god; now men preferred evasion or the oblique reference. And certainly there was not in Makor any old gray woman like Gomer who was personally willing to confront the general of the Egyptians and the might of Nebuchadrezzar. Now there was only Jehubabel, a pudgy, bearded man of forty-five, who made his living from a string of dye vats and was therefore principally worried about getting enough purple dye from the cities to the north or red dye from Damascus. It was by default that Jehubabel had become leader of the Jewish community, for he was not a forceful man nor was he particularly religious. In fact, he had only two qualifications for the job into which he had been thrust: he lived next door to the synagogue and he was what was known as a man of wisdom; that is, he had read the great Jewish classics and had forgot them, but he remembered several score of pithy sayings accumulated by the Jews over the centuries when they were trying to protect their identity from absorption by either the Egyptians or the Babylonians. Jehubabel was a master of this commonplace knowledge, and as he moved from his dye vats to the synagogue he often stopped to converse with his Jewish neighbors, who comprised about one third of Makor's population. If they invited him to their homes he said, 'Keep your foot from your neighbor's house lest he weary of you and so come to hate you.' The aptness of the proverb and the ponderous manner in which he delivered it, his round face beaming as if light were upon his inner mind, convinced his friends that he was a wise man. When an acquaintance said something appropriate, Jehubabel might quote, '"A word fitly spoken is like apples of gold in pictures of silver."' And when news reached him that his precious dyes had reached port in Ptolemais he often cried, '"As cold waters to a thirsty soul, so is good news from a far country."' In this pedestrian manner Jehubabel moved about his daily tasks, and if Antiochus had not appeared on the scene his store of familiar proverbs might have sufficed to guide him through an uneventful life. But against the brute force of the emperor, Jehubabel's homely wisdom availed little and against the sophisticated Greek schooling of Governor Tarphon he was powerless.

His name Jehubabel summarized his history, 'YHWH is in Babylon,' for the men of his family had borne that name since the days of captivity. When the time came for the Jews to return to Israel, a group formed under the leadership of the charismatic prophet Rimmon, then in his nineties, who led them from the canals of Babylon to the hilltop of Jerusalem–about which he had been preaching for fifty years–but when he delivered his people to that city, to everyone's surprise he gathered his own family about him, including his son Jehubabel and his old wife Geula, and these he had led onward to Makor, where he re-established his line. The present Jehubabel was descended from these valiant people, and if the fat dyer had lost most of their fury, he had lost none of their dedication to YHWH. For him to kiss the stony neck of Antiochus Epiphanes was profanation, but when Governor Tarphon assured him that this was a minor requirement that could do no harm, Jehubabel told his Jews, 'Rivers send forth mist so that the sun will take that offering and not dry them up.' And for the sake of peace he obeyed. For him to acknowledge Antiochus as a god was abhorrent, but when Tarphon argued as an old friend that the Jews could do this and at the same time worship YHWH in their synagogue, he did not see the essential conflict. And for him to caress the sacrificial pig was an abomination, yet he had complied because the governor had convinced him that to do so would save lives. He was willing to trust Tarphon, for he liked the red-headed Greek and had never known him to abuse their friendship; yet the tremendous differences that existed between Greek and Jew, between paganism and Judaism, seemed to have escaped him. He could see that Tarphon loved athletic contests and theater, while the Jews clung to a plainer life. He knew that at the palace there was avid discussion of books and plays of a profane nature, whereas the Jews in their homes lived simple and uncomplicated lives. Most of all, he could see that Greek life centered on the temple of Zeus, which no one took seriously, and on the gymnasium which everyone did, whereas the Jews clung to their plain old synagogue; but he did not appreciate the fact that these differences were fundamental. Therefore, when the final edicts came against which the Jews of any other age would have rebelled, Jehubabel was prepared to believe Tarphon when the governor reasoned, 'I better than most men know Antiochus, for does not my preferment stem from him? He is vain but never stupid, and when he sees that his new laws are repugnant to the Jews he will climb down from his arrogant position. Believe me, Jehubabel, the only sensible tactic for you Jews is to humor him now, even to the extent of the pig, and then to make formal protests through me. You can be sure he'll rescind the laws.'

So as a result of Jehubabel's fumbling acceptance of the pig, when Antiochus later struck at the very heart of Judaism with his persecution of Makor's three hundred and fifteen Jews, all but one accepted the new rules; but one old man who could see things for himself refused to do so, and as this stubborn martyr died he stared at Jehubabel with his one remaining eye, charging him with having betrayed his people, so that long after the old man's death Jehubabel would be haunted by his accusing, bloodstained face.

Governor Tarphon, after having watched the obscene execution–so alien to things truly Greek–left the porch of the temple and wandered slowly down the broad avenue that led to his gymnasium, at whose main doors stood two handsome statues of Heracles as a wrestler and Hermes as a long-distance runner. The gods were tall and white and naked, bespeaking the divinity that lay in any man who trained himself to physical perfection. It was Tarphon's custom, as he passed between the statues, to turn left to Heracles and flex his shoulder muscles as if he were wrestling with that god, then right to Hermes, testing his own leg muscles, which were still firm and resilient. But this day the gods seemed to accuse him, and he lowered his eyes, muttering, 'I must advise Antiochus how wretchedly his laws were received.'

Ashamed of what he had been required to witness, Tarphon entered the gymnasium, where he was greeted with the reassuring smell of men sweating at games and washing themselves clean with scented oil and steaming water, and he was about to undress and enter the games room at once, but he rejected that idea and turned toward a small room which he maintained in the spacious building; and when he did this he was brought before a towering white statue of Antiochus Epiphanes in his assumed role as discus champion. The emperor had never been good at games, but it pleased his fancy to be depicted as one skilled in sports, so here he stood gigantic and naked, posing not only as the man who had supplanted Zeus but also as one who had defeated ordinary mortals in discus throwing. Tarphon had to recognize how unenforceable the new laws were, and he muttered, 'This time Antiochus must retreat.'

He went to his room, where he spent some time drafting in classical Greek a report which advised the emperor of how the old Jew had resisted the law to the point of death and of the probable effects on the community. Then, looking into the future with unusual clarity, he added a brief section in which he predicted that if the new laws against the Jews were rigidly enforced they might provoke an armed rebellion; but when he was finished with this unsolicited analysis he considered it presumptuous and pushed it away. Closing his eyes he tried to visualize what had frightened him, and he came remarkably close to seeing the revolution that was about to explode among the Jews, but he refused to come to grips with the problem; for although he sensed the terrible forces that had been ignited that day in Makor, he was not willing to trust his own judgment, and he could not decide whether or not to send the report. Seeking to compare his ideas with what others might think, he summoned one of the slaves who served the gymnasium and directed him to fetch the Jewish leader Jehubabel, and when the slave was gone he undressed and went into one of the smaller games rooms where for some weeks he had been coaching a group of Makor boys in wrestling, it being his intention to send them to a series of regional competitions later in the year; and in the wholesome conflict of the wrestling room he forgot that day's ugliness.

Naked, he walked among the equally naked young men, commenting upon their skill, and he came at last to the dark-haired youth Menelaus, who had unusual strength in his shoulders. He pulled aside the young man's opponent, saying, 'Watch me for a moment,' and he engaged Menelaus; and as soon as he had done so he felt the youth's power bearing down upon him, forcing his practiced knees almost to buckle, and he grunted, 'Good lad, keep pushing,' while he himself began to respond to the contest and the other wrestlers halted to watch their gymnasiarch fighting with Menelaus.

Had the young man sought preferment from Tarphon he would surely have allowed the gymnasiarch to win, but this was an even contest, and the powerful youngster ripped and grabbed at Tarphon's trim body, trying to catch him off guard; while the older man, recalling many such conflicts in the past when he was a major competitor in Athens, tried to lead the eager youth into one trap or another. Once Tarphon felt he had the boy, and with a grab he reached for his right leg, but Menelaus deftly pivoted and not only escaped but put himself in position to grasp the gymnasiarch by the neck, almost jerking him off his feet. Then the older man's experience asserted itself, for having anticipated what might happen, he moved partly forward as if he were under the young man's power, and this caused Menalaus to throw all his weight into the fight, whereupon Tarphon skillfully tossed him into the crowd of watchers, where he stumbled and fell to his knees.

The athletes crowded about the red-haired governor, applauding him as if he were one of their own age, and some older toadies who had been watching the wrestlers began crying, 'There are few in Seleucia who could defeat our gymnasiarch in wrestling.' Upon this, Tarphon called young Menelaus to him and in a slow recapitulation which all could follow explained where the over-eager young athlete had made his error. As Tarphon outlined the steps those in the steaming room could see the muscles of the two men stand out and could understand what must happen next in such and such a case. It was a beautiful exhibition, controlled and effective. 'Demetrius!' Tarphon called. 'Protect yourself!' And he threw his naked body at a tall young man less skilled than Menelaus had been, and they re-enacted the maneuver, but this time the younger man was no match for the governor and when he made his first error Tarphon spun him against the wall, whereupon Menelaus jumped into position, crying, 'Gymnasiarch, protect yourself!' And he slammed at the older man with such vehemence that he forced Tarphon back and would have thrown him solidly, except that Tarphon began laughing and slapped his vigorous challenger on the shoulder.

'You win!' Tarphon conceded, but the watching sycophants said in loud voices, 'Had our gymnasiarch really wanted to win, he would have thrown the boy easily.' So that none could hear, Tarphon told his young opponent, 'We know better. At the games in Ptolemais you will surely win easily. And you could win at Antioch, too.' He paused as if about to say something of importance, but changed his mind.

It was a moment of rare fraternity, of sweating bodies tired to exhaustion, of muscles pulled almost beyond the point of resilience, and slaves appeared among the wrestlers with strigils which the men used to scrape away the dirt on their bodies before they went to the baths, but as Governor Tarphon drew the rough-edged strigil across his bare thighs, relaxing in pleasure as the bronze metal scraped his tired leg, another slave came into the room to say, 'Gymnasiarch, the Jew Jehubabel is here,' and Tarphon said to Menelaus, 'You'd better go to the baths before your father comes.' The room emptied. The toadies went elsewhere to praise lesser men, and Governor Tarphon stood alone, completely naked, with not even a strigil in his hand. The door opened and out of the steamy heat loomed the incongruous bearded figure of Jehubabel, completely covered in a long unkempt robe. The two men stared at each other, epitomes of the struggle that had been joined that day: Tarphon the Greek, whose ancestors had built the walls around Makor making the town as it now was, a naked athlete who thought of his finely trained body as a temple; and Jehubabel the permanent Jew, to whom the grandeur of Greece was an unopened book and the naked body an insult to YHWH. Looking now at the undraped gymnasiarch Jehubabel recalled the saying current among his people: 'Only a fool takes pleasure in the swiftness of a horse or the strength of a man's leg.' Few Jews in Makor bothered with the gymnasium or its pagan rites.

Tarphon, aware of Jehubabel's abhorrence of nakedness, deferred to the older man by grabbing a robe left behind by one of the wrestlers and throwing it over his shoulders; but as soon as he had done so he was sorry, for the robe was both long–which made him look awkward, which he tried never to be–and smelly, which made him seem unclean, which he never was. But he had taken it and could not easily discard it, so he wrapped himself in it and led the way to his room.

No sooner, however, had Jehubabel left the nakedness of the wrestling room than he found himself facing the absurd statue of Antiochus Epiphanes as a discus thrower, and the towering expanse of white marble with the godlike head and the huge genitals appalled the Jew. He could not forget that today's execution and its savagery had been ordered by this fool who had decreed himself to be so represented, claiming to be both a god manifest and a naked discus thrower. The round-faced, pudgy Jew was disgusted, but he could not speak, for in the past he had picked up the suspicion that his friend Tarphon hoped some day to be represented in Makor by a similar statue, and he thought, turning his back on Antiochus and his glaring nudity: No one can understand a Greek.

Tarphon led him into the small room where on a table lay the report he had been writing, held in place by what Jehubabel considered a curious object: a life-size marble hand, broken off at the wrist and holding an instrument which the Jew had not seen before. 'How was the statue broken?' he asked in the Koine.

Tarphon smiled indulgently. This was the kind of question one might expect from a Jew, for although he found the Jews of Makor industrious and well behaved, he also found them notoriously deficient in a sense of beauty. The Greeks had not been in Makor a dozen years before they began building the lovely temple of Zeus, but the Jews were still content with their squat and ugly synagogue. Greeks loved silk, the cool feel of marble, the smell of spices and the sound of lyric poetry being read at night, while the Jews remained a peasant people to whom beauty and luxury were equally abhorrent. With condescension Tarphon explained that no statue had been broken. 'The artist carved the hand this way,' he said, also in the Koine.

'Why would he do that?' Jehubabel asked.

'From little, much,' Tarphon replied. When Jehubabel looked blank, he added, 'By looking at the fragment you can imagine the whole statue.'

'But if he wanted you to see the whole statue, why didn't he carve it?'

Tarphon was irritated but he was also amused. 'In the spring haven't you ever tasted just one bite of a Damascus plum? It was so good that you could sense all the plums for that year?'

'I don't eat plums,' Jehubabel said.

'But this carving? Doesn't it call to your mind the entire human body?'

The round-faced Jew drew back suspiciously to consider this preposterous theory, and he found that to him the broken wrist conveyed no such language. He saw a rather lifelike hand holding an object he had not seen before, and that was the end of the matter. 'What's he holding?' he inquired.

Tarphon was taken aback. It had never occurred to him that a grown man would not recognize a strigil and he summoned his slave to fetch the one he had left in the wrestling room. When it arrived he passed it along to the Jew. 'Can't you guess what it's for?'

Jehubabel studied the metal scraper for some moments but could not fathom its mystery. 'It has a dull point, so it might be used for digging,' he reasoned. 'But it also has a sharp edge, so it might be intended for cutting. I don't know.'

'It's for scraping your skin,' Tarphon explained. Jehubabel looked at him in astonishment and made the governor feel self-conscious. 'After athletic contests,' he added lamely. In an attempt to demonstrate he reached for some part of the Jew's anatomy, only to find that all of Jehubabel's skin except for the backs of his hands and a small part of his face was covered—either by his robe or beard. There was a moment of embarrassment, during which it became obvious that Jehubabel did not intend to uncover any part of his body, so Tarphon switched to his own, throwing aside one side of the smelly robe and drawing the strigil over his exposed thigh. 'It's most refreshing,' he said, but the round-faced Jew looked at him as if the governor were going out of his mind.

Having drawn aside the borrowed robe Tarphon was reminded of its offensive smell, and while Jehubabel studied the sculpture he took off the robe completely, stretched out upon a bench and called for his slave to bring a container of heated oil, which the latter began applying to Tarphon's body. Spreading the warm oil liberally over the gymnasiarch's back, he massaged the muscles and with his thumbs worked the lotion into the pores, and as he did so the aromatic spices permeated the room, providing a good ending to the day's exercise. 'This oil is the only luxury I allow myself,' he explained to his friend. 'They make it in Macedonia and I used it when I wrestled in Athens.'

'The smell of the rose and the taste of the grape do not abide till the morrow,' Jehubabel observed, and Tarphon winced. The only unpleasant aspect he had found in working with the Jewish leader was this constant barrage of pithy statements in which Jehubabel took refuge whenever intellectual problems were to be faced. The Jew was known in Makor as a learned man, but he never referred to the great books of Judaism; against the works of Plato and Aristotle he never quoted Jews of equal gravity. It was always some cryptic proverb gleaned from the fields or culled from the shearing sheds that was supposed to summarize the Jewish position. Some years ago, when Tarphon promised to protect the Jews against the law of Antiochus, Jehubabel had stated his reaction clearly: 'A friend is a friend at all times, and brothers are born for adversity.' Next year, commenting upon the worsened laws, he had said, 'Whom the gods love they chasten, even as a father corrects the son in whom he delights.' In fact, for a man with the wide-ranging interests of Governor Tarphon, talking with Jehubabel for any length of time was apt to be a bore, and the Greek often wished that his colleague would forget his little gems of wisdom and for once face the reality at hand.

Why did he bother with Jehubabel? Because in the shifting Greek world of Ptolemais and Makor, the Jew was the one completely honest man with whom Tarphon had contact. He wanted nothing of the gymnasiarch, practiced no flattery, kept his word and worked hard for the betterment of the town. He paid his workers at the dye vats well, educated his children and assumed responsibility for the synagogue. Tarphon often told his wife Melissa, 'If we had a dozen more like Jehubabel, governing this district would be a pleasure, but apparently only the Jews can produce such men.' Because Tarphon appreciated the rock-hard constancy of the man he was prepared to put up with his boring, almost niggardly, manner.

Now, from the rubbing bench, Tarphon said, 'Tell me honestly, Jehubabel. The execution today. Was it the end of a difficult period or the beginning of real trouble?'

Jehubabel looked away from the naked body stretched out on the bench, belly up, for it offended him. Also, he could still see the accusing face of the martyred man staring at him as he shouted out the defiant prayer of the Jews, and he was driven to make a somewhat harsher reply than he would have otherwise done: 'Once a river leaves its banks it does not return until the rains cease.'

'What do you mean by that?' Tarphon asked in some irritation.

'If these laws persist there could be serious results.'

'Could be, yes. But will there be?'

Jehubabel wanted to believe that what Tarphon had told him earlier would come to pass–that when Antiochus knew how the Jews felt about the new laws they would be rescinded; so he clung to that hope: 'If Antiochus retreats a little I feel sure trouble can be avoided.'

The slave washed Tarphon with a damp cloth, then brought clothes into which the gymnasiarch slipped, leaving most of his body still exposed. Moving to a chair beside the table he asked, 'If trouble should become inevitable, what will cause it?'

'The swine we can forgive,' Jehubabel said reassuringly. 'And we acknowledge Antiochus as ruler . . . even as god over his own people. But there is one thing . . .'

'That you're afraid of?'

'Jews will continue to circumcise their sons.'

'No! No!' Tarphon protested. 'On this matter I agree with Antiochus. The human body is too precious to be altered whimsically by any religion that comes along. Why do you suppose we outlawed the branding of slaves? And mutilation? And tattooing?' He brandished the marble hand with the strigil as if it were a pointer and demanded, "Tell me this. If your Jewish god, who is as perfect as you claim, made man, why should you try to improve on his handiwork?'

For once Jehubabel did not retreat to an aphorism. He said, 'When the creator finished his perfect work he took Abraham aside and said, "I have made a perfect man. Now I need a perfect people. To prove to the world that you are my chosen people, you shall circumcise your sons." In doing so, we act not contrary to divine will, but in furtherance of it.'

Tarphon was surprised at the Jew's clear statement, but he shrugged his shoulders. 'The law is plain, Jehubabel. No more circumcision.' Then he added, 'Please.'

The stocky dyer considered this appeal, the latest in a long series, and once more he conceded: 'I don't think any Jews would circumcise their sons without first discussing the problem with me.' Tarphon smiled. He knew that within the Jewish community it was only Jehubabel who performed the circumcisions, so if the law of Antiochus were to be broken it would be Jehubabel who would be responsible, but he did not embarrass his friend by admitting that he understood this fact. The long-robed Jew concluded, 'So if the Jews ask me for advice I shall tell them that for a little longer . . .'

Tarphon was relieved. This was all he needed, a little time, for he felt sure that with time he could alleviate the troubles. Taking the second sheet of his report from under the marble hand he tore it up and threw it in a basket. 'I was about to send Antiochus words which he did not need to hear,' he said with a nervous laugh. Then as he led Jehubabel to the door of his room the two men saw looming above them the gigantic statue of Epiphanes, and Tarphon said, 'I'm glad you understand, Jehubabel. Against his great force you weak Jews could not prevail. It is with reason we'll soften his laws.'

Jehubabel preferred not to look at the indecent statue. Instead, he took refuge in a Jewish proverb whose application not even he understood: 'The breath of the king withers the barley, but at the end of winter comes rain.'

Tarphon thought: He's truly a sententious bore, but without him we'd have trouble. Then, to help Jehubabel comprehend the situation, the gymnasiarch said with a certain enthusiasm, 'Don't be misled by that statue. Would you be surprised if I said I thought it preposterous too? But I also know Antiochus the man. As he rules in Antioch. He moves among the common people of that enormous city in a way no tyrant would dare. At night he suddenly enters a drinking place and sings with the sailors. He acts in plays, or wanders unknown in the alleys to see how the poor live. He has one consuming desire. To be loved. And when at the games his people cheer him he becomes in fact a god and dispenses justice to all. Believe me, Jehubabel, when he hears that his laws have made you Jews unhappy . . .'

'As the whirlwind passeth, so is the wicked no more,' Jehubabel said, 'but the righteous is an everlasting foundation.' Tarphon shook his head, as if the middle part of the sentence had fallen out of the conversation, but in friendship he grasped the Jew's shoulder and said, 'When Antiochus reads my letter, the law will be changed.' And he accompanied his friend to the exit.

But as they left the gymnasiarch's room, from the other end of the building appeared a group of seven handsome young men–the athletes with whom Tarphon had been wrestling. They were lean, clear-eyed young fellows dressed in a uniform which the older men of Makor had provided them to wear on their trips to compete with other communities: broad-brimmed hats with low crowns, handsome fluttering capes of light blue fastened at the neck with silver clasps, and white flexible boots whos laces criss-crossed up to the knee. In these gay uniforms the seven athletes looked like seven statues of Hermes, poised for whatever commission Zeus might hand them, and as they clattered noisily past the looming statue of Epiphanes, Jehubabel saw that the tallest of the group was his own dark-haired son Benjamin; but he took no pride in this fact.

When the boys were gone Tarphon walked with his friend to the exit, saying, 'Jehubabel, your son Menelaus will be the finest athlete Makor has ever produced.'

'"A wise son maketh a glad father:"' Jehubabel quoted from Solomon, '"but a foolish son is the heaviness of his mother." Wrestling is foolishness. Discus throwing . . .' He pointed over his shoulder to the statue of Epiphanes. 'Foolishness.'

'No!' Tarphon protested. 'Days when such sayings were true are past. A boy today must have some wisdom, yes. But he must also know games, the social pleasantries. Nothing in excess. Great change is in the air, old friend, and you must change with it.'

But Jehubabel, haunted still by the face of the dead martyr, said, 'Wisdom is still the only thing, if with wisdom you also get understanding.'

'I got my understanding from wrestling,' Tarphon replied, but this the Jew could not believe and he walked alone up the broad avenue leading to the temple of Zeus, where against his will he was drawn to look at the gigantic head of the man who posed as god, illuminated from below by an oil lamp which burned perpetually. '"Vanity of vanities,"' he quoted from an ancient saying. Then he saw the spot where the old man had been flayed; it was still damp. For a few moments he prayed there and then turned east to walk down the main thoroughfare, whose numerous shops contained importations from all parts of the world: flashing ornaments made from the tin of Cornwall, silver beads from Spain and bright copper pots from Cyprus; there was gold from Nubia, marble from Paros and ebony from India. Some shops offered foods that a century before were unheard of in this town: sesame candies from Egypt, sharp cheeses from Athens, figs in honey from Crete, cinnamon from Africa and sweet pannag from Byzantium.

'"All is vanity."' Jehubabel quoted as he approached the synagogue under the east wall. The gaudy shops had never appealed to him; they were run only by foreigners, for the proud Jews of rural Israel were still incompetent in trading and the handling of money, inclining towards the more fundamental occupations like farming and dyeing, except that during the Babylonian captivity a few had acquired technical skills like goldsmithing, which their descendants still practiced. It was not these seductive shops which called forth Jehubabel's reflection on vanity; it was his son Menelaus. The boy's real name was Benjamin, but like many Jewish lads in Seleucia he had early acquired a Greek name by which he was generally known. Tall where his father was stocky, robust where his mother was slim, he had quickly won the attention of the Greeks, who had inducted him into their schools and their games, in both of which he excelled. Now, alienated from his Jewish parents, he spent most of his days in the gymnasium and many of his nights at the palace, where he was being initiated into Greek culture of the higher order. Like Gymnasiarch Tarphon, with whom he often wrestled, he was beginning to find his father's homilies tedious, and like Melissa, Tarphon's clever wife, he found the old-fashioned ways of the Jews difficult to take seriously. In the natural course of events, by the time Menelaus was thirty he would no longer be a Jew, for the empire of Antiochus Epiphanes needed young men of aptitude and it was probable that he would be invited to serve in areas where Jews were unknown. Inducements were being offered, not only to young Jews but to Persians and Parthians as well, to forgo their old inheritances and to become full-fledged Greeks, and as young Menelaus exercised with Tarphon and learned at first-hand the principles of Greek political life, or as he studied with Melissa and uncovered the richness of Greek intellectual life, he found himself increasingly tempted to surrender Jewish ways and to join the large number who had left the synagogue and had become in fact Hellenes.

A fool despises his father's teaching, Jehubabel brooded mournfully as he passed the empty synagogue on his way to his home, which stood next door, but at the entrance to the synagogue his sleeve was caught by a small man with protruding eyes who said, 'Jehubabel, I must speak with you.' It was Paltiel, a farmer with few sheep and a man from whom courage would hardly be expected, but now the scrawny fellow pulled at Jehubabel's sleeve and said the frightening words which made the revolution of the Jews unavoidable: 'My son was born eight days ago.'

Jehubabel trembled. In the gymnasium he had promised Tarphon that there would be no trouble, but now the fatal words were being said directly to him. The fat dyer began to sweat and asked, 'Paltiel, were you at the execution today?'

'I stood two cubits from the old man, and before he died he looked at me with one eye. He looked into my very heart, and I am determined.'

Jehubabel thought: At how many others did the old man look today? To Paltiel he said, 'Then you are committed?'

'Aren't you?' the little farmer asked. 'The old man looked at you, also.'

'You saw?'

'Jehubabel, he looked at us all.'

The trembling dyer's whole inclination was to tell Paltiel to be gone, but the small man could not be dismissed, so Jehubabel said, 'Wait here,' and he walked dumbly to his home where his wife had supper waiting; but he went past her to an inner room, where he took from a chest a small cloth in which he kept a sharpened knife, and this knife he placed on the floor, sitting before it and staring at it, wondering what to do. And after a while his wife came to call him to supper, but when she saw the knife she lost her appetite and sat on the floor beside him.

'It is a terrible thing you contemplate,' she said.

They remained silent for some minutes, staring at the knife, grasping for any solution to the problem of which they had become an unwilling part, and Jehubabel quoted evasively, '"The thoughts of the righteous are right: but the counsels of the wicked are deceit."' To this impeccable statement his wife nodded, and he felt encouraged to add, '"A virtuous woman is a crown to her husband: but she that maketh ashamed is as rottenness in his bones."' She smiled wanly, as if to thank him for his confidence, but refrained from saying anything that might help guide him so he added, '"The integrity of the upright shall guide them: but the perverseness of transgressors shall destroy them."'

Having insulated themselves with these comforting saws, Jehubabel and his wife were about to dismiss the temptation and put away the knife when Jehubabel saw, looming out of the darkness, the monitoring eye of the dead man, and he cried, 'A man already dead mustn't tell us what to do.' His wife asked what he was saying, but a knocking came at the door and the urgent voice of Paltiel: 'Jehubabel, we are waiting!'

In despair the spiritual leader of the Jews looked at his wife, then drew himself full length on the floor, crying, 'Adonai, Adonai, what shall I do?' No instructions came from YHWH and he confided to his wife, 'I don't know what to do. Tarphon suspects my complicity. I saw him smiling at me. If his soldiers catch me in this act I shall be lashed to death.' He shuddered, for he could feel the lead-tipped thongs as they cut into his body.

Then came a rush of hope. He sat up and caught his wife's hands. 'Tarphon assured me that Antiochus was a sensible man. He sings and dances like any Greek. Wants people to love him. Now, when you see that great stone head in the temple you mustn't think . . .'

'Jehubabel!' came the ghostly voice of Paltiel, summoning him to inescapable reality.

And so in that inner room, Jehubabel, one of the first persons in world history to do so, had to face the mystery of the Jew: 'Why does he seek out martyrdom? An insignificant man like Paltiel? Why does he combat the empire?' And Jehubabel felt it wrong that vital decisions should be forced by the eye of a dead martyr and the voice of a man willing to become one.

'Jehubabel!' came the demanding voice. 'Must I alone, sanctify my son? Tell me now if you are afraid.' And to the listening couple the voice outside had become the voice of Adonai.

Slowly, driven by forces which he did not comprehend but which would rule Judaism for the ensuing centuries, Jehubabel picked up the knife, wrapped it in its cloth and tucked it in his belt. 'I must go,' he told his wife. 'The old man is looking at me.' And she accompanied him to the door, where she gave him her blessing, for in his final agony the old man had looked at her, too.

The sweating, dumpy man and the scrawny little farmer hurried past the synagogue and down a dark alley which led toward the main gate, but halfway along that passageway they stopped to dodge quickly into a small house, occupied by Paltiel, and there four Jews were gathered with an eight-day-old baby boy who had been prepared for circumcision. As if it were a routine ritual Jehubabel asked, 'Are we prepared to enter into the covenant of Abraham?' but when the assembled Jews gave their routine replies he looked at them with quivering eyes and asked passionately, 'Neighbors, are we aware of what this means?' And upon interrogation he found that the old man had looked at each face in that room, handing on a commitment that would never die. Each man knew what was involved and was prepared for the consequences.

Jehubabel, trembling with the gravity of what he was doing, stood aside to utter a short prayer, after which he presented his sharp knife and circumcised the infant, who began to howl at the unaccustomed pain, but little Paltiel jammed a wine-soaked cloth into the child's mouth and the crying ceased. 'His name is Itzhak,' the farmer said, 'for Itzhak was the son of Abraham who was offered as a sacrifice to . . .' Here the father reached a difficult impasse. He was not allowed to speak the name YHWH; indeed he did not know how the sacred name was pronounced, for it had been some centuries since the word had been spoken in Makor. But since any deity must be referred to in some manner the custom had grown up of calling YHWH by the arbitrary Hebrew word *Adonai,* which would later be translated into other languages as *Lord.* When the vowel indications for *Adonai* were added to the letters YHWH, a curious symbol developed which German scholars many centuries later would mistakenly read as Jehovah, a word that had never existed and that had never in any way been applied to the austere Hebrew deity. Thus the greatest of gods was called YHWH, which had no pronunciation; he was known to ordinary Jews as Adonai, which was purely arbitrary; and he would conquer the world as Jehovah, a name which had never belonged to him or to anything else. Perhaps only this vague and contradictory nomenclature could indicate the wonder of the concept involved, or explain why a group of Jews in Makor were willing to risk being flayed alive because of their devotion to the god who had sustained them.

Paltiel, the man with few sheep, who was taking the greatest risk—for the Greeks could examine his son at any time and see proof of guilt—held his son aloft and said, 'He is Itzhak, who was offered as a sacrifice to Adonai. But he lived. Tonight all of us offer our lives to Adonai, and may we also live.'

One by one the conspirators, aware that their lives were forfeit if the child Itzhak were inspected by Greek officials, slipped out of the house, but as Jehubabel picked his way back to the synagogue he heard boisterous voices coming along the main street and he thought it might be a group of soldiers who would question him, and he hid. But the noisy ones were the seven athletes in their blue capes returning from an evening at Tarphon's palace, and they marched toward the synagogue to bid his son Benjamin good night. In the fraternity of athletes they brought him to his door, making him swear that he would be at the gymnasium early next day. An ordinary father seeing how welcome his son was among the boys whose fathers ran the town would have felt pride in his acceptance, but Jehubabel, watching from the shadows as his Greek son called farewell to his Greek friends, felt only shame that the boy should have drifted so far from the spirit that had driven Paltiel to the circumcision of his son.

His apprehension regarding Benjamin increased when Governor Tarphon traveled to Ptolemais, where work had accumulated regarding the seaport, leaving Melissa in the palace along the northern wall, for there Benjamin went in Tarphon's absence, and it became clear to Jehubabel that an evil relationship had developed between his son and the gymnasiarch's beautiful Greek wife. For several painful days Jehubabel lingered in narrow streets between the temple of Zeus and the palace, and from his hiding place spied upon the boy's movements. What he saw convinced him that his blue-cloaked son was betraying his benefactor.

On the third night of watching, Jehubabel waited for some hours until Benjamin left the commodious house, his blue cloak over his arm as he headed for the gymnasium, but when the boy approached, Jehubabel stepped suddenly before him, saying in Aramaic, 'You shall not go to the gymnasium. You shall come home with me.'

'The others expect me,' his son replied in the Koine.

'Your mother expects you,' Jehubabel muttered under his breath, and he dragged his son toward the temple of Zeus and then eastward along the main street, whose opulent shops exemplified for him the temptations into which the Jews of Makor had fallen.

At their home Jehubabel sat the bewildered boy on a bench and summoned his mother. Together the two older Jews challenged their son with having betrayed Governor Tarphon, who had so often befriended the family. 'There is the dog that bites his keeper's hand, and there is the young man who seduces the wife of his guardian,' Jehubabel said sententiously, while his son continued to look perplexed.

'Can a man take the fire of adultery into his bosom, and his clothes not be burned?' Jehubabel asked, but still his words made no impression on the boy.

'Her house is the way to hell, leading you down to chambers of death,' the fat face with the beard mumbled, but Menelaus, his ear attuned to the subtleties of Greek thought, could not understand what his garrulous father was trying to say.

'Drink waters out of your own cistern and running waters out of your own well. Let them be yours only, and do not share them with strangers,' the pudgy moralist intoned, and Menelaus grew fidgety, which annoyed his father.

'"Train up a child in the way he should go:"' Jehubabel said with great earnestness, '"and when he is old, he will not depart from it." We warned you that the lips of a strange woman drop sweetness like a honeycomb and her mouth is smoother than oil.'

'Father, you're talking nonsense,' Menelaus said, using the Koine.

Jehubabel was stunned. He had been offering his son the profoundest wisdom he knew and the boy mocked him. He felt that he had to make some powerful statement that would clear the young man's head and force him to see the grievous wrong of adultery, but instead all he could think of was the ancient summary of the Jews: 'What son curses his father, his lamp shall be put out in darkness.' To Jehubabel, trained in the ways of Judaism, the sentence had frightening implications, but to Menelaus it was words only.

'I didn't curse you, Father. I said you were talking nonsense, and you are. Now what is it you're trying to say?'

Jehubabel drew away from his insolent son. 'I am warning you that adultery with the wife of Governor Tarphon . . .'

Menelaus began laughing, easily and frankly. 'Is that what's frightened you?' he asked. Then, pointing with his hands, he said in broken phrases, 'That I go . . . Melissa's house . . . and Tarphon is in Ptolemais?' He laughed again and said, 'Father, Governor Tarphon asked me to do this. Many of us go to Melissa's. We sit and listen to her read.'

Jehubabel sat down heavily. 'You do what?' he quavered.

'Or we talk.'

'About what?'

Menelaus was momentarily baffled. On this day Melissa had talked about a play in Athens, a philosopher from Antioch, and the day when a tame bear had chased her in Rhodes. 'Well, we talk about many things.'

His son's hesitancy satisfied Jehubabel, who could see Tarphon's palace only as a pit into which his son had stumbled in his sexual debauchery. Ponderously he said, 'Stolen waters are sweet, Benjamin, and the bread you eat in secret is pleasant, but death is there.' To Jehubabel it was tantamount to malediction, but to Menelaus it was quite irrelevant.

Once more the boy tried to explain: 'We seven are like the sons of Tarphon, and Melissa cares for us. When we talk with her she tells us what to do.'

'You have entered the house of evil, and the servants have closed the doors,' Jehubabel said, and Menelaus looked at him in bewildered silence. The boy knew that he would not be able to explain to his father, so without speaking further the young athlete picked up a few articles of clothing and left. When Jehubabel asked where he was going, Menelaus said, 'To the governor's. Long ago he asked me to live with him, and now I shall do so.' And he was not seen again in the house by the synagogue.

When Tarphon returned from Ptolemais he was required to do two things which displeased him. On orders from Antiochus Epiphanes he announced that all Jewish households must be searched for male children, and if any under the age of six months was found to have been circumcised, that child's parents would be flayed alive. When the order was given he summoned Jehubabel to the gymnasium and said, 'I trust you have not broken the law.'

The bearded dyer looked at Tarphon in silence, for he was praying that the farmer Paltiel might somehow hide his son, but Tarphon interpreted the Jew's refusal to speak as animosity stemming from the fact that Menelaus had moved to the palace. 'Believe me, Jehubabel, when your son is champion of the empire you'll thank me for taking over his training.' But Jehubabel continued to pray, and Paltiel succeeded in hiding his son Itzhak among his sheep, and that day the Jews were spared.

When the soldiers reported to the gymnasium that no circumcisions had taken place, Jehubabel regained his composure; it was Tarphon who sat down heavily in a chair, and the Jew realized how eager the governor had been to find no guilt. 'We want no further executions in this town,' Tarphon said. Then he rose and clasped Jehubabel about the shoulder. 'Thank you, old friend, for having spared us all.'

When the pudgy, long-robed Jew left the gymnasium—the most unathletic-looking person who ever did so—Tarphon undressed and went to the wrestling room, where he asked Menelaus to fight against him, and as they moved about, grappling for holds, Tarphon had to explain the second bit of unpleasant business, but first he encouraged the young man by saying, after a vigorous sequence of thrusts and grabs, 'In Ptolemais I met a group of wrestlers from Tyre. Claimed to be champions of the north.'

Casually Menelaus asked, 'You wrestled against them?'

'Yes.'

Menelaus was breathing heavily. 'Did you defeat them?'

'Easily.'

Tarphon watched Menelaus carefully, and what he saw reassured him. A slight quiver came to the young man's lips and the governor knew what he was thinking: If Tarphon can defeat them, and I can defeat Tarphon, it means that I could be champion.

But Menelaus was cautious. Hesitating lest he offend his patron, he inquired, 'Were they really champions?'

'They claimed to be. Said they were certain winners at Antioch.'

Tarphon was pleased with what happened next. Menelaus smiled. It was the relaxed smile of a young man who senses victory ahead. It showed neither arrogance nor conceit, but rather the anticipation of a contest in which there was reasonable chance for success. Men who had never played games would not have recognized this smile, but anyone who, like the gymnasiarch, had engaged in athletic contests most of his life would observe it with respect, because it was from such self-confidence that victory was built. At that moment Menelaus was very much a Greek and he said quietly, 'I am eager to compete at Antioch.'

'And I want to take you there,' Tarphon answered. 'But in Ptolemais I heard bad news to go with the good.'

Menelaus stopped smiling. 'What was it?' he asked, and again Tarphon was impressed with his sober willingness to face reality. He's an authentic Greek, Tarphon thought.

Slowly Tarphon tried to explain the ugly facts: 'For a Jew to win at Antioch would be extremely popular. I know the emperor would like to see one of your people capture a major trophy. It would . . . I mean it would prove that in the empire we do not discriminate against any man . . . that we can all become good Greeks if we try. Now I'll grant there have been minor differences between Antiochus and the Jews . . . take even your own father . . .'

'What are you trying to say?'

Tarphon brushed the sweat from his forehead and continued, 'I'm saying that we all want you to go to Antioch . . . and to win.'

'I also,' Menelaus replied, preparing himself for bad news.

'But Antiochus has decreed that no contestant may stand naked before him who is circumcised. It would be offensive to the spirit of the games.'

In the steamy room there was silence, and the two athletes were forced to look down at the visible proof of Menelaus' covenant with YHWH. In his first days in the gymnasium Menelaus had been conspicuous because of this sign, and other boys had taunted him, for he was the only Jew who came to the place, and he had fought alone; but with his later victories had come self-respect, and the other athletes now looked upon his circumcision with the impersonal interest they might have directed toward a boy who had lost a toe. To them Menelaus was three things: a Greek, a Champion, a circumcised Jew—and the first two outweighed the last. But the Seleucid capital of Antioch had seen no Jewish athletes, and there the fact of circumcision would be scandalous as a profanation of the human temple. Menelaus understood all this even more clearly than Tarphon and it was he who suggested the solution: 'In Ptolemais isn't there a doctor who can cover the sign?'

'There is, but it's terribly painful.'

'If I were able to bear the pain?'

'Then it could be done.'

Cautiously Menelaus weighed the choices growing out of what the governor had just said, and he could not decide between them. Tarphon, appreciating the boy's perplexities—for who would reject the essence of his inherited religion?—did not press him to speak at that moment. Instead, he found Menelaus a strigil and the two athletes sat on benches and scraped themselves, after which they went to the baths, where slaves immersed them in tepid water, then massaged them with scented oil and dipped them into very hot water, from which they came out exhausted and relaxed. This was the finest moment of the day, when the fruits of vigorous exercise were found in cleanliness and the expulsion of irrelevant worries. It might almost have been called 'The Greek moment,' for it so perfectly epitomized the Greek ideal; and in this period of unusual mental clarity before he fell asleep on the padded benches, Menelaus faced up to the full implication of what he had been discussing with the gymnasiarch.

'Speak honestly to me, sir. Have I chance to win at Antioch?'

'I tested all the strangers from Tyre, and none could damage you.'

'And if I win at Antioch, will Athens follow?'

'As day follows night,' Tarphon said. He liked the pragmatic sequence in which this young Jew faced problems. The operation which the doctor in Ptolemais had developed in order to erase the sign of circumcision was bitterly painful and must not be undertaken lightly. One misguided Jew from Jaffa had committted suicide because of the agony, which proved so much greater than he had anticipated. But if there was a chance for some great prize, that might justify pain. So Tarphon considered it honourable to give his young friend that straw's weight of encouragement which men often require in order to reach a decision: 'Menelaus, when a young man wrestles he is striving not only for the immediate laurel. When I was your age I fought like a warrior, but I also studied and the time came when the empire needed a governor, and I was chosen. But I had won the office long before. Some day I'll be promoted, and this governorship will be vacant. Now, I know that Antiochus wants to appoint a Jew to some important position. To reconcile your people to his rule. That Jew could be you.'

Menelaus was sleepy. The exercise and the warm bath and the penetrating smell of the oil combined to overcome him, but before he lost consciousness he said, 'When you race to Ptolemais next week I should like to be among your challengers.'

'You shall be,' Tarphon said.

On the morning of the annual race trumpeters summoned spectators to the main gate of Makor, where Governor Tarphon stood in military uniform, sword at his side, helmet on his head. About him clustered the seven athletes in their special uniforms, looking like gods, and beyond them stood four or five younger competitors who had not yet proved themselves sufficiently to have earned costumes but who hoped that in this eight-mile race to Ptolemais they might take the first steps toward such recognition. Beyond them stood the townspeople, including Canaanites and Jews, Phoenicians and Egyptians, all with their wives and daughters.

The runners now sat on doorsteps to unlace their formal shoes, replacing them with sandals that they tested by running a few steps, which made them look even more like gods as their blue capes moved in the morning breeze. When they were satisfied that their sandals fitted, trumpets blew and the men took off their head coverings, handing them to friends, who were thus honored. Each man tied a small white cloth about his forehead, after which the trumpets again sounded, whereupon the contestants took off all their clothing to stand naked in the sunlight. They were a handsome group, bronzed, muscular and marred by no disfiguring fat. They were probably as fine a body of men as the Greek empires could have provided that morning, and none excelled the figure of the gymnasiarch as he stood naked before his people—a man extremely well controlled and capable, somewhat past the age of competition but able to defeat most of the young fellows amongst whom he stood. As if they intended the general public to marvel at them, the athletes moved about for some moments, during which all could see that of the contestants only Menelaus was a Jew.

Then Governor Tarphon casually took a breechclout and wrapped it about his middle. The others followed suit, and soon all were ready for the race. The gymnasiarch signaled for the trumpets to sound once more, after which he addressed the runners in tones loud enough for the citizens to hear: 'Any of you who fail to beat me into Ptolemais will get no wine in that city and no sweet oil for your baths when you return to Makor.' The runners laughed, and he moved among them, punching them on their strong shoulders and testing their firm belly muscles with his fist.

Melissa came forward, kissed her husband, then kissed Menelaus and another young man who lived at her house. To the rest she said, 'If you do not defeat Tarphon this day he will prove unbearable. For my sake, please, do not let him win.' Everyone laughed, and she gave the signal which started the race. Down the ramp the athletes went and onto the Damascus road, heading west toward Ptolemais, and as they ran it was easy to see from the long, rhythmic stride of the red-haired gymnasiarch that he would not be easily defeated this day.

Among the spectators who watched the beginning of the race was Jehubabel, who had to stand in shame among his silent Jews as they followed the abhorrent spectacle of a Jewish boy parading naked before the wide-eyed young women of the town as they stared with fascination at the peculiarity which marked him from the others. The more naked Menelaus had seemed, the more closely other Jews had drawn their robes about them, as if to compensate for the young man's defection. And all felt sorry for Jehubabel.

In the days following the departure of the runners, the town soldiers, obedient to a plan laid down by Tarphon before he left, launched another search of Jewish homes to see if any were disobeying the laws of Antiochus Epiphanes, and without warning they descended on a group of widely scattered families, including the home of Paltiel the farmer, and there they discovered that his infant son had been circumcised. Grabbing both the child and his parents they hauled them to jail and sent a runner—an official messenger who ran alone bearing an ebony wand of authority—to Ptolemais with news for Governor Tarphon: 'The Jew Paltiel has been caught flagrantly disobeying the law. In accordance with plans approved by you, he and his wife should be executed within two days. But do you wish the executions delayed until your return?' That afternoon the same messenger returned with the expected reply: 'It is impossible for me to leave Ptolemais. Proceed as planned.' The soldiers had accurately guessed that their governor, who had initiated the search, would want to be absent when the executions took place, and it was for this precise reason that the search had been carried out while he was away.

It was one of those days of incredible beauty that come to the Galilee toward the end of autumn, when the summer heat has ended and the winter rain has not yet started. The earth stands refreshed with heavy dew and the olive trees rest from their burden of fruit. The vines are empty and the oxen are idle. In the sky not a cloud appears, not even haze from the sea, but cool breezes move casually across the landscape, bespeaking the cold weather that lies ahead. In all seasons of the year the Galilee is a masterpiece of nature, an area to make the heart glad that man is an animal who can love the earth as a deer loves the cool highlands or as the bee eater loves the fields over which he skims; but in autumn, when the seasons are about to change, it has a special beauty, and if great thoughts have sometimes come from this small region it is partly because this magnificence of the land–the magnificence that lies in familiar things rather than in great waterfalls or towering mountains–has always impressed itself upon the people who lived in the area. Never was the Galilee so lovely as in this fateful year when the empire of the Seleucids seemed so securely entrenched not only in the Galilee but in all of Israel, even to Jerusalem. It was as if nature herself were holding her breath to see what would happen in the conflict between the imperial might of Antiochus Epiphanes and the unarmed resolution of a few Jews.

That autumn, in Makor at least, it seemed obvious that Antiochus must win, for when the Jews of the town were assembled before the temple of Zeus they were a terrified lot. There the guards had erected two pillars and had provided two lashes fitted with lead-tipped thongs. In the hush of an exquisitely beautiful morning, the family of Paltiel was led forth, the little farmer with protruding eyes, his wife who could have moved unnoticed in any crowd, and their infant child, The swaddling clothes of the latter were ripped away and the child was held aloft by his feet to demonstrate that it had been circumcised in defiance of the law.

With hideous swiftness a sword flashed and the child was split in two.

Before the parents could express their anguish, they were stripped and tied to the poles, where they were lashed fifty times. The effect of a lead-tipped thong upon a man's body was terrible, striking fear into the hearts of all, but upon a woman's body the effect was overwhelming. Those required to watch lowered their heads.

The mutilated bodies were thrown to the ground, where knives cut away any remaining skin, and then the torsos were hacked apart and thrown on a heap of rubbish outside the town where dogs and jackals came to feed. But in the late afternoon of that perfect day, a solitary soldier, who had broken some minor rule, appeared with a bucket and a broom to wash away any stains that might remain before the temple of Zeus, for the Greeks were a meticulous people to whom cleanliness and beauty were imperative.

That night the crushed Jews of Makor sent a few of their men to the synagogue, where they met in silence, merely to pray. Jehubabel, who should at that moment have stood forth as the spiritual leader of the community, was mute, caught in the grip of self-condemnation. He had permitted Paltiel to circumcise his son. Indeed, he had himself wielded the knife that completed the covenant, and it should have been he who stood at the lashing post, not Paltiel. He had allowed his own son to go over to the Greeks and had permitted him to stand naked in the sunlight like a young pagan who knew not YHWH. It had been Jehubabel's counsel that had persuaded the Jews to allow pigs to be sacrificed in this synagogue, defiling it forever, and the words he had spoken with Governor Tarphon, his friend, had come back to crush him. But even now, in this hour of humiliation, he was unable to call forth any vigorous statement that would enlist his Jews in a rebellion against their oppressors. When at last younger men asked what must be done, Jehubabel answered sententiously, 'We must be prudent, for he that is slow to anger is stronger than the mighty, and he who controls his temper is more powerful than he who rules a city.'

But his commonplaces received a bold challenge when toward midnight the next voluntary martyrs stepped forth; the baker Zattu and his wife Anat appeared with their infant son to repeat the terrible words: 'Our son is eight days old.'

'You were at the execution,' Jehubabel mumbled.

'We were,' they said.

'And you're willing to take this risk?'

'If we are not faithful to Adonai, we are nothing,' the couple recited in a phrase they had memorized together.

Jehubabel looked about the synagogue. 'Is there a spy among us?' he asked apprehensively, and each man knew that the life of the community lay in his hands, so the baker Zattu went to each and asked, 'Have I your permission to circumcise my son?' and each man was required to acknowledge his own complicity in what the Jews were about to do.

Against his own better judgment Jehubabel went home to procure the small knife; and again his wife asked what was afoot and he brought her back to the synagogue with him, that she, too, might be a part of that solemn covenant; and finally all commonplace words were driven from his mouth and he announced simply, 'What we are doing tonight puts us at war with the kingdoms of the Gentiles. There can be no turning back. We shall have to flee Makor, to live among the swamps like the beasts of the field. Do you wish me to proceed?'

There was a murmur of assent, but after his brave start Jehubabel lost courage. Turning to Zattu and Anat he asked pitifully, 'Do you know what you are doing?'

Together they repeated their formula: 'If we are not faithful to Adonai, we are nothing.'

And then a transformation came over Jehubabel, and one not of his directing: At the first circumcision he had been forced by the martyr Paltiel to perform and had he been left alone he would have avoided that confrontation. But the moment had come when he must stand by himself before YHWH, without the protection of aphorisms or evasions. The leader of the Jews must now lead, and as he faced the congregation, not knowing what to say, he remembered those solemn words which YHWH himself had spoken to Abraham and he began to recite the oath which bound the Jews to their special destiny:

'And I will establish my covenant between me and thee and thy seed after thee in their generations for an everlasting covenant, to be a God unto thee . . .

This is my covenant, which ye shall keep . . . Every man child among you shall be circumcised . . .

And he that is eight days old shall be circumcised among you, every man child in your generations . . .

And the uncircumcised man child whose flesh of his foreskin is not circumcised, that soul shall be cut off from his people; he hath broken my covenant . . .

And Abraham was ninety years old and nine, when he was circumcised in the flesh of his foreskin . . . And all the men of his house, born in the house, and bought with money of the stranger, were circumcised with him.'

So in a kind of martyr's defiance, ennobled by a force he did not understand, Jehubabel threw off his fear and performed the circumcision. The Jews had taken the step from which there could be no retreat.

THE TELL

One cool sunny day in October, while John Cullinane watched the hoopoe birds make believe they were archaeologists, Eliav and Tabari stood behind him on the mound with a pair of field glasses inspecting the sea off Akko, where white specks were appearing, and the Arab asked, 'You ever see this, John?'

Cullinane took the glasses and focused them on the lovely minarets of Akko, then shifted them downwards to the Mediterranean, where against the blue sea a cluster of white specks appeared, dancing upon the water like uncertain birds. 'Are they sails?' he asked.

'The annual race from Akko,' Tabari said, and the men passed the glasses back and forth to follow the distant competitors.

'It must have been quite a shock to the Canaanites and the Jews when the Greeks introduced games on a large scale over there in Akko,' Cullinane suggested.

'We Jews watched their exhibitionism with disgust,' Eliav said. 'The Old Testament looks with a fairly cynical eye at games.'

'But not the New,' Tabari said as he followed the white dots spreading out across the sea, the abler to the fore and those less skillfully handled already behind. 'I remember at school in England our headmaster used to recite with tears in his voice the statement of St. Paul commending games.' Mimicking a toothy Church of England dignitary, he recalled the motto of his school: '"I have fought the good fight, I have finished the race, I have kept the faith. Henceforth there is laid up for me the crown of righteousness, which the Lord, the righteous judge, will award to me on that Day . . ."'

'The Greeks and the English,' Eliav reflected. 'They're the ones who took games seriously. Gave us an ideal of sportsmanship. And not only in games. You fight with an Englishman in war or politics, fight him fairly, and when the war's over you shake hands. I wish we Jews and Arabs had learned that kind of discipline.'

'I was always out of place in my school,' Tabari recalled. 'There was one swine from Leeds who used to knock me down eight times running in boxing, then say with his ruddy sportsmanship, "You fought the good fight, Tabari." Under my breath I used to mutter an old Arab curse, "I hope, you bloody bastard, you break every tooth in your head but one," Between those two concepts there's quite a difference.'

'Why didn't the Greek ideal catch hold in these parts?' Cullinane asked.

'For the same reasons it wasn't acceptable in Rome,' Tabari explained. 'It's fun to chase after a running man, but it's more fun to sit in a comfortable stadium and watch lions chase him. The Greeks and the English developed sports. The Romans and the Americans degenerated them into spectacles. And the Arabs and Jews said to hell with the whole silly mess.'

'But the sense of fair play, extended truce, that comes from games. We all need that,' Eliav said. 'From what experience will we in this part of the world learn those lessons?'

'"He kicked me in the back when I wasn't looking,"' Tabari quoted from the motto of his family, '"so I kicked him in the face, twice, when he was."'

'How do you explain the big difference between Old Testament and New on these matters?' Cullinane asked. 'I can remember dozens of quotes from St. Paul on athletics.'

'Could only have been the Greek influence,' Eliav said. 'Paul attended the great games at Antioch. He speaks constantly of wrestling and running and gaining the prize. It was from him that Christians gained their idea of the moral life as a struggle against competitors, whereas we Jews abhorred the idea of competition in such fields. From the over-all point of view, I suppose the Christians were right.'

Cullinane tried to recite a passage from St. Paul dealing with athletes, but he bogged down and went to his office for a Bible, where in Corinthians he found the words which had been hammered into him as a boy: '"Know ye not that they which run in a race run all, but one receiveth the prize? So run, that ye may obtain. And every man that striveth for the mastery is temperate in all things. Now they do it to obtain a corruptible crown; but we an incorruptible. I therefore so run, not as uncertainly; so fight I, not as one that beateth the air: but I keep under my body, and bring it into subjection: lest that by any means, when I have preached to others, I myself should be a castaway."' He closed the book and asked, 'Isn't that the sportsman's ideal, fight to win but control yourself in doing so?'

'I'm rather pleased these days,' Eliav said, 'when I see Jewish men and women competing in the Olympic games. Very late we're discovering that in these matters the Greeks were right.'

'Now if the Arabs will do the same,' Tabari added, 'and if we'll both go the rest of the way and indoctrinate ourselves in the British attitude toward fair play when the game's over, we might pick up where the Greeks left us more than two thousand years ago.' Through the glasses he studied the distant racers and reported, 'The triangular sail's far out in front, proving that St. Paul was right. In every race there can be only one winner. The question is what filthy tricks can you play on the other fellow, without being caught, to make sure he loses?'

The Ptolemais to which Gymnasiarch Tarphon led his runners in that gracious autumn of 167 B.C.E. bore no resemblance to the ancient Akka of the Egyptians or to the Accho of the Phoenicians. Those settlements had huddled inland upon a mound overlooking the Belus River, but Ptolemais, one of many cities throughout Asia Minor encouraged by the forward-looking Antiochus Epiphanes, stood boldly upon a peninsula jutting out into the sea, while the hinterland reached back to encompass the older site as well. Within an ambulating wall Ptolemais stood as one of the subtlest political inventions of man, a free Greek city-state with its own assembly, its right to mint its own coinage and its own particular system of government with elected officials subservient to Antioch and Antiochus only in matters of foreign policy and the higher reaches of religion. Along the waterfront it contained a noble theater built of marble, where the tragedies of Aeschylus and Euripides were seen and where the comedies of Aristophanes were offered to amuse the mob. Exquisite temples dotted the city, one to Antiochus Epiphanes but many to the local gods like Baal, and there were baths dedicated to Aphrodite. Factories produced glassware that would enchant all subsequent generations who loved beauty; silver from Asia and gold from Africa were worked into local jewelry that was famous as far away as Spain.

To explain in one instant the superiority of a true city-state, as compared to a town like Makor, which was ruled from Antioch, Tarphon took his runners to a bench-lined square where a tall, white-bearded Negro from Nubia stood majestically on a podium, arguing with any who cared to contest his intelligence. 'He's a sophist,' the gymnasiarch whispered to his athletes. 'Listen.'

Tarphon stepped forth from the crowd and said, 'Sir, I hold the earth is flat.'

'It must be round,' the dark sophist replied, and in a series of brilliant and logical deductions the former slave, trained in Athens, proved to any sensible man that the earth must be round. He cited Aristotle, travelers to Arabia, the common sense of men who could see the ocean and the flight of birds. When he paused for breath, Tarphon whispered to Menelaus, 'Tell him it's round.' And Menelaus did so, whereupon the sophist cast his luminous eyes at the youth and said, 'Hold now! How in reason could the earth be round?' And one by one he demolished his own former arguments, calling again upon Aristotle and common sense to refute the idea that a thing so essential to life as the earth could be round, allowing men to fall off.

'Then it must stand on end,' a listener from Egypt suggested, and this proposition the sophist demolished with witty evidence until all had to confess that they were listening to a brilliant man whose white beard and black skin lent dignity to their city.

Ptolemais in those days contained some sixty thousand people, including businessmen from Rome, who sent secret reports back to their senate, and as the young athletes from Makor watched these rich and varied persons at their work they came to understand how precious Greek citizenship could be and what a treasure they would gain for themselves could they become citizens, too. Of the sixty thousand, only five thousand were citizens, some thirty thousand were slaves, and the remaining twenty-five thousand were residents possessing no rights of voting or claims to consideration by the city-state. Jews fell mostly into the latter category, but as Tarphon explained to Menelaus, 'This is the essential reason why it's prudent for you to visit the doctor. For if you win at Antioch, you will be made a full citizen of Ptolemais. Only citizens can compete in the Olympics at Greece.'

'Are you a citizen?' Menelaus asked.

'I won my citizenship in the wrestling arena,' Tarphon said with visible pride.

'I shall be a citizen of this city,' the youth vowed and he asked the gymnasiarch to lead him to the doctor.

In a side street, not far from the theater, an Egyptian doctor accepted the two strangers, listened as Tarphon explained, then said, 'Gymnasiarch, now you shall go, for this must be a matter between the boy and me.' Tarphon nodded, gripped his protégé by the shoulder and whispered, 'This is the path to citizenship,' and he was gone.

As soon as the door closed the Egyptian startled Menelaus by ripping aside a curtain to disclose the marble statue of an athlete, naked and powerful. Grabbing a knife the doctor took the statue's penis in his left hand and pretended to slice it with four sharp, deep cuts, crying, 'This is what we do.' He was watching not the statue but the patient and saw with satisfaction that although Menelaus flinched, and blood left his face, he did not look away but kept watching the marble penis so as to judge whether he could bear the pain. Satisfied that he could, he bit his lip and waited. 'Under this pain,' the doctor explained, 'a Jew older than you, from Jaffa, committed suicide.'

'He was not seeking the prize I seek,' Menelaus retorted, whereupon the Egyptian moved swiftly at him with the knife, seeking to terrify him, but the young Jew did not flinch.

'I think you are ready,' the doctor said, 'and you may scream as much as you will, for it will exhaust the pain.' And he made ready a table upon which the young man would lie, and called three slaves to hold him.

When Tarphon received satisfactory reports from Makor stating that the disobedient Jewish family had been executed and that any uneasiness resulting therefrom had subsided, and when the Egyptian doctor assured him that Menelaus had been unusually courageous and would soon mend, he assembled the rest of his team and led them home, where they were received in triumph, but it was soon noticed that Menelaus, the Jew, was not among them, and this, coming so soon after the executions, caused comment which the gymnasiarch allayed by announcing that a great honor had come to Makor: 'Our young champion Menelaus had been invited to the imperial games at Antioch.' When the crowd stopped cheering he added, 'He's training in Ptolemais, but he will soon be home.'

He took three of the young men to the palace, where Melissa had a feast prepared for them, and there he announced that the young man Nicanor, who had triumphed over him in the race to Ptolemais, would henceforth be permitted to wear the town's uniform, and ceremoniously he handed the young Phoenician the coveted garb. Melissa kissed the youth and then Tarphon said that he was going to the gymnasium, where he asked his slave to fetch Jehubabel.

The meeting was unpleasant. Tarphon began by explaining to the Jewish leader that in the case of the Paltiel family his hands had been tied. During his absence in Ptolemais the orders had come from Antiochus Epiphanes, and since he had not been able to return to Makor in time . . . Jehubabel looked at him with disgust, and this irritated Tarphon, who reminded him, 'If I had been here I might have arrested you, too, for you must have been involved in this thing.' But Jehubabel, a timorous man in the beginning, was no longer to be frightened, and Tarphon, seeing this, tried to regain his friendship by other means, for the governor knew that if there was to be open enmity between them the control of Makor might become difficult. 'Let's forget Paltiel,' he suggested. 'The important news is your son. He performed brilliantly. Wrestled with the best and defeated them all.' He pointed his finger at the pudgy Jew as if he were prophesying: 'One day that boy will stand in the victor's circle at Olympia.'

Jehubabel looked at Tarphon as if the latter were an imbecile, and he began to say what folly it was for the leader of a people to take pride in standing naked before them, as if athletic ability had any bearing on integrity; but instead he launched into an attack on Tarphon's wife: 'How can you presume to govern when you can't control your own wife?'

Tarphon was stunned. 'What do you mean?'

'My son. Your wife.' The round-faced Jew was scarcely intelligible, but Tarphon guessed that Jehubabel must have placed some ugly interpretation on a matter with which he was not acquainted.

'What has happened between your son and Melissa?' he asked.

'He's in your house. At the gate she kissed him while you were watching. Have you no shame?'

Governor Tarphon looked down at his folded hands. How could one explain anything civilized to the Jews? All during his years in Athens, Tarphon had moved from one principal home to the next, where beautiful women patronized promising young men and suffered no compromise in doing so. Sensible Greek matrons knew how to conduct themselves, and Tarphon had found that one of the finest rewards of his marriage was the spacious room in which his beautiful wife met with young men of varied accomplishments and encouraged them to further attainment; it was this interchange of philosophy and art and politics that sustained life, and Tarphon pitied the narrow-minded Jew who interpreted the process otherwise.

'You should guard your wife,' Jehubabel warned. 'Like a jewel of gold in a swine's snout is a fair woman without discretion.'

'What are you trying to say?' Tarphon asked in some exasperation.

'A man whose wife is a whore, what peace can he know?'

'Get away from here!' Tarphon cried, rushing from his chair to push the dumpy Jew from his room. He had tried, the record would prove how desperately he had tried, to conciliate Jehubabel, but it was now obvious that there could be no fruitful discussion between them. When he had Jehubabel at the door he warned, 'The law will be enforced. And when we find the next circumcised child, you too will die. For you shared in the guilt of Paltiel.'

He shoved his guest through the door, but this placed Jehubabel under the statue of Antiochus, and with a courage new to him Jehubabel said scornfully, using the joke of the Jews, 'Antiochus Epimanes,' meaning the fool, after which he spat upon the discus thrower, crying, 'This vanity will perish,' and he left the gymnasium.

That evening Tarphon repeated the conversation for Melissa, and she was distressed that the Jew had made such a fool of himself. That he had misunderstood her actions she was willing to forgive, for Greek ways must seem strange to austere Jews, but she could not understand his failure to appreciate his own son. 'In Menelaus he has the finest youth in Makor, but he seems determined to crush his spirit. Why can't he simply accept the wonderful thing the gods have given him? And not see him as a criminal?'

She became so agitated that she insisted upon talking with Jehubabel, there and then, but Tarphon refused to argue any further with the Jew; so exercising her freedom as a Greek woman she summoned two of her slaves, who bore small lamps into the street, and thus she made her way to the home of Jehubabel, surprising him by insisting upon coming inside and sitting like a familiar neighbor on one of the kitchen chairs.

'Jehubabel,' she began in the Koine, 'I am distressed at the enmity which has grown up between you and Menelaus.'

The Jew thought: She has ensnared my son, and now she wishes to entrap me. But for what purpose?

'And I am even more distressed that you have opposed my husband. Truly, Tarphon is the best friend you Jews could have. He has tried to soften every law.'

The Jew thought: Ah! There's some new edict which Tarphon is afraid to discuss with me face-to-face. He's sent his wife to trick me.

'My husband and Menelaus have both told me what you think of me. Believe me, Jehubabel, you are wrong. I have tried to help Tarphon bring Makor a good government and I have tried to show your son the greatness of our empire. But I am not important. Menelaus is. Don't you realise what a magnificent son you have? That he could one day be governor of this district?'

Jehubabel drew back from this tempting woman. Now he could understand why Benjamin had fallen victim to her allurements: she was graceful and desirable and it was appalling that such a woman should talk of empire and the education of young men.

'Unless you work with us,' she was saying, 'we'll have difficult times in Makor. Next week there's to be another search. For the circumcised ones.'

Jehubabel heard no more of what she had to say. He could think only of the baker Zattu and his wife Anat. With them he had conspired to break the law and if they were apprehended it was certain that this time he too would be executed. It seemed to him that Melissa was speaking of the trivial manipulation of society—if the Jews behaved, a boy like Benjamin might one day become governor—while Jehubabel was being driven to consider the ultimate relationship of the chosen people with YHWH. In his moral arrogance he could not understand that Melissa was speaking of neither politics nor society but of something quite different: the hungry yearning felt by many Greeks for a stern moral structure to accompany their exquisite sense of artistic and philosophic beauty. 'Don't you suppose we're ashamed of the flayings?' she asked. To his deaf ears she made an impassioned plea for harmony between Jew and Greek, but Jehubabel now saw the latter merely as an oppressor of savage malignity; she pleaded with him for a further temporizing with Antiochus IV and his aspiring plan to Hellenize the eastern world, but for the Jew there was only Epiphanes, the would-be god who slaughtered infant boys. She tried to depict the world that could result when present religious irrationalities were controlled, but he would not hear. She spoke of a Greece that was reaching out to encompass the world, but he thought of a Judaism that was retreating within itself, seeking to purify itself for the tests ahead. The time for dialogue between Hellenism and Judaism had passed; briefly there had been a chance that between intellectual Greeks and moralistic Jews some kind of fruitful alliance might be achieved, with the lurid insights of the former uniting with the rugged power of the latter to create some new and vital synthesis, but the Greeks had behaved so stupidly and the Jews so stubbornly that now the rupture was beyond repair. Two hundred years from this night, not far from this very spot, Hellenism still searching would discover a more pliable religion arising in Galilee, and that union of philosophical Greek and Christian Jew would provide a spark which would ignite the world. Unaware that this was to happen, Melissa went sadly home, satisfied that in her generation the attempt would accomplish nothing.

When she was gone Jehubabel did not hesitate. He sent his wife to summon the leaders of the Jewish community, including the baker Zattu, and when they were assembled in his kitchen he said, 'Next week there will be an inspection of all male babies.' Zattu paled, but he had known that sooner or later this moment must come, so he was prepared for it, but he looked to the older men for guidance, and Jehubabel was ready. He said, 'We must leave Makor.'

'For where?' Zattu asked.

'The swamps. The mountains.'

'Can we live there?' the baker asked.

'Can we live here?' Jehubabel countered.

There was earnest discussion of how the Jews might survive outside the town, and all were apprehensive until Jehubabel reminded them, 'For centuries our people lived in that manner, and we can do so again.'

'But we will be so few,' Zattu argued, even though it was he who risked the sentence of death.

Then for the first time in his life Jehubabel became prophetic: 'I believe that other Jews in other towns must realize that with the Greeks there can be no hope. I believe other Jews are holding discussions like this . . . tonight . . . now.' He stood silent, and his listeners could visualize the perplexity with which their fellow Jews were facing the great persecution. And after midnight they agreed that at the first sign of the next general search, those in that room, and their families, would flee Makor to make their lives in any way they might among the swamps and the hills; and as each man left, Jehubabel inspected him and asked, 'Is it a pledge?' And it was so pledged.

At the end of the week, when tension was high and no one knew where the next blow would fall, a welcome diversion came with the return from Ptolemais of Menelaus, accompanied by a team of wrestlers who had come by ship from Cyprus. Tarphon announced happily that he would sponsor a public exhibition between the Cypriots and the men of Makor, at which he would wrestle the second man of the Cyprus team. 'Their champion will be met by our champion, Menelaus!' Proudly he placed his arm about the shoulder of his returning protégé, and the young athletes filed off to the gymnasium.

That afternoon the gymnasium was thrown open, and the stone seats of the exhibition hall quickly filled with townspeople. Jews were forced to attend, it having been found that otherwise they would refuse to participate in what they held to be pagan rites, so in the front row, across from Melissa's box, sat Jehubabel, his arms folded stubbornly across his fat stomach, his eyes fixed on the sanded floor of the arena. To have to watch one's own son parade his nakedness was humiliating, but to attend on this particular day, when the fate of the Jewish community was in jeopardy, was abhorrent, and he would not try to hide his sense of insult.

Trumpets sounded, and from a door leading to the dressing rooms the six young men of Cyprus marched out, naked, tanned from their life aboard boats, and confident. They had come from a major island of the Ptolemaic empire to show a small provincial village on the outskirts of the Seleucid empire how men from a cosmopolitan center conducted themselves, and they paraded a certain appealing arrogance. Melissa, looking at their superb bodies, thought what a handsome lot they were, and how surprised at least the first two were going to be when they struck young Menelaus and her husband.

Another flurry of trumpets caused a different door to open, and from it marched the six local athletes, led by the red-haired gymnasiarch, manly and stalwart as he had been during his championship days in Athens. He was still a superb human being and the local audience applauded, but as the men lined up in the center of the arena a murmur began in the front rows, then climbed through the stone seats and at last erupted into cheering applause as the population saw the transformation that Menelaus had undergone. All evidence of his circumcision was gone, and since many knew how painful this operation was, cried of approval began to greet the young champion.

'Menelaus! You are one of us!'

An old man who had once been champion in Tyre shouted, 'He is a Greek! He is a Greek!' And young women who saw with interest the transformation began to applaud and call the name, 'Menelaus!'

At first Jehubabel had refused to look at the entrance of the athletes, but when he heard his son's name being shouted with approval he had to look up, and he saw his son standing not far from him, relaxed and marvellously handsome, his skin lightly rubbed with oil. At first Jehubabel could not understand why the people of Makor were applauding him, and then the baker Zattu, who might at any moment be flayed for having consecrated his son to YHWH, nudged Jehubabel and pointed to the result of the operation. The Jew's eyes rested with astonishment upon the visible proof of the boy's disgrace, and he was so appalled at what Menelaus had done that he pressed his hands over his face, and as the crowd called the boy's name Jehubabel heard the words of YHWH himself saying as of old: 'And the uncircumcised man child whose flesh of his foreskin is not circumcised, that soul shall be cut off from his people; he hath broken my covenant . . .' and it seemed to him a commandment, and he leaped from his seat, grabbing the walking stick of a crippled Jew, and with this knotted club he struck his son with such force that the boy fell to the ground. With four crushing blows he beat his son about the head, shattering his skull. Then with a loud cry, 'The pledge! The pledge!' he ran from the gymnasium and without halting dashed through the main gate, shouting, 'The pledge! The pledge!'

As planned, he headed for the swamp, and by nightfall a few Jews had joined him. Some of the leaders had managed to flee the gymnasium. Lesser ones, hearing the battlecry, had lowered themselves over the town walls with ropes, and there were undoubtedly others who had escaped but who had not yet joined up with the fugitives. Jehubabel's wife had not received word in time, and she would be lashed to death, but Zattu, his wife Anat and their son had escaped.

They were a sorry lot, a handful of unarmed Jews hiding in a swamp without food and led by a man who had just murdered his son. They could hear the heavy splattering through mud of Greek soldiers trying to seek them out, and they could catch words of the Koine as the Greeks passed by, but at dusk the sounds halted and they were left alone. When they were satisfied that their persecutors had gone, Jehubabel assembled them in prayer, and without recourse to the tedious proverbs of his commonplace life, said, 'Adonai, this day we place our lives in your hands. We are nothing. We are a miserable, lost group of Jews with no food and no weapons. But we are convinced we shall prevail against the madman who dares to call himself God-Made-Manifest. Adonai, show us what we must do.'

And this prayer brought to the huddled Jews such an honest realization of their plight that no man spoke, but they clung each to the other, and in the silence of the swamp they heard anew the splashing and whispered, 'The soldiers have come back,' and Jehubabel prayed, 'Adonai, if the Greeks capture us tonight, let us die in your arms.'

The searchers came closer and might have passed on, except that the child of Zattu began to whimper, and this betrayed them, and the retreating sounds returned, bringing terror to the swamp, and in Hebrew a voice whispered, 'Jehubabel!' We know you are here. Present yourself, for we have been in the swamp for six days. All over Israel, Jews have risen against the oppressor. In Jerusalem. In Modi'im. In Beth-Horon.'

No one spoke. It could be a trap planned by the clever Greeks, but with a desperation he had never known before Jehubabel wanted to believe. He wanted to believe that his pitiful remnant was not alone in that swamp. And then the voice came again: 'Jehubabel, we know you are here. If you are zealous for the law, if you stand by the covenant, come out with us, for we are not a rabble. We are an army, obedient to Judah the Maccabee.'

LEVEL IX

King of the Jews

Found at Makor–glass phial, hand-blown at Caesarea, 20 B.C.E., by a Roman artisan. Erroneously known as 'a tear glass' and supposedly used for collecting tears at the death of a loved one, it was actually a phial for the storing of expensive perfumes, since the narrow opening delayed evaporation. Of clear glass when blown, now beautifully tinted by amber, green and aquamarine discolorations. Deposited at Makor in the spring of 4 B.C.E.

I have always held the town of Makor to be one of the most charming Roman colonies in our Jewish kingdom, and I do not speak from any narrow provincialism, for I have worked in all the great cities of the east. It was my good fortune to supervise the adornment of Jericho and I spent three years at Antioch rebuilding that well-regarded street first laid down by Antiochus Epiphanes. I paved it with marble and roofed it with an arcade resting on colonnades so extensive that the eye could not follow them to their end. My happiest period came, of course, when I constructed Caesarea, that admirable city, and I also assumed responsibility for rebuilding the Jewish temple in Jerusalem, but frankly I never derived much pleasure from that assignment, for I am no more a Jew than the king himself and I cite the temple merely to prove that I was involved in some fairly important projects.

If, therefore, I say that in my opinion our frontier town of Makor combines the best of Roman architecture with an exquisite physical setting commanding both the mountains and the sea, I am comparing my little town with the finest of Jericho and Antioch. I am even bold enough to discuss it in terms of Caesarea itself, and that's saying much. When I rose, a few moments ago, in the cool dark hours before dawn on what will probably be my last day on earth, I looked out upon the beauty I had helped create here in Makor, and although I am not a sentimental man I cried involuntarily, 'If we could only preserve this as it now stands! We'd have a memorial of the best that Rome accomplished.'

From my prison in the Venus temple I can see in the darkness the white façades that have brought a kind of perfection to this forum. To my right stands the small Greek temple erected, I am told, to honor Antiochus, the benefactor of this area. It stands low against the earth, with six flawless Doric columns, reminding us of how much we owe the Greeks. In the Roman plan for Makor, I retained this gemlike structure as the focal point, but converted it to our Jupiter temple. Local citizens claim it stands upon a spot that was sacred for the past three thousand years, and this I am ready to believe, for the little building has an inherent poetry that could not have sprung entirely from the hands of an architect.

Facing this Greek edifice, which I altered in no detail, stood the sprawling palace of the governors, which I rebuilt completely, adding a new façade with sixteen niches in which the king placed statues of the great men of Rome. When the impressive marble heads were put into position the Jews of Makor rioted, for statuary was an offense to their belief, and my wife Shelomith, who is a member of their religion, wept. But the king came, and against my judgment and my wife's tearful pleading, assembled in the old gymnasium all Jewish dignitaries, and when he had them trapped, coldly sent his mercenaries among them with naked swords, and the Jews were hacked to death until the floor of the gymnasium was red and slippery.

I remonstrated with the king, telling him, 'This slaughter is not required,' but he replied, 'I have learned how to control Jews, and you have not.' And he was right, for after that first killing our Jews of Makor behaved, even if those in the rest of the kingdom did not.

When I was through with the old Greek palace no one could tell it had once been a Hellenistic construction, and from it the governors assigned by the king gave our region good government. In one sense it was foolish to speak of us as a Jewish town, for the kingdom of the Jews lay to the east and south; we were perched off to one side where the border of Phoenicia intruded, and we took our basic coloring from that region of the Roman empire. Like it we spoke Greek; we worshipped the Roman gods; we went to the Roman theater or to the arena in Ptolemais, where I had built a masterwork for gladiatorial combats. But structurally we were a part of the Jewish kingdom, and families like that of my wife's played a respectable role in the town, even though the better jobs were held by Romans like me.

The dimensions of the forum were thus determined by the temple of Jupiter to the south and the governor's palace to the north. Along the western side I built a series of three small temples, excellent work the king said, the central one of which we dedicated to Venus. It was always my favorite, a small marble thing with six Ionic columns that seemed to float in the air. It is ironic that I should now be imprisoned in this temple, but if it is true that each man in his life builds his own prison, and inhabits it the way crawling fish inhabit shells along the beach at Caesarea, then I have built for myself an exquisite jail exactly suited to the kind of man I have always wanted to be. In the dark hours of this dawn I am content to be immured within the Venus temple, for it is a work with no error. Its stones fit without mortar. Its columns are precisely related to the façade. The view from any point within the prison is exactly as I had wanted it to be, and if I must die this day I would rather die here than anywhere else in the kingdom. Nor do I know of another spot within the empire where any of the potential prisons I built would suit me better. The palaces at Antioch are too large. The graceful forum at Jericho is too impersonal. And the loveliness of Caesarea belonged always to the king and never to me. But this quiet spot, and the edge of the empire, seems to have been planned from the beginning as a proper place for me to die.

I look out from the Venus temple, past the half-sleeping guards, and see across the forum the building of which I am most proud. It runs almost the entire distance from the old Greek temple to the governor's palace, a grave, heavy building containing neither preliminary columns nor niches for statuary. It is simply a mass of rock, perfectly proportioned, with straight and simple lines, ponderous perhaps but with that dignity I once saw when the legions of Julius Caesar were marching from Damascus to Egypt. They came forward not as ordinary soldiers but as a massive group having its own intention outside the men who comprised it; and from that day when I was in my early twenties, I tried to build into my structures the same sense of weight and dignity. In

Jericho I did not succeed; the king interfered with all my plans and I made compromises whose ill effects could not be hidden. But when I decided to erect the great, solid building in Makor, the king was not at my elbow. He told me simply, 'Build something to remind us of those first days when we fought together at Makor.' I am certain in my heart that the king wanted this excellent building to be named after him, but when it was finished he was apprehensive about his relationship with Rome—since he was not a Jew his kingship over the Jews depended solely upon the pleasure of Rome—so he imported a boat-load of dignitaries from that imperial city and held a three-day feast during which he announced the name of my latest building. I see it know, as the sun lightens, a low, formidable work marching toward me like the leather-shielded legions of Julius Caesar, but it does not bear his name. It is called by the sycophantic name our king gave it that day—the Augusteana—and in it we have long worshiped Caesar Augustus as our god. This is my wife Shelomith has refused to do, as have other Jews, but no trouble grows out of their rejection: in our town Roman and Jew live as they do in our kingdom; in a kind of armed truce, each holding to his own gods and to his own beliefs, as do my wife and I. She loves Jerusalem and the Jewish god, and is never so happy as when I am commissioned to do additional work at the temple; I, as a Roman citizen, keep mostly to Caesarea and the worship of Caesar Augustus, and it seems to me that we Romans have the better of the bargain, for there is no city in the empire, not even Rome itself, more enticing than Caesarea, that remarkable city which we have built of white marble and the sweat of slaves.

Between my jail and the Augusteana stands the Makor construction for which I alone am responsible: a double row of marble columns, tall, with heavy Corinthian bases and beautiful capitals on which nothing rests, for I placed these columns here only to add grace to the forum and to link the various buildings one to the other. Looking at them now, I think that my life has been a series of columns, marching along like days, and I have never had enough either of columns or of days. How many marble columns did we use at Caesarea? Five thousand? Ten thousand? They were the unifying beauty of that city, and they came to us in ship after ship sailing from Italy. One night the king and I walked through Caesarea, and he said to me in Greek, 'Timon, you've made this a forest of marble. I shall send for a thousand more columns and we'll build an esplanade to the theater.' In Antioch, in Ptolemais, in Jericho, how many columns have I erected—those silent marching men of marble who bring grace to the roads they walk?

Our forum has only eight, extending in two lines from the Greek temple to the palace, but they summarize the thousands we used elsewhere, for without the king's knowing it I inspected a hundred ships coming from Italy, seeking out the perfect pillars: this one near the Venus temple is fluted, and that pair by the Augusteana are purple. A purist, say, the Greek who built the first temple, would shy from the medley I have composed and would seek a single pure note repeated seven times. I wanted this summary of my life . . . how beautiful they are in their variety, how perfect in their proportions. From three thousand columns I chose these eight, and had I three thousand more to choose from I could not improve upon this group. Stand there, my shimmering columns bearing nothing on your heads. If it is today that I must die . . .

What difference does it really make whether the messengers come from Jericho today or six days from now? I am sixty-four years old, still lean as when I fought with the king, white-haired but with all my teeth. I have seen the legions of Julius Caesar. I accompanied Cleopatra for nine days. I knew the glory of Antioch intimately and I have worked hard. More fortunate than most, and infinitely more smiled upon than the king, I found early the one woman I was destined to love, and although there were periods when I discovered joy in the slaves of Jericho or with the graceful young eunuchs of Caesarea, I always returned to Shelomith. How fortunate I was, really. She lies now on her cot, sharing my prison, and even with her whitened hair she is as attractive to me as when I first saw her on the arm of the king. He, poor soul, has known ten wives and has grown to hate them all, while I have drifted along with Shelomith as a man drifts down a river in a small boat, heading always toward the sea of obliteration but finding always new pleasure in the scenery that comes upon the river banks and perpetual new delight in the companion who shares his boat. Shelomith is like a marble column who lives, and if we die this day my eight perfect columns in the forum of this little town will be her monument, for her spirit inhabits them already.

If I go to the southwest corner of my prison I can see down the avenue one of my happiest creations. In my youth I used to play near the old Greek gymnasium, then a building fallen into sad disrepair, and I used to run along the cracked and crumbling walls imagining myself an athlete at the Olympiad and shivering in the mournful memories of the place: at the broken gateway stood two staues which I loved even before I had learned to appreciate the excellence of Greek carving. To the left stood Hercules as a wrestler and to the right was nimble-footed Hermes as a runner, while inside the faded halls stood the statue which impressed me with both its gigantic size and its ugliness. It was Zeus, now called Jupiter, as a discus thrower, but we were told by loyal Jews that it was really Antiochus Epiphanes, the benefactor whom the Jews had driven from the land a century before, but no part of that story did we then believe.

I took this crumbling gymnasium and made of it a thing of beauty. For me it was a work of love, in no way conspicuous among the many temples and stadia I built, but it gave me almost as much pleasure as either the Augusteana or the little temple in which I now rest; because when it was finished, all in white marble, it became the center of life in Makor, and whenever the king had to sail from the port of Ptolemais, he stayed with me and spent hours in the marble baths. He once told me that some of the happiest hours of his life had been spent in Makor, the first town he had conquered and the base from which he had gained control of the Galilee and later of the entire Jewish kingdom.

Because the king had prospered in Makor, he allowed me freedom in rebuilding my little town: the main gate was reconstructed, but I kept the ancient zigzag pattern; and wherever needed, the walls that must have dated back to the time of King David were rebuilt, so that the town seemed encased like a precious jewel in a stout stone setting. The streets were clean and straight, and old houses were torn down to be rebuilt of white limestone. Even the old water system I refurbished, installing a new set of granite steps in the main shaft and placing marble benches about the wall itself.

Under the Roman peace that dominated our kingdom, the environs of our town prospered too. The road to Ptolemais was straightened and paved with stone along which chariots could move with ease if not with comfort. I ordered the old olive press on my family grounds replaced by a superior type developed in southern Italy, and my fields were lined with stone walls, marking their proper limits. There was a neatness in our countryside which I added to whenever I returned home from working in distant cities, and inside the walls we knew an opulence which came to us from all parts of the world: Persia and India were as close to us as Britain or Gaul; caravans reached us from all directions and ships put in to Ptolemais from every port in our sea and from some along the western shore of Africa. Old Jews tell me that today Makor is as big as it ever was, with more than a thousand people living inside the walls and six hundred living in peace outside. I have seen all the rivers of the east. I have sailed into all the seaports. I have worked at Rome and Athens and Alexandria. . .

My wife is waking. I go to her bed and tickle the end of her little nose with my fingernail, so that I may be the first thing she is aware of on this last day. She turns on her pillow and smiles, and I recall what a philosopher once told me in Jericho: 'A man is never old if he can still be moved emotionally by a woman of his own age.' If he was correct I shall die a young man. This morning I could run a race or direct the first steps in the building of a new temple, and I love Shelomith. She smiles and says with a certain gaiety, 'I would not miss a moment,' and places her feet on the marble floor.

'They're getting up,' the guards call one to another, and word is carried to the town officials.

'Is this the day?' Shelomith asks, and I tell her, as she washes at the alabaster laver I had carved in Antioch, that in my judgment the king must surely be dead by now—he could not have lived much longer, not possibly—and that before the day is out the messengers must arrive with the news that will set the soldiers upon us with their swords at the ready.

Some eleven times in my life I have seen the king's mercenaries turned loose upon prisoners. It was a favorite trick of the king's, to have his enemies enclosed in a narrow space, unarmed, and to send roaring through the doors his legionnaires in battle dress, wearing shields and short swords. Why the soldiers obeyed him I never understood, for the slaughter was hideous to watch, and it must have been equally repulsive to those who performed it. But the soldiers were obedient, and their short swords flashed until their military tunics were red with blood; and almost never was any victim killed by a simple thrust. He was always hacked to death, with ears sliced off and legs cut away at the ankle until the carnage was more than I could bear. But the king would stand and watch, his gray-white tongue licking his lips, his fat hands clasping and unclasping in fury as he cried, 'Death to them all, for they have opposed me.'

I first met Herod forty-five years ago at the zigzag gate of Makor. He was twenty-five years old then, and I nineteen. He was the glamorous, daring son of the Idumaean manipulator who was trying to win the kingdom of the Jews away from the rightful heirs of Judah the Maccabee. It seemed impossible to us then that a non-Jew could win the throne, and we who were young did not join Herod because we hoped for preferment if he became our king; we rallied to him, I think, because he was handsome and commanding. In those days there were bandits in Galilee who called themselves patriots, and we wished an end to them. Herod told us, 'If we attack relentlessly we can conquer them. You shall have peace, and I shall have'—he hesitated, then added—'my reward.'

At different points near Makor we rounded up large numbers of the bandits, whom not even Rome had been able to subdue, but whom Herod terrified. At two of the general killings I was present; I carried my short sword among the unarmed prisoners and helped hack them to death. How many did we slay in those first campaigns? A thousand . . . four thousand? I swung my arm until it was leaden, and we crushed the bandits. The worst we burned to death. The seconds-in-command we crucified slowly. Herod, conspiring to win the Jewish throne, started by killing thousands upon thousands of Jews.

Herod chose me as his confidant because at four crises in his life I supported him when others feared to do so. I formed this habit in those early years, when the Jews rose against their tormentor and when it seemed, twice running, that he was doomed. In Jerusalem the leaders of the Jews pointed to his massacres in Galilee and said that he had acted outside the Jewish law, which was true. He had ignored it and had willfully perverted it, killing without trial or judgment, crucifying and burning; so he himself was hauled to trial, and on the evening before the tribunal convened, to sentence him to certain death, he asked me if I was as courageous in the law as I had been on the battlefield, and I said, 'Yes.' So when the austere court of bearded elders assembled to condemn him, I marched my soldiers into the court and threatened to kill any Jew who voted against my general. The judges panicked and Herod was set free.

The second time I supported him was when the Jews, still hoping to keep him from the crown, sought to poison the mind of Antony, who had followed the greater Caesar in the bed of Cleopatra, our southern neighbor. I went to Antony, who ruled our areas, and spoke on Herod's behalf; and partly because of my pleading Antony accepted Herod as his regent for the Jews, and in this manner my red-cheeked young general attained the highest power. I must say that he did not forget the assistance I rendered him in those first two tests.

Timon Myrmex he called me, for when we spoke together we used Greek, and when he saw my love for building he sent me from one city to the next, but our principal joy came when he summoned me to Caesarea, then an open sand dune behind Straton's Tower, where together we planned one of the world's great cities. 'This is my Timon Myrmex,' he announced to his generals, 'my digging ant. He is to do the building,' and never did he stint in his support. When I warned him that the Caesarea we had planned would absorb the revenues of his kingdom for ten years, he spurred me on, and later when I calculated that to rebuild the temple at Jerusalem along the plans he wished would cost an equal amount, he encouraged me to go ahead. If when I die tonight, with the soldiers hacking at me, I leave behind a Judaea more beautiful than it was before, it is not because I was a master builder, for in Antioch or Jericho there were men more capable; Judea is a locus of the magnificent principally because King Herod had an unfaltering sense of beauty.

There are many—I have heard them in Athens and Rome—who ridicule the Jews and charge them with having no sense of beauty. They point to the ugly synagogues of the Jews as compared with a jeweled temple like the one I am in at this moment. Or they compare the ugliness of Jewish worship with the stately intonations of the priests of Jupiter. Or they ask where the Jewish statues and the Jewish architecture are. Or the beautiful songs that mark even a seaport like Ptolemais, where the Greek ships come. And it is widely held that the Jews do not know beauty. But for a while the Jews had a king who knew what grandeur was. My wife condemns him as a non-Jew and will not accept my praise; if I understand correctly he was a half-Jew, but he led his people to beautify their land as none other in my experience is beautified.

I remember when we first started building—at Jericho it was—long before Caesarea had been dreamed of, and we were watching slaves dress large chunks of granite for a wall, and Herod took a chisel and demonstrated an idea he had spoken of some days before. 'If on every stone you leave the central part protruding, but cut the edges back to a uniform depth and uniform width, like this . . .' He directed the masons to cut a huge stone as he directed, and when it was done he had slaves twist and turn the stone in the sunlight, and when I saw the fascinating play of light and shadow across the uneven stone, I understood what he had visualized, and we built that wall as he suggested. And when it was finished the sun reflected from its curious rocks as it never had done before from any wall, and throughout the kingdom we set our slaves to cutting rocks in the Herodian fashion.

How many did we cut in those years? It must have been nearly a million. Whole armies of slaves spent their lives cutting away the edges of rocks so that the diamond-like stones could be fitted into perfect walls, with each stone uneven and projecting in the center, but perfectly aligned along the beveled edges. A million such stones? It must have been more like a score of million. Have you ever seen the largest rocks in the walls of the temple at Jerusalem? Some are three times as long as a man's height and proportionately huge in their other dimensions. It required two hundred men to move them from the quarries great distances away, but each monstrous stone fitted into its proper place, and each had its edges cut as Herod had determined.

He loved me not only because I stood by him in his four great crises, but also because I was his boon companion in the years when he knew Mariamne. She was a princess of the Maccabean line, and if he could marry her, he would through her royal blood gain an extra claim to the Jewish throne; but he loved her I know for much different reasons than dynastic ones. She was exciting, marvelously beautiful, witty and well skilled in love. I remember one day when her friend Shelomith walked with her through Makor; Mariamne clung to the right arm of the young king and Shelomith to the left, and they were a handsome trio. The four of us were much together in those days, laughing and talking in Greek, and then one night in Jericho I asked Herod if he thought it proper for me to marry a Jewish girl and he said that he intended doing so. There have been questions in recent years as to whether Herod loved this exquisite Jewish princess, or whether he married her to insure his claim to the throne of Judaea, but Shelomith and I know. We were with them in those early years, when Herod's love for Mariamne so far excelled my love for Shelomith as to make me wonder if I were a normal man. He doted upon her and was enraptured when she presented him with two strong sons, Alexander and Aristobolus. I was present when the boys were named and I know the love that surged between the parents.

I could understand, even then, why Herod loved his slim Jewish princess. She was truly radiant as she moved about the kingdom, bringing to herself and her husband the love of the Jewish people. Even Selomith forgot in those happy years that her king was not Jewish and that he had usurped the throne through guile, for those whom he had dispossessed were now repossessed in the person of Mariamne; and during those excellent years the executions ceased, and the soldiers with their short swords were not turned loose upon the Jews, neither in Jerusalem nor elsewhere in the kingdom. Herod and Mariamne were destined to become the fortunate lovers of ballads, and if Shelomith and I have developed between ourselves a profoundly satisfying love, I think it is partly because we shared with Herod and Mariamne their unparalleled affection.

'What is your most persistent memory of the lovers?' I ask my wife as she joins me at breakfast on this last day.

'That morning in Ptolemais,' she replies without considering any other.

Herod had been to see Cleopatra in Egypt and had sailed back to Ptolemais, which was not even in his kingdom, for Caesarea was not then built and we had to use an alien seaport, and we three went to greet him. 'I see him as he came running down the wooden pathway from the ship, leaping over bales of cotton and greeting his queen as if he were a boy. It was spontaneous, an act of love, and I have forgiven him many things because of the honesty he showed that day. How long ago was it, Timon?'

I cannot remember the years accurately, but we four were together again, here in Makor, on the eve of the gravest test, when the world of Herod hung in the balance. In the terrible struggle between Antony and Octavian we had sided with the former, principally because we were closer to Egypt and knew Cleopatra and her power. But at the battle of Actium, Antony lost, and it was rumored on good suspicion that Octavian would send a Roman army against Herod, dispossessing him of the kingdom and dragging him off to Rome for execution.

'I am sailing to Rhodes in the morning,' Herod informed us. 'Timon Myrmex shall come with me and I will throw myself on the ground at Octavian's feet. I shall plead with him for mercy as no man has ever pleaded before.'

That night we prayed at the old Greek temple over there, then walked to Ptolemais and boarded a small boat which took us to Rhodes. There, with a few of us at his side, Herod marched to face Octavian, the solitary inheritor of Julius Caesar, the man who had driven both Antony and Cleopatra to suicide, and in a few fateful sentences which were to determine the history of Judaea for generations, Herod said manfully, 'It was Antony who set me on my throne, and I freely admit that to him I have rendered every possible service. Not even after his defeat at Actium did I desert him, for he was my benefactor. I gave him the best possible advice and told him there was only one way of retrieving his disasters. Kill Cleopatra. If he would only kill this woman I would give him money, protection of my walls, an army, and my active help in waging war against you. But there it is! His ears were stopped by his insane passion for Cleopatra. With Antony, I also am defeated. With his fall I lay aside my crown, for it is yours, Octavian, and not mine. I come to you placing all my hope in my unblemished character, for I know that you will not ask whose friend I was but what sort of friend I can be.'

Octavian, whom now we worship as Caesar Augustus, watched with fascination as Herod prostrated himself, uncrowned and with no mark of dignity upon him, and on impulse the victorious emperor of the known world caused him to be raised up, saying 'It was a very good thing for me that Antony listened to Cleopatra's advice and not yours. Through his folly I have gained your friendship. Henceforth you shall be my king of the Jews.' Thus Herod, with a bravery not equaled in my lifetime, regained his throne from an enemy who normally should have slain him.

As in so much that he has done, Caesar Augustus acted wisely, for Herod has proved one of the great kings of the Roman provinces. I've worked for the proconsuls of Antioch and Spain, and they did not compare in either character or energy with our king Herod. He has kept peace in his part of the empire while extending our borders to their natural limits. To the Jewish kingdom, which had known war and desolation under the later Maccabees, he has brought tranquility if not acceptance; during his reign no bandits and no extremists have plagued our land, and some years ago when I stopped off in

Rome on my return from Spain, Augustus himself told me, 'I remember that day when you came to Rhodes with Herod. It was an impudent gesture he made, but I wish I had always chosen my kings so wisely.'

How then, in spite of these successes, has Herod degenerated so miserably? Was he haunted by some evil spirit determined to destroy his grandeur? Or did his hatred and suspicion of the Jews slowly derange his mind? Some say that a snake wormed its way into his belly, gnawing at his vitals, but Shelomith and her Jews claim that their god has placed a special curse upon him for having usurped the throne of David. I have my own theory.

I should have foreseen that these things might happen, for thirty-one years ago he came to my quarters in Jericho, where I was building him a temple, and threw himself upon my couch, whispering with horror, 'Myrmex! You must kill a man! I have proof that Aristobolus has conspired against me.' I drew back in surprise, for Mariamne's brother was only seventeen and the darling of the Jews, for in him they saw a prospect for the re-establishment of Maccabean rule.

'The young schemer has plotted to steal my kingdom and must die,' Herod whispered, and when I warned him not to kill the queen's brother, he cried in a mad frenzy, 'Don't mention their names together. Mariamne's a goddess and her brother a viper.' Then he added significantly, 'This afternoon he goes swimming.' He summoned the captain of his Cilician guard, who explained the plot: 'Myrmex, the young man trusts you. When he enters the pool, you move forward to embrace him, but in doing so, grab his arms. My men will swim under water and catch his feet.'

It was a lovely pool, one that I had edged with marble, and I made believe that I was swimming when Aristobolus appeared, moving through the sunlight as if he were a Roman god. 'Greetings, Timon,' he called, and when he came down the marble steps I waded forward to embrace him and pinioned his arms, so that when the Cilicians grabbed his feet I could feel the tremor pass through his body. He gave me a wild stare, his eyes less than a cubit from mine, but I set my teeth and brought my hands upward until they grasped his neck, and in this manner we dragged him under the water.

I had nearly forgot the murder of Aristobolus—for dynasties must protect themselves, and the young Maccabean had proved himself too popular with the mob—when Herod climbed the steep path to Massada, where I was converting ruins into a fortress-palace unmatched in the east, and there as we sat like eagles looking down upon the Dead Sea and the hills of Moab he whispered again, 'Myrmex, how can I bring myself to do it?' He became a man distraught, almost insane I judged, and when he began moaning like a witch I dismissed my helpers and as they filed down the rocky footpath like ants I asked what he was required to do that so agitated him.

'I must kill Mariamne,' he said, looking up at me like a wild Essene from the desert.

'No. No,' I protested as if her were my brother, but on his mountain peak he ranted on with circumstantial evidence against his blameless wife. I truly intended to kill her, for in some way she had conspired against him. I deafened my ears and said, 'Get down from here and tell me no such madness,' and he drew back with fearful suspicion, his hand on his sword, for we were alone at the edge of the cliff, and he cried, 'You are in league with her too. Augustus protect me! Myrmex intends murdering me.' I slapped the mad king and led him slowly down from the cliff, saying, 'If you cannot trust me, Herod, your world is indeed crumbled.' And when we were on safe ground I said, 'Now tell me your fantasies.'

I took him back to Jericho and during each portion of the trip he recited her guilt. He had proof without question, he said, and for three days he raved, unable to bring himself to kill her. But finally he gave the signal and his mercenaries marched implacably to Mariamne's room—they rarely ran to such assignments—and slaughtered her.

When his faultless wife was dead he loved her more than he had when she was alive. He stormed about his vast palaces, screaming for mercy from the ghosts that haunted him. He would come rushing to my apartment and sit staring at Shelomith, then break into passionate tears, crying, 'I killed the fairest Jewish princess the world has known. I am condemned.' In grotesque sequence he married a chain of other women. He had many children who may already have inherited his kingdom, and he stormed among his female slaves, pointing to this girl or that and shouting, 'You are not Mariamne,' but he took them nevertheless.

On the ship that brought me back from Spain there had been a wench well used by sailors, an attractive girl whom I in my loneliness fancied, but the captain of the vessel warned me, 'She has the seaport sickness,' so I contented myself with watching from afar, but one day as Herod walked along the quays at Caesarea he saw this girl and cried, 'You are Mariamne,' and she did indeed look like our dead queen. 'Not that one,' I pleaded, but he was obsessed with her regal beauty and had his way, but later when the sickness struck he railed at me, 'I told you it was Mariamne! She has come back to curse me,' and he fell ill, but an Egyptian doctor cured him for a while.

When his anguish was greatest, when something reminded him especially of Mariamne, he would come to me distraught and say, 'We shall build a superior temple at Antioch,' and for a while his energies would be diverted into this channel. But soon ugly suspicions of other plots against him would develop. One day he ordered thirteen women placed upon the rack for such tortures as no human body could stand, and when in their agony they confessed to fantastic crimes and implicated men they did not even know, the suspected ones were dragged to an arena where the mercenaries were sent among them swinging their short swords, hacking and killing the innocent until we who watched were sickened.

Then he came to me, whispering again, 'They are plotting against me.' And this time it was his own children, the sons of Mariamne whom Shelomith and I had helped name. We had been present at the circumcisions, and now they were accused of attempting to poison their father. This time, praised be the gods, Caesar Augustus intervened to warn Herod that he must not kill his own sons, and there was a pathetic reconciliation in which Alexander and Aristobolus—the latter had been named for his uncle whom I had helped drown—tearfully swore filial love for their demented father and promised him their loyalty.

But within a short time he came to me once more: 'The fiends are still planning to kill me,' and this time he brought me proof of their guilt. I therefore accompanied him to Berytus, the city that Caesar Augustus had appointed for the trial, and on behalf of my king I made an impassioned plea before the judges. Herod himself followed with a hideous series of charges and at last the court gave him reluctant permission to kill his sons, should he upon reconsideration wish to do so. Clutching the permissive papers like a maniac,

Herod returned to Judaea with a list of three hundred principal citizens who were suspected of being involved in the plot, and when I saw the names I realized that many of the victims could not possibly have been implicated and I started to argue with him, but he shrieked, 'They have conspired against me and they shall die.'

For some time Herod shivered alone in his palace in Caesarea, undecided as to whether or not he should murder Mariamne's sons, and Shelomith and I tried to persuade him not to do so, but whenever he looked at my wife waves of regret swept over him and he would subside into tears, bewailing his lost princess and his queen; but when this sorrow overtook him it served only to intensify his determination to kill her sons as well, so I forbade my wife to see him again, trusting that by myself I could restrain his vengeance.

'Turn your sons loose,' I pleaded. 'Release the three hundred Jews.'

I might have succeeded except for an old soldier who frequented the palace. Herod gave him trivial jobs out of gratitude for the old man's help in earlier campaigns, and this veteran grew bold enough to warn Herod face-to-face against his plan for murdering his sons: 'Take care! The army hates your cruelty. There isn't a private who doesn't side with your sons. And many of the officers openly curse you.'

'Which ones would dare?' Herod cried, and the foolish old man rattled off their names.

When this occurred I lost all chance of controlling the king. He dispatched his bodyguard to arrest everyone named, then threw the old soldier upon the rack, torturing him beyond endurance, twisting and turning his body, jerking him until his joints came apart and bones cracked. The veteran made confessions that were valueless, but Herod accepted them. Assembling a mob he had the accused officers brought before him. In a wild speech, bursting with passion and lust, he built up a story of conspiracy and guilt that terrified the populace. 'Your kingdom is threatened,' he told them, and at the height of his oratory he screamed, 'These are the guilty ones. Slay them!' And the mob swept in with clubs and wrenching hands. Dozens who knew no guilt of any kind were torn apart that day, their heads crushed while their king danced up and down, screaming, 'Kill them! Kill them!'

How many Jews did Herod slay in his years of madness? How many columns did he erect during his years of greatness? Neither number can be identified. I, who attended only a few of the massive slaughters, must have witnessed with my own eyes six or eight thousand of the kingdom's best people hacked to death. One senseless incident: a woman getting her hair curled by slaves spoke against the massacres. A maid reported her and she was put to the torture. She spewed out the names of sixty accomplices, to what, no one knew. These in turn were tortured upon the rack, with African and German soldiers leaning on the screws, and they implicated hundreds of others. So all were slain without trial for a crime that had not even been contemplated or named. Their wealth went into the coffers of the king, for their families even down to children two months old were also slain.

How many Jews did Herod slay? How many great minds did he drive to oblivion? How much of the power of our kingdom was destroyed? I could not even guess, but the slain great ones are not to be numbered in thousands. We must think, rather, of tens of thousands, and always the best men and the best women of our nation. I am amazed that the Jews still have persons capable of collecting taxes or drafting laws, but I am not amazed that Shelomith and I have finally been caught in Herod's web. Who informed upon us? I cannot guess. What was our crime? It's impossible even to speculate. Perhaps a woman grew tired of her lover, and on the rack, as the Circassians bore down upon her, she uttered names from some distant recollection. I ask Shelomith what she thinks of this theory and she replies, 'It's as good as any other we've proposed.'

How terrible the tragedy became! Of my friends, one in three fell to the tyrant: Antigonus dragged down by the rumor of a fishmonger; Barnabas slain because he held land the king wanted; Shmuel, the uncle of my wife and a trusted Jew, beheaded on the accusation of a drunken Greek sailor; Leonidas, Marcus and Abraham, all dead for no reason that I know; the poet Lycidas and the songwriter Marcellus slain as members of a conspiracy whose outlines were not defined; Isaac and Yokneam dead merely because they owned silver. I could continue but the roll call is meaningless, for any family in Judaea could equal it, with different names sacrificed to different charges.

Why have the Romans allowed this madman to persecute his own people in this manner? Judea is far from Rome and of little consequence, really. Years ago with my help Herod charmed Caesar Augustus, and in the intervening decades the Roman emperor has been willing to support Herod so long as the latter maintains discipline along the borders of the empire. Reports filter back to Rome, of course, but they are charges made against a king of the scarlet and lodged before an emperor of the purple, so Augustus always sides with Herod. Once a commissioner sent out to Caesarea confided to me, as a fellow Roman, 'Does it really matter, one way or the other, if most of the brilliant Jews are killed off? Won't it be easier for us to rule if they're eliminated?' So Herod was not only permitted to destroy the nation but actually encouraged to do so.

A few weeks ago, however, events took a turn that will probably make even Rome notice the terror that has overtaken its stiff-necked Judaean outpost. Long ago Herod as a gesture of ultimate defiance to the Jews, who hated him as much as he despised them, caused to be erected over the main gate of the temple a wooden image of a Roman eagle, the first statuary that had defiled the temple since the days of Antiochus Epiphanes, and for years the faithful Jews were impotent to do anything about the infuriating symbol. When it was first erected I did not understand Jews as well as I do now, and I did not anticipate their permanent resentment against this affront to their religion; now, thanks to Shelomith, I think I understand.

At any rate, some days ago two loyal priests harangued their students to the point where a group of young men suspended themselves by ropes from a high point and chopped down the Roman eagle. Throughout Jerusalem the devout began to cheer, and I think there might have been a riot except that Herod's African and German mercenaries descended upon the mob and arrested the two priests and about forty scholars, who were dragged before the king. His rage was beyond reason, for he saw that what the Jews were doing against him would place them into direct conflict with Rome, and this would put his crown in jeopardy. When that wooden eagle toppled he could feel his crown tottering. In blind fury he struck back. The two priests and the three boys who chopped down the eagle were burned alive before the temple gates. The other forty were to be herded into a small enclosure, where African soldiers were turned upon them until all bodies were hacked apart. The eagle would be replaced with a larger one, Herod informed Augustus, so that Rome need not fear. Herod would kill a million Jews, if it were necessary, to keep Caesar Augustus placated.

Publicly he bragged to Rome, but secretly he was embittered by the antagonism of his Jews, and he declined into his fatal illness. Sensing that he was about to die he begged me to accompany him to hot baths on the other side of the Jordan, at a spot where sweet waters issued out of the rocks and flow into the Dead Sea, that lake of bronze, Callirhoe, the place is called, and as our entourage paraded along the bleak, deserted lands east of Jerusalem in search of it, I felt that we were dead men marching across the landscapes of hell, and Herod must have shared my thoughts, for he forced the soldiers to draw the blinds about his litter so that he need not see the desolation which so precisely matched the mourning of his spirit. At night, when our camp was pitched, he talked with me in Greek of the philosophers he had known, of the Greek beauty that had impressed him so deeply throughout his life, and he said with a dry cackle in his throat, 'You and I were the best Greeks of all, Myrmex. Rome thinks of us as Romans, but we fooled them. Not even Caesar Augustus could buy my soul, for it is Greek.' I was surprised at his use of the word *soul*, for this was a Hellenistic word not familiar to Jews, nor was the concept it represented, but it summarized his attitude toward life. Inspired by our hopeful conversations, he gained strength as we marched, but at Callirhoe, that lovely oasis with the musical name, which sick men reach after days in the desert, the local doctors prescribed a hot bath in a tub of almost bubbling oil.

I tried the simmering liquid with my fingers and protested that the heat would kill him, but the doctors persisted, and Herod said, 'If we have come this far, old friend, let us explore the heat,' and he was lowered into an oily furnace, and I was right. The heat was so tremendous that he fainted. His throat croaked and his eyes turned up in death. I shouted that the doctors were killing him, but they assured me, 'The whitened eyes are a good sign,' and after some minutes in the scalding bath the disease-racked body of Herod was hauled out, and as the doctors predicted he revived. Temporarily he was improved by the experience, but after some days under the date palms of Callirhoe he worsened, and ordered, 'Take me back to Jericho. I have some urgent business with my son Antipater.' And we returned across the landscape of death.

I last saw King Herod seven days ago. I described him to my wife, and when she heard of the hideous estate into which he had fallen she wept for our old friend. In size he was gross, laden with fat where once he had been lean and handsome. He was mostly bald and three of his front teeth had broken off without having been replaced. Sickness had spread through his entire body, and his legs were great stumps, half a cubit thick at the ankles. He could not eat without agony throughout his bowels, and a dreadful sickness had attacked his genitals, producing worms that lived in the mortified flesh. He had sores elsewhere in his body, but the worst of his affliction was that his stomach had turned permanently rotten and gave off such a stench that even his bodyguards had to be relieved at intervals lest they collapse from the smell. He was a man of seventy on whose dying body had been visited all the crimes of his former years: Mariamne was revenged in his horrible illness, and his sons, his mother-in-law, and his friends by the score and his subjects in their thousands. He was horrible beyond imagination, but he was a man who had been my friend, my benefactor, and when the others had fled I stayed with him, endeavouring to assuage his final hours.

'Herod,' I said boldly, 'I am your oldest friend and I am no longer afraid. You can do me no harm that I have not done myself through working with you.'

'What do you mean?' he sputtered, raising himself on one elbow so that his foul breath, like a dozen privies stirred together, swept over me in repulsive force.

'I helped you drown young Aristobolus . . .'

'He was killed by strangling,' the wild king shouted. He could not remember that there had been two victims named Aristobolus–uncle and nephew. He had forgotten the first great crime.

'I stood by while Mariamne was killed . . .'

'No!' he protested, holding aloft his other hand. 'Her ghost came here and I am forgiven!' He fell back on the bed, cackling like an idiot. 'She has forgiven me, Myrmex! Her ghost comes no more. Oh, Mariamne!' He wept, and as his chest contracted, waves of incredibly putrid air reached me from the corruption of his body, and I was forced to withdraw from his bedside.

'Don't leave me!' he pleaded. 'You are the only friend I can trust.' He spoke with childish longing of the good days we had known together and asked me if I would accompany him again to the northern provinces. 'The Galilee is the only part of my kingdom where people truly love me,' he whimpered. 'I should like to see Makor again with you.' He recalled how he had started his march to the throne from my little town and asked me if it was still beautiful, with cool breezes coming down the wadi in the hot afternoons. 'In Galilee I am still loved,' he told himself.

Seeing that the dying man clung to his perpetual wish to be loved, I decided to play upon his fancy to advance the cause for which I had come to seek him, and I said, 'You will not be loved, Herod, if you proceed with your plans to kill Antipater.' My words revitalized him, as if only hate could activate that disintegrating body.

'My son is plotting against me,' he roared, rising to a sitting position. 'It was his lies that caused me to put to death my other sons. Oh, Alexander and Aristobolus, my true and wonderful sons, why did I murder you so foully?' He fell back upon his cushions and for some moments wept for his vanished sons, but then his bitterness toward his living son returned and he cursed the young man most cruelly, charging him with crimes that were preposterous.

'Herod!' I reasoned with the insane man. 'You know he could not have done these things. Release him and all Judaea will applaud you.'

'Do you think so?' He sought my reassurance that by such reprieve he might at last win the love of his subjects, and I was about to launch an inspired defense of Antipater, such a one as I had uttered years ago on behalf of Herod himself, but a soldier from the prison interrupted with the news that Antipater, prematurely advised that Herod was dead, was offering to bribe the guards into releasing him so that he might lay claim to the throne.

'Kill him,' the putrid man shouted from his deathbed, and a detachment of his guard marched off obediently, their short swords bared for the fifth member of the king's family, and I recalled the bitter jest of Augustus: 'I would rather be Herod's swine than his family, for the pigs have a chance of living.'

'You foolish man!' I yelled. 'The kingdom needs Antipater.'

'I don't,' the old king shouted defiantly. His activity caused him to cough, great convulsions which filled the room with odors, and the ensuing pain affected his mind, for when the spasm ended he lay back exhausted. For a while he wept for the son who was being murdered at that moment, and several times he whispered the name of Mariamne. 'Will she be waiting for me when I die?' he asked pathetically. Before I could reply he continued, 'You were the lucky one, Myrmex, you and Shelomith.' He smiled at me as if I were his brother, and he saw with satisfaction the tears that came involuntarily to my eyes. 'Are any women in the world so beautiful as the young Jewesses we knew? Cleopatra, Sebaste, I saw all the others but there was never one like Mariamne. Why was she taken from me?' He spoke of her as if she had been carried off by some unexpected illness for which he shared no responsibility; then, feeling himself threatened from a new quarter, he whispered to me, 'Have you heard the rumors, Timon? That a true king of the Jews has been born?' When I could not respond to rumors which had not reached me, he called me closer to the bed and whispered in an even lower voice, 'They say it was in Bethlehem. I've sent soldiers to investigate.'

There was nothing I could reply to this latest of his fears, so I remained silent, but of a sudden he rose, left his bed and with his great, stumpy feet puffed out like a corpse three days dead, moved about the room, clutching at imaginary shadows. 'Why have the Jews hated me? Timon Myrmex, you're married to one. You tell me. Why have the Jews hated me?' Spreading his legs far apart to lend himself balance, he stood before me in his nightclothes, shouting, 'I've been a good king for the Jews. I brought peace and justice to their land. Think of the temple we built for them, but they treat me coldly. They call me the Idumaean and say I'm not a Jew. Myrmex, you know that my one desire has been to serve the Jews.' Clutching suddenly at my arm, lest he fall, he cried, 'Shelomith loves me, doesn't she?'

I assured him that she did, and he whimpered like an apprehensive boy, 'She's the only one who does.' Clutching me anew he confided, 'You know that Mariamne never loved me. She held me in contempt . . . said I was no real king.' He looked about suspiciously and whispered, 'I think she had a lover. A man who cut hair in the palace.'

To halt this blasphemy I said, as if he were a child to be got back into bed, 'Only last week Shelomith told me she loved you. However, if you continue killing Jews even she will grow to hate you.'

He stared at me in horror, grasping at his throat. 'Shelomith would hate me? Doesn't she know that everything I've done has been intended to help her Jews? Myrmex, tell me honestly, when I die the Jews will mourn for me, won't they?'

Why did I say it? Why could I not have supported this crazy old man as I had done so often in the years before? What did it matter to me whether the Jews mourned for him or not? But I told him, 'Herod, if you continue to kill, no one will mourn you.'

He staggered back as if I had struck him. He choked on my words, and waves of putrescence flowed from his crumbling body, so that I looked at him with disgust. This infuriated him and he began shouting, 'You are wrong, Myrmex, by the gods you are wrong. The Jews will mourn me as they have never mourned before.' He called for his mercenaries–Africans, Cilicians, Egyptians, Germans, Persians–the men who had coldly killed off the leaders of Judaism, and screamed at them in jumbled, frenzied sentences: 'Go to every city in Judaea. Arrest the leading citizens. Put them in jail and guard them well. Feed them luxuriously. Let them have all comforts. And on the day I die, kill them.' The soldiers were stunned, but Herod continued: 'Go now to every city. None is too small. Go even to Makor. And start by arresting this man!' He pointed at me with a trembling finger. 'He and his wife shall die. Kill them as I have directed you in the past.' He strode about, hacking and thrusting with his right arm. Wrenching a short sword from one of his Germans he slashed it through the air not far from my face. 'Hack him to death. Kill all the great men in the kingdom.' Exhausted, he fell back upon the fetid sheets and grinned at me, his broken teeth making his face grotesque.

'Myrmex, you shall die. Why should you be tall and slim while I am gross? Why should you have your teeth and your hair while your king has nothing but a rotting body? Why should you still have Shelomith while the only woman I ever loved has been taken from me? You shall die. All of you shall die.'

As the soldiers moved in to arrest me he wept on his couch, and I thought of the ancient poem of king David's which Shelomith had often sung to me:

> Each night I make my bed swim.
> I drench my couch with my tears.
> My eye has wasted away from grief . . .

Herod was the legal successor to King David, so it was proper to compare them, but as I stood a prisoner before him I thought of how the earlier king of the Jews had wept for the great sins he had committed, finding consolation in the forgiveness of the Hebrew god whom he had tried to serve in his fumbling way; but Herod wept only for his personal misery, throwing himself upon the mercy of no god, and he found no consolation.

From his bed he shrieked the last words I would hear from this old friend: 'When I die the Jews may not mourn for me. But by the gods they will mourn.' And I was led away.

Under guard I was brought to Makor. I marched, a prisoner, through Sebaste, which I had rebuilt into a city of magnificence, renaming it for the wife of Augustus. With fetters about my wrists I marched to Nazareth and Cana and Jotapata. With the guards behind me I penetrated the swamp and marched through my own olive grove and up to the gates which I had rebuilt in the Roman image. Desperately I wanted to cry out a warning to Shelomith, telling her to flee, but the soldiers had rushed into the town and taken her prisoner. We met in shackles, in the forum I had built, and she was beautiful as on the the day Herod had brought her to me. She did not wail nor did she berate me for the errors which had led us to this conclusion. When the soldier-captain read the proclamation, that Timon Myrmex and his wife Shelomith were to be arrested and kept in a public prison where the citizens could see them, and that on word of the death of Herod armed soldiers were to be set loose upon them, she smiled.

'Tell King Herod,' she told the soldiers, 'that I am sorry he murdered Mariamne.' In those few words she summarized the mad misery of the man.

That was three days ago. In the interval the citizens of our little town have reacted as Herod foresaw. Non-Jews come to the steps of the temple to bemoan my fate, and I advise them that as a Roman I am prepared to die. Jews come to visit Shelomith, for her father was a man of dignity and is well remembered in Galilee, and with equal resignation she assures them that she has lived a good life and a long one and that the ignominy of execution does not humiliate her. My people offer arguments and her people utter prayers, and it almost seems as if Shelomith and I must console the living rather than accept their weeping on our behalf.

But I must not create the impression that we are stoics. Yesterday I came upon my wife as she rubbed her tired face with a sweet oil which she keeps in a small phial: she had before her a tray of these bottles which Herod had given her years ago when we stayed with him at Caesarea, and she was so exquisite as she lifted first one little phial and then the other, creating beauty from them as if we were going to a dinner, that I sobbed, and she put down the tray and took my hand.

'We must not berate ourselves for having served Herod,' she whispered.

'You don't accuse me . . . for having intertwined our lives with his?'

'Of course not! Apart from these last insane years he did far more good than evil. He gave us a harsh administration, but he gave us peace.'

'Why do you Jews always seek out kings like Herod?' I asked.

'We? Rome gave us Herod. We had no voice in choosing him.'

'I meant that if your people had rallied about the Maccabees there would have been no opening for Herod.'

She considered this and replied slowly. 'We Jews always find it difficult to support our own people. We seem to prefer being governed by others.' Then she added, 'It's something you won't understand. But we cannot believe in any kingdom, neither of our own making nor of Rome's. We hold that the true kingdom is of God and will come only with the Messiah, so even if Herod had been Jewish we wouldn't have accepted him. There will never again be a Jewish state in Israel, for we are destined to live under the yoke of others, offering our testimony not to principalities but to God.'

I was unwilling to follow her in these philosophical discussions so I turned the talk to happier days. 'I am nineteen again and you are a child living near the synagogue of Makor. A small ship sails into Ptolemais bearing a powerful young man named Herod who steps down to say, 'I have come to pacify the Galilee.' If we were, to live those years again, would you advise me to stand with him? Defend him before Octavian?'

Again she paused to consider my question, for Shelomith has the Jewish characteristic of looking at life with absolute honesty of purpose, and quietly she said, 'Would we not be craven to reject our history now?' She took my hands and said, 'We followed Herod, and I suppose we'd do so again. But we should have given some thought, Timon, to the greater king whom we should have served with greater devotion.' Before I could respond, she laughed and asked, 'Of all the years we spent together, which were the best? When we were building that beautiful arcaded street in Antioch?'

'No. Caesarea made anything else insignificant. As long as the earth endures, that city will be the capital of Asia, and to have helped launch it was no mean accomplishment.' We sat in our prison and recalled those majestic rows of columns, the palaces and the gemlike theater nestled beside the blue sea. It was a masterpiece that we built, Herod and I, and it will remain as long as men cherish works of beauty.

Yesterday Shelomith smiled when I spoke in this manner of Caesarea, and when I asked why, she said, 'You are so stubbornly Roman! I should have thought that the temple of Jerusalem would be your permanent satisfaction. Even we Jews are forced to admit that there Herod performed a miracle.'

I had never spoken to my wife of this matter, but death was upon us and there was no sensible reason to withhold our thoughts, so I said, 'The temple I have erased from my mind. For me it does not count.'

'Why?' Shelomith cried, for like all Jews she kept a deep affection for this ancient building.

'For a long time I've suspected that sooner or later Rome will have to destroy the temple.'

'But why?'

'Because imperial Rome and the temple cannot exist together within the same empire.'

'Timon! You are talking insanely, like the king. Rome is one thing. It lies across the ocean and is very powerful, but the temple exists in a separate world. Its continuation is permanent.'

'I used to think so,' I said.

'What changed your mind?'

'You weren't in Jerusalem when the priests caused the young men to chop down the wooden eagle.'

'You told me about it,' my wife answered, and her eyes glowed with satisfaction as she recalled the daring escapade.

'You remember the tearing down,' I said, 'but I remember the men who were burned alive. We set up five pillars before the temple and huge piles of brush were placed upon the stones, forming platforms on which the condemned men stood. Herod's soldiers . . . they're always ready to do anything . . . lit the fires and we expected cries of anguish to come from the pillars.'

'What happened?'

'The fires burned unevenly, but as the flames licked about each face, one after the other, the man who was being burned alive cried with his last breath, 'Hear, O Israel, the Lord our God, the Lord is one.'

'At such a moment what else would a man say?'

I looked at Shelomith and realized, after a lifetime of the most intimate existence with her, that I barely understood her, and she must have recognized this, for she said quietly, 'Tomorrow or the next day, when the messenger comes, and the soldiers and sent in to kill us, you will think of Rome and Augustus and the distant buildings you have built. You may even look upon the Augusteana across the way and a marvelous light will go out. Timon, I have loved you so. You have been so brave, so enduring.' She began to weep, not silently but with unstifled sobs that sent tears gushing from her eyes, and as they fell upon her lap she took one of the perfume bottle and with its lip brushed aside the offending tears, so that some fell into the bottle, and she laughed nervously, saying, 'Together we have made the perfume of life, tears and roses and the smell of olive trees in the spring. That perfume has been in my nostrils since the first day I met you.'

She placed the phial on the tray and resumed the line of thinking that the tears had interrupted. 'As we die you will look upon the buildings of this world, but I will whisper, "Hear, O Israel, the Lord our God, the Lord is one." Herod with all his soldiers, with all his flames, will never be able to silence that cry.'

'That's why I say the temple will have to be destroyed. Rome has offered you membership in the world at large. But in your stiff-necked pride you've rejected the world and clung to your temple.'

'Must it perish?' she cried, and we were dealing with such impassioned thoughts that I left her improvised dressing table, so that she might complete her toilet, and went to the entrance of the temple where the guards were waiting for the word to slay us.

Two were Egyptian and two were German, and I asked them how they had entered the service of Herod. The Egyptians had been given him by Caesar Augustus when he dissipated Cleopatra's power, and the Germans had been brought to Judaea as slaves, progressing by one chance or another to responsible positions in the army. 'How many Jews have you slain?' I asked the men. They shrugged their shoulders. 'We do what we're told,' they replied.

'Well, how many?' I insisted. 'We haven't had any foreign wars, so all your activity has been against the Jews. How many would you guess?' And they began recalling their various expeditions against Jerusalem, when there was trouble there, and Samaria before the name was changed to Sebaste, and the trouble in Gaza. Slowly the figures mounted until these four chance soldiers, operating in different areas, found that they had slain more than a thousand leading Jews.

'When the orders come to kill my wife and me . . . won't you wonder what it's about?'

'Orders come and we obey them,' one of the Germans replied. His sharp, dreadful sword hung easily from his left hip.

'But you've known that Herod was insane.'

'Don't speak against the king,' the soldier warned me.

'But he's dead. We're merely awaiting confirmation.'

'I should think you'd want him to live,' the German argued, speaking a colloquial Greek.

'You haven't answered my question. Why should you obey the orders of a dead man?'

'Because if you don't have one king, you have another,' the German explained. 'If Herod is dead, as you say, there's another king in Antioch to give orders and above him there's the emperor in Rome, and it doesn't matter very much who tells us to do what. There's always a king somewhere.'

Jews came to pray with Shelomith, and in their bearded faces, obdurate as iron, I found my solution to the behaviour of the Herodian soldiers. On earth there was always a king giving orders, and frequently they were contradictory or even inhuman, as in the case of a putrefying Herod, but above them there had to be a true king who judged things honestly and who, when the time came, corrected the mistakes of the earthly sovereigns. If there were not such a system, the behaviour of a mortal like Herod would be incomprehensible.

I looked at the Jews, whom I had never understood, for they were always a withdrawn race who showed neither love not toleration for the Romans, and I realized that it was not through the friends of Herod but through these bearded, intransigent men that Judaea and perhaps the whole empire would find its moral stability. Between the Jews and the Romans there would be war–of that I was increasingly convinced–and doubtless the temple as a symbol of Judaism would have to vanish; but the principles these men stood for, the rectitude I saw in their faces, must ultimately triumph. For the first time I was sorry to be dying, for I wanted to witness this great confrontation. For me, Herod had terminated any belief in Rome as a permanent master. There would have to be something else, some force that could control insane men. Why, he had even intimated that if the rumors were true, if an honest king of the Jews had been born in Bethlehem, all Jewish babies in that district must be slaughtered, but from this hideous act he had drawn back. It was essential that some superior power be called into existence to force such men to draw back from their other insanities, and I wished that I could be on hand to greet the messengers of that power when they arrived.

Shelomith and I talked of these things for many hours yesterday and I went to bed with increased respect for her religion, which I had not deeply investigated before. I say, 'I went to bed,' as if this day had merely been another in a long sequence of routine days, but was not. We shall probably never go to bed again. I shall never again see her rise like a flower coming to bloom in the spring, and in the nothingness of death, if I am permitted memory, I shall miss her more than I can say. My three sons, one in Antioch, one in Athens and one in Rhodes, will look like her until they die, some years from now, and then her lovely image will be forgotten. Being a Jewess, she never allowed me to have her portrait made, for like the brave men who chopped down the Roman eagle and who were burned alive for their audacity, she considered portraits blasphemy. Something Moses had told his Jews prevented them from having any likeness made; but I smile, for as long as Makor stands, the eight perfect columns will serve as her memorial. They are closer to her reality than a painting of her face could ever be, for they reproduce her essence: tall, flawlessly proportioned, austere, yet molded to the requirements of her position. Like her columns she stands with her head unadorned, and bearing nothing, for she is a free woman. Only the Jews know how to produce such women, and I have known two of them—Shelomith and Mariamne. Had the queen lived she would have kept Herod sane, but she died prematurely and he died with her.

Messengers come to the gate! Shelomith moves to my side, her right hand in mine. We watch the important men in short military skirts stride down the street and swing into the forum. Between the columns they march, not looking at our prison, and they head for the governor's palace. We watch them disappear with their fateful news and observe, almost against our will, that the four guards stiffen in preparation for the deed ahead.

Shelomith kneels to pray, and some old Jews who knew her father begin rocking back and forth outside the temple, wailing prayers that I do not understand.

I cannot pray. I joined with Herod when I was nineteen and with him I rode to power and to triumph. If his insanity has now enveloped me in death, I cannot decently complain. My ancestors lived in Makor for countless generations, and they studied always how they must adjust to the invading armies, and usually they made the right decision. They were Hebrews or Greeks or Babylonians as occasion demanded, and years ago I decided to be a Roman. I have been a good Roman, and I leave this part of the world—not only Makor but all of Judaea and Syria as well—more beautiful than when I found it, and having offered this as my benediction I am ready to die.

The governor leaves his palace, the one I built, and strides along the forum I erected. He comes to the prison which I built for myself, and the German guards unleash their swords—those fearful short swords that do the king's work. The governor and the messengers stand erect before the temple columns and Shelomith stands bravely beside me as a voice begins to speak.

'King Herod is dead. The prisoners are set free.'

Shelomith's hand falls from mine, and all I can think of is that somehow I must seek out the new king to see if he plans the building of new edifices. But Shelomith has dropped to her knees and I hear her praying, 'Hear, O Israel, the Lord our God, the Lord is one.'

LEVEL VIII

Yigal and His Three Generals

Found at Makor–brass coin, a Roman sestertius worth about 4c
when issued. One fourth of a denarius, the penny of the Bible.
This notable design, celebrating the conquest of Judaea
launched by General Vespasian in 67 C.E., was used repeatedly
during the reign of the Flavian dynasty: Vespasian emperor 70–
79; his son Titus, 79–81; and his second son Domitian, the
persecutor of the Christians, 81–96. This specimen issued in
Rome 72 C.E. by Vespasian to honor Titus, who had destroyed
Jerusalem 70 C.E., thus ending the Jewish War. *Obverse:* T(itus)
CAES(ar) VESPASIAN(us) IMP(erator) PON(tifex)
TR(ibunicia) POT(estate) CO(n)S(ul) II. (Caesar Titus, son of
Vespasian the Emperor, the Great Priest, Owner of the
Tribunician Power, Consul for Two Times.) *Reverse:*
IUDAEA CAPTA (S(enatus) C(onsulto). (Judaea captured.
with the approval of the Senate.) Similar coins were struck in
Caesarea, but on these the legends were in Greek. Such coins
issued until the assassination of Domitian. Lost in the ruins of
Makor by a Roman traveler, October 18, 74 C.E.

Throughout its long history Makor's fate was usually determined by what
happened in remote capitals like Memphis, Babylonia, Antioch and Rome; and
citizens listened for distant rumors that might affect them.

Thus in 14 C.E. they heard that great Caesar Augustus had died and that his
place had been taken by the tyrant Tiberius, a man so debauched and craven
that he fled Rome and hid on small islands until 37 C.E., when he was finally
smothered in a heap of dirty laundry. Tiberius was succeeded by the even
worse tyrant Caligula, who, like others before him, insisted upon being
worshiped as the only god. Crazy with lust and abominations, he ordered his
statue to be placed in all temples throughout the empire, and to this fatuous
command the various nations acceded–except one.

The Jews of Judea refused to accept Caligula as their god, and they likewise
refused to allow his statues to enter their territory; and when the emperor heard
of their obstinacy he left off his immoralities long enough to announce that if
the Jews alone, of all his subjects, refused to acknowledge him as their god, he
would force them to do so with armies, after which he would sell the lot into
slavery–every man and child throughout the Jewish nation. This ominous
edict was delivered in the year during which Caligula caused his horse Incitatus
to be elected a full consul of Rome, and not longer after that day, on which,
having grown surfeited with ordinary killings in the arena, he ordered
hundreds of casual spectators in the stadium thrown to the wild beasts so that
he might enjoy their sudden agony as the lions and tigers sprang upon them.

Caligula sent his edict for disciplining the Jews to a trusted veteran of Roman wars, General Petronius, who was stationed with two full legions in Antioch, and that wise, daring military man took immediate steps to subdue Judaea and impose the emperor's will. Importing a third legion from Italy and gathering three auxiliary groups from Syria, he waited for a Roman ship that was bringing twoscore huge statues of Caligula, and when all were assembled he marched his men southward with startling speed and ordered the ship to Ptolemais, from which seaport he proposed to subdue Judaea.

Eight miles east, in the little frontier town of Makor, which as so often in the past would have to engage the first onslaught of the invaders, lived a young Jew named Yigal, neither priest nor merchant, to whom the simple precepts of his religion were more sweet than the sound of children's laughter. He worked at the olive press south of town and owned no property, not even the house in which his wife and their sons lived. His was a frugal family and the children were never wasteful of the meager drachmas he earned. At the Feast of Tabernacles they begged a few coins so that they might build the booth in which they and their parents would live during the holy days. At Passover they pestered their father to buy a kid, and at the feast celebrating Queen Esther's triumph over the Persian persecutor Haman they required a few additional coins to buy the sweets and trinkets customary on that occasion.

In the year that General Petronius bore down with his legions upon Judaea, Yigal was only twenty-six years old, and he was one of the least important men in Makor, but by some intuitive sense it was he who foresaw with shimmering clarity what would happen to the Jews if the Romans succeeded in erecting their statues to Caligula in local synagogues and in desecrating the great temple in Jerusalem. What was more remarkable, it was Yigal–this undistinguished olive-grove worker–who discovered the only tactic whereby the Jews could halt the Romans; so one morning, to his own surprise, he assembled what Jews he could in Makor's Roman forum and, standing on the steps of the Venus temple, harangued them as follows:

'Jews of Makor, our fathers have told us of that day long ago when the tyrant Antiochus Epiphanes sought to violate our holy places with his image as that of the only true god. Then our forefathers rose against him and drove him from this land. I know we cannot duplicate their feat. The Romans are many times stronger than the Syrians ever were. They march with dreadful legions that have never been defeated, and we poor Jews are powerless to oppose them. Our leaders Simeon and Amran are correct when they advise us not to take arms against the Romans, not to harry or molest them in any way, for if we do so we can be sure that the Romans will destroy this town and Jotapata and every other, even to Jerusalem. Our synagogues will not only be profaned, they will be razed to the ground, and we shall be sold into slavery as we were in the days of Babylon. We are powerless, and the enemy is upon us.'

Yigal was not the kind of Jew to whom townsmen would ordinarily listen. He was neither tall like the oldest of the priests, nor bulky in figure like the governor; nor was he a brilliant man. He was of medium height, frail, brown-haired. His eyes were not blue nor were they brown, but a kind of gray-green, and both his nose and his chin were small to the point of being ridiculous. His teeth were uneven but strong, and his voice was not commanding but it was clear, without rasps or muffled vowels. He was certainly not a man one would choose for a leader, and the reason why he had remained merely an assistant at the olive grove was that he had failed to impress the owner with any ability other than honesty and promptness. If he was paid for twelve hours' work a day he delivered than number or more. Even his love of Judaism did not differentiate him from the other Jews of Makor, for he could never be a zealot. In simple terms, he found in his dedication to the laws of Moses a satisfaction which he knew did not come to Romans who worshiped Caligula–Jupiter nor to Greeks who clung to the Zeus–Baal of the region.

'We are powerless,' he continued that day, 'but we are not without strength. For this night I shall walk to Ptolemais, with my wife Beruriah and my three sons, and there we shall lie down before the legions of General Petronius and we shall tell him that we would rather die than have his men place images of his emperor in our synagogues. If all of us do this, if we are willing to bare our throats and the throats of our children to the Roman swords, Petronius must listen. He may order his men to slay us. Tomorrow night I may be dead, and my wife may be dead and the children I love so dearly. But we will have proved to the Romans that they may not do this wrong thing unless they kill every Jew in this land.'

Simeon, the acknowledged leader of Jews in this part of Galilee, ridiculed Yigal's plan, saying that even nine hundred Jewish throats would not impress a man like General Petronius, but Yigal was not to be silenced. He resumed his argument and to his surprise a farmer called Naaman, older than Yigal but like him a man of no substance, joined the plea and added, 'We have learned in the past that unless we protest with all our energy we will be smothered by the Romans. Here is the final test. If we surrender our synagogues to the statues of Caligula we are doomed. Truly there is no escape, and I agree with Yigal that we must march to Ptolemais and throw ourselves before the Roman legions, telling them to kill us there. I shall go with him.'

'You fools!' Simeon warned. 'The planting season approaches and you're needed in the fields.' For it was the Jews who tended the countryside, Greeks alone serving as merchants in the towns.

To this Yigal replied, 'Those fields can be our major weapon. If we refuse to plant, the Romans will be forced to listen.'

'No!' Simeon said. 'Against the Romans no one can prevail.' And so the town was split into two parts, most agreeing with Simeon that submission was the only way to preserve the Jews but some siding with Yigal and Naaman that opposition must be made now, even though the Roman legions were fully armed while the Jews had nothing.

All that day, while the Roman ship in Ptolemais unloaded its statues of Caligula, the Jews in Makor continued arguing, and at about the time that General Petronius was ready to begin his march to Jerusalem, depositing a statue in each conquered place, but saving the two largest for the temple, Yigal finally persuaded about half the Jews in Makor that the moment of decision was upon them. Standing in the forum he said simply, 'We shall trust that God Almighty will illuminate the heart of General Petronius and prove to him that he dare not kill all the Jews of Judaea. If we accomplish this, even though we lose our own lives, what great work we shall have done for the Lord.'

'You will never halt the Romans,' old Simeon wailed.

'We have no other choice,' Yigal countered. He bowed his head and prayed for a few moments, then gathered up his wife and three sons and started slowly toward the main gate. The farmer Naaman and his family followed, and they were joined by others who understood what Yigal was attempting, but most of the senior Jews and all of the Greeks laughed at the improvised army of four hundred that marched with no weapons and no general to guide them.

Yigal went out the main gate and onto the stone-surfaced road that led westward to Ptolemais, and with slow, patient steps so that the women and little children could keep pace, he started the historic march to the seaport where the Roman legions waited. His ragtag army passed the checkpoints where the old Phoenician guard posts had stood and came late in the day to that barren mound along the Belus River where for three thousand years the original port of Akka had faced the Mediterranean. As dusk approached, the Jews reached the plain leading to the new city, perched on a peninsula, which King Herod had graced with a cluster of delightful buildings, and there, in the shadow of the walls of Ptolemais with its massive gates, Yigal and his people sat upon the ground and waited. Night fell and the shadows of Roman troops could be seen upon the walls, lit from behind by fires that burned in the city. The Jews had no fires, and the night was cold, but they huddled on the ground–fathers and mothers making sleeping circles in which the children nestled–and all wondered what the Romans would do on the forthcoming day.

When the sun was up General Petronius surveyed the rabble from a lookout post on the wall, and making nothing of the scene dispatched some legionnaires to apprehend the leaders of the mob, and when the soldiers arrived Yigal and Naaman offered themselves as hostages. They were marched inside the gates, where in a public square decorated on three sides by handsome Herodian buildings, General Petronius met them, backed up by the sixteen senior centurions of his legions. The Romans wore battle dress, short military skirts, metal-studded sandals, shin-guards, loose-fitting garments about their shoulders, and marks of their rank. They were resolute, relaxed warriors, ready at the command of their general to kill a hundred thousand Jews if necessary for the completion of the assignment. Hardly a Roman soldier in Ptolemais believed that Caligula, an offensive man with ugly habits, was a god; but all believed that if the emperor wished to tell his distant dominions that he was, the provinces had better obey. The soldiers watched with contempt as the two Jews in cheap civilian robes approached.

'Who are those people out there?' Petronius asked in Greek. He was a tall, handsome man, son of a good Roman family and a scholar given to reflecting upon the lessons of history. He always spoke Greek, which he had learned from Athenian slaves.

Using the same language Yigal replied, 'We are Jews. Come to beg you not to bring statues into our land.'

Some of the soldiers laughed, and Petronius said, 'Statues of Caligula are to rise in every land. It has been ordered.'

'We will sooner die than permit them here,' Yigal said quickly. Again the soldiers laughed, not in ridicule of the inconspicuous field hand but at the humor of the situation.

General Petronius said, 'At seven this evening we shall begin marching to Jerusalem, and your Jews had better step aside, for we must deliver our statues.' Behind the officers Yigal could see the first of the huge white images which slaves would haul over hilly roads for many months. With his twoscore marble faces Caesar Caligula, the god, looked benevolently down upon the scene.

'Respected General,' Yigal said, 'if you wish to move those statues into our land you will have to kill all of us on the plain.'

The simple force with which he spoke these words evoked two reactions. At first General Petronius was astonished at what the man was saying, but quickly he recovered his composure and grasped the mild-mannered Jew by the throat. 'Are you challenging the power of Rome?' he demanded.

Naaman interceded. 'Our quarrel is not with Rome, sir. Twice each day we sacrifice to Rome. We serve in your armies and pay your taxes. But we cannot permit in our country graven images, neither of gods nor of men.'

'We shall see about that,' Petronius thundered, thrusting Yigal aside and ordering his legions to move forward. The gates were swung open. The centurions called signals which the decurions passed along to their men and the march began, but as the first foot soldiers reached the gate Petronius capriciously ordered them to halt. 'Bring forth the smallest statue,' he cried, and slaves ran to fetch a handsome black-marble bust of Caligula, with vine leaves in his hair and deep-carved sockets for his benevolent eyes. It was a statue that any museum would cherish or that people a thousand years later would instinctively recognize as a thing of beauty. 'The god Caligula will go before us as we enter Judaea,' Petronius announced, and now, with the slaves moving ahead, the army resumed its march into the land of the Jews.

But when a short distance had been covered, the soldiers came upon the four hundred Jews of Makor–that trivial little town that hardly any Roman had heard of–who resolutely lay across the road and barred the way. The slaves, carrying the offensive statue, halted, not knowing what to do, and centurions of the three official legions ran forward with drawn swords. There was a painful moment as the determined Jews continued to block the way, while the Romans hesitated about killing them without specific orders from General Petronius. No Jew was armed.

Hurrying from the rear, accompanied by Yigal and Naaman as prisoners, Petronius came upon the scene and saw for himself that the Jews of Makor were indeed resolved to die where they lay rather than allow the statue to pass. He judged there were less than five hundred of them, with more than half women and small children, while he had some eighteen thousand armed troops at his command. If he gave the signal the killing could be ended in fifteen minutes, but he was a man of sensitivity; he had won many battles without massacring women and children, so now he hesitated. Turning to Yigal, a man half his age, with neither education nor distinctions, Petronius said, 'Order your people to disperse.'

'We are going to die . . . here on the road.'

'Centurions! Clear the road.'

Eagerly the soldiers ran toward the Jews, swords drawn, but when the nameless people of Makor made no effort to protect themselves, awaiting the cold thrust of the sword, Petronius ordered his men to halt. Sweating, the Roman general said to Yigal, 'Young man, if they do not obey me we shall have to slaughter them all. Tell them to get up and move aside.'

'I have told you . . . we are going to die.'

'For what reason?' Petronius pointed with some dismay at the inoffensive black statue of the new god. 'For a piece of stone you would die?'

'A false god must not enter our land,' Yigal said.

Petronius swallowed. He knew that Caesar Caligula was no god. He also knew that Caligula had become a false god only because he had murdered his predecessor, Tiberius. And he suspected that before long Caligula himself would have to be murdered. The man's excesses–killing decent citizens so that he could sleep with their wives for one night, then sending the women into prostitution and slavery–these things would have to be stopped, but in the meantime Caligula was emperor and he was also god. To defy him in any way or to allow the Jews to defy him would mean death for all. 'I am going to raise my arm,' the irritated general warned. 'When it falls we shall march forward, and if any Jew lies in our way . . . Centurions, cut them to pieces!'

The Roman general, backed by an enormous might, stood in the sunlight facing the two inconsequential Jews, one a helper at an olive press, the other a farmer with no lands of his own, and he raised his right arm, holding in the air an ebony baton. About his arm muscle and his forearm he wore military bands of gold and he made an imposing picture as he stood with the baton aloft. He seemed to be counting, but his voice could not be heard, for from the recumbent Jews opposing him came a mumble of prayer broken by an old man who whispered in a clear, soft voice, 'Hear, O Israel, the Lord our God, the Lord is one.' It was apparent to all that in defense of this basic doctrine–that there was and could be only one God, unbroken and undistributed–the Jews were prepared to die.

The centurions raised their swords. The slaves stepped aside, holding Caligula aloft in the brilliant sunlight, and for a long, long moment General Petronius wavered. With his arm raised he looked at Yigal and Naaman, who would be the first to die, and he saw that they had no intention of ordering their people to move aside. Indeed, each of the Jews was repeating the prayer which the old man was whispering.

'Bring these two back to the city,' Petronius commanded. Keeping his arm aloft he turned his back on the huddled Jews and ordered his men to follow him. Then slowly he lowered his arm, striking his right leg with the baton seven times. Behind him, in the plain, he could hear the Jews chanting, not a song of victory but of praise.

Inside the city Petronius told Yigal, 'We'll starve your Jews into common sense. They'll commit their own suicide.' And he threw a cordon about the Jews, allowing none to leave the plain, and all throught the blazing day the Jews lay in the sun while slaves dragged out from the city walls a gigantic statue of Caesar Caligula, placing it before the thirsty mob. In the cold night that followed, the watching troops could hear children crying as the benevolent visage of Caligula beamed down upon them in the moonlight. When dawn came there was no relief from the torrid sun, and the old man who had whispered the prayer died with its words still on his lips. Children fainted.

At four that afternoon, when the punishment was most terrible, General Petronius led Yigal and Naaman to the scene and asked if they would now order their Jews to disband. 'We have come here to die,' Yigal said simply. Petronius then directed a slave to give Yigal a drink of cold water, and as the Jew drank under duress, standing in the shadow of the great statue, Petronius cried to the prostrate Jews, 'See, he doesn't suffer. He has plenty of water.' With his own hands he poured the remainder on the dry ground at the god's feet, where it was immediately absorbed by the parched earth. Kicking the dust Petronius shouted, 'Do not listen to this fool. Go home. Go home.'

No one moved, and the third cold night came with neither food nor water, and on the next day a child died. The Petronius began to feel his own throat parching as if it were afire. For some time he fought against this strangling sensation, then made his decision. 'Tell the slaves to bring the statue back,' he ordered. When this was done he took Yigal and Naaman to the city gates. 'Lead your Jews home,' he said quietly, 'and three days from now assemble all Jewish leaders in Galilee to meet with me in Tiberias. There we shall decide what to do.'

So Yigal left the walls of Ptolemais and walked like a man in a daze to the plain where the Jews of Makor were near death; and as he saw each dusty face–Shlomo, with whom he had played as a boy; Asher, whose sister he had married; Beruriah, who had borne his children–he wanted to kneel before each one, for these simple people by their faith had turned back the full might of the Roman legions. He could not speak, but then he heard a rustling sound and the cry of children, for General Petronius had sent his slaves out from the walls with buckets of water and food. No adults were allowed to touch the rations but children were to be kept alive, by orders of the Roman general.

Three days later the leaders of the Jews in Galilee assembled in Tiberias–that dazzling new city recently built on the shores of the Sea of Galilee by Herod Antipas, son of Herod the Great–and there General Petronius laid before them his problem. Of course, Yigal and Naaman were not present, for in Makor they were not considered leaders of the Jews. Their place was taken by cautious Simeon, accompanied by Amram and other elders from Makor, but from surrounding villages did come several vigorous young men like Yigal, and all listened as the Roman general pleaded for understanding and compliance: 'I am a soldier, and I am bound to obey the law of my emperor. If I break it and permit you to bar the statues from your land I will be executed. Then it will be Caesar Caligula himself who will make war on you, not I. He will not send water to your dying children. He will kill every Jew in Judaea.'

'He will have to,' one of the younger Jews answered, and the crowd shouted its approval.

'Are you ready to fight even Caesar?' Petronius asked.

'We shall die . . . all of us will die . . . before we allow his statues to enter.'

On and on the discussions went, and in spite of all Roman threats the Jews remained adamant. Petronius appealed to their self-interest: 'Don't you want to form a helpful part of this great empire?' He cited economics: 'What kind of farmer allows his fields to lie idle in the sowing season?' He discussed theology: 'Other nations in the empire accept Caligula as their god while in secret they honor their ancient deities. Can't you do the same?' And because he was a man of honor, trained in the philosphies of Greece and on the field of battle, he sometimes betrayed his position by speaking as a humanist: 'Would you force me to slay women and children–which I must do if you refuse any further?' And when he said this the Jews knew that he had already decided not to slaughter the multitude, even though he himself might not yet realize that he had reached this conclusion.

Each morning this worried gentleman–for Petronius was that in the most significant sense of the word–ate a light breakfast, stood on his palace balcony to study the glorious mountains that surrounded the Sea of Galilee, then went below to conduct his arguments with the stubborn Jews. At noon he ate lunch with his centurions and in the afternoon went on foot to the refreshing hot baths that made Tiberias such a pleasure, and in those bubbling mineral waters that welled up from some deep volcanic disturbance he would lie and try to forget the dilemma in which Caesar Caligula had placed him. He prayed that some miracle might occur to solve the problem for him: The overdue dagger of the assassin might find its way to the tyrant's heart. In the hot baths Petronius muttered such prayers. But no solution came.

Finally at one meeting he shouted at the Jews, 'For weeks you meet with me and don't even have the grace to bring before me the man who started all this.' He dispatched Roman messengers to fetch Yigal from Makor, and when the young Jew reached Tiberias, Petronius took him to the hot baths, which an ordinary workman like Yigal could never otherwise have seen, and Roman laughed when the young Jew refused to undress. 'I've seen circumcisions before,' Petronius joked, and he persuaded Yigal to enter the bath; and there the two men talked with neither the panoply of glory nor the conceit of individual honor.

'Young man,' Petronius pleaded, 'if you Jews obstruct me now, you will have to face Caesar Caligula later. He will be a hideous opponent. He will burn you alive as if you were men of straw. Or crucify you by dozens on every hill.'

'Then we shall die,' Yigal said.

The two men left the steaming waters and were attended by slaves, and when they were dressed again, Petronius said, 'Please consider what you are doing.'

'We can do nothing else,' Yigal replied.

'You damned Jews!' Petronius exploded, and with a mighty blow of his fist he knocked the frail workman to the floor. But as soon as he had done so he stooped and gathered the stunned Jew in his arms. 'Forgive me,' he whispered. 'These meetings are driving me mad.' He helped Yigal to his feet and brushed his garments. 'Is there no hope of a settlement?' he pleaded.

In the marble dressing room of the Herodian baths Yigal replied, 'You will have to kill every Jew in Galilee, after that Sebaste, and then Jerusalem.'

That evening Petronius assembled the negotiators at an inn near the lake—that marvelous body of water so deep in the earth, so crowded by mountains on each side, yet so sweet and marked by repose—and he said, 'Jews of Galilee, your crops must be sown. No land of the Roman empire can lie idle in the sowing season. I am therefore sending you home to plant your fields.' The Jews greeted this with suspicion, for so far he had made no offer to withdraw the statues, and this could be a trick. Then the great general lowered his head and said in a whisper scarce heard above the waves of Galilee, 'The statues I will take away. With the help of your god I shall try to persuade Caesar Caligula that he cannot override the will of his Jews in Galilee. Romans cannot murder an entire population.' He rose, straightened his battle dress and asked for his baton. Then, in full imperial dignity, he said, 'If I fail, I perish. But I shall die gladly if by my action I save so many men of honor.' And he embraced Yigal.

That night he struck his camp in Tiberias, as if he could not bear to sleep again in that obstinate place. Bivouacking in the countryside like a general at war, he rose before dawn and marched back to Ptolemais, but as he came down the Damascus road and spotted the walled town of Makor nestling beneath its mountain, he stopped to study the zigzag gate and the white walls of the gymnasium, and against this background he visualized Yigal. 'The most obdurate man I've ever confronted,' he growled.

And then a torment of humiliation possessed him, a full general of Rome repulsed by an olive worker, and he cried, 'How did such a town defeat three Roman legions? I should put to death every Jew inside those walls and erect ten statues of Caligula to be worshipped by their ghosts.' Behind him he could hear the marching feet of the two legions retreating with him and in that burning moment he decided to turn them loose on the undefended town. 'Centurions!' he shouted. 'We'll teach a gang of Jews to abandon their fields!'

But as the men marched forward he looked at the fields where women had begun to plow and their men to sow, and at the olive grove where work had been resumed, and in these fields of Makor he saw the type of sturdy peasant who had once made Rome strong: men and women who loved freedom, who worshipped their own god in their own obstinate way, who paid their taxes and fed the empire. For a moment he visualized his own farm in Istria and remembered the satisfaction he had known working its fields, and to his centurions he said quietly, 'Proceed to Ptolemais.' It was in this manner that Makor through its reliance on the one God vanquished the full power of the Roman empire.

A man can read ten thousand pages of history and find only the corruption of power and the defeat of hope, but occasionally he will come upon an adventure like that of General Petronius, who, because he was at heart a Greek philosopher, refrained from destroying Makor and returned to the port city of Ptolemais, where he crated the statues of Caligula and marched his legions aboard ships for transportation back to Antioch. There he composed his report to Caesar Caligula: 'Mighty God, Spirit of Power, Light of the World, in pursuit of Your august instructions I invaded Judaea on schedule, but at Ptolemais I found five hundred Jews offering themselves to be sacrificed rather than permit statues of the new god, Caligula, to enter their territories. At Tiberias, I consulted with the leaders of the district and satisfied myself that in order to place the god Caligula's statue in the temple at Jerusalem, I would have to kill every Jew in the Galilee. For generations Your granary would lie barren. The name of Rome would be cursed forever. Unless You wish, August One, to kill on a scale not yet seen in our empire, I must beg You to withdraw your instructions to me. You must allow the Jews to worship as they have in the past.'

The dispatch reached Caligula at an evil moment. He raged at the contempt of the Jews and at the pusillanimity of his Syrian general. By swift messengers he sent news to Antioch that the Jews must be completely destroyed and that Petronius must commit suicide; but on the day his messengers sailed from Podi the patriots of Rome rose up and murdered their vile emperor, as they had known for some months that they must. So another messenger was dispatched by another boat to Syria, commending Petronius and annulling the order of execution, but none dared hope that this reprieving news could reach Antioch before the general was dead.

Sailing across the same sea, eastward from Rome, the competing ships—one bearing death, the other life—traversed the same waters; and unexpected storms caught the ship of death and held it prisoner for three months, while the ship of life sailed calmly to port, informing General Petronius of Caligula's murder and his own salvation.

Thus Petronius and Makor were saved, but Rome was not, for it continued to fall into the hands of degenerate emperors, and murder became the accepted preamble to nomination. In 37 C.E. the tyrant Tiberius had been smothered, only to be succeeded by a worse tyrant, Caligula. Now in 41 C.E. Caligula was murdered, to be followed by Claudius, husband of the incredible Messalina, and both of them had to be murdered for the welfare of the state and public decency; but they were followed in 54 C.E. by the worst tyrant of all, Nero, who having kicked his pregnant wife to death turned his demented attention to the distant Jews at the edge of his empire. 'What is this you say about a Jewish rebellion?' he asked, and his generals explained.

Under the procuratorship of Pontius Pilate, they said, there had been disturbances over the gaudy flags carried by the legions when they served in Jerusalem: golden eagles attached to these flags were worshiped by the Roman soldiers, and Jews insisted that these idols be removed before entering the Holy City. Additional difficulties had arisen because of a crucifixion which Pilate seemed to have bungled. There was also the matter of Paul of Tarsus, a very troublesome Jew, who claimed that his god had spoken to him on the Damascus road and who was stirring up trouble among both Jews and pagans. But primarily, the generals reported, the Jews of Jerusalem were talking of the establishment of their god's kingdom and were beginning to grow contemptuous of Roman rule. 'They are openly challenging us,' the generals reported, 'and the source of their strength is their temple, from whence all agitation stems.'

'Has there been fighting?' Nero asked, and he was told that in November of the year 66 Jewish zealots had driven all Roman forces from Jerusalem and had actually slain more than six thousand Roman troops in doing so. The bull-necked emperor gave two simple commands: 'Destroy Jerusalem. Level the temple.'

It was no ordinary general to whom Nero delivered these instructions for his final solution to the Jewish problem. He chose no Petronius weighed down by the moral burden of Greek philosophy and susceptible to the pleas of Jews devoted to their god; Nero picked the heavy, plodding fifty-seven-year-old commoner Vespasian, who would be assisted by his energetic son Titus. They would be given the Fifth Legion Macedonia and the Tenth Legion Fretensis, two of the best-known fighting teams in the world, composed not of mercenaries but of free citizens of the Roman empire. And one of the first things Vespasian did upon assuming command was to send Titus to Egypt to pick up the Fifteenth Legion Apollinaris as well, a mercenary unit trained for desert-type warfare under the command of a flint-hard strategist, Trajan.

At Antioch this crushing army assembled—the Fifth and Tenth, plus twenty-three cohort divisions, six wings of cavalry, and auxiliary troops from commanding kingdoms, plus engineers, workmen, slaves and servants—a total of nearly fifty thousand hardened men. Swiftly Vespasian marched to Ptolemais, where he was joined by Titus and Trajan, who had brought the Fifteenth Legion, rested after its long inactivity in Egypt.

As he stood poised with this overwhelming force Vespasian was one of the strong generals of Roman history: when required, he could be adamant, as he had proved against the Germans; or conciliatory, as he had shown when serving as military commander in Britain; or a ruthless tactician, as he had demonstrated in Africa. He was stubborn, big of body, heavy of face and generous of mind. His troops idolized him and would in the end make him the first decent emperor Rome had known in half a century; he was a man who had learned to respect both allies and adversaries and to treat each with honor. He was, perhaps, that spring of 67 as he waited in Ptolemais, the outstanding Roman of his generation, the poor son of a poor farmer, a man who had risen to extraordinary heights solely because of his unimpeachable character. Compared to men like Tiberius, Caligula, Claudius and Nero, this leather-hard general was indeed a god, but such claims were a foolishness he would not indulge in.

Nor did he engage in intrigue, but he did realize that even though he was then nearly sixty and Nero only thirty, the emperor had already given so many signs of derangement that he might one day have to be strangled, and if Vespasian could crush the Jews quickly he could well be in line for the purple when Nero vanished. He therefore directed his centurions to sweep directly toward Jerusalem, basing his future upon the chances of a swift triumph. Yet as he studied his maps he saw the same ominous fact that had faced many other would-be conquerors of the Jewish kingdom: to get at Jerusalem he would first have to pass through Galilee, that ancient home of warriors and determined men; and to enter the Galilee he would have to subdue the little walled town of Makor.

Assembling his staff he asked, 'What is the final word on Galilee?' and they replied crisply, 'As difficult as ever. Hilly. Filled with caves occupied by zealots. Little walled towns on hilltops. And all commanded by the best general the Jews have ever produced.'

'Who?'

'Josephus. A young man educated in Rome. About thirty. Brilliant in the open. More brilliant when cornered. So far the Romans have never beaten him. In victory he's arrogant, in defeat brazen. In some miraculous manner he rescues both himself and his troops to fight the next day.'

'Where is he now?'

'Lucky for us he's in Tiberius, wasting his time.'

'You're sure he's not in Makor?' Vespasian asked.

'No. He seems to have overlooked its significance.'

'You're certain he's not in Makor?' Vespasian repeated.

'Our spies from Tiberias saw him on the lake last night. Our spies from Makor say he's never been in that town and isn't now.'

'Then we shall speed with all force to take this point.' And the broad stubby forefinger of the Roman leader obliterated the dot on his map that signified Makor; so on April 4 in that critical year of 67, General Vespasian, assisted by Generals Titus and Trajan, left Ptolemais with nearly sixty thousand men and one hundred and sixty major engines of war. Nero's vengeance against the Jews was about to be exacted.

THE TELL

On one aspect of life in Israel foreigners rarely received a straight answer, not because Israelis practiced duplicity, but because no one living in Israel saw the problem the way outsiders did. By curious accident John Cullinane finally received honest instruction on the matter, but when he did he found that he could discuss it with no one, because the others had not shared his experience.

From his earlier work in Israel, Cullinane knew the outlines of Hebrew history and understood that there were two types of Jews—Ashkenazi from Germany and Sephardi from Spain—but he had supposed that any basic differences between them had long since dissolved. Nevertheless, he kept seeing cryptic references in the press.

'What's this Ashkenazi-Sephardi business?' he asked Eliav.

'Nothing of consequence.'

'Are Jews still divided into the two groups?'

'Yes.' Obviously Eliav wanted to stop the conversation.

'Which are you?'

'Ashkenazi, of course.'

Cullinane got the impression that his pipe-smoking colleague was proud of his Ashkenazi background. Later, when he had asked her about the matter, Vered was even more abrupt than her fiancé had been. 'A trivial difference,' she snapped.

'Which are you?' he asked.

'Ashkenazi, of course.' And she, too, seemed proud of the designation. Then he began seeing short statements in the press to the effect that 'the Sephardi Jews can better their relative position in Israel only by education.' He asked Vered what this meant and again she brushed him off: 'John, it's a minor educational problem that we'll take care of in time.' But a few days later one of the leaders of the Sephardi community–whatever that was–stated: 'In education we Sephardim are outrageously discriminated against, as indeed we are in all aspects of public life in Israel.' Again Cullinane asked what it meant, and again Vered assured him 'It's nothing you would understand, John.'

Unable to get satisfaction from his colleagues, Cullinane went to the library, where the standard histories confirmed his rough understanding: the Ashkenazim were mentioned in the Torah as a minor Jewish people, whose name was ultimately used to designate Germany, and since it was from there that Jews emigrated to countries like Poland, Russia and America, most Jews in the western world tended to be Ashkenazim; whereas the Sephardim were those Jews who had moved first to Spain and thence to countries like Morocco, the Balkans and the less civilized parts of the world. Between the two communities a feud had developed: the Sephardim constituted the aristocracy of Judaism while the Ashkenazim were the uneducated field hands. It was the Sephardim who produced many of the great Jews of history–Maimonides and Spinoza for example–and certainly in America they formed the elite, characterized by men like Justice Cardozo. But when education became available in eastern Europe, the Ashkenazim quickly gained the ascendancy, while the once-honored name Sephardi was denigrated and applied to all Jews who were not Ashkenazi, whether they had any association with Spain or not, so that today Sephardi meant loosely the oriental Jew as opposed to the European, the lumpen proletariat as contrasted to the sophisticated expert from Russia or Germany. The two groups differed in inconsequential ways: Ashkenazim spoke Yiddish based on German; many Sephardim used Ladino, a vulgar Spanish. They also pronounced Hebrew differently, the Sephardi usage representing the world standard; and they followed different synagogue rituals, where the Ashkenazi was often preferred.

Prior to Nazism and the establishment of Israel the differences between Ashkenazi and Sephardi had been diminishing and indeed almost vanishing; of the 16,500,000 Jews in the world, a full 15,000,000 were Ashkenazi, and they controlled all significant movements and committees. 'I doubt if I ever knew a Sephardi Jew,' Cullinane reflected. 'There probably weren't many in Chicago.'

But with the extermination of 6,000,000 Ashkenazim in World War II and the bottling up of another 3,000,000 in Russia, the Sephardim became proportionately more important; and when the state of Israel was launched, its geographical position in Asia meant that it contained more Sephardi oriental Jews than Ashkenazi Europeans. Suddenly what had been a diminishing factor became one of central significance.

'Jews won't discuss it with you,' Tabari warned as he drove Cullinane to Akko for the purpose of picking up supplies. 'They hope it's a problem that will go away if nobody ventilates it too much.'

'Why do you say problem?' Cullinane asked, as the beautiful spires of Akko rose from the sea.

'Well, as an Arab I'm naturally closer to the Sephardim and perhaps I see things from their point of view. But I don't believe I'm being prejudiced when I say that the Sephardim constitute more than half the population of Israel but hold less than five per cent of the good jobs.'

'Education?' Cullinane asked.

'And their easy way of life.' The Arab reflected, then said, 'Let's put it this way. If I were going on a camping trip with a bunch of Jews I'd want them to be Sephardim. Because then I'd be assured of a rollicking time. But if I had a factory where profits were obligatory, I'd insist upon hiring an Ashkenazi manager and as few Sephardi workmen as possible.'

This seemed an improbable situation to exist in Israel, a nation called into being as an answer to discrimination, but Cullinane said nothing. Later he asked, 'Do we hire any Sephardim at the dig?'

'Not on the staff, of course. They don't have the education. And there are none in the kibbutz gang, because they avoid kibbutz life. Among our volunteer students, two of the best. And naturally our Moroccans are all Sephardi.' He drove for a few minutes, then added, 'Good Ashkenazim like Vered and Eliav are worried lest continued immigration change Israel into a Sephardi state.' Cullinane asked if that would be bad, but Tabari countered, 'Look, old man, it's not proper for me as an Arab to be discussing a purely Jewish problem. Ask Eliav. Or Vered.'

'I did. And they said, "It's of no consequence."'

'Being Ashkenazi, they would.' He stated this with no rancor but with a finality that announced, 'I've no more to say.' But before he had driven another hundred yards he added, 'The best clue is this. A heart specialist from America examined one thousand Jews in Israel. Of the Ashkenazim, sixty-four per cent showed signs of potential heart trouble. Of the Sephardim, less than two per cent.'

In Akko, Cullinane was impressed anew at the easy manner in which Tabari moved from one small shop to another, joking with everyone and picking up minor items needed at camp, but after a while Cullinane wandered off on his own to investigate a small mud-walled house from which loud noise was issuing. From the street he listened for a while to singing and shouting, then started to drift on, but he was hailed by a stout woman who cried from the door in Spanish, 'Come on in, American.' He did not speak the language well, but at the dig in Arizona he had picked up a few colloquialisms.

'*¿Qué vaya?*' he asked.

'Elijah's celebration,' she said, offering him a bottle of beer. Jabbing her elbows back and forth she bulldozed a passageway through the crowd and led him into a small synagogue, about the size of a hotel bedroom and jammed with perhaps half a hundred oriental Jews, bearded, happy, shouting. The hallway was overflowing with women and children, babies and barking dogs. Services had not yet started and there was a wild passing back and forth of beer bottles, Israeli sandwiches in which layers of goodies were crammed into a pocket of flat bread, a hideous orange soda pop and plates of paste made from ground chickpeas. The conviviality was extraordinary and the noise increased when a fat beadle started bellowing, 'You!' When people began poking Cullinane in the ribs he realized that the beadle was shouting at him.

'Put your hat on in the *beth knesset!*' the fat man yelled.

Cullinane had no hat, but the large woman found him a yarmulke and popped it on the back of his head. 'Now you're as good a Jew as we are,' she said in good English.

'What's this about Elijah?' he asked.

'We're marching to his cave,' she explained.

'Where's that?'

'In Haifa.'

'Marching? In this heat?' It must have been more than fifteen miles from Akko to Haifa.

'We march twenty feet,' she laughed. 'Rest of the way by bus.' She told him to join the men in the synagogue proper and he said he doubted if any more could squeeze in, but she rejoined, 'You've got muscles,' and she gave him a stout shove in the middle of his back.

There was one thing in the synagogue he would never forget. By the door of the crowded room sat an idiot, a marvelous, gentle-faced young man of perhaps twenty-four, with the fat and happy cheeks of one who has surrendered all responsibility. His face radiated holiness, and those who entered the room bowed down to kiss him on the forehead, and he looked back at them with the compassionate eyes of YHWH. It was a terrifying experience–this group of old, bearded Jews bowing down to kiss God's vicar–and Cullinane thought: At last I know one difference between the Sephardi and the Ashkenazi. No German Jew would humble himself to do that.

The singing was delightful, an echo from the Old Testament when the Hebrews had lived in tents along the edges of the desert. It was oriental, a long-drawn wailing with kinds of sequences that Cullinane had not heard before, passionate music sung with passion. There was, so far as he could detect, no Jewishness about it but only the timeless wailing of the desert. Suddenly his ears were shattered by a different sound coming from the hallway jammed with women. It was a war cry–he could call it nothing less–in which several women uttered shrieks while vibrating their tongues rapidly against the roofs of their mouths. The effect was shattering, and he left the synagogue proper to ask the large woman what the new shouting was about, only to find that she was leading the noisemakers.

'What is it?' he asked.

She stopped the war cry and laughed. 'Call me Shulamit,' she said. 'It's the cry Arab women use when they want to inspire their men at a battle or a massacre.' She put her head back and uttered a piercing rendition, which was joined by other women. Shoving a plateful of the food into his hands, Shulamit said, 'This is a day of joy. Eat!' And as he did so she returned to her war cries.

'If you want to pray,' the beadle shouted in Spanish, 'get inside. You kids!' he added in Hebrew. 'Stop that! Let's have some quiet here.' Six men began roaring for silence and one took to cuffing the older boys on the head, while these in turn abused the younger, who picked on the girls.

'Silence!' the beadle bellowed, wiping his steaming face. Again his call was echoed by his six helpers.

The noise increased. The singing continued and the women punctuated the bedlam with their war cries, trilling their tongues with fascinating speed. The idiot spilled a bottle of orange pop down his front, but a very old man in a long white beard cleaned the young man's clothes with the cuff of his coat. There was more shouting for silence, and a boy struck a girl so hard that she began to cry, whereupon the two mothers involved beat their offspring heartily, after which there was muffled sobbing. An old rabbi started a speech to which no one in the hallway listened, and few in the synagogue.

'Silence!' roared the beadle, but one of the women had appeared with a large tray of cold beer and a bottle of arrack, which passed from mouth to mouth as the rabbi droned on. It seemed to Cullinane that every second sentence contained the word *Sephardim,* which the old man pronounced *Sfaradeem,* and Cullinane, picking out what Hebrew he could understand, said to himself: Eliav and Vered can say that the Sephardim have no real grievance, but they should listen to what this one is saying. It was a lament such as a rabbi might have uttered a thousand years ago, except that then the word *Sephardim* had scarcely been invented. 'Where are our leaders?' the old man wailed. 'Why do we let them abuse us as they do?' If it had not been for the gulping of beer, the shouting of children, the choking taste of the raw arrack, the cries of the women and continued bellowing of the beadle, the address would have had a kind of pathos. In its present setting it was merely a formula: 'What has happened to our beloved Sfaradeem?' What, indeed.

At the end of the old man's harangue the beadle and his helpers took from the holy place four scrolls of the Torah, encased in handsome wooden boxes ornamented with silver horns, and the procession to Elijah's Cave formed up, with women crying, men shouting, the idiot dancing and the old men in beards walking solemnly through the classic streets of Akko, leading a chant which in time became hypnotic. 'Who are the people who serve God?' a man cried. 'Israel!' shouted the crowd. 'Israel, Israel, Israel!' came the cry, a hundred times, a thousand.

The procession went only a few blocks to where some buses waited, whose loading was such a study in frenzy that Cullinane watched with a kind of horrified fascination. 'Come along!' Shulamit cried, dragging the Irishman after her.

'I can't leave my friend,' Cullinane protested.

'Who is he?' the big woman shouted.

'Jemail Tabari.'

'Everybody knows Jemail. You!' she shouted to a little boy. 'Tell Jemail the American's gone to Elijah's Cave.' She threw the child a coin and Cullinane said that he would repay her. She turned around and looked at him. 'Are you crazy?' she asked, grabbing a fresh bottle of beer.

It was a trip that Cullinane would often recall, a voyage to the heart of Israel. Like most Americans visiting the country he had met principally the well-bred, the sophisticated Jews of the political elite. Vered Bar-El and Eliav were typical, but more important was this powerful sub-strata, this lusty, arrack-guzzling mob, so joyous and vital. The round-faced idiot looked back through the bus and clapped his hands clumsily, whereupon a woman again started the Arab war cry and the noise began that would not cease that day. It was a trip not to Elijah's Cave but to some point far back in history, perhaps to the time of Elijah himself, and if Cullinane had not been fortunate enough to make it he would have failed to appreciate a major aspect of Judaism.

'I cannot understand what happened to us,' Shulamit said in Spanish as she munched a huge sandwich while forcing food upon Cullinane.

'You mean the Jews?' he asked.

'No,' she replied. 'The Sephardim. Since 1500 we've been the principal Jews in Israel. At Zefat, Tiberias, Jerusalem, we were the ones who counted. When the state started, in 1948, we were the numerous ones, but our leaders had always lacked force and by 1949 all the responsible jobs were held by Ashkenazim. Since then it gets worse, year by year.'

'Is there conscious discrimination?'

Shulamit considered this for some time, turned aside to join in a series of war cries which threatened Cullinane's right eardrum, then said in English, 'I would like to think not. But I'm worried about the future of this country.'

'You feel yourself being excluded? You Sephardim generally?'

Shulamit gave a wild cry, then asked abruptly, 'You're not a newspaperman, are you?'

'Archaeologist,' Cullinane assured her.

'Because this is an Israeli problem,' Shulamit insisted. 'We don't need advice from outside.'

'I'm giving none,' Cullinane promised, and she continued to speak of the fact that between Ashkenazi and Sephardi there was little social contact and few marriages, that good places in the medical school went always to the Ashkenazi, that business, law, newspapering, cabinet positions . . . all were reserved for the other group.

'I doubt it's as bad as you say,' Cullinane argued, 'but let's suppose that it's half true. Who's at fault?'

'We're not talking about fault, we're talking about fact. And if it continues, this country is in trouble.'

'How'd you get into a mess like this?'

'Don't blame the Sephardim!' she protested.

'I'm not blaming anybody.'

'Because in America, where I used to work, the Ashkenazi have their own problems. A German Jew would not allow his daughter to marry a Galicianer.'

'Who are they?'

'From Poland. The worst part.' And Cullinane got the impression that Shulamit would never marry a Galicianer, either.

The scene at Elijah's Cave, high on a hill overlooking the Bay of Haifa, was a fitting climax to the synagogue and the bus ride. Thousands of people, mostly Sephardim, toiled up a very steep hill to a series of buildings which could accommodate perhaps two hundred. One teetering affair bore the notice:

THIS BUILDING CONDEMNED AS UNSAFE
STAY AWAY

On its roof some three hundred children gathered. But the striking part of the crowd was the old men and women, come to the cave for mystic reasons, shouting and praying in the steaming sunlight. Some were camped on the ground and had been there for two days. Some sheltered themselves under eaves of the condemned building, while thousands of others milled back and forth, listening to anguished speeches in which old men reviewed the life of Elijah and the low state into which Sephardi Jews had fallen. It was a wild, mournful, gay, beer-drinking mob, but its inner significance could be appreciated only when Shulamit led Cullinane into the cave itself, a deep, plastered cavern that looked more like a subterranean room than a cave.

It was jammed with the maximum number of people—perhaps five hundred—perspiring hideously in the dank air, lighting thousands of candles in the prophet's hiding place, and bowing their heads for blessings from the various rabbis and holy men who clustered inside, breathing not air but some strange mixture of ozone, piety and religious frenzy. Cullinane had always thought that only Catholics indulged in priestly blessings, but now Shulamit knelt before one of the purple-clothed rabbis and kissed his hand, which he then placed on her head, giving her Elijah's blessing, while in another corner a group of ten men formed themselves into a congregation, listening to an eleventh who conducted formal prayer services, perspiring, jostling, drowned out by the haunting war cries of some women at the entrance.

'What has happened to our beloved Sephardim?' a man in still another corner shouted, while in the center a group of women from Morocco sang and beat on drums precisely like the ones which had been used at Makor four thousand years before. The music was wild and imperative and four little girls danced beautifully, throwing their arms in the air and captivating the men, including Cullinane, as Jewish girls had done for generations out of mind.

'Where are the great Sephardim?' the man in the corner lamented, and the women at the entrance repeated their mournful cries as pilgrims lighted their candles in the murky cave.

At dinner that night a much-sobered Cullinane sat silent. Tabari explained, 'He got caught up in the celebration at Elijah's Cave.'

'How'd he do that?' Eliav asked, as if the Irishman were not present.

'He wandered into the Sephardi synagogue at Akko,' the Arab laughed.

'Pretty soon we'll halt this wretched business of Ashkenazi and Sephardi,' Eliav said stubbornly. 'It started only because the Jews were driven out of their homeland by Vespasian and forced into separate groups. Now that we're reunited we'll soon be one again.' And Cullinane, looking up, saw to his surprise that the tall Ashkenazi was speaking seriously and believed what he said.

In the spring of 67 c.e., when Vespasian, Titus and Trajan were bearing down upon Makor, the olive worker Yigal was fifty-three years old, still employed at the olive press and still a man of little significance in the community. His three sons were married and his principal joy was in playing with his eleven grandchildren, sitting on the steps of the Venus temple as they ran back and forth across the forum.

In Makor, Yigal's earlier success in protecting Judaea from the statues of Caligula had won him no lasting honor and he was considered by his neighbors to be an honest, simple-minded man skilled neither in business nor in government. He was a respected member of the synagogue, prayed regularly and sought no distinctions in the religious hierarchy of the Jews. In his older years he had become slightly stooped and his frail frame now seemed gaunt where before it had been spare. His hair was thin and gray and his shaven cheeks were hollow. His gray-green eyes often contained the hint of a smile, and he lived happily with his wife Beruriah, showing no envy for the more successful members of his community who were always going off to important meetings in Jerusalem or Caesarea.

By a curious chance it was his companion Naaman, the farmer, who had succeeded Simeon as head of the community, and if one had asked a dozen citizens of Makor who had been the hero of the resistance against the Romans a quarter of a century before, all would have replied, 'Rab Naaman. He marched to Ptolemais and warned General Petronius not to bring graven images into Judaea.' It was understandable that Naaman should be so remembered, for when Yigal returned from that penetrating experience he was able to forget it and to resume his life as an olive worker; Naaman on the other hand had come home transformed by the miracle he had seen God perform. Without hesitating, and without seeking counsel even from his wife, he had abandoned at the age of thirty-eight the life of a farmer and had surrendered himself into the hands of cautious old Simeon, saying to that learned man, 'Make me a scholar, that I may understand the ways of God.' For many years this uneducated farmer had memorized the holy books, had argued their precepts and had transformed himself into a learned sage with a real vocation for religious leadership. He was now, at the age of sixty-five, a venerable old man with a white beard, a muffled voice and clear blue eyes. Throughout the Galilee his wisdom was respected and many from distant villages sought his solutions to the problems that confronted them. He was a learned man and the Jews called him 'Rab.'

He had retained a sort of friendship with Yigal, whom he recognized as one of the stable Jews in Makor, but it would never have occurred even to him to put Yigal into any position of eminence, for whereas Naaman had grown into a new man with new responsibilities, Yigal had remained what he would always be: an honest workman who interfered with no one. In fact, had one been seeking the typical Jew of the Galilee he might have selected Yigal: devout, quiet, dedicated to his family and secure in his relationship to God.

But in the spring of 67 even such phlegmatic Jews were worried. For nearly a year the nation had been in rebellion against Rome, for Judaea had determined to accept no more abuse from its rulers. In response to Roman provocation Jews had revolted in Jerusalem and slain the garrison and had ravaged other areas, and in retaliation the Romans had killed twenty thousand Jews in Caesarea and fifty thousand in Alexandria, the capital of Egypt. Even in a smaller city like Ptolemais two thousand had been slain and darkness hovered over the land. Through the valleys of the Galilee armed bands swept at will, first Jew, than Roman, then zealot, and finally mere brigands, killing and plundering most barbarously.

Because of its effective wall Makor was spared the violence of this period and it was the hope of Rab Naaman that the little town would continue doing so until such time as Emperor Nero's troops appeared bringing order to the district. Makor would then offer its allegiance to Rome, stupid governors would be withdrawn and conditions would be stabilized. In fact, it could be said that Rab Naaman was impatient for the coming of the legions.

But in his plans he did not take into account his friend Yigal, for to Naaman's surprise the olive grower said at a meeting in the synagogue, 'Again we must withstand the might of Rome.' When hecklers asked what nonsense he was speaking, he explained, 'You either protect God or you don't.'

Rab Naaman intervened and said, 'We must not oppose Rome, for it is her duty to put down this Jerusalem revolt. I promise you that when she has done so we'll have peace as before. Jews will live in religious liberty under kings assigned by Rome.'

'There will be no liberty,' Yigal said. 'Bit by bit they will consume us.'

'What does this man know of public matters?' Naaman asked through his venerable beard. 'Has he met with the Romans at Caesarea? Does he know the evil our side has done in Jerusalem?'

'I know only that the fate of our land lies in the balance,' the stubborn little olive grower said. 'I know that if we do not resist now we shall be hauled as slaves from Makor. We must resist Rome.'

Throughout the debate, which encompassed many days in late March, Yigal refrained from alluding to the success he had known in opposing Roman power a quarter of a century before, for he recognized that the two conditions were different: then Rome had sought merely to import statues of a demented emperor and the armies could with honor retreat from such nonsense; but this time the legions had come to punish an armed rebellion, and once Vespasian marched out of Ptolemais it would not be easy to coax him back. Acknowledging the gravity of the situation Yigal engaged in no cheap demagoguery such as crying, 'We turned them back twenty-five years ago and we can do it again.' Instead he spoke as an honest farmer, beseeching his townsmen to face the situation before them.

'If we can resist Vespasian here in Makor, we may force him to reconsider.'

But Naaman countered, 'I've been warned by a merchant from Ptolemais that Vespasian already has three legions there, the Fifth, Tenth and Fifteenth.'

'Three Roman legions are a terrible force,' Yigal conceded, 'but two hundred years ago in this town Jews like us finally had to defend themselves against Antiochus Epiphanes, and under the leadership of Judah the Maccabee they succeeded.'

'Who will lead us this time?' Naaman asked contemptuously.

'A leader is always found,' Yigal said.

'Do you know what three Roman legions mean?' Naaman pressed. 'They could crush Makor like an almond shell. Our only chance is to surrender and to trust in their compassion.'

Stubbornly Yigal argued, 'When evil thunders down upon a town there is only one thing to do. Resist. We have food. We have walls and we have water. I say resist.'

The Jews of Makor, whose lives depended upon the outome of this debate, wanted to know why a mild man like Yigal suddenly wanted to oppose the armed might of Rome, and in a quiet voice, fumbling for words and exact expressions, the farmer explained, 'You know me as a man of peace. My desire has been to see my grandchildren marry so that I might live with four generations in this town. I don't know enough to seek office, and Rab Naaman takes care of the synagogue. I don't want to oppose Rome, but Rome insists upon opposing me.'

'Rab Naaman says that once they punish the zealots in Jerusalem, they'll go back home and leave us in peace. What about that?'

'He may be right,' Yigal admitted. 'But I think they'll stay. And wipe out our faith.'

'What do you want, Yigal?'

'What do I want? To be a Jew. Why do I say, "Fight Rome"? Because if we don't we'll be forced into other faiths. Why am I so stubborn? Because if we can make Rome respect us, we have a chance to remain Jews.'

'Then you think we should fight?'

The perspiring farmer wiped his forehead, for it was no trivial question this man had asked: Should an unimportant town try to resist three Roman legions? Squaring himself he said, 'Yes. We should fight.'

Then Rab Naaman rose, speaking through his beard with the force of a wise old man, and he said deprecatingly to the citizens, 'You and I know Yigal as an honest farmer. Where olive oil is concerned, we respect his judgment. But of Rome he knows nothing. He cannot imagine what a modern legion is like. Macedonia, which swept Europe. Fretensis, which humbled Asia. And he wants us to fight Apollinaris of Egypt as well.' The audience began to laugh as Rab Naaman marched three long fingers of his right hand through the air. Then, with a voice that breathed authority, he said, 'We'll surrender to Vespasian before he reaches the walls. And your children and mine will live in peace with the Romans.' And this was the procedure agreed upon.

Ashamed of his neighbours Yigal followed old Naaman home, and when the two men sat together in a room filled with parchments the olive worker asked, 'Rab Naaman? Why do you forget the valor we once showed?'

'Because a quarter of a century has passed, and I have learned wisdom,' the old man said.

'You've learned cowardice.'

This was an insult which ordinarily the rab would have resented, but tonight the old scholar ignored it. 'You're thinking of Makor, but I'm thinking about the future of the Jews,' he explained, speaking slowly, for he wanted Yigal to grasp his reasoning. 'We live in an age when Rome can eliminate us . . . erase us from Judaea forever. Yigal, do you know what that means?'

'I only know that we are faced with the destruction of our religion. Worship graven images? Strange gods? These abominations I can't accept.'

The old man nodded. 'You're right. We are faced with the loss of our religion, but not if we stay here. But if the Romans move us from this land . . . There'll be no synagogue in the land of our slavery. We're in terrible peril, Yigal, and you want to fight over a little farm.'

'God lives on a little farm,' Yigal said.

Rab Naaman bowed. He supposed that if God were a farmer, a small olive grove would be most precious to Him, but he also knew that this was not the question under discussion. 'Like Gomer, I am afraid that if we Jews are driven from Israel we'll forget Jerusalem,' he said. 'We'll break into groups. In exile we'll be Jews no more, and God will be alone with no people to adore Him. Our only responsibility now is to stay together . . . to keep our foothold in Eretz Israel.' Then he added in a low voice, 'And to protect our foothold in Eretz Israel, the land of Abraham, I will accept any indignity from the Romans.'

'Even Nero as a god?'

Aware of the terrible thing he was about to utter, Rab Naaman lowered his voice and confessed, 'To save the Jews I would accept even Nero . . . as a god . . . but not in my heart.'

'I would accept him never,' Yigal said, and he left the rab.

The gulf between the two men was now too great to be bridged. Throughout Makor, Yigal preached the necessity for resistance, but old Naaman moved persuasively from house to house, explaining the idiocy of the olive farmer's position. 'Macedonia, Fretensis, Apollinaris,' he recited, and the musical names struck terror into the hearts of the Jews.

Rab Naaman would have prevailed and the conflict with Rome would have been avoided had not one of the most extraordinary Jews of all time stormed into Makor–hot and dusty from a long march and accompanied by a cadre of picked assistants willing to undertake any assignment. The newcomer was Josephus, appointed by Jerusalem to govern the Galilee, a man only twenty-nine years old, descended from those Maccabean patriots who had won Jewish freedom from Antiochus Epiphanes, and a priest of the highest order, a scholar trained in Greek, a habitué of the imperial court in Rome, and one of the finest writers the Jewish nation would ever produce. Striding like a young god into the middle of the Roman forum, he cried, 'From this town we will hurl back the Romans.' He looked at the walls approvingly and shouted, 'Men of Makor! You have been chosen!'

Within a few hours he persuaded the citizens that Yigal's plan to fight Rome was sound, and the mob swung from Naaman's counsel of reasoned surrender to one of impulsive belligerency. 'As general in charge of the north, I tell you that if we oppose Vespasian with all our power, the Roman legions can never dislodge us.' The crowd continued to cheer, and before the cautious warnings of Rab Naaman could be voiced, Josephus had divided the citizens into military units, had appointed his captains, had sent Yigal like a lackey to bring all available olive oil from the press, and was identifying new constructions that would strengthen the walls. Houses whose sides projected above the walls were given two severe tests by Josephus: Could their roofs support fighters? Could their sides resist Roman siege engines? If they failed either test he said simply, 'Tear them down.'

To the homeless ones from outside the walls Josephus said, 'Sleep in the Roman temples. We are at war.' When these matters were settled late in the afternoon, he turned to Yigal and explained, 'We've chosen to meet the Romans at Makor because we know you have hidden water. I'd like to see it.' So Yigal led the fiery young leader down the shaft, through the sloping David Tunnel and to the well, where to his surprise Josephus looked not at the sparkling water, clear even by the light of flares, but at the roof.

What's he interested in the roof for? Yigal asked himself.

'Solid?' Josephus asked, tapping the ceiling with a piece of broken water jug. 'Very thick.'

'Good,' the young general said, and he led the way back to town. At the shaft he went up the exposed flight of stairs as swiftly as if he were an athlete, while Yigal trailed behind.

Wherever Josephus moved in the next few days his energy was infectious. On the wall he convinced the workmen that they could build a little faster, a little higher, and he helped them do both. With the women who were passing stones from the dismantled houses he joked, and soon had them laughing. He inspected all water cisterns to see that they were filled and announced that each house must in addition keep jugs of fresh water available in case of fire or the Romans' taking the well. He even went to the synagogue to persuade Rab Naaman and the old scholars that Makor was doing right in resisting the Romans, and although he had no success with Naaman, he was not surprised when he cajoled the other bearded leaders to support him. On the eve of battle there was hope in Makor, generated by this charismatic young general, and the town went to bed on the night of April 4 satisfied that it had a chance of withstanding the legions.

Two citizens of Makor failed to be impressed. The first was Rab Naaman, who sat alone in the synagogue reflecting on the days ahead and praying, 'Almighty God, Your children are about to launch a war which few understand and into which they have stumbled blindly. Destruction is upon us and the scattering of tribes. O God, protect us in the years ahead, and if the Romans are to be the new conquerors after the Egyptians, Assyrians and Babylonians, let us find some way to exist as prisoners within their camps.'

And Yigal, in spite of the support which Josephus had given him, also viewed with suspicion the sweeping success of the adventurer, for he saw in the young general many things he did not like: the man's energy was vulgar; his enthusiasm was of constant force, regardless of the subject; he acted as if he could persuade any man to his conviction, if only he could talk with him long enough; like a clever Greek he could marshal facts to support any position he had taken; and his desire to see the well and to inspect the roof was in some unspecified way suspicious. With apprehensions of disaster, where he had once had hope, Yigal walked through the evening twilight on this last day of peace and entered the small home where Beruriah, their three sons, their wives and the eleven grandchildren were waiting, and there he placed about his shoulders a white woolen shawl in which he conducted family prayers: 'Almighty God, we are about to fight on Your behalf, but I am worried. When I tried to explain this war on Your simple terms nobody understood, but now everybody's ready to follow the young general who gives them no reasons at all. They go to war not from faith but from arrogance, and without appreciating the consequences. Father and director of our destinies, guide us. Let every person in this room gird his courage for the days ahead.' He prayed in silence for some moments, and in the quiet room his wife imagined that she could hear the tramp of Roman feet. She, better even than her husband, realized that Yigal had sought to enlist his townspeople upon a holy mission, and they had refused to comprehend what he was talking about: the defense of their faith, no less. But under the influence of General Josephus they were willing to engage the Romans in an act of plotless warfare, the end of which could only be death. She bowed her head and echoed her husband's prayer: 'In the days ahead let us have courage.' And in the small room the nineteen members of this family prayed that as good Jews they might prove faithful to their God. When darkness came they did not light their lamps, nor did they put away the dishes, but they prayed as a unit, and when the babies fell asleep they were placed on the floor, and all remained in the room.

Midnight came, and the furry owl that lived in the wadi hooted his signals, but the family prayed on. Under Yigal's guidance during the preceding years this group of people had come to know God as their benefactor and friend. They had often speculated on why He permitted men like King Herod and Caligula to rule, and they had never found logical explanations. Now that Nero was imitating the earlier persecutors of the Jews, they were increasingly perplexed, and were forced to conclude that in these matters God was not entirely powerful. He had selected the Jews as His personal representatives on earth and He was well disposed toward them, but when raw evil was set loose against His people, as in the case of Nero and Vespasian, God seemed powerless to prevent the persecutions. Yigal knew, of course, that the prophets Elijah, Jeremiah and Gomer had explained that these recurring visitations of evil were called forth by the backsliding and stiff-neckedness of the Jews, and not by God's impotence to combat evil; in fact, far from being unable to control the tyrants, the prophets had argued that God personally dispatched them to serve His own purposes, but this Yigal refused to believe.

'God is like us,' he told his silent family as the night hours waned and roosters began to crow in the distance. 'He loves good and He wills it to prevail, but the time comes when He requires our help to make it triumph. This day is such a time, and if others fail in their resolve, we must not.'

'Are you afraid that General Josephus won't know what to do?' one of his sons asked.

'I wish that Josephus were more like Naaman—a man of God,' Yigal said, as dawn began to brighten. Then, seeing daylight on the wall outside his home, he was struck anew by the infinite relationship that exists between God and man, and he cried, 'Let us dedicate ourselves this day,' and he caused even the babies to be awakened, and he moved from one person to the next, asking, 'Do you this day dedicate yourself completely to the will of God?' And each member of his family was required to look into the gray-green eyes of this simple man as he posed the eternal question. When he came to the babies he allowed them to grasp at one finger of his hand as he smiled at them and consecrated them to the thundering days ahead. He was at that moment a fifty-three-year-old Jew who, through years of speculation and ritual, had come to believe that God and the Jews were truly bound together in a covenant comprising deity, people and land, and when the press of terror was most acute, that covenant was most meaningful. In his white prayer shawl, marked with blue stripes and knotted fringes, he concluded the prayers: 'Almighty God, we are with You now, and for as long as it is Your will that we shall live, till a hundred and twenty.' As he said these words cries rose in the street that from the walls the lookouts could see the Romans advancing, and the family of Yigal went out into the sunlight to see the latest persecution descending upon them.

Down the road from the west came two troops of light-armed bowmen, soldiers with large muscles in their legs, ready to rush in the direction of any surprise attack that might endanger the following columns. These shock troops were composed of Gauls, Germans, Africans, Syrians, Egyptians, Carthaginians, Greeks and people from the Danube, the most disciplined conscript army the world had so far seen, and when these first units were satisfied that the road was free of ambushes, they did not rest before the town walls but started immediately to clear a large site for the Roman camp.

Next came the detachments of heavily armed Romans, mounted on German and Spanish horses, able to move with dreadful swiftness in support of the scouts, should they uncover stray units of the enemy. These were followed by experts bearing all the necessary instruments for marking out the camp site selected by the scouts, plus a huge detachment of engineers who would build any roads that the army might require. They were closely followed by foot soldiers protecting laborers who carried the luggage of the officers; to reach this essential gear an enemy would have to penetrate eighteen separate files of fighting men, surrounded by eight ranks of cavalry.

Behind this concentration appeared some two hundred horsemen, in the middle of whom rode the generals, Vespasian, his handsome son Titus and his lieutenant Trajan. Close behind came the great units of cavalry whose mules dragged along the multitudinous engines of war, each valuable item being protected by a company on foot. Then came the commanders of divisions, the lesser officers, and some dozen tall men on specially fine horses, bearing aloft the standards of battle and the three golden eagles belonging to the Fifth

Macedonia, Tenth Fretensis and Fifteenth Apollinaris Legions. Trumpeters, drummers, waterboys and cooks followed in a compact nest, protected by many soldiers, and not until this stupendous preamble had passed did the actual fighting men appear, thousands of soldiers, six abreast, marching shoulder to shoulder down an empty road as if they were already in battle.

At the rear came the servants, the mercenaries from Syria and Macedonia, mules, asses, camels, wagons, plus a rear guard of light infantry, an entire detachment of heavy infantry and four swift units of rear-guard cavalry. For more than two hundred years the Romans had been marching like this, and no opposing force had yet been found to stop them permanently. On this sunny day the first obstacle in their path was the frontier town of Makor, guarded by some eleven hundred Jewish troops. But they were not as insignificant as they might have seemed, for the Jews also had Yigal, the devout townsman, and General Josephus, one of the cleverest soldiers of the time.

Stationed on the wall Josephus watched enthralled as the Romans appeared. 'Which one is Vespasian?' he asked Yigal repeatedly, but when at last the elderly, hard-faced Roman veteran rode by on a chestnut stallion, there could be no doubt that he was the great general, conqueror of Germany, England and Africa. 'So there he is,' Josephus whispered in fascination, and as long as the bull-necked Roman was visible the Jewish general stared at him—as if this were to be not a war of troops but a personal encounter between him and Vespasian.

As soon as he was satisfied that the Roman army was in position, Vespasian, in accordance with tradition, spurred his stallion to the main gate, where, under a flag of truce, he demanded, 'Who is your commander?'

To Yigal's astonishment, General Josephus stepped back into shadow and indicated that Yigal was to confront the Roman, and the little olive worker was shoved forward. With dismay he looked down at the Roman might and listened as the rough-voiced general cried, 'Makor, I call upon you to surrender.'

Yigal did not know how to reply to this formal greeting from an enemy, so he remained silent until Josephus prodded him and whispered, 'Tell him you will never surrender.' It seemed inappropriate to Yigal that he should be delivering this message but he stared down at Vespasian and replied, 'We will never surrender.'

Vespasian wheeled his horse, turned his back on Yigal and called to his men, 'Make camp,' and the siege of Makor was on.

It was to be the kind of warfare that Yigal had foreseen during his all-night vigil with God. The Romans prepared each move with meticulous detail: even the troops chosen to make the first assault were selected so that tall men would be available to throw aloft light, agile warriors should a break appear at any point. Each man in the first wave was covered from neck to ankle in leather armor, and was protected from above by shields of iron and cowhide which deflected any rocks dropped from the wall. And when the Romans started forward they came with innumerable ranks, but on this day they had to scale the ancient glacis of Makor, now a very steep slope topped by the rugged wall, and at the end of the first day's fighting the Romans had accomplished nothing but the loss of nearly a hundred men without having killed any Jews.

That night General Josephus passed among the defenders with words of confidence. 'The Romans learned today that Makor cannot be taken,' he told them. 'If we remain ready at every point we shall soon discourage them. Tomorrow is the critical day. Sleep well.'

His prediction was accurate. Shortly after dawn Vespasian hurled his most powerful units against the gate and lesser forces against the walls, but Josephus had his troops so cleverly balanced and armed with such cruel rocks, stones, sacks of broken crockery and iron-tipped spears that he repulsed the Romans on fourteen separate sorties. A truce was arranged so that Vespasian could drag away his wounded, several score being dead, and at dusk the gray-haired Roman sought a conference. Again Josephus moved Yigal to the fore, and from the wall he consulted with Titus and Trajan, listening as they reported that Vespasian was impressed by the fighting spirit of the Jews and wished to offer them an honorable surrender. 'All lives will be spared and your best troops will be invited to join our legions,' young Titus announced, but Josephus whispered, 'Reject the offer,' and Yigal did so. When the deputation was gone Josephus advised his troops as to what he thought the Romans would try on the morrow.

Again he had anticipated their tactics, and again the Romans were repulsed with heavy losses. It was apparent that frontal assault was not going to subdue Makor, so on the third day there was no general attack, but the lumbering engines of war were drawn into position and a siege of serious proportions was launched. It was here that Josephus proved his skill, for he could judge how fast the Romans could move their engines to any given spot and what type of defense would best repel them. With each new Roman assault he varied his tactics, and when Vespasian finally succeeded in moving a tower against the southern portion of the wall, Josephus ordered his men to feign disorder until a maximum number of Romans were on the tower; then he let loose upon it a rain of rocks and spears and burning timbers which set the great structure ablaze, until it toppled back into the road, killing many.

That evening Vespasian himself came to the walls, under a flag of truce, once more offering Makor honorable surrender, but again Josephus avoided confronting the Roman, sending Yigal instead, and for the second time these two elderly men faced each other–Vespasian with a baton amidst a dozen commanders, Yigal in a well-worn cotton robe atop the wall near the gate.

'With whom do I speak?' the rocklike Roman called.

'I am Yigal.'

'With what authority do you represent this town?'

Yigal did not know what to reply. He had no authority except that of an honest Jew whom his neighbors respected. He was neither general nor scholar, merchant nor dyer. He remained mute, and Vespasian cried, 'Yigal, who are you?'

'I work at the olive press,' the small Jew replied.

From the Romans there was much laughter. Even Titus, the son of Vespasian, smiled at the picture of an olive worker negotiating with a general commanding three legions, but Vespasian himself did not laugh. All his life he had suffered ridicule because of the fact that he sprang not from any patrician family but from an ordinary farmer in the Sabine lands; and he knew from personal experience the single-minded moral force that such a man can generate. Respectfully he called, 'Yigal, worker at the olive press, Emperor Nero of Rome demands that you throw open your town.'

'That we cannot do,' Yigal replied. 'We will not accept Nero as a god.'

'Yigal!' the stocky old warrior shouted. 'Open your gates now and let us share this night in peace.'

'That we cannot do,' the stubborn Jew repeated.

'You have seen our might. You know that in time we must crush you. This is the last chance—will you surrender honorably?'

'No. We will not worship your golden eagles.'

'I will see you in death, Yigal,' the great general called from the lowering darkness, and unseen by the Romans, Josephus tugged at Yigal's robe and whispered, 'You answered him well.'

In the darkness Vespasian, perplexed by the soldierly resistance of the Jews, assembled the Roman generals in his tent under the olive trees and asked, 'Where do those Jews find their arrogance?'

'They've always been stubborn,' Trajan said. 'They want few things, but those few things they insist upon.'

'Have you fought them before?' Vespasian asked.

'No, but I've known them in Alexandria. On little points they gave no trouble, but on big ones . . .' The leader of the Fifteenth Apollinaris made a wry face.

'What big things?' Vespasian asked. Like this matter of gods?'

'On religion they're most stubborn,' Trajan reported.

'What is their religion?'

Titus explained, 'Before we left Rome I inquired. The Jews worship an ass, carved of gold, which they keep in their temple in Jerusalem. Once each year every loyal Jew kisses the hind end of this ass.' The generals laughed, and Titus continued, 'Their major god is Baal, whom our ancestors met at Carthage. They mutilate each other through their rite of circumcision, but this doesn't seem to damage their fertility, for they number about three and a half million.'

Vespasian frowned, but Trajan reassured him: 'The number sounds larger than it is. They're a contentious lot and will submit to no regular military rule. At best they're brave. At worst they're a rabble easily disrupted.'

'I see in Yigal of the olive grove few signs of panic,' Vespasian said. He left his tent and wandered among the olive trees which his adversary had tended for so many years, and his farmer's eye noted that they were well tended. Returning to his tent he stuck his head through the flap and asked the younger men, 'Do you suppose this is his grove?'

'Whose?' Trajan asked.

'Yigal's. He's the one we're fighting.' But before Titus could remind his father that Yigal said he worked in the olive grove, not that he owned it, Vespasian closed the flap and returned to his solitary wandering in the dark olive grove, and he came upon an old tree which had been cleverly pruned to increase the yield. He recognized the work of a master farmer. Striking the bark with his fist he muttered, 'Yigal has spoken the truth. He is an olive grower. He cannot possibly know the tricks the Jews used this day.'

He stood by the tree, kicking angrily at the roots, then fell suddenly quiet. He gasped, clenched his fists and shouted into the night, 'By the ghost of my father, the other one got here!'

Rushing back to the tent he tore open the flap and jerked Titus from his cot. 'In Ptolemais you were wrong.'

'About what?'

'Josephus is in that town,' Vespasian said as he moved about the tent, raising a dust in spite of the rugs that covered the ground. 'Somehow he slipped in before we got here. Because no olive grower could know enough to repel our towers as those Jews did today.'

'What are you going to do?' Trajan asked.

'I am going to haul General Josephus of the Jews back to Rome for an imperial triumph. And when the drums cease, I shall have him strangled.'

Vespasian went to bed, but an hour before dawn his servants wakened him, and he in turn went to his son Titus and his lieutenant Trajan, wakening them, for he was a peasant and was willing to humble himself before others. 'We shall not leave this camp until we have crushed Makor. Today I want every available man thrown against it.'

Inside the walls General Josephus warned his Jews, 'This is the second test. He will try to terrify us, but if we get through this day we are saved.'

It was twelve hours of horror, with a rain of spears and arrows and tremendous rocks being thrown at the town while the engines moved forward–huge towers from which spears could be thrown down upon the defenders, powerful ballistas which hurled rocks like small houses–and pressure was maintained throughout the day at all points. Frequently it seemed as if the numbing power of the Romans must prevail, but in these critical hours Josephus was superb. He ran from one exposed danger spot to the next, exhorting his men as if they were a hundred thousand, dodging Roman arrows and inviting death. Of this man's personal bravery none could doubt, for he fought as if he alone were responsible for throwing the Romans out of Galilee, and without his valiant efforts that day Makor would have fallen.

It held. By some miracle the handful of Jews inside the walls built in David's time and repaired by Jeremoth in the age of Gomer repulsed all that Vespasian could mount against them. Rocks crashed into the Augusteana and carried away the roof, but the main gate, which was the important thing, held fast. From the towers rained down much armament which crumbled the glorious pillars of the ancient Greek temple, but the postern gate was not broken, and when night fell it was obvious that the maximum effort of the Romans had collapsed in exhaustion without accomplishing much.

That night Yigal, as always, assembled his family of nineteen in his little home and gave thanks for what God had done for His Jews in that critical period when the death of the town hung in the balance. Placing his woolen shawl over his shoulders he rocked back and forth in the Jewish manner as he prayed prior to eating. Then he talked with his sons about the day's warfare and played with his grandchildren, who were beginning to experience the hunger attendant upon any siege. They were also thirsty, because even though Makor had ample supplies of water from the hidden source, and although huge supplies had been stored in cisterns, General Josephus had prudently ordered rationing against the unlucky day when the well might somehow fall into the hands of the Romans. Other families cheated on this matter and drank what they wanted, but Yigal, as leader of the defense, understood what Josephus was trying to accomplish, and in Yigal's house the rationing was observed.

Beruriah came in with the night meal–a frugal offering of beans and bread and olives–and Yigal ceremoniously served the little children, then watched them severely in the dim light lest they begin to eat before their elders. This was a game he had always played with his children, and hungry though they were they enjoyed participating in it, watching his sharp eyes as they passed from child to child, half smiling, half stern, while his skilled hands continued serving the meager portions. But this evening he was not to finish, for a messenger came running with a summons to the wall. Fearing some catastrophe Yigal put down the crushed olives and left his home, his prayer shawl still about his shoulders.

At the foot of the wall, illuminated by flares held by his Roman generals, stood Vespasian, a great solid man with a warrior's stern insistence upon ending this siege. 'Yigal, worker at the olive press, I have swallowed my pride and I ask you again: Will you throw open your gates?'

'Never,' Yigal replied.

'For the last time, will you accept an honorable peace?'

'This is a town of God,' Yigal replied from the darkness of the wall, 'and there can be no honorable peace with the gods you bring from Rome.'

'Do you intend, then, to sacrifice the people of this town?'

'We are with God, and He will save us,' Yigal answered, and for the last time the determined Roman veteran and the obdurate Jew faced each other at the wall of King David. They were of about the same age, each a dedicated man, each honorable and a man to trust—when the time came for Vespasian to die he would say quietly, 'A Roman emperor should die standing on his feet, ready to face all enemies,' and in this defiant posture he would meet death, of ten successive emperors from Tiberius to Domitian the only one to escape assassination or forced suicide. But between him and Yigal there could be no conciliation.

'When I next face you, Yigal of the olive press, the meeting will be terrible,' and Vespasian was gone.

On the nineteenth day of the siege a fearful thing happened and on the nineteenth night began a sequence of events which, involving as they did Josephus and Rab Naaman, would be remembered in history. Both occurrences were protested by Yigal, but he was helpless to prevent either. On the morning of this critical day General Josephus ordered his professional soldiers to drag out the tuns of olive oil that Yigal had provided, and a large fire was started in the forum between the roofless Augusteana and the wrecked Greek temple. When Yigal saw the fire and realized what was intended he asked Josephus if this was necessary, and the young general nodded.

'But this has been an honorable war,' Yigal protested.

Josephus turned from the fire to reply, 'You wanted the war. Don't come crying when I take steps to win it.'

'Will this cruel step accomplish anything?'

'It may very well drive Vespasian from the walls.'

'It may also . . .'

Josephus became angry and left the fires where the oil was being heated. 'Yigal,' he said with some bitterness, 'you know that if the Romans ever take this town you are immediately dead. You've known this for some time, so why are you now cowardly?'

'For myself I ceased to fear twenty-seven years ago,' Yigal replied, 'when I faced General Petronius with no weapons, and since that day I have never feared to die. You and I are dead, Josephus, but if we fight honorably the Romans may spare our women and children. If you proceed with your present plans they will have just cause to slay not only you and me, but the children as well.'

At Yigal's suggestion that he, Josephus, might also die as the result of what was about to happen, the young general blanched. He caught his breath, as if it were indecent for Yigal to suggest such a possibility. Impatiently he dismissed Yigal and told his men, 'Stoke up the fires. And get those ladders ready.'

Yigal, banished from the scene, hurried to the home of old Naaman to enlist his aid in protest against what Josephus intended, but he found the bearded old scholar lost in contemplation of his holy books and nothing could summon him back to this world. 'Rab Naaman,' Yigal begged, 'a terrible thing is about to be done, and only your authority can stop it.'

'The question, Yigal,' said the spiritual leader, 'is no longer Makor, but that of the entire Jewish nation. How can we survive? Hotheads like you and Josephus insisted upon war, and now we shall be swept away. The synagogue will be destroyed and our children will be led off in cages to be slaves among the heathens. I am not concerned with what General Josephus does or does not do at this moment. I am concerned only with the Jewish people, for what we do in these next months and years may be final.'

In vain Yigal tried to summon the old man to a serious discussion of the burning oil, but the scholar would speak only of the years ahead. 'We survived Babylon because of great Jews like Ezekiel and Rimmon of this town. And also because the Persians rescued us. Who will rescue us this time, for there are no longer any Persians? When we leave Makor this time we leave forever, and the lives of our children and their children's children for all generations will be spent in alien lands.' The old man, terrified by this vision, caught at Yigal's arm and cried, 'How shall we survive?' The olive worker had no chance to reply, for at the wall there was a shouting, and the Jews of Makor cheered as if the victory was theirs, so that Yigal had to leave the old scholar; he knew that his people by their actions at that moment were assuring not victory, but a terrible defeat.

To six different positions on the wall, wherever the Romans had moved up a tower, the men of Josephus had carried tubs of bubbling oil and small buckets for ladling it out. Protected by bowmen they waited on the walls until a Roman soldier in full armor came within reach, and then with surprising skill they drenched him with the boiling oil and shouted with glee as the ghastly stuff crept in beneath his armor, scalding and burning as it went. The Roman, trapped in his gear, could do nothing to escape the punishment, so that no matter where on the tower he stood he had to clutch with both hands at his burning prison, trying vainly to tear away the hides and metal that covered him. Meanwhile the oil kept burning into his skin, and he would lose his balance and fall shrieking onto the glacis, where he would roll down the sloping side and die in an agony of scalding blisters and consuming burns.

The most hideous part of this death was that it occurred in the midst of the man's companions at the foot of the wall. They had to watch as the screaming body rolled amongst them, like a flattened ball used in some brutal game, and at their very feet the writhing man would beg for rescue while his companions were powerless to help. Once or twice kindly friends tried throwing water on the tortured man, but this helped only to spread the oil and deepen the suffering. One soldier from Gaul, watching helpless while his tent companion twisted in mortal pain on the ground, drove a spear through his friend's neck, killing him mercifully.

It was at this point that Vespasian came to a portion of the wall where six Roman soldiers lay dying in their harness, screaming for death to release them from the unbearable anguish, and he knelt at the head of one who had served Rome well and passed his fingers over the man's scalded forehead. Oil, he said to himself as he studied his fingers, rubbing them together as his soldier died. Olive oil. Turning to Trajan he said, 'When we occupy this town I want the maximum number of prisoners taken alive.'

That night Josephus started his digging. He convened a meeting attended by Yigal, Naaman and his professional lieutenants. Baldly, and in few words, he announced, 'It's absolutely essential that the Romans do not capture me. I am needed in Jotapata and in Jerusalem. I do not want to leave Makor at this crucial point, but the welfare of the Jews demands that I go ... to more important duties elsewhere.'

Yigal did not protest, for he had always known that Josephus was an important man, but when the general of the Galilean forces explained how he proposed to escape, Yigal was appalled. 'I've had my engineer study the situation,' the young general said, 'and he thinks that it would be quite safe for us to dig a small upward tunnel leading from the well to some point outside the walls, in the wadi where the Romans do not guard.'

'You would endanger this whole town in order to rescue yourself?' Yigal asked incredulously.

'There would be no danger. We'd penetrate the last bit of earth at night,' Josephus explained, 'then cover the scar with care, and no one would ever know.'

'But if a Roman sentry should happen ...'

'We've studied the area for some nights,' Josephus began, but Yigal did not listen, for he realized that the brilliant young man had decided upon the use of scalding olive oil at the same time that he was planning his own escape. To save himself Josephus was willing to imperil the entire frontier of the Jewish nation, and Yigal could not understand such behaviour. He listened to no more of the intricate plan—how the dirt would not be brought into the town lest it cause panic among the citizens, who might falsely deduce that they were being betrayed—but the final detail of the scheme shocked him back into reality.

'I've decided to take with me,' Josephus was explaining, 'only two people. My trusted soldier Marcus, and Naaman.'

There was discussion of this, and as Josephus had anticipated, the rescue of the old scholar made the plan palatable to those whose co-operation was required. 'Jews always need the leadership of wise men,' Josephus argued, and as he spoke, Yigal gained the impression that the brash young man, so conceited in other matters, truly loved the Jewish religion and the constructive work of leaders like Rab Naaman. Josephus was honestly proposing to rescue the old man because he knew that Naaman was needed if Judaism was to survive.

Finally Naaman himself spoke. 'Yigal, brother of my youth, I will see that the scarred earth is hidden so that my town will be safe.' The old man scuffed his feet about, as if he had well visualized the problem, and Yigal wondered: Did he too know of this plan when I tried to protest against the oil?

Yigal was not to find an answer to that subtle question, for that night the diggers began their small tunnel leading upward from the well. Within a few feet they came upon that powerful criss-cross of monoliths that the Hoopoe had sunk in the earth more than a thousand years before, and these they by-passed with a lateral cut; and finally, when Vespasian and Titus and Trajan were bearing down with all their power upon the doomed town, the moonless night came when a puncture could be made.

Josephus had given orders that no unusual number of men must be on the walls that night, but Yigal felt that he must satisfy himself as to the escape of the three, so at dusk, he put on his prayer shawl and conducted his usual evening prayers at home, playing with his hungry grandchildren till their bedtime. He smiled at his children and watched his wife approvingly as she cleared the table on which food was becoming increasingly scarce. Toward midnight he walked casually to a small house near the well shaft, where a few men were assembled, and there he was finally joined by General Josephus and Rab Naaman, now a bent old man whose bleary eyes could see far into the future. Led by the soldier Marcus the two charismatic Jews moved to the well shaft, where Naaman gave Yigal his blessing: 'Somehow God will save this town and His beloved Jews.' Soldiers helped the old man down into the tunnel.

Then Josephus, at the threshold of that scintillating career which would bedazzle Rome—he would betray the Jews of Galilee and would hide with forty survivors from Jotapata in a cave and enter with them into a suicide compact, manipulating the straws so that he could die last, and when all but one lay about him with their throats cut, he would flee; he would surrender to Vespasian, and at the moment when the Romans were to kill him he would astound that general by shouting like an ancient prophet that he foresaw Vespasian as emperor of Rome, and Titus, too; as a result he would be informally adopted by Vespasian and would take his name, under which he would help the Romans crush the Jews in Jerusalem and destroy the nation; in Rome he would live in a house of Vespasian's as an honorary citizen of the empire with a pension; he would be the personal confidant of three emperors in a row—Vespasian, Titus, Domitian—and he would outlive them all; under their patronage he would write extraordinary books that vilified the Jews and extolled the Romans, but at the same time he would write notable apologetics on behalf of Judaism, so that much of what we know of the Jews during a period of four hundred years comes from his gifted pen; and he would die at last, having described himself repeatedly as trustworthy, brilliant, devoted, and heroic beyond the norm—it was this young general who stood at the edge of the well and extended his hand to Yigal, saying, 'I shall rouse the countryside. My diversions will pull Vespasian elsewhere and Makor will never fall.' He kissed Yigal good-bye and said to the men he was betraying, 'Do not weep for me. I am a brave soldier and I will take the risk of the tunnel.' Then he fled down the hole.

From the wall, hidden so that Roman sentries could not see him, Yigal watched the dark places in the wadi, not knowing where the earth would heave upward, and after some time, in the moonless night, he saw three figures loom out of the earth. He could not differentiate them one from the other, except that the slowest-moving one stayed at the hole, kicking at the earth and trying to mask the marks, but one of the others dragged him away, so that they could make good their escape.

'O God!' Yigal whispered to himself. 'They have not closed the hole.' In anguish he waited till dawn, when in the rising light he could see the betrayal. Even from the wall he could see the tell-tale mound of earth and the dark circle of the opening. 'The Romans will find it within the hour,' he groaned, and he knew that when they did they would follow it down to the well, which would then be lost to the town.

Quickly Yigal summoned all available women and sent them down to fetch extra water, so that all cisterns would be filled and home receptacles too, but that day the Romans did not discover the escape route. Each morning Yigal would walk upon the wall, trying not to stare at the gaping wound in the earth, and each day he would thank God that no Roman had so far spotted it. Once more General Josephus had been proved right: had Rab Naaman lingered at the hole to efface the marks he might have betrayed the entire party; for Josephus had guessed that the Romans would not see such an obvious thing as an open hole.

Now came the last days of the Roman siege. When he was satisfied that the Jews were out of olive oil Vespasian brought his towers back to the walls, and his monstrous ballistas began a systematic bombardment of the town, killing many Jews who tried to protect the battlements. Now there was no calling back and forth between Roman and Jew; there was only the harsh, hard work of assaulters who were determined to knock down tall piles of stone and the resourceful tricks of defenders who were obliged to repulse them. But each day the inevitable end came closer.

With Josephus and Rab Naaman gone, the defense of the town fell wholly on Yigal's shoulders, and although several faint-hearted Jews came to him advising capitulation, he said, 'The life of man is determined when he first places his trust in God. We have been dead ever since we offered our lives to halt Petronius from bringing in his statues of Caligula. What happens in the next weeks can be of no consequence, for if we are dead we have died faithful to our covenant with God.' He would suffer no talk of surrender, and one man who persisted was tied up at Yigal's command. With a grave dignity that few men attain this average little man, who didn't own as much as one square of land, kept alive the spirit of his town, serving as general and priest and counselor alike.

Each night he prayed with his large family, looking upon his many grandchildren with a love that not even he had imagined possible. 'We are the chosen of God,' he said, and if he had been asked why he persisted in the defense of Makor, he would have replied, 'Because no man can understand the kind of work God will allot him in this life, but whatever it is, he had better perform it faithfully.'

On the next day when it became apparent to all that the town must collapse with the next sunrise, Yigal gathered his family for the last time to discuss with them what a good Jew should be: 'You children may live your lives as slaves in some far country,' he said with little outward emotion, 'and it may be difficult for you to remain Jews. But if you remember only two things it will be easy to be faithful. There is but one God. He has no assistants, no separations, no form, no personality. He is God, one and alone. The second thing never to forget is that God has chosen Israel for special duties and responsibilities. Perform them well.' He hesitated and his voice broke. 'Perform them well.'

Placing the prayer shawl about his shoulders he leaned back and closed his eyes and in a low voice began to recite that gracious litany of the ordinary Jewish household, the last chapter of the Book of Proverbs in which the Jewish husband recalls the good life he has known with his wife:

> 'When one finds a worthy wife,
>   Her value is far beyond that of pearls.
> The heart of her husband is confident about her
>   And he does not lack gain.
> She does good and not evil for him
>   All the days of her life . . .
> She rises while it is still night,
>   Giving food to her household
>   And a portion to her maidens . . .
>
> She makes sure that her merchandise is good;
>   Her light does not go out at night.
> She puts her hands upon the distaff,
>   And her hands take hold of the spindle . . .

Her children rise up and declare her blessed,
Her husband also, and he praises her:
"Many daughters have done virtuously,
But you have excelled them all."
Mere grace is delusive and beauty is empty;
The woman who is reverent toward God is worthy of
praise.'

He stayed with his children for some hours, talking with them about the various countries to which they might be taken, after which he gathered all the elders of the family and formed them in a circle about the young ones. The older Jews held hands as Yigal said quietly, 'Wherever you go in slavery, remember this moment. You are surrounded by the love of God. You are never alone, for you live within the circle of God's affection.'

He put the children to bed, then went through the streets of the little town, reassuring all who were awake and encouraging them to behave with dignity on the morrow. At the beautiful forum, now demolished by the Roman ballistas, he talked with the hungry men, and on the ramparts he could see in the moonlight that escape hole which the Romans had not yet found. In the marble-faced gymnasium, where the wounded lay, he comforted them, and at the synagogue where a few old Jews prayed through the night he paused to participate in a discussion of God's law as laid down in Leviticus and Deuteronomy, and the men argued like Jews, as if tomorrow were an ordinary day.

Then dawn began, and he called his men to their positions. To an onlooker he would have been an amusing little man that bright morning, an ordinary Jew making believe that he was a general, but he sustained his men as if he had been a Caesar fresh from triumphs along the Rhine. When the Romans moved forward, when their great machines creaked and groaned with power as they bore down upon the walls, he went from spot to spot encouraging his men as he had seen Josephus do, but by the midmorning the walls began to crumble. Nothing that the Jews could do prevented the crunching force of Rome from triumphing, and by midday the assaulting legions occupied the forum.

Early that afternoon Vespasian gave a command which he would often regret in his later years when as emperor he knew the responsibility that adheres to casual commands. He ordered the crucifixion of Yigal and his wife Beruriah. Tall poles were brought to a point outside the town, at the edge of the olive grove in which the little Jew had worked. Crosspieces were nailed roughly to the poles, and eight long spikes were produced. Yigal and his wife were laid upon the crosses, and their extremities were nailed down with the great square spikes. Then the crosses were raised in the air, but before the bodies of the two Jews were pierced so that they might bleed to death, a scene of horror was paraded before them.

The nine hundred surviving Jews were herded to a spot beneath the crosses, and as Yigal and Beruriah looked down in their own agony, shrewd judges from among the Romans cried, 'That one's of no use to us,' and swords would hack an old man or woman to death. In this way four hundred were disposed of, after which two engineers coldly studied the younger men to judge whether or not they could survive work on the ship canal that Nero had ordered to be dug at Corinth. With practiced eyes they spotted any deformity: 'This one has a bad arm.' And swift swords would slash away both the arm and the head, but some of the sturdier Jews were reserved for transportation to the isthmus. Then the hard-headed slave traders who accompanied all Roman armies stepped forth to appraise the women; only a few were found worth saving and more than three hundred rejects were slain in a few minutes. Finally the children were led before the slavers, and all under the age of eight were automatically killed, for it had been found that these rarely survived the slave camps. An older boy with a harelip, a girl with a limp . . . these were cut down at once, but any who might bring a fair price were thrown into great iron cages for transportation to the slave market at Rhodes.

'O God, preserve them!' Yigal moaned, and then he saw the special hell that Vespasian had decreed for the man who had poured boiling olive oil upon his Romans. The seventeen members of Yigal's family were led forth, and his three sons were cut down as their mother screamed in agony. Then their wives were slain. And finally the eleven grandchildren were taken one after the other to the foot of Yigal's cross, where they were pierced by Roman swords. Eight, nine, ten, they died. The last child was a little boy who could not understand what was happening. From behind two soldiers struck him and he fell a mutilated thing.

The seventeen corpses were then tossed into a pile, after which General Vespasian, arms akimbo, stood beside them, calling to his adversary, 'Observe, olive worker, the fate of Jews who resist Rome.'

His body numb with pain, Yigal found strength to call back, 'But they will resist.' With wonder and contempt the bull-necked Roman stared for the last time at his twisted victim, then left abruptly to supervise the final destruction of the town.

Only then were soldiers with long lances permitted to pierce Yigal's belly and Beruriah's neck. It was obvious that she would die first, and she turned her eyes to gaze with love upon her frightened, retching husband. Her lips moved but made no sound, and as the two Jews looked at each other across the sunlit space, she expired. Yigal, watching her, whispered:

> 'Many daughters have done virtuously,
> But you have excelled them all.'

He turned his head away from the carnage to look once more upon that small town on the hill where he had been so happy. The walls were coming down and in all quarters there was flame.

LEVEL VII

The Law

Found at Makor–stone from a synagogue reused in a church
(see chapter 1). Originally a stone lintel above the west door of
the entrance to a synagogue, with decorations as shown on top:
two groups of vines, leaves and bunches of grapes, beside two
date palms, all symbolizing the richness of the Galilee; in the
center a small four-wheeled flat wagon bearing the holy Ark of
the Covenant, an acacia box containing the stone tablets of the
Ten Commandments. The ark was carried by the Jews on their
forty-year march from Mount Sinai to the promised land.
Captured in war by the Philistines, it brought them only evil
until they voluntarily returned it. Brought by King David to
Jerusalem, finally placed by King Solomon in the temple, from
which it vanished at the time of the Babylonian destruction.
Carved in white limestone, Makor, 335 C.E., reused in 352 C.E.
as part of the southwestern façade of a Byzantine basilica and
recarved in that year by the original artist with three Christian
crosses. Deposited at Makor March 26, 1291, during the
destruction of the Basilica of St. Mary Magdalene.

Jesus Christ was born, so far as we know, in the summer of 6 B.C.E., that being
sometime before the death of King Herod the Great. Jesus lived his early life in
Nazareth, only sixteen miles south of Makor, and conducted his principal
ministry, which covered a span of one year and nine months, along the shores of
the Sea of Galilee, only eighteen miles to the east. He never came to Makor and
about April 7, 30 C.E., was crucified by order of Pontius Pilate, the Roman who
then served as Procurator of Judaea.

It may be surprising, therefore, to know that it was not until the year 59 C.E.
that the name of Jesus Christ, the good neighbor of Makor, was first mentioned
in that little town; but upon reflection this is not so remarkable. In the
turbulent years of Christ's mission on earth there were many young Jews
wandering up and down the Galilee. Some, like General Josephus, tried merely
to rally their people to resistance against Rome, and their motives were
military. Others sought to convince the Jews that an independent government
was needed, and their intentions were political. Some wandered from one
community to the next, preaching stern systems for the redemption or
reconstruction of Judaism, and their dreams were religious. And some went
from town to town prophesying the coming of one messiah or another. A few of
these latter had reached Makor, on the edge of the Jewish lands, but the rabbi
Jesus was not among them.

Nor was it unusual that the town had not heard about His crucifixion on a hill
outside Jerusalem, for that event was in no way unusual; one Jewish king had
crucified eight hundred of his subjects on one afternoon while getting drunk
with his concubines on a public platform in the middle of Jerusalem, to which
his guests had been invited to enjoy the spectacle. In recent years King Herod
had crucified a multitude of Jews, while lesser Roman officials had also used

this traditional punishment with harsh frequency. Furthermore, the major contacts of a frontier town like Makor were never with Jerusalem or Nazareth, nor even with the settlements along the Sea of Galilee; they had to be with Ptolemais, that alien port so near at hand yet almost always in the grip of strangers who followed exotic religions. Thus, when Makor was Egyptian, Akka had belonged to the Sea People. When Makor was part of David's kingdom, Accho was Phoenician. When Makor was ruled by Herod, Ptolemais was held by Cleopatra. And in the time of Christ, when Makor was governed by the procurators of Judaea, Ptolemais belonged to whatever Roman puppets controlled Syria. Makor had to worry about Ptolemais, not Jerusalem.

Yet it was because of Ptolemais, that ancient, ancient seaport to which triremes from Athens and hippos from Tyre had always sailed, that Makor finally heard of Jesus Christ. In the spring of 59 C.E., when the crucified prophet had been all but forgotten even in areas which had known Him well, a Roman corn ship came down from Puteoli and Piraeus to drop anchor in the fish-hook harbor of Tyre, where the captain gave deck space to a frail, baldheaded man in his sixties seeking passage to Caesarea; and next day, when the vessel had wandered down the coast a short distance to the snug harbor of Ptolemais, the traveler took advantage of the unexpected layover to go ashore and harangue any Jews who might be lounging along the waterfront. And among his chance audience at the port that day had been that same Yigal of Makor who had some years before offered his life in this city to halt the advance of General Petronius and the Roman statues, and it was by this accident that Yigal became the first resident of Makor to hear the message of Jesus Christ.

In heavily accented Hebrew the speaker had said with some pride that he was Paul of Tarsus, 'a city of more than half a million lying to the north,' and he explained to the Jews of Ptolemais that although he was a free Roman citizen he was also a Jew, a Pharisee of strict education, but that a greater Jew than he had taught in Galilee and had shown men how the old preaching must give way to the new, how the law must be fulfilled outside the synagogue, and how the salvation of the human soul could be attained by following in His steps.

Paul spoke with clarity, relying upon reason to persuade his listeners. As he stood in the open air, a small man with bandy legs and a great hooked nose that sprang from the point where his thick eyebrows met, he showed signs of nervous exhaustion, as if time were slipping through his fingers; he had much to relate that day in Ptolemais, and the dull indifference of Jews like Yigal, who stood with his hands folded behind his back, trying to calculate what the visitor was trying to say, seemed to infuriate the baldheaded stranger, and he spoke with terrible persuasiveness. He explained to the Jews that they had a chance now, on this sunny day in Ptolemais, to receive into their hearts the man who had been crucified to save the world.

'Was not this Jesus a rabbi?' a Phoenician Jew asked.

'His disciples called Him such,' Paul replied.

'Our rab is good enough for us,' the indifferent man said, and Paul did not bother to argue with him. Instead, he turned his back upon the Jews, and looking toward the sea as if he were addressing the world, explained in tempestuous Greek phrases the tenets of the new religion: 'Why is there evil in the world? Because we are born in sin. How can we be saved? Because Jesus Christ, through His crucifixion, takes our sin upon his shoulders.' For some moments he addressed his impassioned oratory to Yigal, who felt a tingle down his spine as this Jewish convert to Jesus spoke of the new world of Christ in which the law of Moses was fulfilled. But Yigal mastered his excitement. He could not be attracted permanently to any religion that had abandoned Judaism, heading for new directions which he could not foresee, so he left the meeting in Ptolemais and returned to Makor. For some few days the words of Paul of Tarsus disturbed him, and for a while he thought of discussing them with Rab Naaman, but he did not do so; and as we have seen, eight years later in 67 C.E. he was caught up in struggles against the might of Rome and was himself crucified not far from Nazareth–at about the time that Paul was being beheaded for somewhat similar reasons in Rome.

But if Makor was slow to acknowledge the reality of Jesus Christ, the time came when His presence reached the little town with persuasive grace. In the year 313 the Roman emperor Constantine had seen on the eve of a vital battle near Rome a fiery cross bearing the promise '*In hoc signo vinces,*' and when that prophecy proved true, he had by decree ordained Christianity to be the religion of the whole Roman empire, one of the most fateful single acts ever performed by one man. And in 325 he encouraged his mother, an extraordinary woman, to go on a pilgrimage to the Holy Land to see if she could identify the places where Jesus had lived three centuries earlier.

Queen Helena had known an uneven life: a free-and-easy waitress in a Bulgarian inn, she had married a passing soldier, and when he was later offered the Caesarship it was on condition that he abandon his wife and find another more suitable, and to this he agreed. In her loneliness Queen Helena had discovered the consolations of Christianity and had encouraged her pagan friends to do the same; and when her son assumed the purple she moved from obscurity to prominence, so that her pilgrimage to the Holy Land was an event of significance. While sleeping in Jerusalem she had a vision much like her son's: she saw the precise location not only of the cross on which Christ had died but also of the sepulcher in which the body of Jesus had lain for two days. In subsequent visions she identified most of the other sacred spots, and over each one her son caused a basilica to be erected, which would serve as the focus of pilgrimages for as long as men loved Christ.

In 326 Queen Helena disembarked at Ptolemais to begin the overland trip to the Sea of Galilee, hoping to identify there the scenes where Jesus had preached, and once more her visions supplied the answers. 'This must be the place where our Lord fed the multitude with two fishes and five loaves,' she announced, and a basilica was built. 'I feel sure that on this spot Jesus must have delivered his Sermon on the Mount,' she said, and a second church was ordained. From oblivion she rescued those places that would become cherished throughout Christendom, and on her way back from her discoveries she stopped over at Makor, a town without walls perched on a mound, and there as she slept beside the mean little Byzantine church she had a final vision: she saw that Mary Magdalene, following the Resurrection of her Lord, had found refuge in Makor, and Helena rose next morning in great excitement to announce, 'Here we shall build a fine church so that pilgrims on their way to Tiberias and Capernaum may break their journey.' Guided by her vision, she led the townspeople to the exact spot where Mary Magdalene had lived, and in accordance with the curious fate that governs such matters she chose the holiest place for ten miles in any direction, that sacred point where the cave men had erected their monolith to El, where the Canaanites had worshipped Baal and the early Hebrews had prayed to El-Shaddai. Here the priests of King David had offered sacrifice to Yahweh, while Jews rescued from Babylon had prayed to YHWH. Zeus, Antiochus Epiphanes and Augustus-Jupiter had all been worshipped on this slight rise of earth, and now the great basilica of the new religion would follow in its appointed course. Queen Helena knelt on the holy spot and, when she rose, indicated where she wished the triapsidal structure to rest, unconsciously placing her altar directly above the ancient monolith.

It was some years before the rulers in Constantinople got around to building the basilica of St. Mary Magdalene in Makor. By then the saintly old queen was dead, and she never knew whether her church of pilgrimage had been completed or not. Nor did Constantine, who died in 337, only nine years after his mother. But in the family the tradition was kept alive, and even though the descendants of Constantine warred among themselves, brother slaying brother in Roman fashion, it was always intended that their grandmother's wish for a pilgrims' church at Makor should be honored, so early in the year 351 the Spanish priest Eusebius convinced the rulers that the time was ripe. Consequently two ships set out from Constantinople laden with architects, slaves, stone masons and Eusebius himself. They landed at Ptolemais, and like thousands of pilgrims before them and hundreds of thousands later, started the overland march toward the Sea of Galilee, but unlike the others, when they reached the halting point at Makor they stopped permanently, which placed them within the dominion of Rabbi ha-Garsi.

In these centuries when God, through the agency of preceptors like Augustine of Hippo, Origen of Caesarea, Chrysostom of Antioch and Athanasius of Alexandria, was forging a Christian church so that it might fulfill the longing of a hungry world, He was at the same time perfecting His first religion, Judaism, so that it might stand as the permanent norm against which to judge all others. Whenever in the future some new religion strayed too far from the basic precepts of Judaism, God could be assured that it was in error; so in the Galilee, His ancient cauldron of faith, He spent as much time upon the old Jews as He did upon the new Christians.

To build Judaism into its normative form, God had at His disposal the four great planks which His people had hacked from their desert experience and their battles with the Canaanites: the Jews finally accepted Him as the one God, supplanting all others; they worshipped His Torah; they were uplifted by the lyric outbursts of religious poets like King David and his chief musician Gershom; and periodically they reconstructed their society according to the flaming cries of true prophets like Jeremiah and the woman Gomer. But to preserve His Jews during the trials that loomed ahead, God required two additional planks, one common to many religions and one totally unique, and He was now about to create those necessary supports.

On that sunny morning in the year 326 when Queen Helena knelt on the earth at Makor, preparing it for the spectacular growth of Christianity, the leadership of the Jews rested in a remarkable little man named Rabbi Asher ha-Garsi, known through the region as God's Man. From the age of three he had dedicated himself to the service of YHWH and at nine had memorized the Torah; by fifteen he knew by heart the wisdom literature of his people. At sixteen, obedient to the wishes of his parents, he married a country girl whom they had selected, and although in conformance to Jewish tradition governing holy men he restricted himself to sexual intercourse on Friday nights, he quickly fathered a string of five daughters, for whose support he worked diligently. As his name ha-Garsi indicated, he made his living by the purchase of wheat which he boiled, dried and broke into small pieces, producing the cereal so much appreciated by the city residents of Ptolemais. Groats-making was hard work and involved financial risk, for the cost of raw grain could rise or fall suddenly while the price of finished groats might be moving in the opposite direction. Better than most men, Rabbi Asher the Groats Maker understood the pressures of life, and the disappointments too, for he had always wanted a son to project his name and help him in his business, but none came and his two oldest daughters had married men who would not have been helpful in any occupation other than resting; his succeeding daughters were showing no signs of doing much better.

So the little rabbi sweated in the groats mill, worried about his hungry family, and tried to appease the Byzantine tax collectors; but his principal occupation was serving Makor as its unpaid rabbi, for in these years the Jews of the district were not rich, and it was in his conduct of this office that Rabbi Asher had gained the name God's Man, for when members of his congregation came asking him to adjudicate their problems he first smiled at them with his sad blue eyes, which seemed to say, 'You don't have to explain about trouble to me,' then tucked his hands under his black beard, and finally said, 'Before we discuss this matter, let's agree between ourselves as to what God's will is. If we know what He wants, we will know what we want.' In his own life he accepted without question the law as laid down in Leviticus and Numbers–Deuteronomy he held in some suspicion as being both modern and revolutionary–and he wished that his community were willing to imitate him. 'It would be better if all followed the Torah,' he told his people, 'but men and women are weak, so some of us Jews must set the pattern for the rest.' His gentleness had won many to a closer observance of the law, and it was recognized in Makor that in any argument which disrupted the town, if Rabbi Asher the Groats Maker could be brought into the discussion the interests of God would be represented, for even among the Christians he was known as God's Man.

Now, as Queen Helena prepared to leave Makor, Rabbi Asher at the groats mill wiped his hands and looked with compassion at a huge, dark-skinned man with beetling eyebrows and hulking shoulders who had come to consult him on a difficult matter. At first the little rabbi was irritated by the interruption, but he smothered these feelings and said to the big man, 'We'd better talk at my house, Yohanan.'

He led the way to a mean building where his younger girls were playing noisily. As he appeared they withdrew, leaving him a small room crowded with parchment scrolls rolled in the ancient manner and others whose leaves had been cut and bound in the new style. Shooing the children's rooster from his alcove he took his position behind a small table while the hulking visitor, his prognathous jaw jutting out belligerently, waited.

'Yohanan,' the groats maker said gently, 'we must first try to find what God's will is in this matter.'

'I want to get married,' the big man mumbled.

'My reply must be what it was last week. Tirza is a married woman. No man may ask her to marry until we have proof . . . proof.'

The big stonecutter growled, 'Three years ago her husband ran off with the Greeks. He's dead. What more proof do you want?'

Almost as if he understood the symbolism of his act the little rabbi took his hands from beneath his beard and placed them upon a scroll of law. 'In cases where the husband's death can neither be proved nor disproved, we require fifteen years to pass before the woman can be declared a widow.'

'He used to beat her. Must she wait fifteen years for him . . .'

'Until the fifteen years have passed, Tirza remains a married woman. The law says . . .'

'The law! The law! Fifteen years for a woman who's done no wrong?'

'So far she's done no wrong. But if she lives in sin . . . outside the law . . .'

'We don't care,' the big man shouted, rising to his feet so that he towered over the little rabbi. 'I'm going to marry Tirza today . . .'

'Yohanan, sit down.' Without touching the stonecutter Rabbi Asher forced him back onto the chair, saying quietly, 'Remember Annaniel and Leah. He went to sea and the boat foundered. Six witnesses swore that he must have drowned, so against my counsel Leah was permitted to remarry, and five years later Annaniel wandered back. He was still her husband and because we had broken God's law two families were destroyed.' The little scholar replaced his hands beneath his beard, lowered his voice and added ominously, 'And Leah's lovely children were declared bastards. You know what that meant.'

Silence lay upon the small room as the stubborn workman stared at the man who had brought God into the discussion, and Rabbi Asher, thinking that he had convinced the stonecutter, decided to offer consolation. 'God is not selfish, Yohanan. He forbids you Tirza but He has placed here in Makor many fine Jewish women who would be happy to marry a man like you. Shoshana, Rebecca . . .'

'No,' the tormented giant pleaded.

'With any one of them you could build an honest family . . .'

'No!' the big man repeated, leaving his chair for the last time. 'Today I shall marry Tirza.' And before the little rabbi could argue further, Yohanan had left the place of law, rushing into the larger, freer area of the town, where he ran through the streets until he came to the house where the deserted woman Tirza lived, and he swept her into the air, shouting, 'We are married.' From the door of the house he cried into the street, 'Three men of Israel, come to hear me!' And he collected a crowd before whom he held up a band of gold which he had brought from a Greek merchant, and in a proud voice announced, 'Behold, the widow Tirza is consecrated unto me with this ring, according to the law of Moses and Israel.' And they were married; but Rabbi Asher the Groats Maker, watching from the edge of the crowd, knew that they were not married.

As the rabbi returned home from the improvised street wedding, he grieved over the obstinacy of the big stonecutter and was about to enter his study when he was gripped by an irrational desire to leave the passions of the town and walk in the quieter countryside, so in a mood of perplexity he wandered toward the sloping hill that led from Makor down to the Damascus road, and he arrived there just as the procession of Queen Helena the emperor's mother, departed in grandeur for Ptolemais, and the little Jew stood aside as the horses, the donkeys, the palanquins, the soldiers and the bearded priests marched westward to the seaport, where their ship lay waiting. When they were gone Rabbi Asher started to return home, having forgotten in the excitement of their departure his intention to walk among the trees, but he had taken only a few steps when he was gripped by the shoulders, as it were, and turned back to his initial purpose.

He left the ragged town and wandered among the gnarled olive trees; his attention was arrested by one so ancient that its interior was rotted away, leaving an empty shell through which one could see; but somehow the remaining fragments held contact with the roots, and the old tree was still vital, sending forth branches that bore good fruit; and as he studied this patriarch of the grove Asher thought that it well summarized the state of the Jewish people: an old society much of whose interior had rotted away, but whose fragments still held vital connection with the roots of God, and it was through these roots of law that Jews could ascertain the will of God and produce good fruit. He was distressed that the stonecutter had decided to ignore that law, for Asher was certain that disaster of some kind must follow.

His attention was distracted from these matters by a gaudy bee eater flashing through the olive branches, above whose gray-green tips he could see a stork drifting idly on upward currents as if on his way to speak with God in heaven. As the rabbi stood thus, contemplating the mystery, he became aware of a noise at his feet, and he looked down to see a hoopoe bird rustling about in search of worms, and he watched as the industrious digger came upon a colony of ants. The groats maker bent down to study these minute creatures, saying to himself: Whether man looks to the soaring storks or to the tiny ants, what he sees is God. And as he knelt there close to the olive press, vacant now, for the fruit was not yet ripe, his closeness to God brought forth what could be described only as a vision: in the clearing reserved for the press he saw floating in the air a scroll of Torah, and around it–also suspended in air–a golden fence shimmering in sunlight; outside the fence were hundreds of Jews, young and old, male and female, reaching out their hands to encompass or perhaps damage the Torah, but the incandescent fence prevented them from doing either. And while he watched, a woman who could only have been Queen Helena of Constantinople, whom he had seen a few minutes before, knelt and caused a new church to rise from the earth, and about her head shone a radiance which filled the orchard; she vanished and her church, too, but the Torah remained, still protected by its golden fence. With blinding light those two dreamlike realities hung in the air, imprinting themselves upon Asher ha-Garsi's brain; then slowly even the Torah vanished and he was left alone.

To interpret this vision he did not require wisdom. He sat on the stones of the olive press and stared at the gnarled trees with that insight which comes to a man only once or twice in his lifetime, allowing him to see ahead into the structure of the years. His first impression was of the radiance that had surrounded Queen Helena, and the power of Byzantium whereby she had drawn from the earth of the Holy Land a new church, and he foresaw that the Galilee would never again be the same. A new force, represented by Helena and her son, had enetered the world, and Rabbi Asher knew that it would never be turned back. The position of the Jew in relation to this new religion would remain undetermined for some centuries, perhaps forever, but a dominant power had arrived and to ignore it would be folly. If Queen Helena, kneeling in the public square of Makor, said there was to be a basilica on that spot, Rabbi Asher was willing to believe that one would rise, for in his vision the crown of this queen had been neither copper nor brass; it was pure, radiant gold, and he knew that gold carried with it the power to command.

But his more persistent vision was that of the Torah protected by its golden fence, and he recognized this as an imperative to him personally. In wondering what he must do he recalled certain events that had taken place not far from this spot when, two and a half centuries before, General Vespasian had finally crushed Makor, destroying its walls and killing or enslaving all Jews inside. In those fearful days the greatest Jew that Makor was to produce had escaped through the water tunnel at midnight and had gone on to rally the Jews after the traitor Josephus had aided the Romans in their destruction of Jerusalem. Rab Naaman of Makor, the old man was called, a white-bearded rabbi who had lived to be a hundred and three. In his ancient years, when he weighed less than ninety pounds and could scarcely be heard through his ashen beard, he had discovered a student much like himself, a peasant who till the age of forty could neither read nor write but who had developed into one of the leading scholars of Jewish history—the legalist Akiba—and these two self-made men conspired to save Judaism; for they assembled the law whereby Jews could live now that the external focus of their religion, the temple in Jerusalem, was no more. Once all Jews had lived either in Galilee or the south, but now only a small percentage did so, for the Romans had driven the majority to Spain, to Egypt, to Babylonia, to Arabia and to countries not yet named. How scattered they were, how powerless, yet always bound to Israel by the work that Rab Naaman and Akiba had performed.

In the stillness of the olive grove, where the original patriarch Zadok had once talked with God direct, Rabbi Asher listened to the voices of Naaman and Akiba as they were remembered in the Galilee.

'Rab Naaman of Makor said: Build a fence around the Torah, that it may be protected from thoughtless infraction.'

'Rabbi Akiba said: That simple man who gives delight to his fellow creatures gives delight also to God.'

'Rab Naaman of Makor said: To live within the law of Moses is to live within the arms of God.

'Rabbi Akiba said: They came to me crying that since the Romans have destroyed the land, Israel is poor, but I said that poverty is as becoming to Israel as a red harness on the neck of a white horse.'

'Rab Naaman of Makor said: I complained, "There are two men and only one gives to the poor." God said, "You are wrong. There is only one man, because he who will not give to the poor is an animal."'

'Rabbi Akiba said: Jews are born to hope, and in desolation they must hope even more strongly. For it is written that the temple shall be destroyed and then rebuilt. How could we possibly rebuild it unless the Romans had first destroyed Jerusalem?'

'Rab Naaman of Makor said: Like a twisted olive tree in its five-hundredth year, giving then its finest fruit, is man. How can he give forth wisdom until he has been crushed and turned in the hand of God?'

'Rabbi Akiba said: Israel must not be like the pagans, thanking their wooden gods when good happens and cursing them when evil comes. When good comes, the Jews thank God, and when evil comes, they thank Him too.'

'Rab Naaman of Makor said: There is the law, and before that there is the law.'

'But Rabbi Akiba said: He who glories merely in his knowledge of the law is like the carcass of a dead animal lying in the road. To be sure, the rotting beast attracts the attention of all, but whoever passes by holds his hand to his nose, for it stinks.'

For some time Rabbi Asher recalled the homilies of the dead sages, and in the afternoon he rose inspired and returned to town happily like a bridegroom, for he concluded that he understood God's wishes: in the vision Queen Helena had been shown building a Christian church, and obviously God approved, for she had appeared in radiant light. To Rabbi Asher this meant that he, too, must

erect a holy building, and he marched to the area south of that which Queen
Helena had staked out for her Christians, and there he indicated where a small
synagogue should be built. He then assembled his Jews and said, 'For years
we've been worshipping in my house, and it is no longer proper for us to do so.
We shall build a synagogue like those in Kefar Nahum and Biri.' His suggestion
met with approval until one cautious man asked, 'And how shall we pay for it?'

Here Rabbi Asher was perplexed, for the Jews of Makor were an
impoverished lot. Of the thousand people then living in the area—the smallest
population it had known for centuries—more than eight hundred were Jews,
but they controlled none of the major industries. 'How shall we pay for it?' the
man asked again, and there was silence.

Then, from the rear, a big hulking man rose to his feet, the stonecutter
Yohanan, and he said through his jutting teeth, 'Rabbi's right. We ought to
have a synagogue. You feed me and my wife, I'll build one better than Kefar
Nahum's.'

The Jews were aware that only a few hours before this big man with beetling
eyebrows and hairy hands had defied the rabbi, and they expected God's Man
to reject his offer, but to their surprise Rabbi Asher announced, 'From
Ptolemais to Tverya, Yohanan is the best stonecutter, and I will give his family
their groats.' In a few moments he extracted other promises which would
permit the synagogue to be started, and thus began that curious but fruitful
partnership between the groats maker and the stonecutter which was to make
Makor beautiful again.

Prior to this the synagogues of Galilee had usually been drab affairs in the
Jewish tradition of a bleak exterior and a warm interior, but now the hulking,
almost brutal, stonecutter displayed a knack for carving the white limestone his
donkeys hauled in from the quarries, and before long the walls of the synagogue
began to show stone birds and turtles and fish, so that during the second year of
his work the Jews of Makor saw that Yohanan, using the poetry of stone, was
building a masterpiece. It seemed that the uglier his outward life became, the
more delicately he used his chisel, so that if he had not yet found a way to live
within Judaism he at least knew how to create a home in which Judaism could
prosper.

For his outward life remained ugly. After the synagogue was well begun
Tirza gave birth to a son, which disturbed her, for she had to face the fact that
since the boy was a bastard, he could never be a proper Jew; and she began to
imagine that the women of Makor condemned her as she passed. One day she
ran screaming to her husband, 'Rabbi Asher follows me with accusing eyes
wherever I go!' She became obsessed with the idea that he was damning her for
having broken the law and began to whine complainingly to her common-law
husband, 'Yohanan, take me to Egypt or Antioch.' When he asked what good
that would do, she could give no coherent explanation but offered the irrational
suggestion that there they might find her first husband. The stonecutter tried
to reason with her, but nothing he said consoled her, so in perplexity he went to
the rabbi and said stupidly, 'Tell me what to do.'

The anguish of Yohanan's plea impelled God's Man to take over and he
said, 'I'm sure that God holds Tirza to be your wife, even though illegally. I,
too, must accept responsibility for her, and if she thinks that I have personally
offended her, I must assure her otherwise.' And the little man left his study to
apologize to Tirza; but when he reached her house she was gone. Rabbi Asher
trailed her to Ptolemais, but she had already taken ship for Alexandria, and

when he sent an appeal to the rabbis of that city they replied that she had wandered off to Spain.

Now Rabbi Asher proved himself a true Man of God, for he summoned Yohanan and said, 'Even though your bastard son can never be a complete Jew, let us at least do for him what we can,' and he arranged for the boy's circumcision, during which the awkward stonecutter stood holding his son as if the child were an apparition from another world. 'Let his name be Menahem the Comforter,' Rabbi Asher said as he completed the covenant between the infant and God, and when it became apparent that Yohanan would never learn to care for the boy, Rabbi Asher arranged for different women of the town to look after the child so that Menahem, a handsome, square-jawed creature with large black eyes and bright intelligence, might grow as other boys did.

His father, chin drooping on his chest as if he were a confused animal, lounged about the town after his work was done, talking roughly out of the side of his mouth and serving as a focal point for the irresponsible younger men of Makor. 'This town is nothing,' he grumbled. 'If you want to see the world travel inland from Antioch. Edessa! They have wine in Edessa I can still taste. Persia! I was a fool ever to leave Persia. Girls from sixteen nations gather there and they love a man who earns a little money.' He was a bad influence but was allowed to remain because he showed such skill with the chisel.

One evening when Rabbi Asher came to inspect the day's work he had the sensation that his synagogue was growing from the earth like a stone flower, and he was content that in building this lovely place he was accomplishing God's wish as delivered in the vision. Then he saw Yohanan working alone among the rocks chipping casually at a chunk of raw limestone, and as Rabbi Asher watched how skillfully the stonecutter brought beautiful design out of the chaos of the rock he said, 'Can you understand now, Yohanan, how the hammer and chisel of the law bring form to the chaos of life?' The big man looked up and for a brief moment seemed to catch a glimmer of what the rabbi was attempting to explain, but the spark died. At that spot, during a period of ten thousand years, ninety-nine per cent of all sparks struck by either flint or mind had flamed momentarily and died; but know Rabbi Asher saw what his stonecutter was making: a linked series of heavy, squarish wheels, and as soon as the rabbi saw this motif he visualized its effectiveness as a frieze for the inner walls of the synagogue, for the inherent movement of the wheel teased the eye forward from one point to the next.

'Perhaps we could use a line of them? Around the wall?' Asher ventured to suggest.

'That's what I was thinking,' the stonecutter growled.

'What is it?'

'I saw it in Persia. A running wheel.'

'What's it called?'

'Swastika.' And in this manner the notable design, common throughout Asia, became virtually the symbol of the Galilean synagogue, for all visiting rabbis who saw the effective frieze wanted swastikas for their buildings, too.

So the synagogue progressed and Rabbi Asher became smug; he even visited the quarries to pick out superior stones, but one day as he returned along the Damascus road he felt the world suddenly grow quiet, as if all birds had fled and he alone were present. A choking filled his throat and his knees were pulled, as if by giant fingers, to the earth, and as he knelt in the dust he witnessed the same burning light that had accompanied his first vision, and once more it illuminated the Torah and the golden fence that protected it. This time there was not one church but many, with towers and battlements, and the synagogue was in ruins. All the work that Yohanan had completed, under Rabbi Asher's urging, had apparently accomplished nothing. The churches and the ruins faded until there remained only the Torah and the fence, noble and unchanged, so blinding in its power that Rabbi Asher threw himself prone in the roadway, a frail-bodied Jew with a long black beard to whom God was speaking, and he now had to acknowledge that on the former occasion he had not understood.

'Almighty God, what did I do wrong?' he pleaded, knocking his head in the dust. The only answer was the shimmering vision of the Torah and the fence; but from his prostrate position the groats maker saw something that he had overlooked the first time: the fence guarding the Torah was incomplete. God's divine law was not fully protected, and now the intention of the vision was made manifest. Rabbi Asher was being summoned to dedicate the rest of his life not to the building of an earthly synagogue but to the completion of the divine law.

'O God!' the humble little man whispered. 'Am I worthy to go to Tverya?' And as soon as he pronounced that name the golden fence completed itself and he bowed his head to accept the heavenly commission. 'I shall place my feet upon the road to Tverya,' he said.

In the middle years of the fourth century there was in the Roman city of Tiberias, called Tverya by the Jews, a lively community of thirteen synagogues, a large library and an assembly of elderly rabbis who met in continuous session to discuss the Torah and its later commentaries, seeking thus to uncover the laws which would govern all subsequent Judaism. For hours and even months they debated each phrase until its meaning was made clear, and it was to this body of men that Rabbi Asher directed himself in the spring of 329. He had no need to hurry, for the assembly had been in session, off and on, for a hundred years and would continue for another century and a half, if not in Tverya then in Babylonia across the desert.

On his white mule Rabbi Asher rode eastward over the beautiful hills of Galilee and looked out upon the broad plains across which Egyptians and Assyrians had battled. He rode into the cliff-perched town of Sephet, which General Josephus had fortified against the Romans of Vespasian, and it was from that high point that he caught his first sight of Tverya, its white marble buildings scintillant against the blue waters of the lake. 'If men can find truth anywhere,' he said to his mule, 'they ought to find it down there.'

From a distance Tverya was an enchanting city, for the spacious buildings of Herod Antipas had made it a rival of Caesarea, with marble steps leading down to the lake and luxurious baths for visitors, but when Asher rode inside the walls he saw that it breathed an atmosphere of death, as if its future were abandoned. Few new buildings had been added in recent centuries and those which survived had fallen into disrepair behind their marble façades. Thus Rome was dying in its farther provinces. In Tverya there would be no miracles, but there could be the work of honest men, and it was to this work that he now directed himself.

Stopping strangers he asked where the scholars met, and the first four citizens did not even know that the group had been convening in their city for more than a century, but each volunteered to tell him how he might find the hot baths. Finally he met an old Jew who led him to an insignificant building in which the great work was being done; and, tying his mule to a tree, Asher approached the low mud-brick house. He knocked softly on the door, but was left to stand in silence. He knocked again and was admitted by a grumbling old woman who had come from the kitchen. She led him through the house to an extensive courtyard in which stood two pomegranate trees and a large grape arbor, beneath which huddled a circle of old men who did not bother to look up at his approach. At their feet, literally, crouched groups of students, following their words affectionately, while at a table under one of the pomegranate trees sat two scribes making notes of how the argument progressed. When decisions were reached, these scribes would compress into a few pithy lines the debate of months, and that would be the law. This day they wrote little as four rabbis engaged in energetic debate on a minor point.

FIRST RABBI: We are concerned with one question alone. Protecting Shabbat. I say that the man may not wear it.

SECOND RABBI: Speak out. On what authority do you make this claim?

THIRD RABBI: Then listen. Rabbi Meir had it from Rabbi Akiba that if a woman goes out of her house on Shabbat with a bottle of perfume so that she may smell nice, she is guilty of vanity and has broken Shabbat. This case is the same.

FOURTH RABBI: More to the point. The law of the sages prevents a man on Shabbat from carrying in his pocket a nail from a gallows. Why? He carries it only for good luck and it is forbidden.

SECOND RABBI: What nonsense. The man we are talking about does not seek good luck.

FIRST RABBI: Listen to the sages. A woman must not leave her house with braids of cloth. Why not? It makes her hair more attractive, and is forbidden. This is what we're talking about.

FOURTH RABBI: Nor shall she go into the street wearing a hair net. The same case, surely.

SECOND RABBI: But remember this. A woman may go abroad on Shabbat sucking a peppercorn to keep her breath sweet.

FIRST RABBI: Only if she placed it in her mouth before Shabbat began.

THIRD RABBI: Also, the sages always held that if she happened to drop the peppercorn from her mouth during Shabbat, she could not put it back until Shabbat had ended.

SECOND RABBI: To all of that I agree. But our man is not going to drop it from his mouth. And he placed it there before nighfall on Friday.

FIRST RABBI: On those requirements we agree. It must be in his mouth before Shabbat begins.

THIRD RABBI: The real question. Has he any right to have it there at all on Shabbat? No, because it is an act of vanity. Like a woman wearing a gold ornament. Which is obviously forbidden.

SECOND RABBI: Agreed. If it is merely an ornamentation, the man must not have it in his mouth on Shabbat.

FOURTH RABBI: And I insist that it is merely an ornament.

SECOND RABBI: Hold now! He wears his false tooth in order to eat better.

FOURTH RABBI: But he could eat just as easily if he didn't have it. A false tooth for a man is no more, no less, than a gold head-dress for a woman.

SECOND RABBI: That cannot be the case. The headdress is ornamentation. The tooth is a necessity.

THIRD RABBI: False. A gold tooth is just as attractive to a man as a gold . . .

SECOND RABBI: Who said a gold tooth! I said a tooth. A false tooth added to the mouth for the purpose of chewing better.

THIRD RABBI: Is there a difference between a false tooth and a gold false tooth?

FIRST RABBI: Indeed! The gold tooth is worn for decoration only.

SECOND RABBI: Not true! A man buys a gold tooth because it fits better than stone and wears longer than wood. He acts from prudence, not vanity.

FOURTH RABBI: Error! Error!

THIRD RABBI: Is not a false tooth placed in the mouth the same as a woman's curls added to her forehead? And do not the sages say that she may not wear such curls unless they are sewed on permanently?

FOURTH RABBI: Why permanently?

THIRD RABBI: Lest she inadvertently add them to her head on Shabbat.

FIRST RABBI: Sewing she can be trusted not to do because three acts are involved. Needle, thread and sewing. She knows that each is forbidden. But pinning a curl to the head is not a usual act and this she may forget, so it is forbidden.

THIRD RABBI: And a false tooth is not added to the mouth permanently, but must be put in each day, and is therefore exactly like the false curl of the woman, which may not be worn.

During the first four days that Rabbi Asher spent among the learned men of Tverya he was kept standing by the wall, a small, tentative figure, listening as his elders hammered away at the false tooth. As they inspected the problem from all philosophical and material angles, Asher learned that they had been on the subject for two months, hoping to establish from it a broad principle governing the use on Shabbat of objects that were both useful and ornamental, and at several points in the argument he felt that he had ideas to contribute, but the expositors ignored him and modesty prevented him from trying to attract their attention. On the evening of the fourth day, bewildered, he left the convocation. Did the rabbis intend to ignore him permanently? Or had he through vanity misread God's command that he join them?

He sought guidance on these matters at the logical place in Tverya, a small hill northwest of town, which he climbed at sunset until he came to a cave that was already holy but which would become more so as the centuries advanced: the grave of Akiba, greatest of the rabbis and savior of the law. Here Asher sat humbly, hands folded and hoping to receive from the long-dead rabbi instructions concerning his present plight, but none came. Now, whether this cave actually held the bones of the Jewish saint could not be determined, for just as Queen Helena had gone through the Holy Land arbitrarily deciding where the cherished relics of Christianity were, so devout Jews had established categorically where the saintly scenes of their religion had occurred. At Sephet certain of the great men were said to be buried, but Tverya was allotted Rabbi Meir and Rabbi Akiba, and pilgrimages to their supposed graves would continue as long as there was a Judaism.

But if Rabbi Asher was unable to communicate with the great rabbi he did find something equally important: sitting before the cave he watched the sun depart from the lake and the city of Tverya; and the play of sunset colors upon the eastern hills, the panoply of gray and purple and gold upon the grassy cliffs was so ghostlike that he felt the presence of God even more strongly than he had in the olive grove, and he submitted himself to whatever wishes God might have regarding his stay in Tverya. In this state of euphoria, while light diminished and the marble city began to fade, a wind passed down the deep valley, coming from the north, and it rippled the surface of the water as if a figure were moving across the waves. Entranced, Asher watched the progress of the giant steps, and they came directly to Tverya, where they seemed to mount the spacious marble wharf that faced the water front, and whatever it was that had agitated the surface of the lake took residence in the city. Reassured and exhilarated, Rabbi Asher climbed down from the tomb and returned to Tverya, satisfied to remain there until the rabbis took notice of him.

On the fifth day there was no change. He resumed his silent position against the wall and listened as the great men continued their discussion of the golden tooth, and for the entire two weeks that he was kept waiting this tooth remained the only concern; but his observation of how the rabbis worked had one salutary effect: he learned that the exposition of the law was a serious matter requiring both subtlety of mind and mastery of learning, and he understood that in settling the exaggerated problem of the tooth they were automatically deciding all lesser conflicts between utility and vanity. As he stood in the shadows he remembered the old description of a true rabbi, 'that basketful of books,' and he pledged that if the time came when the men of Tverya finally consulted him, he would respond with subtlety and wisdom.

On the nineteenth day, when the guardians of the law had pretty well agreed that if a man wore a gold tooth on Shabbat he was transgressing, and when they were about to formulate a law permitting a stone or a wooden tooth, a rabbi who was trying to make a point about the inherent vanity of man, turned abruptly to Rabbi Asher and snapped, 'You, from Makor. What did Rab Naaman say?'

Softly, without moving from his shadows, the groats maker explained, 'Rab Naaman of blessed memory said, "Why did God create man only on the sixth day? To warn him. If ever he becomes swollen with pride it can be pointed out to him that in God's creation of the world even a flea came ahead of him."' He paused. 'Rab Naaman also said, "The camel was so vain he desired horns, so his ears were taken from him."' Without comment the rabbis listened, and Asher concluded, 'Rab Naaman said, "Man is born with his hands clenched, but he dies with them wide open and empty. The vanities he clings to elude him in the end, so he should not bother himself with them during his life."' The rabbis listened approvingly, and without speaking one old man made a place for Asher to sit, and in this way God's Man became one of the great expositors, laboring to construct the basic framework of Judaism.

To the four great planks which God possessed for the preservation of the Jews—monotheism, Torah, personal lyricism, prophecy—He would now add two more: the Talmud, and rabbis to interpret it, after which He would have a complete structure within which His Jews would henceforth live. God's concept of the rabbi was easy to understand, for he was not much different from the ancient priest of El-Shaddai or the newer ones who were being called forth by the Christian church of Byzantium. The rabbi was apt to be more learned than the former and more personally committed to daily life than the latter, for he was required to have a wife and his congregation was always happier if he had five or six children, for then he would appreciate the burdens of the common man. The rabbi would also work for his living—of the sages meeting at Tverya during Rabbi Asher's apprenticeship one was a fisherman on the Sea of Galilee, one a woodchopper, one a ritual butcher and one a scribe who made copies of the Torah—and no Jewish rabbi would ever accept discipline by a hierarchy of any kind: his contract was a personal one with the community that invited him to guide them. Often, as in the case of the greatest rabbi, Akiba, he would be a brilliant scholar with a memory that would be difficult to match in any other profession. He would serve as conscience, arbiter, monitor and judge of life and death. Rabbi Akiba had warned: 'When you sit on a court which condemns a man to death, do not eat all day, because you have killed part of yourself.' Of every segment of his community the rabbi was a part, and when it suffered its periodic agonies, he suffered more than all, and it was this basic relationship that Asher ha-Garsi exemplified, for in the long discussions held under the grape arbor of Tverya, he quickly established himself as God's Man, for he spoke with but one concern, to ascertain the will of God, and he always spoke humbly, as if he were only a little man incapable of knowing God's wishes directly but able somehow to detect them by lowering his face and catching the passing whisper. Being closer to God than most men he suffered more deeply when ordinary men acted contrary to God's law, and he was always willing to humble himself in trying to bring God and man together.

But even if a devout rabbi like Asher ha-Garsi was in essence the same as a Christian or a Buddhist priest, God's final plank, the Talmud, bore no resemblance to anything else in the world's religions. It was a remarkable achievement, the heart of Judaism, and it consisted of two parts: the Mishna and the Gemara. The first had been assembled by Rabbi Akiba and his followers some eighty years before Rabbi Asher was born; it was the second component upon which the expositors of Tverya and Babylonia were now working. When the two were joined together, some time around the year 500, the Talmud would be in existence.

What was the Mishna? An adroit solution to a difficult religious problem. The wise men of Judaism had evolved the principle that at Sinai, god had handed Moses two sets of laws, one written on the tablets of stone and later transcribed word for word into the Torah, and a second of equal importance which had been whispered to Moses alone, the oral law, which provided specific elaboration of the Torah. For example, in the written book of Exodus, God said distinctly, 'Remember the Sabbath day, to keep it holy,' but He did not stipulate in writing what one must do to observe this commandment. It became the task of the rabbis, depending upon the oral law which God had given Moses, to clarify the commandment and make it specific.

Who knew what this oral law was? Only the rabbis. How did they know? Because it had been handed along from man to man in a solemn unbroken chain: 'Moses received the Torah from God Himself at Sinai, and passed it along to Joshua, and Joshua to the Elders, and they to the Prophets, and they to the Men of the Great Assembly and they to Antigonus of Soko . . . Hillel and Shammai took over from them . . . Johanan ben Zakkai . . . Rab Naaman of Makor . . . the great Akiba . . . Rabbi Meir . . .' and in days to come the rubric would be added, 'From him Rabbi Asher ha-Garsi took over,' and it would pass to Rashi, the marvelous Frenchman, then to the greatest mind of all, Maimonides, and to the Vilna Gaon of Lithuania, and on to the merest rabbi working in Akron, Ohio. These men were custodians of the oral law.

For the first fifteen hundred years this oral law had been carried only in the heads of scholars, but after the two Roman destructions of Judaea–first by Vespasian and later by Hadrian, who erased even the name of Jerusalem and changed Judaea to Palestine–a group of scholars had met in a small Galilean village not far from Makor to codify this inherited law. Thus they constructed what became known as the Mishna, which men like Rabbi Asher were required to know by heart. For example, in extension of the crisp Torah injunction not to work on Shabbat, the Mishna identified forty-less-one principal kinds of labor which were forbidden: 'Sowing, reaping . . . baking . . . spinning . . . tying or untying knots . . . sewing two stitches . . . hunting a gazelle . . . writing two letters . . . lighting a fire . . . carrying anything from one domain into another . . .'

One does not sit down before the barber, close to the time of the Shabbat prayer. A tailor should not take his needle on Shabbat eve just before nightfall; he may forget and go out with it. Nor the scribe take his pen. One should not begin to clean his clothes, and one does not read at the lamplight, because he may tilt it. The schoolmaster may supervise the reading of his children, but he himself must not read. Similarly, a man that is in heat should not eat together with a woman that is in heat, because it may lead them to sin . . .

One must not put bread in the oven on Shabbat eve before darkness, nor may the cakes be put on the coal unless there is time for the crust to form before Shabbat arrives. Rabbi Eliezer says: In time for the crust to form on the bottom . . .

What may one use for lighting on the Shabbat, and what must one not use? One must not use cedar fiber, nor oakum, nor silk, nor a bast wick, nor a desert wick, nor seaweed, nor pitch, nor wax, nor castor oil, nor burnt oil, nor tail fat, nor tallow. Nahum the Mede says: One may use boiled tallow, but the Sages say: Whether boiled or not, one may not light with it.

The Sages, however, permit all oils: sesame oil, nut oil, radish oil, cucumber oil, tar and naphtha. But Rabbi Tarfon says: For lighting only olive oil may be used.

In this way the Mishna inspected each aspect of life and laid down the laws which bound Jews to their religion.

What was the Gemera? When the completed Mishna had been used by Jews for only a short time they began to find that it was not specific enough; it proscribed thirty-nine different kinds of work, but as new occupations evolved, new rulings were required. So the rabbis restudied each category, trying to spread its elastic words over the greatest possible number of occupations and hitting sometimes upon interpretations that were masterpieces of intellectual juggling. For example, during the first month of Rabbi Asher's service as one of the expositors the question arose as to what the prohibited occupation of sowing might include. An old rabbi with experience in farming gave it as his opinion that sowing included such collateral occupations as pruning, planting, bending trees to shape and grafting.

Rabbi Asher said, 'Grafting is clearly the same as sowing, and is therefore forbidden, but pruning is clearly the opposite of sowing, for it is a cutting away rather than a planting.'

The older man said, 'Hear this. Why does a man prune? To lay bare the new growth so that it may spring forward. Thus pruning is sowing.'

Rabbi Asher said, 'You make it clear. Pruning is forbidden too.'

They spent a full year discussing agriculture and the kinds of farm work that may not be done on Shabbat. Using the old farmer's theory that pruning was the same as sowing, they arrived at the extraordinary conclusion that filling a ditch was the same as plowing and that working on a hole near one's house was the same as building, since at some later date a building might grow out of the hole.

Rabbi Asher led the group in a discussion of what might be included under the prohibition against reaping: 'We learned: sheaf-binding, wire-making and cutting stone for a building are identical with reaping. Rab Naaman said they are prohibited.'

A rabbi who worked in the building trades argued, 'I had it from Rabbi Jonah from Meir from Akiba: Stonecutting is the same as plowing. It is already forbidden.'

On and on the arguments went as the rabbis gathered up the loose ends of life and tied them into permanent packages. In the third year they summoned a sailor from Ptolemais to discuss the cryptic passage of the Mishna, 'Tying and untying knots is forbidden on Shabbat.' Just what was involved in the tying of a knot, they asked, and to what other human activities might this prohibition extend? The sailor demonstrated what tying a knot consisted of, and after two months of discussion Rabbi Asher proposed the following general rule: 'Any joining together of two things that are by nature the same is equal to the tying of a knot. Thus, on Shabbat a man may not place additional grapes in a press which already contains grapes, for that is tying a knot.'

A rabbi visiting from Babylonia, where similar discussions were taking place among the Jews of that region, said, 'Why not say simply, knots tied by camel drivers, donkey drivers and sailors?'

An old rabbi said, 'I heard it from Rabbi Zumzum who had it from Rabbi Meir that no man should be held culpable for a knot that could be untied with one hand.' Thus the argument progressed day after day as the great expositors laid down their specific interpretations. Their extensions would be known as the Gemera, and when their work was finished, after two and a half centuries of debate in both Tverya and Babylonia, the Mishna (Repetition) and the Gemera (Completion) would coalesce to form the Talmud (Teaching), that enormous compendium which would in turn be interpreted by the Egyptian doctor, Maimonides, and after him by others of lesser insight, so that in the end there would stand a jumbled, rambling, inspired portrait of Judaism in action. It was this Talmud that provided the fence around the Torah, protecting God's law from unintentional trespass; God had said merely, 'Remember Shabbat,' but the rabbis had staked out their fence far from the actual Shabbat, defending the sacred day behind a multitude of laws. It was on this holy work of building the fence of the Talmud that Rabbi Asher would spend the rest of his life.

This did not mean that he lived permanently in Tverya, engaged only in legalistic discussion. Like his fellow rabbis from Kefar Nahum and Biri, he continued to supervise the spiritual life of his home community, and since he also had a wife and three unmarried daughters, it was his added responsibility to see that his groats mill made a profit. So whenever the crops were harvested he mounted his white mule to ride back through the Galilean forests to his little town in order to purchase grain, and one of his most satisfying moments came when he guided his mule up the incline into Makor to greet his family and to inspect conditions at the mill.

It was with bursting joy that Rabbi Asher reached the privacy of his home at the end of these trips, for he would rush, tired and dusty, to greet his wife and embrace his children. Gathering his family about him he would lead them in singing either psalms or folksongs, and he would toss his youngest daughter into the air, catching her as she squealed with joy at having her father home again. At meals he would stand at the head of the table and look upon his family, praying with sheer happiness: 'God, the journey is ended and I am once more with those I love.'

But when he was alone he would stand humbly in one corner of his room and begin a serious communication with God, thanking Him gravely for having kept the family well and warm, and as he prayed a frenzy would possess him, and he would begin bowing from the waist, left and right, running forward to meet God, then retreating out of respect. At certain passages in his prayer he would throw himself full length upon the earthen floor so forcefully as to bring dust, then he would rise and the bowing would be repeated. At the end of his extended prayer he would have worked his way completely across the room and perhaps halfway back again, a little man in ecstasy, prostrating himself before his God. His attitude to prayer summarized his morality: 'When I am in the synagogue praying for others, I make the prayers short lest my brothers grow tired, but when I am alone with God, I cannot prolong them sufficiently.'

When it was known in Makor that the rabbi was home again, many visitors would come seeking either guidance or charity, and with the former, Asher observed the rule which he had often defended in the discussions at Tvery: 'Deal leniently with others but strictly with yourself.' And he did what he could to soften the harsh blows of peasant life in a town where tax collectors were brutal and Byzantine soldiers cruel. With those who sought charity, he was guided by the unequivocal precept of Rab Naaman of Makor: 'A man who will not give to the poor is an animal,' and in some years the profits of his groats mill were largely dissipated because of the cereal which he gave away. As for the manner of dispensing charity, he had formulated a rule which would be incorporated into the Talmud: 'Take care of the other man's body and your own soul.' If the worst drunkard came to him for food, Rabbi Asher first fed him, then prayed for him and sent him away. 'Lecturing him about his evil ways should be postponed for another day,' he explained. 'Charity and exhortation must not be mixed.'

Wherever he moved in the community he tried to bring joy, telling mothers that their sons would become scholars, assuring young girls that they would find husbands, and encouraging farmers to hope for profitable seasons. He had always been impressed by that teaching of the Mishna which said, 'In the hereafter each man will be asked to explain why he abstained from those normal pleasures of life to which he was entitled.' Songs, dancing, wine in moderation, feasts with one's friends, games for children and young people, courtship in the spring and caressing children were occupations, Rabbi Asher said, which brought joy to life, and those who were in his presence for any time found cause for laughter.

His principal regret came when he resumed work at the groats mill, hauling the bags of wheat, and he had to acknowledge that so far he had found no one to run the place satisfactorily in his absence. He had tried several men, but they had lacked the integrity he required, and so in his absence the place merely struggled along, watched over by his busy wife and earning only half the profit it should have done. Once he had hoped that his two sons-in-law would assume this responsibility, but they showed no inclination to do so, and now when he returned to Tverya it was with the doleful realization that he had still not found a man to make the groats.

This deficiency was regrettable in that Asher's ancestors had devised a special way of making the cereal: they took well-ripened wheat, boiled it in water like the other groats makers, but to their water they added salts and herbs, and when the time came for drying the grains they did not pour the water away, like the others, but allowed it to stand in the sun until the wheat absorbed it, taking back into the grains whatever nutrients would otherwise have been washed away. Asher also allowed his wheat to dry in the sun for at least a week longer then his competitors did, so that when the grains were finally cracked by his stone mill, forming pieces smaller than rice, they had a chewy, nutty flavor that all appreciated. Once when he was about to return to Tverya a Greek merchant protested, 'Rabbi, why do you fool with those white beards? Any man can write down the law, but it takes a man chosen by God to make good groats.' It was a pity, Asher thought, that he had found no manager.

Therefore, in the winter of 330, when his wife announced that she was pregnant again, well past the normal age for conceiving, he experienced a surge of joy, for he convinced himself that by this miracle God was determined to send him a son to inherit the groats mill. He went about town, a little man of forty-eight with a beard that was showing gray, telling his friends, 'You can see it's only reasonable. Five daughters in a row. The last has got to be a boy.' He decided to call the child Matthew, God's Gift, and sometimes in the street when he spoke of his son his eyes would dance and only with difficulty did he keep his feet from doing the same. 'He was sent me by God,' the little rabbi proclaimed, but in the autumn his wife gave birth to a sixth daughter and she was named Jael.

Subdued, Rabbi Asher mounted his white mule and rode down the caravan road to Tverya, where under the grape arbor he was about to begin a specific chain of deliberation which would have a most permanent impact on all Jews: during the nine years from 330 through 338 the expositors would discuss principally one pregnant verse of Torah. God first stated his concept in Exodus and then, because apparently He considered it vital to His plans for the Jews, He repeated the warning twice: 'Thou shalt not seethe a kid in his mother's milk.' That was all God said; possibly He did not want a mother sheep to be abused by knowing that its offspring was to be cooked in her milk, which would double her anguish, as it were. Or the restriction might have been imposed because Canaanites to the north indulged in this practice and anything a Canaanite did was to be avoided. At any rate, God had reiterated the simple directive, and it fell to the rabbis to interpret it.

As they studied the cryptic sentence, three words stood out. *Seethe* was probably meant to include all kinds of cooking. *Kid* was meant to include all kinds of meat. And *milk* was intended to cover all possible variations of dairy products. Under these initial interpretations the expositors began to erect those complicated dietary laws which would set the Jews apart. Extensions made which only men of ingenuity could have deduced, and routines for kitchen and cooking were established which would enable Jews to observe every eventual sanction growing out of God's brief commandment. The dietary ritual had a certain beauty to it and was in conformance with the sanitary laws of the time. Milk and meat must be kept forever separate, for the slightest trace of one could contaminate the other, and a drop of milk carelessly spilled into a kettle used for cooking meat might mean that the pot would have to be shattered lest the community be led unknowingly into error. At first the rules laid down by the rabbis were not intrusive: Jewish kitchens became a symbol of God's covenant and to keep dishes separated was a trivial thing. Jewish women came to enjoy cooking in accordance with divine law, as whispered by God to Moses and conveyed by him to generation after generation of holy men. But now Rabbi Asher advanced the idea that even the cooking vapors from a pot containing beef could contaminate a whole kitchen where milk was being used, and no local housewife could contest him; when in Babylonia other rabbis began to evolve other refinements even more difficult to observe, no one could contest them, either. For what the rabbis were doing, in part consciously and in part unconsciously, was to create a body of law that would bind the Jews together as they went into exile to the Diaspora. Without a homeland the Jews would live within their law and become a nation mightier than those which had oppressed them. Without cities of their own they would as a cohesive unit help determine the destinies of cities they had not yet seen.

Wherever they went—to Spain or Egypt or Argentina—they would take with them the decisions of the rabbis of Tverya, and within the limits established by these decisions they would live, a more permanent group of people than any who had surrounded them in their two thousand years in Israel. Gentiles, observing their homelessness, would construct the myth of the Wandering Jew, but in reality this phrase was meaningless, for no matter where the Jew wandered, if he took with him the Talmud he was home.

Fraught with future meaning though these discussions of cooking were, the consultations which best exemplified the Talmudic process were those ingenious deductions whereby procedures for ritual worship were established. All Jews agreed that such worship must not be conducted by haphazard formula, but what constituted proper ritual was difficult to determine, for on this matter the written Torah was silent; it spoke of a time when worship was conducted at the temple in Jerusalem; and the oral Torah was equally deficient because the transmitters of the secret information had not foreseen the time when Jerusalem would no longer exist. And even when the Romans did finally allow the city to be rebuilt, a new temple was not permitted. Therefore the rabbis were required to legislate for a religion whose externals had changed markedly.

The rabbi of Kefar Nahum, known to the Christians as Capernaum, where the largest of the Galilean synagogues stood, remembered that the Eighty-second Psalm said clearly, 'God standeth in the congregation of the mighty . . .' and from this it was deduced that God was willing to convene with His faithful in a public congregation. How many were required in the forming of a congregation? No man could say. Was it three persons? Or seven? Or twelve? Each of these numbers had mystical value and it was probable that God had preferred one of them. But no one knew.

The rabbi of Biri, the town with the loveliest synagogue—a gemlike building with many columns constructed of white limestone—recalled that in the Book of Numbers, God had asked Moses directly, 'How long shall I bear with this evil congregation, which murmur against me?' and although this referred to an evil group, it was nevertheless one that God had recognized as an officially constituted congregation. The rabbis tracked the reference backward and found that it related to the twelve men who Moses had dispatched into Canaan to spy out the land: 'And the Lord spake unto Moses, saying, Send thou men, that they may search the land of Canaan, which I give unto the children of Israel: of every tribe of their fathers shall ye send a man . . .' So putting the two texts together they deduced that when God spoke of a congregation He was referring to at least twelve men. But the rabbi of Kefar Nahum pointed out that of the twelve evil men who spoke against the Lord, one should be excused, for Caleb of the tribe of Judah had spoken on behalf of the Lord: 'And Caleb stilled the people before Moses, and said, Let us go up at once, and possess it . . .' So this made eleven the proper number for a congregation. But then Rabbi Asher discovered that of these eleven still another, Joshua of the tribe of Ephraim, had also spoken in defense of the Lord: 'The land, which we passed through to search it, is an exceeding good land. If the Lord delight in us, then he will bring us into this land, and give us; a land which floweth with milk and honey.' Thus, in the congregation, evil though it was, there had been twelve men less Caleb and Joshua, so ten was the required number, and the famous summary was evolved: 'God is willing to meet with ten street sweepers but not with nine rabbis.' The question then arose as to what constituted a man, and after years of discussion it was determined that a man was any male child who had reached the age of thirteen; henceforth no public worship was possible without the presence of ten Jewish men above the age of twelve.

In this patient, involuted and often arbitrary manner the great rabbis wove that net in which God would hold His chosen people. Every word of the Torah–even the punctuation mark–was analyzed. A single concept of the Mishna might occupy the rabbis for a year, and their Gemara, when completed, would be further dissected for fifteen centuries. As a result the Talmud would constitute an inexhaustible source of wisdom which men could study all the days of their lives, still finding rewards even if they lived, like Moses, to be a hundred and twenty.

One day in the year 335 Rabbi Asher rode home to find that Yohanan, on his own initiative, had taken a step which altered the appearance of the Makor synagogue. The little rabbi, unprepared for what the surly stonecutter had done, went as usual to the door to inspect progress and found running down the length of the interior two rows of marble columns whose antique beauty gave the heavy room a distinct touch of paganism. 'Where did you get them?' the rabbi asked suspiciously.

Afraid of being rebuked, Yohanan growled, 'My son Menahem . . . he heard the people saying . . . mysteries hidden in the earth.' He hesitated, unsure of himself. 'Columns of gold, they said.'

'Your son? Found these?'

Uneasily the big stonecutter mumbled, 'The other children won't play with Menahem. He went digging . . . out there. Uncovered one end of one column. It wasn't gold.' He waited apprehensively.

Rabbi Asher could see that the pillars were pagan and their shimmering colors could only be interpreted as adornment and he was tempted to order them thrown out, but reflection assured him that at least they were not graven images. 'Who made them originally?' he temporized, but Yohanan could not guess. He was unable to imagine that a Makor citizen like Timon Myrmex had once spent several years selecting these eight choice columns from the thousands that were piling into Herod's Caesarea in order to adorn the Roman forum. How beautiful they were to Yohanan and how earnestly he hoped that Rabbi Asher would allow them to remain.

'They can stay,' the groats maker snapped. 'But don't do things like this again.'

When this approval was granted, Rabbi Asher found that Yohanan wanted to discuss a problem which the rabbi had long anticipated, so with some apprehension God's Man said, 'We can't discuss it here. Stop work and come to my house.' The two men left the synagogue and moved to the cool stone house from which the rabbi's wife managed the groats mill while he was absent. Asher led the way to the alcove where he kept his volumes, and there, surrounded by visual evidence of the law, he sat in a large chair, placed his hands on his table and said, 'Now what do you wish to tell me about your son?'

'How did you know?'

'We will discuss him many times.'

'He's nine. He's growing up.'

'I know.' Rabbi Asher could visualize the boy Menahem as he played in the streets, a vagrant child who seemed likely to become a handsome young man. The rabbi sighed with regret over what he must now say, and postponed his judgment by asking, 'You're wondering what to do with Menahem?'

'Yes.'

'I'm wondering, too,' the rabbi said.

'In what way?'

Rabbi Asher retreated a little, like a legalist seeking protection in documents. Clasping his knuckles firmly, until the tips of his fingers were white, he said, 'Now come the difficult years, when those who break the law begin to reap their rewards.'

'What do you mean?' Yohanan demanded.

Rabbi Asher, having delivered his sermon, relaxed the nervous clasping of his hands and said gently, 'I've been wondering what we shall both do about Menahem, and I find no solution. For he's a bastard.'

'I'll protect him!' the stonecutter insisted.

'He remains a bastard,' Rabbi Asher said softly, 'and he can never marry.'

'I'll buy him a wife.'

'Not a Jewish wife.'

'I'll make him part of this town,' Yohanan shouted, driving his fist against the rabbi's table till the parchments trembled, but the little man did not flinch, for he had anticipated the problem now to be faced by Yohanan, and it could not be dispelled by force.

In Deuteronomy, God's law was stated in clear, cruel terms: 'A bastard shall not enter into the congregation of the Lord; even to his tenth generation shall he not enter . . .' Ten generations was a euphemism for eternity and in Palestine the law was enforced: bastards were outcasts forever and ever. Of course, in simple cases where an unmarried girl had a child by an unmarried father, bastardy was not involved, for the girl could marry any man and make her child legitimate, nor did bastardy result from the frequent instances in which Jewish women were raped by invading soldiers, for such children inherited the Jewishness of their mother and were easily absorbed into Jewish life; but when a man like Yohanan willfully had intercourse with a married woman, the event was a threat to all Jewish homes and the offspring had to be stigmatized as bastard and eternally outcast from the community.

With tears of compassion forming, Rabbi Asher explained this implacable law to the stonecutter: 'Why does Menahem play alone? Because he's a bastard. Why is he marked wherever he goes? He's a bastard. When he grows to manhood, why will he be unable to find a wife? Because of the sin you committed against the law.'

'No!' the distracted workman cried. 'This law I will never accept,' and with this threat he terminated the first of his many confrontations with the rabbi.

During his fourth visit Rabbi Asher asked, 'Why must you fight the law, Yohanan?'

'Because I'm determined to see my son a Jew . . . here in Makor.'

'That he can never be.'

'How shall he live?'

'As an outcast, finding consolation in the fact that those who in this life suffer for the Torah find everlasting bliss hereafter.' This was the second time in recent months that Rabbi Asher had used this concept–a life hereafter–and it was strange to hear a Jewish philosopher speak in this way, for the Torah did not sponsor such belief: immortality, resurrection, heaven as a place of reward and hell as a depth for punishment were largely New Testament doctrine. But the Jews of the Diaspora, because of their long residence among pagan Persians and Greeks, had belatedly acquired these doctrines and now Rabbi Asher felt no betrayal of Judaistic dogma in asserting that Menahem must accept an abominable life on earth in order to win a sweet life hereafter.

'But why must he suffer in this life?' Yohanan demanded. 'A blameless boy?'

'Because you broke the law,' Rabbi Asher said, and before the stonecutter could protest anew, the little groats maker continued, 'In God's Torah there are 613 laws, 365 prohibitive laws, one for each day in the year, 248 affirmative, one for each bone in the body. You are bound by this ancient law. I am bound by it. Even God Himself is bound by its framework, for it establishes order. Your son can find no happiness on this earth and he can never be a Jew, but if he makes himself a slave to the law, he will upon his death win redemption.'

'Why Menahem? Why doesn't the punishment fall on me?'

'It is not within our power,' Rabbi Asher said, 'to understand either the prosperity of the wicked or the affliction of the righteous. Train your son to accept his fate, that he may be an example to others.'

'Is that all you can offer?' the workman asked.

'That is the law,' Rabbi Asher replied.

It was in this year of 335 that the stonecutter began his carving of the lintel over the west door of the main façade, and as he worked he kept Menahem at his side, explaining to him the significance of what he was doing: 'I imagine vines growing out of the earth, and through the floor of the synagogue, and up that wall to bring us grapes. Four bunches. Eight grapes in each bunch. That's enough to make two glasses of wine, one for you and one for me.'

'Do your palm trees grow through the stone floor, too?'

'Of course! And they bring us sweet dates to eat with our wine.'

'And the little wagon? Does it come through the doors?'

'With white horses galloping.'

'What's in the wagon?'

'The law,' Yohanan said. And he was so devoted to the synagogue he was building, this limestone prison that would immure him, that he worked with extra care on the big stone, depicting on its face the things he loved. When it was finally hoisted into place, when the wooden ceiling was thrown across the eight columns of King Herod and the frieze of joyous swastikas was complete, with stone snakes and herons and oak trees to allure the eye, Yohanan concluded that his work in Makor was finished, and he thought that he was free to leave. 'I'll take my son and try some other town. Maybe there . . . with a different rabbi . . .' But when the time came for him to go Rabbi Asher came to see him, and he handed Menahem, now ten years old and a gifted boy, some sweets which he had purchased in a Greek shop.

'Yohanan,' the rabbi said, 'you mustn't leave Makor. You've made this your home and we appreciate you. The people love you.'

'I've been thinking . . . well, a boat to Antioch . . . maybe Cyprus.'

'You can't flee, Yohanan. This is your home . . . your law.'

'The law I won't accept.'

'At Antioch, would you escape it?'

'I'll stop being a Jew,' the stonecutter threatened.

The irresponsible statement Rabbi Asher ignored, saying, 'You and I shall always live in the Galilee. The law and the land bind us to it.'

The idea struck Yohanan forcefully and he broached his next suggestion for the synagogue. 'When I worked at Antioch we made designs with bits of colored stone.'

'Designs?' Rabbi Asher asked suspiciously.

'Not graven images. Mountains and birds, like on the wall.'

'From bits of stone?'

'If we covered the floor with such designs,' the stonecutter suggested, but Rabbi Asher could not visualize what he was talking about, so Yohanan took a stick and outlined a tree on the floor. 'We make it with pieces of stone,' he explained.

As usual Rabbi Asher was apprehensive about unnecessary adornment, but he had just spoken so harshly concerning the law and he was so desirous of keeping the stonecutter in Makor that against his better judgment he approved the floor. 'But no images,' he warned.

So once more Yohanan, seeking a beauty he did not understand, locked himself in Makor. When Menahem was eleven, growing tall like his father, the boy began to suffer from his outcast status, so Yohanan took him on his trips through the Galilee, searching for red and blue and purple limestone. They made a curious pair, a hulking, awkward giant of a man and his handsome son, exploring the countryside. They sought out remote mountain sites and camped beside cliffs which streams had cut through layers of rock, and wherever they probed they found not only colored stone but the absorbing wonder of the Galilee, that timeless habitat of beauty. Crossing swamps they saw the one-legged heron and the gulls which came inland from the sea; Menahem found the cattails, those strange and furry plants which pleased him so much, while his father sat silent, spying upon the jackal and the fox.

When Menahem was twelve, slim and agile where his father was graceless, Yohanan led his workmen to selected sites, where colored rocks were quarried in flat slabs for transportation to Makor. At the quarries father and son saw the inner heart of their land–chips flying from the earth and the roots of large trees cut aside so that the valuable colored strata could be followed–and they caught a new, structural aspect of the Galilee. Looking beyond the dust, they saw the beauty of the valleys, the fall of a stream issuing from the hills or the crest of a mountain they had not seen before, and from these different units a strong design began to take form in Yohanan's stubborn mind. He decided to place in his pavement the soul of the Galilee, no less, and he formulated in vague shapes and weights the final pattern. So far only one part of the design was certain: olive trees and birds would be included, for to him they were the Galilee.

It was in this year of 338 that Menahem, the twelve-year-old son of the stonecutter, first became aware of Jael, the eight-year-old daughter of the groats maker. This occurred when the rabbi's wife, called upon to deliver four extra sacks of groats to a Greek merchant from Ptolemais, could find no men to help her and thought of enlisting Menahem to turn the drying grains and then to grind them between the stones. He enjoyed the work, and when his father disappeared on a tramp through the hills searching for an elusive purple limestone, he stayed on at the groats mill, and one morning as he was turning the stone he looked up to see the rabbi's daughter smiling at him. She was a beautiful child, with blond pigtails, blue eyes and the liveliness of her father, and she had not yet inherited the animosity practiced by the older children toward Menahem.

'Are you the one they throw stones at?' she asked innocently as she watched him work.

'Yes.'

'What's your name?'

'Menahem. My father's building the synagogue.'

'The big man?' she asked, hunching herself over to imitate Yohanan's bearlike walk.

'He would be angry if he saw you making fun of him,' Menahem said with the sensitivity that had been kicked into him by the people of Makor.

She stayed with him, chatting inquisitively, and during the time required for the extra four sacks she watched his motions. 'Father turns the stone the other way,' she advised him. 'Father holds the sack with his knees.' Finally, when the four bags stood ready for the Greek merchant, she perched on top of them, directing Menahem how to clean up.

His work on this emergency job was so much appreciated by the rabbi's wife that she kept him on, and in time he replaced one of the men who had proved to be both lazy and intractable. With Menahem's sober, self-directed energy the mill turned out almost as much cereal as it had under the guidance of Rabbi Asher, and once or twice the perceptive youth caught a glimpse of the future: he would become the foreman at the groats mill and then the contempt that the boys in the streets held for him would vanish. Accompanying this hopeful vision was Jael's presence, day after day; when he went for walks among the olive trees she tagged along, a lovely blue-eyed girl making impulsive observations.

'Sister said I shouldn't play with you, since you're a bastard.'

Menahem did not flush, for the boys of Makor had long since clubbed into him an acceptance of this word. 'Tell your mother you're not playing with me. You're helping me make groats.'

'At the mill it's work,' Jael said. 'But in the olive trees it's playing.'

Often she took his hand as they walked under the benevolent trees, some so old and tattered that they must topple in the next wind, others as young and supple as Jael herself. 'I like to play with you,' she said one day, 'but what is a bastard?'

At twelve Menahem himself was not sure of what the word signified, except that it covered an ugly situation in which he was involved; but at thirteen–that critical age for Jewish boys–he was to discover in full measure the nature of his taint. This was the year of initiation, when he should have entered the synagogue dressed in a new set of clothes, climbed to the rostrum where the Torah was read on Shabbat morning, stood before the sacred scroll and chanted for the first time in public a portion of God's word. At that moment, in the presence of the men of Makor, he would cease being a child and would state with assurance, 'Today I am a man. The things I do from this day on are my responsibility and not my father's.

But when the time came for Menahem to take this dramatic leap from boyhood to manhood, thus entering the adult congregation of Israel, Rabbi Asher, God's Man home from Tverya, had to advise the boy, 'You may not enter the congregation of the Lord, neither now nor to the tenth generation.'

Yohanan began to bellow. He would take his son to Rome. He would halt his work on the mosaic pavement. He contrived other threats that merely made him sound noisy, while his doomed son stood aside–a tall, slender young fellow of thirteen in that agonizing age when the passage of a bird's feather across the hand can cut like a sharpened knife. For three days he listened to his father and Rabbi Asher brawling, and he heard for the first time in brutal clarity the details of his birth. At last he knew what bastardy was and the terrible exclusion it entailed, not for the author of the sin but for the recipient.

Other boys of his age, against whom he had protected himself in the streets, put on their new clothes and made their appearances before the congregation, standing uneasily at attention as Rabbi Asher instructed them in the ways of God. Abraham, the son of Hababli the dyer, a clod of a boy who would never acquire any appreciation of Judaism, to whom the presence of God would never be a reality, stumbled his way through a section of the Torah and proclaimed that he was now a man, and this oaf was accepted into the congregation, but Menahem was not, nor would he ever be.

In despair he fled Makor and for two days no one could find him. Rabbi Asher, sensing the heavy blow that had fallen upon him, was afraid that he might have destroyed himself, as bastards in Palestine sometimes did, but Jael, knowing Menahem's habits, went into the olive grove and found him sleeping in a hollow core of a patriarchal tree beneath which they had once played. Taking his hand she led him back to her father, who said to the outcast, 'You are more of a man than the others, Menahem. On you falls the weight of the law, and the manner in which you accept that burden will determine your dignity on earth and your joy hereafter. My wife says that your work at the groats mill is exceptional. You shall have that job as long as you live, and may God grant repose to your stormy heart.'

'The synagogue?' the boy asked.

'That is forbidden,' the rabbi said, and the sternness of this verdict was so dire, delivered thus to a child of thirteen, that the bearded man wept and took Menahem in his arms, consoling him: 'You shall live as the child of God . . . as the man of God. The sages have said, "The way of a bastard is cruel."' He wanted to say more, but his voice broke with passion, and the two parted.

So his thirteenth year brought to Menahem confusion but also an understanding that many adult men never acquire. At the groats mill he worked intelligently, calculating what must be done to protect the trade, and establishing himself as the practical foreman of the place. It was not unusual that he, an outcast, should be working for the rabbi who had proscribed him; at the dying vats Abraham's father used slaves who were not Jewish, and other Jews hired pagans who still worshipped Baal and Jupiter on the high places back of town. Menahem was happy to have work, and Rabbi Asher was pleased to have at last someone in charge whom he could trust to maintain his high standard.

At the same time the boy's father had reached the stage in building the synagogue when he must begin laying the mosaic floor, and bitter though he was at the treatment accorded his son, he felt inspired to proceed with his work, so whenever Menahem was not busy at the rabbi's mill he helped at the rabbi's synagogue. In these contradictions a youth entirely outside the congregation found both his work and recreation inside Judaism, and in this ambivalent condition his thirteenth year was passed.

Construction of the mosaic had proceeded only a little way when Yohanan found it was necessary to consult with Rabbi Asher, but the bearded expositor had returned to the grape arbor of Tverya, so the stonecutter and his son set out through the forest for Menahem's first trip to the Sea of Galilee; and as they reached Sephet they climbed a steep hill and the boy saw for the first time that radiant body of water and the marble city of Tverya, and they stopped as if the great hand of beauty had halted them: mountains held the lake in a purple embrace; brown fields were as soft as the feathers of birds; gray haze rose from the Jordan; and flowers shone like flickering stars within the meadows. As the stonecutter, in appearance so unlike an artist, looked down at the shimmering lake, he finally visualized the design for his mosaic: mountains, lake, olive trees and birds fell into place and he experienced that consuming urge to create which takes precedence over all other compulsions. So far as Yohanan was concerned, the pavement was complete; now all he must do was spend five years in executing it.

When he entered the gracious, decaying city and led Menahem along the waterfront, he was half pleased, half irritated to notice that many girls lounging near the fishing boats turned to stare at the handsome youth, and he regretted that he had not followed his earlier instinct and taken the boy to a new life in a new land, but building the synagogue had held him captive and his conflicting obligations were tangled in his mind. Finally he found the mud-walled house where the expositors were meeting, and there he sent a messenger to advise Rabbi Asher that visitors had arrived. After an hour the little rabbi appeared, his eyes sad because of some wish of God that he had been unable to explain to his colleagues, but when he saw Menahem standing gravely in the sunlight he was reminded of the boy's honorable acceptance of his burden, and admiration for the youth cleansed his mind of the sorrow it had been harboring.

'I am pleased to see you, Menahem,' he said gently.

'We are ready to start the floor,' Yohanan interrupted.

'All right,' he said with no enthusiasm.

'I lack one thing.'

'Get it.'

'I'll have to go to Ptolemais . . . with money.'

Rabbi Asher frowned. Like the rest of the great expositors he saw little money, but he was willing to listen. 'What's the problem?'

'The design I plan . . .'

'What is the design?'

'The Galilee.'

'What about it?'

'It needs purple. At many points it needs purple stone. And I've found none.'

'I saw some.' the rabbi said. 'Beyond Sephet.'

'I saw that too. It crumbles.'

'In Ptolemais? Have they purple stones?'

'No, but they have purple glass. Cut into squares.'

Rabbi Asher considered this problem for some minutes. He was willing for Yohanan to build the floor but he wanted to spend no money for it. 'What do you need purple for?' he parried.

'Kingfisher's feathers. The hoopoe bird, too.'

Rabbi Asher studied this carefully. 'Use other birds.'

'I thought of that,' Yohanan replied. 'But I also need purple for the mountains.'

'I suppose so.' He turned and addressed the boy as his equal. 'Is the mill making money, Menahem?' The boy nodded, and the rabbi said, 'Buy the glass in Ptolemais.'

'I'll get some golden glass, too,' Yohanan said.

'Gold? That sounds like adornment.'

'It is,' the stonecutter admitted, 'but it will make the pavement glisten . . . in just a few spots.'

Rabbi Asher conceded and was about to dismiss his workmen when he thought of Menahem. 'Wait a moment,' he said and left to consult with his associates, who were discussing whether a housewife was permitted to throw out used dishwater on Shabbat. The argument had been in process for some days, with the Sephet rabbi arguing liberally that throwing out the dishwater was a logical extension of preparing the Shabbat meal, which rabbis had always permitted, but with the Biri rabbi contending that throwing out the water was equivalent to sowing, 'for from the freshly watered earth seeds might spring forth,' and this was specifically prohibited. Now Asher interrupted the expositors with a problem of different gravity.

'The stonecutter of whom I spoke . . . and his bastard son. They're outside and I thought to bring them in.'

The Kefar Nahum rabbi protested against discussing individual cases, but an old man who had come from Babylonia for these sessions said, 'Our great Rabbi Akiba would have stopped discussion even with God in order to speak with children. Fetch the boy.'

So Rabbi Asher returned to the street and summoned Yohanan and Menahem into the cool courtyard, where the scholars saw with their own eyes what a promising youth was among them, and the old man from Babylonia cried, 'With the appearance of such a youth the sun rises!'

Menahem was made to stand facing the great expositors, while his father remained against the wall, listening, and at last the scholars reached a typical rabbinical conclusion: 'A bastard may under no circumstances enter the congregation of the Lord for ten generations. But there is a way.'

The old man from Babylonia explained: 'Rabbi Tarfon, of blessed memory, and Rabbi Shammua, too, said, "Let the bastard boy when he is past the age of twelve steal an object worth more than ten drachmas. He is arrested and sold into slavery to a Hebrew family. Then he is married to another Hebrew slave. And after five years the owner emancipates them both and they become freed-men. And as new freedmen their children will be welcomed into the congregation of the Lord."'

Yohanan heard the words with dumb astonishment. While the rabbis solemnly discussed where the theft must take place to make it an honest theft, and how the boy must be arrested and before what witnesses, the big stonecutter felt that a world of incomprehensibility was crashing about his ears. This was insanity, what the rabbis were saying, and it would take a man with no beard and no learning to tell them so. In bitterness he looked at his tall son as he stood self-consciously before the judges who were counseling this extra-ordinary course of action, and he was inspired to reach out and grab the boy by the hand and lead him from that confused company, but then he heard the old rabbi from Babylonia calling him, and he found himself moving obediently to stand beside his afflicted son.

'Yohanan, stonecutter of Makor,' the saintly old man was saying, 'you see how the irresponsible actions of a headstrong man lead him and his offspring into trouble. Rabbi Asher tells us that you were warned not to contract an illegal alliance with a married woman, but you went ahead. Now you have no wife and your son is in grave trouble . . .'

Up to this point Menahem had stood calm before the judges, accepting their review of his case as a repetition of the abuse he had received since childhood; even Rabbi Asher's talks with him in Makor had been so understood; but now as the stranger from Babylonia droned on with words of an impersonal gravity 'never able to marry . . . an outcast forever from the Jews . . . only recourse is selling himself into slavery . . . he can never be clean, but his children can be saved . . .' the boy caught the full force of their meaning and uttered a convulsive sob, covering his face with his hands to mask his shame. Once he looked up to seek consolation, but the judges had none to offer. Finally Yohanan put his arm about him, saying quietly, 'Come. We must go back to work,' but Menahem could not move, and his father had to drag him away.

If the Talmud which the rabbis were compiling under the grape arbor of Tverya had consisted only of laws as remorseless as the one invoked against Menahem ben Yohanan, neither the Talmud nor Judaism could have long endured, but this was not the case; the Talmud was also a testimony to the joy of Jewish living. Its preaching on the law was hard and clear, but side by side it contained abundant passages which tempered that law to make the finished document a singing, laughing, hopeful summary. The Talmud was a literature of a people, crammed helter-skelter with songs and sayings, fables and fancy; and one of the reasons why the rabbis from Kefar Nahum, Biri and Sephet were so eager to work upon it was that their meetings were so much fun: lively argument sparked by the joy of personal clashes and a sense of being close to God.

Only a massive work could hope to capture the vigor and fellowship of these meetings, and the Talmud became such a masterpiece. Its final size was difficult to comprehend: the Torah upon which it was built was brief; the Mishna was many times as long; the Gemara was much longer than the Mishna; and the commentaries of Maimonides and the rest were in turn much longer that the Gemara, the Mishna and the Torah together. The Torah consisted of five books, the Talmud 523. The Torah could be printed in two hundred and fifty pages, but the finished Talmud required twenty-two volumes.

In a major commentary on this vast, formless work the name of Rabbi Asher, God's Man, appears eleven times, three in connection with legal decisions, eight in those frivolous, lovely passages which evoke the day-to-day life of Jews in Palestine: 'Rabbi Asher ha-Garsi told us: Antigonus the wily seller of olive oil used three tricks. He allowed sediment to gather in the bottom of his measure so that it contained less. At the time of judging he tilted the measure sideways. And he taught himself to pour so that a large bubble of air formed in the middle of his jug. At his death God judged him according to his own measure. The sediment of his sin nearly filled the jug. It was tilted so far to one side that most of eternity slipped from him. And that day God poured with such a bubble!'

Two quotations from the groats maker concerned the wildlife of the Galilee, as he had observed it on his trips: 'Rabbi Asher told us: the hoopoe bird was walking along the ground and the bee eater was flying in the sky. Cried the latter, "I am closer to God." But Elijah, peering down from heaven, warned, "He who works in the soil is always in the arms of God." From which Rabbi Bag Huna deduced, "This proves that the farmer is closer to God than the merchant." But Rabbi Asher replied, "Not so, Huna. All men who work are equal."'

It was this Rabbi Bag Huna who offered the famous definition of a Talmudic scholar: 'He should be able to concentrate so thoroughly upon the Torah that a seventeen-year-old girl could pass his desk completely naked without distracting him.' To which Rabbi Asher said, 'I fear not many would pass that test.'

Rabbi Asher made three comments upon the Torah: 'Get old and get gray, get tired and get toothless, but get Torah.' 'The law is like a jar filled with honey. If you pour in water, the honey will run out and after a while you will have cheapened the mixture until there is no honey left.' 'At the gate of the shop a man has many friends. But at the gate of Torah he has God.'

He is remembered principally, however, for the echo of laughter that hung over Tverya when he was present. 'Rabbi Asher the groats maker said: A man who laughs is more to be cherished than one who weeps; a woman who sings, than one who wails. And God is very close to the child who dances for reasons which he cannot explain.' He argued for a God who loved even outcasts like Menahem, the stonecutter's boy. He punctured sham, upheld the dignity of work, spoke for a happy marriage in which husband and wife shared equally, and bore constant testimony that God was a generous and forgiving deity. 'Rabbi Asher ha-Garsi said: Few have been tested as Rab Naaman of Makor was tested. When the Romans were about to destroy his town, Rab Naaman was offered safety through flight, and he deserted his friends. When he died he threw himself before God, crying, "The scar of that shameful act is still upon my heart," but God lifted him from the ground and said, "When you fled through the tunnel that night you took with you a new understanding of the law, and with Rabbi Akiba you saved My Torah. One shred of the law administered with compassion is more important than a hundred towns, and the scars on your heart I brush away."'

Rabbi Asher's final comment on the Torah was simple: 'He who knows Torah and does not teach it to others is like a single red poppy blooming in the desert.'

His adherence to this last principle made it impossible for him to refuse when the rabbis asked him to instruct students in the yeshiva operated at Tverya for the training of young scholars. Classes convened in an old Roman building by the lake, and there Rabbi Asher would stand, a little old man in a white beard, talking at random about the joy he found in Judaism: 'My guiding light has always been Rabbi Akiba. He saved the Mishna for us, and I love the memory of this man. From childhood I aspired to follow in his steps.' When students asked why he considered Akiba the greatest of the rabbis, he replied, 'He cultivated a personal relationship with God, but he also directed himself to the problems of how his Jews could at the same time be faithful to God who controlled heaven and obedient to the Romans who controlled the earth. Today we could learn much from Akiba.' When his students, some of them hot-headed young men who were growing restless under Byzantine rule, brought the discussion down to the present, asking how he would behave toward the Byzantine invaders, he replied, without equivocation, 'Study the final hours of Akiba. Every possible concession he made to Rome, but in the end he had to proclaim that when the will of God and the law of empire clash the former must prevail.'

It was therefore each student's responsibility to ascertain God's intentions, and to help them in this task Rabbi Asher proposed certain drills: 'If our desire is to uncover God's wishes, we must develop minds that can penetrate shadows, for the mists produced by living obscure the truth and you cannot discern it unless you sharpen your wits.' At this point he would unroll a scroll of Torah and read from Leviticus: 'These also shall be unclean unto you among the creeping things that creep upon the earth; the weasel, and the mouse, and the tortoise after his kind, and the ferret, and the chameleon, and the lizard, and the snail, and the mole. These are unclean to you.' Having read this, he would say, 'God himself forbids His people to eat the lizard. I want you to find one hundred reasons why the lizard should be eaten.' When his students protested that this might be blasphemous, Rabbi Asher explained, 'Again and again the great rabbis have warned us that when God handed Moses the sacred law, He placed it in the hands of men so that it might exist on earth and not in heaven, to be interpreted by men. The Torah is what we say it is, you and I in all our frailty, and if God made a mistake in forbidding us to eat the lizard, we had better find out about it.' He would crash his hands upon the table and cry, 'The Torah exists only on earth, in the hearts of men, and it is what we say it is.' He always told his students of the day on which the Prophet Elijah came back to earth following a great dispute among the rabbis, who asked him fearfully, 'Was God angry when we changed His word?' and Elijah told them, 'No! God clapped His hands gleefully and cried, "My children have defeated Me! They live on earth and they know the problems of earth. O, My beloved children, always be as wise as you were today."' Sometimes students would protest, 'But you speak of God as if He were a human being, and yesterday you told us He is a spirit,' and the little rabbi would thunder, 'Of course He's a spirit. He has no body nor hands either. I'm telling you a story. Accept it as that.' And he would stomp from the room, stopping at the door to shout back, 'Tomorrow! A hundred reasons why Jews should eat lizards.' Then he would add softly, 'Imagine, perhaps one of you, in this little room in this little city, will correct the error of God, and tomorrow night He will clap His hands again and cry, "Once more My children have defeated Me! That blessed city of Tverya."'

He had found that when a man was driven to construct a hundred sophistical reasons for denying Leviticus, the man had to consider the ultimate nature of God. Sometimes the yeshiva students contrived ingenious answers: 'In Exodus it says that after God had created all the animals and before He created man, He reviewed His work and it is written, "And God saw that it was good." Since He made this judgment after the creation of the lizard but before He created man, the lizard must have been good in the abstract, always and forever, without reference to man. And it must still be good, and can therefore be eaten.'

Another student once argued, 'God created first the earth, and as a father loves most of his first-born, so God loves first of all His earth. Of all the animals that live upon this beloved earth, the lizard presses his belly closest to the earth and cannot live away from it. Therefore he is even closer to the earth that God loves than man, and as part of the earth he must be good, and Jews can therefore eat him.'

One year an especially clever student advanced an argument that would be retained in the Talmud: 'We often have to choose between two precepts of our Lord that appear contradictory. Now listen. In the commandments He tells us, "Thou shalt not steal," yet He Himself stole a rib from Adam to give mankind its greatest blessing, woman. Now He tells us not to eat lizards, but if we did we might find them to be a blessing also.'

Day after day Rabbi Asher encouraged his students to pursue their adroit reasonings, and when the last had been proved specious, he surprised everyone by saying, 'Now bring me a hundred reasons why the lizard cannot be eaten,' and when this had been accomplished he felt that his students were beginning to acquire the tenacity required of anyone who presumed to study Jewish law. He loved to tell his students a story which summarized his attitudes on this matter of intellectual inspection: 'A Roman came to rabbi Gimzo the Water Carrier, and asked, "What is this study of the law that you Jews engage in?" and Gimzo replied, "I shall explain. There were two men on a roof, and they climbed down the chimney. One's face became sooty. The other's not. Which one washed his face?'' The Roman said, "That's easy, the sooty one, of course." Gimzo said, "No. The man without the soot looked at his friend, saw the man's face was dirty, assumed that his was too, and washed it." Cried the Roman, "Ah ha! So that's the study of law. Sound reasoning." But Gimzo said, "You foolish man, you don't understand. Let me explain again. Two men on a roof. They climb down a chimney. One's face is sooty, the other's not, Which one washes?" The Roman said, "As you just explained, the man without the soot." Gimzo cried, "No, you foolish one! There was a mirror on the wall and the man with the dirty face saw how sooty it was and washed it." The Roman said, "Ah ha! So that's the study of law! Conforming to the logical." But Rabbi Gimzo said, "No, you foolish one. Two men climbed down the chimney. One's face became sooty? The other's not? That's impossible. You're wasting my time with such a proposition." And the Roman said, 'So that's the law! Common sense." And Gimzo said, "You foolish man! Of course it was possible. When the first man climbed down the chimney he brushed the soot away. So the man who followed found none to mar him." And the Roman cried, "That's brilliant, Rabbi Gimzo. Law is getting at the basic facts." And for the last time Gimzo said, "No, you foolish man. Who could brush all the soot from a chimney? Who can ever understand all the facts?" Humbly the Roman asked, "Then what is the law?'' and Gimzo said quietly, "It's doing the best we can to ascertain God's intention, for there were indeed two men on a roof, and they did climb down the same chimney. The first man emerged completely clean while it was the second who was covered with soot, and neither man washed his face, because you forgot to ask me whether there was any water in the basin. There was none.'''

While Rabbi Asher in Tverya taught this compassionate interpretation of the Torah, Yohanan and his son hiked back to Makor under the heavy burden of their portion of the law, and when Menahem reached home he sought consolation in hard work at the groats mill, where Jael came to talk to him, and he told his father, 'I cannot go to Ptolemais'; so Yohanan went alone and after some days returned with two donkey-loads of purple glass and a small parcel of golden cubes. He was now ready to proceed with his masterwork.

In an open-front shop not far from the new synagogue he installed six men whose job it was to take the slabs of colored limestone which had been quarried from the Galilean hills and to saw them into long strips somewhat less than half an inch square across the face. Then, with chisels, they took the lengths of stone and chopped off half-inch segments, so that at the end of the day each man had about his feet a little pile of colored cubes, and when the reds and blues and greens and browns had accumulated in sufficient quantity Yohanan began building the mosaic.

In his fourteenth and fifteenth years Menahem helped his father place the cubes: on a bed of thin cement spread over the original floor Menahem would fill in the background spaces with ordinary gray-white cubes, while his father sketched the areas where color was required, and gradually the two would bring the large design down to a small focus where some bird or tree was indicated, and here with deft, stubby fingers Yohanan would construct from a bagful of mixed stones the gracious forms that made the pavement come alive. With a small wedged hammer he would strike off slivers of brown rock and with these would build a mid-summer fern, dry and withered as it bent in the wind off the hills, and on the tip of the fern he would place a bee eater, perfectly constructed of pastel blue and yellow squares, with bits of the purple glass for wing tippings; slowly the father and son evoked in the synagogue of Makor the essence of their homeland: the sweeping hills and silvery streams, the crested hoopoe bird in mauve and white, his tail outlined in purple glass from Ptolemais. It never occurred to the two modest workmen that they were creating a masterpiece, but they did sense from time to time that they were composing a muted song to the goodness of the Galilee as they had come to know it.

The day finally came when an olive tree was needed in one corner of the design, and Yohanan stepped aside to watch approvingly as Menahem constructed his first object: with brown and green stones, with a few touches of red and blue, he built a living tree on the floor of the synagogue and Yohanan realized that in his son he had found an artist. But with each stone the boy laid he grew older; he was now sixteen, when Jewish youths could be betrothed, and in the mornings as he worked at the groats mill he would listen while Jael—now a striking child with flaxen hair—chattered about the wedding of such-and-such a couple. If things had been otherwise, a young fellow like Menahem with a good job and clean appearance would have been considered a catch; but no uncles with nieces of marriageable age came to discuss wedding contracts with Yohanan, and the last years of work on the mosaic were spent in deepening bitterness.

Menahem became eighteen and nineteen and the net of the law closed more tightly about him. Now the boys of his age were mostly married and some had children of their own, but no girl in the town would look at him, except young Jael, who was becoming a beautiful young woman. At fifteen she found it embarrassing to wait at the mill, but sometimes she intercepted Menahem as he walked from the mill to the synagogue, where the final stages of work were in progress. Occasionally the two would leave the town and stroll among the olive trees, and there one evening beside the ancient tree in whose cavernous interior Menahem had once slept he kissed the rabbi's daughter for the first time. It was like the creation of a benevolent new world, the first experience of belonging he had known since childhood, and his love for Jael became the cardinal hope of his ugly life.

The ensuing years were as painfully lovely as any that Menahem would know: he could not court Jael openly, but he could kiss her secretly; yet he knew that she was reaching the age when proper suitors must appear with attractive offers. Her marriage was delayed because Rabbi Asher still had one older daughter to marry off before he got to Jael, and this occupied his attention when he was in Makor. Finally, in the year 350, the groats maker found an unlikely family with a son who had a slanted eye and no great prospects, and this fellow agreed to marry the rabbi's older girl, so Menahem knew that Jael's turn was next.

One day as he worked in the mill filling sacks which the rabbi held open, he blurted out, 'Rabbi Asher, can I marry Jael?'

The little rabbi, now sixty-nine years old, snapped his head forward so that his beard interrupted the flow of the groats. 'What did you ask?' he demanded.

'Jael and I want to marry.' the boy said.

Rabbi Asher let the mouth of the sack fall shut, ignoring the groats that Menahem spilled about his feet. Without speaking he left the mill and went to the synagogue, where he upbraided Yohanan. 'What have you encouraged your son to do?' he asked.

'Work hard. Save money. And leave this place.'

'What did you tell him about my daughter?'

'I never spoke to him . . .'

'That's not true!' the rabbi stormed.

Getting no satisfaction from Yohanan, he ran home, where he found Jael working with her mother. Unawed by her father's excitement the girl admitted that she loved Menahem. 'He's so much wiser than the others. He works hard, too.'

Her words had to be respected, for they carried their own justification; in the five unsatisfactory marriages which Rabbi Asher had arranged for his older daughters he had not come close to locating a husband as promising as Menahem ben Yohanan. In a kind of desperation he had been forced to accept men who were lazy, or not observant Jews, or stupid, and now his youngest daughter had discovered for herself a husband who would be an adornment to any household: a young man capable of running the groats mill and likely to prove a good father. Without speaking further the little rabbi left Jael and went to the room where it was his custom to pray.

Throwing himself on the floor he cried, 'God, what must I do?' He rose, dancing here and there, bowing his body, running backward and forward, and again prostrating himself full length in the dust. He then prayed for nearly an hour, struggling with the concepts of God, of Torah and of law. Finally, a little man worn out from his wrestling with the deity, he lay humbly on the floor and accepted judgment. When he understood clearly what was required he rose, returned to where Jael waited and kissed her with a tenderness unusual even for him who had never feared to demonstrate his love for his children. Without speaking he left the house and went to the dye vats, where within a few minutes he arranged a contract for the marriage of his daughter Jael to Abraham, son of the dyer Hababli.

With maximum speed the wedding was arranged. A canopy was erected at the rabbi's house and jars of wine were purchased from the Greek who kept a shop near the old Christian church, but on the morning of the wedding Jael imprudently ran to the groats mill, where she stood before Menahem, sobbing, 'Oh, Menahem. It was you I wanted.'

Her father, having anticipated such rashness, quickly appeared to lead his daughter home, and Menahem spoke to her no more. That evening he watched from the edge of the crowd as Abraham, whom he had known as a graceless boy and a bully, stood with a gold cap on his head, waiting under the canopy as ashen-faced Jael was brought to him: he had not expected his father to acquire for him so lovely a bride. When the improper wedding was concluded, the prayers having been recited by Rabbi Asher himself, when the glass was broken and feet had trod the pieces, Menahem, watching in anguish, swore that he would no longer live in such pain.

He waited until the bride had been carried off by the still befuddled groom, and the guests had drunk the wine and had departed in the night, then sought refuge in the olive grove where he hid in the darkness. When morning came he went soberly to the home of Rabbi Asher and asked to speak with him. The little guardian of the law sat in his alcove, his long beard covering his hands, and he asked, 'What do you wish, Menahem?'

'Am I truly sentenced to such a life?'

Slowly Rabbi Asher took down a scroll of the Torah, unrolling it to a passage whose words he indicated with a thin forefinger: 'A bastard shall not enter into the congregation of the Lord, even to his tenth generation.' He took away his hands and the scroll rewound itself, as if it had a life of its own.

'I cannot accept it. I'll go to Antioch.'

To Rabbi Asher the threat was familiar: nearly a quarter of a century before in this room Yohanan had uttered those same words, but the stonecutter had found himself held fast by custom and had not gone to Antioch. Quietly the little rabbi explained, 'If you did flee to some other city, you would find yourself in the arms of Jews, where the law abides.'

'There's no escape?'

'None.'

It was now that Menahem voluntarily reopened the subject which he had first heard discussed twelve years before under the grape vines of Tverya and which he had often subsequently pondered. With deliberate care he asked, 'But if tonight I steal goods worth ten drachmas . . .'

Eagerly Rabbi Asher replied, 'We would arrest you, sell you as a slave, marry you to another slave, and after five years set you completely free.'

'And I would be clean?'

'Not you. But your children.' The old man paused. He was approaching his final years and was increasingly aware of his responsibilities as God's Man, and something of the joy and love of the non-legal discussions in Tverya flooded his heart, and he confessed, 'Menahem, you are my son, the keeper of my mill. Please, please steal the ten drachmas' worth and win back your place within the law.' Leaving his parchments he ran with short steps to where Menahem stood, and throwing his arms about the young man, kissed him and cried, 'At last you will be a Jew of the congregation.'

In this way Menahem finally submitted himself to the law. Departing from the rabbi he headed back to the synagogue to ask his father to arrange a theft and an arrest before witnesses so that he might be sold as a fictitious slave; but as he went to inform Yohanan of his submission he met coming up the hill into town a caravan of donkeys, architects, stone masons and real slaves led by the priest Eusebius, a tall, sober Spaniard who had served in Constantinople and who was now coming in his black robes and silver crucifix to build the Basilica of St. Mary Magdalene. He was a thin, solemn man of imposing stature, gray at the temples, lined in the face, and he entered Makor with the stately spirituality of one familiar with God. The first citizen he encountered was Menahem, visibly perplexed, and for a moment the two strangers stared at each other. Then, surprisingly, the Spaniard's austere face broke into a warm, enveloping smile; the lines in his cheeks deepened and his somber eyes glowed with a promise of friendship. He bowed slightly to Menahem, who felt himself drawn to this impressive churchman who had come to modify the town.

THE TELL

When John Cullinane lived in Chicago he attended Catholic mass occasionally and funerals rather often, but whenever he worked overseas he tried to attend local Catholic churches regularly in order to see their rich variation in architecture and ritual. For example, at the end of two months' work at Makor he had prayed with the Carmelite monks on Mount Carmel, with the Salesians at Nazareth, with the Benedictines at the Galilean church of Loaves and Fishes, with the Syrian Maronites in Haifa, and with the Greek Catholics at Akko.

He found the strange services exciting, not only from the spiritual point of view but also from the historical; there were some liturgies he could scarcely understand, while others seemed rather close to the Irish church he had known as a boy, but common to all was evidence of Catholicism's ability to accommodate itself to many cultures, relying upon a central core of authority to insure the continuity. The more Cullinane saw of his ancient church in the Holy Land the more impressed he became with its vitality, for although the state of Israel was predominantly Jewish, Cullinane discovered everywhere this vigorous Catholic continuum based upon Arab Christians who, sometimes against formidable tyranny from either Rome or Constantinople, had retained their special rites since the early centuries.

By no means had Cullinane visited all the types of Catholic church available in the Galilee; he hoped especially to see those mysterious branches which had broken off from Rome; the Greek Orthodox in Kefar Nahum, the Russian Orthodox in Tiberias. And he was interested in the Monophysite groups that had rejected both Rome and Constantinople: the Abyssinians, the Armenian Gregorians, the Egyptian Copts. But the nature of his work halted Sunday excursions, for at Friday noon each week all digging at Makor stopped, and none of course was permitted on Saturday, which was the Jewish Shabbat. Then on Sunday digging resumed, and since this was the first workday of the week, he felt that he must be present. He was thus kept from exploring further into the local life of his own church, and although this irritated him somewhat as an archaeologist, he felt no loss as a worshiper, for had he been at home with a free American-style Sunday he would rarely have gone to the local cathedral.

What he did do was what he had done wherever he had been engaged in excavations: each Friday afternoon he climbed into his jeep, usually alone, and drove to some nearby village to participate in the Jewish sunset services which welcomed Shabbat. There he would mingle with the crowd, put an embroidered yarmulke on the back of his head, and try to penetrate the mystery of the ancient religion into which his workmen were digging. He did not do this because he was inclined towards the Jewish interpretation of life—although he found it congenial—but rather because as a man who would spend ten years excavating at Makor it behooved him to know as much as he could about the civilization that he was exhuming.

He had behaved in this way when excavating in Egypt, where he had been a faithful worshiper in the Friday mosques, and when digging in Arizona, rising before dawn to participate in the evangelical rites practiced by the Mesa people. If in the future he were called to dig in India he would there become a sympathetic Hindu, and in Japan a Buddhist. His instinct in this matter was good: a man who would later presume to write about the successive layer of life in Makor required to know as much as possible about all aspects of that life, and he had already spent a dozen years studying the languages, ceramics, metal ware and numismatics of the Holy Land, none of which was so instructive as the religion.

So as the summer passed, John Cullinane became less a Catholic and more a Jew, immersing himself in the weekly ritual that had kept the Jews together through dispersions that would have destroyed a lesser people. In fact, he grew to love the coming of Friday sunset, when Jewish men, freshly washed and dressed, walked like kings to their synagogues to go through the rites of welcoming Queen Shabbat. More sacred than any other day of the Hebrew calendar was this Shabbat, when the creation of the world and God's compact with the Jews were remembered, and it occurred once each week, more sacred perhaps than Easter to a Christian or Ramadan to a Muslim. Inside the synagogue Cullinane waited with a kind of joy for the arrival of that moment in the ceremony when the Jews began to sing the powerful hymn composed many centuries ago in Zefat. The cantor would be chanting some quite ordinary passage whose words Cullinane could not understand, and then of a sudden the man would throw back his head and utter the joyous cry:

> 'Come, My Beloved, let us meet the Bride.
> The presence of Shabbat let us receive.'

Nine long verses followed, but after each the cry of joy would be repeated, with all the congregation joining, and Cullinane memorized the words of both the cry and the verses, singing them under his breath as the cantor intoned the mystical words which reported the love of the Jews for this sacred day:

> 'Come, let us go to greet Shabbat,
> For it is a wellspring of blessing.
> From the beginning it was ordained,
> Last in production, first in thought.
> And they that spoil thee shall be a spoil,
> And all that would swallow thee shall be far away.
> Thy God shall rejoice over thee
> As a bridegroom rejoiceth over his bride.'

One aspect of the Shabbat hymn Cullinane could not get into focus. At the beginning of his stay he rarely went to the same synagogue twice, for he wanted to savor the full range of Jewish custom, and just as Protestants assumed that there was only one Catholic church, forgetting the rich variation that marked the east where the religion was born, so he as a Catholic had supposed that there was but one Judaism; yet here in the land where that religion was also born he had an opportunity to see the great diversity, for in six different synagogues the great Shabbat hymn would be sung in six wildly different ways: as a German march, a desert wail, a Polish burial lament, a Russian huzza, a modern syncopated melody and an ancient oriental chant. Part of the pleasure of the Shabbat service, Cullinane found, lay in trying to guess what tune would be used for the central song.

He asked Eliav about this, and the tall scholar put down his pipe to say, 'They tell us that the Lecha Dodi has been fitted to more varied tunes than any other song in the world. I think a man could go to Shabbat services for a year and hear a new melody every time. Each cantor has his own version, which is right, because this is a most personal cry of joy.'

'Am I free to come up with my rendition?' Cullinane asked. 'Heavy on the Irish lilt?'

'I'm sure the Jews of Ireland must have their own Lecha Dodi,' Eliav said.

It was disappointing to Cullinane that he could not get any of his staff to attend synagogue services with him: Eliav refused; Vered excused herself, 'As I said before, the synagogue's for men'; Tabari said, 'I find that if I enter a local synagogue dressed in full Arab robes, bow toward Mecca and cry, "Allah is Allah and Muhammad is his Prophet," I am apt to cause resentment. You go.' And of course none of the local kibbutzniks ever attended worship, having outlawed even the building of a synagogue on their property. So Cullinane was forced to go alone.

Toward the end of the digging season, after he had visited perhaps two dozen different synagogues, he settled upon three that exemplified for him the essential spirit of Judaism, and to these he returned. Along the ridge of Mount Carmel stood an ugly, corrugated-iron building served by a cantor, a small fastidious man with a handsome silver beard, who could sing like an opera star, and worship here was especially pleasing when the cantor brought with him a choir of seven little boys, all with side curls, to sing the Lecha Dodi in piercing falsetto while he underscored them with his baritone. Often, as they sang, a cool breeze would come up the wadi from the sea and it took no effort for Cullinane to imagine that God was present at that moment. But whether the Irishman visited this synagogue for that sense of a very ancient Judaism which the mean building conveyed or for the music, he would not have wished to say.

He also enjoyed going back to Zefat to the tiny synagogue he had visited with Paul Zodman, that jumbled, noise-crammed room where the Vodzher Rebbe huddled in the corner while his handful of fur-capped Russian Jews worshiped in the undisciplined manner of the past. It was indeed – as Cullinane had once said – 'like seventeen orchestras and no conductor,' but it was also a fundamental, haunting experience of the reality of God. In this synagogue, when the time came for men to chant the Lecha Dodi, they did so in seven or eight different tempos, melodies and accents, and one evening when the strange fury of the place caught him unexpectedly, Cullinane found himself bellowing at the top of his voice, to an Irish tune that he had composed while working on the dig:

> 'Come, my Beloved, let us meet the Bride.
> The presence of Shabbat let us receive.'

And the Vodzher Rebbe, so old that he seemed immortal, looked up from his corner approvingly.

But the synagogue which in the end enlisted Cullinane's steady patronage was the small Sephàrdi one in Akko, into which he had stumbled that day when he joined the procession to Elijah's Cave. It was neither spacious like the one in Haifa, nor emotionally intense like the Vodzher Rebbe's in Zefat, but it was a warm, congenial place of worship. The Sephardi ritual, more lyric than the Ashkenazi, was to Cullinane's liking and its tune for the Lecha Dodi became his favorite, for it moved along with a spirit that seemed the essence of Judaism: these Sephardim were actually welcoming God's holy day, and when at the height of the song all in the congregation turned to face the entrance, as if Shabbat herself were about to join the singing, it was a moment of transcendent joy that Cullinane had not experienced in other religions.

Once, sitting in the Akko synagogue on Friday evening, he thought: As a place of worship this is really a dump. The other day I drove to the top of Mount Tabor to attend mass at the Franciscan basilica. It must be one of the most exquisite churches in the world. And now this. I wonder why synagogues are physically so unattractive? Judaism must be the only major religion that doesn't stress beautiful temples. Perhaps it has something more important . . . a sense of participating brotherhood, of unity in diversity. On this Friday, as the sun moves across the earth from Fiji where the day begins, to Hawaii where it ends, when sunset comes Jews everywhere will be chanting this same song of welcome . . . each to his own preferred tune.

The next day as he sat worshiping with the Sephardim in this small synagogue, Cullinane received a strong rebuke which he would not forget during the remaining years at the dig. Jewish congregations did not take public collections the way Christians did; they clung to the very old custom of gathering money to run their synagogues by selling off certain ritual functions: in most synagogues of the mid-twentieth century these contributions were arranged in private, but the Sephardim of Akko–following an ancient tradition–actually conducted a Shabbat auction during holy worship, and it disturbed Cullinane to find the synagogue taken over by a brazen-voiced auctioneer who shouted, 'Come now, who will pay fifteen lira for the honor of reading Torah?' And by such public bidding he sold off seven or eight of the holy functions, with the congregation aware of how much each man was willing to pay for his privileges. By some movement of his face Cullinane must have betrayed his disapproval of this profanation of a religious rite, for at the end of the worship the big woman, Shulamit, who had taken him to Elijah's Cave, came up and asked in English, 'Disgusting, wasn't it?'

'What?' Cullinane asked, trying to appear innocent.

'That auction . . . in a house of God.'

'Well . . . '

'It's almost as bad as the bingo games I used to attend in your churches . . . in Chicago.' And she threw her big arm about him and they went to an Arab restaurant by the sea, where they got drunk on arrack.

The first person in Makor whom Father Eusebius met officially was the military commander of the Byzantine garrison, under whose jurisdiction he placed the workmen he had brought with him; in Makor the relationship between church and army would be intimate and Eusebius was determined that it start correctly. He then proceeded to the existing Christian church, a sorry affair at the east of town, where he greeted the uneducated Syrian priest with gentle condescension; he intended no familiarity with this schismatic. And then, because he knew that a large portion of Makor's population was Jewish, he picked his way carefully through the narrow streets to the groats mill, where he drew his black silk robes about him and stared down at Rabbi Asher, bare-armed and white-bearded as he sweated over sacks of cereal.

The tall Spaniard nodded graciously, half-smiled and said, 'I'm told that you're a scholar, honored by your people.'

Rabbi Asher wiped his forehead and tried to find a seat for his visitor, but the mill was disordered and he could locate nothing suitable. The austere visage of the Spaniard relaxed as he said, 'On the boat I sat for many days.'

'Fetch a chair from the synagogue,' Asher directed his foreman, and for the second time the slim visitor noticed Menahem.

'Your son?' he asked as the young man disappeared.

'I wish he were,' Asher said, feeling an instinctive liking for the Spaniard.

'As you know,' Father Eusebius began, 'I've come to build a basilica.' He hesitated. 'A large basilica.'

The acceptance that Rabbi Asher had begun to feel vanished. Why did he have to say a big church? he thought. But Father Eusebius continued, assuring the rabbi that it was his hope not to disrupt Makor but to bring it prosperity. 'We shall build rapidly,' he explained, 'and will import no more soldiers than we already have.' He paused. 'I shall hope that you will instruct your Jews . . .' He left the sentence unfinished. Nodding graciously he left just as Menahem ran up with the chair. 'We shall save that for another day.' He said charmingly as he went off to inspect the town which would occupy him in the years ahead.

The Makor to which Father Eusebius had come to build his basilica looked far different from the way it had in its days of beauty under King Herod, and almost nothing that the meticulous Spaniard saw could have reminded him of the Greek charm that had once invested this place. The walls were down, so that the settlement lacked any external unity: houses now perched precariously on the steep slopes and were propped up by timbers that gave the impression of a village hanging out its wooden washing. The lovely forum was gone; not a temple stood nor even the walls of a temple. The residential palace had long since been torn apart for building stone, and here and there throughout the town one could find the base upon which the statue of an emperor had once stood, now perched on end to form part of a kitchen wall. The gymnasium was gone: where were the statues of naked Epiphanes posing as a discus thrower or of fleet Hermes the runner?

Even the two components that had best characterized Makor were vanished: the well was forgotten and the David Tunnel was no longer used. Its deep shaft was almost completely filled in, for during the past three hundred years it had served as the town dump. Now women of the town walked down a steep flight of wooden stairs that descended into the wadi, where a completely new well had been dug; Makor did not even remember the sweet source from which the town had taken its name.

Father Eusebius, accustomed to the grandeur of Rome and Constantinople, did however find one structure with a kind of peasant charm, a building he could respect. It was the synagogue standing near the middle of town, and as he came upon it this first day he stopped at the southern end to study the heavy, stately façade shaped like that of a Greek temple but lacking the perfection that marked all true Greek architecture. The portico was supported on six rather ugly stone columns, and Eusebius remarked to his architect: 'Whoever carved those pillars was no Greek.' But he had to grant that the effect was strong. Under the portico stood three doors topped by carved lintels, and the excellence of the western one showing grape clusters, date palms and a small wagon, intended no doubt to represent the holy ark, impressed the Spaniard and he stepped reverently upon the porch to peer inside; and there for the first time he caught a sense of Palestinian grandeur equal in its rough way to the fine things being built in Constantinople, for the interior ceiling was supported by eight columns of perfect proportion, differing in color and obviously stolen from some Greek or Roman building, for no Jew could have carved such pillars. They gave the synagogue a poetic beauty, but what impressed Eusebius more was the mosaic floor, in which he saw before him composed in cubes of local rock the design of Galilee: birds resting on an olive tree, sly foxes waiting in the rushes, and formalized little streams running down from purple mountains, a gathering of diverse elements into an artistic unity.

'Demetrius!' he called. 'Look at this.'

A Byzantine assistant came to inspect the mosaic and was impressed, for it was finer than his workmen were able to produce. 'Who did it?' Demetrius asked.

'They must have imported someone from Byzantium,' a workman in mosaic suggested.

Eusebius went back onto the portico and asked in Greek of a passing Jew, 'Who built your floor?' The man did not understand, but Menahem, returning the chair to the synagogue, moved forward to say, 'My father made it.'

The priest and the Jew regarded each other in silence, then Menahem added, 'He's working inside,' and he led the tall Spaniard back into the synagogue, where in a corner Yohanan was mending a clay pipe. 'This is my father,' Menahem said.

'Did you make the floor?' Eusebius asked.

'Yes.'

'You learn in Constantinople?' Demetrius inquired.

'Antioch,' Yohanan replied, and for the first time since he had begun working on this floor he experienced the satisfaction of watching experts who understood what he had accomplished accept his design as a work of art.

'Exquisite.' Father Eusebius said with controlled enthusiasm, and he could visualize such a pavement gracing his basilica, so on the spur of the moment he turned to Yohanan, saying, 'Your work here seems done. In our basilica we have need for your skills.'

'That glass costs money,' Yohanan warned.

From a bag carried by an assistant Father Eusebius handed him more gold coins than he had ever seen before. 'Buy the glass . . . now. We shall need a floor three times this big.' He turned to consult his experts, and they referred to their forthcoming basilica in such specific terms that Yohanan realized that in their minds it already existed. 'Could we fit a floor this size into the space before the altar?' Eusebius asked, and his architect replied, 'If we moved two of the pillars . . .'

'The pillars we won't touch,' the Spaniard said abruptly, 'but between them . . . Wouldn't there be room?'

'Ample,' the architect agreed, but Demetrius pointed out. 'In that case we couldn't use a square design like here.' With his hands he indicated the dimensions available, and Eusebius nodded.

The Spaniard turned to Yohanan and asked cautiously, 'Could you produce just as fine a work? In these dimensions?' and he moved his hands in the air as Demetrius had done.

Yohanan thought: These determined men have come to build, and I would like to work with them. Quietly he said, 'I'm a Jew.'

Father Eusebius gave the dry, ascetic laugh of a Spaniard descended from a long-established family and said, 'There may be sections of our church hostile to Jews, but not here in Makor. Have no worry. This one,' and with a slight nod he indicated his architect, 'is from Moldavia and still worships trees. There's a Persian who prays to fire. Our German troops are followers of Arius, who hold that the substance of God . . . ' He stopped, reflecting that Yohanan did not require to know these matters, but as a man secure in his own strength he added gravely, 'As a Jew both you and your skill will be welcome.' And he took

Yohanan by the arm, leading him persuasively from the synagogue.

The next days were exciting. Father Eusebius relaxed his aloofness long enough to allow the local Syrian priest to identify the traditional spot where Queen Helena had knelt and this determined the altar area of the new basilica. Yohanan then watched as the Christians stepped back and forth across the area north of the synagogue, seeking the best position for their building, and since these were the days before the church insisted upon altars oriented to the east, many different locations were tested, but in the end Eusebius summoned Yohanan and asked him what he thought of a solution that would place the basilica at an angle to the synagogue, reaching toward the northeast. 'Is the earth strong there?' the architect inquired.

'Of course, but you'll have to tear down . . . ' And Yohanan called off from memory the names of men occupying the houses of that area: 'Shmuel the baker, Ezra, Hababli the dyer, his son Abraham . . . thirty houses!'

Eusebius nodded. 'In the years ahead many will use this church. Pilgrims from lands you've never heard of.'

'But thirty homes!'

'What would you prefer?' the Spaniard asked, endeavouring to be conciliatory yet determined to be firm. 'That we knock down your synagogue?'

When Yohanan realized what was involved he sent Menahem to Tverya, advising Rabbi Asher that he had better return to Makor at once, as decisions were being made which would alter radically the future of his town; and when the young man reached Tverya he found his rabbi and spelled out for him what was happening: 'Thirty houses will be torn down. Most of them Jewish. Shmuel's, Ezra's, your son-in-law's . . . ' He ticked off the families who had been named for eviction. Rabbi Asher sat with his hands folded beneath his white beard and listened patiently, then said to his surprised foreman, 'The discussions here in Tverya will not recess for three days, and for me to leave before they end would be impossible. Go, return home, Menahem, and tell the families that they will have to vacate as the priest has indicated. I'm sure the Christians will find them new land and new homes.'

'But, Rabbi Asher . . . '

'We've known for a quarter of a century that it was God's will that this church be built,' the old man said, 'and we should all have been prepared for this day. I was.' And feeling no panic he returned to the grape arbor, where the great expositors were tackling the question of the remarriage of a widow, a concern that could occupy them for several years.

But when the groats maker informed the other rabbis of what was happening in Makor they broke their legal discussion to inspect briefly the problem which had been encroaching upon them for some years. The rabbi from Sephet spoke for the majority: 'I see no need for alarm. This so-called Christian church of Constantinople is merely Judaism in another guise. We've seen many such deviations in the past, and most have vanished.'

But the old Babylonian rabbi understood what was happening, for from his two rivers he had followed the impact of Christianity on the ancient religions of Persia and he appreciated the engulfing vitality of this new movement. 'It is not as you say,' he warned. 'Jews have one God, Christians have three, and their church is not a deviation but a new religion. Furthermore, in the past no major emperor embraced any of the earlier deviations, but Constantine did, and there's the practical difference.'

'Have they such force, these Christians?'

'I saw their armies. They fight with a spiritual fire.'

The rabbi from Kefar Nahum said, 'The only thing that disturbs me is the fanaticism of the pilgrims arriving in our town. Before Queen Helena's visit we saw a few wanderers each year, but she stirred things up. Now hundreds come and ask, "Isn't this Capernaum where the Jews rebuked Jesus?" And they spit at the synagogue.'

'It isn't the pilgrims that concern me,' the rabbi from Sephet reported. 'It's the tax collectors. They've been forced to become Christians. And feel it their duty to annoy us.'

The young rabbi from the white synagogue at Biri said he felt sure that the relations between Judaism and the new religion would stabilize satisfactorily. 'As Rabbi Hananiah has just said, they are really Jews. They accept our holy Torah. They accept our God. We should regard them as any other minor sect . . .'

'No sect is minor,' the old scholar from Babylonia repeated, 'if it enrolls the emperor.'

'We have outlived many emperors,' the Biri rabbi said.

The discussions now turned to a series of troublesome incidents which had begun to disturb the Galilee, and when the rabbis finished exchanging information it was found that in all towns except Makor there had been disturbances in which young Jews had resisted the Byzantine tax collectors, whose demands had become indeed excessive. In Kefar Nahum resistance had been so vigorous that Byzantine soldiers were required to put down the protests, but open fighting had not developed. When viewed together, as part of an emerging pattern, the brawling was ominous.

And then the Biri rabbi broached the fundamental problem: 'The tax collectors say they must raise more money to build churches for the new sect. My Jews cannot accept such impositions, and the soldiers cry, "You crucified Jesus, didn't you?" and tempers are inflamed.'

At this point Rabbi Asher, now one of the older members of the group, proposed the working rules which were to guide the rabbis: 'God asks us to share this land with a vigorous sect of His religion. Children who are growing into manhood we treat with dignity; let us treat this new movement in the same way. Gently, gently.' And of the expositors present that day, only the Babylonian referred to Christianity as a new religion; the others saw it as a continuation of that series of Jewish particularist movements which had included the Essenes and the Ebionites. At best, they considered Christians as comparable to the Samaritans: Jews who accepted only the Torah and refused to believe in the divine inspiration of the rest of the Old Testament. As the Biri rabbi rationalized: 'The Samaritans cut our holy book in half while the Christians double it with a new book of their own. At heart each remains Judaism.'

It was in this unsettled mood that Rabbi Asher said farewell for the last time to the expositors of Tverya. Unaware that he would meet with his colleagues no more, he departed without pausing for a last look at the grape arbor beneath whose protection the fence around the Torah had been built, or at the bearded faces who had argued with him so passionately during the past twenty-two years. When his white mule ascended the hill to Sephet he did not turn to inspect the autumnal splendor of Tverya, with its Roman buildings slipping silently into desuetude, but next morning as he started for Makor he did catch a final glimpse of the Sea of Galilee, and along its western shore he saw for the last time Tverya, that beautiful city, home of the Herods, haven of those who loved quiet nights, sacred to the birth pangs of two religions, where Jesus slept and rabbis argued, where Peter fished and great Akiba lay in death, the city where soft waves whispered along the shore as the Talmud was being born, Tverya, Tverya.

For some moments Rabbi Asher sat astride his mule, gazing down upon the gray-white city where he had worked for so long–how sweet those conversations had been, how elevating–and he entertained the unhappy thought that some day, since he was now sixty-nine, he must reach the point when he would be too old for this constant traveling. But he had no idea that he was to be halted neither by age nor by faltering faculties, but by the maturing of forces which as yet he only dimly perceived, and it was to the cauldron where those forces were being brewed that he now directed his mule. The animal shook his withers, then moved ahead and Tverya was no more.

As he rode that summer's day through the quiet forests of the Galilee, Rabbi Asher ha-Garsi was the epitome of what God had intended when He called forth the rabbis to guide His people through the dark centuries that loomed ahead. He was a hard, thin man with a white beard and gentle blue eyes; as a descendant of many generations of Jews who had lived in or near Makor, he carried in his body reminiscences of Egyptian warriors who had stayed in the area, of long-nosed Hittites who had served as mercenaries, of Phoenicians who had drifted down the coastline from Tyre and Sidon, and of Romans and Greeks who had married with local girls. Rabbi Asher liked to think of himself as a pure Jew, and he was–just as seventeen hundred years later, kibbutzniks in this same area who looked like Russians or Germans or Americans or Arabs would also be pure Jews–for to be so required an inheritance of mind and not of blood. Rabbi Asher, being a descendant of the notable Family of Ur, had begun as half Canaanite, half Habiru, though what those terms meant no man had ever been able to say, but he was also all the other strains that those two vital groups had absorbed through the millennia. He was, in short, a Jew.

As his white mule wandered down the road between the encroaching trees, birds of summer darted through the shadows, saluting the bearded old man who was passing by. Asher smiled. He was thinking of the earthy saying of Akiba: 'When their love was strong they could sleep on the edge of a sword, but now when they have forgotten, a bed sixty feet across is not sufficient.' He also remembered the summary of all philosophy which Akiba had offered his disciples: 'My teacher Eliezer told me that only one rule was required by a Jew if he wished to live a good life. "Repent the day before you die." And since no man knows when he shall die, he is prudent if he lives each day a life of true repentance.' Rabbi Asher had tried to live as if on the morrow he were dead.

When the old man approached his little town he saw as he had anticipated the Byzantine workmen were building small homes near the olive grove, for here the thirty families to be dispossessed by the Christian basilica were to be resettled. Asher hoped that the removals were being made without incident, and he kicked the mule's flanks to speed him up the incline leading into town.

He found Makor in ferment. When his arrival became known, representatives of the thirty families crowded into the small stone house attached to the synagogue to launch their protests. Shmuel said, 'I've worked forty years building my shop. People won't leave the town to buy bread.'

'We'll have to find new quarters in town, that's obvious,' Rabbi Asher promised.

Ezra the shoemaker had a different problem: on each flank of his old home he had built additional rooms for his two sons and their wives, but the house provided by the Byzantines at the new site lacked space for three separate families. 'For our one house inside the walls we should receive three outside.' 'That's reasonable,' the old man said. 'I'm sure the Byzantines will listen.' 'Not to me,' Ezra said.

'To me they will,' the rabbi assured him, and when he had heard all the complaints he thought: There's no problem here that men of good will cannot adjust, and he left the small house by the synagogue and walked around to the rear, to where Father Eusebius was directing his workmen as they staked out the actual lines of the basilica, and when he saw how enormous it was to be–almost twice the size of his substantial synagogue – he gasped. Was this an accurate measure of Christianity? No wonder his Jews were protesting.

But when he approached Father Eusebius to question him about the demolitions, the tall Spaniard forestalled any complaint by striding across the rubble and extending both hands. 'I'm glad you've come back, Rabbi Asher! I want you to see what we've done to protect your synagogue.' And before God's Man could reply, the black-robed Spaniard led him to the square-cut wall of the synagogue to demonstrate how the basilica was leaving an open space of nearly ten yards as protection to the Jews. 'We shall exist side by side in peace,' the Spaniard said.

Then, before Rabbi Asher could comment on this gesture of conciliation, Father Eusebius led him away from the demolition area and into his office, a single lime-walled room with an earthen floor and on the spare walls a silver crucifix from Italy and a wooden icon panel from Constantinople. It was a quiet, austere room marked by a rough wood desk and two chairs, and if it did not reflect the patrician derivation of its owner it did bespeak certain hard manliness. As soon as Rabbi Asher was seated, feeling chilly and out of place in the presence of the graven images, Father Eusebius smiled and said, deprecatingly, 'I've been remiss in one matter, Rabbi Asher. I did not keep myself informed about the removal of your Jews to their new locations outside of town. Certain injustices have developed, about which I heard only last night. I've directed my man Yohanan . . .'

'The stonecutter?'

'Yes. I directed him to find a place in town for the baker. People can't be forced to walk long distances for their bread, can they?' He raised his thin white hands gracefully above the desk in a gesture of supplication. 'So if the baker comes complaining to you, tell him he's justified and will be cared for.'

Finally the little rabbi found a chance to speak, and his first concern was not about general principles nor the large issues that were beginning to loom over the Galilee. He discussed the human problem of the stonecutter. 'Did you say that Yohanan was working for you?'

'Yes. We'll need a large mosaic in the basilica.'

The words aroused suspicious implications. Why large? To make the basilica more impressive than the synagogue? Why mosaic? Because the Jews had trained a fine workman who was now available at no preliminary expense? And why that ominous phrase 'we'll need'? For what reason was there this need? Why did any religion need so large a building?

As if he had anticipated the rabbi's questions, Father Eusebius said quietly, 'We're building what must seem a great church because many pilgrims will be coming to Makor. You know that in the years ahead . . .'

'Are you here permanently?'

'Yes. I'm to be bishop. I've been sent here to . . .' The stately Spaniard hesitated. He had been about to say 'convert the area,' which was his specific commission, but tactfully he concluded, 'build up the area.' Then, as if his unconscious mind were at work, he added, 'You mustn't think harshly of Yohanan.'

'For quitting his work at the synagogue?'

'No. For taking his son away from your groats mill. The young man's working here, too.'

For Rabbi Asher this was a hard blow. In his business he needed Menahem, but this was not his first thought. From infancy he had looked after this forsaken child, finding him homes, seeing that he was cared for. He had given him a job and an almost fatherly love and had lately sponsored the process whereby Menahem might be drawn back into Judaism, and now to find that he was working in the basilica was a shock; but Father Eusebius did not propose discussing this personal matter. 'Rabbi Asher,' he began in his official voice, hands folded severely before him while his gaunt, handsome face was outlined against the white wall, 'I'm glad you came home . . . most glad.' He paused, but his guest was still thinking about Menahem and the mill. 'I'm glad you returned, because you're needed here.' Again the slim priest hesitated, but the rabbi said nothing. 'You're needed because some of your quick-tempered young Jews are beginning to cause trouble. Over taxes, I believe. So far our governor has proved most lenient. Possibly because I have cautioned him to be so. But, Rabbi Asher . . .'

The Jew rose as if he were about to leave the room. He wanted to talk directly to Menahem, to see if the young man had stolen the ten drachmas so that he could be sold into slavery and restored to Judaism. He nodded respectfully to the priest, as he had nodded to his colleagues in Tverya when he took leave of them, and started for the door.

'Rabbi Asher,' the Spaniard said, not raising his voice but speaking in a tone which required attention. 'Sit down. Your son-in-law Abraham is among the leaders of this hot-headed group. You must command him to cease his provocations or they will lead to trouble.'

'Abraham?' For a moment Rabbi Asher could not visualize anyone to go with the name. He had little respect for his son-in-law, even if the young man had married Jael in a moment of crisis, but at least he could respond to the legal aspect of the problem. 'Oh yes! The rabbis at Tverya were discussing this matter. Excessive taxes and quick tempers.'

'I've directed our tax collectors to ease the burden,' Father Eusebius said. 'And I've diverted our workmen to build new homes for your Jews. Now you, Rabbi Asher, must co-operate by instructing your son-in-law Abraham and his cronies to stop their dangerous agitations.'

'Abraham?' the little rabbi repeated in a kind of daze. It was not likely that Abraham ben Hababli posed any threat to Byzantium. 'I'll reprimand him,' he promised.

'Please do,' the Spaniard said.

Rabbi Asher left the austere room with its graven images and hurried to his mill, where he found one elderly workman turning the stones while unfilled bags lay about the floor. 'Where's Menahem?' he asked.

'He's left us,' the man replied, slowly revolving the upper stone so that small amounts of cereal fell onto an earthenware platter.

Deeply worried, Rabbi Asher went by small alleys to the large area where the basilica was to rise, and there he saw Yohanan and Menahem piling the rubble of destroyed homes into sacks which slaves from the African desert hauled to the edge of town, emptying them into the wadi. Father and son spoke politely to the rabbi, who asked, 'Menahem, may I speak with you?'

The young man, taller and huskier from his work in the open, followed the rabbi to a spot where the slaves were not working, and there God's Man asked, 'Have you done as we planned? Ten drachmas' worth, before witnesses?'

As if that bizarre episode were a nightmare from his irrational past, Menahem moved away and said apologetically, 'I've been so busy working here . . .'

'Have you left the mill?'

'Yes. I'm helping to build a large mosaic here.'

Rabbi Asher thought: Again that word large. Why should largeness seduce sensible men? But Menahem was speaking hurriedly, as if ashamed of his defection: 'At first I'm to be in charge of finding the colored stones. My father's to be an architect. But when the floor's ready we'll both work on the design.'

'But, Menahem! Your plan to become a legitimate Jew?'

The young man wished to say, If you had honestly wanted me as a Jew, I'd be one now, but out of respect for the old rabbi he said, 'I've much work to do, Rabbi,' and he walked away. At this moment there was shouting at the eastern wall and signs of flame, so both Menahem and Rabbi Asher ran to that quarter, where Byzantine soldiers were thrashing a young Jew while workmen tried to extinguish a fire which was eating at a storehouse in which tax collectors kept the produce paid by the citizens of Makor. Before Rabbi Asher could intervene to protect the boy being beaten he saw the tall figure of Father Eusebius stalking through the crowd, pushing citizens aside as if they were chaff, and with a cold, dark visage, looking at the fire.

'You! You!' the Spaniard shouted at various Jews. 'Halt that blaze!' It was no use. Flames had caught hold of the contents of the building, grain and olive oil, and it was obvious that all must be consumed. In white-lipped fury the priest looked at the latest outrage of the Jews, then moved to where the soldiers were beating the supposed arsonist. For a long moment Eusebius watched the punishment, then cried, 'Enough!' But the culprit was dead.

A great sigh rose from the assembled Jews, accented by the crackling of the flames and the hopeless shouts of the fire fighters. Father Eusebius, satisfied that the building was lost, left the scene, but as he passed Rabbi Asher he said coldly, 'This is what I meant when you would not pay attention. Now the German army will march down from Antioch, and it is your doing.' Like a sword unsheathed he moved through the crowd to his white walled room, where he prayed for some time, then sent messengers to Ptolemais with a report that the Jewish insurrection was getting out of hand: 'I am afraid you must bring down the German army stationed at Antioch.'

That fateful night the two religious leaders of Makor, Father Eusebius and Rabbi Asher, each conducted meetings which would have strange results in the town. Rabbi Asher's was with his son-in-law Abraham, a stocky, dull-minded young man who sat close to his wife Jael and argued with surprising vigor against his father-in-law. 'The Byzantines have gone too far,' the young man said. 'No, we will not turn back. Jael will tell you why. If we must fight, we'll fight.'

Then Jael, twenty-one years old, explained to her father, 'Abraham's right.

We can have no peace with the Byzantines. The tax collectors . . .'

'Father Eusebius promised me that taxes would be lowered.'

Jael laughed. 'They've been increased. Somebody has to pay for that church.'

'But . . .'

'Wait till you see the new tax on your mill,' she said contemptuously. 'The soldiers grow more arrogant. You saw what they did this morning.'

'But the boy had set the warehouse on fire.'

'I set the fire,' Abraham said boldly. His wife took his hand and held it during the rest of the conversation.

'You?' Rabbi Asher asked, and the incredulity in his voice betrayed his low opinion of his son-in-law. Were callow fools like this challenging Byzantium?

'And with the coming of Father Eusebius,' Jael continued, 'the repressions have speeded up.'

'No!' her father protested. 'Father Eusebius wants us to live together peacefully.'

'Yes! Yes! On his terms. He is very gentle when Menahem leaves the groats mill and goes to work for him. If our people stand by quietly when their old homes are destroyed he'll build them new ones out of town. He does nothing wrong, but those who do wrong are encouraged by his presence.'

'We shall not halt our war against the Byzantines,' Abraham repeated stolidly, and Rabbi Asher, looking at the almost brutish young man, realized for the first time that a younger generation was on the move in Makor, one over which he had little control.

While this gloomy discovery was being made in the rabbi's home, a meeting of mystical significance was under way in the austere room occupied by Father Eusebius, who sat behind his rough-hewn desk while Menahem occupied the chair facing him. 'Tell me again, slowly and with no exaggeration,' the Spaniard said.

In his work with Father Eusebius, Menahem had come to respect the cool efficiency of the Spaniard. He had watched him weigh facts, such as which houses to tear down, and reach a conclusion on the evidence. And once he spoke, the dark-haired priest was willing to abide by the responsibility he had taken upon himself. Menahem found him a just, courageous man, dedicated and hard-working, not easy to know but solid like a rock when known. He now stared at Menahem, deep lines in his cheeks, a cold but just face resting on his left hand. 'Slowly and with no lies,' he repeated.

Menahem swallowed and said, 'My father married a woman who already had a husband.'

'He sinned,' Father Eusebius said. 'Grievously he sinned.'

'That made me a bastard.'

'Without question.'

'I could not be a Jew nor take part in any services.' Menahem hesitated and said a boyish thing, recalling an old hurt, 'When I was thirteen I was not allowed to read the Torah.'

Father Eusebius made no comment, so Menahem continued, 'I could not marry. I could not pray. At Tverya the rabbis told me what to do.' He could not continue.

'Go ahead,' the Spaniard said, his face betraying neither compassion nor concern.

'They told me . . . I myself could never be saved. But if I stole ten drachmas' worth . . .' The words came with great pain, for they recalled the spiritual crisis he had suffered when Jael was married. 'They would arrest me, sell me into slavery, marry me to another slave, later set us both free, and while we would not be restored, our children would be.'

For some time Father Eusebius sat silent, reviewing this incredible tale which he had refused to believe the first time he heard it. He dropped his hand from his chin and gradually lowered his austere head until no part of his face was visible, and Menahem realized he was praying. Then slowly he looked up at the would-be Jew and tears of compassion stood in his eyes. As if from the depth of a great basilica he said in a whisper, 'The salvation you sought, Menahem, has always been at hand.' He turned and pointed at the crucifix. 'When He ascended that cross, when He gave His life for you and me, He took upon Himself the burden of sin that you have been carrying. The moment you accept Him, Menahem, you are free.'

The priest rose, came to where the Jew was sitting and knelt beside him on the beaten earth. Placing his hand in Menahem's he brought him to his knees also, and in this position the Spaniard prayed, 'Jesus Christ, our Lord, smile upon this young man Menahem ben Yohanan, who has carried such a dreadful sin upon his shoulders. Not his sin, Jesus, but the original sin of the world. Smile upon him and transfer from his shoulders to Yours the burden which he has so manfully borne.'

In the quiet room a miracle took place. The crushing weight under which Menahem had struggled drifted from his back, the clouds of obscurity from his mind. He felt the actual burden slipping from him, as if he had been carrying three sacks of groats, and he began to sob with joy, as if he were a child to whom something fine had happened.

'And now, Lord Jesus,' the Spaniard continued, 'invite this outcast into Your brotherhood. Tell him, now, that he is free to join us.'

The priest turned on his knees to face Menahem, then rose and with extended hands drew the young Jew to his feet. 'You need be outcast no more,' the priest cried joyfully, and he embraced Menahem as if he were his son. Seating the young man on the chair, he returned to his own, and with a countenance radiant with love, with the gray at his temples shining like silver in the light of the oil lamps, he said, 'Rabbi Asher was right in all he did, Menahem. There is sin in the world, and your father created more by his willful actions. Sin was indeed upon you, too, and you were properly an outcast. But the old law that kept this sin permanently upon your soul is abrogated.' He saw that the young man did not understand this word, but he was inspired and hurried on. 'The harsh old law is no more and in its place has come the new law of love and redemption. If this night you tell me that you are willing to join Christ, your sin will vanish forever.'

Finally Menahem spoke: 'I can join your church?'

'You will build it. It will be yours.'

'I helped build the synagogue, but it was never mine.'

'The church of Jesus Christ is available without restraints.'

'I can sing with you? Pray with you?' He did not see Father Eusebius nod agreement, for he was looking at the floor. In a soft whisper he asked, 'Would you allow me to marry?'

'Any girl in our church would be pleased to marry with you, Menahem,' and the priest led the young Jew to the crucifix, before which the Spaniard knelt in the dust, drawing Menahem with him, and after the two had prayed for some moments Eusebius said, 'Lord Jesus Christ, I bring You tonight Your servant Menahem ben Yohanan, who offers his soul and his life to Your care.' He nudged Menahem.

'Lord Jesus Christ,' the outcast said in a whisper. 'No longer can I bear my portion of sin. Accept me.' His voice choked and on a mighty impulse he prostrated himself full length before the crucifix. 'I cannot bear it any longer . . . I cannot,' he repeated many times. 'Oh, Jesus, help me.'

When Menahem had lain thus for some time, Father Eusebius rose, went to him and raised him to his feet. When the handsome young man, ashen-faced like a ghost, stood before him, the Spaniard kissed him twice and said, 'Tonight you are Menahem ben Yohanan. Three days from now when you receive the sacrament of baptism and the mass you shall become Mark and your new life begins from that moment.' He gave his first local convert his blessing and sent him into the night, a man whose once unsupportable burden no longer existed.

For some time Father Eusebius had been aware that he had a chance of winning Menahem as his first convert, but he had not anticipated what was to happen the following morning. Before work started on the basilica Menahem knocked at the priest's door, and when the Spaniard rose from his prayers he found not only Menahem awaiting him but Yohanan as well, and on a less emotional level than he had used with Menahem he rephrased the hopeful message of his church: 'You have been a grievous sinner, Yohanan, and your sin has reached down to your children and your children's children. You are powerless to erase this sin, but He,' and he pointed to the crucifix standing out like a light from the bare wall, 'He came personally to save you. Accept Him–place your burden on Him, and you shall be free.'

'My son, too?'

'He is already free.' To demonstrate this truth the tall Spaniard placed his arm about Menahem's shoulder, and the gesture was so honest, so without reservation, that Yohanan had to accept its veracity. He saw the radiance in his son's face as Menahem stood free of the burden placed on him by the law, and the reality of salvation was so persuasive that Yohanan fell to his knees, crying, 'Accept me, too.' In this way his feeling of guilt because of what he had done to his offspring vanished, and he was swept along to the sweet mystery of conversion. Enemies of the new church might scoff, but in that white-walled room that morning a burden of sin was actually shifted from the sloping shoulders of the stonecutter and onto the shoulders of Jesus Christ. Yohanan mumbled the formula recited by Father Eusebius and rose a new man. There was no other way to put it: when he knelt he was a man weighed down by the old law, but when he rose he was freed within the new.

The public baptism of Yohanan and Menahem was set for Friday, an unfortunate choice, for although the day had no special significance for the Christians it was for the Jews the beginning of their Shabbat and the loss of two of their members on that particular day seemed an added insult. Curiously, the very Jews who had refused Menahem a place in their synagogue now protested most vigorously against his abandoning it. 'He mustn't be allowed to do this thing,' they protested and a committee was appointed to dissuade the young man from his error, but Menahem could never have anticipated which member of that committee would be the first to plead with him.

It was Jael, and her message was simple: 'You can't leave us now, Menahem. You can't go over to their side. There's going to be trouble with the Byzantines and you must fight beside your own people.'

From his new-found platform of hope he smiled at her lack of comprehension. 'Your father never allowed me to be a Jew. Don't make me one now.'

'But you are one of us. This is your town.'

'This is a new town,' he said accurately. 'Warn your husband to make peace with the Byzantines.'

'Menahem!'

'I am now Mark. A new man, reborn in Jesus Christ.'

Jael drew away from him, as people do instinctively from things they cannot understand, and as she left she asked, 'Have you placed yourself against your brothers?'

'They placed themselves against me. When I was born,' he replied. 'Ask Abraham . . .' He was about to remind her of the ugly years when her husband and a group of his friends had chased him through the streets, shouting, 'Bastard, bastard!' but in his redeemed existence as Mark he chose to forgive those memories; they no longer had authority over his life. 'On Friday I become a new man,' he said, 'and then I shall be a Byzantine, standing against your husband.'

Jael left the hut and walked with sickness in her heart to the groats mill, where she told her father that Menahem was obdurate in his decision; she glossed over the real reason why she had gone to see him, for she did not wish to bother the old man with problems of the growing revolt, but what she did reveal was sufficient to arouse Rabbi Asher. Leaving her he ran dusty and disheveled to the building area, where he found not Menahem but Yohanan. Grasping the stonecutter by the shoulder the little rabbi swung him around and demanded, 'Have you left the synagogue?'

'I'm working here now.'

'I mean Judaism?'

'I'll be baptized on Friday.'

'No!'

'And Menahem with me.'

'You must not!'

The stonecutter brushed away the rabbi's hand and growled, 'The synagogue could find no place for him. This church can.'

'You were born into Judaism, Yohanan. You'll live in it forever.'

'Not if my son is kept out.'

'But we were working on a plan to save him.'

'Five years a slave?' Yohanan looked with disdain at the rabbi and pushed him away.

'But we are all saved only through the law.'

'With such a law I have no further dealings,' Yohanan said, turning to resume his work.

This time Rabbi Asher did not touch the big man; he ran in a ridiculous circle so that he could face him again, and when he did so he said forcefully, 'You cannot escape the law. You'll always be a man of the synagogue.'

The repetition of this word had a curious effect upon the stonecutter. He stood rooted among the debris and stared at the nearby synagogue which he had built with such devotion: he saw the native stone that he had chopped from the Galilean hills, the walls that he had raised tier after tier, and although the lines were not poetic like those of the Greek temple which had once stood on this spot they were the hard, true lines of a man who worshiped God in his own stubborn way. It was a building that would make any workman's heart proud, and suddenly the torment in which he was trapped proved too much for this simple man, and with his apelike hands he covered his face. Rabbi Asher, sensing his conflict, moved toward him, but the stonecutter knocked the old man aside, shouting, 'You ordered me to build it . . . that floor . . . how many pieces did we cut at night? The golden glass . . . Menahem paid for that with his own earnings. No, you hadn't enough. Those walls.' He ran to the synagogue and beat upon the austere limestone rectangles; how beautiful they were, cut from the heart of the Galilee, and against them he fell weakly to his knees.

'Am I to build this synagogue and find in it no place for my own flesh and blood?' he mumbled, striking his head against the stones until it looked as if in his confusion he might kill himself and when Rabbi Asher went to him, seeking to mitigate the law's harsh attitude, the huge stonecutter shouted, 'Do you want me to live in that sin forever?' and he grabbed a rock and would have killed his rabbi, had not Father Eusebius, who had been watching the mortal agony that overtook many converts before their moment of baptism, intervened to lead his trembling workman away.

That night Rabbi Asher delegated Abraham his son-in-law and Shmuel the baker to bring him Menahem but not his father–and when the young man stood before his judge, the groats maker asked, 'Is it true that you are joining the Christians?'

'Yes.' To himself Menahem said: Tonight let him shout what he will. This is the last time he will order me.

But Rabbi Asher asked quietly, 'How can you find the courage to abandon your religion?'

'You've given me no choice.'

'Can you not see that it is God who has punished you?'

'You still advise me to steal ten drachmas' worth and become a slave?'

'That's the law, and through it we find salvation.'

'Now there is a simpler way.'

'By denying God? Who personally chose us as His people?'

Menahem laughed. 'No one believes that any more. Neither my father nor I nor any of them out there.'

'Then you deny God?'

'No. But I accept Him on much gentler terms,' he said. Against his resolve he was being drawn into conflict with the old man who had supervised his life, and that so stringently.

'Do you think that God established the law intending it to be followed easily?' In these words Rabbi Asher, on this quiet night when oil lamps guttered, threw down the perpetual challenge of the Jews: Did God mean life to be easy? Or compliance with His law agreeable?

And Menahem, who at twenty-five had been driven to consider truth for himself, threw back what would become the timeless answer of the Christian: 'God intended salvation to be within the reach of anyone: even me. He sent Jesus Christ to die for me . . . a bastard . . . to tell me that the cruel ancient law was no more . . . that now mercy reigned.'

This concept, so simply stated, stunned the rabbi, cutting at his concept of the law, and he was driven back to being simply God's Man: 'Menahem, when you were born there was none to care for you, and I saved your life. Because I loved you . . . because God loved you. How can you now cease being a Jew?'

'I ceased when I was born,' he said, 'because your law would not permit me to love God.'

'You cannot break God's law and later love Him,' the old man reasoned.

'Christ offers us a way,' Menahem said, and he turned his back on the old rabbi, never to speak with him again.

The public baptism of Yohanan and his tall son provided Father Eusebius with his first opportunity for a religious celebration, so on Friday morning a canopy was erected over the spot where El and El-Shaddai and Antiochus Epiphanes had once been worshiped, and there the tall Spaniard in robes of purple silk stood to receive the supplicant Jews while a chorus chanted Byzantine rituals and Rabbi Asher learned the hard facts of life. Certain faithful Jews had come to him with plans for disrupting the baptism of the renegades and he had counseled them to abandon such ideas, but when these hotheads saw the two Jews actually move forward to join the new church their tempers were inflamed and they began to murmur in protest. From nowhere, it seemed, Byzantine soldiers stationed for that purpose moved in and with silent efficiency muffled the would-be troublemakers. When Rabbi Asher stepped forward to intervene two Byzantines who had been detailed to watch him grabbed him as if he were a sack of groats and tossed him back into the rear ranks.

'You behave, old goat, or . . .' They jabbed him in the belly with their spears. He tried to protest this too, but a coarse hand smothered his mouth and the soldier growled, 'Shut up, damn you!' And the solemn ritual of baptism began.

Father Eusebius, refusing to acknowledge the commotion, approached the kneeling Jews with a phial of holy water, and as the choir sang in Greek, dipped his fingers in the water and touched father and son on the head, telling them first in Latin and then in broken Hebrew certain religious facts which would later become important: 'With this water you are joined to the holy Christian church of west and east. You are forever a part of that seamless robe and nothing can wash away this sacred baptism. It cannot be burned away, nor cut away. Neither punishment nor threat of death can reverse this decision, for you are now full members in the brotherhood of Christ. You are set-free from the old law and you embrace the new.' He raised the two former Jews to their feet and kissed each on the cheek, presenting them to the congregation, to whom he said, 'John the stonecutter, who is helping us to build our basilica, now belongs to that basilica. His son Mark, who was an outcast among you, is outcast no more. Accept these two as your brothers,' and Christians cheered as Rabbi Asher and his Jews stood silent.

It was now the eve of Shabbat, and no further protest was made, for all who might have caused trouble were in synagogue. But on Saturday when nightfall ended Shabbat, young Jews led by Abraham and Jael gathered and decided on a gesture of defiance. Creeping silently past Byzantine guards they drenched a tax collector's home with oil and set it afire. As stars appeared over the sea the beacon of Jewish resistance flamed in the sky and was noticed by the night watch in Ptolemais, whose governor dispatched a ship to Antioch, requesting the German army to march south with all speed.

In Makor relative peace descended upon the troubled community, thanks principally to Father Eusebius, who showed Christian forbearance as his response to the disturbances. Masking any bitterness he might have felt he did not summon Rabbi Asher but went to him at the groats mill, saying, 'I was told this morning that the German troops are on their way to Ptolemais, and unless I halt them there, they'll come here to punish the trouble-makers. Now neither you nor I want those hard-handed Germans in Makor. So I will order them to stay away if you will order your Jews to end these disturbances.'

Rabbi Asher, already distressed by the brazen behavior of his Jews, could visualize the German army leaving Antioch for the march to Ptolemais, from which like their Roman predecessors they would fan out across the Galilee–as if history, like a folk-song, never tired of repetition–and he promised Father Eusebius, 'I will do my best to discipline the Jews.' So he explained to his younger members how they should react to the sudden ascendancy of the Christian church: 'We must exist in harmony, and this we cannot do if there is misunderstanding or envy. In Makor today we see two daughters of God, the old Jewish religion and the young Christian church, and for a while there may be contention, but the two religions remind me of old Rabbi Eliezer and his young pupil Akiba. There was drought and the old man prayed nine times for rain without success. So Rabbi Akiba prayed once, and with his first words came rain. The Jews hailed him as the true prophet and this deeply wounded Eliezer, but Akiba went to him and said, "There was a king who had two daughters, one old and wise, the other young and headstrong. When the gentle sister came before him with some request the king would be reluctant to grant it, hoping to keep his daughter near him, for her voice was pleasant to his ears. But when the harsh and noisy younger child screamed for something, the king gave it to her right away, for he wanted to get her out of the palace." God has by no means forgotten you merely because He grants the requests of your younger sister.'

When Rabbi Asher was satisfied that he had quieted his headstrong Jews he decided to return to Tverya, where his permanent responsibility lay: he could remember how once he had been misled into thinking that the building of a synagogue was the chore God demanded of him, and he did not propose to be diverted now by minor political troubles; his job was to build a fence around the Torah and to explain both the fence and the Torah to the young students at the yeshiva. But when word of his intended departure reached Father Eusebius the Spaniard was astonished that his colleague could think of leaving Makor at this crucial moment and he sent a soldier to the groats mill, and the Christian said, 'Father Eusebius wants to see you. Now.'

The words were ominous, but in a spirit of conciliation Rabbi Asher brushed the dust from his clothes and followed the soldier, standing at last, a little man in a long white beard, before the Spaniard, who smiled and said gently, 'I heard this morning that you intend returning to Tiberias.' He used the Roman name. 'Is that wise?'

The question surprised the little groats maker, for no one had the authority to review his movements. Patiently he explained, 'In Tverya there are discussions which require my attention.'

'In Makor there are rebellions which also require your attention.'

'But my major responsibility . . .'

'Is here!' Father Eusebius said quietly. With persuasion he added, 'Rabbi Asher, in this town we are close to tragedy. Two nights ago I received news from Capernaum. Riots have occurred, and believe me, they were put down with great severity. When your Jews burned the tax collector's office I could have duplicated that severity, but I acted with restraint.'

'I know.'

'But your Jews must accept the fact that from now on this is a Christian

empire. Our religion is to prevail. Do you know that if desired, I could knock
down your synagogue tomorrow? I left Constantinople vested with that
power.' He changed his voice and said with real love, 'But the Holy Land
contains many Jews and I insist upon living in harmony with them.'

'I've seen to it there will be no more trouble, and now I must go to Tverya.'
'Rabbi!' the Spaniard said with quiet, terrible anxiety. 'You don't seem to
understand. Last night there was an uprising in Tiberias. Six people were
killed. The Germans are marching south from Antioch right now. We are in
most serious trouble, and I must command you to remain here.'

The little man nodded, acknowledged the advice without further comment,
paid his respects to the Christian priest, and decided that if there had indeed
been trouble in Tverya it was his duty to hurry there; but when he tried to leave
town soldiers halted him. 'Father Eusebius forbids you to go,' they said, taking
the mule from him. And in this way Rabbi Asher discovered that the
government of Palestine, both civil and religious, was now in the hands of the
self-controlled Spaniard. That night a group of young Jews, heartened by news
of rebellions in Kefa Nahum and Tverya, and deceived by Eusebius' apparent
impotence in the face of their last burning, set fire to a shed in which fodder was
stored, and there was night fighting and a Byzantine soldier was killed; but
Father Eusebius, still hoping to avoid war, maintained control over his troops.

It was during these suspenseful days that the stonecutters John and Mark
adjusted to their new lives as Christians. The father reacted in a way that might
have been foreseen: he nestled within the arms of his new religion as if he were a
tired old animal who sensed the ending of his days and wanted only warmth and
security. When Father Eusebius came to inspect the site of the basilica John
followed him with affection; he worked harder than ever, went regularly to the
humble little Syrian church to mass, and visualized many ways in which to
beautify the basilica when its walls were up. He discovered that an unexpected
change had come over his life, and it had little to do with religion; while
working on the synagogue his attempts to beautify it were always made against
the grain of the Jewish religion and the wishes of Rabbi Asher, whereas among
the leaders of the Christian church he found a desire to express holy ideas in art
which seemed an inherent part of their religion. Now, when John suggested to
Father Eusebius some additional device that would enhance the grace of the
basilica, the Spaniard's eyes would glow and no matter what the cost he would
encourage his convert to proceed. 'The money we'll find somehow,' he
promised, and John experienced what he had not known before; men who
loved beauty as an enhancement of life.

But if John found snug refuge in the church, Mark did not: in a series of
confusing revelations he was learning that his new religion involved a good deal
more than the easy conversion which he had been offered, for although the
Christians presented a solid front against Jews and pagans, among themselves
they were sorely divided, for they could not agree upon the nature of their
religion and their divisions cut deep; those who believed one way were
prepared to slay those who believed another. The brotherhood of all Christians
which Father Eusebius preached was certainly not operating in Makor.

Workmen who came from Egypt explained that Jesus Christ was at the same
time a man and a deity, 'and therefore the Virgin Mary was the Mother of God.'
But workmen who came from Constantinople argued that Jesus was born a
man but lived such an exemplary life that He became a god, 'and so you can see
that the Virgin Mary was the mother of a great man, but certainly never the

Mother of God.' Mark, listening to these arguments about the nature of Jesus, thought: My new Christians fighting over whether Mary was the mother of Christ or the Mother of God sound just like my old rabbis fighting over whether throwing out dishwater was cooking or plowing.

Then one evening as Mark sat with soldiers discussing the burning of the tool shed, a workman from Egypt said casually, 'I hear that a ship has landed in Ptolemais, bringing us a statue of Mary, the Mother of God.'

A soldier from Constantinople corrected him: 'Mary, the mother of Christ.'

The Egyptian, whose ancestors had long worshiped the goddess Isis and whose love was now transferred to Mary, repeated without raising his voice, 'I said Mary, the Mother of God.' In a flash the man from Constantinople threw his spear at the dissentient and riot was avoided only because the point passed the Egyptian's head and broke itself against a stone wall. Mark sat appalled as men leaped into battle positions, then retreated when Father Eusebius, hearing the clatter, walked into the area. Quickly he saw the broken spear, the flushed faces, and with aristocratic skill eased the situation, pretending not to know what had caused the animosity.

Nor did Mark understand. He knew only that the rupture separating Egyptian from Byzantine was apparently irreconcilable, and as the days passed he learned how abiding the hatred was. One night the men of Constantinople came to him, whispering, 'You must believe that Jesus Christ was an ordinary man . . . a Jew like you.'

'I'm a Christian,' Mark said.

'But you're still a Jew. And Jesus Christ, who was a man just like you, died on the cross to save you. Now unless He was a real man, the whole meaning of His crucifixion by you Jews is lost.'

'Did the Jews kill Christ?' Mark whispered.

'Of course. Christ the man. And because He offered Himself as the supreme sacrifice two things happened. We were saved and He ascended to Godhood.' This Mark could understand, for it made Christ a later copy of the Prophet Elijah, who had also ascended bodily to heaven and who often interceded for the good of men. It was this redemptive quality of Christ that appealed to Mark, for only Christ had rescued him, and when he fully grasped the doctrine he discussed it with Father Eusebius, asking, 'Am I right in believing that Christ was first a man and later a god?' and the Spaniard smiled until the lines in his cheeks deepened into warm shadows, and with compassion he said, 'My son, these are difficult matters which do not concern ordinary men.'

'But what do you believe?'

Father Eusebius was about to dismiss the complex matter when he saw that Mark was indeed concerned, and in a decision that would have lasting significance in the life of the young convert, he started their discussion of Christian dogma: 'The Egyptians and the Byzantines are both wrong.'

'Then what must I believe?'

'Always accept what the holy church has decided,' Father Eusebius said. 'The decisions are sometimes difficult to comprehend, but they are always right.' And he sat for a long time unraveling the mystery of the Trinity and explaining how Christ had had two complete natures, appearing on earth as a complete human being while having existed always as a deity coequal with God.

But a few nights later the workmen from Egypt took Mark aside and whispered, 'You're new to our religion, so don't get started wrong. You're a

simple, honest man and reason tells you that Christ couldn't have had two
natures at the same time. He had only one, a mixture of human and divine. He
was never divided nor can He be. And since He was born divine, Mary has got
to be considered the Mother of God.'

'I can't follow you,' Mark said.

'Christ was perpetually of one nature, a man like you and a god like God,' the
Egyptians argued, but when they parted, Mark was more perplexed than ever.

Next day he had proof of how serious the debate was, for the Byzantine who
had thrown his spear at the Egyptian was not content with having escaped
being a murderer. As the gangs were working at the destruction of Jewish
homes this loud-mouthed theologian observed to no one in particular, 'I wish
the Egyptians who argue that Christ was born a deity would explain just one
thing. Do they enjoy the image of God sucking on a human breast?'

He had barely uttered this blasphemy when an Egyptian struck him with a
rock. He fell, and before Father Eusebius could halt the riot other defenders of
Mary hurled additional rocks, so that when the Spaniard did get to the fallen
man the Byzantine was already dead and the triumphant Egyptians were
chanting, 'Mary, the Mother of God! Mary, the Mother of God!'

Father Eusebius suspended work for two days while he tried to end the
theological warfare, and during this truce Mark had an opportunity to watch
how each side refused to consider the arguments of the other and he caught a
foretaste of the bitterness that would in time split his new church. Even when
grudging peace was established, with both parties promising Father Eusebius
to brawl no more, adherents of each persuasion continued to visit Mark,
whispering, 'Be one of us. You know that Christ must be as we say.' It was his
Jewish monotheism that determined his choice, for in the end he cast his lot
with the men of Constantinople, for in spite of Father Eusebius' logic he found
it impossible to believe that Jesus Christ had been an ordinary man and at the
same time the coequal of God.

While Mark thus took his first plunge into those theological speculations on
which he would spend the greater part of his life, his father devoted his
evenings to the problem which more than any other accounted for his
conversion to Christianity, and one night after work he washed carefully, put
on his best clothes, pared his fingernails and combed his graying hair. As he left
his quarters on a mission which frightened him he was much different from the
man who, a quarter of a century before, had fought with Rabbi Asher. He was
still a round-shouldered, apelike man, more powerful than most, but the
aggressiveness which had marked him then was gone. The defeats of life had
chastened him and he no longer thought that he could force decisions;
furthermore, the placid creative work in which he had been engaged at the
synagogue had left its mark, for as he walked through the cool evening his face
showed a kind of rocklike beauty, the rugged, scarred dignity of a quarry when
the overlying earth has been scraped away and the stones laid bare. Perspiring
like a nervous schoolboy he went to the home of the wine merchant whose shop
faced the old church. There he sat uncomfortably as the Greek poured him a
welcoming glass, and after he had gulped it down, said, 'Gregorio, I've come to
ask for your daughter's hand. For my son Mark.' Before the Greek could
interrupt he added quickly, 'He's got a good job. I have a bag of drachmas. I'll
build him a home. He's a fine boy, Gregorio.'

The answer came straight and simple: 'I'd never let Maria marry a Jew.'

'But now he's a Christian.'

'Yes, a Jewish Christian.' And there the discussion ended.

The words hurt John more than he could have explained, but he did not bluster. Nor did he threaten to solve things in his own way, but like a dumb beast went home, laid aside his good clothes and stared at the wall. On succeeding nights he washed, fixed his nails and combed his hair, approaching three different Christian homes with marriageable daughters. In each he was received honorably, offered wine, extended the pleasantries common in a small town like Makor, and then rebuffed as a Jew.

After the fourth such humiliation he returned to his room and folded away his good clothes. Once he said to himself in a stumbling unreal voice, 'I think I'll take the boy to Antioch. They're always building there. It'll be easy to find him a job and a wife . . .' He stopped and buried his face in his hands, like an animal that has been wounded from an unknown quarter, and he knew then that he would never be free to leave Makor, since he was now as firmly bound to the basilica as he had been to the synagogue, for when a man builds a place of worship he walls himself inside.

Mark heard rumors of his father's expeditions but he ignored them, for in the barracks he had entered upon another area of argument among Christians, less critical perhaps than the first but of greater ultimate importance to him. In these early years, when Christianity was fighting the outside world to protect its physical existence and its own membership in an effort to achieve a permanent theology, a group of ultra-dedicated men took their guidance from St Paul, who had preached both poverty and the principle that truly religious men ought to live without women. These devout followers, first by the hundreds and later by the thousands, took vows both of poverty and of chastity, and some, like the great Origen of Caesarea, to whom the Christian world would owe much of its Bible, went so far as to base their lives upon what they thought to be the teaching of Jesus regarding castration: 'For there are some eunuchs, which were so born from their mother's womb: and there are some eunuchs, which were made eunuchs of men: and there be eunuchs, which have made themselves eunuchs for the kingdom of heaven's sake. He that is able to receive it, let him receive it.' Citing these words of Christ, the great Christian ⟨ had castrated himself.

'No man can give greater proof of religious faith than that,' an old Byzantine sergeant argued, and one day the grizzled veteran disappeared. He had gone into the Syrian desert, where he joined one of the small monasteries which were then beginning to flourish throughout the east, and it was rumored in Makor that before vanishing he had followed the example of Origen. The workmen spoke of his act with hushed respect, and before long a hawk-faced Egyptian disappeared too.

Mark was surprised when Father Eusebius spoke out sharply against monasticism. Following the general opinion in Constantinople the intellectual Spaniard, who respected art and the comforts of moderate living, preached, 'Within the monasteries men obey laws which help them to lead lives of contemplation, and this God probably loves. But other men of equal piety live in the noise of the world, building, rearing children and helping to govern the earth, and this God certainly loves.'

This problem of monasticism fascinated Mark and one evening, when the tensions in Makor were at their greatest and when Father Eusebius awaited momentary notice of the Germans' arrival in Ptolemais, the young artist sought out his priest and in the austere white-walled room asked him what had

motivated men like Origen and the old Byzantine sergeant to castrate
themselves in honor of Jesus Christ. 'As human beings they were misled,'
Eusebius said frankly, 'but as devout men trying to subject themselves to God's
law . . .'

'His law?'

'Yes. All religions must create a law and sensible men must live within that
law. It is the glory of Christianity that the law was made simple by Christ our
master, who took upon Himself its major burdens.'

'But God's law remains?' Mark asked.

'Of course,' the Spaniard said. 'Origen and the sergeant were wrong in their
interpretation of the law, but they were correct in seeking to place themselves
within that law.'

'Is there a law that priests like you may not marry?'

'Yes. The law of St Paul. But for ordinary Christians, like you, marriage is a
boon. Even a crown.' The tall Spaniard lowered his chin upon his thumbs and
smiled. 'My father had eleven children and he was closer to Christ than I will
ever be. We lived in Avaro . . .' He reminisced for some time concerning that
lovely town in central Spain and it was his opinion that both the olive oil and the
wine of Avaro were superior to Palestine's. His reflections were broken by the
arrival of a messenger from Ptolemais, and when Eusebius read that the
Germans had arrived from Antioch and would march eastward in two days, he
knew that the time for sentimental recollections of Spain had passed. Directing
the messenger to available food, he bade Mark an abrupt good night. 'Marry a
Christian girl and have eleven children. That's the pathway to heaven.' And he
disappeared to consult with the captain of the local garrison.

Thus in his first weeks as a Christian, Mark found himself engaged in various
controversies which would torment his church for centuries; and even though
he was confused by the contradictions he was nevertheless able to see the true
nature of this church: a vital, stormy meeting place for contrasting cultures and
conflicting beliefs, in which an Egyptian could spontaneously crush the head of
a Byzantine who mocked the Mother of God, and in which through the
centuries one heresy after another would have to be suppressed and schisms
healed, but in which Greeks, Romans, Persians and former Jews would be free
to battle for an acceptable theology. Mark saw that the struggle to establish the
essentials of faith for Christianity was going to prove as difficult as it had been
for Judaism; but when the law was finally agreed upon, the church would
possess a miracle of wisdom whose structure no one, certainly neither the
Rabbi Jesus nor the Apostle Paul, could have foreseen. The difference between
Christian law and Jewish would be this: to enforce their law the Jews who
would never be in supreme political control, would be limited to public opinion
including such punishments as ostracism, as great minds like Baruch Spinoza
would discover; but the Christians, to enforce theirs, would be free, since they
would enjoy supreme power, to use strangulation, burning and the extirpation
of entire provinces. But the basic problem would remain the same, and it would
be in the unraveling of this Christian law that Mark, the son of an illiterate
stonecutter, would eventually gain a kind of immortality.

But in the moments when he was first probing these matters other young
Jews his age in Kefar Nahum, Tverya and Makor were deciding that the
moment had come to throw off the Byzantine yoke, so one night rebellion of a
most serious magnitude erupted in all three communities. It was past midnight
when Mark was awakened by Abraham, Jael's husband, who took him to a

secret meeting where Jael was speaking. When she saw Mark enter she
hesitated, then said to him above the heads of the crowd, 'Menahem, will you
join us on the eve of victory?'

Her use of his real name struck with curious effect. He felt dizzy, as if a last
chance were being offered him to preserve his true existence. 'I am a Christian.'

Jael came to him, her pigtails swaying in the flickering light. She was more
beautiful than he had remembered, an extraordinary girl who had once kissed
him, who had wanted him as her husband. Extending her hands in a gesture of
complete acceptance she said, 'We are not Jews seeking a synagogue. We're
men and women seeking freedom.' And she pointed to several conspirators
who were still pagans worshiping Serapis.

But Mark, son of John, had chosen another path which made it impossible
for him to join Jael and her husband. When he refused her invitation to
participate in the revolution she ordered two Jews against whom he had fought
as a boy to grab his arms. 'We can't let you run away to warn the Byzantines,'
she said, and he remained their prisoner as teams fanned out across the town
setting fire to many buildings. He stood with his guards as enthusiastic
messengers came back with reports of initial successes.

'A skirmish by the church. We killed four soldiers.'

'Abraham was captured, but we freed him.'

Toward morning Abraham appeared, with a gash across his forehead, and
later Jael joined him. 'We're driving them from the town,' she cried and then,
seeing Mark, she told his guards, 'Let him go now. He can do us no harm.'

Through the rubble of dawn Mark went to the room of Father Eusebius,
finding it untouched and vacant. The priest had fled to refuge in an improvised
Byzantine camp under the olive trees, to which Mark now reported. The
Spaniard was relieved to see him and with deep emotion embraced him like a
son. 'When you didn't appear to help us,' Eusebius said, 'I was afraid you'd
reverted to the Jews.'

'They're not all Jews,' Mark said, 'and they're not fighting you. Only the tax
collectors. I was in your room. The church, too. Nothing was touched.'

This honest report reminded the Spaniard of lost opportunities, and he
placed his fingertips over his eyebrows as if he was praying, then said, 'Now it's
too late. Down that road from Ptolemais the German army is already
marching.'

'Can you stop them?' Mark asked.

'I could, but the Jews have asked for war,' the priest said, 'and war they must
have.' He returned his fingers to his eyes, saying, 'It was not planned to end this
way. Neither Rabbi Asher nor I wanted this,' and he sat beneath the trees as his
Byzantine soldiers took steps to protect the camp; but this was unnecessary, for
the rebels were occupied in looting the town.

The Germans, on their route-march east, reached Makor at one that
afternoon, and before Father Eusebius could instruct them otherwise, swept
into the town, battering down the improvised resistance of the Jews and
launching a systematic destruction of all Jewish homes, killing any occupants
who did not surrender promptly. With fearful efficiency the soldiers, trained
on western battlefields and hired as mercenaries by Byzantine emperors,
cleaned out one area after another until they succeeded in pushing the last of the
Jewish rebels down the steep northern flank of the town, pursuing them into
the deep wadis, where they killed recognizable fighters. It was in this melee,
deep in the wadi, that Abraham, son of the dyer Hababli, lost his vain and

reckless life. His wife Jael, who tried to defend him against four Germans, fled deeper into the brush.

Other German units attacked the area in which Rabbi Asher had his groats mill, and the white-bearded old man tried to protect his property, but it was easily set ablaze by the soldiers, who began cuffing him about. John and Mark, having been sent in the wake of the troops by Father Eusebius, witnessed the abuse that the rabbi was taking and the blood that appeared on his beard as he ricocheted from one laughing soldier to the next.

'Stop it!' the big stonecutter cried, pushing the Germans away, but by the time he rescued the rabbi the old man was in pitiful condition, so with one sweep of his arms John lifted him and sought to carry him home. But Rabbi Asher's home had disappeared with the others, so Mark led the way to Father Eusebius' study, where the wounded old man was laid on the floor beneath the crucifix.

'Your day is over,' John told him bluntly as he wiped away the blood. 'Go back to Tverya and build your law.'

'The law will exist here, too,' the battered old man whispered, but as he reiterated his basic belief the soldiers who had been deprived of their sport began shouting, 'Why should Jews who crucified our Lord be allowed a synagogue?' And a mob turned toward the rugged, low building and began tearing it apart.

Father Eusebius, hoping to preserve something of his town, tried to halt the devastation, but the Germans would not recognize his authority and proceeded to rip down the fine slabs of limestone and to tear out the windows. By the time John and Mark reached the scene the structure was doomed and the two new Christians were sickened by what was happening; they had rejected the synagogue but were appalled that strangers should defile it as a building.

'No!' John shouted as he tried to protect what he had created, but now even the townspeople had joined in the riot, and when he ran into the building he saw that a team of Syrians had ripped down a lintel and were rushing with it toward one of the pink stone pillars to see if they could smash the lovely column, and they succeeded. Like a wounded animal, a thing alive and breathing, the precious column tottered, broke in the middle and crashed in pieces. A corner of the roof, set free, began to fall, and as it collapsed the final destruction was at hand.

'You, stand back!' the rioters warned John as he tried to halt their sacrilege, while others with poles and gouges began ripping up the mosaic.

'Death to the Jews!' the men shouted, wrecking in minutes the work it had taken John years to execute. With a frantic thrust he leaped at the men destroying the mosaic, but one saw him coming and jabbed him in the stomach with a pole. The stonecutter fell backward and the rioters left him where he lay.

The destruction could not be halted, for the hatred of the imperial troops was directed against abstract ideas: not Jews but the places where they worshiped, the homes where they lived. After a few hours no Jewish buildings remained in Makor, and it was apparent that henceforth there would be no place in the town for Jews. The Germans made this decision inevitable when, after having been brought under control by Father Eusebius, they trooped solemnly to the old Syrian church for prayers, after which they dragged the local priest to the ruins of the synagogue, where they made him sprinkle holy water about the shattered stones, consecrating the wreckage as a Christian church. They then paraded formally to Father Eusebius and said, 'We've erased a synagogue and given you a basilica,' after which they stormed down the road to Tverya, where the destruction would be even more complete.

Night fell, and the punished town tried to re-establish itself. In his quiet room Father Eusebius did what he could to revive Rabbi Asher and was relieved when the bearded old man recovered. The Germans had knocked out two of his teeth and cut him about the mouth, but he was able to walk, and after midnight he left Eusebius to assemble and console his Jews. He found only desolation: of his six sons-in-law four were dead; the groats mill was no more, and when he saw the synagogue, only its gaping walls remaining, he felt as if his own life had been destroyed.

There were no homes standing to which the Jews could go, so they gathered in small crowds, looking to their rabbi for guidance, but he was too overwhelmed by the tragedy to tell them anything. But then from the wadi his daughter Jael appeared, accompanied by two of her widowed sisters, and the three girls seemed so heroic in their quiet willingness to proceed with life on whatever terms remained, that he gained courage from them and prayed aloud: 'God of Israel, again you have chastised us for our sins but in the ruins we announce that it is You we love, it is You we serve.' When he ended his lamentations he consulted with the older men of the community, asking their advice as to where the Jews should now move.

At dawn there came a flurry of hope. Perhaps it would not be necessary to move after all, for Father Eusebius climbed on a trestle and announced, 'As head of the Christian church in Makor I apologize to you for what happened yesterday. Our local soldiers, it is true, helped punish your rebels but they did not destroy your synagogue. My men did not burn your homes. You are welcome to live among us as before, and my workmen will build you a new synagogue.'

All who sought to avoid exile were inspired by this gesture, and an excited Jew cried, 'We'll rebuild the synagogue where it stood.'

'No,' Eusebius had to say quietly. 'That site was consecrated as Christian ground. We'll shift our basilica there, but you are welcome to the land we were going to use.'

'Consecrated?' the Jew asked. He had no home but he was worried about the synagogue.

Another protested, 'A bunch of drunken soldiers forced a priest to scatter holy water . . . '

A Byzantine soldier struck the Jew across the mouth, and Father Eusebius explained, 'Once a person or a building has been consecrated . . . '

'It's not a building,' the first Jew cried. 'It's a ruin.' Again the soldier slapped him as a blasphemer.

'Ruin or not,' Eusebius said, 'it was consecrated. And as I warned you when John and Mark were baptized, once the water has been placed, nothing can remove it.' He was about to speak further when Rabbi Asher, in one of those penetrating visions that sometimes reveal themselves to God's Men, realized that it had been God's wish that this synagogue be destroyed. It had been started in the first place only because Asher had misinterpreted the vision in the olive grove, and it had been finished by a profane man who had later turned renegade. It had been too arrogant, too beautiful with graven images to be a synagogue, and God had wiped it out; for the essential religious structure of the Jewish faith would never be an ornate or garish building. It would be the law. If ten Jews assembled in a mud hut and the law was there, then God was also there; and Rabbi Asher saw that if the Germans destroyed Tverya, too, the expositors who were collecting that law would be forced to gather in Babylonia, where the Talmud could be completed. It was not his responsibility to mourn over a lost synagogue, but to get ahead with the compilation of the law. In his extremity he remembered his own parable about God and Rab Naaman: 'One shred of law administered with compassion is worth a hundred towns.'

Therefore he turned his back on Father Eusebius and to the astonishment of his Jews announced, 'This day we march to Babylonia.'

Some refused to follow his leadership; they would go into exile through Ptolemais, shipping to Africa and Spain. Others would try to remain in Makor, but they would not be permitted to do so; there would be no synagogue and since they did not wish to accept Christianity, they would drift down the coast to Egypt. A few did convert, but most bundled up what clothes they could borrow from their Christian neighbors and in the afternoon of that mournful day gathered at the slope where the zigzag gate had once stood. A few stopped to weep at the shattered synagogue; a few said farewell to Christians who had befriended them; but most turned their faces resolutely towards the east–to Babylonia, where Jews would still be free to follow the teachings of the Torah.

Among those who assembled to make the long march was Jael, and when Mark saw her about to leave forever he went to her, and in view of all, said, 'Jael, don't go. Stay here with me.'

With contempt she looked at the renegade and drew away from him as if he were contaminated. He repeated his pleas, while Jewish women in small groups moved back so as to avoid contact with him. 'Jael, on your wedding day you came to me,' he said. Like a child he pointed towards the ruins of the groats mill, as if to remind her of the exact location of her visit.

She scorned him, turning away with loathing, and her widowed sisters formed a circle about her, as if to provide protection although she needed none. For the third time he appealed to her, and now she spoke: 'I would not touch you with my foot. When we needed your help you whined, "I am a Christian," and you allowed real men to face death alone.' She made a horrible rasping sound in her throat, an animal utterance of complete rejection. The Jews began to spit at him, old women with no teeth and young children with no fathers. With her slender hands, which had once caressed him, leaving their fingerprints on his heart, she bade him leave and he did so, with the jeers of his people echoing in his brain.

He went to the bare white room of Father Eusebius, where for some hours he prayed before the crucifix, a tortured man who had not been allowed to be a Jew and who was not accepted as a Christian; and at the end of his vigil he understood that it was his destiny to seek out the solitary ones who served God in the deserts of Syria.

At the edge of the town he had loved so much Rabbi Asher ha-Garsi mounted his white mule and led his Jews into exil. On the first night the rabble slept by the roadside, on the second in Sephet, and on the following morning the old rabbi did a remarkable thing: during all the time that the ruins of Tverya were visible from the road leading out of Sephet he refused to look at them. Hababli the dyer walked beside the white mule and said, 'I can see no houses in Tverya, Rabbi,' but the old man stared ahead. If the lovely city was in ruins, he would not honor the destruction by looking, and by mid-afternoon the lake and the glory were gone, and he had not said farewell; but in the evening, when the exiles were lost in low valleys from which Tverya could no longer be seen, the old man went apart from the others and turned his face toward where the city of the Herods had once stood—that glorious site by the hot baths and the lake, where the expositors had argued under a grape arbor—and he knelt in prayer, directing his thoughts neither to God nor to his memory of Tverya, but rather to that cave which lay in the hills above the town: Rabbi Akiba, in the years ahead let me have the courage you had. In Babylonia let me have the insight into God's love that you had. And in the morning the little old man led his Jews out of Palestine and into the long Diaspora that would extend itself through nearly sixteen hundred years.

Thus Makor, for the fourth time in its history, was for the moment stripped of Jews. Sennacherib had destroyed them. Nebuchadrezzar had led them into captivity and Vespasian into slavery, but each time stragglers had returned to rebuild petty settlements. Now the Byzantine expulsion threatened permanent results, for it had involved religious motivations, and these were apt to be longer-lasting.

When the final Jew was gone, when Mark had disappeared into the Syrian desert from which he would emerge years later a theologian of great power, John the stonecutter took charge of leveling the synagogue to make way for the church, and with each rock he shifted, an ache moved in his heart. The little animals he had carved with such love had been smashed by the rioters; the decorated lintels were knocked down; the marching swastikas were gone; the pillars were upended; and his poetic floor had been gouged out. The only sensible thing to do was to erase all memory of the place, setting aside such stones and pillars as might be used again. Accordingly, the hulking stonecutter directed his workmen to salvage the unbroken pillars and to make bands of iron to restore those that had been fractured. He organized teams of women to gather in baskets the mosaic cubes and to clean them for reuse, but when the new basilica was completed, usurping the site of the synagogue, and when the time came for designing the mosaic floor, John found that even though he had at his disposal the same colored stones as before, he was unable to re-create those joyous memories of his youth.

LEVEL VI

A Day in the Life of a
Desert Rider

Ornamental work carved in white limestone to decorate the
Chapel of Omar set aside for Muslim worshipers in the Basilica
of St Mary Magdalene at Makor. Installed October 18, 644 C.E.
(A.H. 22). Defaced with a panel of crosses by Crusaders from
Germany, May 24, 1099 C.E. Deposited on the afternoon of
March 26, 1291, during the siege of the town.

Jews had been living in Makor for two thousand, eight hundred and thirty-
seven years before the first Arabs settled there, but the soldier who brought the
Muslims to this town was a singular person and his arrival was an affair of
moment.

In the city of Tabariyyah, on the cold rainy morning of November 22, 635,
two different squadrons of Arab raiders saddled their camels in the pre-dawn
light that sifted down upon a crowded caravanserai standing beside the lake.
They were about to participate in a meaningful experiment whose results
would go far to determine the nature of Islam in Palestine and Africa. The men
of the first squadron, reflecting from their white robes the lights of a campfire,
were agitated and noisy, moving this way and that with curved swords
gleaming as they prepared to embark upon a dangerous mission. They were led
by a small, wiry Arab of marked energy, the captain Abu Zeid, whose fiery
commands, whispered like the utterances of a serpent, bespoke the violence
with which he had led his desert troops in their conquest of rich Byzantine
cities. As he strode among his men, testing their saddles and their swords, his
face was sometimes illumined by red flames from the fire and he seemed an
avenging demon hovering at the edge of Tabariyyah, ready to strike with great
fury. Finally he could control his impatience no longer, and without awaiting
official orders from the silent headquarters building, sprang into the saddle of
his gray mare, kicked her flanks vigorously and led his troops through the gates
and into the darkness, crying, 'To Safat! Allah will lead us!' Stragglers
lounging by the camp cheered as the troops rode forth, while warriors who
watched them go said with practiced judgment, 'By nightfall Safat will be
Arab.' There might be no residents surviving in the city, and houses might be
roofless, but they would be Arab.

When that first violent squadron was gone another became gradually visible
in the dark shadows encompassing the caravanserai: these men were not
mounted, nor were they nervous. They moved with quiet determination
among their camels, tying down burdens and tightening saddle straps as if they
were about to depart on a trading expedition where all things were known
except the price of cloth. They were Arabs, all of them, and like the first group
had proved themselves in the capture of Damascus and the occupation of

Tabariyyah. They constituted one of the finest segments of the Arab army, and whereas the riotous troops of Abu Zeid had been thrown against Safat to kill and burn, this second contingent had been held in reserve for the more significant part of the test.

Their leader stood by a pillar of the caravanserai, a tall, slim man wearing a gray headdress that reached to his waist and a multicolored robe composed of many strips of cloth sewn together. He wore heavy sandals and a wide belt of woven goat's hair which supported a leather loop from which hung a medium-sized sword. He was a man of dark countenance, in his mid-thirties, and he said little. Keeping to the shadows he observed his men as they checked their battle equipment, then directed one to find out whether all animals had been watered. He studied with approval the forty-odd horses that stood easily in the midst of the caravanserai, excellent beasts which had proved their mettle at Damascus. They wore no saddles, but three large camels stood nearby loaded with their equipment, including spare saddles, and the tall man in the many-colored robe moved slowly, like a merchant on an ordinary day, to inspect these camels, assuring himself that his own red-studded saddle was included in the luggage. He then returned to his pillar, from which he studied the eastern sky, where above the Sea of Tabariyyah the stars were fading and the light of sunrise was beginning to show.

He was Abd Umar, and his first name signified that he had been born a slave: his father had been some unknown desert warrior, his mother a black Abyssinian slave captured on some raid to the south, but he had never known either of his parents. He had grown up in the Arabian city of Yathrib and had spent his early years leading camel caravans from that trading center over the seven hundred miles to Damascus and back. He spoke Arabic and Greek, and when the Arabs burst out of the desert with a new message for the world he had found a place among the armies and a position of responsibility among the chiefs of the tribes. In what other nation could a half-Negro slave win a post of such honor? For the Prophet had said that when God created men he lifted dust from all parts of the earth, and some was black and some red and some white, but all men were made of that dust and all were therefore brothers.

It was this slave who had been picked for the day's important mission. The Arabs hoped that while Abu Zeid and his ruffians were subduing Safat in the hills, the disciplined troops of Abd Umar might succeed in capturing Makor without much killing, for if that town could be occupied peacefully, the crucial seaport of Ptolemais, which the Arabs knew by the ancient name of Akka, might surrender without a siege, and retention of this port was necessary if places like Tyre, Cyprus and mighty Egypt were to be invaded. It was with knowledge of these strategies that the slave now walked among his men, whispering, 'It's almost dawn.'

Silently, as if they too appreciated the gravity of the day, his men mounted their camels, keeping the forty riderless horses under control: those handsome brown-flanked beasts would be used by a picked group for the final assault on Makor and must be kept rested during the initial part of the expedition. Now the warriors atop the camels became visible in the gray light which spread over Tabariyyah, bringing the hills into relief: they were hardened fighters who had met the best mercenaries that Byzantium could throw against them. Many wore short beards but most were clean-shaven like their leader. They wore robes of every hue and dimension; when their clothes were of a dun color the men seemed to merge into the bodies of their camels, but when the robes were alternate lengths of purple, red, yellow, brown, green and blue, the Arabs were like bright birds that had flown in from the desert, seeking the valleys of Palestine. In eight years this resolute body of men had not known defeat and they were now quietly determined that this day would see both their victories and their faith extended. Waiting quietly for Abd Umar to mount and lead them forth, the Arabs relaxed on their camels as if they were sleeping centaurs, while their horses stood with equal patience.

But Abd Umar was not ready to depart. Leaving his men he walked with military grace out of the caravanserai and across to a small hut standing by the lake, where the light of an oil lamp showed a mean interior: bare mud walls, no furniture, a few cracked dishes and some clay pots. This was the headquarters selected by the general of the Arab troops when he captured Tabariyyah, and now he slept soundly on the floor, a rugged man in his fifties, with the ends of his beard trailing in the dust, his right cheek cradled on his right palm in the manner used by Muhammad when he slept.

'General,' Abd Umar whispered. There was no response from the sleeping warrior, so the former slave remained kneeling beside his superior, not certain what he should do next. Like Abd Umar the general had invaded Byzantium not to gain wealth or comfort for himself; a hovel with a dirt floor was sufficient, for he rode only to extend the spiritual dominion of the Prophet.

'General, we go,' Abd Umar whispered, still reluctant to touch the sleeping man. In seven major battles the general had led his troops to spectacular victories, but now he refused to rise when his subordinates were setting forth on important engagements. He had instructed them well and he trusted both the wild-headed Abu Zeid and the sagacious slave Abd Umar. There was nothing he could tell them now and he needed sleep, for if Abd Umar succeeded in capturing Makor, all the Arabs would rush westward to besiege Akka, and the coming days might be exhausting.

Finally Abd Umar shook the general. 'Tomorrow you may ride to Akka,' he told him. 'By nightfall Makor will be yours.'

Grudgingly the sleeper raised himself on one elbow, intending to berate the slave, but when he saw Abd Umar's intense, dark face he realized how eagerly the young captain had wanted to speak before marching westward. 'You have your instructions,' he growled. 'No killing.'

'I shall obey,' Abd Umar said, and he rose to go, but the general caught his sleeve.

'You wanted to talk about the battle?'

'Yes,' the former slave replied.

'I can repeat only what the Prophet told me when we approached Mecca that first time. "Be merciful . . . if you can. Spare the aged, the women, the children . . . if you can. Give every man an honest chance to join you, and if he submits, accept him as he is, but even if the enemy resists, kill no sheep, no camel, no ox–unless you intend to eat it. And let no man harm a palm tree or an olive."'

'I have my instructions,' Abd Umar said.

The general dropped back to the ground and returned to sleep.

Thus Abd Umar, the servant of Muhammad, received his commission to explore the possibilities of compassion and conciliation as weapons of empire, and as he walked thoughtfully toward the caravanserai he thought of that morning when he had stood at the gates of Yathrib, watching as the Prophet, accompanied by a few devotees from Mecca, came seeking refuge in the northern city. It was an ugly day, Abd Umar remembered, with enemies eager to jeer the bearded, thick-set man with lustrous eyes and black hair reaching to his shoulders who claimed to have heard God speaking to him, and at that time Abd Umar had not appreciated the significance of Mohammad's arrival either in Yathrib or among the Arabs. For some years he had known vaguely of the man's existence, and after the arrival he had heard that Muhammad was adding to the revealed writings which he had brought with him from Mecca, but for Abd Umar the actuality of the Prophet had not been great.

Then war came, with the people of Mecca trying to invade Yathrib, that they might kill the Prophet, and Abd Umar had volunteered to defend him and had engaged in many bloody encounters in which as a half-Negro slave he rode in the personal entourage of the Prophet, thus seeing at first-hand the brilliant generalship of the holy man. Once Abd Umar told his own fighters, 'Three times in those days our side was surely defeated, except that Muhammad rallied us with clever moves, and each time he succeeded in throwing a superior enemy off balance and defeating him.' Any successful military tactics that Abd Umar now possessed he had gained from watching Muhammad.

It was through this military service that Abd Umar had first come to respect Muhammad, but it was not long before he began to feel the man's spiritual force as well. Abd Umar had been too young to be termed a friend of the Prophet's, but he had been close enough to know the impact of what Muhammad had preached—a lesson whose five steps were so simple that any human being could understand: the old gods were dead; there was only one God; He had been discovered by the Jews; He sent the great prophet Jesus Christ to reveal His views; and now He had sent the final prophet, Muhammad, to complete them. On one point Muhammad had always insisted when Abd Umar heard him speak: he had not come out of Arabia with some strange new doctrine, but only with the fulfillment of what the Jews and Christians had started before.

Thus when Abd Umar walked toward the caravanserai in the cold morning air, preparing to invest a town he had never seen, he moved with a confidence that the defenders of the town could not have; for they were either Jews whose religion had grown old and meaningless or Christians who had misinterpreted their Jesus as the final prophet. In no way did Abd Umar hate his adversaries; he felt sorry for their temporary blindness and he intended to help them find God. It was true that in the capture of both Damascus and Tabariyyah some Jews and Christians had been slow to grasp the message of the Prophet, and there had been killings, but those days were past. Starting now, with Makor, there would be no more killing of either Jew or Christian, for the three faiths must live together in tolerance; the leaders of Islam now realized that if Jews and Christians were kept alive they would not only help to make the land rich, but after a few years would acknowledge the moral superiority of Muhammad's revelation and their conversion would be accomplished as a matter of course.

In this reflective mood Abd Umar re-entered the caravanserai and without speaking climbed aboard his camel, signaling that he was ready. There were no shouts, no clattering of swords such as had marked Abu Zeid's departure for Safat; the troops responsible for this new type of Arab policy moved quietly out of town, avoided the established roads and sought a path that would take them quickly onto high ground, from which they would traverse the mountains and swamps separating them from Makor. It would be a punishing cross-country ride, but they would come at last upon the Damascus road, down which they could make their final dash on horseback. The first part of the journey, climbing the steep hills to the west of Tabariyyah, would be the most difficult, and Abd Umar led the way, encouraging his men until they had scrambled to the top of the curious camel-shaped hill called the Horns of Hattin, where he halted his troops to inspect the horses. There he delivered his last instructions.

'You are to kill no one. Set no fires. And no man may touch a palm tree or an olive.' He waited until these new orders had had time to be understood, then rode to each of his lieutenants, reminding them personally, 'Tonight Makor must accept the Prophet, and its people must be our friends.' The grim-faced men agreed, and he led them westward.

As he rode into the heart of Palestine he recalled the first time he had heard of this rich land: he had for some years been leading desert caravans between Yathrib and Damascus, six weeks in the saddle each way, and he had been vaguely aware that off to the west lay a small land occupied by Greeks and Romans; but it had made no impression on him until on one trip, made before he knew Muhammad, he was returning to Arabia with a cargo of gold from Byzantium when he overtook the caravan of a trader from Mecca and with him traveled south for several days. Finally the Meccan had said, 'I must turn westward toward Jerusalem,' and for the first time Abd Umar had discussed that city.

'It's torn by strife between the Christians,' the Meccan said.

'The Christians against whom?' Abd Umar inquired.

'Themselves,' the Meccan replied, shaking his head in confusion, and he had led his camels toward the hills which protected the Jordan.

Now Abd Umar himself was involved in Palestine and he was finding it as perplexing as the long-ago Meccan had indicated: when the Arabs ventured into Tabariyyah following their conquest of Damascus they had met with little armed resistance, but the leaders of three different Christian churches had come bearing complaints one against the other so that brawling had broken out with loss of life. Spies had come to the caravanserai at Tabariyyah with reports that similar conditions prevailed in both Safat and Makor, while Akka was bitterly divided over which church had the right to collect money from pilgrims arriving from Rome and the west to visit the Sea of Galilee. At Damascus, of course, the contentions between the Christian churches had been disgraceful, and as a result of these confusions, plus the desire to keep Christian pilgrims visiting their holy places—for they brought much wealth—Abd Umar had begun to make a study of the Christians and their habits, gathering what information he could from spies and the leaders of churches in captured Damascus and Tabariyyah.

In this work he was encouraged by something Muhammad had once told him: 'There are only three permissible religions—Judaism, Christianity and ours—and these are acceptable because each relies upon a Book which God had personally handed down.' He pointed out that the Jews had their Old Book delivered to them through Moses, while the Christians had their New called forth by Jesus Christ, but the Arabs had the Koran, and since the latter summarized the best of the preceding two, the former were no longer essential. On one memorable day Muhammad had told his companions, 'You are to follow the traditions of the Jews and Christians span by span and cubit by cubit . . . so closely that you will go after them even if they creep into the hole of a lizard.' Later, when there had been much discussion of this teaching, the Prophet had predicted in Abd Umar's hearing, 'You will always find that our most affectionate friends will be those who say, 'We are Christians,' for they like us are people of the Book.' At Tabariyyah, after Abd Umar had halted the brawling among the various sectors of the Christian church, he had asked the priests to instruct him in their faith and he was relieved to find that what Mohammad had said was true: these Christians accepted three of the Prophet's favorite predecessors, John Baptist, Mary the Virgin and Jesus Christ. In fact, he discovered that the Christians revered Mary almost as much as the Arabs did, and this was reassuring.

At the same time, however, he discovered that the Christian church was so badly split between Byzantine, Roman and Egyptian factions–regarding points of theology which he could not untangle–that any hope of reconciliation was impossible. He suspected that because of its hateful fights Christianity would soon wither like a rootless plant exposed to sunlight in a desert wadi, and it was his job to make the last days of the religion as pleasant as possible. At Makor he was determined to accord the Christians every courtesy, hoping that they would of themselves see their error and join Islam.

Was he arrogant in these assumptions? Not especially, for in those springtime years of Arabian faith, when leaders like Abd Umar had known Muhammad personally, Islam seemed a marvel of cohesion and order; when compared to the confusions that tormented the Christian church and the inadequacy that had overtaken the Jews, it had both commitment and direction, so that Abd Umar could be excused if he believed that the future lay with his kind. For the days had not yet come when Islam was to be shattered into worse schisms than even the Christians knew, but the great separation into hostile camps was even then building. Before Abd Umar was dead the saintly Ali, cousin of the Prophet and husband of his daughter Fatima, would be slain; his sons would be hounded into near-divinities around whom would rally many of the greatest minds of Islam and much of its propulsive power, forming a breach that would never be healed.

If Abd Umar had looked closely at his own religion he could have seen these strains developing, but like most religious persons of his day he was more concerned about the divisions that rent other religions than about the strife that would soon shatter his own, so as he pressed his troops toward the forest that separated him from Makor, he cautioned himself: Under no circumstances must we become involved in the quarrels of the Christians, for they will soon fall apart and join us.

Within the vanished walls of Makor the Christians waited. They were a sorely divided lot torn into four fragments which reflected the various schisms that racked Christianity in this period. Not even the loss of Damascus to the Arabs and the consequent halt of trade had inspired the sects to unite against their common enemy. The fall of Tiberias had ended the rich pilgrim traffic to Capernaum. And now it looked as if the approach of Islam would terminate Makor's profitable trade in relics: each year several dozen thigh bones pertaining to St. Mary Magdalene were peddled to believers who carried them home to adorn small European churches, and the loss of this income could prostrate the town. But still the Christians quarreled.

Of course, the basic argument–was Jesus man-and-God-at-the-same-time as Egyptians argued, or was He man-then-God as those of Constantinople believed?–had long been settled precisely as Father Eusebius had foreseen: each side was wrong and all good Christians now acknowledged that Christ owned two complete natures, one forever human, the other forever divine, though the Egyptians still refused to abandon their contention and on it had constructed a separatist church. But with the problem of Christ's physical nature thus solved to most people's satisfaction debate was moved onto a higher level, for the problem which now tormented the church was this: Was the spiritual nature of Jesus human or divine?

In the Basilica of St. Mary Magdalene, built nearly three centuries before and well known in Europe for the mosaics which pilgrims visited on their way to and from the holy places, a bishop reigned, appointed by the emperor in Constantinople and obedient to the desires of that imperial ruler. He was an ineffectual man who had at first tried to bring some kind of peace to Makor, but in making this attempt he had insisted upon the orthodox opinion that Christ had two separate natures, human and completely divine; but this doctrine was not acceptable to the simple-minded people of Makor, who knew in their hearts that Christ could have had only one nature, human and divine at the same time. So the two-nature bishop in his basilica preached the ideas of Constantinople to an ever-dwindling congregation, while in the ramshackle church east of the main gate the one-nature citizens worshiped according to the popular rites of Egypt. They were sometimes threatened by the bishop, who imported imperial troops from Constantinople, and when these soldiers appeared, the one-nature people filed meekly into the basilica to promise both the bishop and the mercenaries that they would henceforth accept the orthodox contention that Christ had two natures, but as soon as the soldiers disappeared they would go roaring back to their own church, shouting:

> 'The body of Jesus is one,
>   Holy forever.
> The Mother of Jesus is God-like,
>   Holy forever.'

When this provocative song erupted outraged Byzantines would try to murder the Egyptians, so that Makor was often splashed with blood; but the schism could not be healed, nor would it ever be. Like the great split that was about to engulf the followers of Muhammad, this one between Egypt and the west would endure forever.

In addition to the Byzantine and Egyptian sects Makor owned two additional Christian churches, one supported by Rome for the use of its pilgrims coming from Europe and another for the strange Nestorians of the east, and between these two groups there was also frequent brawling, so that in this little village one could observe a microcosm of the theological anarchy that characterized the church in Asia: the Byzantines from Constantinople, the Romans, the Egyptian separatists and the Nestorians.

It was into this cauldron that one of the noblest emperors of Byzantium had recently tossed an attractive new theology. Heraclius was soldier, scholar and saint, and in the first of these capacities had recently defeated the Persian Chosroes to win back the True Cross, which had originally been discovered three centuries before by Queen Helena, and this accomplishment had made him the world's premier Christian. So in his second character he studied the dissensions that threatened his church and was now ready as a saintly man to suggest an ingenious compromise acceptable to Byzantine, Roman, Egyptian and Nestorian alike, if only they approached his proposal with good faith. In those fateful years when the Arabs were stealing Damascus and half his empire

Heraclius was busy developing his grand compromise, which reached Makor in this provisional form:

Eager to end the strife that mars our church, we have decided that there shall be no more argument as to whether the nature of Jesus Christ was one or two. The matter is unimportant and we hereby decree that regardless of how a man believes, he is welcome in our church. Forgetting the nature of Christ's body, we hereby announce that He had but one will, which faultlessly represented the will of God. This is now the belief of all true Christians, for we have spoken.

The emperor's edict was read at dawn one summer's morning, and by nightfall three men were dead in the ecclesiastical rioting. In succeeding days the bishop wailed in his basilica, 'There are two natures in Christ and one will. That is the law.' But the stubborn Egyptians countered, 'There is one nature and two wills,' so that the emperor's gesture, intended to bring conciliation, had brought only a new schism to agitate the community.

And so as Muslim troops approached from the east on that mighty conquest which would terminate the power of Byzantium in the Galilee, the citizens of that contentious area continued their bitter arguments over the nature of Christ, not realizing that they were engaged in an extension of the same argument that had agitated Makor in the days when the young Jew Menahem ben Yohanan joined the new church as Mark, and the debate was no more trivial now than it had been then: it was an effort to build a base from which Christianity could conquer the world. If one considered Jesus to be all man, His divinity was rendered meaningless, while the miracle of Mary as the Mother of God vanished; on the other hand, if one argued that He was all God, the significance of human redemption was diminished and the crucifixion could be interpreted merely as a device adopted by God to prove a point: no human suffering or agony need be involved. However, if a concept of Jesus could be evolved whereby His substance, His nature and His will could all be accepted as both divine and human, then Christianity would have acquired a subtle unifying principle upon which enormous structures of faith and philosophies of life could be built. It was in this historic battle over the meaning of Christ that the Christians of Makor were engaged, but the adroit proposal of Emperor Heraclius helped little, for within a few weeks of its reception pickets came from Tabariyyah with news that the Arabs were planning to capture Makor, and Ptolemais as well.

Now, as Abd Umar, the servant of Muhammad, led his squadron away from open fields and into the forests of the Galilee, he might be somewhat confused by the conflicting claims of Christians; but he was totally bewildered by the Jews, for he would never be able to understand why they had failed to accept Muhammad, and he approached this problem with love, for in any essential meaning of the word he could have considered himself a Jew.

As a half-Negro slave he had for a time been the property of one Umar, hence his name Slave-of-Umar, but that man had disappeared and he had passed into the hands of a robust, red-headed Jew named Ben Hadad, whose ancestors had wandered down from Palestine during the turbulent years when General Vespasian of Rome was crushing the rebellious Jews. Ben Hadad's people had arrived in a caravan from the Galilee and had found a pleasing welcome in Arabia among the sand dunes and the white-walled cities. The Jews had lived alone, obedient to the Torah, and had gradually established themselves as traders, especially in Bed Hadad's city of Yathrib, to be known in history as Medina.

Ben Hadad was a large, jovial merchant whose caravans had prospered and who had acquired, during a trip to Damascus, a portion of the Talmud brought there from Babylonia, and his possession of these sayings of the Jewish fathers had made him a kind of spiritual leader of his people; but he fell into no traditional category of rabbi, sage or teacher. He was an easygoing man who loved the hurly-burly of trade and who sent his adopted son, Abd Umar, into the desert with a caravan by himself at the age of eleven.

'Take care of the camels and God will take care of you,' Ben Hadad had said to the dark boy. 'If a man asks for fifteen pieces, give him sixteen . . . if you expect to do business with him again.' Where the other Jews of Medina refused to engage in any work on Shabbat, Ben Hadad argued, 'If my camels are half a league from home at Friday sunset, God Himself wants to see them properly bedded down.' He also taught Abd Umar, 'If you abide for three days in the desert tending a sick camel, God will somehow repay you.' He was a man of forty-eight who had four wives and numerous children, but of them all he loved Abd Umar best, for the slave was quick and had the same love of good living as Ben Hadad. 'When a young man goes to Damascus and fails to see the girls from Persia, he might just as well have stayed at home with the women packing dates.'

Better than most Arabs, Abd Umar appreciated how much of the Koran had come to Muhammad through the teachings of Jewish sages, and he approved when the Prophet, hoping to bind the old and the new into one force, made generous efforts to win the Jews to his side. Muhammad had nominated Jerusalem, the city from which he had ascended to heaven, as the locality toward which his followers must turn when they prayed; he had reassured his Jewish neighbors repeatedly that he like them was descended from Abraham–through Ishmael in his case; and he had incorporated into his religion all matters which the Jews held most precious: the concept of one God, the visions of Moses, the rectitude of Joseph, the glory of Saul and David and Solomon, and the practical wisdom of Job. To any intelligent mind the religion of Muhammad must be the logical next step in the growth of Judaism, and the Prophet waited for the Jews to join him. It was symbolic, perhaps, that when he fled from Mecca to Medina, it was the hospitable Jew Ben Hadad who first welcomed him coming through the Medina gate, and one of the first gestures Muhammad made in his new home was to invite Ben Hadad's people to join him.

Why had the Jews refused? Why? Abd Umar often wondered, for he could recall the derisive manner in which his father, Ben Hadad, had laughed when Muhammad suggested that he lay aside the Old Book and accept the Koran. When pressed, Ben Hadad said 'I agree with you that there is only one God, but prophecy has ceased.' Argument had followed, and Muhammad was as persuasive a logician as any who had ever crossed Arabia, but the Jew had repulsed him with his rocklike faith: 'The Torah is all we need.'

Abd Umar could recall the mornings on which he said good-bye to Ben Hadad for the last time: he was twenty years old and about to start his caravan on a trip to Damascus when Muhammad and some followers launched a discussion under a nearby tree, and as he heard the inspired message that came from the Prophet's lips he delayed the departure of his camels and listened, realizing for the first time that he–the dark slave of a Jew–was being summoned to a lifelong mission. He lingered far beyond the prudent time for starting, hearing with awe the revelations of the man from Mecca:

> 'When the sun is overthrown,
> And when the stars fall,
> And when the hills are moved
> And when the camels big with young
> Are left by the wayside,
> And when the wild beasts are herded together,
> And when the seas rise,
> And when souls are reunited,
> And when the girl-child that was buried alive is asked
> For what sin she was slain,
> And when the pages are laid open
> And when the sky is torn away,
> And when hell is lighted,
> And when Paradise comes near,
> Then every soul will know what it has done!'

At the conclusion of this apocalyptic vision he had prostrated himself before the seer, crying, 'I am your servant.'

'Not mine, but God's,' the Prophet had replied, and at that moment Abd Umar entered into the covenant which had subsequently guided his life, transforming him from a slave into a captain of the faithful.

In his new-found exaltation he had gone to Ben Hadad, saying, 'Father, I've surrendered to the Prophet.'

At first the red-haired Jew had scowled, but then had said generously, 'I hope you find comfort.'

'Will you join me?'

'No, there's one God and for Jews He speaks through the Torah.'

The conviction of Ben Hadad's reply caught his son off guard, but finally the slave understood. 'You're a leader, so you have to remain a Jew. But the others . . .'

'Will they join Muhammad?' The merchant laughed. 'Son, we're Jews because we believe certain things. None of the others will join.'

The Jew's reply disturbed Abd Umar and he felt obliged to say, 'Then this may be the last time I'll take your caravan to Damascus.'

'Son,' Ben Hadad replied with humor, 'I brought you up to be a man of God. In Damascus the Christians are men of God, too. So is Muhammad. We'll all work together somehow.'

Yet Abd Umar's prediction was correct. That was the last trip he would make to Damascus for the Jew, but how could one explain, even to himself, the reasons that had ended their relationship? In spite of every overture made by Muhammad, the Jews of Medina had remained obdurate. In Abd Umar's absence they had even joined an enemy in war against Muhammad. They had ridiculed his Koran publicly and had co-operated with pagans in attempts to halt his acceptance, so on one dreadful day which the new religion would long try to forget, the eight hundred Jewish men of Medina were marched into the market place, led to an open trench and beheaded one by one so that their skulls and torsos pitched into the waiting grave. At the moment of death each Jew was offered his life if he was willing to answer one question correctly.

'Will you forswear your religion and join us?'

Ben Hadad laughed at the question and his head rolled one way while his body tumbled another.

That day seven hundred and ninety-nine Jews rejected Muhammad; only one saved his life by converting, and when the tragedy had ended, two facts were clear: Jews were not going to join the new religion, but it was impossible to execute them all. They were good farmers and they were needed on the land, so a grudging truce was arranged: if they behaved themselves they could cling to their Book, but they would have to pay higher taxes and would no longer be free to move about.

To demonstrate his own willingness to forgive, Muhammad took recourse to a dramatic gesture. When the sickening massacre was over and repentance was in the air he moved among the five or six hundred Jewish women who had been made widows that day and selected a beautiful girl whom Abd Umar had known well, Rihana, a merchant's wife, and the Prophet married her. In the next year, when he was forced to execute another rebellious Jewish leader, he married that man's widow as well, the gracious Safia, and with his two Jewish widows he had lived amicably, depending upon them to mitigate the opposition of the Arabian Jews.

As Abd Umar's soldiers were riding through the Galilee forest their captain reviewed these gloomy memories, and the trees, to which the Arabs were not accustomed, depressed both him and the troops and he recalled that mournful day when he had returned from Damascus to find that Ben Hadad had been slain. He had run to the long grave to honor the good Jew who had taught him so much and there he had reflected: Of every ten boys I played with as a child, nine are buried in that grave. The weight of ugliness he had experienced that day would never leave him; it moved with him through the Galilee.

His attention was taken from these matters, however, when the road through the forest opened to display a view of the surrounding hills, and on one, where Safat hung like a star in the sky, the Arabs could see fires burning. They watched with strange emotions: their brothers had reached the town, but they were destroying it in the manner that was to be forbidden in the future. A soldier said matter-of-factly, 'Abu Zeid got there.'

Abd Umar turned brusquely in his saddle and snapped, 'The days of fire have vanished.' After staring again at the rising smoke he added, 'We'll take Makor with none of that.' As he urged his camel back into the gloomy forest, rain began to fall and he knew that the transit of the swamp would be difficult, but he thought not of these immediate matters; his mind remained focused on that afternoon when he had first seen the long grave of the Jews. It was there, at the place of death, that he had become the kind of man he was now: willing to fight and a courageous leader, but a man who would never condone vengeful killing.

Within the mean and narrow streets of Makor, Jews awaited the ominous coming of Islam. They knew of the fall of Damascus and the capture of Tverya, their once-sacred city on the lake, and they shivered, for this was the season of storms, when rabbis added to their prayers a phrase giving thanks to God for having sent the rain: 'You, O Lord, are mighty forever. You cause the wind to blow and the rain to fall.' Once more a third of Makor's population was Jewish, and in the surrounding valleys were many additional families working their farms, for the Jews still preferred rural life to the business ventures in town, where money matters remained in Greek hands. But these Jews were allowed to play no significant role in the Christian town, for Constantinople had laid down the rule that no new Jewish buildings could be started nor improvements added to those already standing. Furthermore, even if a synagogue were in existence, it must not compete in either height or appointments with Christian churches in the same community, and since the Nestorian minority in Makor could afford little, the synagogue was truly a hovel.

Nor was the Jewish deficiency expressed only in externals; the bewildered rabbi who led the community was as bedraggled spiritually as his synagogue was physically. He was neither an old man wise in the traditions of Palestinian life, nor a young scholar imbued with the inner potential of the Talmud; he was merely a forty-year old man subservient to the Byzantine majority and a blind adherent of the legalistic formulations of the Talmud. He was a kind of moralizing bookkeeper who considered it his job to keep his Jews obedient to the civil law of Constantinople and the religious dictates of the Talmud. In the long history of Judaism there would be many such rabbis, and in spite of them the religion would survive, but a real rabbi, like Akiba, who faced with Rome the same problems that the Makor rabbi faced with Byzantium, and who in the process enlarged the whole scope of Judaism, making it nobler than it had been when he received it, would have been appalled at the pettiness of mind that characterized the local rabbi. Only one favorable comment could be made of the man: he was no worse than the Christian priests who served this little town during the death throes of the Byzantine empire in Palestine.

Where had they come from, these Jews of Makor? Following the general expulsion of 351, when Tverya was laid waste and the compilation of the Palestinian Talmud brought to an end, in each remote valley a few rural families had survived, and when the fury was over, these remnants began to assemble in towns like Makor, where they formed ineffective groups lacking both funds and leadership. Once or twice every decade some Jew of Ptolemais or Caesarea, where the communities were strong, would make the long trip to Babylonia, where the center of Judaism now lay, to refresh himself as to what was happening among the leaders, and he would return to explain to neighbouring villages the decisions that Babylon had recently handed down. And occasionally a ship from Spain would bring some wandering scholar on a visit to the holy places of Judaism, and he would report to the gape-mouthed Jews of Makor on the wonders of Europe.

In this year of crisis, when Islam was on the march and when only a unified land could hope to withstand the assault, their foolish rabbi had sorely split his community over an incident so timeless that it could have sprung from the scroll of Genesis. Like most of the classic tragedies of the Torah it began simply: There were two brothers. One married a beautiful wife. The other did not.

Throughout Palestine, for the last two thousand years and regardless of who controlled the country, there had always been one occupation monopolized by Jews, the dyeing industry, and in Makor the dye vats that lay west of the basilica were owned by two brothers, Judah and Aaron, the older of whom had some years before married Shimrith, a stately, beautiful young woman whose father had traded by donkey with the markets of Ptolemais, while the younger brother had married a local farm girl, stodgy and hard-working. The marriage of Judah and Shimrith had been a productive one, for although they had no children they had established a loving, observant Jewish home from which they radiated what little enlightenment Makor knew in those bleak years. In fact, when Jews compared their fumbling rabbi with Judah, they often observed among themselves: 'How much better off this town would be if Judah were our rabbi.'

But this year his attention had to be focused elsewhere. With the fall of Damascus to the Arabs, stragglers began arriving in Makor with tales of Arab invincibility, and fear settled over the town. Trade with Damascus halted and a worrisome surplus of dyed goods began to accumulate, so that the brothers were faced with a difficult choice: close down the vats and throw their Jewish workers into starvation, or visit Ptolemais to see if more lengths of cloth could be pressed upon the merchants coming there from Venice and Genoa. Accordingly, in early November, Judah did what thousands of men from his little town had done in centuries past: he dressed in his best clothes, found himself a staff and set forth upon the journey to Ptolemais, which still seemed the most exciting and romantic settlement in the world; and it was while he was gone that his wife Shimrith became vaguely aware that her brother-in-law Aaron had begun to look upon her with unaccustomed interest, even though he had a wife of his own.

The brothers had always lived together in a cluster of cramped buildings at the western edge of town: the dye vats stood in the middle, with the mean synagogue to the north and a home for two families to the south. Aaron and his large family kept to one half of the house, while Judah and Shimrith held the other. Often the two households ate together, so that Aaron had many opportunities to know Shimrith, who respected him as the gruff, powerful man he was, beardless and slope-shouldered from the heavy work at the dye vats. His big hands were unusually stained with the signs of his occupation and he was careless of his general appearance, so that he was not the kind of person Shimrith would normally seek out, and now in her husband's absence she began to fear him, for it was obvious that he had become obsessed with her.

Whenever she was in sight he stared at her, lasciviously. Ignoring his own wife he tried to place himself so that Shimrith would have to pass close, and at each opportunity his red-stained hands reached for her legs. She avoided him when possible, but the proximity in which they lived made contact inescapable, and she grew to loathe his sudden, grabbing appearances from behind doors. One day he cornered her when his own wife was absent and was so disgusting in his behavior that Shimrith cried, 'I shall tell Judah when he returns.'

'Do so and I'll kill him,' Aaron threatened, but Shimrith beat him about the face until he had to let her run panic-stricken to her own portion of the house.

While she huddled there alone she heard the rising of the wind as a storm came in from the sea, bringing the reality of winter to the Galilee. That night there would be frost and on the higher mountains snow; farmers would hurry with their winter plowing and citizens of the town would don their warm clothes and cluster together about small fires, listening to the winds howling down the wadis. Makor, on its exposed height, was especially susceptible to these wintry storms, and pilgrims from Europe who had always imagined Jesus and Moses as living in the sweltering heat of the desert were often bewildered when they found the Galilee as cold as their homelands.

For Shimrith it was a miserable, lonely period. During the bleak winters she had always loved being with her husband, in the warmth of his arms and safe in his protection. Now, alone, she felt afraid to leave her own cold rooms lest her brother-in-law molest her, and even when she heard the children playing and calling for her she kept to herself, praying for the swift return of her husband from Ptolemais. But the storms kept him in the port city, and the day came when Aaron felt free to make a direct attack upon her.

He was impelled to do so by a curious logic with which he had convinced himself that she was hungry for his advances: Look at her! That big, wonderful woman with wide hips and me the only man in Makor strong enough to satisfy her. She's alone and she must want me to come to her. One look at her smooth olive face tells me she wants to be loved, and her hands twitch nervously when I'm nearby. He honestly believed that he would be doing his sister-in-law a favor by approaching her, and this led to the conviction that she had, by sly glances, invited him to do so.

Consequently, in the middle of a morning, when he should have been at the dye vats, he slipped out the rear of the workshop, scurried along the edge of town and darted into the back door of his home. Assuring himself that his wife was occupied with her children in the open area between their house and the basilica, he burst into Shimrith's house, appearing before her suddenly, grabbing her and kissing her with much vigor.

She tried to push him away, but with a skill that he must have practiced in imagination he pinioned her arms with his body, used one hand to cover her mouth and another to throw aside his loose-fitting robe, so that he stood naked and furious before her. He then proceeded to tear away her clothes, while she kicked and struggled vainly against his superior force. When he had her nearly nude he forced her to the floor, still keeping his hand over her mouth, and in a violent scene of tearing and brutality tried to force his massive way into her body.

When the struggle reached its final stage she was afraid that she must faint, for she was barely able to breathe, but when she felt his body stabbing at her and his animal-like breath enveloping her she made a supreme effort to protect herself, kicking at him with her knees and scratching her nails across his face. This unexpected pain enraged the dyer, and with an uncontrollable blow of his fist he bruised her face and knocked her nearly unconscious. Unable to resist any further she fell back exhausted and in a kind of wintry haze felt him ravage her.

When he was gone she whispered to herself, 'God of Moses, what must I do?' and like many women who face this ultimate indignity she made a fatally wrong decision. Alone and bleeding on the floor she was so mortified by what had happened that she did not immediately cry out. During the rape she had tried to do so; she had done all that a woman could possibly do to defend herself, but her mouth had been smothered so that the cries she did utter were not heard. Now, when others were within hearing distance, she remained mute in terror and shame, and the hours passed, confirming her silence. A cold rain fell on the Galilee and winter was at hand.

That night Aaron reported to the evening meal with scratches across his face, but glowing with an animal contentment. Satisfied that the silence of his sister-in-law proved her enjoyment of the morning tussle he smiled at her with open longing, and she was distraught when she realized the interpretation he was placing on her muted behavior. His daughter asked what had scratched his face, and he replied, leering at Shimrith, 'A kitten with an olive face.'

The next two days were marked with terror. Outside, the storm continued, with dark clouds riding in from the sea so that Ptolemais was hidden in darkness, while inside the house of the brothers Aaron stalked his sister-in-law as primitive hunters in this region had once stalked the lioness. Finally he trapped her near the kitchen, where with a grandiose gesture he opened his robe, revealing himself naked and hungry for her, confident that she too had been plotting for this moment, and he had so convinced himself that Shimrith

loved him that he ignored her anguished retreat. Moving toward her he offered
to repeat the game, but this time she was prepared. Producing from her dress a
brass knife she stood ready to stab him if he touched her, and for a moment he
was halted by this surprising development.

Then, with bewildering speed, he threw aside his robe completely, and with
a deft feint toward her head caught her off guard, and with one hand wrested
away the knife and with the other silenced her mouth before she could scream.
It could have been a game, Aaron thought. It could have been that she had
grabbed the weapon only so that she could be disarmed and overpowered, as if
that were her pleasure, heightening her wild responses to the sexual act.
Responding to her strange sense of play he struck her across the chin, and
before she fainted undressed her and threw her upon the floor.

Too late, too late she ran sobbing from her violated home to seek refuge with
the rabbi, but when she entered his disheveled room and found him nesting
behind a clutter of scrolls she had a premonition that she had come to the wrong
man for help. Sitting with his pale hands folded beheath his beard he listened as
she gave her account of Aaron's behavior, and before he was willing to
comment either yea or nay he rummaged among his scrolls until he found one
to his liking, and after having consulted it, asked simply, 'So Aaron raped you?'

'Yes.'

'How many times?'

'Twice.'

'The first time?'

'Two days ago.'

'And you didn't cry out?'

'I couldn't.'

'And later you told no one?'

'I was too ashamed.'

The rabbi tugged at his beard and asked a most significant question. 'Where
did the attack take place?'

'At our house?'

'By the synagogue?'

'Yes.'

The rabbi sat back and studied the distraught woman with what he thought
was understanding. It was an old story, familiar to all judges, of the woman who
had half eagerly, half hesitantly encouraged her lover, only to react with shame
and humiliation some days after the experience. The Torah was filled with
account of wild sexual behavior, for the patriarchs were men of lust and their
women were worse, tricking and seducing and procuring. It had taken nearly a
score of centuries to subdue the wilder impulses of the Jews, and rabbis had
spent much effort trying to formulate logical codes, but of one thing they were
certain: even the most circumspect woman could trap herself into seducing a
man one day and charging him with rape the next. The essential test had always
been, even in the Torah: 'Had she cried out to protect herself at the first
opportunity?' The Jewish moralists knew that when a woman did not make this
normal and primitive response any subsequent behavior must be viewed with
suspicion. The present case of Shimrith, wife of Judah, merely presented new
proof of this old truism.

'An evil thing has been committed,' the fumbling rabbi granted, 'but it is not
the evil that you charge against your brother-in-law. It is the evil you did in
luring a man and then charging him with rape.'

'Rabbi!' The stunned woman let her shoulders slump as if she had been clubbed across the back.

'Yes,' the legalistic man continued, fumbling among his scrolls for a passage to fortify his judgment. 'I have the words right here some place,' and finally he found what he wanted, the determinative passage in Deuteronomy: if 'a man find her in the city and lie with her; then ye shall bring them both out unto the gate of that city, and ye shall stone them with stones that they die; the damsel, because she cried not, being in the city ...' Putting aside the scroll he said gravely, 'The Torah continues that if the supposed rape took place in the country, the woman shall not be stoned to death, for there perhaps she cried and no one heard. By your own confession, Shimrith, I could condemn you to death. For you enticed your husband's brother in the city, and had you cried out even I could have heard you in the synagogue next door. You seduced your brother-in-law twice and now come complaining. This time I shall let you go, but keep away from Aaron, for whom you have conceived this lustful desire. And when your husband Judah returns from Ptolemais try to be a good wife to him.'

Having delivered his judgment the rabbi rose amid the dusty jumble of his life, but Shimrith could not. She was stunned and unable to move. 'If I go home,' she said, 'Aaron will force me again.'

This posed a new problem and the rabbi sat down, searching his folios until he found a section of the Talmud covering this eventuality, which he summarized for the supplicant: 'If a woman be faced with rape, against her virtue and against her will, it were better that she should die.' Smiling at her in a kind of greenish compassion he said gently, 'You had the knife, didn't you? You knew the law, didn't you? Confess, Shimrith. You did tempt him, didn't you? You were gratified, in a womanly sort of way?' He hesitated, then asked, 'Was it perhaps because you knew that Aaron could have children and Judah not?'

She drew back from the ugly man, realizing at last how gravely she had compromised herself by having remained silent. She had an excuse. Silence had been forced upon her by physical choking and by mental confusion, but that it was silence she had to admit. At the door of the rabbi's cluttered room she looked back with dismay. She had come to him with perhaps the gravest problem a woman could present to a spiritual guide and had received no consoling response. She fled the place, not appreciating the fact that the pettifogging rabbi had given her the sagest advice on this matter of rape that the world had so far evolved, and one that would never be superseded. If women did not entice timid men by every subtle trick used by birds and beasts, how would the human race be perpetuated? And if men did not force their way upon timid women, within the rules of decency, how would the hesitant female every find a partner? In this animal-like swamp of human passion the most careful rules had to be drawn, and once drawn, observed. Rape had been scientifically described in the Talmud, and no woman who had entertained her husband's brother once, waited two days, entertained him again, and had then decided to cry 'Violation' could claim protection under that careful description.

That night the cold rains continued, and at dawn the next morning Shimrith, aching with confusion and shame, climbed to the roof of her house, where she studied with longing the distant church towers of Ptolemais, and as she watched them change their shapes and colors when the wintry sun played upon them she prayed that her husband would return that day to rescue her. If he did not she would walk to Ptolemais to find him, for she was abused in spirit and could find no consolation.

As if in response to her prayer, Judah did leave Ptolemais late that afternoon, hoping to reach Makor at dusk, but halfway home a most heavy storm whipped across the flatlands leading from the shore and he was required to take refuge in a sheep shed, where he spent more than an hour talking with the shepherds, and this meant that he reached Makor after dusk, but Shimrith, still watching from the roof, saw him coming and ran through the rain to find solace in his arms. While they were still outside the town she told him of the wretched events and he stopped in the roadway like a man with a heavy burden to question her as to what had happened.

'Where was Aaron's wife?'

'Outside, playing with her children.'

'Was there no one in the synagogue?'

'There might have been.'

'Why didn't you cry out?'

'I was stunned. I was ashamed.'

Standing in the dark rain Judah considered this carefully. It was the same evidence that Shimrith had presented to the rabbi, but this time it was listened to with compassion. Judah remembered how shy his stately wife had always been, how modest in her appraisal of her own beauty. He knew her extraordinary honesty, even about little matters, and he believed her, yet he felt obliged to be fair to his younger brother. 'Did you entice him in any way?' he asked.

'No.'

Satisfied with his wife's account, Judah put his arm about her and kissed her. 'On you there is no sin,' he said consolingly. 'Your body has been insulted but not your spirit. If you have the courage to come to me and to tell me these things, you have the courage to accept their consequences.' He kissed her again and said with his mouth smothered in her dark hair, 'I love you with all my heart, Shimrith, and while I was absent in Ptolemais I longed for you each moment. Now go back to our house and wait.'

'What are you going to do?'

He pushed her toward the winding road leading up to Makor, then started toward the olive grove, but she followed him, tugging at his arm and demanding, 'What are you going to do?'

'I don't know!' he cried in anguish. 'It's no small thing.' He stalked alone into the olive grove, trying to find an honorable solution to this situation, and while his frightened wife returned to her cold home, he pondered the various facts that confronted him, and possibly in his compassion he found the solution he sought, but if so he explained it to no one, for as he walked beneath the ancient trees strong hands reached out and strangled him.

It was never known who murdered Judah the dye master. Some held that the shepherds with whom he had taken refuge had trailed him through the dusk, striking him down when darkness fell, but this made little sense, for he had not been robbed. Others argued that ruffians set loose from Tverya after the capture of that city by the Arabs had done the job, but Shimrith knew otherwise, for early on the morning of the murder, while she was still on the roof praying, she had looked down into the streets of Makor and had watched as the rabbi came quietly to the dye vats, where he had taken Aaron aside to upbraid him. If the rabbi had treated her harshly as a vacillating woman, he spoke in even stronger terms with Aaron, who had abused his brother, lusting after his wife while the brother was absent. Although she could not hear the voices of the two men she could deduce with fair accuracy the fact that the rabbi had told Aaron of her formal complaint, and she could see her brother-in-law's strong hands clasping and unclasping in rage.

All that day she had succeeded in hiding from him, lest he take vengeance against her, and towards evening she was gratified when she saw him leave the house. Later, when men came shouting that Judah lay murdered on the road, she looked at Aaron's feet and they were muddy, smeared with the dark earth of the Damascus road. There had been one awful moment when she had stared at his sandals, and when he caught her doing so, she had screamed. He knew. She felt sure that he knew she had screamed not because of her husband's death but because of the dark mud which proved him to be the murderer.

Judah had been buried only two days when the rabbi came to the house of mourning to talk with Shimrith. Fortified by three scrolls of law he sat in the chair that Judah had used, folded his hands under his black beard and said unctuously, 'Your husband died leaving no children. Is that not so?'

Yes, she nodded.

'You know our law. When a childless wife becomes a widow she must immediately marry her dead husband's brother ... to prolong his name in Israel.' There was a protracted silence during which Shimrith could hear cold rain dripping on the roof. 'It is your duty,' the rabbi said, scarcely audible above the rain, whose constant fall seemed the symbol of duty.

'I will not marry the man who killed my husband,' Shimrith said.

'I could order you to be stoned. For bearing false witness.' The rabbi trembled, then added, 'Shimrith, marry Aaron as the law commands. You will have children to honour Judah and this present ugliness will be forgotten.'

She refused to speak. What the law was requiring of her was morally offensive and she would discuss it no further. Standing in silence before the rabbi she kept her hands pressed close against her sides, so that her woolen dress covered her trembling fingers. In this stubborn position she waited.

The rabbi chose to ignore her temporary obstinacy, for he had learned in the past what a shock it was to young widows to be told that they must immediately marry their brothers-in-law, but this sensible rule had been evolved when Moses guided his Jews in the desert, where the continuation of the clan was more important than any personal consideration, and although under present conditions of settled life there might be doubts as to its continued necessity, it was still the law and therefore to be obeyed. 'This obligation is put upon you by the Lord,' the rabbi mumbled. 'For by your sacrifice the continuity of your husband is assured.' He hesitated, for his words were obviously making no impact on Shimrith.

Shimrith refused to comment on this extraordinary verdict, and the rabbi saw that it was useless to argue further while she was still distraught by her husband's death, so he left; but that afternoon he found that the Jews of Makor were beginning to separate into two groups. The first said, 'Rabbi, you know very well that Aaron murdered his brother. Why do you insist that Shimrith marry him?' To these the ineffectual rabbi mumbled, 'I could order you stoned for saying that.' The second group said, 'The law requires a widow without children to marry her husband's brother. Why do you allow her to dally?' And to these the rabbi said, 'I do things in my own good time.' But even he could see that each day the rift widened as partisans became more convinced of their position.

Finally, in late November, the rabbi marched to the house of the dyers with a scroll of law under his arm and delivered to Shimrith a stern judgment: 'I order you to marry your brother Aaron this day.'

Prepared for this moment, Shimrith chose to remain silent, determined never to obey this offensive order no matter if it meant expulsion or even stoning. She listened not to the rabbi but to the rain, and from its insistent fall she gained the courage she required to support her resolution. She felt the cold grayness of this November day seeping into her heart, making iron of what had once been blood. She would never marry her husband's murderer, and the fence around the Torah could crash down upon her before she would yield.

But still she did not speak, and just as Aaron in the aftermath of having raped her had misinterpreted her silence as acquiescence, so now the rabbi made the same mistake.

'It is written here,' he said reassuringly as he unfurled the Torah, '"If brethren dwell together, and one of them die, and have no child, the wife of the dead shall not marry without unto a stranger: her husband's brother shall go in unto her, and take her to him to wife, and perform the duty of an husband's brother unto her. And it shall be, that the firstborn which she beareth shall succeed in the name of his brother which is dead, that his name be not put out of Israel." It is not my command, Shimrith. It is the will of God.'

Not even then did she speak. As a powerful Jewish woman, intelligent beyond the average and capable in many untested directions, she began to find reassurance in her unexpected resolve, which she expressed only to herself by keeping her hands pressed tightly against her sides until her fingertips grew white with controlled fury, and in this insolent pose she stared back at the rabbi until the pusillanimous lawgiver left the room. At the door he mumbled, 'We should all submit to God's law with humbleness. I'll arrange the wedding.' And he was gone.

Alone in the desolate room, with cold rain striking the roof while her husband's murderer crouched on the other side of the wall, his ear pressed close to catch what the rabbi had been saying, Shimrith whispered to herself, 'There will be no observance of the law. For if the law says that I must marry my husband's murderer . . .' She did not finish the sentence, for she knew how impossible it would be for her to prove that Aaron was the murderer, and she foresaw that the rabbi could enlist a considerable pressure, forcing her finally to accept the red-stained master of the dye vats. As a Jewish widow with no living parents, what could she do? She now belonged legally to her brother-in-law, and the rabbi could command her to marry him even though he already had a wife. Even Byzantine soldiers were available to enforce such a decision, now that it had been formally delivered, and in the end there could be only tragedy unless she complied. But this she would not do; so while Aaron remained with his ear to the wall she slipped away and climbed to the roof, where she stood in the rain staring toward Ptolemais and wondering how to escape.

Now Abd Umar, servant of Muhammad, brought his camels and his horses out of the brooding forest trails to begin his transit of the Galilee swamp. As his animals approached that morass, rain fell and because of overhanging branches all riders were forced to dismount and lead their beasts along the bypass that skirted the northern edge of the swamp; and as the Arabs entered this unfamiliar world, where the sky was dark and the earth filled with crawling things, Abd Umar began to wonder whether this adventure was sensible.

As long as their wars had been conducted in the open desert, those gallant areas where vast stretches of sand allowed camels full range, Abd Umar had been confident in the Prophet's destiny; even the conquest of Damascus had been within reason, for in that battle the Arabs had been able to ride their camels across traditional sand except for the final approaches to the city. The occupation of Tabariyyah had been largely the same: a free camel raid over the empty spaces east of the Jordan, then a swift drop to cultivated land and the occupation of the city. But with the attack on Makor came a new kind of warfare, the unpleasant ride through forested land, then this frightening march on foot to skirt the swamp, ending in a gallop on horseback down an established road. It was not the kind of warfare an Arab preferred, and Abd Umar would be content when it was finished and he could return to the clean and open desert.

He was thinking in this gloomy mood when the riderless horses began to whinny and then to panic. He ran back along the marshy path to where the beasts were shivering in fright, and he saw that they had come upon a large snake which one of them had chopped to death with his hoofs. The serpent lay writhing even after death, and Abd Umar shivered like his horses. Then his own beast, which he was trying to reassure, leaped aside and whinnied pitifully. Abd Umar, catching a flash of movement from the corner of his eye, turned swiftly to confront an enemy. It was a frog, and as the Arab chieftain watched, it leaped into the swampy water, leaving a green splash as it disappeared.

Abd Umar quietened his horses, then regained his position at the head of the file, leading his camel and listening to the huge beast's soft, plopping feet as they sucked in and out of the mud. Now for the first time the Arab chieftain actually studied the formidable terrain through which he was passing: he saw the strange birds, the water rats, the reeds with feathery tips and the incredible herons, standing knee-deep in water like statues, waiting till the lumbering camels came upon them, then lifting themselves awkwardly into the air, where they flew in lazy circles as if climbing on evanescent circular stairs.

To a man from the desert it was terrifying, this swampland, and for a moment he had a wild desire to flee the place. He wanted to be with Abu Zeid on the heights, storming a town like Safat and putting the defenders to death in an orgy of fire and slaughter. Most of all, he longed for the desert, that vast clean empire of the soul. In the depths of the swamp he remembered the time when alone he had brought the remnants of a caravan back to Medina; his companions had lingered in Damascus. It was on this trip that he had accompanied the other caravan to the point where the road to Jerusalem cut off to the west, and after that separation he had traveled for nine consecutive days without seeing a man, an animal, or any sign of human cultivation. How notable that trip had been, traveling into the heart of the desert, where men felt the presence of God. With an effort he suppressed his insensible desire to be with Abu Zeid at the burning of Safat, but he could not control his instinctive hatred of this swamp and the forest that encroached upon it. He walked rapidly, hoping to quit the ominous area, but his camels could move no faster, for the swamp caught at their cumbersome feet, and Abd Umar thought impatiently: Camels may be fine for the desert, but here they accomplish nothing.

He was forced to lag behind with his animals, and this gave him opportunity to reflect upon the radical changes that had disrupted his life: For thirty years all I wanted was the two black ones. He referred to dates and water, the only requirement of the true desert rider, for with them and a good camel a man could exist almost indefinitely in the sands. Once he had lived with his men for nineteen days with only the two black ones, and at the end of the period, when other food was available, he ate a little but finished his meal with some black dates.

Black. He thought of his unknown mother and then of the sacred stone in the heart of Mecca–that small reddish rock sacred to the Prophet and referred to as the black rock. When Muhammad died, Abd Umar left on a pilgrimage to the Ka'bah and walked seven times around the solemn rock, whispering, 'God of this Ka'bah, I bear witness that I have come in pilgrimage. Charge not, "You did not come to my Ka'bah, Abd Umar," for You see me now, a humble man walking in the shadow of Your rock. Forgive me. Forgive Ben Hadad the Jew. For I have made my pilgrimage, as You must see.' As he now recalled the ominous black rock, where God was present, he happened to see the black water of the swamp, and it was not like the sweet dark waters he had known; it was alien, and for a fragment of a second he entertained a partial vision of the future in which black and various other colors were mingled as Muhammad had once said they would be; but it was fugitive, and at this time he was not able to comprehend the message of this day.

Instead, he plunged ahead hoping that soon his contingent would break out of the swampy land, and as the trees–those menacing emblems of this strange land–crept down upon him he promised himself one thing: If we conquer this land I shall certainly cut down these trees. A man needs open space. And again he longed for the desert where a man could see ahead of him and behind. 'There are only two trees in this world worth keeping,' he muttered to himself. 'Olives and date palms.' He was oppressed by the trees, and when birds exploded out of them, frightening his horses and startling his men, he saw yet another reason for getting rid of them. 'I want to sleep tonight where there are no trees,' he instructed his lieutenant when they stopped to rest the camels. Those lumbering beasts, having drunk that morning in Tabariyyah, looked upon the swamp water with disdain, but the horses tasted of it, drawing back in fear when frogs jumped past them.

'*La ilaha illa Allah,*' Abd Umar repeated softly to himself as he resumed his transit of the swamp. 'There is no God but Allah.' It was a rubric of Muhammad's which fascinated men, its poetry matching its philosophy, and it summed up all that Abd Umar now believed. As he wandered along the last portion of the distracting swamp he repeated the formula automatically, '*La ilaha illa Allah,*' satisfied that it would protect him from the dangers of the forest, and it was in this kind of hypnosis, thinking of things permanent, that he led his men around a final bend in the path to a spot where the dark waters ended and where there were no more snakes or frogs; and as he saw firm land opening before him, and the approaches to Makor, his mind at last apprehended in solid form the vague intimations that had been formulating in the swamp.

Like most of the early followers of Muhammad, Abd Umar had begun by interpreting the Prophet's religion as no more than a personal experience undergone by Muhammad–no one could stand near this charismatic general, this servant of God, without acknowledging his leadership–but there had been much speculation as to what would happen when he died; and Abd Umar had been among those who had expected the movement to collapse. He would never forget that mournful day on which the Prophet had actually died: he had wept like a child, for his world had come to an end, but old Abu Bakr had come from the death tent bringing the words that made continued life possible: 'Those of you who worshiped Muhammad must know that he is dead like any man, but those of you who worshiped God know that He lives forever.' And it was this continuity of God that had given Arabs like Abd Umar the power to go forward.

'I shall never return to the desert,' he whispered to himself as he left the swamp. 'Today we shall conquer Makor and, in a little while, Akka, and there I will take a boat and sail to islands and to kingdoms . . . I, who have never seen the sea.' And he visualized in general terms the magnitude of the venture upon which he was engaged: the extension of Arabia's religion throughout the world. If he was saying farewell to the mysterious swamp which terrified his camels and horses, he was likewise saying farewell to the desert, where his camels and horses had roamed hopefully toward endless horizons.

'Those deserts I shall see no more,' he said, accepting the finality of God's decision. '*La ilaha illa Allah*,' he intoned, for if there was but one God, and if He directed all, it was best to accept His dictates. If God led a half-Negro slave through the dangerous swamps and trees, He had the right to say where that slave should go next.

Will I ever see my wives again? Abd Umar wondered, visualizing those women who had always remained with his children in Medina. Like Muhammad he had married a Negro woman from Ethiopia and she was his beloved, but he also protected the daughter of Sulayman and the sister of Khaled Yezd the warrior. Would they, in some mysterious manner, be able to follow him across the seas, running to him in some unknown city, with bare feet and children clinging to their skirts?

The Damascus road lay just ahead and scouts were shouting from their newly mounted camels that all was well. Makor must lie beyond that hill, the one covered with trees. The forced march through the swamp had succeeded, and the battle, if there was to be one, would be engaged in a few minutes. '*La ilaha illa Allah*,' Abd Umar muttered, climbing aboard his own camel and checking the horses. But as he entered upon that most ancient of roads upon which the invaders of this region had always traveled, he found its solid footing reassuring, and only briefly did he reflect upon his discovery that the years ahead were to be remote and battle-filled and lonely: When we take the town I'd like to find a good slave girl . . . or perhaps a young widow. He added this afterthought because Muhammad himself had taken eleven wives, and ten of them had been widows, and few men in Arabia had known a happier domestic life than the Prophet.

Within the doomed precincts of Makor the pagans waited, and even the dullest realized that for them the coming of Islam could signify only the end of one world and the beginning of a new. Who were these pagans who had resisted the pressure of Judaism and the proselytizing zeal of Christians like Father Eusebius? Some had joined the fire worship of the Persians when the latter swept through Palestine some twenty years before, holding it briefly as part of their empire. Others, slaves imported from the upper reaches of the Nile, remained faithful to their river god Serapis, and a sturdy few, whose ancestors could be traced back to the cave men who had sprung from this rocky mound, remained faithful to Baal.

Incredible as it may seem, these resolute men and women of Baal had withstood the full onslaught of Egyptian, Jewish, Christian and Persian persuasion, plus the temptations of a dozen other religious powers, including Antiochus Epiphanes and Caesar Augustus, remaining loyal to the primitive god of the mountain. On dark nights, at the equinoxes and at the ripening of the olive groves, these determined pagans still climbed the mountain back of town where monoliths remained only in memory, and there they worshiped the permanent god of Makor.

When the Byzantines stationed soldiers on the mountain with orders to kill any pagans coming to worship Baal, the tough old Canaanites stayed inside the town and whispered to each other the oldest and best-kept secret of the village: their fathers had been told by their fathers that directly under the altar in the large basilica, hidden permanently in the bowels of the earth, stood the everlasting altar of Baal, a monolith of black stone which had existed on that spot from the time when men first knew Makor.

So the pagans cheerfully attended Christian worship in the basilica, listening to the priests and bowing reverently to the altar rather more frequently than Christian ritual demanded. Of course, when the Byzantine guard was withdrawn, the priests having informed Constantinople that all worshipers of Baal were now eliminated, the hard-headed pagans again slipped away at night to climb their sacred mountain.

What had been the secret of their extraordinary longevity? It must have been that any sensible man who lived in close contact with nature, as the people of Makor did, knew in his heart that the forces which guided the rain and the thunderstorm were mysterious, and not mysterious in some subtle way that brings war over the matter of whether Jesus Christ had one body or two, one will or two, or whether a Jew might wear a gold tooth on Shabbat, but in a fundamental, perceptible way. In the spring, when new buds began to unfold at the tips of branches, some to form leaves and others blossoms from which fruit would develop, even the most stupid man in Makor could perceive that something mysterious was afoot, and he required neither priest nor rabbi to initiate him into the basic mystery. It was simplest, perhaps, to allocate the mystery to Baal, who lay hidden in the earth under the Christian altar, for it could not have been by accident that the priests of the basilica had chosen that precise spot for the heart of their structure. Baal, in his ancient wisdom, had directed them there.

In a sense, the old pagans were right. It was not by chance that the altar of the basilica stood over the spot where Baal had reigned, but rather by the sensible logic that pervaded all religions: the Jews had borrowed from the Canaanites, and the Christians had borrowed from the Jews. Now there was approaching from the desert a newer religion that had borrowed even more extensively from both Jew and Christian, but all went back to those primitive urgings which had found expression in Baal, and before him in the primogenitive divinity of all, the mysterious and self-effacing El.

But harsh judgment was at hand for the pagans. Muhammad had differentiated sharply between 'the people of the Book,' which included Jews and Christians, and those who knew no Book, the pagans. The former would always have an honourable place in the Arab religion; the latter were to be offered either conversion or extirpation, and word of this final choice had filtered through to Makor, so that the pagans knew that when the Arabs came clattering down the road a moment of decision was upon them.

In the hours of waiting the citizens of Makor made their various decisions. The orthodox priests of Byzantium wanted to defend the town, but the schismatic Christians, whom they had abused for so long, let it be known that they would refuse to fight; indeed, they welcomed the coming of Muhammad, for they suspected that under the Arabs they would know greater toleration than they had under the Byzantines. The Jews looked forward to another dispersion; where they would go this time they did not know—perhaps overland to the newly forming countries of Europe. In the meantime their community was divided between those who held that the widow Shimrith should be forced to marry her brother-in-law Aaron, and those who felt that in view of that man's rape and probable murder she should be exempt. To the warring Jews the advent of the Arabs was merely another incident which they hoped they could survive. But to the pagans the new religion represented the end of the road, and they waited in terror.

In this demoralized condition the little town of Makor prepared to confront the Arabs, who came united as no preceding conqueror had ever come, unified by one religious ideal as none had been unified before. It was a most curious chance of history that the Arabs arrived when they were strongest, in the throbbing flush of self-discovery and unification, and that they reached Makor when it was at its worst and weakest. In nearly six hundred years no one had thought to rebuild the town walls or to dig out the well.

Why had such sterile days befallen a civilization once capable of producing men like Tarphon the gymnasiarch, Timon Myrmex the architect, Bishop Eusebius and the young Jew Menahem ben Yohanan, honored in church history as St Mark of Antioch? The only logical explanation was that the Greek concept of life had simply run out of inspiration. After nearly a thousand years of control its polity had become rigid, its art moribund and its military capacity deficient. Even its marvelous new religion, Christianity, which Greeks had molded upon the divine presence of Christ and the theological statesmanship of Paul, had grown formalized and sterile, bringing to its Palestinian followers neither security nor inspiration. Christians inclining toward the more liberal policies of Rome were tyrannized; those who clung to Egypt were persecuted; while the poor Nestorians were periodically tortured, one emperor after another convincing himself that if he could only punish the Nestorians enough he could stamp out their abominable heresy. It was in this faltering and pathetic posture that Hellenism was required to confront the rising power of the Arabs. The consequence was bound to be humiliating and perhaps in the interests of world history it was proper that it should be so.

Now Abd Umar, the servant of Muhammad, brought his squadron out of the swamp and ordered all to remount camels for a gallop to the Damascus road, where he had barely time to notice that the wintry sky had cleared and was flecked with clouds, when scouts reported that the olive grove of Makor lay ahead and the town must be close at hand. The tall slave ordered his camel to kneel, and when the beast had done so, dismounted and ordered forty of his best men to do the same. The swift and rested horses were brought forward, and swords were unsheathed while the unnecessary camels were led to a grazing area off the road. Abd Umar, adjusting his striped and many-colored robe and tightening the cords of his headdress, sat easily upon his small sand-colored horse, his long legs looking awkward as his feet fitted themselves to the basketlike stirrups, and in this position of battle he surveyed his men, knowing that he had no need to address them in words of courage. He gave only one battle command, 'Kill no one,' after which he wheeled his horse, spun in a tight circle and started galloping down the road; but at the bend where he first saw the unprotected town, he also saw, to the left of the road, a sight which distracted his attention and reminded him of the confusions he was encountering on this cold, damp afternoon. At the edge of the olive grove stood an ordinary farmhouse: the owners tilled a small plot of land, raising grain which they sold to the groats maker, and such farms had always constituted the backbone of Jewish Palestine, and Roman as well; but to the hard-riding Arab the little establishment was an affront. Like most men from the desert he held in contempt any man who would tie himself to a piece of land instead of remaining free to roam wherever trade or battle took him. Farmers were the despised creatures of this world, the cowards, the conservatives, the shameless ones who knew nothing of sword or camel, and for Abd Umar suddenly to find that the town he was about to invade was the center of such farmers was repellent. Even more than the trees and the swamp, this farmhouse unsettled him . . . made him ill at ease in ways he could not have described.

But much as he despised the farmhouse he could not keep his eyes from it, so as he galloped toward the town that loomed ahead on the foreboding hill, Abd Umar glanced sideways at the menace and swore that if he succeeded this day in capturing Makor, he would destroy every farm within the radius of a day's journey. He remembered that the Koran mentioned little about farming but spoke at length regarding merchants and warriors; yet even as he rode past the farmhouse he realized that his initial idea of burning such places was ridiculous; he was talking like Abu Zeid and was ashamed of himself. The Arabs had come out of the desert to bring Muhammad to strange lands, and the customs of those lands must be respected, insofar as they did not controvert the teachings of the Prophet. But even this philosophical concession did not erase from Abd Umar's mind the contempt he held for whatever men lived inside that miserable house. 'If this is a town of farmers,' he muttered to himself as he galloped toward Makor, 'it's hardly worth conquering.'

A lieutenant 'leading a contingent of men sped past, shouting, 'Abd Umar, I shall ride into the town first.' The ex-slave understood that his subordinate was trying to protect him from the first flight of arrows, but he held the offer to be humiliating and spurred his sand-colored horse until he was again in his lead position, and in this formation the Arabs galloped up the winding road and into the town. There was no first flight of arrows, nor any, and within a few exhilarating moments the Arab horsemen had stormed unopposed into the heart of the town and were milling about the square before the basilica, wondering what to do next.

The easy conquest had caught Abd Umar by surprise: he had supposed that in the first clash of swords his brain would clear and he would sense what steps to take, but when the citizens refused to fight and merely presented themselves like cattle, he was caught off guard and was as perplexed as his men. Then, as his own horse whinnied in agitation at the sight of so many people, he remembered the instructions of the Koran, and he shouted to one of his lieutenants, 'Tribute, on the backs of their hands,' and Arabs who could speak Greek dismounted to instruct the Jews and Christians that in accordance with the Koran they were to kneel, bow their heads and offer tribute on the backs of their hands held out parallel to the earth, in the humiliating posture reserved for slaves.

So all four congregations of the Christian church knelt in the dust to offer tribute, and both factions of Jews did the same, Aaron kneeling in one group, Shimrith in the other, so that Arab soldiers could move among them, collecting the submission money. And when it was placed before him Abd Umar–using the Greek he had learned while trading at Damascus–announced to these two groups, 'Allah is gratified that we have met in peace, and we shall live that way forever. You are people of the Book, and you may rise and face me honorably.' When all had done so he made the simple offer under which the followers of Muhammad would rule their conquered territories, now that the first savage blood-slaughters had ended: 'Surrender your arms. All Greeks and other robbers must leave the country, but others may remain and keep your own religion. Pay a modest tax and we will grant you full protection. Or if you prefer, accept Islam now and become a full member of our community, in which you will have the same rights as we do.' Having said these words, he waited.

At this critical moment a Christian named Nicanor, a follower of Byzantium and the theory that Jesus Christ was of two natures, cried, 'Do you accept Jesus Christ?'

'He is revered in our Koran as a mighty prophet,' Abd Umar replied, and the Christian threw himself on the ground, crying, 'I accept Islam,' but when he did so, one of the Byzantine priests stepped forward to forestall him. A sword flashed and the priest's thumb was cut off. It could just as easily have been his head, and all appreciated this act of mercy.

Coldly Abd Umar announced, 'At the moment this man said, "I accept Islam," he became one of us, and it is forbidden for any of you to speak to him against the faith he has chosen. Who else accepts the Prophet?' A large number–truly a surprising number–came forward to accept the conquering faith, but the Egyptians who held that Jesus Christ was of one body only and that Mary was the Mother of God, approached Abd Umar and through their unkempt little priest asked, 'Did you speak the truth when you said that if we obey your laws we are free to keep our own religion?' The soldier who had sliced off the thumb of the Byzantine priest was offended by this oblique suspicion of dishonesty and would have struck the Egyptian, but Abd Umar interrupted: 'It is difficult to know the truth, and you do well to investigate. But I did speak honestly. You will be free to live as you wish.'

The Egyptian priest bowed his head, then said boldly, 'Son of Allah, we of Egypt choose to pay your taxes and to keep our little church.'

'It is done,' Abd Umar announced. Then he addressed the Christians. 'You shall live with us in peace, and I shall protect you as I have just done. You may not prevent those of your followers who wish to join us from doing so. Nor may you ride either horses or camels, but donkeys and mules you are allowed. You may have no building, neither church nor home, that is taller than ours, nor may you build any new churches beyond those that you already have.' He stopped. 'I see no children,' he said.

'They are hidden,' the Egyptian priest explained.

'Bring them all forward,' Abd Umar announced, and terrified mothers scattered through the town to bring their offspring out of hiding.

When the little ones were assembled, Abd Umar said in Greek, 'Now let each child go to his true-born parents and let each father and mother certify that this child was born of his body.' The children scattered to the arms of mothers, who clutched them hungrily, but some fourteen were left standing alone, the orphans of the town.

Abd Umar now dismounted and walked among the fourteen as if they were his sons and daughters. Of each one he asked, 'Where is your father,' and when none could reply he said, 'These childen are from this moment the children of Allah, for Muhammad had said that all children are born in our faith. It is only their parents who lead them astray.' And he kissed the children, one by one, and they were his.

The last child he embraced was Jewish, with a Jewish name, and Abd Umar asked, 'Where are the Jews of this town? What is their decision?'

The fumbling rabbi stepped forward to say that the Jews offered their submission. They would pay the tax but would keep to their faith. At this Abd Umar asked, 'Are there none among you to join us?' Silence. 'I was raised by a Jew. Ben Hadad of Medina, a merchant. It is a newer and a better faith that I bring you. Will none join?' Again silence, and he said no more, for he had not expected the Jews to convert, but as he was about to remount he thought that one Jewish woman, prettier than the others, had started to make a motion as if she were inclined to join the conquerors. If that was her intention it was forestalled by the rabbi, who looked commandingly at her, so that she said nothing. Had a soldier witnessed this apparent interference he would have killed the rabbi, but Abd Umar, hoping to avoid bloodshed, thought: That problem we can deal with later.

Mounting his horse he uttered a series of short commands directing the various priests to take to themselves all members of their congregations, and the rabbi to do the same with his Jews. When this maneuver was completed he rode to the small body of pagans left standing unclaimed and shouted, 'You, each of you. Do you not belong to the people of the Book?' The pagans remained surly, some staring defiance, some looking at the ground. To the first in line Abd Umar rode, asking in a loud voice, 'You? Do you in this instant accept Islam?' The man hesitated, trembled, replied that he remained faithful to the fire gods of Persia. Before he had completed his sentence he was killed from behind, a powerful sword slicing through his neck until his head toppled sideways before his body fell.

Ignoring the corpse Abd Umar rode to the next pagan, a tall Negro from Sudan, and allotted him five seconds to determine his future, but this man also held fast to his own god–in this case Serapis–and Arab foot soldiers were about to kill him when Abd Umar interceded. Reining in his horse before the Negro he said, 'I am dark like you, and the Prophet found a place for me. Join us.'

The tall Negro, appreciating what must follow, answered, 'I am faithful to Serapis,' and Abd Umar looked aside as he was struck down.

But the third pagan he approached was a member of the great Family of Ur, and although this man had clung to Baal through many former vicissitudes, it now required him less than one second to decide in favor of the new religion. 'I accept the Prophet!' the man of Ur called out in a clear voice, and the warmth with which he was received by the Arabs encouraged the remaining pagans to accept Islam. As they knelt to do so the man of Ur stood aside at a spot from which he could see both the basilica where Baal lay buried and the top of the mountain where he reigned, and he reassured himself: It won't be any more difficult under the Arabs than it was under the Byzantines.

That day Abd Umar was required to kill only two pagans, and when the rest had completed their conversion and he realized how simple the conquest of Palestine was to be, he spurred his horse toward the western part of town, from which he looked across the fields to the distant walls of Akka. How dazzling the sea-girt city was that cold afternoon, gleaming in the late sun, its many towers pointing downward to the riches that awaited the conqueror. Abd Umar smiled. Capturing that city would be as easy as taking Makor, for the same savage divisions could be depended upon to paralyze the Christians, while ritual-bound Jews could provide no leadership. 'An empire is falling apart!' he cried. 'And we ride in to gather up the pieces.'

Now at last he could visualize the specific steps beyond Akka: the voyages across that sea out there, the battles in lands whose names he did not know, his swift rise to general and the extension of his faith until it encompassed half the known world. No man before had ever stood on the mound of Makor faced by such a boundless horizon, not even the young Herod who was to accomplish so much, and the ex-slave breathed deeply of the sea air. His experiment had succeeded; he had taken Makor by compassion, and he whispered to himself, 'The killing has ended. The fires have gone out and we have a world to win merely by leading our horses up to the city walls.'

Saluting the waiting gates of Akka, Abd Umar wheeled his horse back toward the center of town, and as he did so he happened to see, standing by the dye vats, the Jewish widow Shimrith, afraid to enter her own home because her brother-in-law lurked there. The Arab captain, recognizing her as the pretty woman whose indecision he had witnessed, dismounted.

LEVEL V

Volkmar

Found at Makor—headstone carved from native limestone by
guildsmen from Genoa working at St Jean d'Acre, 1124 C.E.,
under orders from Count Volkmar II, who thus honored his
father. (Here lies Volkmar of Gretz, whose soul rest in peace
amen.) Stone put into place at Ma Coeur, December 21, 1124
C.E., nineteen years after the count's death. Deposited in the
ruins May 17, 1291.

Shortly before dawn on Thursday morning, April 24, 1096, the priest Wenzel
hurried to his master's room in the castle of Gretz and banged on the door.
Inside, the sleepy count merely growled, but repeated knocking roused him
from his sleep and at last he grudgingly threw open the iron-studded door.

'Now what?' he grumbled. He was a stalwart man with thick shoulders,
heavy neck and sandy-red hair. Although he was nearing fifty he appeared to be
in his early forties, and his nightrobe showed hairy legs and big feet to match
his capable hands projecting awkwardly from lace wristlets.

'Sir!' the gray-haired priest cried in joyous excitement. 'They're coming!'

'Who?' the sleepy count demanded.

'The ones I told you about.'

'The rabble?'

'I didn't call them that.'

'If they're rabble, why wake me?'

'You should see them, sir. They're a miracle.'

'You go back to bed,' the drowsy count ordered, 'and I'll do the same.' But as
he spoke he heard in the morning air a rustle. It sounded like the waves of the
sea against his boat when he was returning from the war in Sicily, and as he
listened it grew. A rooster crowed, dogs began barking and he heard the sound
of feet running through the narrow streets of his city. And then he heard the
sound itself, outside the walls: a rushing of many bodies, the soft swirling of
dust and the slow creaking of wagons drawn not by horses but by men.

'What is it?' he asked his priest.

'The ones from Cologne,' Wenzel replied.

'I'd better see them,' the count surrendered, and while the priest watched he
threw off his robe, revealing a powerful, hairy body, and slipped into his
woolen clothes, ending with a pair of rough leather boots. The priest led him
through the chapel and onto a battlement from which they could see below
them, coming up the road that led from Cologne to Mainz, a huge collection of
moving objects not fully discernible in the dawning light.

'What's that in front?' Count Volkmar asked.

'Children,' the priest answered. 'They run ahead from town to town, but
they don't belong.'

Volkmar leaned against the battlement and watched in amazement as through the dust raised by the scrambling children came file after file of men and women, undisciplined and unarmed. They moved through the cold early light like ghosts, their eyes transfixed and their feet shuffling with no apparent purpose but with a constant forward impulse. Volkmar cast his eyes backward along the interminable lines until the marchers were lost in dust.

'How many?' he asked his priest.

'At Cologne they estimated twenty thousand.'

'They have no arms! No knights!'

'They propose to have none,' Wenzel replied. 'They say that with God's aid they will conquer.'

Volkmar stood silent in the face of this strange army, marching forward as no other had done in the remembered history of the Rhine. Men and women loomed out of the darkness, shuffled silently past and others took their places. At times the procession was modified by clusters of wagons drawn by men or miserable horses, and each vehicle was piled with bags of clothing or remnants of food. On some, babies rode or old women, while in the wake marched a group of children much different from the wild ones who led the procession. These were tired. They had been marching for many days and no longer found energy for play or make-believe.

'Are those children ...' Count Volkmar didn't know how to finish his sentence.

'Those are the ones who belong,' the priest explained.

'They look starved,' Volkmar grumbled.

'They are.'

The count made a hasty decision. 'Wenzel, when they enter the city, see that the children are fed.'

'They're not stopping here, sir,' the priest told him, and Volkmar looked toward the head of the procession and saw that this was correct. The gates of the city were closed and the marchers were heading silently toward Mainz.

'Stop them!' the count ordered, and he dashed back into the castle to alert his wife and children so that they could see the amazing sight.

Wenzel, a thin man nearing sixty, hurried through the city, calling for the watchmen to open the city gates, and when the huge iron hinges had creaked in their sockets and the wooden slabs had swung aside, the priest moved into the midst of the marchers, waving his arms. The first part of the procession paid no heed, and passed on, but the marchers in the middle area saw the priest and came slowly to a halt. As they did so Count Volkmar and his wife, accompanied by a son and daughter in their teens, came purposefully through the gate, dressed in the fine garb of city dwellers. In a loud voice Volkmar announced, 'We will feed all children.'

The crowd cheered and mothers began shoving forward twice the number of children Volkmar had anticipated, until more than a thousand were clustered about the gates of Gretz. Matwilda, the count's pretty wife, was touched by the obvious hunger showing in the little faces and bent down to talk with some of the older girls, but they spoke no German.

'Can we feed so many?' the priest inquired.

'Feed them,' the count snapped, and men inside the city were summoned to bring out what food could be made quickly available. Volkmar tried to speak with the younger children but found that they also knew no German.

As he knelt to question one small boy he saw for the first time, sewed onto the shoulder of the child's blouse, a pair of rudely cut strips of red cloth put together to make a cross. Pointing to the emblem he asked Wenzel, 'Is this it?'

'Yes,' the priest replied, and Volkmar looked about him to find that most of the crowd pressing upon him were similarly decorated. The cross was usually small, the cloth ragged and of many colors, but the effect was impressive.

Count Volkmar was about to query a husband and wife regarding their insignia, when there came a shouting from the rear and the motley crowd opened a path for someone of apparent importance. It was a scrawny priest riding barefoot on a gray donkey. The little man had piercing eyes, sunken cheeks and matted hair. He wore a dirty black robe over which he had thrown a brown surplice lacking sleeves but marked with a flaming cross in red. Sensing from experience that Volkmar was the essential man in Gretz, the little priest kicked his donkey and rode directly to the count, crying in a cracked voice, 'God wills it! You are to ride with us, for your salvation is in the balance.'

Suspiciously Volkmar asked his own priest, 'Does this one represent the False Pope?'

'Yes,' Wenzel nodded.

'Get away from me,' Volkmar cried, drawing back from the man on the donkey.

'God wills it!' the little priest shouted, urging his tired animal forward.

This big German knight looked down at the inconsequential rider and said scornfully, 'You serve the False Pope.'

'But the true God, and He commands you ride with us.'

Not only did Volkmar refuse to ride with this rabble; he was sorry that he had volunteered to feed the children who now pressed in from all sides. If the little man on the donkey were indeed a servant of the False Pope it could be embarrassing for the Count of Gretz to be caught assisting him, and he seriously considered canceling the order so as not to implicate himself. But at this moment events were swept out of his hands, for from the gates of his city a mob of his town folk began rushing out to greet the little priest.

'Peter! Peter!' they shouted as one wave after another crowded to touch his robe or to caress the donkey. Some tried to pull hairs from the beast's coat, but these were driven back by men protecting the priest.

'It is God's will,' the priest shrieked in his high, cracked voice. He was a thin wisp of a man, about forty-five years old, driven by some tremendous inner compulsion which flashed in his eyes. 'I have been sent to call you to your duty.'

The people of Gretz listened in wonder as he told them that they could be saved from the impending end of the world only if they marched with him. Listening to his wild words Count Volkmar became more convinced that the man must be avoided, and he led his family back through the ranks of his own townsmen until he was safe within the city wall. 'Let none of that mob enter Gretz,' he commanded the guards.

His bailiff now came up. 'Sir, if you want food for all those children you'll have to give me extra money.' Volkmar considered this for a moment, then shrugged his shoulders.

'We said we'd feed them,' he replied with no enthusiasm. He left the gate, where the children were making a fearful noise, and retreated in some confusion to his castle, from which he continued to look down on the growing mob. 'There's a lot more than twenty thousand people down there,' he told his wife, after which he prudently summoned the captain of his guard and instructed him: 'Without attracting attention, close the gates, and if any should try to force entrance your bowmen are to shoot them down.' It would not be said of him that he had trafficked with the False Pope.

Since food had already appeared, the pilgrims did not protest when the gates swung shut. Posterns were opened through which more food was passed, and finally the feeding of the children was completed. Parents, obviously starved, were allowed to grab the last scraps, while the cooks–looking over their shoulders lest the count see them–passed bundles of food to the little priest and his immediate entourage, whereupon the great mass started to move slowly onward toward the towns of Mainz and Worms and Speyer.

'It's surprising how well the little priest maintains order,' Volkmar said grudgingly to his wife as they watched the dusty mob move off, but Matwilda uttered a sharp cry when the carts bearing families appeared at the rear of the procession, for she could see the privation under which the women and babies attached to this congregation moved. Surrounded by scrawny cattle, only a few of which were giving milk, these unfortunates lived in dust and danger.

'I'm sorry for them,' she sighed. 'They shouldn't be attempting such a journey.'

'Damn!' her husband shouted. 'Who's that at the end?' His wife followed his pointing finger and saw six or eight families from Gretz taking their places among the pilgrims.

'They're our people,' she confirmed.

Thundering down the castle stairs Volkmar rushed to the gates, ordered the guards to follow him, and ran bareheaded out to intercept his travelers. 'Hans!' he asked one. 'Where are you going?'

'To Jerusalem,' the slow-witted field hand replied.

'Do you know where Jerusalem is?' the count demanded.

'Over there,' the man replied, pointing towards Paris.

'You get back behind the walls,' Volkmar growled impatiently. He summoned his guards, who cut the would-be pilgrims off from the disappearing mob. 'What's that on your shoulder?' the count asked one of the men.

'The cross of Jesus Christ our Saviour,' the man replied.

'Take it off,' Volkmar said, brushing at the offensive bits of frayed cloth, but his hand was stayed by that of Wenzel, who had followed the count to check on what might happen.

'Sir, if these men wish to follow the way of our Lord, they must be permitted.'

Volkmar wheeled to confront his priest, shorter by a head than he. 'These men and women are needed to work my fields. Guards, get them back inside the walls.' The guards started to do so, but the priest continued his argument.

'Would you oppose the will of God?' he asked.

The question stunned Volkmar, for he was a man obedient to the law of Christ, but now his priest was asking him to reach conclusions on matters which he did not comprehend and he reacted roughly. 'Inside the walls!' he shouted, and placing himself in the roadway with his arms spread wide like the branches of a cross, he barred the way. Grudgingly the would-be Crusaders filed back through the gates as Priest Wenzel blessed them for their holy effort, and when the gray-haired churchman finally turned to reprove the count, Volkmar growled, 'No people of mine follow the commands of a False Pope.'

But his voice carried little conviction, for he had begun to weigh the words of Wenzel: were his peasants, in trying to join the marchers, acting in accordance

with Christ's wish? Perplexed, he was about to retreat to his castle when he saw
his bailiff dragging back into the city the pots that had been used for feeding.
'How much did it cost?' the count asked.

'We'll need six gold pieces to pay the merchants,' the red-faced bailiff
estimated.

'I should have watched my tongue,' Volkmar commented ruefully, and
as he spoke he saw in the square near the gates a group of people obviously
agitated by something that one of their members held, and he elbowed his way
into the mob. 'What's this?' he demanded.

'Klaus caught a hair from the priest's donkey,' a woman explained, pointing
with local pride to a man who stood with his hands cupped as if they contained
gold.

'Let me see,' Volkmar commanded, and the man moved forward and slowly
opened his hands, disclosing one gray donkey's hair. The count was about to
sweep away the blasphemous relic, but he saw the joy of it had brought Klaus
and the admiration it elicited from the mob. Disturbed, he turned his back on
the stupid peasants and their donkey's hair.

He walked to the southeastern corner of his city in search of someone with
common sense with whom he could discuss the perplexing events of the
morning, and he came at last to a fine house, cross-timbered in front and four
stories high, nestled against the protecting wall of the city. 'Anybody awake?'
he shouted outside the front door, and in a moment a young girl, obviously
pregnant and contented with that fact, threw open the heavily barred door and
cried, 'Count Volkmar! Come in. Father's here.' She led the count through a
hallway containing massive pieces of furniture and into an inner room where a
remarkable man sat waiting in a long robe of Venetian material edged by a fur
collar. He was in his mid-forties, a congenial, quick-eyed Jew with a black
beard and a gold-embroidered cap, and the impression he created was one of
unusual competence: in negotiation this one would be alert, in discussion
judicious, and in physical crisis courageous. He nodded to Volkmar as the girl
announced, 'Father, it's the count.'

To this impressive room, lined with folios, Volkmar was no stranger. Often
he had come here to borrow money, more often to discuss gossip or to pick up
bits of political information, for the man in the gold cap could read and write
and in his earlier years had traveled to many lands. 'Hagarzi,' Volkmar said,
speaking as friend to equal. 'I need six pieces of gold until the crops are in.' To
this proposal the moneylender nodded, as if that part of the visit concerned him
little.

'For that you could have sent your bailiff. What really brings you here?'

'I need to know whether a rabble like the one that passed Gretz this morning
has any chance of reaching Jerusalem?' The Jew made no reply, and Volkmar
asked, 'Did you see them?'

'Of course,' Hagarzi said, implying that it was his business to see whatever
passed Gretz at dawn. Then he added slowly, like a general reviewing his
ancient battles, 'I've never been all the way to Jerusalem. To Antioch, yes.'

'You went to Constantinople?'

'Several times. While the Hungarians and Bulgarians were still pagan I used
to captain companies of traders on their way from Gretz to Constantinople, and
we got there with only a few battles.' He leaned back and traced signs in the air,
reconstructing the travel routes to the east. 'It can be done. If you don't arouse
the Hungarians . . . or the Bulgarians.'

'Then you think there's a chance the foolish priest on the gray donkey may succeed?'

'All the way to Jerusalem?' The cautious trader pondered this. 'I saw no knights to protect them,' he said. 'They carried few provisions.'

'What road will they take?' Volkmar asked.

'When we went,' the former captain replied, closing his eyes and holding his beard with both hands, 'we followed the Danube to the point where the road turns north to Novgorod.' He began to reminisce about the vigorous days of his youth, when he had led his caravans to Smolensk, Kiev . . . 'We traded with them all.'

'Suppose the rabble reaches Constantinople,' Volkmar interrupted, and the trader opened his eyes. 'Could they possibly continue to Jerusalem?'

'They could start,' the moneylender replied. Obviously he did not care to discuss this aspect of the problem, so he launched a diversion: 'I remember one year when we tried to go from Kiev to Constantinople . . .'

'You don't think they'll reach Jerusalem?' the count persisted.

'Volkmar,' Hagarzi said, laughing brusquely as he used the count's familiar name, 'this is a venture summoned by the Christian church. Would it be proper for a Jew to comment on its progress?'

'You and I are the oldest of friends, Simon,' and he also used the familiar name.

'They won't get there,' the banker said. 'When I was last in the east the Turks were becoming very strong. I wanted to revisit Antioch. Goods from Cyprus and Egypt. Impossible.' Quickly he added, 'However, if I'd had a thousand well-armed men . . . knights . . . like you.'

Volkmar did not want Hagarzi to think that he was contemplating any crusade to Jerusalem, so he changed the discussion abruptly: 'Which Pope will prevail?'

Again the Jew closed his eyes. 'Only a close friend would deem it proper,' he reflected, 'to ask a Jew's opinion on that problem.'

'Only an old friend would know that you've been trading with Rome and· probably have the answer.'

'From what the merchants in Rome tell us, our German emperor has backed the wrong man. His German Pope Clement is not going to gain acceptance. The French Pope Urban will.'

This was not what Volkmar had wanted to hear. For some time he had assumed that his emperor would get his headstrong way and that of the two contenders Pope Clement would be declared the rightful pontiff; but Volkmar had much respect for the opinions of the well-informed Jew and had rarely found him to be in error, and what Hagarzi was saying disturbed him.

'How can the French Pope win,' he argued, 'if England, Germany and much of Italy are against him and if our Pope Clement holds Rome?'

'This idea of a crusade, which Pope Urban proposed . . .'

'You saw the mob, Hagarzi. What could it accomplish?'

'That mob, nothing. But my news from Normandy and Toulouse is quite different. Real leaders are sewing the cross to their tunics.'

Before the men could discuss the matter Hagarzi looked to his door, where his daughter appeared with a salver of spiced drinks and German cakes. Volkmar pointed to her belly and asked, 'When?'

'In four weeks.'

'Am I supposed to give the little wretch a present?'

'As always,' Hagarzi laughed, and the men drank their wine of friendship.

In those years the Jews in cities like Gretz lived pretty much as they wished. Fanatic Christians sometime howled against the commingling of Jew and Catholic, but no restrictive measures had yet been promulgated, so that a distinguished banker like Hagarzi could be accepted as one of the city's important citizens. His sturdy house had become a center of city life to which many Germans like Count Volkmar came not only to borrow, but also to talk.

They came to borrow because of contrasting interpretations which had been placed by Christianity and Judaism upon two critical verses from the Old Testament. Catholics held that the stern commandment in Exodus meant exactly what it said: 'If thou lend money to any of my people that is poor by thee, thou shall not be to him as an usurer, neither shalt thou lay upon him usury.' This was interpreted as meaning that no Christian–on pain of excommunication or death–was allowed to let money at interest, and this ruling came at the precise time when trade was beginning to be international and when borrowing substantial sums to finance such trade was essential. What to do? It was then discovered that Jews, looking not to Exodus but to Deuteronomy, took their instructions from Moses, who had commanded them:"Thou shalt not lend upon usury to thy brother; usury of money, usury of victuals, usury of any thing that is lent upon usury: Unto a stranger thou mayest lend upon usury.' So at the instigation of the Christians a curious agreement had been worked out: Christians would rule the world, but Jews would finance it–so to them was handed responsibility for all banking transactions, and it became customary for even cardinals and bishops to borrow openly from Jews at commonly understood rates of interest, while foreign traders had to do so in order to stay in business. In this manner Jews like Simon Hagarzi of Gretz prospered, but it was ironic that many did so against their own better judgment. Hagarzi, for example, sprang from a family which had wandered into Germany from Babylonia, settling themselves along the Rhine centuries before the present Germans had straggled down from the north. Like his predecessors in the little Palestinian town of Makor, Simon Hagarzi had begun life as a groats maker and he would have been happy to remain so; but in pursuit of grain he had come to know many distant cities, so that he was logically pushed into the business of banking. Now his transformation was complete; what Canaanites, Egyptians, Greeks, Romans and Byzantines had been unable to accomplish–taking Jews from the land and making merchants of them–Europe had achieved. Jews were now the money-manipulators, and without their services the new Europe could not have matured.

But even if Hagarzi had not controlled the credit of Gretz, Germans would still have come to talk with him, for in an age when few could read and when news traveled slowly, Hagarzi was perhaps the best-informed man in the city. Yet he was humble in his knowledge, and if he knew much of the Talmud by heart, he kept it to himself and his family, for he knew that the Christians had their own Book, and he never intruded his religion upon them. Even so, he was known to Christian and Jew alike throughout the city as a man who united in his person not only sagacity but also a radiant personal charity which had confirmed him in the title God's Man, a name by which the men of his family had been known through many generations in Makor and Babylonia; even devout Christians found spiritual profit in knowing this particular Jew.

As always, when Count Volkmar left Hagarzi he had his money, which he handed over to his bailiff. He then walked disconsolately to his castle and slowly climbed the stairs to where his wife sat at breakfast with the children, but he had not had time to tell her of Hagarzi's prediction about the competing Popes when a servant ran in to inform him that strangers were riding down the road from Cologne. The family went onto the battlements, from which they saw a cloud of dust sweeping energetically toward the city. 'It must be half a dozen horsemen,' Volkmar estimated, and as he studied the approaching cyclone he craned his neck forward to see who might be causing it.

At last, as the men drew close to the wall, he discerned that the foremost rider was dressed in a light suit of mail, his helmet and shield at his side. Over the metal suit he wore a long tunic of white upon which had been stitched a large cross in blue. Then the man's head became discernible, a handsome, commanding blond head with clean-shaven chin and blue eyes.

'It's Gunter!' Matwilda cried happily as she ran down to greet her brother.

When the seven knights from Cologne were seated in the hall, with Gunter clanking his metaled feet, the exciting news was broken. 'We've taken the cross,' the young German announced. 'Within the month we'll march to Jerusalem. When we leave we'll have fifteen thousand men with us, and you're going along.'

'Me!' Volkmar ejaculated.

'You! And Conrad of Mainz and Henry of Worms. Everyone.'

'I do not follow the commands of a False Pope,' Volkmar protested.

'To hell with the Pope!' Gunter shouted. 'Clement, Urban? Who gives a damn? Brother, in the Holy Land there are kingdoms to be won, and no quarrel about Popes must separate us from such booty.'

The knights who had ridden forth with Gunter on his conscripting tour nodded, and one asked Matwilda, 'Wouldn't you like to be Queen of Antioch or Princess of Jerusalem?'

'I'd like to see Gunter with such lands,' she replied, for she knew how strenuously her younger brother wanted a fief of his own.

'But I'm quite content here in Gretz,' Volkmar insisted.

'Don't you want to go crusading?' his brother-in-law shouted. 'Everyone else in the Rhineland does.' He dashed to the platform overlooking the public square and bellowed, 'You down there? How many of you want to march to Jerusalem and rescue it from the heathen?'

A shout welled up and echoed through the castle. One man cried, 'Klaus has a hair from the donkey of Peter the Hermit.'

At mention of the little priest's name Gunter scowled, then yelled to the crowd, 'In one week all able-bodied men who want to march with me to Jerusalem. . .' Now the shouting grew frenzied and the blond knight waved his arms, but when he returned to the table he slumped noisily into his chair and muttered, 'That damned monk. He hasn't a chance of getting to Jerusalem.'

'You think not?' Volkmar asked.

'You saw him. Were there ten men in his twenty thousand capable of fighting? Peasants, old women.' The young man rose and stamped about the room, his mailed feet clanging on the stones. 'Volkmar, to recapture Jerusalem for Jesus Christ we need soldiers, men trained to war. The Turks are terrible fighters . . .'

'And you are determined to go against them?' Matwilda asked.

Gunter leaped across the room and knelt beside her. 'Sister! Some fighting man who leaves Europe this month is going to be crowned King of Jerusalem. Half a dozen others are going to hack out great marches for themselves. I intend to be one of those men.' Then, somewhat ashamed of his personal outburst, he pointed to one of his companions, adding, 'And Gottfried here will gain another.' Volkmar and his wife looked at Gottfried, a chinless fool. The knight grinned and nodded. He, too, intended to win a barony in the Holy Land.

Then Gunter's wild ambition again surged to the fore and he cried, 'One month from today, on May 24, we shall march forth from Gretz, fifteen thousand, twenty. And you shall be with us.' He kissed his sister good-bye and swept down the castle stairs, eager to spread the word of his crusade to the other Rhenish cities. At the gate he saw Klaus still clutching his donkey hair, and he shouted, 'Can you get a horse, man?'

'Yes,' Klaus called back.

'Then ride with us,' Gunter cried. 'I need a servant who is lucky.' And when the seven knights rode off to the south Klaus of Gretz rode with them.

When they were gone, and the excitement had subsided, Wenzel of Trier came quietly to his lord and said, 'It is my opinion, sir, that you should take the cross.'

'Why?' Volkmar asked in deep seriousness.

'Because it is the will of God,' Wenzel replied.

'Those are the words of the False Pope's man,' Volkmar countered.

'In this great matter, believe me, Volkmar, there is no false Pope, there is no true. There is only the call of God. The holy city, the land of our Lord Jesus Christ, is held by the infidel and we are summoned to redeem it.'

Count Volkmar leaned back, disturbed. 'You speak as if you . . .'

'One month from today,' the hard-eyed priest announced, 'I shall ride with the others.'

'But why?' Volkmar pressed. 'You have a chapel here. We need you.'

'And we need you in Jerusalem.'

For a week Count Volkmar pondered the invitation that Gunter had so forcefully laid before him, and each day Wenzel of Trier, his stern face staring out from beneath the gray hair he wore in bangs, added his priestly pressure; a spiritual movement without comparison was under way and any man of courage who missed it would be forever ashamed. Wenzel never spoke of kingdoms or principalities; in his heart was the call of God and he did not want his master to ignore that call.

On the succeeding Saturday, Count Volkmar, who could neither read nor write, summoned Wenzel to draft a cautious letter of inquiry to the German emperor, asking whether a Rhenish knight could properly respond to the crusading summons of the False Pope, who also happened to be French; and this was a more delicate question than it might have seemed, since the French Pope had recently excommunicated the German emperor and there was personal bitterness between them, and while Volkmar waited for a reply he went to discuss the matter with Hagarzi, God's Man, and the Jew listened as the big, awkward count explained his dilemma: 'I want to serve God, but I do not want to anger my emperor. How can a German emperor give permission to his knights to follow the orders of a French Pope, who isn't even legal?'

The moneylender laughed, and grasping the edges of his robe with both hands, said: 'Count Volkmar, if you've decided to go on the Crusade . . .'

'I have no intention of going,' the count protested.

Ignoring the disclaimer Hagarzi continued, 'Be guided by the story of one of our great rabbis, Akiba. The question arose of blowing the ram's horn in a new city, because Jerusalem, which alone had the right to sound such a horn, had been destroyed by the Romans. What to do? Akiba and his liberals argued,

"Let us sound the horn here and establish a new Jerusalem." But the conservatives countered, "Only in Jerusalem may the horn be sounded. And Jerusalem is no more." So Akiba made this proposal: "The hour is upon us. Let us blow the horn now and resume the argument later." So they blew the horn. Then came the conservatives to argue, but Akiba pointed out, "What's to discuss? The horn has been blown. A precedent has been set. In the future we must like good Jews observe that precedent."'

The two men laughed, and Hagarzi said, 'Believe me, Volkmar. Don't wait for the emperor's reply. Decide now what must be done, then do it.'

'Even though I may infuriate my own emperor?'

'Governments are made to be infuriated,' the Jew replied, but in spite of this daring advice Volkmar decided to wait.

Before a reply could reach Gretz, Gunter and his six knights rode back from their foray up the Rhine, and the party had grown to fourteen enthusiasts, including an attractive girl whom Gunter had acquired in Speyer. At the castle of Gretz he indicated that from now on the girl would be sleeping with him, in one of Matwilda's rooms, and his sister was outraged, but Gunter ignored her.

'Wherever we rode,' he cried in flushed excitement, 'men of great reputation signified that they would join us at the end of the month. Volkmar, you've got to come.'

The count refused comment, but Wenzel confided, 'At least he's written to the emperor for a judgment.'

'Volkmar!' the excited young knight cried. 'You're one of us. The emperor gave Conrad of Mainz permission to go.'

'He did?' Volkmar asked cautiously.

'Yes! Conrad's bringing a troop of nine hundred.'

The words stunned Volkmar. How could the city of Mainz, no larger than Gretz, spare nine hundred men? Who would tend the fields? And for the first time he realized that a sweeping, all-embracing movement was afoot, one which ignored plow fields and ordinary husbandry.

'From Gretz we'll take away twelve hundred men,' Gunter predicted. 'I've got Klaus circulating tonight. We'll need horses and carts, too.' He had discarded his mail suit and appeared in light robes, covered by the tunic which bore the large blue cross, and as he spoke he kept his left arm about the pretty girl whose name no one knew. 'It's an enterprise of great danger, and perhaps I have spoken too much of the principality I intend carving for myself with this right arm. For there is also the matter of God's will, and Wenzel here can tell you that it is shameful to have the holy places of our Lord in infidel hands. By God,' he cried, striking the table, 'it shall not continue.'

He led his strange girl to bed and in the morning assembled his group and rode off, taking with him three more horsemen from Gretz. He had been gone only a short time when from the south a messenger rode in with the emperor's reply: 'We have passed far beyond the matter of Popes. We must win Jerusalem for our Lord Jesus Christ. So if you find it in your heart to fight for the recovery of His homeland, proceed.' When Volkmar heard the words he knelt on the stone and asked Wenzel to bless him; for if his brother-in-law was marching to the Holy Land for a broad mixture of reasons, Volkmar would go for one only: to strike the infidel and drive him from the holy places. Looking up, he laid hold of his priest's hands and swore, 'I take the cross. It is God's will.'

But when he came to ask Matwilda to sew upon his tunic a red cross he found himself confronted by a problem which he was quite unable to solve, and he walked through the city to Hagarzi's house, where he was again greeted by the Jew's pregnant daughter. As soon as he was closeted with the moneylender he burst out, 'Hagarzi, I need help.'

'Money?' his friend asked.

'Much more difficult.'

'The only thing more difficult is a man's wife.'

'Correct. I've pledged myself to go crusading . . .'

'I hope you reach Jerusalem,' Hagarzi replied solemnly.

'We've a good army,' Volkmar assured him.

'Then you have a chance.'

'But when I informed my wife I found her sewing the cross on her own garments and on those of our children.'

The moneylender leaned back in his chair and opened his eyes very wide. 'She intends going too?'

'Yes, her brother has infected her with his strange dreams.'

'Volkmar,' the banker said earnestly. 'I've been four times to Constantinople and never were we able to take a woman. It's a hundred days through dangerous country.'

'She insists.'

God's Man looked with compassion at his count. The two had worked together on numerous projects and the amount of gold that Hagarzi had contributed to works initiated by the count could not be calculated, for the Jew had long since stopped keeping accounts. Of Volkmar's friends only Hagarzi could appreciate what decisions the count was now facing. In such crises the experienced Jew had found it was best to speak frankly: 'Volkmar, if a hundred men leave Gretz headed for Jerusalem and back, fighting Hungarians, Bulgarians, Turks . . .'

'Last time you said that Hungarians and Bulgarians are now Christians.'

'They are, but you'll still have to fight them.'

'It's the infidel we intend fighting,' Volkmar protested.

'Of a hundred men who leave, nine will be lucky if they return.'

Volkmar was stunned. He had thought that fighting the infidels in Jerusalem would be much like fighting the Normans in Sicily. A few would die on each side, but most would come home with here and there a scar. The Jew continued, 'So if you leave us, there is little chance that I'll ever see you again.' He hesitated. 'Or that your countess will, either.'

'You would take her?' Volkmar asked.

'Yes. But not your son. We'll need a count in Gretz.'

Volkmar sighed and looked at the row of folios above the moneylender's head; the castle owned not one. He asked, 'Could you lend me gold on the fields across the river?'

'Of course. But if you go you must leave a will protecting me.'

Without deciding then, the count left the banker's house and walked through the market, where women sold the first fruits of spring—fine onions and beans—and when he reached the castle he did something that he had not done for a long time. He kissed his son, then ripped from the boy's shoulder the red cross which his mother had that morning sewed to the tunic. 'You are not going.' The boy began to weep and Volkmar summoned his family. They gathered in a cold, bare room, for the German castle of that period was little better than a commodious barn with stone flooring. The chairs were rough, the table unsmoothed and the linen coarse. A damp smell of horses and urine permeated the place and there were no fabrics to soften the effect of the sweating walls. Painting and music were unknown, but an open fire kept the dank rooms reasonably comfortable in winter, and there was plentiful food, cooked pretty much as barbarian forefathers had cooked it six centuries before.

'Matwilda and Fulda will ride with me,' Volkmar announced. 'Otto will stay home to hold the castle with his uncle.' He drew his son to him and held the boy's chin to keep it from trembling.

Matwilda, then in her middle thirties and as attractive as when Volkmar had ridden north to court her, was pleased with the news that she could make the trip, and she understood why Otto had better stay at home. She consoled her son, then listened as her husband summoned Wenzel and a scribe: 'If I should not return, the fields across the river are to become the property of the monastery at Worms, which shall first discharge the debt I owe to the Jew, Hagarzi, known in Gretz as God's Man. The castle, the town and all lands pertaining to both shall become the property of my good wife Matwilda, or if she do not return, to my son Otto.' The detailed description continued, the thoughtful words of a man who loved God, his family and his fief, concluding with a final paragraph that was to be much quoted in later years when men tried to penetrate the motives which had inspired the Crusaders: 'Let it be known that I am marching to Jerusalem because the will of God should be respected in this world and because the scenes in which our Saviour, the Lord Jesus Christ, lived should not remain in pagan hands. I am marching with a goodly band, and we have placed ourselves entirely in the hands of God, for we go forth as His servants to accomplish His will.' When the words were read aloud to him he nodded and made his mark, which as it appears on the document today resembles the red cross he was wearing as he signed.

The next weeks were filled with unusual activity. If Count Volkmar of Gretz was going to Jerusalem, along with more than a thousand of his people, he would leave little to chance. For his wife and daughter, eight wagons and sixteen draft horses were provided filled with enough equipment to serve them and the six servants who would care for them. Eight additional wagons carried foodstuffs, implements and armor. Besides the servants for the countess, an even dozen serfs marched on foot to care for the count and Wenzel of Trier. In addition, eight grooms brought along some two dozen riding horses for the minor knights associated with the count, and these were followed by about a thousand consisting of merchants and farmers, monks and ordinary serfs. About a hundred women wanted to join the procession, but this number diminished after Matwilda had weeded out the known prostitutes.

On Sunday morning, May 24, 1096, the Gretz contingent formed up outside the city gates, an orderly crowd of peasants waiting for the arrival of Gunter and his men from the north. At about ten o'clock outriders appeared, soon followed by a host of some six thousand, and it was quickly apparent that the care which Count Volkmar had given to the selection of the men from Gretz had not been duplicated by Gunter when he chose the volunteers at Cologne; for he appeared with a rabble. Thieves, men sprung from jail and notorious prostitutes were conspicuous. There were gangs of debtors who had shaken free of their creditors, and peasants who would hoe the fields no more. Boredom was banished and the frenzy of unknown adventure was high as Gunter, now splendid in new armor and a red tunic with a blue cross, spurred his horse through the wagons and the cattle. He was attended by eleven knights, and these were not rabble but hardened young men capable of defending themselves and the unruly crowd they led.

'Did you ever see such an army?' Gunter cried with animal joy as the knights rode up to welcome the new recruits.

Volkmar made no reply, but as the mob pressed in upon his own well-disciplined people he suggested, 'Let Wenzel bless us as we start,' and all uncovered as the priest intoned, 'Dear God, protect this holy army as we march to Jerusalem to recover it from the infidel. Strengthen our arms, for we fight Your battle. Sweet Jesus, lead us, for we wear Your cross. Death to the infidel!'

The multitude echoed, 'Death to the infidel!' and at this unfortunate moment a Jew of Gretz who sold clothes in the market happened to pass the gates, and Gunter cried, 'Great Jesus! Why should we ride to Jerusalem to fight His enemies there and leave His greater enemies here to prosper?'

And in the heat of the moment he dashed with a loud cry through the gates and with one swipe of his great sword slashed off the head of the unsuspecting Jew. The mob howled its approval, and men from the north started spurring their horses into the city, followed by thousands on foot.

'Kill the Jews!' they bellowed.

A Jewish woman was coming to market, and a lancer ran her through, using his tremendous strength to toss her in the air, where she hung suspended for a terrible moment, her eyes still seeing the sudden mob beneath her. The crowd shrieked and she descended sickeningly toward the street, where they trampled her to death.

Volkmar, sensing what must follow, tried to fight his way back into the city, but he was powerless. 'Stop!' he begged, but none would listen.

The mob was after Jews but could not have explained why. In the obligatory Easter sermons they had listened to ill-informed priests crying, 'The Jews crucified Jesus Christ and God wants you to punish them.' From learned discourses delivered by bishops they had discovered that in the Old Testament, Isaiah himself had prophesied that a Virgin would give birth to Jesus Christ, and that the Jews had stubbornly rejected the teaching of their own Book: 'For this sin they shall be outcast forever.' And in their daily life they watched as the Jew lent money, which honest men were forbidden to do, and some had known at first-hand the interest which moneylenders charged. But stronger than any of these complaints was the inchoate suspicion, not often expressed in words, that in a world where all decent men were Christian, there was something intolerably perverse in a group who clung obstinately to an earlier religion which had been proved an error. The Jews were a living insult to the trend of history, and if one helped exterminate them, he must be doing God's work. Therefore, when Gunter pointed out the folly of marching to Jerusalem to confront God's enemies while the greater foe stayed here in Gretz, he awakened a score of latent hatreds.

'Kill the Jews!' the mob roared, storming its way through the gates, and local residents—who had no specific cause for cursing Jews—were caught up in the frenzy and suddenly turned informer. 'In that house a Jew lives!' Like locusts the mob descended upon the house, killing, pillaging and laying waste.

'Get the moneylender!' cried a man who had never borrowed from any Jew, and like a monstrous animal the crowd turned with one accord and swept into the southern corner of the city, where a Christian led them to Hagarzi's four-storied house. Fortunately the banker was absent, but soldiers flushed out his daughter, whom they ran through with two lances, throwing her far over their shoulders. As she flew in the air it became evident that she was pregnant, and women shrieked approvingly, 'With that one you caught two!' And they stamped her to pieces.

'The synagogue!' they shouted, and this low building so unlike a church infuriated them, for when they came to that holy place they found that some sixty-seven Jews had taken refuge inside. 'Burn them all!' the mob screamed, and about the entrances chairs and scraps of wood were placed, drenched with oil, and set afire. When gasping Jews tried to fight their way free they were greeted with lances jabbing them back into the flames. All perished.

They were the lucky ones, for now the Crusaders started flushing out Jewish women. Old ones they killed on the spot, running them through with daggers. Younger ones they stripped naked and raped time after time in the town square, with all applauding. Then, in disgust, they hacked off the girls' heads.

For two sickly hours the Crusaders stormed through the streets of Gretz, killing and maiming and defiling. When at last they leaned weary on their swords, with blood on their tunics and smoke in their eyes, they justified their slaughter to each other: 'It would have been folly to leave for Jerusalem when the men who crucified our Saviour stayed behind to grow rich.' When they withdrew from the city they left behind eighteen hundred dead Jews and the beginning of a heritage that would haunt Germany forever.

In the dreadful silence that followed, when the great knights were gone and the priests, one sturdy Jew wearing cloth from Venice and a fur collar crept out from the refuge into which he had fought his way some hours before and started moving cautiously through the alleys. He saw the gutted synagogue with its sixty-seven charred skeletons. He saw his offspring strewn across the streets. He saw the smoldering memorials and the frightened, bewildered faces of the neighborhood Christians whom he had often befriended. They recognized him as a Jew, one of the great men of their city, but they were so sated with killing that no one raised his hand against the pitiful man. We leave him there–an honest banker–beginning to pick up the hideous shreds of his life, moving with glassy eyes through the alleys of Gretz; but we do not abandon him, for he will be with us again and again. His name is Hagarzi of Gretz, a fugitive groats maker from the town of Makor, and to his neighbors, when the grandeur of his courage is recognized, he will continue to be known as God's Man.

When the Crusaders camped that night beside the Rhine, Count Volkmar left his wife and went to the tent of the captains, where he accosted his brother-in-law, who lounged in a chair, demanding, 'How dare you kill the Jews of my city?'

Gunter, relaxed after the exciting day, had no desire for argument. 'They are the known enemies of God,' he explained, not raising his voice, 'and in this tent we have just sworn that when we have passed none will live along the Rhine.' The knights showed that they supported this resolve.

Volkmar, appalled by the coldness of this evil decision, grasped Gunter's arm. 'You must not encourage the men,' he pleaded. 'Look at the madness they performed in Gretz.'

Patiently Gunter brushed away his brother-in-law's hand. 'I'm sorry the fire from the synagogue burned some of your city,' he apologized, determined that no argument should mar the profitable day.

Volkmar dragged him to his feet. 'You must prevent such riots,' he commanded. 'You're not to kill Jews.'

Gunter was annoyed. He was taller than Volkmar, heavier, younger. But he merely removed his brother's arm and slumped back into his seat. 'It would be folly to leave the Jews behind. They crucified Christ and they must not grow rich while we are absent fighting.' He turned from the count, dismissing him, but such contempt Volkmar would not tolerate, and he roughly dragged Gunter to his feet; but the young blond warrior had had enough. Raising his powerful right hand he pushed it into his brother's face and shoved with force. Volkmar was driven back. He staggered and fell. Reaching for his sword he would have unsheathed it, but was prevented from doing so by Gunter's knights, who closed in on him and lifted him to his feet, rushing him from the tent. Gottfried, the foolish one with no chin, found bravery and shouted from the tent flaps, 'Bother us no more. Gunter leads this army and we shall leave not one Jew alive.'

Up the Rhine surged the Crusaders, led by Gunter with his cross of blue, and wherever they struck, Jews were slaughtered. At Mainz, at Worms, at Speyer there were killings to make a man sick. At the head of the murderers rode Gunter, shouting that God Himself had ordained the destruction of His enemies. In small towns Jews huddled together in one house and were burned alive. In cities they crept into protected quarters and were chopped to death as bold knights coursed among them. In one town the Jews assembled, and with knives sharpened as the Torah demanded for ritual slaughter, methodically cut their own throats so that the floors were slippery with blood when the Crusaders crashed down the door.

'Filthy infidels—to do such a thing!' the knights protested, but their rage reached its apex when Jewish mothers slit the throats of their own babies rather than wait for the crusading lances.

'They're animals,' Gunter bellowed. 'What mother would kill her own babe?'

We can speak accurately of these matters because Wenzel of Trier recorded them in his chronicle of the German Crusade:

Most strange in this chain of death was the fact that except for a few Jews who were killed in the heat of first assault, all could have saved their lives and their souls by the simple act of converting to the True Faith, but this they obstinately refused to do, preferring to maintain their abominable error rather than to accept salvation. I myself offered not less than four thousand Jews the love and peace of my Lord Jesus Christ, but obstinately they turned their backs upon me, crying, 'Hear, O Israel, the Lord our God, the Lord is one,' and our Christians had no other choice but to slay them. Sickened by the killings my Lord Volkmar tried repeatedly to break away from the army and return home, but I was forced to remind him that he had sworn an oath to capture Jerusalem and if for any reason he refused to honor that oath he would be forever excommunicate, so he had no escape but to keep with us and I consoled him: 'Is it not better that an honest man should ride with Gunter, endeavoring to restrain him?' But even so, I believe that my Lord Volkmar would have left us had not his wife Matwilda pleaded with him that it was his duty to remain, so that what later happened to the countess was in a sense of her own doing.

The slaughter of the Jews continued until one afternoon two girls about seventeen years of age stood side by side until the rapists were upon them, then carefully slit each other's throats. It was impossible for two people to kill each other in this manner, but the Jewish girls had done it.

'For God's sake, stop!' Volkmar pleaded for the hundredth time, and when his wife saw the two dead Jewesses, of the same age as her daughter Fulda, but prettier even in death, she ran to them and kissed their ashen lips; and the killing ceased—but thirty thousand Jews were dead, and the great Crusade had been launched in blood.

The march through Austria was more peaceful, for when the attention of the knights was no longer distracted by Jews they were free to look among the women who had accompanied the march, and each found one or two who promised well on the long journey. And there were pleasant nights in the hayricks and under the stars. Gunter kept the young women he had picked up on his initial survey as well as a prostitute from Speyer; but Volkmar stayed with his wife and daughter, praying that somehow the rabble of which he found himself an unwilling part would finally stumble into Constantinople, where the real armies would be assembling.

But in Hungary, Gunter and his Germans ran into trouble. Barely a month had elapsed since the hordes of Peter the Hermit, marching without money, had caused ill will by trying to live off the land, snatching what they needed from Hungarian peasants, and Gunter's men were about to harvest the hatred thus engendered. At the first town the Crusaders found that local merchants had closed their shops, knowing that they would not be paid if they kept them open, and there was no food. Gunter solved this by shouting an order: 'Break open the shops and help yourselves.' There was moderate fighting and some two dozen Hungarians were killed.

'By God!' Gunter cried as he assembled his men at the far end of town. 'They meant to give us trouble and we are the Lord's men!'

'Let's go back and destroy the place,' one of his assistants proposed, and for a moment the angry mob hesitated on the verge of another slaughter, but Count Volkmar succeeded in luring them down the river and a massacre was avoided. Of the leading knights, he was the oldest, and certainly the sagest, so he pointed out to his younger associates that their main job was not to brawl with Hungarians but to reach Constantinople with as many fighting men as possible. 'The enemy is in Asia,' he kept reminding them.

But when at the second town the citizens–prewarned by messengers from the first–barricaded the gates, refusing to allow any Crusader to enter, Gunter shouted, 'Open the gates now or we'll burn them down.' The Hungarians refused and a great fire was started, and whenever a Hungarian tried to escape he was shot with arrows and the town perished.

From that day on, it was war between Hungary and the Crusaders. When the latter reached a town they found it evacuated, with all food gone. Starvation threatened. Ruthless Hungarian raiders stalked the stragglers, killing off the weaker Germans. Horses and wagons were destroyed and such constant pressure was maintained that Gunter lost one man in eight.

With groans of relief the disorganized columns finally straggled into Bulgaria, where those recently converted Christians were willing to extend the Crusaders one chance: the first Bulgarian town sent emissaries to welcome the marchers, but a priest warned Wenzel: 'Tell your knights to behave, or there must be trouble.' Wenzel summoned Gunter and Volkmar and said, in words which he later recorded in his chronicle:

'My Lords, we have seen in Hungary what ill returns a want of Christian grace can bring, and I pray you, direct your men to behave as an army of God should, and let us be gentle with the Bulgarians, for they worship the same Jesus Christ that we do, and let us be an example to them of what the brotherhood of the cross signifies.' But either they did not heed my words or their men did not listen, for after the gates were opened and the market made available, our men, sore and famished from the wars in Hungary, descended upon the poor Bulgarians like heathen, taking their wares for the asking. The townsmen, a vigorous people, defended themselves ably, and a fighting began in which many were killed, and the Crusaders became enraged and chased through houses seeking for women, which they treated most shamefully, killing many. It was a pity that day to be wearing the cross of God.

The retaliation was inexorable. If the raiders of Hungary had been remorseless, those of Bulgaria were worse, and on the afternoon of July 15, 1096, a barefoot crowd of peasants swept down and isolated the contingent in which Count Volkmar and his family travelled, taking some seven hundred Germans prisoner. To his horror the count watched as the Bulgarians started methodically to chop off the heads of all, but he was saved by a knowing peasant who cried, 'For this one and his family we can get ransom.' And Volkmar was led away to prison at Sofia.

In some ways this was the best thing that happened to him during the Crusade, for while he languished in jail with his wife and daughter, waiting for Wenzel to appear with the ransom money, Gunter and his knights struggled and slaughtered their way through Bulgaria, losing almost a third of their army. And when they finally did reach Constantinople they found their way barred by the great wall of that city.

'Open the gates, or we'll tear the city down!' Gunter blustered, whereupon the Byzantine Christians dispatched a skilled army which punished the Germans badly, killing off another nine hundred. Much chastened, the Crusaders were admitted to the marvelous capital of the east just in time to join up with Peter the Hermit as he boarded a small fleet which would ferry him from Europe to Asia. With deep emotion Gunter stood in the bow of his boat, waiting to leap ashore in Asia and start the real march to Jerusalem. Of the sixteen thousand pilgrims who had started with him from the Rhine less than nine thousand remained, but as the boats touched shore these cried with great voice. 'It is God's will! Let us crush the infidel.' The Crusade was formally under way.

On October 1, longer after Gunter had crashed into Asia, Wenzel of Trier returned to Sofia with a bag of ransom money, and as the governor of the prison accepted it he told the priest, 'If all Crusaders had been like your Count Volkmar we Bulgarians would have given them no trouble.' With seeming regret he bade the count and his family farewell and dispatched an armed escort to lead them to the capital. 'May you destroy the infidel,' he called as the little convoy headed for Constantinople.

They reached the massive walls on October 18, 1096, and Volkmar ordered the escort to halt so that he could examine the impressive fortifications, and he found that where his castle wall at Gretz had a thickness of four rows of stone, the Byzantine had twenty. 'I should not like to be assaulting this fort,' Volkmar remarked to the priest.

'Sire,' the Bulgarian guard interrupted, 'this is not the fort. This is only the outer wall.'

With growing astonishment the Germans entered the city, and when they came at last to a real fort Volkmar said flatly, 'From an outside assault this could not be taken,' and the Bulgarian told him, 'The forts held by the Turks in Asia are stronger by far, and you will have to take them if you wish to reach Jerusalem.' For the first time Volkmar sensed the kind of struggle he was engaged in.

He continued, wide-eyed, to where the roadway offered a view of the Golden Horn, with many ships moored to its twisting, resplendent shores, and he caught sight of the opposite bank, teeming with shops and merchandise. This was no rural Rhine; this was the heart of a great empire; and then he saw to the right the many-domed splendor of Sancta Sophia, radiant beside the sea, and he knew how special the city was.

When he was delivered to the underlings of the emperor he asked where his fellow Crusaders were, and was told, 'We have word that Godfrey of Bouillon will arrive shortly and Robert of Normandy is coming.'

Relieved to hear these impressive names, Volkmar explained, 'I meant Gunter of Cologne and Peter the Hermit.'

The man's face darkened and he said, 'Concerning them you must ask others.'

Late Wenzel prowled about the market and found that Gunter and the Germans had crossed into Asia in August and were already engaged in fighting the Turks. The news depressed Volkmar not because he was afraid that his brother-in-law would get to his dreamed-of realms before he, Volkmar, could catch up, but rather because if fighting were at hand all men of honor should attend, and he voiced his disappointment to Matwilda. But the next day Wenzel returned with the rumor that the rabble in Asia had stumbled upon the Turkish army and had been annihilated.

For three gloomy days conflicting reports ricocheted across the shores of the Golden Horn, and at last Gunter of Cologne was ferried back from Asia, so gaunt and hollow-eyed that his sister hardly knew him. The once ebullient fighter had lost forty pounds and his blond hair was matted. His tunic was shredded and the brave cross of blue was torn half away. He was pleased to see Volkmar, but only so that he could collapse onto a brocaded bed, where he asked for water, refusing to speak.

During the first full day the haggard German slept and said nothing, and finally he stared at Wenzel, who had waited patiently by the bed, and said, 'Seven of us got back.'

Wenzel called for the count, repeating to him and Matwilda what the Crusader had muttered.

'Only seven knights got back?' Volkmar asked.

'No knights but me,' Gunter replied, twisting his shoulders as if to avoid interrogation. 'Of the rest, six peasants.'

'Where did you leave the women?' Matwilda asked.

Her brother lifted his head to look at her, then broke into a thin-lipped grin. 'The women?' he repeated. 'Have you ever watched a band of Turkish foot soldiers rush a camp of children and horses and women?' He flicked his right hand four or five times, indicating sword thrusts. He continued to grin stupidly, his face out of control.

'They were all lost?' Volkmar asked.

'Brother,' the shaken knight replied, 'of all who marched with us seven survived.'

The priest knelt beside the bed and began to pray, while Volkmar tried to visualize the small army that had marched past Gretz only five months before. Ultimately it had contained more than twelve thousand men plus three or four thousand women and children, and Gunter had lost all but seven. 'Merciful God,' Volkmar prayed, 'what kind of crusade is this?'

Then Gunter insisted upon talking: 'It wasn't always defeat. Oh no! We had one stirring victory. We were marching inland from the sea and came upon a village from which issued a small army of men well armed and dressed in flowing robes. With great cries we fell on them and killed them all.' He began to giggle nervously—a great blond man behaving as if he were a child, so that Volkmar and Priest Wenzel looked at each other in consternation, but after a moment he regained control and said, 'When all were dead we discovered from their women that they were Christians marching to join us. But they looked like Turks ... the long robes ...' He half sat in bed and pleaded with Volkmar: 'What right has a Christian to wear a turban?' No one spoke and he fell back on his pillow, staring at the ceiling. Where had his knights gone? the lovely women? dumb Klaus clutching his donkey hair? But Volkmar could see only chinless Gottfreid, grinning vacuously that first morning at Gretz. It was he who best represented the sixteen thousand dead.

Volkmar recalled that the monks who had preached the Crusade had honestly warned, 'We are going to fight for the Lord and some will die, but all who surrender their lives in the great attempt will be granted remission of sin,' so it had always been understood that there would be losses; furthermore, Hagarzi had warned that of a hundred who left not more than nine would return. The count therefore had known that the proud venture entailed the risk of death, and as a man in his late forties–an advanced age for that day--he was prepared for his own; but he was not prepared for only seven survivors out of an army of sixteen thousand. Now it was his throat that was dry.

'What error did you make?' he asked his brother-in-law.

The young knight looked up at him with astonishment. 'Error?' he repeated incredulously. 'You mean what one thing did we do wrong so that the Turks won?' He laughed almost hysterically. 'What did we do wrong?' he repeated over and over until his sister drew Volkmar and the priest away.

One of the other survivors, a freeman from Gretz, discovered where his count was staying and came by to submit a more coherent report, and again Volkmar was appalled at the man's condition, for he was so haggard that he must have been starved for months. 'No organized supply,' he growled. 'No discipline. Women in the way and guards at night sleeping with the women. Gunter insisting that his two whores get full rations. Priests praying where we needed cavalry.' It was a sorrowful picture relieved by only one report: 'In the final battle at Nicaea the few knights we had were marvelous. Gunter killed ... how many?' In admiration the freeman recounted the blond knight's conspicuous bravery: 'And after performing all this he cut his way through the Turkish lines, and since I had stolen a horse, I was able to ride after him. But the courage was his, not mine.'

Volkmar fed the man and asked why the Turks were such powerful men, and to his surprise the man became excited: 'Sir, the Turks can be beaten. They're ordinary soldiers with fast horses and good arrows. But I watched ... a hundred real knights ... you ... Gunter ...' He was so enthusiastic that he stuttered, but his eyes flashed.

'You think we can win?' Volkmar probed.

'Of course! So does Gunter. All the way back from the battle he kept telling me of how we would fight next time. He spotted every weakness of the Turk.'

'Then why did you lose so horribly this time?' the count insisted.

'Because we had no soldiers, sir. We had only men like me who believed that God would open a way for us and feed us and blunt the sword of the enemy.' He raised his thin face and looked with a certain calm content into Volkmar's eyes and said, 'What we needed in addition to our faith in God was armed soldiers and knights like you to lead them.'

In the next month both began to arrive–soldiers led by Hugh of France, tough, tested warriors obedient to Godfrey of Bouillon. Then came the wiry Normans following their Duke Robert and the insolent northern Franks led by Stephen of Blois. The streets of Constantinople rattled with the armor of these

disciplined men, and in the afternoons when they sat together looking across
the straits at Asia they did so with well-prepared plans in mind. This was no
rabble led by a barefoot priest on a donkey. This was the most powerful army
that had ever poised on the edge of Europe, and as the warriors gathered they
listened attentively to each detail of Gunter's disastrous engagement with the
Turks. Some of the newcomers were frightened by this dismal account, but
most bolstered their confidence as he reported soberly: 'We must have a
disciplined group, moving in precision, and the best men shall ride at the
rear–for that's where the Turk likes to strike.'

On May 24, 1097, twelve months after his departure from Gretz, Count
Volkmar, attended only by his wife, his daughter and his priest Wenzel–for all
the rest who had ridden with the sixteen wagons were dead–crossed over from
Constantinople into Asia on the first dramatic step of the real Crusade, and as
he sat in his small boat, eager to be first ashore on the holy battleground he
thought: 'It's perplexing. I've been fighting for a year and have yet to see an
infidel. We have slain so many and all were Christian . . . except for those first
thirty thousand Jews. Sickened by his reflections he turned on the spur of the
moment to Wenzel, crying, 'Good priest, bless the completion of this venture,
for we have begun so poorly.' And he knelt in the boat, a thick-shouldered,
heavy-necked, sandy-haired German seeking God; and his wife Matwilda
knelt beside him and his daughter Fulda; and that night Wenzel of Trier
recorded in his chronicle how the Crusade had started on the edge of Asia:

> While the sea was about us, my Lord Volkmar and his lady knelt and I asked upon his pure head
> God's blessing, saying, 'This is your honest servant Volkmar of Gretz, who has set forth to
> accomplish Your bidding. Bless him. Keep his arm strong and bring him at last to the gates of
> Jerusalem for his whole desire is to support You and to destroy Your enemies. Amen.' And when
> the boat touched land my Lord Volkmar leaped ashore, raising his sword above his head and
> crying, 'Lord, let me be worthy of Your Holy Land.'

In this benediction Gunter did not bother to participate, for nine months
earlier he had leaped ashore in similar fashion, burning with equal zeal. This
time he stayed in the rear of the boat entertaining a group of French women
whom he had acquired from the camp of Hugh, brother to the French king.

THE TELL

Whenever John Cullinane faced intellectual problems relating to the dig he
found inspiration by visiting Akko, where he spent his mornings in the loveliest
mosque of Israel, admiring the peaceful courtyard with its numerous date
palms and hibiscus bushes. It was a seductive place, a Muslim enclave in a
Jewish state, made doubly attractive by the six giant columns that some
Turkish robber in the eighteenth century had dragged to this spot from the
Roman ruins at Caesarea. In the courtyard surrounding the mosque were half a
hundred smaller columns from the same place, and inside the brightly colored
building stood many more, and as Cullinane studied them he was able to
convince himself that King Herod had known these particular pillars during

those years when Caesarea flourished.

Never did the beauty of the Akko mosque fail to assert its subtle dominion over Cullinane, so that if he considered all the Jewish and Catholic remains in Israel–from the superb white synagogue of Baram to the soaring Franciscan church on Mount Tabor–he derived his greatest pleasure from this Muslim mosque. This was partly because he usually took with him Jemail Tabari, who apparently felt the same affinity for the place, for he used to lounge about the courtyard making acidulous comments which Cullinane enjoyed.

'You come here,' the sharp-witted Arab suggested one day, 'because when you stand among the date palms and the pillars you can imagine yourself living with the Arabs. Confess. Isn't that right? Well, I created quite a stir at Oxford in my second year with a scatterbrained theory I think you ought to consider. I developed–half daydream, half history–the theme that the Crusaders doomed themselves when they failed to establish an alliance with the Arabs. Everybody at Oxford was like you, Cullinane. They thought that Richard the Lion Heart fought his battles against gallant Arabs from the desert. They were quite hurt when I had to tell them Saladin wasn't even one tenth of one per cent Arab.'

'I thought he was.'

'Pure Kurd,' Tabari said with no further comment. He argued in Arabic with the caretaker of the mosque, who finally admitted the two archaeologists to the minaret, inside whose tightly twisting innards they climbed in darkness until Tabari broke free onto a platform from which they could see the timeless beauty of this remarkable city, and Cullinane had nothing to say. He could only stand and look down at the scarred land. The Turkish walls, so wide that in spots ten chariots could have stood side by side, had in Crusader times contained twenty-two towers, some of whose roots were still visible. Squares and docks and ancient buildings dating back nearly a thousand years stretched in all directions, while to the east rose the silent tell of prehistoric Akka, from which Napoleon had tried in vain to capture the city . . . a tell as yet unexcavated but containing the mysteries of at least five thousand years. Farther to the east lay Makor, with two gaping wounds in its flanks through which inquisitive men were peering into its secrets, while to the west lay the immortal Mediterranean across whose stormy bosom had come the Phoenicians, the Greeks, the Romans and later the English.

Cullinane was about to make the kind of extravagant statement that archaeologists should avoid, like, 'This is my favorite town in Israel,' when Tabari joined him and, pointing down at the vast walls, said, 'When King Richard the Lion Heart camped by that tell, trying to capture St Jean d'Acre, there were damned few Arabs inside the walls trying to stop him.'

'I'm surprised,' Cullinane said, for although he knew the history of the Holy Land better than most, he had not previously heard this thesis advanced, and he suspected that Tabari was wrong.

'Let's go down to the café,' the Arab proposed, and he led the way to a spot where drinks had been served for some twenty centuries and asked the waiter to fetch a bottle of arrack. As Tabari poured two glasses of the clear anise-flavored stuff, he said, 'The Crusaders held Acre for about two hundred years, but in that time they rarely fought Arabs, because just before the Christians arrived the Turks had moved in and had crushed us pretty badly. So it was always Turks you fought, never Arabs. As a matter of fact, except for that minor matter of religion, we Arabs were always much closer to you than we were to the Turks. The sensible alliance, of course, should have been the humiliated Arabs plus the resurgent Christians against the upstart Turks.' He shook his head mournfully over the lost chances of history, then surprised Cullinane by saying, 'I suppose you know that we Arabs tried time and again to effect such an alliance.'

'I never gave much credence to that thesis.'

'We tried. Repeatedly.'

Cullinane poured a few drops of water into his arrack, watching with pleasure as the clear liquor turned a milky white. Tabari summoned the waiter, explaining in the exaggerated simplicity he would have used with a retarded child, 'My friend's an American. And as you know, Americans must have ice. Don't stand there like a fool. Fetch some ice for the American.'

'We have no ice,' the waiter protested.

'Find some!' Tabari cried. 'He's an American.'

Then he turned to Cullinane. 'When your men finally captured Antioch they were surprised to find Arab ambassadors there, proposing an alliance against the Turks.'

'What queered it?'

Tabari strummed his fingers on the ancient table top, then suggested tentatively, 'When you once describe a venture as a holy war you surrender all capacity to judge honest alternatives.' He stopped and looked up at the clean and beautiful mosque etched against the palm trees.

At this point there were many avenues into which Cullinane might have taken the conversation: Was Tabari saying that in October, 1097, when the Crusaders reached Antioch they were too imbued with Christian zeal to weigh the actual situation confronting them, just as the Arabs in 1964 in the nations surrounding Israel were so infatuated by the concept of *jihad* that they could not rationally accept the fact that Israel existed as a sovereign state? Or was he slyly charging the Jews with an error of which they were not yet guilty: constructing a religious state with such enormous blinkers that the world's reality was prevented from shining through? Or did he perhaps refer to the larger religious war which he had sometimes discussed, in which the United States and Russia were ideologically engaged, each subject to the same infirmity that had struck the Crusaders: an inability to see through the heat waves which they themselves were generating? These were not matters which Cullinane wished to explore at this moment, for he was concerned only with the actual history of Acre during the Crusades and not with what might have been. He was gratified, therefore, when the waiter returned with a piece of ice, but it was very dirty.

'My God!' Tabari cried. 'You can't put a thing like that in the glass of a hygienic American.' He took the filthy ice and started washing it with water, then brushing it with his coat sleeve, but no amount of cleansing would make that ice acceptable, and in frustration he put it in his own glass. Addressing a group of amused Arabs sitting on their haunches outside the mosque he cried, 'This will never be a first-class country until a self-respecting American can get ice for his arrack. What kind of people are we?'

Turning to Cullinane he said provocatively, 'My point is this. The first nine thousand men your Crusaders killed in Asia were Christians. Your gallant Frenchmen and Germans would kiss their crosses, storm into some town, shouting, "Death to the infidel!" and meet there a bunch of Arabs wearing turbans. When the slaughter was over they found that they had killed perfectly good Nestorians and Byzantines and Egyptian Copts who had wanted to help them. It must have been confusing. When this was finally straightened out your boys did get around to killing real Muslims, but this time unfortunately you killed only the Arabs who wanted to join you as allies. Only very late in your invasion did you kill any Turks, who were always your real enemies.'

'How do you explain it?'

'The fundamental unfairness of life,' he laughed. 'How dare a Christian look like an Arab? Or today, how dare so many Jews look like Arabs? Or you could ask it another way. Why does that damned pipe-smoking Eliav look so much like a Christian German while I look so much like an Israeli Jew?'

This lively nonsense Cullinane was willing to explore, but toward the end of the morning Tabari returned to his main theme: 'The real tragedy of the Crusades has always been the fact that the Turkish barbarians could have been eliminated . . . They were nothing but a gang of murderers, you know, surging out of Asia . . .'

'You sound as if you didn't like them,' Cullinane suggested.

'I despise them. They ruined our Arab civilization and it may never recover.' For some minutes Tabari reviewed with sadness the eight-hundred-year Turkish domination of the Arabs, concluding, 'And the hell of it is that all the while you Crusaders battled these Turks, we Arabs were waiting on the sidelines, willing to patch up some kind of alliance with you, but your leaders lacked the imagination to achieve it. So the moment passed. And in the end you Christians were defeated. And we Arabs went down the drain with you.'

Mournfully he sipped his arrack, adding a final point that Cullinane had not heard before: 'How do you explain, John, that in the final days even the Mongol descendants of Genghis Khan offered to become Christians if the Pope would allow them to enlist in the Crusade and attack the Turks from the rear? That's right. And no one in Europe even answered the Mongol letters.' He shook his head reflectively, then stooped to pick up three small pebbles which he tossed one by one into the plaza. 'So we were all lost together. Christians, Arabs, Mongols. Because when men ignite in their hearts a religious fury, they inflict at the same time a blindness upon their eyes.'

If Count Volkmar wanted to engage the true enemy, he would not have long to wait, for from the east came Babek, the mighty spearhead of the Turks, driving in from the plains of Central Asia where the horde had gathered strength for its assault some decades ago upon the Arabs and now upon the Christians who had intruded upon the area. He was a violent general, willing to fight on any terrain, but preferring to pick his battleground with the delicate precision of a lady choosing the right thread for an embroidery. He watched with amusement as the Crusaders stupidly assaulted one Christian settlement after another, killing the bearded converts in the mistaken idea that they were infidels.

They're destroying their own allies, he thought, shaking his head at the folly.

He intended setting the same trap for the Frankish knights that he had used to destroy the little priest on the brown donkey, and from a distance he followed the great army as it stumbled its massive way into the same danger. But then his spies warned him of a significant difference: 'This time there are many armed knights,' and he decided not to attack frontally. Instead, he waited until the captains of the force separated their troops and sent a detachment of some ten thousand to ride eastward to protect that flank, and for three days Babek remained hidden from this smaller army until he judged it to be so far removed as to provide an isolated target which the main army would not be able to rescue.

At the head of this eastern force rode Count Volkmar of Gretz, and at the rear, obeying the advice he had given others, roved the captain-in-charge, Gunter of Cologne, with a cadre of picked knights whose job it was to protect the wagons containing French and German women. Ponderously the caravan groaned forward–one hundred and eighty tested knights, twice that number of mounted squires and freemen, seven thousand well-armed foot soldiers, and some two thousand stragglers, including Priest Wenzel and the Countess Volkmar. A wind puffed the dunes of Asia Minor and grass on the barren hilltops quivered.

On July 1, 1097, Babek was satisfied that his trap had been properly set, so when the day's heat was approaching its apex he signaled his sixty thousand hard-trained troops to attack Gunter's outnumbered Crusaders. With paralyzing speed and fury the Turkish hordes swept out from their hidden positions, dashing in on swift horses and loosing as they rode a blizzard of iron-tipped arrows which began to strike the Frankish horses. There was a wild whinnying, the harsh cries of the disorganized European knights, and the frenzied shrieks of the Turks as they struck at the soft middle of the army, hoping to demoralize all and to effect a complete route in the first few moments of the battle.

But the Turk Babek had not foreseen that he would be encountering Gunter of Cologne, who took one sweeping look at the developing battle and made an immediate decision which would be long debated: he calculated accurately the number and power of the approaching Turkish army; he saw that if it followed its present trajectory it must overrun the wagons and thus cut the Crusader line in two, whereupon the superior numbers of the enemy could encircle first Volkmar's forward group, then his own rear contingent, cutting each to pieces at leisure; but he also saw that if the two groups of knights were able to join now, this instant, they could present a front which not even Babek could penetrate. With no further calculation and with no wavering Gunter of Cologne shouted to his men, 'To Volkmar! Now! Now!' And he led a furious charge through the first of the Turkish riders, bringing nine tenths of his force unto union with Volkmar's.

Of course, his decision left the women, the children and the baggage train exposed to the Turks, who, infuriated by the escape of the knights, swarmed into the abandoned wagons and launched a massacre which would forever haunt the Crusaders. Horses were lanced, old men were chopped down by a dozen swords, while from a distance the Crusaders had to watch as their women were carefully inspected. Any who might bring even a bezant in the slave markets of Damascus were shoved aside. The rest–the old, the not-so-old–were mercilessly slaughtered. Knives and hands ran red as heads were chopped off. The Countess Matwilda was stood against a wagon while five Turkish foot soldiers used her as a target for their arrows. She fell grotesquely.

The younger women, who for their fairness would bring prize money from men seeking to improve their harems, were stripped in the sunlight and raped repeatedly. Fulda, the daughter of Count Volkmar, was among them, and of her father's agony Wenzel of Trier wrote in his chronicle:

My Lord Volkmar, seeming to hear the screams of his naked daughter as the Turks dragged her from man to man, went as one crazy and would have ridden alone into the heart of the Turkish army, wreaking death, but the strong hand of Gunter restrained him and others argued, 'Sir Volkmar, there is nothing we can do.' And Gunter said, 'Save your fury for the Turks. They will be here for many days.' And so my Lord Volkmar was imprisoned by his own, and when the afternoon was upon us, Gunter led forth a foray of only forty knights, and the Turks thinking to overwhelm them launched pursuit; and when all was confusion my Lord Volkmar gave the signal and we who were left rode among the Turks like reapers in August rushing through a yellow field, and we killed and we killed until the end of day, and at night we counted only a few of our men dead but endless numbers of the infidel. And for the pity of my Lady Matwilda and her fair daughter I myself took a great mace and like the others I killed and killed.

General Babek reeled back from this crushing defeat. He could not understand how the blond knight at the rear had been so quick to appraise the situation nor how the German had succeeded in effecting a consolidation of the two halves of his army. He was similarly perplexed by the cunning strategy of the two leaders who later in the day had willfully separated their troops a second time, thereby operating a pincers which had crushed his demoralized footmen. Surveying the battle he found that he had annihilated the old men and the women but had not harmed the effective fighting force, whereas he had lost more than ten thousand of his best men. For the better part of an hour he considered launching a surprise attack at the still outnumbered Crusaders, but he decided against this and was about to order a retreat when his lookouts shouted that the Crusaders were attacking yet again. 'They must be idiots!' he cried, hastily forming his men to meet the insane charge.

For we had decided [wrote Wenzel of Trier] that the Turks would be trying to understand what had occurred in our victory, and Gunter argued, 'Let us destroy them now, for they will not think we would dare,' and my Lord Volkmar, like one demented, shouted, 'Aye! Aye!' and the charge was formed, but before we started down the hill toward the Turks, Sir Gunter took me aside and said, cunningly, 'You must see that your master does not reach the Turks, for if he does we shall not stop him,' and it was my duty to hold the count back, but this I could not do, for as we launched the charge he sped to the fore and was first among the enemy, swinging his mighty arm and taking his black helmet into the very heart of the Turkish camp. That he was not killed was a miracle, and at the conclusion of our mighty victory we found a remarkable thing: my Lord Volkmar sitting alone on his horse, his sword dropped in the dust and his hands folded in his lap as he wept.

Babek retreated to the east, from whence he reported to his superiors: 'These men are much different from what we were told,' and the Turks, who had been misled by their first easy victory over the peasantry that followed Peter the Hermit, began to consider seriously the new war that confronted them.

Between Volkmar and Gunter there could never again be peace, for Gunter had knowingly sacrificed the women to the infidels; but the leaders of the Crusade, Godfrey, Hugh, Baldwin and wild Tancred, listened to reports of the stirring battle and properly concluded that only the daring action of Gunter in the first moments accounted for the victory. And when they reviewed the manner in which he had organized the feint and the final charge, they announced that he was the hero of the day and that henceforth he must ride with them and help them plan their assault on the infidel. But Volkmar would never forget the sight of Gunter willfully abandoning his own sister. 'To reach us,' Volkmar swore, 'he had to gallop directly through the women's camp. He almost ran down my daughter' his own niece, as he sped to us.' Nor could the Count of Gretz erase from his memory the vision of his wife standing against the broken wagon, nor of Fulda dragged from man to man.

A sullen bitterness took possession of the German leader. He stayed alone, would talk only with Wenzel, and then only of religious matters, and when his brother-in-law found some extra women in the entourage of Baldwin and brought Volkmar a fifteen-year-old French girl, advising him, 'Go to bed and forget,' Volkmar rose in fury and would have killed him but for Wenzel's interposing himself and sending the girl away. Some days later Volkmar saw the child, already a brazen, riding behind Gunter, her arms clasped over the blue cross, and he felt ashamed of the Crusade. How many women has this monster delivered to the enemy? he mused in disgust. In Hungary, in Bulgaria, and in the first two great battles Gunter had succeeded in losing something like two thousand women, many of whom had been his temporary mistresses, but he was always hungry for more and always he found more.

But at Antioch, the third largest city of the Roman empire, frequented by Caesars and adorned by them, that sainted city where the word *Christian* was first used, Gunter proved himself a valiant general. The siege of this tremendous fortress-city, whose thick walls never did surrender to the machines of the Crusaders, was initiated on October 21, in 1097, and it continued with battle and brutality until June of the next year, when the impregnable walls still mocked the invaders. The painful siege was marked by three critical periods, and in each Gunter distinguished himself.

As the Crusaders drew their forces into a knot about the walls an unforeseen emissary approached from the south—a Muslim from Egypt whom Volkmar leaped forward to kill. But Gunter stayed his brother-in-law and led the Egyptian to the leaders, where the Muslim proposed an alliance between his people and the Crusaders to smash the Turkish upstarts, and Gunter argued warmly that the Crusaders should accept the offer and bind themselves to the Egyptians.

'With infidels?' Volkmar stormed.

'With anyone who has an army,' Gunter countered.

'It would profane the Crusade,' Volkmar reasoned.

'When we have won,' Gunter proposed, 'then we can cleanse ourselves of profanation.'

He worked with the Egyptians, evolving a plan whereby they would capture Jerusalem from the Turks while the Crusaders took Antioch, breaking the back of Turkish power along the chain of seaports, but the proposed union accomplished little, for when the Egyptians, true to their part of the bargain, proceeded to capture Jerusalem from the Turks—so that the Crusaders could have occupied the city without a battle had they been partners in a true alliance—the Christian part of the bargain was not pursued, because bitter men like Volkmar who had seen Muslims kill their families could not believe that other Muslims might have other interests; and the momentary promise of a powerful eastern alliance vanished.

Of Gunter's second accomplishment, Wenzel of Trier wrote:

My Lord Gunter met with great good fortune when the fate of our crusade hung in the balance. As our knights stood facing the weak walls of Antioch powerless and near starvation, General Babek decided that the moment was proper for him to move in and revenge his defeat, so he sped down upon us from the east with near fourteen thousand, and our captains decided, 'If we wait, we die. Let us therefore ride out to see what can be done,' and my Lord Gunter rode forth with only seven hundred knights, singing as they approached the enemy, where victory was deemed impossible. But with the aid of God the seven hundred crushed the fourteen thousand and Gunter rode back to Antioch singing once more and sharing his saddle with the mistress of the Turkish general, the dark-eyed girl who taught him the Arabic.

And finally, when it became apparent that the ancient Roman walls of Antioch, now strengthened by the engineers of Byzantium, could not be pierced in any manner, it was Gunter who established contact with a Turkish spy who for the proper amount of gold arranged to open the gates for Count Bohemond of Taranto. It was an unlikely offer, one which Gunter had been able to arrange through his knowledge of Arabic, but which he himself scarcely believed. On the night of June 3, 1098, the spy made good his deal, swung open the impregnable gates and admitted the Franks to the city, where an unparalleled slaughter took place.

At one point Volkmar, surging through the fallen city with his men, held back his sword just in time to keep from killing two girls in Arab dress who knelt pitifully before him making the sign of the cross. To his surprise he found that they were Christians, faithful to Rome, and he shouted to his men to wait, but before he could act the girls were slain—as were thousands of their fellow worshipers.

It was at this senseless point, when all were being killed indiscriminately, even Christian girls the same age as his daughter, that Volkmar withdrew from the mighty surge of the movement. He leaned against a mosque which was being gutted by his own men and deadened his ears to the screams of the dying. He thought of the distant days when he had planned his march in the cool castle of Gretz, and he longed for that uncomplicated German sanctuary.

And in those hours [wrote Wenzel of Trier] while others were gaining the riches for which we struggled, the jars of incense and the chests of gold, my Lord Volkmar wandered empty-handed through the streets of Antioch until he came to what had once been the Church of Peter and Paul and was now a mosque, and he entered there and took his place on the stones before the spot where the altar had stood before the Muslims tore it down, and he prayed that God would lead him in peace to Jerusalem, for he was sick unto death of killing. But even as he prayed, men from Gunter's army chased three Turks into the mosque, cut them open and threw their entrails over the carvings sacred to their god Mahmoud.

When the great, twisting, tumbling Crusade resumed its march toward Jerusalem, Count Bohemond was left behind as Prince of Antioch, while Baldwin of Bouillon, an ordinary knight, was sent to distant Edessa with the title of count; and from these developments all men like Gunter of Cologne who had intended carving their kingdoms from the Holy Land gained encouragement, looked hopefully toward the next battle and discussed their dreams with their associates. But Volkmar of Gretz rode alone. He was now an old man of fifty-one and his sandy-red hair showed signs of white. His neck was still stocky, but his arms moved more slowly and sometimes in battle he felt that he lacked the strength to ride forward. Three of his mounts had died in battle and in his loneliness he had premonitions that a fourth would go down and take him along, cutting him short of Jerusalem, which he no longer expected to see. The armies were bogged down in Syria and typhus raged through the camps, so that the future was obscure.

But then, in the spring of 1099, as the end of his third year at war approached, events began to move with startling speed. The Arab town of Ma'arrat fell, and when the squat fortress of Arqah gave signs of proving even more difficult than

Antioch the Crusaders discovered the simple expedient of letting it stand. Leaving a small siege group they by-passed the thorny fort, then did the same with the lovely chain of ancient Arab seaports: Tripoli, Bairut and Tyr. All were by-passed with their Turkish armies intact; and the Crusaders found themselves poised for the final dash to Jerusalem. 'If we win the city,' Gunter of Cologne insisted, 'we can come back and pick off the seaports one by one, like grapes,' and the original allure of the Crusades revived. It was of this exhilarating period that Wenzel wrote:

On that May afternoon when we marched south from Tyre toward the city that was to become St Jean d'Acre, leaving the inhospitable lands of the north and entering upon those sacred grounds of Palestine, where our Lord Jesus Christ had lived and died, a great exultation seized our men, and each spurred his horse forward so that he might be the first to cry, 'We have come to the land of our sweet Lord Jesus.' And in this spirit we came to a small hill from which we could look down upon the pagan spires of Acre, nestling within tremendous walls, and I feared that this formidable place would dampen our spirits, but our leaders cried, 'We shall not war against that Seaport, we shall leave it as did the others. On to Jerusalem.' And right willingly did we by-pass those enormous walls.

My Lord Volkmar and I were in the left, or eastern flank, riding midway toward the Sea of Galilee, when we chanced to see some Turks in the distance. We spurred our horses up a small hill, thinking to give them chase, when Gunter of Cologne swept past us on a French horse he had acquired, shouting, 'Let us enter the Holy Land of Jesus,' and he so excited us with his movement, urging us on to follow him, that we forgot the Turkish soldiers, and rode furiously southward until we came to the crest of a hill from which we saw the most pleasing sight to greet us since the day we left Gretz. To the west rose the pagan spires of Acre, shimmering beside the sea, and there the great lords were parleying, agreeing to spare the city. To the east we saw the rich and wooded hills, leading down to the Sea of Galilee, where our blessed Lord had lived and taught.

But straight ahead, on a small mound, with gray olive trees to the south, stood the little town of Makor, its mosques bright in the sun and the holy cross of our Lord rising from the steeple of the basilica. My Lord Volkmar cried, 'Behold that sweet town and its green fields.' But before we could move forward Gunter shouted, 'This town is mine!' And he galloped his horse down the hill madly, riding up to the town and shouting for all to hear, 'This town is mine! It shall be the capital of my kingdom!'

Among the infidels of Makor who had been watching for some months the southward progress of the Crusaders, none was more shrewd in estimating their final victory than the current head of the great Family of Ur. Shaliq ibn Tewfik was a hawk-eyed man of forty-two who could calculate success and failure with all the skill of his Arab training; but whether he was entitled to be called an Arab remained a moot point, not always agreed upon by the people of Makor when they sat together discussing their dealings with him. Shaliq was a Muslim, as all had to admit, and for the past four centuries his family had been Muslim too; but small-town memories are long and it was not forgotten in Makor that Shaliq's family had once been pagan, then Jewish, and for a while Christian, so that at best his heritage was spotted. On the other hand, of a hundred men in Makor who termed themselves Arabs, not many had ridden in from the desert with the true faith; most had sprung from Hittite and Egyptian and Canaanite stock, but today all were good Muslims and they passed as Arabs, so it ill behooved any to question Shaliq ibn Tewfik.

Regardless of his ancestry, sharp-eyed Shaliq traded wisely and listened well, and he had discovered that as the Crusaders moved down through Asia from Antioch to Ma'arrat it became a matter of chance whether a local resident survived or not. As Shaliq explained to his frightened family: 'When a town is taken the Crusaders are so embittered that they slaughter Jew, Christian, Muslim alike. But as soon as the heat of battle ends—let's say the third day—any local citizens who have survived are treated well.' He paused. 'So well, in fact, that the knights will begin picking their wives from the very women that three days earlier they were spitting on their lances.' He looked at his trembling family and said harshly, 'Our job is to survive for three days. But where?'

He scouted the town, working alone so that no other family could profit from what he might discover. For a few hours he thought he might choose the cellar under the hay, but he rejected this because he had heard that the Crusaders always set fire to hay, worrying later about food for their horses. The shed hidden behind the wheat stacks was surely a trap, for the soldiers would be hungry and would haul the bags away. But in his anxiety he remembered an abandoned shaft, now almost filled with rubble, which he guessed might once have led to some well deep inside the town, and this was a cool place not known to other citizens, for the ancient tunnel to which it had once led was no longer remembered; and it was in this shaft, on May 21, 1099, that Shaliq ibn Tewfik dug a small cave and hid his wife Raya and his sixteen-year-old daughter Taleb bint Raya and his sons, taking with him water and food for three days. Pressing themselves into the cramped refuge they heard the first shock of troops in the streets, the brief fighting and the surge of feet across the square. There were screams, as Shaliq had foretold, and the smell of smoke. But the Family of Ur held fast while their father counted, 'One day, then two days, then three.'

When Gunter captured Makor—not a difficult task, for the Turks were not defending the city and there were no walls to protect it—he put to the death every visible inhabitant. Christians and Muslims alike went down, and in a pocket near the ruins of the eastern wall he cornered the last Jews ever to live within the walls of Makor—the final descendants of Joktan and Zadok and Jabaal—and he slew them all, man and woman and child. His men wanted to keep one young girl for themselves, but Gunter would not have it so. 'Let there be no traffic with the enemies of Christ!' he bellowed, and the eradication was complete.

But during this final slaughter a dismal thing occurred. One Jew, a farmer, decided not to surrender his life easily and grabbed an axe, so that when Count Volkmar of Gretz came by, this Jew leaped at him and cut a deep gash down the German's left leg. As the blood spurted out the Jew tried to swing the axe again, but men from Gunter's group saw the assault and killed him. That night, when it looked as if the white-haired Count of Gretz must die, Wenzel wrote sorrowfully:

The great perfidy of Jews was proved once more when, the subjection of the city having been assured, one crafty fellow nevertheless armed himself with an axe and lay unjustly in wait for my Lord Volkmar, and sprang at him most fiendishly, near severing his left leg. We took the count to a clean room where we lay him on a bed, and his eyes came to rest on a local crucifix, for unfortunately that day we had killed many Christians, which can be forgiven, for they looked much like Arabs and in the heat of battle we could not tell saved from damned, and when Count Volkmar saw the crucifix and knew that once more we had slain Christians, he would have died, but I stayed with him that night, binding the leg and praying for his soul. On the morrow Gunter of Cologne came to see us and to say, 'Brother, I must join the others lest they take Jerusalem without me and I am not present to claim my kingdom.' I said, 'Dare you leave your brother so?' and Gunter answered, 'I marched from Cologne to capture Jerusalem, and not the devil himself shall keep me from the Holy City.' I begged him not to desert his brother, who was dying, but he replied, 'His leg will have to be cut away and he will surely die, but I will leave him six good men.' And Count Volkmar heard these words and cried from his bed, 'Go to hell with your men and your kingdom,' but Gunter grew not angry and said softly, 'Brother, it is this land that I intend taking for my own, and if you live you may share it with me,' and he rode off, with all his soldiers, leaving not even the six that he had promised. And I thought that my lord would die, except that on the third day from a cave appeared a man named Shaliq who had wisely escaped the slaughter, and he claimed to be a doctor and showed me how to cut off Count Volkmar's leg and when the putrid thing was hauled away the count grew better, and the mysterious doctor said to me, 'I and my family are truly Christians, but the Muslims forced us into infidel ways, and we would like to be again baptized.' And with tears in our eyes we baptized him and his wife and three sons and daughter. His name was infidel, and I said to him, 'In the name of the Lord, drop thy infidel ways,' and because he was a doctor who knew how to cut a leg I told him that henceforth his name was to be Luke and he ended his baptism by repeating his new name many times, with approval from his family. His appearance and signs of saintliness I declared a true miracle, and judged it a good omen for our occupation of this city.

But while Wenzel and Luke, the merchant-turned-doctor, were hacking away at his leg, and cursing Jews for their perfidy in striking a Christian knight with an axe, Count Volkmar lay in a delirium of pain, biting the handle of a dagger and seeing before him Simon Hagarzi, and he could hear again the Jew predicting, 'Of a hundred men who leave Gretz, nine will be lucky if they get back,' and he knew in his madness that he would not be one of those. He would see the Rhine no more, and thinking of the Jews his men had slain along that river he forgave the solitary Jew who had attacked him. 'It was God's revenge,' he mumbled to himself as the Arab sawed on his leg bone. 'May God forgive us for the things we have done.' And the leg was gone.

For several years the re-established settlement at Makor did not see Gunter of Cologne, for he rode on to help capture Jerusalem, then participated in the siege of Ascalon, continuing to the protracted wars against Tripoli and Tyr and finally, in 1104, to the subjugation of the critical port city of Akka itself. When the solid walls of that fortress were reduced through siege and the town renamed, Gunter finally returned to Makor, where Luke, serving as bailiff-judge-treasurer of the town, welcomed him on behalf of the governor, Count Volkmar.

'Where is my brother?' the now-slim warrior asked, and Luke led the way to a large house which served as the rude palace from which Volkmar ruled the surrounding territory.

Gunter rushed through the door to greet his brother-in-law, who stood an old, white-haired man of fifty-six, one-legged and frail. 'The fighting is ended,' Gunter announced, 'and I did what I said. The fief is mine.'

'What fief?' Volkmar asked.

'This one. The land between Acre and Galilee.'

Carefully choosing his words Volkmar said, 'But here I rule.'

'And so you shall!' Gunter cried expansively, shocked by his brother-in-law's general feebleness. 'And you shall continue to rule on my behalf until you die – I'll be out extending our borders.'

'But when I die this land passes on to my son Volkmar.' The old count signaled to Luke, who fetched an attractive dark-haired boy of three. The child ran to his father, who balanced himself on his one leg so as to catch the boy, swinging him in the air.

'They told me you were married,' Gunter said, evading for the moment the question of inheritance. 'Where'd you find a Christian girl?'

'Here,' Volkmar replied. 'One that you missed killing.' Again the count motioned to Luke, and the bailiff disappeared to return shortly with his daughter Taleb, now an attractive woman of twenty-one. Bowing to Gunter she said in lilting German, 'Welcome to Makor, brother.'

The battle-worn knight bowed and replied, 'It is I who welcome you to my fief, sister.'

This time it was Volkmar who chose to evade the question. He directed Luke to prepare a welcoming feast, and Luke, clever as always, managed to find a sheep, some good wine from the local grapes and lesser items from as far away as Damascus. 'The caravans had resumed,' Volkmar explained, passing his brother-in-law fresh dates and honey from the Muslim capital. 'It's true that Damascus remains in Arab hands,' he continued ruefully, 'but we both need the trade.'

'That's sensible,' Gunter growled, licking his fingers. 'Where'd you find Luke and his daughter?'

'Here in Makor. They hid . . . in a cave, till you were gone.'

Gunter bowed to the countess. 'I'm glad you survived. To tell the truth,' he confessed, 'if I were starting afresh I'd kill far fewer.' Uneasily he shifted his weight and leaned forward to face the father and daughter he might have slain that first day. 'I learned my lesson in Jerusalem. We killed everyone in sight . . . Arabs . . . Jews . . . but the next day we found that half the dead were Christians just like ourselves. No one had told us. Have you heard about the way we took Jerusalem?'

'Many times,' Volkmar said with disgust.

'I explained that if we were doing it again . . . You know, brother . . .'

'I am no longer your brother,' Volkmar answered quietly.

'You are more,' Gunter replied, taking no offense. 'You are my essential friend. I was about to say that after Jerusalem we discovered how rich we would have been had we kept the local people alive.' Here again he bowed to the countess and her father. 'In Jerusalem, after the slaughter, we discovered vats of purple dye worth a hundred thousand bezants with no one left alive who knew how to use it. All the Jews were dead.'

'Here we behaved differently,' Volkmar replied. 'In the villages we killed no one, and now the farms are prosperous.'

'I'm glad you kept them that way. I'll need them in my fief.'

'It will never be yours,' the older man said firmly.

'It will,' Gunter responded without anger. 'With my sword I have won it, and it is mine. You're welcome here as long as you live, because I need your help. But when I have sons of my own they shall rule, and your boy Volkmar will have to find his life elsewhere.'

The two German knights looked hard at each other, and thus began the test of wills, with Gunter asking bluntly, 'Volkmar, why don't you take your son and go back to Germany?'

The question startled the old man, for in the years since his wife and daughter were taken from him at the battle of the wagons he had thought little of Germany. More than eight years had passed since he last saw the Rhine. His son Otto now ruled the city of Gretz, and Volkmar no longer considered himself a German. Pointing to the modest, yet convenient room in which the feast was being held he asked, 'Who would leave this warm place for a cold castle in Gretz?' He indicated the good food that Luke had procured, the wine, the merchandise already pouring in from Damascus, and these things he compared with the manner in which German knights lived in their frugal, drafty castles along the Rhine. His wife Taleb wore silk and embroidered stuffs, whereas his first wife Matwilda had been happy to find coarse goods. In Makor he had gold and silver to replace the lead and brass of Germany. Through the ingenuity of Luke he had access to medicines unknown in Germany; in fact, he declared, 'If I had lost my leg in Gretz, to be cared for by German doctors, I would now be dead. I have no desire to go back to that barbarous land.'

'Then stay here and help me rule,' the younger knight urged.

Thus Gunter moved permanently to Makor, and during his first week initiated changes of a spectacular nature, the most lasting of which was his decision to build on the crest of the mound a huge fortified castle: 'Every man from Acre to Galilee will work sixteen days a month on this fortress till it's finished. At the quarries we'll need a thousand men. Permanently. To haul the rocks, five hundred horses.' While Volkmar tried to follow on a crutch that Luke had carved for him, Gunter strode forth to mark the limits of his castle, and the older man was astonished at the magnitude Gunter proposed.

'It will be immense, because from it we shall rule an immense principality.' He began that day to use the word *principality*, for this was what he intended to carve for himself. Finally he returned to where Volkmar stood on his crutch and asked, 'You've lived here for five years. Which part of town will be best for our castle?'

Volkmar explained that the northwest segment, abutting the basilica, would be best, for from that spot one could both catch the cool evening breezes that came down the wadis and enjoy the sea beyond Acre, and for these reasons Gunter was tempted to build there, but in the end considerations of defense led him to select the rugged eastern end, for there the wadi to the north showed a more precipitous face. 'Some day there'll be a siege,' Gunter predicted, 'and that gully could be what saves us.'

So northeast of the basilica he staked out an enormous castle, and when Luke saw that one third of the town's houses stood in the marked-off area he protested, but Gunter said simply, 'Tear them down,' and it was done.

From having besieged nearly thirty fortifications–Nicaea, Antioch, Jerusalem, Ascalon, the names were like dreams, with Greek fire pouring down upon his shoulders and he loading the mangonels with the chopped-off heads of Turkish prisoners to be lobbed inside to taunt the defenders–from such experiences Gunter knew how a castle should be built. No square corners would be allowed, no neatly squared-off towers, for those he had found susceptible to assault. 'With a battering ram you can always knock out the corner stones,' he explained to Luke, 'but with a rounded tower where do you start your attack?' He also insisted that throughout the castle each rock be fitted snugly to the next, so that grapples could find no purchase to support scaling ladders. Each wall was sloped and situated so that all parts could be protected by interlocking arrow fire from two towers. 'And the bottom of each wall,' he explained, 'must slope sharply outward . . . at this angle . . . so that when a rock is dropped from the battlements it will ricochet sharply forward, crushing any men trying to hide under protecting cover.'

For two years, 1104 through 1105, Gunter worked feverishly to complete his masterpiece, and as it drew to a conclusion workmen began to look forward to the time when they could once more turn their attention to their fields, but he forestalled this by announcing that now the real work would begin, a massive wall, twenty feet thick, around the entire crown of the hill. 'These farmers should go home to their families,' Volkmar protested, but the younger knight growled that if the town was not fortified the day would come when nobody in the area would have families to go home to, and he began those enormous constructions which converted the long-feeble Makor–for the thousand years since Vespasian it had known no wall–into the archetype of a Crusader town, with the castle, the basilica and the mosque all neatly tucked inside gigantic fortifications.

The new Crusader walls, of course, had to stand well inside the lines followed by the earlier Canaanite and Jewish walls, for as the mound had risen in height its available building area was constantly constricted and was now much smaller than before, so that when the giant walls were completed a new pattern of life had to develop. Inside the cramped town no more than three hundred peasants could now live, for the castle and the religious buildings usurped most of the free space, but since the fortified town brought peace to the area, more than fifteen hundred villagers and farmers could live in security outside the walls, knowing that in time of trouble they could retreat to safety within the battlements.

When the work was completed Gunter found comfort in the brooding power of the mound, but Volkmar, hobbling one day to the olive grove so that he might see the turrets soaring aloft like insolent challenges to the countryside, became depressed and reasoned with himself: We've used the farmers for two years and have built only a prison. We've buried ourselves in a tomb of stone. Cut ourselves off from the people who will have to support us if we're to live. And he saw the castle and the walled town not as a haven of security but as a monstrous error that would confine and crush the Crusade, and on his crutches he limped back to remonstrate with Gunter, who was even then causing fresh towers to be erected along the northern wall which overlooked the wadi. 'The castle's finished,' Volkmar said, 'so there's nothing to do about it. And you've walled in the town, so that's done too. But what plans do you now have for bringing the countryside into the heart of our structure?'

Gunter looked at his former brother-in-law as if the cripple were mad. 'Countryside?' he laughed. 'We take refuge behind these walls and we let the countryside do what it will. This is a cruel land and will always be. Down that road from Damascus the countryside will come against us some day. Or invaders will come at us along this road from the sea. Or up through the olive grove from Egypt. The countryside? Let it try to get at us!' And in a frenzy he acted like an enemy trying to scale the great walls of Makor, and he clawed at the rocks with his fingernails, but he and Luke had set the stones so cunningly one upon the other that his fingers could find no purchase and his hands slid from the wall.

'To hell with the countryside!' he shouted. 'When they're swarming down here my men will be up there pouring oil on them. We'll crush the countryside if it tries to attack this wall.' And he stood back to admire the faultless rocks, but Volkmar was still held captive by the sensation that these were the walls of a mighty prison into which the Crusaders had willfully built themselves.

When the defenses were completed, the finest south of Antioch, Gunter should have relaxed but he could not, for one nagging fact kept him awake at night, and this he could not dispel. The fundamental weakness we haven't solved, he reflected continuously. We've no water. Of course, he had done all possible to minimize this fault, causing deep cisterns to be dug and lining them with rock and plaster until they were watertight, then directing every roof to carry a channel which threw its rainfall into these deep reservoirs, but that fatal year could come when drought and siege would be allies, forcing surrender from within. One day Gunter spoke of this to Luke, who now supervised all operations, and the Christian convert said, 'Sir Gunter, when I was hiding in the cave . . . from you . . .' The two friends nodded. 'I had the feeling that I might be in a shaft leading to a well.'

Gunter's breath caught. If there was a secure supply of water . . . within the castle. 'Where's is this cave?'

'It was filled in when we paved the floor,' Luke explained, pointing to a room in the castle living quarters.

Gunter was about to strike his lieutenant, but stayed his hand. 'Why didn't you tell me?'

'I could not visualize this final plan,' Luke said.

'Get me twenty of your best men,' Gunter commanded, and that day he began ripping up the paving stones which had been laid in place only a few weeks before. His miners went down for ten feet, then fifteen, then twenty, and Luke became uneasy; but at last they came to squared-off rocks that had not been placed in position by accident but according to design: they had reached the wall of the ancient shaft built by Hoopoe more than two thousand years before. As soon as Gunter edged his way down to this rock work, and saw for himself its excellence, he recognized what his men had found, but in order to make sure, he had them dig their way around all four sides of the long-vanished shaft, and when it was exposed he saw evidence of the concentric stairways and knew that if he dug straight down through the accumulated rubble he must find water.

All available men were put to the job of cleaning out the abandoned shaft, and when they had excavated it for more than a hundred feet straight down, with Gunter impatient but never wavering in his conviction that water was at hand, they came to the solid rock bottom and found nothing. The disappointment embittered Gunter and he descended into the shaft, hammering on the massive rocky base with his bare hands, bellowing, 'Where in God's name is the water?' but finding only dust.

He came out of the barren hole and brooded for some days about the ill chance that had led him on this fruitless chase, and it so happened that these were days of drought, when there should have been rain but wasn't, and he became frantic with apprehensive visions of the future when such a drought would coincide with an Arab attack and he would stand helpless and dying of thirst inside the walls. He raved at Volkmar, 'How could a well dry up when it once flowed?' And he made his brother-in-law descend the steps on his crutches to where the shaft began, so that Volkmar could see for himself that Gunter's original idea had not been crazy, and it was a chance remark that Volkmar happened to make that solved the mystery. Looking at the grooved stairs that lined the shaft he said, 'They were worn down by thousands upon thousands of bare feet.'

'What's that?' Gunter cried in the darkness.

'Look. Where the feet of women wore down the stones.'

The idea fascinated Gunter, and for more than a week he was haunted by the vision of an endless chain of barefooted women descending to the bottom of the shaft, bearing water jugs ... 'Where would so many have stood?' he asked himself, and then one night he screamed, 'They weren't going down the shaft at all. They were going to something!'

In a frenzy he had himself let down to the solid rock of the bottom, where he watched in his imagination as the monotonous line of women filed past him heading somewhere. He scratched at the walls, trying in vain to ascertain where they had gone, but he found no clue. He signaled to the men aloft to haul him out, and he walked the streets of Makor, followed by the barefooted ghosts. Once he stopped sharp and turned on them. 'Where did you go?' he railed—at Kerith the devout Jewess who had gone down those steps to admire her husband's work, at Gomer who in those depths had spoken directly to God—'Where did you vanish to?' he screamed at the phantoms, but they waited silently behind him.

He then did what perplexed men had done in Makor throughout the millennia: he climbed to the top of the half-built wall and surveyed the setting of Makor itself. In the west he could see the fires of Acre and beyond it the moon-glistening sea of grandeur; to the south were the olive trees and the unseen swamps; and to the north, where the hills came down like invading ranks, only to be halted by the deep wadi . . . He stopped. He wondered if that wadi had anything to do with the water. 'Why did they dig the shaft so deep?' he asked, but the facts before him were not yet clear, and in despair he knelt upon the walls and prayed, 'Almighty God, where have You hidden the water?' He became angry as he called the words and beat the cold stones with his hands. In the end he shouted defiantly, 'God! God! Where did you hide the water? I need it now!' And because God does not necessarily prefer soft men who chant in basilicas, moonlight shone in the wadi and Gunter leaped to his feet like a man whose bed has caught fire, and he shouted, 'They dug so deep because the water's out there!'

In the pre-dawn he rushed back to the shaft and summoned Luke, bawling at him, 'I know where the water is!' And he took five good diggers down with him and tried to calculate where north lay, and by luck he came close, and in that direction he caused his men to dig. All day they worked, with him goading them at their elbows, and fresh teams were brought down, with men hauling baskets of rubble aloft; and after night had fallen a Greek workman plunged his shovel through a soft layer of dust and struck nothing. Like a madman Gunter dashed at the hole and with a small taper looked ahead, and saw the long-vanished David Tunnel dug by Hoopoe and his Moabite slave. Disregarding the possibility of accident or surprise he dashed along the tunnel, silent for so many centuries, until he saw the walls of the far end looming up to halt him, and at their base he found the ancient well.

When he returned to the castle that night he was in no way exultant, for although he knew that now his castle and his town were secure against even the strongest enemy, his descent into darkness and his close brush with God reminded him of how transient life was and forced him to consider the future. When Luke came to congratulate him he found not a roistering German knight but a man much humbled, who said softly, 'It's time I found a wife.'

That night Luke waited till Count Volkmar, who insisted upon remaining in his original quarters, had gone to bed, and then the bailiff called softly to his daughter Taleb, asking her to talk with him, and looking down at the floor he said to her, 'Sir Gunter speaks of taking a wife.' Silence . . . 'Today I examined my Lord Volkmar's leg. It will never heal.' Silence . . . 'He cannot live long.'

'Each morning he has a fever,' Taleb reported.

Luke felt it necessary to speak with great bluntness. 'I've been wondering about Sir Gunter. Have you not thought it strange that he sleeps with so many women . . . he has a harem . . . Egyptians and that whore from Acre. But I've never heard that any of his women became pregnant.'

The two Christians looked at each other for some moments, after which Luke continued, 'I've come to the conclusion that Sir Gunter couldn't have sons . . . even if he wanted them.'

Taleb placed her folded hands on the table before her father and said, 'You must not forget that young Volkmar is your grandson . . . as well as my son.' Silence . . . 'What is it that you are proposing?'

Luke swallowed. 'For the next two or three weeks Gunter will remain preoccupied with cleaning out his well. But when that is done he shall have to turn to other matters.' Silence . . . 'If I were you, I would place myself so that when he turns you are plainly visible.' From the bedroom Volkmar called for his wife; he was having trouble with his leg and wanted her to fetch his crutch.

In the next days Taleb bint Raya, the twenty-two-year-old Christian convert, found numerous occasions to inspect the water system and the new castle. When a caravan of merchants came in from Damascus and Gunter decided to christen his great dining hall, which in succeeding centuries pilgrims to the Holy Land would characterize as the most beautiful room in the east, Taleb volunteered to serve as hostess, and she sat between the two German knights as the boar and venison were served along with the spiced wines, the dates, the honey and the exotic vegetables. At the height of the feast Gunter cried out to the Damascenes, 'You men travel a lot. I've been thinking of getting married. Tell me, are those Armenian princesses from Edessa as pretty as they say?'

A merchant replied, 'Your Baldwin married one, and when I saw them in Edessa she seemed a fine lady.'

'They are Christians,' Volkmar observed.

'I'm thinking of sending to the King of France,' Gunter said. 'For one of his sisters.'

'The King of France?' Volkmar repeated. 'Do you think he would reply?'

I believe he would,' Gunter replied. 'For one day I shall be king of this area.' Then he looked directly at Taleb and added quietly, 'But I think I shall allow the King of France to worry about his sisters. I may not go so far afield.'

Volkmar could not avoid seeing this glance, nor its implication, but on that night he elected to say nothing; thereafter he stayed away from the new castle, remaining in his old quarters from which he sought to govern the district; but gradually he found that his prerogatives were being removed. Luke, as leader of the accommodating Family of Ur, quickly deserted his old employer and transferred his allegiance to the castle, where he installed the political machinery which actually governed the region. One morning Volkmar summoned Luke to the basilica, as a neutral meeting place, to ask him directly what was happening, but Luke explained that with so many peasants reporting from the outlying villages it was easier for him to meet them in the castle. 'They expect it,' he added.

'But the taxes will still be paid over to me?' Volkmar asked.

'Of course! Of course!' Luke assured him.

Volkmar limped home intending to ask Taleb to explain truthfully what was going on, but this he could not do, for when he entered the house he found his wife wrestling with Gunter, and her dress was mostly torn away, so that her body was exposed to the waist–and it was not at all clear whether she had been resisting or not. It was a dreadful moment, after which Gunter stood behind Taleb with his arms encircling her, his hands grasping her breasts while she fell easily back toward his protection.

'You're an old man,' Gunter cried impatiently. 'Your leg never mended and you've got to die soon. When you do I'll take your wife, and we'll have children of our own. I'll send your bastard back to Germany, and if he doesn't want to go I'll strangle him.' And with these words Gunter kissed the half-naked woman on the neck.

Volkmar had only his crutch, but he lunged at Gunter and there was a scuffle during which the old man fell to the ground, while Gunter, still holding Taleb by the breasts, kicked at him contemptuously, causing the leg stump to break into fresh bleeding.

When the lovers were gone Volkmar called for his servants, asking them to fetch Luke the doctor, but that man having heard what had occurred, could not be found, so the bleeding continued. Of this bleak day Wenzel wrote in his chronicle of the German knights:

I carried my Lord Volkmar to his bed, for he was much wasted from his early days, and he said, pressing his hands against his white beard, 'I feel new pains and I shall not live long,' but he lasted through that night and in the morning called for his son, who came to him but did not understand how gravely ill his father was. His wife Taleb, whom I myself had baptized, would not approach his room but made merry in the castle with Sir Gunter, for whom she had even then a notable affection, and I did not wish to remind her of her duty. In the evening I said to Volkmar, 'Poor sir, you never did get to Jerusalem,' but he replied what I knew to be the truth, 'You are wrong, Priest, for on the morning I set out from Gretz I was in Jerusalem.' He ordered me to pray for his good wife Matwilda and asked, 'How could she have had such a brother?' and then he prayed with me for his daughter Fulda, sharing with me a secret I had never before known. 'I am convinced that she is locked up somewhere east of Damascus,' and I realized then why he had always been the first to greet the caravans that came from that city, hoping that he might discover some news of her. 'Pray for my daughter, Wenzel. Pray for her.'

At twilight Count Volkmar's fever increased, and he could hear revelry in the castle. He asked again for his son, but Wenzel had to report that Luke had stolen the child and was keeping him hidden in the castle. To this sad news Volkmar said nothing, and it seemed certain that he must soon die, but at midnight he was still alive.

LEVEL IV

The Fires of Ma Coeur

Found at Makor–seal of the town of Ma Coeur. *Obverse:*
'VKMR VIII GRET S M CUR COND DOV REAVME
DACR' (Volkmar VIII of Gretz, Sire of Ma Coeur, Count of the
Kingdom of Acre). *Reverse:* 'CE EST LE CHAST DE MA
COVER DE JESUS' (This is the castle of Ma Coeur de Jesus).
Issued at Ma Coeur, June 11, 1271, upon the investiture of
Volkmar VIII. Cast in bronze at St Jean d'Acre by German-
speaking artisans unfamiliar with the French used officially in
the kingdom of Acre. Deposited at Makor April 2, 1291 C.E.

In the spring of 1289, when the spiritual fire that had sustained the Crusades had
died away to an ember, when Jerusalem was lost forever to the infidel, when the
lovely chain of seaports reaching southward from Antioch had fallen
permanently into enemy hands, and when a sense of doom hung over the land like
a searing cloud of sand particles blown in by the khamsin, the walled city of St
Jean d'Acre still remained as the Crusader capital and the eighth Count Volkmar
of Gretz still defended the castle of Ma Coeur as a bulwark of the faith, trusting
that some miracle would permit him to retain it for another generation.

Then, on April 26, 1289, a miracle caused his prayers to be answered. The Mamelukes, a handful of slaves imported from Asia to serve the Turks, had somehow gained control of the vast Muslim empire and unexpectedly volunteered
to extend their truce with Acre for the traditional period of ten years, ten months
and ten days; and when this reassuring news sped across the Holy Land, caravans
started moving once more between the Mameluke stronghold of Damascus and
Acre. French and Italian newcomers, struggling ashore at the latter seaport after
tedious voyages in dangerous ships, were frequently astonished to find that
among the first persons to greet them upon landing at Acre were beturbaned
merchants from Damascus, trying to earn an honest bezant by sharp trading
with the Christians. It was difficult for these new arrivals to understand when the
resident Crusaders explained: 'Of course, it's your duty to kill infidels, but not
these infidels, because with them we conduct a very good trade from which
everyone makes a profit.'

Among the first of the Muslim merchants to drive his camels across the
overland route from Damascus was the old Arab Muzaffar, who in the fall of 1289
made one of his accustomed stops at Ma Coeur to peddle his pepper and nutmegs,
his China silks and Persian brocades and, most importantly, to hand Count
Volkmar a document from the Mameluke officials in Damascus. As always, the
residents of the castle extended old Muzaffar a brotherly welcome, for through
the years he had handled much business for them and was considered a member
of the family, especially since years ago at the wedding of Volkmar VII, the

present count's father, the old Arab had advanced the castle a goodly sum toward the festival expenses.

He was short for an Arab and inclined toward fatness, so that when he stood against Count Volkmar, who like his ancestors was red-headed and rugged, he seemed flabby; but when properly dressed in fawn-colored robes, with a black and gold cord about his headdress, and with his white beard standing out from his tanned face, he was handsome; and when he delivered the official document he smiled warmly. 'The Mamelukes grant you permission to go on pilgrimage,' he said in French, making himself comfortable in the castle hall.

'You've read it?' Volkmar asked in Arabic.

'Of course.' Abruptly he abandoned the count and hurried forward to greet the countess, who kissed him warmly on both cheeks. She was a slight, winsome creature whose plaited locks hung in two strands forward over her shoulders and reached to her waist. After studying her with approval Muzaffar observed in French, 'Almost every garment you wear has reached Ma Coeur on my camels, and today I have a worthy successor.' He called for one of his men, who brought a leather box containing a long-trained dress made of samite, adorned with wide sleeves and decorations of pearl. 'For a lady who is going on a pilgrimage,' he said graciously, and she realized that this beautiful garment was being offered as a gift.

'The Mamelukes have given permission?' she asked.

'After a little help, here and there,' he laughed, twisting his right hand this way and that to indicate bribery.

'You're our dearest friend,' the countess cried, kissing him again, 'but I'm not going.' The old Arab made as if he were taking back the dress, and she caught his hands. 'But in my new dress I'll make a little pilgrimage right here,' and from a window she pointed down to the basilica, the Maronite church and the Roman. The latter stood across from the mosque.

'But our son's going,' the count explained.

'How excellent!' the old trader cried in French. 'Volkmar! Take your pilgrimage next spring. We can meet in Saphet and ride across the hills together.'

The count, a tall rugged man in his forties, clean-shaven and sharp of feature but dark of face like his Holy Land ancestors, studied the proposal for some moments, then countered cautiously, 'It would be appropriate to see Saphet with you, Muzaffar, but there are two drawbacks. In spring the Galilee grows warm, which would not of itself stop me, but from Saphet I'd planned returning over the hills to Starkenberg to show my son the German castle there, and that would take you far out of your way.'

'Not at all!' the old man protested. 'I'll send the camels along the trail with a driver. I'll ride across the hills with you and catch up with the camels here.'

'Will you bring your own horse?' Volkmar asked.

'It might be better if you brought one for me . . . No! I'll buy the best horse I can find in Damascus, then sell it when I reach Acre.'

'Agreed?' Volkmar asked.

'Saphet in April.' As the two friends shook hands, the Arab added, 'And if I'm to do that I must be moving.'

'Not until you've eaten,' the count protested, and he called for an early lunch.

The great hall in which the two men sat had been finished in 1105 by Gunter of Cologne, and it was a masterpiece of Crusader art, its thin rock ribbing rising in a series of high arches into which narrow windows had been let. The stone floor was of excellent workmanship, each stone abutting tightly against its neighbor, so that in nearly two hundred years it had required resetting only once. When the paving was freshly oiled—as it was this day—it looked more like soft carpeting than hard stone.

About the room were placed statues of some of the famous owners of the castle, silver candlesticks from Damascus and Aleppo, items of gold from Baghdad and enameled boxes from Persia. Because wood was beginning to be scarce in the Holy Land the huge chests that lined the walls and the long table had come to Acre on Genoese ships from the forests of Serbia, but the spectacular tapestries that hung on the eastern wall had been woven in Byzantium.

It was a beautiful room, and much life had passed through it, for in the preceding hundred and eighty years the Volkmars had contracted family alliances with most of the great Crusader families, except only the Bohemonds of Antioch and the Baldwins of Jerusalem, who had always refused to marry with the line of Ma Coeur. Marriages had been performed in this room and coronations, and in August 1191 month-long celebrations were launched when the castle was recaptured from Saladin by Richard the Lion Heart of England and restored by him to Volkmar IV. Richard had stayed in the castle for two weeks, recuperating from his siege of Acre. The princes of Galilee had graced this room, the Embriacos from Genoa and John of Brienne. Here the emissaries of the Comnenus emperors of Constantinople had come, and the Ibelins, a local nobility, and the queens of Armenia. How great they were, the lords of Tyr and Cesaire, the counts of Tripoli; but in the history of the distinguished room one name stood out above the rest.

'Let us drink to Saladin, cursed be his memory,' Volkmar proposed, and the old trader raised his glass, even though as a Muslim he should not have taken wine.

'I love wine,' the old man said, adding, 'Saladin was so noble he should have been an Arab.'

'He killed two of my ancestors,' Volkmar observed.

'If both sides had listened to him,' the old man reflected, 'we should have long ago devised a way of living on this land.'

'That much I grant you,' Volkmar agreed.

At this point the count's son, a boy of eleven, came in from his studies and greeted the Arab, who had often brought him unexpected gifts from Damascus. The two spoke in Arabic, and Muzaffar asked the count, 'Have you ever shown your boy the Horns of Hattin?'

'No,' the count laughed. 'Our family prefers to stay away from there.'

'You should do it next spring,' Muzaffar suggested. 'The more we know about history, the better.'

Countess Volkmar interrupted to summon the men to a smaller room where a generous meal was spread across a heavy wooden table. The principal dish was roebuck, taken from the hills opposite Acre, but there was also grouse brought to the castle by Muslim traders from Jerusalem. About the table were placed bronze bowls of damson plums and apricots from Syria, oranges and late melons from fields near Ma Coeur. Volkmar judged that Muzaffar's men must have already sold the castle new supplies, for he was offered a small silver dish from Athens containing Persian violets crystallized in transparent sugar. These were flavored with cinnamon and were intended for dessert.

'I have always loved to eat from your plates,' Muzaffar joked. 'They almost make me feel a Christian.' He lifted the proud old plate, designed in Jerusalem years ago but baked in the potteries of Egypt, and studied it again. It was handsomely crazed and bore only one design, in red: a large, stupid-looking, gape-mouthed fish, and for nearly two centuries each Crusader fortress in the Holy Land had owned a set of such dishes, for they had become the most popular emblem of Christianity: centuries before, someone had discovered that the Greek letters for the word fish, *ichthys*, formed an acrostic which could be translated 'Jesus Christ, Son of God, Saviour.'

As they ate, Muzaffar looked at the folios that stood in cases along one wall of the room. Ma Coeur owned seventy volumes, a notable library for that day, and most had been brought there by Muzaffar. In Aleppo, Smyrna or Baghdad, wherever he had happened to be, he had acquired old works for his friend, for like many Arabs of his day he thought it strange that the unlettered Crusaders took so little interest in learning.

When the leisurely meal ended he took one final gulp of wine, kissed the countess farewell, gave young Volkmar some coins from beyond Persia, and took the count's arm, walking him out to the camels. When they were alone he asked quietly, 'And at the end of the truce?'

Count Volkmar considered for some moments, then said, 'The men at Acre are hopeful, but I'm cautious. The Mamelukes may drive us from the land.'

'I think so. What will you do?'

'I shall not leave this castle.' The count suspected that Muzaffar might have come as a spy; if he did, the Mamelukes had driven him to it. On the other hand, if they had sent him they had better know the facts. 'I'll resist,' he repeated stubbornly.

'And the boy?'

'There's the question,' Volkmar replied in undisguised perplexity.

'Why don't you send him back to Germany?' Muzaffar suggested.

'My father made a visit to Germany and I can remember his telling us that compared to the way we lived at Ma Coeur, the Germans lived like animals. And for their part, the Germans felt that he had become an Arab and they wondered if his religious attitudes could be trusted. He told us that between him and his cousins there had been little understanding: he loved learning and they couldn't read; he liked philosophical discussion, but all they knew about was hunting. In short, he had been civilized by the Arabs while they had been allowed to remain suspicious barbarians. At the end of his uncomfortable visit everyone was relieved to see him go—he most of all. I don't think my son would like Germany.'

'But I warn you, Volkmar. He should leave.'

'I know. But where?' The two old friends embraced and the Arab returned to his camels.

On a sunny morning in late April, 1290, Count Volkmar rousted his eleven-year-old son from bed and took him to a room where waiting men had spread upon the floor the boy's first full suit of armor. 'We shall be riding over dangerous countryside,' the count explained. 'A safe-conduct is no protection against stragglers and robbers.' After the men had dressed the boy in his usual underclothes, they fitted him with a padded tunic made of thick folds of linen stuffed with cotton wadding that had been soaked in vinegar. This would withstand arrows. Over it they put a light, flexible coat of mail whose joints worked easily and whose edges fell to the boy's knees. It was slit in the back, so that he could sit astride his horse. His feet were slipped into iron shoes from which a long tongue extended upward to protect the shin bone. And because the pilgrims would be riding in hot sun, over all was thrown a thin gauze cloak upon which had been stitched in blue silk the seal of the castle: a round tower flanked by another.

Proudly young Volkmar clanked in to greet his mother and to kiss her farewell. He carried no lance, but he was allowed a token sword and a stout wooden shield covered with hard leather and studded with iron. In the courtyard he saw with satisfaction that each of the knights was dressed like him, except that they were heavily armed, and all wore iron helmets which looked like buckets but which allowed them to see and breathe through small slits.

The drawbridge of the castle was lowered, the iron gates were swung open, creaking in sunlight, and the entourage spurred their horses across the moat and down into the mud-walled town, past the Catholic church of Rome, past the Maronite church of Syria, and up to the old Byzantine basilica called Sancta Magdalena, at which pilgrims had been halting for nine hundred years, seeking blessing before they headed east to the Sea of Galilee on a visit to the scenes of Christ's ministry. Resting their horses by the entrance the knights dismounted and made their way into the darkened chapels, where they knelt and asked blessing on their venture. A faltering priest in ragged vestments mumbled Greek words over their bared heads, and they crossed themselves, returning to their horses and the lovely green countryside of the principality of the counts of Gretz.

How beautiful it was, how achingly beautiful to the senses was Galilee that spring morning. The forests of cedar and pine had not yet been completely chopped away; olive orchards and the far vineyards still flourished; fields produced rich harvests of wheat and oats and barley, while small plots were kept aside for sesame, from which sweet candy was made for children. And at every fifth or sixth mile some new village of Volkmar's fief would appear, each with its ninety-six Muslims and four Christians working together. It was a land, Volkmar thought as he surveyed it for what he sensed might be the last time, which truly flowed with milk and honey, and he was depressed to think that no way could be devised for holding on to it. As a descendant of the Family of Ur, Volkmar loved the land not only because it was his principality, but also because it was a good and beautiful thing of itself. It was worth preserving in its richness, and he knew that when the Mamelukes captured such land they took no pains to keep it productive. They killed the farmers, chopped down trees, destroyed the irrigation and abandoned the valleys to the Bedouins and goats. It would be cruel to see these fields laid waste, Volkmar reflected.

As the pilgrims headed toward Nazareth the count explained to his son, 'The secret of wealth is to have many people working, but in the old days we did not understand this, so we slaughtered all who lived on the land because they were of a different religion. But we quickly learned that in doing so we were killing ourselves, and the land lay idle until we could find hands to till it. Our first count was among the earliest to discover this truth, and that was why through the years our family prospered whilst others did not.'

'Is that why we were able to build the castle?' the boy asked.

'Well,' his father hedged. He thought: In his own time the boy can read what Wenzel of Trier wrote and it would be difficult to explain now, but to his own memory the words of the old chronicler came back with all the muted force that had accompanied them when he had first read them:

And after the death of my Lord Volkmar, rest his Christian soul, unforeseen events took place in the castle of Makor. Sir Gunter of Cologne quickly took my Lady Taleb to wife but placed her son, Volkmar, in a prison, where the boy had little food and no sunlight and where none instructed him, and there the boy languished for seven years. For Gunter announced that he would have his own son who would inherit the principality, but when the lady became not pregnant, the knight swore at her in my presence and shouted, 'Damn thee, thy womb swelled for him.' And one night at a banquet he roared to all that he would lie on his wife every night for a year until she bore him a son, and from her end of the table she said quietly that since she had already proved that she could have a child, and had done so, the matter must rest with him, and at his discomfiture we all roared. So Gunter found many women and lay with them, one after another, but none bore him a son and he was past forty years of age, and he saw that he was not to have a child and that when he died the only person to inherit his fields and his castle would be the boy who lay in prison, so the prisoner was brought forth, eleven years of age of which seven had been lived in darkness, and now my Lord Gunter turned to this child as if he were his own precious son and taught him all he knew of warfare and of defending castles and of governing peasants so that their yield would be improved. He required me to teach the boy Latin and Greek and the boy's grandfather, Luke the Bailiff, perfected him in Arabic and Turkish, so that when the boy was sixteen Gunter contracted a marriage for him with the noble family of Edessa and the old knight was impatient, walking up and down the battlements, until the princess bore a son, for then my Lord Gunter cried, 'Now, by God, you are worthy to own this land,' and it was this Volkmar who extended the boundaries.

They camped that first night on the edge of the swamp that filled the middle areas between Ma Coeur and Nazareth, and in the morning one of the guards wakened the sleepers with the cry, 'The storks are rising!' The pilgrims rushed to view one of the memorable sights of Galilee: five storks from a large flock that had been resting near the swamp during their migration north had found a current of hot air rising from the land, and these five had already entered it and were being carried speedily aloft without using their wings at all. Their huge black bodies were canted upward and their white wings were extended motionless to their fullest extent, so that the rising air swept them aloft in wide spirals. Their pink bills were thrust straight forward and their long reddish legs trailed after them like rudders.

Those storks remaining on the ground understood from the manner in which their fellows soared into the air that an upward current had been found, and with awkward, lumbering jumps they loped across the meadows and projected themselves, wings outspread, into the column of rising air, allowing it to loft them far into the sky toward those highest currents along which they would migrate to Europe. When Volkmar and his son hurried into the morning sunlight they could see a mysterious pillar of more than a hundred storks, apparently motionless yet rising upward, one above the other, until the topmost ones were lost in the sky, and Volkmar quoted from Jeremiah, who had once watched these birds rising over the Galilee: '"Yea, the stork in the heaven knoweth her appointed times."'

'It's an omen for us,' one of the knights avowed, for as the birds soared aloft, wings and necks and legs extended, they formed a series of supernatural crosses reaching from earth to heaven.

'An omen of good!' other warriors echoed, and all bared their heads and crossed themselves, but Volkmar, watching the topmost storks start flapping their giant wings as they left the rising current, said to himself: No omen, but a warning. They are flying to Germany and soon they will nest in the chimneys of Gretz. The storks had been sent to warn Volkmar and his family to leave the Galilee and go back to Germany. For many days his thoughts would be tormented by that column of majestic crosses, motionless in the sky.

One of the warriors experienced in the swamp now took command, and the file of pilgrims threaded its way southward through the mysterious waters that had always been such a challenge to the adventuresome men of the district. Leading their horses along the solid footpaths they startled egrets and the striking purple herons. The marshes were alive with flowers, tulips and lupine and cyclamen and orchids, and the one that had always so delighted the children of Ma Coeur: the slender olive-green plant with brown stripes whose leaves looked like the heart of Jesus and whose canopy protected a little gray-green man. 'Priest-in-his-pulpit,' the children called the plant, and it was young Volkmar's favorite.

At the far end of the swamp they regained firm ground and began their final march to Nazareth, but as they proceeded, the full richness of Galilee broke over them: bee eaters flashing through branches, olive trees shimmering in sunlight and red poppies marking their way like beacons. Let the storks head for Germany, Volkmar said to himself. What man would leave this paradise? And he determined to stay on his land.

At Nazareth, which seemed a sturdy anchor of Christianity in a land already become infidel, Volkmar left the others and went alone to the grotto where the archangel Gabriel had announced to the Virgin that she was to become the Mother of Jesus. It was a portentous spot, more nearly a deep cave than a grotto, and its walls were damp. As Volkmar stood in the narrow space the actual presence of Mary and Gabriel was made manifest. It was for this that the Germans, the French and the English had fought: that the Christian world might come in peace to such sacred spots and worship; but after two hundred years of warfare a knight of Ma Coeur could come to this holiest of spots only on sufferance of a Mameluke slave. What had gone wrong? Why had the various Volkmars been unable to hold Nazareth, or the Baldwins, Jerusalem? Why should the scenes of our Lord's passion be in infidel hands, lost forever to the Christians? He could not understand, and he lowered his strong head and whispered, 'Mary, Mother of God, we have failed you. For some reason I cannot comprehend we have failed and soon we shall be driven away. Forgive us, Mary. We did not find the way.'

For nearly an hour he remained alone in the sanctuary, then climbed gloom-ridden back to sunlight and told his son, 'You must go down to see the spot where the Word became flesh,' and he spoke no more of that holy place.

They rode then to Mont Thabor, where the appearance of Jesus had been transfigured from that of an ordinary mortal into the reality of a deity, and they stayed with the monks who ignored Mameluke threats and operated on top of the mountain; and next day they rode to the gentlest of the holy places, Cefrequinne, the Cana of Bible times, where a Muslim and his wife showed them the very cot on which Jesus had rested during the wedding feast. Young Volkmar asked in Arabic if he might lie on the Lord's couch, and the Muslim replied, 'For one coin anyone may lie on it,' and the boy did so. He also saw two of the six jars which had held the water which Christ had turned into wine, and touching their rough clay the boy experienced a historic sense of Jesus. 'Are these the real jars?' he asked, clasping his fingers about the handle that Jesus might have used.

'Yes,' the count said, and when the others were not looking he, too, grasped the heavy clay pots. This turning of water into wine had been the first miracle, the initial step taking a Nazarene carpenter to Calvary, and Volkmar heard the long-ago words which Wenzel had written of the first Volkmar: 'For I was in Jerusalem on the morning I set out from Gretz.'

What had been the deciding point in the Crusades? Volkmar wondered as he stood in the house at Cefrequinne. When had failure become inevitable? He supposed it must have been at some unrecorded date early in the 1100s, in the time of Volkmar II, when it became obvious that no great number of European settlers were going to make the long trip to Jerusalem. We never had enough people, the count mused. How often do we hear of this king or that whose wife died or whose sons wasted away with no one coming along to take their places? We were always so few . . . so few. In the rude hut where Jesus had begun his mystical life the names returned: Baldwin and Bohemond, Tancred and Lion Heart, and that false Reynald of Châtillon who had destroyed so much. 'God! I would like to have that man's throat between my hands right now!' Volkmar cried, and instantly he was ashamed of his passion in such a holy place, but the Muslim caretaker took no notice, and Volkmar muttered, 'There are two things for which I respect our enemy Saladin. He destroyed nothing in our castle and he killed Reynald with his own hands.'

A true sadness came over Volkmar, and he sat upon the couch of Christ and lowered his head. How had men so essentially good in heart permitted catastrophes like Reynald and his kind? Than the saintly Louis, the French king in Acre, there could be no sweeter man; and the greatest of them all, Baldwin IV of Jerusalem, who, when his body was rotting away with leprosy and his eyes were blind and his feet gone, insisted still upon being carried into battle one last time against Saladin, whom he had defeated time after time.

> We rode out to battle in the desert [wrote the Volkmar who was to die at the Horns of Hattin] and the purple tent of Baldwin went with us; and when the enemy saw this tent once more on the march they fled, and when they were gone I went in to tell the leper king of his latest victory and he turned his sightless eyes upon me and thanked me and I drew away lest he hear my tears, for I had forgot that he was but a boy of twenty.

Why had they gone, the great ones, leaving the lesser behind? Baldwin the Leper was one of the superb kings of the east, but he had died a boy, leaving a creature like Reynald of Châtillon to contest for his throne. We needed fresh blood from Europe, and it never came, Volkmar reflected. His own family had remained strong–eight Volkmars in a row, and his son seemed as promising as the others–but perhaps it was because they had often brought their wives from afar. His own countess had come from the noble family of Ascalon, but his mother had been raised in Sicily. If, after the First Crusade, we had never allowed another knight on this soil, Volkmar decided, but if we had brought instead farmers and shoemakers, we could have held the kingdom. In his gloominess an ironic thought came to him and he laughed, pressing his hands against the couch of Jesus: A better idea, each year we should have imported a dozen shiploads of French and German milkmaids, for the European men, unable to find wives of their own background, had married wantonly into the local population. Any girl who would step before the priest and allow herself to be baptized was termed a Christian . . .

He stopped. His judgment was ungenerous, for it had been Taleb, wife to the first count and the worst kind of cynical convert to Christianity, who had really saved the principality for the Volkmars. Of this extraordinary woman her son had told the whitehaired Wenzel of Trier:

> In the long years when I lay in the dungeon without seeing sunlight, two people came to mean the entire world to me–the jailer who brought my food, throwing it on the stone table without

speaking–and my mother who slipped through the gates I know not how. Once I saw the jailer kissing her and perhaps that was the coin she used, but she came as often as she could escape Gunter's detection and she talked with me. How simple that statement is, how much it signifies. She talked with me. Unlike my father and Gunter, she could read, and she told me of all that she had learned, and this I prized more than the bits of food she smuggled to me. And I remember that each time she sat with me she said three things: 'I am not pregnant.' 'Soon the brute must awaken to the true situation.' And, 'Volkmar, you shall be the amir of this principality.' If it had not been for her, when I finally was taken from the dungeon I would have been an idiot.

This second count later testified that during his long reign it was his mother who had advised him on how to deal with Arabs and on ways to enlarge the fief by invading lands loosely held by incompetents. Yet at her death she had outraged the kingdom by replying to the priest when he asked her if she was not happy that she had left off being a Muslim and become a Christian: 'I was never either. Both ways are folly.' And in spite of the priest's pleadings and those of her son, she died in this belief, so that no statue of her, nor any plaque, was permitted in the chapel of Ma Coeur.

We never had enough people, Volkmar mourned in Cefrequinne as he visualized the map. We held the cities of the coast from Antioch to Ascalon, but the sources of real power, like Aleppo and Damascus, we left in the hands of the Turks. And now the Mameluke. And even with that condition facing us we still refused to do the two things necessary for our survival. We never became a sea power with ships of our own, for we depended upon the men of Venice and Genoa, who bled us white and betrayed us whenever it suited their interests. Nor did we achieve an alliance with the Arabs, binding their land to ours. So in the end Syria combined with Egypt and we were left an enclave on the edge of the sea. He reflected on the lost glories and concluded: We produced men of vision like Volkmar the Cypriot, but whenever they were about to effect some kind of compromise new fools landed from Europe to slay the Arabs and to destroy what the wise men were attempting.

He snapped his fingers and the Muslim caretaker hurried over. Volkmar apologized: 'I was thinking ...' and the Muslim shrugged his shoulders. There's the contradiction! Volkmar thought as the man left. And I never perceived it before. We needed the settlers from Europe ... couldn't exist without them. But all we got were warriors determined to kill the very friends we had to depend on for survival. Ah, well. He sighed ruefully and assembled his men for the ride to the Sea of Galilee; but as they saddled up he said, 'We are thirteen–the number of those who dined at our Lord's Last Supper.'

He was unaware, at that moment, of the contradiction in which he was caught, for on leaving Cefrequinne he and his men knelt in reverence to that hallowed spot, not realizing that the true Cana of Christ's miracle lay seven miles northwest at a site now remembered only by coyotes. In the year 326, when Saint Helena, the mother of Constantine, had come this way identifying the scenes of Christ's life, even the name of Cana had been locally forgotten, and in answer to her inquiries helpful peasants of Nazareth had shown her a mud-walled village, saying, 'This is Cana,' and Cana it had henceforth been. The Lord's couch, the water jugs, were the inventions of Muslims who collected pilgrims' coins thereby. In many similar externals the Crusaders had been deceived by the Holy Land and had failed to grasp the realities that confronted them, but in their dedication to a religious principle they had not wavered, and when these men now prayed in the false Cana, they prayed to a real Saviour.

They rose and for some hours traveled eastward through the fallow countryside, and wherever the earth was exposed it looked damp and dark, the kind that grows its weight in food. The trail was still marked with flowers: the purple thistle and the yellow daisy and that blue five-petaled beauty which winked with pollened eyes as men rode by. It was a land of exquisite loveliness, well suited for the birthplace of a Saviour, and then the men riding ahead cried, 'The lake!' and all spurred their horses, and the knights in armor paused in wonder at the beauty of the scene below.

It was the Sea of Galilee, now known by its Latin name, Mare Tyberiadis, sunk in its deep depression among surrounding hills whose red and brown coloring played across the surface of the water, so that sometimes the lake was its own blue—a deep, pulsating blue of vivid quality which made the heart cry out with joy—while at other times it was red or brown, or, where the trees were, green. But always its colors were in motion, a living, twisting kaleidoscope, as marvelous a body of water as there was on earth.

'This is the lake of Jesus,' Volkmar explained, as his son gazed down upon the water on which the Lord had walked. 'To the north is Capharnaum, where we shall travel later. The city with the castle is Tabarie. Years ago it belonged to your uncle's family, but now it's Mameluke.' And the men rested their horses for a long time, surveying the incomparable scene which for so many years had been denied them because of Turkish conquest.

Young Volkmar was eager to ride down to Tabarie, for the walled city was inviting, but his father indicated that they must postpone that visit for a while and ride to the north in the direction of a strange hill composed of two projections. 'The Horns of Hattin,' the count said, 'and I would our house had never heard the name.' His knights crossed themselves, for of the twelve men riding that day from Ma Coeur, each had lost an ancestor at the great battle and some, like Volkmar, had lost four: great-great-uncles and great-great-grandfathers and men, who, had they lived, might have held the kingdom together.

'It was in July, 1187, more than a hundred years ago,' Volkmar explained. 'Saladin was in Tabarie with all the water and wall he needed. At Ma Coeur were the king and the greatest knights of the day, and in our hall the argument began. What would you have done, Volkmar? You're safe inside your castle. You have thousands of strong men and more than enough armor. You have water at hand and food. To defeat you, Saladin must leave his walls and his water, march up this hill, come far across the plains we've just traveled and then try to fight you in your own castle. What would you do?'

'I'd get lots of food inside the walls and wait,' the boy answered.

'Great God!' the count cried, smiting his mailed chest. 'A child understands. But what did the fools around the king propose? That we leave our tight castles. That we leave our water supplies and our food, and that in the middle of summer we put on our coats of mail and march here to fight Saladin on ground of his own choosing.'

'That's what we did,' one of the knights muttered, surveying the improbable battlefield.

'The men of Volkmar pleaded against the folly,' the count recalled. 'Our grand hall echoed with their arguments, but after they had explained how easy it would be for Saladin if we left our castle and fought him here at Hattin, Reynald of Châtillon . . .' The Count of Ma Coeur looked away and muttered, 'May God damn his infamous soul. May God curse him afresh in hell.' He took his son's hands and said gently, 'Next morning when Volkmar IV and his son rode to battle they told their wives that they would not be coming back.' The gloomy descendants of that day looked at the Horns and were mute.

'Did they fight here?' the boy asked, for he had grown to like the gently falling field, with its protecting Horns and fine view of the lake below.

'I suppose you'd call it a fight. Twenty thousand Crusaders left Ma Coeur on July 3, the hottest day of the year, and in full armor—much heavier than we wear today—marched without finding water to this spot, where Saladin had more than a hundred thousand men waiting. We had one thousand horsemen. He had twenty thousand. On the final night before the battle our men were dying of thirst . . . there was a well over there, but they didn't find it . . . the moon shone on the lake and they could see the water. It sent them mad, and Saladin knew it, so he set those fields on fire and sparks and smoke blew across our people, and at dawn he began to tighten the net. It was the worst battle that men have ever fought in this land. Cruel . . . cruel.'

'Why did our side do such a thing?' the boy inquired.

'Because it was the turn of stupid men to lead us,' Volkmar replied. 'We lost Tabarie and the Galilee and Jerusalem and Ma Coeur, and even St Jean d'Acre.' He turned away from the others and stared at the hills. 'We lost so much,' he muttered to himself. 'Later on we won back Ma Coeur and Acre but Jerusalem was gone forever, and now the twilight deepens.' He began to hum a chant from the Catholic liturgy *Tenebrae factae sunt*, 'The shadows are falling.'

Behind him he heard the knights explaining to his son, 'Count Volkmar broke through the ring of iron and died leading his men toward the lake. They reached here,' and the men showed young Volkmar where his ancestor had fallen.

'Was his son with him?' the boy inquired.

'Of course,' the knights answered, 'Volkmars always seek the enemy,' and the company saddled again and resumed their march to Tabarie, where the Mameluke guards were astonished to see them riding like ghosts out of the hills in which their ancestors had perished, so that an alarm was sounded and the governor himself, a Mameluke with fierce mustaches, left the fort and came to the gate, where he inspected the order from Damascus and allowed the pilgrims entrance.

It was an inviting little city they had come to, close-walled on three sides and with the lake on the fourth. Since Galilee stood far below sea level the air was heavy and hot, but the cool breeze from the lake was welcome and the food was excellent. The Arabs who inhabited the town—there were not more than six Mamelukes and a hundred Turks—were hospitable, and all were eager to hear news of Acre and Nazareth.

The warriors laid aside their armor and lounged in comfortable chairs beside the lake, drinking beverages which the garrison supplied, after which the Mameluke governor, pressing down his mustaches, proposed that all go down the road to the hot baths which had made the city famous in Roman days, and for the first time young Volkmar saw springs gushing from the ground bringing water far too hot to touch. The dusty men indulged themselves in the humid rooms and felt the tedium of the saddle seep away in the heat. Then they dressed and rode back to the city, Count Volkmar experiencing pangs of regret when he thought: Once it was ours. Once a prince lived here and gathered fees from lands ten miles away. To come to Tabarie in winter and take the baths, that was the best that Galilee offered.

He thanked the Mameluke officer for his courtesy and the former slave bowed, and as he did so Volkmar cried to his son, 'Look! Look! There's a Jew.' And for the first time in his life the boy saw a Jew.

'A few returned from the lands of the Frank,' the Mameluke explained, studying the stranger as if he were a new kind of horse, useful but not customary.

Young Volkmar stood fascinated as the strange man walked slowly through the streets, bearded, cap on head, shuffling a little, looking for something or somebody. The Mameluke called out to him in Arabic, and the man came over to the knights. His Arabic was not good, but he was able to explain that he had come from France.

'Why?' the mustachioed governor asked.

'Because this city is holy to the Jews,' the man replied.

'Why?' Volkmar inquired.

'Because the Bible was written down in this city and because the Jerusalem Talmud was, too.'

'What's the Talmud?' the knights asked.

'The Jewish book of law,' the man explained, and he was allowed to walk on.

For a perverse reason Volkmar was pleased that his son had finally seen a Jew, for none had stopped in Ma Coeur for two hundred years, yet when the boy grew older and read the chronicles he would surely come upon that cryptic passage that had caused the Volkmars so much irritation. An unknown priest had put his suspicions into writing, nearly two hundred years before:

And after a while men reasoned thus: On her deathbed the Countess Volkmar said only that the religion of Christ and the religion of Muhammad were folly, and in the great halls the rumor circulated that this was because she was herself Jewish, in a secret way, and it was recalled that often friends had asked her, 'Why do you not drop your name Taleb and take a Christian name? and she had oft replied, 'Because I was born Taleb and it would be foolish to change.' And then others remembered that her father, known as Luke—for he did take a Christian name—had borne all the signs of a true Jew. He was good in medicine. He ate no fat of the meat. He could read and write. He knew mysterious matters. And he was unusually skilled in handling money, which he did for Count Volkmar so long as the count lived, then for Sir Gunter. And the suspicion grew and it was for this reason that some of the great houses like Antioch and Jerusalem refused to marry with the Volkmars, but others, seeing how the principality prospered, above all others, were in great speed to ally themselves with it.

Count Volkmar laughed at the old tale and recalled 'the great houses' which had refused to intermarry with his ancestors. 'Where are they now?' he asked. 'They vanished so long ago.' Then he chuckled. 'Taleb is about as perfect an Arab name as you can find. She wasn't Jewish. She was stubborn, and would to God her descendants had been more stubborn that night when they allowed the idiots to argue them into fighting at the Horns of Hattin.' He shook his head as if loose things—ideas, memories—were floating therein, unconnected, and then he fell back in his chair and stared at the lake.

From Tabarie the pilgrims rode north to Capharnaum, a lovely deserted spot where rich fields drifted down to the water and where Jesus Christ had fed the multitudes by hundreds and by fifties, with only five loaves of bread and two small fishes: 'And they did all eat, and were filled. And they took up twelve baskets full of the fragments, and of the fishes. And they that did eat of the loaves were about five thousand men.'

'Could it have happened?' the boy asked.

Volkmar looked at his son in astonishment. 'Of course!' he said. 'If you had caught a fish from the lake you'd have seen that it was only half a fish, swimming around with a piece bitten out. It was thrown back into the lake by Jesus after the fragments were collected. Of course these things happen. That's why we come on pilgrimages.'

The boy studied Capharnaum with new interest, whereupon his father explained, 'The five thousand men were seated here. The two fish were carried in a basket up that path. And Jesus stood exactly where the altar of that ruined church used to be. When I was a boy you could see on the floor of the church a picture of the fish,' and he led the knights into the ruined sanctuary and rummaged about the rubble until he found the mosaic which once had been kept polished by priests of Byzantium; and the two stone fish were as real to him as the living flowers of the fields outside. Here Jesus had stood. Here He had fed the five thousand with the two fish represented in the panel.

'This is why our land is called holy,' he said quietly, and the knights resumed their climb into the steep hills until they came at last to the mountain village of Saphet, where they were to meet Muzaffar coming his own way from Damascus.

This was the most painful moment of the trip, more so even than the silent Horns of Hattin, for that battle had occurred a century before, whereas the loss of Saphet was still a gaping wound in Crusader memory, and after the knights had presented their safe-conduct to the Mameluke garrison they passed into the courtyard of what once had been a notable Christian castle. High on a hill, with precipitous falls on each side, the soaring castle of Saphet had been a beacon to the surrounding countryside. From its battlements one could see the Sea of Galilee far below, and the plains of the north. It commanded the road from Damascus to Acre and dominated a dozen lesser passes. When the signal fires in its highest turrets were lighted they were seen on the seacoast, and Acre could be assured that all was well along the eastern marches. It was the hilltop castle par excellence, and in 1266 one of the real tragedies of the Crusades had occurred here—one that still struck terror in the European heart.

The first Mameluke sultan had laid siege to Saphet, and after a brilliant initial resistance the defenders were driven to realize that the winds of history had changed and that they would no longer be able to hold such outposts. Gallantly they offered to surrender so that no more lives need be lost, and terms were faithfully agreed upon: open the gates and each man would receive safe-conduct to Acre. The Mameluke sultan gave his binding oath, and the long siege ended. But not according to the pact. As soon as the sultan was within the gates his men pinioned the defenders and every knight was beheaded on the spot. 'We wanted them to know the kind of enemy they faced,' one of the Mameluke generals explained, and thus the war of extermination was launched.

Now Saphet was a ghost town. The lovely settlement that had once clung to the flanks of the hill, outside the fortress walls, had been erased by the Mameluke attackers and had not yet been rebuilt, so that the fortress stood alone, its massive walls beginning to crumble. 'We'll pull them down one of these days,' the officer-in-charge stated. He seemed a likeable person, not one given to beheading prisoners. His head was shaven and bore a deep scar at which young Volkmar stared. He ordered refreshments to be served on the battlements, where cool breezes drifted across the mountains.

'It's a marvelous spot,' one of the garrison said in Arabic as he pointed to a village that nestled below on the flank of a hill. 'I often wonder about that village. In all the wars that have been fought over Saphet I suppose it's never been touched. But up here . . . battles . . . bugles . . . beheadings.' He looked directly at Volkmar as if he regretted the facts of history.

Crusaders and Mamelukes enjoyed two fine days at Saphet. Archery contests were held, with the Mamelukes winning by a consistent margin, but in sword play the Crusaders prevailed. 'That's how I got my scar,' the Mameluke officer explained to the boy. 'One of your swords at Tyr.' Horse races were arranged within the castle walls, and here the smaller Turkish mounts had such advantage that the Crusaders could scarcely keep up on their lumbering beasts. 'But on a long march to be followed immediately by a battle,' Volkmar said, 'our horses are better every time.'

The baldheaded Mameluke replied, 'For your tactics, yes. For the quick dash and retreat of our warfare, your horses would be too heavy to handle.' The men traded a big horse for one of the swift Turkish animals, and young Volkmar was given the beast to ride back to Ma Coeur.

Then the Mameluke captain asked a most bold question: 'How long do you suppose the sultan will allow your fortress and Acre to exist?'

Volkmar scratched his clean-shaven chin and said slowly, 'The truce agreed upon last year runs beyond the end of the century. I would suppose . . .'

'Do you think a truce can be observed that long?' the Mameluke persisted.

'Yes, I rather do. After all, both you and we gain real advantage from having Acre available to ships . . .'

'Agreed!' the Mameluke replied whole-heartedly. 'You and I know that we ought to prolong the truce. Between us there's no trouble. But we've been told by the Genoese . . . I heard it myself in Cairo from a sea captain's lips . . . Your Pope is preaching a new Crusade.'

'Yes,' Volkmar said disgustedly. 'Back there they don't understand . . .'

'And if ten shiploads of knights eager for battle . . .'

The two leaders looked glumly down at the waters of Galilee, now red, now green, and a younger Mameluke broke the silence by observing, 'I doubt the truce can last ten years.'

'I doubt it, too,' Volkmar concurred gloomily.

In the morning the old castle sounded as it must have in days past, for men were shouting on the battlements, and all came out to see the first camels of Muzaffar's caravan picking their way along the mountain road. There was cheering, for his arrival meant that the garrison would have fresh food, and the gates were thrown open to admit the seventy-odd beasts and their armed attendants. True to his word Muzaffar appeared on a fine horse, from which he dismounted as if he were a young man. Moving easily across the stones in his long robes he saluted the garrison commander, then embraced Volkmar and kissed his son.

He had a dozen bits of news. He, too, had heard that a new Crusade was being preached in Europe. 'Will they never learn?' he expostulated. 'Seriously, this may be the last trip I'll dare to risk. And when you see all the goods in Damascus waiting to be traded and all the things that the Genoese ships are bringing to Acre . . .' He spat into the wind. 'We're all fools.'

The baldheaded Mameluke wanted the old trader to stay with them for several days, for he was like a troubadour, filled with gossip, but he refused: 'I've got to get the camels to Acre.' Then he suggested, 'But I could do this. If you'll send a guard as far as Ma Coeur, I'll send the camels off now and I'll stay here overnight and we can ride to Starkenberg in the morning.'

It was agreed, and the two young Mamelukes who wanted to see Ma Coeur were dispatched with the caravan while its owner relaxed on the sunny terrace, chatting about the rumors of empire. 'What we can't understand in Damascus,' the old man remarked, 'is why the Pope should cry for a Crusade from Europe when he has a perfectly good one alive right here in Asia and does nothing to support it.'

'You mean the Mongols?' the Mameluke captain asked.

'Yes!' the old Arab insisted. 'The other day I was talking with a Mongol trader down from Aleppo. He says the whole swarm of them are ready to become Christians if the Pope says the word, and they'd be an army of hundreds of thousands smashing at you Mamelukes from the back door while the Europeans hammer at the seaports. They'd have you caught in a trap.' He squeezed his wrinkled hands together with force.

'We used to worry about that,' the Mameluke confessed, rubbing his scar. 'For years we wondered when the Mongols and the Christians would combine against us. But now we don't worry. It can never happen.'

'Why not?' the old man asked.

'It's difficult to explain,' the Mameluke answered. 'Look how the Turks let us steal their empire. We were one man in ten thousand and slaves at that. At any point they could have stamped us out, but now we own the world. I suppose you've heard that Tripoli has fallen.'

'Yes,' Volkmar said with the sensation of doom settling upon him.

'Look down there,' the Mameluke said, pointing to the hillside village over which a cloud was passing while the rest of the world remained in sunlight. 'We can see the shape and direction of the cloud, but the villagers can't, because they're in it. We can also see what the Pope ought to do, but he can't, because he's in it.' The cloud drifted off.

'I'm really worried,' the old trader broke in. 'When the recent truce was arranged I thought: I'll be trading with Acre for the rest of my days. But with Tripoli gone, with the Christians behaving so blindly . . .' He rose in agitation. 'I'm afraid you Mamelukes will destroy Acre within the year.'

'We may have to,' the captain agreed, and as he spoke Muzaffar saw that, undetected, young Volkmar had approached the group and was listening.

Next morning Mazaffar and the two Volkmars rode north to Kafr Birim, where a settlement of Jews returned from Spain clustered about the ruins of that once-noble synagogue, and while the boy ran about gawking at the first group of Jews he had seen, his father spoke secretly with Mazaffar: 'On your trip back to Damascus would you take my son with you? Get him to Constantinople and somehow to Germany?'

'You're so concerned?' Muzaffar whispered.

'I am.'

'Then I'll confess what I've told no one else. This is my last trip, old friend.'

'You think the Mamelukes will strike so soon?'

The Arab nodded, and the company started mournfully westward across the finest hills of Gaililee, but at Starkenberg they found only ruins. That fair, poetic castle, perched on its crag like a solitary eagle, had once been the beau ideal of Crusader castles, but it had been overwhelmed by the Mamelukes, and now its jagged turrets and crumbling walls seemed like the broken teeth one finds in a weathering skull. Count Volkmar rode apart from the others to study the ruins, for here as a boy he had come to meet the Germans whose companionship his father enjoyed. Here he had learned to speak German and had kissed his first girl, and the lustful knights had followed the young couple as they tried to lose themselves in the surrounding hills, asking them when they returned, 'Did you? Did you?' Impregnable Starkenberg–castle that could never be subdued–how had it fallen? Sheer cliffs protected it on three sides and on the fourth the Crusaders had chopped their own cliff, down through living rock, until the castle was protected on that flank, too. The German knights had seemed so powerful and their cisterns so deep–forty feet cut into the heart of rock and splashing with sweet water–how had such defenses crumbled? For some time the count spoke with the ghosts of those he had known, and then the horsemen headed south.

There had always been a sense of excitement as one rode home from Starkenberg, for the path was mountainous and the horses kept coming to one rise after another, and at each summit the rider was certain that this time he must see Ma Coeur, but always some new hill interceded until . . . 'It's there!' the boy cried, and on his swift Turkish horse he dashed down the trail, throwing sparks, and through his dust the knights with longing in their eyes saw the tall round towers of Ma Coeur.

THE TELL

John Cullinane, brooding one day as he sat on the walls of Akko, trying to reconstruct the city as it must have been during Crusader days, thought: Everyone I know studies the wrong men when they want to understand that period. They take Richard the Lion Heart to represent the Christian side and Saladin to be the noble Muslim. They contrast the two and end with nothing. But I was lucky. When I was a boy doing my first reading about the Crusades I came upon the two men whose lives sum up the whole business, and I wish Plutarch had lived long enough to compare them. I'm certain he wouldn't have used Richard and Saladin. He'd have used my friends.

Frederick the German, the Holy Roman Emperor, was a grandson of the noble Barbarossa, with whom he had nothing in common. After shrewdly gaining control of Sicily and much of Italy, he found himself without a wife and looked around for a likely match, hitting upon the idea of wedding the fourteen-year-old queen of the moribund kingdom of Jerusalem; and on their wedding night she found him seducing her cousin. Frederick, after a few days with his child-bride, packed her off to his harem in Sicily, where she had a baby and died, leaving him Jerusalem, if he could get it from the infidel. Was there ever a worse king than Frederick? And for a place that called itself the Holy Land? He was short, fat, bald and myopic. He was humpbacked and had watery green eyes. As a young man he had sworn to go crusading to recapture Jerusalem, but he was so cowardly that he deferred year after year until at last the Pope had to excommunicate him, which enraged him so much that in 1228 he finally made the long trip to Acre, where the local barons found to their astonishment that he respected Islam just about as much as he did Christianity. He brought with him a Muslim counselor to whom he spoke Arabic, and he preferred Muslim customs. He was also suspected of being in the pay of Jews, for when plotters came with the oft-circulated myth that 'two Christian children were found this morning dead outside a synagogue,' he disappointed them by refusing to sanction a massacre. Said he, 'If the children are dead, bury them.' As he had suspected, there were no dead children. Frederick was a difficult man to understand because he understood so much. Wherever he went his shrewd, inquiring mind sought information about history, architecture, medicine, philosophy and local custom. He was the most brilliant church historian of his day and a radical improviser in economics and government, and by force of personality he bulled through the founding of the University of Naples. He had a rude, German honesty but was one of the most sexually corrupt men of his time, and his knights said of him, 'He studied Islam and learned all the wrong things.' Early in his stay at Acre he accepted as hostages two young sons of a local lord, waited till their father was gone, then strung them up to an iron cross so that they could not move and kept them there until their father honored his promises. His own son he drove to suicide. Because he was excommunicated his colleagues despised him, and no more pathetic man ever came crusading than this watery-eyed German. Nor did the Muslims respect him. In spite of his numerous gestures of friendship they described him in their chronicles as a red-faced, myopic little fellow who didn't have the manhood to grow a beard and who would bring no more than a few bezants in a slave market. They also suspected him of being an atheist, since they had heard him proclaim that his study of history had pretty well convinced him that Moses, Jesus and Muhammad were imposters. This impiety also repelled his own people, so that when he inherited the kingdom of Jerusalem after his child-bride's death, he could find neither churchman nor knight who would place the crown on his head; he went almost alone to the Church of the Holy Sepulchre, had a servant put the crown upon the altar, from which he raised it with his own hands, announcing that he was crowning himself King of the Holy Land. He was an arrogant man, self-seeking, ugly in manner and in all conceivable aspects a travesty of the crusading spirit.

Opposed to him, Cullinane reflected, stood Louis of France, the positive beau ideal of knighthood. Saintly in personal character, a devoted husband and father, he was a king without a known blemish, and after a life dedicated to good works he was joyously canonized by the church and became one of its most popular saints. If I were a Frenchman, Cullinane mused, I'd have to choose St Louis as my ideal. In battle he was courageous, in negotiations honest, in thought pure, in government just. Whom else can you say that of? There's no record of his ever having broken his word, and in settling disputes he listened to the other man's point of view; and often said without sanctimoniousness that his one ideal in life was to bring into the affairs of men and nations the rule of Christian love. We have some of his speeches on the eve of battle–glowing challenges to his troops to live up to their knightly vows, for if they did he was confident that victory would be theirs. He was a tall, handsome man, thin and on the sickly side, but of a noble appearance when decked out in armor, and in each of his battles the chroniclers agree that he fought in the front line, leading his men with outstanding heroism. Looking at him now Cullinane thought, as he stared down at the city of Akko where King Louis had lived for nearly five years, he seems too perfect, but it's hard to pick a flaw in him. No Pope had to excommunicate Louis to make him undertake a Crusade. As a young man he had come close to dying of malaria, and on his presumptive deathbed had sworn that if God saved him he would go crusading. God heard, and as soon as

Louis was able to walk he assembled an enormous fleet and in 1248 sailed for Egypt and the Holy Land, to which he brought dignity, faith and a kind of living poetry. As Cullinane looked at the narrow streets he thought he could see the tall king, dressed in armor and flowing robes, moving through the shadows, for he was the man above all who epitomized the strange malady that sent saintly men from France and Germany to these shores.

It was confusing, therefore, to remember that everything King Louis attempted in the Holy Land ended in disaster. He fumbled and bumbled his way into one catastrophe after another, needlessly sacrificing hundreds, thousands and scores of thousands of the finest soldiers of Europe. On one disgraceful afternoon he ineptly lost so large an army that the Egyptians simply had to chop off the heads of most of his knights because there was nothing else to do with them. Later, by gross error, he allowed himself to be captured, and his faltering Crusade had to dig up one million bezants to ransom him. He squandered armies the way a careless lieutenant loses platoons, and when he was through, the Holy Land was near prostration and recovery was impossible. Frantically seeking allies this saintly Christian stumbled into the hand of the Assassins, the most disreputable of Muslim factions, and he found himself financing the murder of his own people. He was the worst disaster ever to strike the Holy Land, yet his knights worshiped him as their ideal commander; and many, on the eve of battles in which his ineptitude would cost them their lives, penned letters home which still breathe the sanctity he inspired. The Muslims recognized him as a truly good man, but their generals must have prayed that fate would pit them against Louis rather than a real general. In fact, his string of disasters raised embarrassing questions throughout the east: if this greatest of God's servants could lose so constantly when vistory was assured, could it honestly be said that God was on the side of the Christians? You still wonder, Cullinane mused. King Louis at last had to leave St Jean d'Acre, a dejected man who had failed to accomplish a single aim, but he marched out of the city with flags flying as if he had been a great victor—which in some respects he had been. Years later the crusading zeal again obsessed him and as an old man he convened another great army. Due to some incredible aberration he persuaded himself that he could free Jerusalem by invading not Acre, but Tunisia, and to those inhospitable shores he led one of the most pathetic Crusades ever put together in madness and a love of God. In blazing summer heat he took his reluctant warriors to Africa, where no battles were fought, for plague struck the ships, mercifully killing the saint, who died muttering, 'Jerusalem, Jerusalem.' In a lifetime of effort he had never come close to rescuing that city. Most prodigally he had wasted lives and money. Yet he lived on in memory, and still does, as the ideal Crusader.

Frederick the Second, on the other hand, should have been a calamity but instead succeeded in all he tried. With his knowledge of Muslim ways he coldly surveyed conditions in the Holy Land and quickly decided that it would be a waste of manpower to fight the Muslims, who at this point wanted crusading no more than he did. Therefore, in a series of shrewd negotiations, the German king arranged a truce in which the Christians got everything they had been fighting for: control of the three holy cities of Jerusalem, Bethlehem and Nazareth, with corridors leading to each, plus protection of Christian pilgrims, plus ten years of guaranteed peace. Few Crusaders—no matter how large their armies or their stacks of bezants—had ever gained more; so after only a few months in the Holy Land the green-eyed, humpbacked German went back to

Europe, having demonstrated how a war between equals should be conducted.

It's the damnedest thing, Cullinane reflected, but Frederick's peaceful negotiations so outraged the knights who had been fighting for a cause that they openly reviled him. 'A true knight should not capture Jerusalem without a battle,' they raged. 'We should have killed every Muslim in the city.' Others contended that they should have laid waste the countryside and taken many slaves. 'God's blood! We should have marched like men and had an honest clashing of swords.' So impassioned did the outcry become, that when the crook-backed king scuttled out of Acre, citizens lined the streets and threw pigs' guts at him and cursed him. At one corner they even threw slops over him, for he had done what no leader is allowed to do: by negotiation he had achieved the national purpose, but in doing so had cheated the citizens of an exhilarating war, and for this he could not be forgiven.

In the early summer of 1290 the position of the Crusaders seemed to improve and a restrained optimism could be felt creeping across the countryside. Crops promised to be above average. Olive oil and wine were being produced in abundance. The Mamelukes were at rest and word reached Acre that the call of Pope Nicholas IV for a Crusade had been ignored throughout Europe, and men could reasonably hope that the present truce would not be disturbed.

When Volkmar of Ma Coeur observed this optimism rising in his principality he dropped his plan for sending his son to Europe. After inspecting the walls of his town and their glacis he concluded, 'If some kind of minor trouble does erupt, these outside walls will surely hold for five or six days.' Then he studied the moat and the massive wall which protected the castle itself, and he judged that they could hold for at least half a year, as they had done in the past; their surfaces were as smooth as ever and their outward-sloping bottom sections were as well prepared to ricochet boulders among the attackers. 'When the next century comes we'll be in this castle,' he whispered to himself.

In early July he decided to visit St Jean d'Acre to see if the leaders of the kingdom agreed with his hopeful assessment, and as he approached the famous city, its towers rising from the sea, his sensation of security increased, for in some mysterious way Acre communicated its strength to all who saw it. Disaster the city had known, but always it had recovered. After his crucial victory a hundred years ago at Hattin, Saladin had taken it; but four years later Richard the Lion Heart had thrown eighty thousand of his men to death against its gates and forced them open. Volkmar felt content that Acre was destined to remain in Crusader hands.

It was a town on a peninsula, surrounded by the sea; its strength came from the sea, and its fortresses stood with their great stone feet in salt water. Across the peninsula ran a massive wall, and the heart of the city was protected by a second. It was the noblest town of the coast, and as Count Volkmar led his party to the iron gate leading beneath the towers his men shouted proudly, 'Volkmar of Ma Coeur!' and the ponderous doors swung open to admit the dusty knights to the security of Acre.

But as soon as he entered this stronghold of the Crusaders, Volkmar was hailed by a Venetian merchant, who cried, 'Sire, sire! Don't sell your olive oil this year to the Pisans. They're robbers.' And he found himself drawn back into that frustrating whirlpool of conflicting interests and cross purposes that characterized Acre in the days of its death. 'Oh, God,' he muttered as the angry cries of competing groups reached him. 'This city can't survive another week. We are indeed doomed.'

For in those lovely days, as the Crusades ground to their mournful halt, Acre summarized the reasons why this movement was crumbling in disaster, for few cities in history had been so sorely divided as was Acre in 1290. Nominally it was ruled by the Franks of Henry II, King of Jerusalem, who controlled neither a kingdom nor Jerusalem, but actually it was a sorely divided Italian city, torn by the feuds of Guelph and Ghibelline. The heart of Acre was divided into three commercial quarters, each completely walled off from the other, with its own churches, town hall, magistrates and unique body of law. Each of these Italian areas centred upon its fonduk, a large, open-square warehouse from which the quarter took its name, and from which it maintained an open warfare, featuring soldiers and assassinations, against its competitors. The largest fonduk, running along the eastern waterfront and commanding the best industrial area, belonged to Venice and was subject only to laws promulgated in that Adriatic mother-city, for the functionaries of King Henry were not even allowed inside the walls. In the heart of Acre, well fortified on all sides, stood the fonduk of Genoa, whose residents obeyed only Genoese law. And at the southern tip of the city, enjoying a windswept spot along the sea, stood the autonomous fonduk of Pisa. The relationships between the quarters in this critical year of 1290 epitomized a basic weakness of the Crusades: differences in Europe determined behaviour in the Holy Land, for in Italy, Genoa had declared war on Pisa, and Venice was maltreating Genoese merchants; so in Acre local Venetians had driven Genoese from the city, and Genoese ships were retaliating by capturing both Venetian and Pisan sailors and selling them to the Mamelukes as slaves. It was war, conducted solely for economic advantage, and if it ever became profitable for the factions to betray Acre to the Mamelukes they would do so without a twinge of conscience.

That was the first division, but not the most important. The city was defended not by a traditional army but by monks who had entered one or another of the military orders—Templar, Hospitaller, Teutonic—and each of these stubborn units was also self-directing, self-paid and dedicated to warfare against the others. The monkish knights who led the orders were permitted to make their own treaties with the Mamelukes and to determine when and how they would do battle. To get all three to agree on any plan of defense was difficult if not hopeless. In Acre each had its own fortified section of the town, not included in the Italian quarters but equally distinct and self-governing; monks and merchants looked at each other with contempt, but since each was essential to the other, a grudging truce was maintained.

The third division, while of lesser importance militarily, was probably of greatest significance where morale was concerned. There were thirty-eight churches in Acre: Latin churches loyal to Rome; Greek Orthodox obedient to Byzantium; Greek Catholics who supported Rome but retained their own rites; and the stubborn, colorful Monophysites who ignored both Rome and Constantinople in their adherence to the old belief that Christ had but one nature. These included the Copts of Africa, the Armenians, and above all the Jacobites of Syria, whose priests made their sign of the cross with one bold finger, proclaiming to the world the oneness of Christ. Among these groups flourished bitter hatreds, with the priests of one confession ignoring or hampering the presence of the others. There were four sets of churches, four rituals, four competing theologies. In any crisis the interests of the four groups were almost sure to be divergent and any hierarchy might try to throw its enemies into confusion or even into the arms of the waiting Mamelukes.

And so the turreted town of Acre, so powerful when seen from a distance, was actually eleven separate communities bound together only by their fear of the encroaching enemy: the Venetian, Genoese and Pisan fonduks; the Templar, Hospitaller and Teutonic orders; the Roman, Byzantine, Greek and Monophysite churches, plus the fragile eleventh, the kingdom of Jerusalem, ruled by a handsome, ineffectual young king whose intimates had succeeded in hiding from the public the fact that he was an epileptic.

In this confusion there was only one redeeming feature, the bells of Acre, and now as the time for evening prayers approached, their magic quality drifted across the walled city. First came the deep iron bell of the SS. Peter and Andrew, the Roman church near the waterfront, establishing a stately rhythm which was soon joined by the dancing bronze bell of the Coptic church and then by the tinkling chatter from the Syrian church of St Mark of Antioch. One by one the other thirty-five bell towers sent forth their messages until the sea-girt peninsula was throbbing with sound. No city in the kingdom of Jerusalem—so great a name now signifying so little—had ever known an assembly of bells like those of Acre, and from his childhood Volkmar had loved them. Now as he looked aloft toward the azure sky from which they sounded, his hope revived for a moment and he listened to their noble symphony, the only thing their churches could agree upon, but then a Pisan merchant tugged at his sleeve and whispered, 'Sire, don't listen to the Venetians if they promise to buy your oil for more than we paid last year. Words, words. You know Venetians.'

Disgusted with the interlocking feuds that surrounded him, and feeling the old sense of doom returning, Volkmar rode to the Venetian fonduk, whose entrance was marked by the statue of a pig placed there to insult the Muslims, and went to the caravanserai, a spacious courtyard whose bottom rooms contained fodder for camels and whose upper floor served as a kind of inn. He looked for Muzaffar, hoping that the old Arab might still be trading with the Venetians—and there the old man was. Volkmar grabbed his hands and led him to the church of SS. Peter and Andrew, which Volkmar preferred because these men had been fishermen of Galilee; and there the Crusader went to one of the Christian chapels to give thanks for his safe arrival, while Muzaffar went to a chapel reserved for Islam, where before a delicately carved screen with a mark indicating the direction of Mecca, he prostrated himself on the pavement to whisper his Muslim prayers.

This was an arrangement guaranteed to startle hot-headed visitors from Europe—this business of sharing a consecrated Christian church with the enemy one had come to slay—but it was justified on the logical basis that outside the town walls stood a Muslim mosque in which a chapel containing a statue of the Virgin Mary was set aside for Christian use. There were other confusions for the stranger: most of the internal trading was in Arab hands, so that trusted Muslims like Muzaffar of Damascus were courted by the Italian merchants: and if one finally did meet a Catholic priest, he was apt to be a bearded Syrian with long oriental-looking garments, and it was this which helped bring about the final catastrophe in Acre.

For the time being the town was delightful. The boy-king, Henry II, and his recent bride were in residence, and in the long afternoons the knights dressed in ancient costume and rode horses caparisoned with ribbons and flowers. Those in men's clothes pretended that they were Lancelot or Tristram or Parsifal, while the others, dressed as women, were their ladies; and mock-jousts and tournaments were held, men against women, and there was much singing. The sight of real women, dressed handsomely and seated with the young queen, reminded Volkmar of the exciting days he had enjoyed in Acre when he was young and when all the families—the Volkmars were rich then and the Jewish rumor was forgotten—wondered which young girl he would select as his countess; and he had tried many. Those were the good days, before the Mamelukes took Saphet.

He thought of them now as he walked through the narrow streets of the town, and he recalled the girls, the lovely girls of Acre. There was Bohemond's niece and the Ibelin girl who had crept out of any castle her parents had ever tried to lock her into, and the grandniece of the King of Cyprus, who loved wine. Did anyone ever live as we lived then? Volkmar asked himself, and he turned away from the Venetian fonduk where Muzaffar waited, and went into the Pisan district, where he had been known as a young man, and at the pillared caravanserai he inquired, 'Are they upstairs?' and a man with no teeth replied that they were. He hurried up to the second level, two stone steps at a time and walked along the cloisters to a small door which opened cautiously, throwing a light. 'You may come in,' a voice whispered.

Inside were girls from many different lands, but the tall white-skinned one from Circassia was the most expensive, and Volkmar's eyes lighted as he saw her. She smiled, recognizing him as a man of importance who might leave an extra present, and he bypassed the French girls and the Egyptians and the Ethiopian who had been a slave, and took the tall Circassian by the hand and she led him to a room of manifold delights. In the hour before dawn they were awakened by the bells and he said, 'When I come back to Acre I'll ask for you again,' and in Arabic she replied teasingly, 'If you've found joy, why risk losing it?' and he had crushed her to him and had not gone, but had stayed with her for three days, saying as he finally left, 'At least I remember what it was like.' This time she did not tease him but said, 'I would be pleased if you returned tomorrow.'

It would have been difficult for Volkmar to explain why he lingered on in Acre during that hot midsummer. He loved his wife and was proud of his son; not many of the noble families had been able to survive for two hundred years in one line and increase their holdings while doing so, and he had cause for pride. But as a man of forty-five, strong in the arm and courageous, he felt that he ought to be doing something creative with the productive years of his life, yet what he saw in Acre proved that his world was slowly falling apart, gasping to its death without commitment to any ideal; and he could find the vital reassurance he needed only in the primitive relationship of one man and one woman in bed. Night after night he drifted back to the Pisan quarter to spend his hours with the lovely Circassian girl, and when the bells wakened them they talked aimlessly and he discovered that she was a Christian, captured by Muslims on the edge of Kiev and sold by them to a slave dealer in Damascus. There a Pisan trader, seeing no wrong in the transaction, had bought her for the caravanserai of his fonduk, where she entertained men from Europe or Persia. Like the Acre in which she worked she was content with current arrangements and joked, 'I've been sold four times and each was an improvement.' When she discussed the wars which loomed ahead she was actually gay, for she felt confident that she would survive. 'With a good chance of improving my fortune if things go well,' she added, and her optimism encouraged Volkmar. And so these two drifting, laughing people came to bed.

One morning when he was walking idly back to his lodging place he happened to pass through the fonduk of Genoa, now largely empty because of the war between Genoa and Pisa, and he discovered that a group of Jews, newcomers from France, had taken residence in one of the unused caravanserais. He had never really spoken to a Jew, nor had any of his ancestors, since that day in 1099 when Volkmar I had tried vainly to save some of the Jews found in Ma Coeur, but Gunter had slain them and for nearly two hundred years no Jew had lived there.

Having nothing better to do Volkmar wandered over to the newcomers, who had set up a dyeing plant which produced handsome fabrics, and began chatting with them in French. To his surprise one of the men, thin and with a dark beard, showed a willingness to talk–even an eagerness–and Volkmar lounged against a pillar and tried to discover why the Jew and his friends had adventured into Acre.

'This is our homeland,' the Jew explained.

'Where were you born?'

'Paris.'

'I should think Paris would be your homeland,' Volkmar suggested.

'This is the land of the Jews,' the bearded one said, tapping the stones of Acre.

Volkmar laughed. 'It's the land of the Italians, that much we know. And the Franks. And the Germans . . .' He hesitated.

'And the Arabs,' the Jew added laughingly. 'They seem to own more of it than anyone else.'

'In spite of this, you call it home?' Volkmar continued.

'Yes. All during my life in Paris we said each night, 'To next year in Jerusalem.' So one day I decided to come.'

'What is a Jew?' Volkmar asked, in sudden concern.

The dyer looked up from his work, wiped his hands and came to the knight. 'Maimonides says . . .'

'Who's Maimonides?'

'A great thinker . . . lived here in Acre in the last century.'

'Were there Jews in Acre . . . then?'

'Of course. Maimonides came here after fleeing from Spain.'

'Were there Jews in Spain?'

'Of course. After they were driven from the Holy Land they went to Spain.'

'Who drove them from the Holy Land?' Volkmar asked. He knew that his ancestors had killed enormous numbers but he had never heard . . .

The Jew ignored the question and said, 'Maimonides drew up a list of thirteen marks which identify the Jew. They are . . .'

'Why do you remember the rules? Are you a priest?'

The bearded Jew looked at the knight and smiled. For two centuries this Crusader's family had lived in the Jewish homeland, yet he did not know that Jews no longer had priests. The Jew made no comment, but returned to his list,

ticking off the marks on his fingers: 'A Jew believes in God. That He is one
alone, has no physical form, and is eternal. Only God may be worshiped, but
the words of His prophets are to be obeyed. Of these prophets Moses our
Teacher was greatest, and the laws which came to him at Sinai came directly
from God. The Jew obeys this law of Moses. He believes that God is all-
knowing, all-powerful. He believes in reward and punishment, both in this
world and hereafter. He believes that the Messiah will come and that then the
dead shall rise.'

'I believe most of that,' Volkmar said, 'Where's the difference?' The Jew
looked hesitantly at the Catholic church of SS. Peter and Andrew and was
inclined not to reply lest he offend the knight, but Volkmar sensing this said,
'Go ahead. I'm not a priest.'

The Jew moved closer, wiped his hands again and said, 'You believe that
God is three, that in the body of Jesus He took human form, and that in such
form God can be worshiped. We don't.'

Instinctively Count Volkmar drew away from the Jew. Blasphemy had been
spoken in his presence, and he suffered at the utterance of the intemperate
words. He was at first tempted to leave the man, run away, and then he, too, saw
the church at which he and Muzaffar had prayed, and it seemed strange that the
Christians could share a church with Muslims, whom they were fighting to the
death, but could not possibly do so with Jews, from whom Christianity had
sprung. He stemmed his impending flight and asked, 'Why do we hate you
Jews so deeply?'

The bearded one replied, 'Because we bear testimony that God is one. We
were placed among you by God to serve as that reminder.'

The discussion continued for some time, after which Volkmar walked
thoughtfully to his room in the Venetian fonduk. He sought out Muzaffar, and
they went together to pray, after which they ate in a house run by Italians from
a town near Venice. During the meal Volkmar asked, 'How do Muslims treat
Jews?'

'Muhammad was very just in his attitude,' the old trader answered, throwing
the end of his turban back as he prepared to drink wine. 'You know, of course,
that Muhammad had a Jewish wife.' The conversation continued with truths
and half-truths and Damascus folklore. It was Muzaffar's opinion that much
Islamic teaching had been borrowed directly from the Jews.

Acre grew increasingly hot, and each morning Volkmar said, 'Today I must
go home,' but he found excuses for discussing military matters with the leaders
of the religious orders, and there was the constant invitation of the Circassian
girl, long-legged and vibrant in bed, and he remained in the city, always hiding
from himself the real reason for his delay: he was finding intellectual pleasure in
his random conversations with the Jew at the dyeing vats. Of all the residents of
Acre in that vital, doomed summer only this Jew seemed to be contemplating
the universal problems of life and death, of God and the humility of man; and
Volkmar wanted to talk about these things.

'Do the thirteen rules of your Maimonides keep me from heaven?' he asked
one day.

'Oh no!' the Jew cried eagerly. 'While he was living here in Acre,
Maimonides said plainly, "God is near to everyone who turns to Him. He is
found by anyone who seeks Him and turns not aside."'

'You are more generous than we,' Volkmar replied.

'Maimonides also said, in a letter to a man much like you–a non-Jew who loved God–that this man was as much the charge of God as any Jew. He wrote, "If our descent is from Abraham, your descent is from God Himself."'

'Do you believe that?' Volkmar asked.

'I believe that you are the personal child of God, even though you spend your nights with the Pisan whore.'

Volkmar was tempted to strike the Jew, but he spoke with such authority that to molest him would be a sin. 'How do you know these things about me?' the knight asked.

'Because I have wondered who you were, what trouble haunts you,' the Jew said.

'Acre haunts me,' Volkmar replied. 'How long shall you and I be here?'

'Not long,' the Jew said. 'And when the Mamelukes storm through the gates'–he looked at the small stone gate leading into the deserted caravanserai–'you may perhaps escape. Not I.'

'Then why don't you flee Acre now?'

'Because this is my homeland,' the Jew replied.

That day there was no more talk, but on the next morning, as Volkmar wandered back from the Pisan fonduk, the Jew remarked, 'You and I look upon death with such different views that I wonder if you would care to see one of my manuscripts?'

It was a peculiar question, for the two halves did not seem to correlate, but Volkmar, having nothing better to do, assented and the Jew led him to a mean hovel which the Genoese had deserted at the beginning of their war with the Venetians, but the meanness was only external. Inside, the Jew's wife had made a clean, good home, along whose farthest wall rested a collection of manuscripts which even in that day were practically beyond price. The bearded Jew took down one and showed its pages to Volkmar, parchment leaves on which not Hebrew but Arabic letters had been beautifully written from right to left. Pointing to a special page the Jew said, 'These words are for you and me in this hot summer.'

Volkmar took the folio and read the remarkable passage in which Maimonides considered the case of Rhases, the cynical Arab who had written down a list of every evil thing in the world: war, famine, lust, betrayal, the Arab had listed them all, and at the end he had concluded that evil in the world outweighed good, that hope was irrational and that it would have been better if man had not been created. Volkmar laughed and said, 'Seeing the anarchy in this city I would agree with Rhases.'

The Jew took back the folio and read what Maimonides had replied to this reaction: '"Such reasoning stems from narrow parochialism. A man looks at his own fate, or at what happens to his friend, or at the disasters facing the whole human race, and he thinks: This is decisive in the vastness of things. Or a man finds that in his life unhappiness predominates, and he judges the universe from that experience."' The Jew's voice rose to heights of power as he thundered: '"But we are not the center of the universe, you and I, neither as individuals nor as the representatives of the whole human race. God's universe must be considered as one great whole composed of interrelated parts, and its majestic purpose is not the gratification of our puny selves."'

Impulsively Volkmar wrested the manuscript from the Jew and read the words with his own eyes. 'What do you call yourself?'

'Rabbi,' the Jew replied.

'And you are a follower of this Maimonides?'

'No. He was merely a Jew who once lived in Acre, no better than you or I, but more intelligent perhaps. I am a follower of God, Who is one, Who sees us as we stand here, Who has the future of this town in His hands.'

'I have been growing more hopeful, recently,' Volkmar lied. 'The crops are good. Trade's good. I've begun to think the truce will hold.'

'This city?' the rabbi laughed. 'With eleven armies and seven foreign policies? I don't worry about truce with the Mamelukes. I worry about truce with ourselves.' He shrugged his shoulders.

'Then why do you stay?' Volkmar pressed, and as he spoke, the great iron bell of SS. Peter and Andrew began tolling.

'Because this town, such as it is, is Eretz Israel.' The ponderous iron bell was joined by one of bronze pealing at a merrier tempo from the Coptic church.

'What do those words mean?' Volkmar asked.

'Maimonides explained it. "Eretz Israel, the land of the Jews, accepts no foreign nation or language. It reserves itself for its own sons." So your castle, even when the Mamelukes besiege it, can never be . . .'

'Don't!' the count cried, putting his hands over his ears to keep out words which he himself had uttered: the castle was not his home nor had the Crusaders made Palestine theirs by any sensible occupation; but as he stood thus with his ears covered, the bells of Acre began pealing from all directions and he realized that news of moment had arrived. He could hear clamor in the street and regardless of its significance he wanted to be with his own people; and he left the house of Judaism, so battered on the outside, so clean and perceptive inside.

He ran toward the Venetian quarter, where many were gathered while the bells rose to a paean of jubilation, and soon he saw knights running from the various quarters, shouting. 'The Crusaders have arrived!' And he joined the cheering, for there, rounding the Tower of Flies which protected the anchorage, came the fleet from Europe. At the critical moment, as had so often happened in Acre's history, substantial reinforcements were at hand.

As the bells danced in their steeples with noisy glee the first ship tied up to the Venetian dock, and Volkmar noticed an ominous fact: the captain and crew showed none of the elation customary at the end of this dangerous voyage. Mechanically, they tied the ropes and sighed as at the conclusion of a dirty business, and soon the knights of Acre were to understand why.

At Rome, Nicholas IV, the first Franciscan Pope in history, had hoped to make a name for himself by preaching a fiery Crusade that would finally wrest Jerusalem from the infidel, but he was unlucky in his timing, because none of the kings he had hoped to attract had any intention of leaving home. England, which in the past had provided many stalwart knights, offered no response whatever, for the English ruler was preoccupied with Scottish matters. In France, the birthplace of Crusaders, business was good and after the death of St Louis the French had lost all stomach for Jerusalem. Aragon was engaged in open war with the papacy, while relations between Genoa and Venice had again degenerated into warfare. From all the countries of Europe, Pope Nicholas had been able to find only one nest of volunteers, and these came not from knightly families but from a cluster of backward villages in northern Italy, so this culminating Crusade consisted not of warriors but of sixteen hundred illiterate peasants who knew nothing of Jerusalem and less of Acre.

When the gangplanks were lowered and the triumphant army straggled ashore, the citizens of Acre gasped. Slack-jawed men, bowed from toil in field and shop, the Italian peasants straggled onto the Holy Land. Without leadership, without any arms but knives and clubs, the riffraff landed, listened to the bells, stretched their still wobbly legs and asked, 'Where's the infidel?'

Through one of God's inscrutable stage directions, some of the mob fanning out through the city happened onto the church of SS. Peter and Andrew, where they entered to give thanks for their deliverance from the sea. As they knelt they saw in the chapel opposite the prostrate figure of the Damascus merchant, Muzaffar, praying at the little Muslim mosque. One of the Italians dashed back to the door of the church, screaming, 'The infidels are upon us!' on which the others unsheathed their daggers and lunged at Muzaffar, slashing him severely across the right shoulder. The startled Arab ran crying from the church, pursued by the Crusaders, whereupon others, seeing the Muslim with his sword arm covered with blood, concluded that the Arab had killed a Christian and leaped at him with their daggers and swords, and would have killed him had not Volkmar jumped forward to save the old man.

The local knights, apprehensive over what might develop if the peasants got out of hand, moved among the rioters and tried to calm them, but the crusading spirit was alive and they burst out of control, storming through the town, for on the day they had sailed from Europe they had been promised certain heaven if they killed an infidel, and they could see that the infidel was among them. 'Hold them off!' the leader of the Templars shouted, and his knights formed barriers while bells lent music to the confusion, but the mob swung unexpectedly to the north, where two Syrian priests happened to be leaving the church of St Mark of Antioch and their unfamiliar robes convinced the mob that here were infidels, and the two were slaughtered.

The massacre, that hot August day, was paralyzing. Armenian Christians whose families had lived in Acre for two centuries were slain. Mameluke ambassadors from Cairo, Mameluke emissaries in town to arrange trade treaties with the Venetians, were beheaded amid scenes of fire and cheering. Arab merchants on whom the prosperity of the city depended were stabbed to death, and churches which could not be easily identified as either Christian or Muslim were sacked. The delicate balance on which Acre existed, attained after so many decades of patient adjustment, was shattered in an afternoon.

At the height of the riot Count Volkmar thought of the improvised Jewish settlement in the fonduk of Genoa, and for reasons which he could not fully have explained he gathered some Templars and hurried there, only to find that the new Crusaders were storming through the place and screaming, 'Kill the Jews! They killed Jesus!' Volkmar rushed to the mean hovel in which the rabbi lived, but he arrived too late. The rabbi was dead. The manuscripts were burned.

The Italians, riotous with victory and still unaware of what they had accomplished, were finally herded into the Pisan quarter, where they sang Crusader hymns while the iron bell of SS. Peter and Andrew concluded its dirge. When they sought the king, so that he could praise them for their fidelity, some of the older knights began arresting the leaders of the mob, hoping that by delivering them to the Mamelukes disaster could be forestalled, but the Italians resisted arrest, crying, 'We were sent to kill Muslims and we've killed them. Take us not to jail but to Jerusalem.'

When news of the massacre reached Cairo the Mamelukes refused even to discuss resumption of the truce; ambassadors sent from Acre with apologies were allowed to die in prison. Any possible reason for allowing Christians to

remain in the Holy Land had been surrendered in the massacre, and St Jean
d'Acre must be finally eliminated. When this fiat reached the city the knights
knew that barring a miracle their days in the Holy Land were ended. 'Oh, God,'
prayed the surviving priests, 'why did those fateful ships not sink in the harbor
before leaving Italy?' And all inside the walls made preparation for the final
tragedy.

Count Volkmar, nursing a cut left arm which one of the new Crusaders had
given him as he rescued Muzaffar, summoned his men and prepared for the
doleful journey home, but before he left he felt that he must say good-bye to the
tall Circassian girl, so he climbed the stairs of the Pisan caravanserai, but found
there that the Italians had come upon this lively Christian as she wore a
Circassian robe and had of course slaughtered her. Gravely he bowed to the
other girls, then walked to the castle, where from the king's general he obtained
a basket of pigeons which he carried with him as he went to SS Peter and
Andrew for his final prayers. As the bells of the city pealed their litanies he led
his men out through the walls of Acre, that cherished city, that strange
abomination, and each man suspected that he would not again visit those walls,
those gleaming turrets that so captivated the imagination.

At Ma Coeur, Volkmar and his knights launched a day-and-night activity.
All peasants living outside the walls were ordered to make ready to move inside
and to bring their beasts, and when this was done, Volkmar told them, 'If any
are afraid, you may leave now.' A few Muslims headed south to join the
Mamelukes; but where could the Christians go, even if they so desired?

The knights were perplexed when Volkmar paid considerable attention to
brushwood, but without discovering his purpose they humored his whim and
directed peasants to lug large piles of the brush inside the castle walls. Other
men were let down on ropes to check the huge cisterns, thirty and forty feet
deep, and they reported that thanks to the secret well, the castle had enough
water to serve two thousand people for two years, should the siege last so long.
Comparable supplies of food were also in storage: fruits, nuts, dried fish and
meat, chickens, some pigs whose very shadows alarmed the Muslims, and
immense stores of grain. Few Castles in the Holy Land over the past two
hundred years had escaped sieges, and some had held out for thirty or forty
months unassailable behind their walls. But in those happier days there had
always been the assurance that sooner or later relief would come from Antioch
or Cyprus. But this time where would the rescuers be?

When supplies were checked Volkmar and his knights inspected the lines of
defense. The outer wall of the town no longer seemed so stout as when Gunter
of Cologne had built it two centuries before, but it was in good repair and was
protected by the glacis; if properly defended this wall could frustrate an enemy
for five or six days. The narrow alleys of the town also presented opportunities
for defense, and the mosque and the three Christian churches would provide
strong rallying points: indeed, the Basilica of St Mary Magdalene could be
converted into a minor fortress which ought to hold for several weeks. The
deep moat protecting the castle wall would be hard to cross, while the wall itself
was surely impregnable. Behind it rose the castle, a self-contained unit with its
own ponderous walls well able to withstand an enemy for months. And all was
in repair.

Satisfied on these points Count Volkmar next turned to the most difficult
question facing him: what to do with his wife and son? He assembled his
knights and said, 'If there is one who would prefer sailing from Acre, perhaps

to Germany . . .' The discussion had gone no further. The countess said that she had been born in the Holy Land, that her father had withstood seven sieges, and she four. And her son said, 'At Saphet I heard what the Mameluke captain said and at the Horns of Hattin young Volkmar stood with his father, didn't he?'

'He did,' Volkmar replied. He then asked, 'Do any of the knights prefer Acre?' None did, and the waiting began.

On a stormy morning in late February, 1291, the man on the watch-tower announced, not loudly nor with excitement, 'They are coming.'

Dispassionately the knights lined the battlements to inspect the Mamelukes as they rode easily up from the southern plains. There was no great dust, no shouting. The vast columns moved slowly for they felt no excitement; when they finished with Ma Coeur they would proceed to Acre and one siege was pretty much like another: generals stayed in the rear and half-naked foot soldiers went up against the walls. Any Ma Coeur peasants who happened to be working outside the town moved quietly within, except a handful who set off across the fields to join the Mamelukes. No one tried to prevent them.

By noon the purposeful column was nearing the walls of the town, but no one on either side fired arrows or launched spears. The impressive thing was that the columns kept coming forward in staggering numbers. 'There must be fifty thousand people down there,' one of the knights calculated. The figure was not unreasonable.

As soon as the horde was sighted, Volkmar went to the quiet room where he and Muzaffar had dined at the beginning of the truce, and he wrote to Acre:

A Mameluke army of considerable size is now approaching from the south. It seems to be accompanied by so many siege engines that I cannot believe they are all intended for Ma Coeur, so I suppose you must expect them next. All here is well, and we shall withstand until we have been slain on the last battlements. We shall send you the customary signals, but we do not expect your few knights to ride to our defense. To do so would be folly. May God bless us both in these hours of trial, and may He send divine rescue from some quarter that we cannot now perceive.

He carried the message to one of the keeps, where it was tied by a silken thread to the leg of a pigeon, which, as soon as it was released circled higher and higher above the castle until it established a reckoning, then sped for Acre.

All during the day the columns moved forward, the largest army Count Volkmar had ever seen, and at dusk his knights agreed that it must number well over a hundred thousand—while Ma Coeur had only some sixty knights and a thousand unarmed peasants. He posted his sentries, then went to bed and slept well.

For two days nothing happened, except that the Mamelukes sent their slaves fanning out across the countryside, chopping down all trees except olives, stripping the trunks and moving into separate depots both the resulting posts and the broken branches. At the same time the soldiers pushed up from the rear the great wooden engines of war, creaking noisily and moving slowly: the monstrous ballistas which could be cranked tight, then sprung to arch rocks of two hundred pounds into the castle compound; lighter sheitanis, the Satanic ones, for lighter loads; enormous swaying towers with retractable drawbridges which would be dropped across the walls of Ma Coeur; wooden bridges to throw over the moat; rams with bulbous iron heads to smash down gateways; ladders, scaling hooks, grapples and buckets for burning pitch; next, the most effective weapon of all, the mangonel, a rope-wound bow which required three men to operate and which, when sprung, released an arrow capable of crashing through the strongest shield; and finally, the most frightening, the slow-moving turtle creeping steadily forward as if it had a life of its own. In the days ahead the men on the battlements would come to know each of these weapons well, and already they held them in respect.

It was not only the presence of the engines that impressed the Crusaders; it was their astonishing number. Where an ordinary siege might have one tower, the Mamelukes had five, plus two dozen turtles, and so many horsemen they could not be counted. When all was in readiness the Mameluke general signaled by three white flags his desire for a parley, and in accordance with the custom of the age the gates of the town were opened, the drawbridge was lowered across the moat, and the main gate to the castle was thrown open to admit the general and six of his top assistants, who thus had a chance to study carefully the nature of the defenses they must finally subdue. With a kind of grim fascination Volkmar noticed that among the six were the mustachioed governor who had treated the pilgrims so graciously at Tabarie and the baldheaded man with the scar who had captained the garrison at Saphet. The Mamelukes looked straight ahead.

Their general was a short, red-faced man of forty, bearded and with long mustaches. He wore a turban beset with jewels, and no metal armor, but a costume of heavily quilted brocade richly adorned with gold and silver. His shoes were similarly decorated and came to sharp points that rose at the tip. He was armed with a short curved sword whose handle was encrusted with jewels, and he carried in his right hand an ebony baton, also bejeweled. He was a man of considerable importance and wished to get right down to work, for he had been given a terminal date by which Acre must fall and he wanted to waste no unnecessary days at the preliminary siege of Ma Coeur.

Count Volkmar mustered his knights in the courtyard so they could be seen, and directed peasants bearing lances to move about the other portions of the castle. Then he waited till the enemy general appeared, dismounted and approached, extending the hand of friendship. Volkmar took it. The men shook hands, whereupon the other Mamelukes dismounted. The leaders gathered at a table near the parapet and the Mamaluke spoke first, using Arabic, which he handled awkwardly.

'Our preparations you see. You wish to surrender? Now?'

'Under what terms?'

'Your peasants, Muslim, Christian, can stay. They'll farm their land as now,' the Mameluke began, and Volkmar smiled, thinking: They aren't going to make the same mistakes we made at the beginning. The little general continued, 'No knights killed. You select four. The rest become slaves.' At this Volkmar drew back, and the general concluded, 'You, your wife, your family and the four knights. Safe-conduct to Acre.'

Coldly, and with a courage he was not aware he possessed, Volkmar asked, 'The same safe-conduct that you gave the defenders of Saphet?'

The Mameluke general masked his anger– if indeed he felt any. 'Since then we learned,' he said.

'To each of your proposals, no.' Volkmar spoke without accenting any word.

'The sultan directed me. I must ask you a second time.'

'And I am bound by my conscience to answer for the second time, no.'

The red-faced Mameluke bowed. Contemptuously he surveyed the castle and the assembled knights. 'You may delay us perhaps one week.' He bowed again, and at the gate called back, 'No man up there will come through this gate alive.' And he was off.

Still he made no move. His mangonels were primed and his turtles were ready, but he spent two more days bringing the towers up to the walls of the fortress, after which he signaled for another parley; but when the gates were opened he did not ascend to the castle but directed an assistant to speak with the villagers, after which some sixty peasants followed him out through the gates. The Christians among them were started on their way to the slave markets of Damascus and Aleppo.

Shortly after dawn on the twenty-fifth of February the siege began. The fat general in the padded suit gave signal for his trumpeters to sound alarms, and the vast army inched forward, all engines moving at the same time toward the main gate and applying such a steady pressure that by mid-afternoon the enemy was within the walls of the town. Stunned by the failure of his outer defenses, which he had calculated could resist for at least five days, Volkmar ordered his troops to fight in the streets, where determined cadres occupied the mosque, the Roman and Maronite churches and the basilica, while their companions retreated across the bridge, which was raised behind them. All who did not make their way into the castle were methodically butchered by the Mamelukes, almost without passion. The invaders did not even bother to save attractive young girls for harems; they raped them in the streets, then slaughtered them. To prove to the defenders how mortal this siege was to be, Mameluke slaves were then given the job of beheading all corpses. The ballistas were cranked up and one by one the heads were lobbed into the castle compound, where Volkmar's men saw the grinning, rolling faces of their friends.

Count Volkmar retired to draft his next report to the men of Acre, and in it he reported his dismay at the easy collapse of the city wall:

It was a wall such as I have seen withstand an ordinary army for many days, and it was courageously defended, but the Mamelukes have summoned an army of a size not hitherto known in these parts. At first, our knights estimated them to be near a hundred thousand, but I thought more like sixty. Now we are agreed that they are more than two hundred thousand, with so many engines that they cast solid shadows. They will find our castle difficult indeed and I am not apprehensive about an early defeat. We pray to God each day, and to the sweet Jesus Christ who brought our ancestors to these shores.

And with this message the next pigeon was dispatched.

Of the four defenses upon which the castle depended—glacis, town wall, moat, castle wall—the first two had given way, but knights still controlled the three churches and the mosque. Early next morning the Mameluke general inspected the town and gave orders for the reduction of those four religious buildings, and before the sun was well up the attack began. At the same time slaves began throwing rubble into the moat at those points where the wooden assault towers would be hauled into position against the castle wall. Where the moat protected the main tower the outer edge of the moat was chopped away, forming a steep path leading to the bottom of the ditch, and down this path crawled, at a hauntingly slow pace, the ominous turtles.

They were low sheds, not more than three feet high and neither wide nor long, but of immensely strong construction. Under them miners, protected from rocks or Greek fire from above, could gnaw out a tunnel beneath the foundations of the main tower. An ordinary tunnel would be so narrow that when it opened on the other side of the tower, men crawling through could easily be killed as they emerged, but it was not an ordinary tunnel which the men beneath the turtles were digging.

To the edge of the moat were moved the largest ballistas, and when they were in position they began lobbing huge rocks into the castle buildings, and the Mamelukes cheered as one giant boulder crashed through the stone lacework of the grand hall, ripping away part of the wall. Next the mangonels were cranked up and their lethal arrows placed against the strings, and when the machine let go, the arrows winged with sickening force against the men of the wall, and if a defender was caught by such an arrow it went completely through him and he toppled backward from the parapet.

Count Volkmar's men were not powerless. When the slaves approached the moat to cast their rubble, arrows and rocks drove them back and many were killed; when the turtles tried to work their way into the bottom of the moat the defenders dropped large round rocks down the face of the wall, and the flange at the bottom would send the rocks careening through the massed troops, tearing away legs and arms. But their most effective weapons were the clay jugs of Greek fire—naphtha and sulphurous compounds, set ablaze by red-hot flints—that burned even on water and could be extinguished only by vinegar or talc. It blinded soldiers or burned away their faces, and constantly, from each round tower so carefully positioned by Gunter, a stream of iron-tipped arrows sped at any Mameluke who tried to approach the glassy-surfaced walls. At this point Count Volkmar decided to conserve his pigeons, so as midnight approached he directed his men to haul onto the highest tower of the castle a pile of brush, and he and his son climbed the winding stairs with a torch, throwing vast shadows on the rock; and they lit the brushwood in the ancient manner so as to signal throughout the hills of Galilee and across to Acre itself the fact that at the castle of Ma Coeur all was well.

The arrogant boast of the Mameluke general that he would invest the castle within a week had long since been proved empty: he had leveled the mosque; he had taken the Roman and the Maronite churches and had torn them down, but the Basilica of St Mary Magdalene still resisted, and at the end of the third week the siege had bogged down in the bottom of the moat, except for three towers that had been inched close to the main walls, where for the time being they rested, inactive. Each morning the ballistas would hurl great rocks and the mangonels would let fly their piercing arrows, but the siege seemed to have ground to a halt; so each night at midnight the count and his son sent the signal: 'The fires of Ma Coeur are still burning.'

But the miners were at work. Deep in the heart of old Makor, down below the level of the Roman times, below the potsherds of the Greeks and Babylonians, the Mameluke slaves were digging a tunnel under the main tower of the outer wall. As they inched forward, other slaves came behind bearing stout wooden props which they forced into position to support the tunnel. And at the close of each day one of the Mameluke captains entered the tunnel with a white string to measure how far the digging had proceeded, and when all were satisfied that it must have gone well beyond the inner face of the wall, the general ordered a huge cave to be widened under the tower foundations.

Now the miners dug rapidly, and hundreds of posts were lugged through the darkness to shore up the cave until the vast emptiness looked like a forest that had died. At this point all work ceased and attacks on the castle were halted, while the three white flags were once more prominently displayed, after which the red-faced Mameluke general and his assistants rode over the drawbridge and into the beleaguered fortress. Nodding gravely he dismounted and ordered the scar-headed captain from Saphet to stretch out the measuring string, while another drew with chalk the circumference of the underground cave. Then he said, 'Knight, our cave lies under this tower.'

Count Volkmar looked at the ominous circle and said, 'I believe you.'

'We have not yet moved in the brush,' the Mameluke said in his broken Arabic. 'We offer one last chance. Then the brush.'

'The terms?' Volkmar asked.

'As before.' There was a pause, 'Your answer?'

'As before.'

'Farewell. We shall not speak again.'

'Yes, we shall,' Volkmar contradicted. 'For when you get through that wall you must also get into the castle. And every night at midnight I shall speak to you with my signal fire. It will take you much longer than the week you said.'

The Mameluke made no reply, and that afternoon the defenders of the castle watched as long lines of slaves carried brush into the cave. But the torment of the digging had stopped, and in the quiet respite Volkmar dispatched one of his last pigeons, bearing fatal news that would be correctly interpreted in Acre:

> The basilica has fallen. The mining has ended, they have shown me the circumference of the cave under the principal tower, and the brush has been moved in. We wait in silence, but we cannot hope. The tower must fall, and then we shall be forced into the castle. Go to the church of SS. Peter and Andrew, the patrons of Galilee, and pray for us. We shall hold out for weeks but seek your plea for divine help.

That night the Mamelukes lighted the brush in the cave, and in a sighing, smoking fire the wooden posts began to burn away, producing a final blaze that heated the tower walls and cracked them, so that when the under-supports were gone the foundations began to collapse, and there came a shudder in the wall and a wild shouting from the Mamelukes as the long-impregnable tower of Ma Coeur came crashing down. Turbaned warriors leaped across the hot stones to drive the Crusaders away from the outer battlements and into the castle; but at midnight from the highest parapet the signal fire blazed forth, assuring Acre that all was still well.

Now came the grim days when the hand of defeat was close to the throat of the defenders, for the Mameluke general methodically directed his thousands of slaves to smooth out the stones of the fallen tower and to build a level road over which his huge wooden structures could be wheeled, along with the ballistas and the mangonels. Patiently the turtles were moved against the castle itself and miners began their laborious job of undercutting the gate, and with no display of haste or bitterness the Mamelukes proceeded to bite away at the foundations. The siege was now in its fifth week, and since the ballistas and sheitanis were closer, the Crusaders began to lose more men. Worst of all, throughout the day, throughout the night, those who survived could hear the tapping of the hammers and the picks far below them, while the castle's supplies of Greek fire diminished and had to be used more sparingly, so that the attackers grew more bold.

Now came the sickening part of the siege, the subtle, fearful whisper that could creep through the strongest walls of a castle and into the minds of everyone defending it. When this sound first arrived no man was exempt from fear; and later, no matter how casually he came to live with the sound, in the base of his mind there lurked always fear. It was the distant noise of pickaxe against stone, of men digging deep in the earth, and because they tapped against the fundamental wall the sound was carried through all the stones of the castle, not echoing madly as when a rock plunged through a roof, tearing all away with it, but insidiously, like the aching of a tooth that does not yet require pulling but which warns: 'This ache is not going to stop.'

How persuasive the sound became. The count would look at his wife, and she would say nothing, but he could see in her eyes the reflection of each tapping sound as it carried to her feet and up through her chair and into her brain. On some bright mornings, when the tapping stopped for a moment, the Crusaders would look at each other in alarm and then return to normal as the almost noiseless echo resumed.

So far the great rocks tossed skyward by the Mameluke engines had not penetrated the circular chapel, and here the countess and the women spent most of their days, contemplating the errors which had brought their men into this grave position and wondering as to what might happen in the last hours of the siege, for none had hopes that she would escape; the tapping was too insistent and too close. Countess Volkmar, leaving the chapel now and again to help care for the wounded, thought: It wouldn't have mattered if I had married into some other castle. They're all doomed. But I wish we'd sent Volkmar to Germany.

The boy, less susceptible than others to the psychological pressure of the tapping which echoed through the castle, busied himself about the inner ring of turrets, running from one group of defenders to the next, as the knights fought to keep back the giant wooden towers that seemed to inch forward by themselves and were now almost touching the outer faces of the wall. Several times in recent weeks men had been killed near where young Volkmar stood, and he must have known that his castle was doomed, but he displayed no fear. For him—as for his father—the best part of each anxious day came at midnight, when they climbed together to light the fires which always seemed at first to give only a feeble blaze but which in the end illuminated the countryside in an eerie light, disclosing the Mameluke tents in the olive grove and the rolling hills of Galilee.

At the end of the fifth week the besieging forces halted offensive operations and once more raised the three white flags, but this time the red-faced general took no part in the parley. He sent the Saphet captain, who said simply, 'The tunnel under your gate is ready for its brushwood. Do you now surrender?'

'Do you guarantee safe-conduct for all to the city of Acre?'

'Your family and four,' the scar-headed captain repeated. 'The rest sold as slaves.'

'No.'

The envoy turned abruptly and strode from the castle, making no boast about how quickly it would fall. That night the cave was set fire, and after the blaze had eaten away the supporting logs the gate towers swayed toward the Mamelukes, hesitated, then came apart and crashed grotesquely in the dust. The Crusaders retreated into the central keep while the methodical Mamelukes put their slaves to building the warm rocks into a roadway, and their engineers to the task of pushing the engines of war into position until turbaned faces could look almost into the narrow windows of the keep. The defenders had lost two cisterns and most of the animals but they still controlled the David Tunnel, and their remaining tower contained enough food to sustain them for months in case a miracle was on its way across the Mediterranean. But no ships were coming; the futile Italians had been the last gasp of the crusading effort, and they had destroyed, not helped.

So at the start of the sixth week the defenders of Ma Coeur were contracted into the final tight knot of men and women protecting themselves inside the enormous walls of the keep itself, and it would be only a matter of time until one of the great Mameluke engines was maneuvered against some door. So sure were the Muslims of victory that they no longer sent miners beneath the walls. Ma Coeur must now fall through sheer brute pressure.

It was fascinating, hideously fascinating, to watch the first wooden turtle edge forward to perform a new function. It crept ahead until the men beneath could place their hands against the keep. Rocks from above careened down the slanting walls and spurted outward, but the roof of the turtle was so constructed that the boulders skimmed across the top, killing men standing behind but not those crouching beneath. Next Greek fire was poured on the machine, but the Mamelukes had covered this turtle with the bloody hides of freshly slaughtered cattle, so the wood did not burn—and the flames were extinguished with vinegar. And when the turtle had crept into position ropes were passed back and lashed to one of the great assault towers, and by pulling from the turtle and pushing from behind the enormous engine was edged into position.

A crash. A scream. A cry of 'Over here!' and Crusaders rushed to intercept the Mamelukes who had stormed their way into the keep—twenty of them, forty, dropping down from the tower.

'Protect the gate!' Volkmar shouted, and knights converged suddenly from all sides, fighting the powerful invaders hand to hand; and gaspingly the forty-three Mamelukes were slain and the keep was spared: so that again at midnight the fires of Ma Coeur could be seen at Acre, where men prayed both for the defenders and for themselves.

Before dawn the defenders beat back that first enemy tower and toppled it into the courtyard, killing many slaves, but with daylight the Mamelukes moved forward two other turtles which in turn started drawing two new towers against the keep. But when these were in position no assault was made, for the turtles crept along the wall to new positions from which they drew up three additional towers, until the keep was ringed. 'They will come at us from all sides,' young Volkmar said, more with a boy's interest in mechanical things than with fear.

The castle priest, looking at the ominous towers, knew that this day must mark the end of the siege and he summoned Count Volkmar and his family to the roof, where they looked out upon the glorious fields of the Galilee, red and gold in their spring flowers. The olive trees in which the Mameluke had staked his innumerable tents, were silvery gray, and in the distance beyond the spires and minarets of Acre gleamed the blue Mediterranean. It was an April day, the kind that had always made the hearts of men glad in this region, and the priest told the knights and their ladies, 'Beloved children of Christ, we have come to the day when we shall meet God Almighty face to face. We have fought well. We have been crusaders of the spirit, and if there are among you those who ask, "Why has this tragedy overtaken us?" I cannot explain, but centuries ago that great man St Augustine, surveying a similar period, spoke thus to all who are perplexed: "For the world is like an olive press, and men are constantly under pressure. If you are the dregs of the oil you are carried away through the sewer, but if you are true oil you remain in the vessel. But to be under pressure is inescapable. Observe the dregs, observe the oil, and choose, for pressure takes place through all the world: war, siege, famine, the worries of state. We all know men who grumble under these pressures and complain, but they speak as the dregs of oil which later run away to the sewer. Their color is black, for they are cowards. They lack splendour. But there is another sort of man who welcomes splendor. He is under the same pressure, but he does not complain. For it is the friction which polishes him. It is the pressure which refines and makes him noble.'''

As the priest finished these words the Mameluke general waved his ebony baton and the final pressure against Ma Coeur commenced, but with an additional terror for which the Crusaders were not prepared. The mangonels and sheitanis they knew, and when the latter began lobbing bundles of burning fagots onto the roof Count Volkmar helped his men throw down the fiery embers, but in addition to these ordinary machines the Mamelukes had brought a special weapon: a corps of drummers banging nearly a hundred drums of various sizes and constructions, all with animal skins drawn tightly across reverberating heads, and as the soldiers and the slaves began their final push against the walls these drums thundered a wild beat of encouragement and gave us a sense of inevitability to the stormy scene, while from the captured basilica bells clanged furiously to mock the doomed Christians.

In the first terrifying burst of sound Count Volkmar ran back to the center of the roof, where the priest and the women waited, and throwing himself on his knees, cried, 'Good Father, bless us now,' and above the throbbings of the drums the priest intoned his last benediction: 'Forgiving Jesus,' his thin voice came, scarcely audible above the thunder of drum and bell, 'accept our souls this day. In our castle we have been a Godly family and each man has trusted his brother. We have fought as we can, and in our last hour we find great love in the presence of each other. King Jesus, accept us as we are.'

From behind came a cry: 'They are upon us!'

The fight was hideous. Each of the five towers crawled with archers who fired point-blank at the Crusaders, often from a distance of inches, while powerful Mameluke swordsmen, intoxicated by the drums, leaped like animals from the towers and swept the turrets with their scimitars. This day there were to be no prisoners, not even women to be sold as slaves, for the general had determined to wipe from the earth this annoying castle.

Count Volkmar would have preferred making his last stand on the ramparts, but the wildly charging Mamelukes forced him below, and with the increased tempo of the drums echoing in his ears he found his wife standing quietly with her son, keeping his hand in hers lest he join the battle. 'Let the boy fight with me,' the count cried and he stooped to lift a sword from the hand of a dead knight, and while he was in this position three Mamelukes leaped into the room and stabbed him many times, so that he fell forward without having struck a blow. His death prevented him from seeing the Mamelukes swarm upon his wife and son, after which they sought out the inner rooms, launching a systematic slaughter of the remaining women. As this was happening the first group of drummers climbed the towers and came into the keep, where, over the dead Volkmars, they beat out their triumphant rhythms while bells clanged brazenly from all remaining steeples. Thus ended the Crusades at Ma Coeur. In blood the iron men of Germany had come and in blood they went.

At midnight, in gruesome jest, the round little general ordered the signal fires of Ma Coeur to be lighted, and they flamed as in the past and were hopefully seen at Acre, but in the silent morning, when the great engines of war were needed no more, the general ordered that Ma Coeur be leveled: 'No tower here will ever again cause us trouble.' The slaves began, stone by stone, to throw down the turrets and to destroy this most powerful of the small Crusader castles. Work on which Gunter of Cologne had spent years was destroyed in days, and when it was clear that slaves could be trusted to complete the task the red-faced general ordered the mangonels and the ballistas and the turtles and the walking towers to be moved westward until they reached the walls of Acre, where the miners resumed their patient underground tapping until the sound echoed ominously throughout that city.

At Ma Coeur the slaves continued their work for the better part of a year, disassembling the castle as children might break apart a toy. Many of the larger stones were hauled away to build new Mameluke castles and smaller ones were broken and scattered over the landscape. The well shaft was filled in, and shortly there were no towers and no walls to betray where the castle had stood. The slaves withdrew and the spot was desolate. The once-lovely fields were barren and remained so; the ancient olives were untended and no human being lived where the town had existed for so long.

On his yearly trip in the winter of 1294 Muzaffar, a one-armed Arab still operating caravans out of Damascus, had difficulty identifying the mound of Ma Coeur, for the Galilee was covered with snow. He found the location only by spotting the roadway which had always climbed the hill to the zigzag gates, and here he halted his camels for a moment, bowing in reverence to the knight who had saved his life. 'Poor men,' he whispered when his prayers were done. 'They knew nothing of the land they occupied, so they built huge walls to lock reason out.' And he plodded his way westward to ruined Akka, where no bells rang and where the harbor was silting up.

In summer searing khamsins from the now treeless hills blew across the plains, bringing minute dust which eddied into the crevices, imperceptibly solidifying the fallen mass and slowly covering it. In 1350, half a century after the fall, numerous rocks were still evident, and shepherds remembered that there had been a castle; but by 1400–a century after the annihilation–only a few rocks were visible and people were beginning to forget what they pertained to.

Now the only visitors to Makor–for the Frankish name was forgotten, having passed into history with the last of the Volkmars–were jackals, which sent forth their strange, penetrating howls when the moon was full, and which picked over the area for things that might be trapped in their swift rush. Birds flew over the mound and sometimes nested among the last of the whitish rocks strewn haphazardly in the dunes of sand. There were snakes and toads coming up from the malarial marshes that had taken the place of the irrigated fields which for twelve thousand years had fed the people of Makor. And there were a few rodents seeking for the wheat which once again grew wild.

By 1450 the wind had moved enough blowing earth into the area to cover completely every sign of human occupancy, and there were now none who recalled the name by which the place had been known. In fact, it had neither name nor visible existence. It was a mound rising from the foothills of the Galilean mountains, grass grew upon it and flowers, and three or four times a year some camel caravan from Damascus passed on its way to Akka–now a dismal port town in no way distinguishable from the other rotting towns along the once-noble Phoenician seacoast.

By 1500 the mound was higher and the obscurity greater. There was then probably no living human being who knew that Makor had ever existed or where Ma Coeur, that notable stronghold of the Crusaders, had stood. Historians and archaeologists had not yet begun to tantalize themselves with such concerns, but of course the name did continue to exist in that ancient list of towns, and occasionally some Christian scholar in Bologna or Oxford would idly speculate on where Makor, like the other vanished cities of the past, might have stood, while Talmudic scholars remained familiar with the name Rab Naaman of Makor but not with the village from which he came. For all practical purposes the name and the mound were lost. Only the olive grove existed.

Winds blew in from the desert. Inch by inch the tell grew, and the solitude increased. The silent mound slept beneath the sun, hiding the sweet well that through ten thousand years had brought life to so many. Its waters trickled away through subterranean channels until they entered the malignant swamp which extended itself year after year over the no longer fertile ground. How great the desolation was, how crushed and puny the grandeur that had existed here. Even the birds came no more, for the grasses that had grown centuries before now perished in the desiccated air; the mound had become part of a desert.

This land of richness and great orchards. This land where bees had made a honey famous before the Bible was composed. These far, sweet lands that had gladdened a man's heart and made his wife sing. These sacred valleys where men had wrestled with the concept of God, and with God Himself. These marvelous hills where the baals had stood and the fair girls had danced naked, all slept under dust.

How contradictory it was: the swamps spread, wasting their waters, while at the same time the land became desert for want of water. Occasionally a tribe of Bedouins would sweep through the area, senselessly killing any farmers who might be trying to revive the soil, then passing on. Their coming was meaningless and their going was unrecorded; and the mournfulness of the land increased.

Then, in the early 1500s, a few men and their families began returning from the far ends of the Mediterranean and from ports in between. They were Jews, and they came not to Makor, from which they had sprung but of whose existence they knew nothing; they came to Safed, seventeen miles to the east, and a new cycle was begun which would later encompass Makor, too.

LEVEL III

The Saintly Men of Safed

Found at Makor–Menorah made of gold in accordance with
instructions laid down by God in Exodus 25: 31–40. Cast by
Moorish workmen in Avaro, Spain, about 1240 C.E., during the
period when Judaism was still permitted in that kingdom.
Deposited at Makor June 21, 1559 after sunset.

It was an age of expansion. Constantinople, under Ottoman rule since 1453,
was offering Europe such riches drawn from India and China as to make the
dreams of Marco Polo seem unimaginative. Columbus had presented the world
with a new hemisphere to balance the old, and daring Portuguese navigators
were proving that cargo ships could reach the wealth of Asia by doubling the tip
of Africa. Spain was amazing Europe with the wealth of Aztec and Inca, and all
the world's horizons were being expanded so that the center of power was no
longer the Mediterranean; for on the Atlantic hitherto unimportant nations
suddenly found themselves possessed of empires so enormous as to be
indescribable. Even a trivial kingdom like England, beset on three borders by
hostile Scots, Welsh and Irish, could visualize acquiring territory a thousand
times larger than itself, while the Dutch were about to prove that they could
establish commercial stations wherever their daring captains located safe
anchorage and fresh water.

It was an age of intellectual discovery. From the cellars of forgotten
monasteries, from the long-unused libraries of princes, and most often from
Arabic scholars who had preserved the wisdom of the west, the books of
Aristotle and Thales, of Plato and Euclid were rescued from the past to astonish
men and enlarge their concepts. Dante and Boccaccio reminded a forgetful
world of Virgil and Ovid, while the glories of Sophocles and Seneca awakened
new appreciations of the drama. And not only was the intelligence of the past
being discovered; each ship returning from Java or Peru brought with it,
packed among the spice and silver, fresh discoveries of the mind, and thus the
way was prepared for that succession of world-changers who followed
Gutenberg, Copernicus and Galileo.

It was an age of religious explosion. For centuries Christian Europe had been
united into one all-embracing Church, devout, competent and far-seeing.
Recently Christians had been inspired by two victories: the expulsion of Islam
from Spain and the first conversions of the Aztecs; now there was reason to
hope that millions in Asia and Africa would join the Church, since missionaries
of great dedication were on their way to these areas. For a brief moment it was
logical to believe that the known world might soon unite under the leadership
of Rome. And then Martin Luther strode with rude and giant steps across the

boundaries of Europe, awakening men like Calvin and Knox who would destroy old associations and establish new.

It was an age of political invention. City states gave way to national units and barons surrendered to kings who found their support in the new middle class. Secular governments displaced religious as leaders began to study Machiavelli instead of Thomas Aquinas. The barbarians from the north were finally brought under control and Europe, having expelled the Muslim Arabs from Spain, now girded to fight back the Muslim Turks as they threatened the approaches to Vienna.

It was an age of growing freedom. Men who rebelled against the confinement of Europe were now free to try America and Asia. Any who had chafed under papal rule were welcome to adopt Lutheranism, and peasants who had silently borne the tyranny of landlords were now free to attempt a revolt. Law courts were strengthened and in the realm of writing and art men could break away from medieval restriction to follow Petrarch or Michelangelo. Each year brought new horizons, for this was the age of freedom.

But not for the Jews. In 1492, after more than seven hundred years of faithful service to Spain, the Jews were expelled from that state. They fled to Portugal, where they were scourged, forcibly baptized and later exiled. In Italy and Germany they were forced into inhuman quarters where they wore inhuman costumes. At almost rhythmic intervals they were charged with murdering Gentile children for blood to be used at Passover. They were accused of poisoning wells, of spreading cholera, of knowing how to infect rats with the plague to decimate Christian communities; and they were particularly accused of posing as Catholics, accepting the holy wafer of communion and hiding it slyly under their tongues until they could produce it for blasphemous black masses. In an age of growing freedom they were constantly restricted as to where they could move, what they could wear and especially what occupations they could engage in.

In this golden age of discovery the Jews discovered only the rope and the fagot. Each time a Jew was accused of having murdered a Christian child—and never once was the charge substantiated—some Jewish community would be wiped out in one ghastly slaughter. Each time a crime occurred near a Jewish quarter, that district would be stormed by indignant Christians and its inhabitants burned alive. And throughout the Christian world, come Holy Week, the friars would preach such sermons against the Jews that the enraged churchgoers would storm from their cathedrals to kill and maim any Jews they met, thus hoping to honour Him who had been crucified on Good Friday and risen in resurrection on Easter.

Why did not the Christians, since they held supreme power, simply annihilate the Jews once and for all? They were restrained because Christian theologians had deduced from passages in the New Testament the ambivalent theory that Jesus Christ would not return to earth bringing with Him the heavenly kingdom until all Jews were converted to Christianity, but at the same time 144,000 unconverted Jews were needed to be on hand to recognize Him and bear witness to His arrival. On this ambivalent theory two courses of action had been built: Jews must be converted; and those necessary few who refused must be kept in such obvious misery that all who looked could see what happened to people who denied Jesus Christ. So the Jewish districts multiplied, the harsh laws increased, and each year the Jews suffered unbelievable repressions. It was as if the Church kept them alive to remember the coming of the Messiah, the way a man keeps an aching tooth in his head to remind him of mortality.

In only two ways did Jews share in the expanding spirit of the age: they were still encouraged to serve as moneylenders, which enabled them to keep alive; and in 1520 in Venice a printer struck off a complete printed copy of the Talmud. So bitter had been the Christian hatred of this Jewish masterwork, so often had it been burned by the authorities in Italy, Spain, France and Germany, that when it was finally put into type only one manuscript copy was known to exist. It was by a miracle that this summary of Jewish knowledge was saved . . . and the Venetian printer who thus rescued the law of Judaism was a Christian.

But in those dark days, when the Jews of Europe sighed at the stake and smothered in their districts without any moral protest from the Christian world, one gleam of hope began to shine from a most unlikely quarter: the inconspicuous hillside town of Safed in Galilee.

I

Rabbi Zaki the Shoemaker was a fat Jew, and this was his undoing.

In the Italian seaport of Podi, where he had taken residence after his marriage in 1521, the coming of spring brought moments of anguish to Jewish men who were overweight, because starting in March they could feel the eyes of their Christian neighbors probing their rolls of fat and calculating whether Zaki was fatter than Jacopo or Jacopo slightly fatter than Salman; and each man and his family began to worry. Nevertheless, the calculations continued, and as the twenty-first of March approached, the apprehension of the fat Jews became very real indeed, and each family asked in secret, 'Will our father be chosen this year?'

Rachel, Rabbi Zaki's wife, really had no cause for uncertainty, because Zaki was so gross that he was automatically selected, year after year. It was only a question of which five additional Jews would be chosen as his teammates, so that Rachel, freed from the calculations that tormented the other wives, could spend her whole energy castigating her unfortunate husband.

'Why are you so fat?' she plagued him throughout the year. 'Moses isn't fat. Is Meir fat like you?' She had lived with Rabbi Zaki for twenty years and had come, not without cause, to the conclusion that he was a poor specimen of manhood. He did not provide well for his family. He never charged enough for his shoemaking, allowing clever Italians to outwit him. And it was obvious now that he was not going to become a famous rabbi leading his congregation to fame. He was merely a fat man who most of the year seemed pathetic, and in March positively degraded.

The Jews of Podi were a close community, for during the expulsion of 1492 they had fled in a body from Spain to Portugal and then–after the shocking mass baptism ordered by the Portuguese government–from Lisbon to Italy. In the strictest sense Rabbi Zaki, his sharp-tongued wife, Rachel, and all the Jews of Podi were Christians, for they had been forcibly baptized–some bleeding from the mouth, some screaming–in Portugal; but a series of considerate Popes had decreed that the Christian Church could not accept the fruits of such baptism and that the Jews of Podi were therefore free to revert to their original religion, which was after all an offshoot of the Holy Bible. The generous Duke of Podi had welcomed them as industrious merchants who brought much income to his territories and had even encouraged them to have their own synagogue, so that gradually the persecution of Spain and Portugal were forgotten in the kindlier atmosphere of Italy.

One of the leading merchants of Podi was Avramo the redhead, Rabbi Zaki's father-in-law, and as the Jews of the port looked at their pathetic little rabbi they often wondered how he had been able to catch the merchant's daughter. Rachel had hoped for a better marriage than hers had turned out to be, for, as she frequently reminded both her father and her husband, 'I knew even before we were married that Zaki would amount to nothing.' But her father had argued, 'I think Zaki will become a fine rabbi, and you should be honored that he takes you as his wife.'

But Rachel was not honored. As a child in Portugal she had known Zaki as the fat one whom the others teased, and as an adolescent girl she had watched him grow even fatter, so that none of her friends looked on him with longing. Left alone, he had read Talmud and apprenticed himself to an Italian shoemaker, who had warned his parents, 'You're wasting your money. Zaki has such fat fingers he'll not be able to hold the nails.' Still the amiable fellow had managed somehow to become both a rabbi and a shoemaker.

The Jews of Podi were never able to understand why a man like Avramo had agreed to give his daughter to such a clod, and when in later years Rachel herself raised the question, he explained, 'When I looked at Zaki's fat face and rolling eyes I knew that he was a good man, and good men make good husbands.'

The wedding had gone forward, and Rachel found herself tied to a man of no distinction who each March brought upon himself and his family an almost unbearable disgrace. 'Why do you eat so much?' she screamed at him with increasing desperation as the years passed. 'Does Meir eat like a pig, day after day? Tell me that.'

Zaki could only reply, 'God must have wanted me to be fat.' He was an amiable hulk, a man who loved his shrewish wife, adored his three daughters and found joy in eating with his family and fulfillment in serving as a rabbi. Since he was a short man, enormously round, none need envy him and all could find amusement in him. What they saw was a kind of gelatinous good will, an oleaginous buffoon of the spirit. He did not consciously make himself ridiculous, but since he knew that he was so, he did not fight against his nature.

'God wanted someone He could laugh with in the afternoon,' he told his wife one day.

'He got someone the whole town laughs at each spring,' she stormed.

'I didn't make myself fat,' he said weakly.

'You did, too!' she cried. 'For years you've been eating like a pig.'

'Rachel,' he pleaded. 'Not that word.'

'I withdraw the pig,' she snapped.

'But you are fat,' his unlovely daughter Sarah complained.

'I am the rabbi,' he said quietly. 'Even if I were as thin as Meir, the Christians would still choose me.'

The idea—a new one that Rabbi Zaki had developed subconsciously at that moment—hit his wife with some force and she stopped feeling sorry for herself. She looked at her grotesque husband and for a fleeting second half understood the point he was making, but even as he spoke he had fish sauce on his jowls and his logic was destroyed.

'Go ahead!' she lamented. 'Eat and grow fat and make us ashamed of you.' The girls wept.

In humiliation Zaki listened to the grieving, then said, 'They will choose me again, and again you will stand in the sun and watch me, and there is no escape. But they choose me because I am the rabbi, and I think it is better that I am fat and that they laugh at me because of my fatness and not because I am the rabbi. Would you have it otherwise?'

Of course they chose him. For several hundred years the dukes of Podi had provided sport for the community by assembling, at the spring equinox, a carnival of mountebanks, jugglers, fools and dancers. There was gaiety for one day, even if it fell in the midst of Lent, and in recent years the climax was reached by the race between the fat Jews and their next-street neighbors, the town prostitutes. For this race, which had grown famous in eastern Italy, the six fattest Jewish men were chosen, stripped down to a pair of thin underpants and driven barefoot to the starting line, where they took their places among the frowzy, boisterous whores.

The excitement of the race, which drew thousands of people from towns as far distant as Ancona, arose not only from the joy of seeing the fat Jews puffing nearly naked through the streets while the populace threw things at them—not hurtful things like rocks, for that was forbidden, but harmless items such as eggs and chicken feathers smeared with honey—but also from the fact that the little pants which the fat Jews had to wear were so constructed that along the route there was always a chance for the Christian women to get a fleeting glance at what the mysterious rite of circumcision did to a man.

To the Jews, nakedness in any form was humiliation, but to run in the Podi pants, with the penis popping in and out, was abhorrent. Not only Rachel, but the other wives as well, and Jewish men who did not run, wept for Israel.

In 1541 the twenty-first of March was a hot, bright day, and during the morning hours the mountebanks and jugglers did good business. Members of the ducal family moved austerely through the crowd, nodding somberly as townspeople assured them, 'This year it's to be a fine race.' In the mid-afternoon there were games of football and the offering of free drinks, ending with a horse race through the streets and across the public square. It was a day of relaxed festivity, much relished in the midst of Lent.

But it was the late-afternoon spectacle that the people wanted, and toward five o'clock the town constable aroused cheers by bringing from the jail six notorious prostitutes, assuring them that any who finished within the first three places would have the remainder of their jail sentences remitted. 'But to win,' he warned them with broad winks, 'you must pull and trip the fat Jews or they will finish ahead of you.' The six bawds said they understood.

The crowd cheered the girls and began betting on them, but everyone waited for the real contestants; and at five, when the first sunset of spring began to throw gold on the cross of the cathedral, the duke ordered a bugler to sound the trumpet. Now the crowd roared and formed a path which led to a roped-off section of the piazza. A hush fell over the rabble as the Duke of Podi signaled to the cathedral, out of which issued a stunning procession of clergy dressed in the vestments of the Christian Church. Impressive both in detail and mass the body of clerics moved in regal fashion across the piazza, taking its position beside the improvised ducal throne. Again the trumpeter blew, and again the crowd cheered, for from a narrow lane leading to the Jewish quarter came a motley crowd led by six men in long brown robes, each marked by a bright yellow star.

In the lead was Rabbi Zaki, ridiculously fat, a man not over five feet three inches tall and weighing at least two hundred and twenty pounds. His bare feet padded across the stones and his dunce's cap, tall and red, bobbed in the late sunlight. The mere sight of him caused the mob to shout with joy. Behind the racers, each sick with apprehension, even though the brown cloaks still covered them, came the entire population of the ghetto, for each Jew unless he were near death and excused by a Dominican friar was required to witness the humiliation of his people.

The contestants were led to where the six prostitutes waited, and one of the girls elicited shrieks of approval when she pulled Rabbi Zaki's robe apart, peeked at his trousers and screamed, 'I saw it.' She made an indecent gesture to the crowd. Rachel and her three daughters, who had been herded into the front ranks of the Jewry, kept their eyes on the ground, but a barefooted friar in charge of the Jews shouted that they must look up. The girls did so in time to see their ridiculous father stripped of his robe, so that he stood almost naked in the fading sunlight while the crowd shrieked with delight.

The duke himself addressed the contestants: 'This is to be a fair race three times around the piazza, down the Corso and back to the cathedral. Any girl who finishes in the first three will have her sentence excused.' At this the crowd cheered. 'But if any Jew finishes in the first three he is granted privileges for one year. Race well. Ignore the crowd. And I shall wait for you at the finish.' He bowed handsomely to the racers, signaled the trumpeter and retired.

At a sign from the Dominican, prostitutes and Jews started running, and a gasp of joy rose from the crowd when one of the fat Jews fell right at the start. 'Clumsy! Idiot!' they screamed, pelting him with vegetables. He stumbled to his feet and tried to overtake the others. With outrageous irrelevancy Rachel thought: Thank God it wasn't Zaki.

Three times around the piazza the racers went, with prostitutes screaming and the six fat Jews silent. The audience, having cheered the start, was quiet now, waiting for something memorable, the Christian women watching dry-lipped as the inadequate pants flapped open and shut. Then it happened. Rabbi Zaki was in second place when one of the whores leaped forward, clutched at his pants and pulled them down about his knees. His fat legs, completely incapable of stopping, tangled themselves in the cloth and he went tumbling across the stones, skinning his knees and exposing his nakedness.

'Whoever that girl is,' the duke cried, 'set her free, whether she wins or not.' The crowd, staring minutely at every motion of the fat rabbi in recovering his pants, cheered and whistled. Zaki, hurt and far behind the others, tried to withdraw, but the Dominican poked him and informed him that he, like all the others, must finish the course.

Down the Corso, Zaki went, then back toward the cathedral; but as the runners re-entered the square the same girl pulled down the pants of another of the Jews, and the race ended in an obscene scramble, with firecrackers exploding, music playing and the crowd screaming its approval. Minutes after the others had finished Rabbi Zaki waddled up to the cathedral door.

Along with the five other racers he was handed his brown robe and red dunce's cap. Dressed thus, he was shepherded into the cathedral, where the Jews of the community were assembled on wooden benches set off from the rest of the church by rope, and while the citizens of the town and many from outlying villages–for their small locales provided no such spectacles–crammed in to stare at the Jews and surround them with hostility, the prelates of the Church assembled and took their places on a wooden platform. The duke and his escorts went to other specially erected seats and all listened as a haggard friar began a conciliatory sermon intended to show the Jews the glories of a gentle and forgiving Christianity.

'You swine, you pigs, you filth of the gutters,' he shouted at them, 'you abominations, you unspeakable dogs of the outhouse why do you persist in your contumacy? With your hooked noses you smell out the filth of the world and are content to lie in darkness and wallow in your own defecation. Your women are all whores. Your men are circumcised criminals. Your daughters are the bawds of the nation. You are the Anti-Christ and your sons shall perish in eternal hellfire. Why are you so obdurate?' For twenty minutes the friar, whose job it was to convert the Jews to a higher form of religion, hurled at them thunderbolts of scorn and poured over them the vials of his abuse. No crime was too contemptible for them to have committed, no malpractice too abominable for them to wallow in. It was a sermon that was being preached throughout the Christian world in those years and it was based upon a perverse logic, for with each fresh insult the Jews, roped together in their special area, knew that what the fiery man said was preposterous, and they concluded that if his Church were as ignorant of Judaism as he was, there was truly no sense in listening to its plea for conversion. If the Jews of Europe had had even the slightest inclination toward apostasy, their obligatory attendance at the yearly conversion sermon would have hardened their hearts against it.

Now the friar came to the second part of his plea: 'You argue in the filth of your despair that God is one, whereas we know that He is three. How can you be so blind? So stupid? So contumacious? Why do you persist in holding to your Old Book when we have proved that it is faulty? Why do you refuse to accept the glorious New Book, which clearly contains the truth? God is three and all the world proclaims this fact. Can you not see that your Old Book was given you only temporarily so that the way might be prepared for the true words of the New? Why do you cling to your error? Why?'

And every Jew sitting by sufferance in the cathedral that day knew that he persisted in his error, his oftentimes fatal error, because he had been taught from the days of Abraham and Moses and Elijah that God is one, indivisible, alone and unknowable.

From the pulpit the friar now launched into the final portion of his sermon, using at last the soft voice of reason: 'Come, Jews, who were once Christians, come back to the true Church while there remains a chance. Forswear your error. Surrender your blindness. Come back with singing hearts to that seamless robe where you will find peace and gentleness and love.' He paused. From inside the roped-off section faces of stone stared back. The friar, seeing the obdurate Jews and sensing their unwillingness even to listen, decided to remind them of the special condition in which they lived. 'You are not ordinary Jews, men and women of Podi,' he began quietly, 'you are people upon whom the baptism of Christ once rested. You are people who have gone astray, and unless you return quickly to the fold events of a terrible nature are bound to overtake you.' His voice rose to a dreadful, premonitory wail: 'For if you do not return to the Church you will be dragged into the cellars to taste the rope, the fagot and the choking water. Your bodies will be broken and your hearts torn with anguish. The peace that I offer you this day will no longer be available, and you will march across the piazza not in the spirit of friendly sport as you did this day, but bearing a fiery brand which will be used to light the fires which will consume you. Fiends, idiots, sons of hell–repent now. Join the true Church now. Abjure the blasphemies of Moses and the old ways. Now, now!' He ended in a paroxysm of religious fervor, and Rabbi Zaki, who knew something of these matters, was terrified.

That night, after Rachel had belabored him again for being so fat and for having allowed the whore to tear down his pants in the race, Zaki started to speak seriously of his fear, but at this point his daughters took up the complaint and insisted that by next spring he lose his weight and not humiliate them. The sorely tried man was tempted to bang the table and cry, 'We are not talking about humiliation! We are talking about our lives.' Instead, he waited for his womenfolk to complete their condemnation, which he knew they had a right to deliver–for they were wounded in spirit–and when they were done he said quietly. 'The friar meant what he said. We shall be allowed a few more years. Then the burnings will begin.'

'Zaki!' his wife snapped. 'Are you an idiot?'

'I am saying what I know to be true. We must leave Italy this week.'

'What do you mean, burning?' his wife heckled. 'Because you are so fat that you fell down? Because the friar made his usual ugly speech? You grow suddenly afraid?'

'I am desperately afraid,' Zaki acknowledged. 'That angry man meant what he said.'

'Where would we go?' Rachel demanded. 'Tell me, where?'

Zaki lowered his voice, looked about the room and said, 'Salonica. There is a letter from a German Jew who fled to Salonica, and he says that the Grand Turk . . .'

'To Salonica!' his wife repeated. She began laughing hysterically and pointing at her daughters. 'Do you think I want them to marry Turks?'

Zaki waited for his wife's contempt to die down, then said quietly, 'Rachel, we are in trouble. I think we should sail for Salonica immediately.'

This was too much for Rachel. She rose from her chair, stormed about her husband's mean shop and cried, 'Has not the Pope himself assured us that we can live peaceably in Italy for as long as we wish? Are you a coward that you doubt his promise?'

'This Pope promised. The next Pope can revoke,' Zaki argued carefully.

'But he gave the promise because he knew that we were baptized forcibly. We were never true Christians, and like the good man he is he has allowed us to be Jews again. I do not wish to go to Salonica. I refuse.'

'Rachel,' the fat rabbi pleaded, 'you asked me if I was a coward? Yes, I am. I listened to that man today and he was on fire. He sounded like the priests of Spain and Portugal. He will not rest until Jews like you and me are burned. Rachel, listen!'

But Rachel would not listen, and she refused to permit her daughters to listen, either. Tormented by that day's confusions the rabbi's family went to bed, but he did not, and in the morning, after prayers, he went to the ducal palace, where he waited for five hours until the duke allowed him to enter. 'I want permission to take a boat to Salonica,' Zaki said.

'What!' the duke exploded. 'You want to leave?'

'Yes,' Zaki replied.

'But why?'

'I am afraid.'

'Of what? Zaki,' the duke laughed thinly, 'you mustn't worry about the fun yesterday. We meant no harm. As for the girl who tore down your pants, the jailer put her up to it. Women are curious about these things, you know.' He chuckled at the harmless teasing. 'Zaki, we meant no offense. There's nothing for you to be afraid of.'

'But I am afraid.'

'All right! Next year you won't have to race.'

'It's the sermon I'm afraid of.'

'That?' the duke laughed. 'We have to do that. Once a year. Pay no attention to him. I rule this city.'

'Excellency, the friar meant what he said.'

'That fool? That clerk? He can do nothing, believe me.'

'Excellency, I am terribly afraid. Let me take my family to the Grand Turk.'

'No, by God! Not to that infidel.'

'Please. Evil days are coming here, of that I am sure.'

The duke found this statement offensive, for Pope Clement himself had promised that Jews baptized under force would be forever under the protection of the papacy and were free to practice their religion as they wished. It was expected that future Popes would repeat this promise. Therefore, when Rabbi Zaki expressed his wish to leave Italy, heading for the realms of the Turk, his plea could be considered only as an insult to the Church. 'You cannot go,' the duke said, and the interview was ended.

At home the women deduced where the rabbi had been and they chided him for his faint-heartedness. Other Jews were summoned to ridicule him, and all pointed out that whereas the fears he expressed might have been logical in Spain or Portugal, where there was an Inquisition determined to uncover Jews masquerading as Christians, there was no logical ground for fear in Podi. 'This is Italy!' they pointed out, taking refuge in the constant rationalization of the Jew: 'It won't happen here. The people are too civilized.'

Rabbi Zaki for once in his life could not be swayed by either his friends or his family. He had a clear vision of what must inevitably happen in Italy, either with the arrival of a new Pope or with a change in the prosperity of the peninsula. 'I am afraid,' he repeated stubbornly. 'I saw the faces of the people yesterday. There was hatred in the cathedral.'

'He's been making the same speech every year,' a cautious merchant repeated. 'We'd feel the way you do, Rabbi, if we'd raced half-naked with the women laughing at us.'

'But you didn't have to race, did you?' Rachel stormed. 'Because you're not fat like a pig.'

Zaki was stunned that his wife should have used this word again and in front of his congregation. With a pleading voice he whispered, 'That is not a word to use against a rabbi.'

'But you do eat like a pig!' she cried, and he looked at the floor. It was a mark of the little rabbi that even in his humiliation he never once thought of leaving Podi without his nagging wife, even though he could easily have done so; two men from the city had fled to Amsterdam without their families, but he could not understand their behavior. He knew there was going to be terror in Italy and he could not abandon his stubborn wife and his unlovely daughters to face it, obstinate though they were.

'I am taking my family to Salonica,' he said quietly, 'and if you men are wise, you'll do the same.'

His wife was so irritated that she refused to discuss the matter, and the meeting broke up with a sense of frustration and fear. But in the morning Rabbi Zaki was back arguing with the duke, and after apologizing for any possible insult to the Duke, to the Pope or to the Church he again asked permission to emigrate.

'Give me one reason,' thundered the duke.

Zaki, during the night, had pondered half a dozen good reasons, but on the spur of the moment dismissed them all and said, 'Because I have three daughters, Excellency, and like a good father I wish to marry them to Jewish men, whom I can find in Salonica.'

The duke considered this unexpected reasoning and began to laugh. 'You have to find three husbands, Zaki?'

The rabbi said 'Yes,' and sensing that he had enlisted the interest of the duke, added, 'It's not easy, Excellency. To find one good husband these days is not easy.'

'And you think that in Salonica . . .'

'Yes.'

The duke called in his younger brother, for whom he had obtained the appointment as Archbishop of Podi, and when that amiable prelate heard of Rabbi Zaki's request to leave the city he did his best to quieten the Jew's fears. 'The duke commands here,' the archbishop reasoned, 'and you should know that he will tolerate no act against his Jews.'

'I need you for my commerce,' the duke said.

'But I heard the friar say we were to be burned,' Zaki said. 'I believe him.'

'That one?' the archbishop asked, laughing like a man recalling a pleasant day in the field. 'You certainly know that my brother and I found his silly sermon as repugnant as you did, Zaki. Consider it only as a part of the Easter celebration and pay no more attention.'

'I cannot put it out of my mind. I am afraid.'

The tall archbishop summoned Zaki to the window and pointed toward the center of the piazza, where from a granite plinth rose a statue of the Duke of Podi astride a white stallion, The sculptor had caught the condottiere, sword in hand, at the moment of his conquest of Podi, and his manly bearing lent dignity and courage to the city he ruled. 'Do you suppose a warrior like the duke would ever permit a preaching friar or even a Pope to determine his behaviour?' The churchman laughed at the absurdity, but when Zaki repeated that he wanted to go, the archbishop shrugged his shoulders. 'In Podi we hold no man against his will,' he said compassionately. 'But regulations covering departures are administered by the friars,' and he sent for the very man who had preached the Lenten sermon.

The Dominican bowed to the duke, acknowledged the archbishop and looked with disgust at the Jew who defiled the ducal rooms. 'He should not be allowed to leave,' the friar warned. 'He was baptized a Christian and it's abhorrent that he should join the Turk.'

'He's determined,' the archbishop said, whereupon the Dominican asked for pen and paper and began listing the restrictions under which Zaki might depart: 'He may take with him no papers proving that Christians owe him debts. Nor any books written or printed, no money minted in this state, no lists of names which might help the Turk, nor any instruments for the Christian sacraments.

And at the pier, in view of all, he must kneel and kiss the New Testament, acknowledging its divine inspiration.'

When the terms of departure were agreed upon, the Duke of Podi signed the paper and in later years this fact would be remembered against him. The archbishop signed, too, and this was also recorded. Finally the Dominican thrust the document at the Jew, warning him, 'If one item is transgressed, you may not depart.'

But Zaki had his permission, and in a kind of mysterious terror he fled the room where he had always been treated so justly by the duke and his brother, for he sensed the deepening of a tragedy whose outlines he only vaguely understood; but as he crossed the piazza on his way to talk with a ship captain about passage, he stopped at the marble statue of the condottiere and muttered a prayer, 'May God, Who allowed you to conquer this city, allow you to keep it.'

Then, as he neared home, he began to sweat, for although he had convinced the duke, the archbishop, the friar and the ship captain, he still had to convince his wife, and this would prove most difficult of all. But on one point he felt not the slightest uncertainty: even though he knew that tragedy was about to engulf Podi, if his wife and daughters refused to flee with him he would have to remain with them. 'Rachel is sometimes a trial,' he muttered to himself, 'but no man can desert his wife. Besides, she's given me three lovely daughters.' For her sake he prayed that he could persuade her to leave the city.

When he reached his shoemaker's shop he tried to put on a look of firmness and he must have succeeded, for Rachel saw that a decision of moment was about to be announced.

'I've been to the duke's,' he began.

'Yes?'

'And he has agreed to let us go.'

'Where?'

'I've also been to see the captain and he has agreed . . .'

'Where?'

'There's no turning back, Rachel,' the fat rabbi pleaded. 'Evil days are ahead in this city . . .'

'Where?' she screamed. 'Salonica?'

'Yes,' he said bravely, raising his arms to fend off the attack that must take place.

To his surprise Rachel sat down. She breathed heavily, made no other sound and hid her face in her hands. After a while she gave a low sob and summoned her daughters from the other room. 'We're going to Salonica,' she announced softly, like the whisper of a volcano afraid to explode. The oldest girl, Sarah, gasped and her mother leaped from the chair. 'Yes!' she shouted. 'Your father's taking us to Salonica!' The youngest child began to cry and Rachel slapped her. 'We're going to Salonica,' she shouted in a hysterical giggle. 'You're all going to marry Turks.' She collapsed in the chair; even the older girls began crying, whereupon she stormed about the room, shouting, 'We're going to Salonica, oh, my God!' Then she slapped each of the girls harshly and announced calmly, 'We shall do as your father says. No one in this room will ever again argue about his decision.'

She kept her word. With demonic frenzy she applied herself to packing the family goods, but as she tied each parcel the Dominican friar would come to inspect it, reminding her that many of the things she wanted to take belonged, by agreement, to the Church. Once Zaki was afraid that Rachel would fly at the Dominican, but she patiently surrendered even the toys of her children. When the friar had completed his third scrutiny Rachel declared war, muttering, 'Very well.' Digging up a secret hoard of forbidden gold pieces she sewed them adroitly into unlikely places, so that when the rabbi's family was given its final searching she succeeded in smuggling so many coins that she could support the family for some years in its flight.

The Jews of Podi came to the pier to bid their frightened rabbi farewell, and to him they seemed like a necklace of beautiful pearls strung along the dock, causing tears to well up in his eyes as he listened to their farewells; fortunately he could not hear their whispers: 'Look at our crazy rabbi. Lost his head because a whore pulled down his pants.' And then, like the shadow of death crossing the waves, a darkness came over Zaki's vision and he saw his beloved congregation as it was to be. There stood fat Jacopo, who had been in the race, and he would be burned alive in 1556. Beside him stood thin Meir, a cherished friend who would be burned alive in 1555. There were the sisters Ruth and Zipporah; the elder would be burned alive in 1555, but the younger would die in prison almost torn apart by torture. There was also the gentle Josiah, who would die at the stake in 1556, but because he was dim-witted he would escape death by flame, because at the end he would say uncomprehendingly, 'Of course I accept conversion,' and the executioner would mercifully strangle him before the fires began.

The cloud passed, and the doomed Jews stepped aside as the smiling Duke of Podi came onto the dock, crying, 'Good-bye, Zaki. No one in Podi had bitterness against you. You're being very stupid.' And one day this generous-hearted man would be humbled and hounded from his dominion because of the assistance he would give his Jews in their time of trial.

It would not be proper to claim that on this day in 1541 Zaki foresaw these precise events in the darkened faces of his friends, but he knew with a certainty that similar things were bound to happen. To no one could he confide, not even to his bewildered, faithful wife, the reasons for his insight: 'If men repeat often enough their hatreds the evil comes to pass.' He looked at his dear friends, his lovely companions doomed in their goodness, and he wept.

His wife, ashamed of his latest display of cowardice, refused to weep. But as the ship started to move she cried hysterically, 'We are going to Salonica.' During the first days of the tedious voyage she and her daughters kept to themselves, but when Muslim pirates threatened the ship she began to wail, 'Is this what you are taking us to Salonica for?' And she made so much commotion that the captain bellowed 'Rabbi, shut that woman up or I'll let the pirates catch us.' Zaki went to his wife and pleaded, 'Rachel, if we have escaped Italy, God will not abandon us to slavery now.' His wife looked at him with blank amazement and forgot the pirates: her husband was still talking gibberish, and she was so appalled to have married such a fool that she kept her mouth shut.

The pirates were outdistanced, but the ship was forced to land in northern Africa, where shoemakers were not needed and where Rachel and the girls had to work. And after many years they came to Safed.

2

On a cold, wintry morning in 1540 the citizens of Avaro in central Spain found on their doorsteps a printed broadsheet commanding them to report to the Holy Inquisition anyone who had publicly accepted baptism as a Christian and had then secretly continued to practice as a Jew. To aid informers in spying out this crime, a series of ingenious tests was provided:

Put before your neighbor morsels of food such as pork, rabbit and conger eels, and if he refuse to eat, he is a Jew.

Watch with great care everything your neighbor does on Friday. Does he put on fresh linen? Does he light candles at least an hour before honest men do? Does his wife clean the house that day? If you catch him doing these things, you have a Jew.

Go to your roof on Friday two hours before sundown and watch all the chimneys of the city. Any that stops smoking suddenly as the sun sets betrays a Jew. Run and catch his name.

When you visit your neighbor's home spy out to see if he washes his hands more than most. When his wife kneads bread does she throw a small bit into the fire? If you detect any of these matters, report your neighbor at once, for he is a Jew.

In church does your neighbor, while professing to be a true man, rock his head back and forth and bend occasionally at the waist? Does he recite the Psalms like an honest man, then refuse at the end to repeat the *Gloria Patri?* Does he attend with special reverence whenever testimony from the Old Testament is mentioned? Does his tongue seem to gag in his mouth when he is called upon to recite the phrase, 'Father, Son and Holy Ghost?' If he does any of these things, you have caught a Jew.

At Holy Communion watch your neighbor with redoubled vigilance. Does he swallow the wafer with forthright honesty like a true Christian, or does he try to hide it in his mouth for deliverance later to Satan? Or does he linger with it on his lips, then swallow it swiftly when he catches you looking at him? If he does either of these tricks, remember his name.

Be vigilant ever. If you are present when your neighbor dies, see if at his last breath he turns his face to the wall. When a son is born to your neighbor see if his wife delay for forty days before returning to normal life. Watch if the new child is called secretly by a name from the Old Testament. Try diligently to see if his son is circumcised. And inspect all that your neighbor does, because you may succeed in routing out a Jew, and if you triumph over this devil, great grace is yours.

A few days later the distinguished advisor to King Charles of Austria and Spain, Counselor Diego Ximeno, whose ancestors had for eleven hundred years lived in Spain as Jews, and for the last century as converts to Christianity, happened to choke as he was eating a piece of pork. Inadvertently he allowed the pork to fall to the floor, where, seeing it ruined, he absent-mindedly ground it into the dust with his heel. A jealous neighbor detected him doing these things and next day satisfied himself beyond question that Diego Ximeno was a secret Jew because he spotted the robust, handsome counselor washing his hands three times in the course of one day, whereas a believing man would not have done so.

Accordingly, this trusted friend went quietly to the office of the Inquisition and reported: 'I have strong reason to suspect that Diego Ximeno is a Jew.' The Dominican in charge of recording accusations raised his eyebrows, for although in recent years some rather prominent citizens of Avaro had been caught in the nets of the Inquisition, no one of Diego Ximeno's importance had yet been apprehended, and to catch a man of his dignity would bring the local office into national prominence. Senior officials of the Inquisition were therefore summoned and the informant was questioned avidly. 'For some time,' he told them, 'I have suspected Diego of being a secret Jew, but not until the paper arrived telling me what specifically to look for did I know how to trap him.'

The committee itself had a much longer list of ways to catch a Jew than the one which it had sponsored in print, and one by one these questions were put to the excited witness and he was led to review his years of friendship with the counselor, until all reached the conclusion that Diego Ximeno at one time or other had been guilty of almost every act that betrayed a secret Jew. It was safe for the informer to make his nebulous accusations, for under the codex of inquisitorial procedure he would never face the man he was condemning, nor would Ximeno ever be told who had informed against him or what had been the charge. At the end of several hours the priests conducting the interrogation thanked the neighbor, and when he was gone, concluded, 'At last we have caught a truly great one. Honor is ours.'

That afternoon uniformed guards of the Inquisition marched to Ximeno's office and without advising him of any particulars arrested him and hauled him away to a cramped, dirty subterranean cell, where he was kept in absolute silence for four months. The inquisitors knew that they must prepare their case against such a man with care, for even though he had had Jewish ancestors a hundred years ago he also had great influence with the court, and his arrest had already caused many horsemen to ride between Avaro and Vienna. Finally the Inquisition was ready to interrogate the prisoner, which it did with secrecy and solemnity, but since Ximeno was not told what the specific charges against him were, he confessed to nothing. On the second day no progress was made, nor on the third, so on the fourth the court convinced itself that in Diego Ximeno they had a secret Jew who was going to prove exceedingly difficult.

Accordingly, he was returned to solitary confinement, where he languished for the rest of 1540 and all of 1541, during which time he was required to pay substantial sums for his keep and for the marshaling of further evidence against him. Regardless of the eventual outcome of his trial he was being financially ruined, and he knew it.

The Avaro chapter of the Inquisition could afford to move so deliberately because of the significance of the work in which it was engaged. Before it became powerful in Spain the Inquisition had been in existence as a necessary arm of the Church, for some six or seven centuries, during which it had served to protect Christianity from numerous heresies. For the first half-thousand years of its operation it had been a generally benign office, but with the ascendancy of Tomás de Torquemada as Inquisitor-General of Spain and his elevation of the Inquisition to a position independent of both Pope and emperor, the policing powers of the body had degenerated into a kind of panic and terror: in a period of seventeen years, some 120,000 of Spain's inquisitive intellectuals were killed. And then, with Torquemada dead and the Faith apparently secure against false movements, a time was reached when the terror could be relaxed, but at this moment Martin Luther in Germany launched the most dangerous heresy of all, so that even a fool could see that the true Christian Church was imperiled by Protestantism. What was almost as disturbing, certain Christians like Erasmus of Rotterdam were writing books that cunningly mocked the Church, and as if this danger were not enough, Jewish families who had some centuries before accepted baptism into

Christianity were discovered to be secretly adhering to old Judaic rites. Thus the Church was beset from without and within, and only the Inquisition, superior even to the Pope, could hope to root out the heresies, burn the incriminating books and track down the Lutherans and the secret Jews.

The official figures for the Inquisition of Avaro illustrate the Church's response to the peril it faced. In the two centuries before the arrival of Torquemada, Avaro beheaded only four persons, and these were grievous enemies of the Church who refused to recant gross sin. But from 1481 to 1498, under the whip of Torquemada, the Avaro judges executed eleven thousand heretics. In the quiet period that followed, the number dropped to less than twenty a year, but in 1517, with the appearance of Luther as a mortal threat and with the influx of works by Erasmus, the number of executions rose sharply.

It is significant that in this period of sixty years, from 1481 to 1541, not a single professed Jew was executed by the Avaro Inquisition. If any man, upon arrest, could say boldly, 'I am a Jew and have always been known as one,' he was banished from the realm, but he was not burned. The Spanish Church had to despise him and send him on those mournful wanderings which the New Testament had predicted, but it never touched him. At the same time, however, the Avaro Inquisition had rooted out some eight thousand people whose families had once been Jews but who had converted to Christianity, accepting baptism and full membership in the Church while secretly continuing to practice Jewish rites. And of these eight thousand faithless ones more than six thousand had been burned alive. There was the girl Maria del Iglesia, whose family had been Christian for three centuries, who fell in love with the young man Raimundo Calamano and in a moment of courtship confidence confessed to him that she and her family observed Passover: he ran straight to the Inquisition, and three days before she was to marry, troops broke into the Del Iglesia home to find forty-one Jews eating matzoth, and all were burned alive. There was the renowned scholar Tomás de Salamanca, who taught the youth of Avaro, and one day his nine-year-old son burst into the street, shouting, 'My father whipped me. He fasts on Yom Kippur.' So after investigations extending over a period of seven years, sixty-three close associates of Tomás had to be burned alive. What was especially frightening was the fact that among the confessed Jews were seventeen nuns who had held Jewish rituals in their convent, thirty monks, seven priests and two bishops. The Church was being dangerously corrupted from within, and only the most painstaking investigation could protect it. For that reason the case against Diego Ximeno, counselor to the king, moved slowly.

At the beginning of the third year Ximeno was again summoned before the tribunal, which now had in its possession a voluminous file of material linking him to Judaism. Informants as far away as the Italian city of Podi and the German city of Gretz had made depositions damaging to him, and the judges were completely satisfied that they had a secret Jew. Now the problem was to force him to confess and to incriminate others in Avaro who might have masked their evil practices as successfully as he had done. Over a period of four days he was interrogated in minute detail, and when he proved obdurate the tribunal had no alternative; they had to commit him to the torture.

He was dragged immediately to the subterranean vault long used for the purpose of extracting confessions, but he was not, as some might suspect, thrown into the hands of brutal men free to abuse him at will. He was delivered to a skilled and patient priest who had been conducting such interrogations for many years and who was assisted constantly by a knowing doctor who had learned from experience what torment the human body could absorb without expiring. There were few deaths from torture in the dungeon of Avaro.

On the other hand, the ordinary workmen who administered the three tortures which were allowed had become callous experts who had acquired a score of tricks guaranteed to break down the resolve of any secret Jews, so at the moment when Diego Ximeno was thrust into the dungeon these men already knew that he was someone special sent to test their skill. If they extracted a confession, they would be rewarded; if they failed, they would be rebuked. It was therefore a poignant moment when the handsome man of fifty, stalwart even after two years of imprisonment, stumbled into the torture chamber, gained his footing and stood in quiet defiance before the interrogating priest.

'Do you confess, Diego Ximeno?' the priest asked. The prisoner looked at the Dominican with contempt, whereupon the priest, who had often seen that particular look at the beginning of his interrogations, but never at the end, said to the doctor, 'The prisoner refuses to speak. Is he qualified for the question?' The doctor studied Ximeno and thought: He's arrogant and he's in strong health. This one may take a long time.

The doctor nodded to the scribe sitting at the feet of the priest. It was this man's job to record confessions and to confirm in writing that humanitarian safeguards were observed in the torture room. 'Write down,' the priest directed, 'that the prisoner was found qualified for the question.'

With this the Dominican signaled to the workmen, who with lightning force grabbed Ximeno, pinioned his arms and stripped him naked before he knew what was happening. With equal speed they lashed his hands behind his back, fastened twenty-pound weights to each ankle, and by means of a heavy rope attached to his wrists hauled him some forty feet into the air. From below, the foreman of the workmen shouted, 'You'll talk, Counselor.' They left him suspended for nearly an hour, while his arms, wrenched upward from behind, slowly pulled his shoulders from their sockets.

The ache throughout his body had become almost more than he could bear, and the Dominican, seeing his anguish and sensing that he might be ready to speak, came below him and called, 'Diego Ximeno, do you now confess?'

Still uninformed as to the specific charges against him, Ximeno bore his pain in silence.

'Diego Ximeno,' the priest pleaded, 'if you are in pain now, believe me it is only a beginning. Please confess or we must apply the question.' The prisoner made no response, so the priest returned to his small dais, instructing his scribe to record the fact that the prisoner had been offered mercy.

Suddenly, with terrifying shouts, the workmen dashed at the rope which suspended Ximeno and by means of prearranged holds allowed it to slip so that the prisoner dropped thirty feet, ending with a shattering halt which tore each of his major joints apart with maximum pain. His wrists, elbows and shoulders were mutilated, while the weights on his legs, magnified many times by the precipitous fall and the sudden stop, pulled apart his ankles, his knees and his hips.

Before Ximeno could identify his new pains the workmen pulled him back to the ceiling to initiate one of the worst features of the torture. At times they would shout and drop the rope. At other times they would shout and not drop it. Again, without warning, they would drop it only a few inches. At other times there would be the sickening fall almost to the floor and the hideous wrenching.

Ximeno was now beyond pain, and when the Dominican again begged him to confess the stalwart prisoner refused even to listen, so the rope was let go and he was dropped in a heap, quickly lifted onto a table and subjected to an entirely different kind of torment; for if the hanging and falling had constituted gross pain, which men like Ximeno could school themselves to resist, what was now at hand was psychological torture that few could withstand.

The table upon which he was laid had a small log across the middle, so that his back was severely strained and his stomach drawn flat in a position which of itself induced strangling. Then a funnel was placed in his mouth and his nose was closed. Huge draughts of water were poured into the funnel from an earthenware jar, and as his taut lungs gasped for air he alternately strangled, choked and gulped the water. It was an agonizing, shattering torture.

Before the second jar was poured, the priest returned and begged the prisoner to recant. 'The tortures will cease,' the Dominican assured him, but apparently Ximeno was prepared to die and said nothing. The priest departed and the scrivener recorded the fact that the merciful offer had been made.

'This time you'll speak,' the workmen promised. One leaned hard upon Ximeno's distended stomach as it arched over the log, and the sudden movement of water throughout his internals almost killed him. Another placed in his mouth a cloth which long experience had proved to be of exactly the right mesh, and through this the water was now poured. Gulping, fighting for air, Ximeno sucked the cloth into his throat, where it embedded itself as the water trickled slowly through. It seemed that he must surely strangle, but at the end of the long agony the workmen suddenly jerked the cloth from his throat, tearing away the membranes and bringing blood.

'Now speak,' the workmen whispered, and when he refused, the bloody cloth was again inserted in his mouth. Six jugs of water, six strangling, terrifying, mortal jugs, were poured into him while strong hands pressed on his stomach, so that his lungs, his bowels and his heart seemed to explode.

He did not talk. So he was hauled at last to the final torture, where, spread in complete agony on the cold stones, his joints inflamed and his throat torn, he was given a few minutes of respite, during which he heard the priest begging him yet once more to avoid the worst agony which was now at hand. He remained silent, whereupon the soles of his feet were smeared with a mixture of pepper, oil, menthol and clove, and when the unguent was well into his pores fagots from an open fire were brought and passed back and forth across his feet, raising horrible blisters and sending throughout his body pain of an absolute magnitude. He fainted.

He awakened some time later in his cell. His mattress had been removed and he was lying naked on the stones, his heap of clothes beside him. He was unable to move either his arms or legs. His feet ached beyond human endurance, and his mouth had already become so scarred that each breath was agony. For four dreadful days he lay there hoping to die, and on the fifth, when his blisters were at their worst, his joints inflamed and his throat a mass of sores, he was dragged back to the vault, where the priest said, 'Diego Ximeno, we have proof beyond question that you are a Jew. Please, for God's mercy, confess and let us end this business.' Ximeno said nothing.

The Dominican honestly wanted to save the accused from further pain, so he pointed to the door of the torture chamber and said, 'Diego, believe me, of a hundred misguided people we have to bring down here, we set at least ninety free. To resume their normal lives. To rejoin the Church as corrected

Christians.' He waited but Ximeno said nothing. 'It's true, we punish them here, but when they confess they go free with nothing worse than an unhappy memory. Diego, if you tell us now the names of the other Jews, you will go free, like the ninety, with nothing worse than a few scars on your ankles. Please, please speak.' But Ximeno said nothing.

This time the workmen used different tactics. Pulling him to the ceiling they eschewed tricks and set about dropping and raising him as rapidly as possible, until it seemed that his heart must be torn out of his body. Then, after a few minutes, they lugged him like an inanimate object to the water table, pressed him down upon the log until his back nearly cracked and proceeded immediately with the cloth and six jugs of water. Later, at the fire, they went right to work and burned him so horribly that again he fainted. With disgust they dragged him, unconscious, back to his cell and heaved him through the air, smashing him against the wall.

'Let's hope we killed him,' they muttered, for his obstinacy was a reflection upon them. They had proof that he was a secret Jew, and his refusal to confess was preposterous.

Of his tortures on the third day he remembered nothing, but they were in no way different, for the Inquisition did not permit its workmen to cut a man's flesh, to blind him or to meddle with his private parts, and if a prisoner remained silent in the face of rope, water and fire, as Ximeno had done, it was permissible nearly to kill him with these means but it was not permissible to do more. At the end of the third incredible session the doctor stood over the inanimate hulk by the fire and said, 'This one can stand no more.'

The Dominican looked at the distorted, blistered body and cried, 'Why don't they confess and save themselves this agony?'

The doctor asked, 'Do you suppose this one really is a Jew, Father?'

'At first I was sure,' the Dominican replied. 'But after this . . .' He turned away.

Toward the end of 1542, when Ximeno had been nearly three years in solitary confinement, for which his estate still had to pay rent week after week, the sad-eyed Dominican came at last to see him: 'Diego, tomorrow your day of judgment is at hand. You are to be burned at the stake.'

The prisoner still made no response, and the priest begged, 'Diego, please, for the mercy of God, confess, so that when you reach the stake the executioner will be permitted to strangle you before the fire begins.'

Again there was no comment, and the distraught priest cried, 'Diego! Do not force us to do this horrible thing. Your soul is already in the hands of God. At least allow your body to go in peace.'

But the resolute prisoner said nothing, and the priest departed.

At four on Sunday morning two young Dominicans entered the cell bearing a sackcloth uniform into which Diego Ximeno was forced to climb. Over it the priests threw a long yellow robe on which had been painted little red devils throwing into the fires of hell heretics and secret Jews. Finally they jammed on the prisoner's head a tall conical hat, yellow and adorned with swirling flames. 'You must follow us, Counselor,' said the two young friars of Avaro, who in happier days had often sought his assistance, which he had freely granted.

At the door of the prison Ximeno was handed a lighted taper, which signified that he was to be burned, and he came at last to the barefoot procession itself: sixty-three who had confessed minor crimes against the Church, like reading Erasmus, and who would escape death to live the rest of their lives in dismal isolation—pauperized, forbidden employment, anathematized; nineteen who had confessed major crimes, like naming their sons Moses or refusing to eat conger eels, and these would be burned, but at the last moment they would be strangled so as to escape the fire; and six like Diego Ximeno, who had refused to confess either to Judaism or Lutheranism, and they would be burned alive without strangling.

It was a long procession, headed by the dignitaries of the Church; and a longer day, marked by sermons, pleas and accusations. More than forty thousand persons packed the plaza to hear the solemn proceedings, for the day had been widely advertised throughout the region and all who attended were granted special dispensation, for that day they would see where the path of heresy led.

Late in the afternoon the inquisitors came finally to the cases of those to be burned, and justification for this act was cited from the specific words of Jesus Christ Himself as reported in the holy gospel of St John: 'If a man abide not in me, he is cast forth as a branch, and is withered; and men gather them, and cast them into the fire, and they are burned.' But once the verdicts of death had been read, the Church dignitaries solemnly washed their hands of the matter and left the scene, while the prisoners were turned over to the secular arm of the state with the plea that they be treated kindly and that no blood be spilled.

The secular arm then marched the condemned to an entirely different part of the city, where stakes had been set into the ground and fagots piled high, and as the prisoners marched, the populace screamed at them, threw things, cursed and reviled them. Those prisoners suspected of being Jews went through a particular Gehenna, for they were tormented with special taunts: they had known God and had turned their backs on Him; they had crucified Jesus; they were worse than the swine they refused to eat. And with each step that the suspected Jew took, two friars clung to him, crying, 'Jew, confess that your religion is false. Confess that God is three and not one.' And to many Jews on the death march this vilification of their religion was worse than the taunts of the crowd. At the burning place the citizens watched with horrified fascination as Diego Ximeno, silent and austere, climbed unaided onto the pile, ignoring the pleas of his accompanying friars that he save himself from the final agony. Below him secretaries waited with pen and book, ready to write down whatever he might scream in his torment. This had become a matter of some importance, for there were many in the town who were beginning to believe that Ximeno was not a Jew, and such a belief might become embarrassing if it led to local sanctification. But as the flames leaped at his throat Ximeno summoned forth the same iron control that he had shown in the torture room, and he died confessing nothing, so that at the moment of his death the people who had known him well began to whisper, 'He was not a Jew. He was a saint,' and the first steps of his canonization began, much to the disgust of the Inquisition, which had intended something quite different.

Of all the watchers who saw the burning of Diego Ximeno, none witnessed it with greater apprehension than Dr Abulafia, a distinguished medical man whose Jewish ancestors had become Christians in 1391 and who, as a good Christian himself, had risen to a place of prominence in the city. He was married to a Christian lady of impeccable lineage. He ate pork, was not circumcised, nor were his sons, and he had never been suspected by anyone, not even during the worst rigors of the Inquisition, of being a Jew. Upon the distribution in 1540 of the list of signs whereby secret Jews could be trapped, some of his acquaintances had jokingly reviewed the items with him, saying 'At least nobody can accuse you of being a Jew, Abulafia,' and not even his friends had considered reporting him to the inquisitors. He was a flawless man.

With horror he had stood in the public plaza to hear the formal charges against his old patient, Diego Ximeno, and during the procession to the burning grounds he had twice stationed himself in positions where the condemned man would have to pass close to him; but Ximeno, in a kind of mortal trance, had stared straight ahead, refusing to see the doctor. When Ximeno climbed to the stake Dr Abulafia positioned himself with the secretaries waiting to catch any words the doomed man might utter, but again nothing happened. Yet at the last moment, when Ximeno's hair was ablaze and his skin had begun to char, he did cast one final, lingering glance at Dr Abulafia, and their eyes met through flame.

When the fires burned down and there left only iron chains soiled with greasy soot, Dr Abulafia walked dumbly homeward, and it was now he who was in a trance. At home Doña Maria asked, 'Why are you so pale?' and he replied, 'I've just seen Diego burned,' and his wife replied, 'He must have been guilty. These are not things for us to worry about.'

Abulafia was unable to eat supper, nor did he wish to play with his two sons. He went to his study to examine patients, but he became dizzy and thought he would faint. By exercising will power he succeeded in maintaining control, saying to himself: If I faint now it might be fatal. Who knows which of these patients was sent to spy on me this night? So he worked on.

Dr Abulafia was a tall man with dark, sympathetic eyes. Handsome and much respected by the people of Avaro, he had a gentle manner with the sick which enabled him to earn more money than most of the doctors in town. He was a skilled surgeon, enjoying a favorable reputation in cities as far distant as Toledo, where he had once treated Emperor Charles. He sprang from a family whose contributions to Spain dated back to the year 400 c.e., and he should have felt secure this ghostly night, when the smoldering fires of the burning still hovered above the city, but he did not. The execution of Diego Ximeno haunted him, so at the earliest chance he closed his office. Avoiding his family he went to a small inner room containing no books, no papers, no pictures. The walls were white, the table and chair rudely made, and he sat staring straight ahead and thinking. He was afraid to write anything down, which he desperately wanted to do, for his wife or some spy might find his writing and give it to the inquisition. He was afraid to mumble the words his brain formed lest someone be listening and overhear un-Spanish syllables. He was not free to recite any litany, nor to consult books, nor to read manuals, nor to do anything other than sit.

He stared at the wall for nearly an hour, trying to cleanse his mind of the terrible things it had seen that day, but flame and the penetrating eyes of Diego Ximeno haunted him; when he tried to concentrate he saw only the eyes of the counselor, but finally the dreadful visions faded and the letters of the Hebrew alphabet began to form in space before the whiteness of the wall, and they began to move hither and about, forming in alternation consoling or condemning patterns. Still he stared, as the letters took meaningful patterns recalling concepts which he had suppressed for many months; then they assumed the form of symbols which evoked other meaningful concepts, and still he sat, motionless, wanting to write down the letters with pen and paper but terrified of doing so; and after a long interval of watching, the Hebrew letters turned to fire and marched purposefully across the wall, and he began to breathe in short gasps. His stomach contracted and these preliminary letters started to fade from sight until the wall was lonely and bare.

Then, from an immeasurable distance behind the wall, came four letters of extraordinary force, too powerful to be looked at directly. He dropped his eyes. The letters came through the wall and across the room right to his forehead; and now without using his eyes he could see them in all their terrible majesty, and they were broken, YH on one side and WH on the other, and try as he might he could not bring them together to form the unspoken, the unspeakable Name; and slowly the letters receded until they stood again upon the wall, and now he could look upon them with his eyes, and they stood accusingly there, YH to one side and WH to the other, and he had not the power to fuse them into one word. For the word he sought was the sacred Name of God Himself, and this Name Abulafia could not speak; for he felt himself to be a man of sin: he could have joined Ximeno at the stake but through cowardice had not done so. After a long while he stopped looking at the accusing letters and found himself muttering an ancient Hebrew prayer, and it was for the salvation of Diego Ximeno's soul; for Dr Abulafia knew with certainty that the counselor had been a secret Jew and that the Inquisition was therefore justified, according to its rules, in burning him alive.

On the day in 1540 when he heard that Ximeno had first been arrested, Dr Abulafia had said to himself, trembling in this white room, 'Diego will confess, and he will tell them that I, too, am a Jew.' Then his agony of cowardice began. With unmanly apprehension he watched the prison where Ximeno was kept, expecting each day to be called before the Inquisition with word that the counselor had incriminated him. The three years that Ximeno had lain in silence were to the doctor an eternity, for he could visualize the tortures that his friend was suffering. In recent years several patients, having been set free after preliminary questioning in the torture chamber, had come to Dr Abulafia with distended joints or horrible scars on their feet and they had wanted to tell him how they had acquired these marks, but he had refused to listen. 'The sacred Inquisition does its duty and does it justly,' he told them, for he could never be sure which were spies saved from their own burning in order to trap him.

In the refuge of this silent room he had prayed: 'God of Moses our Teacher, save Diego.' And when weeks passed and the Inquisition did not come to arrest him, he said to himself: Maybe Ximeno is not going to confess, and he grew ashamed at having entertained such self-seeking thoughts. A few days ago the broadsheet had come fluttering through the streets, announcing that the next burning of heretics would be headed by Counselor Ximeno, and Dr Abulafia had suffered fresh moral confusion until at last he had been driven in a kind of self-sacrificing mania to station himself along the path of Ximeno's march to the fagots, willing to step forward and identify himself if the doomed man gave the signal; but with a fortitude Abulafia considered impossible, Ximeno had marched in silence, protecting the names of others that he alone knew to be secret Jews. Yet as he passed, Abulafia saw something that he would never forget. Ximeno's face was a mask which revealed nothing, but his bare feet were marked by gaping scars which could have come only from burns. And at the end there had been the last fraternal glance.

Now on the night of death Dr Abulafia sat again in the white room and asked himself: How many other secret Jews in this city did Ximeno protect through his courage? And when he contemplated the fortitude of the martyred man he had to cry aloud, whether spies heard him or not, 'Praise God for those who have the strength to die for the sanctification of the Name.' And he continued with a soaring, poetic invocation to the good Jew who had that day allowed himself to be burned alive rather than escape his agony by incriminating others who would be hounded to death after he was gone.

Dr Abulafia had met Ximeno twenty years ago, in the winter of 1522. It was an accident, an accident of words: at a formal dinner celebrating the patron saint of Avaro he had asked innocently, 'What is this Kabbala the Jewish people speak of?' And after a series of cautious probings the counselor had revealed himself as a master of the Kabbala, that esoteric body of mysticism that had grown up in Germany and Spain as a pathway to the understanding of the Hebrew God. Ximeno had given Dr Abulafia a manuscript of the Zohar, the arcane book of Kabbalism, believed to have been composed centuries before by a mystical Jew in Granada, and had initiated him into its mysteries. Abulafia had found much to his liking, for while he had never been able honestly to accept the Christian principle that God was of one substance and three manifestations, he found the austere monotheism of Hebraic teaching equally difficult. There was in life, and his Spanish nature sensed it, an additional spirit of flight, the wild movement of the human soul seeking some kind of further identification with God; and only in the Zohar did Abulafia find a solution that satisfied him.

Between the immensity of God and the insignificance of man the Zohar postulated ten spheres of divine manifestation, each of which man can approach or even encompass: the supreme crown of God, the wisdom of God, the intelligence, the love, the power, the compassion, the everlastingness, the majesty, the root foundation and the kingdom of God. These ten spheres, through which God emerges from his unknowable state, can be represented in the form of a tree, but it is known that the sap of this tree, the vitalizing power, is and must be the ultimate spirit of God.

It was through the exploration and contemplation of these spheres that Ximeno and Abulafia reached the mystical point at which sometimes, after having manipulated the letters of the Hebrew alphabet for hours, they would come close to the ultimate secret of God Himself. Then the four separate letters of the mystical tetragrammaton, YHWH, would appear on the paper before them, properly fused into the Name, and they would become aware of the actual presence of God Himself.

But when the searching fingers of the Inquisition began to clutch at one secret Jew after another, Ximeno had warned, 'Companion, we had better burn our books,' and with moral confusion they had burned their copy of the Torah, even though it was a holy book for the Christians, too, and their tracts from the Talmud, but when it came time to burn the Zohar, Abulafia had promised, 'I will burn it tonight,' and without telling Ximeno he had secreted it in a wall of his cellar, for the book which had illuminated his soul he could not burn. Later Ximeno had cautioned, 'We must no longer write Hebrew letters. A child might find an unburned scrap or your wife might see scratches on the desk.' And they had formed the habit of sitting together in absolute silence, two secret Jews, each contemplating the mystery of God in his own way.

It was surprising, Abulafia thought, that the Inquisition had not identified him as one of Ximeno's friends, but he remembered that Diego had wisely refused ever to meet Abulafia socially; he had come always as a patient, claiming a persistent nasal condition. 'I will not tell even you who the other Jews are,' he had once said, 'for the day may come when we shall be called upon to resist harsh tortures and we must not know who our neighbors are lest we prove not strong.'

Now, in the white room, Dr Abulafia tried to reconstruct what he knew of Ximeno's habits: He came frequently to visit me, and I was a Jew. He also visited the shop of Luis Moro. Could it be that . . . He slammed his hand across his lips to stop even the speculation, because if he were called to the torture he must not even have suspicions to give the judges. He would strike the name Luis Moro from his memory forever and if . . .

'Oh, God! Oh, God!' he cried aloud. Then he quieted himself and wondered: How did Diego have the courage to keep my name from his lips? Abulafia wanted to utter lamentations in the streets for Ximeno, to pray for this great soul whose life had expired in flame, but he was afraid. Silently he wept, not even allowing the tears to form in his eyes lest his wife come suddenly upon him.

Choking on his grief and sense of sin Dr Abulafia reached a decision: I will flee Spain, I can no longer endure this horror. He hoped to find some quiet spot where he could study the Zohar in peace, seeking to find some way whereby the ten spheres of Godhood might lead ordinary men to an awareness of Him. But where could a Jew find freedom? And how could he escape Spain to get there? To Abulafia's rapidly moving mind came the memory of a letter he had once seen from a German Jew who claimed that in the empire of the Grand Turk, Jews could live without persecution, and he began constructing an involved plan for reaching Constantinople.

It was amateurish and almost impossible of execution, but he was in such a state of panic that he could be excused for his grotesqueries. First of all he would abandon his wife and children, and this was a grave decision of itself, for Maria Abulafia was a beautiful, compassionate wife whom he had loved deeply and his two sons were sturdy, laughing boys; but he reasoned: Even if they wanted to be Jews I couldn't get them out of the country. And if they preferred to remain Catholic how could I trust them to keep my secret? He decided to tell them nothing, unable to realize that his own flight must surely bring them before the Inquisition as his suspected accomplices.

Next he took another equally foolish step. He slipped down into the cellar, moved aside two stones and took out Diego Ximeno's manuscript of the Zohar and a small seven-branched candelabrum, an heirloom menorah which Ximeno had given him on the day in 1522 when they had mutually confessed to being secret Jews. To try to smuggle these two items out of Spain, especially through the port of Seville, was madness, for detection would mean certain death, but he would not leave without them.

In the morning he kissed Maria and the boys good-bye, informing them that he had been called to Seville on medical matters, and at an inn along the way he coldly forged documents directing him to proceed to Egypt on behalf of the Crown to investigate medicines developed by the notable Spanish doctor, Maimonides, who had served the Fatimid Caliph in Cairo. A more clever man would have produced a document so perfect that it must look suspicious; Abulafia's was so patently absurd, with the royal seal–transferred from another order–upside down, that it passed as honest.

In Seville he was nearly trapped three times: once at the inn where a suspicious clerk wanted to inspect his luggage and actually had the Zohar in his hands; once when he presented his forged sailing orders at the citadel; and finally when the Dominicans interrogated him, as they did all passengers, for final clearance. 'Wasn't this Maimonides a Jew?' they asked.

'Yes,' Abulafia replied, clenching his whole body to keep from trembling. 'Hundreds of years ago. But he is treasured as a Spaniard.'

'Why does the king want you to study Jewish medicine?'

'You know what they say about Maimonides. If the moon had consulted him, it wouldn't have spots on its face.'

The Dominicans laughed. 'Have you any Jewish blood?' they asked.

'None.'

'What are you carrying?'

'Medical books.' And thus he fled Spain.

As soon as his ship touched Tunis, Dr Abulafia went ashore to find a butcher shop, where he slashed his outer garments and smeared them with blood. He paid a Muslim to carry the evidence back to the captain with word that the Spanish doctor had been stabbed by robbers and that his body lay somewhere at the bottom of the bay. He then carried his precious luggage to a small inn and waited nervously until he saw his ship sail back to Spain. His childish plot had worked.

He summoned the innkeeper and asked to borrow a pair of scissors and a candle, after which he locked the door to his room and broke the candle into seven parts. Placing them in Diego Ximero's menorah he lit them, prayed in Hebrew and symbolically washed the water of baptism from his head. Then with trembling hands he took the rusty scissors and started to circumcise himself. The first cuts were so unexpectedly painful, the rush of blood so sudden, that he came near to fainting, But he strengthened himself, whispering, 'Fool! Think of Ximeno's feet,' and with a fortitude that had not previously been tested, he proceeded with his commitment. In exultation he threw open his window, crying in a loud voice the sanctified prayer of Judaism, 'Hear, O Israel, the Lord our God, the Lord is one.' Passers-by looked up at him as if he were a Jewish muezzin calling them to his mosque, and he shouted, 'Ximeno, I am a Jew? I am a Jew!'

And after many years he came to Safed, bearing a book.

3

The third Jew who made the long pilgrimage to Safed came not from raw fear, like Rabbi Zaki, nor from a love of Kabbalism, like Dr Abulafia; he came impelled by a force greater than either of those: the moral outrage of a man disgusted by his society.

In 1523 Germany represented an anomaly among the nations: Spain, Portugal, France and England, as rising national states, had expelled their Jews; but Germany, not to be united for several centuries, found no way to act as a unit and so began to accumulate those historic hatreds that were to erupt so savagely in later periods. For example, Cologne had expelled its Jews in 1426 but Frankfort had not. Augsburg, Nuremberg and Ulm had banished their Jews long ago, but the Rhineland city of Gretz, secure within its wall, still preserved a Judenstrasse where Jews were permitted to exist; and no resident of that quarter was more respected than Rabbi Eliezer bar Zadok, a descendant of the great family Hagarzi ha-Ashkenzax, whose ancestors had come from

Babylonia as groats makers about a thousand years before. In 1523 Rabbi Eliezer was a tall, scholarly man who surprised strangers with his boyish jokes and love of good beer. At his wedding to the prettiest Jewess in Gretz, Leah the weaver's daughter, he astounded the Judenstrasse by dancing all night, drinking beer with any who would join him and then in the cold dawn leading a group of scholarly Jews to the synagogue, where he lectured on the Talmud till nightfall, never mispronouncing a word. Friends asked, 'But what of the bride?' and he replied with an extraordinary smile, 'Leah and I are married for eternity. One night spent dancing with friends, one day spent honoring the Talmud we shall never miss.'

He was the acknowledged leader of the Jewish community, the judge of the Judenstrasse. More than any other Jew in Gretz he was free to move about, and although he was forced to observe all normal laws governing Jewish quarters, he alone managed to accept them with a certain dignity. For example, although he was a tall man he was forced by law to wear a Jew-hat almost three feet high, conical in shape, red in color and with a brim twisted to form devil's horns, so that when he moved about the city he could be identified as a Jew. He was also required to wear a coarse woolen coat 'which must reach to within two inches of the earth,' and this gave him the figure of a witch and was an invitation for the rabble to chase him through the alleys; but Eliezer wore his coat with such dignity that on him it became a kind of uniform, honored by the man who wore it. In the middle of the coat's back, like a target, was sewed a bright yellow ring signifying—as if additional signs were needed—that the wearer was a Jew, and the same ring, smaller in diameter, was repeated in front over the heart. It was this loathsome stigma that invited the Gentile community to despise even a dignified Jew like Rabbi Eliezer, for wherever he walked the yellow badge proclaimed, 'Here comes a Jew!' The circle was interpreted by some to represent a coin, ridiculing the only profession allowed the Jews; but most knew it to be a reminder of the holy wafer used in communion, which Jews were accused of stealing to profane in their obscene rites. It was this symbol, more than any other infliction, which kept the Jew apart from honest people; and if boys threw stones at Jews, it was partly because the slowly moving circles made irresistible targets.

There were other irritations. Eliezer, as a rabbi, would normally have grown a long beard, but since beards were a sign of German respectability, he must keep his short. He was not allowed to walk near the cathedral, to be on the streets during Holy Week, to converse aloud where others could hear him during church services, or halt at any time to speak with children lest he lure them into apostasy. Worst of all, he was required both by law and by custom to live within the Judenstrasse, which in Gretz was a concentrated horror. In the twelfth century two rows of large houses had been erected for Christians, and because enmity had developed between the owners, a space was left between the rows, and here brawls used to occur. The authorities were forced to build two walls sealing the houses off from each other, thus creating an empty space, forty-four feet wide, into which had been squeezed two rows of Jew houses along an alley six feet across. On the street level the houses seemed almost to touch; but as more and more Jews were crowded into the area, each narrow house had to be built higher and higher until finally only a small section of sky was visible: the Judenstrasse was permanently in shadow, its rooms gasping for air and its inhabitants crowded beyond belief.

One end of the street was blocked by a house which rose five stories, cutting off the sun, while the other was guarded by a stout iron gate, above which rose another house, so precious was the space. Thus the narrow area was closed at all points, and at dusk each day the iron gate clanged shut to be locked by a Christian guard whose salary the Jews were forced to pay. Inside the gate, where each Jew must see it daily, rose an obelisk commemorating a crime supposed to have been committed by the Jews of Trent some years before. Each of the four sides contained bas-reliefs showing details of how a saintly child had been tortured to death by hideous Jews in long cloaks, while above ran the legend: 'Sacred to the memory of the Christian boy, Simon of Trent, whose body was used as a blood sacrifice by the Jews of that city in the year 1475, for which unnatural crime all the Jews of Trent were burned to death.' It was a solemn reminder of the volcanic passions that might erupt at any moment against Jews, made more poignant by the fact that sometime after the mass burning, it was proved beyond question that Simon had not been touched by the Jews, and that the whole affair must be excused as another unfortunate mistake.

In each narrow room of the Judenstrasse lived an average of six persons, so that the number of Jews in the city was not insignificant, but they were not allowed to work in the Christian areas of the city, nor to join any of the guilds where men worked as artisans, nor to buy or sell merchandise of any kind except amongst themselves, nor to engage in any kind of enterprise except moneylending, which the Church still forbade to Christians; and it was not unusual to see the Christian dignitaries of Gretz come furtively to the Judenstrasse money shops, seeking loans, and then some months later to lead the rabble in to kill the moneylenders, burn the account books, and thus erase all debts.

Apologists for the system pointed out: 'Having the Jews assembled in one place affords them protection in case of trouble.' and perfectly sincere Christians who had never seen the incredible conditions believed this. They also argued: 'Jews like to live in a Judenstrasse. They thrive on it, don't they?' This reasoning was, in a perverse way, proved true by the Jews themselves, for when they found their families crowded into loathsome quarters, they adhered even more stringently to their strict sanitary laws, and at the same time Jewish medicine, which Christians ambivalently scorned and sought, protected them from any of the plagues which swept the free population. The Talmud itself had said: 'No Jew may live in a city that lacks a good physician.'

In the middle of the Judenstrasse stood one narrow room, musty and cramped, the center of Rabbi Eliezer's joy. It was his synagogue, and few houses of God have ever been so mean as this ugly little hovel in which the Jews of Gretz were forced to worship; it had no benches, no windows, no shelves for manuscripts. Jews who wished to pray sat on the floor, or, when the room was crowded, stood. There was a raised desk from which on Shabbat the rabbi's uncle, Isaac Gottes Mann, read the Torah, and there was one small shred of adornment: in front of the cupboard where the scroll of Torah was kept, hung an embroidered cloth. And that was about all, except that in one corner, for use on weekdays, there stood a patched and rickety table more than a hundred years old, plus one chair and a candelabrum; it was here, day after day through the long years, that Rabbi Eliezer studied Talmud, endeavoring to identify the legal and moral bases of his faith. Among the Jews of Germany it was recognized that if he were permitted long life he must surely become one of Judaism's luminaries.

In another corner of the synagogue was an area in which Rabbi Eliezer conducted school for the young boys of the Judenstrasse, and all under his care learned to read, for repeatedly he told parents, 'Teach your son to read and you give him four arms.' To Eliezer it was offensive to use the synagogue in this way, for boyish recitations interrupted the reading of older scholars, but in all the Judenstrasse not one additional corner could be found.

It was not by preference that the Jews of Gretz occupied so mean a synagogue; under existing law they were allowed no better: 'The Judenstrasse may contain a synagogue providing it be not large, nor so high as the cathedral, nor adorned in any way. Once built, it may never be changed in any detail, no matter how slight, without approval of the bishop.' The Jews did not like to see their learned rabbi studying at his rickety table, and some years ago had built him a better, but the guard at the iron gate had gotten wind of their move and had alerted the officials, who had confiscated the new table, fined the Jews and ordered the old one returned.

It was curious, Rabbi Eliezer reflected, that these degrading restrictions had originated not with civil legislators but with the Church. As he explained to his congregation: 'The same religion which seeks to win us to its bosom through conversion also forces this Judenstrasse upon us to prove how merciful it is.'

Actually, in Gretz there was little attempt at conversion, for no Jew would leave the guidance of Rabbi Eliezer and no Christian would welcome him if he did. Centuries before, Gunter the Crusader, in his rough German manner, had summed up the local attitude about conversion: 'A converted Jew is like chicken manure, hot when it leaves the bird but cold when it hits the ground.'

Furthermore, at this particular time in Gretz there was little reason for Jews to envy Christians, for the latter religion was shattered by contention. Though in 1517 the Jews had watched with indifference as Martin Luther, a monk who spoke Hebrew, launched his first shafts against the parent Church, now in 1523 a surge of hope sped through the Judenstrasse when Isaac Gottes Mann brought home a copy of Martin Luther's first public statement regarding Jews.

'It's unbelievable!' he cried as Jews assembled in the alley.

'What does he say?'

'He calls it *Jesus Was Born a Jew*. And I could not believe my eyes when I read it.' Carefully he recited the singing words:

'Our fools and jackasses, these priests, bishops, sophists and monks have treated the Jews in such a fashion that if a man wanted to become a true Christian he might better become a Jew. Were I a Jew and saw what blockheads and windbags rule and guide Christendom, I would rather become a sow than a Christian. For they have treated the Jews more like dogs than men. Yet the Jews are kith and kin and brothers-in-blood of our Saviour. If we are going to boast about the virtues of race, Christ belongs more to them than to us. To no other people has God shown such favor in entrusting them with His Holy Word.'

Isaac looked up, and the hope that he saw in the eager faces infected him and he cried, 'May God give Luther victory! If he wins he will abolish the Judenstrasse, because listen to what he says next: "My advice, therefore, is to deal decently with this people. So long as we resort to violence and lies and slander, and so long as we forbid them to work and trade and mingle at our side, thereby forcing them into usury, how can we expect to win them or better them? If we wish to help them we must employ not Papist law but Christian love. We must give them a friendly hand, letting them work and thrive in our midst, in order that they may have reason and occasion to become of us and with us.'''

The compassionate words caught the imagination of the Jews, and one summed it all up: 'He will let us work.'

But at this moment Rabbi Eliezer came through the iron gate, and seeing the crowd of people, joined them to hear the last words of the monk's message. In him, too, a surge of hope rose, but being a cautious man he asked to see the pamphlet, and as he studied it in silence and tried to formulate a guess as to what had been in Luther's mind as he wrote, he came to the sobering conclusion that the Jews would be wise not to pin their hopes too strongly to the Lutheran banner, and he said so.

'What do you mean?' Gottes Mann asked. 'He says right here that Jews are to be treated like human beings.'

'Yes, he does,' Eliezer agreed.

'Then I think we should support him,' Isaac said, and his suggestion gained some support.

'False,' Eliezer objected.

'How can you say that?' his uncle asked. He was the principal moneylender and a man of prudence.

'We know the Church,' Eliezer replied. 'And how it treats Jews. But we don't know this monk, Martin Luther.'

'Read his words, Rabbi!' one of the men pleaded.

'I have,' the tall man replied, 'and I know what Martin Luther means now, when he wants to use us against his own Church. But what will be his position if he wins? Will he not insist that we convert to his religion?'

At first Eliezer's argument made no sense. As one Jew argued, 'After this long night of oppression Martin Luther comes along and says, "In your treatment of Jews you are more like animals than Christians." I say, "Trust Luther and hope for his triumph."'

'No,' Eliezer warned flatly, 'there will be no support for Luther from the Jews of this city. We must not create a new opponent to supplant the old.'

He asked to borrow the pamphlet, and as he walked to the two tiny rooms in which he lived, airless and cramped, with his wife, his baby, his mother-in-law and two aunts, he felt certain that his decision was correct; but when he had gone over the pamphlet word by word he called his wife, and since she could not read, he read the words to her and watched as she sat with her hands clasping her knees, the most beautiful woman he had ever seen; and at the end of the reading he asked, 'What do you think of the message?'

'He says a lot that I like to hear,' she replied.

'But what does he mean?'

'I suppose that he has two things in mind. To use us now and to convert us later.'

'Exactly,' Eliezer cried. He had been married to Leah for two years, and his joy had not diminished. She was as perceptive as she was beautiful, and as affectionate with the people of the Judenstrasse as she was with her own son. She wore her hair parted in the middle and drawn down over her ears, so that her clear, bright face was framed in black. She had lived most of her life inside the locked gate of the quarter, for her father had wisely anticipated trouble if so lovely a Jewess were allowed to be seen by the young men of the city; and after her marriage to the rabbi, Eliezer had also asked her to stay close to home for the same reason. There had been many incidents in which attractive Jewish girls were raped or killed, and the authorities could find no way to punish the malefactors, principally because judges were reluctant to interpret rough play with Jewish girls as in any way criminal.

So for the next ten years Leah, the young rebbetzin of Eliezer bar Zadok, knew only the Judenstrasse, and here she shed a kind of radiance which made the narrow street livable. She was not a midwife, but most pregnant women wanted her to be with them during the toils of childbirth, and she had helped many. She was gifted with the needle, and in the semi-darkness of the Judenstrasse homes she taught young girls how to care for their fathers' clothes. Best of all she had a vivid imagination and loved to tell old stories about the heroes of Judaism, and mothers of the narrow street grew to expect their children to be at Rabbi Eliezer's, listening to the rebbetzin as she embroidered fabulous backgrounds to stories which in the Bible required only a few sentences.

'Now you must not think that Jael was any ordinary wife,' Eliezer heard her saying one day as more than a dozen children listened. 'Oh no! She was tall and she had red hair, and when she was no older than you she went into the Sinai Desert and tamed a lion, for she was never afraid. She knew how to weave and had many dresses of red and gold and blue, and she found colored stones to make for herself a necklace. Believe me, when Jael was married to Heber it was one of the biggest weddings you've ever seen. People came from villages far distant. They rode on horses and on camels, and Jael's younger sister—she was about your age—came riding on the tame lion, and some of the guests had to walk for three days to get to the wedding.'

'Were they allowed to leave the Judenstrasse?' a boy asked. 'Moishe!' she cried. 'In those days we had no locked streets or iron gates. Don't you know how we lived then? We had beautiful villages under the open sky, and palm trees bending with dates, and men like your father had horses on which they rode for miles along green fields. Maybe your father, Rachab, would have tended bees, and wherever he went on his white mule there were flowers, and in the woods there were lions for brave men to hunt, and at the edge of the desert there were camels which you could ride—if you were clever enough to catch them. And everywhere there was beauty. The lakes . . . the lakes were so big you could not possibly walk around them, and a man named Nethaneel had a boat on one of the lakes, and after the wedding he took all the children on the lake for a boat ride.'

Rabbi Eliezer studied quietly in a corner of the room, and after a while one of the older girls who wore pigtails asked, 'But why did Jael take a hammer and drive a nail into Captain Sisera's head?' The rabbi leaned forward to catch his wife's explanation, for the Talmud taught that Jael, in order to trick her enemy, engaged with him in seven acts of sexual intercourse, after which she drove a nail through his skull.

'If I explained to you now, Miriam, you could not possibly understand. So believe me when I say that Jael was one of the gentlest women of the Jews. Tell me, Miriam, do you think that a woman who could tame a lion would be other than gentle?'

'What does a camel look like?' one of the little boys asked.

'You've never seen a camel?' Leah cried. 'It's got fur like a lion and a tail like a tiger and four fast feet like a horse, and big teeth that tear down the tops of trees, and it sleeps in a little ball, like a kitten. You should have seen Jael and her husband Heber and their children when they rode on camels through the flowers. They would wave to people on the lake, and in the evening they would have dances in great open spaces under the stars. Did you really think that in the old days we proud Jews lived in narrow alleys like this?'

Frequently Rabbi Eliezer felt tempted to halt his wife's storytelling, for later the children would have to unlearn most of what she told them, but he never spoke to her about it. For later when the children grew up and married and went to live in the corner of some crowded room, to have their own children who would know only the Judenstrasse, it was desirable that they had at one time known of open spaces and self-respect; and the errors did no harm, for later they would remember only that Jael was a heroic woman who had killed a man in order to save Israel.

But the day came when even Eliezer realized that he must put a stop to his rebbetzin's wild storytelling, for as he sat on his bed one morning apparently reading, he heard Leah telling the wide-eyed children, 'The ark Moses found in the desert was as long as this house and twice as big, all covered with gold like Gottes Mann's cane, and in it he put the tables of the law and carried them for forty years across the desert. The desert?' She paused. 'It's as big as all the land from here to the city wall, flat and with lovely grass growing out of the sand, and flowers as far as you can see. And each night it grows a loaf with dark crust beside each flower, and in this way God kept his Jews alive for forty years.'

'What happened to the ark?' a boy asked, imagining himself on the flowering desert.

'It was lost,' the rebbetzin said, smoothing her hair back from her forehead, 'and we were all sorry. We wept. We tore our clothes. And then one day King David found it, tucked away in a small village, and he was so happy that he began to dance and to sing and to drink great mugs of beer. And he danced all night. And as he danced what do you suppose he did?'

'Kissed the girls?' Miriam in pigtails asked.

'Yes. He did that too. But he also composed more than a hundred psalms of joy.' It was at this point that Rabbi Eliezer felt obligated to halt his wife, but for some reason he did not do so, and Miriam asked, 'Is it true, Rebbetzin, what my mother says? That on your wedding night your husband danced all night?'

'Oh, yes!' the rebbetzin said. 'When we Jews lived freely, under the open sky, with the flowers of the desert about us, we danced all the time. It's only here that we've forgotten, Miriam, and when the rabbi danced at our wedding he was restoring the days of King David.'

And Rabbi Eliezer looked above the heads of the little children and saw his wife looking at him with love, and he said unexpectedly, 'Children, you must go home now,' and when they had left he sent his son from the crowded room too, and he embraced Leah as if it were the first time he had been alone with her. 'You are my lovely psalmist,' he whispered. 'In your distorted and contrary way you bring me truth.' He kissed her ardently and felt her cool hair tumbling about his face, and from the crowded alley they could hear the cries of children.

In late 1533, as a result of this tender interruption, it came Leah's turn to summon the midwife, and a girl was born named Elisheba, and now with two children of her own Leah was hardly ever seen without a cluster of young ones about her heels, and almost every day she had to tell them another story from the Hebrew past: of Samson and the far fields he had owned, where a man could ride in any direction for days without coming to the boundaries; and of Miriam, the great dancer, who had an orchestra of maybe seventy musicians and not less than sixteen different costumes; and finally of a shepherd boy named Samuel, who used to wander along paths that took him through fields and into forests and along lakes and across a land that was memorable. Whenever Leah told her stories children were able to visualize their Promised Land.

These were the happiest years that the Judenstrasse of Gretz ever knew, and none of the inhabitants had greater cause for joy than Rabbi Eliezer and his wife. His congregation was attentive to his leadership, and conflict within the quarter was scarcely known. His family constituted an almost ideal Jewish home, except that now four additional people from another family were cramped into the back room. He had no space to study, but he could always retreat to the synagogue and the rickety table with its candle and Talmud.

But in 1542 Isaac the moneylender came forth with a proposal: 'I have made profits and would like to contribute a new synagogue to the Judenstrasse, one of which we could be proud.'

Rabbi Eliezer rebuked him: 'The city law says we must live with the synagogue we have.'

'The new one could have benches,' Isaac argued, 'and a study place for you. It would be a credit to the Lord.'

Eliezer argued against the proposal, telling the would-be donor to give his funds to the poor, but Isaac pointed out that in the present period of religious uncertainty the town burghers might be more lenient. So against his better judgment Eliezer went before them and announced, 'The Jews of Gretz request permission to build a cleaner synagogue.'

He got his answer quickly: 'It would be an insult to the city, and would constitute a challenge to the supremacy of the cathedral. Since the Jews must already have the money in hand to commit this sacrilege, we hereby fine the Judenstrasse a sum equal to cost of building a new synagogue.'

Rabbi Eliezer had to protest the unfairness of this fine, and the city elders turned their wrath on him: 'And for his contumacy, the rabbi of the Judenstrasse is to be tried for opposing the operation of holy law, because the Bible says that Christians were abused in the synagogue, hence it must be an abomination of wickedness.'

A court was convened and Eliezer was summoned to trial, but Church officials protested that no Jew could properly swear to tell the truth, especially not on the Bible, which they denied, so an ancient Germanic custom was invoked, and into the court was hauled the bloody hide of a freshly killed pig. The rabbi was required to cast off his shoes and stockings and to stand barefooted in the pig's bloody skin and repeat, 'May the skin of this pig envelop me if I lie, may its meat choke my mother, may the head of the pig be transformed into the head of my daughter and may the swinish blood be smeared upon the foreheads of my children for three generations if I do not tell the truth.'

Rabbi Eliezer, who had taught himself to read seven languages, stepped like a criminal onto the pigskin and swore. The officials then required him to repeat after them the routine confession: 'I am a filthy Jew whose people crucified the true Christ. I am a wanderer who has no home save where the benevolence of the Church provides one. I am evil and corrupt and an abomination to all men. I poison wells, spread the plague and kill Christian children for their blood. My women are whores and my fate is everlasting hell, for I am the enemy of the Church and of all good Christians.'

Next Rabbi Eliezer publicly admitted that this description accurately characterized him, after which he was required to attest, on the blood of the pig in whose skin he stood, that he came before the court not as a rabbi, the leader of a congregation, for to admit the presence of such leadership might be interpreted as acknowledging the lawful presence of Jews, but as a man alone, asking for an intemperate request. He was forced to kneel down, placing both hands in the pig's blood, and he did so.

Not only was the denial of a new synagogue confirmed, but the synagogue already standing in the Judenstrasse was ordered to be torn down, since it was a source of evil and an offense to Christ. And as penance for his personal effrontery Rabbi Eliezer would be required next Shabbat to kiss the hind end of the Sow of Gretz in front of the assembled citizenry.

Defiled and torn in spirit the rabbi returned to the Judenstrasse and informed his Jews that they were about to lose their synagogue. In the narrow alley he announced, 'It is a judgment upon us because of our arrogance. When will we learn, O Israel, that we serve the Lord not in buildings but in our hearts? The sin is upon us, not upon them who destroy the building. The lamentations are ours, for we caused them with our vanity. When the building is torn down we shall all watch, and we shall wear mourning, for the sin is upon us.'

He went to the ritual bath to cleanse himself of the defilement he had suffered in the Christian court, but as he lay in the consoling waters he heard children shouting, 'Here come the men with the axes!' He reached the street in time to see a score of workmen start their demolition of the synagogue. With crowbars they ripped down the door and with fire borrowed from the kitchen of a Jewish home they started a conflagration into which they threw the door, Eliezer's old table and the rickety chair. The raised desk from which the Torah was read they pitched into the flames and then Eliezer watched with dismay as they tore down the embroidered covering of the cupboard and tossed it irreverently onto the fire; it was as if they had thrown a woman there, for the fragile cloth was beautiful, and a man tried to rescue it but was driven back.

Then Eliezer's dismay became unbelieving tragedy when the workmen ripped down the cupboard and shook it to dislodge the parchment scroll of Torah. As the holy book rolled in the dust, the destroyers kicked it toward the flames. Deftly one of the men caught the scroll with his toe and lofted it in a graceful arc so that it fell into the fire, where flames quickly reached for the sheepskin and consumed it.

From the Jews came a long wail: 'God of Moses, take back your Torah!' And they began to rend their garments as if death had visited that place, and Rabbi Eliezer, tearing his long-coat, prayed aloud, reciting from the Psalms of David: '"Our fathers trusted in thee: they trusted, and thou didst deliver them. They cried unto thee, and were delivered: they trusted in thee, and were not confounded."' Thus in their moment of humiliation he tried to console his people, but in the midst of his prayer his voice dried up, not from fear and not because of the flame, but because from the synagogue the workmen had brought the precious scrolls of the Talmud, and these rare books they now threw into the laughing fire.

A young boy whom Eliezer had been teaching the Talmud saw the precious works strike the flame, and he was so desirous of knowing the secrets of these books that he broke away from his mother and tried to rescue them. He rummaged among the brands, clutching futilely at the parchments, and the Christians, seeing that he could accomplish nothing, indulged him; but at last the flames drove him back and he stood beside the rabbi, not yet aware that his hands were badly charred. '"Be not thou far from me, O Lord,"' Eliezer prayed. '"O my strength, haste thee to help me."' And the men with the axes worked on.

When the fires were burned down, when the charred hands of the would-be scholar were bound, Rabbi Eliezer stood looking at the gutted synagogue, recalling those wintry nights when candles had lighted the faces of old men studying the Talmud and those bright, hopeful Shabbat mornings when frightened boys of thirteen had stood before their elders to announce in piping voice, 'Today I am a man.' Where now would the old men read, where now would the young proclaim? He looked with affection at the roof, to which each year for many centuries the storks had come in spring from the Holy Land, to the gaping door at which travelers had always found a welcome, and at the hollow interior, where generations of Jews had learned the principles by which men can live together in harmony. This synagogue had been a force for great good in Gretz, and in destroying it the Christians had weakened themselves.

With these gloomy thoughts Rabbi Eliezer went slowly home like a man walking knee-deep in ashes, and there he found his wife sitting calmly among the chilren, sharing with them the only lasting reality the Jews had ever known: 'In those days we owned a city on a hill to which men of every kingdom were welcomed in friendship. Jerusalem it was called, and inside its walls King Solomon built not a small synagogue but a temple standing upon an open space so great you could not walk around it. Not two of you together, Moishe starting at one end and Rachel at the other, could have run around that field in a whole day. There were trees with birds in them, and camels watering themselves beside the cool streams. It was a temple so beautiful that King Hiram of Tyre sent down a shipload of two hundred people to inspect it and tell him if it was as beautiful as the temples of Tyre; and two of his men cried, "Put out my eyes so that I need not tell the king that I have seen this perfect thing." and two other men said, "Let us stay in the land of the Jews, for we would be afraid to tell our king how great their temple is," and two other men, very important men in the city of Tyre, said, "Give us brooms that we may stay here the rest of our lives and sweep this temple, it is so beautiful." And in that way King Hiram lost six good men.'

'Were there stables for the horses?' a boy asked.

'Not in the temple itself,' Leah explained, 'but along the edges of the fields nearby there were many stables filled with swift horses, and boys and girls like you used to mount the horses and ride swiftly . . . Oh, you rode so swiftly over the meadows and down the roads and when you came to a brook you would lean forward like this and spur your horse and . . . Oh!' Leah threw her hands in the air. 'You and the horse flew over the brook and you landed safely on the other side and you rode on and on in the free air and after a long while you stopped and turned your horses around—and what do you suppose you saw?'

'The temple?' a boy asked.

'Yes,' she said.

Rabbi Eliezer sat on a chair in the corner and buried his face. Leah, seeing him, thought that he might be weeping and she asked the children to go out and play, but Christian horses had been led into the narrow street to cart away the remnants of the synagogue, so she hid the noisy children in another home, that they might not witness the desecration, and then rejoined her husband.

He was not weeping. Rabbi Eliezer was not the kind of man to weep, but he did sometimes feel upon his shoulders a force greater than he could struggle with, and now he felt it, and seeing him thus his wife burst into tears. 'Our lovely, lovely synagogue,' she cried. It had been a travesty of a place of worship, an obscene hovel, really, but it had been too large for the Gentiles to tolerate, and now it was gone. 'Oh God of Israel, what did we do wrong?' she wept.

Coldly, because he did not dare set loose his thoughts, the rabbi said, 'On Shabbat they are repeating the obscenity of kissing the Sow's rump.'

'You?' she asked in an ashen voice.

'Yes.'

'No!' she screamed, and flung herself on the floor, clutching at his knees. 'No!' No!'.

He smoothed her hair and began to laugh. 'Yes, your husband. On Shabbat at noon. And you and all the Jews of Gretz will be there to watch. For me it will not be a humiliation, but for the men who have ordered it, yes.'

She looked up at her husband and he was strangely composed. She rose from the floor and sat beside him, asking, 'What shall we do about the synagogue?'

'We will make this room our synagogue,' he explained, and he sent her into the street to ask the Jews to join him in prayer; and when the men were jammed in he recited from memory one of the great passages of the Torah, for in the community there was no longer a copy: 'This is the promise of Moses our Teacher: "If from thence thou shalt seek the Lord they God, thou shalt find him, if thou seek him with all thy heart and with all thy soul. When thou art in tribulation, and all these things are come upon thee, even in the latter days, if thou turn to the Lord thy God and shalt be obedient unto his voice; (For the Lord thy God is a merciful God;) he will not forsake thee, neither destroy thee, nor forget the covenant of thy fathers which he sware unto them."'

On Shabbat, when they should have been in synagogue, the Jews in their tall red hats, long cloaks and yellow circles were marched through the iron gate of the Judenstrasse and up to the front of the cathedral, where they faced two of the most artistic stone statues in Europe, the 'Triumph of Church over Synagogue.' To the left of the entrance stood the Church Triumphant, a graceful woman of exquisite features standing at rest and bearing in her right hand a stave adorned by banners, and in her left a cross topped by a crown of thorns. The excellence of the carving was demonstrated in her face, but the spirit of the Church as it showed in her eyes and firm chin was not peaceful, but condemnatory; not marked by conciliatory grace, but harsh and unforgiving.

The coldness of the statue was understandable, for it looked across the great entrance of the cathedral to a similar statue representing the Synagogue Defeated, and this woman was not beautiful. Her eyes were blindfolded and her mournful, humiliated head was bowed. In her right arm she carried a broken spear with no triumphal banners, and in her left a most curious object. It was the two-part stone tablet of Moses on which God had given him the law, but in this case the stones were broken, and the entire figure of the synagogue was one of desolation. Rabbi Eliezer, as always, studied only the broken tablets of Moses and wondered: What theology could construct a theory that a new Church could be built upon the destruction of all which had made that Church morally strong? Do they think they rescind the law of Moses by shattering his tablets?

His tormentors that day had little thought for the law of Moses, nor for anything else except the hearty horseplay of the Middle Ages, preserved in Germany long after it had vanished elsewhere; for after a perfunctory sermon which reminded the Jews of the merciful quality of the Church, they were herded to the northern side of the cathedral, where a robust statue more famous than either that of the Church or of the Synagogue at the entrance had been set into the wall. It was the notorious Sow of Gretz, and now as the populace saw the Jews herded before it, shouts of joy and festivity filled the old city.

The Sow of Gretz was a huge recumbent stone pig of evil visage lying on her side with some two dozen teats exposed. At half the stations little stone devils with amusing tails and saucy horns fed, while at the remaining teats Jews in disgraceful caricature feasted, the intended concept being that from the poisonous sow of Judaism all Jews sucked in contamination from the day of birth. If the carving had ended there it could have been accepted as rather vigorous religious homily, suited to the rougher tastes of an earlier day; but on the right-hand side of the statue the argument became more vicious. Here a devil lifted the tail of the sow to show to a Jewish rabbi the origin of the Talmud, for from the anus of the beast could be seen projecting the edge of the Jewish book, while the bowels ejected a heavy stream of defecation which struck the stone rabbi in the face. Throughout the centuries it had become customary for the Christian children of Gretz to paint the lines of defecation yellow and to continue the coloring across the face of the rabbi.

'For his arrogance the rabbi will now kiss the hind end of the Sow,' an official announced, and Eliezer was led to the rear of the statue and forced to bow down. But as he did so his revulsion was so great that he jerked backward and his tall hat fell off, and there was a scream of protest from the populace. 'Hat, hat!' they shouted, and he was directed to replace it, but as he returned to the Sow the hat again fell off, so an official produced a string with which he tied the hat to Eliezer's ears. The crowd cheered.

Now the rabbi prepared to kiss the Sow's rump, and as he bent down he found that pranksters had smeared the statue with real excrement, and those in the crowd who knew what had been done giggled with knowing delight; but he kissed the Sow and then instinctively wiped his lips. The crowd protested, and officials decreed that he must perform his obeisance again without wiping his lips, and he complied.

That night he assembled in his home-synagogue some of the leaders of the Jewish community and read them a letter which had circulated secretly in Germany for some years. It had been written by a Jew from Gretz who had escaped the Judenstrasse and made his way to Turkey:

> In the realm of the Grand Turk even the poorest Jew can live like a human being. Constantinople lacks nothing, and is one of the finest cities in the world. I dress as I please and wear no special mark. My children do the same and are not beaten on the streets. We have built a fine synagogue, and one of our men is counselor to the sultan. Any man who can work is welcomed by the Turk.

'I think we should go,' Rabbi Eliezer said.

'You're agitated by the dirty business of the Sow,' Isaac Gottes Mann argued. 'They didn't humiliate you, Eliezer.'

'I cannot even remember that I kissed the Sow,' Eliezer honestly replied. 'But I do remember the looks of hatred on the German faces. It is for their sakes that we should leave.'

'Why do you worry about the Germans?'

'If we cause such hatred in Catholic hearts, then we should go,' Eliezer replied simply.

'Those people today?' Isaac countered. 'If they didn't hate us they'd find somebody else.'

'I no longer want to be the cause of Christians' committing sin,' Eliezer said, and his wife noticed that in three sentences he had moved the argument upward from German to Catholic to Christian; and when the men argued further, he said firmly, 'I will not live with my brother if I cause him to outrage God.' Leah thought: This great, good man, constantly he lifts matters up to where they truly rest.

There was a change in the discussion when Isaac, still hopeful that the Jew would find an honorable place in Germany, argued, 'The dominance of the Church over us is limited, Eliezer. Before long Gretz may be a Lutheran city,' and spurred by these words the Jews in the crowded synagogue reopened the speculation begun twenty years earlier at the publication of Luther's conciliatory letter on the Jews: Was there a possibility that a new kind of Christianity might replace the old?

'We must pray for the triumph of Luther,' one of the hopeful Jews reasoned. 'In all parts of Germany he is humiliating the Church, and with his victory our freedom will come.'

A matter of real hope had been raised, a breath of fresh air sweeping down the centuries of persecution and entering even the crushed houses of the Gretz Judenstrasse. No Jew dared openly say that he prayed for the downfall of his ancient oppressor, for the Church had proved remorseless in its punishment of renegades, but it was agreed against Rabbi Eliezer's advice to wait a little longer; and that night when the congregation had departed, even Leah whispered, 'We should not go to Turkey, husband. Our children are happy here and we have a good life.' But Eliezer knew that she was not right. No life that involved the hatreds he had seen that day, even though no man had been killed or no house burned, could possibly be termed good.

'Leah,' he said sharply, 'it's proper for you to create the dreams of children and to tell them of open fields, but don't tell your husband that this rotten life is good.' He pointed at the bedroom in which he stood. 'A synagogue of half a room, in which the rabbi sleeps.'

Leah replied, 'I am hoping that some day things may be better.'

'The Jews of Germany always hope,' he said harshly, kicking his bed into position.

Leah took him by the hands and asked, 'Eliezer, tell me the truth. Why are you determined to leave?'

He thought for a moment, then said, 'Because to live as we do in the Judenstrasse is a moral outrage.'

The simple truth stunned Leah and she said quietly, 'I shall go with you.'

Cryptically Eliezer added, 'We may have to leave very soon. The books of the Jews are being burned, and unless my work is done quickly they may perish.'

Then in 1543 even optimistic Jews like Isaac Gottes Mann learned what the future was to be, for Martin Luther, their one-time champion against the Church, turned on them with a fury that only a sage like Rabbi Eliezer could have predicted. Having tried vainly to convert the stiff-necked Jews to Lutheranism, and having found them as obdurate against Protestants as they had been against Catholics, Luther surrendered all hope for them and lashed out in rantings that came close to monomania or downright idiocy. 'Well-poisoners, ritual murderers, spreaders of the plague, practicers of black magic' were some of the milder forms he flung at them. Jewish bankers, he said, stole the life-blood of the community while Jewish doctors poisoned Gentile patients. Synagogues must be destroyed, the Torah burned wherever it could be found, homes torn down brick by brick and Jews sent into the fields to live like Gypsies. 'I would threaten to rip their tongues from their throats,' said the prince of Protestantism 'if they do not accept the proof that God is three and not one,' and he urged all God-fearing men to hound the Jews like wild beasts from the land.

It was a shattering blow, the final closing of the door, for these charges would reverberate along the Rhine for centuries, finding voice at last in strange and hideous quarters. So that night Rabbi Eliezer announced to his family, 'Tomorrow we start for Turkey.'

'Do you know where it is?' the rebbetzin asked.

'We shall go up the Rhine,' he replied, 'cross over into Hungary, and go down the Danube to the capital of the Grand Turk.' And only his wife could visualize the terror and loneliness encompassed in those words.

But Eliezer could not leave Gretz without discharging a final obligation to his community, and to that end he assembled the leaders in his narrow room, saying, 'I think you ought to leave Germany now. Those who cannot risk the long journey to Constantinople should move on to Poland, where there is freedom.'

This suggestion was greeted with protest, so he added, 'I know how deeply you love Germany and how you hope one day to find peace here. Isaac Gottes Mann has consented to become the leader of those who stay behind, and under him may you find the peace you seek.'

'Reconsider!' Gottes Mann begged his nephew. 'This madness will pass and we Jews will know centuries of wonderful accomplishment in this beautiful land, for we are Germans.'

'I feel myself charged with saving the soul of Judaism,' Rabbi Eliezer said, and next morning he was off. But as he led his family for the last time through the iron gate his rebbetzin looked back with longing at the little children who were weeping to see her go, and she uttered the lament of all Jewish mothers who left the ghettos which they had tried to make endurable: 'Our little street, what a kingdom of love it was.'

When the family of Bar Zadok approached the border of Germany they were overtaken by a gang of men on horseback who noticed the beauty of the two women, Leah and Elisheba, then nearing eleven, and they began to molest them, so that the rabbi and his son had to defend their womenfolk against the horsemen, who shouted, 'Let's have fun with the Jewesses!' A heavy fight ensued, with the men lashing out at the four Jews and finally knocking Leah to the ground.

When Eliezer saw his wife fall he leaped at one of the assailants, caught him by the leg and tried to pull him from his mount; but the others rode back furiously and their horses trampled the fallen Leah so badly that she died. With anguish greater even than he had ever known, Rabbi Eliezer buried his wife and led his children toward Hungary.

In that country the rabbi's son fell ill, and there was no money to buy his cure, and he, too, died. But after a long time the tall scholar and his daughter Elisheba came to Safed.

THE TELL

'Jesus Christ!' Cullinane cried, bursting from sleep and finding himself bolt upright in bed at three in the morning. He was covered with sweat, and the vision he had been having of the two trees remained as clear as the stars shining through his tent.

The first tree he had seen as Major Cullinane, flying his bomber into the Atsugi air base in Japan at the end of World War II. One March morning at an inn where he had taken a charming Japanese girl he had lain in his bed after a session of exquisite love-making and had idly spotted a cherry tree which an early warm breeze had teased into sending forth the first flowers of spring. It had been a different kind of tree from those he had known in America: a huge, gnarled trunk several feet across and apparently dead, except that from it sprang one splendid branch which was vitally alive and about to be covered with flowers.

'Why don't they cut the old tree down?' he had asked the girl.

'Cut?' she had echoed in disbelief. 'I bring you here ... the best tree in Japan ... very famous.' And with gestures she had explained that the Japanese prize such a tree above all others, for it reminds the viewer that it is ancient and near death, but that one powerful strain of life still pulsates through the bark; and as he had lain there, enjoying the girl and the quiet inn and the old tree, he had caught something of the spirit of Japan and its strange values.

'In America,' he had said, 'any self-respecting farmer would cut down an old crock like that. But I see what you mean.'

Later the same girl had taken him to the bonsai mart in Tokyo, where he had seen dwarf trees, sixteen inches tall and two hundred years old; and his pleasure in their beauty had been so evident that she had taken him to her uncle's, and for the first time he had become aware that she was not a prostitute but a sensitive girl with a college education, caught up in the aftermath of an imperial war. And she had shown him her uncle's bonsai, famous in Japan—a dwarf cherry tree more than three hundred years old, with a trunk even more dilapidated than the one at the inn. It was almost hollow, black and lifeless, with numerous holes worn through it where branches had once grown; and again one single bright limb flourished, covered with blossoms.

'It's a miracle,' the old man had said, 'the foundation and the flower.'

The second tree he had found at Makor, that very old olive, a gaunt, dismembered relic whose trunk existed only as a dead cavity surrounded by fragments of life, but like the cherry in Japan this patriarchal thing—perhaps two thousand years old—sent forth from its always-dying body persistent branches of great beauty, and they bore fruit. On first seeing this miraculous olive he had not remembered the cherry in Japan, but one day in August while sitting beneath its branches and trying to evoke the Makor of Emperor Vespasian, he happened to look at the tree in a new way, and he had snapped his fingers, crying, 'It's just like that cherry tree Tomiko showed me in Japan.' He had remembered the girl's name, and the inn, and her uncle's bonsai.

Now, in the dark tent at Makor, he remained sitting in bed and saw the two ancient trees before his eyes, plus a conceptual vision as clear as the diagram in a book. He thought: I was raised to believe that the Old Testament was dead, and that whatever it contained worth saving had been transplanted into the New. In the same way I was taught that Judaism was dead, except for a few obstinate Jews, and that true religion had been handed on to the Christian church, which had produced a flowering.

He shook his head, as if he had been knocked dizzy, but the two trees remained before him, and they represented the modified view of religion which he had been developing without having consciously verbalized it: We have the great, primitive trunk of Judaism and we also have the branch-tip flowering of Christianity, and I intuitively thought that the first was dead and that all life had passed into the second. I never really considered whether the Christian church had direct roots into the soil or not. If anyone had told me that the flowering branch had no roots except those which extended through the forbidding old trunk of Judaism, I'd not have known what he was saying. But now I see.

He was fascinated by the persistence of his vision and was amused when he reconstructed how the trees had come to him. He had gone to sleep thinking of Vered Bar-El in Chicago and this had led to an erotic dream about Tomiko, probably the most exciting girl he had ever known—or it may have been that he was younger then—and she had passed naked into the old trunk of the cherry tree, and it in turn had become the olive tree under which Jesus could have sat; and in this way he had come to the question of God. It sneaks up on you in the damnedest places, he mused, and the trees slowly vanished, but their enigma remained.

Freed of the vision he tried to sleep but found this impossible, and in the dark hours before birds sang he thought of the work he was doing. Until Makor he had never seriously considered the merits of Judaism. He had not understood how anyone could find in the stalwart obstinacy of the Jews a way of life, nor had he approved the awkward procedure of the synagogue with its lack of harmony and appeal to the senses. It seemed to Cullinane—and in this he was without rancor or blind adherence to his own faith—that the Christian church had brought to the religious experience an extraordinary beauty and a personal involvement that far exceeded what he had found in Judaism. It was like comparing, he thought, a beautiful singing young woman filled with life to an old woman . . .

He choked. There, by God, it was! The stony, unyielding religion he had been unable to understand deserved all the unfavorable descriptions he had given it; but it was also like the old woman, knowledgeable, patient, immortal and close to God. He closed his eyes and saw again, the olive tree of Makor: so terribly powerful, so close to the soil, and old, old, old, with holes through it and emptiness and a forbidding sense of time. Yet it was alive.

Remaining in a sitting position he took a hard look at himself and asked: After this digging in the heart of religion, what do I honestly think of Judaism? And because he was a bookish man his conclusions centered on three books: Judaism was an unresilient, gnarled body of primordial belief founded on the Torah; plus a Talmudic ritual equally unyielding but very efficient in providing man with specific guidance; and the Zohar. This trio of books, Torah, Talmud, Zohar, had produced a unified religion with tremendous powers for survival; in fact, the religion seemed to have a built-in determination to survive, for throughout history, whenever its contemporary form had seemed doomed, some new primitive force had evolved which had given the religion another thrust forward. Even the dates of these thrusts were significant, Cullinane thought. By the year 1100 B.C.E. the characteristics of Old Testament Judaism had been fairly well evolved, and to a surprising degree it had existed unchanged for about thirteen hundred years, when in the years following the final destruction of the Jewish state, say, around 200 C.E., the Talmud began to take shape. The period of Talmudic domination had lasted for another thirteen hundred years until around 1500 C.E., when the Kabbala of Spain was transported to the heights of Safed, where it suddenly exploded in a mystical radiance which spread throughout the Jewish world with enough vitality to keep the spirit of Judaism alive for another thirteen hundred years, say, until the year 2800 C.E. What the Jews will come up with then, Cullinane mused, is no concern of mine.

Again he lay down and tried to sleep, but he could not, so he asked himself: If I had to characterize Judaism in simple terms for someone who knew nothing about it, what words would I use? And almost against his willing it to be so, the symbolism of the olive tree returned and he replied: Ancient, gnarled, unresilient, a powerful religion which takes man back to his fundamental nature and experience. He laughed. In two thousand six hundred years Judaism had been able to accept only two changes, the Talmud and the Kabbala, whereas Christianity, with masterful resiliency, had spun off a dozen staggering modifications whenever the spirit of the times demanded: trinitarianism, transubstantiation, the infallibility of the Pope, the near-deification of Mary. There lay the difference between the two religions; there lay the explanation of why Christianity had conquered the world while Judaism remained the intransigent, primordial religion of the few.

'Hey, Eliav!' he called. 'You still asleep?' There was no reply, proving that Eliav was still sleeping and would no doubt wish to remain so, but in spite of this Cullinane crossed over to Eliav's bed and shook him.

'You asleep?'

'Not now,' the Jew replied.

'I can't sleep. I've been hammering at some ideas and I'd like to try them out on you.'

'Shoot.' Eliav sat up and grabbed his knees to his chest, while the Irishman sat on the foot of his bed. Only moonlight illuminated the tent, and the men spoke in low voices so as not to disturb Tabari.

'I've been perplexed ... '' He hesitated, as if in embarrassment. 'By a matter of religion.'

'Why not? We've been digging in it for long enough.'

'And I wondered what a believing Jew ...'

'Don't look at me. I'm no orthodox rabbi, spending his time in the synagogue.'

'I'm no priest, spending his time at mass.'

'You mean,' Eliav suggested, 'that we're both illiterates?'

'Exactly, except that it's people like us who keep the thing moving.'

'Agreed.'

'So let me ask it again. What does an average, non-orthodox Jew like you think of the parallel development of Judaism and Christianity?'

Eliav let go his knees and leaned backward on his pillow, thought for some time, then drew himself forward and said, 'I've always thought that classical Judaism was about ready for a new infusion sometime around the year 100 C.E. The old patterns were ready to be enlarged. For proof, look at the concepts we get from the Dead Sea Scrolls. Or the development of the Talmud. So I've never resented the eruption of Christianity. The world was ready for it.'

'Why?'

'Possibly because Judaism was a hard, tough old religion that didn't give the individual enough free play. It could never have appealed to the world at large. The bright, quixotic religion of Christianity was ideally suited for such a proselytizing need.'

'Is brightness the difference between the two?' Cullinane pressed.

'Partly. Because, you see, when Judaism did reform by means of the Talmud it went backward toward its own nature. It became harder and more irresponsive to modern change, whereas the Christian church moved forward psychologically, and in a time of wild change an organism that is retracting has less chance than one which is expanding.'

'Seems to me it was unfortunate for Judaism that in the years of decision you had the inward-looking rabbis, whereas we Christians had outward-looking church fathers.'

'Right there you beg the question,' Eliav said slowly. 'You say you were lucky that in the critical years between 100 and 800 C.E. Christianity went forward, and we were unlucky that during the same years Judaism went backward. Don't you see that the real question is forward to what, backward to what?'

Cullinane reflected for a moment and said, 'By God, I do! That's what's been bugging me without my knowing it, because I hadn't even formulated the question.'

'My thought is that in those critical years Judaism went back to the basic religious precepts by which men can live together in a society, whereas Christianity rushed forward to a magnificent personal religion which never in ten thousand years will teach men how to live together. You Christians will have beauty, passionate intercourse with God, magnificent buildings, frenzied worship and exaltation of the spirit. But you will never have that close organization of society, family life and the little community that is possible under Judaism. Cullinane, let me ask you this: Could a group of rabbis, founding their decisions on Torah and Talmud, possibly have come up with an invention like the Inquisition—an essentially anti-social concept?'

Now it was Cullinane who rocked back and forth, and after a while he confessed, 'I'm afraid that in those days we did treat you rather badly.'

Eliav groaned. 'Why do Christians always use that marvelous euphemism, "treated rather badly"? John, your Inquisition burned to death more than thirty thousand of our best Jews. I read the other day that a leading German had confessed that his nation had "treated the Jew rather badly." He had fallen back upon this inoffensive term to cover the destruction of a people. Judaism would simply not permit its rabbis to come up with solutions like that. Judaism can be understood, it seems to me, only if it is seen as a fundamental philosophy directed to the greatest of all problems: how can men live together in an organized society?'

'I would have thought,' Cullinane suggested, 'that the real religious problem is always "How can man come to know God?"'

'There's the difference between us,' Eliav said. 'There's the difference between Old Testament and New. The Christian discovers the spirit of God, and the reality is so blinding that you go right out, build a cathedral and kill a million people. The Jew avoids this intimacy and lives year after year in his ghetto, in a grubby little synagogue, working out the principles whereby men can live together.'

'About the euphemism, "treated rather badly." What does a Jew like you feel about that ... now?'

Again Eliav relaxed his hold on his knees and fell back into the darkness. 'I think it was very good for the world,' he said slowly, 'that Martin Luther came along.'

'What do you mean?' Cullinane asked.

'I mean that up to then you Catholics had really treated us Jews, as you say, rather badly. If one made a simple list of all that your church did to mine it would quite destroy any moral justification for Catholicism to continue, and if a man like me felt that what your people had done to us was an essential characteristic of Catholicism, then I don't see how we could co-exist. But fortunately for world history, Martin Luther came along to prove that Protestants could behave with equal savagery. After all it wasn't misguided Catholics in Germany in 1939 who fired up the furnaces. It was good, sober Protestants. It wasn't Catholic political leaders who shrugged off the whole affair. It was Protestant prime ministers and presidents. So a man like me reasons, "What happened in Spain was no part of Catholicism. And what happened in Germany wasn't Protestantism. Each was merely an expression of its times, a manifestation of the deadly sickness of Christianity." Do you understand what I'm saying?'

'That it's the Christians who kill Jews, not Catholics or Protestants.'

'Yes,' Eliav said. 'The tremendously personal religion that evolved around the figure of Christ was all that He and Paul had envisaged. It was brilliant, penetrating and a path to personal salvation. It was able to construct soaring cathedrals and even more vaulted processes of thought. But it was totally incapable of teaching men to live together.'

There was a stirring in the other bed and Tabari came over to Eliav's cot. 'Don't believe a word of what he's saying,' the Arab said. 'The only reason the Jews haven't behaved like the Christians is that for the last two thousand years they haven't had anyone they can kick around. That's primarily because whenever they form a kingdom it quickly comes apart at the seams. How long did the empire of Saul and David last? A little over one hundred years. In an area as small as Palestine they broke up into the Northern Kingdom and the Southern. John, you've heard what they say about Jews? Two Jews get together, they build three synagogues. "You go to yours, I'll go to mine, and we'll both boycott that son of a bitch on the hill."'

Eliav laughed. 'You may have something there, Jemail. Historically, we've found it just about as difficult to get together as you Arabs have.'

'About the same,' Jemail agreed. 'But as I listened to you two fellows argue I thought: Why should I lie here silent, when I have the solution?'

'What is it?' Cullinane asked.

'Simple. Judaism had its day, and if the Jews had been smart, when Christianity came along they'd have joined up. Christianity has had its day, and if you were intelligent you'd both join the newest religion. Islam!' He bowed low and said, 'Soon all Africa will be Islamic. And all Black America. I see India giving up Hinduism while Burma and Thailand surrender Buddhism.

Gentlemen, I represent the religion of the future. I offer you salvation.'

The easy nonsense of his statement pleased the men and they began to laugh, while from the other tent the photographer called, 'Coffee,' and a day began, little different from the fifteen million days which had dawned over Makor since the first organized community had been established in its cave.

4

In the early years of the 1500s Safed was an undistinguished village of one thousand people who lived in a collection of mud-walled houses perched along narrow alleys that climbed up and down the southwestern flank of a hill in the Galilee. At the crest of this hill, wasting in sunlight and inhabited only by eagles and crawling things, stood the gaunt remains of a Crusader fort, its once-soaring turrets fallen and its walls collapsed.

Winds from the north had deposited upon the humbled fortress a freight of blowing silt in which trees had taken root, so that the once-proud castle was now merely a mound of earth with only here and there a rock projecting, sometimes with a bit of carving, to indicate how majestic that hilltop had once been. Of the thousand residents some two hundred were Jews, a few were Christians and the rest were Muslim, with only one or two men who remembered hearing from their grandfathers that their hill had once been a bastion of the Crusaders.

The town, which nestled on the hillside well below the ruins, contained two mosques, a synagogue, a small church, some dark covered souks and a nest of small Jewish shops. The Turkish governor, ruling on edict from Constantinople, maintained peace among the various communities and allowed qadis to judge the Muslims, rabbis to rule the Jews and priests to govern the Christians. Once each year a small caravan straggled in from Damascus, bringing a few bales of shoddy goods in sad memory of the silks and spices of former times, and Turkey collected few taxes, for there was no substantial trade. In fact, if one had looked dispassionately at Safed in those early years he would surely have predicted, 'This little village will continue sleeping forever. The only good thing here is the mountain air.'

Then in 1525 several events, apparently unrelated, conspired to change the history of Safed, transforming it for some ninety years into one of the most significant communities in the world: a manufacturing city of sixty thousand, a trading center known through Europe and the spiritual capital of the Jewish people. The drowsy little town was about to enter an age of gold so luminous that its memory would be cherished by nations then not even in existence. The revolution was achieved by three unlikely conspirators: the camel, the spinning wheel and the book.

The miracle of Safed began with the camel. As the wealth and power of the Turkish empire grew, with Constantinople replacing Genoa and Venice in control of merchandise passing from Asia to Europe, the new prosperity affected centers like the manufacturing city of Damascus and the ruined port of Akka. Since the highway between these two communities had always passed through Safed, the latter town became a post from which to protect caravans and a stopping point for merchants. Each body of travelers left behind in Safed some of its wealth and occasionally a few of its personnel, for the enchanting location of the town, perpetually cool with snow in winter, appealed to men tired of the desert. Most who reached Safed by this means were Arabs, and they occupied the southern and eastern sections of town, building new mosques and additional lines of covered souks.

But without the spinning wheel the camels could have accomplished little, and it reached Safed in an ironic way. When Jews were expelled from Spain and later from Portugal, many of the best and most courageous were drawn not to new refuges like Amsterdam but back to Eretz Israel, the land of their longing. Disembarking at Akka they were told by sailors in the one inn still existing along the waterfront, 'Jerusalem is a hovel and Tubariyeh is no more. The real Holy Land exists only in Safed.' By foot and by donkey these strong-minded Jews made the overland trip to Safed, where they began to swell the western quarter of the town, building small stone houses on the beautiful slopes which overlooked both a wadi and a mountain. Seldom have the victims of a religious persecution found a refuge so gentle as did those Jews of Avaro and other Spanish cities who escaped to Safed.

They brought with them the spinning wheel, which they had used in Spain to spin merino wool, and with it they initiated in their new home what was to become the foremost weaving center in Asia. Huge caravans began to assemble in the ruins of Akka, waiting for ships bringing the raw wool of Spain and France, and in Safed the Jews produced from this wool an excellent cloth, dyeing it by ancient processes and shipping it back through Akka to the markets of Europe. Unexpectedly the income of Safed rose from ten thousand florins a year to two hundred thousand and then to six hundred thousand, and its Jewish population from two hundred Jews to well over twenty thousand. It had become what the sailors of Akka had said, 'The leading town in Palestine.'

But caravans of camels have come to many towns, and riches have multiplied for a while, leaving no world-memories. And the same would have happened in Safed had not the Jews who carried the spinning wheel also brought a book, one of the most extraordinary in history, and it was the impact of this book that spread the name of Safed to the remotest Jewish community in the world, luring to the hillside center scholars from a dozen nations as different as Egypt and Poland, England and Persia.

But again, many towns have received books and done little with them. It was the glory of Safed that it received in addition to its book three rabbis prepared to give that book significance: Rabbi Zaki from Italy, Rabbi Eliezer of Germany, and the charismatic Rabbi Abulafia from Spain.

The first of the three rabbis to reach Safed was Zaki the Shoemaker, who, after seven years of painful struggle through Africa and the shores of Greece, landed with his wife and three daughters at the ruined, rock-strewn port of Akka. A caravan set forth intended for Damascus, and camped the first night at the uninhabited mound of Makor, from which the ancestors of Zaki had fled more than a thousand years before; but the houses his people had lived in lay beneath a Crusader fort, and it lay beneath a heap of sand and flowers.

On the next day, at about four in the afternoon, the caravan reached the pass separating the plains from the hills of Safed, and for the first time Zaki and his family saw the lovely town that was to be their home. On the summit a few great blocks of stone from the Crusaders' fort reflected back the bright sunlight, while below them, spreading out across steep slopes, flowed a collection of little houses, like petals falling from a flower.

Zaki, his heart bursting with the wonder of what he saw, uttered those singing words which God had used in urging Lot forward: '"Escape for thy life; look not behind thee, neither stay thou in all the plain; escape to the mountain, lest thou be consumed."' He had been in the plains and now the mountain beckoned.

'It looks as if it would be cold,' Rachel warned.

'In Salonica they assured us,' he reminded her. 'Life is good here.'

'It looks as if the people would fall out of their houses and roll down the mountainside,' she complained.

'It only looks that way,' he said convincingly.

The road entering Safed led to a public square which spread out from the foot of the ruined castle, and this area served as the commercial center of the town. Here the camels were unloaded and their cargoes sorted for delivery to merchants. Turkish officials clustered about the muleteers, asking of news from Akka, and Rabbi Zaki was left alone, staring down at the heart of Safed; and whispering a prayer for his deliverance he looked beyond the limits of the town and saw between the hills to the south the sunset-colored waters of the Sea of Galilee.

His arm was grabbed by a strong hand, and he heard a rough, peremptory voice asking, 'Are you intended for Safed?' He turned to find himself facing a burly, good-looking man with a stout black beard and workman's clothes.

'I am sent here by Rabbi Jemuel of Constantinople,' Zaki replied.

'Blessed be his memory,' came the brusque reply. 'That your family?'

'My wife Rachel and my daughters.'

'You'll need a big house,' the Safed man said. 'Right now we have none.'

'I told you not to come to Safed,' Rachel began to lament. 'We were happy in Salonica.'

'But until we find one,' the bearded man added, ignoring the complaints, 'you shall live with me. All the newcomers do at first. My name is Yom Tov ben Gaddiel.' And he led the family–they had scarcely any luggage–down a steep path and through alleys only a few feet wide until Rachel was dizzy, and she reminded Zaki: 'I told you people would fall off this hillside.'

They came to a square, not a European plaza but a halting place on the hillside, perhaps twenty feet across, and here the little group rested, hemmed in by houses, and Rabbi Zaki was able to study Safed: a warm, tightly knit town where Jews were at ease. They then proceeded down the hill until they reached Yom Tov's home, and from his door they could see the western hills and the pass they had negotiated, and extensive fields reaching to the horizon. Zaki covered his face and thought: It's this we've been searching for; but his wife thought of Podi and Salonica and Izmir and all the other good places they had known, and she was disconsolate.

Next day, when the Jews of Safed learned that a rabbi from Italy was among them, they crowded Yom Tov's house to question him, and many wanted to know why a Jew who had lived in Podi would have left such a well-regarded haven–and Rachel echoed the question: 'Yes, why?' Zaki explained what his fears had been and told of how for seven years he had longed to get to Safed. He said that the fame of the hilltop town had spread throughout Jewry and that he had wished to make himself a part of the brotherhood.

His simple explanation was received in silence, as if the men of Safed knew that they did not merit such praise, and in the long moment of hesitation Zaki had a chance to inspect the faces about him: they were bearded faces, marked by deep-set eyes which seemed to express the quiet exaltation of the town. The men wore oriental-style gowns and some wore turbans as well; and there was a stateliness about them, as if they had spent many years learning to control both their emotions and their fugitive thoughts. They were men, Zaki thought, with an intellectual power far surpassing his own, and he wondered if he could hold a place amongst them.

This fear was increased when Yom Tov said, 'Shall we explore the alleys?' And leaving the women behind, Zaki set out to see his new home. First he was led back to the square at which the family had stopped the evening before, and from there he moved along a narrow lane to the south, where to his surprise he was brought to a yeshiva where a man in his late fifties was expounding the Talmud to a class of nearly a hundred devotees. It was the great rabbi of Safed, Joseph Caro, who spoke in a cold, deliberate manner, interpreting the law of Judaism. Never before in his life had Zaki seen so big a yeshiva, nor had he been aware that so many Jews were interested in philosophical discussion.

Yom Tov then led him down to a lower level and back to the west, where in a large house he was introduced to an even more persuasive teacher, the learned Moses of Cordova, the man of Safed who knew most about the mysteries of the Kabbala, and he, too, had a student body of nearly a hundred, listening to intricate speculations which Zaki knew he would not be able to comprehend.

Yom Tov then led his fat guest to another level of the town, where he found in close proximity four different synagogues, each with its teacher and sixty or seventy scholars. 'It's a town of wisdom!' he cried in the Ladino which he had picked up in Izmir and which served as a lingua franca in all except the German quarters of Safed.

'It's also a town of work,' Yom Tov reminded him, leading the way to a large building through which a mountain stream tumbled, causing devices of various kinds to operate, and here Zaki became aware that his guide was both a respected rabbi, Yom Tov ben Gaddiel, and the leading cloth manufacturer of Safed. His plant employed three hundred men who were engaged in combing, fulling, washing and dyeing processes.

'In Safed we say, "Without work there is no Torah,"' the rabbi explained. He spoke of one famous rabbi who kept a shop, of another who was a barber. 'I'll find jobs for your women.'

'Doing what?' Zaki asked, for in the factory he saw only men.

Yom Tov led him back to the center of town, where they stopped at several homes, and in each, women were spinning wool imported from Turkey or weaving it into the stout cloth which accounted for Safed's fame throughout the Mediterranean. Yom Tov explained that he owned the mill, another dyeing establishment at the edge of town and the warehouses.

'You must be very rich,' Zaki observed without envy.

'No,' the local rabbi corrected. 'The money we make on cloth goes into the yeshivas and the synagogues.' Zaki stared at the black-bearded man in laborer's clothes and said nothing, for the words he had just heard were difficult to believe.

When they returned to Yom Tov's home Zaki was perspiring, and Rachel observed, 'At last! You'll climb up and down these hills so much you'll lose some of that fat.' And she proceeded to describe in much detail how embarrassed she had been when her husband had lost his pants in the spring races at Podi, but none of the listeners felt embarrassment, because most of them, during their lives among the Christians, had suffered equal indignities.

'I shall give you four spinning wheels,' Rabbi Yom Tov explained to the women of Zaki's family.

'What for?' Rachel asked suspiciously.

'To work,' Yom Tov answered sharply, and before Rachel could reply that she had not come to Safed to learn spinning, he added, 'Here we all work. I'll find you a house where the women can spin in the back and the rabbi can be a shoemaker in front.' And such a house was found.

As the family settled into its new life Rabbi Zaki confided to no one the principal reason for his joy in having reached Safed, but to himself he often thought: It's wonderful! So many young men here without wives. If I don't get the girls their husbands here, where in the world could I?

So wherever he went, whenever men gathered together to talk religion, Rabbi Zaki could be depended upon to cite either the Torah or the Talmud regarding the desirability of marriage. 'As the Talmud says,' he used to quote in his shoemaker's shop, '"The unmarried person lives without joy, without blessing and without good. He cannot be called a man in the full sense of the term."' And always in the course of talking with his customers he would remind them of the pregnant words of Genesis: 'male and female created he them.'

It would have been difficult to find a poorer propagandist for marriage than Rabbi Zaki; Safed required very little time to classify him as uxorious and his wife as a shrew. As for the three girls whom the fat rabbi offered as God's blessing to unmarried men, they were ill-tempered, petulant and bad-complexioned. It seemed unlikely that the older girl, Sarah, would ever marry, for she had a sharp tongue and a drawn face, while the two younger girls, Athaliah and Tamar, though prettier in feature were equally acid in nature.

And then one day a muleteer from Damascus, a stolid Jewish lad who had never read the Talmud or heard of the yeshivas of Safed, climbed down the many levels of the town to sit with Zaki at the shoemaker's bench: 'On the trip from Akka I watched your daughter, Rabbi.'

'You did?' The fat shoemaker leaped. 'Which one?'

'Athaliah. She has a better manner than the others.'

'She's a wonderful girl!' Zaki cried impulsively. 'Oh, this girl .. she can cook ... she can weave.' He became so excited that his words stumbled over themselves, for his daughters were getting old and this was the first time that anyone had even obliquely discussed marriage ... He stopped cold. 'You do want to marry her, don't you?' he asked bluntly.

'Yes,' the muleteer mumbled. 'I've told my mother.'

'Oh, Rachel!' the fat rabbi cried. And he summoned his family; and when the girls were lined up he announced, 'This fine young man from Damascus ... What's your name?' He choked, grew red in the face and grasped Athaliah by the hand, delivering her to her suitor.

As soon as it was decently possible the muleteer led his bride away to Damascus, and that night Rabbi Zaki initiated the tradition that was to make him beloved in Safed and renowned throughout the Jewish world. He went to bed at dusk, for it was written in the Talmud that men should not be abroad after dark, but he could not sleep, for he was possessed by a great happiness at having found a husband for one of his girls; and when he thought of the way doomed Jews were living that night in Podi and Portugal and Spain, he felt driven to rise from his bed and dress and go out into the narrow streets of the town, and to walk up and down, crying, 'Men of Safed! How can you sleep in your tranquillity when Jews throughout the world are unhappy and miserable? Do you appreciate the magnitude of your blessing? Jews of Safed, you happy, happy Jews, let us rise now and go to the house of God and give thanks.' And he routed out the scholars and the leaders and the men who would always know more than he and drove them to the synagogue, and there, in the light of a few candles, he recited the triumphant passages of Deuteronomy, and in his simple way brought many of the citizens of Safed closer to God than did all the Talmudic scholars and all the Kabbalists.

Two or three nights each month this sensation of absolute happiness would overcome Zaki, and he would roar through the narrow streets, summoning the Jews of Safed to praise their God for His bounty; and whereas it had been obvious to the scholars that Zaki of Italy would not attain a place of eminence in their schools—not even as a student, for he could not understand what men like the legalist Caro or the mystic Cordovero were talking about—he could, by the sheer simplicity of his faith, become one of the memorable rabbis of Safed. Although he left no writings, he so impressed his humanity upon the town that he modified subsequent religious behavior.

The keynote of his teaching, repeated again and again in his midnight discourses, was charity. 'Gold does not grow out of the land,' he taught. 'It is found in man's labor. And those who profit from the gold must give a fair share back to the poor.' He used simple explanations, saying, 'The mills of Rabbi Yom Tov could not run for a day if God stopped the mountain streams that feed them. If we live on God's charity, should we not share what God gives us?' He argued that a man should distribute at least twenty per cent of his income to the needy, saying, 'And if he gives less than one part in ten he may not call himself a Jew.' Again and again he pleaded with his listeners to be generous, and the joke was circulated through Safed: 'Rabbi Zaki wants more than anything else in the world to give things away ... especially his daughters.'

Outside the synagogue Rabbi Zaki was even more effective, for from his workbench he reviewed the homely precepts of the Jewish sages: 'The great Akiba tells us: "Whosoever neglects the duty of visiting the sick is guilty of shedding blood." Have you been to see Rabbi Paltiel's wife since she fell sick? Go now, and you can have your shoes when you return.' His round face and luxuriant beard became a trademark of humanity throughout the Jewish section of Safed, and he was the favorite Jew of the Arab quarter, too, for he offered his Muslim friends no religious argument, only laughter and mended shoes.

The young men of the town, watching his jovial passage, argued, 'If his daughter Tamar has lived with him so long, she can't be as bad as she looks,' and one day a man came to the shop and said, tentatively, 'Rabbi Zaki, I've been thinking that I might like to marry your daughter.'

'Sarah?' he cried. 'She's a fine girl.'

'I meant Tamar.'

'She's a fine girl, too!' the shoemaker said enthusiastically, but after the marriage was celebrated he asked his son-in-law, 'About Sarah. Do you happen to know any other men ...'

'No,' the groom replied firmly, but that night Zaki again coursed through the alleys, calling for the Jews to celebrate the paradise they knew in Safed, so that the more cynical observed, 'Watch! When he finally gets rid of that oldest daughter we'll have midnight services for a month.' But Safed enjoyed the exuberance of their fat rabbi, for everyone acknowledged–even the great scholars–that from time to time someone ought to call the attention of the people to the everyday joys and triumphs of a decent life. 'And there is no greater triumph imaginable,' dour Joseph Caro opined, 'than finding a husband for a daughter like Tamar.'

If charity was the pragmatic heart of Rabbi Zaki's preaching, the philosophical core was found in a passage of Maimonides which he revived for Safed: 'Everyone throughout the year must regard himself as if he were half innocent and half guilty. And he should regard the whole of mankind in the same way. If then he commits one more sin, he weighs down the scale of guilt against himself and against the whole world. And he himself causes the destruction of all. But if he fulfills one commandment, he turns the scale of merit in his favor and perhaps he saves the entire world. He by himself has power to bring salvation and deliverance to all the men of the world.' He frequently recited this passage, adding, 'And every man in Safed tonight, Arab and Jew alike, has this divine opportunity. The charity you do tomorrow, you, Muhammad Iqbal, may save the world.'

The gentle teaching of the little rabbi was the more impressive in that his personal life was such a shambles. In retrospect Rachel had grown positively fond of Salonica, the largest Jewish city in the world thanks to the Spanish expulsion, though when she had first landed there from Africa she had assured her daughters that it was a stinking place where the Turkish governors were despicable, the Greek citizens inhospitable and the Jews irreligious. In Safed the same people who listened with deepening respect as their humble rabbi talked of the good life, heard that same man's wife berate him as a fool; but the one did not seem to affect the other.

Rachel's ill temper was understandable She had convinced herself that if the family had remained in Salonica, Zaki would by now have found a husband for Sarah, but when the rabbi looked at that unfortunate girl, now twenty-five and with a worsening complexion and disposition, he wondered. He sympathized with Sarah. With her two younger sisters married she was bound to be miserable, but she made herself so disagreeable that Zaki had pretty well stopped offering her to the young men who came to his shop.

Then one day in 1547 he came puffing home with the titillating news that a new rabbi had come to Safed. 'A tall man, very handsome. His name is Abulafia and he has been wandering through Africa and Egypt. He has no wife.'

Rachel jumped. 'Speak to him right away, Zaki! It's your fault your daughter has no husband.'

Zaki agreed to this remarkable thesis. These days he agreed to almost everything, so Rachel continued, 'It's a father's duty to find men for his daughters, and it reflects sorely on you, Zaki, that your oldest daughter is unmarried. Look at her–a splendid woman.'

Zaki looked at her and thought: I could name six things that girl could do which would help her more than any of my efforts. Nevertheless, he looked forward to an intimate talk with the newcomer, for no rabbi should be without a wife.

Dr Abulafia created excitement in more than the Zaki family. His years of wandering had made him thinner; his beard was gray; he wore a turban; and his constant search for the mysterious meanings of man's relationship to God had caused his features to assume a remote beauty that was disturbing to men and women alike. There was a sensuousness about him, manifest in all he did, a mixture of Spanish grace and Hebrew insight; and before he had been in Safed a month it was clear that the Kabbalist group had found a new teacher and possibly their leader.

To the public and to the large number of students who crowded to hear him lecture on the essence of God, Abulafia was impressive, for he taught that even the humblest Jew, by strict concentration and a longing for the infinity of God, could lift himself to levels of comprehension much higher and more complex than those which now engaged him; but it was with the select group of experts who met with him each dawn that Abulafia was radically effective, for to these trained philosophers the Spanish doctor expounded the inner mysteries of the Kabbala itself.

Abulafia's introductory beliefs, which he expressed in words of almost flowing purity, were twofold: 'To live in harmony with himself a man must labor to unite the knots which bind his soul, and this is a personal matter between man and himself; then he must seek through contemplation an understanding of the Name of God, which is the timeless relationship between man and God.'

Abulafia's teaching on the apprehension of God was easy to understand: 'You must sit in a quiet room with a sheet of clean white paper and a brush, and you must begin to write at random the letters of the Hebrew alphabet, which is the language in which God wrote the Torah; and without associating these flowing, moving letters with specific words, you must permit them to come and go of their own will, nor must your mind direct your arm to direct your fingers to direct the brush to form this letter or that or to put it either here or there. And after several hours of this march of letters, if your concentration is of sufficient intensity, the pen will fall away and the paper will move from you, and you will be in the presence of endless thought in which the letters move of themselves, free and in space, and after a while your whole body will be seized by a trembling and your breath will come in short gasps and perhaps not at all, and there will be a bursting of your chest and you will feel that you are about to die – and then an enormous peace will come, for your soul will have untied the knots that bind it and the veil will have passed from your eyes; and after some time in this state of light you will see new letters of a radiance unknown before, and from them will appear the ineffable four, and you will see them, not on the paper nor on the wall nor in the room, but in the endless fathoms of your soul, the sacred name of God, Y H W H.'

That was the primary level of Abulafia's teaching, available to any scholar who took the trouble to study one of the handwritten copies of the Zohar circulating in Safed. This was a book as mystical as its teachings, for great contention had arisen as to its authorship. Perhaps because of local pride, the men of Safed believed that it had been written by the immortal Rabbi Simeon ben Yohai, who for thirteen years in the second century had hidden from the Roman soldiers of Emperor Hadrian. He had lived in a cave in the nearby village of Peqiin, where Elijah had visited him, bearing the secrets of the Kabbala, which Yohai had written down in the Zohar, the Splendor.

But as Abulafia knew, the book, which consisted of a commentary on the Torah, had been composed around 1280 by an adventurous Spaniard who had written it in ancient Aramaic to lend it credence: it was a mélange of mystical formulae, probably gathered from many original sources, plus a compelling explanation of the way a poetic mind can sometimes hypnotize itself into an apprehension of the reality of God. In secrecy, in well-thumbed copies which passed at night, the Zohar had traveled from Granada in Spain to all parts of Europe, treasured as much by mystical Christians as by Jews.

It was in the mountain village of Safed, however, that its power was to be most clearly demonstrated, for here had gathered, almost by accident, the half-dozen men who were to give the book its philosophical vitality, after which it would enjoy long life in Germany, Poland and Russia, forming the basis of a radical new interpretation of Judaism. It was a book which influenced all who touched it, and Dr. Abulafia, as the leader of the Safed group, expounded its first levels in lucid and seductive prose, but when he progressed to the second and third levels he became incoherent so far as logical exposition was concerned, but burning in his brilliance of metaphor and suggestion. Once, when a flood of incomprehensible words had tumbled from him like a stream issuing from the hills of Safed, he apologized. 'To utter one word from the world of ultimate mystery is to break down the keystone of an arch so that no one knows from which side the next stone will fall.' He was asked by his pupils to put his words down in an orderly system, but he countered, 'Where would a man start in a field that has no beginning, no end and no definition? But if you listen to me long enough you will gain a sense of what I am trying to say, and that is all that I know myself.' At other times he spoke with a clarity that was almost agonizing, and with an insight gained partly through rejection and personal tragedy, partly through an all-absorbing contemplation of God: 'If seventy of us in this room study the Torah we find that it has seventy different faces to present to us, for each of us will see his own creation of beauty shining through the words of God. But I say to you that the Torah has not one face, nor seventy faces, but six hundred thousand faces, one for every Jew who was present when God gave Moses our Teacher the law; and if the cords that bind your soul are untied, you are free to find your own Torah among the six hundred thousand.'

In the group of listeners influenced by Dr Abulafia's teaching was Rabbi Zaki, but he was affected in a different way. When the more abstruse explanations were reached he was apt to fall asleep, and occasionally he snored, for Kabbalistic flights of thought were quite beyond him; and one morning when the students were inclined to laugh at the dozing shoemaker, Rabbi Abulafia rebuked them, saying, 'I think our sleeping fat man describes better than my words what I am trying to say. Rabbi Zaki has seen not the face of the Torah but through to the heart of the Torah itself, and there he found the one commandment of God upon which Torah and Talmud and Judaism rest: "Thou shalt love thy neighbour as thyself." I happen to know that Rabbi Zaki spent last night sitting with the sick wife of Rabbi Paltiel and he requires to sleep, and there is no man in this room worthy to waken him.'

The reason why Rabbi Zaki loved to attend Abulafia's lectures, which he rarely understood, was that he could sit in the synagogue and think: A fine rabbi like Abulafia ought to have a wife. I can imagine no woman in Safed, nor in Salonica either, who would make him a better wife than my Sarah.

So one day in 1549, after the Spanish doctor had finished a soaring exhortation, Zaki waited for the scholars to ask their last questions. Then, alone with Abulafia, he asked bluntly, 'Doctor, why don't you take my daughter Sarah as your wife?'

Dr Abulafia sat down. 'Sarah?' he asked. 'Do I know Sarah?'

'You must have seen her. She appears often with my wife.'

'Oh, Sarah! Yes.' There was silence.

'The Talmud tells us that a rabbi must have a wife, and I assure you that Sarah is as fine a girl as her mother.'

'I'm sure she is,' the Spaniard said.

'And even if you cannot accept my daughter, Dr Abulafia, you must find a wife somewhere, for many of us feel that your influence in Safed would be greater if ...'

'If I were married?'

'Yes. For a rabbi it's practically an obligation.'

The handsome Spaniard sat looking at his hands for some minutes, then said quietly, 'For your daughter I would be an old man. After all, I'm fifty-seven, till a hundred and twenty.' This was the Jewish way of stating an age, derived from the promise of God as given in the Torah: 'Yet his days shall be an hundred and twenty years.'

'I assure you Sarah would not worry about that.'

Again there was a protracted silence which neither man knew how to break, but some heavy burden was on Abulafia's heart, and when he looked at the simple, round face of his friend he was inspired to speak with this man as he had never spoken to another, and he suggested, 'Shall we climb the hill to the old fort?' And the two bearded rabbis walked slowly through the narrow streets of Safed, those winding, wonderful streets that never ran in one direction more than a hundred feet, and after considerable climbing past seven synagogues they came to the broken rocks of the fort, and there Abulafia pointed to the distant hills and to the Sea of Galilee.

'This is paradise, Zaki, and I agree with you that any man who lives here should have a wife.'

'Doctor, believe me! Sarah would make you a perfect wife. She's neat, and her mother has taught her how to cook.'

'But in Spain ...' Abulafia halted, afraid to conjure up revolting memories, except that the reassuring presence of Rabbi Zaki encouraged him to do so. Laughing nervously he said, 'Zaki, you want to get rid of a daughter who clutters your house. And that's a big problem. But I must get rid of the devil who rides my soul, and that's impossible.'

The little rabbi looked at the Kabbalist in amazement. 'But it's you who tells us each morning that we must untie the cords that bind our souls.'

'I do,' Abulafia said. 'And I cannot unbind my own.'

The two rabbis looked at the sweeping beauty of upper Galilee; in the days when it was wooded, say, when the great rabbis of the third and fourth centuries were meeting in Tverya to compile the Talmud, it must have been even more inspiring. And Abulafia whispered, 'In Spain I was married. To a Christian woman whom I adored. We were marvelously happy, but I was afraid to tell her I was a secret Jew. We had two sons. They didn't know I was a Jew either. When the worst of the persecutions struck ...' He hesitated. He rose and walked about for some time, looking down at Tubariyeh, where the soul of Judaism had been saved by a group of dedicated rabbis much like the ones who had now gathered in Safed on a somewhat similar mission. He wondered if any of those great old men like Rabbi Asher the Groats Maker had been burdened with a sin as terrible as his. Then he looked down, and Rabbi Zaki was waiting.

'The best friend I had in the world,' Abulafia continued, 'better even than my wife, was a secret Jew named Diego Ximeno. He introduced me to the Kabbala, and anything I've been able to accomplish ...' He thought of Ximeno looking at him through the flames. 'The Inquisition trapped him. Through what trick, I don't know. They tore his joints apart, ripped out the lining of his throat, burned holes in his feet. And on the day they dragged him through the streets to the place where he was burned alive, he passed as close to me as . . .' His ancient sense of sin choked him.

'Burned?' Zaki asked. 'Alive?'

'Yes. Well, that night I decided to flee Spain, because Diego Ximeno had shamed me with a courage I could never have. He was as close to me as you are, in his mortal moment, and he looked at me but refused to betray me. So I forged papers ...'

Abulafia's students, who envied his gray-haired grandeur and his mastery of language, would have been surprised could they have heard him in these next moments: he was a man at the apex of his power, unable either to form words or look at a friend. He sat with his head between his hands, mumbling, 'In my ignorance ... well, I wanted to spare my wife ... it never occurred to me ...' Syllables came, but no sense; then: 'I reached Tunis ... circumcised myself with a pair of old scissors ... shouted from the window, 'I'm a Jew! I'm a Jew!'

For a moment Abulafia collapsed completely. Then he re-established control and forced himself to say, 'Years later a Spaniard coming through Alexandria fell sick and they brought him to me. He said, "Abulafia? Wasn't there a renegade Jew from Avaro named Abulafia?" And although I was safe I began to tremble. "This Abulafia ran off and left his wife and children to the Inquisition." I clutched the man's arm to keep from fainting and he guessed who I was. Sick though he was he fled from me in horror. I ran after him, grabbed him and threw him to the street. A crowd gathered and he fought me off. He pointed at me ...'

Remembering that day in Egypt the tall rabbi broke into uncontrollable tears, and until fat Rabbi Zaki comforted him, could not speak: 'My wife was burned alive. My eldest son was burned alive. My youngest son died in the torture. They did not even know the name of Jew.'

Like the sick man in Alexandria, Rabbi Zaki drew away. In Salonica he had met many Jews from Spain and Portugal who had undergone the tortures of the Inquisition and he was no longer affected by the horror of any narration; but he had never met a man, no matter how degraded, who had saved his own neck at the expense of his wife and children; indeed, he could not imagine, judging from his own experience in leaving Podi, how any man could abandon his family. But in spite of his automatic disgust he did not feel qualified to pass judgment on a man like Abulafia, who had done so, and he refused to make any moral comment. He was therefore unprepared for the tall rabbi's next question: 'Zaki, am I entitled to marry your daughter?'

To his own astonishment Zaki heard himself say, 'No.'

That day they said no more. But when Zaki reached home and saw his unlovely daughter Sarah, he experienced pangs of remorse. My God! he cried to himself. I had a chance to catch her a husband and I said no! He was thrown into a world of self-recrimination and remorse. As a rabbi he could not escape taking a harsh view of Dr. Abulafia's behavior; to desert a wife and children and to be the cause of their being tortured to death; it was a graver sin than he had ever heard of, more serious perhaps than apostasy, for this was an abdication of all human principles. Yet the more he brooded upon the matter the more confused he became.

His perplexity was heightened when Dr Abulafia came to his home and in an act of moral despair asked Rachel and Zaki, 'May I have your daughter Sarah in marriage?'

'Yes!' shouted Rachel.

'It is for him to say,' Abulafia replied, pointing to Zaki.

'He says yes!' Rachel cried joyously.

'No,' Zaki said.

'Study your heart,' Abulafia pleaded and left. As he climbed sorrowfully up the narrow street he could hear Rachel screaming at her husband.

For three days the shoemaker's shop was a scene of hell. Sarah, who from the first had been bedazzled by the gracious rabbi from Spain, wept until her pasty face was an ugly red. She accused her father of destroying her life. Rachel was more to the point: 'He's insane. We should hire an Arab to stab him.'

Zaki bowed his head before the storm he had aroused, but the moral problem facing him he did not avoid. Abulafia, by his abandonment of his Christian wife, had put himself outside the sphere of love, and even though rabbis were supposed to marry, the handsome Spaniard had been well advised not to do so; Zaki was sorry he had raised the question that day, and he was even sorrier that he had involved his daughter.

It was Zaki's habit, when faced by such conflict, to consult the sage whose writings he had found most helpful when guidance was required; so he went to the synagogue and took down his favorite book, turning its pages idly until he came upon the sentence in which Maimonides discussed the passage from the Talmud which summed up his philosophy: 'The Torah speaks in the language of living men.' The law was given to men, not men to the law. In the abstract Abulafia's behavior made him unfit to enter into a second marriage, but this was no longer a case of abstracts. Human beings were involved–a lonely rabbi who was doing God's work, an unmarried woman–and common sense cried, 'Let them marry.' Still unconvinced that he was doing right Zaki puffed up the hill to Abulafia's medical office, stood in the doorway and announced in a halting voice, 'The wedding can proceed.' He turned, went down the hill and told his daughter, 'Rabbi Abulafia will marry you.'

On the day of the wedding the Jews of Safed joked, 'Since Zaki got rid of that one, he'll have us rejoicing in the synagogue all night,' and after the wedding feast they went home to wait for the sound of their fat rabbi running through the alleys to summon them. But nothing happened. Midnight passed and one o'clock, and finally some men came to the shoemaker's shop and called to him, 'Rabbi Zaki! Are we not going to celebrate tonight?' And he would give no answer, so the men went back and reported, 'The fat old fellow was in a corner praying. And he wouldn't look up.' So others came and cried, 'Rabbi Zaki, please call us to the synagogue!' But in this marriage he found no joy and could not respond, so a third time they called, 'If we summon the crowd, will you also come?' And he was about to refuse even this when Rachel came from the kitchen. It had not occurred to her before that the people of Safed actually loved her ridiculous husband, and to hear them begging him to join them gave her a new view on their marriage: in his fumbling way Zaki had found good husbands for each of his daughters, and tonight she had to admit that the girls had not been prizes. His accomplishment was not a mean one, and she looked at him with respect. Awkwardly she placed her hand upon his shoulder and said, 'They want to celebrate, husband. And I want to celebrate, too.'

'You can't go in the streets,' he said solicitously.

'I've poured myself a glass of wine in the kitchen.' Zaki could say nothing, so she tugged at his arm. 'They're calling for you,' she said and opened the door. This invitation he could not refuse, and when he came sore-hearted to the synagogue he saw a gaunt, bearded stranger standing at the wall next to a beautiful girl, and it was Rabbi Eliezer from Gretz, newly arrived with his daughter Elisheba.

The appearance of the German rabbi, last of the three whose work in Safed would modify subsequent Judaism, had a sobering effect upon the city. He was neither a simple good man like Zaki, nor a mercurial mystic like Abulafia. Nor was he any longer a handsome young rabbi who loved dancing and good German beer, for seven years of exile had aged him noticeably. He was now an austere man burned out by the fires of persecution and personal misery. All that remained was a vision crystal-clear as to how the Jews of the world could be salvaged from the chaos which must overtake them in the years ahead, and it was his undeviating dedication to this one concept that would make him immortal.

In Safed he did not teach, nor did he build his own synagogue, as did many of the other leading rabbis. When wealthy Rabbi Yom Tov offered to erect one for him he refused. Instead, he gathered all the books available in the Galilee and applied himself to them, day after day, year after year. Anyone who wished could consult with him, and as the years passed, practically the whole of Safed did so, even the Arabs, for he was acknowledged the leading legalist of the Galilee. The Kabbala he refused to investigate, saying, 'That is Dr Abulafia's field. He has the mystic vision and I do not.' Nor did he concern himself with the daily ministry of a man like Rabbi Zaki, of whom he said, 'He is the greatest of the rabbis, and I hope that in the future every community finds one like him. But I must tend my books.'

Eliezer's self-appointed task was the codification of Jewish law: he would put down in simple terms those things a Jew must do in order to remain a Jew. The Torah contained 613 laws, the Talmud scores of thousands, and the decisions of later rabbis like Maimonides and Rashi hundreds of thousands. On any given topic, say, marriage, no Jew could any longer know what the law was and this confusion Rabbi Eliezer proposed to remedy. Furthermore, in his travels through Germany, Hungary, Bulgaria and Turkey he had seen many communities where knowledge of even the Torah law was dying out and where the Talmud was not known, let alone Maimonides. The legal structure of Judaism was vanishing, and if this continued, the Jewish people must perish. For all such Jews, Eliezer would provide one massive book containing a summary of all law. His ambition was to save Judaism, no less.

He had started his work in Constantinople in 1546, but that city was not conducive to systematic thought; the Jews had few books and the Turkish government put men of obvious talent like Eliezer under considerable pressure to accept administrative posts. Three times the gaunt rabbi had been invited to become a counselor at court, and doubtless his talents would have insured him advancement, but he felt called to serve in a different capacity. 'In Safed,' his friends had told him, 'you'll find both books and a spirit of scholarship.' And they had collected a purse of gold which would last him for many years, and promised him more if he needed it, so that he was free to concentrate his whole energy on the question: 'What must a Jew do to remain a Jew?'

On the question of marriage alone he had already filled two notebooks, and his researches had reminded him that each man must have a wife, so in Constantinople he had married a Jewish widow who found her fulfillment in

looking after his books and his attractive daughter. He was now codifying the
laws of inheritance, adoption and divorce, and this would require another two
books. After that would come land tenure, the clean and the unclean, business
practice and each intimate detail of human life. For every conceivable human
action there could be found a law, and the Jew must know what that law was.

In later years certain liberal philosophers of Judaism would deplore the fact
that the iron-willed German ever reached Safed, for after he completed his
codification the Jews of the world were hemmed in by a body of law so specific
and rigid that any normal growth seemed impossible; harsh critiques were written of Eliezer bar Zadok's deadening influence on Jewish thought, but in the
end even his censurers had to acknowledge that only his iron will had brought
order into chaos; if it was true that he had forged chains of bondage, it was also
true that he had built those sturdy bridges on which Jews marched from past to
present and on into the future. It was not forgotten that the first problem to
which Eliezer bar Zadok addressed himself was one of the most permanent in
world history: 'How can a man and woman live together in harmony?' And his
second problem had been: 'What are the duties and privileges of children?' If
Jewish family life grew constantly stronger while that of its surrounding
neighbors weakened, it was because Eliezer the German Jew had spelled out
the most intimate laws regarding these matters: 'There is no aspect of sexual
relationship between husband and wife that may not be discussed, but we have
found that there are four things which a man ought not ask his wife to do, and
there are three which no wife must ask of her husband.' And in simple language
he stated what those seven restrictions were. He also gave the most succinct
reason for abandoning plural marriage: 'Torah and Talmud agree that a man
may have more than one wife, but the law says that if a man does have three
wives, each has a right to sleep with him one night in turn, and if he begins to
show favoritism either sexually or emotionally to one at the expense of the other
two, the latter have a right to complain that they are being neglected, and if he
cannot serve each properly and in her regular turn, which few men can do,
then let him have one wife only.'

The world knows about this golden period of Safed, when Zaki taught love
and Abulafia mysticism and Bar Zadok the law, because of an accidental
traveler. In 1549 a Spanish Jew who had fled to Portugal and then to
Amsterdam foresaw the Spanish-Dutch war that was about to sear his new
homeland, and he concluded that this was as good a time as any to visit Eretz
Israel, so after two years of dangerous travel he reached Jerusalem, where all
men spoke of Safed as the jewel of Israel, and in the winter of 1551 he came
north to Tubariyeh and then over the hill to Safed. Dom Miguel of Amsterdam
was a perceptive traveler, one much concerned with Judaism, and the
comments in his journal, while sometimes naïve, were always enlightening:

From afar I had heard that the great rabbis of Safed earn their living by doing
each in his own way manual labor, but I was not prepared to find that Abulafia
the Mystic holds daily doctor's hours or that Zaki the Good mends shoes. One
saintly man from Portugal, much respected by his fellows, cleans chimneys,
and the poet who wrote *Lecha Dodi*, which all in these parts sing, makes his
living selling fodder to the caravans bringing wool from Akka.

And wives work too. At home they are expected to clean, sew, cook and care
for their children. But many go to the factory of Rabbi Yom Tov ben Gaddiel
ha-Ashkenaz, where they spin and weave. Others work in the fields of farmers,

but all who work expect to be paid in Turkish coins which, to my disgust, proclaim Allah, the God of Moses, is God.

If I were asked to name the glory of Safed it would be the children. Those who recall the pale-faced youth of the Jewish quarters in Europe would be surprised to see the children of Safed. During the recent snowstorm I saw them rolling in the drifts with ruddy cheeks and now that summer has come I watch them playing games with Arab children and their faces are brown. They're noisy. They sing songs brought here from all parts of Europe, but at ten or eleven the girls become proper household helpers and boys begin their study of the Talmud. I would that the Jews of Germany and Portugal might produce such children.

The daily life of Safed, I am happy to report, is governed by the commandment which Moses our Teacher gave us after he had delivered the tablets of the Ten Commandments: 'And these words, which I command thee this day, shall be in thine heart: And thou shalt teach them diligently unto thy children, and shalt talk of them when thou sittest in thine house, and when thou walkest by the way, and when thou liest down, and when thou risest up. And thou shalt bind them for a sign upon thine hand, and they shall be as frontlets between thine eyes. And thou shalt write them upon the posts of thy house, and on thy gates.' These warnings were observed by all Jews in Safed, for the Torah was constantly in the heart of the great rabbis like Zaki and Abulafia. I found that it also governed the behavior of businessmen like Rabbi Yom Tov. Even children were taught the laws, for the words of God were discussed in each home I visited. If I met Rabbi Zaki walking through the streets, he was reciting the Torah. The first thing we did each morning and the last each night was to pray, and I wish the Jews of Amsterdam did the same. I am pleased also to report that when a man prays he binds the leather phylacteries, one about his left arm, the other to his forehead. And each Jewish home I saw in Safed bore on its right-hand doorpost a small metal container in which rested the great law of the Jews: 'Hear, O Israel, the Lord our God, the Lord is one.' It was a most sweet and pleasant experience to be living within the law, and to be reminded of it at all times, both in the going out and at the coming in.

Like most strangers who visit Safed, when I walked into town cold and dirty from my travel, I was taken at once to the shoemaker shop of Rabbi Zaki, for he used to have three daughters, but all are married, and he finds pleasure in entertaining strangers. His good wife Rachel complains at times, but Zaki takes no notice of this nor do his guests. Sharing a home with this simple man is like living with the sages in the old times, and the seven days of his week are a string of amulets, each with its peculiar significance.

Half an hour before dawn each day throughout the year, a messenger from the synagogue comes tapping down the alleyways and at our door calls softly, 'Rise, Rabbi, and greet the dawn.' Zaki dresses, brings a candle for me, and leaves his house in darkness to join with other men who head for the synagogue, where candles have been lighted and where in brief joyous ceremonies, joyous that is, except on Sunday, the new day is hailed. 'O God!' Rabbi Zaki cries at these dawn services. 'We men of Safed dedicate ourselves to Thee.'

Tuesdays and Wednesdays, Rabbi Zaki sets aside for hard work, applying himself to the making of shoes. But on Mondays and Thursdays he looks forward to additional religious services. He is so faithful in fasting on these days, touching neither water nor food till sundown, that I wonder at his fatness. Sometimes he spends the better part of Thursday at the synagogue, either

reading or leading his Jews in prayer. In Safed, as in all Jewry, Monday is also
the market day, observed since the time of Ezra, and Zaki enjoys moving along
the stalls and greeting his friends.

But for Rabbi Zaki, Friday is the memorable day, complex and encrusted
with those hidden meanings we Jews love. It is, in many ways, the best day of
the week, not even excepting Shabbat with its special responsibilities. On
Friday, Rabbi Zaki lies awake in the darkness, listening for the running feet and
the knocking at his door, and he says to himself, 'What joy! Another Friday.'
He comes to my room and kisses me, crying so that his breath makes the candles
flicker, 'Rejoice, Dom Miguel! It's Friday.' Then he takes me to the synagogue,
where he sings in a loud voice, after which he stands at the door and breathes
deeply, saying to himself, 'Same sun. Same breeze. But somehow this day is
different.' He spends his morning winding up his week's business, and tries
always to attend one of the yeshivot, where by tradition each Friday the great
teachers sum up the principal truth of the week's discussion or expound the
basic tenets of Judaism.

In this report I have spoken much of Rabbi Zaki, and perhaps you would
rather hear about Dr. Abulafia or Bar Zadok, but when I tell you what Zaki
does at Friday noon, before he lunches, you will understand. He leaves the
synagogue where the great ones are expounding and he goes to his shoemaker
shop, where he studies the box in which he keeps the money earned by mending
shoes. 'This week, Dom Miguel,' he tells me, 'we can spare a little more,' and
he takes from the box almost half of what he has earned. Hiding the coins in his
long-coat he starts walking through the narrow streets, and wherever he finds a
poor man, or a widow who has not with what to make Shabbat, he pauses and
asks how this person is and as he talks he quietly places a few coins in some
inconspicuous place. But when the meeting ends he always says, 'Shmuel, you
are a man who bears misfortune with dignity. You must know God better than
I do. Give me on this happy Friday your blessing,' and he makes the man feel
that it is he who is doing the rabbi a favour. And thus he disposes of his
wealth.

His charity completed, Rabbi Zaki goes home, where Rachel has been
cleaning her house and doing much cooking, with all her pots bubbling at once.
Carefully Zaki lays out fresh clothes, from stockings to robes, then walks to the
ritual baths, where he cleanses himself for the moments that lie ahead. His
lunch on Friday is always frugal and he grows impatient for the hours to pass,
but by mid-afternoon a kind of benediction settles over him, and over the town
itself, and he takes down his handsome prayer shawl, white with black stripes
and knotted fringe, and he leaves his home and begins to walk sedately toward
the edge of town, then out toward open fields, saying to me, 'Keep up, Dom
Miguel. You are going to meet your Bride.' As he moves through the narrow
alleys, men join up with us until he leads as many as sixty or seventy into the
countryside – a fat, round little man with a black beard, whose neighbors trust
him. We are not in the fields long before we see Dr. Abulafia coming, tall and
princely, his graying beard long and his manner of walking courtly. He is
always attended by students of the Kabbala. Then Rabbi Yom Tov, dressed in
expensive robes and with an air of command, comes marching toward us with
his business assistants; and finally through the fields comes a man alone, Rabbi
Eliezer bar Zadok ha-Ashkenaz, his eyes wearied from reading. Four times
since I came to Safed I have been told that in Germany, Rabbi Eliezer was a
man who could dance all night and drink endless amounts of German beer, but

if that was ever the case, sorrow has changed him much in the intervening years.

In the shadow of the mountains we sit upon the ground and speak of holy things. We sing hymns composed by poets of the town and study the flowers of the meadow, but as the sun drifts toward the west Rabbi Zaki feels himself gripped by an acute excitement, and he rises and returns to town, first in a slow walk, finally in a donkey-like gallop, his gown flapping about his fat legs as he calls behind, 'Run faster, Dom Miguel! Your Bride is coming!' Through the narrow alleys of Safed he hurries, up and down the hills, crying, 'Queen Shabbat is about to appear. Let us go forth in our finest clothes and in our sweetest breath to greet the Queen!' He knocks on doors and cries at street corners, lest any miss the Queen. Then, in a kind of ecstasy, he waits as the other rabbis return from the fields singing songs of praise to the imminent moment of our joy. Each man proceeds to his own synagogue, the Sephardim like Zaki to one of the many Spanish congregations, the Ashkenazim like Eliezer to one of the two German synagogues, and men sit upon the floor, while women give praise in the balcony masked by gauze curtains, and after the evening prayers have been chanted, all join in the great Safed hymn that we would do well to sing in Amsterdam: 'Come, my Beloved, let us meet the Bride. The presence of Shabbat let us receive.' And as the sun sinks, the day of the Lord begins in Safed, that mysterious day on which the communion between God and man is reaffirmed.

In a later passage that some Jews wished Dom Miguel had omitted, because of its frank discussion of sex in Safed, he wrote:

Shabbat in Safed is a day of extreme joy, and after the twilight service ends on Friday evening Rabbi Zaki invites some two dozen of his friends and all travelers from far places to his home, where the food prepared that morning by the rebbetzin is laid out and where wine from the Safed hills is poured. We sing old songs of Italy and Spain till nearly midnight and if a stranger gets drunk, more from the singing than the wine, Zaki does not rebuke him. One Friday during our singing he told me, 'You will have to put them out, Dom Miguel, for I must go to bed. Since I was first married in Podi I have lain with my wife every Friday night, even aboard ship when we were both seasick, and she would take it unkindly if I missed now.'

On Shabbat itself three synagogue meetings are held: dawn, morning, afternoon. During this holy time all but religious life halts completely. Men are allowed to carry nothing, not even a string, lest inadvertently they work upon the Lord's day. No food is cooked, no fire lighted, no lamp lit. Rabbi Zaki spends this day close to a window, even when in the synagogue, with his eyes fixed toward the lake below, for he tells me that when the Messiah arrives on earth he will make his appearance some Shabbat morning on those waters and then walk over the hills to Safed. 'It would be a thing of error,' Rabbi Zaki says, 'if we were not ready to greet him as he enters town.' It is a custom in Safed, and one I have grown to love, as Shabbat ends on Saturday at dusk–when a man can see three stars in one glance at the heavens–for the rabbis to gather as if to prolong the day, holding a feast, singing old songs and speaking of the goodness they have known. Rabbi Zaki prays almost till dawn, clutching, as it were, at the garments of the Bride as the day passes into history. How sweet Shabbat can be those last moments!

But I have never seen a more doleful day than Sunday in Safed. Now Rabbi Zaki awakes with the taste of ashes in his mouth. I hear him in his bed, fearful of the messenger's footfall. Reluctantly he dresses and we go in silence to the cold synagogue, so different in spirit from what it had been only a few short hours before. This dawn Zaki looks at no one and he prays alone, as do the rest of us. And then, when the day has well broken and the sun is upon us, the rabbis of Safed meet glumly on street corners and try to decide what went wrong last week. 'If we had been truly God's men throughout the entire week,' Rabbi Yom Tov complains, 'the Messiah would surely have come. What did we do wrong?' And the rabbis discuss the errors of the past, the faults of Jews who keep barring the Messiah from his Holy Land. I have often heard Rabbi Zaki say, 'Here in Safed we are so engaged in a struggle for our personal happiness that we forget our responsibility to the greater world.' And often he leaves these informal Sunday meetings to preach with new dedication his simple formula: 'More charity. More love. More submission to God's Torah.' And so, as each new week begins, the Jews of Safed again try to live such devout lives that through their example the Messiah will be lured down to earth, for as Rabbi Zaki never tires of reminding us, 'It is written in the Talmud that if a single community repents, the world will be saved.' But it is my opinion that if the Messiah is ever brought down to earth it will be by the efforts of one man, and that man will be Rabbi Zaki the Shoemaker.

As for the worldly government of Safed, twenty-three thousand Jews, thirty thousand Arabs and I don't know how many Christians are ruled by Turkish pashas sent down from Constantinople. The Turks collect taxes, set rules for the wool trade and provide soldiers now and then if bandits, called bedawi, move too close in their raids. The day-to-day life of Jews rests in the hands of their rabbis, while the Arabs are governed by their qadis, or judges, and the Christians by their priests. Since the arrival of Rabbi Zaki and Rabbi Eliezer there has been no death sentence and little divorce. I heard of some adultery but of not a single pauper who failed to receive charity. If the rabbis find time they teach the children to read, but here I do not find those systematic schools which were a credit to the Jews of Germany. Nor have I heard of any offences against the civic peace. I was pleased to see that businessmen are not allowed extravagant profits, for during my visit Rabbi Zaki publicly rebuked Rabbi Yom Tov for not increasing the pay of his women workers when profits rose, and by public demand the wage was raised. I would that all Jews lived as just lives as I lived in Safed.

Curiously, now that I am removed from the city I recall only one sound as my lasting memory of that hillside paradise. It is the call of the muezzin from the Arab minarets which surround the Jewish quarters, and as I hear it echo I remember how easily Jew and Arab existed in this city and wonder at the bitterness with which the Portuguese insisted that they could not live with Jews, and at the ugliness in German towns, and especially at the hatred which Spaniards in Amsterdam feel toward their Jews. One man told me, 'Arab and Jew share Safed in peace only because each is ruled with equal harshness by the Turk. If Arabs ruled they'd abuse the Jews, and if Jews ruled they'd be intolerable.' I hope the rabbis of Amsterdam will advise me on this matter.

Because our Jews in Europe are forced to lead far from perfect lives, I must not leave the impression that Safed is a paradise. If we must depend upon the purity of this city to lure the Messiah back to earth we may have to wait a long time. The men of Safed like women and they like wine. The latter they import in large tuns from Damascus, and the former they arrange for in a most ingenious and satisfactory way. Along the line where the two communities meet, the Arabs keep a house where Jewish men pay to visit girls brought down from Damascus, while the Jews maintain a house in which Arabs come to visit Jewish girls from Akka and Nazareth. I myself visited the Arab house one night, and it was a credit to the city. The rabbis themselves were lusty men and I was told in secret that Dr Abulafia, much tormented at home by a shewish wife, kept a mistress near the yeshiva where Joseph Caro taught, and I shall never forget hearing Rabbi Zaki recount with pleasure the story of great Rabbi Akiba, who, lusting for knowledge, once followed his teacher into the privy itself, 'and from what he saw him do there Akiba picked up three good habits which he used ever after.' And when I asked, 'What were the tricks of hygiene that Akiba learned in the privy?' Rabbi Zaki told me bluntly, and we would not do poorly if we adopted them in Amsterdam. Many of the poems we sang in the synagogues told of passionate love, and the women of Safed like fine fabrics and get them. Jewelry we could buy from the Arabs, and any man was considered miserly who did not buy his wife some, so when I left the city I gave four presents, and they were better made and cheaper than any I could have bought in Antwerp.

Dom Miguel of Amsterdam concluded his remarks on Safed with a passage that would be quoted often in later centuries as a kind of ideal toward which Jews might aspire:

I have traveled across the hills to Peqiin, and am seated in the cave where Simeon ben Yohai wrote the Zohar while hiding from the Roman soldiers, and I think I now understand Safed. If in the future men tell you that we Jews were intended to be homeless, without a land of our own, or that we cannot govern ourselves or live side by side in peace with others, send such liars to Safed, for there you will see Jew and Arab living in peace. You will see Dr Abulafia ha-Sephard existing easily with Rabbi Eliezer bar Zadok ha-Ashkenaz, and you will see a hillside living happily under the law of Moses, and getting rich while doing so. But most of all you will see a fat little rabbi from Italy puffing up and down the steep alleys, bringing love to all men. In Jerusalem they told me, 'In Safed you will find the captial of Judaism.' I did not, for to me Jerusalem will always be the capital, but I did find Rabbi Zaki, and he is the heart of Judaism.

In only one respect did Dom Miguel fall into serious error regarding Safed: though the years were golden, the city was far from finding the secret to permanent civic harmony, for in early 1551 a severe contention broke out, and between the very rabbis whose harmony Dom Miguel had praised. Before long it involved the entire Jewish community and could in time have destroyed it had not prudent steps been taken to heal the breach. It began when a Jewish woman from Damascus wanted a divorce from a man who had lived briefly in Safed and whose family antecedents were uncertain. Rabbi Abulafia, still tormented by his own sin and unhappy in his marriage with Sarah–who grew more like her mother as the years passed –was inclined to aid others who had fallen into domestic trouble. So even though the legal position of the claimant was unclear, he granted the divorce. Rabbi Eliezer, who was not involved in this case, noted with some apprehension that this was the fourth time that Dr. Abulafia had ignored a strict interpretation of the Mosaic law, and Eliezer felt

that the spiritual foundations of Judaism were under attack. Accordingly, he
retired to the library which the Jews of Constantinople still maintained for him
with their contributions and composed a harsh letter, filled with legal citation
and the kind of blunt Germanic sentences he used in his codification of the law.
The essential paragraphs read:

Does Rabbi Abulafia think that he can issue such faulty divorces without
censure? Does he plan to issue others in the future? If he does, we cannot see
how the rabbis of Safed can any longer place credence in his decision in these or
other areas. Surely a man who cannot understand the simple law of divorce can
hardly be trusted to judge graver problems. By his arrogant and intemperate
decisions Rabbi Abulafia raises in all minds three serious questions: 'Does he
know the law? Does he respect it? Will he in future observe it?'

These are matters which go far beyond Safed. We who have been allowed by
God to see the sad state of Judaism throughout the world, know that Jews are in
Peril and can be saved only if they live according to the law. Any rabbi like Dr
Abulafia who abuses that law helps to destroy Judaism. In circulating this
necessary but unpleasant letter we are not concerned with his faulty decision in
the Damascus case. That was an error which can be forgiven. But we are
concerned with the majesty of law as it operates to save Judaism. And we say to
Dr Abulafia, 'If your arbitrary decision in this case becomes a precedent, the
basis for Jewish family life will be destroyed.' We know he cannot intend this,
so in charity we must conclude, Dr Abulafia does not know the law. Surely he
does not wish to lead the Jews of Safed into those twilight areas where each man
is his own judge, where all are free to write the law according to their own
desires, and where the hard, clear light of Torah and Talmud is obscured.

The letter, when it reached the alleys and synagogues, occasioned a fury of
comment. It was the kind of document intended to make men take sides, and it
succeeded. Rabbi Abulafia's students were outraged and started drafting an
answer which would show Rabbi Eliezer to be an idiot, but the doctor refused
to be distracted by personal invective and halted his associates. He better than
they understood the heart of Eliezer's challenge, and he wished to place only
the basic issue before the people. Therefore, in the weeks that followed Rabbi
Eliezer's distribution of the letter Abulafia worked quietly, saw his students
each morning, prayed more than usual and spent his evenings discussing legal
precedents with learned friends. Finally, when the tempers of his followers had
cooled, he handed them a letter to circulate through the synagogues. It was a
statesmanlike document, free of acrimony but filled with legal citation.
Abulafia had dug out cases from six different countries supporting his decision
in the Damascus divorce. He arranged his precedents so as to verify each
procedure that Rabbi Eliezer had questioned. He showed that the practical law
of divorce, as it now operated in the Jewries of Spain, Portugal, Germany,
France, Egypt and Turkey, clearly supported his decision, so that any charge of
arbitrariness or ignorance could not be sustained.

Yet even as he had compiled this part of the letter, he had confessed to himself
that any scholar who analyzed his precedents would become aware that step by
step, from Spain to Turkey, a chain of distinguished rabbis had been moving
slowly and perhaps unconsciously away from a strict interpretation of Torah
and Talmud. Encouraged by liberalists like Maimonides a group of rabbis had
begun to evolve a tradition of their own, and Abulafia knew that it was at this

revisionist tradition, and not at Abulafia himself, that Rabbi Eliezer had been striking in his letter. But this aspect of the controversy the Spaniard chose to avoid; his clear eye was focused on still another battleground existing between the two men, and it was to this fundamental topic that he addressed himself in the final pages of his letter:

I deny that the argument of the learned Rabbi Eliezer bar Zadok ha-Ashkenaz concerns me personally; indeed, I believe he has done Safed and Jews of the world a favor in raising the abstract points he has. Nor does the legalistic problem of adhering too much to Maimonides or too little to the Talmud involve me. Here again I believe that Rabbi Eliezer has performed a service in pointing out these divergencies. The real problem upon which we are engaged, and upon which I shall be happy to remain engaged, is this:

Can Judaism prevail if it is tied to a narrow interpretation of the law as conceived and administered by a body of older rabbis? Must we not in the years ahead revitalize our religion by infusing it with the day-to-day revelations experienced by common men? I believe in strict observance of the law, as I have shown in the preceding citations, and I would be shamed in my own eyes if I felt that I had strayed from one iota of that law as it has evolved in the lives of real men and great rabbis. I render no decision before I know what is being done in Paris, Frankfurt and Alexandria, for I am a servant of the law as it develops in the lives of men. But I also believe that Judaism, to prevail, must avoid becoming the preserve of a few men who, by their legalistic approach, stamp out the ordinary joy of life and its mystical appreciations.

With this courtly letter the battle was joined. It never became a personal brawl between Eliezer and Abulafia; the other rabbis and the good sense of the two participants prevented that. But it did become a fundamental confrontation between the two dynamic forces of Judaism in that age: Ashkenazi legality versus Sephardi mysticism; or, to put it another way, the conservative force of the rabbi versus the expanding social vision of the community; or, the great restraining tendency of Talmud versus the explosive liberation of Zohar. On these grounds the battle was fought.

The men around Dr Abulafia—and they were the most persuasive in Safed—had a clear vision of what might happen to world Judaism if the rabbis prevailed. 'It will become,' one of them predicted, 'a religion much like the yolk of an egg. The meat will all be there, clean and pure at the center, but it will be protected from common understanding by the crystallized white of the egg, legalism, and by the impenetrable shell, rabbinical force. All that can save us is the lifting of this vital yolk clean out of the shell and the sharing of it with average men.'

Abulafia himself did not reason in this manner. He said, 'The mysteries of the Zohar are no more understandable by the common man than is the law of the Talmud. We shall always need rabbis, in the future more than in the past. But the exhilarating beauty that is found in the Zohar must be left free to illuminate the souls of all men, and if laws prevent this, then laws must be modified.'

Rabbi Eliezer, alone in his study, cut off from the popular rabbis by his austere nature and from the masses by his lack of a synagogue, talked mostly with his eighteen-year-old daughter Elisheba, who had her mother's intelligence as well as her beauty. To the girl he said, 'It isn't a matter of

Abulafia or me. Nor of law and mysticism. He is very right in his refusal to argue on either of those levels, but his experience has been only with Spain, where Jews lived wherever they wished and where persecution, when it did come, came to each man of himself. On the other hand, I know what happens in lands like Germany, where Jews are driven into narrow streets. And, Elisheba, most of the Jews in the world are going to live that way from now on. What can it mean to such people, freedom? We're not concerned with the personal happiness of Uncle Gottes Mann, the honest businessman, may God preserve him wherever he is. We're concerned with how four thousand Jews, living on top of one another, can exist. And they can exist and preserve their religion only through the most careful observance of the law.' One night he shouted in anguish, 'They keep talking about Safed! I'm talking about the world. Without the law, what will bind the Jews together?'

As the argument grew keener, the rift down the middle of the community widened. The camel caravans kept hauling finished cloth to Akka and continued to bring raw wool back, so that everyone was making money, but Rabbi Zaki was worried. In his simple, clumsy way he saw more clearly than either of the main protagonists that this rupture must be healed, but neither man would make a conciliatory gesture. So he went at last and humbled himself before Rabbi Eliezer, but when the interview began he was distracted by the arrival of Elisheba, her hair drawn straight against her ears and tied at the back in a long pigtail; and like the fool his wife had claimed he was he forgot the main purpose of the meeting and said, 'Rabbi Eliezer, you should be finding your daughter a husband.'

The rebuke was so honest, and so unexpected, that the austere German Jew began laughing. 'You're right,' he chuckled. 'I've been diverted to less important things.'

'We all have been,' Zaki agreed. 'The whole town's been talking about Talmud and Zohar, Maimonides and Abulafia. Don't you honestly think we ought to get back to work, all of us?'

'Do you understand what the argument's about?' Eliezer asked.

'I try to. Dr Abulafia is worried about the present. You're worried about the future.'

Again Eliezer laughed and drew his daughter beside him. 'You come awfully close to the truth,' he confessed. Then he grew grave. 'But I can foresee a day not far off when the Jews of the world, distraught and each with his own vision of God, will hear some crazy man shouting, "I am your Messiah! I have come to save you!" And unless at that moment the God-struck Jew is standing firmly on the law and protected by it, he is going to dance in the air and cry, "The Messiah is at the gates and I am saved from the Judenstrasse."'

'From what?' Zaki asked, and the German drew back as if the man he was talking to had not his alphabet, knew not the basic words he was speaking.

Then he said, 'We Jews can be stupid people, Zaki. Only the law keeps us strong. We are a people of the Book and the day will come when only the Book will preserve us from ourselves.'

'I believe you, Rabbi Eliezer, and now can we have peace?'

'Yes. I have made my statement and I will keep silent.'

'I'll go see my son-in-law,' Zaki said, and when he had left, Eliezer said to his daughter, 'There goes a saintly rabbi. To Rabbi Zaki, Dr Abulafia is not a man who has torn Safed apart and endangered Judaism. He is his son-in-law.'

At the home of the Kabbalist, Zaki was assured by Sarah that she 'had told the rabbi a hundred times to stop writing letters.' Dr Abulafia laughed uneasily, whereupon Rabbi Zaki suggested, 'I think it's time you leave the coolness of your library and come down the hill to my shoemaker shop.'

'Perhaps so,' Abulafia said, and he reached for his prayer shawl. As he left the house Sarah yelled at him, 'And listen to what my father has to say,' and Rabbi Zaki thought: Now I'm a prophet!

He sent a boy to fetch Rabbi Eliezer, who came down the hill, and the three men sat in the shoemaker's shop and discussed the altercation. Rabbi Zaki said, 'I think we have all stated our positions clearly.'

Eliezer corrected him: 'You haven't said anything, Rabbi Zaki. What is your position?'

'That there are six hundred thousand faces to the Torah and that two of my dearest friends on earth, Rabbi Eliezer and Rabbi Abulafia, have each seen one of the faces and from it gained great illumination.'

'We have been arguing about fundamental differences,' Abulafia protested.

'Is there anything more fundamental than the Torah?' Zaki asked.

'No,' Eliezer replied. 'I shall write no more letters.'

'Nor I,' Abulafia promised.

Rabbi Zaki asked Rachel to bring some wine, and said, 'You have each wondered if I understood the argument. I do. Abulafia is fighting for the right of the individual Jew to approach the Torah on his own level and to find joy therein, and to this I agree. Eliezer is fighting for the right of Jews as a group to exist, and of this I approve. The job of a poor rabbi like me is to see that each of these desirable goals has a chance of succeeding. But the word "Judenstrasse" I do not understand, and I wish someone would explain it.'

'It's a street, hideously narrow, where Jews in Germany are forced to live,' Eliezer explained. 'And soon we shall all be living there.'

'When we do, may we have the courage of Diego Ximeno,' Dr Abulafia prayed, and the feud ended.

It would be incorrect to claim that in this critical debate the town itself had remained neutral. Safed was a place of singular beauty; from the edge of the fort crumbling on the hill down to the open fields that lay beyond the synagogue, sixteen narrow streets hung one below the other, connected by alleys which cut through at odd and inconsistent angles. In many places the streets were so narrow, scarcely three feet wide, that above them the houses joined and one walked as in a tunnel; there was an essential mystery about the place. Its location was such that frequently a cloud would drift into town and hang capriciously over some houses and not over others, and a neighbor could stand at his door and see the home of his friend mysteriously disappear—then reappear in sunlight as the cloud passed. The air of Safed was different, too—a clear, penetrating air that seemed to affect the lungs, causing one to breathe deeply with a kind of exhilaration—and through this clear air one could see unusual distances with almost ghostlike penetration. In short, Safed was a town which enhanced the mystical interpretation of life, and it is quite possible that had the Kabbalists chosen some other spot in Galilee, their success might have been limited.

It was Elisheba who first noticed this partiality of Safed. One day she said to her father, 'The town fights against you.' He laughed grimly, but she added, 'Here I could almost become a mystic. The alleys are just as narrow as the Judenstrasse we left in Gretz. Why, then, do they seem so lovely?'

'Because here there is no iron gate keeping you from the fields,' he replied matter-of-factly.

Elisheba was now twenty and resembled her mother more than ever; she was tall and had her father's dignity of movement but her mother's love of children and fantasy. She had become the object of speculation, and even Spanish-speaking Jews began attending the German synagogue to see if Elisheba was in attendance. Many young men thought of marriage with the rabbi's daughter, and some came to Zaki's shop to discuss the matter with him. 'Ask her father,' the fat rabbi told them.

'I'm afraid of Rabbi Eliezer,' they explained.

'I'll speak to him if your parents ask me,' Zaki said. But to one young man, shorter even than himself, Zaki said, 'Forget Elisheba. She's tall and you're short, and men and women who marry should fit together in all ways.' He arranged a different marriage for this suitor, and later the man said that the fit was good.

Twice Rabbi Zaki went to Eliezer to speak on behalf of suitors, but the German Jew, reluctant to lose his memory of Leah, told him, 'Elisheba can wait a little longer. Besides, I like to watch her as she brings the books.'

In the next years Rabbi Zaki was struck by two personal tragedies which diminished his ebullience; the only consolation he found was in the fact that the first took place before the second, sparing his wife additional sorrow. In early 1555 Rachel fell ill. Dr Abulafia was called and could do nothing for his mother-in-law; and some men claimed, 'She's poisoning herself with her own bile.' For some time she had gone back to heckling her husband as to why he didn't build a big synagogue of his own plus a yeshiva in which to teach.

'I have nothing to teach,' he replied.

'You would have if you weren't so fat,' she said irrationally. In bitterness and unfulfillment she approached her death, for the three marriages of her daughters were not working out well, but on her last morning she whispered, 'Husband, I'd like a little glass of wine,' and for a while as he sat by her bed she relaxed her animosity and said, 'We should have stayed in Salonica. But I agree that Safed is better than running half-naked through the streets of Podi. It was better this way . . . since you insisted on being so fat.' And with her death Zaki became lost in tragedy and for half a year was little seen in Safed.

At the end of 1555 his mind was taken from his loss by the arrival of a refugee from the Jewish community in Ancona, the Italian seaport north of Podi, and this man convened a meeting in the largest synagogue to report on the disaster that had befallen his city. 'For long years,' he said, 'we Jews who fled from Spain lived happily in Ancona and even had grandchildren born on Italian soil. I had a weaver's shop.' He hesitated as if recalling some insupportable sorrow, then said softly, 'Of eighteen who lived on my street, only I escaped.'

'What happened?' Rabbi Zaki asked.

'Four Popes in a row had confirmed our right to live in Ancona, even though we had been forcibly baptized when passing through Portugal. But this year came a Pope who announced that the Church must now solve the Jewish problem once and for all. We believe his nephew wrote out the new rules, but he issued them.'

'Are they much different from before?' Zaki asked.

The refugee turned to study the fat rabbi and said, 'Aren't you Zaki, who fled Podi?'

'Yes.'

'The new rules are different. First, no city in the world may have more than one synagogue, and if a city does, the others are to be torn down at once. Second, every Jew in the world must wear a green hat. Men and women. Sleeping and waking. Inspectors may break into the home at any moment to see that Jews are wearing their green hats. Third, all Jews in a town must live on one street.'

'For years we did that in Germany,' Rabbi Eliezer said. His prophecy was coming true.

'Fourth, no Jew may own property. If he now owns land he must sell it within four months for whatever the Christians wish to offer. Fifth, no Jew may engage in any kind of commerce, save the resale of old clothes.' He droned on through additional proscriptions: no Christian may work for a Jew; no Jew may apply medicine to a Christian; no Jew may work on a Christian holiday; nowhere at any time, not even in synagogue, may any Jew be addressed with a title like Messer or Rabbi or Master.

Rabbi Zaki, listening to the recital, tried to find what hope he could. 'These are simply the old laws made harsher,' he said.

'But now we have two new ones,' the man from Ancona said, 'and it was from these I fled. Thirteenth, all previous laws which granted Jews any kind of protection are abolished, and the fathers of each town are invited to impose any additional restrictions they desire. Fourteenth,' and his voice dropped to a whisper, 'if the Jew protests at any point he is to be punished physically, with great severity.'

In the silence practical-minded Yom Tov ben Gaddiel asked, 'But when the laws were announced did anything happen?'

'No,' the Ancona man said, and throughout the synagogue the Safed rabbis could be heard breathing with relief. 'But on my last night in the city a Christian who owed me much money came quietly to my house and said, "Simon ben Judah, you've been a good friend. Here's half the money I owe you. Flee the city this hour because at dawn there will be many arrests." I asked, "What for?" And he shrugged his shoulders: "After all, you are heretics." And as I hid on the hill behind Ancona I saw, toward four in the morning, torches moving out through all the streets where Jews lived.'

'So what happened?' Rabbi Yom Tov asked.

'I don't know. I escaped to Podi.'

'Were Jews arrested there?' Zaki asked, his big face wet with perspiration.

'No. Your duke said that in Podi the new laws did not apply and in this defiance he was supported by his brother, the cardinal. Agitated messengers came from both Ancona and Rome to argue with the brothers, but they stood firm and allowed no arrests. Nevertheless, I grew frightened and took passage on a Turkish ship.'

'Tell me,' Zaki asked. 'Jacopo ben Shlomo and his wife Sarah, were they well?'

'They were well,' the Ancona man reported. 'They still have their red house by the fish market.'

That night Rabbi Zaki returned to his lonely shoemaker shop and prayed, but his lips moved heavily, for he could see his Jews of Podi standing on the wharf that day so long ago, with signs of fire on their foreheads. And then, in the summer of 1556, Safed received, along with a shipment of wool, another of the terrifying broadsheets which cities in Europe found morbid pleasure in circulating during the middle years of the century. The new printing press in

Podi had produced this one, which, with harrowing woodblock prints providing details, told the world than in 1555 and 1556 the Holy Inquisition had saved Podi by burning alive twenty-nine Jews, and the name, the description, the heresy of each was reported in detail, with twenty-nine woodcuts showing how each Jew had reacted to the fire.

Fat Jacopo, who had run in the last race with Zaki, had died praying. Thin Nethaneel had begged for mercy. And Sarah, the wife of Jacopo, had died with her hair a living torch. In horror Rabbi Zaki read the predicted history of his congregation; it was as if the Inquisition had reached across the Mediterranean, calling him back to the punishment he had escaped by flight.

It was then that Rabbi Zaki, the amusing rotund man, fell into that sense of guilt which characterized his last years. The two blows coming together affected him profoundly, for he felt that if he had been a better husband Rachel might not have grown so bitter; and in fleeing Podi he had abandoned his congregation to the stake, just as surely as Dr Abulafia had abandoned his family to its torture. For some months he was a man partly deranged by self-recrimination, and in neither Torah nor Talmud could he find consolation. He tried sharing his sorrow with Rabbi Eliezer, who had done the same in fleeing Gretz, but the austere German was so preoccupied with the law that he had no time to offer comfort, nor did the law itself, which stated what a man must do when mourning for the dead but not what to do when those dead were hung about his neck, burning in perpetual fire, so that the smoke blurred his vision. In his extremity he found aid in an unexpected quarter. Dr Abulafia came to him in the shoemaker shop and said, 'Zaki, father-in-law and friend, the time has come in your perplexity for you to study the Kabbala,' and the devout Spaniard explained in simple terms certain concepts of the mystical world that learned Jews had been perfecting in recent years. 'The mystic perceives with his heart what his mind knows to be true . . . but cannot prove,' Abulafia began. 'And we know that prior to creation God must have been immanent in all things. Without God there could be nothing. But if a merciful God is all things and is responsible for all things, how can we experience events like the burning of the Jews of Podi? Because just before God created the world, He voluntarily withdrew to make space for the physical world we see. But to remind us of His presence He left behind the ten vessels of which you have often heard me speak. And into these ten vessels He poured His divine light so that His presence might be amongst us. But after the first three vessels had caught their portion of the light and saved it for us, the lower seven were struck with such a flood of splendor that they could not retain it, and the vessels were shattered. Thus came confusion and tragedy into the world. Today you and I stand among the shattered vessels and the memory of our betrayals in Podi and Avaro. Sin is upon us and it becomes our responsibility, through dedication, prayer and extra-human effort, to reconstruct these shattered vessels, so that the light of God can exist in its intended receptacles. Zaki, you must co-operate with all men of goodness in their task of gathering together the shattered pieces and reconstructing the vessels.'

At last Rabbi Zaki understood what his handsome son-in-law had been teaching since his arrival in Safed. There was an evil in the world which God was powerless to combat without the help of men; a mystical partnership was being offered, stunning in concept and in its power to elicit the best in life. Like thousands of other Jews who in these years were piercing the mysteries of Zohar, Zaki discovered that he was not the kind of man to find spiritual solace through routine memorizing of Talmud or a sterile codification of law. He could find that mystical solace only through the Kabbala.

'What must I do to help rebuild the broken vessels?' Zaki asked in a spiritual daze.

'No man can tell you,' Abulafia replied. 'Contemplate and pray, and He will warn you when He needs you.'

So Rabbi Zaki started to concentrate, but he found it difficult; usually he fell asleep. Nor was he the kind of man to whom God spoke, so he went back to the simple things he could do best: he prayed for the Jews of Podi, and then suddenly the world opened up for him in full mystical radiance. It began one day in November when the dignitaries of Safed came to him and blunt Rabbi Yom Tov said, 'Zaki, it's not proper for you to remain unmarried.' Zaki replied that he was then fifty-seven years old till a hundred and twenty and that his life with Rachel . . . 'That's no excuse,' Yom Tov reasoned. 'When God finished creating man, what was the first great commandment God gave him?'

Yom Tov waited, then recited in powerful voice, '"So God created man in his own image, in the image of God created he him; male and female created he them. And God blessed them, and God said unto them, Be fruitful, and multiply . . ."'

At the first two meetings Zaki refused to heed his peers, but at the third meeting the force of God's original commandment struck him when Yom Tov said, 'For His first words to the human race God could have chosen any of His commandments, but He chose the simplest of all. A man must find a woman, they must enjoy themselves in each other, and they must multiply. God later said many other things to his stiff-necked Jews, and we rebelled against Him at almost every point, but on this one principle there was agreement.'

Another rabbi said, 'So, Zaki, you must find a wife.'

And the little plump man surrendered: 'I will look among the widows of Safed.'

Then into his shop came Rabbi Eliezer, saying, 'Zaki, my daughter Elisheba wants to marry with you.'

It was like a thunderbolt that struck but one house in a village, and that house was Zaki's. 'But I'm fifty-seven till a hundred and twenty and she's twenty-three.'

'How do you know her age?'

'Because from the day she arrived in Safed I have followed her in all she's done.'

'Then why are you surprised?' the German rabbi asked.

'But a dozen young men have sat in that chair and asked me, "Speak to Rabbi Eliezer that I may have his daughter." You know that yourself–I've been to see you several times.'

'And why do you suppose Elisheba has always asked me to say no?'

Rabbi Zaki wanted to believe what his ears were hearing, but he was afraid. Before him he saw not Rabbi Eliezer, but his own complaining daughter Sarah, who never bothered to mask her disenchantment with her courtly Spaniard, who seemed so attractive to the other women of Safed. Zaki guessed shrewdly that his daughter's disappointment stemmed from the age-old problem which was discussed with disarming frankness in the Talmud: 'The marital duty enjoined upon husbands by the Torah is as follows: every day for those that are unemployed, twice a week for laborers, once a week for donkey-drivers who lead caravans for short distances, once every thirty days for camel-drivers who lead caravans for longer distances, and once every six months for sailors, but disciples of the sages who study the Torah may stay away from their wives for thirty days.' Rabbi Zaki thought: Dr Abulafia is an elderly man, sixty-six till a hundred and twenty, and I am an old man, too, and if he has run into trouble, why may not the same happen to me?

With compelling simplicity the fat rabbi confessed, 'Rabbi Eliezer, I'm afraid to marry your daughter.'

Compassionately the German replied, 'I'm sure my daughter knows your fears, but she holds that in these matters God directs us. She's willing to take the risk. She wants to marry you.'

Three times Rabbi Zaki started to speak, but no words came, so finally Eliezer said, 'Little Zaki, you're a saint. And women are more apt than men to recognize saints when they see them.' So the marriage was held in the German synagogue.

Then came the days of heaven on earth. Rabbi Zaki, who had pleaded with so many men to marry, discovered that he had not understood the meaning of the word, for those participations, which with complaining Rachel had been a duty, became with the tall, poetic Elisheba a joy beyond imagining. Being an uncomplicated man and one not committed, like Dr Abulafia, to wrestling with spiritual problems, Rabbi Zaki encountered no difficulty in fulfilling or even exceeding his Talmudic quota; there was in fact only one problem: one Friday afternoon in the abounding joy of his new marriage he started to say that at last he understood the invocation of the Shabbat hymn, 'Come, my Beloved, let us meet the Bride,' but as soon as he had uttered the first words he dismissed them as blasphemous, for he knew that the Bride Shabbat was greater even than the Bride Elisheba, and in this radiant concept he found assurance. In the quickest possible time she was pregnant, announcing to Safed, 'Rabbi Zaki and I are going to have two dozen children.' And as soon as her first son was born she became pregnant again, so that in three years she had three children. She laughed all the time, and when the young men of the town said, 'We notice that Rabbi Zaki doesn't call so many midnight meetings any more,' she shocked Safed by asking demurely, 'Would you?'

What Zaki remembered most about his faultless wife, when he was absent from her, was a silly thing. On Fridays, as Shabbat approached, she took white paint and outlined all the cracks where stones joined in the floor of their home, and out into the street as well. It was a German habit and made the home look squared-off and neat, and one day as he recalled these lovely whited squares with which his wife praised God—he saw them in his mind's eye against the sky to the west—he first saw the figures 301. They came upon him as burning symbols, more real than the earth on which he walked, the flaming figures 301.

That night as he sat by candlelight, moving the Hebrew alphabet about his paper, hoping that he might convoke the mystical letters YHWH, a feat he had not yet accomplished, for his mind was not disciplined enough for that ultimate of mysteries, the ordinary letters suddenly began falling away and he saw at last only the two which designated the number 301. Again the letters stood forth in flame.

During the happiest period of his life, when Elisheba was walking proudly with her three children and when his own influence in Safed was at its height, the fat rabbi found the number 301 rushing out to confront him at unexpected places. On Friday afternoon he would go with the rabbis to the fields to sing of the coming Shabbat, and when he departed from them to announce Shabbat through the streets from one white wall after another, the burning figures 301 stood forth to terrify him. He could not escape them, and in the third month of this visitation a day came when, embracing his wife, he saw them emblazoned on her forehead and then on the heads of his children. It was a moment of terror.

For three days he spoke to no one, and on Friday he neither took a ritual bath nor went into the fields to welcome Shabbat. Instead, he crept quietly to the German synagogue, a man unable to acknowledge the divine summons which had come to him, and as the voices of singers rose about him, he could hear Elisheba chanting behind the curtain that separated the women:

> 'Come, my Beloved, let us meet the Bride.
> The presence of Shabbat let us receive.'

And then on the embroidered curtain covering the Torah he saw the flaming figures 301.

Above the voices of the singers he cried, 'Oh, God, what must I do to help?' And the figures burned in fire, as if they must consume the synagogue, and to the surprise of the worshipers he prostrated himself on the floor, crying, 'God, have You called me at last?'

Rabbi Eliezer heard these words and interrupted his chant to run to the fallen rabbi, and when he saw the ecstasy on the fat man's face he sensed that some dreadful thing had come to pass through meddling with Kabbala, and he did an extraordinary thing. He slapped Zaki three times and cried, 'It is not so!' But the fallen man ignored the blows and looked only at the cupboard of the Torah, where the mystical figures burned for some moments, not to disappear until Zaki cried in full submission, 'I shall go.'

At the end of the service he ignored Rabbi Eliezer and hurried home, where he said evening prayers with his wife and children, almost breaking down when he saw their four loved faces. He closed his doors to the habitual visitors who liked to sing with him on Shabbat evening and went instead to his room, where he prayed all night. In the morning he waited till Elisheba had fed the children, then said, 'I must talk with you.'

Like an uncomplicated girl she smiled and said, 'Speak.'

'Can we walk to the old fort?' he asked solemnly, and she, having feared this moment for some days, assented. Calling an old woman to mind her children she joined her husband and they climbed the narrow streets leading to the Crusaders' fort, where they sat on old rocks and surveyed the marvelous landscape in which they lived.

Rabbi Zaki said, 'It is a matter relating to the will of God.' His wife said, 'I knew it must be.'

'I am not learned like your father, and I cannot pierce mysteries like Dr Abulafia, but long ago, when I first read Talmud as a boy, I found the message which has guided my life. It was in the words of the great Akiba, who was also an uncomplicated man like me. Akiba said, "Everything in life is given against a pledge, and a net is cast over all the living; the shop is open, the shopkeeper extends credit, the ledger is open before you, the hand writes, and whoever wishes to borrow may come and borrow; but the collectors make their rounds continually and exact payment of every man, with his consent or without."'

There was silence. Elisheba had long known this greatest of passages from Akiba; she knew that all human beings lived under a net which bound them to certain limits of activity, and she knew also that the bill collectors circulated each day, lifting the payment of those who had borrowed against the future. These understandings were the basic morality of Judaism and she did not flinch from them. She wondered what was in her husband's mind.

'For many months,' he said, 'I have felt the number 301 summoning me, and recently it has appeared on your brow and on the brow of our children.' He trembled and drew back. 'It's there now, Elisheba.'

'What does it mean?' she asked softly.

'Fire,' he said.

For some moments she looked at the fat little saint with whom she had been allowed to live in such simple happiness, and slowly the meaning of his vision came to her and she rejected the great words of Akiba. 'No!' she screamed in terrible anguish. 'Zaki, no! No!'

'It means fire,' he repeated dully.

For some hours they sat peacefully among the Crusader ruins, an old man and a beautiful young wife, and finally each had to accept the fact that there was no escape, no alternative. Finally Elisheba, with an anguish greater than she had imagined could exist, turned to her husband and said, 'If you must, may God strengthen you for the sanctification of His name.'

'I must,' he said, and like ghosts, treading on unreality, they went down the hill.

Elisheba took it upon herself to notify the other rabbis, and they came running through the streets to the shoemaker's house. 'Is Zaki dying?' the neighbors inquired, seeing the sudden convergence.

The little shoemaker, then sixty years old and with a white beard, sat sternly at his bench as the leaders of Safed gathered about him. He said, 'All my life I have wondered why I was made so fat. To please Rachel I tried to eat less, but God kept me fat. It was for a purpose. So then when I march to the stake for the sanctification of His name I shall make a blaze that will burn for a long time.'

And now the spiritual solidarity of Safed manifested itself. Rabbi Eliezer, torn from his legal studies, did not remind his colleagues that such egocentricity was the end product of Kabbalism, nor did he cry that seeking out martyrdom was arrogance and a matter not approved by law. He reasoned, 'Zaki, my beloved son-in-law, has God directed you to do this thing, or is it merely your own vanity?'

And Dr Abulafia, whose encouragements to Zaki to study the Kabbala could have been responsible for the fiery message, felt himself rebuked by Zaki's determination to compensate for his abandonment of his congregation. 'Zaki,' he asked, 'is it a true vision you've had or something you imagined because you were with others who had honest insights?'

Patiently Rabbi Zaki put each of his friends at ease. 'This happened to me long before I heard of Kabbala, for on the day I fled Podi, God showed me on the faces of the friends I was deserting the mark of fire. And it is a true vision, for in a dream a voice spoke to me and said, "Zaki, if you try to divide this number 301 by two or three or four or five or six, which are the ordinary days of the week, there is always one left over, which is you. But if you divide it by seven, which is the number of our Shabbat, there is no remainder, and you are one with God."' In a whisper he added, 'And if you sum the letters used in writing *fire* they come to 301.'

Among the Kabbalists there was serious discussion of these mystical facts, for obviously they portended something arcane, but the discussion was broken by blunt Rabbi Yom Tov, who reminded Zaki, 'There is one supreme reason for not going. If your bones are buried here in Safed, on Judgement Day you will rise to greet the Messiah; but if they are buried overseas you will have to burrow underground like a mole to reach the Holy Land.' This was a belief held by many Jews, and it was their dread of a long twisting journey in darkness which inspired them to return to the Holy Land to die.

Of equal weight was Rabbi Abulafia's reminder: 'You are not an ordinary Jew, Zaki, going to Rome on a mission to defend the Torah. Some have done so and escaped. But you are a Jew who was once baptized in the Christian Church, and like the Jews of Podi who were burned, you are in the eyes of that Church a heretic, and they believe they have a duty to burn you. If you go to Rome, you invite your own certain death.'

But what Rabbi Zaki said next was of greater weight: 'We live within the net of God, and though I swam to the farthest end of the Mediterranean I could not escape. Had I stayed with the Jews of Podi, I would have burned with them. They call me and God calls me.'

The discussion was broken by the arrival of Zaki's two oldest daughters, Sarah and Tamar, who demanded to know what the meeting was about. When they were told that their father proposed going back to Rome to argue for Judaism and to offer himself for martyrdom, they began to protest bitterly. Like their mother they had been against his leaving Podi, Africa and Salonica, and they were now against his leaving Safed. 'If Mother were alive . . .' they shouted harshly.

'She is not alive,' Elisheba interrupted. 'But I am, and I say that if Rabbi Zaki is called by God to this terrible mission, he shall go with my blessing and the blessing of our children.'

'They're not old enough to know anything,' the sisters whined.

'I know what they will believe on such matters,' Elisheba said, 'because they are the children of a saint.'

'If our mother were here . . .' Sarah wailed.

'Order your wife out of here,' one of the rabbis told Abulafia, but he said resignedly, 'She is his daughter. She is allowed to stay.' And the matter was put up to Zaki, who said, 'You may stay, Sarah, but do not speak so loudly.'

The discussion went on and on, but nothing could shake Rabbi Zaki from his determination to go to Rome, and it was at last agreed that he should do so. He spent two weeks in finishing his affairs and selling his shoemaker shop to a young man he hoped would marry Elisheba when he was dead. He held long conversations with his children, trusting that they might remember something of the old, white-bearded man who had been their father.

From one synagogue to the other he went, praying with the people who had grown to love him, and on the last Friday he went to the fields with the rabbis and sang joyously at the approach of Shabbat. Then he left them and marched slowly through the streets, calling the Jews to their duty of greeting Queen Shabbat, and it was supposed that he would go to the German synagogue, which his wife attended; but he went instead to that of Rabbi Abulafia, a man who also carried a burden of sin, and the two old rabbis looked at each other across the heads of the congregation.

On Sunday he said farewell to his wife. No more would he embrace those lovely breasts or know her enchanting thighs. Her womb would grow no more with his seed and at night he would not feel her white leg creeping across his. The exact structure of her marvelous face framed in black hair would slowly recede from his memory, except that in the last moment, through the flames, he would see not YHWH, but Elisheba, the daughter of Eliezer bar Zadok.

Early Monday morning the people of Safed, led by their rabbis, walked into the countryside after Rabbi Zaki as he started on his pilgrimage. They gave him money and prayers. He kissed his wife and his children, then kissed his wife again, but the last citizen of Safed with whom he spoke was Dr Abulafia, who came bearing a small parcel. 'You know the sin under which I live,' the Spaniard said. 'Help me. When I fled I brought with me this menorah. Take it back to the land of persecution. Someone may cherish it.'

Rabbi Zaki looked at the turbaned man and said with humility, 'I judged you harshly. Now God forces me to behave in the same way. Forgive me.' But when he camped that night at the mound of Makor he argued with himself: Taking Rabbi Abulafia's menorah back to Europe is an act of arrogance, if not of idolatry. He therefore buried it deep in the earth, trusting that at some later date a Jew of the region would find it and consider it a miracle.

On the next morning he rose early and resumed his march toward Rome.

LEVEL II

Twilight of an Empire

Found at Makor—Turkish gold coin (see chapter 1) issued by
the Fatimid Dynasty of Egypt. Original reads in part—*Obverse:*
'In the name of God, this dinar was struck at Tiberias 395 A.H.
(1004 C.E.). Ali al-Mansur Abu Ali being Imam. Al-Hakim bi-
Amr-Allah being Commander of the Faithful.' *Reverse:* 'There
is no God except Allah alone. He has no partner. [This phrase
was included to irritate Christians.] Muhammad is the Apostle
of God, sent with instructions to demonstrate the true faith in
its entirety, even though the pagans hated this. Ali is the friend
of Allah.' It was this Caliph ai-Hakim who ordered the
destruction of the Christian Church of the Holy Sepulchre in
Jerusalem in 1009, thus initiating the series of events that
culminated in the Crusades. Deposited at Makor August 21,
1880 C.E., sometime after six o'clock in the afternoon.

It was hot in Tiberias, both within the city and without. A blazing sun beat
down upon the molten surface of the lake and hammered at the barren hills like
a great torch seeking to set the world afire. Inside the massive black walls of the
town the heat was more than a man could bear, so that during the suffocating
hours of midday few could be seen in the narrow alleys, down which ran open
sewers throwing a hideous stench.

Tiberias was the earth's lowest settlement, cowering more than six hundred
and eighty feet below the level of the sea, and in this torrid summer of 1880 it
was also one of the world's most miserable communities, a somnolent, cramped
and dirty little town overburdened with filth and fleas. In the remorseless sun it
dozed as if ashamed to show its face to the world.

Legend of the countryside claimed that the king of insects held court in
Tiberias and hither summoned his subjects each summer to devise new means
of tormenting human beings, their shrewd inventions being first tried out on
the citizens of this wretched town. Certainly something in the hot, low place
was conducive to the breeding of insects, for each house was alive with fleas and
scorpions and bedbugs.

For nearly a thousand years Tiberias had been the butt of jokes, because as
early as 985 an Arab traveler, forced against his will to spend some time in the
town, reported to his friends: 'For two months in the year the citizens gorge
themselves upon the fruit of the jujube bush, which grows wild and costs them
nothing. For two months they struggle with the numerous flies that are rife
there. For two months they go about naked because of the fierce heat. For two
months they play the flute, for they suck pieces of sugar cane which resemble
flutes. For two months they wallow in mud, for the rains soak their streets, and
for the last two months they dance in their beds because of the legions of fleas
with which they are infested.' The people of Tiberias enjoyed a reputation no
more favourable than that of their insects. A drowsy, undistinguished lot, they
drifted through the years with no accomplishments, and a stranger, looking at

their town in its present condition, could not have recognized the once-proud city of the Herods nor the center of learning from which the Talmud and the written Bible were given to the world. It would have been impossible to imagine that within these walls a Crusader court had once held sway, for now only a few Arabs huddled in their district, a few Jews in theirs, the Sephardim remaining strictly aloof from the Ashkenazim while a handful of Christians clung to the southern edge of the town, and on stifling days like this, when the thermometer on the kaimakam's balcony stood at 124 degrees and when no breeze came from any quarter, the citizens of Tiberias lay panting in their beds, hoping that the night would bring relief.

In this flea-bitten town only one man was cool. In an underground room perched over a cellar which had been packed during the winter with ice lugged down from the mountains, a handsome, portly man in his early forties reclined in a bamboo chair, his fat feet higher than his belly and a wet towel about his head. He was naked except for a small breech-clout and he was drinking grape juice into which had been placed chips of ice from the cellar below.

Even so, this amiable man with the long mustaches was sweating, not because of the heat, but because of intricate and dangerous plans in which he was involved. Two different groups of plaintiffs had petitioned him for exactly contrary decisions regarding a matter of land: the white-robed qadi and the red-faced mufti had joined forces to plead for one solution, while Shmuel Hacohen, a sway-backed Jew from Russia, sought an opposing judgment. And Faraj ibn Ahmed Tabari, the kaimakam of Tubariyeh, as Tiberias was now called, had devised a trick whereby he could extort baksheesh from each side while appeasing neither, and such a solution appealed to his sense of administration.

Tabari lay back in his chair and imagined the plaintiffs as they would stand before him in a few hours. The red-faced mufti would bluster: 'As religious leader of the Muslims I demand.' The white-robed little qadi, afraid of his judgeship, would wheedle: 'Excellency, I do think you should.' And Hacohen, a man of incorruptible determination, would stand with his left foot awkwardly forward and plead: 'A boatload of Jews has landed at Akka.' And each would have in his pockets, to bolster his petition, a handful of gold coins, dependable, negotiable English sovereigns. It was the kind of situation the kaimakam could appreciate.

But the real reason he sweated was not this exacting duplicity regarding land nor the oppressive heat of this unbearable day. Governor Tabari was nervous because he felt himself being edged closer to that moment when he must take a stand regarding the future of the empire, and this he was afraid to do. Before the recent war the sultan had arbitrarily offered a constitution and the hearts of young men like Tabari had surged with hope; but just as arbitrarily the sultan had revoked the constitution and young men could see that despotism and tyranny were to be indefinitely prolonged. This was a matter on which men of character should take a stand, and Tabari, at forty-two, could logically place himself either with the young idealists or with the established officials who were satisfied with no change. Normally he would have procrastinated on a matter of such importance, but his brother-in-law was on his way from Istanbul to urge that Tabari side with the reformers who were planning a direct appeal for the restoration of law. Trying to decide which way to jump in such circumstances was enough to make a man sweat.

Kaimakam Tabari's inability to make a decsion should not be construed as defectiveness in character; one of the few Arabs permitted to attain high position within the Turkish administration, he had to be cautious where policy was concerned. In fact, his presence in government had been a fortunate accident and he would allow no mistakes to jeopardize it. Years ago, as a sharp-eyed Arab boy growing up in Tubariyeh, he had captivated the interest of the then kaimakam, a Turkish scholar of extraordinary quality who had invited young Faraj to play with his son and daughter, and who, in watching the Arab boy at games, had developed an insane passion for the youth.

Strange years had followed, in which Faraj traveled with the kaimakam from Safad to Akka to Beirut, thus .acquiring his insight into Turkish administration; and then, as suddenly as the passion had arisen, it waned, and the kaimakam allowed Faraj to marry his daughter and arranged for him to attend the school for administrators in Istanbul. There Tabari had been a lone Arab in classes dominated by Greeks, Bulgars and Persians, and had learned with what contempt the Turkish rulers held all Arabs, those least and lowliest of the empire. He dedicated himself to proving what an Arab could accomplish and he so impressed his instructors that after graduation he was assigned to exploratory positions in Salonica, Edirne and Baghdad. It was to that latter city, in 1876, when he was thirty-eight and his strange father-in-law was dead that his wife's brother had come with exciting news: 'Faraj! You're being sent to Mecca. And if you can somehow get together baksheesh in the amount of six hundred Maria Theresas you'll be allowed to buy the kaimakam's office in Tubariyeh.'

At that stage in his career, with three children, Tabari had been able to accumulate through extortion, theft and bribery only two hundred Maria Theresas toward the purchase of his next appointment, so the secret offer posed a difficult problem, but his brother-in-law would accept no objections. 'Get hold of the kaimakam's office, one way or another,' he counseled, 'for then you'll be able to accomplish great things.' And for the first time Tabari listened to one of the young idealists explain what the Turkish empire might become. 'Faraj! When you're back in Tubariyeh you can open a school. Maybe a hospital. We have plans for a system of military service which will also teach peasants to read and write.' They had talked for many hours, at the end of which Tabari said, 'I'll find the money somehow,' and they had shaken hands, not as conspirators but as two men, one a Turk, one an Arab, who perceived the reforms that must overtake their tired old empire.

What Tabari did not know as he traveled south to Mecca was that the sultan's men, seeking a new crop of officials who could be trusted to defend the old order, had selected him for preferment and were sending him there to see if an Arab with no funds could be relied upon to protect himself in an emergency. They found out. Within a month Faraj Tabari had set in motion an intricate plan which would enable him to steal twice four hundred Maria Theresas in less than a year, and all from impoverished Arabs who could not protest. It would not be wholly accurate to describe his manipulations as stealing; in those somnolent years the Turkish empire operated on the principle that each government employee ought to be able to put aside each year, in one manner or another, four times his official salary: one to pay baksheesh on the job he already held, one to pay for the job he wanted next, one to help his superior pay for his job, and one to hold back for emergencies. Any Turkish official who did not know how to extort, lie, squeeze, blackmail and defraud without creating scandal was obviously unqualified to help run the empire, and Faraj Tabari was ready to prove himself one of the best officials sent to Arabia in recent years.

He started by going down from Mecca to Jidda, where Muslim pilgrims arrived for their journeys to the holy places of Islam, and within a few days he initiated a system whereby each pilgrim was milked of an additional tax. All ships putting in at Jidda harbor were required to pay unexpected port duties, and when they protested, unanticipated difficulties arose which could be solved only by the payment of more baksheesh. Next the energetic young Arab saw to it that all caravans putting in at Mecca were taxed on their oil and dates, and transfers of land were inexplicably held up until fees of an unspecified nature were paid.

What was exceptional about Tabari's operation was that he accomplished it with ease and even urbanity. Each underling who collected baksheesh for him was allowed to keep a portion for himself, while those in superior positions found themselves receiving unexpected contributions. Maneuvering as if he had headed governments for years, Tabari won the respect of all, kept the friendship of most and certainly demonstrated that he was prepared for a command position within the empire.

When the six hundred Maria Theresas had been accumulated he took them to Istanbul, handing them to the official in charge of appointing kaimakams and then spending memorable weeks revisiting his school and forming those friendships which would control his destiny in the years ahead. His brother-in-law, who had insinuated himself into a good job, met him frequently at cafés along the Bosporus, with reports of progress among the younger men. 'We have key positions in every department,' the enthusiastic reformer said. 'When you get back to Tubariyeh there will be so much to do.'

During his first weeks in Istanbul, Tabari was almost convinced that the younger men would succeed in forcing the promulgation of a new constitution and he felt strongly drawn to them, but in the fourth week a cab called for him and he was driven out along the Bosporus to the splendid Dolma Bagcheh Palace for an audience with the sultan, and he found Abdul Hamid, destined to be the greatest ruler of modern Turkey, to be a shrewd, calculating man, cruel in decision and obviously determined that his empire should not again be molested by constitutional reform. Tabari was one of several newly appointed kaimakams whom the sultan was receiving that afternoon and at one point the group moved to a dark room of the palace, where Abdul Hamid said, 'In the old days, if one of our kaimakams betrayed his office, he was invited here for a consultation, and as he waited . . .' Abdul Hamid giggled, and in the ensuing silence a huge black eunuch slipped into the darkened room and caught Tabari by the neck. The other governors gasped, and Tabari could feel the slave's fingers tightening about his throat. Then the negro dropped his hands and everyone laughed nervously. Abdul Hamid added, 'Without a trace the faithless ones were strangled and pitched into the Bosporus. Of course, today we no longer use such punishments.'

And so, properly instructed on how to rule an empire, Faraj ibn Ahmed Tabari, the most successful man yet produced by the Family of Ur, returned to govern his home town of Tubariyeh. He allowed no strife, visited his outlying districts faithfully and paid regular baksheesh to the mutasarrif in Akka and to the wali in Beirut. Furthermore, as a result of insistent pressure on everyone who did business with him, he was able each month to put aside a sum of money toward the purchase of his next job, which ought to be of such importance that he could steal enough to retire on. When that time came he planned to return to

Tubariyeh and buy a portion of the town for himself.

For he loved the grubby little settlement in which he had been reared. Even when serving in remote districts he had been able to recall the snow-capped mountain to the north, the lights of Safad nestling in the hills and the beauty of the lake. The quality of government he gave Tubariyeh was by no means inferior, if judged by the standards of the area, say, from India to Morocco, for he kept his people happy. He initiated no oppression and allowed each minority, like the Christian or the Jewish, to govern itself in matters concerning religion and family life. He supervised a rough justice and maintained civil peace in which the tedious years could pass with no disruptions and little change. Throughout the east thousands of people lived under conditions far worse than those provided by Governor Tabari, and if along the lake there were no schools, if women of all creeds lived like animals, it was simply that no alternatives had been suggested. During the two years he had sat in his office staring out at the barren hills of the Galilee, it had not once occurred to him that the reforms spoken of by the eager young men in Istanbul could be applied here if only he would spend a little energy upon them. When he saw the barren fields he did not understand that they could be otherwise or that they ever had been so. He lived beside a lake which contained some of the finest fish in Asia, a lake which had once fed multitudes even without the miracle of Jesus, yet he never thought it strange that contemporary Tubariyeh had no boat and no food from that plentiful reservoir that stood right at the edge of town. It did not occur to him that it might be a good idea to purchase a boat somewhere and bring it to the lake so that the citizens of Tubariyeh could again enjoy fish. The last vessel to sail that lake had rotted away four hundred years before, and where there had once been fleets of a hundred and two hundred craft there was now not even a rowboat. On the edge of plenty his people starved, and he could not visualize a solution.

'My job,' he once explained to the wali in Akka, 'is to maintain order and to watch at night lest the Bedouins attack the walls.'

Kaimakam Tabari had one simple rule of administration, and it was understood by his subjects: In Tubariyeh positively everything was for sale. If an Arab youth was summoned to military service it was obvious that there was no possible escape; but if his father paid the kaimakam enough, he could escape. Alien Jews were forbidden under the most severe penalties reaching almost to death from owning land in Arab areas; but if the Jew could get together enough baksheesh he could buy the land. When the qadi found a man guilty, it was arranged between the qadi and the kaimakam that the former would impose an excessive sentence; then the guilty man could appeal to the latter, and if he had enough money to pay the baksheesh he went free. For the issuance of the simplest government paper, an established scale of bribes was in force, and in either the civil court of the qadi or the religious court of the mufti any decision that was wanted could be had by paying the proper baksheesh to the kaimakam.

Of course, the income thus gained was by no means all his. He was generous in paying off his subordinates and in splitting fees with the qadi and the mufti. Furthermore, he had to send regular bribes to Akka and Beirut. As a result of this constant drain on the people of Tubariyeh, there was no money left for schools, or sewers, or water supply, or a jail in which a human being could survive. There were no hospitals, no adequate policing, no fire-fighting and no roads. There was the wall, and this kept out the Bedouins, and there was the smiling, amiable kaimakam who made things as easy as possible for his people.

For such a system of general bribery to work, there had to be relative honesty among the principals, but recently the kaimakam had found that the red-faced mufti was cheating on baksheesh and undermining him in Akka. Such behaviour was not surprising, for Tabari's brother-in-law had warned him that Arabs like the qadi and the mufti would be unhappy with a fellow Arab for kaimakam: 'They'd prefer outsiders. A Bulgarian, for example. They would fear him and know where they stood.' As usual, the young man proved right, and as this hot day drew to a close Tabari resolved to settle matters with the mufti. He finished his grape juice, wiped his body for the last time and donned the Turkish uniform in which he conducted the business of government.

From behind a curtain on the second floor of his home he spied with fatherly interest upon the life that began to move once more through the alleys of his town. Muslim shopkeepers lounged at the doors of their shops. An old Jew passed through the market, seeking rags, while through the entrance of the synagogue other Jews passed to resume their study of Talmud. A Christian missionary, unable to convert either Muslim or Jew, walked in perplexity beside the lake, wondering what secret power Jesus and Paul had possessed that they could unlock hearts which were barred to him. Finally the kaimakam saw what he was looking for: from the door of the mufti's house slipped the little qadi, dressed in white and very nervous. Looking furtively in all directions the judge darted across the alley and started to walk in innocence toward the government buildings. After he was safely gone the portly mufti, dressed in black and with a red face on which his emotions could not be hidden, appeared from the same door and casually walked by different streets to the building where the meeting was to be held.

'They don't want me to know they've been conspiring,' Tabari laughed. In a way he was pleased that they had been laying plans behind his back, and he was careful to give them time to reach his office, so that if necessary they could conspire further; for he judged that the more secure they felt, the better chance he had of squeezing from them a sizable chunk of baksheesh. This was contrary reasoning, for usually one would expect only a man alone and in desperation to offer real baksheesh; but Turkish administrators had discovered that it was men who felt sure of themselves, men who had substantial funds at their disposal, who paid for what they wanted. Such men could not be bullied, but they could be tricked.

Kaimakam Tabari put out his Turkish cigarette, adjusted his tarboosh, went in to kiss his wife, to whom he owed so much, and started his walk to the office. Arabs and Jews alike drew back to pay him respect, and he moved slowly, majestically past the mosque, but at the caravanserai, which occupied a central area, he paused to inquire whether the messenger had arrived from Akka with the dispatches from the mutasarrif, and he was disappointed to find that no horseman had come.

'If one does,' Tabari directed, 'speed him to me,' and with this he could no longer delay facing his visitors, so with feigned eagerness he burst into his office, hurried up to the two conspirators and embraced them warmly.

'Good friends, be comfortable on this hot day.' He arranged chairs for them and asked, 'Now what's your problem?'

The little judge gaped. 'Excellency! For two years we've been discussing our problem.'

'Of course,' Tabari agreed amiably. 'But have we any new solutions?'

'What word from Akka?' the mufti asked bluntly.

'None.'

'Then you will make the decision?'

'Of course.'

'And what have you decided?'

'I am inclined toward your point of view.'

The hopeful qadi assumed that this meant victory and was obsequious in his praise: 'Excellency, we knew in our hearts that a man of your wisdom . . .'

But the mufti, one of the ablest men in Tubariyeh, was better schooled in the tricks of Turkish administrators, and sought to pin Tabari down: 'Can we rely upon your word?'

If the kaimakam was insulted by the mufti's crudeness, he restrained himself by recalling his main objective: Today I want money from this man. Revenge can wait until tomorrow. He smiled blandly and said, 'Of course you have my word.'

Again the qadi was delighted. 'Then the Jew gets no land?' he asked.

'I didn't exactly say that,' Tabari hedged.

'What did you say?' the mufti snapped.

Once more the governor stifled his anger. He thought: Sooner or later I must cut this man down. But not today. To the mufti he explained, 'I said that I shared your opinions.'

'But what are you going to do about them?'

Tabari thought: Let the red-faced dog get madder. Then it will be easier to goad him for the money. He said easily, 'What am I going to do? Exactly what you two gentlemen have recommended.'

The little qadi showed his relief that the uncertainly had been erased. 'This is a memorable day, Excellency. Then the Jew gets no land?'

'Not under any possible circumstances,' the governor promised, and with a gesture of transparent honesty he threw his hands on the table, palms up, as if to say: 'There you have the whole matter before you.'

The qadi laughed nervously, as if a burden had been lifted from him, but the dour mufti realized that the squeeze was on. Whenever a Turkish official used that ominous phrase, 'under no possible circumstances,' every wise man knew that the matter was at last up for hard discussion and that the verdict would go to the claimant who paid the largest bribe. The mufti thought: Look at that damned Arab, waiting for me to make an offer that would seal the bargain. Well, he can wait.

Kaimakam Tabari did wait. He saw that the stupid qadi had missed the point, but he knew that the mufti had understood what was expected and was remaining silent in order to humiliate his superior. But the mufti controlled the money that Tabari wanted, so it was the kaimakam who had to swallow his pride and say, 'I've been thinking'; and when he used this universal phrase of Turkish corruption even the dim-witted qadi knew what was up.

'I've been thinking,' Tabari repeated, 'that since the three of us have agreed that the Jew should have no land, I'd better inform the mutasarrif in Akka.' The mufti, a willful man but one eager to protect his Muslims, looked at the slippery kaimakam with contempt, so again Tabari was forced to spell out the negotiation: 'But for me to go to Akka will require money.'

'How much?' the mufti asked scornfully.

'Thirty English pounds,' Tabari said unflinchingly. When he saw the qadi blanch he added suavely, 'I say English pounds because I know you stole more than forty from the last group of pilgrims to Capernaum.'

As the mufti glared at the governor his red face became nearly purple. It was infuriating, the mufti thought, to be treated in this manner by an Arab playing the role of a Turk. Moreover, if he did give Tabari the thirty pounds, little of it would reach Akka, and this idea spurred a crafty thought: Why not give Tabari the thirty pounds, wait for him to steal half, then inform the mutasarrif in Akka that Tabari had stolen from him? By such a trick he might get rid of Tabari altogether, and that would be worth thirty pounds.

The qadi was not equal to such duplicity. The best he could do was sell legal decisions to the highest bidder and then split with the kaimakam, and the concept of springing a trap as far away as Akka was quite beyond him. But the moral problem in the case before him was not; and to everyone's surprise he turned to Tabari: 'Kaimakam Tabari, it seems clear that if you allow the Jew to buy land outside the wall he will bring in other Jews to work that land, and if they succeed, still other Jews will follow them, and soon we poor Muslims . . .' He waved his hand futilely, as if trying to stem the inevitable.

'Oh, I agree with you thoroughly,' Tabari cried enthusiastically. 'That's why I do hope you can find the money for Akka.'

'Will the mutasarrif be qualified to make the decision?' the mufti asked, lured against his will into discussing the case on its merits.

'Of course!' Tabari said in all seriousness, but even as he spoke he reflected: Two years ago the papers were started on their way from Tubariyeh to Akka to Beirut to Istanbul. The decision has surely been made by now, and somewhere along that chain a firman from the sultan is headed this way. Now the European governments had been insisting upon more liberal land laws throughout the empire, and if the sultan grants privileges to Russians and Englishmen, he must do the same for the Jews. So if I want to get my baksheesh from the qadi and the mufti I'd better get it now, before they learn that the sultan's decision has gone against them.

The mufti was speaking in a low growl: 'Aren't you afraid of having Jews buy land?'

'I am indeed,' the kaimakam replied with honest passion. 'It would change everything. Open the gates for . . .' He didn't know for what, but he suspected that the easy old days of accommodation and the quiet passage of years would vanish. He felt an honest sorrow, which he quickly suppressed, for time was passing and the firman might arrive at any moment without his having got the money.

'If we give you the thirty pounds?' the qadi asked plaintively.

'I'd work diligently to keep the Jews off the land.'

'And we could rely on this?' the qadi pleaded.

'You have my word of honor!' the kaimakam expostulated. 'In fact, I'm riding to Akka tomorrow. I'll hand the mutasarrif your money myself, and there'll be no Jews in Tubariyeh.' To himself he reasoned: If the sultan's decision is otherwise, I'll insist I did my best to halt it.

This wily thought, as it came to him, must have betrayed its duplicity in some way, for the canny mufti, watching Tabari's face, gasped to himself: That dirty swine! He already knows what the sultan decided and he's trying to steal our money. Damn him! I'll give him the money and strangle him with it. Tonight I'll send a message to the mutasarrif telling him what's happened. And before the week is passed, our friend Tabari will be in jail.

But now something of the mufti's trickery betrayed itself to Tabari, who was well schooled in the basic rule of Turkish administration: When you have forced a man to pay a bribe, study him carefully to see how he plans to take his revenge. It became clear to Tabari that if his mufti paid the bribe he would do so in hatred and only because he saw some way of hurting the kaimakam. What could the mufti do to endanger me? Tabari asked himself. Only one thing. Pay the money to me, inform the mutasarrif that he's done so, and count on me to keep the money for myself. Smiling genially at the red-faced religious leader, Tabari thought: You illegitimate pig. I'll take your money and I'll give every piaster to the mutasarrif, then tell him what a swine you really are. In two weeks you'll be in Yemen.

Now the qadi and the mufti looked at each other in consultation, and the qadi delivered their decision: 'We'll give you the thirty pounds, Excellency.'

'To be used as you suggested,' the mufti growled. 'For Akka.'

'Of course,' Governor Tabari cried pleasantly, and by great good fortune something inspired him to go to the two men and throw his arms about them, as if they were his friends, because at that moment an Egyptian servant appeared at the door behind them carrying a dispatch case; but because the governor gripped the two men tightly in an embrace, they could not turn to see the servant, and when they were able to do so he had disappeared on a signal from Tabari, taking whatever messages he had with him.

When the embrace ended Kaimakam Tabari cried to the servant, 'Hassan, accompany the mufti to his home. He has a package for me.'

The Egyptian, his hands now empty, returned casually to the room. The mufti looked at him suspiciously and suggested, 'I'll bring the money over tomorrow.'

This called for Tabari to apply the second rule of Turkish administration: When a man agrees to a bribe don't let him out of your sight till he delivers. He may reconsider. 'You forget,' Tabari reminded the mufti, 'I leave for Akka in the morning, and to be effective, your money should reach the mutasarrif promptly.'

The mufti bowed, extended his hand in friendship, then led the qadi from the room. As soon as they had parted from the governor the angry mufti drew the judge aside, so that the servant could not hear, and whispered, 'Did you have the feeling that someone entered the room while the old bastard was embracing us?'

'I didn't notice anything,' the bewildered qadi replied.

Suddenly the powerful mufti whipped about, caught the servant by the arm and demanded, 'You just brought the kaimakam a dispatch from Akka, didn't you?'

'No!' the startled Egyptian replied. In silence he accompanied the mufti to the latter's home, where he checked and rechecked the thirty English pounds which the religious leader handed him.

At that moment Kaimakam Tabari was opening the dispatch case which the servant had been about to hand him a few minutes before. The routine papers Tabari laid aside, shuffling through the others until he found what he had suspected would be in the pouch. Hastily he took out the precious firman, inscribed in gold and sealed with red silk, and read:

The petition of the Jew Shmuel Hacohen of Tubariyeh, to purchase land at the foot of Bahr Tubariyeh, said land now in possession of Emir Tewfik ibn Alafa, native of Damascus, is hereby granted. The further petition of Hacohen to purchase additional land giving direct access to the

Bahr Tubariyeh and the River Jordan is hereby denied. Under no circumstances shall Jews be allowed to acquire land with water frontage.

As Kaimakam Tabari finished reading the firman he smiled, for it meant that the mufti's bribe had been ineffectual even at the moment of being paid, and as an official of the Turkish empire he relished such sardonic contradictions. But now his servant entered with the thirty pounds and news that was less pleasing: outside in the waiting room stood the Jew, Shmuel Hacohen, eager to discuss with the kaimakam the land which he had for the past four years been trying vainly to purchase.

THE TELL

It was singular, John Cullinane thought, that twice in modern history the Jews had been saved by the Turks. It had happened in the sixteenth century when Turkey had offered the outcasts such refuges as Salonica, Constantinople and Safed; and it had been repeated in the nineteenth century when pogroms ravaged Poland and Russia. Why had it been the Muslim Turks who had salvaged the Jews when Christian nations tried to extermine the religion from which they themselves had sprung? One might reason that Islam had been tolerant because it valued Old Testament traditions more highly than Christians did, for Muhammad had specifically directed tolerance toward Jews, while Christianity never did; but this was specious reasoning, and Cullinane dismissed it.

And why was it only the Jew whom the Turk tolerated? During the periods when the Turk was showing his greatest consideration to the Jew, he was at the same time persecuting the Druse and the Armenian, the Bulgarian and the Greek. The same kaimakam who on Monday aided the Jew, on Tuesday hung the Armenian, and on Wednesday shot the Greek.

It was necessary, Cullinane thought, to look outside the field of religion for an explanation, and when he did he found certain ideas which made sense. The Turk did not favor the Jew because he preferred him to the Christian; on the contrary, the Turk, like God, found the Jews to be a stiff-necked people, most difficult to manage. But the Jew stood alone and could be treated alone. He had no outside nation pressing to intervene on his behalf, and so long as he behaved himself reasonably well he was welcomed in Turkey and treated generously. This was not so with the Christians or the Arabs. With the former there was the constant threat that they might summon to the Holy Land nations like France, England or Russia to protect them; while with the Arabs there was the insidious possibility that they would somehow unite to throw off Turkish rule. Consequently, neither Christians nor Arabs were allowed freedom to expand.

At first glance, Cullinane thought, the situation seemed contradictory. One would normally argue that since the Jew was friendless he could be persecuted with impunity, whereas the Christian, surrounded by friends, had better not be touched. The Turks had reasoned otherwise: they did not wish to persecute anyone for his religious beliefs, but they did want to hold their shaky empire together and would tolerate no one who might in the future pose a threat to its continuance. Thus in Tubariyeh there was no possibility that the sickly students of the Talmud might one day coalesce into rebellion against the empire, whereas there was always the danger that the Arabs might do just that, so it was not illogical for a devout Muslim kaimakam to render decisions unfavorable to his mufti.

On the other hand, Cullinane learned that he must not interpret Muslim indifference to the Jews as constituting approval. The tragedy that was allowed to overtake Safad in 1834 was a classic example of Muslim administration, although in this instance it had been the invading Egyptians and not the Turks who were involved. On May 31, 1834, a sizable earthquake struck Safad, accompanied by much loss of property, and some weeks later word reached town that the Egyptian army was going to conscript Arab men. Superstitious Arabs concluded that some malign influence was working against them, and the Jews were blamed. The logical solution was to massacre them, which the Arabs started to do. For thirty-three unhampered days the Muslims were allowed to riot, destroying synagogues, killing rabbis and defacing over two hundred scrolls of the Torah, each worth more than a man's home. The remnants of the great Jewish settlement were driven into the countryside, where for more than a month they lived on grass and slaughtered sheep, after which the government came back, caught the Arab ringleaders and hanged thirteen of them.

This was the way the Turks ruled: Start no pogroms yourself, but if the Arabs went to massacre the Jews, let them; then sweep in and execute the Arabs. Thus each community lost its leaders and relative quiet was maintained. But certainly in this cynical system the Turk treated the Jew no worse than he did the Muslim.

To Cullinane this impartiality was not surprising. He had found that most people, in their study of history, evaluated religion as a rather more important political force than it was. In the abstract one might expect Catholic France and Catholic Spain to recognize common interests, but they rarely did. Once when Cullinane was inspecting a dig in Persia he developed the attractive idea that the Muslim religion would some day unify western Asia, but before he had time to perfect his theory he found that Muslim Afghanistan was an ally of Hindu India, but wanted to go to war with Muslim Pakistan, which was an ally of Buddhist China. A little later Muslim Egypt tried to destroy Muslim Arabia. Even more spectacular to anyone digging in Israel was the example of the Crusaders, who set forth as a Christian army but who found their first enemies in Catholic Hungary, in Orthodox Constantinople and among the Christian communities of Asia Minor.

Cullinane had learned not to expect Catholic Ireland and Catholic Spain to share common views, and he doubted that Muslim Turkey and Muslim Syria ever would, either. For religion was not a solid basis upon which to construct either a nation or a congerie of nations, and he could foresee the distant time when Pan-Arabism, not religion, would unite true Arab states like Syria, Iraq and Arabia, while surrounding non-Arabic states would go their historic ways: to the west Muslim Egypt would assume a position of leadership among the nations of Africa; to the east Muslim Iran would concentrate on Asia; while to the north Muslim Turkey would associate herself with the problems of Europe. Nationalism, not religion, would decide, and he often caught himself wondering whether the new state of Israel had been wise to commit herself so completely to one faith, no matter how ancient and deeply rooted in the local soil that faith might be. He was surprised at the power of religious parties in the government, at the religious emphasis in schools and at the fact that Israel, like Turkey of old, had handed civil problems like marriage and inheritance to religious courts composed of rabbis if one were Jewish, priests if one were Catholic, or ministers if one happened to be Protestant. As a good Christian he could not help concluding: This is where Byzantium was sixteen centuries ago. Why would a new nation of its own free will insist upon repeating such mistakes? He felt that one of these days he ought to ask Eliav about these matters, for apparently Jews felt that their religion contained special features which exempted it from errors which had overtaken other faiths.

Shmuel Hacohen wanted land. He had to have land. More than any other man in Palestine this sway-backed, hard-working Jew from Russia had to find land; and as twilight ended on this hot summer day he became desperate, for the same messenger who had brought the dispatches from Akka to Kaimakam Tabari had brought word to Hacohen that the first shipload of Jews from Europe had landed two days earlier at that port. Tomorrow they would begin marching to Tiberias, and unless there was land awaiting them Hacohen would face disaster.

Four years ago, when he first came to Tiberias, he had thought that buying land for a Jewish settlement would be a simple task, but months and years had slipped by in tantalizing negotiation, in bribery and confusion, and Hacohen found himself in 1880 no nearer to having acquired his acres than he had been in 1876. For example, two full years had elapsed since his last petition had been forwarded to Istanbul. How could any government postpone making such a decision for two whole years?

At six o'clock on this very hot day Shmuel sat in his miserable room, wondering what to do. He lived in a hut that marked the border between the Ashkenazi and Sephardi sections, and not even in the worst of Russia had he known such a room, for in Russia one had at least a floor and—if he tried hard enough—a freedom from bedbugs; but here in the hopeless filth of Tiberias there was nothing except old men studying the Talmud, women living their pointless lives like animals, and children growing each year in ignorance. It was a hideous perversion of the way a Jew ought to live in his homeland, and Shmuel Hacohen was morally outraged.

He groaned in the heat. Obviously he must again implore the kaimakan to release the land needed by the incoming Jews, but as he visualized the kaimakam he shook his head: I can't understand him at all. He recognized that Tabari was corrupt beyond any standard existing in Russia, and he knew that the kaimakam intended to squeeze out of the Jews every piaster possible. He was also aware that Tabari used the mutasarrif in Akka and the wali in Beirut as convenient excuses for extracting additional baksheesh, but what Hacohen could not understand was the man's apparent lack of any moral base from which to operate.

Shmuel was willing to concede that Kaimakam Tabari was at heart a good man; otherwise he could have played Jew against Arab, and Christian against both, generating rifts within the community as Russian governors did, but this Tabari refused to do. He handled each religious group in his community in the same corrupt manner, thus preserving a kind of happy-go-lucky peace, and after Hacohen's experiences in Russia he knew how to appreciate such peace. In his homeland Hacohen had learned to work with men who were mostly good or mostly bad, and with such men he knew where he stood. But with Kaimakam Tabari the problem was more complex, for the man could never bring himself to announce forthrightly what was to be done. Even when Hacohen bought him off with many pounds, things could not be considered settled, for the next man who brought the Kaimakam a few more pounds could buy him back the other way. Trying to purchase land through such a man was frustrating to the point of despair, and Shmuel Hacohen had reached that point.

In his steaming, filthy room, not fit for sheep or goats, the wiry little Jew pulled on his western clothes, jammed his feet into hot leather shoes and prepared to wrestle yet again with the slippery, smiling kaimakam. But this day was going to be different. He was determined to get land. He would get the land he had paid for or . . .

He did not finish the sentence, because even in his state of anxiety he knew that he had no weapon with which to threaten the amiable official. A Jew could not protest to Akka or go to Beirut. He must deal only with Kaimakam Tabari. Nor could a Jew, like a Frenchman, appeal to his ambassador for aid—because the Jew had no ambassador. All Shmuel Hacohen could do was to pay more baksheesh to Tabari, and then more, and then still more.

Consequently, on this last desperate day Hacohen knelt in the dust at the head of his mattress and rummaged among some stones, from which he withdrew his final cache of funds. He had nearly a thousand English pounds, the last of his money from Russia, and this must close the deal. He brushed his trousers and started for the door, then stopped, considered for a long time, and returned reluctantly to the foot of his bed, where he dug into the earthen floor, coming up at last with a beautiful, shining gold coin. He studied it with love and regret, concluding that on this day of judgment even that coin was expendable.

He had found the ancient piece on one of his first scouting trips along the southern end of Bahr Tubariyeh where he had stopped to kick at the soil to see if it was promising. When he uncovered a dark, rich earth, capable of yielding fine crops if properly farmed, he took a stick and continued digging as if the land were already his, and in so doing turned up this antique coin covered with Arabic writing. It was waiting for me, he told himself.

It had been Shmuel's intention to spend this lucky coin toward the purchase of his own home in the new settlement, and he had resisted all temptations to waste it otherwise, but now he was trapped. He must have land for his Jews, and if this gold coin could help him get it, the coin would have to be spent.

Into his right pants pocket he put what little Turkish money he had left. Into his coat he put the roll of English bills. And into his left pants pocket, where he could feel its reassuring weight against his leg, he placed the gold coin. Putting on his Turkish fez he brushed his suit again and prayed, 'God of Moses, lead me out of this wilderness.'

Shmuel Hacohen had been born Shmuel Kagan in the little village of Vodzh along the western boundary of Russia. His father was a thin, pious man who collected rents for Russian landlords, and Shmuel's first arguement came when he was nine: his orthodox father had forced him to wear soft curls dangling down beside his ears, the Hasidic mark of piety as demanded by the Bible, but young Shmuel, a sickly and sway-backed child who walked with his left shoulder thrust forward, was learning that boys with curls were apt to be set upon by the Russians, so, borrowing his mother's scissors, he had shorn himself. At the time his mother said nothing, but when Kagan senior returned from collecting rents she burst into tears and Shmuel's father took him into a darkened room, where he recited the terrifying admonition of Moses our Teacher: '''If a man have a stubborn and rebellious son, which will not obey the voice of his father, or the voice of his mother, and that, when they have chastened him, will not hearken unto them: Then shall his father and his mother lay hold on him, and bring him out unto the elders of his city, and unto the gate of his place; And they shall say unto the elders of his city, This our son is stubborn and rebellious, he will not obey our voice; he is a glutton, and a drunkard. And all the men of his city shall stone him with stones, that he die.''' His father had paused before adding, 'You let your hair grown in curls.'

Shmuel had been impressed by his father's threat, and was for some weeks haunted by a vision of the punishment recommended by the Torah, but even this failed to make him pliable to his father's ideas. He refused to wear the curls. The conflict became intensified when his parents wanted him to enter the yeshiva to prepare himself for a lifetime of study, since they recognized that he was an able boy. Again Shmuel refused, for he had already decided to enter some kind of business.

'There's no business nobler than studying Talmud,' Kagan said.

'It's not for me.'

'Shmuel, listen. Each morning when I pass the synagogue I ask God to forgive me. That I'm collecting rents. For Gentiles. And not reading Talmud as I should.'

'Me, I want to work.'

The senior Kagan, knowing the disappointments that Jews faced in Russia, fearing the pogroms that were becoming frequent along the Polish border, said with certainty, 'Son, you're a weak boy with a swayed back. For a Jew like you there's only one safe course. Study Talmud. Become a pious man. And trust in God.'

This reasoning the stubborn boy could not accept, so in their impasse father and son agreed to place their differences before the holy man of Vodzh and to abide by his decision. Accordingly, they left their home and walked along the muddy road until they reached the village pump, across from which stood a courtyard surrounded by a rambling wooden house. Hasidic Jews, with fur caps, long black gowns and side curls, clustered about the door, and through them Kagan led his son. Without knocking he entered the house, announcing, 'Rebbe, we come seeking judgment.'

The saintly man before whom they stood scarcely seemed a religious leader. He was a tall, robust man in his forties, with a ruddy face, smiling eyes and a bushy black beard, a rabbi who loved dancing and the shout of folksongs; at weddings he would sometimes throw the bride on his massive shoulders and race about his courtyard, kicking his heels and bellowing marriage songs until his congregation cheered. If at midnight some wanted to halt the festivities, it was he who kept the musicians playing, and once when he was reprimanded for continuing a marriage celebration till dawn he said, 'The Jews of Vodzh have neither carriages nor gold nor expensive wine. If we cannot be lavish with our dancing and our music, how can we celebrate?' And when his questioner remained quizzical, the big rebbe grabbed him and shook him, saying harshly, 'Jacob! This bride has not the dishes to lay a table. All her life she will live in poverty, consoled only by the memory of this night when she was beautiful. For God's sake, dance with her now, before the roosters make us finish.'

He was known simply as the Vodzher Rebbe, a Hasidic rabbi who alleviated the misery of his Jews by the joy of his religious experience. In Vodzh he maintained a court, which the rebbes of his family had conducted for three generations, a house in which transient Jews could find a place to sleep or local Jews a center for discussion. It was a holy place from which he dispensed justice among his people, who could not find it in the local courts. In all the villages of western Russia and eastern Poland the Vodzher Rebbe was recognized as one of the saints of Judaism, and often on Saturdays he would have at his table as many as fifty Jews from different communities who had come to hear wisdom from his lips, but what they usually heard was his lively voice singing old Jewish folksongs.

Across his left cheek he carried a scar which further detracted from an appearance of saintliness, but this was his badge of honor about which Hasidic Jews would speak for generations: 'One Friday afternoon the woodcutter Pinhas ran to the Vodzher Rebbe, saying, "Poor Mendel! He does not have with what to make Shabbat." That winter our rebbe had no money, for he had given it all away. But the idea of a pious Jew unable to celebrate the coming of Queen Shabbat was too painful to bear, so he put on his fur cap and marched to the great house of the nobleman, saying, "Sir, your poor Jews of Vodzh have no money to make Shabbat. What can you give me?" The nobleman was insulted by this interruption and with his sword cut the rebbe across the face. Without flinching the rebbe said, "That blow was for me. Now what have you for the needy Jews?" And in this brave manner he got the kopecks so that Mendel could make Shabbat.'

Now, as the Kagans stood before him, this huge saintly man smiled at the close-cropped boy and asked, 'Shmuel Kagan, what have you been up to?'

'My son refuses to wear his curls,' the father complained. 'He will not enter the yeshiva.'

'He won't?' the rebbe asked.

'I want to work,' Shmuel replied.

The big rebbe threw back his head and laughed. 'How many fathers in Vodzh would be happy if their lazy sons once said, "I want to work."' He reached out and grabbed Shmuel, saying, 'Sit on my lap, son,' and with one enormous hand he clutched the frail boy to him, rumpling his short hair with the other. 'I noticed that you were running through the village like a lamb newly shorn.' At this witticism the Hasidim in the room laughed, as courtiers should, but the rebbe ignored them, saying to the boy, 'Your father is right, Shmuel. Israel can't exist without a fresh supply of new scholars each year. My own son is at the yeshiva, and he makes me proud. Your father would be proud if you were studying Talmud.' He hugged the boy and asked, 'What's the matter? No mind for studies?'

'I want to work,' Shmuel repeated.

'And so you shall!' the rebbe cried joyously. 'Kagan, Israel needs not only scholars but practical men as well. Shave your hair, Shmuel. Go to the Russian schools. Go on to Germany and attend university. Do the wonderful things that Jews are capable of. But never forget your God.' He rose, and keeping the boy in his arms, began to dance, jumping up and down in one place so that his beard brushed across Shmuel's face, and the Hasidim began clapping their hands. One by one stately men with long beards and side curls joined the dance, and the rebbe's court echoed with shouts of praise as the holy men danced.

'We are dancing for Shmuel Kagan!' the rebbe cried. 'For he is the child of God and in the world he is to do great things.' Toward the end of the long dance, when all were chanting and beating their hands, the big rebbe kissed Shmuel on the cheek and whispered, 'You are the child of God, the son of Abraham.'

The dancing ended, and with reverence the big man placed Shmuel beside his father, to whom he said, 'The paths to God are manifold.' Then, as if he were experiencing a visit from God, he clutched the boy to him and burst into tears, great animal-sobs coming from his beard as he mourned, 'You will do all these things, child, but in them you will not find happiness. Nor you,' and he pointed to one of the visiting Hasidim. 'Nor you. Nor you.' He returned to his chair and sat trembling like a child, for he had been allowed a vision of the tragedy that faced his Jews.

So Shmuel Kagan, with his father's consent, avoided the yeshiva and went instead to the Russian school; he was a good student, but no small village like Vodzh could provide the funds to send a boy to university, so at the age of twenty he found a job as timber buyer for the government, an in this capacity traveled much of western Russia, a small Jew with an odd way of walking, who went from town to town, acquainting himself with the strange winds that were beginning to blow across that vast land. In Kiev he met young men who argued, 'The only hope for the Jew is to join the socialist movement and build a new Russia in which he can find an honorable home.' In Berdichev he came upon a group who met in the home of a poet who insisted, 'Jews will come into their own only when they return to Zion and build there a new state.' But at the end of each trip he returned to Vodzh, where he sat like a penitent in the court of the rebbe, listening as that bearded saint developed his view that the true salvation of the Jew could lie only in sanctity and the Talmud. To his surprise young Kagan found himself more attuned to the rebbe than to the voluble men in Kiev and Berdichev and he was always pleased when the spiritual leader ceased talking and began chanting some Hasidic song. Shmuel joined in, and the rebbe's court would echo with their noisy voices: this was permanent, the joy that poor Jews could find in praising their God.

But at the rebbe's court there was contradiction: although he himself relied solely upon the Talmud, he did not deny validity to men who thought they had found alternative routes for the Jews. One day in 1874, when Shmuel was twenty-eight, the rebbe surprised the young timber merchant by observing, 'What the poet in Berdichev told you is correct. The day is coming when we Jews of Russia and Poland must combine with the Jews of Eretz Israel to build a new land for ourselves. We shall till the soil and work in cities like other men, and if I were younger I would elect this new life.'

That year Shmuel was further perplexed by the arrival in his father's home of a bearded, unctuous middle-aged Jew named Lipschitz, who nodded to everyone, kept his mouth in a fixed smile and shook hands limply like a woman. He hiked from village to village through Russia, carrying with him a list of Jews who could be counted upon to give him lodging, and in Vodzh he had thrust himself upon the Kagans. 'I am from Tiberias,' he announced. 'Tiberias, in Eretz Israel, and I shall be living with you for a few days.' He made himself at home, ate voraciously, and visited all Jewish families, begging funds with which to support the Talmudic scholars of Tiberias.

Shmuel disliked Lipschitz and suspected that he was keeping much of the money for himself, but the man's mention of Eretz Israel so close upon the rebbe's comments excited Shmuel's imagination, so that while the guest fed himself Shmuel asked many questions. Between mouthfuls the visitor explained how the holy town nestled beside the Sea of Galilee, how Arabs dominated the town, how the Turks governed, and how the Jews lived.

'What work do they do?' Shmuel asked.

Astonished, Lipschitz replied, 'They study.'

'All of them?'

'Yes,' and he recited the Jewish legend which said that on the day when holy men no longer studied the Talmud in Safad and Tiberias, Judaism would perish. 'You give your money in Vodzh so that the Messiah can be protected in Tiberias,' he explained, but Shmuel thought that much of what he said was nonsense.

In succeeding months the young timber merchant spent many nights talking with his rebbe, who picked his way like an agile deer through the complexities Shmuel was encountering: 'Joining a revolution I could not approve, for when the new Russia comes, you and I will still be Jews and our position will not have been improved. Emigrating to Eretz Israel might be right for you, with your energy, but it would be wrong for most of my court. Holding fast to ancient Jewish custom is still our salvation.' As the big man talked, Shmuel acquired his understanding of what Jewish rectitude meant. There was a right way to perform any act and a wrong way, and honest men clung to the former. Each aspect of business life had its moral tradition, which to ignore meant distress. Human relationships were governed by inherited law, which in the long run proved just. At times the rebbe experienced a mystical apprehension of the future, for in late 1874 he warned Shmuel, 'One day our Jews in Poland and Russia will again face the days of Czmielnicki. I'm too old to escape. I'll stay here and help my court survive whatever strikes. But others should ponder the future and act upon it.'

One warm spring evening in 1875 Shmuel discovered what his rebbe had meant, for in a nearby village a casual group of Russian peasants were sitting at an inn getting happily drunk after the day's planting, and as the sun set, a sense of moroseness overcame one of the farmers and he observed, with no intention of harm, 'Every kopeck I get falls into the hands of some Jew.'

'That's right,' a second farmer said. 'Either we give them to Kagan for rent or to Lieb for vodka.'

The farmers turned as a body to study their Jewish host, and Lieb, recognizing the look, began to put away the glassware. He signaled his son.

'Lieb,' the first farmer shouted, 'what do you do with our money?'

'I run this place only for the landlord,' Lieb said apologetically, hiding his employer's money.

'And Kagan?' the second farmer asked. 'What does he do with our money?'

'Like me. Gives it to the landlord.'

The men had to admit that Lieb was right, and the second farmer said, 'You Jews are as bad off as we are,' and Lieb breathed easier.

But then the first farmer said idly, as if reflecting upon some critical event in his life, 'Jerusalem is lost.'

Like a spark this mournful observation lit up the eyes of the half-drunk peasants. A man who had not spoken repeated, 'Jerusalem is lost.'

There was a long moment of hesitation, during which Lieb the inn-keeper prayed while the sun went down. The farmers watched it go, waiting. The signal came from a youth, drunker than the others, who uttered the fatal word, that hateful word which once pronounced could never be recalled.

'Hep,' he said quietly, and Lieb turned white with fear.

'Hep,' the first farmer repeated as Lieb looked to see if he could reach the door.

'Hep!' the peasants began to chant, and villagers hearing the ominous word began boarding up their windows. Lieb, with panic on his face, shrank into a corner among the bottles.

'Hep!' the drinkers repeated, and of a sudden the young man leaped from his chair, flung himself upon the bar, sliding down to where he faced the innkeeper. Grabbing a knife from a leg of meat he threw himself upon the white-faced Jew and cut his throat.

'Hep!' roared the growing crowd as it surged toward the Jewish section of the village, bellowing the ancient cry of the pogrom: 'Hep!' *Hierosolyma est perdita*. And somehow the fact that Jerusalem was lost, a distant city which they did not know, became an excuse for murdering Jews. If any people in the world had a right to mourn the loss of that sacred city to Islam it was the Jews, but its surrender was used as a reason for exterminating them.

There were some in the crowd who recognized the irrelevancy of their cry and these substituted another of equal potency: 'The Zhid crucified our Lord.' But whichever cry was used, it fed the wild spirit of the pogrom and all united in the culminating wail, 'Kill the Zhid.'

The peasants, having destroyed the ghetto of their own village, stormed into the countryside, gathering strength from every farm until they reached Vodzh, where someone screamed, 'Let's get the rent collector!' They rushed to the Kagan home, shouting with approval as a swordsman tore off the head of Shmuel's father with one blow. They cheered again when the same sword slashed open the belly of the old woman. With axes and hoes the Christians gained revenge for the loss of Jerusalem, hacking to pieces four bearded Hasidim who were trying to reach the rebbe's court.

The mob then stormed into the court, where they found the big man dancing ecstatically with nine of his steadfast friends. For a moment the peasants hesitated, unprepared for this strange scene of men cleansing their minds for death. But then a young drunk sprang at the rebbe, screaming, 'He crucified Jesus, didn't he?' And so the Vodzher Rebbe was slain, and his beard set on fire, and his body dragged through the streets to a spot where more than sixty children, women and old men were being slaughtered and tossed through the air like sheaves of harvested wheat. Jerusalem was lost, Christ was dead, and somehow the shedding of this Jewish blood consoled the bereaved peasants in their drunken sorrow.

Shmuel Kagan returned to Vodzh in time to bury his parents and his rebbe. That night he determined to quit Russia, for he understood at last that what the rebbe had said was true: 'when the new Russia comes, you and I will still be Jews and our position will not have been improved.' A vision of Tiberias, beside its lake, grew strong in his mind and he spent the following days consulting with Jews, numbed by the inexplicable ferocity of their neighbors, and he collected from them funds for the purchase of community farm land at Tiberias. Finally he approached the Vodhzer Rebbe's son, now graduated from the yeshiva, and asked him to lead the exile, but the religious young man refused to leave the village of his ancestors. 'I shall stay here and be the rebbe. Last week my father told me that pretty soon you would be going.' So the new rebbe prayed with Kagan and at the end they repeated the litany of all Jews in the Diaspora, 'To next year in Jerusalem.'

When Shmuel reached Akka in 1876 he did not, like many Jewish immigrants, fall upon the ground to kiss the soil in which he would be buried, for he saw Palestine not as the end of life but as a beginning, and in this spirit he performed an act even more symbolic than kissing the soil: he dropped his Russian name Kagan and assumed its Hebraic original, Hacohen, and as Shmuel Hacohen—Samuel the Priest—he entered upon his new life.

His trip from Akka to Tiberias was an adventure in disillusionment, especially to one trained as a timber buyer, for both the Old Testament and the Talmud had taught him that Israel was a land heavy with trees: he found only bleakness. In the entire thirty miles from the Mediterranean to the Sea of Galilee, Shmuel Hacohen found only one small group of trees, the ancient olives at Makor, and he wondered who had destroyed the homeland of the Jews.

His apprehensions were increased when he reached the hillside where Rabbi Akiba lay buried, for from this eminence he looked down to see not the spacious marble fronted Tiberias of the Romans nor the beautiful Tverya of the Talmud but mud-walled Tubariyeh of the Turks, a mean little town huddling within Crusader walls. What impressed him most, however, was the utter barrenness of the land; he could find no fields under cultivation, and he recalled the lush, dark loam of Russia. Doesn't anybody down there farm? he asked himself, and when he descended to the town and entered the stone gates he found a desolation equal to the fields outside. It seemed to him that he was returning to the hatreds he had fled in Russia, for Turks ignored Arabs while Sephardi Jews did not speak with Ashkenazim. He tried to establish friendship with the latter group, many of whom were from Russia and Poland, but they rebuffed him as an intruder who might be trying to share in the charity they collected from Europe. When he explained that he did not want this charity, that he wanted to associate himself with those Jews who worked for a living, he found that what Lipschitz the collector had said in Vodzh was true: Jews in Tubariyeh did not work. To protect the sanctity in the rest of the world they spent their years reading Talmud, and had he tried to explain that he carried in his pocket funds for the purchase of farm land outside the walls, they would have considered him three times a liar: 'No Jew has such money. Nor this one in particular. And if he had, to spend it on land outside the walls would be insane.'

On the afternoon of his arrival he started looking for tillable land, but none lay near the walls, so next morning he went to Capernaum, at the northern end of the lake, where he spotted extensive areas that would be acceptable, and all along the western shore of the lake he found other land that could be tilled. Back in his room, he dispatched an excited letter to Vodzh: 'Here empty land is waiting which could be made as fine as any in Russia. I shall inform you as soon as I have completed my purchase.'

Two days later he hiked to the southern end of the lake, where the River Jordan begins its steep descent to the Dead Sea, and beside this bountiful river he found both the land he wanted and the ancient gold coin. After that first acquaintance he sought no other land; here the persecuted Jews of his village would build their farms and replant the vineyards that had lain vacant since the days of Rome. In his second letter to Vodzh he reported in Yiddish: 'I have named our land Kfar Kerem, the village of the vineyards, and here we shall make wine, for did not Solomon himself sing, "Come, my beloved, let us go forth into the field; let us lodge in the villages. Let us get up early to the vineyards; let us see if the vine flourish, whether the tender grape appear . . ." Start packing now.'

Shmuel found his land in February, 1876, but when he tried to buy it he encountered such confusion that he quickly warned his villagers: 'You'd better not leave Vodzh until I find who owns our land.'

It took him eighteen months to discover this simple fact, and not until he had bribed three different officials was he allowed to know the owner's address: 'Emir Tewfik ibn Alafa, well known in Damascus,' but when he paid an Arab letter writer to send the emir a message, offering to pay a good fee for the idle land, he received a curt reply from a secretary: 'Emir Tewfik has never seen this land, receives no rent from it, it not certain where it is located, and has no desire to sell.'

So in late 1877 Shmuel taught himself Arabic and walked to Damascus, where he tried for two months to see the landowner, but the emir refused to meet him. A tall dignitary in tarboosh and white robes explained, 'Emir Tewfik ibn Alafa has never spoken to a Jew and has no intention of starting now.'

'But doesn't he wish to make a profit on his land?'

'Emir Tewfik never buys or sells.'

'Doesn't he care that the land is idle?'

'Emir Tewfik has thousands of acres of idle land. They are no concern of his.'

Shmuel was forced to leave Damascus without having seen the landlord and was about to decide that the enchanting fields could not be his, when on his way back to Tubariyeh he fell in with a delightful Arab, who advised, 'Handle it through the kaimakam. For enough money he can do anything.'

'Even buy me the land?' Shmuel asked.

'Anything.'

So Hacohen spent the next three months learning Turkish, and in early 1878 presented himself at the kaimakam's office, petitioning for an interview. To his surprise, the kaimakam, a tall, thin Turk in his seventies, admitted him and listened sympathetically to his problem. The situation was this: the kaimakam knew that in two months he was leaving Tubariyeh, but no one else did, least of all Shmuel Hacohen. So the governor teased the little Jew along, milked him of considerable baksheesh, and retired from active service without having written a single letter regarding the land purchase. When Hacohen discovered the duplicity he also found that the delightful Arab traveler who had suggested that he take his problem to the kaimakam was the latter's cousin and had collected ten per cent of the baksheesh.

Shmuel's disappointment was so great that he could not have continued in Tubariyeh, badgered by corrupt officials and outcast by the Jewish community, had he not in the spring of 1878 gone on a pilgrimage to Jerusalem; and while it was true that sight of this noble city on the hill inspired him with Jewish longing, its great stone blocks in the temple wall reminding him of the Vodzher Rebbe, it was not this spiritual adventure which was to sustain him. In Jerusalem he encountered something more significant than racial memories: he met young Jews from Russia and Poland who were convinced that Jews had a chance of one day controlling their homeland; he met others who predicted that in years to come the Jews of Israel would speak not Yiddish but Hebrew, 'as the prophets spoke to us three thousand years ago'; he met businessmen who had started factories and others who were erecting houses outside the wall; and one night which he would long remember he met six young Jews who had begun to build a Jewish village near Jaffa.

'The Gate of Hope, we're calling it,' they announced. 'It's to be the first of many.' One of the men turned to Shmuel. 'You? From Tubariyeh? Are you starting any villages there?'

The men reminded him of the young Russians he had met in Kiev who were planning to rebuild that moribund nation, and of the poet in Berdichev who dreamed of a Jewish homeland; and as he discovered the vitality which these Jews had brought to Palestine he found new determination and replied, 'When I get back to Tubariyeh I'm buying some land ... Near the Sea of Galilee. We're building a village there. Kfar Kerem.' And he returned to his hovel restored in his belief that he could do it.

In the summer of 1878 the new kaimakam, Faraj Tabari, took office, and when Shmuel reported his predecessor's trickery in taking baksheesh for services never performed, the official laughed disarmingly and promised, 'With me you'll get the land,' and with these honeyed words Tabari had launched an agonizing period in Hacohen's life. Postponements, lies, chicanery, these were the rule in Tubariyeh now, while in Russia the Jews of Vodzh, having concluded that Kagan had absconded with their funds, were making plans to arrive en masse in Akka. In frustration Hacohen went to the kaimakam and asked, 'When can I get the land?' But Tabari merely stroked his mustache and said, 'Mmmmmmmmm, on a matter as grave as this I'd better consult the mutasarrif in Akka,' and Shmuel understood that this would require more money. To approach the wali in Beirut would cost much more, while a letter to the sultan in Istanbul was prohibitive.

At the end of 1879, improbable as it seemed, Hacohen, this inconspicuous Jew from Vodzh, had seven different officials of the Turkish empire in his employ, one way or another, but the land was not yet his. By applying constant pressure and bribes whose number he had lost count of, Shmuel had advanced his case to a point where Emir Tewfik in Damascus was willing to sell the useless acres for the not exhorbitant sum of nine hundred and eighty English pounds, but the baksheesh required to reach this agreement already totaled more than seventeen hundred pounds. And still the Turkish government would announce no decision.

Yet Hacohen did not lose faith in Kaimakam Tabari, for in a curious manner the thieving Arab had demonstrated an unquestioned friendship for the Russian Jew. One night, as Shmuel sat in his filthy room wondering whether or not to abandon Tubariyeh, he heard muffled footsteps on the cobblestones and intuitively checked to see that the places where he had hidden his money were secure. He had barely done so when his door burst open and eight Jews in fur caps, side curls and long coats rushed at him, pinioned his arms and dragged him off to a rabbinical court convened in the Ashenazi section of town.

It was a gloomy, portentous scene, with three rabbis waiting to judge the prisoner. In Yiddish the charges against Hacohen were read: 'He is not a part of our community. He does not observe our laws strictly nor does he study at the synagogue. He has been heard speaking against Lipschitz, who knew him is a suspicious one in Vodzh, and he disturbs the district with his folly about land purchases and Jews working as farmers.' As the preposterous phrases rolled forth Shmuel thought: The real charge they don't make. That I endanger their way of life.

Then came the sentence, incredible for the year 1880, but made possible by the Turkish custom of allowing each religious community to govern itself: 'Shmuel Hacohen is to be fined to the amount of his possessions. He is to be stripped, stoned and banished from Tubariyeh, and may he leave Eretz Israel without further disturbing the ways of Judasim.' Before Shmuel could protest, the first provisions of the sentence were carried out.

Jewish men who had come to fear the little Russian who lived outside their narrow world laid hands on him and stripped away his clothing until he stood naked. Pockets in his torn garments were searched for money, which was handed to the court, after which he was hauled to a corner of the wall, where the general population began hurling rocks at him, not caring whether they blinded him or killed him, and he might have died except that one of the rabbinical judges interceded and the bleeding prisoner was dragged to the main gate of town and thrown outside the walls. The mob then proceeded to his hovel, where they started digging up the floor to find any gold he might have hidden.

It was at this point that Kaimakam Tabari interfered. His gendarmerie, hearing that a Jewish punishment was under way, had paid no attention, for this was a matter concerning one of the religious communities, and how they discplined their people was not a governmental concern; but word of the unusually harsh sentence reached Tabari: 'Did you say Hacohen? The Jew from Russia?' When he knew that it was the little land buyer who was being stoned he summoned his guard and went to the town gate, where torches showed the naked and bleeding Jew wandering vainly outside the walls.

'Take him home,' Tabari ordered. 'You, you and you, give him your clothes.' When gendarmes reported that officers of the rabbinical court were wrecking Shmuel's hut, Tabari hurried there and said to the mob, 'Go home, all of you.'

As Shmuel regained his mournful room he saw with gratitude that the searchers had not reached the money intended for the purchase of his land. He fell on his mattress, too bewildered to cry. The sentence of the court had been so unexpected, the punishment so harsh, that he was content to have escaped with his life, and as for the kaimakam's intervention, this Shmuel could not explain, but as he wiped his sores with a dirty cloth he asked himself: Did he keep me alive only so that he could rob me of what I have left? The thought was unworthy, for Shmuel could remember that as he had stood naked outside the walls the torches had shown him the kaimakam's face, and it was that of a man who could not tolerate such punishments. If in the forthcoming months Tabari stole all of Hacohen's savings, this would not alter the fact that tonight he had acted as one human being toward another. Why had he done so? Shmuel fell asleep before he found an answer, but Faraj Tabari, sitting alone in his room overlooking the mosque, asked himself the same question and replied: He was little and he had a swayed back, but he looked like my brother-in-law, so I had to save him. And for the first time the kaimakam expressed the hope that his brother-in-law might soon visit Tubariyeh to explain which of the new ideas could be put into practice here.

The next days Shmuel would not remember. In a daze of pain from the stoning by which Eretz Israel had rejected him, its mountains falling upon him in his nightmares, he lay upon his mattress while insects came to inspect his wounds. Each of the Jewish communities left him alone, the superstitious

Sephardim viewing him as a curse and the vengeful Ashkenazim hoping that he would die. By tradition Arabs did not come into the quarter where he lay, so his fever and nightmare were allowed to run their course and for two days of delirium Shmuel imagined that he was back in Vodzh, through whose cool lanes he went seeking timber.

When he recovered, unaided by anyone, he went into the alley to buy food, but the stares he met from the Jews were so hateful that he retreated to his hovel more wounded than he had been by the rocks. Was he wrong? Was it impossible to bring European Jews to this district and with them to build a new way of life, independent of charity? Weak though he was, he said to himself: It can be done! And he went back into the streets of Tubariyeh determined to resist his tormentors, but when he saw the bearded faces staring at him, waiting till they could catch him away from the kaimakam's protection, he returned to his hovel and whispered, 'God of Moses, I can accomplish nothing in this evil town.' And he prepared to flee.

From the earthen floor he dug up his money, and in the ill-fitting clothes which the kaimakam had forced his tormentors to give him he slipped out of town. Children saw him going and ran to tell their fathers, who left their studies to taunt the fugitive as he headed toward the north. At Safad he found conditions even more repellent than in Tubariyeh; old, suspicious Jews huddled over their Talmuds while young men took to robbery: the spiritual glory of the hilltop town was not even remembered. He left it behind and climbed over the hills that lay to the west, and what he found there saved him for the work he was destined to accomplish, for one evening as he wandered across a barren hillock, where he knew that trees must once have flourished, he came upon a little settlement that changed his perspective on what Jews could do in Israel.

It was Peqiin, at first sight merely another mountain village with narrow paths clustering about a central well and a synagogue hidden in a distant quarter, but when Shmuel came to know the place better he found it had distinguishing characteristics. For one thing, the Jews of Peqiin did not stay in their synagogues reading Talmud, for they were so remote from centers like Safad and Tubariyeh that no European charity reached them; they grew crops or they starved, and Shmuel found their fields in excellent condition. Nor did the Jews of Peqiin hide behind a wall, lest the Bedouins attack; they lived in the open and set men with rifles to guard the mountain passes. Four times in the 1870s Bedouins had thought to ravage the settlement and had retreated with their dead. The Jews here were a sturdy lot and for many weeks Hacohen found refuge with them, working in their fields and repairing the lacerations of his mind.

But the principal quality of the village he did not discover till late. It was a long evening in spring, when grape arbors were showing promise of a good crop, and as he sat gossiping in the village square he remarked, 'Jacob, you've never told me where you came from.'

'From Peqiin,' the farmer said.

'I mean your parents. What part of Europe?'

'From Peqiin,' the man repeated.

'No. I mean Russia? Poland? Lithuania?'

'I'm from Pequiin. Aaron's the same. And Absalom.'

A look of astonishment came over Hacohen's face, for he had never met Jews who were not from some place abroad. 'Egypt or Spain?' he asked.

'We're Jews,' Aaron said. 'Our families never left this land.'

'But during the Diaspora?'

'The sons of Jacob went down into Egypt,' the Peqiin farmers explained, 'but we didn't. Nehemiah and Ezra lived in Babylonia, but not us.'

'Where did you go when the Romans drove us out?'

'We didn't go.'

He could not believe that hidden in these hills the people of Peqiin had never fled: it was unreasonable, yet in persistent questioning he could find no Jew who remembered Russia, none who had returned with memories of Baghdad. These were Jews whose families had lived here for four thousand years, and the subservient habits of exile they had not acquired. One evening in July, when the men he was working with were at dinner, he walked upon the hills that had always known Jews, and as he did so the giant steps of the Vodzher Rebbe seemed to be striding along beside him: the huge and ghostly rebbe broke into a dance and once more gathered Shmuel to his arms. 'You are the child of God, the son of Abraham,' the rebbe said. He kissed Hacohen the man as he had once kissed Kagan the boy, and cried to the hills, 'You will gain your land, Shmuel, but in it you will find death.' With the rebbe's words ringing in his ears, Hacohen went in and said good night to the Jews of Peqiin.

'I must go back to Tubariyeh,' he said.

'But why? If they stoned you?'

'To buy land.'

'You can buy land here, Shmuel.' The recognized him as a worker and wanted him to stay with them.

'My land is beside the lake,' he said, and when he reached Tubariyeh he found his hovel occupied by chickens. Chasing them away and turning his mattress over so that their manure would fall to earth, he dug a fresh hole at the head of the mattress and there he hid his English pounds, while at the foot he buried the gold coin. As soon as this was done he began applying pressure on the kaimakam, nor would he stop until he had bought his land where the River Jordan left the lake and vineyards could be planted.

It was with the memory of these lonely and frustrating years, plus the present knowledge that the Jews from Vodzh were already in Akka, that Shmuel began his march on this hot afternoon to face the kaimakam in a final effort to buy the land. As he walked through the streets where Jews ignored him, he was not an impressive figure. Even when wearing his tarboosh he was only five feet four inches tall, and his borrowed clothes hung awkwardly. His pants were too short and his shoes creaked from their country tramping. He was still a sway-back, so that his belly moved ahead of him down the alleys, and he walked with his left shoulder forward as if he were trying to edge his way through life. He smelled of the evil room in which he was forced to live and he had suffered so many disappointments that he was beginning to look like the furtive Jews who scuttled through back alleys in cities like Kiev and Gretz; but these appearances were only outward, for his mind had found a kind of peace: at Peqiin, Jews had proved they could live on the land and could make it prosper. Bedouin raiders could be kept off with guns, and he marched through Tubariyeh determined to come away from this final meeting as the owner of land.

The kaimakam, who had hoped to postpone seeing Shmuel until he had perfected his plan for mulcting him of additional baksheesh, now that the firman had been promulgated, disarmed Hacohen by meeting him at the door of his office as if he were a friend and asking pleasantly, 'Why do you come out on a day as hot as this?'

'Did the firman arrive from Istanbul?'

'Not yet, Shmuel,' Tabari lied. Then, seeing Hacohen's shiver of despair, he added, 'These things take time, Shmuel. There's the mutasarrif in Akka, and the wali . . .'

'I know!' Hacohen snapped, almost losing his temper. 'Excuse me, Excellency. I've had disturbing news from Akka.'

Kaimakam Tabari became suspicious, reasoning to himself: I know the Jews have arrived, but Hacohen doesn't know I know. So why does he tell me something that makes his position weaker? He must be doing it for a reason. Probably plans to throw himself on my mercy. To Shmuel he said, 'Now what could possibly happen in Akka that would be bad news? You know the mutasarrif's on your side.'

'The Jews who are buying the land . . . they've landed.'

When Shmuel said this the kaimakam allowed his face to form a scowl. 'They have? This is serious, Shmuel.' He waited to see what approach the Jew would take.

He had guessed right. Without replying Hacohen reached into his coat pocket and produced a roll of bills. Pushing them to Tabari he said, 'Nine hundred and eighty pounds. For Emir Tewfik in Damascus.' The kaimakam did not touch the money, but watched carefully as his visitor continued to unload his right pants pocket. Out came a few paltry coins, some foreign bills, the kind of bribe a desperate man would offer for the recovery of a horse. Tabari waited.

'Excellency, this is every piaster I have in the world. Take it, but let me have the land.'

'This is a grave thing you suggest,' Tabari replied. 'You want me to authorize the Jews to settle on the land before we hear from Istanbul. If I did that I could lose my job, my reputation.' He paused to let Shmuel study the matter, then added softly, 'If we could wait a few months . . .'

Again Hacohen pushed the money at the kaimakam and said with passion, 'If they come here and find they've been cheated they'll kill me.'

Kaimakam Tabari leaned back and laughed in a consoling manner. 'Shmuel, Jews don't kill other Jews! They might abuse you or ostracize you, but even that other night they didn't kill you.' He felt sure that Hacohen controlled more money, somewhere, and he intended getting it. He stood up and moved a chair closer to his desk. 'Sit down, Shmuel.'

This gesture astonished Hacohen. Never during his four years in Tubariyeh had he been allowed to sit in a kaimakam's presence and he became doubly cautious. Tabari was saying, 'I've been meaning to ask you for some time, Shmuel. What about the Bedouins? The raids? That is, supposing your people do get their land.' The kaimakam caught himself. 'I mean, supposing we can work something out.'

Hacohen tried not to betray his feelings. The firman from Istanbul had arrived! He knew it from the way the kaimakam was acting. The Jews were going to get their land! He deduced what had happened. The messenger who had brought him news of the landings in Akka had at the same time brought Kaimakam Tabari the firman. Speaking very slowly, because he could not guess what Tabari would propose next, Shmuel said, 'At Peqiin I discovered how to handle the Bedouins. First you offer to buy their friendship. And if you fail, you take a gun and fight.'

'Fight?' the amiable kaimakam laughed. 'Shmuel, your bunch of pale scholars? Fight men of the desert?'

'There's nothing else we can do, Excellency. In Europe, in Spain, we didn't fight and we were burned alive. Here at Tubariyeh we'll fight. But I don't think we'll have to.' He thought of the resolute farmers in Peqiin; for three years there had been no attacks.

The kaimakam smiled indulgently and asked, 'I suppose the newcomers are all Ashkenazim?' With his fingers he drew curls down his cheeks. 'They don't seem like fighters to me.'

'You've only seen one kind of Ashkenazi, Excellency.'

'I'd be pleased to meet some other kind,' the kaimakam joked. 'The Ashkenazim we see here in Tubariyeh ... Mean, little-minded. Now the Sephardim, on the other hand ...'

Hacohen had no intention of allowing Tabari to sidetrack the main issue. Istanbul had granted the Jews their land and its transfer must not be delayed. He tried to bring the discussion back to that point, but Tabari rambled on: 'I've always preferred the Sephardim.'

Hacohen thought: Regardless of what the kaimakam thinks he sees here in Tubariyeh, the future of the Jew lies with the Ashkenazim. It'll be the hard, dedicated men with German educations and Russian determination who'll determine the future. Let my friends in Akka get hold of their land, and we'll see. To the kaimakam he said quietly, 'The Sephardim are more pleasant to know.'

'Yes!' Tabari agreed. 'In Tubariyeh every Jew I respect is a Sephardi.' He corrected himself. 'Everyone but you, Shmuel.'

There followed an awkward silence, for obviously the kaimakam was leading to something, but what it was Hacohen could not guess. He waited, and Tabari added, 'So what with the newcomers all being Ashkenazim, whom I don't like anyway, why should I risk my position?'

'It's all the money I have,' Hacohen insisted stubbornly.

Kaimakam Tabari looked hurt. 'I didn't want more money from you, Shmuel. It's just that we have to have more funds from somewhere to buy the right judgment in Istanbul.'

It was a moment of hard decision. Shmuel could feel the gold coin pressing against his leg and he was tempted to bang it onto the table as a last wild gesture; but he had learned in these matters to trust his intuitive judgment, and this reassured him that the firman was already in Tubariyeh and that he need only be insistent. He therefore held back the coin and waited.

Finally Tabari spoke. 'So what I thought was'–there was the horrible phrase again–'that if you could give me the names of the leaders of your group now in Akka, when I go there tomorrow I can see them and explain the gravity of the situation ...'

From a cesspool of disgust Shmuel Hacohen looked at the kaimakam, and each man was aware of what the other was thinking. The Jew thought: He'll go to the ship with an interpreter, some tough from the Akka waterfront, and they'll confuse and bully the immigrants. The Jews will think he's threatening their land and they'll surrender every kopeck they have. The bastard. The bastard.

But Hacohen was wrong about what the kaimakam was thinking, for Tabari was saying to himself: This bewildered Jew. He thinks I'm doing this merely to tantalize him. Extortion. He doesn't realize that right now I'm being the best friend he ever had. I'd better show him.

'You won't give me the names?' he snapped.

'Find them yourself. Steal from the immigrants in your own way.'

'Stupid!' the kaimakam cried. With anger he took from his desk the firman and slammed it on the table. 'Read that, you stubborn Jew.'

'I can speak Turkish. I can't read it.'

'Do you trust me to read it?' Tabari read the first part and watched Hacohen's face start to break with tears of joy. Then he read the harsh final proviso about keeping the Jews from water and he saw dismay take the place of joy.

'Without water the land is nothing!' Hacohen protested.

'Obviously. That's why I must have extra money.'

Hacohen thought: It's a lie. It's a lie. He wants the money for himself. Then he heard the kaimakam saying easily, 'The fact is, I suspect the sultan had nothing to do with that last clause. Some friend of mine tacked it on to help me out.'

'What do you mean?'

'So that I could do just what I'm doing now. Get a little more money for myself . . . and give him half.'

The duplicity of what Tabari was saying was too much for Hacohen to absorb. In Russia government officials were cruel. But a man grew to understand them. In Turkish lands . . . His anxiety was too great and he started to laugh. The kaimakam joined him and explained jokingly, 'So our position is this, Shmuel. I want you Jews to have your land, and the water too. I suppose the sultan feels the same way. But in view of that last clause I must interrogate Istanbul, and that takes . . .'

'Money?'

'A lot of money. More than you have left. Now, may I have the names?'

Feeling morally depleted by developments two and three times more devious than he could follow, Shmuel Hacohen took the kaimakam's pen and wrote down the names of the Vodzher Jews who could be depended upon to get the money together, if they had any. As he penned their names the faces of his friends came before him: Mendel of Berdichev, with beard and fur cap; Solomon of Vodzh, an outspoken man; Jozadak of the next village, a fighter and a man who hated rabbis. As he finished recalling the names he dropped his head on the desk and wept.

Kaimakam Tabari appreciated the anxiety under which Shmuel had been working and he left him alone for some moments. Then he reached out and touched Shmuel on the shoulder, asking, 'What good would the land be without water?'

'I wasn't weeping for them,' Shmuel replied. 'I was thinking of those who are dead and will not see the land.'

Then began a curious negotiation, an exchange that neither Kaimakam Tabari nor Shmuel Hacohen would ever forget. Tabari was convinced that the tough little Jew had more money somewhere, reserved for an emergency, and he suspected that after the land was secured he would not see Hacohen again; one of his most fruitful sources of baksheesh would thus dry up, and he hated to see anyone come into his office with money and escape. So on the spur of the moment, without really thinking, he did the thing that he would never afterward forget.

He said, 'By the way, Shmuel, I have something in the other room you might like to see.'

'What?'

'Come, look.' And the portly governor threw open a door and led Hacohen to a shelf on which stood a row of twenty-two tall books bound in leather and stamped in gold. Hacohen recognized them as a fine Lithuanian printing of the Talmud, for he had seen such books in Berdichev while collecting money for the land purchase; and when Tabari handed him a volume to inspect he opened the pages reverently and before him stood the glorious, singing Hebrew that his father had wanted him to study.

'What I'd like to know,' Tabari was saying, 'is why this book has such an effect on Jews?'

Shmuel looked at the large pages—more than twenty inches tall and nearly fourteen wide. This was a book unlike those that a Muslim or a Christian would know, for each page was a separate work in itself, composed of six or eight distinct kinds of type varying in size from very large to very small. The organization was unbelievable: in the center of the page would appear in bold type a short phrase, surrounded on all sides by blocks of different-sized type explaining and elaborating what the central phrase intended. Down margins would appear columns only three quarters of an inch wide, printed in minute letters. It was a jumble, a confusion, a thing of beauty, and no two pages were alike.

'What does it mean?' Tabari asked.

'Well, this bold sentence in the middle is an opinion handed down by the great Rabbi Akiba.'

'Who was he?' Tabari asked.

'A rabbi. He's buried here in Tubariyeh.'

Tabari studied Akiba's material, then pointed to one of the surrounding blocks of type. 'What's this one?'

'A judgment of Rabbi Meir, who came later. He's also buried in Tubariyeh.'

'And this big block over there?'

'Greatest of them all. Maimonides of Egypt.' He studied the beautiful, complicated page and said, 'Excellency, you've chosen a page most appropriate to Tubariyeh, for Maimonides is also buried here.' Then, to his dismay, he realized that Kaimakam Tabari wasn't taking his discourse on the Talmud seriously, had not even wanted to know what the great Jewish book was about. Tabari had much earthier ideas in mind and in pursuit of them he slammed the big book closed and stared directly at his little guest. 'Shmuel, will you have a synagogue in your new settlement?'

'Yes.'

'Well, wouldn't a set of the Talmud like this . . . real leather. Wouldn't that be a great thing to give the new synagogue?'

At first Hacohen thought that Tabari, in gratitude for the baksheesh he would extract from the Jews, was proposing to give the newcomers this expensive gift of books, and the little Jew almost made an ass of himself. He started to express his gratitude, then caught himself: My God! He expects me to buy them.

Tabari, quick to notice changes in the faces of people who came to consult him, caught the incipient smile and underwent the same degree of shock: My God! I do believe the little Jew thought I was giving him the books.

It was Tabari who spoke first. 'So I thought that if you had—well—even a little extra money . . .'

The rest of the things Hacohen said that hot evening he could not later recall, for it was not he but some power greater that spoke through his voice. 'Where did you get the Talmud?' he asked coldly.

'There was an old rabbi with some papers that had to be signed . . . in Beirut.'

'Did he offer you that Talmud? For some papers?'

'They were exceedingly significant papers ... involving his whole community.'

'But did he offer you his Talmud?' In some strange way it was now Shmuel Hacohen's office. It was he who was posing the questions.

'Well . . . it wouldn't be exact to say that he offered the books.'

'You asked him what he had of value?'

'I expected him to come with money . . . gold pieces. When he arrived with only books . . .'

'You took them?'

'It was a matter of vital significance,' Tabari insisted.

Shmuel could not speak. He opened one of the volumes and studied the title page: *Wilno, 1732.* He wondered what dreadful pressure had been put on the old rabbi to make him surrender these volumes. Jews had died for these books, had been burned at the stake, had seen their children and their sisters killed. What had the old man wanted for his people so desperately that he would divorce himself from his own conscience? To the kaimakam he said, quietly, 'These are rare books, Excellency.'

'I thought they were.'

'And you'd like to convert them into cash?'

'Of course. I know you said you had no more gold. But a man always keeps a little back.'

Without argument Shmuel Hacohen took from his left pocket the precious coin. Ceremoniously he placed it on the table where the kaimakam could see it. 'I don't know what it's worth, Excellency, but it's yours. Maimonides has said, "If a man build a synagogue let him build it finer than the house in which he dwells." I shall live with rats and lice a little longer. But the synagogue . . .' He looked at Tabari as if to ask: What kind of man would steal the holy book of another, then try to sell it back for profit?

Shmuel started piling the massive volumes onto his arms, but Tabari, seeing the impracticability of this, summoned his Egyptian servant. Hacohen pushed the man aside and at last balanced the twenty-two volumes on his forearms and left the room. The kaimakam hurried ahead to open his office door for the burdened man, and for a long moment the two stared at each other, the moral gap between them so tremendous that no comprehension could bridge it.

As he walked through the hot night Shmuel kept repeating the words of Moses his Teacher: 'And what nation is there so great, that hath statutes and judgments so righteous as all this law, which I set before you this day?'

THE TELL

For Cullinane the problem of the Jews' moral right to Israel was simple. It was a question of custodianship. When Herod was king, the Galilee held a population of more than half a million; in Byzantine times, more than a million. But at the end of Arab, Crusader and Turkish rule the same land supported less than sixty thousand, a visible loss of sixteen out of every seventeen persons. From what he could now see about him, Cullinane guessed that in another twenty years of restored Jewish control the rebuilt soil would again maintain its million people.

This was the staggering, incontrovertible fact: the other custodians had allowed the once sweet land to deteriorate, the wells to fall in and the forests to vanish; the Jews had brought the land back to productivity. He could not avoid wondering whether such creative use did not confer a moral right to possess the land, previous negligence having forfeited such right. The more Cullinane asked himself this question, the more he realized that he was basing an entire moral structure on land alone, and this was not logical.

Yet one by one he had to discard alternatives. Israel's religious claim he dismissed without much consideration. Israelis, as Jews, had no more claim to a free Israel than Quebec's misguided Frenchmen had a right to a separatist state merely because they happened to be Catholics. 'One hell of a lot more goes into the making of a viable state,' Cullinane assured himself, 'than religion,' and he said this even though he, as a Catholic, sympathized with his co-religionists in Canada who felt that they were being discriminated against. To establish a state wholly on religious foundations led to historical perplexities like Jinnah's Pakistan or the problems involving northern Ireland. As an Irishman, Cullinane felt that his ancestral island had a right to be united, but surely not on religious considerations only.

Nor was Israel's historic claim to the land impressive; to Cullinane it was irrelevant. Once a man started opening the historical-rights barrel of eels, no one could predict where the slippery evidence might run. The Sioux and Chippewa would reoccupy the United States, which might be an improvement but which might also entail difficulties; ninety-nine per cent of Englishmen would have to evacuate; and the composition of France would be completely changed, which might also be a turn for the better but which would probably create as many problems as it solved. History was neither logical nor moral, and whether one liked it or not the passage of years did establish a pragmatic sanction which only egomaniacs like Benito Mussolini or ghostly fools like the wandering dauphins of France tried to revoke.

One by one Cullinane could tick off the lines of reasoning which failed to impress him regarding the Jewish claim to Israel–language, race, hurts endured abroad, the authority of the Bible, the historical injustice of being the only organized people without its own land–all of these made no substantial impression on Cullinane; but when he had dismissed them logically and in order, there remained one towering consideration, and as the first year's dig approached an ending this problem of moral right returned to perplex him.

'What do you think?' he asked the men in the tent one night.

To his surprise, Tabari defended the Jews. 'I place maximum importance on this matter of historical claims,' he said. 'I believe that any organized people which has demonstrated a cohesiveness and common purpose has a right to its ancestral lands. So even though in this instance the Jews have recovered that land at my expense, they are nevertheless entitled to it. Perhaps they took too much too fast. Perhaps the present modus vivendi will require adjustment in minor points. But the Jews' basic right to be where they are can't be controverted.'

Dr Eliav was, as always, careful and reflective. He lit his pipe, looked at the doors and said quietly, 'Since no reporters are present I will confess that Jemail's reasoning about adjusting the modus vivendi makes sense. Throughout history this bridge-land of Israel has been able to exist as a viable nation only when it maintained sensible economic relations with neighboring lands like Syria and Lebanon or neighboring empires like Egypt and Mesopotamia. We'd be idiots if we argued that some miracle in the twentieth century has changed that fundamental truth. So the present enmity between the nations of this area has got to be considered a temporary interruption of an historic process, and I have found that where temporary interruptions go against the grain of history they do not long endure. Now, how the necessary rapprochements are to be achieved I can't say, but some weight must be given to the fact that we have made the land ours by demonstrating that we understand it and can make it productive. History usually takes such accomplishments into account, also.'

'But the real problem that worries Cullinane,' Jemail suggested, 'is whether such custodianship does in theory as well as fact create ownership. Isn't that your problem?'

'Precisely,' Cullinane agreed. 'From what I said earlier, you know that I think it does. Superior husbandry gave the Anglo-Saxons custodianship of America. Superior English governance gave England temporary title to Ireland.'

'That word "temporary" frightens me,' Eliav interrupted. 'You mean that we Jews shall be here for a decade, then . . .'

'Certainly more than a decade,' Jemail laughed. 'After all, how long did the English hold Ireland?'

'Six or seven hundred years,' Cullinane replied. 'That's what I mean when I say temporary.'

'I breathe easier,' Eliav said. He noticed that Jemail was about to speak, but apparently reconsidered and sat with his hands in his lap.

'Can we agree on this?' Cullinane asked. 'The custodianship of Arab and Turk was a disaster, at least so far as land surface was concerned.'

'No argument from this Arab,' Jemail agreed affably. 'Some years ago an Englishman named Jarvis pointed out that for centuries the world has been misled by a phrase. We called the Bedouins "the sons of the desert," whereas they were really "the fathers of the desert."'

'What did he mean?' Cullinane asked.

'Wherever the Bedouin took his camels and his goats he destroyed good land to create his own desert. After all, very few people in the course of world history have been able to build deserts out of such fruitful areas as the Nile, the Euphrates and the Galilee.' He laughed, then added, 'It's our special talent, but of course we have others. And persistence is one of them. You know the maxim we Arabs are taught. "A man who gains his revenge after forty years is acting in haste."'

'The question as I see it,' Eliav suggested, puffing at his pipe, 'is whether the world is entitled to prevent the Bedouin from doing what he damned well pleases with his land. Are we justified in insisting that any segment of creation–a human life, a river, a horse that might run well if trained, a corner of land–must be utilized to its top capacity? Perhaps, in God's strange way, the Bedouin who created deserts was acting more in harmony with the divine plan for this area than was the Jew, who proved he could eradicate those deserts.'

'It's just possible,' Tabari said, 'that God, having seen what you Jews and we Arabs did with this land, and the strange fruit we grew here–Islam, Judaism, Christianity–cried, "Turn that cursed place back to the desert so that no more religions are raised up in My name." Perhaps the way of the Bedouin is the way of God.'

The men relaxed as the photographer appeared with a pot of coffee. 'What's the argument?' he asked as he spread the cups.

'I asked if Israel's constructive custodianship of land conferred on her a moral right to ownership,' Cullinane explained.

'Sounds like the pragmatic sanction of the imperialists,' the Englishman said brightly. 'What we were tossed out of India for.'

'You're right,' Eliav said. 'If you judge the Jew in Israel solely from the point of custodianship you come close to charging him with imperialism. So we've got to consider moral right, but having admitted this I want to ask one question. Is there any nation on earth that can come before the bar of justice claiming that it exemplifies moral right? On this spot the Canaanites drove out the original owners, and the Jews expelled the Canaanites and Egyptians and Persians and Babylonians, and God knows who else. You Arabs,' he said, pointing to Jemail, 'came into the act very late. Very late indeed. You just barely got here ahead of the Crusaders and the Turks. So why suddenly should Israel, of all nations on earth, be summoned before the bar of international justice to explain its moral right? You know, when there was a town on this tell years ago a girl who married had to be sure that on the morning after the wedding her mother could parade through the town a bloodstained sheet, proving that her daughter had been a virgin. What kind of sheet do you propose that the Israeli government parade through the world? And to whom? To Peru, for example, which disinherited its Indians and accomplished nothing in doing so? To Australia, which conscientiously set out to kill every Tasmanian and succeeded? To Portugal? To the United States with its Negro problem? Let us first see parading through the streets of Jerusalem the bloodstained sheet of Russia, proving that she was a virgin. Or the sheets of Germany and France.'

Eliav had spoken with rather more force than he had intended, and the Englishman said, 'I always think that bedding is a great topic for coffee,' and Tabari suggested, 'Why don't you throw their own Book at them? "He that is without sin among you, let him first cast a stone."'

Eliav laughed and said that he apologized, then in his slow manner concluded, 'What I was leading up to was this. Israel's ultimate justification must be moral, but not in the way that nations have used that word in the past. We will not appeal to history nor to custodianship of land nor to the persecutions we suffered abroad. We'll stand before the world and say, "Here in a small land we have shown how people of many backgrounds can live together in harmony. With us, Arab and Druse, Muslim and Christian know social justice." John, you're wrong when you justify everything by custodianship of land. Anyone can attain that with a police force and some agriculture specialists. But Israel's custodianship of people, of human rights, is going to be spectacular.' He hesitated, then pointed at each of the men with his pipe. 'That's to be our moral justification.'

Tabari clapped him on the shoulder and said, 'In a land noted for noble speeches, that hit a fairly high standard, Eliav. But I'm afraid you won't have time to prove your point, because what I see happening is this, after some years we Arabs will unite, impossible as that now seems. With leadership from some unsuspected outside quarter like Persia or Morocco, or perhaps from central Asia, as in the past, the united Arabs will drive the Jews into the sea. Just as we did the Crusaders. Of course, the entire civilized world will be aghast at the slaughter, but it will do nothing to stop us. Absolutely nothing. Spain, once again a monarchy perhaps, will accept some of the refugees. Poland and Holland will take some, as before. But then in the United States horrible pogroms will begin. I can't see the reasons too clearly now, but you'll think up some. All the Jews in New York will be marched into a gigantic space ship and shot off into the air on a no-return rocket, and good Christians led by your President will applaud. From San Francisco, from Cleveland and especially Fort Worth, other rockets will shoot forth. And off in space these lonely ships will circle the earth, and light will reflect from them so that at night you'll be able to see them pass the moon, and people will cry, "There go our Jews." And after many years the conscience of the world will be aroused, and citizens of great soul in Germany and Lithuania will make it possible for surviving Jews to come back once more to Palestine. And when they reach this spot and see how their irrigation plans have been allowed to lapse, and when they see how the Arabs permitted the schools and the vineyards to perish, they'll say, "Things have sure gone to hell in our absence." And they'll begin building all over again.'

Both Eliav and Cullinane started to comment on this summary, but neither could think of anything relevant to say.

For Kaimakam Tabari to travel from Tubariyeh to Akka in August his caravan had to depart at sunrise so that a safe halting point could be reached by noon, thus permitting the tents to be pitched before the worst heat of the day. Consequently, at four in the morning a sizable entourage convened at the caravanserai, where horses and provisions were checked.

Along the edge of the lake moved flickering lights, soft in mystery, as people from various quarters of the town came to watch the caravan's departure. Children from Arab and Jewish families ran through the narrow alleys, each group keeping to itself, while mothers stood silent and their husbands asked knowing questions of the muleteers. The morning, already steaming and airless, was filled with the good smell of horses, and the gates of the town were being opened.

At this point the kaimakam appeared, a big, handsome man in flowing Arab garb, while from the government building near the fort came four armed soldiers to mount their horses and take their places along the caravan. A drum began to beat and cheers rose from the crowd as the expedition headed for the light-tipped hills to the west.

It was prudent, in 1880, to move within an armed body, for solitary travelers were apt to be murdered, and even groups of three or four if not accompanied by riflemen might be assaulted by Bedouins. Along the very road which Jesus had walked alone and in security the Turkish kaimakam scuttled like a frightened schoolgirl; for the route which had once contained inns and numerous cities now crossed only bleak and dangerous lands. What was worse, if the hills were safely passed, one entered upon extensive swamps, much larger than they used to be and ridden with malaria; two thousand years ago most of the area had been irrigated land producing the grape and olive which had made the Galilee rich.

Shortly after eleven that morning the armed caravan reached the barren knoll of Makor, the customary halting place, for from its height the guards could protect themselves from bandits, and on this high spot Kaimakam Tabari's tent was pitched. By noon, when the sun was savage, he was asleep.

At six that afternoon he was awakened by loud laughter. Sticking his head out of the tent to see what was happening, he detected nothing, but since the laughter continued, he threw a robe about his shoulders and went onto the knoll. On the path below he saw a sight which would have made anyone laugh.

Coming down the road from Akka, traveling alone and on foot, was a frail man wearing an outrageous costume; and from time to time, from either joy or insanity, he stopped, executed a little dance and leaped high in the air, uttering all the while unintelligible words. Then adjusting his shoulder pack he would resume his journey.

'What is he?' Tabari asked. No one knew. 'Go fetch him,' Tabari directed, and three riflemen ran down the knoll to confront the surprised stranger.

He must have suspected that the men intended to kill him, for with an ecstatic indifference he stood before them and bared his breast, waiting for the shots. Fear he did not display; some other emotion possessed him, and when the Arabs made it clear that they meant him no harm he danced again, then dutifully followed them up the hill.

The frail man stood before the kaimakam and waited, as people on the knoll chuckled, for he was an amazing sight, a consumptive Jew bent in the shoulder and bearded. Beside his ears dangled long curls, and over his body hung a black coat gathered at the waist. His pants were extraordinary and the kaimakam could recall none like them: they were made of a gray fabric containing a bold vertical stripe, and, hanging free like a boy's, reached only to his calf. Below them were exposed white-ribbed stockings, which ended in shoes with silver buckles. The costume was completed by a large flat hat trimmed with brown fur, and since the man had obviously been walking in the heat of the day, his face was lined with sweat and dirt; but more memorable than trousers or fur hat or dirty face were his piercing blue eyes.

'Ask him who he is,' Tabari commanded.

Members of the caravan tried Turkish, Ladino and Arabic, with no results, but a horseman who knew Yiddish uncovered the fact that this was Mendel of Berdichev, come to settle on his new land.

Kaimakam Tabari recalled that this was one of the men identified by Shmuel Hacohen as a leader of the proposed colony, and it was from men like this that he was supposed to extort additional funds for the appeal on water rights. 'Ask him what he's doing on the road alone,' Tabari growled.

The interpreter could comprehend little of what the pilgrim replied, but he made an attempt to explain: 'He could not wait for the others. He wanted to see the land.'

'Why is he dancing?'

'For joy.'

'How does he know where he's going?'

'He has a map.'

The kaimakam asked to see it, and from a Russian printing of the Torah, Mendel of Berdichev produced a map of Old Testament days, and it was about as good as any that the Turkish government had produced in recent years. At least the path from Akka to Galilee was indicated, and it was this path that the Jew was following.

It was obvious to Tabari that any attempt to mulct this demented man of baksheesh was hopeless, so he asked, 'Doesn't he know that he may be killed by bandits?'

The interpreter discussed this with the stranger, but the latter either did not understand or did not care. A positive radiance suffused him, and if death were to be his lot before he reached his land, there was nothing he could do to forestall it. 'He says,' explained the interpreter, 'that in the Russian troubles he nearly died, that in Danzig they stole his money, and that on the ship he came close to drowning, but he is now in Israel.'

The kaimakam and the immigrant stared at each other for a moment, the enchanted blue eyes of the Jew looking deep into the dark eyes of the Arab, and there was no understanding. Nor was there enmity. Grudgingly Tabari said, 'Tell him he can sleep with us.' There was no point in sending him into the guns of the Bedouins.

But the Jew could not halt. He bowed to the kaimakam, to the horseman, to anyone in sight, then started dancing down the hill. Give him some water,' Tabari directed, and when the man's canteen was filled, he ran to the road, turned his face toward Galilee and leaped joyously like one demented, as if he felt coming through the soles of his feet the strange and lyric message of the land.

In the twilight he headed east, and as Tabari watched the disappearing figure, wondering what he signified, he had the strange feeling that this stranger from Berdichev had been looking at him with the same hard eyes that Shmuel Hacohen had used the night before. Haunted by these two pairs of eyes, Tabari began absentmindedly toying with the gold coin that Hacohen had paid him for the Talmud; but he was not aware of doing so, for his attention was still focused on the dancing Jew.

Next morning, as Tabari approached Akka, he intended to proceed immediately to the immigrants to see how much baksheesh he could squeeze out of them for handling their water problem with Istanbul, but he found that the impact of the dancing Jew had driven aside such concerns and he had no wish to meet with the newcomers at this time. He therefore procrastinated, diverting himself with unimportant matters, but in the afternoon he forced himself to the ancient caravanserai of the Genoese, where the waiting Jews were encamped, and there he found Solomon and Jozadak to be more sensible negotiators than Mendel had been; but his heart was not in the business and he extorted only a tithe of what he would otherwise have managed. He was glad to leave the caravan, and made his way to the popular and spacious Turkish baths in the old building opposite the citadel; and there he found a pleasant surprise awaiting him. The large Negro attendant, naked except for a small towel, greeted him and said, 'In the far room is someone you may wish to see.'

Tabari undressed hurriedly, eager to get the dust of the journey from his bones, and stepped into the small, well-remembered room where the stone seats were always clean and the steam abundant. At first he could not see who waited, then gradually through the steam and shadows he saw sitting on one of the benches the massive figure of the mutasarrif of Akka. The man was enormous, with a big, dark Turkish face and rolls of fat from chin to ankle; he seemed an enormous bullfrog waiting for a fly.

'Mutasarrif Hamid Pasha!' Tabari cried. 'What an extreme pleasure of pleasures!' The fat man grunted, and Tabari continued. 'I've come all the way from Tubariyeh to see only you, and here you are!'

'I was expecting you,' the fat man said, as if from the bottom of a well. He indicated that Tabari was to sit beside him, and since the mutasarrif of Akka was a pure Turk and Tabari only an Arab, the gesture was more than merely polite.

For the kaimakam the moment had extra meaning, for it was to this room of perpetual twilight, with its dark and mysterious shapes looming up through the steam, that the old-time kaimakam of Tubariyeh had brought him while he was still a young boy, and it was here that the infatuated Turk had barred the door and explained his passion for the young Arab. In later years, when the madness had passed and Tabari was the kaimakam's son-in-law, they had again come to this same room, but in a different relationship.

How old Mutasarrif Hamid looks! Tabari thought. The bullfrog resembled Tabari's father-in-law in the years before he died.

The big Negro brought in fresh water, throwing some on the walls to increase the steam. 'Would you care for some grape juice?' the mutasarrif asked, and when Tabari assented, the Negro disappeared, returning shortly with cool glasses.

Tabari, as he drank the purple juice, reviewed the delicate problem before him: if he could depend upon the fact that the mufti of Tubariyeh had not informed Mutasarrif Hamid of the thirty English pounds, he, Tabari, could keep all thirty for himself. On the other hand, if he were sure that the mufti had betrayed him, he could make a gesture of offering Hamid all the money before the question was raised, thus gaining credit for himself. And, finally, if the mufti had been afraid to approach the mutasarrif himself, but had somehow conveyed the impression than an unknown amount of money had changed hands, Tabari could keep a good share and give Hamid the rest.

But he must also remember that the mutasarrif controlled his chances for promotion, so it was necessary to retain not only his good will but also his active enthusiasm. What to do? It was precisely the problem that faced all officers of the Turkish empire: How honest should I be . . . this time?

He made up his mind. With a burst of frankness he told his host, 'Excellency, I bring you good news. The mufti of Tubariyeh has given me thirty English pounds. For you. To enlist your aid in keeping the Jews out of Tubariyeh.'

'I know,' the fat old man mumbled.

Tabari was not fooled by this reply. There was a very good chance that the old man did not know and was claiming that he did only to keep Tabari honest in the future. In this tricky business a man could be certain of nothing.

The old bullfrog continued, with steam condensing on his face and dripping onto his paunch, 'But as you well know, Faraj ibn Ahmed, the sultan has already decided to let the Jews have the land. So the mufti's gift . . .' The two rulers had to laugh, and the old man raised his hands in a gesture of helplessness.

'I'm sorry for the mufti,' Tabari said cautiously.

'He's a vicious man,' Hamid grumbled in the gloomy twilight, 'and I took it as an affront when he came to warn me personally that he had paid you the money.'

'Did he do that?' Tabari asked in surprise.

The fat old bullfrog smiled to himself and thought: You know very well that he got to me with his story first. Else why should you have given me the full thirty pounds? But to Tabari he said, 'Yes, he came running to me like a schoolboy . . .'

'How could he?' Tabari asked in real perplexity. 'He paid me only two nights ago, and when I rode out of Tubariyeh I saw him in the crowd.'

'After you left he and the qadi came the back way by Safad. The mufti wants you out of Tubariyeh.'

The canniness of the red-faced mufti impressed Kaimakam Tabari. He was a redoubtable enemy and something had better be done about him, now: 'Excellency, that mufti must be replaced.'

'I've already sent a letter to the wali in Beirut. But these things, as you know, Ibn Ahmed . . .'

'Cost money,' Tabari concluded. 'I know, and with that in mind I've brought you a special gift, a gold coin issued eight hundred years ago. I found it in Tubariyeh.'

The old man's eyes opened in greediness, then flashed a warm smile through the murky steam. 'A generous gift, Ibn Ahmed. I don't think the mufti will bother you in the future.'

The two officials relaxed in the pleasing heat and watched with casual interest as the Negro brought in wet towels to place about their heads. He also sloshed warm water onto their shoulders and rubbed their bodies with his powerful hands. When he was gone the old man observed, 'In two years I shall retire.'

'So soon?' Tabari asked.

After a long silence the old mutasarrif grumbled out of the twilight, 'I'm returning to a farm near Baghdad. A beautiful spot it is.'

'I like Baghdad,' Tabari said. More silence followed, during which the young man tried to guess at what the older intended.

'It will be costly to man the farm . . . to do the things required.'

Oh, God! groaned Tabari to himself. The ancient thief wants more money. But this time he was wrong. The old man was reflecting on his long years as an official and for once required nothing but an attentive ear.

'I've been haunted the last few weeks, Ibn Ahmed, by memories of the places I served in. Baghdad was the best. Aleppo the most interesting. And Bulgaria was the worst. If I had my way I'd turn Bulgaria loose and tell them, "Rule this damned place yourselves. It's your punishment."'

'I always understood that Greece was the worst,' Tabari suggested.

'Never served in Greece,' the old man said. 'But three days ago when I watched the ship come into harbor with those Jews I had the strange feeling that they were going to prove more troublesome than Greeks or Bulgarians. Faraj ibn Ahmed, are we making a great mistake in allowing so many to enter the country?'

'The firman has been signed.'

'Sometimes the wrong firman is signed,' the old man said cryptically. Wringing out the towel he placed it over his huge, wet face.

Kaimakam Tabari recognized thise statement as one made to trap him, but he did not know where the trap lay. Had the mutasarrif uttered his mildly disloyal statement as a means of luring him into anti-imperial sentiments? If so, it ought to be rebutted, for it was a reflection on the sultan. Or had the old man finally awakened to the dry-rot in the empire and did he honestly believe that changes were necessary? If so, Tabari ought to agree with him, for the mutasarrif had it in his power to determine what promotion Tabari would get next, and he would be capable of holding him back if disagreements arose.

It was essential that Tabari say something, and in trying to decide which way to jump he began to sweat with a copiousness not justified by the steam. In spite of the moist room his throat went dry, and in panic he looked to see if the mutasarrif's countenance would betray any clue to the old man's thinking, but the bullfrog remained passive, with the towel hiding his face as he had planned. Desperately Tabari racked his mind for guidance, but none came. In his heart he wanted to be a courageous man like Shmuel Hacohen, willing to challenge obstacles if necessary, but when he saw the great hulking mass of the mutasarrif he lost his courage. Almost certainly the old man was trying to trap him into radical disclosures, so Tabari clenched his hands and said, 'I've found the sultan is usually right in the firmans he signs.'

Beneath his towel the mutasarrif wheezed approvingly. Uncovering his face he stared at Tabari with huge drooping eyes and said, 'It's good for an Arab to think that way. This morning the mufti tried to tell me that you had gone over to the reformists.'

'That swine!' Tabari was outraged by the treachery yet pleased that his assessment of the mufti had been correct.

'Normally I'd not have listened to him,' the flabby mutasarrif continued, 'but two days ago your brother-in-law was hung in Beirut. Conspiracy.'

Tabari sagged as if the tense ropes in a torture chamber had been relaxed. The old bullfrog had nearly trapped him. Had he given the wrong answer, he might now be on his way to death, but it was not this escape that caused his body and his conscience to sag. He realized that in masking his slowly developing opinions in order to protect a possible promotion he was surrendering them forever. Other men would lead the Turkish reformers, not he. Shmuel Hacohen would ride with the future, not he. Perhaps this was why he had saved the Jew that night, to serve this purpose. His limp hand reached for the towel and now it was he who covered his face, for at this moment he wished no one to see him.

'You were wise, Ibn Ahmed,' the old man said, 'to resist your brother-in-law. Never again will the sultan allow any constitution foolishness. What we must do is permit no change and hope that things work out for the best.' At that moment his desk was heavy with petitions covering matters of health, schools, Catholic missionaries and an ingenious plan for clearing the harbor of silt, but during his remaining tenure none would be moved forward.

The old bullfrog shifted his enormous belly so that steam could work its way into a new set of folds, then, unexpectedly, grabbed the towel from Tabari's face and stared at him, saying, 'When I leave Akka you're getting my job.'

Tabari sighed. Somehow the flavor had vanished from the promotion.

'Promise me one thing, Ibn Ahmed. Keep things as they are. We have a happy city here. Be sure that Christian pilgrims are allowed to visit their holy places without molestation and keep the Bedouins away from towns. But above all, when the wali comes down from Beirut be certain that things are in good shape. Spend money to fix them up, your own salary if necessary. Because in a place like Akka you can always get it back later, one way or another.'

The silent Negro slipped in to suggest that perhaps the two officials would like to move into another room for their massage, but the mutasarrif refused: 'Let's stay here a little longer, Ibn Ahmed.'

Later, as they were dressing, Tabari sought to deliver the gold coin, only to discover that he had lost it, and as he vainly searched his belongings he became aware that the fat old man was irritated and suspected him of some kind of double dealing. If this suspicion were allowed to persist, Mutasarrif Hamid might change his mind about the promotion, for the old bullfrog could be vengeful. So feigning generosity and love Tabari cried, 'Excellency, I've lost your coin. But here are some funds I've collected for another purpose.' And he handed over the money which he had extorted that day from the incoming Jews.

As soon as he was free of the mutasarrif he dispatched two horsemen to Makor with instructions to search for the gold coin which he must have dropped there, but it was not found.

LEVEL I

Rebbe Itzik and the Sabra

Found at Makor–bullet manufactured in New Haven, Connecticut, February, 1943 C.E., and intended for use in World War II. Fired from a rifle manufactured in Manchester, England, April, 1944 C.E., and also intended for use in World War II. Deposited at Makor sometime past midnight on the morning of Friday, May 14, 1948 C.E.

The three had this in common: that each loved the land passionately as a man loves a woman, joyously as a child loves the dawning of a day when there is to be a picnic on the land; the sabra loved Galilee as the soil from which her people had sprung through generations uncounted; the soldier loved Palestine as a refuge after years of fighting; and the little blue-eyed rebbe loved Israel as the land that God had chosen as a site for testimony. It was during the turbulent spring days of 1948 that their three loves came into contact.

To Isidore Gottesmann, the soldier, the instructions of Moses our Teacher were clear beyond necessity for debate: 'When thou goest out to battle against thine enemies . . . the officers shall speak unto the people, saying, What man is there that hath built a new house? . . . let him go and return to his house, lest he die in the battle . . . And what man is he that hath planted a vineyard? . . . let him also go and return unto his house, lest he die in the battle . . .' Gottesmann especially liked another commandment: 'When a man hath taken a new wife, he shall not go out to war . . . but he shall be free at home one year, and shall cheer up his wife which he hath taken.'

Thinking ruefully of his own situation, Gottesmann looked up from the almanac on which he was working and reflected: I have a new house. I've planted a vineyard. And I've a new wife. Moses Rabbenu must have had me in mind specifically, and I want to stay at home lest I die in battle.

Then he laughed nervously: And I'm particularly covered by this injunction. Here Moses surely had me in mind: 'And the officers shall speak further unto the people, and they shall say, What man is there that is fearful and fainthearted? let him go and return unto his house . . .'

He leaned back from his desk, where he had been compiling data from the almanac, listened to the sounds coming from the kitchen as his wife prepared supper, and shook his head. He was a tall, thin, ascetic Jew with sunken cheeks and deep-set eyes peering out from beneath dark eyebrows. He did not seem an unusually sensitive man; he was rather more reserved and self-directed than most, and he had the habbit of biting his cheek and drawing his lips back from even teeth. When he quoted the Torah he used Hebrew, but his personal reflections were in German, for that had been his native tongue. He also spoke an excellent English with only a slight German-Yiddish accent: And God knows that on that last command I qualify, because I've grown quite cowardly. 'Fearful and fainthearted' describe me exactly.

He shook his head and called, in a heavily accented Hebrew, 'Dinner about ready, Ilana?'

From the kitchen of the new white-walled house came a hearty, almost masculine cry: 'Tend your figures. Leave the kitchen to me.'

Gottesmann returned to his almanac and completed his calculations, placing them meticulously within the columns he had ruled in his note-book: Tonight, April 12, 1948, sun sets at eight minutes past six. Tomorrow morning, April 13, 1948, sun rises at thirteen minutes after five. Now, if we allow an additional forty-five minutes of visibility both after sunset tonight and before sunset tomorrow, we have left . . . He paused to do some subtracting, then noted the critical answer: We have about nine and one half hours of darkness in which to do whatever needs to be done. Carefully he put his pencil down and slumped over the almanac. He could guess what needed to be done and who would be ordered to do it.

It was some time before he raised his head, and then he did so wearily: Moses our Teacher could have summed it up in one simple command. 'What man is sick of war? Let him return to his house.' He bit his cheek and muttered, 'I'm fainthearted and fearful and can do no more.'

As a sensitive boy of eleven in Gretz he had watched the great madness of 1933 sweep the Rhine, and had understood when his father shipped him to Amsterdam in 1935. When the war started he had joined a hit-or-miss Jewish underground that operated along the German border rescuing refugees. English agents, penetrating into Holland, had stumbled upon the group and had provided a hard-core leadership, giving them the job of blowing up bridges. These English had quickly spotted Gottesmann's ability and had pushed him through their underground to Antwerp, from which he was ferried across to Folkestone and a good English education. In 1942 he had joined the British army as a stores corporal, handing out Lysol for latrines, but soon he was switched to a secret unit headed for Syria to keep Damascus out of Vichy and German hands. Later, when the fear of Rommel had evaporated, he fought in Italy; and there, meeting for the first time members of the Jewish Brigade from Palestine, he acquired their vision of a free Israel and volunteered to work in the smuggling of illegal immigrants. For nine years, 1939 through 1947, he had been at war, and now he had had enough. He was beginning to lose his nerve—if he had not already lost it—and he wanted only the creative relaxation of tending his vineyards at Kfar Kerem.

He had first seen these lovely vineyards under unusual circumstances: one winter's day in 1944 when the German threat to Syria had dissolved, thanks to the English victories in the desert and the Russian triumph at Stalingrad, Gottesmann's special unit was sent by truck from Damascus to Cairo, and since the convoy had been directed to use back roads it came by way of Safad, where it was halted in the mountain town by an unexpected snowstorm. The English soldiers piled out to inspect the fairy-tale corridors, crying, 'Look at that old fellow from the ghetto.' But Gottesmann went by himself down the narrow alleys, thinking: This is how the Judenstrasse of Gretz must have looked when Simon Hagarzi lived there. And it was with keen pleasure that he stumbled upon the small house marked by the reverent sign:

HERE LABORED THE GREAT RABBI
ELIEZER BAR ZADOK OF GRETZ
WHO CODIFIED THE LAW

Later, when he had climbed to the hilltop, the snow ceased and in the ensuing sunlight he saw for the first time the majestic hills of Galilee; how extraordinary they were that wintry morning, brown in their barrenness yet golden in the unexpected sunlight and tipped on each rise with silver from the snow. The convoluted hills twisted and turned in harmonious folds like the intricacies of music, dropping at last to the lake itself, now crystal-blue in the distance. All his life Gottesmann had known of Galilee, but he had not known that it was beautiful.

'Is this the land they spoke of?' he cried with soaring joy. 'Is this what we Jews used to own?'

As he looked at the goodness he saw that clouds had begun moving in from the deserts east of the River Jordan, clouds super-heated from their thirsty march across waterless sands; and as they drifted across the mountains which protected Galilee they struck the cold air of the snowstorm, so that above the lake they leaped and spun in wild confusion, reaching far into the heavens and breaking into violent patterns. And for a moment Gottesmann had the feeling that nature was showing him a summary of the future with hordes from the desert striking at the Jews of the Galilee, and the turbulence in his heart was reflected in the sky, premonitory of the violence to come, yet consoling in the towering beauty and promise of peace also to come. It was Galilee at its finest—that turbulent area in which states and religions were born; and in a kind of exaltation he climbed into his army truck and rumbled down the mountainside to Tiberias, where the captain in charge suggested, 'Let's celebrate at the hot springs,' and they had piled out to enjoy the old roman baths at the southern end of the town. Feeling unnaturally clean and fresh-eyed, Gottesmann had left the baths to walk slowly southward, coming finally to the end of the lake, where he discovered the rich fields and the sleeping vineyards of Kfar Kerem. Some men were planting grape-vines, and he asked them in Yiddish, 'Who owns this land?' They replied in Hebrew, 'The men of Kfar Kerem.'

'What men are they?'

'We're the men,' the farmers had replied.

'Jews? Like you?' he had asked.

'Yes, Jews like you,' the men had joked in Yiddish, which they spoke poorly.

At that moment the idea struck him: After the war I'll never go back to Gretz. And England's not my home. Carefully he asked the farmers, 'What did you say the name was?'

'Kfar Kerem. Village of the Vineyard,' one of the men translated.

'We're the oldest Jewish settlement along the lane,' another said. 'Built years ago by a man named Hacohen,' and Gottesmann had remembered the names, the fields, the vineyards.

When his convoy reached Jerusalem on its way to Cairo, Gottesmann experienced for the first time the mystery of that city so pregnant with meaning for a Jew—'To next year in Jerusalem' the prayer of his family had been—and while the English troops explored the Arab bazaars which gave the city charm he went with a few Jewish soldiers to the Hebrew University, on Mount Scopus, and there as he looked across the hills at the wonder of his land he became aware of three pretty Jewish girls who were speaking to the soldiers in Hebrew. He indicated that he did not know the language, and the leader of the students said in imperfect Yiddish, 'We hope that when the war ends you'll come back to help us capture our homeland.'

She was a girl of seventeen, broad-shouldered, sun-tanned, with her heavy hair cut short and her khaki dress even shorter. She was the tough, muscular girl of the impending state of Israel, a true sabra–'flower of the cactus,' as those born in Palestine were called, 'prickly on the outside, sweet on the inside'–but there was about her lovely face something that was unmistakably Russian. Her upper lip was thin but her cheeks were full. Her cheekbones were high and her stubborn chin was squared off, so that she did not look Jewish, and when she smiled her teeth were unusually big and white. She was like no other Jewish girl he had ever seen, strong and confident as she asked, 'You will come back to help us?'

'To do what?'

She became solemn, most unlike a girl of seventeen who is flirting with strange soldiers, and said, 'There's to war. There's to be much fighting and we shall need your help.'

He remembered the turbulent clouds over Galilee and said, 'You can't fight all these Arabs.'

'We don't want to fight them,' she replied, 'but they'll insist. They'll think they can destroy us. But after we capture Jerusalem . . .'

'After you what?'

She looked at him with wide, lovely brown eyes. 'We'll capture Jerusalem,' she said with assurance. 'We'll need help, of course.' And she grasped his hands eagerly, crying, 'Soldier, please come back.' Ashamed of her outburst she stepped back, asking, after a while, 'Where is your home, soldier?'

'Germany.'

'And your family?'

'I have none.'

She took his hands again and kissed them. 'In Germany you have no home. In our free Israel you do.' He was startled, and in Hebrew she spoke words that he could not comprehend but whose passion he grasped: 'Here is our home! Jerusalem shall be our capital, and if they mean to war with us, we shall show them war as they have never seen it before.'

Caught by the poetry of her words, he asked in Yiddish, 'And where is your home?'

'In the greatest of all Jewish settlements,' she said quietly. 'At the foot of the Sea of Galilee, where my grandfather proved that Jews . . .'

'Kfar Kerem?'

'You've heard of it?' she asked proudly.

He took her handsome square face in his two hands and kissed her. 'Kfar Kerem will be my home,' he said in Yiddish, 'and you will be my wife.'

Like lovers from the Crusades, speaking in Bordeaux on the afternoon when the knight must sail to the Holy Land to be absent for ten years, they spoke that afternoon of the historic days facing the Jews, and her soaring patriotism communicated to him the spirit of Kfar Kerem. 'I train in the army, and we shall win from the English,' she predicted confidently, 'and from the Arabs, too, if they insist. We'll have a great city here in Jerusalem and our university . . .'

'You'll never hold Jerusalem.'

'We will hold Jerusalem,' she said firmly, and she walked with him to the army trucks, where she gave him her address, although he did not need it: Ilana Hacohen, Kfar Kerem. But as the trucks drew away she cried suddenly with an impassioned voice, 'Jewish soldiers! Please, please come back!'

Now, on April 12, 1948, as he sat in his new house among the olive trees, he listened to the untutored clatter of pots in the kitchen. It sounded as if a child were playing at a toy stove, and he thought fondly of Ilana, his reluctant housewife. The Galilee, remote from the centers of power, seemed to be falling apart and the Jews didn't know what to do. There was idle talk about an attack on the town of Tiberias, held by the Arabs, but bolder spirits argued that the first assault should strike at Acre, also in Arab hands. And as for Safad, the situation there was worse than desperate; it was hopeless.

The situation was this. On November 29, 1947, the United Nations meeting at Lake Success in New York, had voted 33 to 13 to accept England's decision to hand back the mandate given her by the old League of Nations, under which she had been responsible for the government of what came to be known as British Palestine. The problem of what to do now with this vital territory reverted to the United Nations, and the responsible committee had already decided that the land be divided into three parts: inland an Arab state containing mostly Arabs; along the Mediterranean a Jewish state containing mostly Jews; and in between, the internationalized city of Jerusalem to be shared by Muslims, Jew and Christian alike, since that city was holy to all three religions.

On the morning following the announcement of this decision, the Arabs in Palestine had shown the world how they intended to comply by sweeping down upon an unarmed Jewish bus, killing five and wounding seven. Of course, this was not the first disturbance on either side, but it helped ignite an undeclared Arab-Jewish war, with each combatant fighting to gain territorial advantage against the day when division came into effect and an open war could start. During their final months of custodianship the English tried honestly to maintain some kind of peace, but as the bullets increased, as Arab village and Jewish market went up in smoke, the English made it clear that they were determined to leave. On May 15, 1948, they were quitting the land, and Arabs and Jews could partition it in warfare. As a result, in the difficult months at the end of 1947 and the beginning of 1948 the English were beset with irritating problems for which they blamed the Jews; the government in London tried to maintain a façade of impartiality, but their men on the job in Palestine found themselves increasingly partial to the Arabs, and it became obvious that all day-to-day decisions attendant upon withdrawal were going to favor the Arabs and impede the Jews.

This was only natural. The average Englishman had a personal affinity for Arabs and a distrust of Jews; but more important to the dispassionate Englishman was the fact that the Jews were pathetically outnumbered– 600,000 Jews against 1,300,000 Arabs in undivided Palestine, plus 36,000,000 others determined to attack from Egypt, Transjordan, Syria and Lebanon, all of whom had common boundaries with Palestine, and from Saudi Arabia, Yemen and Iraq, which did not. English politicians could be excused if they believed that within two weeks after May 15, 1948, the last Jew in Palestine would be pushed into the sea; it would be therefore unwise to aid these misguided people in prolonging their suicide. Wherever possible, existing fortifications, equipment and physical advantages were being handed over to the Arabs. By mid-April, 1948, the outlines of the transition were clear: The British would go; the Arabs would come; the fleets of the world would stand by in the eastern Mediterranean to rescue whatever Jews escaped the final massacres. Where the survivors were to find refuge, the U.N. would have to decide.

The raw figures facing Isodore Gottesmann were disheartening. In all of upper Galilee, which he and his group were supposed to hold, there were not more than five thousand Jews. Opposed to them were not less than a hundred thousand Arabs, with some two hundred thousand more available from the contiguous Arab countries to the north and east. For example, in the villages between Safad and Acre there were exactly thirty-four Jewish boys and girls with rifles. In Safad itself, where the first blow would probably be struck, an accurate census of Jews had been made: 1,214 Jews surrounded by an estimated 13,400 Arabs. Since Gottesmann had been trained in German gymnasia and English universities, he knew that one must not associate accurate figures and estimates; nevertheless, he had worked out the fanciful ratio of 11.1 Arabs to every Jew. It was an easy number to remember, 11.1. But even it was misleading in that it represented the Jewish strength as greater than it actually was, for the Arabs not only held every high and strategic point, so that their superior weapons could be aimed downward, point-blank at the Jewish quarter, but the 1,214 Jews who were in Safad were composed largely of elderly religious people who either refused to defend themselves or were incapable of doing so. Many were convinced that God still intended to punish Jews for unknown sins and that this time He had chosen the Arabs to do His work, as in the recent past He had chosen the Germans, and before that the Cossacks under Czmielnicki and the Spaniards under the Inquisition. The Jews of Safad were doomed to die; the Torah said so. And they would sit in their synagogues and wait for the long knives as they had waited in the past.

Gottesmann looked at his gloomy figures: Of the 1,214 Jews in Safad, only 140 are armed, and only 260 in all are capable of fighting. The real proportion as between Jewish defenders and Arab attackers, augmented by reinforcements from without, must therefore be considered to be about forty to one. Yet the capture of Safad by Jewish forces was essential to the preservation of a Jewish state or to the winning of the war that would accompany its establishment. For Safad commanded the hills, and just as it had been vital to the Crusaders in 1100 C.E. as a salient protecting Tiberias and the roads to Acre, and to the Mamelukes in 1291 C.E. as a point from which to control the rest of Galilee, so now in 1948 it was again a site overlooking the jugular vein of the area. Taking into consideration the overwhelming superiority of Arab numbers, the United Nations had logically awarded Safad to the forthcoming Arab state, but if it were allowed to remain in Arab hands the viability of any Jewish nation would vanish. As the days of the mandate drew to an end, Safad became the vital target for Jews in the area, and it was held by the Arabs, 11.1-to-1.

As he completed his notes he used the contemporary spelling, Safad, pronounced Sfat in one syllable to rhyme with *spot*. Like all the places of Galilee this fortress town had known many different names: it had originally been Sepph, then Sephet, then Safat; Crusaders had known it as Saphet, historians as Safed, the Arabs as Safad, map makers as Tsefat, and Hebrew nationalists as Zefat. In similar manner Acre had been Akka, Accho, Ptolemais, St Jean d'Acre of the Crusaders, and now purists were calling it Akko; but the most notable of the variations had occurred with the Sea of Galilee: at first it had been known as a sea called Chinnereth, from the resemblance of its shoreline to a harp, then Kinnereth, then Gennesaret, Galilee. Tiberias, Tverya, Tabariyyah, Tyberiadis to the Crusaders, and to the Turks, Bahr Tubariyeh. For the English it became Lake Galilee and was to be Yam Kinneret, with the second word accented on the second syllable.

Isidore Gottesmann, satisfied that his figures on Safad were in final form, closed his folder and leaned back. He was sure that later on that evening, when Teddy Reich and his Palmach lieutenants came to review the situation, Teddy was bound to say, 'We've got to capture Safad. Get going, Gottesmann.' The unhappy soldier smiled wryly: Everyone calls him Teddy but they call me Gottesmann. Because I look like a skinny Englishman. And because I like it that way.

He thought back upon the times when the calling of his name by some Englishman had been of critical significance: That night after we blew up the bridge inside the German border. The English major heading the underground had said in his crisp, unemotional manner, 'Splendid show, Gottesmann. You're for Antwerpen.' And that had been the difference between life and the extermination camp, for those who had not made it to Antwerp had been caught and killed. Or the night in the Belgian port when another English underground operative had called, 'One more place in the lorry. Look lively, Gottesmann,' and this, too, had been the selection between living and dying, for on the following week this Antwerp ring had been penetrated by the Nazis. He also remembered the time when he had stood at attention in dirty civilian clothes as a professor announced to a motley crew, 'And for the University of Norwich, Gottesmann. You did well in your papers, lad.' At graduation his German-Jewish name had been called crisply and he had moved into the British army, then into Syria and later into Italy—always at the command of British Gentiles who were generous in recognizing his merit and in granting him their approval.

But later the voices calling him had changed to Yiddish, the hard, tough voices of small, tough men: 'Gottesmann, we've got to ship these refugees to Eretz Israel. Rent a boat at Taranto. I don't know where you'll get the money. Get it.' And the voice of Teddy Reich, who was even tougher and smaller than the others, all brain and sinew: 'Gottesmann, you'll take this dynamite to Tiberias and wait till the lorry . . .' Just before the suitcase exploded a British voice had cried with agonizing despair, 'My God, Gottesmann! What have you done?'

It had been while hiding from the British after this dynamiting that he had been smuggled into Kfar Kerem, where he had made his way to the home of Netanel Hacohen. Tapping softly on the door he had aroused a tall, square-jawed Jew, who said gruffly, 'If they're chasing you, come in.'

'I met your daughter in Jerusalem.'

'She's not here. But you must be Gottesmann and I suppose you blew up the lorry. Welcome, son.'

That night he had seen for the first time the haunting portrait of little Shmuel Hacohen, his left shoulder protruding as if he wanted to fight, his eyes flashing with notable vitality. 'He was killed by Bedouins while fighting to protect this land,' Netanel explained. 'When the first trouble started the others wanted to give up the vineyards and retreat to the walls of Tiberias, but Shmuel preached, 'We'll build walls greater than any Tiberias has seen. Out of our love for the land!''

'Preached?' Gottesmann interrupted. 'Was he a rabbi?'

Shmuel Hacohen's son laughed. 'Shmuel? A rabbi? When he died he was fed up with rabbis. There were no rabbis in this family. The Jewish state will be born when enough men like my father take enough guns and shoot down the bastards who are threatening us. When my father was fifty he organized his own little army to protect this settlement and he bought himself a donkey so that he could ride from one watch station to the next, firing his men up. The Bedouins announced to the whole countryside, "We'll kill the little Jew on the donkey, and the others will run away." So they killed him. When we recovered his body it had nineteen bullet holes. But his faith had been so strong that no one dared run away, and after two or three battles the Bedouins left us in peace. Gottesmann, to hold this land we had to fight for it. If we want a state for the Jews we'll have to fight for it. You did a fine thing when you blew up the lorry.'

'I asked about the rabbi business because I saw these volumes of the Talmud,' Gottesmann said.

'Those?' Netanel laughed. 'Somebody sold them to my father and he kept them for good luck. Shmuel Hacohen . . . you could sell him anything. His preaching was simple, Gottesmann, and you remember it. No state is given on a silver plate. You buy with blood. Rabbis and governments and fine ideas will not win this land. Guns will. You get the guns, you'll get Israel.'

And then one day, as Gottesmann lay hiding, Netanel hurried into the room, explaining, 'You've got to get out of here. My daughter's coming home from university,' and Ilana appeared, somewhat thinner than when he had seen her in Jerusalem, lovelier when she smiled but more serious and totally dedicated to the ideal of a Jewish state. When she saw Gottesmann packing she said, 'Don't go,' and later, when he recalled that first meeting, he remembered principally the great tenseness of her mind and body. She stood forward against her toes, not back on her heels. Her chin was held forward too, like her stubborn grandfather's in the picture, and her eyes, unlike those of girls Gottesmann had known in other countries, were marked by lines of concentration. Above all, he remembered her tough, rounded knees as they popped out from beneath her very short dress, and he recalled how delightful it had been, in his hiding, to touch those knees and to feel this vibrant girl, so eager for life and the day's challenge pressing against him.

Now he laughed easily as he heard her banging about the kitchen in her last stages of preparing his evening meal. She was a dreadful cook, a typical Israeli she called herself, burning her thumbs and the meat, and she slapped food on the table as her ancestors must have slammed it on the wooden boards in their tents four thousand years ago in this very spot, when returning from their sheep in the wilderness. How excellent a human being she was, this Ilana, how strong in her resolves, and how desperately her husband wanted to stay away from the war that was engulfing him . . . how he longed to stay with his wife among the vineyards.

Yet in his longing Gottesmann had to admit that not even under the humane law of Moses Rabbenu was he excused from this war, for although he did have a new house and a new vineyard, he did not actually have a wife. He and Ilana were not married. In the tempestuous fashion of the day she had simply moved in with him, announcing to the settlement, 'Gottesmann and I shall live together.' He had expected some kind of protest from her father, but tough-minded Netanel had summoned two witnesses before whom the lovers recited the ancient formula: 'Behold, thou art consecrated unto me according to the law of Israel,' after which Netanel boomed, 'You're married. Have lots of children.' Certain cautious neighbors had suggested that perhaps Gottesmann and his girl would like to have a rabbi from Tiberias authenticate the marriage, but Ilana had cried contemptuously, 'We're through with rabbis and all that Mickey Mouse crap.'

The phrase had struck Gottesmann as inappropriate to the discussion at hand and he had asked Ilana, 'Where did you pick up the words "Mickey Mouse crap"?' and she had explained, 'When you go to the movies and watch the cartoons the hero gets into all kinds of trouble, but at the end, when terrible things are bound to happen, Mickey Mouse swings in from nowhere and saves the world. Gottesmann, it doesn't happen that way. And for sure it's not going to happen that way in Israel'–Ilana always spoke as if her new homeland already existed–'because nobody is going to come swinging in from anywhere, not God nor Moses nor some rabbi. So let them keep that Mickey Mouse crap to themselves. Fifteen thousand Arabs are going to come down out of those hills some day, and we'd better be ready.' Her eyes flashed and she repeated, 'We'd better be ready. Not Mickey Mouse. Not some rabbi wringing his hands and wailing, "Israel is lost. Israel is being punished."' Recalling that outburst Gottesmann looked down at his folder and smiled.

Behind him the door banged open. There was a clatter of feet. A tray was banged onto the table and a chair was squealed backward over the stone floor. 'Food!' a husky-harsh voice shouted, and supper was served at the Gottesmann home.

Ilana Hacohen was twenty-one, not tall, not plump. Her big white teeth sparkled as ever, and as usual she looked quizzical. She obviously loved the security and repose of living with a man and she took pride in her new home. With heavy yet loving hands she pushed the crockery about the table and splashed a generous helping of food onto her husband's plate. It was meat and vegetables, cooked as if by accident, and it made him long even for the food of English restaurants. 'Eat it all,' she said. 'I'm saving some for Teddy Reich.' Then, on the impulse of the moment, she leaned across the table and kissed her tall, serious-browed husband.

'You worried about Safad?' she asked.

'For every Jew in Safad there are 11.1 Arabs,' he said glumly.

'If they're the right Jews,' she reflected.

'And the Arabs hold all the favourable positions.'

'They always do,' she said.

'And in honest fighting strength they outnumber us forty to one.'

When Ilana chewed she kept the food in small portions in the right side of her mouth and moved her jaws only slightly, so that she seemed unusually reflective, with her thin upper lip drawn tight and the lines about her eyes contracted. She thought of the odds, forty to one, and of the position of Safad as she had known it, now so critical to the Jews. 'It looks to me,' she said slowly, 'as if Teddy Reich ought to move his Palmach in there tonight.'

Isidore Gottesmann visibly stiffened. He stopped chewing and looked down for a moment at the white boards of the table. Ilana regarded linen as ridiculous in time of war; she didn't propose washing table covers when there was other work to do. When her husband did not speak she said quietly, 'And if Teddy decides to send his men in, you and I are going too.'

'I guessed we would,' her husband said, and they continued eating.

Ilana Hacohen knew Safad well. Her grandfather had been killed by the

Bedouins long before she was born, and she had never known him, but she remembered well the happy days when her father used to take her on horseback up the steep trail to Safad, from which they could see the Sea of Galilee and Tiberias. As they stood on the old Crusader ruins her father would explain how from this spot the Jews had looked down upon the great Roman city of Tiberias, when large fleets had stood out into the lake, and of how, in later days, a group of misguided bigots had assembled in Tiberias to write the Talmud, 'thus binding the world in chains.' He said that some centuries later, around 900 C.E., a much finer body of rabbis had also worked in Tiberias, 'compiling the only honest text of the Bible, so that Tiberias is just as important for the Christians as it is for the Jews.' But it was his opinion that the only rabbi from these parts whom one could love was Rabbi Zaki the Martyr. 'He was a great and honest man,' he said, 'and all could trust him.' Of contemporary rabbis, except for Rabbi Kook, he did not know many who could be so described. He told his daughter, 'Always remember, in this country we have the best rabbis that money can buy.' They were a grubby, contemptible lot and old Shmuel Hacohen had decreed that none should be allowed in Kfar Kerem.

This did not mean that Ilana had grown up without religion. In her father's house the reading of the Torah was exactly equivalent to the reading of Shakespeare in the home of an educated English family, or the reading of Goethe among Germans—except that because of its antiquity and historical power the Jews of the settlement felt that their great literary masterpiece was somewhat more effective than Shakespeare was for the English or Goethe for the Germans or Tolstoy for the Russians. Rarely a day passed in Ilana's childhood when she did not hear some practical discussion of the Bible as the historical background of her people. She knew that Kfar Kerem stood where Canaanites had once ruled and that on their victorious return from Egypt the Jews had surged northward through the valleys to the west. She could imagine them still marching, just beyond the ridges back of Tiberias. To Ilana, God's division of Canaan among the twelve tribes, which had taken place some three thousand years ago, was as real as the proposed United Nations division that would occur within a few weeks; Kfar Kerem stood at the junction of the portions given to Naphtali, Issachar and Manasseh, and it was from these lands that the citizens of Israel had been driven into captivity. Mount Tabor still stood as the perpetual beacon of the north, and the Sea of Galilee remained as Isaiah had described it. To the sabras of Ilana's generation the Bible was real indeed. In her father's vineyard she had found Jewish coins that had been issued by the Maccabees, and she could recall that day on which her father had taken her to see the recent excavations at Beth-shan, pointing toward familiar places on the Plain of Jezreel. 'Why did he do it?' he had cried.

'Do what?' Ilana had asked.

'Keep his troops here at Gilboa while the enemy was camped over there at Shunem.' And he explained why the man had been a fool, a blunderer.

'Who was?' she asked again.

'King Saul,' her father replied. To the Jews of Kfar Kerem, Saul was a man of history, not a shadowy figure in a religious chronicle, and so with Gideon, David and Solomon.

Like most of her friends, whose parents were either non-religious or actively anti-religious, Ilana Hacohen bore a non-Biblical name. Hers meant *tree* and spoke of the soil. Other girls bore evocative names like Aviva (spring), or Ayelet (fawn), or Talma (furrow). Young men were apt to be called Dov (bear), or

Arieh (lion), or Dagan (cereal). Ilana was determined that when she and
Gottesmann had children there would be no Sarahs or Rachels among them, no
Abrahams or Mendels; she wanted no part of the old Biblical names nor of the
Eastern European ones either. In fact, her only disappointment with her
husband was that he kept his German name of Isidore, one relating in no way,
she felt, to a modern Jewish state.

It would be difficult to say whether Ilana and her father were religious or not.
On the one hand they loved the Bible as the literary textbook of their race. On
the other, they despised what the rabbis had made of it. 'A prison!' Netanel
Hacohen cried. 'And the Talmudic rabbis who worked here at Tiberias were
the worst of the lot, codifying into ugly little categories all things that God
intended to be free.' He also looked unkindly at the work of the later rabbis who
had lived in Safad: 'In their exile in Spain and Germany they picked up many
bigoted ideas and came back here to force them down our throats.' There were
others in Kfar Kerem who were so disgusted with rabbinical Judaism that they
went much further than Netanel Hacohen. These Jews were prepared to throw
out God and Moses, too.

Ilana knew some of these latter thinkers and she found their reasoning
persuasive. 'We are Jews,' they argued, 'and it is our job to reconquer Palestine.
When we do we won't require a lot of rabbis from Poland and Russia to tell us
how to govern ourselves.' Women of this group were apt to be especially
vehement in their denunciation, and it was from one of these, a girl at the
university who had lived in America for some time, that Ilana picked up the
phrase which seemed to her the best summary of the religious problem; 'that
Mickey Mouse crap.'

Among Ilana's friends a curious cult had developed which could be
explained only as a combination of deep love for the Bible and an equally deep
distrust for institutionalized religion as they had seen it operating among the
Jews of Galilee. Many girls flatly refused to get married in the old rabbinical
patterns. 'Me take a ritual bath?' Ilana had protested. 'I'd sooner jump in cattle
water ten days old than step naked into that Mickey Mouse crap.' Her girl
friends sought out the men they wanted to live with and in swift progression
became pregnant, fine mothers and good heads of their families. They also
refused to wear make-up, that being the prerogative of purposeless women in
decadent countries like France and Argentina. It became an act of faith not to
shave under the arms, to avoid make-up, to wear very short skirts, to bob the
hair and to take advanced training in the management of machine guns and field
mortars – if any were made available by the men who needed them. These girls
also spoke only Hebrew, fluently and with an earthy lilt. Yiddish they deplored
as an echo of the eastern European ghettos, and Ladino was as bad. Those
whose parents knew no Hebrew consented to talk with the old folks in whatever
language was native, Russian with the Russian immigrants, Polish with the
Polish newcomers, but Yiddish was frowned upon. 'It's a ridiculous mark of
servitude,' Ilana protested, 'and Gentiles are correct in laughing at it.'

They were a tough, wonderful, exciting group of young people, and if they
had surrendered formal religion, they had found a substitute equally
demanding: they were dedicated to the creation of a Jewish state that should be
called Israel and that should be founded in social justice. There were no
communists in Kfar Kerem, and there were actually those who preferred
capitalism with its ever-present chance for a man to become rich, but most were
like Ilana: 'Our house is not really our house. It belongs to the settlement, and if

we should move away the house will go to someone else just like us, which is only right. I work in the vineyard and I think of it as mine, but it really belongs to the settlement, too, and if I leave, other hands will tend the grapes. The important thing is that the land will continue.'

This was the real mystique of the group: the land will continue. 'There were Jews on this land four thousand years ago,' Ilana often said, 'and I am proud to be a part of that chain. When I'm gone more Jews will live on our land, for another four thousand years. It's the land that counts.'

She often recalled the teachings of her grandfather, which were kept alive in Kfar Kerem in a small book which was published after his death and in which he spoke of his great difficulty in acquiring land, and of its significance to the Jews who first realized that it belonged to them:

I met them as they came overland from Akka and the Arabs gathered at the gates of Tiberias to watch them struggle through, and everyone began to laugh, for they were thin and undernourished, and many of the men's backs were bent from much study in the yeshivas of Berdichev. Not even the Jews of Tiberias thought that such people could live on the land, beset by drought in some years, floods in others, and Bedouins all the time. But I swore that the Jews of Kfar Kerem–as I had named the new settlement–would master the land. And to that purpose I drove them constantly to watch how the Arabs tilled the land, to remember what tricks the Russians had used on their fields; and weeks and months would go by without my ever hearing the word *Talmud*, but the word *land* was before us at every waking hour.

Ilana explained to her husband, 'After it was evident that my grandfather was going to succeed, many religious Jews tried to join the settlement, but when they saw how determined Shmuel was to keep Kfar Kerem a farm and not a countryside synagogue, they left in disgust and went up to Safad. My grandfather never allowed a synagogue in Kfar Kerem nor any merchants, and this was the first new settlement to use Hebrew. Shmuel never mastered the language . . . he spoke it like a little boy, some of the old people told me. But before he died he was conducting the settlement meetings in Hebrew. My own father refused me permission to speak Yiddish, and I'm thankful now. Of course, I've picked up the usual number of words and I understand it, but I'd be ashamed to speak it.'

Land was the goal, the land of Canaan and Israel, the ancient fields awarded by God to Naphtali and Issachar and Manasseh. One day when Ilana was riding in an armed truck with her husband toward Acre she saw those once-great farm lands that had deteriorated into malaria-ridden swamps, and she broke into tears: 'It's a crime against the land. This is what happens when Eretz Israel falls into alien hands. We Jews have got to win back all this land, and in three years we'll make it fertile again. We shall have to fight for it, foot by foot, but we shall win because I can't believe that God intended . . .'

'You confuse me when you speak of God,' Gottesmann had interrupted.

'Why?'

'Well, yesterday you said some pretty forceful things against religion. Today you speak as if God were going to give you the swampland.'

'Don't you believe that God has chosen us to tend this land?'

'No,' Gottesmann replied.

'I do,' she snapped, and her husband decided to drop the matter. Yet it was apparent to him that Ilana had come to identify God with the land, not differentiating between the two, and as the truck bounced along he thought: This must be the way people believed five thousand years ago when the long progression to monotheism started. 'God is the land, therefore we shall worship this hill,' and almost at once they discovered that between God and His land there had to be some agent of mediation, whereupon they invented priests and the priests led to rabbis, and the rabbis led to all that Ilana hates.

Now, in his new home, waiting for Teddy Reich and the decisions about Safad, Gottesmann acknowledged to Ilana that he had come partly around to her way of thinking. As he ate the last of the meat—it was a matter of pride among the sabra wives not to serve dessert—he confessed, 'In the last few days I've decided that you're right. The land comes first, and after we get it we can worry about the other problems.'

'You're talking sense!' she cried excitedly, pushing the dishes aside. Propping her elbows on the table she leaned forward and the lines of anxiety about her eyes disappeared. 'When we get hold of the land, Gottesmann . . .' Like many sabras she always addressed her husband by his last name, but in her case this custom also reflected her dislike for his first name.

'I have a feeling,' he continued, 'that the next six weeks will decide whether we get the land or not.'

'Whether!' she cried. 'Gottesmann, we must get the land. Are you afraid we won't?'

'I'm a soldier,' he explained. 'I know what it means . . . in a town like Safad . . . forty on the other side to one on our side . . .'

'But we must,' she said quietly. In great agitation she left the table and stalked about the room, a husky girl, handsome in feature and explosive in her new-felt power. She was not a tall girl, but she seemed to encompass in her tense body the strength of the fields her grandfather had conquered and protected. 'God of Moses!' she whispered. 'Let us recapture our land.'

Then Teddy Reich exploded into the new house, and all things changed. He was a young, one-armed German Jew of twenty-four, without an ounce of fat or a shred of illusion. He moved like a charged wire, sputtering and jerking as if animated by some writhing inner force. He had keen, cold eyes, a spare chin and a close-cropped head of black hair. He was only slightly taller than Ilana, which made him much shorter than Gottesmann, and he possessed one of the most daring minds in Galilee. He was accompanied by four men like himself, all tough German Jews, and a fifth who seemed noticeably out of place. This young fighter was actually rotund, had a soft round face, drooping shoulders and a perpetual grin. He was Nissim Bagdadi, and his last name betrayed both his origin and the fact that he alone, of all the eight in the room, was a Sephardi Jew.

'The word on Safad?' Reich demanded. Throwing himself urgently into a chair he grabbed a pencil and listened.

'I was there two days ago,' Gottesmann began.

'Difficulty?'

'Shot at going in and out.'

'In the countryside?'

'No. In the town.'

'That's to be expected,' Reich hurled back. Ilana gasped. Gottesmann had not told her he had been fired at by the Arabs. He rarely spoke of his war experiences. Reich noticed the gasp and looked at Ilana. 'What's the place look like?' he snapped.

Gottesmann took one of Ilana's steep-sided bowls and inverted it on the table. 'Looks like this,' he explained in bad Hebrew. 'This flat part on top, the

Crusader ruins, held by Arabs. From here they dominate everything. Now imagine the sides divided into six segments–a pie. The Arabs hold five. We hold one . . . this little one. At this upper corner of our segment there's a rugged stone house which the British have turned over to the Arabs, and here there's a police station which we're afraid the British will give them, too.' Glumly the eight Jews studied the impossible situation: only one section held by their people, and it dominated by the Crusader ruins, by the stone house and by the police station.

Then Gottesmann placed a tall book in back of the bowl. Jamming his fist on top of the book he said, 'And back here, commanding everything, is the big new fortress built by the British. The Arabs are already moving in.'

Impatiently Teddy Reid reached out with his one arm and swept everything aside. Book and bowl swept across the table, and the impregnable fortress, the stone house and the concrete police station were gone. 'How many people are involved?' he barked.

'We have a definite count–1,214 Jews against about 13,400 Arabs. That's 11.1 of the enemy to one of us.'

'Standard,' Reich grunted. 'Will the Jews fight?'

'Two hundred and sixty might . . . if we can get them some guns.'

'How many have guns now?'

'One hundred and forty.'

'Better than I thought,' Reich cried. 'Allon says Safad must be taken. We'll move in that platoon hiding north of town.'

'Can a platoon do the trick?' Gottesmann asked.

'Simple,' Reich said, not looking up as he jotted notes. 'Safad must be taken. To do it we can spare one platoon.' There was silence, then he added, 'Gottesmann, if you left now, could you get to that platoon in the hills before dawn?'

'There's no moon. If we push, we can make it.'

'Start now,' Reich directed as he continued his note-taking. 'Tell them they must fight their way into Safad tomorrow night.'

'Very good,' was the reply, in German. If he had any emotional reaction to the difficult assignment he had just been handed, he showed nothing.

'You need any of my men?' Reich asked.

'I'll take Ilana,' Gottesmann replied. Then he studied the four tough Ashkenazim, but decided against them. 'And for our guide, Bagdadi.'

No one in the room spoke. Ilana, standing near the table, made no move.

Teddy Reich looked up from his writing, turning to inspect Ilana and Bagdadi, then nodded, after which he rose, kicked open a door and went into the bedroom, where he threw himself on the unmade bed and said, 'While you're gone we'll use this as headquarters.' Before Gottesmann and his wife were out of the house he was asleep.

It was customary for members of the Palmach to carry, when engaged in military operations, loads of at least forty kilos each, but in view of the unusual difficulty to be encountered on this trip to Safad, Gottesmann gave himself and Bagdadi only thirty kilos each, sixty-six pounds, while Ilana volunteered to carry forty-four pounds. Normally a hike from Kfar Kerem to Safad could be handled with comfort by the well-trained Jews of the Palmach–an abbreviation for the Plugat Machatz, 'striking force,' organized in 1941 to resist the threatened German invasion–for the roads were pleasant, the uphill climb invigorating and the distance only twenty-two miles; but tonight the three soldiers could not use the roads, for they were patrolled by armed Arabs who had killed several Jews attempting night missions. It was Gottesmann's plan to start due west from Kfar Kerem, then to head north to the eastern flanks of the Horns of Hittim, cross the flat lands west of the lake and finally to penetrate the mountains on which Safad stood. It was an uphill trip of twenty-seven miles. The chances for success were not good, since four main roads had to be crossed. The countryside leading to them was rugged, and all had to be completed before four-thirty, when daylight would begin to break. If the travelers were caught in sunlight, the waiting Arabs could pick them off one by one, as they had the thirty-five Jews trapped in sunlight at Hebron.

But Gottesmann had picked Bagdadi as his third man for good reasons. The plump Iraqi was both skilled as a scout and valiant as a fighter. He knew the terrain well and had an animal sense of where an enemy might be attempting to spring a trap. Starting at a dogtrot, he quickly had his team heading away from the Sea of Galilee. Ilana, lugging a rifle and much ammunition, found no difficulty in keeping pace with the men, and whenever Gottesmann caught sight of her, head back, mouth tightly closed, he felt a rush of love for this exceptional girl who in normal times would have been at the university.

With deft maneuvers Bagdadi got his people across the first two roads leading into Tiberias from the west, then launched the hard climb up toward the Horns of Hittim, and as the sturdy trio reached the old Crusader battleground they could see below the sleeping city of Tiberias, which other Jews would try to capture within the next few days. When Gottesmann remarked on this, Ilana whispered, 'May God give them victory,' but Gottesmann had already dismissed Tiberias and was thinking, as he ran, of the historic battle at Hittim which had determined so much history in this part of the world. It's possible for a nation to make one wrong guess and lose its existence, he reflected. Is this attempt on Safad such a mistake? Bagdadi, apparently unbothered by history, pressed on, and the ancient battlefield was left behind as they headed north.

'Slow!' Bagdadi whispered, and the three Jews froze against the spring earth while a British scouting truck moved down the third of the main roads, its searchlight flashing aimlessly across the fields, Bagdadi kept everyone flat, and Gottesmann realized how much he appreciated the involuntary rest. When the light drifted harmlessly above them he noticed that Ilana had closed her eyes and was breathing deeply, but as soon as the truck passed, Bagdadi whispered, 'We're behind schedule,' and when they rose Gottesmann had to smile as his wife automatically brushed the sand from her khaki blouse and short khaki dress.

They now began a steady dogtrot along a fairly level course which carried them toward the hills but kept them well west of the main Tiberias-Safad road along the lake. These were the hours after midnight, and by pressing steadily Bagdadi recovered some of the time lost earlier, so that when they approached the stern hills on which Safad perched they knew that they had at least a chance of getting to the Palmach village before the sun came up. But now the going became brutal, for Safad lay nearly thirty-five hundred feet higher than Kfar Kerem, and they had to make their way through rocky fields, tempting though the nearby roadway was, but no one protested, for all could feel the still-sleeping sun almost pushing on their backs. When it rose it must not catch them in some gully.

They were now in the heart of Arab country, with small villages on every side, and Bagdadi was proving his skill in leading his team as far as possible from likely Arab marksmen. He halted the march and whispered, 'From here to the last road will be difficult. Crossing it will be worse. Then we have a very steep climb. If we run into Arabs, what?'

'No firing,' Gottesmann warned. 'Absolutely no firing.' He gave this order more to Bagdadi than to Ilana, for he knew her to be extremely cool under such conditions.

'No firing,' Ilana repeated, knowing what worried her husband.

'No firing,' Bagdadi promised as he started toward the road with swift head-down strides. It was difficult and painful work.

They passed one Arab village, then another, hearing only the dogs barking at the night. They came in sight of the road but held back, for it looked unusually ominous, as if snipers might be waiting, and as the three huddled in the darkness they saw something that was both exhilarating and frustrating. Above them, so close that it looked as if it could almost be touched, lay Safad, the lights of its Arab quarter brilliant in the night air. Each Jew wanted more than anything else to climb directly to the inviting town, to the critical focus of their movement, but each knew that he must duck and dodge for several more hours, must cross the dangerous road and then work his way silently into the safe hills north of the town where the Palmach waited. It was as difficult as turning away from the gates of a brightly lit dance when one was young.

'We go!' Bagdadi whispered, and they cut quickly across the exposed road and disappeared into the brown hills on the northern side, where Bagdadi kept his team running up the steep incline that would lead them eventually to the hills behind Safad.

It was now three in the morning, the eighth hour of their march, and Ilana was nearing exhaustion, but she took a small drink from a canteen that Bagdadi carried and shifted her rifle ... 'I'll take it,' Gottesmann offered, but she grabbed it fiercely, bent forward and continued up the hill.

'Keep together,' Bagdadi warned. 'Arab villages all around.' And for an hour, till his watch showed four, he maintained his killing pace. Even Gottesmann was finding it difficult to stay up with the astonishing Iraqi, but to fall behind would be fatal, and they pressed forward as behind them the first gray light of dawn began to break.

Now Bagdadi's judgment became crucial. Somewhere ahead lay the village held by the Palmach, but in between stood others filled with waiting Arabs, and to pick an accurate track through the intervening land, to avoid alerting Arab sentries and at the same time to prevent Palmach scouts from firing random shots, required delicate skill. The Iraqi moved slowly, testing the route, until Gottesmann, whose nerves were almost out of control, snapped, 'God, man! Move!'

Gently, as if he were rebuking a child, Bagdadi said, 'This is the time when we dare not choose wrong,' and like a clever fox smelling out the terrain he picked the only path that would take them between the waiting villages.

But as they reached a spot in the center of the Arab holdings an ugly period came when the sun, weary of night, began reaching for the horizon. It was four-twenty and twilight was about to begin. It was a moment of terror, for each of the three Jews could see the visible shape of the others ... far too clearly. Ilana, wanting nothing more than to rest where she was, grew frightened as she saw her husband's face looming out of the vanishing darkness: it was the face of a man who had driven himself to the edge of endurance, and he stopped running. He could go no more.

'We must go,' Bagdadi warned.

Gottesmann refused to move. He could drive his legs no farther, and he intended staying where he was, within the nest of Arab villages.

'We've only fifteen minutes!' Bagdadi pleaded.

Gottesmann could not respond. He saw a depression among some rocks and sat down, while the growing dawn formed a silhouette around him.

'Get him up,' Bagdadi pleaded with Ilana. Tired as she was she went to Gottesmann and pulled on his arm, with no success.

The leadership of the venture now rested solely in Bagdadi's hands, and emotionally he was ill equipped to exercise it, for his life had been spent, it seemed, in following directions laid down by Ashkenazi Jews: as a boy of two, the son of a large Iraqi family living in Hebron, he had watched the unbridled massacres of 1929, when Arabs had swept over that town, slaughtering all Jews in an apocalyptic fury. In the room where he lay hidden under the bed seven of his family had had their throats cut and their bodies mutilated, and although he was mercifully spared from remembering precisely what had happened, he did vaguely recall pools of blood across which he had crawled when the screaming ceased and Ashkenazi Jews came to rescue him.

He had grown up an orphan in Tel Aviv, where the superiority of the Ashkenazim went unchallenged, and of the older boys who thrashed him on the city dumps, all had been from the superior group. When he applied for jobs he found that Ashkenazim had them, and the few vacancies in schools went to them, too. In the Palmach he had received orders only from Ashkenazi officers, but now, with death imminent, responsibility for one segment of Israel's future had passed to him.

Realizing that Gottesmann was determined to commit suicide, Bagdadi pushed Ilana away and with two sharp blows struck the fallen German Jew across the face. 'You'll run!' he said. With one jerk of his powerful arm he dragged Gottesmann to his feet and gave him a shove that started him staggering zigzag across the final half-mile separating them from the Palmach village. Turning to Ilana he barked, 'Follow me,' and he twisted his way through the last of the Arab territory.

Gottesmann's irrational behaviour had wasted precious minutes and now sunrise was upon them. A shot rang out from the hills, frightening Ilana but awakening her husband, and in the next minutes his clearing eyes began to see puffs of dust as bullets struck ahead of the running Jews, and he thought: Maybe they'll keep missing. He was not aware that it was his near-breakdown that had thrown his team into this predicament, and a bullet came close to his head, whining in protest as it missed, and ricocheted among the rocks. His lungs were heavy and his legs grew increasingly difficult to manage. He thought: This must be hell on Ilana. He looked ahead to where she was running and saw something which brought him fully back to reality. Ilana, determined to reach the village, was running as fast as she could, but in a straight line. A series of bullets was beginning to zero-in on her, and in a few more steps she was sure to be hit.

In this brief second of agony Gottesmann remembered a man named Pinsker in the German underground. Effective, cold, he had been a little man who expected to fight Nazis the rest of his life. 'So when you're running you will think yourself a rabbit,' he instructed all his men. 'For the rest of your life you're a rabbit and must run as if you knew that someone was looking down a rifle at you. You cannot imagine how a dodge to the left, a dodge to the right, will upset that man looking down the rifle. Gottesmann!' he had screamed. 'You're a rabbit.'

'*Nieder!*' Gottesmann himself now screamed, but to his horror Ilana kept running straight ahead. A bullet kicked dust at her left heel. He felt sick, then realized that he had intuitively used the German command *nieder* and not the English 'take cover!' He panicked. What he wanted was the Hebrew *artza!* But before he could call again, Bagdadi looked back, instantly sized up the situation, and with a slight flicking of his hand indicated to Ilana what she must do. As soon as she saw his signal she threw herself flat, rolled over three times and resumed running on a new course. The next bullet struck where she would otherwise have been, and the three darting, dodging, twisting Jews escaped the Arabs and approached the village held by the Palmach.

Now it was Bagdadi's turn to know anxiety, for in the uncertain light the chances were good that some Jewish soldier would begin firing at anything that was moving; so as he ran Bagdadi unfurled a small white flag containing a hand-stitched blue Star of David and began shouting at the top of his voice, 'Palmach! Palmach!'

A quick-thinking sentry in the village sized up the situation and launched a barrage of fire at the Arabs along the ridges. The enemy was driven back and the three messengers from Kfar Kerem staggered the last hundred yards without any Arab bullets coming close to them.

When they approached the rude headquarters, gasping and pressing their ribs together, the sun was well up and they cast clear shadows on the earth. Gottesmann freed one hand and grasped Bagdadi by the Iraqi's wet shoulder. 'You know land,' he said, and before he had finished reporting to the local commander Ilana had found a place on the floor and had curled up like a little animal. After an hour's talk he and Bagdadi lifted her, and without waking her carried her to a real bed. She slept all day.

At dusk on the afternoon of Tuesday, April 13, the Palmach men roused Ilana and her two well-rested companions. In the small village there was an air of commitment. Teddy Reich's command to move forward, infiltrate Safad and take over the local defense forces had been so thoroughly discussed, and its difficulties so accurately assessed, that excitement and fear were pretty well spent. Now everyone knew that a platoon of thirty-three men and girls would creep through the countryside at midnight, crawl on its belly for about three miles and try to sneak into the town through Arab patrols. If the maneuver degenerated into a pitched battle, the Palmach were to return fire but to keep moving forward.

The unit was led by MemMem Bar-El, a sinewy young man who wore a beard and prided himself on his somewhat flashy appearance, his sabra birth and the fact that he spoke no language but Hebrew. He was blue-eyed and red-headed, with the controlled instincts of a true fighting man. His title, MemMem, was derived from the Hebrew initials for platoon commander, and for this job he was nearly ideal. His judgments were swift and clearly communicated; in their execution he was usually in the lead. In normal times Bar-El might have been a lady-killer chewing a toothpick; now he was a battle-tested leader, twenty years old.

He was accompanied by a beautiful girl of seventeen, thin, with dark eyes and clear skin. In all respects she was small; her face and body seemed more a child's than a young woman's, and she came only to Ilana's shoulder, but she piled her hair high on her head, like a Frenchwoman, hoping thereby to make herself look taller. She also wore a boxlike soldier's cap which always seemed about to topple backward, for she kept its visor pointed skyward to steal additional height. She was unlike Ilana in that she dressed with the flair of a girl who enjoyed clothes, but she was obedient to the other rules of the sabra: no lipstick, no rouge, no shaving. She served as Palmach secretary and was known simply as Vered, the Hebrew word for rose. She had joined Bar-El's unit in the simplest way: she appeared one morning, volunteering to serve in any capacity, and now she lived in whatever quarters the MemMem could find for her. When questioned she insisted, 'At the end of the war I shall attend university.' Bit by bit the men pieced together the fact that she had come from the family of some important doctor in Tel Aviv, but her parents did not know where she was and she intended not to tell them until victory had been won. Sometimes the men found her crying, and this embarrassed her, but the improbable thing was that delectable as she was, she had no boy friend and permitted none to touch her; Bar-El served merely as her watchdog. Gottesmann was surprised, therefore, when this frail child slammed shut the folding table-desk used by the Palmach as its headquarters, hefted it easily in her left hand, then reached with her right for a rifle and loaded on her back additional gear until she had the normal thirty-kilo marching load for girls. He felt an impulse to lean down and kiss her as he would a child, and say, 'You can put the toys down, Vered,' but she let him know that she intended marching through the wadis to the relief of Safad.

The Jews ate a late meal, then closed down the village as if they had gone to bed normally. Some members who were not making the assault on Safad paced the outskirts on normal guard duty, stopping occasionally so that they could be seen by Arab patrols. A few dogs raced through the alleyways, barking sharply, and in all possible respects the village was kept ordinary; but shortly before midnight MemMem Bar-El assembled his unit and with swift, quiet movements the twenty-six men and seven girls disappeared from the village and lost themselves in a deep wadi running north and south from Safad. No Arab had seen them.

Working silently the Palmach moved single file down the steep banks of the wadi, lugging one Sten gun, a Vickers machine gun stolen from the English, a Mauser, a Garand, an armful of Czech rifles and revolvers from many sources. In the middle of the unit plodded a small donkey loaded with four Hotchkiss guns. Three of the younger boys were covered with web equipment stolen from a Scottish unit. Gottesmann, in charge of the rear, thought: I'd enjoy hearing what an English sergeant-major would say of this troop. Then he looked up to see the lofty lights of Safad as he had seen them the night before, and he realized that the unit was well below the elevation of its starting point and far below its objective. The rest of the operation would be uphill with eighty-eight pounds of equipment.

Now came the first danger. All the Jews were in the bottom of the gully, working their way cautiously southward toward the Jewish section of Safad, and if anything went wrong they would be trapped, with the enemy holding all the high positions. Furthermore, the bottom of the wadi was a natural pathway, so that any patrols that might be operating from the Arab part of Safad must surely intercept them. Yet Gottesmann approved the perilous disposition of the Jews. If they were going to penetrate Safad, they could do so only by this method. In the meantime, if one were religious, he could pray. None of the men

Gottesmann knew was doing so, but each held his rifle at the ready.

Silently the Jews moved down the wadi. At one point Bar-El muttered to Gottesmann, 'Now for the hellish part. Maximum stringing out.' If the Arabs were alerted, this would be the time for them to strike.

Bar-El jumped. Gottesmann felt his throat tighten in an involuntary spasm. A weired, terrifying cry sped through the wadi, echoing back and forth from one wall to the other. Ilana gasped and reached out to grab Gottesmann's arm. The sound was sickening, fearful. Only Bagdadi was at ease. He chuckled: 'Jackals. They smell the donkey.' Any Arabs who were listening found the sound familiar and in no way suspicious. Sweating, the Jews moved forward.

They were now ready for the quick move toward Safad, and it was necessary to consolidate the strung-out troops, so the MemMem halted while the rear caught up. After consulting with his guides Bar-El whispered, 'Cemetery.' The prior briefing had been so thorough that each segment of the platoon knew what to do.

In three units the Jews fanned through the old cemetery: one to the left past the tomb of Rabbi Abulafia, the greatest of the Kabbalists; one to the right past the tomb of Rabbi Eliezer of Gretz, who had codified the law; and another toward the honorary tomb of the greatly loved Rabbi Zaki the Martyr, who had died in Rome. Perhaps it was because these long-dead saints protected the Jews, perhaps it was because the Arabs could not believe that such an attempt could be made, but more likely it was because the Arabs had been lulled by the British announcement that they were withdrawing on April 16–the day after tomorrow–and taking all Jews with them ... for one of these reasons MemMem Bar-El was able to sift his men silently across the cemetery without detection.

Crash! A shot rang out from the Jewish sector. It came from the sturdy old synagogue of Rabbi Yom Tov ben Gaddiel. From the Arab quarter random replies were made, and Gottesmann thought: Damn, there's going to be a real fusillade. The Palmach men, cursing, dropped. Bar-El dispatched two guides into the town to halt the Jewish firing.

Silence. The men and girls inched forward. They were almost safe ... almost in Safad.

'Now!' Bar-El shouted, and the remaining thirty-one scrambled madly out of the cemetery and into the sanctuary of Safad.

As soon as the Jews hit the narrow alleys Vered's high, girlish voice broke into song, wild, exulting:

> 'From Metulla to the Negev,
>   From the desert to the sea,
> Every youth is bearing arms,
>   Every boy should be on guard.'

Up and down the streets of the Jewish quarter the Palmach went, shouting its battle songs.

'Break into three groups!' Bar-El cried, and toward the edges of the Arab quarters the soldiers marched, singing the song of the Jewish fliers:

> 'Batsheva, Batsheva, the song is for you,
>   From Dan to Beersheba we shall not forget.
> From the heights we will send you a song.
>   Let us drink "L'hayim" with the whole Palmach.'

'Start someone shouting that two thousand Palmach have arrived,' the MemMem directed, and little Vered went running through the streets, her childish voice crying, 'We're saved! Two thousand brave men. Through the Arab lines.' Soon the citizens of Safad were repeating the cry, but Isidore Gottesmann was standing silent, his eyes and ears filled with love as Ilana Hacohen and Nissim Bagdadi directed a group of Palmach and Safad youngsters in a parade led by the donkey. Ilana sang the song which so hauntingly caught the spirit of the Jewish movement in which girls like Vered, no more than children, offered their lives for freedom:

> 'Danny-leh, Danny-leh,
> Eat your banana-leh.'

It was the pleading voice of the indulgent Jewish mother, coaxing her fat little boy to stuff himself one mite more. As she sang the nonsense words Ilana's voice was like that . . . filled with love and the joy of having made it to Safad.

As dawn broke that Wednesday morning a surge of hope echoed through the narrow streets of Safad: 'The soldiers have arrived!' And Jews who the previous afternoon had been choosing between massacre or exile were now free to weigh a third alternative, victory, and throughout the town men resolved to hold out a little longer. In all Safad there was rejoicing.

In all Safad, that is, except in the Ashkenazi synagogue controlled by Rebbe Itzik of Vodzh. In its narrow confines ten old men with long black cloaks and curls dangling beside their ears stood praying. The previous afternoon the British government had offered them safe-conduct to Acre, but they had determined not to leave Safad.

Their leader was a thin, small man, a Russian Jew who forty years before had brought his flock from Vodzh to Israel so that its members could die in the Holy Land and, when the Messiah came, escape the dark and tedious underground burrowing from Russia. He had piercing blue eyes and bushy eyebrows, long white curls and beard. His flattened hat was trimmed with fur and his drooping cloak repeated in every detail the garment decided upon by Polish Jews three hundred years before. His hands were white and wrinkled, and when a young boy came bursting into the synagogue, shouting, 'Rebbe! Rebbe! Jewish soldiers have arrived. A whole army,' the little man ignored the news, merely clasping his hands more tightly and bowing his head. His nine followers did likewise, their ankles and knees pressed closely together, as the Talmud directed. They prayed that the children of Israel might be patient when the Arabs fell upon them. They prayed that God would accept their souls when the long knives flashed. And they prayed that they might soon be one with Moses our Teacher, with great Akiba and with the gentle Rabbi Zaki, who had known the meaning of God.

After a moment the boy shrugged his shoulders and ran off to cry his good news elsewhere.

THE TELL

Excavating was interrupted, insofar as Cullinane was involved, when a team of archaeologists from Columbia University dropped down from a dig they were conducting at the ruins of Antioch in southern Turkey to check the finds at Makor. At a luncheon meeting at the kibbutz the director of the Columbia team caused considerable pleasure by stating, 'Word of what you're doing down here has circulated through the profession. What with levels reaching all the way back from Crusader times to the beginnings of agriculture, you have a good chance to make this a classic dig.'

Cullinane nodded and said, 'With two assistants like Eliav and Tabari we're not going to lose much material that could be salvaged.'

'Are you an Arab, Mr Tabari?' one of the Columbia men asked.

Cullinane deferred to his Arab assistant, and when Tabari merely smiled, he explained, 'If you understand Arab names you'll appreciate it when I tell you that Mr Tabari's real name is Jemail ibn Tewfik ibn Faraj Tabari. His family gave him those names to remind the world that he was not only the son of Sir Tewfik Tabari, the top leader of the Arab community during the English occupation, but also the grandson of the great Faraj Tabari, the governor of Akko. He was famous for having rebuilt much of that city.'

'Doesn't Tabari come from the same root as Tiberias?' one of the Columbia men asked.

'In Turkish it's the same word,' Jemail explained.

'But you decided to stay with Israel?' the New York professor continued.

'Yes,' Tabari said abruptly. He had no objection to discussing the matter of his allegiance, but he knew that to Cullinane and Eliav it was old hat, and he himself was bored with it.

The New Yorker studied the three archaeologists in charge of the Makor dig and changed the line of conversation completely: 'Don't you men find it . . . Well, with fifty-five million Arabs or whatever it is breathing down your neck . . . Well, I've been reading the inflammatory pronouncements coming out of Cairo and Damascus and Baghdad. That they're going to drive you into the sea? Massacre every Jew. If they did this, wouldn't it go pretty hard on an Arab like you, Tabari?'

And suddenly Cullinane realized that this reasonably intelligent professor was aware that those who worked in Israel lived under the hammers of history, under the constant threat of annihilation, but he seemed not to be aware of the parallel fact that he in New York and his brother in Washington lived under precisely the same threat.

Next afternoon began the long debate that would determine the character of the state that was struggling to be born. It started because Ilana Hacohen and Isidore Gottesmann were assigned living quarters in a small house that stood next to the historic shoemaker shop that had once been used by Rabbi Zaki the Martyr. By the people of Safad this shop was regarded with affection, and by tradition it was reserved for the home of some rabbi. In 1948, when the Jewish-Arab conflict was drawing to its climax, it was occupied by the Rebbe of Vodzh.

The Yiddish word *rebbe* had originally signified an elementary-school teacher who taught religious classes in Hebrew in the villages of Poland and Russia; but later it had become a specialized word identifying those gifted rabbis who operated within the tradition of Rabbi Abulafia of Safad: the mystics, charismatic leaders and inspired tzaddikim of eastern European Hasidism, the unique rabbis who gathered about them devoted followings. Two men would speak: 'My rebbe can uproot mountains with his interpretations.' 'Yes, but my rebbe can cure all manner of sickness.' The Jews of Vodzh said, 'Our rebbe understands the Talmud better than any other rebbe. He is the well that gives water without losing a drop.'

Even as a young man in Vodzh the rebbe had been recognized as one specially destined for a holy life, and word spread among the Jews of Russia and Poland that a worthy successor had finally been found to the great Rebbe of Vodzh, who had died a martyr in the pogroms of 1875. The young man's piercing blue eyes seemed to cut through to the essential moral problems that men faced, and he became widely known as Itzik, Little Yitzhak. At twenty-four Little Isaac felt no hesitation in condemning the richest Jew in Vodzh for a miserly act which contravened the teaching of the Talmud, and it had been his energy alone that had organized the mass exodus of his loyal followers to Safad. How difficult that had been, to bring those seventy people back to Eretz Israel, except that thirty years later most of the Jews who had not followed him from Vodzh were dead in the gas chambers of Oswiecim.

In Safad, Rebbe Itzik had established a new home for his followers. Along the narrow alleys his Jews had found abandoned houses which they rebuilt into clean homes. Living on alms from America they had acquired one of the ancient Ashkenazi synagogues, not the sturdy one of Rabbi Yom Tov Gaddiel's but an adequate refuge, and through the years they had prospered in their modest way. The Vodzher Jews they were called, and although some of the younger people had left for livelier towns, the rebbe's group still contained some sixty people determined to worship God according to the Torah as interpreted by their Vodzher Rebbe.

His theology was simple. He believed literally the great commandment of Moses our Teacher: 'Now therefore hearken, O Israel, unto the statutes and unto the judgments, which I teach you ... Ye shall not add unto the word which I command you, neither shall ye diminish ought from it, that ye may keep the commandments of the Lord your God which I command you.' To Rebbe Itzik this commandment was lucid and all-embracing. It meant exactly what it said. A Jew should keep the law as handed to Moses by God. That law was found in the Torah, which contained 613 specific orders ranging from the first noble words at the beginning of Genesis, 'Be fruitful, and multiply' to the last tragic commandment to Moses our Teacher as he lay dying in sight of the promised land: 'Thou shalt not go over thither.' Encompassed between this nobility and tragedy lay all the law that man required, the lists in Leviticus, the repetitions in Numbers, the final summations in Deuteronomy. These laws

Rebbe Itzik knew by heart and their words were sweet: 'And if a stranger sojourn with thee in your land, ye shall not vex him.' 'If a man vow a vow unto the Lord, or swear an oath to bind his soul with a bond; he shall not break his word, he shall do according to all that proceedeth out of his mouth.'

Upon these laws of the Torah a man must build the general pattern of his life. The ritual to accompany his birth was explained and the manner of his burial was laid out. His love for a woman was hedged with decent precautions, and his relations with his son, his business and his king were set forth; and Rebbe Itzik was satisfied that a Jew must live precisely within this body of law, and he had put together a congregation of sixty people prepared to do so.

The life that Rebbe Itzik had devised for them was somewhat different from that followed by the other Jews of Safad. In dress they were conspicuous; they looked like archaic ghosts in long black cloaks, flat fur-rimmed hats, shortened trousers and heavily ribbed stockings. They wore beards and black skullcaps and for some perverse reason preferred walking with the stoop that had characterized them when they were forced to live furtively in ghettos. Their daily life was much the same as that followed by Jews in Safad four hundred years before, with frequent synagogue attendance and strict devotion to complex dietary laws. And on Shabbat, starting on Friday afternoon, they stood especially apart from the rest of Safad, a little group of devout Jews living around Rabbi Zaki's old shop.

No fire could be lit, no light used. No food was cooked, no vehicle moved. A man could walk only two thousand paces from his home and he could carry nothing; if he had a cold and needed a handkerchief he could tie it around his wrist and make believe it was a piece of clothing, but carry it he could not. On this day a man could not even carry his prayer shawl to the synagogue. The boy children of Rebbe Itzik's group were especially differentiated from other young Jews by the long and often delicate curls dangling in front of their ears and by the four-cornered shawls which they dropped over their heads and wore under their shirts. The shawls bore fringes in accordance with God's Torah: 'Speak unto the children of Israel, and bid them that they make them fringes in the borders of their garments . . . that ye may look upon it, and remember all the commandments of the Lord, and do them.'

But powerful as he was in dictating the life of his community, Rebbe Itzik was not arrogant; he never assumed that he was wise enough, by himself, to interpret God's Torah, and it was his constant responsibility to study the Talmud, finding therein the guidance that had kept Jews together for more than fifteen hundred years. Each day of the year, excepting only the Ninth of Ab, when they mourned the loss of Jerusalem by staying up all night to read Lamentations, the male adults of the Vodzher group assembled at the synagogue to study Talmud, and since all lived on charity contributed from abroad, the men were free to sit in circles about their rebbe as he expounded passages from the massive volumes. One of the Vodzher Jews once wrote to Brooklyn: 'If I have a dream of paradise, it's to sit in the synagogue on a wintry night in Safad, when snow is on the ground, and the lamp is flickering, while our rebbe expounds Talmud.'

Rebbe Itzik knew the great book virtually by heart, and members of his congregation liked to boast: 'Our Vodzher Rebbe can do this. You take a volume of the Talmud and pierce any six pages with a pin. Our rebbe can look at the first page, close his eyes and tell you what eleven additional words your pin has gone through.' The Talmud by which he lived provided answers to any conceivable problems, although sometimes, in the middle years of the twentieth century, one had to wrench meanings a little here and there to uncover a relevant legalism, but he was not averse to doing so, for he found the great compilation surprisingly contemporary: 'Rabbi bar Mehasia said in the name of Rabbi Hama ben Goria who said in the name Rab: If all the seas were ink, and all the reeds were pens, and all the skies were parchment, and all the men could write, these would not suffice to write down all the red tape of this government.'

But the most remarkable characteristic which set Rebbe Itzik and his little group apart from the other Jews of Safad was their determination never to use Hebrew except as a holy language. From the Torah and Talmud they had derived the conviction that Hebrew would be used for common speech only after the arrival of the Messiah and that until such time it was reserved for religious purposes; and in furtherance of this belief Rebbe Itzik pointed out: 'Observe that in the Talmud itself, only the Mishna, the law of God, is written in Hebrew. The Gemara, the explanation of ordinary rabbis, is inscribed in Aramaic. What the Talmud refused to do, we also shall refuse to do.'

Therefore, outside the synagogue, the Vodzher Jews spoke only Yiddish and they held it to be offensive when others spoke to them in Hebrew. Occasionally Rebbe Itzik had scolded people who addressed him in that language, and he went so far as to refuse his followers permission to ride on any train run by the English government, since the tickets were printed in Hebrew as well as in Arabic and English.

As long as Palestine remained in British hands the peculiarities of Rebbe Itzik's group occasioned no difficulty. In Jerusalem, Jews of similar persuasion in obedience to the Talmud sometimes stoned ambulances that tried to move on Shabbat, but in the Vodzher part of Safad the streets were so narrow that no car could enter, and even that cause of irritation was avoided. But in 1948, with the likelihood of an eventual Jewish state, problems developed.

Rebbe Itzik viewed with apprehension the idea of such a state in Palestine, and to imagine one bearing the name of 'Israel' was repugnant. He told his associates, 'The idea's an outrage. It must not be permitted.' He became so violent in his rejection of statehood for the Jews that he threatened to become a nuisance, and when some young men of his congregation actually ran off to Kibbutz Makor to fight with the Palmach he deplored them as if they had converted to another religion. 'There must be no Israel!' he protested.

To support these curious reactions Rebbe Itzik found authority in the Torah. Repeatedly God had condemned the children of Israel to exile among other nations: 'And I will scatter you among the heathen . . . and your land shall be desolate, and your cities waste.' Jerusalem was to be occupied, which meant that the Arabs, in holding the Holy Land, were acting as God's agents, and to oppose them was sacrilegious. Furthermore, the Holy Land would revert to the Jews only when the Messiah appeared; then Hebrew could be spoken generally, and for ordinary human beings like the Palmach to try to force the coming of the Messiah was presumptuous. There must be no state of Israel, no Hebrew, no resistance to the Arabs. There must be submission, prayer and resignation; and if Arabs chose to massacre, that also was God's will.

Fortunately for MemMem Bar-El and his Palmach, only a handful of Vodzher Jews held these extreme views, for even among the little rebbe's immediate followers about half listened when other leaders like Rav Loewe and Rabbi Goldberg advised: 'The Palmach serves as an instrument of God's will.

Co-operate in every way, for this time we shall fight the Arabs.' When Rebbe Itzik was advised of what the other rabbis had said he folded his hands and looked at the ground. 'They do not understand God's will,' he whispered sorrowfully.

The argument started toward noon on Thursday, April 15, when Ilana Hacohen, refreshed from hours of victorious love-making with her husband, came into the narrow street that ran past Rebbe Itzik's home. As she left her new quarters, a rifle slung across her shoulder, she brushed back her bobbed hair, straightened her very short skirt, and happened to see the mezuzah nailed to the doorpost in conformance with the law of the Torah. Sensing the days of trial that lay ahead she reached up and touched it. As she did so, she happened to see in the street the tense little figure of Rebbe Itzik.

'For good luck!' she said in Hebrew. 'We're going to need it.'

To the little rebbe, everything this brazen girl had done was an outrage. She appeared like a wanton. She carried a rifle. Obviousiy she was fighting for a state of Israel. She had touched the mezuzah as if it had been an ordinary Christian idol. She had referred to it as a mere good-luck omen. And she had addressed him in Hebrew. With contempt he turned his back on her and walked away.

Ilana Hacohen, reared on the fighting principles of her grandfather and her anti-rabbinical father, reacted on impulse. To the astonishment of the benevolent dictator, she grabbed him by the shoulder and wheeled him around so abruptly that his hat fell off. 'Don't you rebuke me,' she warned.

Rebbe Itzik was not accustomed to opposition, and the unprecedented action of the sabra stunned him. He stooped, tried to recover his hat but awkwardly kicked it farther from him. As he rose he found his eyes opposite the brazen bare knees, then staring up at the girl's tanned, insolent face. Irrelevantly he cried, in Yiddish, 'You're not even married to that man in there, are you?'

'If you speak to me,' Ilana snapped, 'use the language of the land.'

The infuriated rebbe started to reprimand her and she started to answer back. Her defiance attracted a group of the rebbe's congregation, and an old man cried, 'Whore! Don't dare to address our rebbe.'

Ilana swung to face her accuser, and as she did so the butt of her rifle whipped close to the rebbe's cheek, and he drew back. The newcomer thought his rebbe had been struck and he started to reach for Ilana. Deftly she grabbed her rifle with two hands and parried the clumsy effort.

The noise drew Gottesmann to the narrow street, and he quickly deduced what was happening. He knew Ilana's feeling toward the ultra-orthodox, whom her grandfather and father had derided, and he could guess the rebbe's reaction to her, a soldier of the emerging state. He caught his wife and pulled her back into the house. Then he took her place in the street and tried to mollify the outraged Jews.

Speaking Yiddish, which quietened things somewhat, he told the patriarch, 'Rebbe, we've come to save your town—if we can.'

'Only God will determine whether Safad stands or falls,' the rebbe replied.

'That's true,' Gottesmann agreed.

'But we'll help Him along,' a young passing Palmach fighter cried in Hebrew.

Gottesmann, seeking to ease this new blow, assured the rebbe in Yiddish, 'The important thing is, we must work together.'

The insulted rebbe retreated to the shoemaker's house, where his loyal supporters consoled him. At the same time Gottesmann retired to the house next door, where he told Ilana, 'We're here for one job, Ilan. Don't be sidetracked.'

'We're here for two jobs,' she corrected. 'To win a nation and to see that it gets started right. You let that old fool . . .'

'That's not the word,' her husband protested. 'Just stay away from him.'

'I will, if he stays away from me.'

But on the next day fresh trouble broke out. It was April 16, 1948, and the English were evacuating Safad. The captain in charge of trucks, a fed-up veteran from one of the mill towns in England who understood neither Arab nor Jew, marched wearily into the heart of the Jewish section, attended by four tough Tommies with submachine guns. He summoned Rebbe Itzik and some of the other elders, while MemMem Bar-El remained hidden behind a wall as Gottesmann translated the English for him.

The British officer shouted, 'Jews of Safad, in one hour we're leaving. Your situation is hopeless. You're a thousand. The Arabs waiting over there are fourteen thousand. Fresh troops moved down last night from Syria. If you stay, dreadful things are going to happen. We offer you—all of you—safe-conduct to Acre.' He waited.

Rebbe Itzik moved forward. 'We've held a meeting,' he said, indicating the ten Jews of his congregation. 'And we have decided that the Vodzher Jews will stay here.' The British officer groaned and wiped his forehead. Then Itzik added, 'But the people of Rabbi Goldberg and Rav Loewe are free to leave with you.'

The Englishman turned to these two rabbis and said, 'You've made the right choice.' He started shouting orders under which all the Jews could ride his trucks into Acre, and after his instructions had been repeated in both Hebrew and Yiddish a few old men and some mothers with babies began preparing themselves to move through the Arab lines to the trucks.

'All of you!' the officer bellowed. 'Get going!' He started pushing the people toward the protected exit route but he was peremptorily halted by MemMem Bar-El, who appeared dramatically with a rifle, backed up by ten Palmach men.

'No Jew will leave Safad,' he announced quietly in Hebrew. There was consternation. When the British officer heard Gottesmann's translation he showed his incredulity. As for the would-be refugees, they took the command as a death sentence, while Rebbe Itzik held it to be insulting for a man with no authority—a stranger in Safad—to contradict the decision of the rabbis that the old and young could leave.

'No Jew leaves Safad,' Bar-El repeated.

'This is highly irregular,' the Briton fumed. 'Who are you?'

'MemMem Bar-El,' Gottesmann interrupted. 'Palmach.'

'How'd you get in?' the Englishman asked.

'Right through your lines,' Gottesmann laughed.

'But, man! You're overwhelmed.' The tired Englishman indicated the four compass points. 'Surrounded. Outnumbered. Starving.'

'That's right,' Gottesmann said. 'All the Arabs have to do is come in a few steps and capture us.'

The officer shrugged his shoulders and pleaded, 'At least let us take out the children.'

'You heard him,' Gottesmann said, indicating Bar-El.

The Englishman ignored the MemMem and asked Gottesmann, 'You educated in England?'

'Norwich.'

This seemed to make a difference to the Englishman, and he pleaded, 'You know they intend to kill you all? They've told us so.'

'We're not evacuating.'

'Let us take the cripples and sick.'

MemMem Bar-El understood the plea and snapped, 'We stay together. As we did at Massada . . . at Warsaw.'

The Englishman licked his dry lips and said, 'I've been trying to prevent a massacre. Now it's on your head.'

'It's on all our heads,' Bar-El replied simply. 'Your mother's and my uncle's. You English have done everything possible to destroy Palestine. When you leave . . . in a few minutes . . . you'll turn all the installations over to the Arabs, won't you? Arms, food, everything.'

'I've been ordered,' the Englishman explained apologetically. 'It's been agreed that the Arabs should have this town.'

'And you worry about a massacre.' Bar-El spat contemptuously.

'In these matters we have to be impartial.'

'Goddamn your impartial soul,' Bar-El said hoarsely. Gottesmann refused to interpret this, but one Englishman who understood Hebrew started forward. A Palmach girl stopped him.

Gottesmann said, 'You're so dreadfully wrong about Safad. It will not fall.'

Bitterly the MemMem added, 'Turn the keys over to the Arabs and when you're back home remember the name. Safad. Safad. Safad.' He spat on the ground and led his men away.

Gottesmann walked with the Englishman to the edge of the Jewish quarter. 'I meant what I said,' he repeated. 'We're going to take this town.'

'May God bless you,' the Englishman replied. He could say no more, for now he must turn all fortified positions, the food supplies, the field glasses and the extra armament over to the Arabs. Nearly two thousand additional troops had moved down from Lebanon and Syria to be in on the kill. Six thousand well-armed Arabs were determined that not one Jew should escape.

Immediately after the parting two things happened. The tired Englishman said to one of his assistants, 'It's the first time I've ever seen Jews ready to fight back. They'll last three days. Pray for the poor bastards.' And an Arab sniper, seeing Gottesmann neatly framed in an alley, fired at him, but the bullet missed and the final battle for Safad was engaged.

THE TELL

In the dining hall one clear October morning Cullinane asked, 'What did a Jew who had served with the English think of their behavior in 1948?'

It was an ugly question which most people avoided, for if the British had succeeded in their plan for turning Palestine over to the Arabs, Jews would have hated them forever; usually the topic was side-stepped. But Eliav had often considered it and had developed certain generalizations which he was willing to discuss.

'Normally,' he began, puffing at his after-breakfast pipe, 'I don't mention the matter, so I'm not sure my thoughts are consistent, but the English did represent a goodly portion of my life and I'd be stupid not to have acquired some ideas. Briefly, when the English picked me up I was a rough, uneducated tyke and they made a man of me. During their war against the Germans they treated me with dignity, and I grew almost to love them. During our war against them they behaved with notable crassness, and I had to fight them. Looking back on everything, I'm perplexed.'

'Let's take your ideas one by one,' Tabari suggested. 'First, they gave you manhood.'

Eliav nodded. 'You could make it stronger. They gave me life. They rescued me from Europe. Educated me, gave me this Oxford accent which helps me so much in impressing American archaeologists. Imagine what you could do with it in Chicago, John!'

'I do very well with a fake Irish brogue, thank you,' Cullinane observed. 'Remember, Chicago is an Irish Catholic city, not an English one. But tell me this, did the English ever admit you to full partnership?'

'I've thought about that. You know, some Jews have risen to positions of great power in England. Disraeli reached the top. Sir Herbert Samuel did pretty well. Leslie Hore-Belisha. It's remarkable, really.'

'But did they accept you?' Tabari asked bluntly.

'For a few moments during the war, I thought so. But I was fooling myself.'

'Rather curious,' Tabari reflected, 'because we Arabs who went to Oxford always considered ourselves full-fledged English gentlemen. Still do.'

'You didn't fight them later,' Eliav said.

'Correct. We fought on their side, so our feeling was strengthened. There was another curious factor . . .' He was about to offer an obiter dictum but apparently thought better of it and pointed to Eliav. 'Your second point. That during the war they treated you well.'

'They did,' the Israeli said. 'They taught me how to fight a guerilla war, how to organize a military unit . . . everything. In the War of Liberation I had to do some fairly ugly things against the English, but I always said, "Tommy, old boy, you taught me how to do this." And I found that they had taught me right.'

'You've no bitterness?' Cullinane asked.

'None,' Eliav said. Then, after drawing on his pipe, he added, 'And I suspect I speak for most Israelis.'

'Wait a minute!' Cullinane protested. 'I've been reading some Israeli books and their scorn for the English pro-Arab policy . . . Why do you suppose a bunch of Jews blew up that lorry full of English soldiers at Tiberias?'

Eliav took a deep breath, studied his pipe which now rested between his palms, and said, 'Let's talk about that lorry. It was blown up, as you may recall, in retaliation for English blundering at Akko. I don't believe you should leap to the conclusion that the lorry could have been destroyed only by Jews who hated Englishmen. The men who did the job may have respected England very much.'

There was a clatter of dishes as the kibbutzniks cleared away the tables, then Tabari resumed: 'You said that during World War II you grew almost to love them. That's a funny statement for a Jew.'

'I meant that after my escape from Germany . . . When I appreciated what horrible things were happening . . .' Eliav paused, then added matter-of-factly, 'We were a large family. Few survived.'

Cullinane gripped his chair and thought: Sooner or later it smacks you in the face. I've known Eliav for all these months and now he tells me that he lost most of his family. In a restaurant you start to give a crude waitress hell. Then you see tattooed on her arm a Bergen-Belsen number. He bit his lip and said nothing.

Tabari, possibly because he had been educated in England, was not affected by Eliav's last statement. 'So everyone has a sorrowful story. What's it got to do with the discussion?'

Eliav, like most Israelis, appreciated this impersonal reaction and said, 'This. In the worst days of the war, when I was serving here in Palestine . . .'

Tabari interrupted. 'You're one of the few Jews I know who calls it "Palestine." I thought that was frowned upon.'

Eliav smiled. 'When I'm speaking as a member of the British army I use their name. As an Israeli I'll take it most unkindly if you call my homeland "Palestine." Well, anyway, when I served here and watched Rommel's Afrika Corps coming at us through Egypt, and other Germans trying to reach us through Syria . . .' He stopped, puffed his pipe and said with great reserve, 'If the British had not held desperately–you might also say heroically–six hundred thousand Jews would have been gassed to death in Palestine.' He relaxed and added lightly, 'I rarely pray, and when I do I usually leave God and Moses out of it. But I have frequently asked blessings for Field Marshal Montgomery. I'm sure neither of you can imagine how I feel about him.' He tapped his pipe and said, looking at the floor, 'It was a very near thing, gentlemen.'

Cullinane asked, 'Then you're able to differentiate between Englishmen who fought with you and Englishmen who fought against you?'

'Of course. Because I must differentiate between my two selves. The Jew who learned all he knows from the English and the Jew who later fought them with all his dedication.'

'You're able to keep your many selves straightened out?' Tabari asked sardonically.

'You go nuts if you don't,' Eliav laughed. 'How do you keep your various responsibilities as an Arab Israeli . . .'

Cullinane interrupted. 'It's good hearing a Jew speak of these matters. As an Irishman I feel just about as you do. I must acknowledge that in the world at large the English have accomplished wonders, but in Ireland . . .' He threw up his hands. 'I'm sounding like an Irish politician in Chicago, but what I mean is, in Ireland they never had a clue. They operated from an entirely different intellectual base.'

'You've made my speech,' Eliav said, 'and now let's heckle Tabari.' He relit his pipe.

'One more thing,' Cullinane protested. 'I know why they went wrong in Ireland, but why did they go wrong here?'

The Jew finished lighting his pipe and in the interval Tabari leaned forward as if he were going to speak. Eliav, noticing this, deferred, but Tabari bowed and said, 'Hyde Park is yours.'

'To understand the English in Palestine,' Eliav reflected, 'you've got to understand which Englishmen came here. Then you've got to study those

Englishmen against the Arabs they met, and against the Jews.'

'Precisely,' Tabari said with malicious pleasure. 'Point is, Cullinane, we saw two types of Englishmen in Palestine. The poor, uneducated second-raters who couldn't be used at home and who weren't good enough for important posts like India. Don't forget, our little Falastin was truly a backward place of no importance, and we got the dregs.'

'True,' Eliav nodded. 'The other group, of course, were absolutely top-drawer. Biblical experts, Arabic scholars, gentlemen of broad interests. Now how did these two different types of Englishmen react in Palestine?' He deferred to Tabari.

'On this I'm the expert,' Tabari joked, 'because my family used to hold drills ... I'm serious. My father would gather us together and coach us on how to treat the stupid Englishmen. I can still hear him lecturing: "Words are cheap, Jemail. Use the best ones you have. Effendi, honored sir, excellency, pasha." He advised us to call every army person colonel unless we recognized him as a general. I had an Oxford education, but I used to take real delight in calling some pipsqueak from Manchester effendi. I developed an exaggerated ritual of touching my forehead and chest as I bowed low and said, "Honored sir, I would be most humbly proud if you would so-and-so."'

'What do you mean, so-and-so?'

'Well, I judged whether or not he knew Arabic, and if he didn't, I ended my sentence, "Kiss me bum," and the stupid fool would show his teeth and grin and give me anything I wanted. The Arab corruption of the average Englishman was criminal.'

'And on the same day,' Eliav added, 'this befuddled Englishman would meet a Jew from Tel Aviv who dressed like an Englishman, acted like an Englishman. Except that the Jew was apt to be better educated. Here there was no effendi nonsense, no floor-scraping. The Jew wanted to talk legal matters or Beethoven or the current scandal. And there was one additional thing the Englishman could not forgive. The Jew insisted upon being treated as an equal.'

Tabari laughed. 'Under the circumstances, who can blame the lower-class Englishman for preferring the Arab?'

'With the upper-class Englishman the problem was different,' Eliav said. 'They came with good degrees. Usually they spoke Arabic, but rarely Hebrew. And all had read the great romantic books which Englishmen insist upon writing about the Arabs. Doughty—you ever read any of his daydreams? T. E. Lawrence, Gertrude Bell.'

Tabari said, 'Yes, we Arabs have enjoyed about the best public-relations men in the world, all Englishmen. And tell him about the photographs.' The Arab fell into an exaggerated pose, right arm over chin, fingers extended poetically. With his left hand he threw a napkin over his head as a burnoose, and all in all looked rather dashing.

Eliav said, 'The other day Jemail and I were reviewing some two dozen books on this area and in every one the English author was photographed in full Arab regalia. Robes, turban, flowing belt.' The men laughed, and Eliav concluded, 'One of the worst intellectual tricks pulled on England was that photograph of T. E. Lawrence in Arab costume. Damned thing's hypnotic.'

'Helped determine British policy in this area as much as oil,' Tabari suggested.

'If the truth were known.' Eliav said, 'I'd bet that even roly-poly Ernie Bevin had hidden somewhere a photograph of himself in Arab robes.'

'But can you imagine any self-respecting Englishman who'd want himself photographed as a Palestinian Jew?' Tabari held up his hands in disgust.

The archaeologists winced at the image as a kibbutznik slammed up, growling, 'You gonna sit here all day?'

'We may,' Cullinane said drily.

He did not embarrass the kibbutznik, if that had been his hope. 'Just wanted to know,' the boy said, sweeping away the dishes in a clatter.

'I'll keep my cup, if you don't mind,' Cullinane protested.

'No point,' the kibbutznik said. 'Coffee's all gone.' Cullinane drummed on the table to control his anger and the boy went off whistling.

'There was one additional factor,' Tabari began hesitantly. 'It doesn't appear in official reports, but in this part of the world it was rather potent.' He leaned back, then continued, 'Many Englishmen who came here had enjoyed homosexual experiences. At school. In the army. And they were predisposed to look at the Arab of the desert, who had always been similarly inclined, with fascination if not actual desire. If one was a practicing homosexual, what could be more alluring, I ask you, than an affair with an Arab wearing a bedsheet? You and he on two camels riding to the oasis. A dust storm raging out of the desert and only two date palms to protect you. One for him, one for you. Blood loyalty and all that. Some very amusing things happened in this part of the world in those years. I can assure you.'

'I wouldn't have raised the subject,' Eliav said quietly, 'but since Jemail has, I must say he's not joking. Now suppose you were an avid homosexual, John . . .'

'We'll suppose nothing of the sort,' Cullinane protested. 'You forget it was Vered who interested me, not Jemail. Please to keep the names straight.'

'What I was saying,' Eliav continued, 'was that if you were a young Englishman filled with romantic ideas and you stepped off the transport in Haifa, where would your sympathies . . .'

'Sympathies, hell!' Tabari protested. 'Who would you want to go to bed with? Mustaffa ibn Ali from the Oasis of the Low-Slung Palms or Mendel Ginsberg who runs a clothing store on Herzl Street?'

Cullinane found the conversation preposterous, so he asked, 'Considering the circumstances, you agree that the English did a reasonably decent job in Palestine?'

'Yes,' Eliav said.

'Speaking as an Arab,' Tabari added, 'I think only the English could have handled things as well as they did.'

'Then you've no bitterness?' Cullinane asked the Jew.

'With history I never fight,' Eliav replied. 'With the future, yes. And when I was fighting the English they represented the future. I had to oppose them.'

'Tell us the truth,' Tabari pleaded, as if he were a child. 'Aren't you generous in your present judgments because of the fact that when you served with the British army . . . wasn't some officer . . . let's say, a little extra nice to you? Come on, Eliav. We'll understand.'

'Curious thing is,' Eliav replied, 'they were all damned decent and I shall never forget it.'

Through the middle of Safad, running from the concrete police station down the hill to the cemetery containing the graves of the great rabbis—Eliezer, Abulafia, Zaki—stands a handsome flight of stairs built of finely dressed limestone. Its 261 steps, arranged in twenty-one separate flights, are wide and its whole appearance is one of solidity and permanence. These stairs will be long discussed in Israeli history, for they were built by the English for the express purpose of separating the Arab quarter from the Jewish, and there have been some to argue: 'See! The English went out of their way to erect an official barrier between Arab and Jew. They made the division permanent, for by keeping the two groups apart they were able to play upon the fears of each, thus retaining for themselves the right to govern. The steps created new differences that would not otherwise have developed, and maintained old differences which would otherwise have dissolved. If you want a monument to English venality in Israel, look to the 261 steps of Safad.'

But it was also possible to argue: 'We have historical records of Safad dating back to shortly after the time of Christ, and many different governmental systems have operated during that time, but so far as we can ascertain, there was always a quarter in which Jews lived by themselves and another in which non-Jews lived. There were synagogues and churches, then synagogues and mosques, and each held to his own. All that the English did in building their flight of stairs was to acknowledge existing custom and externalize in concrete form a tradition as old as the town itself. The handsome flights of stairs did not divide Safad. The divisions of Safad called forth the stairs. Perhaps the time may come when the stairs can be dismantled, but this could not have been done during the English occupation.'

And the impartial voice of history could have argued: 'The truth lies somewhere in between. I can remember periods extending into centuries when Jew and Arab shared Safad in easy harmony. In the early days of Muhammad this was so. In the period of the Kabbalists there was no friction. And even in this century, prior to the great massacre of 1929, Jews felt free to live in the midst of the Arab quarter. On the other hand, I can recall periods of desolation. The Crusaders killed off every Jew in Safad. In 1834 there was a pitiful slaughtering, and I do not believe that Englishmen were governing in Saphet at that period. At this date who can remember exactly why the beautiful stairs were built? All I know is that from 1936 through 1948 the stairs kept two warring people apart; and at night, when the revolving searchlight on the police station flashed down the stairs, Jews and Arabs alike were afraid to cross over and molest the other.'

But on April 16, 1948, things changed swiftly, and as the English, in a stirring ceremony, handed the Arabs the keys to all the fortresses, all the high, protected points in town, and marched away with bagpipes playing, it became obvious that the war for Safad would begin at the stairs. If the Jews could hold there, they had a chance to hold the town.

Whiiiiing! Zaaaaah! Across the fine gray stairs the Arab bullets began to whine. The withdrawing English had assured London that all Jews would be massacred within three days. The Arabs believed they could overrun the area —in two. From all sides a constricting, dense, concentrated pressure began to strangle the Jewish quarter and during the first half-hour of fighting many Jewish families had evacuated the houses nearest the lovely stairs. Arab spotters cried, 'They're falling back.'

Zaaaaaah! Unnnnnnh! The bullets splattered into the mud walls of the Jewish houses and after an hour of fighting no Jews could be seen on the other side of the flight. The Arab commander, knowing what a psychological shock the capture of a bridgehead across the stairs would be, gave the order to move out, and in company force the assault was launched. '*Itbah il Yahoud*—Slaughter the Jews!' cried the Syrians, the Iraqis and the Lebanese as they leaped across the open space.

In the next few minutes Jewish boys and girls seemed to appear from everywhere, for MemMem Bar-El, anticipating this Arab move, had his people well stationed. Moving out from a deserted house Ilana Hacohen fired with deadly calm. Little Vered in her boxlike hat came darting in with her submachine gun spurting. Gottesmann and Bar-El loomed up from a pile of rubble, throwing grenades, while from a roof smiling Nissim Bagdadi fired with cruel effect. The astonished Arabs fell back. They tried to drag their wounded across the stairs, then abandoned them.

'Cease fire!' Bar-El shouted, and the Jews retired. Along the stairs there was no sound but the whimpering of a young Arab from Mosul. And in the Arab quarter men were whispering, 'Girls were fighting. With guns.' That night each side acknowledged that if there was going to be a massacre of Jews in Safad, it would not come easily, as in the past.

In the days that followed, MemMem Bar-El issued orders which mobilized the Jewish population of Safad for the task of fortifying the outer rim. Trenches were to be dug connecting vantage points; houses had to be torn down to deny them to Arab snipers; roadblocks were required; and one hundred and seventy-three armed Jews dug in to hold off the assault of some six thousand Arab fighters. Every man and woman had a job to do, and Bar-El sustained in the town a kind of stubborn optimism.

But he failed to impress Rebbe Itzik, who refused to participate in the ungodly work. Each dawn he and his ten fur-hatted elders repaired to the Vodzher synagogue to contemplate the imminent destruction of Safad, and from a repetitious history they were able to select precedents for the manner in which a doomed body of Jews should behave in the last minutes before they perished. Judaism was the only religion with a specific prayer to be uttered 'when the knife was at the throat, when the flames were at the feet,' and through the centuries this final reiteration of belief had been used 'to lend sanctification to the Holy Name of God.' Peculiar grace had always been accorded those who died at alien hands while still proclaiming belief in the oneness of God, and Rebbe Itzik determined that when the Arabs finally overran the Vodzher Jews a new chapter would be added to the glorious record of Jewish martyrdom.

He was therefore disturbed on Monday morning when he found at his synagogue only seven Jews. 'Where's Schepsel and Avram?' he asked. He noticed that Shmuel was the other absentee. One of the old men said, 'They're breaking rocks,' and the little rebbe rushed out of the synagogue to locate his followers. He found them working under the direction of MemMem Bar-El, breaking rocks taken from demolished houses. The resulting stones were to be jammed in between boards, thus providing bulwarks that would stop rifle bullets. Many cartloads of stones were needed to protect the Jewish houses facing the stairs, and the three Vodzher Jews were doing the job with sweat pouring from beneath their fur hats.

'Schepsel!' the rebbe cried. 'Why aren't you in synagogue?'

'I'm working to hold back the Arabs,' the old Jew replied, and no argument that Rebbe Itzik could advance sufficed. Three of his battalion were gone.

Later that morning he received an additional shock, for he found Ilana Hacohen, gun over shoulder, organizing the young girls of his congregation into a defense team, whose job it would be to carry stones to the old men and to provide meals for the Palmach.

'Come back, little Esther!' he called, but the girls had found a more inspiring leader, and the old man shuddered when Esther shouted to him, 'Ilana says that when the next rifles come I can have one.' The girl, Avram Ginsberg's daughter, was thirteen.

But when Ilana had her girls well organized she did an unexpected thing: she stopped by Rebbe Itzik's home intending to explain what was being accomplished in defending Safad, for the MemMem had growled, 'See if you can win the old goat over.' When she pushed open the door to the shoemaker shop she was met by the rebbe's old wife, a Russian peasant woman who was cooking soup. Ilana tried to speak to her, but the rebbetzin knew only Russian and Yiddish, and Ilana refused to use the latter language. In a moment the rebbe appeared, surprised to find the armed sabra sitting in his home. The meeting was bizarre, for as an ultra-orthodox rebbe he deemed it improper either to touch or to look at a woman other than his wife, so that when they finally spoke it was as if each sat in a separate room.

'We drove away four Arab sorties last night,' said Ilana in Hebrew.

'It is the will of God that Israel should be punished for its sins,' he replied in Yiddish.

'But not by Arabs.'

'In the past God used Assyrians and Babylonians. Why not Arabs?'

'Because the Assyrians could defeat us. The Arabs can't.'

'How dare you be so arrogant?'

'How dare you be so blind?'

On Wednesday, during the third day of their renewed discussion, Ilana had the distinct impression that in some contradictory way the little rebbe took pleasure in what she was doing, for apropos of nothing that had been said he cried, 'The daughters of Israel are fair,' and to her surprise she replied, 'We're trying to build an Israel you will be proud of.' He looked at his folded hands and said, 'Can you accomplish this if you are so arrogant? Why don't you marry the tall Ashkenazi?' And her stubborn reply, in Hebrew, distressed the old man: 'We are married.'

Nevertheless, the slight rapport increased when Ilana brought Vered with her, and the rebbe came upon them as they were eating the rebbetzin's herbs and boiled water. 'Of one thing I am proud,' the little man said.

'The barricades we've built?' Ilana asked.

'No,' Itzik replied. 'The fact that in all Safad, when food is so scarce, no Jew operates a black market.'

'If he tried,' Vered said, 'MemMem would shoot him.'

'How old are you?' the rebbe asked, looking out of the corner of his eye at her almost childlike appearance.

'Seventeen,' Vered replied.

'Is your father religious?'

'Yes. He doesn't know where I am.'

'His heart must ache,' the rebbe said, muttering a prayer over the two girls.

Then the rapport was shattered. On the evening of April 23, the beginning of their second Shabbat in Safad, MemMem Bar-El felt in his bones that the Arabs were due to attack, and he feared that the attempt would be made on Saturday, when it was logical to suppose that the Jews would be at worship, so on Friday afternoon he summoned all available hands to erect an additional barrier; and the Jews were silently moving boards and rocks when Rebbe Itzik loomed out of the growing darkness.

'What are you doing on Shabbat?' he demanded in Hebrew.

'Building a wall,' Bar-El replied.

'Stop!' the little man cried.

'Rebbe, go home to your prayers!' Bar-El pleaded. The outraged rebbe sought to prevent the men from continuing their work and it became apparent that his protests might alert the Arabs, so the MemMem clamped his hand over the little man's mouth, swung him around and passed him along to Nissim Bagdadi. 'Get him out of here,' Bar-El ordered.

The Iraqi Jew, weighing at least twice as much as the rebbe, easily carried him away from the urgent work and lugged him to the shoemaker shop, where he called for Ilana, telling her, 'Keep him home. We've got to build a wall.' So Ilana went to the rebbe's house and sat with him, grimly silent, until the emergency work was completed. Toward dawn the old man predicted in Yiddish, 'God will curse that wall. God will curse any army that works on Shabbat.'

But the real crisis came with Passover, when Arab pressure was heavy and MemMem insisted that two critical rows of houses be strengthened with bulwarks, even if other houses had to be torn down to provide the rocks. Work commenced on the eve of Passover, and Rebbe Itzik, hearing the hammers and the shovels, became frenzied. He ran among the bending workmen, the fringes of his shawl brushing across their eyes and reminding them of their own fathers at prayer on this holy day. He pleaded with them to desist from profaning the day, but they pointed out that Rabbi Goldberg and Rav Loewe, recognizing an hour of peril, had granted full permission to transgress either Passover or Shabbat. 'So we're working,' the men replied.

Now the decision of Rabbi Goldberg and Rav Loewe was one honored by nearly two thousand years of Jewish history, for the Greeks and the Romans, knowing of the Jews' refusal to move on Shabbat, had always tried to select that day for their major offensives and by this tactic had won easy victories until the rabbis of Akiba's time had pronounced the principle that when a man or a nation was in peril of its life any provision of the Torah might be put in abeyance, except those regarding murder, incest or apostasy. MemMem Bar-El, relying upon that judicious precedent, had appealed to the rabbis for a declaration that the present siege was such a mortal moment and they had agreed. The soldiers could work. But to Rebbe Itzik the law was holier than the preservation of an unborn state which had no right to exist, and he stormed the streets calling down imprecations.

'Get him out of here,' Bar-El pleaded, and again Ilana was given the job of keeping the old man at home; and in these moments of tension occurred a most regrettable incident, one that Ilana would often wish had been avoided.

She and Bagdadi led the rebbe home, fending off a few of his devoted followers who wanted to know, 'What are you doing with our rebbe?' Bagdadi returned to the front, where the work continued. In the shoemaker's room, where Rabbi Zaki the Martyr had offered his common sense to the people of Safad, Ilana sat with the blue-eyed Rebbe of Vodzh and balked almost all he tried to do.

'I should be at the synagogue,' he protested.

'You were at the synagogue,' she said, 'and you left to make trouble. Sit down.'

'Do you think that God will bless a state that works on Passover?' he threatened.

'We'll get the state, then we'll worry about God and His Passover,' she replied.

The blasphemy was horrible. 'Unless we go back to the old ways, any Israel you get will be ashes in the mouth.'

This kind of reasoning disgusted Ilana and she asked, contemptuously, 'Rebbe Itzik, do you really believe that obsolete ideas generated in Poland three hundred years ago represent the will of God?'

'What do you mean?' the old man sputtered.

'The uniform you wear. There was never anything like that in Israel. It's straight out of the Polish ghetto.'

'The fringes . . .' the rebbe cried.

'That coat,' she interrupted with amused disgust. 'That didn't come from Israel and we don't want it here. That fur hat. That blackness. That gloom. All from the ghetto.'

Rebbe Itzik stepped back, appalled. This brazen girl was challenging the symbols of his life, the honored traditions of ten generations of holy men in Vodzh. 'This is the dress of God,' he began.

'Don't tell me that!' she cried, cutting off his claim. 'It's a badge of shame forced upon us by Gentile overlords.' It was then that she lost her control for a moment, so appalled by what this frightened little man proposed doing to her impending land of Israel. Unfortunately, she chanced to look at the rebbetzin, standing by the fire–where Elisheba of Gretz had stood, caring for her three orphaned children who had later accomplished so much in Israel–and in a moment of fury Ilana brushed her hand across the old woman's head, knocking her hair to the floor. The rebbetzin stood in shame, her bald-shaved head exposed in all its knobs and veins. Her wig lay on the stones.

'May God forgive you,' the rebbe whispered in a voice of anguish, terrified to think that any Jewish girl would do such a thing. He stooped, picked up the wig and returned it to his wife. The rebbetzin placed it clumsily on her bald head, then felt for the edges to adjust them to her temples. She looked pathetic and ridiculous and her husband gave the wig a small twist, setting it right.

'Get out of here,' he whispered hoarsely in Yiddish.

But Ilana, having done the thing, refused to move. 'Where is such a custom in Talmud?' she cried. 'In medieval Poland they used to shave the heads of brides so that Gentile noblemen wouldn't demand to sleep with them on the wedding night. To make them ugly . . . repulsive to everyone but their husbands. So to this day you make your brides shave their heads to make them ugly–then you buy them wigs to make them beautiful. What kind of Mickey Mouse is this?'

'Get out of here,' the rebbe whispered again. 'A Jewish girl who would insult an old woman. What kind of Israel are you building?' With unexpected force he pushed the Palmach girl, the bobbed-haired sabra, from his house.

Ilana stood in the dark street for some minutes and heard from nearby houses the sounds of Passover celebrations, conducted in this hour of travail. What had she done? She saw the baldheaded rebbetzin, with her wig in the dust. Suddenly she pressed her face into her hands and shivered, for she was spiritually alone.

She was standing thus when Gottesmann came back from the building for some food, and he pulled her hands down from her face and saw that she was crying. 'What's happened, Lan?' he asked.

'I struck . . .' She could not form the words, but her husband guessed that they had to do with the Vodzher Rebbe, so he kissed his wife and told her to stay where she was. Gently pushing open the door he entered to speak with the rebbe, and after a while came back, very somberly, saying nothing, to take Ilana's hand.

'Where are we going?' she inquired.

'To apologize.'

'No!' she protested.

'You come here,' he whispered with fire in his voice. He dragged her back unwillingly and placed her before the old rebbetzin. 'My wife wishes to apologize,' he said in Yiddish.

Silence. Twist of the arm. Silence. Another twist. Then in Hebrew, 'I'm sorry . . .'

'In Yiddish,' Gottesmann whispered.

'I'm sorry,' his wife repeated in Hebrew. He twisted her arm again, hurtfully, and she said for the third time in Hebrew, 'I'm sorry. In the street I cried for shame.' She pulled her arm away from her husband's grip and covered her face.

Gottesmann, mortified by the scene, was about to take his wife from the room she had insulted when the old rebbetzin intervened. 'Children, it's Passover,' she said. 'You shall greet Elijah here.' And she forced both Gottesmann and Ilana back into the center of the room to help her celebrate what she suspected would be her last Passover. 'Find the leaven!' she whispered with the excitement of her youth, and Gottesmann felt a great lump rise in his throat as he realized that this old woman on this Passover of doom had secreted bits of leavened bread about her house, even though she could not possibly have known that she would have visitors. So, halfway between panic and fantasy, he poked into obvious places and cried, like a child years ago in Gretz, 'Mother! I've found some leaven you overlooked,' and with embarrassment, as if she were a careless housewife, she burned it in the fire, as the Torah commanded.

Thus the house was purified. She brought her guests rickety chairs and served the pitiful shreds of food she had set aside for this holy feast: the bitter herbs, the unleavened bread, but no meat, for Safad was starving. She had, however, managed to find two beets, from which she had made one weak cupful of the traditional red soup symbolizing the Red Sea: in old Russia she had made bucketfuls for Passover. Then her husband tied his belt tightly, put on his sandals and took a stave, so as to be ready for immediate departure should the Lord command, and the four celebrants wrapped bits of unleavened bread in small parcels to be slung over their backs as if they, too, were fugitives fleeing Egypt. And finally the rebbe poured a little Safad wine into their glasses, after which he prayed, '"Blessed are you, O Lord, our God, King of the universe, who has kept us alive until this moment."'

To Gottesmann the moment was unbearably painful. The last Jewish feast he had attended in Gretz with his large and illustrious family had been the Passover of 1935. His Great-Uncle Mordecai had read kiddush that night and fifty-five glasses of wine had been poured, for Scholem the novelist, for Yitzhak the professor of chemistry, for Rachel who had pioneered social work in Hamburg, for five rabbis, two poets, three musicians and a handful of honest businessmen. It had been a Passover of singing and sorrow, for Gottesmann's father had foreseen what must transpire and later that week had sent his son

Isidore to Holland. Fifty-five glasses had been filled with wine that night as the great family sang, "'One kid, one kid for two zuzim,'" and of the fifty-five all but two were to die in the holocaust. "'Who has enabled us to reach this moment,'" the Vodzher Rebbe prayed, and Gottesmann felt that he could not accept this moment; he experienced a recurrence of the dizziness that had overtaken him that morning in the heart of the Arab villages. Very carefully he placed both hands about his wineglass to control their shaking.

When the prayer ended the rebbetzin left the table and opened the door slightly, so that a stranger passing in the street might have access, while her husband poured a fifth glass of wine and placed it aside, should the stranger enter; and then began one of the profound, sweet moments of Jewish life, which that night saved Gottesmann's sanity. At Passover, which is a joyous feast celebrating the deliverance of Jews from Egyptian bondage and their flight into freedom, it was customary for the youngest male child of the family to ask in a song-song voice four traditional questions whose answers would explain Passover, and having no male children the rebbe and his wife and Gottesmann turned to Ilana, as their loved child, and she blushed.

At the agnostic settlement of Kfar Kerem the Jewish holidays had not been celebrated, for the hard-headed followers of Shmuel Hacohen had come to believe that much of Jewish religiosity was both archaic and an insult to reason; but if individual families wished to observe Passover, which did memorialize freedom, they could. Netanel Hacohen and his wife had never done so, but at the homes of friends Ilana had several times celebrated the noble holiday, so she at least knew the rough outline of the ritual. Hesitantly she whispered the famous preliminary question: "'Why is this night different from all other nights?'" Then in a soft voice she asked the first question: "'Why on other nights do we eat leaven, but tonight only unleavened?'" The other three Jews chanted an answer and she stumbled her uncertain way through the second question: "'Why on other nights do we eat all vegetables, but tonight only bitter herbs?'" Again the listeners chanted the explanation and she started the third question.

She forgot what it was. Gottesmann blushed as if he were a nervous father whose child was being watched by hundreds. The rebbe fidgeted. Finally the rebbetzin pointed openly to her hands, whose washing was the subject of the third question, but Ilana thought she was indicating a chair. 'Oh, yes!' she cried brightly, like a happy child. "'Why on other nights do some sit relaxed and some sit uneasily, while tonight all sit back in comfort?'" It was the fourth question but no one corrected her, for a burst of gunfire came from the Arab quarter and Gottesmann leaped to his feet, grabbed his rifle and was gone through the open door.

Acting on reflex Ilana also jumped from the Passover feast and reached for her gun, but she was halted by the rebbetzin. 'This is the night of Passover,' the old woman said, forcing Ilana back into her chair. Then she went to the door, and again cocked it open as her husband passed on to that portion of the feast at which he asked, "'Why do we leave the door open? Why do we pour the extra glass of wine?'" and Ilana was required to answer in the lovely fairy-tale nonsense of tradition that the door was left open for the Prophet Elijah to join this feast, and by tradition all turned to watch the half-opened door to see if just once Elijah might appear; but when Ilana looked she prayed that it might be not Elijah but Gottesmann. The firing grew heavier.

When the legendary songs were ended, with the rebbe's high voice singing of the joy the Hebrews had known when escaping to freedom, even though it was the freedom of the desert without water or food, the celebration reached that strange and very Jewish moment when all present chanted what appeared to be only a nursery rhyme:

> 'One kid, one kid
> That father bought
> For two zuzim.'

With a joy unbroken by the hammering of Arab bullets the rebbe and his bewigged wife sang of 'the angel that slew the butcher that killed the ox that drank the water that quenched the fire that burned the stick that beat the dog that bit the cat

> That ate the kid
> That father bought
> For two zuzim.'

Neither Elijah nor Gottesmann came through the door that night, so the three waiting Jews sat at the table through the long hours and inaugurated that probing dialogue between the blue-eyed rebbe and the sun-tanned sabra which was to continue through the eight days of Passover and into the beginning of May, days when it seemed as if the compressing Arabs must crush the Jews at last, days during which only an extraordinary heroism kept the Jewish quarter of the old town viable. That the Jews of Safad resisted was a miracle, truly it could be called only that, for from all vantage points the Arabs poured down a steady rifle fire, picking off any Jew who moved unwarily. Yet somehow the stiff-necked Jews hung on, outnumbered, outgunned, outmaneuvered; and during this heroic defence of an area that could not possibly be held, but which all were determined to hold, Ilana and Rebbe Itzik talked.

REBBE in Yiddish: Do you really believe that against God's expressed will you can establish a state of Israel in the Holy Land?
SABRA in Hebrew: Yes. Men like my husband . . .
REBBE in Yiddish: How do you dare to call him your husband? You're not married.
SABRA in Hebrew: I call him my husband because my father summoned two neighbors, and in their presence announced, 'My daughter is married. Have lots of children.' Isn't that the way Jews were married on this land four thousand years ago? Were there rabbis then?
REBBE: Years pass and people grow wiser. Through many centuries the Jews found it best that their daughters marry in a certain way. Formally. With community sanction. You're not strong enough to live by your own laws. But you will be strong if you follow our sacred traditions. If you marry your tall Ashkenazi legally. As wise persons do.
SABRA: You keep speaking of traditions. It's I who am going back to the great traditions of this land. To the traditions of the patriarchs . . . Moses . . . Aaron . . . Jacob, men who lived in freedom. It's you who want to ignore those traditions and substitute ugly little tricks picked up in Poland and Russia, where Jews lived like pigs.
REBBE: You may not respect countries like Poland and Russia, but for two thousand years the Jews of the world have been forced to live in such countries. What happened to them there has determined their history, their character.

Would you erase Maimonides, who lived in Egypt? And Baal Shem Tov, who lived in Poland? And the Vilna Gaon, who lived in Lithuania?

SABRA: Yes. We're going to build a new state here, not a pale copy of something that was pitiful even when it existed in Poland and Lithuania. We want new laws, new customs, new everything. And we insist that this newness be based upon the Jews as they were in ancient times. On this land.

REBBE: But what existed then has meaning only in terms of what took place in the intervening years. Of all the Jews who have ever lived in the world, nine out of ten never saw Israel. Are you going to pick your tradition only from the one-tenth who happened to live here?

SABRA: Yes. If the nine-tenths got so badly off the track we'd better forget their errors.

REBBE: And you're willing to throw over all the wisdom accumulated in the Talmud?

SABRA: Yes. You rabbis have made of the Talmud a prison of the spirit, and if we have to surrender what goodness there is in the Talmud to break out of that prison, we'll do so. Then go back to pick up what's good and necessary.

REBBE: Do you believe that one generation of Jews will have sufficient wisdom and moral insight to rebuild what it took our greatest minds, Akiba, Maimonides, two thousand years to construct?

SABRA: These are radical times. If we choose wisely we can rebuild.

REBBE: Don't you respect the Talmud?

SABRA: No. When my grandfather came to Tiberias nearly seventy years ago he was stripped naked and beaten by the Talmud scholars in that town. They said his idea to put Jews on the land was folly. When he brought over a settlement from Russia the Jews took one look at the land he had selected and they all wanted to run in behind the walls of Tiberias and study Talmud. They had escaped one Talmudic ghetto but sought refuge in another. Anything that does that to a people is wrong.

REBBE: Have you forgotten what Maimonides said about Jews as they built a nation? 'Attach your nation to a true thing which shall not alter or be destroyed, and raise your voices in a faith that shall never fail. In this covenant stay, in this religion hold fast, in this your faith remain.' Is there a better counsel?

SABRA: No. But you have said that you're against the state, so why worry about its form?

REBBE: I am always concerned about what Jews do.

SABRA: So if we have a state, you want it to be as old-fashioned as possible?

REBBE: I want all Jews to live within the fence of the Talmud. Have you forgotten what the great Rabbi Akiba said? The fish were having a difficult time with the nets in the stream and the fox called, 'Leave the dangerous water. Come up on land,' and the fish were about to do so when their leader asked, 'If we are having a difficult time in the water, which is our element, how much more dangerous will be the land, where the fox waits to eat us?' If Jews have difficulty within the Talmud, which is their element, how much worse will they be without it?

SABRA: My real complaint against the Talmud is my father's . . . and my grandfather's. That rabbis with narrow consciences interpret it. The Torah says simply, 'The seventh day is the sabbath of the Lord thy God: in it thou shalt not do any work . . .' That's straightforward. But the rabbis write whole books about what a man shall not do on Shabbat, and when Safad is about to fall to the Arabs you bring out those books to halt sensible work. If we win an Israel for you, do you expect to enforce each detail of those many books?

REBBE: Whether I leave Safad alive or not is God's will. If we die, we shall die as we have died in the past. But if I am to be saved, I shall insist that Israel observe every law that God gave us.

SABRA: As interpreted by you?

REBBE: You frighten me when you rely so arrogantly upon your personal judgment as to what will be good for the state you plan.

SABRA: Not my judgment. The judgment of all who bring the state into being.

REBBE: Don't you know what has happened to Jews when they relied upon their own illumination? When they by-passed the Talmud? Up this street used to live one of the most alluring Jews of history, Dr Abulafia. Assisted by others of similar power he developed a mystical insight into the nature of God. An insight which he made available to every man. Each man his own rabbi. God talking personally to each man as he talked to Moses our Teacher. Perhaps new commandments to be delivered direct from God without the searching analysis and intervention of the rabbis.

SABRA: Would you as a rabbi veto what God himself has spoken?

REBBE: Of course. God tells us what is good for the world and the rabbis study his word to determine what is good for man.

SABRA: Then if our state has an elected parliament like England, or a congress like the United States, you would be willing for a group of rabbis to review their laws and say what should be obeyed and what should not?

REBBE: Of course. Someone must do it, and this is what rabbis are trained to do. Because in the days following Dr Abulafia, when each man was his own rabbi, who came upon us offering his credentials and crying that he was the Messiah but Shabbetai Zevi? A Turkish Jew from Smyrna. Given to fits of exhilaration and depression. And his movement swept through the Jews of Europe, so that men in Vodzh were convinced that in 1665 the world would enter paradise in compensation for the Czmielnicki massacres of the decades before. Those were exciting days, wonderful for Jews ... and then you know what happened? Shabbetai Zevi, the savior of the Jewish people, was captured in Constantinople and before even one torture was applied he converted to Islam. Our great savior had the courage of a mouse, and the damage he did to Jews of the world cannot be calculated.

SABRA: You believe the rabbis could have prevented the debacle?

REBBE: Only rabbis can keep Judaism pure. The rabbis of Jerusalem knew that Shabbetai was an imposter and said so. The rabbis where he first spread his poison gave the same warning. And a hundred years after Shabbetai Zevi vanished from history as a good Muslim, he was followed by another who was worse, Jacob Frank. He, too, was the Messiah and he, too, was opposed by the rabbis. But he was persuasive and gained great power. He taught that to know goodness man must first know evil, and under his spell the poor men of Vodzh initiated abominations of the body, and all in the name of the Messiah. And when Judaism was well corrupted, what did Jacob Frank do?

SABRA: I don't know of him. What did this one do?

REBBE: He said that the Talmud should be publicly burned, which it was. And then?

SABRA: What?

REBBE: He led his whole congregation to the Catholic cathedral, where they were baptized.

SABRA: He did?

REBBE: But even the Catholics found they didn't want him. They discovered that when his Catholic Jews prayed to the Trinity they meant God, Shabbetai Zevi and Jacob Frank, so they locked Frank up in a monastery. Why, even Safad has produced its own false Messiah. The legendary Joseph della Reine, who followed in the footsteps of Shabbetai Zevi in that he, too, converted to Islam. So you see, we Jews cannot be trusted if we stray too far from our rabbis.

SABRA: Then you see a people permanently bound by the old laws of the Polish ghetto?

REBBE: I see, when the Messiah comes, a Jewish state. In France or America agnostics are free to build any kind of state they wish. But a Jew who believes in the one God is not. It must be a Jewish state, and it must take into account the totality of Jewish law. And that law is what the rabbis say it is.

SABRA: Ours will be a Jewish state, but it will go back to the Jewishness of four thousand years ago, before your eastern European corruption.

REBBE: Jews are alive today to fight for your state only because the ghettos you despise kept them alive. And they were kept alive only by the force of rabbis administering the Talmud in every tiny community. You exist today because my grandfather existed in Vodzh and fought the Poles and the Russians and the Germans before them. Without him you would not be. And what sustained him? What sustained the Jews of Vodzh against oppressions that the mind of man prefers not to recall? An unalterable faith in the laws.

SABRA: If we are to keep ghetto Judaism alive, I would sooner see the Arabs win.

REBBE: There is no other that can be kept alive. For it is the inheritor. And Jews above all people exist on their inheritance.

SABRA: We're making a new inheritance. In Vodzh your grandfather and his good Jews waited in the synagogue and bared their throats for the pogrom. And his grandfathers waited for Czmielnicki and his gang. No more, Rebbe. If the Arabs are to kill us in Safad, they shall have to kill every goddamned Jew, and before they get to you, they'll have to shoot me down, because I'll be killing them to the last minute with this rifle. We are the new Jews.

REBBE: *Mein tochter*, you do not make a new tradition by blaspheming. You girls, so proud of your rifles and your drills. Standing side by side with your men, where you should not be. This is no brave new tradition, but a very old one, and of it Moses himself said, 'When men strive together one with another, and the wife of the one draweth near for to deliver her husband out of the hand of him that smiteth him, and putteth forth her hand, and taketh him by the secrets: Then thou shalt cut off her hand.'

SABRA: I have never heard a more preposterous straining of a text to prove a point. If an Arab reach out his hand to strive with my husband, I shall shoot that Arab between the eyes. I am a daughter of Deborah, and when we win Safad I shall dance and sing as she did.

REBBE: I am distressed when you speak of power and force of arms. You forget what Moses our Teacher said: 'The Lord did not set his love upon you, nor choose you, because ye were more in number than any people; for ye were the fewest of all people.' It is our task to illuminate the rest of the world by our allegiance to the one God.

SABRA: It's our task right now to win a nation, and we're going to do so.

REBBE: You speak with such contemporary arrogance that I have trouble in reminding you that perhaps we rabbis are the ones who best understand the world. My brother in Vodzh is more orthodox than I, more removed from life, as you might say. May I read the response he wrote in 1945? It has done more to save the lives of girls like you than anything you will ever do.

Question: Two fair Jewesses of Vodzh have come to me much distraught because their husbands and their families refuse to accept them back into the bosom of their homes, and the reason is that each girl has tattooed in bold letters on her right forearm the words FIELD WHORE FOR THE GERMAN ARMY. Their husbands argue, say the girls, that their marriage bonds are dissolved because of the use to which the girls were put in the slave camps. Their families argue that the girls should have died in their shame, and an uncle says that they should have cut off their arms before allowing Jews to see the uses to which they were put. What to do?

Response: The law on this matter is so clear that any man can understand it. Any married woman who becomes a prostitute shall, like the wife of Hosea, be put aside. The husbands are correct in thinking their marriages dissolved. And the law says that any daughter who becomes a prostitute shall be taken to the edge of the city by her own father and there stoned to death. The families are therefore also correct in thinking that their daughters have dissolved the family relationship, according to the law.

But that cannot be the end of the matter, for in the cases of these two Jewish wives ordinary words do not apply. It is 1941 that we are talking about, and we see four young Jewish brides brought before a tribunal of the cruel ones. The judge says to the two who are not beautiful, 'Go to the boxcar,' and to the other two, who are, 'Have your arms tattooed and go into the whorehouse.' To defy either command means instant death. Had these girls a choice? Does a Jewish girl of good family offer her arm to be tattooed or her body to be abused? Was there one of us in this little town who did not know the terror of the evil ones? How can we forget and today say that this girl should have behaved so, and that this man's wife should have done thus?

I therefore direct that these two women return to their husbands and to their families, and that all receive them as thank offerings of the Lord, that we have been spared. To my synagogue they shall come with honor, to my house with praise. We have all come back from the brink of the grave but few with so clear a mark of God's divine forgiveness as these girls wear. If any man in Vodzh shall speak against them, either husband or father, that man is forever excommunicated from the Jewry of this town and from any other town where this letter can reach.

Now, as to the uncle who advised the girls to cut off their arms, he is right in part and wrong in part. They must wear long sleeves to hide the awful thing that was done to them and they must take no pride in their humiliation. But on the other hand they must take no step to remove this contemptible sign, for God sends signs amongst us for a purpose, and all of us in Vodzh who have survived bear some sign, but none of us a sign so hellish; and when these women move among us they are a walking testimony to the fact that God punishes us Jews terribly, yet redeems us with His love.

The point is, that we must have in society someone who can speak on such matters, and he will have the authority to do so only if he speaks from the Book and only if the Book is old and sacred.

SABRA: Seems to me your brother took a long time to say a simple thing: 'Take the girls back, you fools. They fought the war in their way, you in yours.'

REBBE: You miss the point. You could say it as simply as that, but the listener could believe you or not. When my brother said it the Jews of Vodzh had to listen and to obey. They required some higher authority, some moral authority if you wish, to remind them what the law was and then to say, 'In this case it must not be obeyed.'

SABRA: What you say applies to the ghetto. But not to Israel.

REBBE: What I say applies to the human heart . . . to the continuity of Judaism.

SABRA: There's a famous Jewish saying which I like better than your brother's response, Rebbe Itzik. I think it applies to us in 1948. 'In the palace of the king are many rooms and for each room there is a key, but the best key of all is an axe.' We're in the age of the axe.

REBBE: In Jewish history each age is the age of the axe, but we seek something more permanent. I wonder if you consider what you may be doing to the man you call your husband? The Talmud has a proberb about the man who was studying Torah and came to a cool tree. In Hebrew *ilana.* And he cried, 'How lovely is this tree,' and in pausing under it, in disrupting his study of the Torah, he had not only committed a great sin but has also put himself in danger of death itself.

SABRA: This, of course, I do not accept. Gottesmann and I will have children, and they will inherit a noble land, which we will rule together without rabbis.

REBBE: The rabbis you will have with you always, for your heart will call after them.

SABRA: Not this heart.

REBBE: Not until you come home with your arm tatooed . . . in Arabic.

On the morning of Thursday, May 6, the dialogue ended. The final partition of Palestine was only nine days distant and the Arabs besieging Safad received an order from the Grand Mufti's high command in Jerusalem:

Safad must be immediately cleared of Jews and converted into our permanent headquarters for northern Galilee. Once we are secure there, we can move out to conquer all of northern Falastin.

So that afternoon the final push on the Jewish quarter began. Sniping was intensified and Jews began to die. House by house the Arabs tightened the noose, even crossing over the stairs to do so, and in the Vodzher synagogue men prayed.

THE TELL

John Cullinane, as he retraced the ground that had been involved in the battle for Zefat, told Eliav and Tabari, 'It was during the height of this battle that I just escaped making an ass of myself in Chicago. One of the newspapers discovered that I had worked in this area and knew a little Arabic. The editor asked me for an article about what was going to happen when the Arabs began throwing the Jews into the Mediterranean. I got out my maps, asked our reference library for the latest statistics, and wrote a fairly impressive article pointing out how the enormous Arab superiority in manpower, weapons, training and terrain meant that within three weeks of their initial push they would automatically succeed. I assured the paper and its readers that from my investigations on the spot–I threw in quotes from English experts and a lot of figures–thirty-seven million Arabs against six hundred thousand Jews: "Obviously, the war will be short, savage and for the Jews disastrous."'

'Most experts agreed with you,' Eliav reflected sardonically.

'How was your Arab propaganda received in Chicago?' Tabari joked.

'Fortunately for me I had the good sense ... Moses or Muhammad must have been watching over me. Anyway, on a hunch I took my article around to the chaps at the British consulate to check the figures, and the two top men said they couldn't spot any errors, but when I got home I found that the chap they call the Cultural Attaché had been phoning frantically and insisted upon seeing me right away. He came over and with no formality blurted out, "My God, Cullinane, you haven't submitted that article yet, have you?" I said no, and he fell into a chair and asked for a drink. "Thank God, old man. You've saved your neck." I asked him what he was talking about, and he said, "Well, the Jews are going to win and I don't want you to look a bloody fool in public." I remember that I stopped pouring the drink and gasped, "What? Jews win?" He looked at me with surprise and said, "Of course. Everyone knows that!" I pointed out that his own superiors hadn't known it, and he laughed, "They don't know their bums from third base. They think that because some dotty English colonel has been teaching the Arabs how to ride camels that somehow an army has bloomed in the desert." He said a lot more, most of it profane, then told me something that helped make me a prophet in Chicago. He said, "Look at it this way, Cullinane. It's positively impossible for the Arabs to move a motor cavalcade of petrol and ammo from Cairo to Gaza." I called up in my mind's eye the map of the area ... saw the roads and the various conditions and corrected him. "You forget. There's a good paved road now. They're not driving over rocky wadis any longer." He banged his glass down and cried, "You miss the whole bloody point. So do the military blokes at the office. They see the figures on paper. Egyptians, eighty thousand armed troops. What the bloody hell good are they in Cairo if the fighting's in Gaza? They see on paper, Egyptians, eight hundred heavy guns. What are they going to fire at from the pyramids? Take my convoy of essential military hardware. It's moving up to the front under the command of two colonels. It forms up in Cairo one night, and before it leaves the city Colonel One sells to his cousin who's operating in the Cairo black market all the spare tires. Every one. At the first inspection point Colonel Two allows his uncle to steal half the reserve supplies of gasoline. At the second inspection point Colonel One sells off two thirds of the ammo. At the first village a large operator in the black market, a nephew of Colonel Two, offers to buy half the trucks and pay in cash. And at the border the drivers of the remaining trucks decide to steal the machine guns and sell them to the Jews." I remember how he dropped his arms and made his fingers flutter like leaves falling from a tree in November. "So you see, Cullinane, it's morally impossible for that convoy ever to leave Egypt." His argument was so seductive that I tore up my essay and we got stinking drunk together and collaborated on an analysis of the war that gained me some notoriety. In fact, Paul J. Zodman read it and he was so gratified to find someone who thought his Jews might win that later on he put up the money which is now paying my salary, and yours, and yours.'

The three men walked to the flight of stairs that had once separated the Arab and Jewish quarters, and to the left they could see the deserted mosque, so marvelously proportioned and with such pleasing juxtapositions of wall and dome and minaret; it was a minor work of art gracing the hill and lending character to the deserted Arab houses that clustered about its base; while to the right they could see the blunt, squat old synagogue of the Vodzher Rebbe. It lent neither the countryside nor its encroaching mud-walled houses any artistic dignity, but it did cry out the fact that to its doors had come, through the centuries, stubborn men who believed that there was a God who was one, and who in the affairs of men played a significant role. if the men would permit Him to do so.

Tabari sat on the stairs with his elbows on his knees and his chin propped on his knuckles. He said to Cullinane: 'Have I ever told you about the defense of Acre? You know, as Sir Tewfik Tabari's son I was handed the job of defending the old city, and I certainly had the men and the machines to do it. I was particularly pleased about the fact that in the caravanserai of the old Venetian fonduk we had ammunition enough to blow up all of Falastin. In particular, we had two million rounds of British ammunition. Two thousand ammo cases of a thousand rounds per case. And other goodies to match.'

'I fought at Acre,' Eliav said.

'What happened?' Cullinane asked.

'You ever read about the fall of Acre in 1291?' Tabari asked. 'That time it was Mamelukes attacking and Christians defending. But the Christians were broken into about ten different autonomous groups: Venetians, Genoese, Templars, Hospitallers ... This time it was Jews attacking and Arabs defending, and we were broken into four thousand groups.'

'Four thousand?' Cullinane asked.

'Yes. I'm the only general in history to command four thousand one-man armies. We had Iraqi Arabs who had slipped in for the kill. We had Lebanese Arabs who had come down to open shops as soon as we had won. We had some Egyptians, some Jordanians, a lot of Syrians, a few Arabians. I had Falastinian Arabs from Jerusalem who wouldn't speak to the Arabs from Haifa, and I must have had about three thousand valiant tigers whose sole ambition was to loot Jewish stores. They were willing for the other Arabs to fight the Jews, but their job was looting.'

'Was it that bad?' Cullinane asked.

'Worse. Because on the ground floor of the caravanserai there was a thin, ugly, mean-tempered Arab whose uncle knew the Grand Mufti, which gave him peculiar powers, even over me. He had the key to the ammunition depots in the Crusader vaults, and he refused to hand out a single cartridge unless his uncle said it was all right, and his uncle refused to act unless he felt that the Grand Mufti of Jerusalem would approve. He drove me mad. I'd plead for more ammunition ... a raiding party ... two hundred men. He'd refuse to issue it. One day I thought: I'll shoot that ugly bastard and take his key; but he must have guessed what I was thinking, because he warned me: "Don't think that you can get the ammo by shooting me. Because I keep the key hidden."'

'What happened to him?'

'When the Jews approached the city as if they intended to fight, he jumped into a sailboat and fled to Beirut.'

'The key?'

'He took it with him.'

The Arab push on the afternoon of May 6 would have ended the Jews had it been followed that evening by a house-to-house mop-up, but for some reason which Gottesmann could not understand, at dusk the Arabs halted their advance, providing the Jews with time to regroup. But it was apparent that the defenders could not hold out much longer, for MemMem Bar-El was exhausted and Gottesmann was near to falling apart. His nerve was quite gone, and Ilana wondered if he could last another day. Of the small command group only Nissim Bagdadi was in good shape, and he seemed to be living off his fat.

That night the Palmach held a gloomy meeting in Ilana's house and the plans discussed were those of a prostrated remnant, courageous enough to go through the final motions but lacking the energy to devise any tactics other than wait and hold; and as they talked in the midnight hours they heard frightening sounds coming out of the wadi below the cemetery, and Gottesmann shivered. If the Arabs were launching their final push, he'd have to go but . . .

Then voices were heard, as if the red-capped Iraqis and the white-robed Lions of Aleppo were cheering one another on for the kill, and petite Vered grabbed her submachine gun and pushed open the door. Through the starlit night the voices grew stronger. They came from people singing, men . . . women. Now even Gottesmann could hear the words, the defiant words in the night:

> 'From Metulla to the Negev,
> From the desert to the sea,
> Every boy is bearing arms,
> Every girl is standing guard.'

It was Vered who spoke first. 'There must be hundreds.' She dashed from the room. Bagdadi followed her and Bar-El, finding a strength he thought had vanished.

'Come on, Gottesmann,' Ilana cried.

'I'll wait.'

'All right.' She left him sitting there, staring at the open door, and hurried to overtake the excited Jews running down the narrow streets toward the cemetery, but at the corner of the Vodzher synagogue she stopped dead and stood alone in the night. 'It's a trap!' she said. 'They're Arabs, and when we've gone down to meet them the others will attack across the stairs.' On the spot she turned, lowered her rifle and sped alone to the vital sector, but when she got there, ready to fire, she found nothing; for any would-be invaders were paralyzed by the sounds rising from the wadi.

Two hundred Palmach troops arrived that critical night and leading them came Teddy Reich to add a new dimension to the Jewish effort. Wiry, alert and charged with that intense fire that came from knowing there was no alternative–'We capture Safad or we're pushed step by step into the sea'–he characterized the impassioned Jewish command as it was to operate for the next eight months. Dressed in faded khakis, with hand grenades hanging from his webbed belt and a revolver convenient to his right hand, he somehow managed to handle with his one arm a small Shmeisser submachine gun. His left sleeve he kept neatly pinned at the shoulder. He was a short man and his tense body seemed to have been transmuted into rock, for when he assembled the local leaders it required only his appearance to reassure them. 'We've come to do a job,' he said.

After brief introductions of his lieutenants–'Gabai, Zuchanski, Geldzenberg, Peled, Mizrachi'—he marched out to a night reconnaissance of Safad.

'There are the stairs,' the MemMem explained. 'Up there the concrete police station.'

'How many Arabs inside?'

'About four hundred.'

'Machine guns?'

'At least thirty. Left by the English.'

He moved swiftly to the other end of the Jewish holdings and pointed to the ominous stone house, three stories high with a flat roof. 'Defended the same way?' he asked.

'Yes,' Bar-El nodded.

He then returned to the middle of the line and stood for some time looking up at the menacing Crusader ruins dominating the entire town; then he climbed to the roof of a Jewish house to view the most forbidding of all the Arab installations, the great fortress on the mountain back of town, built solidly by the English and impregnable. It had thick walls, abundant food and a sure supply of water. Looking out of the night this fortress was foreboding in a special way. It seemed so powerful, so unassailable by ordinary men. Gottesmann, trying to control his nerves, thought he heard even Teddy Reich gasp when he saw the monstrous thing.

If Reich did suffer shock at seeing the Arab positions, he hid the fact. 'Back to headquarters,' he snapped, and in the quiet hours of the night he held a commanders' meeting that none who attended would ever forget. Taking a steep-sided bowl he inverted it on the wooden table and said, 'Men, this is what we face. The flat part is the Crusader hill. The flanks of the hill are divided into six parts. The Arabs hold five of these parts. We hold one.' Gottesmann closed his eyes. Somewhere he had heard those words before: 'Stone house . . . cement police station . . . Crusader ruins.' Once someone had shoved such a bowl across a table and the sound echoed in his ears . . . echoed. He was about to shout something when the incredible words of Teddy Reich struck him.

'So,' the one-armed German said, 'that being the case, what we shall do, as promptly as possible . . .' The wiry commander stopped, looked directly at each of his lieutenants, focusing at last on Gottesmann, to whom he said, 'We'll move out every man, every woman, and capture those three strongholds.'

'Capture?' Bar-El gasped.

'Yes. Up the hill. Across the Arab road. And we'll smother each of the three points.'

Even the men he had brought with him were astounded and for a moment no one spoke. Then Bar-El pointed to the area above the bowl. 'And what about the fortress? Up there?'

Now it was Teddy Reich who had nothing to say. He took a deep breath, leaned back, then came forward slowly and grasped Bar-El's hand as it indicated the massive fortress. 'About this we shall think later.' He caught the looks of fear and with a sudden leap grapped Bar-El by the shirt. 'We'll leave it!' he stormed. 'Because I tell you that when the Arabs up there hear that we've taken the stone house . . .' His fist crashed onto the table. 'The concrete police station . . .' Another crash. '. . . and the top of that bowl. Men,' he shouted, 'it's the Arabs up there who will be worried. Not we Jews in Safad.'

He knew that it was essential to convince his handful of men that this quixotic scheme of taking the fight to the Arabs could succeed, so before they could discuss it among themselves he started working with dizzy speed. 'You,

Zuchanski. You saw the stone house. How many men? You'll have to take it floor by floor. Lot of fighting . . . same as Haifa. How many?'

Zuchanski mumbled, 'Well . . . with Gabbai and Peled . . .'

'They're yours. How many?'

'Thirty.'

'Pick them out.' Zuchanski hesitated, and Reich snapped, 'Pick them. Now!' The detachment for the stone house was chosen.

'You, Bar-El. How many men to capture the Crusader ruins?'

'If I had Gottesmann, we could use forty-five . . . fifty. It's spread out, you know. Trenches.'

'Fifty men. You have them.' Then Reich looked at the remainder and said, 'The police station . . . at the head of the stairs. That's for me. And for Bagdadi. Can you still dynamite a wall?'

'Yes,' replied the placid Iraqi.

Then Teddy Reich saw Vered and stopped the military planning. 'Aren't you Pincus Yevneski's daughter?'

'Yes,' said Vered shyly.

'Why haven't you written to your parents?'

'They'd make me come home.'

'Where are you staying?' Vered pointed at Bar-El, handsome and bleary-eyed, and Reich smiled at the dashing man.

'Wait a minute!' Bar-El protested.

'Oh, not sleeping!' Vered blurted out.

The men of the Palmach burst into nervous laughter, hilarious and bawdy. 'Not sleeping!' some of them echoed, and they began poking their fingers into Bar-El's cheeks.

'All right! All right!' he growled.

'Ilana,' Teddy commanded, 'you see that Vered stays with you. Understand? Now as to the girls, they're not to be in the attack positions, but they are to protect the flanks. I suppose you want to be with Gottesmann, Ilana?'

'Of course.'

Reich asked the others, who attached themselves to one unit or another. Finally he came to Vered Yevneski. 'Where do you want to fight?' he asked.

'With MemMem,' she said quietly.

Reich closed the meeting by saying that he wanted six young boys–under thirteen–right now. Ilana knew where she could find some, and in a few minutes the six little boys, two with lovely curls dancing beside their ears, stood before the Palmach commander, who asked, 'Which of you six is the bravest of all?' Each of the boys stepped forward. 'Good. Now if you had a very difficult job to do, in two teams, who would you want for your partners?' The two boys with curls moved together. The four without curls made their group. 'Good,' Reich continued. He reached forward and grabbed the fringes that peeped from beneath the shirt of one of the orthodox boys. 'Your name is?'

'Yaacov,' the boy answered.

'Yaacov, I want you to take your friend and go as close to the Arab quarter as you dare. Geldzenberg and Peled here will stay in the shadows and protect you with their guns. And you're to call out to some make-believe friend . . . You're to cry as loudly as you can, "The Palmach have brought a great cannon." If anyone should happen to ask about the cannon, you make up whatever answer you want. Understand?' The boys nodded, and Reich said, 'Good. Now let's all go in the street and let me hear how loud you can shout.'

The six boys went with Reich into the darkness, and Gottesmann could hear them crying, four in Hebrew, two in Yiddish, 'The Palmach have brought a cannon,' and by the time the thin little voices had faded in the direction of the Arab quarter Gottesmann felt sure that the enemy must hear. But then he himself heard Teddy Reich whispering to Ilana, 'You think Gottesmann can pull himself together for the attack?'

'I think he'll make it,' she replied.

The secret weapon which the Palmach had lugged into Safad was the kind of implement that terrifies soldiers, especially those who must operate it. When Bagdadi inspected it, and he knew more about explosives than any of the rest, he came back to tell Ilana and Vered, 'It may not frighten the Arabs, but it scares hell out of me.' He took them to the housetop on which the home-welded device was installed: a triangular base about thirty inches wide at one end had supports rising from its point, and from them was slung an adjustable length of steel casing cast somewhere in Germany by one H. Besse. It bore the number 501 and was about five inches across and twenty-eight long, making a rude kind of mortar into which could be dropped a massive shell that looked like an oversize potato masher–big and blunt on the far end, trim and narrow in the handle–which fitted in the barrel of the mortar. 'It's these fins that make the noise,' Bagdadi explained, pointing to the four steel projections jutting out from the business end of the crude weapon. 'When the shell flies through the air these whine as if they were alive. Sounds awful but doesn't do much damage.'

'What's it called?' Vered asked.

'Davidka,' Bagdadi explained. 'Little David. It's to help in our fight against Goliath.' He pointed toward the concrete police station, which in a few days he would have to assault.

That night the davidka was fired. As Bagdadi had foreseen, the cumbersome shell made a hideous noise as it flew through the air, and it must have frightened the Arabs, but it did no harm, for it failed to land on its nose, so its fuse did not explode. The Jew in charge therefore came up with an expedient that horrified Bagdadi: before the davidka was fired, a length of ordinary fuse was jammed into the nose and lit with a match. Then the firing charge was ignited and the burning potato masher was sent through the air. If it landed on its nose, it went off. If that missed, the burning fuse would explode it. The first two shots worked. What worried Bagdadi was this: 'What happens if the firing charge backfires and leaves the potato masher in the barrel–with the fuse burning?' The Palmachnik in charge pointed to a girl. 'If that happens, she runs out and jerks away the fuse. We hope she makes it in time.' The girl was about sixteen.

The futility of davidka became apparent when the Arabs wheeled into position some real artillery pieces and began pumping heavy shells into the crowded Jewish quarter. The results were sickening, for when the large English shells exploded they ripped mud-and-stone houses apart and crumbling was excessive. Some Jews were buried alive. Survivors ran into the street, abusing the Palmach and crying, 'Until you came with your davidka the Arabs left us alone.'

Rebbe Itzik went through the narrow alleys, pointing out, 'It is God's judgment upon a willful people,' and as the Arab shelling increased, new gloom settled upon the Jewish district, whose residents could not know that soon Teddy Reich intended to rush out and silence the insolent artillery. At this critical moment support reached Reich from an unexpected quarter.

There was in Safad in those final days a Rabbi Gedalia, a sallow-faced, black-bearded man of forty, somewhat stoop-shouldered from much study of the Talmud. He was a withdrawn man and normally one would not expect him to be of much help in these critical hours, but after a searching review of the situation Rabbi Gedalia had reached the conclusion that the Jews had a chance to gain a state in Palestine but only if the holy city of Safad were kept in Jewish hands. He therefore gave the pious Jews of his synagogue directions quite contrary to what Rebbe Itzik was saying: 'Go out and help the fighters. Do anything they demand of you, for with God's help they shall win.'

He himself moved among the Palmach, counseling Teddy Reich, Bar-El and the others: 'You must not think of the odds against you as forty to one. Because most of the Arab soldiers are not fighting for a cause in which they believe. What do the Iraqis and Syrians really care for Safad? They're good fighters and I'm sure they're good men. But this holy place is not their home. It is ours.'

As Rabbi Gedalia talked, the tough young fighters gained strength from his quotations from the Torah, which they accepted as history if not as religion: 'Moses our Teacher foresaw days when his Jews would have to storm up a hill to capture a town like Safad, and he said, "If thou shalt say in thine heart, These nations are more than I; how can I dispossess them? Thou shalt not be afraid of them: but shalt well remember what the Lord thy God did unto Pharaoh, and unto all Egypt."'

As time for the assault approached, he quoted God's heartening promise to His people when they faced trials: '"And ye shall chase your enemies, and they shall fall before you by the sword. And five of you shall chase an hundred, and an hundred of you shall put ten thousand to flight."' As he spoke, this thin, sallow man of forty communicated to all his conviction that the Jews would win.

On the afternoon of May 9, when Arab artillery looked as if it must knock out all Jewish resistance in Safad, Teddy Reich convened his last meeting of the men who were to storm the Arab heights. He spoke confidently, reviewed tacts, and advised everyone to get some sleep. 'Till eight o'clock,' he said quietly, after which he lay flat on the floor and slept.

At Ilana's the old gang met for the last time: Bar-El, Bagdadi, Gottesmann and Vered Yevneski. Ilana slapped together some food and studied her husband apprehensively: 'You seem tired, Gottesmann.'

'I am,' the veteran confessed. 'I wish it were ended, the whole war.'

'Gottesmann!' Ilana laughed. 'It won't be over for years. After we take Safad we get right on a truck and move down to Jerusalem and from there we march to Gaza.' Her husband lowered his head.

Bagdadi chuckled when he thought how surprised the Arabs at the police station were going to be: 'They must believe those concrete walls will protect them forever. Wait till the dynamite starts!'

'You think you can take it?' Gottesmann asked, looking up.

'Of course,' the Iraqi cried. 'Don't you think you can capture the ruins on top?'

'No,' Gottesmann said.

Bagdadi expressed no surprise at this assessment. Instead, he drew up a chair and placed his fat hands on the table. 'To tell the truth, Gottesmann, I don't have much hope, either. That is, not unless a miracle happens. But I'm sure one will.'

'What kind?' Gottesmann asked sullenly.

'Don't mind him,' Ilana laughed from the kitchen of the old house. 'Before a fight he's always pessimistic. Remember how he was the day we bombed the lorry. I'll bet you this, Bagdadi. He'll capture the ruins before you take the police station.'

The five friends, the kind of young Jews upon whom the fate of Israel depended in those lonely days, ate a meager meal, then sat talking of the hours ahead. Ilana, still perplexed by her dialogue with the rebbe, said, 'I wonder what kind of Israel we're building tonight?' And the MemMem said in his pragmatic way, 'Kill enough Arabs now and worry about the state later.' She looked to Gottesmann for help to combat this grievous error, but he was staring at his knuckles.

'The Israel I have in mind,' Bagdadi offered, 'is one where the Jews of Iraq and Iran and Egypt would be welcome. To work with the better-educated Jews of Germany and Russia. Believe me, Gottesmann, you may not think so now, but this state really needs the Sephardim. To build bridges with the Arabs when the war's over.'

Bar-El yawned and said, 'We need you, Bagdadi, but we need sleep more,' and the three men found places to catch a little rest before launching their assault up the hill. When they were well asleep Vered asked softly, 'Is it nice, Ilana, living with a man?'

The older girl looked down at her tall German husband, twitching nervously in his sleep, and replied, 'If you're lucky enough to catch one like Gottesman . . .'

'What is there . . . I mean especially?'

Again Ilana studied her sleeping fighter. 'I can't say,' she replied.

Vered was silent for some minutes, then asked, 'Is going to bed . . . I mean, is it so important?'

Ilana laughed. 'How important do you think it is?' she asked.

Vered blushed and smoothed her hair. 'I suppose it's very important.'

'Ten times that much,' Ilana said quietly. 'Maybe fifty times.'

'I'm ashamed I made such a fool of myself the other night . . . when Teddy Reich came.' Neither girl spoke, then Vered asked shyly, 'If you were me, and if MemMem . . .' She hesitated, and the girls looked down at the sleeping dandy. He was a most attractive young man. Ilana could think of nothing to say, so Vered observed, 'The trouble is, after the war's over I want to go to university.'

'I'm going back,' Ilana assured her.

'Even if you have children?' Vered asked.

'Especially if I have children.' She grew excited and moved her hands as her grandfather had done when explaining to others what Kfar Kerem would one day be. 'We mustn't have the women of Israel a dull lot.'

And when the hour came, and the fighters moved out toward their horrifying targets, from the house next door appeared Rebbe Itzik's wife in her wig, calling, 'Go on, children. God will lead you as He led us out of Egypt,' but the rebbe himself did not hear his wife's blasphemous words, for he was in the Vodzher synagogue praying with two old men, the last of his congregation to support him in opposing the battle that was about to start.

At eight o'clock all units were in take-off position. The night was dark and Teddy Reich was hoping that a surprise rush might carry the Jews well into the front lines of the Arabs before the latter knew what was happening; but as he was about to give the signal to move out, an ominous thing occurred. A drop of rain fell. Then another. Rain in mid-May was impossible. It rarely happened, but here it came, drop by drop. Frantically the Jews looked at each other, trying to assess this unexpected development, then Rabbi Gedalia whispered to Teddy Reich and Bar-El the tremendous commandment of the Lord to His Jews: '"Behold, I have set the land before you: go in and possess the land which the Lord sware unto your fathers, Abraham, Isaac, and Jacob, to give unto them and to their seed after them."' Reich whistled and the attack moved forward.

To climb from the Jewish quarter to the police station was difficult even in times of peace—one had to twist and turn up narrow alleys before attaining the upper plateau—but to negotiate this dangerous terrain on a rainy night, with Arabs blazing away at point-blank range, called for true heroism, and Reich's men displayed it. When necessary they fired with cold resolution, astounding the Arabs by pressing forward until, at nine o'clock, they reached the gray concrete walls of the police station itself. Bagdadi and his team of dynamiters brought their stuff into position against the stout walls, but when they ran back to protect themselves from the blast, nothing happened. The unexpected rain had put out the fuses.

'In again!' Bagdadi shouted, and he led his angry men back to the wall. Two were killed.

Once more the rain put out the fuses, and for the third time Bagdadi called, 'Here we go!' His fat, clumsy courage was the inspiration his men needed, and this time Teddy Reich's team held off the Arab fire, and Bagdadi lost no one. Nor did he manage to ignite the stubborn dynamite. The Iraqi thought of the number of times he had seen dynamite go off almost by itself, and it made him curse.

Reich called his team back and tried to ignite the explosive by rifle fire, but nothing happened. From the Crusader ruins directly above the police station came many rounds of frenzied fire. 'How does it sound up there?' Teddy shouted to no one in particular.

'Sounds like Ilana's winning her bet,' Bagdadi replied.

'What do you mean?'

'They're going to take the top before we get the station,' Bagdadi growled. He was off for the fourth time to assault the wall, again without result. 'Damn the rain!' he cried, as drops ran down his fat face like tears.

At four-minutes after ten the team handling the davidka threw potato masher number one into the far end of the Crusader ruins, and the whine and subsequent explosion were horrendous to hear, for to insure firing, the Palmach were using eighteen pounds of black gunpowder where an ordinary gun would have used two. 'You can smell the cordite down here,' Bagdadi said in disbelief.

At ten-twenty-five potato masher number two headed for the Kurdish quarter, with equal noise but with little effect, except that when it exploded it seemed to make the May rain turn into a real downpour. Reich called to Bagdadi, 'Any use trying to explode our dynamite?'

'Let's wait,' the Iraqi replied, and through the rainstorm the police station remained in Arab hands.

Then davidka launched shots three, four, five at the Arab souks, at the mayor's house and at the ammo dump behind the girls' school, and as the last explosion died away, Bagdadi screamed in unsoldierly fashion, 'Teddy! Look!'

Through the gloom, down the side of the Crusader hill, came Isidore Gottesmann and Ilana Hacohen. They were running like children, and Ilana was shouting, 'Teddy, we've taken the whole hill. It's ours!'

For a moment Teddy Reich held his hand over his face, muddy rain running down his wrist. Then he kissed Ilana and asked, 'The stone house?'

'Great difficulty.'

'Take it,' he said, and as the two ran off to that stubborn house, he said to Bagdadi, 'Now we knock out this station.'

The dynamiters, exhilarated by the news from above, darted once more through Arab bullets, reached once more the face of the concrete stronghold, but try as they might, they accomplished nothing. It was frustrating, bitterly disappointing. From above they could hear the Palmach song of victory, yet if the police station were held by the Arabs all would be lost. The Arabs inside, knowing this, fired back with cruel effect and the Jews were driven off.

At about three that morning Ilana and Gottesmann returned to the plateau.

'The stone house is ours!' they cried, and Teddy shouted, 'Everyone here!' and with desperation the reinforced Jews rushed at the powerful concrete installation, again accomplishing nothing.

The rain halted, and Bagdadi promised, 'Now we can explode the place,' but again the fuses failed to work and his valiant effort came to naught. Of his original team only he was left. He was crying.

It was now a few minutes after four and Teddy Reich was in despair. If dawn came, lighting the streets, the Arabs in the police station–not to mention those in the dread fortress on the high hill–could pick off the Jews with ease. 'Everybody!' Reich begged. 'Let's get this cursed place.'

Isidore Gottesmann felt his nerves going, and Ilana knew that her husband could stand no more. Both wanted to retreat to the Jewish quarter, but neither would do so. 'Once more,' she begged her tall German, and he who had led the fight both on top and at the stone house bit his cheeks and accompanied the next charge on the concrete walls. Nothing happened and Teddy led his men back.

It was now dawn and the Jews could expect from the Arab quarters a violent counterattack at any moment, but as Teddy stood disconsolately at the head of the stairs he began to laugh hysterically. Others ran to him, and they laughed too, like idiots, for halfway down the stairs, in the soft gray light of morning, an old Jewish woman with a shawl over her head was coming out of the Arab quarter, lugging a sewing machine.

'They've all gone,' she called hoarsely.

'They've what?' Teddy screamed.

'They are no more,' she cried, disappearing with her treasure.

Four Palmachniks leaped down the stairs, five, six steps at a time. With rifles ready they moved into the Arab quarter. Soon they fired, but in the air.

'See what's happened!' Teddy shouted. There was no need. From the Crusader ruins Bar-El cried down, 'They've fled from all positions,' and from the direction of the stone house other Jews came running with news that the Kurdish quarter, the sites on the hill, all were empty.

But the key position was not, and stubborn Arab shooting rang out from the police station, so that the Jews had to take cover down the stairs, and there Teddy Reich looked grimly at Bagdadi and asked, 'Ready?' The plump Iraqi nodded, and with quick signals Reich sent many troops against the flanks of the building while he and Bagdadi ran zigzag to the front wall, where they tied down a massive charge of dynamite. Retiring to a corner of the building, where Arab bullets whined at them, they waited, and this time the fuse worked. There was a low, ugly roaring explosion, after which Reich and Bagdadi darted boldly through the dust and into the gaping hole. Jews were at last inside the concrete police station.

The fighting was brief and hideous. In one room a Jew and an Arab, having exhausted their weapons, scratched and bit each other until the Arab finally strangled his opponent, but Bagdadi came blazing in to spray the place. Then he and Reich, in a compelling partnership of German and Iraqi, went heavy-footed room by room, with one-armed Reich swinging his Shmeisser in deadly fashion, until at last Bagdadi stuck his head out the top window, bellowing, 'It's ours! All but the roof.' And in this manner the impregnable station fell.

Only then could the Palmach believe that Safad was theirs. Men came running in from all quarters of the town to report, 'There is no enemy,' and Reich led his leaders on a quick tour of the place to find it mysteriously deserted except for a few old Arabs too weak to run away. From one of these he pieced together what had happened. The old man said, 'My son Mahmoud read about it in the paper.'

'About what?' Teddy asked in Arabic.

'Hashiroma,' the old man said. He didn't understand the word, but he explained, 'When the atoomi bomb fell at Hashiroma the rains came.' He moved his hand through the air simulating a bomb. He mimicked the whining of the davidka and mumbled, 'Don't let the rain touch you, young man. It can eat right through your body.'

The unbelievable had happened. The miracle that Nissim Bagdadi had hoped for had taken place. The Arabs of Safad, that powerful multitude, had heard the ugly whine of davidka, had listened to the unprecedented rain, and had recalled the Jewish children crying, 'A new weapon . . .' In the darkness dilated eyes spread terror, whispers crashed louder than explosions, and finally some fool had cried, 'Atoomi bomb!'

'Where's your son?' Reich asked the old man in Arabic.

'He ran away.'

'He left you? Like that?'

'It was the atoomi,' the old man cackled. 'Be careful of the rain.'

From the safe homes by the mosque of Jama el-Ahmar the Arabs had fled. In the hours before dawn they had abandoned the strong points at the ends of the Heart-Purifying Bridge, where no Jews fought. From solid entrenchments the red-capped soldiers of Iraq, the black-and-white-crowned Lions of Aleppo and the warriors of the Grand Mufti fled. Outnumbering their enemy by more than forty to one, the Arab forces had constructed their own panic, and had then obeyed it.

But Reich's sense of victory was shattered when Vered Yevneski came crying, 'Gottesmann's gone out of his mind!' She said that at the edge of town he had found an abandoned English Land Rover and was now driving down the road to Damascus, pleading with the fleeing Arabs to come back to Safad. It was an act of lunacy and would surely get him killed.

Reich sent Bagdadi to investigate, and the Iraqi Jew, trailed by Ilana and Vered, ran out of town, where they finally overtook the English car, and just as Vered had reported, Gottesmann was driving slowly along the road, pleading with the Arab refugees to come back to their homes. 'We need you,' he said over and over in Yiddish, but the frightened Arabs continued their flight.

Patiently Nissim turned the car around and drove the Jews back in triumph, but Gottesmann sat silent, for he knew that if the Arabs had left permanently, the triumph was somehow tarnished.

In only one spot in all of Safad did the Arabs hold fast—in the great fortress on the mountain back of the town; and when Bagdadi and Gottesmann rejoined Teddy Reich they stared across the wadi at this ominous monster, and Reich could not repress a cry of triumph. 'I told you!' he exulted. 'Right now they're the worried ones, not us,' but the Jewish lieutenants were also worried, for they knew that before long they would have to storm that final fortress, too.

At seven that morning Reich and his leaders met at the head of the stairs, and Bagdadi confessed to Ilana, 'You won your bet. Gottesmann took the plateau before I entered the station.' Then he asked, 'How'd it go up there?'

'You know Gottesmann,' she said with pride. 'Start him down a trench . . .' Quietly she added, 'He was responsible for the Arab collapse. Jumped into the middle of a headquarters area, blazing.'

At this moment one of the Arabs who had been left isolated on the roof of the police station drew a fine bead on Nissim Bagdadi, and the men about Reich heard a soft ping, following which Bagdadi slumped to the ground. Ilana quickly bent over him as Jewish marksmen shot down the Arab, but as she drew her hand away from the unconscious Iraqi Jew's chest, Gottesmann saw the fatal blood and cried, 'No! No!'

He fell on Bagdadi and began tearing away the fat soldier's clothes, but the blood kept coming. 'Nissim!' he cried in a agonizing wail. His hands were smeared with the blood and he shouted, 'Nissim! We need you! The fortress . . .' He continued with incoherent phrases until Ilana persuaded two Palmach men to carry him home, where they placed him on a bed; then they returned to help celebrate the victory of 1,214 stubborn Jews over a final force of some 19,000 Arabs.

For three days Isidore Gottesmann lay in physical and moral stupor. His body was worn out and his mind no longer tried to bring into clear focus the death of Bagdadi, who had symbolized the common destiny of Sephardim and Ashkenazim; the tall German sought the escape of sleep. But on the morning of May 13 Teddy Reich burst into the house, his eyes dancing with joy, whispering, 'Ilan! We've got to waken Gottesmann. Such news!'

'Let him sleep,' Ilana replied, and little Teddy grasped her two hands in his one, danced giddily for a moment, then kissed her. She sat him in a chair.

'It's unbelievable, and I wanted Gottesmann to know,' the wiry leader whispered. 'The fortress . . .'

'What about it?' Ilana asked. Although she would not tell Teddy Reich so, she suspected that Gottesmann had fled reality because the prospect of assaulting that great stone monster was more than he could face up to.

'Remember how the fortress terrified us?' Teddy looked at the sleeping man. 'Maybe that's what's driven him to sleep.' Suddenly, out of compassion which he could not normally express, the driving commander of the Palmach lowered his head and placed his one hand over his face. An ordinary man would have had tears in his eyes. Teddy Reich merely wanted to cover the uncontrollable twitching of his chin. Then came a whisper: 'This morning two boys from a village in the hills went to the great fort . . . door was open . . . nobody inside. They brought us secret papers . . . documents you wouldn't believe. I went up there myself.' He started to laugh. He rose and walked with explosive passion about the narrow room. Then with his solitary hand he produced from his map holder a sheaf of papers which he spread before Ilana. They were secret orders to Arab field officers directing them to evacuate from Palestine all Arab civilians: 'Command them to create maximum confusion and disrupt normal services. Assure them that within seven days Arab armies will capture all Palestine and they can then return to claim not only their old property but any Jewish holdings they desire.'

Reich jammed the incriminating papers back into his pouch, muttering, 'It wasn't the atom bomb that drove them away. It was their own corrupt leadership.' And he stood, feet apart, facing Ilana and swore, 'You and I and Gottesmann could have held that fort for thirty days. But at the first sign of attack, they ran away.' He burst into idiotic laughter, the only time Ilana had heard him do so, and with disgust he pointed at himself: 'The great general! For three days I've been biting my fingernails over that goddamned fort, and it's been standing empty. It was finally occupied by my heroic troops . . . two little boys.'

Possession of the fort brought Ilana a moment of elation, but it could not extend for long, for these were the culminating days when any local victory meant not termination but the beginning of some new responsibility, and Teddy came to the point of his visit: 'They need us at Acre, Lan. We're leaving after sunset.'

Ilana, anticipating what was to be said next, protested: 'Why Acre?'

'Safad all over again,' Teddy explained. 'A key point. Lots of Arabs. No Jews. We've got to take it quickly.'

'You ordering us to help?' Ilana asked.

'I must. Is Gottesmann equal to it?'

'He will be,' she said, and when Teddy left she wakened her husband and told him, 'Tonight we go to Acre.' He said nothing, but he was able to dress, and it seemed to his wife that his long sleep had restored his self-control. His nerves, at least, were steadier.

That afternoon the lovers strolled through the town they had done so much to save. They climbed to the old Crusader ruins from which they could see the lake where they had first made love, and then walked down to the mosques which the Arabs had abandoned. The arts which the Muslims had used in decorating their holy places seemed finer than anything the Jews could show in their synagogues, and Gottesmann said, 'We must preserve these buildings until the Arabs come back.' They sat for some time looking at the Galilee, and Ilana whispered, 'I've only one regret, Gottesmann. I wish I were pregnant.' Her husband started to comment, but she said, 'I'd like to leave Safad tonight thinking that while you and Reich were giving birth to a new state . . .' He tried to say that she and Vered were doing at least as much to win the new Israel, but he could not phrase his ideas, so finally they went back to the Jewish quarter to say good-bye to Rebbe Itzik, whom they had come to think of as their friend, 'our difficult friend,' Ilana called him; but on the way they passed the plaza of the police station, and when Gottesmann saw this formidable building, when he recalled how Nissim Bagdadi had taken it by force of will alone, and when he stood at the spot where Bagdadi had fallen, he trembled and again lost coherence. Then, forming fists, he quieted himself and said, 'We needed him so much,' and Ilana wondered if Reich would want Gottesmann at Acre; but after a while the storm subsided and they left the spot which had affected him so harshly.

Rebbe Itzik bade the couple farewell. 'Get married,' he said, still unwilling to look at Ilana directly.

Ilana answered, 'On one thing you were wrong. We took Safad.'

The Vodzher Rebbe smiled. 'God's miracle did it. Well . . . miracle plus natural force.'

'You mean the rain!' Ilana asked.

'No,' the rebbe replied. 'That God should come down to aid His Jews in the rainstorm was natural. The miracle was that so many Jews could fight together in a common cause.'

'We shall see you again,' Ilana said. 'In Israel.'

'Then we shall begin the real battle,' the rebbe said. 'For the soul of Israel.'

That night Teddy Reich and a group of tested fighters rode out of Safad in a truck to reinforce Jewish troops trying to capture the important Arab stronghold of Acre, and they drove without lights lest they arouse Arab patrols operating between Safad and the coast. All went well until the truck approached the old tell of Makor, which for millennia had guarded this road, and there some Arabs were engaged in an assault on the kibbutz and turned to fire upon the truck. A lively skirmish ensued, at the height of which MemMem Bar-El cried, 'They're running. Knock them out.'

The Jews fanned out across the tell, each shooting at the retreating Arabs, when one of the enemy whipped about and fired rapidly. He hit Ilana Hacohen and she pitched head-first down the far slope of the mound. When Reich got to her she was dead, and he said, 'Fetch Gottesmann,' and two fighters overtook the German Jew, who was climbing back up the mound, his self-control restored by the skirmish.

'Over here,' Bar-El's voice called, and Gottesmann moved through the darkness to where his friends huddled over a fallen body.

'You capture an Arab?' he asked. And when he came to the spot the silent figures separated, allowing him to pass, and he saw that the dead fighter was Ilana Hacohen, her hands still gripping her English rifle.

A terrible cry rose from his throat, involuntarily, a long-drawn wail of anguish. He clutched his chest as if he were a madman and the accumulated passions of ten years broke over him. He rejected the self-discipline he had only just regained and threw himself on the ground beside the stalwart girl who now lay dead. He could not fully comprehend what had happened; the death of Ilana coming so soon after the death of Bagdadi was more than his distraught nervous system could tolerate: a man could bear ten years of war, absorbing one shock after another – family dead, underground partners betrayed, English companions shot by Germans, Jewish refugees drowned off Italy, smiling Bagdadi dead when needed most – a man could stand ten years of that, but not ten years and one day. His convulsive hands reached out to grasp Ilana, the perceptive, the lovable Ilana of Galilee, but all that his fingers could reach was the soil of the mound, the soil from which his ancient people had sprung; and as that earth sifted through his fingers, as he felt its cool impartial existence, he slowly gained strength, and a terrible fury – worse even than his initial wail of despair – possessed him, and he pushed himself up from the soil and turned his back on the dead. Shoving the others aside, impelled by an agonizing vision of the future, tormented and glorious, like the apocalyptic visions that Gomer and the psalmist had known on this mound, he cried, 'I'm no longer Isidore Gottesmann. I'm no longer a German Jew. I'll be the tree that was cut down. My name is Ilan. I'll be God's Man. My name is Eliav, and I shall fight for this land . . .'

Mechanically he started down the steep side of the mound, firing his rifle idiotically, aimlessly, like some mechanized avenging angel gone berserk, and

Teddy Reich said with cold calculation, 'Let him go. At Acre we can use a hundred like him.'

And so the Jew Ilan Eliav left Makor, blazing in fury and setting his feet upon a trail that would lead not only to Acre, but beyond it to Jerusalem and to definitions he could not then have foreseen, blinded as he was by incoherent pain.

The Tell

Schematic diagram of Tell Makor from the south on the afternoon of Monday, November 30, 1964, at the conclusion of the first year's dig. Horizontal scale accurate; vertical scale extended. Solid lines indicate certain sites which will be excavated during subsequent campaigns of 1965–1973 C.E. Observe that the actual distances between levels vary considerably. (For example, as can be seen in the chart on page 700, the distance between Levels XV and XIV is twenty feet, whereas the distance between Levels X and IX is only two feet.) Observe also that the monolith to El, perhaps the most significant of the remains buried in the tell, will be missed by the excavators.

With the approach of November and its threat of rain Cullinane could feel the work at the dig grinding to a halt. His own thoughts were in Chicago, where Vered Bar-El was delivering her series of unnecessary lectures on 'The Candlestick of Death.' Paul Zodman airmailed batches of news clippings showing Vered posed with the fatal menorah, accompanied by captions which explained that six of the king's enemies had been slain and finally the king himself, because, in the timeless words of the Australian journalist, 'he was his own worst enemy.' But when Cullinane read the articles he found that Vered had been honest enough to confess that the story was a fake.

Nevertheless, the clippings disturbed Cullinane because they reminded him of how much he loved this delightful woman: when she peered at him from behind the menorah she was positively enchanting and he longed for her return. I'll propose the minute she gets off the plane, he vowed, but his preoccupation with Vered was interrupted by a newspaper story which altered radically the course of the excavation, not only in 1964 but also for the years ahead.

ILAN ELIAV FOR CABINET POST
FOLLOWING KALINSKY RETIREMENT

J'LEM SOURCES INSIST APPOINTMENT
CERTAIN IF RELIGIOUS PARTIES AGREE

When Cullinane read the news his first reaction was: This is what's been keeping Eliav and Vered apart. But what the relationship was he could not guess and before he could ask Tabari to untangle it, Schwartz from the kibbutz appeared to ask if Cullinane would see one of the women who worked in the dining hall. It was big Zipporah, and Cullinane guessed that she was seeking his help in finding a job somewhere, for she was Rumanian and as such was apt to be ambitious. He doubted that he could be of much help, but against his better judgment he allowed her to enter.

She was a handsome woman of thirty, strong and lively, and he recalled how vigorous she was in the kitchen, how rudely amiable in the serving. When she extended her large hand and smiled he knew he was lost. 'What is it, Zipporah?' he asked.

The pleasant woman sat down, pointed to the headline about Eliav and burst into tears, not feminine tactical tears but great sobs of perplexity and grief. 'Oh, damn,' he growled so loudly that she heard him.

'I sorry, Dr Cullinane,' she sobbed. 'I needing help.'

'I'm sure you do,' he replied banally and even with sarcasm. But as soon as he said the words he felt ashamed and took a quick look at her arms to see if they were tattooed with German slave numbers. They weren't. It wasn't going to be one of those cases, thank God! Relieved, he rose, walked to her side of the desk and offered her his handkerchief. 'I'm sorry, Zipporah. Now, what can I do?'

She blew her nose and looked at the door. 'Can I closing it?' she asked.

'Of course.' He got to the door before her, then escorted her back to her seat. 'Now, tell me what's happened.'

Without speaking she took from her pocketbook the inevitable sheaf of worn papers that every Jew in Israel seemed to have. He groaned. It was to be one of *those* cases. An appeal to the American Embassy, no doubt. When she had her papers in a neat pile she asked quietly, 'Is it true, Dr Eliav going to cabinet?'

He pointed to the headline in the English-language paper. 'I know nothing. But the story seems real.'

'What I wanting to know . . .' The Rumanian woman could not finish her sentence because tears, which she could not control, dripped off her nose and struck her papers.

Cullinane waited for some moments, wondering how Ilan Eliav's putative promotion could cause such a flood of grief. Was the husky girl in love with him? Was she jealous of Vered Bar-El? It was too deep for him, so he shrugged his shoulders and waited.

After a while Zipporah blew her nose again and fought to regain control. 'I so ashamed,' she apologized. 'Usually not crying but the world . . . I wanting help.'

'Now put your papers up here, take a drink of water . . . You smoke?'

'Oh yes!' she cried with relief. After the first puffs she relaxed and asked formally, 'Will you do me the honour to listening, Dr Cullinane?'

'I sure will,' he assured her.

'Here is Zipporah Zederbaum, born Rumania thirty years ago. Married to Isaac Zederbaum nine years ago Tel Aviv. Widow. I working very hard . . .'

'I've seen that. I wish I could find a housekeeper like you in America.'

At this unfortunate word the stalwart girl's composure left her, and she wept for some minutes. 'I sorry,' she apologized. 'My husband . . . I know you hearing many things like this too much . . . but he no good. Really. Not give me one agorot to feeding myself. Ran away with Yemeni girl. Left her and going to America. Never send me no money and while he walking along a road'–she consulted her papers–'in Arizona. He killed by truck. So now my friend Yehiam Efrati . . . maybe you know him? He working in dairy.'

'I don't know him, but he wants to marry you?'

'Yes,' she cried brightly, as if he had solved a puzzle. 'It's so hard, Dr Cullinane. A widow my age. Not easy to finding a man who will to marry her. But he is good man.' She dropped her head and repeated quitely, 'Yehiam, a very good man.'

'You're lucky, Zipporah, to find a man like Yehiam,' Cullinane said enthusiastically. 'Now, what can I do to help?'

'Would you speaking to Dr Eliav for me? If he going onto the cabinet . . .'

'We're not sure of that yet, but let's suppose he does. What am I to do?'

'He must speaking with the rabbis,' she whispered. 'They must changing what they say.'

'What have they said?' Cullinane asked, and the inevitable papers were pushed before him.

'This my birth paper. Good Jewish parents. This my wedding paper. Signed by rabbi. This is a photograph my husband's death paper. Notary public

American here, rabbi's name here. And this Yehiam Efrati's birth paper. Also good Jewish family.'

'Everything seems to be in order,' Cullinane said brightly, checking off the various documents.

'And this,' she said dully, 'what the rabbis in Jerusalem saying.'

Cullinane took the document, obviously official, and read the pertinent parts:

In the case of Zipporah Zederbaum, widow, who wishes to marry with Yehiam Efrati, bachelor, the judges find that a brother of the deceased husband of said Zipporah Zederbaum is still living in Rumania, and that this living brother, Levi Zederbaum, refuses to grant his brother's widow permission to remarry. On this point the law is clear, as stated in Deuteronomy Chapter 25: 'If brethren dwell together, and one of them die, and have no child, the wife of the dead shall not marry without unto a stranger: her husband's brother shall go in unto her, and take her to him to wife, and perform the duty of an husband's brother unto her . . . And if the man like not to take his brother's wife, then let his brother's wife go up to the gate unto the elders, and say, My husband's brother refuseth to raise up unto his brother a name in Israel, he will not perform the duty of my husband's brother. Then the elders of his city shall call him, and speak unto him: and if he stand to it, and say, I like not to take her; Then shall his brother's wife come unto him in the presence of the elders, and loose his shoe from off his foot, and spit in his face, and shall answer and say, So shall it be done unto that man that will not build up his brother's house.'

Long ago the rabbis determined that the widow of a dead man must not remarry until her dead husband's brother give his consent, and it was further agreed that this consent must be given in writing, testified to by proper rabbinical authorities. In this case, all that Zipporah Zederbaum needs do is to obtain in writing the permission of her brother-in-law Levi Zederbaum in Rumania. She would then be free to remarry. But since her brother-in-law refuses to grant her this permission she is not legally free to remarry. And her petition to do so is denied.

Cullinane looked up from the amazing document. His first thought was: She's playing a joke on me. A medieval joke. Then he saw that she wasn't. 'What does it mean?' he asked.

'As it says,' she replied. She was angry and there were to be no more tears. 'In Israel a widow has to get written permission from her dead husband's brother . . .'

'Yes.'

'But why?'

'Our law. Husband's family still has interest in dead man's wife.'

'Does that mean your brother-in-law in Rumania is offering to support you?'

'Support?' she echoed contemptuously. 'No Zederbaum ever helping another.'

'Then why doesn't he sign the release . . . let you get married?' The sturdy young woman handed Cullinane a translation of a letter and sat back clothed in fury as he read it:

Brasov, Rumania
Sept. 3, 1964

To the Rabbis of Jerusalem,

I understand from the incredible document delivered to me yesterday that my sister-in-law, Zipporah Zederbaum, whose husband is dead, is not free to remarry unless I sign a paper indicating that I do not want to marry her and that she is free to marry someone else.

I also understand that if I were in Jerusalem my sister-in-law would have the obligation, when she heard that I did not want to marry her, to take off my shoe and spit in my face.

This is the twentieth century, and if I participated in any way in such medieval rites the authorities in Rumania would be justified in considering me a fool. I refuse to sign any such nonsense and I advise you to forget it too.

In disgust,
LEVI ZEDERBAUM

Cullinane folded the letter and thought: It's about what I'd have written. 'What can you do now?' he asked Zipporah.

'Nothing,' she said.

'What do you mean, nothing?'

'That's why I coming to see you,' she explained. 'After this letter, nothing to do.'

'You mean you have to live the rest of your life unmarried . . . while a man is willing to marry you and support you.'

'Yes,' she said simply.

'It's inhuman.'

'It's the law,' she said, stuffing the papers back into her purse.

'Law, hell!' Cullinane snapped. 'You wait here.' He ran out to the dig, calling, 'Eliav? Can you come in for a minute?' When Eliav approached, Cullinane asked, 'What's this about a cabinet position?'

'These things come up from time to time.'

'But this time it's serious?'

'Could be, but don't tell anyone I said so.'

'Your first constituent is in my office. Woman by the name of Zipporah Zederbaum.'

At the mention of the name Eliav stopped . . . cold . . . refused to move. 'No, Cullinane. It would be most improper for me to see her. Not at this point.'

'You won't talk to her?'

'Look! I know more about her problem than she does. I sympathize. But it would be highly improper for me to speak with her now when I may have to judge her case later.'

'But goddamn it, Ilan. This girl . . .'

'John!' the Jew cried with great force. 'You get in there and give her what consolation you can. And don't meddle in things that don't concern you.'

'I'm sorry,' Cullinane apologized. He watched as his friend stomped off; then he returned to the waiting woman. 'I'll speak to Dr Eliav later,' he fumbled.

'He refused to seeing me, eh?' Zipporah asked.

'Yes, and I understand why.'

'No one seeing me,' she said. 'Nothing I can do.'

'There's no way for you to get married in Israel?'

'None. Here we are having only rabbi marriage, and if they refuse . . .'

'Somewhere I heard that if the rabbis refused, people fly to Cyprus.'

'Who can flying to Cyprus? The money! And if we go Cyprus . . . our children bastards. When they growing up they not marry neither.'

'I don't believe it. You honestly mean that there's no way you . . . Hell, you haven't done anything wrong.'

'There is no way, Dr Cullinane.'

'Then I'll tell you what I'd do. I'd get my things together and I'd move in with Yehiam Efrati . . . now. And if you need help packing, I'll come along.'

The powerful girl, so hard-working, so robustly attractive, obviously longed for a husband, but she was forced to say, 'Unless we married right, what the purpose?'

At lunch Cullinane sought out Eliav, intending to raise hell, but whatever castigations he had in mind were quickly forestalled: 'John, please don't lecture me in this case. Because one of the reasons why I might be taken into the cabinet is to handle just such complexities.'

'Who said complexities? Inanities.'

'As you wish, but this is the law of Israel, and ninety-nine per-cent of our laws are humane.'

'But this poor girl . . . marriageable age . . .'

'I know.'

'Didn't you sympathize with the brother-in-law's letter?'

Ilan Eliav took a deep breath, then said slowly, 'No, because I'm working to establish that Levi Zederbaum'–Cullinane was impressed by Eliav's knowledge of the case–'wrote his letter in the way he did so the local Rumanian censors wouldn't turn him over to the Russian authorities.'

'Suppose you do prove duress?'

'Zipporah can marry.'

'If you fail?'

'She can't.'

'But, my God . . .'

'Shut up!' Eliav cried, and in distress he left the tell and stalked back to the dig, but apparently he was ashamed of his rudeness, for later he returned and said, 'These are difficult days.' He thrust forward a sheaf of papers. 'You think I'm indifferent to Zipporah's case. Look at these.' And Cullinane studied the documents that Eliav would face if he took the cabinet position:

Case One: Trudl Ginzberg is a Gentile German woman from the city of Gretz, along the Rhine. Brought up a Lutheran, she fell in love with Hyman Ginzberg and against her family's predictions of disaster married him. With the coming of the Nazis she suffered grievous persecution. Inspired by some inexplicable love of humanity she volunteered to sew the Star of David on her own clothes, fought to protect her children from Storm Troopers and was kicked in the right eye. Now partially blind. By heroic efforts she saved her children and for four years hid her husband in a cellar, providing him and her family with food by working in a factory kitchen. After the war, when she could no longer believe in God, she scraped together money which enabled her to bring Hyman Ginzberg and their three children to Israel, where the rabbis proclaimed, 'Trudl Ginzberg is a Gentile. Worse, she is an atheist, and we cannot permit her conversion. Therefore, neither she nor her children can be Jews.' No effort on her part, neither her offer to convert nor her willingness to live according to Jewish law, has succeeded in changing the rabbis' minds. She is not a Jew and her children cannot be Jews, either. Can you propose a solution the rabbis would accept?

Case Two: The minute you see Esther Banarjee and Jaacov Jaacov you will know them to be Indian. They came from Cochin and have dark skin, limpid eyes and slim bodies. But they are also Jews. In the fifteenth century their ancesors fled from Spain to Portugal to Syria to Turkey and thence to the coast of India, where they inter-married with dark-skinned natives. In 1957 when Esther and Jaacov emigrated to Israel they were informed by the rabbis that because of some technical difficulty they could not be Jews. Their problem is this: they want to marry but since they are not Jews they cannot do so in Israel. If they were Christians, no trouble. They could marry in one of our Christian churches; but they are not Christians nor do they want to be so. They want to be Jews. In India their ancestors were Jews for more than four hundred years, sharing in the trials and triumphs of our people, but in Israel, because they are unable to provide written records reaching back four generations, they cannot be Jews. What to do?

Case Three: Leon Berkes is the son of an orthodox Jewish family in Brooklyn. He made a lot of money running a string of kosher hotels in the Catskills, and when the state of Israel was proclaimed, felt an inner compulsion to join us, but his business was prospering and required his supervision, so he lingered in America, secretly ashamed of himself and muttering to his friends, 'If I had any guts I'd be over there helping the real Jews.' On his sixtieth birthday he abruptly turned his hotels over to his two sons-in-law, 'fine Jewish boys,' he called them, and came to Israel to invest four million dollars in the Jewish state. Naturally he decided upon a hotel, in Akko, and as an observant Jew announced that it would be kosher. For nearly forty years he had been operating such places and he respected the ancient dietary laws of the Torah, but when he approached the Israeli rabbinate for a certificate he encountered many original problems. The Talmud stated that one could work on Shabbat only in case of dire need, which included the serving of food; but waiters were forbidden to write out meal checks, for that was not essential. Berkes complained, 'It means more work, but if it's the law, okay.' Then the rabbis warned, 'All religious holidays to be strictly observed,' and Berkes assured them that in America he had done so. On holidays he did not allow his hotel band to play music, but the rabbis said, 'We think it would be more respectful if you kept your band silent for nine days before the Ninth of Ab.' Berkes said, 'It's terribly expensive, but if that's Jewish, okay.' Then the rabbis pointed out that the Torah said explicitly, 'Ye shall kindle no fire throughout your habitations upon the Sabbath day,' and Berkes said, 'I never have a fire,' but they explained that in recent years this passage had been construed to mean that no electrical switch, which might accidentally throw a spark, could be operated. They demanded that he stop all elevators throughout the hotel from Friday night through Saturday. He said, 'People are going to grumble, but if it's the law, okay.' But when the rabbis insisted that the automatic doors leading from the dining room to the kitchen must also remain inoperative lest the mechanism accidentally produce a spark, Berkes said, 'This is too much.' The rabbis warned, 'If one door moves, we'll take back your certificate.' So Berkes said, 'You're making it too complicated to be a Jew,' and returned to America. The question: Can we get this good man back to Israel?

'You're taking everybody's problems on your shoulders,' Cullinane said with respect.
'And the most complicated is my own.'
'What do you mean?'
'Remember the day we went to the Vodzher Rebbe's . . . with Zodman?'
'Yes.'
'And the attendant asked "Cohen or Levi"? And we all answered "Israel"?'
'I still remember the Cohens putting the shawls over their heads.'
'And I said I'd explain later.'
'You did. Cohens are priests. Levis are temple attendants. Israels are the common herd.'
'Every Jew is automatically one of these three, tracing back in unbroken lines to the days of the Torah. All Jews named Cohen, Katz, Kaplan, Kaganovsky . . . you can guess the others . . . they're all priests who even today enjoy certain

privileges. Now your Levys, Levins, Lewisohns, Loewes and the rest ...
they're all Levis, and they also have a few privileges.'

'But you poor Israels ...' Cullinane began.

'I'm not an Israel,' Eliav said.

'At the Vodzher Rebbe's you said you were.'

'I did, because I don't take this Mickey Mouse ...' He stopped. 'That is, my
wife ... I never told you about Ilana, did I? She died over there.'

'She what?'

Eliav pressed the warm pipe against his chin and tried several times to speak.
Finally in an offhand way he said, 'I was married to a girl who could have served
as the flag of Israel. She was Israel. She had a very special quality. She was shot.
Right over there. Right ... there.'

'I'll be damned,' Cullinane said. He remembered that first night when he and
Tabari had seen Eliav kneeling on the tell and he was now inclined to say
nothing, but intuitively he knew that silence was not wanted. 'So we've been
digging ghosts?'

'That we have,' Eliav agreed. 'And one of the ghosts has come home to roost
... in a particularly mean way.'

'How?'

'I'm a Cohen ... really. I come from a wonderful line of holy men in the city
of Gretz, along the Rhine. One thing about a Cohen, he's never permitted to
marry a woman who's been divorced ...'

'How's that?'

'Under Israeli law a Cohen is forbidden to marry a divorced woman. It just
can't be done.'

'But you and Vered are engaged.'

'That's right. And if we want to get married we have to fly to Cyprus, get
some English clergyman to marry us according to his law, then fly back to
Israel and live in local sin.'

Cullinane started to laugh. 'We've been trying to dig up ancient history and
all the time we've been living in it.'

'You're wrong,' Eliav protested. 'You've been digging in Judaism but you
haven't tried to understand it. John, we're a special people with special laws.
Why do you suppose I asked you to read Deuteronomy five times? Damn it,
you stupid Irishman! I'm not a Catholic. I'm not a Baptist. I'm a Jew, and I
come from a most ancient people with most ancient laws.'

'I'm beginning to realize that,' Cullinane apologized. 'But this Cohen
business ...'

'You saw Leviticus. The priests "shall not take a wife that is a whore, or
profane; neither shall they take a woman put away from her husband ..." There
it is. And there's no way we can get married in Israel.'

'Wait a minute! Vered's a widow.'

'More important, she's a divorcee.'

'I don't get it.'

'I knew her husband well. We fought together at many places ... a handsome,
dashing young lady-killer. Vered was captivated by him and on the day we
broke the siege of Jerusalem she married him. But when peace came he couldn't
seem to fit in. Never understood that things had changed, so they got divorced.
Then, with the Sinai campaign in 1956, came his second chance. You wouldn't
believe what he accomplished with a column of armored cars, and I suppose
God was gracious, for he died in battle.' He paused to remember a gallant,

undisciplined friend. 'Bar-El was one of the few heroes I've known. An authentic hero.'

'But if Vered's a widow ...'

'The critical thing is she was once divorced. If I intended staying on this dig, that would be one thing. We'd fly to Cyprus, get married there, and if later on the rabbis judged our kids to be bastards, when the time came for them to marry they'd fly to Cyprus too. But I can't join the cabinet and flout Jewish law.'

'You'd give up Vered for a cabinet job?' Cullinane asked in astonishment. And the explosive form of his question satisfied Eliav that the romantic Irishman would face any problems to marry her. His uncle, who was a Catholic priest, his father, who still spouted nonsense, his sister, his friends could all go straight to hell if he wanted to marry Mrs. Bar-El, which he did.

The honest shock of Cullinane's reaction forced Eliav to reply carefully. He said, 'For an Irishman, with an Irishman's secure history, the question is the way you phrased it. But I'm a Jew, and my history is much different. We were two thousand years without a country, John. I and a few ... really, we were a handful ... my wife ... Vered's husband ... and a marvelous Sephardi named Bagdadi, whom I think of very much these days ...' He stopped, and after a long moment said, 'We built a state to which the Jews of the world can repair for the next thousand years. Today that state faces critical decisions concerning its basic structure, and Teddy Reich's convinced me that I'm needed ...'

'Where?'

'In the most critical areas. The question you just asked would make sense if you posed it to an Irishman. But the question to ask me as a Jew is this: Would you, in conformance to Jewish law, surrender Vered Bar-El to help preserve the concept of Israel?'

'Would you?'

Eliav evaded the question: 'The night my wife was killed on this tell our detachment was on its way to Akko. Vered and her man took care of me, because I was pretty much out of my mind. We stormed into Akko, which Tabari held with his Arabs, and about thirty of us Jews went up against ... well, God knows how many Arabs. And somehow I got far ahead of the line and I would surely have been killed, except that this little seventeen-year-old girl came blazing up with a submachine gun. She cleared the street and led me back as if I were her idiot child. I can feel her hand in mine now.'

'Why didn't you marry her?'

'She's a lot more primitive than you think. She was fascinated by the gallantry of Bar-El. When he was gone there was the Cohen business. Who wants to flee to Cyprus? And I was never the dashing buccaneer type.'

The two archaeologists stood for a moment, looking at the minarets of Akko, where Vered Bar-El had fought her way to save Eliav, and finally the Irishman said, 'You've taught me a certain humility this afternoon. I withdraw my question.'

'Thanks.'

'But I pick up yours. Do you intend to marry Vered or to serve Israel?' There was no reply, and after a while Cullinane added, 'Because I'm giving notice right now, Eliav. You marry that girl ... before I leave for America ... or I'm taking her with me. And so help me God, that's it.'

'Vered fought for this country,' Eliav said quietly. 'She'd never leave Israel. She'd never marry a non-Jew,' and by their separate paths the two men left the tell.

Next morning the first of two disruptive visitors arrived, Professor Thomas Brooks, traveling through the Holy Land on one of his regular photographic trips, and since he was an influential board member at the Biblical Museum, Cullinane was obligated to care for him while he was in the Galilee. This was not an unpleasant task, for Professor Brooks was an amiable man, teacher of church history in a small Protestant college in Davenport, Iowa, who made additional income by lecturing through the west on 'Old Testament Times' and 'Scenes from the Life of Christ.' He illustrated his lectures with color slides, which, accompanied by his careful explanations, served better than motion pictures. He was a good scholar, tried to keep au courant with the latest archaeological research, and imparted to his audiences a vivid sense of that tiny area of the world from which the great religions had sprung. He was not allowed, of course, to lecture in Catholic churches, but he suspected that when his screenings were held in public halls rather than Protestant churches many Catholics attended, and he took pains to include in his slides scenes that would have special interest for them.

He was in his late fifties, a fleshy man to whom life had been good, and he traveled with his wife, some years younger than himself, who managed the cameras and the checkbooks. They were a congenial pair, as beloved in the Holy Land as they were back home, and often they had helped rich widows write wills that bequeathed inheritances to the Biblical Museum for its excavations. They were honest people, the Brookses, and they believed in a simple, honest God; but as they finished their photographing tour in 1964 they were disturbed, and they conveyed their apprehension to Cullinane.

'John, I can't approve what's been going on here in Palestine,' Brooks said. As an older man, and as a member of the board that employed Cullinane, he always referred to the director as John, while as a fundamentalist he continued to refer to the new state of Israel as Palestine. 'I don't like it at all.'

'What's wrong?'

'Who wants to see a great gaping ditch running smack down the middle of the Holy Land?'

'They've got to have water,' Cullinane said.

'Granted, but Grace and I reflected many times that all these factories ... these macadamed roads. Really, they destroy the feeling we used to get from this land.'

'They do, John,' Mrs. Brooks agreed. 'I remember when we first came here ... the British administered it then, and it looked just as it must have in Bible times.'

'We took some of our greatest photographs in those happy days,' Brooks sighed. 'I only wish Kodak had had a better color film in those years. The reds have faded from our best slides and we can't use them any more.'

'But today,' Mrs. Brooks continued, 'you can hardly take a photograph anywhere that tells an audience clearly that you're in the Holy Land. Now it's all towns and building developments.'

'I take it you're rather strongly opposed to progress?' Cullinane suggested.

'Oh, there ought to be some progress in the world,' Brooks conceded, 'but it does seem a shame to ruin a land that is so much beloved by people everywhere. I can remember when we first came here, you could find in almost any village a water well which looked exactly as it must have in the time of Christ. We got some of the most extraordinary pictures of women walking to the well with great earthenware jars on their heads. You could have sworn it was Miriam or Rachel. Now it's nothing but deep artesian wells.'

'Your home's in Davenport, isn't it?' Cullinane asked, leaning back in his chair.

'When we can find some time for ourselves,' Mrs. Brooks said. 'Mostly we travel.'

'Hasn't Davenport changed pretty much ... in the last thirty years?'

'Davenport's different. It's not a holy land to anyone. But Palestine ... I hate to say this, John, since you're working on this side, but Mrs. Brooks and I felt much more at home on the other side of the border. In Jordan. They've kept their land pretty much as it used to be. One gets a much better sense of the Holy Land in Muslim Jordan than he does over here in the Jewish sector.' Cullinane noticed that Brooks clung to the old English terminology: the Jewish sector.

'What we mean,' Mrs. Brooks explained, 'is that in Jordan today you can still find hundreds of scenes with people in Biblical costume ... little donkeys ... heavenly-faced children playing by the open wells. You can point your camera almost anywhere and catch a Bible picture. It makes your heart feel warm.'

'You don't get that feeling in Israel?' Cullinane asked.

His use of the current name for the new nation seemed to offend the Brookses, and the professor quickly re-established the accurate terminology. 'This part of Palestine is frankly disappointing. I might almost say irritating. You go to a historic spot like Tiberias, hoping to find something that will evoke for people in Iowa the romantic quality of the place, and what do you find? Housing developments ... bus stations ... a tourist hotel ... and on the very edge of that sacred lake, what? A kibbutz, if you like.'

'And if you do try to take a photo that will catch the essence of the place, you don't find people dressed as they are on the other side. Those wonderful garments that make you think of Jesus or the disciples. No, you find men and women dressed just as they would be in Davenport. Carrying plastic bags back from the supermarket. I saw not a thing in Tiberias that reminded me of the Bible.'

'There were a lot of Jews,' Cullinane said.

'I don't think that's funny, John,' Brooks said. He tried to avoid using the word *Jew*; he had been instructed that the people of that religion preferred to be called Hebrews.

'Aren't you saying, Cullinane asked, 'that the Muslims on the other side look more like Biblical Jews than the living descendants of the Biblical people do?'

'I'm not saying that at all,' Brooks protested. 'But when a land has a special meaning for so many, it ought to be kept ... well ... rural.'

Cullinane bit his lip and tried to keep from smiling. 'A good deal of Christ's ministry must have been spent in cities,' he pointed out. 'Jerusalem, Jericho and Caesarea Philippi. And when you get to St Paul, he seems to have spent most of his time arguing Christianity in the great cities like Corinth, Antioch and Caesarea.'

'That's true,' Brooks said, 'but I believe that most Americans like to think of Bible figures as living in the countryside. It seems to make them more ... well ... reverential.'

Cullinane thought that that might be one of the reasons why Christianity was having such a difficult time with some of its urban adherents, that they could not visualize Christ as inhabiting cities, where more and more of the population chose to live. He said, 'When Jesus was in Jerusalem or Paul in Athens those cities must have been much like New York. I know that when we dig here at Makor we have to remind ourselves all the time that this was an urban settlement, while Akko down the road was always a fairly substantial city. And I'm not at all sure that Jesus went around, or Paul either, looking like a modern-day Arab.'

'I'm fairly well satisfied that they did,' Brooks said. Then, to ease the tension a bit, for he felt that Cullinane was being obstinate in not understanding his basic argument, he said, 'The trip wasn't a failure. Grace and I caught some wonderful shots at Jericho. What a marvelous spot. You could almost feel Old Testament people moving among those ancient ruins.'

'I suppose you got some Arabs to pose for you,' Cullinane said.

'Two handsome fellows. When they took their shoes off they looked just like prophets from the Old Testament.'

'I still wonder if Jeremiah dressed like an Arab.'

'Our audiences think he did,' Mrs Brooks retorted. 'Now, I'm sure you're doing some excellent work here, John, but we couldn't photograph it. Not for our purposes. Because the young people I see out there look like ordinary Americans. It would kill the atmosphere.'

'I suppose in years to come,' Cullinane said, looking up at the ceiling, 'you'll take more and more of your photographs outside of Israel.'

'We'll have to,' Professor Brooks said. 'The Hebrews here simply don't look right. And every new town or factory eliminates one more possible landscape. We're forced to work in the other side.'

'But when Jordan succeeds in transforming itself into a modern nation, then what?'

'I've thought about that,' Brooks said. 'As a matter of fact, right outside Jericho there's some building going on that pretty much spoils that landscape. So next year we're coming back with a great deal of film, and we're going to shoot everything we can and keep it on file.'

'And after that?'

'We'll probably find some backward area of Arabia,' Brooks suggested. 'I think we'll still be able to get some great shots of water wells and caravans down there.'

At the airport, when the Brookses were about to climb aboard the jet that would fly them home to Davenport in less than fourteen hours, Cullinane experienced an irrational urge that he knew at the time would get him into trouble. As his board member started toward the huge airplane, loaded down with cameras and color slides that would evoke the Holy Land for thousands, Cullinane asked, 'Did you get a good shot of our airport?'

The humor of the question escaped the professor, who took it as a personal insult. He was about to say something but the sudden vision of a color slide of the large airport, with taxis delivering Jewish officials with briefcases and soldiers in Israeli uniform, overwhelmed him. He remembered when he had first seen the Holy Land, at the old port of Haifa, where his ship had docked and where a shrouded figure dressed much as Jesus must have dressed two thousand years before, had come ambling along the quay. In that pregnant moment Professor Brooks had sensed what his life mission was to be: to lecture throughout America with slides of the Holy Land showing people how the great religions had originated. And he was not convinced that this could not be done by showing slides of cities or modern developments. The Bible was something ancient. The men who composed it, or who participated in its adventures, were different, and he doubted that he would ever again bother to return to the Jewish portion of Palestine. This brash young digger, Cullinane, irritated him, too, and he thought: I'll speak to the board about him when I get home. Is he really the man we want representing us in the Holy Land?

Cullinane, watching the bewildered man waddle onto the plane, thought: It would break his heart if he knew that when the disciples met in Tiberias St Peter probably said, 'Look, James. We can't possibly get to Jerusalem in three nights,' and James had probably replied, 'We can if we scramble.' He thought of Makor, and reflected on how difficult it was to comprehend any past age: If a town of a thousand people exists for six thousand years, as Makor had, this means that nearly a quarter of a million different human beings must have lived inside our walls. How impossible it is to remember that they were ordinary people, who helped evolve and diffuse Judaism and Christianity and Islam. They didn't go through life posing in bedsheets, and many of their greatest decisions must have been made when they traveled to mighty cities like Antioch and Caesarea, or to significant ones like Jerusalem and Rome.

'God,' he cried, as he uttered the prayer of the archaeologist, 'I wish I could see Makor for one day as it actually was.'

But the vast plane thundered in its chocks. Its jets reverberated. Men covered their ears and the great machine lumbered down the long runway, gaining speed until it rose from the Holy Land, turned gracefully toward the sea and headed for Davenport, Iowa.

As he drove back to the dig, brooding upon Professor Brooks' image of religion, which would condemn an area and a people to ancient ways of life, he became aware that a car was following him and he looked back to see a red-painted jeep that was famous throughout the Holy Land. At the wheel, hunched up like a giant flying through space, sat a very tall blond man, hatless and wearing a dark brown sackcloth clerical habit. His hands grasped the steering wheel as if they were going to crush it and his jeep bounced along at a careless speed. Obviously it was headed for Makor, and Cullinane was pleased to see it coming. He sped ahead, parked his own jeep at the door and ran into the office, crying, 'Father Vilspronck's coming! Tell the architect to get the drawings ready.'

In a moment the door slammed open and the huge brown priest began greeting Eliav and Tabari in the comradeship established through years of working with them at one dig or another. He dropped into a chair, leaned across the desk and caught Cullinane's two hands. 'What contradictory things have you been digging out of my ground?' he demanded, and the question was not preposterous, for by dint of continued intellectual effort Father Vilspronck had made the Holy Land his own in a strange and meaningful way. Nineteen years before, as a young priest from Holland, to which he would return one day a cardinal, he had arrived in Palestine on the same boat that had brought Professor Brooks, and he had asked himself: Would it be possible to determine in a non-hysterical way what happened in the Holy Land during the first four hundred years of Christianity? He had started then to piece together all fragments of knowledge relating to the problem, and as the years progressed he became the world's leading authority on this subject. During one period he had served as a parish priest in Germany, and this had kept him from his chosen work; other years he had spent in Rome close to the powerful cardinals, who had spotted him for preferment, and although he was able there to study the great Vatican documents on Christianity's beginnings, he was unable to proceed with his digging. But always he had managed to find some wealthy Catholic layman who would provide him with the funds necessary to return to

Palestine for his researches. Now he smiled at Cullinane, whom he had known years before in the Negev when they both had worked for Nelson Glueck, and he said in the manner of a bad little boy cajoling his father, 'Well, John, you know what I want.'

'I have them coming,' Cullinane replied, and he asked Tabari to speed up the architect, but before the Arab could do so, the expert from Pennsylvania entered the office with rolls of drawing paper, which he spread upon the desk. They were, as Father Vilsponck had hoped, detailed drawings of the foundation lines uncovered at Level VII, where a Byzantine basilica had ridden over a Jewish synagogue. Giving only a cursory glance at the former, Vilspronck carefully traced out the relationships of the synagogue stones. When he had done this he asked to see the lintel stone that had been found in the basilica wall, and for some minutes he studied the remarkable find in silence. Then he asked, 'Where'd it stand in the wall?' Photographs were produced and the giant priest reconstructed what the men had seen that day. Finally he turned to the architect and asked, 'Have you attempted any projections?'

The Pennsylvanian coughed and said, 'After all, the length of wall we uncovered was only . . .'

'I know,' the priest interrupted. 'But I take it you did make some guesses.'

And the architect flung out a large sheet of paper on which the two walls were shown as found, rock by rock, prolonged into fullscale guesses as to what their finished edifices must have been. If an observer had wanted to witness the true mystery of archaeology, the manner in which living men fight to penetrate the minds of men long dead, he should have seen that drawing of the Pennsylvania architect. As a basis for his deductions, the architect had merely twelve feet of basilica wall running from northwest to southeast; below that he had a right angle marking the earlier synagogue, and using only these slight clues he had drawn the completed buildings, and in doing so had come very close to what the future digs at Makor would uncover.

Father Vilspronck studied the synagogue and asked, 'Why do you make it this size?'

The architect replied, 'Judging from all the synagogues we've uncovered so far, our lintel stone is not large enough for a main entrance. So I must conclude that it rested over one of three small doors. That yields a façade like the one I've drawn. The thickness of the walls is exactly what we've found elsewhere. Working from these hints, I've spent a lot of time in the old synagogues at Baram, Kefar Nahum and Beit Alfa. This is about what we're going to find.'

'I agree,' the priest said, twisting the paper so that he could study the synagogue from fresh angles. He was paying no attention to the later basilica, and Cullinane received the distinct impression that as a priest the big Dutchman was disappointed in what he was uncovering at Makor but as an archaeologist he was gratified. 'Remarkable,' he said finally. 'It bears out what we've found everywhere else.' He shrugged his shoulders, then asked abruptly, 'You done any carbon dating?'

'No need to,' Cullinane said. 'Our date of 351/2 C.E. for the destruction is as good as if they'd left a signed copy of the orders. Our guess as to 330 for the original building of the synagogue . . . plus fifteen or minus fifty as you wish.'

'That's what I thought,' Father Vilspronck said. Brushing away the architectural drawings he asked, 'I suppose you've made a table of probable populations?'

'We have,' Cullinane answered guardedly.

'Care to let me take a look?'

'We'd rather not . . . at this point.'

'How about the synagogue level?'

Cullinane smiled. 'I said we'd rather not, but you knew we would. Usual restrictions?' The priest agreed and Cullinane drew from a locked drawer a document which in the army would have been classified *Top Secret*. He handed copies to each of the archaeologists and watched with amusement as Father Vilspronck darted his eyes directly down to Level VII, where he checked the population figures. As soon as he had completed this, the big man studied the other figures casually.

PROVISIONAL ESTIMATES OF POPULATION

AT SITE 17072584

LEVEL	PERIOD	DATE	HEIGHT OF TELL	TOTAL POPULATION OF GALILEE	MAKOR INSIDE WALL	POPU-LATION OUTSIDE WALL	TOTAL JEWS AT MAKOR
XV	Cave	9800 B.C.E.	0	4,000	0	46	0
XIV	Canaanite	2200 B.C.E.	20	70,000	700	300	20
XIII	Patriarchal	1400 B.C.E.	35	125,000	1400	500	700
XII	Davidic	960 B.C.E.	43	280,000	800	900	1100
XI	Babylonian	605 B.C.E.	44	220,000	500	90	480
X	Hellenistic	167 B.C.E.	48	400,000	720	290	300
IX	Herodian	4 B.C.E.	50	600,000	1000	600	950
VIII	Vespasian	66 C.E.	53	750,000	1100	100	900
VII	Byzantine	351 C.E.	56	1,000,000	600	440	850
VI	Muslim	635 C.E.	60	500,000	700	600	450
V	Crusader	1099 C.E.	60	110,000	600	30	150
IV	Mameluke	1291 C.E.	67	150,000	300	1600	0
III	Kabbalistic	1560 C.E.	77	74,000	0	0	0
II	Turkish	1880 C.E.	72	58,000	0	0	0
I	Independence	1948 C.E.	71	400,000	0	65	65
	Kibbutz	1964 C.E.	71	650,000	0	1485	1485

'I notice that in 1560 C.E. you have the tell standing six feet higher than it does now?'

'Probably did,' Cullinane said. 'Bedouins seem to have mined the place for cut stones in later years, and the height must have dropped considerably.'

The blond priest asked a few more irrelevant questions, then came back to Level VII. 'Would you say that these figures for the Byzantine period are pretty accurate?'

'Just educated guesses,' Cullinane confessed. 'But if the synagogue was that big, it had to serve about eight hundred and fifty Jews. Of course we're extrapolating from Kefar Nahum and Baram.'

The perplexed Dutchman placed the sheet of figures, which summarized so much learning, on the table and slapped it with his big hands. 'At least you're consistent!' he growled. 'Every dig for the last thirty years has confirmed this story of Jewish persistence, and sooner or later we'll have to adjust to it.'

Eliav lit his pipe and asked, 'But you adjusted to it years ago. It's your discovery.'

The priest laughed. 'Half of me accepts. The other half doesn't.'

'Is it so difficult?' Eliav asked.

Father Vilspronck returned the estimates to Cullinane, who collected the other copies and locked them in his desk. For any level the figures might be wrong by fifty per cent, but as the years passed and refinements were made, savants throughout the world would have to adjust their theories to these Makor facts, as the Dutch priest now prepared to do: 'When I went to university the professors had an absolutely clear understanding of the Holy Land. A group of excellent Hebrews lived here for some two thousand years. Their religion grew stagnant and Jesus Christ appeared, luring about half the Jews to Him. The others clung on desperately and in 70 C.E. rebelled against Rome, and Vespasian destroyed both them and their temple. In obedience to God's command that they be a perpetual witness, they wandered homeless through the world while Christianity took over, and it was their punishment to wander until they finally converted to Christ. It was a neat, clean theory and that's what the world believed. My first shock came when I found that in 135 C.E. the Jews, none of whom were supposed to be here, launched an even bigger revolt against Hadrian, and the recent discovery of letters actually written by Bar Kochba, who led the revolt, have had a startling effect on all of us. Once more we were told, "All Jews were driven out," but now we begin to excavate these synagogues of the fourth century and we find there were more Jews here than before. The synagogues were big, handsome buildings. Serving a very large population. Kefar Nahum, Barum, now Makor. All tell the same story. And three hundred years after that, when the Muslims come, we still find large Jewish populations. And four hundred years after that, when the Crusaders came, there were still Jews around.' He stopped and his face revealed his perplexity. 'Something was going on here that the history books did not tell us.'

Father Vilspronck had begun his labors in the Holy Land intending to assemble the testimony that would reinforce Christianity, and it had become the major irony of his life that his work served primarily to tell the world more about Judaism; yet he persisted in his researches, for he knew instinctively that when the honest relationships were revealed, both Christianity and Judaism would be more meaningful and the ultimate conversion of the Jews closer at hand. He also knew something which he buried in his conscience, leaving it to others to develop: the arrival of Jesus Christ in the Galilee did not mysteriously signal the disappearance of competing religions; they survived with stubborn vigor, and if the testimony of the synagogues could be trusted, actually increased their power. It was not until the Greeks, doubling back with the great messages of St Paul, reached the Holy Land that Christianity got much of a hearing in its place of birth. But that was for others to narrate.

The husky priest asked if he could visit the dig, but Cullinane soon discovered that Vilspronck had no real interest in the excavations; he had already visualized most of what had been done. His real desire was to talk with a fellow Catholic, and the two men sat on top of the mound looking toward the minarets of Akko while they discussed one of the prime intellectual mysteries of the world. 'I don't suppose you've found any clues that would relate to Flavius Josephus?' the Dutchman began.

'None. We know from the scars that there was a general destruction of Makor about 66 C.E. It's probably safe to guess that it was burned by Vespasian.'

'Yes, there's that tantalizing passage in the commentary on Josephus: "Jewish tradition claims that Flavius Josephus escaped by night from Makor."' He threw pebbles toward the ravine into which the great Jewish general had fled, abandoning the town to its destruction. 'I'd give a lot if we could find some tangible proof that that rascal had been involved in a site which he had later refused to write about.' The Dutchman clenched his hands and studied the vacant trenches into which he could partially see. 'Isn't it logical to suppose that if Makor were the first Jewish town that Vespasian reached, General Josephus would have been here to fight him? How did he escape by night, and why didn't Josephus himself speak about it? I know why.' The priest rose and stalked about the tell, trying to visualize the town as it must have been two thousand years earlier. 'Josephus refuses to mention Makor because here he behaved in some craven way. He writes at length about Jotapata, only a few miles south, because there he was heroic. I tell you, Cullinane, the man always picked and chose. Always!'

By this means Father Vilspronck hoped to explain away the mystery of Josephus. For a score of years this learned Jew had wandered back and forth across the land that Jesus had trod, and during the very years when the actuality of Jesus must have been greatest. In his books Josephus discusses all aspects of Jewish life, the good things and the bad, and he probes into relationships that were not known until the discovery of the Dead Sea Scrolls; and what the archaeologists are uncovering supports the fundamental accuracy of this vivid reporter.

Yet never once does he mention Jesus Christ, the greatest Jew of his age, nor does he refer to Nazareth, although he writes extensively of cities not more than nine miles away. It is a nagging, gnawing fact that the most acute observer Palestine produced saw fit to ignore the major occurrence of his lifetime, the impact of Jesus Christ upon the world. An honest researcher like Father Vilspronck was therefore driven to ask, 'Was that impact less than we have been led to believe?'

This question the priest was willing to ask, but he had an answer. 'I think that Flavius Josephus consciously suppressed all mention of Jesus Christ and Nazareth, just as he suppressed facts about himself. We know he was a liar,' Vilspronck said. 'Time and again we catch him in falsifications. If he says there were eighty thousand Romans, we find there were forty thousand. If he claims to have been a hero, we discover later that his behavior was despicable. In Josephus we have the case of a loyal Jew who convinced himself that Jesus never existed. He had probably seen the followers of our Lord face to face, yet he tried to erase Him from history.'

Silently the two men watched the sun sink behind the minarets of Akko, and a sense of the immensity of the problems they were discussing descended upon them. Finally Vilspronck said, 'I used to hold Sigmund Freud in contempt. An enemy of my church. Now I find young priests reacting the same way to me. They feel I shouldn't inquire into these matters. But when you start digging into a human soul, or a tell, or a historical concept, you quickly find yourself at levels of rawness you did not anticipate. But they confront you and you follow them to their conclusions.'

He rose to his full height, stalked over to Trench B and accidentally stood above the still-buried water shaft through which General Josephus had fled in the night. Turning to Cullinane he said, 'The complexity of God is so profound and the mystery of Jesus so great that the addition of one more historical problem like the silence of Josephus must be a minor matter. If your faith is capable of encompassing Jesus it can certainly absorb historical contradictions.'

But he was about to be tested by an experience much more difficult to absorb than mere historical contradiction: he was to encounter an exceedingly difficult theological problem. The confrontation happened by accident. He was parking his jeep after having driven Cullinane from the administration building to the mess hall when he said, 'I'd better wash up. I seem to have picked up a lot of dirt on the tell.'

Unluckily, as things turned out, his remark was heard by Schwartz, who said,

'Use my room,' and he led Vilspronck into the darkness.

They had been gone only a few moments when they returned angrily and it was obvious that something serious had happened, for Vilspronck was flushed and Schwartz belligerent. An awkward silence followed, broken by the Dutchman, who said quietly, 'I think I'll skip supper tonight.' He stalked from the hall, wedged himself into his jeep and with a flurry of dust turned it around in a tight circle, a future cardinal who had been able to adjust to whatever new historical evidence the tell was producing concerning Jews in ancient Palestine or Jesus in the Holy Land, only to find himself unprepared to face the reality of either condition as exemplified in a modern kibbutz. As the jeep sped away, Cullinane shouted, 'What happened?' and the big priest called back, 'You'd better look at the signs in your world.'

Perplexed by this reply Cullinane returned to the mess hall and asked for Schwartz. When the secretary appeared, Cullinane asked, 'What did you do to Father Vilspronck?'

'He had a ticklish digestion. Found he wasn't hungry.'

'What did he mean—the signs in my world?'

Schwartz hesitated, not because he was embarrassed by what had happened but because he preferred not to involve Cullinane. Then, shrugging his shoulders, he said, 'Something he saw in my room.'

'Maybe I'd better see it too.'

'Why not?' Schwartz asked indifferently, and he led the way to a dormitory building in which he had been allocated a one-room apartment. As an unmarried member of the kibbutz he was entitled to no more, so that even if he served as secretary for many years, he would still be allotted this one room. It was in no way unusual—desk, chair, bed, water jug, and of course the three essentials: a large bookcase jammed with publications, a record player with its stack of classical records, and a colored reproduction of a painting by Marc Chagall—except that across one wall hung a carefully lettered banner which read: *We did* so *crucify Him.*

This was the banner of younger Jews who had survived Germany and Arab invasion and who no longer cared what the rest of the world thought about them. In early 1964 their motto had become notorious, in an underground sort of way, for at that time Pope Paul VI's visit to the Holy Land drew attention to the possibility that the Catholic Church might issue a pronouncement absolving present-day Jews of blame for the crucifixion of Jesus, and it was widely hoped that this generous gesture would remove the stigma under which Jews had suffered for nearly two thousand years. Some well-intentioned people actually thought that such a statement would deprive anti-Semitism of its moral base and would make it difficult for future hate-mongers to initiate pogroms. Throughout Israel a surge of hope attended discussion of the matter and one hopeful group had attended even written to the newspapers: 'It will be a glorious day when the Christian Church finally exonerates us of our guilt.'

That letter was certainly not signed by Schwartz of Kibbutz Makor nor by any of his friends. They held the offer of absolution to be insulting to the Jewish people and the Pope's visit to be an act of condescension. They drafted a different letter, which Israeli newspapers considered inflammatory and refused to publish: 'It is preposterous for any Pope to come here distributing a forgiveness which is not his to dispense. For two thousand years we Jews have been abused by Christians and it is not their prerogative to forgive us. For them to do so is humiliating both to them and to us, for we are the ones who should forgive them.' As proof of their intention to remain stiff-necked, as God had commanded Schwartz's Jews flaunted their unyielding banner: *We did* so *crucify Him.*

'Take it down,' Cullinane said.

'Are you kidding?'

'Take it down!' the Irishman roared, unable to maintain his placid nature.

Schwartz laughed and this infuriated Cullinane, who grabbed at him as if to catch his mocking head and punch it, but Schwartz easily evaded him and the two stood facing each other. Cullinane controlled his anger and said, 'Right now in Rome the bishops are meeting to correct an ancient wrong. All that you Jews hope for depends on men of good will like Father Vilspronck. And.you insult him.' It was obvious that Cullinane was including himself among the men of good will who sought to improve and protect Jewish-Christian relations, and to him also the sign was offensive.

Schwartz ridiculed his well-meaning counselor and said, 'Nobody takes that good-will crap seriously any more.'

Cullinane flushed and said grimly, 'Then accept my ill will. Take down that sign.'

'Nobody in this room can make me.'

With a leap Cullinane reached the wall, thrusting his fingers behind the cloth and ripping it into two parts. Schwartz rushed up behind him, grabbed at his arms and wrestled with him. Finally Cullinane broke loose, but as he did so, Schwartz got his right arm free and with a wild swinging blow clipped Cullinane along the head and jaw.

The blow so astonished the men that they forgot the torn banner, dropped their arms and stared at each other. Schwartz was ashamed of what he had done and Cullinane was stunned both by the blow and by the furiousness of the struggle, yet he was unable to control his loathing for the sign, so while Schwartz watched he returned to the wall and tore the banner to pieces. 'Neither of us can afford hatred,' he said.

Impassively Schwartz watched the destruction of his sign, then said coldly, 'I don't hate anyone. I don't intend insolence to decent men like Vilspronck. It's just that I no longer give one good goddamn what you think about Jews. Either of you. For nineteen centuries well-intentioned Jews like me tried to accommodate ourselves to what people like you wanted. And where did it get us? We were attentive to kings and Popes. And what did they do in return? Now we've won our own land and we're going to keep it. And what you or Vilspronck or the Pope or General de Gaulle thinks about it is of no concern to me. Not one little bit.'

Responding automatically Cullinane shot out his right fist and caught Schwartz on the point of the chin. Like an amazed oak that had paid no attention to the first chipping axe blows, the dark-skinned Jew tottered, then fell in a heap.

This was the first time Cullinane had ever knocked a man unconscious and he was appalled: 'My God! I've killed him!' But to his relief Schwartz easily recovered, rose to one knee and rubbed his jaw.

'I suppose I deserved it,' he said. And as they walked back to the mess hall Cullinane lavished attention on him as if he were a sick child. Earnestly he said, 'It does matter what we think . . . Vilspronck and men like me . . . because at the time of crisis we might be the ones who will rescue you.'

Schwartz paused to look at the eager Catholic and said, 'For Jews it's always the time of crisis. And no one ever rescues us.' But that night the two men ate together.

Next morning Vered flew in to Lod Airport on her return from Chicago. When she ran down the ramp like a bright little wren come back to resume control of the tree outside the kitchen, Cullinane thought: What an adorable person.

It had been his intention to ride back to Makor with Vered, so that he might propose again, but this was neatly forestalled by Eliav, who pulled her into his car and drove off, leaving Cullinane and Tabari to bother about the luggage. When Cullinane finally overtook them he and Tabari could see in the car ahead the pert figure of Vered speaking rapidly, interrupted now and then by some sharp rejoinder from Eliav, who kept pointing at her with his pipe stem, as if he were a college professor.

'You think this Cohen business will wreck the marriage?' Cullinane asked.

'Something's wrecking it. And remember the particular job they're offering him. He certainly couldn't accept that job on Monday and marry a divorced woman on Tuesday.'

'What do you think of such rigmarole?'

'I take it seriously.'

'How can you?'

'By looking at history. For something like three hundred generations my family has lived in this area. And in that time we've seen a lot of people come and go. But the Jews hang on forever. Because they've had that tight body of God's law binding them together. Today our boy Eliav, who was one of the heroes in the creation of this state, is trapped by the very law he helped preserve.'

'If he had any guts he'd get on the first plane to Cyprus and tell the government to go to hell.'

'John!' the Arab cried. 'You're talking like a liberal Catholic. If the Pope tried to hand you a deal like this Cohen-widow business, you'd ignore him and fly to Cyprus. As a Muslim so would I. But can't you see the difference? Nobody on the outside is forcing Eliav to respect the ancient law. He did it to himself . . . by establishing Israel. I'm sure he didn't intend to set up a state where such law would operate . . . but that's what he's done.' The two men relapsed into silence, which Tabari broke by predicting, 'Within two weeks, John, you're going to have a wife. That girl up there's not going to marry Eliav.'

'You think not?' Cullinane asked hopefully.

'And then the real funny business begins. Out of sentiment you'll probably want to marry Vered at the tell, with the kibbutzniks and old Yusuf as witnesses . . .'

'That would be ending the dig with a bang. You in robes giving the bride away!'

'I'd do it, too,' Tabari laughed. 'But haven't you heard? In Israel such weddings are forbidden.'

'What do you mean? I'd get papers from the American Embassy.'

'Completely impossible. The rabbis say that in Israel no Jew can marry a Christian. Never. So when you propose to little Vered, get yourself two airplane tickets to Cyprus, because you'll never get married here.'

'Outrageous!' Cullinane cried. 'When the Catholic Church tries a trick like this in Spain, the *New York Times* has front-page articles about it. You mean that I . . .'

'I'm in the same boat,' Tabari protested. 'As a Muslim I couldn't marry Vered, either, though I'd like to. We'd have to fly to Cyprus. Matter of fact I did . . . when I married my wife. She's a Christian Arab. And Christians and Muslims aren't allowed to intermarry either.'

'From the way you talk, half the people in Israel who want to get married fly to Cyprus. I don't believe the rabbis issued these rules at all. I think the airlines did.'

In the forward car the conversation was brisk, with Vered saying, 'You needn't be so superior. There are many things about America I liked.'

'Did you see any American Jews?' Eliav asked.

'Yes. And some impressed me very much.'

'Such as?'

'Jews who run hospitals, and endow libraries, great art museums, universities. Of course, I also saw the fat, overdressed dowagers. Plenty of them. But somebody's been giving us a very bum steer about the American Jew. He can be a most powerful person.'

'Would you want to live there?' Eliav asked.

'No. I want to live here . . . where I helped build a nation. And I want to live with you. And I want to get it all settled by the end of this week.'

'Teddy Reich's meeting with the prime minister . . .'

'I don't want Teddy Reich to be involved, or anyone else. Ilan, you're to tell me now. Are we going to get married? When are we going to get married?'

'How can I decide until I hear what Teddy has to say?'

'I'll help you,' Vered said primly, and she handed him a small slip of paper. 'On Tuesday there's an Air France plane to Cyprus. On Wednesday there's Cyprus Airlines. On Thursday there's B.E.A. And on Friday morning there's El Al.'

'And on Saturday I suppose there's something else.'

'There will be no Saturday . . . no Sunday . . . ever.' She folded her hands and kept her eyes straight ahead. When Eliav pointed at her with his pipe she was not looking.

'Is this an ultimatum?'

'The last plane that we will ever consider flies out of here Friday morning. If we aren't on it . . .'

'You'd marry Cullinane? A non-Jew? And leave Israel? I don't believe it.'

'There's an easy test. It comes Friday morning.'

In silence Eliav drove toward Akko, then asked bluntly, 'If I chucked the cabinet and took a teaching job . . . England . . . America . . . would you marry me?'

'Ilan,' she said softly, and her folded hands left her lap and clutched his forearm, 'on the night Ilana died I should have taken over. When I went forward in Akko to save you, it wasn't because you were a valuable soldier. You were a man, a splendid man, whom even then I loved.' She began to cry, and whispered, 'We should have married sixteen years ago, but then I didn't understand. Now I do. Make up your mind, Ilan. I'm proposing to you. Marry me now.'

Eliav kept his hands on the steering wheel and his pipe clenched between his teeth. Staring at the minarets of Akko he turned the car eastward along the Damascus road, and the moment when he should have made his decision passed, and in various airports around the world the four planes that would fly that week to Cyprus tested their engines and were swept out by women wearing overalls. It was Monday.

When the archaeologists reached the dig the mood was autumnal: only Yusuf and his family of twelve worked at the job of closing down the installations and it was obvious that the old man was beginning to find himself isolated in Israel. Already his children were learning Hebrew and adopting kibbutz ways. His three wives were accommodating themselves to Israel, and the pregnant one was even going by herself to the Kupat Holim doctor to discover how to have a baby in a modern way. From their children the mothers were learning Hebrew, and the old patriarch was left alone, a man out of place in a world that he would never catch up with. His eleven underlings, once so subservient in Morocco, now assumed easy control of the family; no longer was he a man of authority, and as the years passed, the half-blind old man would grow in bitterness, while his new land stole from him his dignity, his language and his comprehension. On Tuesday the Air France plane took off for Cyprus and Morocco.

Ilan Eliav did not laugh at old Yusuf in his deepening solitude, for he felt himself to be in a comparable prison. Vered was proving unpredictably difficult; she still insisted upon an immediate answer. 'The last plane leaves on Friday,' she warned. Wednesday came and Thursday, and B.E.A. made its flight. On Friday morning Cullinane, watching two people whom he cherished caught in such a vise, intruded against his own best interests; waiting till he found them together in the ceramics room, he joined them casually and said, 'I'm not using a phrase when I say that what you two are doing to yourselves is breaking my heart. Eliav, if you decide to chuck the cabinet business, if you do fly to Cyprus, I will personally guarantee you work for ten years here at Makor and a teaching position in the Chicago area for the rest of your life. And I'm certain we can find Vered a job teaching archaeological ceramics. I make this offer because I don't want you to reach decisions due to economic pressure.'

'I've been asked to teach at Oxford,' Eliav said dryly. 'Knowing my background you must appreciate how enticing that would be.'

'I spoke only as a gesture of honor. I don't want to marry Vered because you couldn't . . .'

At this moment Vered was consulting her watch, and she seemed to be marking off the minutes one by one, until finally she rose and said quietly, 'The last plane has gone.' Looking at Eliav she placed her hands in his and stood tiptoe to kiss him. 'I wanted you so much,' she said haltingly.

She broke down and Eliav was unable to console her, so Cullinane, moving quietly, placed his arm about her shoulder and drew her away. 'We'll come back to Makor in the summers,' he said. 'When he can, Eliav will leave Jerusalem and work with us.'

She pushed him away and looked at him as if he were a stranger. 'What are you saying, John? I warned you I'd marry only a Jew.' Then, seeing the shock on his face, she muttered, 'Damn, damn,' and ran from the room.

The meaning of her behavior did not become clear until three o'clock that afternoon when Paul J. Zodman arrived unannounced in Israel, jumped into a car supplied by the U.J.A. and roared up to Makor. Bursting into an end-of-week staff meeting he said crisply, 'I stayed out of this for a week. To give Dr Eliav the time he needed to make up his mind. He hasn't married Vered. Neither has Cullinane. So I'm going to. Sunday morning.'

It was Cullinane who said the asinine thing. He stared at Vered, who had regained her composure and was again a little Astarte, her eyes modestly downcast, and then he looked at Zodman, expensively dressed in blue sharkskin, freshly shaved, committed and eager. 'But you already have a wife!'

'Had,' Zodman corrected.

'Oh, my God!' Cullinane cried. 'Is that why you sent me the cable "Come to Chicago"? You knew I couldn't leave and you gambled that Vered could . . .' He saw Zodman and Vered smile, and to his surprise he cried, 'Zodman, you're a plain son of a bitch!'

The merchant brushed this aside and said congenially, 'Look, John! I came here two months ago an unmarried man. I saw two other unmarried men, you and Eliav, allowing an adorable widow . . . So I brought her to Chicago to see if she'd marry me.' There was silence, after which Zodman said quietly, 'She said "No." Wouldn't even let me romance her. Said she was engaged to Eliav and that if he wouldn't marry her because of the Cohen business she might marry you, John, and to hell with being a Jew.'

The group gasped, even Vered. She looked appealingly at Zodman and reminded him, 'You were not to speak of that.'

But Zodman continued, 'Somewhere along the line all of you have loused things up, so on Sunday, Vered and I are getting married and flying back to Chicago.'

Cullinane looked at the various people and said plaintively, 'This dig is going to end just like Macalister at Gezer. My executive goes into the government. My pottery expert flies to Chicago. Tabari, you and I are going to dig this tell all by ourselves.'

'We'll find you somebody,' Zodman joked; but as Eliav had pointed out, it was never easy to be a Jew, and the Chicago millionaire was about to discover this in a most painful way. He proposed to drive Vered that night to Jerusalem to get a permit for their marriage, but Eliav reminded him that he couldn't drive because it was Shabbat. 'Who gives a damn about Shabbat?' Zodman snapped, and he roared his borrowed car southward across the Galilee.

In Jerusalem no one would speak to him on Shabbat and on Sunday he was advised by the rabbinical board, 'Sorry, Mr Zodman, but you can't get married in Israel.'

Without raising his voice he asked, 'And why not?'

'Because we have decided that no divorce granted by an ordinary American rabbi can be trusted.'

'Rabbi Hirsch Bromberg is scarcely average.' Zodman had been on the committee that selected Bromberg.

'He's not on the approved list,' a secretary reported.

Still keeping his voice low Zodman said, 'I also have a perfectly good civil divorce from the state of Illinois.'

'Israel recognizes no civil divorce,' the rabbis replied.

'You mean to say that from this little room you're going to judge all the Jews of the world?'

'In Israel it is our responsibility to say who can get married and who cannot,' the rabbis insisted.

In a very low voice Zodman asked, 'And I can't?'

'No.'

'I'm a large contributor to the Republican party,' Zodman said ominously. 'I know Senator Dirksen and Paul Douglas.' His voice rose to a roar. 'And I will not accept this insult.'

He stormed down to Tel Aviv to see the American ambassador—the state of Israel claimed Jerusalem as its capital and governed the country from there, but foreign powers, still holding that under the United Nations agreement all of Jerusalem was inter-nationalized, insisted upon keeping their embassies in Tel

Aviv and recognizing only it as the capital–but the legal aide to the ambassador assured him that the situation in Israel was precisely as the rabbis had explained it: there was no civil marriage; the local rabbis refused to recognize divorces issued by most American rabbis; and there was no conceivable way by which Zodman could marry Vered Bar-El. 'Of course,' the young man suggested, 'what many do is to fly to Cyprus. Such a wedding does leave the status of the children to be born of the marriage uncertain, insofar as Israel is concerned, but if you don't plan to live in Israel . . .'

'Me? Live in Israel? Are you kidding?' And Zodman drove Vered back to Makor, cursing most of the way.

There it was agreed that Zodman and Vered must fly to Cyprus, as so many other Jewish couples were doing, and in the days required for Vered to clean up her work on the first year's dig, the five leaders of the expedition had repeated opportunities for extended cross-questioning, during which Vered made her position clear: she was leaving Israel not because she liked large cars and air-conditioning, which her friends would charge, saying that she had sold out to the fleshpots of Egypt; not because she was afraid of the future, for she had given ample proof of her courage; not because her allegiance to a Jewish state had flagged, for she knew Israel to be the only tenable solution in a world where other sovereign states had been unable to protect the Jew or give him any honorable alternative to a homeland of his own; but rather because she felt that as a human being aged thirty-three she could no longer bear the burdens of a religion in the throes of becoming a state, with its military problems, social problems, economic problems and especially its complex religious problems. 'I've done my part for Judaism,' she said without bravado. 'I risked my life in more than a dozen battles, lost my husband, lost most of my friends, and I really do believe that I'm entitled to say, "Rachel, from now on you be the Jewess. Little Vered is just too damned tired."'

Her words had such a startling effect on Eliav that Cullinane thought the new cabinet minister might strike her, but he clenched his hands and asked coldly, 'How can you turn your back on all we fought for? Can't you remember Safad?'

And Vered, speaking softly as one who has discovered her portion of truth, however meager, said, 'Do I remember? Eliav, it seems to me we Jews spend our lives remembering, and I've suddenly discovered that I'm sick and tired of living in a land of remembrance. My year in Jerusalem begins with Rosh Hashana when I remember Abraham, four thousand years ago. Then comes Yom Kippur, and we remember everything. The Feast of the Booths and we remember the desert years. Like a great bronze bell tolling over the churches of Jerusalem, we tick off our days and remember our grief. Of course, there are a few happy days. Simhat Torah, Hanukkah, when we remember the victory of the Maccabees, Arbor Day for remembering trees. At Purim we remember Persia three thousand years ago and at Passover we remember Egypt even longer ago. Lag Ba Omer, Shavuot. And on the Ninth of Ab we mourn the loss of Jerusalem. When did we lose it? Two thousand years ago. We have special days to remember Herzl, students, socialists, the United Nations, the brave men who fell defending Jerusalem in 1948, and Independence Day. For years I dutifully remembered and thought it was natural to spend one's life weeping over the dead past, uttering lamentations for things that happened so terribly long ago. It was a burden, but it was our special, inescapable Jewish burden and I accepted it.

'And then I went to Chicago. And I lugged that lousy Candlestick of Death up and down Illinois making speeches to Jewish women's clubs, the kind Israelis like to joke about, and do you know what I discovered? That some of the finest people this world has produced are the Jewish women of Illinois. They live wonderful, satisfying lives without remembering Persia and Egypt and the Maccabees and the Sinai Desert and Jerusalem. They work for the local art museum and build new wings for the hospital and serve on the board of education and pay the deficit for the symphony orchestra and do all they can to make their world a better place to live in. Take away from Illinois what the Jewish women do, and that state would be a dump. And the only thing those women are required to remember is when to make the next payment on the television set. And you may be surprised to hear it, but I can hardly wait to become one of them.'

Eliav clenched his hands and pulled them against his stomach. In pain he asked, 'For this emptiness you'd sacrifice Judaism? For the fleshpots of Egypt, stainless-steel version?'

'Stop it!' Vered cried, beating her palms against the table. 'Stop throwing those old clichés at me. I raise a clear, well-defined issue and you mumble what sententious Jews have been mumbling since the time of Moses. The fleshpots of Egypt. I refuse to accept that any longer.' She waved her hands and placed them over her ears. 'I refuse to spend the rest of my life remembering. I will not remember.'

Eliav, again in control of his bitterness, said quietly, 'Your Gentile neighbors in Illinois will do your remembering for you,' and it was on this point that Eliav and Zodman initiated their acrimonious debate.

ISRAELI: Does Vered think that by going to America she escapes being a Jew?

AMERICAN: She certainly does.

ISRAELI: She escapes until that moment on her honeymoon when the hotel clerk says, 'No Jews allowed.'

AMERICAN: We learn how to avoid such hotels.

ISRAELI: Or until the medical school tells her son, 'Our Jewish quota is filled.''

AMERICAN: They don't put it that way any more.

ISRAELI: Or until a new Senator McCarthy comes along. And fails in his economic promises. And has to use you Jews as his scapegoat.

AMERICAN: Now we have safeguards against that sort of thing.

ISRAELI: Or until some new international tragedy like Nazi Germany . . .

AMERICAN: The world will never again allow a thing like that to happen.

ISRAELI: It will happen before your first son is born. South America? South Africa? Quebec?

AMERICAN: Something will be worked out, I'm sure.

ISRAELI: You sound just like my uncle in Gretz, 1933. And he was right. Something was indeed worked out. And they hung Adolf Eichmann for having worked it out.

AMERICAN: You can't go on scaring the Jews of America, Eliav.

ISRAELI: I don't do the scaring. History does.

AMERICAN: In America we have guarantees that protect us from history. Besides, you overlook one important fact. In America that natural hatred which exists in all people is directed not against the Jew but the Negro.

ISRAELI: If he perishes, you perish.

AMERICAN: You can't apply European experience to America. It's the greatest error I hear Israelis make, and you make it all the time. We Americans are different. Of my non-Jewish neighbors more than half have come from outside countries. We're all minority groups.

ISRAELI: And they brought their anti-Jewish prejudice with them. You say you're different, but it's not because you're an American. It's because you're a Jew, and America will never let you forget that difference. Neither you nor your children.

AMERICAN: Years go by without my experiencing a shred of anti-Semitism.

ISRAELI: You experience it every day, but have become hardened to it.

AMERICAN: Seems to me you're angry with us American Jews for two reasons. We've built a new way of life that's the best the Jew has ever known in this world. And we refuse to emigrate to Israel.

ISRAELI: Let's take your reasons one at a time. As for your new way of life, it's a false old dream in a golden ghetto. A religion that isn't Judaism. A synagogue that's a mere social center and a third generation that thinks it's been accepted by the majority if it names its son Bryan. It's a shallow, ugly, materialistic pattern of life, and it leads to one clear goal: assimilation. The rate of inter-marriage among young Jews in America is over ten per cent and climbing toward twenty-five. A new way of life? No, an old delusion leading to oblivion, when there will be no more Jews.

AMERICAN: That doesn't frighten me. If following Moses for four thousand years has got us where we are, a people totally apart, I think it's time we tried the American pattern. I'll be a good Jew. Vered will be. But if my son Bryan, as you call him, wants to lose himself in the main stream, I say let him do it.

ISRAELI: In that case Israel is really needed to preserve Judaism, and you've been very remiss about sending us immigration to help save the Jewish state.

AMERICAN: Our job is to stay in America and make it the safest home in the world for Jews. And then to share our goodness with our fellow Jews in Israel. And if I may be forgiven a personal reference, I have been careful to share that goodness and have advised my rich neighbors in Chicago to do the same.

ISRAELI: You've been generous with everything but human beings. Have you ever watched an immigrant ship arrive? Mostly uneducated people from Africa. People call them Arab-Jews. Strong-minded Ashkenazim fear that if such immigration dominates for the next hundred years, Israel can only become another Lebantine state. A Middle East backward country in which a handful of European Jews ran things for a while before submerging their state in some kind of honorable alliance with Lebanon or Egypt. And so the vision of a Jewish homeland perishes once more. I'm not so pessimistic. I'm dedicating my life to the proposal that we can establish some kind of Jewish-Arab federation in this area, to the benefit of both. But to do this we must have more highly educated western Jews. And men like you accept no responsibility.

AMERICAN: Indeed I do! I send you every nickel the law allows.

ISRAELI: But people you won't send? Yourself, for instance.

AMERICAN: Me? Live here?

ISRAELI: Yes. Instead of contributing manpower, you take away one of the most highly educated women we have. And next year you'll take away half a dozen of our best-trained young Jews. As a matter of fact, you'd like to take me, wouldn't you?

AMERICAN: Last time I said I'd be proud to have both you and Tabari.

ISRAELI: And you see nothing immoral in this? Using Israel as an intellectual quarry from which to dig the brains your system has failed to produce?

AMERICAN: I believe that a man of talent must go where he can make the best living. And when he's done so, he must share his bounty with others. You can

be sure that when Vered becomes an American we'll send large sums of money
each year to Israel.

ISRAELI: We . . . don't . . . want . . . charity!

AMERICAN: You damned well ask for it hard enough. Every year the U.J.A. man
perches on my desk. 'We must do more for Israel! It's a brave country, fighting
our battle.'

ISRAELI: So you want to keep us a minor Montenegro? A little enclave that
thrills the world because its fighters defend themselves against the Arab circle?
So that Jews in America can feel pride? What would be the moral justification
for such an Israel? But if we can become a beacon of pure, burning light,
illuminating this entire area, forming an alliance with a prospering Arab world
. . . making it a true fertile crescent . . .

AMERICAN: You sound like the U.J.A. man.

ISRAELI: There's no other way to sound. And what I want Israel to become she
cannot become if the Jews of America steal our talent and return only money.

AMERICAN: Where the hell would you be, Eliav, if we didn't send the money? If
there's one thing you Israelis had better quit, it's your flippant charge that the
Jews of America are interested only in material things. I drove to Jerusalem to
see the rabbis, God forbid, and I passed forests planted by Americans,
hospitals paid for by Americans, university buildings bearing American
names, rest homes paid for by Jews in Montana, kibbutz buildings paid for by
Jews in Massachusetts, and, I might add, archaeological sites being excavated
by Americans. If that's materialism, you'd better hope your citizens develop
some, because if you took away the gifts of our selfish, materialistic Americans
this would be a shabby land.

ISRAELI: And if the gifts weren't tax deductible, you wouldn't send us a penny.

AMERICAN: But they are tax deductible because that's the generous kind of
country America is.

ISRAELI: Your money we appreciate. It's your people we need.

AMERICAN: Men like me you won't get. Life in America is too good. Besides,
who would want to live in a land where rabbis have the power they have here?

ISRAELI: You better make up your mind. On your first visit you complained
because our kibbutz had no synagogue. Now you complain because in marriage
we follow Jewish law. What is it you American Jews expect of us?

AMERICAN: I expect Israel to preserve the old customs. I like it when your hotels
are kosher. And no buses are allowed to run on Saturdays. It makes me feel like
a Jew.

ISRAELI: And to keep that feeling alive–somewhere else in the world, not in
America–you're willing to send us ninety thousand dollars a year?

AMERICAN: How do you know what I send?

ISRAELI: It's my business to know. For the money I'm grateful. For the men you
don't send, I hold you in contempt.

AMERICAN: Look here, Eliav!

ISRAELI: Contempt, I said. If you and Vered have a son, would you send him to
Israel?

AMERICAN: Of course I would. I'd want him to work in a kibbutz some summer.
For two weeks.

ISRAELI: You stupid . . .

AMERICAN: You don't seem to understand the fundamental nature of American-
Israel relations.

ISRAELI: Do you?

AMERICAN: A damned sight better than you seem to. Israel must exist. As the focus of our religion. The way the Vatican exists for Catholics. But good Catholics don't emigrate to the Vatican. They stay in Boston, Massachusetts, and Chicago, Illinois, and Los Angeles, California, not to mention Sydney, Australia. And they work like hell and build good Catholic lives and send the money rolling back to Rome. You forget that we have more Jews in New York City than you do in all of Israel. If you take the whole United States, we have three times as many as you do. We're the important part of the Jewish world. And our job is not to come here. Our job is to be the best damned Jews in the world, right in Chicago, and to support you with every expression of good will we can muster ... with money, with tourists, with American votes at the United Nations, with arms if necessary. This country is our Vatican, and if I hadn't seen the Vodzher Rebbe up there in the hills, I'd never give Israel another dime, because he's what I expect of this country. Piety. Kosher restaurants. Men who keep the spirit of Judaism alive. Do I make myself clear?

ISRAELI: It would be a good day for Israel if you never returned and if you forgot us completely. Let us find our own level. Let us make peace with history and subside into a minor colony with an excellent university from which our best minds emigrate each year to Buenos Aires, Damascus, Chicago and other backward areas. Let the rabbis brood over the Torah and Talmud, but let Israel as a vital state perish, because as it is it imposes too terrible a burden. Vered can no longer sustain it in its present form, and you refuse to help. You want us to go back to the old days. When my wife's grandfather reached Tiberias, out of a Jewish population of more than a thousand he found only two or three men at work. The rest waited for the dole from Europe, and when it came they prayed extra hard, insuring sanctity for the Jews who could not live in Israel. Are you proposing to re-establish that system?

AMERICAN: I'm proposing that Israel remain just as it is. That it be the spiritual center of Judaism. That I accept a responsibility for keeping it alive.

ISRAELI: For a man who's made several million dollars, Zodman, you're incredibly stupid. Don't you see that for Israel to prosper is far more important to you and Vered, living in Chicago, than it is to Tabari and me, living here? That Israel protects you from the next Nazism? That Israel gives the Jew dignity you've never had before. How many Jewish taxi drivers in New York have said to me, as I rode to the United Nations, 'You characters over there make me proud I'm a Jew.' You boast of your contributions. You know what I think? I think the state of Israel ought to tax men like you about forty cents on the dollar. To pay for the services we render you.

AMERICAN: How can you expect to hold the good will of a man like me if you talk like that?

ISRAELI: I don't want your good will. I don't want your condescension.

AMERICAN: What do you want?

ISRAELI: Immigration. Your help to stay alive.

AMERICAN: I'm an American and I owe Israel no allegiance. If you keep talking like this I'll stop being a Jew.

ISRAELI: Ah, that's not for you to decide. Cullinane can stop being an Irishman and no one cares. He can announce one morning, 'I'm no longer a Catholic,' and it's his decision. But if you shout for the next ten years, 'I'm not a Jew,' it signifies nothing, for that's a problem which your neighbor decides. Not you. No Jew can ever cease being a Jew.

AMERICAN: In America we're writing new rules.

ISRAELI: But your new rules will be judged by old standards. In Spain hundreds of thousands of Jews said, 'We're no longer Jews. We're Spanish Catholics,' but even after two hundred years Spain said, 'Sorry, you're still Jews.' In Germany the followers of Mendelssohn said, 'We're integrated Germans. We're no longer Jews,' but the Germans said, 'Sorry, your grandmother was a Jew, so are you, forever and ever.' But if you seek a classic application of your theory, go to the island of Mallorca. In 1391 a fearful massacre of Jews swept the place, after which those remaining converted to Catholicism. Study what happened to them. Massacred, burned alive, proscribed, jammed into a ghetto, always loyal Catholics but unable to escape being Jews. The story is too terrible to repeat, but remember this. Each Shabbat those one-time Jews used to eat pork on the public streets to prove that they were no longer Jews, but after five hundred years no real Catholic of Mallorca had ever married one of them, for they were still Jews. And it's our burden to bear this testimony.

AMERICAN: You try to argue that history never changes. America proves that history does change. What happened in Mallorca bears no relationship to what will happen in America. We are free, and our freedom is assured. The whole constitution of our society confirms that freedom, and I trust it.

ISRAELI: I do too, Zodman. Until the day when China becomes a major power and humiliates you in some way. Until the day when A.T. and T. drops to forty and you have another economic crisis. Until Senator McCarthy's successor comes along. Those days will be the test. Some time you should talk with the secretary of this kibbutz. Last year he went back to Russia on a visit. For forty years Russia claimed that it was the new paradise for Jews, and many Jews agreed. You know, when he got to Russia last year not one of his relatives would even speak to him. They looked at him and slammed the door. They paid a trusted friend to visit him in the hotel. At great risk. To tell him, 'Go home. Tell no one that you are related to us. And when you get to Israel, put nothing in the paper against Russia or we will disappear and never be heard of again.' Don't you suppose that if Russia allowed Jews to emigrate, millions would fly to Israel?

AMERICAN: I must believe in the goodness of my country. I want Israel to be here, for others. I want the Vodzher Rebbe to have his synagogue, for others. And I'll pay to keep his synagogue going. But my home, my entire future, must be in America.

ISRAELI: But your spiritual home will be here.

AMERICAN: I'm not so sure. The decisions of your rabbis on cases like my divorce will probably drive us further and further apart. We'll have two Jewries: the spiritual one here, the great effective one in America, and between them little contact.

ISRAELI: No job is more important for each of us than preserving that contact.

AMERICAN: Now Vered and I must leave . . . for the best home the Jews of the world have ever had.

ISRAELI: And when the trouble strikes, Israel will be waiting.

This final exchange took place one night as Schwartz lingered at the table to listen, and when the conflicting points of view were neatly tied into gentlemanly packages, as in a formal debate between men dressed in black ties, he startled the group by voicing the hard truth of the matter they had been discussing: 'You talk as if the future were going to be like the past. It's all changed, Zodman. You live in a much different world. So do you, Eliav.'

'What do you mean?' Zodman asked.

'Just this. A couple of years ago a lot of synagogues were bombed in Florida. Remember?'

'What has Florida to do with me?'

'And it looked as if a strong anti-Semitic wave was beginning. My group here in Israel followed it very closely. And it may shock you to know that if those bombings had continued one more week we were prepared to smuggle armed volunteers into Florida. To train the local Jews. And to shoot it out . . . for keeps.'

Zodman gulped. Cullinane leaned forward to ask, 'You were going to invade Florida?'

'Why not? Germany killed six million Jews and the world has never stopped asking, "Why didn't somebody fight back?"' He rubbed his forearms and for the first time Cullinane saw that each had been badly broken. 'I fought back. So did a lot of others. They're mostly dead now. But if the good people of Miami, or Quebec, or Bordeaux decide some day to liquidate their Jews, I personally shall appear in that city to fight back again.'

A shocked hush fell over the room as Zodman and Cullinane tried to apply this challenge to America, but they were unable to do so because Schwartz was speaking: 'You won't fight back Zodman, because your kind never does. You didn't in Berlin or Amsterdam or Paris. And you won't either, Cullinane. You'll pray and you'll issue most moving statements and you'll regret the whole mess, but you won't raise a finger. And Eliav as a trained seal of the government will announce, "The responsible nations of the world really must do something," but he won't have a clue as to what.' With contempt Schwartz looked at the three men and said, 'But no one will ever again have to ask, "Why didn't the Jews do something?" Because my group will be doing just that.'

He moved to Zodman and said, 'So when trouble starts in Chicago and you're positive it will go away if Jews keep the governor and the chief of police happy, nobody expects you to do anything, Zodman. All we ask is this. If in that time of trouble you see me on the street and you realize that I have come over from Israel to lead the Jewish resistance, don't betray me. Look the other way and pass on in silence. Because I shall be there to save you.'

He nodded brusquely to the three men and left the discussion, a hard-disciplined man who cultivated an unemotional view of the contemporary world. He was a man whom Cullinane had grown to respect and actually to like, a tough-minded man who stood ready to take on the whole Christian church, the united Arabs, the diffident Jews of Florida, the vacillating Gentiles and anyone else who wanted to break into the act. It was reassuring to know that such men populated the new Israel, and Cullinane offered a benediction to Schwartz's self-contained arrogance: 'If you can harness his courage, Eliav, you'll build a great land here.'

Zodman said, 'If I ever meet him walking the streets of Chicago, first thing I'll do is call a cop,' but Vered said quietly, 'You may think differently, Paul, after we've talked awhile.'

The following morning Zodman, the American Jew, took Vered, the sabra, to Cyprus, where they were married by a Church of England minister who made a lucrative business out of uniting couples who were honestly in love but who, under Jewish law, were not permitted to marry. He was a wizened little man with ill-fitting teeth, and when he blessed the Zodmans he said, 'Tell all my good Jews not to be disturbed about this monkey business. Years ago my church used to have the same kind of silly laws, which made people run away from England to get married in Gretna Green, but we got over it. Bet you didn't know Gretna Green was in Scotland.' He made the marriage a deeply tender thing, a true religious ritual, and at the end he asked shyly, 'Since there is no one to give away the bride, may I be permitted to kiss the beautiful lady?' He was barely as tall as Vered.

The unpleasant manner in which Zodman and Vered departed from Makor left a residue of bitterness, and it was Cullinane who observed, 'In 70 C.E., after General Vespasian captured Makor, his son Titus captured the symbols of Judaism and hauled them off to Rome. Today Zodman buys them for immediate transhipment to America.' Eliav added glumly, 'Maybe he was right. Maybe the leadership of Judaism will pass to American hands.' And the unhappiness of the two men was so depressing that Cullinane was relieved to invent an excuse for running off to Jerusalem. Explaining to no one he banged out of his office, calling over his shoulder, 'You fellows better start boxing up the papers,' but Tabari, aware of Eliav's gloom, thought: It would be a lot better if Cullinane stayed here and let Ilan get away for a few days.

The thoughtful Arab therefore scouted around for some fresh work to divert Eliav's attention from Vered, and one morning as he stood on the bedrock of Trench B, under which there could be nothing, he chanced to notice that at the northwestern end of the uncovered rock there was a barely perceptible dip to the west, and taking a small pick he began gingerly to undercut the perpendicular west wall of the trench, finding, as he had suspected, that the falling away of the rock continued in the direction of the wadi. Satisfied on this basic point, he sat in the trench for some two hours and did nothing but look at the massive rock; and as he visualized the various settlements that had occupied the tell he was constantly left with a mystery. Where had the original well stood? And he began to direct all his speculation to the earliest settlement—Level XV, about eleven thousand years ago, as man was just beginning to farm—and he came again and again to the conclusion that the original families must have lived somewhere off the face of this gently sloping rock and closer to the fugitive well, wherever it was. His thought processes were not entirely conscious: as a member of the Family of Ur he had a keen sense of land and he somehow felt that the earliest farmers must have sought fields at the bottom of sloping land, so that what rains fell would irrigate their crops and bring down each year fresh sediment to serve as fertilizer for soil which would otherwise be quickly depleted. Near the rock of Makor, where would such land have been?

He stopped his thinking, made his mind a blank, and tried to conjure up the bedrock of this tell as it had existed, not eleven thousand years ago, but two hundred thousand, three hundred thousand . . . He began to perspire as his body grew one with the ancient land. His hands grew clammy and he breathed hard. For if he could calculate where this sloping rock had ended he might deduce where the missing well had been, and if he found that, he might project the history of the tell backward sixty or a hundred thousand years. Perhaps Makor would turn out to be one of the great archaeological sites, a classic that scholars would refer to as they now spoke of Carmel, Jericho and Gezer.

'Eliav!' he called at the end of three hours. The Jew was working at Trench A but a runner summoned him, and soon from the top of the cut he looked down.

'Find something interesting?' he asked, using the archaeologist's constant inquiry.

'Come on down here,' Tabari said, masking the excitement he felt. When

Eliav saw the pick work at the base of the west face of the trench he asked what was up, and Tabari said, 'Study it. See anything?' The Jew dropped to his knees, inspected the unbroken rock closely and said, 'No tool marks. No inscriptions.' He drew back and looked at the whole area for some minutes, then dropped to his knees again and studied the level. He rose in great excitement and said, 'The whole thing slopes definitely that way.' He paused, looking at Tabari with flashes of excitement in his eyes and said, hesitantly, 'And if the slope continued, it could easily be that somewhere out there, outside the tell . . .' He stopped.

'Ilan', the Arab said cautiously, 'I think this slope may lead us to the well.'

'There's a chance,' Eliav agreed, with even greater caution. 'If so, the well would have to be down in the wadi,' and he pointed in exactly the direction that Tabari had deduced.

Controlling their eagerness the two men climbed down the steep bank to inspect each likely site for a well, but so much detritus had accumulated in that area that any source which might have been there had long since been smothered and now sent its water off through subterranean channels. The men therefore ranged far afield through the bottom of the wadi, searching for some undetected outcropping of water, but none showed. Finally Tabari said, 'I think we've got to follow the slope of the rock. See where it leads.'

Eliav agreed, but protocol demanded that they get permission from John Cullinane, who was, after all, the man in charge. Eliav side-stepped this by saying slowly, 'I think our responsibility permits us to make a little dig on our own,' and with timbers to shore up the ceiling behind them, the two men started a small boring which led them down past the edge of the basic rock. The timbers were not really needed, for over a period of some twenty thousand years the limestone from the waters that had seeped off the rock had transformed the once-soft earth into breccia, a kind of semi-rock which was easy to cut through but which held its own form, and on the fifth day of this digging Jemail Tabari encountered a small pocket of this breccia and realized that the dig was fundamentally altered.

'Get Cullinane back here at once,' he called as he stuck his dusty, dirty head from the minute tunnel.

'Find something?' Eliav asked nonchalantly.

'Not the well . . .' Tabari held out his hands and in them he carried a chunk of breccia containing a human bone, some sharp pointed flints and a substantial deposit of charred fragments. 'I think I've struck the edge of a large cave that had its opening on the face of the wadi.'

With controlled excitement Eliav studied the find and said, 'Let's get a girl in there to sketch it.'

'I touched only what my pick broke off,' Tabari explained. 'The main part is encased in solid breccia, but I did see something that seemed indicative. The corpse was buried with these flints. It wasn't an accidental burial.'

Eliav raised his eyebrows. ''This could go back thirty thousand years,' he suggested.

'That would be my guess,' Tabari agreed cautiously. 'And that's not all. Right beyond the cave . . . It's all filled up, you understand. I thought I was running into a rock that echoed. As if on the other side it were empty.'

'Unlikely,' Eliav replied.

'I thought so too. But go on in and take a sounding. I'll call the photographer.'

So Ilan Eliav wormed his way through the low tunnel until he came to the end; and there, to the right or northern side, he saw imbedded in the hard breccia the cache which Tabari had come upon. His first thought was: It'll take two years to excavate this properly. He felt a pang of regret to think that he would not be there to help; but then his imaginative mind started to dress in living flesh the ends of bone which projected from the breccia, and he wondered who this ancient thing--this man, perhaps--had been. What hungers had he known, what security from realizing that when he died he would carry with him stone beads? How had he gone finally to earth and with what immortal longings? Here in the darkness of the tunnel thousands upon thousands of years later, another man, much like him perhaps, still wearing his flesh for a few more inquisitive years, met him face-to-kneebone and knew only that there was mystery.

Eliav crawled a few paces beyond the imbedded skeleton and found himself facing the end wall of which Tabari had spoken. Using a fragment of the breccia which had held the bones he tapped on the wall ahead. In some strange way it echoed. He was convinced it echoed. He therefore tapped the side walls and the roof and the floor on which he knelt, and from them there returned a different sound. He tapped the end wall again, and there could be no doubt: perhaps it wasn't really an echo, but it was something different.

He reached back for Tabari's pick, left where the important bones had been found, and with it tapped cautiously at the facing semi-rock. The point of the pick dug in easily, and when it was pried backward, broke away a small chunk of the soft rock. Carefully he placed the rock behind him for the basket men to haul out, and with another cramped blow chipped away some more. On the third strike he was startled by the clarity of the echo sound, and he began to dig with some force, throwing the broken rock over his shoulder. His lantern was now obscured by the debris which he was accumulating, and he knew that he should stop to clear it, but he was gripped by a most intense excitement. Swinging his pick with un-archaeological vigor he felt its point bite through a thin layer of semi-rock and then leap forward into nothingness.

He began to perspire copiously, even though the tunnel was cool and he was lean, but he mastered his excitement and became again the professional archaeologist. He left the pick where it was and started slowly to back away, crawling over his own rubble. When he reached the spot where the bones projected he stopped and began flattening the rubble out, piece by piece, until his lantern again threw light on the face of the tunnel, from which the pick suspended at a curious angle. When the tunnel was again in order he returned to the pick and gently rotated it in various directions. Its hidden point contacted nothing and he was tempted to withdraw it and strike again, opening a real hole into the mysterious void, but he felt that this would be unfair to Tabari. He therefore left the pick in position, placed the lantern so that it illuminated not the pick but the projecting bones, and started the crawl back to Trench B.

When he got there Tabari had the girl artist and the photographer waiting, but Eliav in a businesslike manner called for a basket man to go in first and haul out the rubble. 'And don't touch the pick,' he warned. When the man was gone he instructed the artist and the photographer to get the most complete data on the breccia-held bones, and also to catch the details of the pick as it pierced the end wall. When the briefing was completed he took Tabari aside and said, 'I dug out a little more of the end wall, and on the last blow your pick cracked through a thin facing of the soft rock. It struck emptiness.'

'You're sure?' Tabari asked.

'I tested it in different directions. Nothing. But I left it for you.'

'A cave? A well?'

'I don't even have an opinion,' Eliav said.

Level XIX
About 70,000 B.C.E.

Burial
(shells and necklace flints enlarged)

Scale 1:30

At lunchtime the girl who had crawled in to do the sketching took one of Cullinane's cards and drew the probable disposition of the skeleton embedded in the breccia. There was hushed excitement as the card circulated, and Tabari asked, 'Where'd you dredge up the date 70,000 B.C.E.?'

'Educated guess,' the artist explained. 'The flints in the breccia seem to correlate with ones shown for such dating in Garrod and Stekelis.'

When the matter had been well discussed Eliav ventured the opinion that carbon dating would probably place the skeleton at no earlier than 30,000 B.C.E. and Tabari supported him. 'Our bones aren't going to be as old as those found in the Mount Carmel caves by Dorothy Garrod,' he predicted.

'You think the breccia indicates a cave?' the photographer asked.

'We'll know better after lunch,' Eliav assured the group.

'What's the mystery about the pick?' the photographer asked.

Tabari pushed back his food and leaned forward on the table, whereupon talking ceased and the kibbutzniks drew closer, for it was their tell, too. 'When I found the bones,' he said, 'I did a little more digging and thought I heard an empty echo. When Dr Eliav went down to check the bones he did some digging on his own. His last blow . . .' Tabari swung an imaginary pick. 'On the other side . . . emptiness.'

'Another cave?'

'Let's consider that for a moment,' the Arab said. 'If it had originally been a cave, say, fifty thousand years ago, and the entrance was filled in, wouldn't it now be filled in, too? How could there possibly be any empty space left?'

'He's probably right,' Eliav confirmed, and the kibbutzniks dissected the theory for some time, concluding in the end that it could not have been a cave.

'Not an original cave,' one of the kibbutzniks agreed, 'but why not a dug cave, like the ones Kathleen Kenyon found outside the walls at Jericho?'

'Let's consider that too, Tabari said. 'In your opinion, what would be the oldest date we might logically assume for such a dug cave . . . one that wasn't now filled in with breccia?'

'Kenyon's graves were 2000 C.B.E.,' the kibbutznik volunteered. 'And they were certainly not filled in. So ours could be . . . what? Maybe 3000 C.B.E. at the most.'

Eliav listened with pleasure. In Israel everyone was an archaeologist, and the kibbutznik had his dates right, but Tabari pointed out, 'You're a little early. Remember that Jericho is very dry and we're very wet. In wet areas caves fill in much faster.'

'Then what is the empty space?' the kibbutznik demanded.

Tabari thought for some time, then said cautiously, 'Since some of you want to work here for the next eight or ten years, let's try some pure deduction. I'll tell you categorically that I've ruled out caves. Now what else might it be?' There was silence. 'What major component of a tell are we lacking here at Makor?'

'Water supply,' a kibbutznik suggested.

'Correct.' He still pronounced it koe-rect. 'And what does that suggest?'

'The source was either at the base of the tell, which at Makor seems unlikely because of the bedrock. Or it was outside, as at Megiddo and Gezer.'

'Correct. And where does that lead us?'

'Judging by what happened at those two places, sometime around 1100 C.B.E. they dug a vertical shaft through the tell, then a horizontal tunnel to the well.'

'Correct. And which have we hit?'

'If it were the vertical shaft,' a girl volunteered, 'it would surely have been filled solid in three thousand years. Therefore it's got to be the horizontal.'

'Correct, but what if I tell you that the horizontal would also be packed solid in that time?'

This stumped the kibbutzniks and there was silence. The English photographer asked, 'Is your assumption accurate? Would it be packed solid?'

'Correct.'

General Teddy Reich's daughter asked in a very small voice, 'But we know there was a Crusader castle on the tell. They had to have water to withstand sieges. Couldn't they have redug the tunnel? About a thousand years ago?'

'I wish I could say "correct," because that's my theory, too,' Tabari laughed, 'and I pray that we're both right.'

The meal ended and he rose casually, sauntering out to Trench B with an insouciance he did not feel. Everyone who could get away from work tagged along with equal casualness but flushed with excitement, and kibbutzniks in the fields, sensing that something important was about to happen at their tell, quit their work to become archaeologists. At the site the Arab offered Eliav the lantern, saying, 'You found the opening. Go ahead.'

The Jew would not accept. 'It was your deduction.' He reviewed for the crowd Tabari's shrewd guess regarding the sloping rock. 'And it's your deduction about the tunnel. Besides,' he added, 'there may be one hell of a drop on the other side.' He led Tabari to the small tunnel and stepped away.

In this manner the latest scion of the Family of Ur crept back into the earth from which his prodigious people had sprung. He went past the bedrock on which the Canaanites had built; past the sixteenth and seventeenth levels where his ancestors had come upon the pre-primitive settlement which they had destroyed around the year 13,000 B.C.E.; down past the eighteenth level of men who had developed the concept of religion; to the nineteenth and twentieth levels where women had discovered that their dead could be buried with affection; and on to the face of the rock from which the pick handle projected. He was breathing hard, tense with the feel of his ancient earth, and he took the handle gently, twisting it in various directions. Eliav was right. The hidden tip was free.

Harshly he pulled the handle backward, dislodging a large chunk of semi-rock which started to come toward him, then teetered and disappeared in the opposite direction. Ominously, its fall made no sound. With four vigorous blows of the pick, using it head-on as a ram rather than as a pry, he knocked in the face of the wall and found himself with a jagged hole leading into nothingness.

His lips were parched and his breathing forced as he grasped the lantern, and thrusting it before him, crawled halfway into the opening. At first his eyes could see nothing, for the falling rocks had aroused an ancient dust which obscured all, but as it gradually subsided he saw that his prognostication had been correct. He had come upon a long tunnel cut through the limestone accretion. To left and right the partially filled tunnel ran, its beautifully arched ceiling still showing the careful work completed in the year 963 C.B.E. by his ancestor, Jabaal the Hoopoe, and later reworked in the year 1105 C.E. by his other ancestor, Saliq ibn Tewfik, called Luke. The falling stones had made no sound because they had dropped into soft dust which had been filtering into the tunnel since that April day in 1291 C.E., when the Mamelukes had killed Count Volkmar and had started the destruction of the Crusader castle.

To the right or to the left? Which way lay the well? Stuck halfway through the opening he began patiently reconstructing his orientation, and he had such a keen sense of the land, even when lost in its bosom, that he could deduce that the well must lie to the right, or north, of the accidental junction he had made with the tunnel; so he eased himself through the opening and started lifting his feet slowly, quietly, so as not to disturb the dust, moving toward the phantasmagoric darkness which dissolved like the passage of time as his lantern brought light where for seven centuries there had been no light.

Through those years the dust, thick and silent, had sifted down, and now it rose revitalized by the touch of a living foot, only to fall back as the unaccustomed beams flashed upon his ankles, and at last he came to a silent place where things ended, dust and footfall alike; and as he looked down into the darkness he could not estimate how far below him lay the water, but he dislodged a fragment of the roof and dropped it. After a while water splashed. The well of the Family of Ur was found, that sweet source from which all had sprung.

In the days that followed, Tabari and Eliav tried several times to acquaint Cullinane in Jerusalem with the stunning developments, but the telephone operators were unable to track him down, so on their own initiative the men strung lights which enabled them to work at the well, and after digging about the rim and finding only fragments of Crusader pottery—water jars broken by careless Christian women seven hundred years before—Tabari happened to notice in the wall, slightly above eye level, a discoloration of soil which previous visitors had failed to find, for they had been Canaanites or Jewish women like Gomer or Crusaders, and not archaeologists. But on a hunch Tabari began digging into the darkened earth and thus uncovered the original level of the well, finding a few charred stones on which men had sat around one of the world's first intentional fires, and it was among these stones that Eliav found imbedded the item that was to give Tell Makor its prehistoric significance: a piece of flint the size of a large flat hand, shaped into an obvious weapon, slightly convex on

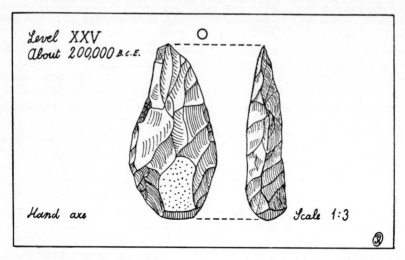

Level XXV
about 200,000 B.C.E.

Hand axe   *Scale 1:3*

the sides and sharpened along the pointed end. It was a hand axe dating back some two hundred thousand years to that nebulous period when beings walked half-erect and hunted animals with simple rocks, cutting the flesh apart with precious hand axes like the one the Englishman was now photographing in situ.

'My God!' he cried. 'What's that?' His flash bulbs had disclosed in the darkness a monstrous shining object, as big as a plate, serrated in many ridges. He had found a petrified elephant's molar, relic of a great beast slaughtered at the water hole when the climate of Israel was different and the wadi a deep river.

To call them men—those walking creatures that had killed the elephant—was in some ways repugnant, for they could neither farm, nor fish, nor tend fruit trees, nor tame a dog, nor build a house, nor make clothes, nor even form words with their apelike lips; but neither could they be called animals, for there were these things which they could do: they could make a tool; they could grasp it in a hand; and by grunts and shoves they could organize a team and plan a system for killing a huge thing like an elephant . . . and for these reasons they were men.

When Cullinane finally returned to Makor he wore a black patch over his left eye, which he explained merely by growling, 'Hospital.' Then he added, 'The nurses told me you were trying to phone, so I knew you'd struck something great, but there was nothing I could do about it.' He climbed down to the first cache of bones, then on to the well and the charred stones. It was more than he had hoped for, more than any archaeologist had a right to expect. When he crawled back to sunlight he assembled the group and said, 'We'll be working here for years, and when Ilan Eliav becomes prime minister of Israel, say, about 1980, we'll invite him to deliver the closing-down address.' The kibbutzniks cheered, after which he said, holding aloft the hand axe, 'Whenever you think Israel is moving too slowly, remember that our ancestors used implements like this for more than two hundred thousand years before they reached the next big invention. Small flints shaped to a point that could be used in subtler weapons.'

The first year of the dig was ending in a blaze of accomplishment.

When he was alone with the staff, 'Tomorrow we must airmail carbon samples from Level XIX to Sweden and America. And I want everybody to pray that they prove out to some date before 30,000 B.C.E.'

A moment of silence followed, after which the photographer ventured, 'There's got to be one stinker in every show. Where'd you get the shiner, boss?'

Cullinane did not laugh. 'It was Saturday morning and I was riding in a taxi to an informal meeting with the minister of finance. About getting our spare dollars cleared for transfer to Chicago. And suddenly out of hiding came a gang of boys and young men in fur caps, long coats and curls about their ears, screaming at us 'Shabbos' and hurling rocks—not stones, rocks. The taxi driver shouted, "Duck," but I didn't catch the Hebrew soon enough, and by the time he repeated his warning I had taken one hell of a rock right in my eye. The doctors thought I might lose it.'

'I didn't read about it in the paper,' Eliav said, half defensively.

'The government wanted no publicity. The cab driver said it was nothing unusual. Orthodox Jews insisting that no vehicle move on the streets of Israel during Shabbat.'

'So they've started the stoning business again?' Eliav groaned.

'I almost lost my eye. And the police made no arrests. They say that when they do the rabbis fight with them, pointing out that the Talmud condones the stoning of Jews who break Shabbat.'

'It's your problem,' Tabari said to Eliav. 'You're in the government now.'

'Not quite,' the Jew argued. 'But when I am I'll do what I can to halt this Mickey Mouse stuff.'

'This what?' Cullinane asked.

'A bad phrase I picked up,' Eliav explained. 'I'll have to drop it now.'

'That Shabbat the young hoodlums broke lots of taxi windows,' Cullinane said. 'The taxi men are becoming afraid to drive on Saturday.'

'That's what the religious group is after,' Eliav explained. 'They argue that Israel can exist only if it goes back to the laws of the Torah . . . in every detail.'

'Preposterous!' Cullinane said.

'As a Catholic you know it's preposterous,' Tabari laughed, 'and as a Muslim so do I. But the Jews don't, and even Cabinet Minister Eliav isn't quite sure. Because pretty soon he's going to have to face up to that problem.'

'While I was in the hospital,' Cullinane said, 'I had the gloomy feeling that one of these days all of us were going to have to face up certain moral problems. And we just don't seem to be willing. I had a long talk with an official of the Italian government. Up to arrange with the Jordanians for the entry of Catholic pilgrims into Bethlehem. He told me how close the Italian voters had come to electing a Communist government. Explained how a small swing of the total votes would have done it. He asked, "Supposing this happens? What does the world then do with the Vatican? Does it go to Russia? Or to the United States? Or does it stay locked up within the walls, impotent, in Italy?" The day could come when we'd have to face that problem.'

'Religions are always in trouble,' Tabari said. 'In adversity they grow honest. It's good for them.'

'And I also had the feeling,' Cullinane added, 'that perhaps at the same time the world might have to face up to the problem of Judaism. "To what extent are we prepared to protect Judaism as our parent religion?"'

Eliav caught the significance of this question, but Tabari did not. The Arab spoke first: 'The other day I joked about putting the world's Jews into orbit, but seriously, I suppose the day is past when you can exterminate six million Jews.'

But Eliav said, 'You're equating Israel with Judaism and you wonder what the world will do if the Arabs try to eliminate Israel altogether?'

'Yes,' Cullinane said. 'For the first time since I've been in Israel ... lying there in the hospital with the crazy cut across my face, thinking of the distorted ideas behind the religious hoodlums who threw the rocks ... What I'm trying to say is that if such zealots represent the new Israel, you can't expect people like me to come to your aid if the Arabs attack. And the death of Israel would raise the moral problem I spoke of.'

'You're wrong and you're right,' Eliav said. 'You're wrong in equating the state of Israel and the Jewish religion. No matter what might happen to Israel, Judaism would continue. Just as Catholicism always continued when the territory of the Vatican was held by others. But you're right that all of us, Catholics, Arabs, Jews, have got to work out some sensible pattern of life for the world, or new alignments will occur so radical that no one here can visualize them.'

'One afternoon,' Cullinane said, 'the doctors gave me a shot of something and I had one of those visions ... of a Jerusalem that had been agreed upon by all the world as an isolated zone of ghosts in which the Pope had his little Vatican because he was no longer welcome in Italy, and the chief rabbi had the area around the Wailing Wall, because he was no longer acceptable in Israel, and the new prophet of Islam had his territory, because no one in the Muslim countries wanted him, and the Protestants and Hindus and Buddhists each had their corner, because nobody wanted them either, and all the rest of the working world was, as you say, realigned into radical new patterns. And over each gateway to Jerusalem stood an arch with a bold sign which read in sixteen languages: MUSEUM."

'It was no vision,' Eliav said, 'and it's our job to see that it doesn't become fact.'

On Friday the cable from Stockholm arrived, and three excited archaeologists gathered in the arcaded building to read the news which would determine whether the human bones imbedded at Level XIX were of crucial importance or not. The Swedish scientists reported:

YOUR SAMPLE NINETEEN STOP REPEATED TESTS YIELD SIXTY-EIGHT THOUSAND B.C.E.
PLUS-MINUS THREE THOUSAND STOP SOUNDS EXCITING

Tabari cheered. 'I've got a job here for the next fifteen years, plus-minus five.'

'Were we lucky!' Cullinane said. 'Of all the available tells we picked the good one.'

Eliav, always practical, reminded the men, 'But to dig out that solid breccia will cost money.' The planners looked up from the cable, and Eliav made it clear that the Israeli government could not advance the funds, exciting though the find promised to be. After the men had explored various alternative avenues Tabari said glumly, 'Well, let's say the ugly word.'

'Zodman?'

'Correct.'

'After the way I gave him hell?' Eliav asked.

'I'd never ask Zodman and Vered for the dough,' Cullinane protested.

'My Uncle Mahmoud,' Tabari said slowly, 'once wangled money for the same dig from the chief rabbi in Jerusalem, the Catholic bishop in Damascus, the Muslim imam in Cairo, and the Baptist president of Robert College in Istanbul. His rule was, "If you need money, shame has not yet been invented." I'll send Zodman a cable that will break his heart.' He began to play an imaginary violin.

Cullinane advised, 'Let's wait till we get confirmation from Chicago on the carbon dating,' and the three leaders spurred the workmen to close down the dig, but each day one or the other crawled down the tunnel to sit beside the well of Makor where living creatures had crouched two hundred thousand years before. For each of the archaeologists it was a mystic rite, huddling there in the cavern: to Tabari it was a return to the ancient sources of his people; to Eliav it was the spot where man had begun his long wrestling match with the concept of God; to Cullinane it was the beginning of those philosophical analyses with which he would be engaged for the balance of his life; but to all it was the source, the primeval spot where the growth of civilizations had begun. At the end of the week Chicago reported:

YOUR LEVEL NINETEEN STOP WE GET A FIRM SIXTY-FIVE THOUSAND PLUS-MINUS FOUR STOP CONGRATULATIONS

As soon as he read the confirming report Tabari drafted a hearts-and-flowers cable to Paul Zodman, begging him for money. When Cullinane read it he growled, 'It's repulsive. I forbid you to send it.'

So Tabari prepared an alternative which said that since Cullinane and Eliav were absent in Jerusalem he was forwarding the laboratory reports, and he trusted that a man as generous and as far-seeing as Paul Zodman . . . 'It's still repulsive,' Eliav grimaced.

'It's how we handled the British,' Tabari joked.

'You really have no shame, do you?' Cullinane asked with admiration.

'You ever hear about my father, Sir Tewfik, when he was judge at Akko? One night he slipped in to see the litigant in a crucial case and said, "Fazl, I know I shouldn't be here, but I just want to point out that you have three lawyers to choose from: an Arab, a Greek and an Englishman. Be sure you choose right." Fazl replied, "Ya-effendi, I was going to use the Englishman, but if you say so, I'll switch to the Arab." My father said, "You misunderstand. Be sure to use the Englishman, because when he bribes me it's in pounds sterling." I'll bet my cable gets us another half-million dollars.' Two days later they had their answer:

I SEE THAT CULLINANE AND ELIAV DIDN'T HAVE THE GUTS TO CABLE AND AFTER THEIR INSULTING BEHAVIOR NO WONDER STOP BUT YOU HAVE THE GALL TO ASK FOR AN ADDITIONAL HALF MILLION DOLLARS TO COMPLETE EXCAVATION DOWN TO LEVEL TWENTY-FIVE STOP YES STOP YOU HAVE GIVEN VERED AND ME A TREMENDOUS WEDDING PRESENT STOP MILLION THANKS

'A man like that, it's easy to hate,' Tabari laughed. 'I should have asked for a million.'

'He has style,' Eliav granted. 'Wedding present!'

Cullinane broke out some champagne and announced, 'I'm going to crawl down there and give those old bastards at the well one of the best parties they ever had.' He lugged the bottle down the tunnel shaft and splashed the liquid against the bones protruding from the breccia of Level XIX. 'My God, we're glad to find you,' he whispered. Then he proceeded to the well, where he sprinkled the champagne as if he were a priest. 'To all of you. We'll be back.' And as he made this flippant remark the echo of his voice came back to strike him, and he fell heavily on one of the marble benches set there by Tomon Myrmex in the time of Herod. He put the bottle aside and covered his face with his hands. 'Vered!' he whispered, and where no one could see him except the ghosts he admitted how forlorn he was, how deep had been his need to marry the little Jewish scholar. He had the vague feeling, at that lonely moment, that he was not going to find a Catholic wife in Chicago, nor would Ilan Eliav find a Jewish bride in Jerusalem; like huge Father Vilspronck they would move about the Holy Land for some years, respected and even loved, but men apart—a Dutchman married to a church, a German Jew married to a state, and an Irishman obsessed by the philosophical analysis of history. 'Vered! Vered!' he muttered. 'You could have saved me.'

At the surface he reported lightly, 'The old reprobates lapped it up. They said that if civilization could produce something as good as champagne they were going to have children like mad so as to speed up the process.'

'How did they communicate those sensible ideas,' Tabari asked, 'seeing that when they lived speech hadn't been invented?'

'To the silent ones,' Cullinane proposed, 'deep in the earth.' And that afternoon he took a plane for Chicago.

The last man to go down the tunnel before things were locked up for the year was Ilan Eliav, who felt regret at leaving the dig just as the exciting years were beginning. Descending to the well he sat in the gloom beside the cool water that had brought life to so many. It surely didn't start a mere two hundred thousand years ago, he reasoned. Below this must lie the plain where animals had always come to drink, and over there, hiding behind a tree, waited some creature who had wandered up from Africa a million years ago, holding in his hand the first rock of Israel that had ever been formed into a weapon. That had been the beginning, that ancient first, and it would never be known, that hairy hand waiting in the reeds as the animals came to drink; nevertheless, Eliav felt communion with that hunter. At Zefat we Jews held the rock in our hand and damned little else. At Akko and Jerusalem, too. He patted the cool wet earth. And now we're climbing our way once more. And he started the long crawl back to where Tabari waited.

As soon as he saw the Arab he said what was on his mind: 'Get your records in shape, Jemail, because Cullinane's got to finish this dig by himself.'

'Why?'

'I'm taking the cabinet job. The prime minister announces it tomorrow. And my first appointment will be you. Director-general.' He extended his hand to the Arab.

Tabari drew back. 'You know what you're doing?' he asked suspiciously.

'I sure do,' Eliav said. He threw his arm about Tabari's shoulder and led him to the edge of the dig, where they sat on stones that had once served as part of a synagogue-basilica-mosque church, and there the Jew and the descendant of Ur fought it out, as their ancestors had done ages ago. They were two handsome men in the strong middle years of their lives: the ascetic Jew, tall and serious, with hollow cheeks and cautious manner; the man of Ur, with his five children, heavier, browner, with a quicker wit and a more congenial smile. At the dig they had formed a constructive team, assuming responsibility for decisions and sustaining the creative mood on the tell. Now they were about to grope for a reincarnation of that fruitful if tempestuous partnership which Hebrew and Canaanite had shared four thousand years ago and which Jew and Arab had known for thirteen hundred years following the arrival of Islam.

'It's about time we Jews and Arabs made some real gestures of conciliation,' Eliav began. 'Looks like we're going to share this part of the world for quite a long time.'

'I have no wish to serve as an experiment.'

'And since in the matters I'll be handling, you're the best-informed man I know . . .'

'If you appoint me there could be all sorts of hell.'

'There will be. But we've got to encourage the day when Nasser will appoint a Jew to some job of similar importance. And he will.'

'I don't want to see you get in trouble, Ilan.'

'Trouble I can take. If they fire me I'll come back here and live off Paul Zodman.'

'But you'll be up to your neck in Arab-Jewish relations, and I could hurt you.'

'No. You'll help. To prove that even in these difficult areas Jews and Arabs can work in harmony.'

'There aren't six people in Israel prepared to believe that.'

'You're one of the six, and our job is to increase the number.'

'I was always much impressed,' Tabari said, 'when your Jewish God halted human sacrifice. Here you are, restoring it.'

'I'm trying to restore something much older. The brotherhood that used to exist on this land. Want to help?'

Tabari studied the invitation for some moments, then said, 'No. I'm an Arab, and the fact that I stayed behind to help rebuild this country doesn't make me any less an Arab. I'll become your assistant, Eliav, on the day your government gives one sign that it understands Arabs, wants them to stay here, and is willing to accept them as full partners . . .'

'Haven't I proved that this summer? Haven't you and I been full, respectable partners?'

'You and I? Yes. Your government and we Arabs? No.'

'What do you want?'

'Take out your pencil. We want better schools, hospitals, roads to our villages, nurses, a place in the university for our best young men, a partnership in which our talents are respected. We want you to see that on this land there can be a fruitful association of equals. Your intellectuals have got to stop patronizing us as if we were idiot children. Your businessmen have got to accept us as men who can count and who are as honest as they are. Eliav, we want to feel that as Arabs we have a home in your society.'

'Haven't I conveyed that promise in everything I've done this summer?'

'And there's one other reason why I can't accept.'

'Do I know what it is?' Eliav asked.

'I think you can guess. In those long discussions we had with Cullinane on the nature of the moral state, I noticed that there was one topic which he often led up to but always shied away from. Americans are taught to be so sensitive about other people's feelings. Yet this is the problem which really tests the moral foundations of Judaism.'

'You mean the Arab refugees?'

'I do. Those refugees on the other side of the border were in Cullinane's mind every time he fell silent in our discussions. They're in mine, too.'

'What would you have us do?' Eliav asked in frank perplexity. 'In 1948, against every plea of the Jews, some six hundred thousand Arabs evacuated this country. They did so at the urging of their political leaders. On the promise that within two weeks they would come back as victors, take over all Jewish property and do what they liked with Jewish women. Now it's sixteen years later. They tell us the number of refugees has multiplied to a million. Arab governments have not allowed them to find new homes in Arab countries and the time has passed when they can recover their old homes here. What do you want us to do?'

'I'll join you, Eliav, on the day Israel makes proper restitution for . . .'

'We've agreed to do that! In my first speech I'm to announce that Israel, before the bar of humanity and world opinion, is willing to discuss compensation for every refugee who can prove he left old Palestine, if such a settlement becomes part of a total peace treaty. I'll go through the world begging Jews in every land to help us pay off that self-imposed obligation. I'll propose taxes here at home higher than we've ever had before. Tabari! Work with me to reach this honorable solution.'

'And what about repatriation?'

Eliav fell silent. Uneasily he moved about the tell and from some distance said, 'After we took Zefat I personally went out . . . in a captured English Land Rover . . . begging the fleeing Arab refugees to come back to their homes in Zefat. Twice I was shot at but I kept on, because I knew then that we needed those Arabs and they needed us. But they wouldn't listen. "We'll come back with an army," they boasted. "We'll take everything. Our homes. Your homes. And all the land." And they walked over the hills to Syria. A couple of nights later, right where I'm standing, other Arabs killed my wife, yet the next morning, after we had the big fight in Akko . . . where I met you for the first time . . .' He looked across the tell at Tabari and asked in a low voice, 'What did I do that morning, Jemail?'

The Arab remained silent, and with a sudden leap Eliav was upon him, grabbing his shoulders and shaking them. 'What did I do?' he shouted. 'Tell me . . . now!'

In a soft voice, barely audible above the November breeze that was coming down the wadi with the first hints of winter, Tabari said, 'You went to the beach, where the boats were filling up with Arab refugees, and you pleaded with every man you could reach: "Don't run away. Stay here and help us build this country." '

'And did any stay?'

'I did.'

Eliav looked at his friend with the kind of quiet passion that history instills in men of perception. He sat down, burdened by the impossible complexity of the refugee problem, and recalled those fateful days when the Arabs had fled the country. 'More than twenty thousand left Akko that day,' he said, 'and I went from man to man, but of them all I was able to persuade only you.' He bowed to Tabari, then said with increasing bitterness, 'And now they want to come back. When the land is fertile and the shops are filled, when the schools are productive and the mosques are open, they want to come back. It may be too late. In Cyprus we're seeing what happens when you try to force two different peoples to live together in a majority-minority status. Would you have us create a second Cyprus here?'

'I want a state which preaches morality to practice it.' Tabari said. 'Bring back at least a token of these refugees to prove . . .'

'We will!' Eliav cried. 'In my speech I'm also to make that offer again. More than a mere token we will bring back. And we'll absorb them in full brotherhood. But a million? Dedicated to destroy us? When only six hundred thousand left? No, dear friend, you cannot demand that we commit suicide.'

'I won't take the job in Jerusalem,' Tabari said finally. 'But I will say this. When we were digging at Crusader levels I remember telling you that just as we Muslims drove out the Europeans after two hundred years, so we would push you into the sea. Now I'm beginning to believe you'll be here for a long time.'

'I'm sorry you won't help us,' Eliav said with deep regret.

'I'll always be an Arab,' Tabari replied.

'On that day in Akko in 1948? Why didn't you run away too?'

'I belong to this land,' the descendant of Ur said, 'this well, these olive trees. My people were here before yours were formed. When it was prudent to be Canaanites, we were Canaanites. For the same lofty reason we were Phoenicians, and when Jews ruled the land we were Jews, or Greeks, or Romans, or Christians, or Arabs, or Mamelukes or Turks. If you allowed us to hold the land we never gave a damn as to which church we worshiped in or what flag we saluted. When my grandfather was governor of Tiberias he spent most of his time looking after his own affairs, and my father, Sir Tewfik, served the British in the same impartial manner, because all we wanted was the land.'

'Why this land, Jemail? What's so special about this land?'

'Here the pressures of the world are vital. After all, if this land was good enough for God to choose, and Moses and Jesus and Muhammad, it's good enough for me.'

'You don't believe in God, do you, Jemail?'

'Indeed I do. There must be a god of the land, who lives in wells like ours, or on hills like that, or in olive groves that replenish themselves forever. He may even live in the religions which grow out of his land. But he cannot exist alien from the land which bore him.'

'We Jews believe in the same partnership of God, and a particular land, and a chosen people. We're very old brothers, Tabari, and in the future we shall meet many times, for we understand each other.'

Distressed at not having enlisted Tabari for the difficult job ahead, Eliav said good-bye to the dig and made his way eastward along the Damascus road and in time reached Zefat, where he intended spending a few hours with the Vodzher Rebbe reviewing a group of legal cases like Zipporah Zederbaum's. He had convinced himself that he had a chance of winning the old man over to a more liberal interpretation of Judaism, but he found him a shriveled wraith with a beard even longer and whiter than before and a fierce determination to resist any encroachment on the law. So Eliav retreated and turned the discussion to the heroic days of Ilana, Bar-El and Bagdadi.

'They're all dead, aren't they?' the little leader asked in Yiddish.

'Yes, but their ideas won.'

'And you've taken another name.'

'Yes, I'm part of Eretz Israel now.'

'And everything has worked out as I predicted, hasn't it?'

'With modifications.'

'And you're to be our minister in charge of the very ideas we used to argue about?'

'Yes, and I hope you'll help me find some sort of compromise.'

The rebbe's face darkened and with both hands he clutched his beard. 'Compromise there can never be,' he said. 'Israel has no right to exist except as a religious state.' And when Eliav fought to gain a concession that would allow Zipporah Zederbaum to marry, the rebbe refused to listen. 'There is the law,' he said stubbornly, and more he would not say. But he did take Eliav by the hands invitingly: 'Come to the synagogue. Stay by my side throughout this night. And you'll discover what Israel is.' Eliav protested that he must move on to Tiberias, but the rebbe would not allow it. 'Your life is at stake,' he said, forcing Eliav to the synagogue, where the services were as moving as ever, except that now more than sixty men attended instead of a mere seventeen. And all roared the Lecha Dodi in some two dozen different styles.

After the evening service the old man returned home but he did not eat, nor would he allow Eliav to do so, but at quarter to midnight the two men said good night to the rebbetzin and walked out into the lovely crooked streets of Zefat to a barren hall where more than a hundred Jews in ceremonial garb were waiting: tall lean men in fur caps, short round businessmen in long robes, and numerous young men in white shawls. They were the Hasidim of Zefat, men violent in their love for God, and now they ranged themselves silently about a U-shaped table as their beloved rebbe made his way to the head position, where he sat alone like a king. Only he had a plate before him at this feast and only he would dine.

At midnight a senior assistant who acted as servant brought him a bowl of soup, and since no spoons or forks were allowed at this ritual the rebbe raised the bowl to his bearded lips, drank a little of the soup, then ceremoniously pushed it away. As soon as he had done so the silent Hasidim leaped from their seats and a hundred struggling hands dived for the bowl. Fingers were dipped into the sacred broth and then conveyed to the mouths until the bowl was dry.

Next came one fish, of which the rebbe ate only a morsel, whereupon the hundred waiting hands tore at the remains till nothing was left on the plate but a few bones, for it was a cherished thing to be able to say in Zefat, 'I ate of the rebbe's fish.' Now the servant brought a bowl of mixed vegetables, the ancient kind that King David had eaten with his bare hands when he traveled from Jerusalem to the Galilee, and again there was the ritual tasting by the rebbe and the mad scramble for a bean or a grain of groats; to Eliav the fight to thrust even one finger into the bowl was disgusting, even though he knew that such feasts were weekly affairs with the Hasidim.

Now came the meat, a large piece of roast lamb cooked precisely as it had been for more than three thousand years by the Jews of this region, but this time there was to be a variation in the eating procedure, for after the rebbe had tasted the lamb he did not push it away. Instead he rose, nodded his wintry head three times and said in a whispering voice, 'To my beloved son Ilan Eliav, who has been chosen to help guide Eretz Israel, I give this meat.' And from the bone he tore off a small piece and with his trembling fingers pushed it into Eliav's mouth. This done, he moved the plate away and his followers struggled for the fragments until the bone lay clean.

The rebbe's midnight meal was ended and the devout silence which had marked it was broken by one old Jew who started clapping his hands. When he had set the rhythm he was joined by others until the room echoed to the commanding sound. A voice started chanting in Yiddish, and now the hall was filled with those wild songs of religious joy that had originated in Russia and Poland. The ecstasy of God was upon this shouting congregation and for more than an hour the songs reverberated, not stately hymns in the Catholic or Protestant tradition, but cries of violent praise to the God who had shepherded them through another week.

At two in the morning a surprising thing happened: an elderly Jew, whom Eliav had noticed earlier as one of the more decrepit ancients, began to dance and quickly the floor filled with gyrating bodies, fur caps awry and coats standing out from hips. If the Hasidic songs were not hymns, neither were the dances customary religious posturings; they were wild prancings of abandonment which gave the impression that the dancers were drunk. Those steps are much too vigorous, Eliav thought, for the old men who are performing them, but at three o'clock the rebbe himself rose to dance, and for some minutes the others stopped to watch him. Incredible, Eliav said to himself. He must be eighty. For the rebbe was captured by the religious fervor he had learned from his grandfather in Vodzh, and he cavorted like a child, kicking his legs high and whirling about until his fur cap traced a brown blur across Eliav's eye.

At first Eliav was afraid the old man might hurt himself, but as other dancers formed about the rebbe, Eliav realized that these men were in a kind of catatonic trance and if they were to be struck dead now they would die in maximum joy: they were truly children of God reveling in His goodness.

After the rebbe had continued his violent dance for some fifteen minutes, all the men of Zefat joined hands in a big circle that reached out to the four walls, and slowly this circle began to move counter-clockwise while Eliav remained in the middle, watching. An elderly Jew began singing and soon the hall throbbed with the sound of voices and feet which halted only when the rebbe stopped the dance.

'Tonight my son Eliav will dance with me,' the old man said, 'that he may gain an understanding of this land he is to govern.' And the ancient rebbe left the circle, took Eliav by the hand and brought him into the group. With the old man's hand clutching his, Eliav danced till morning.

As dawn came over the hills of Galilee the fur-hatted Hasidim began straggling out of the hall to wander home in groups of five or six, and as each group moved into the saintly streets of Zefat the rebbe gave them his benediction. When he and Eliav were alone he said quietly, 'Eliav, we are depending on you to keep Israel a nation dedicated to God.' He asked the young minister to walk home with him, but Eliav said, 'No, I have a mission to carry out,' and perhaps the old man guessed what it was, for he said, 'Your true mission to Zefat you have completed. You've seen that we religious ones intend to fight for this nation. Not a single paragraph of the law may you change.' Then, as if he realized that he had not much longer to live, he reached up and kissed Eliav on both cheeks. 'The dead are dead,' he whispered, 'but they rely on us to fulfill their hopes.' And he followed the others through the narrow, arched streets of Zefat.

Then Eliav was alone in the city he had fought for, and he walked by twisting paths and alleys down to the foot of the English stairs to make a pilgrimage which in recent years had come to mean much in his life. Ahead lay twenty-one separate flights to be climbed, and reverently he began his ascent.

One, two, three: to the left stood the stalwart Jewish house pock-marked

with bullets and unrepaired since the war; here Vered Yevneski had helped
hold off three Arab assaults that would otherwise have taken the house and led
to the collapse of the quarter; she had been so young, so brave.

Four, five, six, seven, eight: to the right he saw the Arab mosque as he had
seen it on the morning of victory, and to the left stood Rabbi Yom Tov
Gaddiel's blunt synagogue, still standing in opposition.

Nine, ten: he stopped in pain, for this was the spot at which Ilana Hacohen
had fought off the first Arab attack across the stairs. Children were playing in
the area now, and he wondered if, when they grew up, they would have the
courage to do the things Ilana had done, that wonderful girl: she had been so
powerful in her dedication; where would her like be found again?

Eleven, twelve, thirteen: he paused to look at the Arab homes, still painted
blue to ward off danger, and the blue had protected them for thirteen hundred
years—but in the end it had been powerless. How lovely the blue Arab homes
were, with their unexpected arches and little gardens; how empty they seemed
now, staring up without roofs toward the impartial sun. He had never hated
Arabs, Eliav reflected, and he wished that they had remained to make their
singing arches and their gardens part of his land as before.

Fourteen, fifteen: he was on the small plaza where the trees grew so
charmingly, flowers on each side, and grapes running up the Jewish wall, and
on the Arab side the six tall evergreens, which gave the plaza distinction and
beauty; here Ilana and Vered had held off the enemy for three hours and in the
trunks of the slim trees one could still find bullets. Beyond were morning-
glories prolific in their blue loveliness; and if the stairs of Zefat contained only
this one small area, they would be memorable.

Sixteen, seventeen, eighteen: now as he neared the head of the stairs he could
see the brooding gray walls of the police station, still marked with bullet holes
where Teddy Reich and Nissim Bagdadi had tried so vainly to assault the
fortress; he still wondered how they had managed to take this forbidding
stronghold.

Nineteen, twenty, twenty-one: he found no words, only the terrible ache of
lost companionship; here Bagdadi had fallen; there Ilana and Bar-El had stood,
and they were dead; what a terrible burden a man must bear if he climbs the
stairs of the years, if he survives and attempts to govern as his dead companions
would have wished.

On this crisp dawn he would ascend beyond the last flight of stairs, for his
mind was carried upward to the Crusader ruins, from which he had first seen
the Galilee in snow, and as he climbed he saw to the east that impregnable
fortress against whose capture his mind had rebelled, and he chanted, as David
did when making his ascent to Jerusalem: "'If it had not been the Lord who
was on our side, when men rose up against us: then they had swallowed us up
quick, when their wrath was kindled against us.'" Beyond the fortress, which
had fallen as miraculously as any in the Torah, he could see once more the
flawless land whose sweeping hills moved in majesty and whose towering
clouds still twisted in violence above the lake hallowed to so many.

He saw the lake itself and, toward the far end, that bit of land which Shmuel
Hacohen had finally purchased from the emir in Damascus, the land where
Jews had proved that they could not only read Talmud but also farm their
inheritance. I suppose you have to be like Shmuel, Eliav reflected. You stake
out your land. You ride around it on a donkey to protect it. And if somebody
shoots at you, you fight back. And if in the end you're killed, you trust that your

granddaughter Ilana will carry on where you left off. He bowed his head and whispered, 'How can any man have the courage to govern a land like this?'

Then, as he raised his head, he discovered, from an unexpected quarter, the answer to his question; for he looked down upon Tiberias, that insignificant, that precious town which had given the world both the Talmud and the Bible. Outside the old Crusader walls he could discern the tomb of Moses Maimonides, of whom it was said, 'From Moses to Moses there was no one like Moses.' Eliav thought: I hope I find one tenth the wisdom he did; and he promised himself that this afternoon, when he passed Tiberias, he would pause to light a candle at the tomb. He doubted that any part of the great philosopher's corpse had reached this burial ground. The tomb could only be a cenotaph, for legend explained that as Maimonides lay dying in Egypt he asked to be buried in Israel, whereupon his corpse was lashed to a donkey and the beast headed north. The animal had died at Tiberias, so there the tomb stood, reminding ordinary men that even they could attain reason if they applied themselves. 'I'll light three candles,' Eliav said.

Then his eye climbed the hill back of Tiberias, toward those fatal Horns of Hittim, and he could imagine the cave in which another legend placed the grave of Rabbi Akiba, and as he paid homage to this great leader he thought: I wish we had him with us now.

For there was beginning to be an outcry, both in Israel and in the world, against the arbitrary structure of contemporary Judaism: Zipporah Zederbaum unable to marry because of an out-worn law four thousand years old; Eliav forbidden to marry Vered because of the Cohen legalities; Zodman's divorce not legal because modern-thinking American rabbis could not be trusted; the German woman, faithful to Judaism even at the cost of her eye and her life, with children who were not accepted as Jews; the Indian Jews who were disbarred; and Leon Berkes who could not work as a Jew. Eliav was particularly worried by such rigid crystallization because he had read enough history to know that if it were continued, the revolt of the kibbutzniks and people like Ilana and Vered could become damaging. In any other nation a typical official like Eliav would find himself allied against the priests who insisted upon such irrefrangible law, and even he had begun to echo the warning voiced by Ilana Hacohen: 'this Mickey Mouse crap.'

But Ilan Eliav was not in 'any other country,' nor could he ever be 'a typical official.' He was a Jew, aware of the unique history of his people. They had survived persecution, as the Vodzher Rebbe knew, only because their stern rabbis had kept them faithful to the law, and if now this law raised certain difficulties, that was nothing new; it had always done so. The law need not be abrogated; what was needed was some new leader to refight in the twentieth century the battles that great Akiba had fought in the second. The law must be humanized, brought up to date. Eliav felt sure that were Akiba alive today he would long since have simplified it, adjusting it to modern life as he had once adjusted it to Roman.

But the law would continue, for only it could keep Israel alive. Where were the Chaldeans and the Moabites, the Phoenicians and the Assyrians, the Hurrians and the Hittites? Each had been more powerful than the Jews, yet each had perished and the Jews remained. Where was Marduk, great god of the Babylonians, and Dagan of the Philistines; and Moloch of the Phoenicians? They had been mighty gods who struck terror in the hearts of men, but they had vanished and it was the conciliatory, sometimes awkward God of the Jews

Who not only persisted but Who also vitalized two derivative religions. And God exercised His power through the law.

It was no mean thing to be a Jew and the custodian of God's law; for if His law was exacting it was also ennobling. It demanded respect if not blind obedience. There could be no larger task, Eliav thought, then devising procedures whereby the Jews of Israel and their more numerous cousins in America could share this vital law and the responsibility for keeping it vital. He recalled a cynical joke: 'The function of the American Jew is to send money to a German Jew in Jerusalem, who forwards it to a Polish Jew in the Negev, who makes it possible for the Spanish Jew in Morocco to come to Israel.' There was more to it than that.

On the day he left, John Cullinane had asked in his easy Irish manner, 'Ilan, why do you Jews make life so difficult for yourselves?' At the time Eliav had thought of no reply, but now, having lost Vered for a Jewish reason and having been projected into the heart of Jewish responsibility, he understood: Life isn't meant to be easy, it's meant to be life. And no religion defended so tenaciously the ordinary dignity of living. Judaism stressed neither an after-life, an after-punishment, nor heaven; what was worthy and good was here, on this day, in Zefat. We seek God so earnestly, Eliav reflected, not to find Him but to discover ourselves.

From where he stood at that moment he could see the spot in Tiberias where he blew up the English lorry, the streets of Zefat in which he had used his machine gun, and he vowed that violence was behind him; he would try to be the kind of Jew that Akiba had been, a peasant who had passed the age of forty before learning how to read, a self-taught man who had become the legal master of his day, a man who at seventy launched a whole new way of life and who, when the Romans finally executed him by tearing away his flesh with hot pincers – a man ninety-five years old and perhaps not legally a Jew, for it was believed that he descended from Sisera, that lascivious general whom Jael had slain with a tent pin – proved himself so dedicated to God that when the Roman soldiers gripped the flesh near his heart, he forced himself to stay alive until he could finish his defiant cry, 'Hear, O Israel, the Lord our God, the Lord is one,' to die on the long, wailing pronunciation of the word 'one'.

HE BRIDGES AT TOKO-RI

JAMES·A·MICHENER

TO MARSHALL U. BEEBE
Jet Pilot

SEA

The sea was bitter cold. From the vast empty plains of Siberia howling winds roared down to lash the mountains of Korea, where American soldiers lost on patrol froze into stiff and awkward forms. Then with furious intensity the arctic wind swept out to sea, freezing even the salt spray that leaped into the air from crests of falling waves.

Through these turbulent seas, not far from the trenches of Korea, plowed a considerable formation of American warships. A battleship and two cruisers, accompanied by fourteen destroyers to shield against Russian submarines, held steady course as their icy decks rose and fell and shivered in the gale. They were the ships of Task Force 77 and they had been sent to destroy the communist-held bridges at Toko-ri.

Toward the center of this powerful assembly rode two fast carriers, the cause of the task force and its mighty arm. Their massive decks pitched at crazy angles, which for the present made take-offs or landings impossible. Their planes stood useless, huddled together in the wind, lashed down by steel cables.

It was strange, and in some perverse way resolutely American, that these two carriers wallowing in the dusk bore names which memorialized not stirring victories but humiliating defeats, as if by thus publishing her indifference to catastrophe and her willingness to surmount it, the United States were defying her enemies. To the east, and farther out to sea, rode the *Hornet*, whose predecessor of that name had absorbed a multitude of Japanese bombs and torpedoes, going down off Guadalcanal, while the inboard carrier, the *Savo*, would forever remind the navy of its most shameful defeat in history, when four cruisers sank helpless at Savo Island, caught sleeping by the audacious Japanese.

Now, as night approached the freezing task force, the bull horn on the *Savo* rasped out, 'Prepare to launch aircraft!' And it was obvious from the way her deck was arranged that the carrier already had some planes in the skies over Korea, and every man who watched the heaving sea wondered how those planes could possibly get back aboard.

The bull horn, ignoring such problems, roared, 'Prepare to launch helicopter!' and although the deck pitched in abandon, rotors began to turn, slowly at first and then with lumbering speed.

Now the great carrier struck a sea trough and slid away, her deck lurching, but relentlessly the bull horn cried, 'Move jets into position for launching,' and the catapult crew, fighting for footing on the sliding deck, sprang swiftly into action, inching two heavy Banshees onto the catapults, taking painful care not to allow the jets to get rolling, lest they plunge overboard with some sudden shifting of the deck.

'Start jet engines,' roared the insistent bull horn.

The doctor, who had to be on deck in case of crash, looked at the heaving sea and yelled to the crane operator, 'They may launch these jets, but they'll never get 'em back aboard.'

The craneman looked down from his giant machine, which could lift a burning plane and toss it into the sea, and shouted, 'Maybe they're planning to spend the night at some air force field in Korea. Along with the ones that are already up.'

But at this instant all ships of the task force swung in tight circles and headed away from the open sea, straight for the nearby cliffs of Korea, and when the turn was completed, the deck of the *Savo* mysteriously stabilized. The effects of wind and sea neutralized each other, and planes returning from the bombardment of Korea now had a safe place to land.

But before they could do so the bull horn cried eerily into the dusk, 'Launch helicopter!' and the crazy bird, its two rotors spinning so slowly the blades could be seen, stumbled into the air, and the horn cried, 'Launch jets!'

Then, as the great carrier rode serenely amid the storms, the catapult officer whirled one finger above his head and a tremendous, almost unbearable roar arose and twin blasts of heat leaped from each Banshee, burning the icy air more than a hundred feet aft. Now the officer whirled two fingers and the roar increased and white heat scorched the deck of the carrier and the twin engines whipped to a meaningless speed of 13,000 revolutions a minute and the Banshee pilot, forcing his head back against a cushion, saluted and the catapult officer's right hand whipped down and the catapult fired.

Nine tons of jet aircraft were swept down the deck at a speed of more than 135 miles an hour. Within less than 150 feet the immense Banshee was airborne, and by the time it reached the forward edge of the carrier, it was headed toward its mission. Four times the catapults fired and four times heavy jets leaped into the darkening sky and headed for the coastline of Korea.

As soon as they had left, the bull horn wailed, 'Respot planes. On the double. We must recover the Korea jets immediately.'

When this announcement was made thirty old-fashioned propeller planes were already lashed down on the after part of the flight deck in precisely that area needed for landing the jets which now appeared overhead. The prop planes had been stowed there to permit catapult take-offs, and now they must be moved forward. So on the wooden deck, swept by icy winds, hundreds of young men in varicolored uniforms sped to the task of clearing the landing space. Men in green stowed the catapult gear so that no remnant of the powerful machine was visible. Other men in yellow leaped upon the deck and began to indicate the course each plane must follow on its way to forward stowage. Dozens of tough young men in blue leaned their shoulders against the planes, swung them laboriously into position and pushed them slowly into the biting wind. In blazing red uniforms other men checked guns or fueled empty craft while plane captains in brown sat in cockpits and worked the brakes to prevent accident. Darting about through the milling, pushing, shouting deck hands three-wheeled jeeps of vivid yellow and lumbering tractors in somber gray hurried to their jobs, while over all towered the mighty arms of the enormous black and sinister crane. Behind it lurked two weird men in fantastic suits of ashen gray asbestos, their faces peering from huge glassine boxes, ready to save the pilot if a crashed plane should burn, while in back of them, clothed in snowy white, the doctor waited, for death was always close upon the carrier deck.

So in an age of flight, in the jet age of incredible speed, these men pushed and pulled and slipped upon the icy deck and ordered the heavy planes with their bare hands. Upon trailing edges burdened with ice they pushed, their faces open to the freezing wind, their eyes heavy with frozen salt and the knuckles of their hands covered long since with protecting scars. And as they moved, their bright colors formed the pattern of a dance and after they had swarmed upon the deck for some minutes the *Savo* was transformed and from the lowering shadows the jets prepared to land.

This intricate operation was guided by one man. From the admiral's country he had directed the task force to run toward the communist coast. The last four jets had been despatched at his command. He had placed the ships so that the operations of one would not trespass the allotted space of the other, and it was his responsibility to see that his carrier faced the wind in such position that smoke trailed off to one side rather than directly aft and into the faces of incoming pilots. Now he stood upon his bridge and watched the mountains of Korea moving perilously close.

Admiral George Tarrant was a tall narrow man with a sharp face that was sour and withdrawing like those of his Maine ancestors. Battle-wizened, he had fought the Japanese with his own carrier at Saipan, at Iwo Jima and at Okinawa, where his austere and lonely presence had brought almost as much terror to his own fliers as it had to the enemy.

He was known through the navy as George the Tyrant, and any aviator who wanted to fetch a big laugh would grab a saucer in his left hand, a coffee cup in his right, lean back in his chair and survey the audience sourly, snorting, 'Rubbish.' Then the mimic would stare piercingly at some one pilot, jab the coffee cup at him and growl, 'You, son. What do you think?'

But men who served with Tarrant soon forgot his tyranny and remembered his fantastic skill in operating a task force. His men said flatly, 'He can do it better than anyone else in the world.' He knew the motion of the sea and could estimate whether a morning swell would rise to prevent recovery of afternoon planes or subside so that even jets could land freely. He was able to guess when new gales of bitter Siberian air would rush the line of snowstorms out to sea and when the snow would come creeping softly back and throw a blizzard about the task force as it slept at night. And he had a most curious ability to foresee what might trouble the tin-can sailors serving in the remote destroyers.

He fought upon the surface of the sea and in the sky. He sent his planes inland to support ground troops or far out to sea to spot Russian submarines. His was the most complex combat command of which one man's mind was capable and on him alone depended decisions of the gravest moment.

For example, the position he was now in, with mountains closing down upon him, was his responsibility. Early that morning his aerologist had warned, 'Wind's coming up, sir. You might run out of ocean by late afternoon.'

He studied the charts and growled, 'We'll make it.'

Now his navigator warned, 'We can't hold this course more than sixteen minutes, sir.' The young officer looked at the looming coastline as if to add, 'After that we'll have to turn back and abandon the planes.'

'We'll make it,' Tarrant grumbled as his ships plowed resolutely on toward the crucial hundred fathom curve which he dare not penetrate for fear of shoals, mines and submarines. But he turned his back upon this problem, for he could do nothing about it now. Instead, he checked to be sure the *Savo*'s deck was ready and in doing so he saw something which reassured him. Far aft, standing upon a tiny platform that jutted out over the side of the carrier, stood a hulking giant, muffled in fur and holding two landing-signal paddles in his huge hands. It was Beer Barrel, and if any man could bring jets surely and swiftly home, it was Beer Barrel.

He was an enormous man, six feet three, more than 250 pounds, and his heavy suit, stitched with strips of fluorescent cloth to make his arms and legs easier to read, added to his bulk. He was a farmer from Texas who before the perilous days of 1943 had never seen the ocean, but he possessed a fabulous ability to sense the motion of the sea and what position the carrier deck would take. He could judge the speed of jets as they whirled down upon him, but most of all he could imagine himself in the cockpit of every incoming plane and he seemed to know what tired and jittery pilots would do next and he saved their lives. He was a fearfully bad naval officer and in some ways a disgrace to his uniform, but everyone felt better when he came aboard a carrier, for he could do one thing. He could land planes.

He could reach out with his great hands and bring them safely home the way falconers used to bring back birds they loved. In the Pentagon they knew he broke rules and smuggled beer aboard each ship he served upon. Carrier captains knew it, and even Admiral Tarrant, who was a terror on navy rules, looked the other way when Beer Barrel staggered back after each drunken liberty, lugging his two ridiculous golf bags. The huge Texan had never once played golf and the two clubs sticking out were dummies. Once a deck hand, fearful that drunken Beer Barrel might slide back down the gangplank, had grabbed one of the outsize golf bags to help, but the surprising weight of it had crumpled him to the deck. Beer Barrel, barely able to heft the bag himself, had got it onto his massive shoulder, whispering beerily to the boy, 'Thanks, Junior, but this is man's work.' And he had carried the bags full of beer into his quarters.

For he believed that if he had a can of cold beer in his belly it formed a kind of gyroscope which made him unusually sensitive to the sea and that when this beer sloshed about it harmonized with the elements and he became one with the sea and the sky and the heaving deck and the heart of the incoming pilot.

'Land jets!' moaned the bull horn.

'Let's hear the checks,' Beer Barrel said to his spotters, staring aft to catch the first jet as it made its 180° turn for the cross leg and the sharp final turn into the landing run. Now the jet appeared and Beer Barrel thought, 'They're always pretty comin' home at night.'

'All down!' the first watcher cried as he checked the wheels, the flaps and the stout hook which now dangled lower than the wheels.

'All down,' Beer Barrel echoed unemotionally.

'Clear deck!' the second watcher shouted as he checked the nylon barriers and the thirteen heavy steel wires riding a few inches off the deck, waiting to engage the hook.

'Clear deck,' Beer Barrel grunted phlegmatically.

He extended his paddles out sideways from his shoulders, standing like an imperturbable rock, and willed the plane onto the deck. 'Come on, Junior,' he growled. 'Keep your nose up so's your hook'll catch. Good boy!' Satisfied that all was well, he snapped his right paddle dramatically across his heart and dropped his left arm as if it had been severed clean away from his body. Instantly the jet pilot cut his flaming speed and slammed his Banshee onto the deck. With violent grasp the protruding hook engaged one of the slightly elevated wires and dragged the massive plane to a shuddering stop.

Beer Barrel, watching from his platform, called to the clerk who kept records on each plane, '1593. Junior done real good. Number three wire.' Never did Beer Barrel feel so content, not even when guzzling lager, as when one of his boys caught number three wire. 'Heaven,' he explained once, 'is where everybody gets number three wire. Hell is where they fly wrong and catch number thirteen and crash into the barrier and burn. And every one of you's goin' straight to hell if you don't follow me better.'

From his own bridge, Admiral Tarrant watched the jets come home. In his life he had seen many fine and stirring things: his wife at the altar, Japanese battleships going down, ducks rising from Virginia marshes and his sons in uniform. But nothing he knew surpassed the sight of Beer Barrel bringing home the jets at dusk.

There always came that exquisite moment of human judgment when one man—a man standing alone on the remotest corner of the ship, lashed by foul wind and storm—had to decide that the jet roaring down upon him could make it. This solitary man had to judge the speed and height and the pitching of the deck and the wallowing of the sea and the oddities of this particular pilot and those additional imponderables that no man can explain. Then, at the last screaming second he had to make his decision and flash it to the pilot. He had only two choices. He could land the plane and risk the life of the pilot and the plane and the ship if he had judged wrong. Or he could wave-off and delay his decision until next time around. But he could defer his job to no one. It was his, and if he did judge wrong, carnage on the carrier deck could be fearful. That was why Admiral Tarrant never bothered about the bags of beer.

On they came, the slim and beautiful jets. As they roared upwind the admiral could see their stacks flaming. When they made their far turn and roared downwind he could see the pilots as human beings, tensed up and ready for the landing that was never twice the same. Finally, when these mighty jets hit the deck they weighed well over seven tons and their speed exceeded 135 miles an hour, yet within 120 feet they were completely stopped and this miracle was accomplished in several ways. First, Tarrant kept his carriers headed into the wind, which on this day stormed in at nearly 40 miles an hour, which cut the plane's relative speed to about 95 miles. Then, too, the carrier was running away from the plane at 11 miles an hour, which further cut the plane's speed to 84, and it was this actual speed that the wires had to arrest. They did so with brutal strength, but should they miss, two slim nylon barriers waited to drag the plane onto the deck and chop its impetus, halting it so that it could not proceed forward to damage other planes. And finally, should a runaway jet miss both the wires and the barriers, it would plunge into a stout nylon barricade which would entwine itself about the wings and wheels and tear the jet apart as if it were a helpless insect.

But it was Beer Barrel's job to see that the barriers and barricade were not needed and he would shout curses at his pilots and cry, 'Don't fly the deck, Junior. Don't fly the sea. Fly me.' An air force colonel watching Beer Barrel land jets exclaimed, 'Why, it isn't a landing at all! It's a controlled crash.' And the big Texan replied in his beery voice, 'Difference is that when I crash 'em they're safe in the arms of God.'

Now he brought in three more, swiftly and surely, and Admiral Tarrant, watching the looming mountains of Korea as they moved in upon his ships, muttered, 'Well, we'll make it again.'

But as he said these words his squawk box sounded, and from deep within the

Savo the combat intelligence director reported coolly, '1591 has been hit. Serious damage. May have to ditch.'

'What's his position?'

'Thirty-five miles away.'

'Who's with him?'

'His wingman, 1592.'

'Direct him to come on in and attempt landing.'

The squawk box clicked off and Admiral Tarrant looked straight ahead at the looming coast. Long ago he had learned never to panic, but he had trained himself to look at situations in their gloomiest aspects so as to be prepared for ill turns of luck. 'If this jet limps in we may have to hold this course for ten or fifteen more minutes. Well, we probably can do it.'

He studied the radar screen to estimate his probable position in fifteen minutes. 'Too close,' he muttered. Then into the squawk box which led to the air officer of the *Savo* he said, 'Recovery operations must end in ten minutes. Get all planes aboard.'

'The admiral knows there's one in trouble?'

'Yes. I've ordered him to try to land.'

'Yes, sir.'

The bull horn sounded. 'All hands. We must stop operations within ten minutes. Get those barriers cleared faster. Bring the planes in faster.'

The telephone talker at the landing platform told Beer Barrel, 'We got to get 'em all aboard in ten minutes.'

'What's a matter?' Beer Barrel growled. 'Admiral running hisself out of ocean?'

'Looks like it,' the talker said.

'You tell him to get the planes up here and I'll get 'em aboard.'

So the nineteen dark ships of the task force sped on toward the coastline and suddenly the squawk box rasped, 'Admiral, 1591 says he will have to ditch.'

'Can he ditch near the destroyers?'

'Negative.'

'Is his wingman still with him?'

'Affirmative.'

'How much fuel?'

'Six hundred pounds.'

'Have you a fix on their positions?'

'Affirmative.'

'Dispatch helicopter and tell wingman to land immediately.'

There was a long silence and the voice said, 'Wingman 1592 requests permission stay with downed plane till copter arrives.'

The admiral was now faced with a decision no man should have to make. If the wingman stayed on, he would surely run out of fuel and lose his own plane and probably his life as well. But to command him to leave a downed companion was inhuman and any pilot aboard the *Savo* would prefer to risk his own life and his plane rather than to leave a man adrift in the freezing sea before the helicopter had spotted him.

For in the seas off Korea a downed airman had twenty minutes to live. That was all. The water was so bitterly cold that within five minutes the hands were frozen and the face. In twelve minutes of immersion in these fearful waters the arms became unable to function and by the twentieth minute the pilot was frozen to death.

The decision could not be deferred, for the squawk box repeated, 'Wingman 1592 requests permission to stay.'

The admiral asked, 'What is the absolute minimum of gas with which the wingman can make a straight-in landing?'

There was a moment's computation. 'Assuming he finds the carrier promptly, about four hundred pounds.'

'Tell him to stay with the downed man . . .'

The voice interrupted, 'Admiral, 1591 has just ditched. Wingman says the plane sank immediately.'

There was a moment's silence and the admiral asked, 'Where's the helicopter?'

'About three more minutes away from the ditching.'

'Advise the helicopter . . .'

'Admiral, the wingman reports downed pilot afloat.'

'Tell the wingman to orbit until helicopter arrives. Then back for a straight-in landing.'

The bull horn echoed in the gathering dusk and mournful sounds spread over the flight deck, speaking of disaster. 'Get those last two jets down immediately. Then prepare for emergency straight-in landing. A plane has been lost at sea. Wingman coming in short of fuel.'

For a moment the many-colored figures stopped their furious motions. The frozen hands stopped pushing jets and the yellow jeeps stayed where they were. No matter how often you heard the news it always stopped you. No matter how frozen your face was, the bull horn made you a little bit colder. And far out to sea, in a buffeted helicopter, two enlisted men were coldest of all.

At the controls was Mike Forney, a tough twenty-seven-year-old Irishman from Chicago. In a navy where enlisted men hadn't much chance of flying, Mike had made it. He had bullied his way through to flight school and his arrival aboard his first ship, the *Savo*, would be remembered as long as the ship stayed afloat. It was March 17 when he flew his copter onto the flight deck, wearing an opera hat painted green, a Baron von Richthofen scarf of kelly green, and a clay pipe jammed into his big teeth. He had his earphones wrapped around the back of his neck and when the captain of the *Savo* started to chew him out Forney said, 'When I appear anywhere I want the regular pilots to know it, because if they listen to me, I'll save 'em.' Now, as he sped toward the ditched pilot, he was wearing his green stovepipe and his World War I kelly green scarf, for he had found that when those astonishing symbols appeared at a scene of catastrophe everyone relaxed, and he had already saved three pilots.

But the man flying directly behind Mike Forney's hat wasn't relaxed. Nestor Gamidge, in charge of the actual rescue gear, was a sad-faced inconsequential young man from Kentucky, where his unmarried schoolteacher mother had named him Nestor after the wisest man in history, hoping that he would justify everything. But Nestor had not lived up to his name and was in fact rather stupid, yet, as the copter flew low over the bitter waves to find the ditched plane, he was bright enough to know that if anyone were to save the airman pitching about in the freezing water below it would be he. In this spot the admiral didn't count nor the wingman who was orbiting upstairs nor even Mike Forney. In a few minutes he would lean out of the helicopter and lower a steel hoisting sling for the pilot to climb into. But from cold experience he knew that the man below would probably be too frozen even to lift his arms, so he, Nestor Gamidge, who hated the sea and who was dragged into the navy by his draft board, would have to jump into the icy waves and try to shove the inert body of the pilot into the sling. And if he failed–if his own hands froze before he could accomplish this–the pilot must die. That's why they gave Nestor the job. He was dumb and he was under-sized but he was strong.

'I see him,' Nestor said.

Mike immediately called to the wingman: '1592. Go on home. This is Mike Forney and everything's under control.'

'Mike!' the wingman called. 'Save that guy.'

'We always save 'em. Scram.'

'That guy down there is Harry Brubaker. The one whose wife and kids are waiting for him in Yokosuka. But he don't know it. Save him!'

Mike said to Nestor, 'You hear that? He's the one whose wife and kids came out to surprise him.'

'He looks froze,' Nestor said, lowering the sling.

Suddenly Mike's voice lost its brashness. 'Nestor,' he said quietly, 'if you have to jump in . . . I'll stay here till the other copter gets you.'

In dismay, Nestor watched the sling drift past the downed pilot and saw that the man was too frozen to catch hold. So he hauled the sling back up and said, 'I'll have to go down.'

Voluntarily, he fastened the sling about him and dropped into the icy waves.

'Am I glad to see you!' the pilot cried.

'He's O.K.,' Nestor signaled.

'Lash him in,' Mike signaled back.

'Is that Mike? With the green hat?'

'Yep.'

'My hands won't . . .'

They tried four times to do so simple a thing as force the sling down over the pilot's head and arms but the enormous weight of watersoaked clothing made him an inert lump. There was a sickening moment when Nestor thought he might fail. Then, with desperate effort, he jammed his right foot into the pilot's back and shoved. The sling caught.

Nestor lashed it fast and signaled Mike to haul away. Slowly the pilot was pulled clear of the clutching sea and was borne aloft. Nestor, wallowing below, thought, 'There goes another.'

Then he was alone. On the bosom of the great sea he was alone and unless the second helicopter arrived immediately, he would die. Already, overpowering cold tore at the seams of his clothing and crept in to get him. He could feel it numb his powerful hands and attack his strong legs. It was the engulfing sea, the icy and deadly sea that he despised and he was deep into it and his arms were growing heavy.

Then, out of the gathering darkness, came the *Hornet*'s copter.

So Mike called the *Savo* and reported, 'Two copters comin' home with two frozen mackerel.'

'What was that?' the *Savo* asked gruffly.

'What I said,' Mike replied, and the two whirly birds headed for home, each dangling below it the freezing body of a man too stiff to crawl inside.

Meanwhile Admiral Tarrant was faced with a new problem. The downed pilot had been rescued but the incoming wingman had fuel sufficient for only one pass, and if that pass were waved off the pilot would have to crash land into the sea and hope for a destroyer pickup, unless one of the copters could find him in the gathering dusk.

But far more important than the fate of one Banshee were the nineteen ships of the task force which were now closing the hundred fathom mark. For them to proceed farther would be to invite the most serious trouble. Therefore the admiral judged that he had at most two minutes more on course, after which he would be forced to run with the wind, and then no jet could land, for the combined speed of jet and wind would be more than 175 miles, which would tear out any landing hook and probably the barriers as well. But the same motive that had impelled the wingman to stay at the scene of the crash, the motive that forced Nestor Gamidge to plunge into the icy sea, was at work upon the admiral and he said, 'We'll hold the wind a little longer. Move a little closer to shore.'

Nevertheless, he directed the four destroyers on the forward edge of the screen to turn back toward the open sea, and he checked them on the radar as they moved off. For the life of one pilot he was willing to gamble his command that there were no mines and that Russia had no submarines lurking between him and the shore.

'1592 approaching,' the squawk box rasped.

'Warn him to come straight in.'

Outside the bull horn growled, 'Prepare to land last jet, straight in.'

Now it was the lead cruiser's turn to leave the formation but the *Savo* rode solemnly on, lingering to catch this last plane. On the landing platform Beer Barrel's watcher cried, 'Hook down, wheels down. Can't see flaps.'

The telephone talker shouted, 'Pilot reports his flaps down.'

'All down,' Beer Barrel droned.

'Clear deck!'

'Clear deck.'

Now even the carrier *Hornet* turned away from the hundred fathom line and steamed parallel to it while the jet bore in low across her path. Beer Barrel, on his wooden platform, watched it come straight and low and slowing down.

'Don't watch the sea, Junior,' he chanted. 'Watch me. Hit me in the kisser with your left wing tank and you'll be all right, Junior.' His massive arms were outstretched with the paddles parallel to the deck and the jet screamed in, trying to adjust its altitude to the shifting carrier's.

'Don't fly the deck, Junior!' roared Beer Barrel and for one fearful instant it looked as if the onrushing jet had put itself too high. In that millionth of a second Beer Barrel thought he would have to wave the plane off but then his judgment cried that there was a chance the plane could make it. So Beer Barrel shouted. 'Keep comin', Junior!' and at the last moment he whipped the right paddle across his heart and dropped the left.

The plane was indeed high and for one devastating moment seemed to be floating down the deck and into the parked jets. Then, when a crash seemed inevitable, it settled fast and caught number nine. The jet screamed ahead and finally stopped with its slim nose peering into the webs of the barrier.

'You fly real good, Junior,' Beer Barrel said, tucking the paddles under his arm, but when the pilot climbed down his face was ashen and he shouted, 'They rescue Brubaker?'

'They got him.'

The pilot seemed to slump and his plane captain ran up and caught him by the arm and led him to the ladder, but as they reached for the first step they stumbled and pitched forward, so swift was the *Savo*'s groaning turn back out to sea.

As soon as the copters appeared with little Gamidge and the unconscious body of the pilot dangling through the icy air, Admiral Tarrant sent his personal aide down to sick bay to tell the helicopter men he would like to see them after the flight doctor had taken care of them. In a few minutes they arrived in flag plot, Forney in trim aviator's flight jacket and Gamidge in a fatigue suit some sizes too large.

The admiral poured them coffee and said, 'Sit down.' Forney grabbed the comfortable corner of the leather davenport on which the admiral slept when he did not wish to leave this darkened room of radar screens, repeating compasses and charts, but Gamidge fumbled about until the admiral indicated where he was to sit. Pointing at the squat Kentuckian with his coffee cup, the admiral said, 'It must have been cold in the water.'

'It was!' Forney assured him. 'Bitter.'

'I hope the doctor gave you something to warm you up.'

'Nestor's too young to drink,' Forney said, 'but I had some.'

'You weren't in the water.'

'No, sir, but I had the canopy open.'

'How's the pilot?'

'When me and Gamidge go out for them we bring them back in good shape.'

'They tell me he wasn't able to climb into the sling.'

'That pilot was a real man, sir. Couldn't move his hands or arms but he never whimpered.'

'Because he fainted,' Nestor explained.

The admiral invariably insisted upon interviewing all men who did outstanding work and now he pointed his cup at Gamidge again. 'Son, do you know any way we could improve the rescue sling?'

The little Kentuckian thought a long time and then said slowly, 'Nope. If their hands freeze somebody's got to go into the water to get them.'

The admiral put his cup down and said brusquely, 'Keep bringing them back. Navy's proud of men like you.'

'Yes, sir!' Forney said. He always pronounced *sir* with an insinuating leer, as if he wished to put commissioned officers at ease. Then he added, 'There is one thing we could do to make the chopper better.'

'What's that?'

'I got to operate that sling quicker. Because it seems like Nestor goes into the sea almost every time.'

'You know what changes to make?'

'Yes, sir.'

'Then make them.'

The two enlisted men thanked the admiral and as they went down the ladder Tarrant heard Forney ask, 'Nestor, why'd you stand there with your mouth shut, like a moron? Suppose he is a mean old bastard. No reason to be scared of him.'

'By the way,' the admiral called. 'Who was the pilot?'

'Brubaker, sir,' Forney cried, unabashed.

The name struck Tarrant with visible force. He backed into the darkened flag plot and steadied himself for a moment. 'Brubaker!' he repeated quietly. 'How strange that it should have been Brubaker!'

Shaken, he slumped onto the leather davenport and reached for some papers which had been delivered aboard ship by dispatch plane that afternoon. 'Brubaker!' He scanned the papers and called sick bay.

'Doctor,' he asked, 'any chance I could talk with Brubaker?'

A crisp voice snapped back, 'Admiral, you know the man's suffered exposure.'

'I know that, but there's an urgent matter and I thought that when he found himself in good shape . . .' He left it at that.

Then he thought of Brubaker, a twenty-nine-year-old civilian who had been called back into service against his will. At the start of the cruise he had been something of a problem, griping ceaselessly about the raw deal the navy had given him, but gradually he had become one of the two or three finest pilots. He still griped, he still damned the navy, but he did his job. The admiral respected men like that.

But Brubaker had a special significance, for on recent cruises Admiral Tarrant had adopted the trick of selecting some young man of about the age and rank his older son would have attained had the Japs not shot him down while he was trying to launch a navy fighter plane on the morning of Pearl Harbor. Tarrant found satisfaction in watching the behaviour of such pilots, for they added meaning to his otherwise lonely life. But in the case of Harry Brubaker the trick had come close to reality. The Banshee pilot had the quick temper of his sons, the abiding resentments, the courage.

Admiral Tarrant therefore desperately wanted to leave flag plot and go down into the ship and talk with Brubaker, but custom of the sea forbade this, for the captain of any ship must be supreme upon that ship, and even the flag admiral who chances to make his quarters aboard is a guest. So Admiral Tarrant was cooped up in flag plot, a tiny bedroom and a special bridge reserved for his use. That was his country and there he must stay.

There was a knock upon the door and the aide said, 'Sir, it's Brubaker!'

The good-looking young man who stuck his head in was obviously a civilian. He wore two big bathrobes and heavy woolen socks but even if he had worn dress uniform he would have been a civilian. He was a little overweight, his hair was a bit too long and he wasn't scared enough of the admiral. Indelibly, he was a young lawyer from Denver, Colorado, and the quicker he got out of the navy and back into a courtroom, the happier he'd be.

'You can scram now,' he told the medical corpsman who had brought him up to the admiral's country.

'Come in, Brubaker,' the admiral said stiffly. 'Cup of coffee?' As he reached for the cup Brubaker didn't exactly stand at attention but the admiral said quickly, 'Sit down, son. How's the Banshee take the water?'

'All right, if you fly her in.'

'You keep the tail down?'

'I tried to. But as you approach the water every inclination is to land nose first. Then from way back in the past I remembered an October night when our family was burning leaves and at the end my mother pitched a bucket of water on the bonfire. I can still recall the ugly smell. Came back to me tonight. I said, "If I let water get into the engines I'll smell it again." So I edged the plane lower and lower. Kept the engines up and the tail way down. When the nose finally hit I was nearly stopped. But I was right. There was that same ugly smell.'

'How was the helicopter?'

'That kid in back deserves a medal.'

'They handle the rescue O.K.?'

'This man Forney. When I looked up and saw that crazy hat I knew I had it knocked.'

Admiral Tarrant took a deep gulp of coffee and studied Brubaker across the rim of his cup. He knew he oughtn't to discuss this next point with a junior officer but he had to talk with someone. 'You say the green hat gave you a little extra fight?'

'You're scared. Then you see an opera hat coming at you out of nowhere. You relax.'

'I would. Forney was in here a few minutes ago. Put me right at ease. Implied I was doing a fair job. You've got to respect a character like that. But the funny thing . . .' He looked into his cup and said casually, 'Captain of the ship's going to get rid of Forney. Says the hat's an outrage.'

Brubaker knew the admiral was out of line so he didn't want to press for more details but he did say, 'The pilots'd be unhappy.'

The admiral, far back in his corner of the davenport, studied the bundled-up young man and jabbed his coffee cup at him. 'Harry, you're one of the finest pilots we have. You go in low, you do the job.'

Brubaker grinned. He had a generous mouth and even teeth. His grin was attractive. 'From you, sir, I appreciate that.'

'Then why don't you stay in the navy? Great future here for you.'

The grin vanished. 'You know what I think of the navy, sir.'

'Still bitter?'

'Still. I was unattached. The organized units were drawing pay. They were left home. I was called. Sometimes I'm so bitter I could bitch up the works on purpose.'

'Why don't you?' Tarrant asked evenly.

'You know why I don't, sir. The catapult fires. There's that terrific moment and you're out front. On your way to Korea. So you say, "What the heck? I'm here. Might as well do the job." '

'Exactly. The President once rebuked me publicly. I'd had that big fight with the battleship boys because they didn't think aviation was important. Then the brawl with the air force who thought it too important. I know I'll never get promoted again. But you're here and you do the job.'

'It would be easier to take if people back home were helping. But in Denver nobody even knew there was a war except my wife. Nobody supports this war.'

At the mention of Brubaker's wife the admiral unconsciously reached for the file of papers, but he stopped because what the young pilot said interested him. 'Every war's the wrong one,' he said. 'Could anything have been stupider than choosing Guadalcanal for a battleground? And look at us today!' With his cup he indicated on the chart where the permanent snow line, heavy with blizzards and sleet, hung a few miles to the east, while to the west the mountains of Korea hemmed in the ships. 'Imagine the United States navy tied down to a few square miles of ocean. The marines are worse. Dug into permanent trenches. And the poor air force is the most misused of all. Bombers flying close air support. Militarily this war is a tragedy.'

'Then why don't we pull out?' Harry asked bluntly.

Admiral Tarrant put his cup and saucer down firmly. 'That's rubbish, son, and you know it. All through history free men have had to fight the wrong war in the wrong place. But that's the one they're stuck with. That's why, one of these days, we'll knock out those bridges at Toko-ri.'

Flag plot grew silent. The two men stared at each other. For in every war there is one target whose name stops conversation. You say that name and the men who must fly against that target sit mute and stare ahead. In Europe, during World War II it was Ploesti or Peenemunde. In the Pacific it was Truk or the Yawata steel works. Now, to the navy off Korea, it was the deadly concentration of mountains and narrow passes and festering gun emplacements that hemmed the vital bridges at Toko-ri. Here all communist supplies to the central and eastern front assembled. Here the communists were vulnerable.

Finally Brubaker asked, 'Do we have to knock out those particular bridges?'

'Yes, we must. I believe without question that some morning a bunch of communist generals and commissars will be holding a meeting to discuss the future of the war. And a messenger will run in with news that the Americans have knocked out even the bridges at Toko-ri. And that little thing will convince the Reds that we'll never stop . . . never give in . . . never weaken in our purpose.'

Again the two men studied each other and the admiral asked, 'More coffee?' As Brubaker held his cup the old man said gruffly, 'But I didn't call you here to discuss strategy. I'm supposed to chew you out.' With the coffee pot he indicated the file of papers.

'They crying because I wrecked that wheel?'

'No. Because of your wife.'

The astonishment on Brubaker's face was so real that Tarrant was convinced the young man was unaware his wife and two daughters were in Japan. Nevertheless he had a job to do so he asked, 'You knew she was in Japan?'

'She made it!' A look of such triumph and love captured Brubaker's face that the admiral felt he ought to look away. Then quietly the young man said, 'This is more than a guy dares hope for, sir.'

'You better hope you don't get a court martial.'

'I didn't tell her to come,' Brubaker protested, but such a huge grin captured his face that he proved himself a liar.

Tarrant kept on being tough. 'How'd she get here without your help?'

'Politics. Her father used to be senator from Wyoming.'

Brubaker closed his eyes. He didn't care what happened. Nancy had made it. In the jet ready rooms he had known many pilots and their women troubles but he kept out of all bull sessions. He loved one girl. He had loved her with letters all through the last war in New Guinea and Okinawa. The day he got home he married her and she'd never given him any trouble. Now she was in Japan. Quietly he said to the admiral, 'If she's broken a dozen rules to get here it's all right by me.'

The old man didn't know what to say. 'War's no place for women,' he grunted.

Then Brubaker explained. 'If my wife really is in Japan, I know why. She couldn't take America any longer. Watching people go on as if there were no war. We gave up our home, my job, the kids. Nobody else in Denver gave up anything.'

This made the admiral angry. 'Rubbish,' he growled. 'Burdens always fall on a few. You know that. Look at this ship. Every man aboard thinks he's a hero because he's in Korea. But only a few of you ever really bomb the bridges.'

'But why my wife and me?'

'Nobody ever knows why he gets the dirty job. But any society is held together by the efforts . . . yes, and the sacrifices of only a few.'

Brubaker couldn't accept this, Tarrant realized, and he was getting mad in the way that had characterized the admiral's sons. The old man had learned to respect this attitude, so he waited for the young pilot to speak but Brubaker happened to think of his wife waiting in Japan and his anger left. 'Look,' he said. 'It's sleeting.' The two men went to the dark window and looked down upon the silent carrier, her decks fast with ice, her planes locked down by sleet.

'It'll be all right by dawn,' the old man said.

'You ever hear what the pilots say about you and the weather? "At midnight he runs into storms but at take-off the deck's always clear, damn him." '

The admiral laughed and said, 'Three days you'll be in Japan. No more worry about take-offs for a while.' He slapped the papers into a basket. 'I'll tell Tokyo you had nothing to do with bringing your wife out here.'

'Thank you, sir.'

Quickly the admiral resumed his austere ways. Shaking Brubaker's hand he said stiffly, 'Mighty glad you were rescued promptly. Why don't you see if the surgeon can spare a little extra nightcap.'

As soon as Brubaker left, Tarrant thought, 'His wife did right. If mine had come to Hawaii when our oldest son was killed, maybe things would have been different.' But she had stayed home, as navy wives are expected to, and somewhere between the bombing of Pearl Harbor, where she lost one son, and the battle of Midway, where her second was killed trying to torpedo a Japanese carrier, her mind lost focus and she started to drink a lot and forget people's names until slowly, like petals of apple blossoms in spring, fragments of her gentle personality fell away and she would sit for hours staring at a wall.

Therefore it angered Tarrant when civilians like Brubaker suggested that he, a professional military man, could not understand war. Quite the contrary, he knew no civilian who understood war as thoroughly as he. Two sons and a home he had given to war. He had sacrificed the promotion of his career by insisting that America have the right weapons in case war came. And now in Korea, of the 272 pilots who had initially served with him in his task force, 31 had been killed by communist gunfire. Tonight he had come within two minutes of losing Brubaker, the best of the lot. No one need tell him what war was.

He was therefore doubly distressed when the people of the United States reacted like Brubaker: 'Hold back the enemy but let someone else do it.' He felt that his nation did not realize it was engaged in an unending war of many generations against resolute foes who were determined to pull it down. Some of the phases of this war would no doubt be fought without military battles. Whole decades might pass in some kind of peace but more likely the desultory battles would stagger on and from each community some young men would be summoned to do the fighting. They would be like Brubaker, unwilling to join up but tough adversaries when there was no alternative. And no matter where they might be sent to serve, Tarrant was positive that they would hate that spot the way he and Brubaker hated Korea. It would always be the wrong place.

As if to demonstrate afresh how ridiculous Korea was, the aerologist appeared with the midnight weather reports from Siberia and China. Since these nations were not officially at war, their weather stations were required to broadcast their customary summaries, just as American and Japanese stations broadcast theirs. But since Korea weather was determined by what had happened in Siberia and China two days before, the admiral always had the tip-off and the enemy gained nothing.

'All wars are stupid,' the old man grunted as he filed the Siberian reports. 'But we'd better learn to handle the stupidity.' He recalled England and

France, dragging through their Korean wars for more than two hundred years. They had avoided panicky general mobilization and millions of citizens must have spent their lives without worrying about war until something flared up like Crimea, South Africa or Khartoum.

'And their wars weren't even forced upon them,' he growled. Secretly he was frightened. Could America stick it out when dangers multiplied? If Englishmen and Frenchmen, and before them Athenians and the men of Spain, had been willing to support their civilizations through centuries of difficulty when often those difficulties were self-generated, what would happen to the United States if her citizenry abandoned the honorable responsibilities forced upon her by the relentless press of history?

He went up on the bridge to check the rolling sea for the last time. 'What would they have us abandon to the enemy?' he asked. 'Korea? Then Japan and the Philippines? Sooner or later Hawaii?' He walked back and forth pondering this problem of where abandonment would end, and as the sleet howled upon him he could not fix that line: 'Maybe California. Colorado. Perhaps we'd stabilize at the Mississippi.' He could not say. Instead he held to one unwavering conviction: 'A messenger will run in and tell the commissars, "They even knocked out the bridges at Toko-ri." And that's the day they'll quit.' Then reason might come into the world.

Upon that hope he ended the long day. He had checked the wind and the weather and the rolling of the sea and the number of planes ready for the dawn strike and the location of those storms that always hovered near his ships. He had posted the night watches and he could do no more.

LAND

It was the greatest liberty port in the world. It had more variety than Marseilles, more beauty than Valparaiso. Its prices were cheaper than New York's, its drinks better than Lisbon's. And there were far more pretty girls than in Tahiti.

It was Yokosuka, known through all the fleets of the world as Yu-*koss*-ka, and almost every man who had been there once had a girl waiting for him when he got back the second time. For in the cities near the port were millions of pretty girls who loved American sailors and their hilarious ways and their big pay checks. It was a great liberty port.

Now as the *Savo* moved cautiously in toward her dock hundreds of these girls waited for their sailors and thousands were on hand for sailors they had not yet seen. Grim-faced guards kept the invaders away from the ship, but the girls did gather outside the gates, and among them on this windy, wintry day was one especially handsome girl of twenty dressed in plaid skirt from Los Angeles, trim coat from Sears Roebuck, and jaunty cap from San Francisco. She wore her jet hair in braids and kept a laugh ready in the corners of her wide, black eyes. Her complexion was of soft gold and seemed to blush as some of the other girls caught a glimpse of the *Savo* and pretended they had seen her sailor.

'There's green hat!' they cried in Japanese.

'You don't worry about green hat,' she replied, pressing against the fence.

A comic among the girls put her right hand high above her head and swaggered as she had seen Mike Forney swagger on earlier leaves, and excitement grew as the *Savo* approached her berth. But this morning the girls would have to stand in the cold a long time, for there was a sharp wind off the sea and the lumbering bulk of the carrier presented so much freeboard for the wind to blow against that tugs with limited maneuvering space could not hold her from crashing into the quay, and emergency measures were clearly necessary. Accordingly the bull horn wailed the bad news, 'F4U and AD pilots prepare for windmill.'

Every propeller pilot cringed with disgust but none showed such outrage as one of the jet men. Stocky, florid faced, with a cigar jutting from his teeth, this forty-year-old Annapolis man whipped his bullet head and underslung jaw toward the bridge to see what stupid fool had ordered another windmill. As 'Cag,' commander of the air group, he was in charge of all planes and felt sickened as he watched the propeller jobs wheel into position. He was about to storm off the flight deck to raise a real row when Brubaker, standing with him, caught his arm and said, 'Take it easy, Cag. You don't have to pay for the burned out engines.'

'It's murder,' the Cag groaned as his valuable prop planes were lashed down to the edge of the deck which threatened to crash against the quay. Their noses were pointed into the wind and their unhappy pilots sat in the cockpits and waited.

'Start engines,' yowled the bull horn. Sixteen valuable engines revolved and sixteen sets of propeller blades tried to pull the big carrier away from the quay, but the effort was not sufficient, and the *Savo* appeared certain to crash.

'Engines full speed,' moaned the bull horn and the noise on deck became great as the props clawed into the air and magically held the great ship secure against the wind.

This caused no satisfaction among the propeller pilots, for since their planes were stationary on deck, with no wind rushing through to cool them, each engine was burning itself seriously and one plane mechanic rushed up to the Cag with tears in his eyes cursing and crying, 'They're wrecking the planes! Look!'

One of the low-slung F4U's had begun to throw smoke and the Cag ran over to study it. He chomped his cigar in anger and said grimly, 'They're killing these planes.'

'Somebody's got to stop this,' the mechanic said.

'I'm going to,' Cag replied quietly and started for the admiral's plot, but before he could get there Brubaker hauled him down and the two men watched the propeller planes gradually ease up and allow the *Savo* to inch into her berth as gently as a fragile egg being laid into a basket by an old farm wife.

'Cut engines,' rasped the bull horn and the Cag said bitterly, 'Burn those engines up now and next trip over Korea the pilot bails out. This lousy captain thinks he has a new toy to play with.'

'Save it for the hotel,' Brubaker said. 'Take it up with the admiral there.' So the Cag turned away and as he did so Brubaker looked down from the carrier deck onto the quay and there stood Nancy and the two girls, dressed in winter coats and huddling together to protect one another from the wind. A great lump came into his throat and for a moment he could not wave or call, so that Mike Forney, who was marching up and down, impatient to burst ashore, asked, 'That your family, sir?'

'Yes.'

'It's worth bein' saved for them, sir.' The way Mike said *sir* made Brubaker look to see if the cocky Irishman were kidding him, but Forney was staring raptly at Nancy and the two girls. 'Hey, Mrs Brubaker!' he roared. 'Here's your hero.'

Jumping up and down on her toes Nancy called excitedly to her daughters, 'There's Daddy!' And they all threw him kisses.

Mike, watching with approval, said, 'Right beyond that fence, sir. I got the same kind of reception waiting for me.'

'You married?' Brubaker asked in astonishment. Somehow he had never thought of Mike as a family man.

'Not yet, but I may be. This shore leave.'

'Some girl who came out with the Occupation?'

'Japanese girl,' Mike said, adjusting his green hat at a night-club angle, but a messenger from the ship's executive officer arrived to inform Forney that the uniform of the day called for something more traditional and the insulted Irishman went below.

Immediately Brubaker wished that Mike had stayed, for the pain of seeing his women on the quay below was too great. They had come too far, they loved him too much and they reminded him too soon of icy Korea's waters clutching at him, trying to drag him down. For the first time in his life he became desperately afraid and wanted to leave the *Savo* right then, for he saw leading from the deck of the carrier, right above the bodies of his wife and daughters, four bridges stretching far out to sea and they were the bridges of Toko-ri and he was breathlessly afraid of them.

'Nancy,' he whispered. 'You should have stayed home.'

But as soon as the ship's lines were secured, he dashed down the gangplank to embrace his wife and as he did so his youngest daughter caught him by the leg and began to babble furiously and from the way he bent down and listened to the excited little girl–as if he actually wanted to know what she had to say–every married man on the deck of the *Savo* towering above knew that Brubaker really loved his kids.

What the child said was, 'I made a long airplane ride and now I know what you do on the ship.' But Brubaker remembered the icy water and thought, 'Thank God you don't know. And thank God your mummy doesn't, either.' Then he laughed and caught the little girl in his arms and kissed her a lot and she said, 'I like to fly airplanes like you, Daddy.'

For Mike Forney reunions were somewhat less complicated, at first. Attended by silent Nestor Gamidge he strode to the gates of Yokosuka Naval Base, threw the marine on guard a nifty salute and stepped outside to freedom. He was a cocky figure, his fists jammed into his pea coat jacket, his uniform a trifle to tight, and it took him only a moment to find the girls. He stopped dead, thrust his big paw onto Gamidge's chest and cried, 'Look at her, Nestor! Best-dressed girl in Japan!' Then he gave a bellow, rushed forward and caught Kimiko in his arms and kissed her lovely little cap right off her head.

'Hey, Kimiko! Fleet's in!'

To his astonishment she pushed him away, sedately picked up her cap and said, 'Not so fast, big boy. We got to talk.' And she led him to a bar and started patiently to explain the radically new situation, the one which was to cause the two riots.

For the officers of the *Savo* the Tokyo brass had reserved rest and recuperation rooms at the Fuji-san, a meandering Japanese hotel whose exquisite one-storied rooms and gardens hung on a mountain top which commanded a superb view of Fujiyama. In the old days this had been Japan's leading hotel but for the first six years after the war it served Americans only. Now, in the transition period between occupation and sovereignty, it had become a symbol of the strange and satisfying relationship between Japan and America: the choice rooms were still reserved for Americans but Japanese were welcome to use the hotel as before; so its spacious gardens, bent with pine and cherry, held both Japanese families who were enjoying luxury after long years of austerity and American military men savoring the same luxury after long months in Korea.

No one enjoyed the Fuji-san more than Admiral Tarrant. He arrived on the second day of liberty, changed into civilian clothes, gathered about him his younger staff officers and forgot the rigors of Task Force 77. Other admirals, when they reached Japan, were whisked into Tokyo for press conferences where they sat on the edges of their chairs trying to say exactly the right and innocuous thing. They must not, for example, admit that they were fighting Russians, nor must they even indicate that any of our men were being killed. In this special war there were special rules to keep the people back in America from becoming worried.

Admiral Tarrant was not the man for such interviews. The navy tried it once and he had said bluntly, 'We're fighting Russian guns, Russian radar, Russian planes and Russian submarines. And a hell of a lot of our men are being killed by this Russian equipment, manned by Russian experts.' General Ridgway's headquarters in Tokyo had blown a gasket and the entire interview was made top secret and the navy was advised that whereas Tarrant might be terrific as a task force commander, 'Send him to some good hotel when he gets ashore . . . and keep him there.'

Now he lounged in the bar and watched a group of pilots pestering Beer Barrel. Ten minutes after the *Savo* docked, the landing-signal officer had grabbed for the bar stool and he had sat there for almost twenty-nine hours, lapping up the wonderful Japanese beer. 'Look at him!' one Banshee pilot cried. 'He's goin' crazy. Doesn't know whether to claim Texas has the biggest midgets in the world or the smallest.'

Four jet men, themselves pretty well hung over, formed a solemn circle about Beer Barrel and began to chant the carrier pilot's version of the Twenty-third Psalm:

The Beer Barrel is my shepherd
I shall not crash.
He maketh me to land on flat runways: he bringeth me in off the rough waters.
He restoreth my confidence.
Yea, though I come stalling into the groove at sixty knots, I shall fear no evil: for he is with me; his arm and his paddle, they comfort me.
He prepareth a deck before me in the presence of mine enemies; he attacheth my hook to the wire; my deck space runneth over.

Admiral Tarrant laughed at the nonsense. Since his big operation two years ago he drank only coffee, but he often growled, 'Just because I'm a reformed drunk no reason why I should deny pleasure to others.' He poured himself some inky black coffee and looked into the gardens, where he saw Harry Brubaker's wonderfully lovely wife and her two daughters and they reminded him of what wars were all about. 'You don't fight to protect warships or old men. Like the book says, you fight to save your civilization. And so often it seems that civilization is composed mainly of the things women and children want.'

Then the admiral grew glum, for Mrs Brubaker had told him at lunch, 'If the government dared to ask women like me, this stupid war would end tomorrow.' There lay the confusion. These bright, lovely women, whose husbands had to do the fighting, wanted to end the war on any terms; but these same women, whose children would have to live through servitude or despair should America ever be occupied, would be the precise ones who would goad their men into revitalization and freedom. So Admiral Tarrant never argued with women because in their own deep way they were invariably right. No more war . . . but no humiliation. He hoped to see the day when this difficult program could be attained.

But a more present problem was at hand, for the Cag stormed across the garden, his cigar jutting belligerently ahead like a mine sweeper. The tough airman was known throughout the navy as a fireball and this time Tarrant, himself an airman, knew the Cag was right. The *Savo's* use of windmill had been intemperate, a perversion of aircraft engines, but a deeper concern was involved, so the admiral prepared to squelch the likeable hothead.

For the navy high command had secretly asked Tarrant to send in a concurrent report upon this demon flier when his Korean duty ended. It was hinted that a bright and brash young man was needed for rapid promotion to a command of real authority and Tarrant guessed that the Cag was being weighed as an eventual task force commander. 'It's a big job,' the admiral mused.

He could recall that day in 1945 when Admiral Halsey commanded a supreme force built of five components each twice as large as present Task Force 77. It was so vast it blackened the sea with more than twenty carriers. It stretched for miles and ultimately it sank the entire Japanese fleet. One brain had commanded that incredible force and it behooved the United States to have other men ready for the job, should such a task force ever again be needed.

Long ago Tarrant had begun to argue that some new weapon—rockets perhaps or pilotless planes of vast speed—would inevitably constitute the task force of the future. He had seen so much change, indeed had spurred it on, that he could not rely perpetually on ships or airplanes or any one device. But until America was secure behind the protection of some new agency that could move about the earth with security and apply pressure wherever the enemy chose to assault us, it would be wise to have young officers trained to command a sea burdened with ships and speckled with the shadows of a thousand planes.

Perhaps the Cag was such a man. A lot of navy people thought so but no one knew for sure whether he had those two ultimate requirements for vast command: had he a resolute spirit and had he due regard for human life?

The Cag jammed his cigar through the door and asked, 'May I speak with you, sir?'

Tarrant liked the younger man's brusque approach. 'Sit down. Whisky?'

'Please.'

'What's wrong?'

The Cag sailed right in. Chomping his cigar he snorted, 'These lazy carrier captains. They're burning up our engines.'

Tarrant thought he'd better let the fireball have it right between the eyes. Staring coldly he asked, 'You think you could handle a carrier better?'

This stunned the Cag and he fumbled for a moment. Then, fortunately, the bar boy arrived with his drink and he grabbed for it. 'You not having one, sir?' he asked.

'You know the doctor made me lay off,' the admiral explained coldly.

Such treatment threw the Cag off balance, for he knew Tarrant's power in the navy. The old man may have queered his own promotion but he was still known as the incorruptible and his judgment on the promotions of others was prized.

In the embarrasing silence Tarrant asked grimly, 'What's your major complaint against the carrier captains?'

The veins stood out on the Cag's bullet head, but he stamped his cigar out and said firmly, 'They shouldn't burn up our propeller planes.'

'How would you berth a big ship against the wind?'

'In the old days I would have waited. But whatever I did I wouldn't run a lashed-down engine at top speed.'

Admiral Tarrant stared impersonally at Fujiyama, the wonderful mountain, and although he wanted to agree with Cag, he pondered precisely what question would most completely throw this young hothead off balance. Finally he settled on: 'So you'd have a group of complaining F4U pilots dictate naval procedure?'

Again the Cag was staggered. 'Sir, I . . .' He fumbled for words and then blurted out with startling force, 'Sir, an engine has only so many good hours. If you burn them up on deck. . . .' He fumbled again and ended weakly, 'Why can't they use half-power?'

The admiral turned slowly away from Fujiyama and asked bleakly, 'Do you consider an F4U engine more valuable than a carrier?'

The Cag retreated. 'What I was trying to say . . .'

'Another whisky?'

The Cag needed something to restore his confidence but reasoned that if the old man was in an evil mood he'd better not accept two drinks, so he said lamely, 'Thank you, sir, but I have a reservation for one of the sulphur baths.'

'They're fun,' the admiral said mournfully and when the Cag awkwardly excused himself, the old man sagged into a real depression, for he found it ugly to watch a promising young commander back away from what he knew was right. 'Well,' Tarrant grumbled, 'he's popular. He'll be able to wangle a desk job. But he's no good for command. And I'll have to say so when we get home.' Grieved, he decided to leave the bar.

But before he could get away, young Brubaker and his pretty wife approached and it was apparent she had been crying. 'She wants to talk to you,' Brubaker said with the air of a young husband who hopes somebody else can say the magic word which he has been unable to find.

'My husband tells me you can explain why this war is necessary,' she said. 'I sure wish somebody would.'

'It isn't necessary,' Tarrant said. Then, seeing the Brubakers' surprise he added, 'You two have something to drink?'

'May we join you?' Nancy asked.

'Doctor won't let me.' Then, seeing the young people frown, he added humourously, 'I have no vices, no ambitions, no family and no home.'

'That's what I mean,' Nancy said. 'I can understand why you get excited about war. But we do have a home and family.'

'I'm not excited about war,' the admiral contradicted. 'And I don't think it's necessary. That is, it wouldn't be in a sensible world. But for the present it is inevitable.' He poured himself some coffee and waited.

'If it's inevitable, why should the burden fall on just a few of us?' Nancy pressed.

'I don't know. You take the other night when your husband. . . .' Before he could tell of the ditching he saw Brubaker make an agonized sign indicating that Nancy knew nothing of the crash and the admiral thought, 'Like the rest of America, she's being protected.'

He salvaged the sentence by concluding, 'Your husband bombed a bridge. Because he's one of the best pilots in the navy he knocked out two spans. He didn't have to do it. He could have veered away from the bridge and no one would ever have known. But some men don't veer away. They hammer on in, even though the weight of war has fallen unfairly on them. I always think of such men as the voluntary men.'

Nancy fought back her tears and asked, 'So until the last bridge is knocked out a few men have to do the fighting? The voluntary men.'

'That's right. The world has always depended upon the voluntary men.'

Before Nancy could reply, the bar boy hurried up and asked, 'Is Lieutenant

Brubaker here?' The boy led Harry to a back door of the hotel where Nestor Gamidge stood, bloody and scarred.

'I'm sure glad to see you, lieutenant,' he gasped. His blues were ripped and his face was heavily bruised.

'What's up?'

'Mike's been in a terrible fight, sir.'

'Where?'

'Tokyo. I came out in a cab.'

'What happened?'

'He's in jail.'

'A public riot?'

'Yep. His girl's marrin' a bo'sun from the *Essex*.'

'You mean his . . . Japanese girl?'

'Yes, and if you don't come in he'll be locked up permanent.'

Tokyo was sixty miles away and to rescue Forney in person would consume many hours of leave that he might otherwise spend with his family, so Brubaker said, 'I'll phone the M.P.s.'

'Callin' won't help, sir. Mike clobbered two M.P.'s as well as the gang from the *Essex*.'

'You two take on the whole town?'

'Yes, sir.'

Brubaker had to grin at the vision of these two tough kids on the loose and made up his mind abruptly. 'I'll help.'

He hurried back to where Nancy and the admiral sat and said quickly, 'Admiral Tarrant, will you please see that Nancy gets dinner? There's been trouble in Tokyo and I . . .'

'Oh, no!' Nancy protested.

'Admiral, it's Mike Forney.'

'Drunken brawl?'

'Girl threw him over.'

Nancy pleaded, 'On our second night, why do you have to get mixed up with drunken sailors?'

Brubaker kissed his wife and said tenderly, 'Darling, if Mike were in China I'd have to help.'

'But, Harry. . . .' It was no use. Already he was running down the long hallway.

When Nancy realized that her husband actually was on his way to Tokyo, she looked beseechingly at Admiral Tarrant and pleaded, 'Who's this Mike Forney he thinks more of than his own children?' Her eyes filled with tears and she fumbled for a handkerchief.

The admiral studied her closely and asked, 'If you were freezing to death in the sea and a man brought his helicopter right over your head and rescued you, wouldn't you help that man if he got into trouble?'

Nancy stopped crying and asked, 'Did Harry crash at sea?'

'Yes.'

She looked down at her white knuckles and unclasped her hands. Very quietly she said, 'You know your husband's at war. You know he's brave. But somehow you can't believe that he'll fall into the sea.' Her voice trembled.

When she regained control Admiral Tarrant asked, 'Has Harry told you about the bridges? At Toko-ri?'

'No. He never talks about the war.'

'You must ask him about those bridges.'

Weakly she asked, 'Is he involved with the bridges?'

'Yes. When we go back to sea, your husband must bomb those bridges.'

In a whisper she asked, 'Why do you tell me this?'

He replied, 'In 1942 I had a daughter as sweet as you. She was my daughter-in-law, really. Then my son was killed at Midway trying to torpedo a Jap carrier. She never recovered. For a while she tried to make love with every man in uniform. Thought he might die one day. Then she grew to loathe herself and attempted suicide. What she's doing now or where she is I don't know, but once she was my daughter.'

Nancy Brubaker could hardly force herself to speak but in an ashen voice she asked, 'You think that . . . well, if thing went wrong at the bridges . . . I'd be like. . . .'

'Perhaps. If we refuse to acknowledge what we're involved in, terrible consequences sometimes follow.'

A strange man was telling her that war meant the death of people and that if she were not prepared, her courage might fall apart and instinctively she knew this to be true. 'I understand what you mean,' she said hoarsely.

'Let's get your little girls and we'll have dinner,' Tarrant said.

But Nancy was too agitated to see her daughters just then. She pointed to the end of the bar where Beer Barrel lay at last sprawled upon his arms, his face pressed against the polished wood. 'Will he fly against the bridges, too?' she asked.

When the admiral turned to survey the mammoth Texan his lean, Maine face broke into a relaxed smile. 'That one?' he said reflectively. 'He flies against his bridges every day.'

When Brubaker and Gamidge reached Tokyo, night had already fallen and there was slush upon the wintry streets that lined the black moat of the emperor's palace. At the provost marshal's office a major asked sourly, 'Why you interested in a troublemaker like Forney?'

'He's from my ship.'

'Not any more.'

'Major,' Brubaker asked directly, 'couldn't you please let me handle this?'

'A mad Irishman? Who wrecks a dance hall?'

'But this man had saved the lives of four pilots.'

'Look, lieutenant! I got nineteen monsters in the bird cage. Every one of them was a hero in Korea. But in Tokyo they're monsters.'

Patiently Brubaker said, 'Mike's a helicopter pilot. The other night Mike and this sailor. . . .'

The major got a good look at Nestor and shouted to a sergeant, 'Is this the runt who slugged you?'

'Listen, major!' Harry pleaded. 'The other night I ditched my plane at sea. These two men saved my life. This runt, as you called him, jumped into the ocean.'

The major was completely unimpressed. Staring at Nestor he said scornfully. 'I suppose the ocean tore his clothes. Did he get his face all chopped up jumping into a wave?'

'All right, there was a brawl.'

'A brawl! A brawl is when maybe six guys throw punches. These two monsters took on all of Tokyo.'

It was apparent to Brubaker that pleading along normal lines would get nowhere, so he asked bluntly, 'You married, major?'

'Yep.'

'Tonight's the second night in eight months that I've seen my wife and kids. I left them at Fuji-san to get Mike out of jail. That's what I think of these two men.'

The major stared at the docket listing Mike's behavior. 'You willin' to cough up $80 for the damage he did?'

'I'd pay $800.'

'He's yours, but you ain't gettin' no prize.'

A guard produced Mike Forney, his face a nauseating blue in contrast to the green scarf. 'She's marryin' an ape from the *Essex*,' he said pitifully.

'I suppose you tried to stop her.'

'I would of stopped the ape, but he had helpers.'

When they reached the narrow streets where hundreds of Japanese civilians hurried past, Mike begged, 'Talk with her, please, lieutenant. She might listen to you.'

He led Brubaker to one of the weirdest dance halls in the world. A war profiteer had cornered a bunch of steel girders and had built a Chinese junk in the middle of Tokyo. He called it the Pirates' Den and installed an open elevator which endlessly traveled from the first floor to the fifth bearing an eleven-piece jazz band whose blazing noise supplied five different dance floors. The strangest adornment of the place was a mock airplane, piloted by an almost nude girl who flew from floor to floor delivering cold beer.

The steel ship was so ugly, so noisy and so crammed with chattering girls that Brubaker wondered how anyone had known a riot was under way and then he met Kimiko, Mike's one-time love. She was the first Japanese girl he had ever spoken to and he was unprepared for her dazzling beauty. Her teeth were remarkably white and her smile was warm. He understood at once why Mike wanted her, and when she rose to extend her hand and he saw her slim perfect figure in a princess evening dress which Mike had ordered from New York, he concluded that she warranted a riot.

'I very sorry, lieutenant,' she explained softly, 'but while Mike at sea I lose my heart to *Essex* man. *Essex* not at sea.'

'But Mike's a fine man,' Brubaker argued. 'No girl could do better than Mike.'

Kimiko smiled in a way to make Brubaker dizzy and plaintively insisted, 'I know Mike good man. But I lose my heart.'

Things started to go black for Mike again and he shouted, 'Not in my dress, you don't lose it?' And he clawed at the dress which represented more than two months' pay.

Kimiko began to scream and the owner of the Pirates' Den blew a shrill whistle and prudent Nestor Gamidge said, 'We better start runnin' now.'

'Not without this dress!' Mike bellowed.

Nestor handled that by clouting Mike a withering blow to the chin, under which the tough Irishman crumpled. Then Nestor grabbed him by the arms and grunted, 'Lieutenant, sir. Ask the girls to push.'

In this way they worked Mike out a back door before the M.P.'s could get to him, but in the alley Nestor saw that Mike still clutched part of Kimiko's dress. He pried this loose from the stiff hand and returned it to Kimiko, saying, 'You can sew it back on.' Upon returning to Brubaker he reported, 'Japanese girls are sure pretty,' But when Mike woke up, sitting in one of the gutters west of the Ginza, he said mournfully, 'Without Kimiko I want to die.'

Gently they took him to the enlisted men's quarters, where Gamidge put the rocky Irishman to bed. When this was done, the little Kentuckian laboriously scratched a note and tucked it into the lieutenant's fist: 'We owe you $80. Mike and Nestor.' Then Brubaker started the long trip back to Fuji-san, where his wife waited.

It was nearly three in the morning when he reached the Fuji-san, but Nancy was awake and when he climbed into bed she clutched him to her and whispered, 'I'm ashamed of the way I behaved. Admiral Tarrant told me about Mike Forney.'

'I wish he hadn't. But don't worry. Nobody ever crashes twice.'

There was a long silence and she kissed him as if to use up all the kisses of a lifetime. Then she controlled her voice to make it sound casual and asked, 'What are the bridges at Toko-ri?' She felt him grow tense.

'Where'd you hear about them?'

'The admiral.' There was no comment from the darkness so she added, 'He had good reason, Harry. His daughter-in-law had no conception of war and went to shreds. He said if I had the courage to come all the way out here I ought to have the courage to know. Harry, what are the bridges?'

And suddenly, in the dark room, he wanted to share with his wife his exact feelings about the bridges. 'I haven't really seen them,' he whispered in hurried syllables. 'But I've studied pictures. There are four bridges, two for railroads, two for trucks, and they're vital. Big hills protect them and lots of guns. Every hill has lots of Russian guns.'

'Are Russians fighting in Korea?'

'Yes. They do all the radar work. We have only two approaches to the bridges. The valley has one opening to the east, another to the west. When we bomb the bridges we must dive in one end and climb out the other.' He hesitated and added quickly, 'At Toko-ri there is more flak than anywhere in Germany last time. Because the communists know where you have to come in from. And where you have to go out. So they sit and wait for you.'

They whispered until dawn, a man and wife in a strange land talking of a war so terrible that for them it equaled any in history. Not the wars of Caesar nor the invasions of Napoleon nor the river bank at Vicksburg nor the sands of Iwo were worse than the Korean war if your husband had to bomb the bridges, and toward morning Nancy could control her courage no longer and began to cry. In her despondency she whispered, 'What eats my heart away is that back home there is no war. Harry, do you remember where we were when we decided to get married?'

'Sure I remember. Cheyenne.'

'Well, when I was explaining to the girls about the birds and the bees Jackie looked up at me with that quizzical grin of hers and asked, "Where did all this stuff start?" and I said, "All right, smarty, I'll take you up and show you." And I took them to the Frontier Days where you proposed and I almost screamed with agony because everything was exactly the way it was in 1946. Nobody gave a damn about Korea. In all America nobody gives a damn.'

When the morning sun was bright and the girls had risen, Harry Brubaker and his wife still had no explanation of why they had been chosen to bear the burden of the war. Heartsick, they led their daughters down to one of the hotel's private sulphur baths, where they locked the door, undressed and plunged into the bubbling pool. The girls loved it and splashed nakedly back and forth, teasing shy Nancy because she wouldn't take off all her clothes, so she slipped out of her underthings and joined them.

They were cavorting in this manner when the locked door opened and a Japanese man entered. He bowed low to both Nancy and Harry, smiled at the girls and started to undress. 'Hey!' Harry cried. 'We reserved this!' But the man understood little English and bowed to accept Harry's greeting. When he was quite undressed he opened the door and admitted his wife and two teen-age daughters, who laid aside their kimonos. Soon the Japanese family stood naked by the pool and dipped their toes in. Harry, blushing madly, tried to protest again but the man said with painstaking care, 'Number one! Good morning!' and each of his pretty daughters smiled and said musically, 'Good morning, sir!'

'*Ohio gozaimasu!*' shouted the Brubaker girls, using a phrase they had acquired from their nurse. This pleased the Japanese family and everyone laughed gaily and then the man bowed again. Ceremoniously, father first, the family entered the pool.

By now Harry and Nancy were more or less numb with astonishment, but the pleasant warmth of the room, the quiet beauty of the surroundings and the charm of the Japanese family were too persuasive to resist. Harry, trying not to stare at the pretty girls, smiled at the Japanese man, who swam leisurely over, pointed to one of the Brubaker girls and asked, 'Belong you?'

Harry nodded, whereupon the man called his own daughters who came over to be introduced. 'Teiko, Takako,' the man said. They smiled and held out their hands and somehow the bitterness of the long night's talking died away. The two families intermingled and the soft waters of the bath united them. In 1944 Harry had hated the Japanese and had fought valiantly against them, destroying their ships and bombing their troops, but the years had passed, the hatreds had dissolved and on this wintry morning he caught some sense in the twisted and conflicting things men are required to do.

Then he sort of cracked his neck, for he saw Nancy. His shy wife had paddled to the other side of the pool and was talking with the Japanese man. 'We better hurry or we'll miss breakfast,' Harry said, and for the rest of his stay they became like the spectators at the Cheyenne Frontier Days and they enjoyed themselves and never spoke of Korea.

Then shore leave ended in one of those implorable incidents which made everyone proud he served aboard a good ship like the *Savo*. Admiral Tarrant went aboard at noon and toward four Beer Barrel staggered up the gangplank with his two golf bags. Brubaker had obtained permission for Nancy to see his quarters but when she found how astonishingly small the room was and how her husband slept with his face jammed under two steam pipes she said she felt penned in and would rather stay on deck.

In the meantime hundreds of sailors and their Japanese girls had crowded into Yokosuka and in the lead were Mike Forney and Nestor Gamidge, accompanied by seven girls from the dance halls of Tokyo, Yokohama and Yokosuka. 'I never knew there were so many girls,' Nestor said to one of the plane captains. 'Best thing ever happened to Mike was losing Kimiko to that ape from the *Essex*.'

Mike agreed. When he had kissed his girls goodbye he swung onto the quay, elbows out, and pointed to the *Savo*: 'Greatest flattop in the fleet.' Then he stopped dead for he saw that the *Essex* was alongside and there stood beautiful

Kimiko, wearing the expensive plaid he had bought her. She was kissing her ape from the *Essex* and things went black. Clenching his fists, Mike lunged toward the lovers but little Nestor grabbed him.

Mike stopped, slapped himself on the head and muttered, 'Sure, what's one girl?' With grandiloquent charm he approached Kimiko, kissed her hand and said loudly, 'The flower of Japan.' Then he grabbed the *Essex* man warmly and proclaimed, 'The flower of the fleet. The best man won. Bless you, my children.'

Then everything fell apart. For some loud mouth in the *Essex* yelled derisively, 'And we could lick you bums in everything else, too.'

Mike whirled about, saw no one, then looked back at golden Kimiko and she was beautiful in that special way and she was his girl. Blood surged into his throat and he lunged at the *Essex* man standing with her and slugged him furiously, shouting, 'You lousy ape!'

Six *Essex* men leaped to defend their shipmate and stumpy Nestor Gamidge rallied *Savo* men and soon M.P. whistles were screeching like sparrows in spring and there was a growing melee with men in blue dropping all over the place. Mike, seeing himself about to be deluged by *Essex* reinforcements, grabbed a chunk of wood and let the ape have it across the ear, laying him flat. At this Kimiko started to scream in Japanese and Mike grabbed her hat and tried to pull off the pretty plaid jacket, bellowing, 'Go ahead and marry him. But not in my clothes.' Three *Essex* men, gallant to the end, knocked him silly.

The captain of the *Savo* witnessed this disgraceful riot and determined on the spot to get rid of Mike Forney, but Admiral Tarrant, surveying the brawl from flag bridge, thought, 'I'd hate to see the day when men were afraid to mix it up for pretty girls.' He called for his glasses and studied Kimiko, who knelt over her *Essex* man and all the sailors aboard the *Savo* and the officers too were a little more proud of their ship.

SKY

The sun had to be well up or the photographs wouldn't be any good, so it was nearly 0945 when Harry Brubaker's jet catapulted violently across the prow of the *Savo* and far into the sky toward Korea. Ahead of him streaked a single Banshee with an extraordinary nose containing nine broad windows through which heavy cameras would record the bridges of Toko-ri.

While the *Savo* was in Yokosuka, other carriers were supposed to photograph the target but they had failed. When Cag bent his bullet head over their muddy films he growled, 'What's the matter? They afraid to go down low? We'll show 'em how to take pictures,' and he assigned himself the dangerous mission, choosing Brubaker to fly protective cover.

Now, as the two Banshees streaked toward higher altitudes Brubaker concerned himself with trivial details: 'Lay off those even altitudes. Use 25,300. Makes it just that much tougher for the anti-aircraft crews. And remember that when Cag goes down for the pictures, keep 3,000 feet above him.'

Then, in the perpetually mysterious way, when he had climbed into the higher atmosphere, he experienced the singing beauty of a jet as it sped almost silently through the vast upper reaches of the world. Sea and sky fell away and he was aloft in the soaring realm of the human spirit.

It was terrible and supreme to be there, whistling into the morning brilliance, streaking ahead so fast that the overwhelming scream of his engines never quite caught up. In this moment of exhilaration he peered into the limitless reaches of the upper void and felt the surging sensation that overtakes every jet pilot: 'I'm out front.' Through the silent beauty of this cold February morning he soared through the blue-black upper sky and thought, 'I'm out front.'

Then, as his eyes swept the empty sky in casual patterns, he uttered a stunned cry, 'My God! There it is!' But when he looked directly at what he had seen it vanished, so he returned to scanning and from the powerful corner of his eye he saw it again, tremendous and miraculously lovely, one of the supreme sights of creation: Fujiyama in morning sunlight towering above the islands of Japan. The cone was perfect, crowned in dazzling white, and the sides fell away like the soft ending of a sigh, and somewhere on the nether slope Nancy and the girls were waiting.

He now looked at the majestic volcano with his full eye, but again it was the omniscient corner which startled him, for it detected the mountains of Korea. Dead ahead they lay, bold and blunt and ugly. Tortured and convoluted, they twisted up at the two fleeting jets, the terrible mountains of Korea. They were the mountains of pain, the hills of death. They were the scars of the world's violent birth, the aftermath of upheavals and multitudes of storms. There was no sense to them and they ran in crazy directions. Their crests formed no significant pattern, their valleys led nowhere, and running through them there were no discernible watersheds or spacious plains. Hidden among them, somewhere to the west, cowered the bridges of Tok-ri, gun-rimmed and waiting.

Brubaker knew the guns would be waiting, for as the Banshees crossed the coastline, a signal battery in Wonsan fired and he could follow the course of other gun bursts across Korea, for the communists announced impending danger exactly as the Cheyennes of Colorado had done two hundred years before.

Now the day's hard work began. As soon as the Banshees came in range of communist guns, Cag began to descend in swift jinking dips and dives to confuse ground gunners, never staying on either course or altitude for longer than fifteen seconds. This threw a special responsibility on Brubaker who stayed aloft, weaving back and forth lest some stray M.I.G. try to pounce upon the preocccupied photographic plane. So imperceptible was Crag's silvery slim Banshee as it skimmed across the mountain tops that Brubaker was taxed to keep his eye upon it.

At Yangdok a flurry of ground fire exploded at almost the right altitude to catch the photographic plane, so the jets increased speed to 560, jinking violently. Below them they spotted the ruins of a less important bridge, four spans rusting in the river. Farther on a communist working party strove to rebuild a major bridge, but this morning Cag ignored them, certain that later flights would halt the work. For now on the horizon rose the peaks that guarded Toko-ri.

Each was pock-marked with many circular red depressions in the snow. These were the gun emplacements and in swift estimate Brubaker decided there must be more than sixty. Lower were gaunt walled nests for the huge five-inch guns, a single shell from which could pulverize a plane before it fell to earth. And deep within the hills, hiding along the river, were the four bridges. On this first fleeting glance he noticed that the two historic bridges were on tall stone pillars and decidedly vulnerable, but that the two emergency alternates were extraordinarily low, scarcely clearing the water.

But most significant of all was one solemn fact: to get to the bridges you really did have to fly in one end of a valley, traverse it and fly out the other end. Brubaker swallowed and thought, 'They got you lined up and going and coming. And when you pull out for rendezvous you're a dead duck.' Then he laughed to relieve his tension and whispered, 'No wonder they saved this one till last.'

At that instant Cag started his bold run into the western entrance to the valley. Pushing his nose down into a 40° dive, he screamed along the shimmering river, held courageously to the hairline railroad tracks, and roared upon the bridges at 580 miles an hour. During each inch of this run more than two hundred communist guns fired at the streaking Banshee, but it howled straight on, its cameras grinding, making no concession to the fire. Cag had one mission only, to bring back photographs, and he ignored everything else. Five-inch guns, three-inchers, machine guns and even carbines blazed at his wailing jet, but at last he pulled away from the mortal pit and with a sickening upward twist sped off to the north.

For a moment Brubaker lost the sleek Banshee as it fled to the hills for rendezvous. In some anxiety he cast his eyes swiftly left and right and thus caught a fleeting glimpse of the plane in the corner of his eye. Quickly rotating his vision in that area he gradually pinpointed the photographic plane, twisting and turning toward the safer hills. He had the sensation of spying upon an animal retreating to some sheltered valley after a wounding fight.

'Drop down and look me over,' Cag called. 'My tail section O.K.?'

Brubaker passed under the long-nosed jet and studied the fuselage minutely, for although both planes were doing more than 400 miles, in relation to each other they were nearly motionless. 'Nothing visible,' he reported.

'Back we go,' Cag said.

The photographic jet heeled over in a tight turn, jinked to a lower altitude and went into a paralyzing dive. Out of the sun it streaked with blazing speed, but the communist gunners were waiting and in monomaniac fury they poured their fire upon the wraithlike Banshee as it screamed upon them. It seemed positively impossible that Cag could writhe his way through such fire but he bore on, clicking his shutters at the doomed bridges.

From aloft Brubaker followed this incredible mission and experienced a resolute desire to be there with his commander, but the instant this thought came to mind it was dispelled by the vision he had seen at Yokosuka: four bridges reaching out into space far above the heads of his wife and daughters, and he grew afraid; for he knew that tomorrow as the sun came up he would be pushing his own overloaded Banshee down, down upon the real bridges. It was then that the great fear came upon him, the one he would not be able to dispel.

Then he heard Cag cry, 'Well, home we go.'

Ecstatically the two jets zoomed to 26,000. Far below them the savage, cheated mountains of Korea began to assume a beautiful countenance. Gone were the tortured profiles and the senseless confusion, for with the bridges of Toko-ri behind him, Brubaker saw Korea with a kindlier eye. To the north sprawling reservoirs glistened like great brooches, holding the hills together. To the south snow hung upon the ridge lines and made the valleys shimmering wonderlands of beauty, while beyond the upcoming range of mountains lay the vast blue sea, bearing somewhere upon its bosom the task force, that fair circle of home, with Beer Barrel waiting on the after deck.

Even Cag was impressed and called, 'Real estate sure looks better on the way home.'

But when they reached home there was dismal news. 'You heard the hot scoop?' Harry's plane captain asked as soon as Brubaker was out of the cockpit.

'We ordered home?'

'Forney and Gamidge are being sent to the barge.'

'The barge?' This was a scow stationed near the Korean coast, and helicopter men with that duty lived miserably and engaged in one dangerous land mission after another.

A destroyer moved in and the last the *Savo* saw of Mike Forney was when he climbed into the bo'sun's chair, green top hat, green scarf and Irishman's pipe. 'I'll send you the eighty bucks, sir,' he yelled, giving the word *sir* its old infuriating touch.

Brubaker didn't care if the captain was watching. He grabbed the disgraced man's hand and said, 'Take care of yourself, Mike. Pilots need you.'

'I go for rough duty,' Mike yelled, clutching his hat as the lines started to draw him over to the destroyer. 'Because I really hate communists.'

The chair dipped perilously toward the sea but Mike kept his legs clear. Instinctively the pilots cheered but the Irishman yelled derisively. 'You apes go into the drink, not me!'

The new helicopter pilot was an officer, a college kid and no doubt competent, but the jet men and propeller crews knew that flying off the *Savo* would be a little tougher now.

The fear that was reborn when Brubaker watched Cag dive into the valley at Toko-ri grew all that day, augmented by the gloom of Mike Forney's dismissal and the briefing. After dinner, in the crowded ready room, the intelligence officer had passed around marked copies of the photographs made that morning and said, 'Take-off at 0900. By then the sun will have driven ground fog out of the valley. Keep well south of the guns at Majon-ni. Cag, you tell them about the approach.'

Cag, cigar in mouth, said briefly, 'On paper it looks like a lot of flak concentrated here.' He jabbed at the map with his right forefinger. 'But it's not accurate. We'll go in low. We'll go in three times. And we'll go in from the east each time. When we're through, there won't be any more bridges.'

There were some questions and then Cag handed them the cold dope. He held his cigar in his left hand and said, 'Marty, you take your four men in at 1000 feet to suppress flak. I'll follow with my four at 1200. Brubaker, you mop up.'

Tightly Brubaker gripped the arms of his chair and fought back his fear. He couldn't fly this mission. He couldn't take his jet inside that blazing rim of hills. His old bitterness at having been called back into service sneaked up into his throat and corroded his courage. Frantically, as if afraid he might break down before his peers, he rose and hurried out.

Stumbling down the narrow passageways of the carrier, he banged against stanchions and bruised his shin upon the damnable hatches. Seeking out his own room he slammed the door shut and climbed up into his bed under the steam pipes. In uncontrolled panic, there in the dark room, he cast about for some way to avoid the strike against the bridges.

'I'll go see the doc. I'll just walk in and announce, "I've lost my nerve."' Impulsively he climbed down and started for the door. Then he stopped and laughed nervously at himself.

For the navy had worked out the perfect way to handle situations like this. Suppose you went in and said you were too jittery to fly, the doc simply said, 'O.K. Don't fly.' It was so easy that a man thought a hundred thousand times before he used that dodge. He stood alone, sweating, in his dark room and recalled the Cag's flight into the valley, and almost without knowing it he uttered the tricky words that bind a man to duty, those simple words that send men in jet planes against overwhelmingly protected bridges: 'If Cag can fly that flak, so can I.' That was what kept the navy system working. You could weasel out any time, but within the essence of your conscience lived the memory of other men no less afraid than you who were willing to tackle the dirty jobs. So you stuck.

But then a late flight returned and he thought ungraciously, 'What mission did they draw? Rail cuts. Up where there are no guns. Why don't they get the bridges? Why does it have to be me?'

He felt ashamed of himself and turned on the light but was appalled by his own gray and ashen face in the mirror. 'Get hold of yourself!' he commanded. Methodically, as if attention to some one job would restore his courage, he sat down to write a letter to his wife, but after he had written only a few lines he drew back in disgust. 'You stinker!' he whispered at his picture in the mirror. 'Scaring Nancy by letting her know you expect to be killed at the bridges.'

He began a new letter and with great composure told Nancy how much he loved the children and of how he longed for the days of peace when they could all go camping again in the Rockies back of Denver. He ended with a paragraph in which he described in detail the suit she had worn that day on the quay at Yokosuka. 'It looked very expensive,' he wrote, 'and I was amazed when you said you made it yourself.'

But when he crawled back into bed things were worse than before and like a stabbing agony in the darkness he cried, 'Why does it have to be me?' He remembered the men he had known in Colorado. Some hated their wives but they stayed home. Others hated their jobs, but they stayed on those jobs. Some of them, he recalled, had always wanted to travel, some had loved airplanes, others were always picking a fight and some good Catholics like Mike Forney hated communism so much they could taste it. Others were poor and needed navy pay. But all of them stayed home.

Through the long night Brubaker wrestled with his fear. Toward morning he was taken with frenzy and leaped from bed, rushing down the passageway to report his loss of nerve, but he never reached the doctor. A shattering sound halted him and in the gloomy darkness he whispered, 'They're launching the dawn planes. It won't be long now.' Then the catapult fired again and he remembered something Forney had once said and he stumbled down the ladder to the port catapult room, breaking in among the crew and crying, 'Where did Mike Forney stand?'

'Here.'

'Is that the piston he told me about?'

'Yep.'

Before Brubaker could ask more questions the engine fired and from its nest forward eleven tons of gleaming metal roared back with appalling force to stop a few inches from his face. Involuntarily he stumbled backward. The enlisted men laughed.

'Forney stood stock still,' they said.

Mike had explained that he came to the catapult room whenever his nerves were getting tight and the explosion of that enormous piston right into his face cured him: 'If a guy can take that, he can take anything,' Mike had said, but before Brubaker got set the monstrous machine fired again and that tremendous gleaming force sprang at him. He fell back.

'Takes a real idiot to stay put' a crewman shouted.

'You ever tried it?' Brubaker asked.

'I ain't no idiot.'

Brubaker rooted himself to a position from which he could not be budged, and like a frightened bull-fighter he mumbled to himself, 'This time I keep my feet here.' While he watched, the mighty piston leaped at him, then stopped with a powerful uuuuush less than four inches from his face.

The catapult crew applauded and said, 'Pretty soon now you'll be as crazy as Forney.'

'Is that bad?' Brubaker asked. Briskly he returned through the darkened ship and climbed into bed. 'Well,' he assured himself, 'at least I'm not yellow.' But immediately he was more afraid: 'Because you know the catapult's got to stop. But the guns at Toko-ri never do.'

So when the messenger called at 0700 he found Brubaker awake and sweating, staring at the steam pipes. When he reported to the wardroom bleary-eyed, Cag asked, 'What were you doing in the catapult room last night?'

There was no use kidding anybody so he replied, 'I was jittery.'

'Does sticking your face in a piston cure that?'

'Yes.'

Cag knew he should have left it at that but this mission was too important so he asked, 'You want to ground yourself? Because today we've got to do a first-rate professional job.'

'That's what I'm here for.'

'Good. I put you in the follow-through spot because I know that if my gang miss the bridges, you'll get 'em.'

'I'm going to.'

At 0730 the pilots moved into the cold ready room where the worst part of the flight took place. Twelve reasonably trim lithe young athletes began to pile onto themselves such a mass of encumbrances that soon they waddled like pigs, completely muscle bound and sweating from every pore. Sometimes even the bravest pilots felt their nerves shiver when they faced the degrading job of dressing for a winter flight.

Brubaker started in shorts. First he climbed into long-handled woolen underwear, then into a skin-tight g-suit, which applied pressure on vital parts of his body so that when he pulled out of steep dives the enormous drag of gravity, the g's, would not suck all the blood from his head. He covered the g-suit with inch-thick quilted underwear, two pairs of short bulky socks and a third which reached his knees. Then came the rough part, for even though the water-tight rubber poopy suit had already saved his life once, getting into it was always murder.

Since the neck band had to be tight to keep out freezing water and since no zippers were allowed, he had to get into the poopy suit in a special way. A long slash ran from the left shoulder across the chest and down to the right hip and he climbed in through this hole, pushing his feet down into the massive boots and his head up through the impossibly tight neck band. Then he grabbed the two flaps of extra rubber along the slash and rolled them together into a bulky, watertight seal which fattened him like a water-melon. And as soon as he closed this final seal he began to sweat like a pig and every minute he wore the poopy suit he was smelly and wet and uncomfortable. From time to time he pulled the neck band out and blew fresh air inside to get some relief. That's why the ready room was kept so cold, to keep the pilots from sweating, but all the same they sweated.

After the poopy suit came the survival vest, the pistol, the bulky Mae West, the hip knife, three cumbersome pairs of gloves, golden crash helmet, oxygen connection, harness straps and heavy goggles. Weighed down like some primeval monster, he waddled to the escalator which lifted him to the flight deck–another trick to keep down sweat–where an enlisted man handed him the board for clamping onto his knee with navigation data, codes, plots and all kinds of miscellaneous papers.

Even when he climbed into his jet there was more gear, so complicated that his plane captain had to crouch behind him and adjust safety belt, shoulder harness, ejection gear, microphone cord and oxygen supply. Harry Brubaker, who was about to soar into space with a freedom no previous men in history had known, was loaded down with such intolerable burdens that at times he felt he must suffocate; just as many citizens of his world, faced with a chance at freedoms never before dreamed of, felt so oppressed by modern problems and requirements that they were sure they must collapse.

As Brubaker adjusted himself to the cockpit he was hemmed in on left and right by more than seventy-five switches and controls. Directly facing him were sixteen instruments and thirteen more switches. He thought, 'If there were one more thing to do. . . .' He never finished the sentence for the mighty catapult fired and he was shot into space, where the suffocating paraphernalia and the maze of switches seemed to fall away and he roared into the upper blue, tied down only by his cancerous fear of the bridges at Toko-ri.

But today he would not see those bridges, for at Wonsan the radio crackled and he heard Cag's disappointed voice, 'Weather scout reports target closed in. Ground fog. Stand by for alternate instructions.'

When Brubaker heard this life-saving news he shouted, 'A reprieve! I knew I wasn't meant to tackle the bridges today.' He started to sing the chorus of *Cielito Lindo* but stopped in embarrassment when he saw that in his surging joy he had unconsciously lifted his Banshee 400 feet higher than the formation.

But ground fog did not save him, for in the next minute a miracle of modern war occurred. Cag received a radio message from Admiral Tarrant, and instantly the twelve jets stopped in midflight, almost as if they were a flock of pheasant searching for a Colorado grain field. Abruptly they turned south, heading for the mountainous battle front, where in the trenches a new emergency had arisen.

At dawn that morning a battalion of South Korean infantry had been hit by a murderous concentration of communist power and it became apparent that the Koreans would be annihilated unless air support could be provided. So a United States army liaison officer serving at the front phoned a Korean general, who called the United States army command in Seoul, who got hold of an air force general, who said he had no planes but would try to get some from a marine general, who suggested that Admiral Tarrant, far out to sea, might have some to spare. The inquiry arrived in flag plot just as the early-morning weather plane was reporting: 'Toko-ri closed in but good. Takusan ground fog. Takusan no see.'

Tarrant, who normally would not see such a message, made a note to chew out a pilot who would use Japanese in a battle report, and replied, 'One flight of twelve heavily armed jets available. Already airborne.'

Seoul immediately ordered, 'Proceed Roundelay. Operate as he directs.'

So by means of field telephone, radio, ship-to-shore communication and ship-to-plane, American jets were diverted to rescue South Korean foot soldiers. As the planes swept south Cag called ahead, 'Roundelay, twelve jets reporting for orders. We're loaded.'

From the bright morning sky came a whispery voice: 'This is Roundelay. I'm flying an S.N.J.'

Each jet pilot was astonished that in today's swift war the out-of-date old S.N.J. would still be used. It had been ancient before they took basic training, but no one had quite the shock that Harry Brubaker experienced. 'An S.N.J.?' he repeated incredulously and he was back in 1935, a gangling boy stretched out upon the floor, quietly and supremely happy, for he had mailed the box tops and the company had kept its promise. Here was the highly coloured put-together of America's latest plane. 'It was an S.N.J.' he recalled.

Then suddenly from behind a mountain, there was the real S.N.J., a rickety, two-bladed propeller job with a high greenhouse, a useless spare seat and six smoke rockets slung precariously under its wings. A slap-happy air force captain was wheeling it slowly around and Harry thought, 'What's an S.N.J.

doing here?' Then he learned.

'This is Roundelay. Get the big guns first.'

'Can't see 'em,' Cag said.

'Follow me.'

And to the amazement of the jet pilots Roundelay trundled his slow plane down almost to the treetops and delivered a smoke rocket against the target. 'See it now?' he called.

'Will do!' Cag cried, and he led his twelve screaming jets into a howling dive, right onto the gun and it fired no more.

'Strictly wonderful,' Roundelay called. 'D'you see the other two?'

'Negative.'

'Watch this smoke.' And the buglike S.N.J. hopped almost at ground level up a narrow valley to deliver another smoke rocket against another gun. Then, when it seemed the midget plane must follow the rocket against the rocks, the pilot twisted free, skipped over a ridge and ducked down upon a third gun.

'Will do!' Cag reported, and when his swift jets had silenced the guns, Roundelay called cheerily, 'You must come back often.'

The jets had zoomed so high they could not keep track of the tiny plane, but then sunlight glinted on the ridiculous greenhouse and they heard Roundelay call, 'I think I see Red troops beginning a new attack. Follow me.' And once more he hurried off like a busy old woman going to market.

Brubaker's division was aloft and he watched Cag's four jets roar low into a column of communists assaulting a hill. With appalling accuracy the Banshees spread their hundred pound bombs, each wound with high-tension steel wire that shattered into small pieces with machine gun fury. The communist advance wavered.

'Next division,' Roundelay called. 'Keep hitting them while they're confused.'

'Will do,' Brubaker replied, but as he prepared for his dive, the S.N.J. wheeled suddenly and Roundelay called, 'Do you see what I see?'

Below, in obedience to some order of incredible stupidity, more than one hundred communists had moved out of a wood and onto a frozen road, and as Brubaker's jets came screaming at them they did an even more unbelievable thing. They fell to their knees in the middle of the road, clasped their arms about their heads and made no effort to escape inevitable death. The tactic so astonished Brubaker that he gasped, 'They're sitting ducks!' And some ancient boyhood training in the mountains back of Denver restrained him.

But when he had zoomed high into the heavens he heard the unemotional voice of Roundelay: 'Clobber those guys. That's their standard trick. Throwing you off balance.'

So the jets wheeled and came screaming back down the road. Not a communist moved. Not one hit the ditch. They huddled and waited. 'Here it comes,' Brubaker whispered grimly, and his finger pressed the trigger. Keeping his eye upon the kneeling troops, he watched his bullets spray a path among them. 'You wanted trouble,' he said weakly.

Roundelay now spotted another column of attacking communists and called in Cag's division. Brubaker, with sickening detachment, watched the merciless jets and thought, 'Those people in Denver who ridicule air force reports of enemy dead ought to see this.' And he remembered Admiral Tarrant's words: 'If we keep enough planes over them enough hours somebody's got to get hurt. And when they hurt bad enough, they'll quit.'

'How's your fuel?' Roundelay asked.

'Can do one more pass,' Cag replied, and the jet pilots, who approached the speed of sound, watched as the slow little doodlebug S.N.J. hopped about in search of far targets. Brubaker, pulling out of his last bombing run, sped past the prop plane and for an instant of suspended time the two men looked casually at each other. Harry saw that the air force man was very thin and wore a moustache but he saw no more, for a five-inch communist gun, hidden until then, fired one lucky shot and blew the frail little S.N.J. completely to ribbons.

In terrible fury Brubaker launched his jet at the gun and tried to root it from its cave. He carried his fire almost into the muzzle of the enemy gun. Then, although his fuel was getting tight, he turned and made another run, pushing his jet to a deadly speed. He saw the gun, saw the wounded crew and the shell casings. On he came, firing until his own guns were silent, and the communists fell away. Then he zoomed aloft to overtake the homeward jets, but except for his wingman the planes were far away.

'You ought to tell me when you're going to run wild,' the wingman protested.

'I really clobbered that one,' Brubaker said grimly, but as the two Banshees soared away from the ravaged battleground with its wrecked artillery and dead bodies huddled along frozen roads, the enemy gun that Brubaker thought he had destroyed resumed firing. Mute with outrage, Brubaker wanted to dive upon it once more but he heard his wingman say, 'Their side has guts, too.'

Finally, when the roar of battle was past and the jets were far in the wintry sky Brubaker called, 'How's your fuel?'

'Thousand five.'

His own gauge read just under a thousand and he thought, 'I hope Beer Barrel is bringing us in.' Then he heard his wingman cry, 'There's Cag, up ahead.'

The two jets increased speed to rejoin the flight and all pilots began the difficult job of trying to spot the task force. Drifting clouds mottled the sea and made the ships almost invisible, but they had to be within a small area, for to the east hung the permanent snow line and to the north a new storm boxed in the fleet, but no one could see the ships.

It was ridiculous. Twelve highly-trained pilots couldn't find a task force of nineteen ships, including carriers, cruisers and a battleship. For some perverse reason Brubaker took delight in this limitation of human beings and thought, 'You never master this business.' Then Cag called, 'There's home!' and where absolutely nothing had been visible a moment before the jet pilots saw the nineteen ships. And Brubaker, seeing them as big as barns on an open meadow, laughed.

But his relief didn't last because when the jets descended he saw that the carrier deck was pitching rather formidably, and this meant many wave-offs because the landing officer would have to wait until the carrier stabilized itself between lurches, so that you might approach in perfect altitude but find the deck in a momentary trough and have to go round again. That took fuel. Because when you got a wave-off you had to pour it on. And there went your fuel.

Then he had a happy thought: 'They probably haven't turned into the wind. The deck'll be better when they do.'

But as he watched, a flight of jets took off from the *Hornet* and that proved the carriers were already into the wind, so he looked at the heaving *Savo*, stern leaping high in the air, bow down and said, 'There's your deck and you'll like it.' Then, although he never prayed, he mumbled, 'Beer Barrel, be out there today!' And as if in answer to this plea Cag announced, 'Beer Barrel's bringing us in on a pitching deck. Anybody short on fuel?'

Brubaker reported, '1591 reporting over ship with 800.'

He listened to Cag forward this news to the *Savo* and then call, 'We'll double up. No trouble getting aboard.'

So instead of the normal interval which would enable one jet to land each 26 seconds, the twelve Banshees formed a tight little circle yielding 15-second intervals so that whenever the deck stabilized there would be some jet diving right for it. But this also meant that one out of every two planes would have to take automatic wave-offs. 'Hope I'm one of the lucky ones,' Brubaker said.

He was. On his outward leg the *Savo* pitched so badly that no landing plane got aboard, but by the time Harry's downward leg started, the big ship was shuddering into stabilized position. 'It'll hold that position for at least a minute,' Brubaker assured himself. 'Time to get three of us aboard.' Nervously he ticked off the jets ahead of him in the circle. 'Seven of them. Just right. First two will have to pass because the deck won't be steady enough, but three, five and seven'll make it. Boy, I'm seven!'

Then he saw Beer Barrel's paddles bringing number three in and the deck crew had the hook disengaged in two and a half seconds and the deck was steady and clear. 'What an outfit when the going's tough,' Brubaker said admiringly.

Then hell broke loose. The pilot in jet number five did what Beer Barrel had warned his men never to do. As his Banshee neared the cut-off point the deck lurched and the pilot tried to compensate. Instead of flying Beer Barrel he flew the deck and missed every wire. In great panic he managed to pancake into the barriers but he ripped them both away and the crucial barricade as well.

Brubaker, screaming over the wreckage, saw instantly that it would be many minutes before the deck could be cleared and he cried feverishly to himself, 'I don't want to go into the sea again.'

His fear was unreasonable. He could see the helicopters waiting to rescue him. He saw the alert destroyers, always quick to lift a downed pilot from the waves. But he also saw the gray sea and he'd been down there once. 'The second time you crack up. You sink and they never find you.' Instinctively he felt to see if his three gloves were watertight at the wrist. That's where the sea crept in and froze you. Then he pulled his hand away in horror and whispered, 'Beer Barrel, don't let me go into the drink.'

Then he got hold of himself and heard Cag's quiet voice say, 'All nylon torn away. At least ten minutes to repair it. Is that critical for 1591?'

Brubaker breathed deeply to drive down any quiver in his voice and reported evenly, 'I'm down to 600.'

Cag said to the ship, '1591 low on fuel. Must land on first pass after barrier is fixed.'

The radio said, '*Hornet*'s deck temporarily fouled. But would landing there in eight minutes be of help?'

Promptly Brubaker said, 'I'd waste just as much gas getting in the circle. I'll stick here.' What he did not say was that without Beer Barrel's help he might lose his nerve completely.

With mounting fear he noticed that the crashed plane still fouled up the landing space and the broken barriers were not being promptly repaired. What made this especially infuriating was that all this time the carrier remained in stabilized position and all the jets could have been landed. Then he saw something that froze him. The towering black crane called Tilly was being moved into position alongside the wrecked Banshee, right where the missing nylon barricade should have been. Then a quiet, reassuring voice spoke to him, offering a choice. '1591,' the impersonal voice said, '*Hornet*'s deck still not ready. Impossible to erect barricade in time for you to land but we must protect planes parked forward. Have therefore moved Tilly into position to stop you positively in case you miss wire. Do you wish to attempt deck landing or do you wish to ditch? Advise.'

He stared down at the monstrous crane looming up from the middle of the deck. 'That'll stop me. Oh boy, will that stop me!' It was a brutal thing to do, to move Tilly out there, but he appreciated why it had been done. Behind the crane were parked $40,000,000 worth of aircraft and they must be protected and he felt no resentment at the maneuver. But before replying he reasoned carefully, 'The last guy missed the wires because the deck pitched. I can too,' and he was about to elect ditching but a compelling instinct told him that his only hope for safety lay with Beer Barrel.

'I'm coming in,' he said.

He made his first turn and prayed, 'Beer Barrel, bring me in. I don't care if the deck is going crazy, bring me in.'

On the down-wind leg he dropped to correct altitude and avoided looking at the pitching deck. He kept his eyes on the screen that shielded Beer Barrel from the wind but for a moment he became quite sick, for the stern was bouncing about like a derelict row-boat.

'Bring me in, Beer Barrel.'

Then as he whipped into the final turn he saw that terrible thing, the crane Tilly filling the end of the landing space and he would have turned aside had he not also seen Beer Barrel. The big man stood on one foot, his paddles up . . . still good . . . still coming . . . oh, Beer Barrel, keep me coming. . . .

Then mercifully the cut sign, the firm hook catching securely, the run of singing wire, the tremendous pull upon his shoulders, and his eyes looking up at the monstrous crane into which he did not crash.

From the flag bridge Admiral Tarrant followed the emergency landing and when he saw Brubaker lunge onto the deck safely he sent an aide to bring the pilot to him as soon as intelligence had checked battle reports. Some minutes later the young man appeared relaxed and smiling in freshly pressed khaki and said, 'Somebody told me there were eight hundred ways to get back aboard a carrier. Any one of them's good, if you make it.'

Tarrant laughed, jabbed a cup of coffee into the pilot's hands and asked casually, 'What were you doing in the catapult room last night?'

Brubaker sat down carefully, sipped his coffee and said, 'I lost my nerve last night.'

'You looked pretty steady out there just now.'

It was very important now that Brubaker say just the right thing, for he knew that something big was eating the admiral but he couldn't guess what, so he looked up over the rim of his cup and said, 'Best sedative in the world is Beer Barrel and those paddles.'

The admiral remained standing, somewhat annoyed at Brubaker's having presumed to sit. Nevertheless, the bonds of sympathy which bound him to the younger man were at work. He didn't want Brubaker to participate in the attack on the bridges, so in an offhand manner he asked, 'Son, do you want me to ground you . . . for tomorrow's flight against Toko-ri?'

Brubaker thought, 'If he'd wanted me to stay down he wouldn't have asked. He'd have told me. This way he hopes I won't accept.' But of his own will and regardless of the admiral he decided to say no and replied evenly, 'If anybody goes, I go.'

Admiral Tarrant was at once aware that he had posed his question the wrong way and said, 'I think you're jittery, son. I think you ought to stay down.'

Again Brubaker thought, 'The old man's wrestling with himself. He wants to ground me but he's afraid it would look like favoritism. So he's trying to trick me into asking. That way everything would be O.K.' But again he said, 'I want to fly against the bridges.'

Certain, and in some ways pleased, that the young man would refuse the order, Tarrant said, 'Harry, I've been watching you. There's nothing shameful in a man's reaching the end of his rope for the time being. You know I consider you our finest pilot . . . after the squadron leaders. But I can't let you fly tomorrow.'

And Brubaker said quietly, 'Sir, if you'd offered me this chance last night I'd have jumped to accept it. Or half an hour ago when I stared at that big black Tilly. But I think you know how it is, sir. Any time you get back safe, that day's trembling is over. Right now I haven't a nerve. Look.' He held out his coffee saucer and it remained rigid.

'You're sure it passed?'

'Positive. Remember when you told my wife about the voluntary men who save the world? I've seen two of these men. It shakes you to the roots of your heart to see such men in action.'

'Who'd you see?' Tarrant asked, the sparring over.

'Yesterday I saw Cag take his photographic plane. . . .'

'Cag?'

'Yes, sir. I saw a man so brave. . . . Admiral, he went in so low that he simply had to get knocked down. Then he went in again . . . lower.'

'Cag?' Admiral Tarrant repeated, amazed.

'And this morning. . . . Did anyone tell you about the air force spotter in the S.N.J.?'

'No.'

Brubaker's voice almost broke but he stammered, 'He was killed by a gun I might have knocked out . . . if I'd really been on the ball.' There was a long silence in which Tarrant poured more coffee. Finally Brubaker said, 'Sometimes you look honor right in the face. In the face of another man. It's terrifying.' His voice trailed away and he added in a whisper, 'So I have no choice. I have to go out tomorrow. If he could fly an S.N.J., I can fly a jet.' He laughed nervously and thrust his saucer out again. It remained immovable, like the end of a solid stone arm. 'No nerves now,' he said.

It was 1145 next morning when Cag, his jets poised aloft for their first run against the bridges, cried, 'Attack, attack, attack!'

With deadly precision, and ignoring the mortal curtain of communist fire, four Banshees assigned to flak-suppression flung themselves upon the heaviest guns at more than 500 miles an hour. Rendezvousing to the north, they swept back in ghostly blue streaks and raked the principal emplacements a second time, but as they reached the middle of this passage communist fire struck number three plane and with a violence few men have witnessed it smashed into a hill and exploded in an instantaneous orange flash.

Before the eight pilots aloft could realize what had happened Cag called quietly, 'Prepare to attack,' and the four jets in his division peeled off for swift assault upon the bridges. They descended at an angle steeper than 50° and for the entire final run of two miles no pilot swerved or dodged until his first huge bomb sped free.

From aloft Brubaker saw that Cag had got two of the bridges. Now he must finish the job. He brought his division down in a screaming dive, aware that when he straightened out the pull of gravity upon him would suck the blood away from his head and drag his lips into grotesque positions, but the fascination of those looming bridges of Toko-ri lured him on. Lower and lower he came. When he finally pickled his bomb and pulled away he absorbed so many g's that a heaviness came upon his legs and his face was drawn drowsily down upon his chin. But he knew nothing of this for he experienced only surging elation. He had bombed the bridges.

Then he heard the dismal voice: 'No damage to main bridge.'

And you had to believe that voice, for it was Roy's, last man through. Tomorrow stateside newspapers might exaggerate the damage. You could kid the intelligence officer. And you could lie like a schoolboy to pilots from another squadron, but last man through told the truth. No damage.

'I'm sure Brubaker got a span,' Cag argued.

'Negative,' Roy replied flatly.

'How about the truck bridges?'

'Clobbered, clobbered, clobbered.'

Cag called, 'Stand by for run number two,' and eleven jets orbited for position. The three flak-suppression Banshees stampeded for the gun-rimmed valley and as they roared in the leader confirmed Roy's report: 'No damage to the main bridge.' But the last of the flak jets reported, 'We really have the ground fire slowed down.'

Then, to the surprise of the communists, Cag brought his men in over the same check points as before and cheated some of the communist gunners, who had been gambling that he would use the other entrance to their valley. Through gray bomb smoke and bursts of flak, through spattering lead and their own fears, the first four pilots bore in upon the bridges. Roaring straight down the railroad track like demon trains they pickled their heavy freight upon the bridge and pulled away with sickening g's upon them, their mouths gaping wide like idiots, their eyes dulled with war and the pull of gravity.

As Brubaker led his men upon the bridges he saw a magnificent sight. Three spans were down and a fourth was crumbling. The two truck bridges were demolished and the alternate railroad span was in the mud. In triumph he called, 'This is Brubaker. All bridges down. Divert to the dump.' And with blood perilously withdrawn from his head he swung his Banshee away from the bridges, over a slight rise of ground, and down upon the sprawling military dumps. Strafing, bombing, twisting, igniting, he screamed on, his three teammates following. Somebody's bomb struck ammunition. Consecutive explosions, each keeping the next alive, raced through the stores.

This time Roy, last man through, said, 'We hit something big.'

Cag, aloft, called, 'All planes, all planes. Work over the dump.'

Brubaker, now higher than the others, watched the dazzling procession of Banshees. Swooping low, they spun their fragmentation bombs earthward and retired into the lonely distance. Returning, they dodged hills and spread deathly fire. Over snowy ridges they formed for new runs and wherever they moved there was silent beauty and the glint of sunlight on the bronzed helmet of some man riding beneath the plexiglas canopy. It was a fearsome thing to watch jets assume control of this valley where the bridges had been, and it was gloomy, for no matter where any of the pilots looked they could see the scarred hillside against which one of their team had plunged to death a few minutes before.

His ammunition nearly spent, Brubaker nosed down for a final run upon the spattered dumps, but Cag called, 'Stay clear of the ammo dumps. We have them popping there.' So he twisted his jet to the south, away from the ammo but before he could launch his dive, two jets streaked across his target and jettisoned their bombs so that again he had to pull away. He was tempted to drop his last bomb where he thought he saw a gun emplacement but promptly he discarded this idea as unworthy for it occurred to him, quite clearly in this instant of decision, that even one bomb more might mean significant interdiction of supplies to the front: fewer bullets for communist gunners, fewer blankets for their trenches, less food. He recalled Admiral Tarrant's words: 'If we keep the pressure high enough something's got to explode over there.'

So in an effort to add that extra degree of pressure which might help to beat back aggression, he turned away from his easy target and picked out a supply dump. He activated his nose guns and watched their heavy bullets rip into valued cargo and set it afire. Then he resolutely pickled his last bomb but as he pulled out of his dive, with heavy g's upon his face, he heard a pinking-thud.

'I've been hit!' he cried and as the jet sped upward chaos took over. He lost control of his mind and of the thundering Banshee and in panic thought only of Wonsan harbor. He felt the irresistible lure of the sea where friendly craft might rescue him and violently he wrenched his nose toward the east and fled homeward like a sea-stricken thing. But as soon as he had made this desperate turn he became aware that panic was flying the plane, not he, and he called quietly, 'Joe, Joe. Just took a hit. So far I'm all right.'

From the dark sky aloft came the reassuring whisper, 'Harry, this is Joe. I have you in sight.'

'Joe, drop down and look me over.'

Now an ugly vibration identified itself as coming from the port engine but for one fragile second of time it seemed as if the frightening sound might abate. Then, with shattering echoes, the entire engine seemed to fall apart and Brubaker whispered to himself, 'I'm not going to get this crate out of Korea.'

A communist bullet no bigger than a man's thumb, fired at random by some ground defender of the dump, had blundered haphazardly into the turbine blades, which were then whirring at nearly 13,000 revolutions a minute. So delicately was the jet engine balanced that the loss of only two blade tips had thrown the entire mechanism out of balance, and the grinding noise Brubaker heard was the turbine throwing off dozens of knifelike blades which slashed into the fuselage or out through the dark sky. Like the society which had conceived the engine, the turbine was of such advanced construction that even trivial disruption of one fundamental part endangered the entire structure.

He had, of course, immediately cut fuel to the damaged engine and increased revolutions on the other and as soon as the clatter of the damaged turbines subsided he cut off its air supply and eliminated the destructive vibrations altogether. Then, in fresh silence, he checked the twenty principal indicators on his panel and found things to be in pretty good shape. 'I might even make it back to the ship,' he said hopefully. But promptly he discarded this for a more practical objective: 'Anyway, I'll be able to reach the sea.'

He laughed at himself and said, 'Look at me! Yesterday I pushed the panic button because I might have to go into the sea. Today I reached for it because I might miss the water.'

As he reasoned with himself Joe came lazily out from beneath his wing and waved. 'Everything all right now?' Joe asked.

'All under control,' he answered.

'Fuel O.K?'

'Fine. More than 2,000 pounds.'

'Keep checking it,' Joe said quietly. 'You may be losing a little.'

Then the sick panic returned and no more that day would it leave. Impeded by heavy gear he tried to look aft but couldn't. Straining himself he saw fleetingly from the corner of his eye a thin wisp of white vapor trailing in the black sky. Knocking his goggles away he tried to look again and his peripheral vision spied the dusty vapor, no thicker than a pencil.

'Joe,' he called quietly. 'That looks like a fuel leak.'

'Don't your gauges show it?'

'Don't seem to.'

'You'll make the sea all right,' Joe said, and both men surrendered any idea of the ship.

'I'll make the sea,' Harry said.

'I'll trail you,' Joe called.

In a few minutes he said, 'You're losing fuel pretty fast, Harry.'

There was no longer any use to kid himself. 'Yeah. Now the instruments show it.'

Joe drew his slim blue jet quite close to Harry's and the two men looked at one another as clearly as if they had been across a table in some bar. 'I still think you'll make the sea,' Joe said.

But Harry knew that merely reaching the sea wasn't enough. 'How far out must we go in Wonsan harbor to miss the communist mines?' he asked.

Joe ruffled through some papers clipped to his knee and replied. 'You ought to go two miles. But you'll make it, Harry.'

The turbine blade that had sliced into the fuel line now broke loose and allowed a heavy spurt of gasoline to erupt so that Joe could clearly see it. 'You're losing gas pretty fast now,' he said.

There was a sad drop on the fuel gauge and Harry said, 'Guess that does it.'

To prevent explosion, he immediately killed his good engine and felt the Banshee stutter in midair, as if caught by some enormous hand. Then, at 250 miles an hour, he started the long and agonizing glide which carried him ever nearer to the sea and always lower toward the mountains.

Quickly Joe cut his own speed and said, 'We better call the word.'

With crisp voice Brubaker announced the strange word which by general consent across the world has come to mean disaster. In Malaya, in China, over Europe or in the jungle airports of the Amazon this word betokens final catastrophe: 'Mayday, Mayday.'

It was heard by communist monitors and by the officers in Task Force 77. Aloft, Cag heard it and turned his jets back to keep watch upon their stricken member. And aboard the scow the newly reported helicopter team of Mike Forney and Nestor Gamidge heard it.

'Mayday, Mayday.'

Silently, through the upper reaches of the sky, the two men flew side by side. They had never been particularly friendly, for their interests and ages varied, nor had they talked much, but now in the dark violet sky with sunlight gleaming beneath them on the hills of Korea they began their last urgent conversation, their faces bright in plexiglas and their voices speaking clear through the vast emptiness of the space.

'We'll make the sea,' Joe said reassuringly.

'I'm sure going to try.'

They drifted down to the sunny spaces of the sky, into the region of small cloud and laughing shadow and Joe asked, 'Now when we reach the sea will you parachute or ditch?'

'I ditched once, I'll do it again.'

'I never asked you, how does the Banshee take the water?'

'Fine, if you keep the tail down.'

'Remember to jettison your canopy, Harry.'

'I don't aim to be penned in.'

'Six more minutes will put us there.'

So they fought to the sea. As if caught in the grip of some atavistic urge that called them back to the safety of the sea after the millions of years during which men had risen from this element, these two pilots nursed their jets away from inhospitable land and out toward the open sea. They were low now and could spot communist villages and from time to time they saw bursts of communist guns, so they fought to reach the sea.

But they did not make it. For looming ahead of them rose the hills in back of Wonsan harbor. Between the jets and the sea stood these ugly hills and there was no way to pass them. Instinctively Harry shoved the throttle forward to zoom higher–only a couple of hundred feet, even fifty might do–but relentlessly the stricken Banshee settled lower.

From the adjoining plane Joe pointed to the obstructing hills and Harry said, 'I see them. I won't make it.'

Joe asked, 'Now, Harry, are you going to jump or crash land!'

'Crash,' Harry said promptly. Back in the States he had decided to stick with his plane no matter what happened. Besides, communists shot at parachutes, whereas the speed of a crash often took them by surprise and permitted rescue operations.

'Keep your wheels up,' Joe said.

'Will do.'

'Be sure to hit every item on the check-off list.'

'Will do.'

'Harry, make sure those shoulder straps are really tight.'

'Already they're choking me.'

'Good boy. Now, Harry, remember what happened to Lou. Unhook your oxygen mask and radio before you hit.'

'Will do.'

'Knife? Gun?'

Harry nodded. Although he was soon going to hit some piece of Korean ground at a speed of 130 miles, his plane bursting out of control at impact, in this quiet preparatory moment he could smile out of his canopy and converse with Joe as if they were longtime friends reviewing a basketball game.

'Pretty soon now,' he said.

'I'll move ahead and try to find a good field,' Joe said. Before he pulled away he pointed aloft and said, 'Cag's upstairs.'

Soon he called, 'This field looks fair.'

'Isn't that a ditch running down the middle?'

'Only shadows.'

'You think I can stop short of the trees?'

'Easy, Harry. Easy.'

'Well then, that's our field.'

'Listen, Harry. When you do land, no matter what happens, get out fast.'

'You bet. I don't like exploding gas.'

'Good boy. Remember, fellow. Fast. Fast.'

Desperately Brubaker wanted to make one run along the field to check things for himself, but the remorseless glide kept dragging him down and he heard Joe's patient voice calling, 'Harry, you better jettison that canopy right now.'

'I forgot.'

Like a schoolteacher with a child Joe said, 'That was first on the check-off list. Did you hit those items, Harry?'

'I got them all,' Harry said.

'Field look O.K.?'

'You pick 'em real good, son.'

Those were the last words Harry said to his wingman, for the ground was rushing up too fast and there was much work to do. Dropping his right wing to make the turn onto the field, he selected what looked like the clearest strip and lowered his flaps. Then, kicking off a little altitude by means of a side slip, he headed for the earth. Tensed almost to the shattering point, he held the great Banshee steady, tail down, heard a ripping sound, saw his right wing drop suddenly and tear away, watched a line of trees rush up at him and felt the final tragic collapse of everything. The impact almost tore the harness through his left shoulder socket but without this bracing he would surely have been killed. For an instant he thought the pain might make him faint, but the rich sweet smell of gasoline reached him and with swift planned motions he ripped himself loose from the smoking plane. But when he started to climb down he realized that his oxygen supply tube and his radio were still connected, just as Joe had warned. Laughing at himself he said, 'Some guys you can't tell anything.' With a powerful lurch he broke the cords and leaped upon Korean soil.

He was in a rice field three miles from a village. Beyond lay other rice fields and many curious U-shaped houses of the Korean countryside, their roofs covered with snow. To the north were mountains, to the south a row of trees, while from the east came a hint of salt air telling him that the sea was not far distant. But even as he surveyed his field he started running clumsily from the plane and before he had run far it burst into flame and exploded with numerous small blasts which sent billows of smoke into the air, informing communists in the village that another American plane had crashed. 'They'll be after me soon,' he thought and ran faster.

Within a few steps he was soaked with sweat inside his poopy suit and his breath hurt as it fought its way into his lungs. But still he ran, his big boots sticking in snowy mud, his intolerable gear holding him back. Finally he had to rest and sat upon a mound of earth forming the bank of a wide ditch that ran along the western edge of the field, but when one foot went into the center of the ditch he drew back in disgust for the smell he stirred up told him this was used for storing sewage until it was placed upon the rice fields. The stench was great and he started to leave but across the field he saw two communist soldiers approach the burning jet with rifles. So he did not leave the ditch but hid behind the mound of earth and reached for the revolver which he had once fired nine times in practice. He inspected its unfamiliar construction and remembered that it contained six bullets to which he could add the twelve sewed onto his holster straps. 'None to waste,' he said.

Then one of the soldiers shouted that he had discovered the American's trail in the snow. The two men stopped, pointed almost directly to where he hid and started for him, their rifles ready.

At first he thought he would try to run down the ditch and hide in the line of trees but he realized the soldiers would intercept him before he could accomplish that. So he decided to stick it out where he was, and he hefted his revolver, for American pilots knew that if they were captured in this part of Korea they were usually shot.

'I'll wait till they reach that spot,' he said, indicating a muddy place. 'Then I'll let 'em have it.' It did not occur to him that he probably wouldn't be able to hit a man ten feet away and that the spot he had selected was ridiculously remote, but fortunately he was not called upon to learn this ugly lesson, for as the two soldiers approached the point at which he was determined to fire, Joe's Banshee whirled out of the noonday sun and blasted the communists. Then, with a wailing cry, it screamed to rendezvous with Cag for the flight back to the *Savo*.

From his filthy ditch, Harry watched the mysterious and lovely jets stream out to sea and cried, 'I'd sure like to be going with you.' They were supreme in the sky, these rare, beautiful things, slim-lined, nose gently dipping, silver canopy shining in the sun. Once he had been part of those jets and now, huddling to earth, he was thankful that he had known the sweeping flight, the penetration of upper space, the roaring dive with g's making his face heavy like a lion's, and final exultant soaring back to unlimited reaches of the sky. Then, as they disappeared completely, he pictured them entering the landing circle and he thought, 'It would be fun, heading in toward Beer Barrel right now.' Then he dismissed the jets.

He was determined to find a better refuge before new communists arrived, for the smell in this ditch was becoming too strong to tolerate, but when he did start to run toward the trees he saw four people standing there. Quickly he brandished his revolver at them, but they must have known he could not shoot them from so far for they stood impassively watching.

They were the family from the nearest farm, a mother, father and two children, dressed in discarded uniforms and brandishing rakes. He stopped to see if they intended attacking him, but they remained still and he saw them not as Koreans but as the Japanese family that had intruded upon his sulphur bath that morning in the Fuji-san and an unbearable longing for his own wife and children possessed him and it was then—there in bright sunlight in the rice field—that he knew he would not see his family again.

He was driven from this brief reflection by the arrival of more soldiers. From the very trees to which he was heading appeared eleven guards, shouting in Korean, so he hastily dived back to his stinking ditch where they could not hit him. They launched a methodical encircling attack but before they could bring him under fire four F4U's appeared overhead, called in by Cag to protect the downed pilot until rescue operations could begin.

Using Brubaker as their focus point, the slow propeller planes established a four-leaf clover in which each flew a big figure eight with such perfect timing as to have one plane coming in over Brubaker at all times, with alternate planes commanding different sectors of land so that no enemy dare approach.

The very first run enabled the F4U men to spot the eleven communists, and with sharp fire they tied the soldiers down. In the respite Brubaker thought, 'With such cover a helicopter might make it,' and he began to hope. Then, thinking to find a better spot from which to dash to the copter if it should arrive, he started to move out, but the Korean family saw him and thought he was moving toward them, so they withdrew. The F4U man responsible for this sector spied the Koreans, saw their tattered uniforms and roared upon them, his guns ablaze.

'No!' Brubaker screamed.

'No! No! No!' He waved his arms, jumped wildly to divert the F4U.

But the pilot could not see him. Focusing his sights grimly at what he knew to be the enemy, he brought his fiery guns a few yards from the faces of the Korean family. For one ghastly moment he thought two of the soldiers might have been children, but by then he was far away, roaring back into the four-leafed clover.

Sick, Harry Brubaker stood in the ditch and thought of his own daughters, and his heavy body was cold with much sweat.

He was standing thus when the helicopter appeared. It had lumbered in from the scow, dodging ground fire and flying so low that a revolver bullet could have destroyed it. Smack in the middle of the rice field it landed and Mike Forney got out. He wore his green top hat, a new Baron von Richthofen scarf of Japanese silk and a carbine. Behind him stumbled sad-faced Nestor Gamidge, also with a carbine. Leaving Gamidge at the copter, Forney ran across the rice field shouting, 'Relax, Harry! Everything's under control.'

Brubaker shouted, 'Better dodge and duck.'

'Why, is there a war goin' on?'

'Look!' He pointed toward the trees and as he did so a volley of machine gun fire spattered the helicopter. Gamidge fell to the ground but rolled over several times and indicated that he was all right, but above his head the helicopter burst into flames.

Forney jumped into the ditch and turned back to watch the fire in silence. No other copter would come onto this field. With flames of noon in their eyes the two men in the ditch looked at each other, unable to speak. Then slowly Mike pulled his right foot up.

'Harry,' he asked. 'Is this what I think it is?'

'Yep.'

Scornfully he said, 'You sure picked a wonderful place to fight a war.' Then he shrugged his shoulders and growled, 'We might as well get Nestor in here. Three of us can stand those apes off for days.'

He hefted his carbine nonchalantly and started across the rice field to convoy Gamidge but when the sallow-faced Kentuckian stood up, communist bullets chopped him in the chest and he fell. Mike, still wearing his green hat, blasted the line of trees in pathetic fury, for he must have known his carbine could not carry so far. Then he ran forward to where Nestor lay but soon he crawled back to the stinking ditch and tried not to look at Harry.

'Is he dead?'

'Yep.'

In silence the two men tried to build protection for their faces, but when they reached into the ditch for stones, an evil smell arose, so that Forney stared back at the ditch and muttered, 'I could have picked a better ...' Then he said bitterly, 'They were goin' to give Nestor a medal.'

'Why'd you bring the copter in here, Mike?'

'I take care of my men, sir.'

'How is it aboard the scow?' Brubaker phrased the question so as to imply that Forney would be returning there when this day was over.

'It's fair, but carrier duty spoils you.'

'I liked the *Savo*,' Brubaker said, and when referring to himself he used the completed tense, surrendering hope.

Forney caught this and said, 'You know what kills me right now? Thinking of Kimiko going to bed with that ape from the *Essex*.'

'That would be tough,' Brubaker agreed.

The two men looked up at the F4U's and Forney asked, 'How much longer will they be able to stay?'

'Not long,' Harry replied.

'Well, we got nothin' to worry about. The jets'll be back.'

Harry said, 'This morning I had a chance to watch jets in action. They're terrific.'

'Look at those apes,' Mike said, pointing to where communists were starting to move in. From time to time accurate rifle fire pinked the top of the mound and Brubaker thought ruefully of people back in Denver who visualized communists as peasants with pitchforks who overran positions in mass attacks.

'Those guys know what they're doing,' he said.

'But they don't know what they're gonna meet!' Mike laughed. Then he suddenly looked at Harry and said, 'Why didn't you tell me you didn't have a carbine.' And before Brubaker could stop him, he dashed across the rice field, grabbed Nestor Gamidge's carbine and stripped the dead man of ammunition. Two F4U's, seeing what Mike was doing, roared low and held the communists off while the Irishman dodged and ducked his way back to the ditch.

'Boy, now they'll know something hit 'em!' he cried as he jammed the weapon into Harry's hands.

Realization that Mike intended to battle it out here made Harry shiver and he asked, 'You think there's any chance they'd allow us to surrender?'

'Those apes?' Mike asked.

The two Americans piled the last rocks before their faces and Harry asked, 'Why do you hate them so much?'

'Simple. One Sunday morning in the cathedral I heard the cardinal explain it all,' Mike said. A bullet zinged into the mud behind them and Mike grabbed Brubaker's arm. 'You understand, sir, I came out here to save you. I don't want to die. There was a fightin' chance or I wouldn't have come. But now we're here, let's go down really swingin'.'

He watched one of the communists creep forward for a better shot. 'Don't fire too soon at these apes,' he whispered. He kept his hand on Harry's arm for at least two minutes. Then, just as the enemy soldier got into position Mike blasted him right in the face. When Mike looked back he saw that Brubaker was busy with his hip knife, slashing away at his poopy suit.

'What are you doin'?' the Irishman exploded.

'Letting some air in.'

'Have you gone nuts, sir?'

'Ever since I climbed into my first poopy suit I've been weighed down. I've been sweating and unable to breathe. Like a zombie. Today I want to feel like a human being.' He stripped away large chunks of his burdensome gear and stood reasonably free. 'I feel better already,' he said.

Mike was sure the lieutenant had gone off his rocker but there wasn't anything he could do about it so he laughed and said, 'I'm the same way. I couldn't fight these apes without my green hat.'

'Why do you wear that?' Harry asked.

'I want people to know I'm around.'

'That's what you told the captain. But what's the real dope?'

Mike stopped, looked frankly at Brubaker and said, 'When I was a kid we lived. . . .' He stopped abruptly and asked, 'Tell me the truth, sir, wasn't that captain a pathetic ape?'

'The way he used windmill all the time.'

'In about three minutes now,' Mike said, pointing to the trees.

The communists moved slowly and with deliberate plan. Four of them came in from the south, three from the mountain quarter. 'I'm gonna keep my eye on those four out there,' Mike said.

Some minutes passed and there was a flurry of fire from the three soldiers in the mountain quarter but Forney yelled, 'Forget them!' and he was right for the other four lunged forward and tried to overrun the ditch. Calmly Mike and Harry waited until the communists were close upon them. Then they started to fire rapidly. The communists fired back but Mike yelled, 'They're crumblin',' and he chopped them down.

'That'll take care of the boys,' he shouted. 'Now bring on the men.' But as he turned to congratulate Brubaker an unseen communist who had sneaked in from the sea quarter hurled two grenades into the ditch. One of them Mike managed to throw back but as he lifted the second it exploded and tore him apart. His body, motivated by the driving forces that had occupied his mind, stumbled forward toward the unseen enemy and pitched into the snow.

Now the sky was empty and the helicopter stood burned out in the rice field and in the ditch there was no one beside him. Harry Brubaker, a twenty-nine-year-old lawyer from Denver, Colorado, was alone in a spot he had never intended to defend in a war he had not understood. In his home town at that moment the University of Colorado was playing Denver in their traditional basketball game. The stands were crowded with more than 8,000 people and not one of them gave a damn about Korea. In San Francisco a group of men were finishing dinner and because the Korean war was a vulnerable topic, they laid plans to lambaste it from one end of the country to the other, but none of them really cared about the war or sought to comprehend it. And in New York thousands of Americans were crowding into the night clubs where the food was good and the wine expensive, but hardly anywhere in the city except in a few homes whose men were overseas was there even an echo of Korea.

But Harry Brubaker was in Korea, armed with two carbines. He was no longer afraid nor was he resentful. This was the war he had been handed by his nation and in the noonday sun he had only one thought: he was desperately in love with his wife and kids and he wanted to see them one more time.

The memory of his family was too much to bear and for an instant he pressed his right hand across his eyes and thought, 'The girls will be in the garden now. . . .'

He did not complete the picture for the hidden communist who had tossed the grenades had remained close and now with one carefully planned shot sped a bullet directly through the right hand that covered the American's face. In that millionth of a second, while ten slim Banshees roared in from the sea to resume command of the sky, Harry Brubaker understood in some fragmentary way the purpose of his being in Korea. But the brief knowledge served no purpose, for the next instant he plunged face down into the ditch.

Through the long afternoon that followed, Admiral Tarrant haunted his telephone, waiting word of the miracle that would save his son. When Mike Forney left the scow with his helicopter, the admiral had said, 'Well, Mike'll get him.' Then the leader of the F4U's reported the copter burning.

Now, from the clandestine broadcaster near Wonsan came the facts: 'Jet plane crash. Helicopter crash. Three Americans killed by communist troops.'

Shaken, the lean, hard-bitten admiral left flag plot and walked gravely to his tiny room, for he knew that he must report these facts to Nancy Brubaker, in Yokosuka. But as he stared at the paper he asked, 'How do you explain to a wife that her husband has died for his nation? How do you tell that to a woman with two children?' And he thought of his own wife, sitting somewhere in a dark room knitting a child's garment . . . but it was already more than seven feet long.

The job was too much for him. Later, maybe, he would know what to write. Then he thought of the Cag, who had led this ill-starred mission. He burned with fury and summoned the Cag to him, lashing at the bullet-headed commander as soon as he appeared.

'Why was Brubaker abandoned?'

Cag's eyes were red and tired from too much flying but he controlled his nerves and said, 'We kept an air cap over him.'

'If one helicopter crashed, why didn't you send another?'

'Sir, it's not my job to dispatch copters. You ask for volunteers. And there are never enough Mike Forneys.'

'How was Brubaker hit in the first place?'

'He was working over the dumps.'

The admiral pounced on this. 'What was he doing at the dumps?'

Patiently Cag explained. 'Before we took off we agreed. If we get the bridges, we expend our ammo on the dumps.'

Icily, from the empty bitterness of his bosom, the old man asked, 'Was that wise?'

Cag had taken enough. He'd stood this angry old tyrant long enough and there was no promotion in the navy that would make him take any more. 'Admiral,' he said grimly, 'this was a good mission. We did everything just right. I put Brubaker in charge of the third division because I could trust him to fly low and bore in with his bombs. He did just that.'

Cag, trembling with anger, rushed on, 'Admiral, everybody in the air group knows that you selected Brubaker as your special charge. You do that on every command and we know why you do it. Some kid your own boy's age. So today I led your boy to death. But it was a good mission. We did everything just right. And it was your boy who helped destroy the bridges. Admiral, if my eyes are red it's for that kid. Because he was mine too. And I lost him.'

The old man stood there, staring stonily at the shaking commander with the bullet head while Cag shot the works. 'I don't care any longer what kind of fitness report you turn in on me because this was a good mission. It was a good mission.' Without saluting he stormed from flag country, his fiery steps echoing as he stamped away.

For many hours the admiral remained alone. Then toward morning he heard the anti-submarine patrol go out and as the engines roared he asked, 'Why is America lucky enough to have such men? They leave this tiny ship and fly against the enemy. Then they must seek the ship, lost somewhere on the sea. And when they find it, they have to land upon its pitching deck. Where did we get such men?'

He went out to watch the launching of the dawn strike. As streaks of light appeared in the east, pilots came on deck. Bundled like animals awakened from hibernation, they waddled purposefully to their jets. The last to climb aboard was Cag, stocky and round like a snowball. He checked each jet, then studied his own. Finally, as if there were nothing more he could do, he scrambled into his plane and waited. Majestically, the task force turned into the wind, the bull horn jangled and a voice in the gloom cried, 'Launch jets.'

Admiral Tarrant watched them go, two by two from the lashing catapult, planes of immortal beauty whipping into the air with flame and fury upon them. They did not waste fuel orbiting but screamed to the west, seeking new bridges in Korea.

·CARAVANS·

JAMES·A·MICHENER

CARAVANS

TO BALDANZA

I

On a bleak wintry morning some years ago I was summoned to the office of our naval attaché at the American embassy in Kabul. Captain Verbruggen looked at me with an air of frustration and growled, 'Damn it all, Miller, two weeks ago the ambassador ordered you to settle this mess about the saddle shoes. Last night the Afghanistan government made another protest . . . this time official. I want you, by three o'clock this afternoon, to hand me . . .'

I interrupted to report: 'Sir, a much more serious matter has come up. Last night a dispatch arrived. I've assembled the data for you.'

I shoved before him a leather portfolio jammed with papers. Across the face of the portfolio was stamped the gold inscription, 'For the Ambassador,' and since our embassy owned only two such folders, what went into them was apt to be important.

'Can't it wait till the ambassador gets back from Hong Kong?' Captain Verbruggen asked hopefully, for even though he was our acting ambassador he preferred to temporize.

I disappointed him. 'It's got to be handled now.'

'What's it deal with?' he asked, for he was a self-made man who disliked reading.

Carefully folding back the leather cover, I pointed to a cable from Washington. 'Senior senator from Pennsylvania. Demands an answer. Immediately.'

Verbruggen, a rugged, bald-headed man in his sixties, snapped to attention, as if the senator from Pennsylvania had entered the room. 'What's he want?' He still refused to do any unnecessary reading.

'That Jaspar girl,' I said.

With a disgusted reflex Verbruggen slammed shut the portfolio. 'For seventeen months,' he complained, 'this embassy has been plagued by the Jaspar girl. I'm here to help a nation climb out of the Dark Ages, and that's the job I'm trying to do. But I'm pestered with saddle shoes and Jaspar idiots. There's nothing more I can think of to do on this case,' he concluded firmly, shoving the papers to me.

But I forced the papers back to his side of the desk. 'You've got to read the dispatch,' I warned.

Gingerly he lifted the leather cover and peeked at the peremptory message from Washington. When he saw that even the Secretary of State had involved himself in the matter, he snapped to attention and pulled the paper before him. Slowly he read aloud:

'It is imperative that I be able to supply the senior senator from Pennsylvania with full details regarding the whereabouts and condition of Ellen Jaspar. All previous reports from your embassy are judged inadequate and unacceptable. If necessary, detail your best men to this problem as it involves many collateral considerations. Am I correct in remembering that Mark Miller speaks the native language? If so, consider assigning him to this project at once and have him report promptly, sparing no effort.'

Captain Verbruggen leaned back, blew air from puffed-up cheeks and once again shoved the folder to me. 'Looks like it's been taken out of my hands,' he said with relief. 'Better get to work, son.'

I lifted the portfolio from his desk and said, 'I have been working, sir. Ever since I arrived.'

'In a very desultory way,' he suggested pleasantly. My boss could never forgo the obvious, which was why he was stuck off in Afghanistan, one of the most inconspicuous nations on earth. In 1946 it was just emerging from the bronze age, a land incredibly old, incredibly tied to an ancient past. At the embassy we used to say, 'Kabul today shows what Palestine was like at the time of Jesus.' In many ways, our attaché was an ideal man for Afghanistan, for he too was only just emerging from his own bronze age.

Yet I liked him. He was a rough, wily businessman who had made a minor fortune in the used-car racket, and a place for himself in the Democratic party in Minnesota. Four times he had helped elect Franklin D. Roosevelt, and although I was a strong Republican, I respected Verbruggen's tested loyalty. He had given the Democrats some sixty thousand dollars and they had given him Afghanistan.

He was almost entitled to it. While still a civilian he had made himself into a rough-and-ready yachtsman, for boating was his principal hobby, and when World War II struck, he volunteered to help the navy manage its shore installations. By merit and drive he had risen from lieutenant to navy captain and had made significant contributions to the building of our great bases at Manus and Samar. He was a tough bullet-head and men respected him; he had courage, and I could prove it.

My name is not really Mark Miller. By rights it's Marcus Muehler, but in the 1840s when my ancestors fled Germany they decided with that foresight which distinguishes my family that a Jewish name would not be helpful in America, so they translated *muehler* into its English equivalent, and henceforth we were Millers.

As usual, my family was right. The fact that my name was Miller and my face wholly un-Jewish enabled me to succeed at Groton and Yale, so that when in 1942 the United States navy was looking for a few acceptable Jewish officers to avoid having many unacceptable ones forced upon them, they grabbed me with relief and were happy when most of my shipmates never realized that I was Jewish. In how many wardrooms was I assured by amateur anthropologists, 'I can spot a kike every time.'

Captain Verbruggen, under whom I served at Manus, watched me for three weeks, then said, 'Miller, you're the kind of kid who ought to be in Intelligence. You've got brains.' And he personally fought with the brass on the island until he found me a good berth. In 1945, when our State Department also became eager to pick up a few Jewish career men with table manners, my former boss remembered me, and in one exciting week he switched me from lieutenant, junior grade, to State Department officer, very junior grade.

Then came the problem of where State should put me, for the typical embassy doubted that I would fit in. For example, I wouldn't be welcome in Cairo or Baghdad, where the citizens hated Jews, or, as it happened, in Paris, where many of our staff felt the same way. At this point Captain Verbruggen, now serving as naval attaché in Afghanistan, reported that he knew Mark Miller, and that I was a well-behaved Jew who would be a credit to the country. 'In fact,' he said in a cable that was passed widely throughout the department, 'some of my best friends are Jews,' and he got me. His courage gained the gratitude of President Truman and a nod from the Secretary of State. To everyone's relief I was working out reasonably well, so that Captain Verbruggen looked on me with a certain pride. I was one of his ideas that hadn't turned sour, which could not be said for all of them.

'I haven't been a ball of fire on the Jaspar girl,' I confessed, 'But when the cable arrived I got everything together. I've reviewed the files and I think I know what's got to be done next.'

'What?'

'At four this afternoon I'm seeing Shah Khan. At his home. He talks better there, and if anyone knows where the Jaspar girl is, he does.'

'Will he tell you?' Captain Verbruggen countered suspiciously.

'In Afghanistan I expect no one to tell me anything, and what they do tell me, I distrust.'

'You're learning.' The captain laughed. He looked at his watch and said, 'If you've already studied the file, and if you're going to meet Shah Khan at four . . .'

'I'd better get to work on the saddle shoes,' I anticipated.

'You'd better. Those damned mullahs are off again on a big religious kick.' I was always surprised at Captain Verbruggen's use of the vernacular. He read widely—magazines, not books—and acquired strange phrases. 'The mullahs from the mountain districts stormed into town yesterday,' he continued, 'and they got wind, somehow, of the saddle shoes and they're demanding that our Marine guards be sent home.'

'You aren't going to let a few mad priests dictate our policy, sir?'

'The one thing I refuse to get mixed up in is a bunch of fanatic Muslim priests. You don't know them the way I do. Already they're putting a lot of pressure on the Afghan government. I may have to lose my Marines.'

'What am I to do?'

'You speak the language. Go down to the bazaar. See what's actually happening.'

'Very good, sir.'

'And, Miller, if there's any good reason for getting rid of the Marines, let me know right away. Their time's almost up and it might be a friendly gesture on our part to get them out of here. Placate the mullahs at no real expense to ourselves.'

I was equally surprised at the precise vocabulary my boss could use when he wished to. 'I don't like the idea of placating a bunch of mullahs,' I objected stubbornly.

'You won't be,' he replied. 'I'll accept responsibility, and we'll all be further ahead if I do.'

I nodded deferentially and rose to go, tucking the Jaspar papers under my arm, but at the door I was stopped by a command from the acting ambassador. 'Let me know what Shah Khan thinks,' he said.

I laughed. 'There must be twelve million people in Afghanistan who would like to know what Shah Khan thinks. I'm sure I won't be the one to find out.' I left the room, then called back, 'But I'll let you know what he doesn't tell me.'

In 1946 the American embassy in Afghanistan required no large staff, for in those hesitant days the big lend-lease program that was to mark the future had not yet been visualized. We who did serve in the strange and sometimes forbidding city were forced by circumstance to be a closely knit group, because at that time Kabul provided positively nothing for foreigners: no hotels that we could use, no cinema of any kind, no newspapers, no radio with European programs, no restaurants available to visitors, no theaters, no cafés, no magazines. No public meetings were allowed, nor were we permitted any kind of normal social life with our Afghan hosts, for this was prohibited by the Afghans. We were thus driven in upon ourselves and if we wanted entertainment or social life we had to provide it ourselves, looking principally to the personnel attached to the English, French, Italian, Turkish and American embassies. At the end of a long, confining winter during which the city was snowbound, we searched hungrily for any diversion and were delighted when the people at the English embassy, always the most inventive where living overseas was concerned, came up with the idea of reading plays aloud before informal audiences.

Therefore, when I got back to my office in the two-story white building which served as our embassy, I was not surprised to find our pool secretary, Miss Maxwell of Omaha, typing furiously and somewhat irritated when I asked for the well-thumbed papers on the saddle shoes.

'They're over there,' she snapped without looking up.

'Could you get them?' I asked.

'Please, Mr Miller,' she protested. 'I'm just finishing the play for tonight.'

'I'm sorry,' I said, finding the papers for myself.

'The reading's tonight,' she explained, 'and I'm responsible for all of Act Three. The British girls are doing Act One, which is the longest, and one of the Italian girls is typing Act Two. She's finished. I guess they never do any work at the Italian embassy,' she sighed.

'You go ahead,' I said consolingly, and I noticed that she had in her machine not only the original copy but seven carbons as well. 'See that I get one of the first three,' I cautioned. 'I can't read those last carbons.'

'On my machine they're all right,' Miss Maxwell assured me. 'It's the Italian typewriters that won't strike off seven copies.' I noticed that Miss Maxwell was using a German machine, and it did make seven usable copies.

I took the saddle-shoe papers to my inner office and started to leaf through them, but the top page arrested me, for it said briefly, 'Afghan agents have warned us that if the Marines continue to molest the saddle shoes, there will be a murder in the bazaar.' This moved the whole matter up several notches in gravity, so I asked Miss Maxwell to summon my Afghan aide, Nur Muhammad, who came quietly into the room.

He was a good-looking, lithe young man of thirty-two, dressed in a western-style blue suit which fitted badly. He had black hair, dark skin, deep-set eyes, a big Afghan nose and extremely white teeth, which he showed rarely. He was a moody, sensitive person who during the two years he had worked at the American embassy had taught himself to speak English. It was generally known that he was in the employ of the Afghanistan government.

'Sit down, Nur,' I said. With grave attention to protocol he sat in the chair I indicated, smoothed his trousers, then folded his hands in his lap.

'Yes, sahib?' he said with a deft combination of willingness to help and studiousness not to appear too eager.

'It's about the saddle shoes,' I began, and Nur Muhammad relaxed. 'You've heard about the latest intelligence?' I continued.

Nur Muhammad betrayed nothing. He was far too smart to be trapped into admitting that he knew anything. He insisted that I speak first. Then he would react to what I had said. 'What intelligence?' he asked blandly.

I opened the manila folder on the case and looked at the ominous report. 'Some of your people have warned us that if the Marines continue to . . . Well, they say molest. Nur Muhammad, do you think our Marines have molested anyone?'

Before Nur could reply my door was opened by a handsome young American Marine who had won battle stars on Guadalcanal and Iwo Jima and who now enjoyed, as his reward, an easy job as one of our two military guards in the embassy. He stepped in smartly, handed me some papers, turned professionally, and disappeared. His uniform, I remember, was immaculate and his shoes were shined.

When he was gone Nur Muhammad replied cautiously, 'I wouldn't say by your standards the young men have molested. But Ramadan is approaching. The mullahs gain more voice each day. It is they who believe there has been molestation and if they believe this, Mr Miller . . .'

I showed him the report. At the suggestion of murder he drew in his breath.

'Yes I said. 'Murder.' Nur Muhammad carefully replaced the paper, then straightened his trousers once more.

'I would not ignore the mullahs,' Nur Muhammad warned. 'You see, as Ramadan approaches they wish to reinforce their power. To remind us of that power.'

'Suppose these suspicions continued? Suppose the Marine you just saw did . . . well . . . molest?' I added quickly, 'You understand, I'm not for one minute granting that any Marine did molest.'

'You made your position clear on that point,' Nur Muhammad agreed effusively.

'But suppose the mullahs thought otherwise? Whom would they murder?'

Without a moment's reflection Nur replied, 'The saddle shoes, of course.'

'The saddle shoes!' I gasped.

'Of course. I must explain, Miller Sahib. In the past the mullahs loved to murder the ferangi, but whenever they murdered a ferangi it caused much trouble for Afghanistan. So they've had to quit.'

I was always bemused by the Afghan word for *foreigner*. When the first Asian students saw this ugly word, with its even uglier connotations, the unaccustomed combination of *g* and *n* perplexed them, so they invented an expressive pronunciation which included all the letters, heavily fraught with hatred, envy and contempt. Some pronounced it *ferangi*, with a hard *g*, some *faranji*, others *foreggin*, but it meant the same.

'The mullahs will not murder the ferangi,' Nur Muhammad assured me.

'I think we should go down to the bazaar right now,' I suggested.

'I do not think I should go, Miller Sahib. My presence would endanger your effectiveness and mine.'

'I agree, but I'd like to have you there, if danger should erupt.'

'What danger can erupt in a Kabul bazaar?' Nur Muhammad asked deprecatingly.

'We just agreed. Murder.'

'But not to a ferangi,' Nur assured me, and he declined to join me, returning to his regular duties.

When he had gone I called Security to request that our two Marines be excused from duty, and although I met with loud protest, my threat to involve the acting ambassador turned the trick. From my window I watched the two clean-cut battle heroes hurrying toward the exit gate. I summoned Miss Maxwell and informed her, 'I'll be in the bazaar.'

'Good,' she replied, grabbing her hat. 'I'll deliver the copies of the play.'

I went to the exit gate and asked the guard to hail me a ghoddy, and in a few minutes a driver pulled up with the world's most uncomfortable taxi: a horse-drawn two-seater in which the driver perched comfortably in front on a hair cushion, while the passengers clung precariously to a sloping wooden seat that faced backward. Thin strips of old automobile tires tacked to wooden wheels enabled the ghoddy to travel over the rough, frozen streets.

I've been told that diplomats and military men remember with nostalgia the first alien lands in which they served, and I suppose this is inevitable; but in my case I look back upon Afghanistan with special affection because it was, in those days, the wildest, weirdest land on earth and to be a young man in Kabul was the essence of adventure. Now, as I jogged along in the ghoddy on an unbelievable mission, I thought again of the violent land and the even more violent contradictions that surrounded me.

The city of Kabul, perched at the intersection of caravan trails that had functioned for more than three thousand years, was hemmed in on the west by the Koh-i-Baba range of mountains, nearly seventeen thousand feet high, and on the north by the even greater Hindu Kush, one of the major mountain massifs of Asia. In the winter these powerful ranges were covered with snow, so that one could never forget that he was caught in a kind of bowl whose rim was composed of ice and granite.

Kabul, pronounced Cobble by all who have been there, Kaboul by those who have not, was shaped like a large capital U lying on its side, with the closed end to the east where the Kabul River flowed down to the Khyber Pass, and the open end to the west facing the Koh-i-Baba. The central part of the U was occupied by a rather large hill, which in my home state of Massachusetts would have been called a mountain. The American embassy and most European quarters lay in the northern leg of the U, which I was now leaving, while the bazaar, the mosques, and the vivid life of the city lay in the southern leg, to which I was heading.

As we made our way toward the center of Kabul I was reminded of the first contradiction that marked Afghanistan. The men I saw on the streets looked much more Jewish than I. They were tall, dark of skin, lithe, with flashing black eyes and prominent Semitic noses. They took great pride in their claim to be descendants of the lost tribes of Israel, who were supposed to have reached these mountain plateaus during the Diaspora. But at the same time the Afghans remembered that the ancient name of their country was Aryana, and in the volatile 1930s they were adopted by Adolf Hitler as the world's first Aryans and his special wards. The proud Afghans were able to accept both accolades without discrimination and consequently boasted that while it was true that they were born of the Jewish tribe, the Ben-i-Israel, once they reached Afghanistan they had ceased being Jews and had founded the Aryan race. It made as much sense as what some of their friends were propounding elsewhere.

The dress of Afghan men was striking. The few educated men and officials dressed like Nur Muhammad: western clothes with fur-collared overcoats and handsome iridescent caps of karakul, shaped either like American Legion overseas caps or like fezzes. Other men wore the national costume: sandals which allowed the toes to drag in the snow, baggy white pants of Arab derivation, an enormous white shirt whose tails were worn outside and reached below the knees to flap in the breeze, richly patterned vest, overcoat of some heavy western cloth, and a dirty turban, one of whose ends trailed over the shoulder. If they were tribesmen from the hills, they also carried rifles and sometimes wore bandoleers well studded with cartridges. I doubt if you could have found a national capital anywhere in the world where so many men walked the streets fully armed, for in addition to their rifles most of the tribesmen carried daggers as well. Civilization in Afghanistan, as represented by officials who wore the karakul cap, existed on a very narrow margin of survival.

During my first days in Afghanistan I had noticed that whenever I saw a pair of these fierce tribesmen down from the hills, men who had probably killed in mountain ambush, one of the couple behaved in a very masculine manner while his partner was sure to have feminine traits. He walked in mincing steps, kept a handkerchief in one hand, and carried a winter flower between his teeth. Usually the feminine partner wore a little rouge or eye makeup and always he walked holding the hand of his more rugged partner.

A further glance at the streets of Kabul explained why this was so. There were no women visible. I had been in the country more than a hundred days and had yet to see a woman. I had been entertained in important homes, like that of Shah Khan, but never had I been allowed to see any of the women who lived there. It was this phenomenon that accounted for the curious behaviour of the men: having removed all women from public life, the Afghans realized that feminine traits were nevertheless desirable and so allocated them to men. On the frozen streets of Kabul I saw just as many feminine actions as I would have seen on the boulevards of Paris, except that here men performed them.

Of course, it isn't accurate to say that I saw no women. Frequently as the ghoddy plugged along I saw emerging from towering walls, whose gates were always guarded, vague moving shapes enshrouded in cloth from head to toe. They were women, obliged by Afghan custom never to appear in public without a chaderi, the Muslim covering that provides only a tiny rectangle of embroidered lace through which the wearer can see but cannot be seen. We were told by educated Afghan men, most of whom despised the chaderi, that the imposition damaged the health and the eyesight of the women, but it persisted. At the age of thirteen all females were driven into this seclusion, from which they never escaped.

I must admit, however, that these ghostly figures, moving through the city in shrouds that were often beautifully pleated and made of costly fabric, imparted a grave sexuality to life. There was a mysteriousness in meeting them and wondering what kind of human being resided inside the cocoon, and rarely have I been as aware of women, or as fascinated by them, as I was in Afghanistan, where I saw none.

It was midmorning when the ghoddy dropped me at the little fortress-like mosque with two white minarets that stood by the river in the heart of the city, and I noticed at the doorway to the mosque three mullahs – tall, gaunt, unkempt men with flowing beards and fierce eyes – who appeared to be guarding the holy place and condemning me, a non-Muslim, for passing so near. When I looked at them politely, they stared back with undisguised hatred and I thought:

These are the men who rule Afghanistan!

At this moment one of them, obviously down from the hills, spied something behind me that alarmed him, and he began screaming imprecations in Pashto. Encouraged by his protests, the other two mullahs started running at me, and I hurriedly ducked aside to let them pass. When they had gone, like scarecrows in their long gowns and flying beards, I looked after them to see what had so agitated them, and I discovered that our typist, Miss Maxwell, had driven to town in the embassy jeep and was now hurrying along the public sidewalk with her eight copies of the play we were to read that night. The country mullah had spotted her, a woman without a chaderi, and felt obliged to assault her for this violation of faith. He and his companions, giving no thought to the fact that Miss Maxwell was ferangi, bore down upon her screaming and cursing.

Before I could protect her, the three tall mullahs, their beards and hooked noses making them caricatures of religious frenzy, had swarmed upon her and were beating her with their fists. What was worse—then and in retrospect—they began spitting at her, and rheum from their lips trickled across her terrified face.

I dashed through the crowd that had gathered and began grabbing the mullahs, shouting in Pashto, 'Stop it, you fools! She's ferangi!'

I was saved by the fact that I knew the language; the holy men fell back, startled that I could speak to them in Pashto, whereas had I been a mere ferangi who had struck a priest they might have incited the crowd to kill me. A policeman ambled up, never swiftly for he did not wish to become involved with mullahs, and said quietly, 'Look here, men. We're in Kabul, not the mountains. Let the woman alone.' And the three fanatic mullahs withdrew to guard once more the mosque at the river's edge.

Miss Maxwell, terrorized by the sudden attack, proved herself a brave girl and refused to cry. I wiped the spit from her face and said, 'Forget them. They're madmen. I'll find your driver.'

I looked about for the embassy car and discovered the Afghan driver lounging unconcernedly along the river wall, from where he had watched the incident. He was sure that I or somebody would halt the fanatical mullahs and that his charge, Miss Maxwell, wasn't going to get seriously hurt, so he saw no good reason to risk his neck brawling with idiot mullahs.

He now sauntered over. 'Must I take Miss Maxwell back to the embassy?' he asked in Pashto.

'The Italian embassy,' I explained.

'Be careful,' he warned me. 'The mullahs are dangerous these days.'

Before he drove Miss Maxwell away, I congratulated her upon the self-control she had exhibited. People back home made jokes about the softness of Americans, but they should have seen Miss Maxwell that March day in Kabul.

When she was gone, I wandered over to the bazaar, a nest of narrow streets in the crowded section of the city, where almost everything was for sale, much of it stolen from warehouses in Delhi, Isfahan and Samarkand. I derived perverse pleasure from the assurance that new India, ancient Persia and revolutionary Russia were alike impotent to halt the hereditary thieves of Central Asia. When Darius the Persian marched through Kabul five hundred years before the birth of Christ, this same bazaar was selling practically the same goods stolen from the same ancient cities.

There were, of course, a few modern improvements. Gillette razor blades were in good supply, as were surgical scissors from Göttingen in Germany.

One enterprising merchant had penicillin and aspirin, while another had imported from a rifled G.I. warehouse in Bombay cans of Campbell's soup and spark plugs for American cars, of which there were beginning to be a few on the deeply rutted streets of Kabul.

But it was the faces that made me think I was back in the days of Alexander the Great, when Afghanistan, astonishing as it now seemed, was a distant satrapy of Athens, a land of high culture long before England was properly discovered or any of the Americas civilized. In these faces there was a sense of potential fire, of almost maniacal intensity, and wherever I looked there were the mysterious forms of women, shrouded in flimsy robes which hid even their eyes.

I was watching the movement of these alluring figures, wondering as a young man should what form was sequestered beneath the robes, when I became aware—how I cannot even now explain—of two young women who moved with tantalizing grace. How did I know they were young women? I don't know. How did I know they were beautiful, and aching with sexual desire, and gay and lively? I don't know. But I do know that these creatures, whatever their age or appearance, were positively alluring in their mysteriousness.

One was dressed in an expensive, pleated chaderi of fawn-colored silk; the other was in gray. At first I thought they were trying to attract me, so when they passed very close I whispered in Pashto, 'You little girls be careful. The mullahs are watching.'

They stopped in astonishment, turned to look out of the bazaar toward the three gaunt mullahs, then giggled and hurried on. When I turned to look after them, I saw that they were wearing American-style saddle shoes. These must be the girls who had been reported as meeting our two Marine guards in the bazaar, and from my memory of the dashing manner in which the Marines had left our embassy compound, and from the saucy way in which the girls had moved past me, I suspected that matters of substantial moment were afoot, and that the impending meeting of these young people might lead to tragedy.

I therefore set out to follow the girls, and I cursed Nur Muhammad for not being on hand to help. The girls were not moving fast, and from time to time I was able to catch glimpses of them, two figures shrouded in expensive silk, exquisite in their movements, and wearing saddle shoes. They became the personification of sexual desire—attractive, dangerous, evanescent—as they moved gracefully through the bazaar, looking, hoping.

I followed them into the alleyways where karakul caps were sold, those silvery gray hats that made Afghan men seem so handsome and ferangi so ridiculous. 'Sahib, cap! Cap!' the merchants cried, falling back with laughter when I said regretfully in Pashto, 'It takes a handsome man to wear karakul.'

Now the shrouded girls moved lazily, wasting time in the fruit stalls where precious melons from the south were available, and in the dark stalls where cloth from India was on sale. I do not think they were aware of me, following them at a distance, but the movement of those gay, abandoned saddle shoes fascinated me, and I well understood how our two Marines had fallen under the spell of these lively girls.

For a moment I lost them. I turned into a street where there were shops with metal goods—bronze, tin, stainless steel and silver—but the girls were not there. Fearing something not easily described, I hurried back to the fabric center, and finding no one there I turned toward a little alley which led to what seemed a dead end. On chance, I stepped that way and saw a perplexing, haunting sight.

Against the dead-end wall leaned our two American Marines, in bright uniform. Against them, their backs to me, were pressed the two Afghan girls, their chaderies thrown back, their unseen lips pressed eagerly against those of the Marines. The girl in gray had allowed her dress to be pulled partly away, and in the wintry air I could see her naked shoulders. I have never seen human beings so passionately intertwined, and I became aware of the fact that the girls had begun to loosen the uniforms of the Marines and to adjust to the results.

It was at this moment that I saw, from the corner of my eye, the three gaunt mullahs moving through the bazaar, intent upon finding the girls. It would be some moments before they reached this alley, and they might not see it. On the other hand, they might.

'You fools!' I shouted in Pashto, running down the alley. 'This way! At once!'

I tried to grab the two girls, partly, I suppose, in order to see what Afghan women looked like with the chaderi removed, but they eluded me, and when they finally did face me, the shrouds were back in place and the girls were as mysterious, as silent as ever.

'The mullahs?' they asked me in real fear.

'Yes! Hurry!'

I started to lead them to what I thought was safety, but the two couples, having surmounted the language barrier, had somehow planned their own escape routes, for in an instant the girls vanished down a narrow pathway that led away from the approaching mullahs, while the two Marines vaulted the seemingly unscalable wall, and I was left alone in the cul-de-sac. I heard the angry mullahs behind me, whipping up a crowd, and on the spur of the moment I had the presence of mind to start urinating against the wall.

This even the mullahs understood, and I heard them cry in frustration from the other end of the alley, 'The evil girls must be here.' When I made my way through the crowd, I saw along the farther edge two shrouded figures, one in a fawn-colored chaderi, one in gray, drifting easily away from the bazaar. Their silken shrouds flowed in the wintry wind like the robes of Grecian goddesses, and along the snowy footpaths I watched the saddle shoes depart. I was aching with the mystery of sex, with the terrible allure that such undulating figures could evoke. I wanted to run after the girls and protest madly in Pashto that I needed them, that with the Marines gone I would like to make love with them, even in the hurried corner of a bazaar where men paused to urinate.

For the Marines would have to leave Afghanistan. That was clear. Regretfully I watched the girls disappear, then realized with some shame that I was inwardly pleased that the Marines would be sent home. I dismissed the unworthy thought and looked for a ghoddy. To my surprise one appeared promptly, occupied by Nur Muhammad, who had come down to survey matters from a distance.

'Trouble?' he asked blandly, pointing to the mullahs, who were haranguing a crowd near the entrance to the bazaar.

'Just escaped,' I reported. 'A miracle.'

I climbed onto the sloping seat of the ghoddy and we drove back toward the embassy. As the horse clip-clopped over the frozen mud that served as a road in Kabul, I noticed once more the little open ditches that lined most streets in the city. In them ran the public drinking water, since underground pipes were unknown in Afghanistan. But in the same ditches the citizens also urinated, pitched dead dogs, brushed teeth and washed all food that would be later eaten by the citizens, including ferangi stationed in the American and European embassies. I shuddered.

Ahead of me a man from the mountains, carbine slung over his back, squatted over the ditch and defecated, while not ten yards away a cook's helper, dressed like Nur Muhammad, unconcernedly washed the meat that would be served that night in the French embassy.

'A thing like that is a national disgrace,' Nur said bitterly.

'Does the government know who the girls are? The saddle shoes, I mean?'

'Rumors whisper that one is Shah Khan's granddaughter.'

'Does the old man know?' I probed.

'He's the one who protested to the ambassador.'

'Is his granddaughter pretty?'

'They say she's a beauty,' Nur replied. 'I haven't met anyone who's seen her.'

'Is it true that Shah Khan has openly stated he's opposed to the chaderi?' I asked, trying to review our intelligence on the man I was shortly to see.

'Of course. That's why the mullahs tried to murder him last Ramadan.'

'I have to be there at four,' I repeated. Nur said he'd have the jeep ready, and I hurried to report to Captain Verbruggen. We arranged for the two Marines to be shipped out of the country that afternoon. They would ride an open truck down the long, perilous mountain passes to Peshawar, at the Indian end of the Khyber Pass. And in the years ahead they would relate such memories of Afghanistan as would inspire other young men to serve in distant nations.

2

Kabul was superb at the end of winter, particularly when the late afternoon sun rushed toward some rendezvous in Persia, to the west; for then the normal drabness of the miserable mud homes was masked in snow, and the solitary figures with carbines who moved across the empty fields outside of town bore an epic quality which captivated the eye. No stranger, at such a moment, could forget that he was in Asia.

Shah Khan lived well to the west, in a forbidding fortress hidden behind massive surrounding walls at least fifteen feet high. It must have required the forced labor of hundreds of convicts for many months to build the walls alone, for they enclosed many acres. This redoubtable establishment, complete with turrets and its own minaret, lay in the shadow of the beautiful Koh-i-Baba mountains, which were now snow-covered, reminding the foreigner that during the winter this city was practically inaccessible, unless one wished to risk his life on sloping mountain passes where each year many trucks were lost.

At the fortress gate through which one entered to visit Shah Khan there hung a bell cord, at which Nur Muhammad tugged vigorously, sending an echo through the frosty air. Normally the heavy gate would have been operated by some superannuated warrior who had served the owner in his youth, but when Nur yanked the cord a second time I thought I heard the pounding of horses' hoofs. Then, instead of the miserly half-inch through which the guards customarily peered at intending visitors, the gates were slammed violently open and a handsome man of thirty-six, astride a pawing white horse, greeted us.

'Mark Miller! Enter!' he cried in English. He was Moheb Khan, son of the Shah, educated at Oxford and at the Wharton School of Finance and Commerce. He held a responsible position in the Foreign Office, but on this day was affecting the dress of a prosperous mountain man, for he wore sheepskin trousers, an expensive embroidered vest, a long Russian-style fur coat, and a silver-gray karakul cap. He was clean-shaven, sharp-eyed and urbane, the educated Afghan at his best. I had talked with Moheb Khan several times before and had found him sophisticated in learning, dignified in bearing, and arrogant in judgment. He was tall and slim, with a large head marked by wavy black hair in which he took special pride. I respected him as one of the cleverest men I knew.

Whenever I was with Moheb I appreciated anew the fact that the future history of Afghanistan, if left to Afghans, would be determined by the struggle between the many bearded mullahs from the hills and the few young experts like Moheb, with degrees from Oxford or the Sorbonne or the Massachusetts Institute of Technology. I was not at all sure how the contest would eventuate, but it was clear that not only I but also all the people of all the embassies prayed that Moheb Khan and his young associates might win.

'Where'd you get the horse?' I asked, walking into the great compound, which in the nineteenth century had housed thousands of men during the frequent sieges.

'Look at the brand!' he cried, reaching down to shake my hand. 'Pardon the glove,' he added, 'but I'm afraid to drop the reins.'

He pointed to the horse's left flank, where a scrawling W had been burned deep into the hair and skin.

'I don't get it,' I said.

'Think, Miller!'

'W,' I repeated aloud. 'I don't know any ranch with that brand.'

'It's sentimental!' Moheb laughed. 'Think! Think!'

I could not guess what the cryptic brand was intented to signify, and when Nur Muhammad edged the jeep into the compound, the horse shied and darted off across the snowy plain—it would be ridiculous to call that huge expanse of land a garden—and I could well observe the fine horsemanship that Moheb Khan exhibited.

He brought the dashing animal back to the jeep, to familiarize the horse with the sound of a motor car, then leaped with agility to the ground beside me and cupped his hands near my right knee, all in one marvelously synchronized movement. 'You ride,' he commanded.

There was something that no stranger ever became accustomed to in Afghanistan: the peremptory command of the educated Afghan. 'You ride!' a friend said, and you got the feeling that if you didn't leap on the horse immediately one of those omnipresent carbines was going to go off. So I threw my right foot into the cupped hands and, leaping upward to match his strong lift, I was astride the white horse.

At Groton I had taken horsemanship, and I could ride passably well, but it quickly became apparent that I was not going to tell this horse what to do. Yet the semi-wild animal loved the feel of a man on his back, for he tore across the huge field in such a way as to blend his movements with mine. I thought: He wants to frighten me, but he also wants me on hand so that there'll be someone to frighten. He did not exactly ignore the reins, nor did he respond quickly. Like a wilful child he must have thought: If I pay no attention to him, this rider may forget the whole thing. But when I quietly insisted that he obey my commands, he accommodated himself to them, tardily and with a trace of rebellion. He was a superb horse, and I brought him back to the jeep, where Moheb Khan stood talking with Nur Muhammad.

When the horse was close to the idling jeep, Moheb suddenly reached for the accelerator with his hand, jammed it down so that the engine exploded once or twice, thus sending the horse high in the air. Fortunately I had not yet dropped the reins, and I tugged at them fiercely to bring the frightened beast back under control. I was furious with Moheb for this reckless act – training his horse at my peril – and on the spur of the moment I dug my heels into the flanks of the white beast and we tore across the open land, turning and twisting and cavorting for some minutes. At the end of our exciting ride I brought the horse back to the jeep and called sternly, 'Nur Muhammad, turn off the engine.'

But before he could do so, Moheb Khan again jammed the accelerator pedal to the floor. This time I held the horse steady, then threw the reins to Moheb. 'He's a good horse,' I said.

'You're a good rider, Miller. Better than any American I've seen yet.' I laughed and he asked. 'You don't fathom the brand?'

'Who can fathom the brain of an Afghan?' I joked.

'Not I,' Moheb confessed. 'But your failure does surprise me.'

'Where'd you get the horse?' I asked again, as we walked toward the main house, an imposing mud-walled castle around which clustered twelve or thirteen smaller buildings.

'Some traders brought him down from the north. Said they got him over the Oxus in Russia. I had a man from the Russian embassy out one afternoon and the horse did seem to recognize Russian commands.'

'Splendid beast,' I said, 'Russian or whatever.'

Moheb Khan led me through the rugged door of the main house, whose mud walls were more than thirty inches thick. I said, 'They must keep you cool in summer.'

Moheb replied, 'More important, they withstood British cannon for eleven days.' He pointed to spots where there were deep indentations. With an imperial afterthought, he indicated to Nur Muhammad where he should wait, then took me in to see his father.

Shah Khan – his name could be translated as Sir Mister and was hardly a name at all – was a slim patrician who had served as adviser to three successive kings. He was thin and gray, wore a trim mustache, expensive Harris tweeds tailored in London, and a heavy gold watch chain across his vest. Normally he spoke Persian, but in dealing with foreigners, he preferred French, for he had attended the Sorbonne; but he was also competent in English, German and Pashto, the language of the countryside. Like all educated Afghans, Shah Khan looked to France as the source of culture, to Germany as the source of military instruction, to America as the source of canned goods, and to England as the fountainhead of duplicity. Nevertheless, it was with the latter country that Afghanistan had always maintained its closest ties, like a husband who hates his wife yet would be lost if she deserted him.

One of the reasons why Shah Khan had taken a liking to me, and confided in me when he refused to do so with other Americans, was that although I could not speak Persian I did speak French, and he could thus indulge his obsession that diplomacy must be conducted only in that language. Today we would speak French.

The room in which we talked was important in the history of Afghanistan and essential to any understanding of the modern nation. Here had occurred spectacular murders which altered the course of dynasty, protracted sieges, secret councils and, strangest of all, Christian weddings under the sponsorship of Shah Khan. They took place whenever some exile from Europe wished to marry a Christian girl from one of the embassies, for there often were no Christian ministers available in Kabul.

It was a rocky fortress of a room, built by a German architect, furnished by a Danish merchant who sold only the best, and decorated by a Frenchman who spent eleven thousand dollars in shipping charges alone. On one wall there was a Picasso, but nothing the French decorator had devised could alter the Germanic heaviness of the room, and it remained a typical Afghan salon.

On the low table from Copenhagen lay copies of the *London Illustrated News*, the *Manchester Guardian*, *Newsweek*, the *Reader's Digest* and six or seven French magazines. Against one wall stood a huge Gramophone with numerous speakers, for Shah Khan loved music, as did his son, Moheb. Another wall contained the principal British, Italian, French and American encyclopedias, as well as novels in five or six different languages.

Shah Khan, who could be as Afghan as his room, asked bluntly, 'What do you wish to discuss?'

I showed him the leather folder and replied, 'Our government is demanding that we report where Ellen Jaspar is.'

'They've been doing that for the better part of a year,' Shah Khan parried. He sat deep in a leather chair which his grandfather had purchased in Berlin. Not even the French decorator had been able to banish it from the room, but he had succeeded in staining the leather an objectionable red.

'But this time, Your Excellency, it isn't merely the government who demands. It's the senator from Pennsylvania.'

'Is that important?' the old Afghan parried.

'Well,' I fumbled. 'Let's say that in America a senator has the same powers that you have in Kabul. Now suppose you sent the embassy in Paris an inquiry. Wouldn't you expect an answer?'

'I certainly would. Moheb, did you know the senator from Pennsylvania?'

'Which one?' Moheb asked quickly. He rattled off the names of the two senators. 'I liked them both.'

'Are they significant men?' his father asked.

'Very,' Moheb replied. The young man was an unusual Afghan, in that while he was a devout Muslim, he also drank alcohol, and he now poured me a drink of whiskey. His father, a Muslim of the old school, felt obliged to reprove his son because the drinking took place before a Christian. Accordingly he spoke harshly in Pashto, whereupon I replied in the same language, 'Let the blame be upon me, Your Excellency.' This reminder that I spoke not only French but also the Afghan language softened the old man.

'You feel, Monsieur Miller, that this time something must be done.'

'Indeed, or we shall all be reprimanded. Perhaps called home.'

'Let us suffer the evils that we know rather than flee to those we know not of,' Shah Khan replied, paraphrasing Hamlet in French. 'Have you new material about this unfortunate girl?'

I checked with Shah Khan and his alert son the facts that our embassy knew about Ellen Jaspar and Nazrullah. In the autumn of 1942 the Afghan government had sent a fine young man from Kabul to the Wharton School, the business end of the University of Pennsylvania, in Philadelphia. This Nazrullah, who was then twenty-four–eight years younger than Moheb Khan–came from a good Kabul family, was bright, good-looking and endowed with a very comfortable expense account which allowed him to buy, from a Philadelphia used-car dealer, a Cadillac convertible painted red.

The young Afghan cut a swath in Philadelphia society. He was seen everywhere–Merion, Bryn Mawr, New Hope. At the same time, the solid engineering degree he had earned in Germany prepared him to work for high marks at the Wharton School.

Moheb added, 'In spite of his enthusiastic social life, Nazrullah was an honor student. I kept tabs on him, since I was serving in the embassy in Washington at the time.'

'Didn't Nazrullah's time at the Wharton School overlap yours?' Shah Khan asked.

'No,' Moheb explained. 'Don't you remember? You sent him to Wharton because I'd done fairly well there.'

I pointed excitedly at Moheb and shouted in English, 'That's it! The W stands for Wharton!'

'Exactly!' Moheb shouted back, and we raised our glasses.

'What's this foolishness?' old Shah Khan asked from the depths of his red leather chair.

'Your son branded his white horse with a W. In honor of his degree from Wharton,' I explained.

'Preposterous,' Shah Khan growled, plainly irritated by his son's noisy drinking.

'Nazrullah was offered half a dozen jobs in America,' Moheb added, 'but he preferred to help us out here at home.'

'Where'd he meet the Jaspar girl?' Shah Khan asked, fingering his gold chain.

'Those were the years,' Moheb reminded us, 'when there weren't too many American men available. Nazrullah . . .'

'What's his last name?' I interrupted.

'Just Nazrullah,' Moheb replied. 'Like so many Afghans, he has no last name. As to the girl. She was a junior at Bryn Mawr. I think he may have met her while he was playing tennis at Merion. She came from a good family in Dorset, Pennsylvania.'

'Where's that?' I asked, finding it strange to be asking an Afghan about American geography.

'Small town in Penns County,' Moheb explained. 'North of Philadelphia.'

'They didn't get married in Dorset,' I explained to Shah Khan.

'I should say not!' Moheb agreed vociferously. 'Her family raised bloody hell. Bryn Mawr did the same. You know what the girl did? In the middle of the war she went to England, wangled her way to India, and came up the Khyber Pass in a donkey caravan. She was married here in Kabul.'

'It was a brilliant wedding,' Shah Khan remembered. 'Have you a picture of the girl, Monsieur Miller?'

From my files I produced several photographs of Ellen Jaspar. As a sophomore at Bryn Mawr she had played in Shakespeare–Olivia in *Twelfth*

Night—a thin, good-looking blonde and apparently graceful. In her junior year she sang in the chorus that co-operated with Fritz Reiner in doing Beethoven's *Ninth Symphony*, and in her surplice with her blond hair peeking from under her cap she looked angelic. There were pictures of her and Nazrullah, she a lovely white and he a romantic brown. And there was one picture of her when she graduated from high school, wide-eyed and smiling, yet somehow apprehensive. I had known a thousand girls like Ellen Jaspar; they adorned the campuses at Radcliffe, Smith and Holyoke. They all did well in English, poorly in mathematics, indifferently in philosophy. They were the vibrant, exciting girls who would seriously consider, in the middle of their junior year, marrying a young man from Afghanistan or Argentina or Turkestan. Most of them, in their senior year, developed more sense and married young men from Denver or Mobile or Somerville, outside of Boston.

'What made her different?' Shah Khan asked.

'We have the reports. Her father says he begged her not to do this thing, and all she would reply was that she was fed up with Dorset, Pennsylvania, and that she would rather die on the sands of the desert than marry the young man from that town who had been courting her.'

'Is Dorset so bad?' the old Afghan asked. 'I knew many small towns in France, and they weren't exciting, but they weren't bad either.'

'I used to drive out to Dorset,' Moheb Khan replied. 'I remember it as a lovely American town. Rather colonial in architecture, I recall.'

'But you didn't live there,' the old man reflected.

'As a matter of fact, I did,' Moheb corrected. 'For three days. Ellen and Nazrullah drove me up one Friday afternoon. He wanted the Jaspars to see that in Afghanistan we had many young men who spoke well. It was an agonizing weekend.'

'The Jaspars took the whole thing rather dimly?' I asked.

Moheb was about to reply when I received the distinct sensation that some additional person had entered the room. A presence of some kind seemed to hover near me in the heavy battle-room and I thought I saw old Shah Khan looking over my shoulder and shaking his head. I turned in the direction of whoever it was who might be receiving the message, and there was no one. But I did see something I had not noticed when I first arrived in the room. In the hallway, thrown across a chair as an American child might throw her raincoat, lay a fawn-colored chaderi.

'Dimly?' Moheb was echoing. 'The Jaspars looked at Nazrullah and me as if we had leprosy.'

'What did Mr Jaspar work at?' I asked. 'Wasn't it insurance?'

'Yes. He had that sweet, affable nature that insurance men around the world acquire,' Moheb replied. 'I liked him, and his wife was equally pleasant. He was also chairman, I believe, of the local draft board. A position of responsibility.'

'Later on,' Shah Khan inquired, 'didn't you advise the Jaspars against an Afghan marriage?'

'Yes. I met them in Philadelphia, and I brought along our ambassador from Washington, and the four of us . . . Nazrullah and Ellen knew nothing of this meeting and did not attend. We discussed the matter quite frankly.'

'You told them the truth?' I asked.

'Completely. As I recall, our ambassador was rather unhappy and thought the explicitness of my explanation unnecessary. Told me later I might have damaged our nation's reputation. I told the Jaspars that if their daughter married Nazrullah, when she reached Kabul her American passport would be taken away and she could never thereafter leave Afghanistan, no matter what the excuse, without her husband's permission. That she was an Afghan then and forever, and that she surrendered all claim to protection from America.'

'You told them that as clearly as you are telling me?' Shah Khan asked.

'Yes.'

'What did they say?'

'Mrs Jaspar began to cry.'

'Did you warn them about Afghan salaries and living conditions?' I asked.

'I did. Most explicitly,' Moheb assured me. 'I said, "Mr Jaspar, Ellen mustn't be deceived by the fact that in America Nazrullah drives a Cadillac and I a Mercedes. Our government is very generous to us as long as we're abroad, but when we go home Nazrullah and I will get jobs that pay no more than twenty American dollars a month.'

'Did they believe you?'

'They saw the cars and were sure I was lying. In Dorset, Pennsylvania, as in Kabul, cupidity is the same. The Jaspars were convinced that Nazrullah was very rich.'

'What does he earn now?' I asked.

The Khans conversed in Pashto and agreed that Nazrullah and his American bride had begun with a salary of twenty-one dollars a month and that it had now grown to twenty-seven, more or less.

'And I explained the housing,' Moheb continued. 'I said that for much of her life Ellen would live in a hovel, surrounded by women who despised her for not wearing the chaderi . . .'

'Is it true, Your Excellency,' I asked, 'that Afghanistan may soon discard the chaderi?'

The old man leaned back in his red leather chair and replied, 'You Americans seem inordinately preoccupied with the chaderi. Look!' and he pointed to the chair in the hall. 'My own granddaughter wears the chaderi and her mother graduated from the Sorbonne.' I looked again at the fawn-colored shroud.

'Does your granddaughter enjoy doing so?' I asked.

'We do not concern ourselves about that,' Shah Khan replied.

'But the Russians do,' I responded, touching a sore point with the old man. 'They say they will force you to set your women free, as they have done theirs.'

I knew instinctively that he wanted to speak further on this point, that he agreed with me and the Russians that the chaderi must go or revolution come, but he stopped the conversation with this observation: 'I learned today that the young woman from your embassy, Miss Maxwell, was assaulted by three mullahs from the hills. You rescued her, I believe. Then you know how powerful these fanatics still are. The chaderi will remain.'

'I assured the Jaspars,' Moheb continued, 'that Ellen would not have to wear one, but that Nazrullah's family would hate her if she didn't. I also warned them that if Ellen appeared in public without the chaderi, mullahs might spit at her.' His voice grew harsh as he added, 'Miller Sahib, I told the Jaspars of every fact relating to ferangi wives in Afghanistan, and later on I told Ellen herself. I was as honest as a man could be. I warned her that if she married Nazrullah she would become a woman without a country, a woman without a judge to protect her, a woman with no human rights at all, an animal . . . an animal.' He rose and walked with great agitation up and down the fortress room. 'And I remember exactly what I said, Miller, because a year later I had to tell another girl, from Baltimore this time, the same dismal story, and this girl had sense enough not to marry me, but your damned Miss Jaspar went ahead and married Nazrullah, and now senators are trying to find out where she is.'

He fell into a chair, poured himself a drink and reflected, 'This preposterous Afghan government. It says, "When young Afghans go abroad they must live like gentlemen." So the government provides huge expense accounts and we buy Cadillacs. What allowance do you suppose I got when I was at the Wharton School? One thousand dollars every month. No wonder the girls wanted to marry us. But when that same government brought me home, you know the salary I got—twenty-one dollars a month. Right now, Nazrullah heads an irrigation project west of Kandahar and earns twenty-seven dollars a month . . . more or less.'

'Is his wife with him?' I asked bluntly.

'Which wife?' Shah Khan asked.

I was startled. 'What do you mean, which wife?'

'Didn't you tell the Jaspars about that?' Shah Khan asked his son.

'There are some things an Afghan doesn't discuss in a foreign country,' Moheb replied.

'Was Nazrullah married before he went to America?' I pressed.

'He had a family wife, of course,' Shah Khan explained. 'But that signifies nothing.'

'That's not in the file,' I protested.

'Enter it now,' the old man said. 'Nazrullah was married before he met the American girl. That should put the Jaspars at ease.' As soon as he had said this, he apologized. 'I'm sorry, Miller Sahib. That was ungenerous. I'm as worried as the Jaspars must be. Where is their daughter? They haven't heard from her, you tell me, in more than thirteen months? What a terrible burden on good parents.'

The old man began to cry, and wiped tears from his dark eyes. Afghans, I had learned, were very apt to cry on little notice, but these tears were real.

When he had mastered his weeping he added in a beautiful French whisper, 'Our family showed the same prudence as Nazrullah's. Before we allowed Moheb to leave for England we married him to a local girl from a good Muslim family. We reasoned, "Later on, if he also marries an English girl, no harm will be done. When he works in Kabul he'll have a Muslim family and when he's sent to Europe he'll have an attractive English wife." I remember discussing the matter with Nazrullah's parents. We promised, "We won't allow the boys to leave home till they've had one or two Afghan babies." It worked very well.'

'Did you explain that to the Baltimore girl?' I asked Moheb.

'No,' he replied honestly, 'But I suppose it was what drove me to describe so frankly the other drawbacks of life in Afghanistan.'

I put my hands squarely on the leather folder and said, 'All right, where can the Jaspar girl be?'

Shah Khan ordered a glass of orangeade, a foul sweet drink which abstemious Afghans took in place of alcohol. It was brought, of course, by a befezzed man, for in a country adhering to the chaderi, men must do much of the work usually done by women.

'I've been pondering this problem,' Shah Khan reflected. 'It isn't easy to obtain news from a city as far away as Kandahar, but we manage. We find that Nazrullah and his American wife . . . you understand that his Muslim wife stays here in Kabul with the children?'

'More than one child?' I asked.

'Yes, he had one before he went to the Wharton School and one after he got back.'

I pondered this, then pointed out, 'But he must have been living with the Jaspar girl when he had the second child?'

'Of course. But he also had responsibilities to his Afghan wife. She merited consideration.'

'So he gave her another baby?' I asked.

'It's difficult to comprehend our attitude toward women,' Shah Khan confessed. 'We cherish them. We love them. We protect them. And we dedicate most of our poetry to them. But we don't want them cluttering up our lives.'

'I'd think that two wives would do just that,' I demurred.

'My life is one of the most uncluttered I know,' Shah Khan assured me quietly, 'yet I have four wives.'

'Four?' I asked.

Something in the way I looked at the old man amused him, for he said quietly, 'You Americans picture a man with four wives as leaping from bed to bed till he drops of exhaustion. It isn't like that . . . not at all. Fact is, in some ways I'm worse off than the average American businessman. He marries young, outgrows his wife and gets rid of her. I can't. When a girl marries me, she leaves her home forever and I can't send her back. I've got to support her in my home the rest of her life, unless I divorce her, which would be a public disgrace. So as the years go by I move these good women, one by one, into back bedrooms. In energy and money the American and the Afghan systems cost about the same.'

Moheb interrupted, 'The Muslim attitude toward women was a response to historical forces, and the interesting thing is that these same forces are acting now to make America polygamous.'

Before I could challenge this surprising theory, Shah Khan observed, 'Moheb's right. Islam was born in a period when war and ambuscade killed off our men. Each family had a burdensome surplus of women, and Muhammad, with his superbly practical mind, saw there were only three ways of dealing with the matter. Either you converted the needless women into marketplace whores, or edged them into ritual celibacy, or portioned them out as extra wives. Muhammad, always the most moral of men, shuddered at prostitution and gave the women legal status as wives. He chose the flawless solution.'

'How does this apply to America?' I asked.

Shah Khan ignored my question. 'So under our system I've had to take care of many women . . . wives, brothers' wives, grandmothers. By the way, Miller Sahib, do you know anything of a Quaker school near Philadelphia called the George School? We're thinking of sending my granddaughter Siddiqa there. The other girls have always gone to Paris.'

Cautiously I asked, 'How old is Siddiqa?'

'How old is she?' Shah Khan asked.

'Seventeen,' Moheb replied. 'She prefers things American and we thought . . .'

'It's a good school,' I said. 'Coeducational. Boys and girls.'

'It isn't a convent?' Shah Khan asked with some surprise.

'Oh, no!'

'That takes care of America,' Shah Khan growled. 'Off she goes to Paris. But what Moheb said earlier is true. The forces that drove Islam to plural marriage will operate throughout the world. In France, for example, I thought their handling of the problem was pathetic . . . mistresses, liaisons, scandal, murder.'

'But Moheb referred to America,' I pointed out.

The young diplomat sipped his whiskey, then reflected, 'Do you know the thing which impressed me most in America? The frightening excess of women over men. In some cities like Washington and New York the situation was scandalous.'

'You were there during wartime,' I pointed out.

'And peacetime,' he reminded me. 'You not only have more women than men in the population, but you also have an increasing number of young men who remove themselves from the marriage market. Homosexuality, Oedipus complexes, withdrawal from competition, psychological crippling . . .'

Shah Khan interrupted to observe gently, 'The point is, Miller Sahib, that brilliant young men like you come to Afghanistan and say, "Such a quaint land beset by such quaint problems." When I go to France or Moheb to America we make exactly the same observations.'

'And the most quaint,' Moheb laughed, 'is the way in which your society pretends to be shocked when some man is caught with two wives, legal or otherwise. What do you expect a girl to do when she realizes there aren't enough husbands to go around? Grab someone else's . . . I would.'

Since I had not come to Shah Khan's for a lecture on the shortcomings of my country, I asked abruptly, 'Then Ellen Jasper was last heard of in Kandahar?'

'Not exactly,' Shah Khan replied. 'We know she was there, because one day some mullahs attacked her on the street. Not wearing the chaderi. She distinguished herself by fighting back, and her husband joined her. Between them they kicked the devil out of the mullahs, and I'm glad they did.'

'Must have made her popular in Kandahar,' I suggested.

'Didn't matter one way or the other,' Shah Khan laughed. 'Most of us in government are bloody well fed up with mullahs, but we don't know what to do about them. At any rate, her outburst didn't harm Nazrullah's chances, for shortly he was promoted to the best engineering job in the country. Set up headquarters in the old fortress at Qala Bist.'

The old man's eyes misted over at the mention of this great name in Afghan history and he asked, 'Monsieur Miller, have you ever seen Qala Bist?'

I hadn't, but I refrained from comment because I didn't want to get the old patriot off on a tirade about the vanished glories of Afghanistan. My trick didn't work, for he said quietly, 'This fantastic arch rising from the desert and reflected in the river. It's as beautiful an arch as there is in the world. I much prefer it to Ctesiphon. No one recalls when it was built, but the building it was attached to must have been immense. There's a fort nearby which surely housed ten thousand men, and an abandoned city of perhaps half a million. Now we don't even remember what the city was named.'

'What's he doing at Qala Bist?' I asked, for I had learned at previous meetings that when Shah Khan started talking about the lost glories of Afghanistan, reaching back long before the days of Alexander the Great, there was no stopping him. In fact, I had acquired much of my Afghan history from such reminiscences, for unlike those of other men, the reflections of old Shah Khan were founded in fact. If he said Qala Bist had once been a city of half a million, it had been, and now even the history of the city was lost.

'Nazrullah and his American wife went there for preliminary work on our big irrigation project,' Shah Khan explained.

Moheb added, 'We know that she reached Qala Bist, for we had letters from them. But that was nine months ago.'

'What would your guess be?' I asked.

'Judging from what's happened to other ferangi wives'—both Moheb and his father used the word *ferangi* no matter what language they were speaking—'three things could have taken place. Miss Jaspar could have killed herself in despair, or she could have been locked up by her husband with no possibility of escape, not even to send a letter. Or she could have tried to run away. There's a British railroad station, you know, at Chaman, but we've asked there and she didn't reach Chaman.'

'Your guess?' I insisted.

'Putting myself in Nazrullah's place,' Moheb ventured, 'I would suggest these lines of possibility. Nazrullah was very kind to his American wife and tried to soften all the blows her vanity received. He took her as quickly as possible away from his domineering family, where his women must have made her life unbearable. At Kandahar he reasoned with her and helped her adjust to living on mud floors on twenty-seven dollars a month. She wanted to go back to America, but he refused permission, as was his right, and after a series of dreadful scenes she decided to run away on her own account and perished before she reached the frontier. It's happened before.'

'But why hasn't Nazrullah reported these matters?' I asked.

'For two reasons,' Moheb Khan replied, bowing to his father's judgment. 'First, she is only a woman and nothing to get excited about. When he gets back to Kabul he'll explain everything. Second, because he truly loved Ellen Jaspar and still thinks she may have survived and will come back to him.'

We sat silent for some minutes and I noticed that the wintry darkness had enveloped us, stealing down from the Koh-i-Baba on icy blasts of wind that ripped across the plain which lay between the fortress walls. Snow eddied in the darkness like the passage of a white horse, and we were alone in the massive room of a massive fort that had withstood shocks from the Koh-i-Baba and from other quarters.

'Would you object, Khan Sahib, if I went to Kandahar and Qala Bist? Some very important Americans insist upon knowing.'

'If I were your age, Miller Sahib,' the old man replied, 'I should have gone to Kandahar long ere this.'

'I have your permission, then?'

'My blessing. In spite of the rude comments of my son, we Afghans do get excited about beautiful women. And if she is a ferangi woman, we respect those ferangi who get excited about her, too.'

To my own surprise, I asked abruptly, 'Shah Khan, have you a photograph of your granddaughter, Siddiqa? The one who wants to go to school in America?'

'No,' the old man replied. 'We true Muslims don't like photography. It seems a violation of our religious principles. An intrusion on the essence of a man.'

'And especially a woman?' I laughed.

'Yes, it is quite contrary to the spirit of the chaderi. But I will tell you this, Monsieur Miller, she is an unusually pretty girl, and she is the child whom you caught kissing the soldier in the bazaar this morning.'

I was shocked by his knowledge of an event which I supposed that I alone had witnessed. 'The Marines are already on their way to the Khyber Pass,' I mumbled.

'If they had not been expelled,' Shah Khan replied evenly, proving that his intelligence service covered Americans as well as Afghans, 'I would not now be talking with you. Moheb, get Monsieur Miller's jeep.'

When the younger man had left, old Shah Khan rose from his leather chair and walked with me to the door. I looked past him for a moment, staring at the fawn-colored chaderi, and the former sensation of overpowering sexuality repossessed me, and I felt dizzy, as if the shroud were exuding its own perfume.

'These damned girls!' The old man laughed. 'They douse their chaderies with cheap French essence. To make the boys notice them more. Smell this!' And he picked up the fawn chaderi and smothered my face with it. The perfume was heavy and clung to my nostrils after he had withdrawn the silk.

The old warrior put his arm about me and said, 'Monsieur Miller, concerning the Jaspar girl. We do have one bit of additional information. Perhaps I shouldn't call it information. Nothing but absurd speculation, I suspect. Anyway, it's so bizarre, really, that I won't suffer myself to repeat it. perhaps it represents what happened, but when you get to Kandahar you'll undoubtedly hear the rumour. So you judge for yourself.'

'You won't tell me?' I begged.

'I would abhor having in your file my name even remotely attached to such a rumor. I've my reputation to consider. But you're a younger man. You can risk such embarrassments, and I wish you Godspeed.' I was always astonished to rediscover that Muslims shared our God in exactly the form we used Him. There it was, old Shah Khan wishing me Godspeed, and there could be no doubt that he was referring to the One God.

'Papers authorizing your travel to Kandahar and wherever else you may have to go in the area will be at your office in the morning,' the old man assured me.

'Thank you, Shah Khan,' I replied, and when he opened the door leading to the waiting jeep I saw his son, Moheb Khan, once more upon the white horse, leaping and twisting and roaring off across the snow. As he disappeared in a cloud of flakes I thought: That must be the only horse in the world branded with a W for the Wharton School in Philadelphia.

3

In Afghanistan almost every building bears jagged testimony to some outrage. Some, like the walled fortress now owned by Shah Khan, were built to withstand sieges, and did so many times. Others were the scenes of horrible murder and retaliation. In distant areas, scars still remained of Alexander the Great or Genghis Khan or Tamerlane or Nadir Shah, of Persia. Was there ever a land so overrun by terror and devastation as Afghanistan?

Yet of all the buildings which testified to acts of violence none was more evocative than the group that huddled within the British compound, for here scenes of terrible defeat and massacre had taken place, here loyalties were betrayed, here brave men died with daggers across their throats, and the fact that the British still maintained friendly relations with Afghanistan was tribute to English resilience.

In 1946 the British compound was probably the most civilized center in Afghanistan, a fortress of its own well out into the country, with its private gardens, tennis courts and restaurants. It was here that the European community, in which the Americans were grudgingly included, met on long winter evenings to read plays. Tonight, fresh from the typewriters of the English, Italian and American embassies, in that order, the play was to be *Born Yesterday*, a boisterous comedy which had opened in New York only the month before. Ingrid, a stately Swedish girl, was scheduled to read the part of Billie Dawn. An Englishman who imagined that he could talk like an American gangster was to be Harry Brock, and I was to read the part of the *New Republic* reporter.

Italians, Frenchmen and the Turkish ambassador's wife completed the cast, and looking back upon such readings I am still impressed by the intellectual pleasure we had when the snow was so high in Kabul. We were, in a very real sense, cut off from everything that civilized men and women had come to take for granted: books, magazines, theaters, hotels, music. All we had were our own personalities, with what understandings and memories we had acquired through the years; and it was reassuring to discover what a vivid social life was possible under those circumstances. Never have I known better wit nor more exciting conversation than in the crowded little rooms of Kabul. Never have I known a group of people to be so self-sufficient, so enchanting as human beings. In those years I used to see the same two dozen people night after night, and they were rewarding beyond expectation, partly because any escape from them or their individualities was impossible.

On this night our reading–in which we were peremptorily handed pieces of paper we had not seen before and directed to read specific parts, growing into them as the night progressed–was delayed because Miss Maxwell, from my office, was late in arriving, and since she had typed Act Three and was to read one of the minor parts, we felt the least we could do was to wait for her. However, our host, the British ambassador, found Miss Maxwell's tardiness embarrassing since he was at the moment entertaining Sir Herbert Chinnery, the stiff, mustachioed Inspector Ordinary for Asia, whose duty it was to report on conditions at the British embassy in Afghanistan as he had just done for the embassy in Persia, and it was important that Sir Herbert be pleased.

'Don't worry,' Sir Herbert said graciously, putting us all at ease. 'I've learned that Americans are rarely punctual.'

I replied that I was sure Miss Maxwell must have met with some misfortune–temporary, I hoped–for she had that very morning risen at six in order to type her share of the play and had then, at some risk to herself, insisted upon delivering it to the Italian embassy, to which Signorina Risposi could testify, 'As a matter of fact,' I concluded, 'in performing her duty Miss Maxwell was subjected to harsh treatment at the hands of three mullahs . . .'

'The usual?' Sir Herbert asked.

'Spitting, jostling, curses in Pashto,' I explained.

'That's the second time it's happened this week,' the ambassador said.

'I've a mind to advise Whitehall,' Sir Herbert confided, 'that all English girls in Kabul go into chaderi immediately.'

'Oh, dear, no!' squealed a peaches-and-cream English girl called Gretchen Askwith. 'Oh, Sir Herbert. No, I beg you.'

It always seemed to me that the British went a little far in their coyness, but Gretchen Askwith was quite the loveliest of the unmarried white girls in Kabul, and it ill behooved me to think poorly of her, for although there were six or eight eligible young European men among the various embassies, I appeared to be the one most likely to win Gretchen's attention . . . that is, if she didn't discover that I was Jewish, a fact which none of the ferangi embassies yet knew.

There was not good blood between the British and the Americans in Afghanistan. The English tolerated us, and that's about all. Captain Verbruggen was thought to be a great bore and unlettered as well. Our secretaries were too pretty and too highly paid. Our Marines were undisciplined. And men like me were much too brash. In fact, about the only thing American that impressed the British was my ability to speak Pashto, but this was diminished by the fact that three of their chaps did too, including one chinless young man who spoke Russian and Persian as well. Still, we were tolerated because our kitchens served excellent food and our bars were generally open.

'There she is now!' Sir Herbert cried, with that boyish excitement that even the oldest Englishmen often retain, but when the door opened it was not Miss Maxwell but an unexpected guest, Moheb Khan. He was now dressed in a blue Bond Street pin-stripe worsted, with handsome brown leather shoes and a London shirting. He had transformed himself into a most proper diplomat, and in this guise presented himself to the ambassador.

'On three occasions, sir, you've asked me to these readings. May I choose my own time?'

'My dear fellow, you honor us!'

'I hear the play's very funny. I'd not have known about it except that I stopped by the Italian embassy and was told of its merit by Signorina Risposi.' He bowed towards the Italian typist, who was quite plump.

'She told you the truth,' Sir Herbert interrupted. 'Our man in Washington saw it last month. Laughed so much he airmailed me a script.'

There was a moment of emptiness, into which the Swedish girl said loudly, 'Couldn't we start? Miss Maxwell doesn't participate until Act Two.'

'I think it would be better if we waited,' Sir Herbert insisted. 'After all, the dear girl did much of the typing, Mr Miller informs me.'

Miss Askwith added, 'And after her bout with the mullahs . . .'

'Do you think the mullahs are gaining ground in their battle for control?' Sir Herbert asked Moheb Khan.

'No,' the Afghan replied cautiously. 'On the other hand, they're not losing ground, either.'

'Some time ago there was talk of discarding the chaderi,' Sir Herbert suggested, and our discussion proceeded from that point. I had found, even in my short stay, that Afghanistan had two copies of conversation which were positively guaranteed to excite participation: the chaderi and the latest cure for diarrhea, for with the kind of drinking water available in Kabul, this latter scourge was sooner or later bound to infect everyone. Sure enough, not long after the chaderi was disposed of I heard Signorina Risposi advising the group.

'A German doctor has invented something much better than entero-vioform. It's called sulfas, I believe. Developed during the war.'

'Does it work?' the Swedish girl was asking.

'My theory,' Sir Herbert interrupted, 'has always been to fill the lower bowel with some bland bulk producer like one of the new mucils. You'd be surprised how this slows down the bowel action.'

'Really?' the Turkish ambassador's wife pursued. 'I've relied on entero-vioform, and it seems to concentrate rather effectively on the upper bowel. But when it fails, it fails.'

The dialogue now switched to French, for one of the scientists in that country had developed a radically new drug which the French ambassador's wife was explaining, and I thought: This must be the only capital in the world where a sophisticated international audience can discuss with all seriousness the control of the upper and lower bowel. Yet no aspect of Afghan life was more significant than this, for when the virulent Asiatic diarrhea, known locally as the Kabul Trots, struck, it was not like a stomach ache back home. It was a sickness which nauseated, embarrassed, debilitated and outraged the human body. In a land where toilet facilities were not excessive, diarrhea was a scourge, and I was willing to gamble that not a single person in that softly lit room, lined with books, was without his or her secret vial of pills and even more secret roll of personal toilet paper.

'What do you do for the disease?' the French ambassador's wife asked Moheb Khan in French.

'It's very simple,' Moheb replied in lilting English. 'You Europeans are always shocked at our open water supply into which little boys urinate. Or worse. But what happens? From drinking such water most of our children die, and that's neither a curse nor a blessing. They die and that's that. So the life expectancy in Afghanistan is about twenty-three years. But that figure doesn't mean what it says, not really. For if by chance you are one of the babies who does not die, you are inoculated against positively everything. Look about you. See the large number of our men who live to an extreme old age. With the women, I can assure you, it is the same. If you drink our water till you are seven, nothing can kill you but a bullet.' He thumped his chest and laughed.

A rotund English doctor, on temporary duty in Kabul, said quietly, 'You know, of course, he's not teasing. Take poliomyelitis, which strikes so many children in an antiseptic country like America . . .'

'Here no child gets polio,' Moheb Khan insisted. 'But you Europeans who come to us later in life, when you've not had the inoculations our water imparts . . . How many cases have we had of polio among the Europeans?'

'Many, even in my time,' the fat doctor concurred.

There was a sound at the door, and in a moment Miss Maxwell appeared, flushed from the deep cold and from some experience which had left her stunned. 'It's too much!' she cried in a kind of wild exhilaration.

'What happened?' many voices cried.

'This morning,' she said excitedly. 'The three mullahs screaming at me.'

'We know about that unfortunate affair,' Sir Herbert said consolingly.

'I didn't mind it,' Miss Maxwell said. 'I left Omaha to see Afghanistan, and I love it.' Seeing Moheb she ran to him and took his hands. 'What do you suppose I just saw? Not two hundred yards from the embassy?'

'More mullahs?' Moheb asked quietly.

'Wolves!' Miss Maxwell reported. 'Yes, a huge pack of wolves. They were running across an open field where the snow was thick.'

'The storms have driven them down from the mountains,' Moheb Khan explained. 'At this time of the year . . .'

'Would they attack . . . a man?' someone asked.

'They're ravenously hungry,' Moheb replied. 'In the morning you may hear

'... Well, they are wolves, down from the Hindu Kush.'

The concept of wild wolves, running in a pack through the outskirts of Kabul, running until they found a straggler, either animal or human, cast a spell of terror over the group that had gathered to read a comedy. We felt chilly, and Sir Herbert directed his Afghan houseboy to throw on more logs. We felt very close to each other, and our group became more compact. Miss Maxwell, I am glad to say, did not try to monopolize the center of attention. She simply reported, 'They were not at all like the wolves in Walt Disney. They were animals, great shaggy, terrifying animals.'

'Did they have long teeth?' Signorina Risposi asked.

'I don't know. At such a moment ... You know, they dashed right at our car. If I'd been driving I don't know what I'd have done. But our boy, Sadruddin, was in charge and he blew the horn sharply. Like one huge animal with many legs they swerved away and disappeared.'

'Where?' the Swedish girl asked.

'Toward town,' Miss Maxwell said, pointing toward where we all lived.

'It's one reason why we built high walls,' Moheb Khan reflected in French.

'This is a land of startling contrasts,' the French ambassador agreed.

'Do the wolves surprise you?' Moheb asked the general audience in English. 'Before we read the play, tell me. Do the wolves surprise you?'

'No,' the French ambassador replied in English. 'When we come to Kabul we expect ...Well, we expect the Hindu Kush.'

'But we are never prepared for what we expect,' Sir Herbert observed. He, too, was willing to postpone the reading of the play. After all, in winter in Kabul it mattered little when a party broke up ... ten o'clock, or one, or four. 'I remember when I was stationed in India. It was before the war.' He didn't say, 'They were good days, those,' but we knew he intended us to think so. 'I was hunting in Kashmir and I announced one day that I was going out with my native bearers to bag me a Kashmiri brown bear.

'A man in the bar at Srinagar, a total stranger, asked, "Are you quite sure you want to shoot a Kashmiri bear, Sir Herbert?" I replied that I intended doing so, and doubtless my manner implied that I was irritated with his question.'

The Afghan servant came in to place upon the fire a few precious logs, and each of us drew closer to someone else, for the wind outside was audible. 'The stranger rejected my rebuff and asked again, "Sir Herbert, do you know anything of the Kashmiri bear?" I replied, with some irritation, "It's a bear. I've seen it at the zoo in Simla. Roger Whatshisname shot one." The man pressed me, "But have you shot one?"

'"No," I replied, and the man said sternly, "Then you have no right to have an opinion upon this matter. Sir Herbert, you must not shoot this particular bear, really you mustn't." I thanked him for his pains and marched out of the bar, but on the way to the shoot, one of my guides asked me in Kashmiri if I had ever hunted the bears of his country, and when I said no, he suggested that we go back. This so whetted my appetite that I spurred the horses and we came to that part of Kashmir where the brown bears are to be found.

'We hunted for some time and saw nothing, but toward dusk we came upon a thicket, and although I didn't get a clear sight on the beast, I could see it was a bear, and I let fly. I didn't kill the bear, and more's the pity, for I had wounded it mortally.'

Sir Herbert stopped his narrative, and for a moment I thought he had undertaken in his telling rather more than he had anticipated. He did not want to continue, that was obvious, but he took a gulp of whiskey and said, 'I suppose no one in this room has ever heard a Kashmiri bear. He has a voice like a human being . . . like a woman in extreme pain. When he is wounded, he beats his way through the thicket crying like a stricken mother. You can almost hear the words. He moans and wails and is obviously about to die of mortal pain. It is . . .' He fumbled for words, extended his right hand and punched the air. 'It is . . .'

From a place near the fire Lady Margaret said, 'It is shattering to the mind. Sir Herbert wanted to leave the thicket, but the bearers warned him that he must finish off the bear. That was his duty. So he plunged in–the men told me–but the bear had limped off into the deeper woods.' Husband and wife fell silent, and we listened to the rising wind, blowing down the last of the winter's blizzards.

'I tracked that sobbing bear for about an hour,' Sir Herbert said quietly. 'It was easy, because constantly the beast screamed and wept. It was positively uncanny. That bear was not an animal. It was all the grieved things the men shoot, the partridges, the deer, the rabbits. I tell you, that bear spoke to me, crying out in its pain. I finally found it exhausted by a tree. Even as I came upon it, it wept new laments. By God, I tell you that bear . . .'

'Did you shoot him?' the French ambassador asked in French.

'Yes. I don't know how, but I did. Then I rushed back to Srinagar to find the man who had warned me in the bar, but he was gone.'

'What is the point of this story, Sir Herbert?' Moheb Khan asked. 'Surely if tonight we shoot a wolf it will not behave so.'

'The point is, Moheb Khan, that none of us in this room was prepared for what we expected in Afghanistan. You, Miss Maxwell, didn't your government in Washington hand you a neatly typed report on Kabul? Mean temperature. Dress warmly. Expect dysentery.'

'Yes,' Miss Maxwell laughed.

'And it was all the truth, wasn't it?'

'Yes.'

'But did it prepare you for today? Getting up at six to type a play because you wanted to be here with us? Being assaulted by mullahs in the bazaar? Seeing wolves rushing at your car?'

'No,' Miss Maxwell said calmly. 'The reports in Washington did not prepare me for any of that. I never dreamed that I could find a room anywhere in the world as warm, as human as this one. Almost everyone I care for deeply is right here, tonight. As for the mullahs and the wolves, I wasn't prepared for them, either. Right now I don't believe they happened.'

'Exactly what I meant,' Sir Herbert said, holding his hands up toward the group. 'Reality in no way prepared me for the Kashmiri bears. I'm sure that dreadful incident never happened. But, Miss Maxwell, sometime years from now, those wolves will be as real to you as that stricken bear is to me. And to each of us, years from now, Afghanistan will be real, too.'

'You make it sound far too difficult to understand my country,' Moheb Khan contradicted. 'It's very easy, really. All you have to do is read what Colonel Sir Hungerford Holdich said about us in the Eleventh Edition of the *Encyclopaedia Britannica*.' He pronounced the names with exaggerated precision.

'What are you saying?' the Swedish girl asked in French.

'With your permission,' Moheb Khan said, bowing to Sir Herbert and taking down from the library shelf Volume I of the *Britannica*. Opening it to the article on Afghanistan he read in a sardonic accent:

'The Afghans, inured to bloodshed from childhood, are familiar with death, and audacious in attack, but easily discouraged by failure; excessively turbulent and unsubmissive to law or discipline; apparently frank and affable in manner, especially when they hope to gain some object, but capable of the grossest brutality when that hope ceases. They are unscrupulous in perjury, treacherous, vain and insatiable, passionate in vindictiveness, which they will satisfy at the cost of their own lives and in the most cruel manner. Nowhere is crime committed on such trifling grounds, or with such general impunity, though when it is punished the punishment is atrocious. Among themselves the Afghans are quarrelsome, intriguing and distrustful; estrangements and affrays are of constant occurrence; the traveler conceals and misrepresents the time and direction of his journey. The Afghan is by breed and nature a bird of prey. If from habit and tradition he respects a stranger within his threshold, he yet considers it legitimate to warn a neighbor of the prey that is afoot, or even to overtake and plunder his guest after he has quitted his roof. The repression of crime and the demand of taxation he regards alike as tyranny. The Afghans are eternally boasting of their lineage, their independence and their prowess. They look on the Afghans as the first of nations, and each man looks on himself as the equal of any Afghan.

'Now that's all one paragraph, mind you,' Moheb Khan warned us, 'and I used to wonder how long it would take me to acquire the attributes I was, as a typical Afghan, supposed to have. Crafty, lying, deceitful I was, but what do you suppose kept me from qualifying? That troublesome bit about the bird of prey. How does one transform himself into a bird of prey? Well, I gave up on that first paragraph, but the next one offered hope. May I continue?'

'Proceed,' Sir Herbert said.

Moheb Khan smiled, adjusted the heavy volume and read on:

They are capable of enduring great privation, and make excellent soldiers under British discipline, though there are but few in the Indian army. Sobriety and hardiness characterize the bulk of the people, though the higher classes are too often stained with deep and degrading debauchery. The first impression made by the Afghan is favorable. The European, especially if he come from India, is charmed by their apparently frank, openhearted, hospitable and manly manners; but the charm is not of long duration, and he finds that the Afghan is as cruel and crafty as he is independent.

With a flourish, Moheb Khan slammed the encyclopedia shut and stared at the readers. 'You know, there's a funny thing about this. It was written by an Englishman who was totally perplexed as to how we Afghans had managed to thrash the living daylights out of English armies . . . twice. The man who wrote this must have perched himself on a stool in a little room and thought for some time: What kind of men are these Afghans, that they can defeat our armies? And he composed the description of a man who was as unlike an Englishman as possible, and then he wrote it properly in this big book, which I first read at Oxford. And what was my reaction? At that time? I was proud that a ferangi had seen so deeply into my character and had written with such respect. Today, when I am older, these seem like words of hatred or ignorance. They are not. They are profound words of respect from a scholar who simply had to know how we Afghans generated our capacity to fight. Never forget that marvellous peroration: "the charm is not of long duration, and he finds that the Afghan is as cruel and crafty as he is independent."'

'Moheb!' I cried. 'You've memorized the passage, haven't you?'

'Only the favorable parts,' he laughed.

'You think "cruel and crafty" one of the good parts?' Miss Askwith inquired.

'When you use those characteristics to defend the end word of the sentence, they're good,' Moheb replied. 'Always remember the end word, Miss Askwith. Independent.' Then he laughed easily and said, 'But through trying years you English have come to know me as your trusted friend. Otherwise, how would I dare read such an English passage inside these walls, where twice my cruel and crafty ancestors murdered every Englishman resident in Kabul? In 1841 we did that evil thing, and in 1879 we played an encore, and I think it damned gracious of you even to have me here.'

'Don't think we English forget the massacres,' Sir Herbert said gravely. 'It lends a certain spice to life in Kabul. Within these red and crumbling walls. Sort of like living in Hiroshima when an airplane flies overhead.'

'I think we should get on with the reading,' I suggested.

'He's to be a star,' a young British officer teased. He was my principal rival for the attentions of Miss Gretchen Askwith.

'As a matter of fact,' one of the Frenchmen said in French, 'he's supposed to kiss Ingrid.'

'I am,' I said eagerly, 'and I'd appreciate it if we got to that part before morning.'

'Wise boy,' Ingrid laughed. 'In the morning I look dreadful.'

It was in this mood that the reading began. During the first act, the voices seemed strange, for the Englishman who was supposed to be Harry Brock remained an Oxford aesthete, and Ingrid could be no more than a Swedish beauty with prominent breasts, while the others remained themselves, including me, who never transmuted myself into anything but an eager young man from the American embassy. But the fire was warm. The audience was attentive. And outside there was the smell of wolves, and no one could forget that he was in Afghanistan in the deep of winter, far, far from what he knew as civilization. I think even Moheb Khan was affected by the experience, for at the end of the first act he asked, 'Sir Herbert, have the evenings I missed been as good as this?'

'Since I've been here they have,' the Englishman replied. 'Three weeks ago we read *Murder in the Cathedral*. I was asked to be Thomas à Becket.'

'Oh, I should like to have seen that!' Moheb cried. 'American college folk are very fond of T. S. Eliot. They adore him as a fellow citizen who became a poet, and respect him for having had the character to flee America, which they would like to do, but can't.'

I'm afraid I had fallen rather deeply into the part I was reading, that of the intellectual reporter from the *New Republic*, and I said, 'Like Eliot, you fled America, Moheb, but unlike him you regret it every minute.'

'Agreed!' the affable Afghan cried. 'If there's one thing I like it's fast cars and a sense of irresponsibility. In America I had both, and every day I work here in Afghanistan I regret their passing.' He raised his palms in a gesture of submission, then added, 'But at some point in our lives, we must grow up.'

'I am sure your country will,' I replied evenly. Moheb, rather pleased with his earlier remarks, flushed slightly but nodded pleasantly, for he was not the kind of fighter who refused to accept his adversary's blows; he rather respected the man who could strike back.

'Will anyone have more spiced rum?' the ambassador inquired, and as the servants refilled our drinks, and as the fire grew brighter, we reformed our group and the reading of Act Two commenced. By now we were more accustomed to our roles, and the audience accepted whatever peculiarities we exhibited. If tonight Harry Brock spoke not Brooklynese but an exaggerated Oxford—one as bad as the other, I thought—we were willing to accept this convention, and when Ingrid cried, 'Would you do me a favor, Harry? Drop dead?' she sounded exactly like the dumb blonde of all countries, of all time. By the end of the act we had created, there in the old fortress, that ambience which dramatists seek but which so often eludes them. Actors and audience were one, moving together and accepting each other as equals. Partly, I think, it was because each person in that warm, quiet room knew that if he did not achieve some kind of satisfaction from our play, there was nothing else in Afghanistan to which he could escape. Either he attained catharsis now, or he was self-sentenced to days of non-participation. So each of us reached out to the other, made overtures that normally we would not have made, because each knew that for the forthcoming sixteen or eighteen months we would find joy with our repetitive neighbors, or we would find no joy at all. That was why life in Kabul—sans roads, sans movies, sans news, sans everything—was so profoundly meaningful. We probed the secrets of a few rather than glossing over the chance acquaintanceship of many, and each new thing we discovered about our colleagues uncovered new significance. For example, I had never imagined that glamorous Ingrid owned such a naughty wit.

The conversation that developed after Act Two was much different from that which followed Act One. Somehow, the play had insinuated itself into our intellect and had taken command. We poor inadequate readers had transcended ourselves, and the characters we were purporting to create had actually come to life. Harry Brock and his aspiring blonde were with us in the stout-walled embassy.

'We could use a few of your type in our country,' Moheb Khan said to the Englishman playing the part of the junk dealer, and he meant not the actual Oxford boy but his play part, the junk dealer.

'There's a great deal to be said about good old Harry that isn't said in this play,' the Englishman agreed. 'Miller, how much of the building of America is to be credited to men like our Harry?'

'A good deal, I should imagine, and I think it's rather clever of you to discover the fact. You've not been in America, have you?'

'No, but reading this part makes one recall how inevitably one thinks of Harry Brock as the archetype American. We excoriate him, just as this play does, but we forget that he is also the life force of the nation, whether any of us likes him or not.'

Miss Gretchen Askwith threw palpitations into the hearts of various young men by observing, 'Really, Mark, you read your part exceedingly well. Have you studied dramatics?'

'In school I was in *Outward Bound*.'

'We intended reading that,' Sir Herbert interrupted, 'but the younger group thought it terribly dated. Do you agree, Miller?'

'I'm afraid I do, but I also think we should read it. It's fun.'

'British, isn't it?' Sir Herbert asked.

I did not respond to Sir Herbert's question, for I was looking at Gretchen, and there in the crowded room I had a distinct premonition that Gretchen and I would be thrown together increasingly in Kabul ... that it would become automatic for all hostesses to invite 'Gretchen and Mark,' and that sometime in the next years all would be asked to Shah Khan's great compound, where a tent would be erected and where Moheb Khan would ride up on his white horse to serve as my best man while the marriage was performed.

It was an inevitable progression, Gretchen Askwith and Mark Miller to the altar in Afghanistan; but as I looked at her and saw her blushing, for she must have been entertaining the same premonition of inevitability, her face was obliterated and I saw only a fawn chaderi, smelling of perfume, and a pair of American saddle shoes, and I heard the name Siddiqa, and I looked at Siddiqa's uncle, Moheb Khan, and I knew that it would never happen that I should marry Gretchen Askwith, no matter how inevitable our courtship. I longed to see the hidden face of Siddiqa Khan. I was mesmerized by the flowing movement of her chaderi, by the exquisite sense of sex this child had somehow managed to evoke.

Sir Herbert repeated his question: 'Isn't *Outward Bound* a British play?'

'I don't know,' I replied. 'I always supposed it was by a sentimental American who wanted to sound British.'

'You may be right,' Sir Herbert replied with the thin smile that served him as a laugh.

The reading of Act Three recaptured the intensity that we had created in Act Two. The laughter at our jokes was rather more explosive than it should have been, and my courting of Miss Ingrid more emotionally received. A good many people in the room were wondering what was going to happen to Ingrid—the person, not the character—and it gave our play an adventitious prurience to have me, one of the unmarried men, attracted to her, even in make-believe.

As we ended our reading there was genuine applause. Our audience was grateful that for a few hours we had provided them with escape, and when the snowy winds whirling down from the Hindu Kush whistled outside, the gratitude increased. I knew there would arise, as had arisen before, a longing not to shatter the illusion of the night, and that we would sit around for hours and talk, hoping to extend the human warmth we had created.

We were astonished, therefore, when Moheb Khan said rather explosively, 'Miss Ingrid, may I drive you home?'

The Swedish girl smiled graciously at the Afghan and replied, 'Yes.'

Within a moment Moheb had his coat and hers. He summoned his driver from the kitchen quarters where all the Afghan drivers were resting, and from the manner in which Ingrid nestled into her fur coat and then onto the arm of Moheb Khan, we intuitively knew that she had allowed the part she had been playing to influence her normal personality. There could be little doubt that Moheb and Ingrid would be bedded down that night. When the door opened and we caught the snowy blast and saw Ingrid move even closer, that last little doubt was erased.

When the door closed, one of the Frenchmen asked, 'But isn't Moheb Khan already married?'

'He has two wives,' one of the Englishwomen volunteered.

'Both Afghan?'

'Of course. He wanted to marry an American, but it didn't come off.'

No one could have anticipated where this line of conversation might lead, but it was forestalled, and properly so, by Sir Herbert, who said, rather petulantly, I thought, 'We really ought to read *Outward Bound*. I'll offer myself as the bartender.' There was an immediate flurry of casting and a determination as to which secretaries would type out the required copies of which acts. Miss Maxwell, indestructible American that she was, offered to do the longest and others fell in line.

Then Sir Herbert said, 'For the young lovers we'll have Gretchen and
Mark.' The audience looked at us as if we had been set apart, and my former
sensation of the inevitability of love in Afghan surroundings returned.
Gretchen smiled, a wonderful British smile with white teeth and flushed
cheeks. There was a moment of painful indecision, which I fractured by
suggesting, 'May I drive you home, Gretchen?'

My question was so parallel to Moheb Khan's, the situation was so
transparent, that Gretchen flushed again, then laughed prettily and said, 'Sir
Herbert, you must keep them from talking about us, too.'

Sir Herbert grew red, looked at Lady Margaret, then said, 'I think you
should know by now that in Kabul any pretty unmarried girl is fair game for all
sorts of speculation. Are you riding with Mark?'

'Yes,' Gretchen snapped saucily. 'Yes, I am. Just the way Ingrid went with
Moheb.' She did not yet have her coat on, but she grabbed my arm
possessively.

Sir Herbert smiled wanly and said, 'I dare say Freddy and Karl will be
damned unhappy about your decision.'

'At the next reading I'll ride home with Freddy and Karl,' she laughed,
slipping into the coat which an Afghan servant held for her.

Lady Margaret interrupted. 'But at the next reading you and Mark are to be
lovers.'

Gretchen flashed her wittiest smile at her superior's wife. 'Lady Margaret,
haven't you noticed? At the end of a reading the actress is so irritated with her
stage lover that she wishes to have no more to do with him. After all, in our play
tonight Ingrid and Mark were lovers. But she made no move to go home with
Mark. By the time the next reading's finished, I'll be fed to here with dear
Mark.' With her hand she made a line across her eyebrows. 'Tonight, he is my
gallant champion, to keep me from the wolves.' To my surprise, she leaned
forward and kissed me on the cheek.

'Bravo, Gretchen!' Lady Margaret applauded.

'Looks as if you're losing your secretary to the Yanks,' Sir Herbert huffed at
the ambassador, as I led Gretchen to the jeep which Nur Muhammad had
driven up.

Not all the British hands could find quarters in the embassy grounds, ample
though they were, and some lived in Kabul proper, in a spacious walled house
west of the public square. It was quite the liveliest spot in town, filled with
laughter, ponderous jokes which the British overseas so love, and a fairy-tale
kind of make-believe which has enabled them to live in reasonable relaxation in
almost any portion of the globe. I was often in this house and I remember it now
mostly as a center of things hearty. When I first came to know it and its
occupants I wondered how a man ever got an English girl into bed. What did
they do with her hockey stick? How did he halt her from making very witty
jokes about nothing? Now, as I started to ride homeward with one of the
prettiest English girls I had ever met, I was bothered by the same questions.

But as we rode over the winding trail that led from the embassy to Kabul, and
as we saw to our left the soaring mountains of the Hindu Kush, outlined in
snowy moonlight, the trivial problems of courtship left us, and we were two
strangers from alien lands traveling across one of the high plateaus of the world.
Gretchen moved closer to me, and we held hands as our jeep approached the
first houses of Kabul.

Then we saw lights—actual flaming torches—as men hurried to and fro and a waggon with horses approached. There was a crowd in the road, and Nur Muhammad left the jeep to find out what had happened. In a moment he returned to report without inflection, 'The wolves found an old man.'

It must have ended quickly. Fifteen to twenty wolves, by local count, had struck the man and torn him to pieces within a few minutes. Now they were raging somewhere to the east and soldiers were out to shoot a few, after which the others would retreat. Nur Muhammad drove the jeep past the scene of mutilation and we reached the English dormitory.

Pretty Gretchen said, 'Will you come in?' and I said I would, for I knew that on the morning following a reading no one would get to his office promptly, and in the English house there would be fun and good talk and kissing beneath the stairs. But when I started in, I saw Nur Muhammad sitting in the jeep and I said, 'Nur, you can go home. I'll walk across the park.' But he said, 'You mustn't. They haven't shot the wolves yet.' And from the east we heard sounds and could tell that something was rushing down the narrow streets, and I did not want to be in the English house that night.

'I'll take Nur Muhammad home,' I apologized. 'He's been working since dawn.'

Almost as if relieved of a heavy burden Gretchen said, 'I do think that's best,' and I bounded, with improper haste I reflected later, into the jeep.

'Let's find the wolves,' I cried to Nur, and we spurred the jeep east of the American embassy and along one narrow street after another until we were on the edge of town, with soldiers well to the south. They were moving slowly northward, hoping to come upon the animals, and we could see lights moving mysteriously along the edge of the river.

We stayed there in the snowy moonlight for some time, alone on the edge of an ancient city with the Hindu Kush rising to our left and the immensity of Asia all about us: to the east the Khyber Pass, to the north the Oxus River and the plains of Samarkand, to the south the bazaars of Kandahar and the limitless deserts of Buluchistan, and to the west the strange lake that vanishes in air, and the minarets of Shiraz and Isfahan. It was a moment of immensity in which I sensed the hugeness of Central Asia, that semi-world with a chaderi over its face, and just as the chaderi of Siddiqa had contained its own perfume, now the crisp, silent night with the flickering lights along the river possessed its particular power. It was the smell of frozen fields, biting on the nostril, the aroma of the bazaar, great and filthy even in the night, and the clean, sweet smell of pine trees that hid behind garden walls. Those were moments I shall never forget, when the vastness of Asia, whose distant mountain passes had sent us the wolves, was borne in upon me and I wondered how I had been lucky enough to draw an assignment in Kabul, the most remote of capitals.

My reverie was broken by shots to the south; gun-flashes could be seen. The soldiers must be near at hand. I remember distinctly that at that moment, when the light of the guns added illumination to the crystal, snowy night, I thought: It was nights like this that the Russian writers spoke of, the white nights of Russia. It was a vagrant thought, shattered by a rush of sound.

Moving up from the river, across fields that were now barren, came the wolves: fifteen, eighteen, they were so close-packed I could not count. They seemed not to be running. They were moving as one giant animal, its heads looking out from side to side and finding no food. It was a terrifying, possessive animal that moved across the snow, a force driven by forces outside itself, an embodiment of Asia and the great mountains.

One of the wolves must have smelled Nur and me, for the pack suddenly veered directly towards us, but when its leaders saw not men but the mechanical jeep, whose headlights now exploded with brilliance, the animals shifted course without visible decision, and the gray pack slipped off into the frozen night.

'Here they are!' Nur Muhammad shouted, and the soldiers rushed up. Some shots were fired and I remember mumbling to myself: 'I hope they got away.'

The Afghan soldiers came to the jeep and conversed with Nur and me for a few minutes, pleased at meeting a ferangi who could speak Pashto. Their officer arrived later in a staff car and it was agreed to leave two men on watch. 'It will soon be spring,' the officer said in Pashto, 'and we'll have no more wolves. Till next year.'

It was now about four in the morning, but there would be no sign of daylight for many hours, and Nur started to drive me home, but I said impulsively, 'Let's go to the English house!' and we did and as I had suspected the lights were not yet extinguished, and when I knocked on the door the English girls were not surprised to see me. Some men were there talking about the play and I created a stir when I said, 'We've been out chasing the wolves. We saw them on the eastern edge of the city.'

'Were they fearful?' Gretchen asked, and she seemed then immensely pretty, and I told her of the wolves and of the soldier who said it would soon be spring, and as I had anticipated earlier there was fine English fun, and good talk, and kissing beneath the stairs.

4

Next morning I was awakened by Nur Muhammad beating on my door and crying, 'Miller Sahib! Captain Verbruggen has called a meeting for eleven!'

I rose hastily, doused my eyes in cold water and waited for Nur to push open the door with his pot of boiling water for my shave. My face luxuriated in the soothing water, and as I scraped my beard, I asked, 'How much time?'

'It's past ten,' he warned, and I looked into the hall to greet him, brown, well shaved, dressed in western clothes and karakul cap, waiting to lead me to our breakfast. This morning he was bursting with a special pride. 'I'm also to attend His Excellency's meeting,' he confided, and I saw that he had used my shoe box to freshen his shoes as well as mine. Such things he was not required to do. He was my official helper at the embassy, but he was a married man and had asked if he could augment his salary by overseeing the servants at my house. 'Otherwise, sahib, they'll steal you blind. They're Afghans, you know.'

I lived in one of the new houses on the far side of the public park that dominated the north arm of Kabul: to the west lay the British dormitory, within walking distance, while to the east stood the American embassy, also close at hand. When I had finished shaving I slipped into an Afghan robe and went onto the roof of my house to view once more a scene far more important to me than either the British dormitory or the American embassy. I wished to inspect the mountains and thus remind myself of where I was.

I looked first to the west, where the poetic Koh-i-Baba mountains stood shimmering in the sunlight, so near they could almost be felt, so graceful and varied that they seemed like Gothic sculpture rather than real mountains. To the north stood the great, somber Hindu Kush, heavy and foreboding. They had been named, local legend insisted, The Hindu Killers because of what they had done to the natives of India who tried to cross them seeking the profitable trade of Samarkand. Whenever during my working day I caught a glimpse of the Hindu Kush I felt that I was in direct link with the heartland of Asia.

For to the east these master mountains of Afghanistan joined the Pamirs, the impenetrable, mysterious massif that guarded the meeting place of nations; and these in turn led to the Karakorams, most inaccessible of the Asian mountains, on whose flanks lived the Hunza people, the Gilgits and the Kashmiris. South of the Karakorams came the Himalayas themselves on their eastward sweep down the spine of Asia.

Thus each morning when I greeted the mountains I felt myself in contact not only with Afghanistan but with the entire continent of Asia and with my own past: the wartime flights over the Himalayas into China; the intelligence mission into Gilgit, perched in the clouds; the great sea battles off the eastern flank of Asia; and now my job with the State Department in Kabul. I breathed deeply half a dozen times, imagined the ponderous ballet of the mountains as they swept across Asia, and went down to where Nur Muhammad and the servants had arranged breakfast.

For his eleven-o'clock meeting Captain Verbruggen had collected the four members of our staff best informed on the Ellen Jaspar affair. Richardson of Intelligence was there, a tweedy, pipe-smoking gentleman who affected a British-type mustache and who was favorably known for talking sense, primarily because he refused to give any opinion unless it was fortified by documents. He had reached the State Department via the F.B.I. and was an expert in security and Russian intentions. We supposed that he had been assigned to Afghanistan only briefly in order to study the southern flank of Russia where it impinged on Afghanistan. He felt the case of the Jaspar girl to be an intrusion and frequently said so. But now he sat confidently, his hands folded on his own intelligence file, just waiting for us to ask him questions.

Nexler, the subtle brains of the embassy, was also present, a self-effacing man in his late forties and the only one on our staff who enjoyed secure status in the real hierarchy of State. Unlike the rest of us, he had not come to the department from some other job; he had always been a diplomat and found subtle pleasure in reminding us of the gap that existed between him and us. He was an expert in masking his opinions, but we suspected that he deplored the naval attaché as a political hack, held Richardson in contempt as a kind of F.B.I. precinct cop, and regretted me as an unavoidable error in a department that had been forced to recruit untested men to fill new posts. He suffered Kabul in silence, waiting for the day when he would be transferred to a real embassy, say Buenos Aires or Vienna. London and Paris would come later. In the meantime his strategy in Kabul was to speak as little as possible.

Nur Muhammad and I completed the group, and it was to me that Captain Verbruggen spoke first: 'Shah Khan's office delivered the papers, so you're free to head for Kandahar.'

'I'll go down tomorrow,' I said.

'Good. What do you expect to find?'

'Yesterday Shah Khan suggested three different things that could have happened. First theory. She killed herself.'

'Is that likely?' Verbruggen asked.

'It's possible. She must have been shocked by the life she was required to lead in Afghanistan. I know I was shocked yesterday by some of the things Moheb Khan said.'

'He's the one in the Foreign Office?' Verbruggen asked.

'Yes. Moheb told me something that isn't in our reports. Nazrullah married an Afghan wife before he left for America and had a baby with her.'

'We knew that,' Richardson said complacently, tapping the file with his pipe.

I was irritated that he had kept information from me. 'Did you also know,' I asked, 'that after Nazrullah and Ellen Jaspar were married, his Afghan wife lived with them and she had a second baby? This could well have caused Miss Jaspar to kill herself. Remember, three years ago the Allison girl did.'

The Americans in the room winced at the memory of that dismal affair, and Richardson asked, 'Wouldn't we have heard about a suicide?'

'I asked about the lack of information, and what do you suppose Moheb answered? She was only a woman, and when Nazrullah gets back to Kabul he'll tell us all we need to know.'

'What were the other guesses?' Verbruggen asked.

I thought: Look at Nexler wincing. A career diplomat would say, 'What are the other hypotheses?' I prefer Verbruggen's way.

'Second theory,' I said. 'She's been locked up by her husband and we won't see her for some years. Remember that this occurred with that English girl Sanderson and that Dutch girl . . .'

'Vonderdonk,' Richardson filled in promptly.

'Do you take such a hypothesis seriously?' Verbruggen asked as Nexler raised his eyebrows.

'I certainly do. It's happened before.'

Richardson sucked his pipe, then observed cautiously, 'Evidence I've collected supports the belief that Nazrullah loved his American wife, did all he could to make her happy. I find no parallel with the Sanderson and Vonderdonk girls. Their husbands hated them and kept them locked up eight or nine years to prove it. I reject this theory completely.'

'We're rejecting nothing,' Verbruggen said firmly. 'This is Afghanistan and not one of us here can project himself inside the Afghan mind. How do you know what Nazrullah might do?'

Richardson nodded amiably, dragged on his pipe, then asked, 'Let's concede that he's keeping her locked up. Where? A city like Kandahar? An outpost like Qala Bist?' We looked at one another.

'Excuse me, sir,' Nur Muhammad interrupted. 'I've reviewed all recent cases of such personal imprisonment. Without exception the jail turned out to be the home of the husband's mother. If you surround a ferangi wife with half a dozen women in chaderi they not only can keep her hidden, they enjoy doing it.'

Captain Verbruggen looked at Nur Muhammad as if to say: Whatever we pay you, son, it's worth it. Aloud he asked, 'Have we checked the mother's home?'

'Everything possible,' Nur replied. 'Not a single clue.'

Nexler spoke for the first time. 'But didn't your government also check in the Sanderson and Vonderdonk cases?'

'They did,' Nur confessed, 'and they found nothing. But Nazrullah's family is much more modern than the ones involved in those cases.'

'Would you rule out the possibility that she's hidden, right here in Kabul?' Verbruggen pressed.

'No,' Nur responded quickly. 'After all, it was Your Excellency who reminded us that this is Afghanistan. But I do think it most unlikely.' The acting ambassador nodded. American officials were not supposed to be addressed as Your Excellency, and by no stretch of protocol did Captain Verbruggen warrant the honorific, but I noticed that all who were so addressed were pleased with the courtesy and reluctant to admonish.

Nexler asked quietly, 'Is there no way to visit the family home and check for ourselves?'

The naval attaché turned sharply to his colleague and snapped, 'You overlook three factors. In Afghanistan a home is a fort, and if we try to barge in they'll shoot us. The country has no habeas corpus. And most important, Miss Jaspar is no longer of any legal concern to the American government.'

'Perhaps we should tell that to the senator from Pennsylvania,' Nexler observed dryly.

'He can bully us about the girl,' the acting ambassador complained, 'but there's not a damned thing we can do to bully the Afghan government. What's the third guess?'

'Shah Khan advised us to consider an eventuality which has also occurred in the past. Miss Jaspar has run away. Trying to reach the British railway station at Chaman. If so, two things may have happened. She reached Chaman, which we know she didn't do because we've checked. She died in the desert, which is the way the two earlier cases ended.'

'I don't have their cases,' Richardson protested.

'Before your time,' I said, and he retreated behind his pipe.

'That finishes your report?' Verbruggen asked.

'Yes, sir,' I replied with a finality I did not feel. There remained the matter of Shah Khan's implausible rumor, which he had refused to share with me, but for the moment I concealed this because I wanted our group to explore logical conjectures before speculating on wild improbabilities.

'I'd like to point out,' Verbruggen growled with that down-to-earth realism which characterized him, 'that your first alternative contains two alternatives of its own, one of which you overlooked. Miller says Shah Khan suggested Miss Jaspar may have committed suicide. I suggest she may have been murdered . . . by Nazrullah.'

Nur Muhammad, whom I expected to rise in defense of his countryman, quickly agreed with the logic of his hypothesis. 'Not impossible,' he said firmly. Then he added, 'But I've studied Nazrullah, and it's unlikely he would murder a ferangi.'

The acting ambassador nodded. 'From what I know of him, most unlikely. But I raise the possibility.'

'Thank you, sir,' I replied. 'As you know, I've never seen Nazrullah, but from what I've read of him he's not the murdering type.'

'We're leaping to some rather broad conclusions,' Verbruggen cautioned. 'Let's all get back to facts.'

Richardson coughed and said, 'I have a complete report on the Jaspar girl. Naval Intelligence and F.B.I. helped us out.' He opened his file ceremoniously, looked at Nexler, and asked, 'May I start reading?' Without waiting for consent he began:

'Ellen Jaspar, born in Dorset, Pennsylvania, 1922. Father's in real estate and insurance. She has one brother, three years younger. He seems normal in every way. Enlisted in the army and did well. Now a sophomore at Penn State. We include a photograph of the Jaspars taken in 1943, the year before our subject met the gentleman from Afghanistan.'

Richardson detached the photograph and said, 'If you're looking for the All-American family, here it is. Even have a collie and a Buick.'

When the photograph reached me I saw a family which could have come from any part of America: mother a bit plump but well dressed; father taller and solid-looking; son ill at ease in pants a little too tight; collie dog well cared for; Buick recently polished; daughter . . .

'She's much prettier than most foreign women who marry Afghans,' Nur Muhammad reacted.

To my surprise Richardson laid down his pipe and said, 'I'd date that one. She's stunning.'

I looked again. At twenty, Ellen Jaspar was the typical sophomore at a good girls' college like Bryn Mawr. She was lean, well groomed, an attractive blonde, which must have made her additionally impressive to Nazrullah. No one would mistake her for the brain of the campus; she was too good-looking for that. Nor would anyone pick her as the hottest thing at the Saturday dance; she was too intelligent for that. She was, to use a phrase then coming into use, well-scrubbed, for even in the picture she was conspicuously neat, and one felt that she had not prettied herself up for the photograph.

Captain Verbruggen took charge of the picture and asked, 'Is there any possible clue as to why she would marry an Afghan?'

Richardson had seen something in the photograph the rest of us had missed, and he said, 'She looks to me like a girl who would often whine, "Oh, Mother!"' Verbruggen, who had a daughter, chuckled, and Richardson continued, 'We all know that girls of twelve are driven to anguish by their parents' inadequacies. Thank God this passes. But this girl looks as if she'd maintained this attitude right into her twenties.'

I studied the photograph again, and I must admit that I could hear her crying, 'Really, Mother!'

The acting ambassador asked, 'Do the reports substantiate this?'

'Yes,' Richardson replied. 'Ellen Jaspar attended public school in Dorset through her sophomore year, and did well. Then she grew discontented with everything and her parents transferred her to a good private school in Philadelphia, where she also did well.'

'All-around girl?' Verbruggen asked, implying that only such girls did well.

'Oh, yes!' Richardson assured him. 'Hockey, glee club, tried out for the senior play. Boys took her to dances and in the summer she was counselor at a camp. Well adjusted.'

'Any desire to travel?'

'None evident, but she did excel in nature work. Led the camp in this respect.'

'College the same?' Verbruggen asked. 'Hockey, singing, dramatics?'

'You've hit,' Richardson said, as Nexler sat silent, looking straight ahead. 'Except that in college her singing became good enough for her to join a semi-professional chorus that sang with the Philadelphia Orchestra.'

The acting ambassador leaned back and looked at the roof. 'Where does the flaw come in? That she would enter such a marriage?'

'We've gone rather deeply into that,' Richardson replied. 'First clue we get is from an interview with one of her high-school steadies. Boy who did well in the navy. He told the investigator:

'"When Ellen came home from boarding school she was pretty stuck up, not socially I mean, because she always stayed a neat kid and we all liked her, but she said screwy things like, 'This town is a real bore,' and 'Can you imagine living the rest of your life in Dorset and going to the country club every Saturday night? Big deal.' She talked this way so much that I stopped dating her." '

Richardson dropped the paper, smiled reflectively and added, 'That's his version. The facts seem to be the other way around. It was Ellen who stopped dating him. At least that's what the others reported.'

'Is Dorset so bad?' the acting ambassador probed.

'I asked for a report on that,' Richardson replied. 'Fine town. Good families, good churches, good schools. It's no Tobacco Road, that's for sure. Pearl Buck lives in the next county and so does Oscar Hammerstein. He's the one who wrote *Oklahoma*. There's a little theater not far away. I'd say Dorset was way above average. But when Ellen reached Bryn Mawr her antagonism increased. One of her roommates . . . And here's a point I'd like to emphasize. Not a single person we interviewed said, "I knew all along she'd do something screwy." This fact alone is noteworthy. In every investigation you expect to meet the joker who foresaw everything four years ahead of anybody else. In her case, no. Listen to this:

'Miss Jaspar's first college roommate told us, "Ellen Jaspar was a dear, sweet kid. She was loyal, responsive, and trustworthy. We had three dandy years together and whatever she's done, she's done with her eyes open. And if you come back and say she's committed murder I'm not going to say, it was in her all along. Nothing but essential goodness was in this girl."

'Her second roommate gave us a somewhat different version. "Ellen could grow quite bitter about what she called 'the inescapable nothingness' of life in her family. She dreaded going back home to marry or live. I'd been to her home several times and I loved the place. Old town, old houses, real good people with lots to do. I didn't understand her antipathy, but I can assure you it was real. Once she exploded, 'In Dorset they don't turn back the clocks. They shoot the man who invented clocks.' She told me she was determined never to go back there to live, but I used to ask her, 'Don't you think New York and Chicago are just as goopy?' She said, 'Maybe so. But there must be some place in the world that's different.' I never understood her bitterness." '

'I'm terrified!' Captain Verbruggen cried, 'Sounds just like my daughter.' He passed around a picture of an intense, good-looking junior from Sarah Lawrence. 'You see any difference?' he joked.

'There was this difference,' Richardson replied. 'In her sophomore year at Bryn Mawr, Ellen stopped dating. Told her roommate, "I'm not going to marry some jerk whose big vision of life is selling insurance in Dorset, Pennsylvania." We also have an instructive report from a boy who went to Haverford. Did very well in the army. He told us:

' "Ellen Jaspar was a real winner. She had a world of class. I took her to several dances in her freshman year and she was practically what you'd call a clock-stopper. Very popular with the gang. Real human too. If she hadn't turned so difficult in her sophomore year something big could have developed. At least I was willing to make the try. What it was that changed her I'll never know. At first I blamed myself, but later on I ran into a lot of chicks who just couldn't get things straight. But I'll take the blame for the bust-up, because I always felt somebody else might have kept Ellen on the track. But I will admit this. I wasn't the man to do it." '

'It must have been about then that she met Nazrullah,' the acting ambassador observed. 'How'd it happen?'

Richardson, who rather enjoyed the limelight, went through involved motions lighting his pipe, then explained, 'Her first roommate covers that:

' "In March, 1944, there was this Saturday dance at the Wharton School and some joker invited four of us to go in to Philly. Well, actually he called me and asked me to bring along three warm bodies. So even though Ellen wasn't dating at the time I said, 'Come along. You may meet a glamorous Frenchman.' The idea struck her fancy and on the spur of the moment she joined us. We went in by train, and at the station my date met me with a jalopy, but there beside him was this dark-skinned fellow with a red Cadillac convertible and a turban. It was too much. Ellen took one look at him and that was that. They saw one another a lot, then this other Afghanistan gentleman came up from the embassy in Washington and they all went up to Dorset to meet Ellen's folks. It must have been a real fiasco. She came back swearing that she would rather die on the sands of the desert than marry some Dorset jerk. She left college before exams and that was the last I heard of her, except for one week end that summer. She appeared at my home in Connecticut sort of breathless. Nazrullah had gone back to Afghanistan without her, but she had a passport and a couple of hundred dollars. She needed another twelve hundred dollars. Like a fool I let her have it. I've never heard from her since." '

'Neither has anybody else,' Captain Verbruggen growled. 'What did her father say?' Richardson was ready with a summary:

' "My name is Thomas Shalldean Jaspar. I own an important real estate and insurance business in Dorset, Pennsylvania, where my family has lived for seven generations. My wife is Esther Johnson Jaspar, and her family . . ." '

'We can skip the begats,' the acting ambassador snapped, so Richardson casually discarded a page and resumed reading:

' "My wife and I have tried to remember anything that might explain our daughter's behaviour, but we come up with nothing. There is no explanation. She was a good girl, never gave us a bit of trouble till her sophomore year in high school, when she got fed up with everything in Dorset, including her parents.
' "When she reached Bryn Mawr we breathed a little easier, for she fell in with two of the nicest roommates a girl could have and also met some nice boys at Haverford College. Then everything went sour. Refused to date. Didn't go out much, and was downright hateful when she came home, which wasn't often. Her behaviour was ridiculous." '

Here Richardson stopped, drew on his pipe, and observed, 'I'm not going to read all of this, but one thing does strike me every time I review it. Whenever Mr Jaspar comes up against anything unusual, unknown or unfamiliar he describes it as ridiculous. He and his wife seem to have had a rather rigorous definition of what was not ridiculous, and God help anything that fell outside their pattern.'

'Thank you for your profound analysis,' Captain Verbruggen said. At a normal embassy such sarcasm from an acting ambassador could blight a career, but in Kabul, an irregular post at best, we worked under an irregular discipline which allowed a rather broad latitude for jokes. Verbruggen's wisecrack was directed at himself as much as at Richardson, who laughed easily.

'Excuse me, sir,' I interrupted, 'but I think we may have the clue we're looking for in *ridiculous*. Since Mr Jaspar stigmatized everything out of the ordinary with that word, his daughter was compelled by an urge to outrage the system. What was the most ridiculous thing she could do? Find herself an Afghan with a turban and a red Cadillac convertible.'

'My dear Miller,' Captain Verbruggen said slowly, 'when I observed that Richardson's analysis was profound I meant just that, because frankly, what he pointed out had missed me. Now you have made it completely obvious, and I thank you, too.'

Richardson relit his pipe, smiled at me and suggested, 'Perhaps we should get back to Mr Jaspar, who seems to have been a completely dull gentleman. Certainly his report is.'

' "At a well-chaperoned dance held at the Wharton School, a fine institution in Philadelphia, Ellen met a young man from Afghanistan and before we had even heard about him she had fallen in love with him. We put detectives on his trail and found that he had a Cadillac, got good grades in college, and that he had been in Germany during the early days of the war. We reported this to the F.B.I. but they said he was cleared and was not a spy. After his examinations the young man . . ." '

Richardson paused and said, 'You'll notice that Mr Jaspar refuses to use Nazrullah's name. Probably considered it ridiculous.'

Nur Muhammad observed, 'More likely he was confused because Nazrullah had no last name.' Captain Verbruggen looked up in approval and Richardson continued reading from Mr Jaspar's report:

' "You know the rest. Week before exams Ellen ran away from college and we don't know where she went. She wasn't with the young man, because the detectives kept track of him until he sailed for Afghanistan. Later she turned up at her roommate's in Connecticut with a little money and a passport. She borrowed twelve hundred dollars, which I later repaid, and then went to England. How she managed this we don't know, because at this time ordinary people couldn't get to England . . . I suppose the world is impressed by ridiculous adventurers, especially if they're pretty girls. We haven't heard a word from her since February, 1945." '

Richardson shook his head dolefully. 'No use reading the rest. Poor fellow never had a clue.'

'Any reports from Bryn Mawr?' Captain Verbruggen asked.

'Certainly.' Richardson brightened, shuffling a new set of papers into position. 'Deans, professors, counselors all report the same: Ellen Jaspar presented no problems.' Satisfied with the completeness of his responses, the intelligence officer folded his file and smiled.

During the former F.B.I. man's report I had been impressed by the detached air assumed by Nexler, the State Department career man. Now he coughed modestly, produced from an inside pocket a letter which he unfolded with care, and said, 'In this case it isn't quite proper to claim that no one had foresight. I made some inquiries at Harvard University, where a Bryn Mawr professor is spending his sabbatical. A routine check by our people there . . .' He turned condescendingly to Richardson and said in an offhand way, 'After the meeting I'll give you the letter. It could prove relevant.'

Richardson was justifiably furious that information had been withheld from him, but he masked his anger behind the ritual of lighting his pipe. 'I'd like to hear what you've turned up,' he said with studied amiability.

'Probably of no consequence,' Nexler replied deprecatingly. 'Comes from an assistant professor of music your people overlooked at the time. Here's what he says now.

' "I'm not surprised at what you tell me about the behavior of Ellen Jaspar, and without wishing to appear omniscient I must say that I foresaw almost everything that you report. In fact, I shared my predictions with her parents, but they paid no attention.

' "When Ellen first joined our group she struck me as one destined for tragedy, but I was not satisfied then nor am I now that *tragedy* was the word I sought. I saw her as a girl of good intention who was determined to disaffiliate herself from our society, and I wondered if she were strong enough to find something better to rely on.

' "I met her for the first time during the opening of college in 1941. Without my asking she said, 'I want to get as far away from Dorset, Pennsylvania, as I can.' She spoke with transparent hatred, which did not disturb me at the time, for I encounter many young people who feel this way during their first year of college. But Ellen plunged into the field of medieval music with such intensity that I knew it was not the music she sought. I took the trouble to check with her other professors, and they found her to be normal and above average in performance. I therefore had to conclude that what I had witnessed was merely some temporary aberration.

' "But when Ellen returned in her second year with increased bitterness, claiming that the world seemed pointless, as if it were interested only in a perpetual Saturday night dance at some cosmic country club, I began to take her malaise more seriously, and I asked my wife to talk with her. Ellen brought her young Haverford boy to dine with us and we found him charming, but were forced to agree with her that his ambitions were as ordinary as her father's.

' "My wife and I became so convinced that Ellen would fall into serious trouble that in the spring of 1943 we wrote a letter to her parents. We said—and signed it jointly lest it be thought that I was in some way enamored of the girl, as male professors sometimes are with erratic and attractive girls—that we were convinced Ellen might be in for serious psychological disturbance unless a solid attempt was made to reconcile her to her family and her society as represented by her home town. This brought her parents down upon us in full fury. They pointed out that I was not head of my department, that Ellen was doing well in her real subjects, and that it was ridiculous for an assistant professor of music to presume, etc., etc.

' "This was not the first time I had heard this distinction between real subjects and mine, and I confess that I was always irritated by people who raised the issue. Therefore, when Mr Jaspar shouted for the third time that my letter was ridiculous I quickly confessed that it probably was and asked him to forget the whole affair, which he did. In fact, that December he sent me a Christmas card, and three months later, in early 1944, his daughter met the boy from Afghanistan.

' "So far as I know I was the only person with whom Ellen discussed her intention of marrying the young visitor. I took her immediately to talk with my wife, and we in turn called in the young man to interrogate him. He impressed us as one of the finest foreign students we had ever met, and if Ellen has fallen into trouble through her association with him, we cannot say, 'We told you so.' We must say exactly the opposite. We told Ellen, 'He's a fine person, but he will not solve your problem.' 'What is my problem?' she asked, and I said, 'You have the disease that eats at our world. You cannot find peace in old conventions and beliefs, yet you are not sufficiently committed to anything to forge new ones for yourself.' She looked at me and said, 'You may be right. But wouldn't my going with Nazrullah be a step in the right direction?' I told her it would solve nothing, but on the other hand it would not make things worse. That's the last discussion we had.

' "When you find Ellen you will find that it is not Nazrullah who has wronged her but she who has wronged Nazrullah.

' "I'll close this informal report with one observation. Ellen Jaspar is sick with the disease that is beginning to infect our ablest young people. She has disaffiliated herself from the beliefs that gave our society its structure in the past, but she has found no new structure upon which she can rely for that support which every human life requires." '

Primly Nexler handed the letter to Richardson, who accepted it without comment, but Verbruggen blustered, 'I'd have acted precisely as the Jaspars did. If my daughter gets A's and B's in her real subjects and a music professor sends me a letter as garbled as that, I'll be as stupefied as the Jaspars were.' Then he stared at me with his big, blunt face and demanded, 'Miller, does that letter make any sense to you?'

Having heard what he had just said, I didn't want to insult him, so I equivocated. 'It's part of the picture, sir.'

'What a hell of an answer!' he exploded. 'As a father my reaction was the one I just gave. But as an outsider, trying to get a focus on this thing, the music professor's letter is the only one that makes sense.' Nexler smiled with satisfaction.

Abruptly Verbruggen turned to Nur Muhammad and said, 'Nur, we brought you here today for a fresh look at an old problem. Considering what you've heard, what do you make of it?'

Nur Muhammad was one of the indefinable Afghans who turned up at all embassies. He learned English–or French or German or Turkish as required–had a fair education, quickly made himself invaluable, and was surely in the pay of the Afghan government, to which he reported secretly. Nur was an agreed-upon convenience, for he told the Afghans what we wanted them to know; and through him the Afghans leaked official secrets to us. He had been invited to this morning's meeting to warn the Afghan government that we expected full cooperation in Kandahar.

Nur, who acted as if he did not know that we suspected him of being a government agent, cleared his throat and said cautiously, 'Your Excellency, I cling to these fundamentals. Miss Jaspar is not held prisoner here in Kabul. Nazrullah did not murder her. She may be a prisoner at Qala Bist, but that seems unlikely, because remember what I said. Only women can keep a ferangi wife prisoner. Men cannot. I therefore conclude that she has run away to the British at Chaman and has died in the attempt.'

'Why haven't we been informed?' Verbruggen growled.

'Nazrullah hopes that she may still be found alive. And remember one thing, Your Excellency. You're not fighting the Afghan government on this matter. It's not a case of Shah Khan withholding information. He too is perplexed.'

'Well,' Verbruggen warned, 'look after Miller in the south. We haven't time to worry about another missing American.'

'He shall be my special charge,' Nur Muhammad assured him, and from the manner in which the acting ambassador had spoken Nur realized that it was time for him to depart. Graciously, he withdrew.

As soon as Nur was gone, Verbruggen said to me, 'While you're down there, there's another matter I want you to look into. Several of the embassies may go together to hire a doctor. We want a ferangi, of course. We've been advised there's a German practicing in Kandahar. What's his name?'

Richardson consulted a memorandum and replied, 'Otto Stiglitz.'

The acting ambassador continued, 'Seems to be a refugee who fled Nazi Germany. But he might have come here to escape British or Russian courts trying war criminals. Anyway, the Italians recommend him as an excellent doctor and if he is, we might work out something. Check him out. Maybe he'll know something about our girl, too.'

I looked about the room to insure that no Afghan personnel had entered unexpectedly, then said, 'There's one more matter to discuss, sir. Yesterday as I was leaving, Shah Khan took me aside and whispered that he had recently received a rumor regarding Ellen Jaspar so bizarre that he refused even to discuss it. Didn't want it in our files under his name. At any rate, a rumor has arisen substantial enough to survive a trip from Kandahar to Kabul, but so ridiculous ...'

'You're using Mr Jaspar's word,' the acting ambassador pointed out. 'Shah Khan said bizarre. I suppose they mean the same.'

'Anyone care to guess what the rumor might have been?' I asked.

'You've obviously been thinking about it all night,' Verbruggen pointed out. 'You speak.'

'Could Ellen have murdered Nazrullah? And is the Afghan government hushing it up?'

Richardson shook his head. 'Shah Khan is the Afghan government.'

Verbruggen was not so easily satisfied. 'Has any American seen Nazrullah alive?'

'Yes,' Richardson replied, consulting his notes. 'That irrigation expert from Colorado, Professor Pritchard, reported that on his way to ascertain water flow along the Persian border he had talked with Nazrullah at Qala Bist.'

'Would he have known Nazrullah if he saw him?'

'His letter refers to him as a fine young man with a beard who graduated from the Wharton School. Must have been Nazrullah.'

'Next guess,' the acting ambassador snapped.

'Could she have defected to Russia?' I asked. This was 1946 and most Americans would have viewed my question with amazement, for in the States it was not yet recognized that Russia was our major enemy. In Afghanistan, living next door to Russia as we did, we knew.

'The thought's been going through my head,' the acting ambassador replied. The Kabul dispatches of 1946 and 1947, if they are ever published, are going to make our staff look like a group of military geniuses. Partly this was because Richardson, our intelligence man, saw things very clearly; partly because Captain Verbruggen had a feeling for military matters; and partly because all of us on the staff could add two and two.

'We know that the Afghans hate communism,' I argued, 'especially its attitude on religion, but we also know that secret Russian missions have been operating in this country. Now if an American woman let it be known that she was fed up with America and Afghanistan ... well, mightn't the Russians approach her?'

Richardson tried to light his pipe and said off-handedly, 'You'd probably be on better grounds if you investigated the likelihood that she defected to the Chinese. Don't forget that lands controlled by the Chinese Communists touch Afghanistan on the north.'

'I think we're up the wrong tree,' Captain Verbruggen said. 'If she had gone over to either Russia or China, those governments would use that fact to embarrass us. They haven't done so.'

'On the other hand, sir,' I argued, 'this girl's whole personality, her attitude toward her home ... Everything indicates the kind of person who might turn traitor.'

The acting ambassador refused comment and changed the line of discussion radically. 'Any chance she's in Europe? Why couldn't she be toasting her heels in Venice with some Italian grand duke?'

Richardson treated this with contempt. 'The chances of an American girl's entering India without being noticed, then sailing from Karachi or Bombay, are just not measureable. Can't be done. You want to call the British embassy to check?'

'I withdraw,' Verbruggen surrendered. There was silence, after which he turned to me, saying. 'You find out what happened, Miller.'

'I'll do my best, sir,' I said briskly.

'You'll find out,' he growled, 'or you'll damned well be back in the navy.' The group laughed and Richardson left, followed by Nexler. When we were alone Captain Verbruggen put his arm about me and said, 'Miller, it would be a feather in my cap if we could get this Jaspar thing cleared up before the old man gets back from Hong Kong.'

'I'll do my damnedest,' I promised.

'On the other hand,' he cautioned, 'don't rush things. This is your first big mission. Ask a lot of questions. Learn the country. Don't be afraid of looking stupid, because one of these days we could be driven into war across this terrain, and you'd be the only American who'd ever seen parts of it. Keep your eyes open.'

'I will.'

Suddenly he cried, with real emotion, 'God, I wish I was going in your place. Good luck, kid.'

As I left his office I thought: Nexler's dying to get to Paris and Richardson wants to get back to Washington. But Verbruggen and I love Afghanistan. Who cares about the dysentery and the loneliness? For I knew that Afghanistan was the toughest assignment on record. Here was the post which sooner or later tested a man, and for me the preliminaries were over. I was about to plunge into one of the world's great cauldrons.

5

While it was still dark, Nur Muhammad helped me pack the jeep for the trip to Kandahar. We stowed our extra tins of motor oil, the precautionary spark plugs, the rope, an extra jack, sleeping bags and medical supplies. We had requisitioned from the embassy four cases of army K-rations, two spare tires and some jugs of boiled water for drinking. Seeing us on that wintry morning, you would not have guessed that we were embarking on a routine trip from the capital of a sovereign nation to the secondary metropolis nearby. We looked more like adventurers about to set forth in some dubious caravan, which we were.

Before we left Kabul, where wolves had again made forays down narrow streets, I asked Nur if he would drive me past the home of Nazrullah's family, and he obliged. It lay in the southern arm of the city, on the way to Kandahar, and when we drew up before its tall, fast-bound wooden gate, studded with ancient nails and bolts, I realized that I was once more facing the portal of an Afghan fortress. The surrounding mud walls were many feet high, so that nothing inside was visible. No agency in Afghanistan other than force was entitled to break its way into these confines, in which a woman could be kept hidden indefinitely without the assent of any but her jailers.

While we sat in the car inspecting the silent and forbidding gate, we became aware of someone inside the walls who had been alerted by our presence, and after a while a feeble light, obviously from an open flame, was seen glimmering through the chinks in the weatherbeaten gate. The light stopped moving. Someone on the other side was staring at us through the gate. No one spoke.

After several minutes I whispered to Nur, 'You suppose they know who we are?'

'They know,' he replied. 'The jeep means ferangi.'

'Why don't we ask where Ellen is?' I suggested, certain that Nur would dismiss the proposal as fruitless. To my surprise he shrugged his shoulders, descended from the jeep and went dutifully to the gate. Even though the unseen watcher must have followed his approach, nothing happened. Finally Nur surrendered and went through the formality of tugging the bell cord.

Inside the stout wall there was a clangor and the light moved. After the customary interval the small one-person doorway that had been cut into one of the larger gates swung open and a thin man swathed in rags and a dirty turban peered out. While Nur spoke in Pashto he listened impassively, then shook his head no. The little door squeaked shut in the darkness and between the chinks I could see the flickering light disappear.

'They don't know where she is,' Nur reported, and in our strong headlights I caught my last glimpse of the mysterious wall.

The road from Kabul south to Kandahar was about three hundred miles long and had been in existence for some three thousand years. Judging from its condition at the end of winter in 1946, the last repairs must have been completed at least eight hundred years ago, for each mile of the road involved a particular adventure.

The potholes were so deep that we could travel at no more than twenty, and wherever water had seeped under the rocks, the entire roadbed vanished and we had to set out across rutted fields until the antique roadway re-established itself. In the darkness we passed many vehicles disabled, their passengers sleeping unconcernedly until spare parts could be procured from Kabul on foot.

Promptly at six, for we were in the vernal equinox, the sun rose over the eastern hills and illuminated the noble, desolate landscape of central Afghanistan. Far to the west stood the Koh-i-Baba range, white in majesty and completely impenetrable as long as snow pre-empted the passes. Nearer at hand stood an occasional home, a low, mud-brick affair entirely surrounded by walls along whose tops thorns had been trained to grow and broken bottles implanted. Close to the road stretched shreds of fields which in good years might produce scattered crops; but usually rain stayed in the mountains and the farmer's work proved fruitless.

The dominant aspect of the landscape was its color. Everything not covered with snow was brown: the mountains, the mud walls, the land where nothing grew. The human stragglers on their way to Kabul seemed all a dirty brown. Once their shirts, hanging to their knees, must have been white, but much wear and little laundry had rendered them brown. Even the dogs were brown.

We stopped once to watch a group of men playing with one of these dogs, but the beast knew we were strangers and began snarling, whereupon the men picked up small rocks and with prodigious accuracy threw at the animal until he retreated. 'I should think they'd injure the dog,' I protested, but Nur pointed out that none of the stones had been thrown with force.

'They love their scrawny dogs,' he assured me. 'Kill an Afghan's dog and he'll track you through the Hindu Kush.'

To travel from Kabul to Kandahar at the time of equinox–we were starting our journey on the twenty-first of March, the last day of winter, the first of spring–was comparable to traveling from the snowbound mountains of New York to the spring-drenched warmth of Virginia, for as we moved south we rushed headlong into the Asian spring, and we traveled from snow to flowers. Before the first morning had passed we were seeing blue flowers beside the road and yellow birds speeding across brown fields. The great bleak plains, so recently under snow, were beginning to look almost alluring.

Our first stopping point was the ancient capital of Afghanistan, the storied city of Ghazni, and I use the word *storied* with care, because when it was announced that I had drawn Afghanistan as my first diplomatic post I studied what I could of local history and no existing city captured my imagination as Ghazni did, for from its many-towered walls there had issued in the year 1000, a convenient date to remember, a barbaric conqueror of unmatched vigor. He was known as Mahmud of Ghazni, and every year for more than a quarter of a century this fearful Afghan had led his armies down through the Khyber Pass and onto the plains of India, where he was not once defeated nor even successfully resisted.

The chroniclers said of him, 'Mahmud kept the cities of India tethered in the sun like fat cows, which he came regularly to milk.' He murdered thousands, swept up the riches of a continent, and transformed his ugly little Afghan city of Ghazni into one of the contemporary centers of education, wealth and power.

I remember that on the day when I first encountered his name, one of the most lustrous in Asian history—comparable perhaps to Charlemagne in Europe—I interrupted my studies to ask some twenty other graduate students then joining the State Department if they had ever heard of Mahmud of Ghazni, and none knew the name. I think it was then that I realized how completely unknown a land Afghanistan was, and I discovered to my chagrin that even learned people were vaguely of the opinion that Afghanistan was an alternate name for Ethiopia. Many of my friends assumed I had been assigned to Africa.

Well, I learned who Mahmud of Ghazni was, and now with Nur Muhammad's guidance I was approaching his city. What a drab, desolate disappointment it was from a distance, a scrawny collection of mean brown buildings surrounded by an ugly mud wall. From where I first saw Ghazni, it looked like a nondescript collection of cattle barns. There were no trees, no cooling river, no spacious approach. It was to remain my major disillusionment in Afghanistan, this dreary, almost forsaken jumble of mud huts that had once been the capital of much of the world.

But when we reached the wall there were compensations, and I must confess that when I stood before the great south gate I did feel a stirring of imagination and an echo, however remote, of the imperial Mahmud. The gate was huge and excellently built. It was protected by two stout round towers whose battlements were slotted for rifle fire and whose windows were mere slits for the accommodation of guns. To stand outside this gate amid a throng of travelers, seeking admission to the city, imparted a sense of history, and I could believe that it was from the security of these walls that Mahmud had issued on his yearly forays.

And when we had edged our jeep through the gates and into the narrow streets, even the dimmest mind could perceive that we were no longer in Kabul, where the embassies provided a spurious international flavor and where German engineers had at least brought the river under control. In Ghazni there were no German engineers and we were in the most ancient part of Asia.

In the little square in which we finally found ourselves, an earthen, unpaved square border by dusty shops and a filthy restaurant, every man we saw was dressed in dirty white trousers, knee-length shirt, western-style vest, shabby overcoat and voluminous turban. All wore open-toed sandals of ragged leather, and there was not a karakul cap to be seen. Nor were there any women, not even in chaderi. Men walked by lugging skins and furs, bladders filled with goats' milk, grapes and melons from the south, bundles of charcoal, and odds and ends of country produce. Compared to the bazaar at Kabul, this was mean indeed, for color was lacking, and movement, and foreign goods; but it was impressive in a timeless way and I was not unhappy when Nur parked the jeep and told me to guard it while he went searching for a place to stay, for the road was so bad that we could not hope to make Kandahar in one day and to stop south of Ghazni was unthinkable.

I had been studying the mean little square for perhaps ten minutes when I found myself surrounded by Afghans in tattered clothes, ordinary men from the city who were interested in the ferangi. They were pleased when I spoke Pashto and were telling me that in the Ghazni area it had been a bad winter with little food when Nur Muhammad returned. As he did so, the crowd mysteriously dispersed, and I supposed that Nur had reprimanded them, but I saw that what had scared them off was the approach of two mullahs, tall, bearded men in dark robes and scowls of intense hatred. They marched up to the jeep, which they knew to be alien to their interests, and began berating it, not me.

Their fury abated when I spoke to them in Pashto, explaining that I was their friend. Granted this assurance, they relaxed their animosity and began discussing my trip with me. They proved to be pleasant men, and under Nur's careful persuasion they actually started laughing and the crowd regathered. Nur assured them that the ferangi would not molest the girls of Ghazni nor would he drink alcohol. They bowed as they departed, and Nur whispered, 'Mullahs could be handled . . . if we had enough time.'

Nur now called a little boy to lead me to the front of the hotel while he drove the jeep to a compound in the back, where it could be locked up and guarded during our stay in Ghazni. The boy, dressed in pitiful rags, shuffled along a narrow alley and brought me finally to my first Afghan hotel, which I approached with real excitement. I will say merely that it had no glass in any window, no lock on any door, no water, no heat, no food, no bed, no bedclothes, and no flooring but earth. It did, however, possess one characteristic that made it memorable: on the dirt floor of our room were piled five of the most beautiful Persian rugs I had ever seen. They had been woven in Russia at the ancient city of Samarkand and had been smuggled into Afghanistan by itinerant traders who had hauled them over mountains and across deserts. They were poems in thread, three reddish blue and two in stunning white and gold. They had lain on the hotel floor for many years, where the extreme dryness had kept them from rotting, and they seemed now as colorful as when they left the loom. They made the hotel livable and I was dismayed when Nur Muhammad began unloading every item of our cargo, including the two spare tires, onto them.

'Don't lug that stuff in here!' I protested.

'What shall I do with it?' he asked.

'Leave it in the jeep,' I said.

'In the jeep?' Nur gasped. 'They'd steal everything we own.'

'You hired two men with shotguns,' I argued.

'They're to see that nobody steals the wheels,' Nur explained. 'Miller Sahib, if we left these spare tires in the jeep, the guards would sell them in ten minutes.'

I was disgusted and said, 'I'm hungry. Let's go out and get some food.'

'We can't both go,' Nur replied.

'Why not? The mullahs know you're here as my friend.'

'I mean the room. We can't leave it unguarded. One of us has to stay.'

I looked out the back window, a mere slit for rifle fire, and pointed to the two big, bearded guards lolling in the empty jeep. 'Let's put one of them in the room.'

'Them!' Nur exploded. 'They'd steal everything we have and shoot us when we got back.'

'Then why are you paying them?' I demanded.

'To keep the wheels on the jeep,' Nur repeated.

I couldn't hide my irritation, so Nur took me to the front window, another rifle slot, and showed me the hotel courtyard, where forty or fifty hungry-looking tribesmen had gathered. 'Miller Sahib,' Nur whispered, 'they're just waiting for us to leave this room.'

It was decided that I should eat first, and it was about three in the afternoon when I returned to the square seeking a restaurant. I use the word loosely, for all I could find was the filthy corner café I had seen earlier. It contained one rickety table, three chairs and a water bottle whose sides could not be seen for flyspecks. Its aroma, however, was another matter, for I had grown partial to Afghan food and this café had some of the best. The waiter, a man in an unbelievably tattered overcoat and green turban, brought me a chunk of nan, a kind of thick, crunchy tortilla made of coarse, nutritious flour and baked in slabs the size of snowshoes. It was, most of us thought, the best bread we had ever eaten, for it was baked in clay ovens over charcoal and tasted of the fields where the wheat had grown. The waiter also plopped down a large dish of pilau, a steaming mixture of barley, cracked wheat, onions, raisins, pine nuts, orange peel and shreds of roast lamb. On these two dishes, nan and pilau, I would exist during my entire trip, and I would never tire of either.

As I ate, men with whom I had been talking earlier reassembled about me. Two sat on the frail chairs. Others stood behind me, and from time to time I offered them chunks of nan, which they used as scoops to attack the pilau. Perhaps seven or eight men thus dipped their fingers into my meal with me, and we developed that camaraderie which is so marked a feature of Afghan life. As I was paying for my meal and bidding my guests good-bye, some men in long coats ran across the square, shouting. I did not understand their words and was about to return to the hotel so that Nur could eat, when the men around me became very excited and tugged at my sleeve. I was to follow them. Together we trailed the first men across the square and out of the gates of the city. I remember thinking that I should return to Nur Muhammad, but some evil genius kept me running and soon I was in the midst of a mob converging on a spot outside the gates where a heavy stake had been driven into the earth.

On the far side of the stake, which rose to a height of seven feet, stood four mullahs, including the two who had accosted me earlier. They were mournful, aloof and terrifying. In their beards and turbans they seemed like patriarchs of old, and I was assailed by the uneasy feeling that I had intruded upon some Biblical scene which should have terminated twenty-five centuries ago. The lean, angry mullahs were from the Old Testament. The string of camels placidly grazing by the crumbling walls were of an ancient time, and the crowd of turbaned men, their faces brown from sun, their beards gray with desert dust, could have been waiting for some religious rite in Nineveh or Babylon.

As I looked hurriedly about I could detect only one note that indicated we were in the twentieth century. Outside the gates of Ghazni, jammed into a crumbling fragment of wall that may once have formed part of a fort guarding the imperial city, stood a telegraph pole which carried three precarious wires from Ghazni to Kabul. What I was about to witness could thus have been telegraphed to the whole world in a matter of minutes, but no one in Ghazni, except perhaps Nur Muhammad, would have considered it worthy of report.

The mullahs were praying, and the declining afternoon sun threw handsome shadows athwart their faces. The prayer stopped. From the nearby gates marched four soldiers bearing carbines and bandoleers, leading between them a hesitant, barefooted figure covered by a coarse white chaderi. In Kabul I had seen pleated chaderies of exquisite cloth with embroidered peepholes for the eyes, and the savageness of the custom was temporarily overlooked; but in Ghazni this chaderi was a coarse, dirty white shroud and the opening no more than a tiny square of cheap mosquito netting.

I was not told who hid inside the chaderi, but it had to be a woman, for so far as I knew men never wore the shroud. Whoever it was must have seen the looks of bitter hatred that greeted her as she passed.

When the soldiers reached the stake, they inexpertly drove several nails into it and lashed their prisoner's hands to these nails, at the same time securing her ankles to the bottom of the stake. When they stepped back, the dirty white chaderi fell completely over the bare feet and the prisoner was wholly masked. She was still free, however, to look out upon the world of hate-filled faces.

Now the four mullahs prayed, and the crowd responded in a ritual I did not understand; but this was followed by a speech from one of the mullahs who had accosted me in the square, and what he said was in Pashto, and this I understood clearly, though what it signified I was not then competent to guess. He shouted mournfully, 'This is the woman taken in adultery! This is the whore of Ghazni! This is the raging insult to all men who revere God!' He ended and I stared at the shrouded figure, trying to anticipate what her punishment was to be. If she heard the charge, she did not tremble.

Another mullah stepped forward and cried, 'We have studied the case of this woman taken in adultery and she is guilty. We submit her to the judgment of the men of Ghazni.' His companions assented, and the first mullah led the bearded men back through the gates of Ghazni and we saw them no more.

I had turned to watch the mullahs and did not see what happened next, but I heard a thudding sound and a gasp. I looked around quickly in time to see that a rather large stone had apparently struck the woman and had fallen at her feet. The gasp must have come from her.

Now the men at my right, the ones who had eaten with me and brought me to the scene, knelt to find stones, and the smaller rocks they discarded, but soon all were armed, and with the same skill that I had seen directed at the dog, they began throwing at the shrouded figure. From all sides stones whizzed toward the stake, and most struck, and it was obvious that punishment for adultery in Afghanistan was severe.

The woman refused to cry out, but a cheer soon rose from the crowd. One powerful man had found an especially good stone, large and jagged, and he threw this with force, aiming it carefully at her body, and it struck so violently in her abdomen that soon the first blood of the afternoon showed through the chaderi. It was this that brought the cheer, but I remember thinking how indecent it was that a human body which none could see should send its blood through the interstices of a shroud and deposit it in sunlight as testimony of punishment.

Another stone of equal size struck the woman's shoulder. It brought both blood and cheers. I felt sickness in my throat and thought: Who halts the punishment?

Then I almost fainted. A large man with unerring aim pitched a jagged rock of some size and caught the woman in the breast. Blood spurted through the torn chaderi and at last the woman uttered a piercing scream. I wanted to run away, but I was hemmed in by maniacs and I had been warned by many accounts that for a foreigner to make one mistake at such a scene might lead to his being killed. I prayed that the men had had enough, and then I saw why the soldiers had hammered the nails in the stake. They kept the ropes from slipping, and when the prisoner fainted, her bloodstained chaderi going all limp, these nails prevented her from falling to the ground.

Surely, I thought, the soldiers will release her now. But they watched impassively while men from all sides gathered fresh ammunition.

The sagging body was struck eight or nine times in the next fusillade, but mercifully the woman could not have known. Now a burly man shouted that he had found the perfect rock and others must stand clear. The crowd obeyed and watched breathlessly as he took careful aim, whirled his arm, and launched his missile with ugly force. It flashed across the fifteen yards separating the men from their target and sped accurately as intended, striking the unconscious woman in the face. Quick blood marked the spot and the crowd cheered.

The blow was so terrible that it wrenched the prisoner's hands from the nails and allowed her to collapse in a heap about the stake. As she did so the crowd broke loose and rushed to the fallen body, smashing it with boulders which no man, however powerful, could have thrown from a distance. Again and again they dropped the huge rocks on the fallen body until they crushed it completely, continuing the wild sport until they had built a small mound of stones over the scene, as a pauper family in the desert might have marked a burial.

In a state of shock I returned through the gates of Ghazni. I passed the restaurant where the fellowship had been so congenial and was greeted by the men who had thrown the largest rocks. They were gathering to discuss the execution and congratulate each other upon expert performances. I got to the hotel to find that Nur Muhammad, realizing I had been side-tracked, had sent a boy for some pilau, which he had eaten with greasy fingers. He was now asleep on the Persian rugs, but when I entered the room he wakened like a prudent guard.

'Why are you so white?' he asked.

'A woman taken in adultery,' I mumbled.

'Stones?' he asked.

'Yes.'

Nur beat the rugs, then put his hands over his face. 'What a terrible disgrace! My poor country!'

'It was horrible,' I said weakly. 'How can you permit it?'

He sat up, cross-legged on the rug, while I sank down on the spare tires. 'Don't you suppose we're ashamed?' he asked. 'Moheb Khan . . . the king? If they'd seen this . . .'

'Why don't they stop it?' I demanded angrily.

'If they tried to stop it, Miller Sahib, the men you watched today and their brothers in the hills would storm Kabul and kill you and me and Moheb Khan and the king, too.'

'Impossible!' I cried.

'They've done so in the past,' Nur insisted. 'In Kabul we have perhaps two thousand educated Afghans who know that things like this must end. In

Kandahar maybe five hundred. But in Ghazni none. We're outnumbered twelve million madmen to three thousand . . . perhaps five thousand. I'm not sorry you saw the execution, Miller Sahib. You'll understand my country better.'

'Will things go on like this indefinitely?' I asked.

'No,' Nur said firmly. 'Across the Oxus people just like us used to behave the way you saw today. Public executions supervised by mullahs were common in places like Samarkand. But the Communists from Moscow and Kiev said they had to stop. The chaderi was outlawed. Women were freed. Miller, we have ten years to halt these terrible things. If we don't . . . Russia's going to come down and stop them for us.'

'Does the government realize this?'

'Of course. Do you think men like Shah Khan are stupid? The government knows it. But twelve million citizens don't.' Nur rose and stamped impatiently about the room, picking his way through our scattered gear. 'Don't you understand the problems that face a man like me? Right now in Ghazni, a few hours' journey from Kabul, every man who participated in that stoning fully expects to continue doing so for the rest of his life. If you told them tonight that you were going to halt all this, they would kill you.'

I was suddenly assaulted by a terrifying premonition and I leaped off the spares tires to grab Nur by the arm. 'Is this what happened to Ellen Jaspar?'

Nur relaxed and started laughing. 'No, Miller Sahib. If that had happened we'd have known in Kabul.'

I said, 'I feel sick. Let's take a walk.'

'I can't leave the goods,' he protested.

'Call one of the guards,' I said sharply. 'I've got to get out of this town.'

'Go ahead. I'll stay here and guard the things.'

'I'm afraid to go alone,' I said honestly.

'You're wise,' Nur agreed, and against his better judgment he started to summon one of the guards. Then he paused to ask, 'You assume responsibility for this?' I said I did.

Nur told the bearded warrior, with the gun and bandoleer, 'If one thing is missing when we return, you'll be shot. Understand?' The fierce renegade nodded and when we left we heard him piling our goods against the door to keep out would-be intruders.

We walked through the square, where the enthusiastic executioners hailed me again, and down to the gate, where I could see the ominous stake rising from the mound of rocks. Dogs were nosing at the blood.

'How long will the body remain?' I asked.

'They'll take it away tonight,' Nur assured me. Then he said fervently, 'One thing you must understand, Miller Sahib. Today's execution must have looked like a riot. It wasn't. Mullahs study these cases with care and no decision is reached casually. Strictly speaking, what you saw was a planned, legal act of justice. But a horrifying one.'

We turned away from the funeral mound and walked south along an old caravan route until we had lost sight of Ghazni. We must have covered four miles when I saw off to the east an unfamiliar sight: something that looked like a flock of large black birds assembled on an empty plain, and I expected the huge birds to take wing; but as we moved closer I saw that we had come upon a tribe of nomads who move back and forth across Afghanistan with the seasons.

'Povindahs!' Nur exclaimed with marked excitement. Running ahead, he called, 'Look at those women!'

From a distance I watched the nomad women, dressed in black with flashing jewelry. They moved with fierce grace–I can call it nothing else–and wore no chaderi. they were free, the wild nomads who traveled the upland plateaus of Asia. The sun was setting now, and its red rays illuminated their dark faces, lending them an animal quality of absorbed preoccupation with the world about them. For more than three thousand years their ancestors had moved back and forth across the boundaries of Asia and no one had found a way to stop them.

In their annual passage across Afghanistan the Povindahs must have looked with disgust at the way the Afghans imprisoned their women, hiding them in sacks and treating them like chattels, while at the same time the Povindah women were free to move about as they wished.

'They're an insult to your whole system,' I told Nur.

'You're right,' he agreed. 'But the price they pay for this freedom is appalling.'

'They look fairly happy to me.'

'They're completely ostracized. When they move through our country they remain a people apart.'

'Then why were you so excited when you spotted them?'

Nur laughed. 'Afghan men are lured to these black tents like flies to honey. Many of my friends have tried to spend the night in there.' He pointed to the tents where the women moved. 'But the Povindah men are watchful to keep us away.'

One such nomad rode up to us now, on a brown horse. He was a tall dark-faced man with mustaches and a flowing turban. Across his chest were bandoleers and with one arm he pointed a rifle at us casually and said in Pashto, 'Keep away!' Nur spoke with him for a moment and he replied graciously, but at the end he repeated his warning. 'Keep away!' Spurring his horse, he rode back to the tents.

'He suspected we were government officials.'

'Where do they go from here?' I asked.

'They follow the melting snow.'

We started to leave when I saw from the corner of my eye a figure in red dart out from one of the tents and disappear behind another, as a bright-colored bird will flash through trees in spring. I turned to look more carefully and was rewarded when a young girl, dressed all in red and bangles, reappeared chasing a goat, but before I could see her well, she disappeared again and I thought: She reminds me of Siddiqa. Like Shah Khan's granddaughter she seemed a person of unusual grace and sexual suggestion.

Nur Muhammad, who missed little, which was why the Afghan government employed him to be employed by the American government, chuckled and asked, 'Fascinating, isn't she?'

'Why does she wear red?'

'Shows she's not married . . .'

'Look!'' I cried. From behind the tent nearest us the wayward goat burst free and ran directly at us. Hot after him came the determined girl, and some forty yards from where we stood she tackled the animal, rolling him in the dust. I saw her dark skin, her flashing eyes, and two long pigtails which swung in the sunlight as she wrestled with the goat. I could understand the fascination felt by the Afghan men for such a person, and as we watched she skillfully led the goat back to its tether.

'Makes me feel good to know that such people are also a part of Afghanistan,' I observed as we walked away.

'They're not our people,' Nur corrected. 'In the winter they go to India. In the summer they go north. They use us only as a corridor.'

'What country do they belong to?' I asked.

'I never considered the matter,' Nur replied. 'Legally, I suppose they're Indians.'

It was night when we approached the Ghazni gate, on whose ramparts flickering lights moved back and forth. It was a solemn moment, at the end of day, when the ancient city was settling down for sleep, and we paused to watch the towers etched in the glow from some improvised fire where travelers outside the city were roasting a sheep. In after years, whenever I have thought of an Afghan city it has been Ghazni, looming in the darkness.

When we passed the scene of the execution Nur Muhammad begged, 'Don't look again, Miller Sahib. This is our shame.' And we returned to the square, where shadowy lights illuminated the corner café. We took our seats at the table and good-natured men elbowed up to us to discuss the day's events; and against my will I found myself entangled with these bewildered, half-savage men who were fighting the contemporary world, yet who were so hungry to know about America. They ate our nan and shared our pilau. They told us of the problems facing Ghazni–the food supply, the taxes and the cost of horses–and at the end of our meal they walked with us to our hotel, where they entered and sat for hours, cross-legged on the Persian rugs, talking . . . talking . . .

6

Shortly after dawn we left Ghazni, passing on the way the scene of execution, from which the stake had been removed, for wood in Afghanistan was precious. The stones, however, were left conveniently scattered in case another culprit should be apprehended.

We had been on the road for less than an hour when I discovered an important fact about Afghanistan which none of my reading had discussed; yet it was so fundamental that if one missed its significance he missed the meaning of this country. I refer to the bridges of Afghanistan.

When we came to the first one I did not appreciate its importance. It was a beautiful bridge, built in the early 1900s, I judged, by some expert engineer. It was well designed, contained good stonework and was ornamented by four crenelated towers. Unfortunately, a recent flood had eaten away the approaches to the bridge, leaving it an isolated structure that now served no useful purpose. To cross the river we had to leave the road, descend by gullies to the river, ford it, and reverse the process until we climbed back onto the road. Obviously, in time of storm traffic on the road would halt, but I remember thinking, while fording the river: That's a handsome bridge . . . almost a work of art.

Thirty minutes later we came upon an even more beautiful bridge, with eight towers done in the most sturdy style, a kind of military Gothic common to old French and German towns. It was a splendid structure and I studied it with some care, for which I had ample time since its approaches had also been washed away. We were thus forced once more to ford the river, and I could see the bridge from below.

The stonework was exemplary; the joints were interesting because I could not detect how they were sealed. It looked as if the architect had depended upon the skill of his cutters to give him a joint which held of its own friction and weight. Moreover the structure was well designed, with the eight towers adding a striking note. It was a bridge to admire, and only the advent of some unexpected flood had rendered it useless.

But when we came to the third fine bridge and found its approaches gone too, I grew irritated and asked Nur Muhammad, 'Are all the bridges like this?'

'They are,' he said sadly.

'Why?'

'We called them "Bridges Afghan Style." They can't be used.'

'What happened?' I demanded.

'Afghanistan's folly,' he said, and it was obvious that he wished to drop the matter.

At the seventh washed-out bridge we had to ford a river much deeper than we had anticipated and got stuck in the middle with our bottoms wet and our engine useless, waiting till a truck came along to haul us out. We had nothing to do but study the bridge overhead, and it was perhaps the loveliest of all: its arch was graceful, its turrets solid, its brickwork neat, and its impression substantial.

'Beautiful bridge,' I admitted grudgingly. 'Who built it?'

'A German. One of the worst tragedies that ever hit our nation.'

It was a pleasure to talk with Nur, for he spoke idiomatic English while I was fairly competent in Pashto; for practice we liked a system whereby I spoke in his language and he replied in mine, but when discussing complex subjects each used his own language. To an outsider our conversation would be confusing, for often we switched languages in midsentence. Now, with my bottom wet and cold, I was angry and spoke in harsh Pashto.

'What happened with these bridges, Nur?'

He replied in careful Pashto. 'A disaster. We were taking our first step out of the Dark Ages and the Germans said, "It's stupid to have your two major cities unconnected by a road." They arranged a big loan and gave us experts who surveyed the road and showed how it could be built. When the king saw the survey, very neatly drawn with little pictures, he approved and said, "We're a modern country now. We must have a modern road." Then he asked who would build the bridges, and the Germans lent us a learned professor-architect who had built many bridges, and the work started.'

Nur pointed up at the bridge. 'He was a brilliant man who demanded the best. Look at that brickwork. You don't find much of that in Afghanistan. It was his idea to mark each bridge with distinctive turrets and ornamentation, for he told us, "A bridge is more than a bridge. It's a symbol connecting past and present." He said that towers and intricate brickwork were part of the Afghan soul. In a famous speech he gave in Kabul he said that he had taken the idea of towers from the family forts that mark Afghanistan.'

'I didn't see the relationship,' I remarked, but Nur pointed down the river toward a private fort and then I knew what the professor-architect had been after.

'He built some twenty bridges,' Nur explained as we sat in the cold river—and I mean in the river, for the jeep kept settling—'and all the time he was working, a handful of Afghans like Shah Khan and my father kept warning him, "Doctor, that bridge is fine for a well-controlled European river, but has anyone told you about our Afghan rivers in the spring?" He replied angrily that he had built bridges over some of the finest rivers in Europe . . . much greater rivers, he assured us, than these trivial desert streams.'

Nur looked sadly at the bridge and said in English, 'You understand, of course, that this all happened before I was born.' Then he explained in Pashto, 'But I remember my father telling us later, "We went to the government and warned them, 'Those German bridges will not stand up against our rivers in the spring.'" They were told, "You think you're smart enough to tell a German how to do his job? A man who has built bridges all over Europe?" My father replied that he had never seen a European river and it looked to him as if the German had never seen an Afghan river, and there the matter was left.'

The jeep settled deeper and Nur said in English, 'Shah Khan is a learned man and a brave one. In those days he was without the dignity of his present position, but he refused to drop the matter. He told the Germans'—and here Nur Muhammad reverted to Pashto—'"These bridges are far more important to us than they are to you. They're our first contact with the western world. If they succeed, we who want to modernize this nation will succeed. If they fail, dreadful consequences may follow. Now please, Professor-Architect, listen when I tell you that sometimes in the spring what you call our trivial desert streams roar out of the mountains two miles wide. They move boulders as big as houses. They destroy everything not perched on a hill. And the next day they're little streams again. Professor, build us big broad bridges and leave off the pretty towers."

'The German professor was furious that Shah Khan would dare speak to him directly. He insisted that a meeting of government be convened, at which he made an impassioned speech. "I want to tell you that I have sunk my pillars to bedrock. I have built as no bridges in Afghanistan have ever been built before. When the floods that Shah Khan speaks of meet my bridges not one bridge will fall down." I must say that Shah Khan was a fighter. He replied, "Professor-Architect, you're entirely right. The bridges will not fall down. Of that I'm convinced. But the rivers of Afghanistan, like the people of Afghanistan, never attack the enemy head on. Your stout bridges are like the British army. Their soldiers were ten times better than ours . . . better fed . . . better armed. But we didn't march up to the British in double file so they could shoot us down. In a thousand tricky ways we surrounded them. They protested, 'This is no decent way to fight,' and we destroyed them. Our rivers will destroy your bridges, Professor-Architect, because they're European bridges and they're not prepared to fight Afghan rivers. What we want, Professor-Architect, are tricky Afghan bridges."

'The German replied, "A bridge is a bridge," and Shah Khan shouted, "Not in Afghanistan." The quarrel was taken to the king himself, and he ordered Shah Khan to shut up. The German ambassador explained everything by pointing out that Shah Khan had been educated in France and was thus emotionally unstable.

'So the bridges were built, and the next year there were no spring floods. For eighteen months we enjoyed a wonderful road between Kabul and Kandahar, and Afghanistan was spurting to catch up with the world. In that second winter there was a great snowfall in the mountains followed by an unusually warm spring, which sent towering floods down the gullies, moving boulders as big as houses. When these floods struck the bridges, the German was proved right. His stone pillars stood fast, as he had predicted. The bridges were as strong as he said. But they were so narrow in span that our rivers simply went around them. All the approaches were gouged out and the bridges stood isolated.'

'Why not rebuild the approaches?' I asked.

'We did,' Nur replied. 'Another flood took them out. So we rebuilt again. Another flood. My father calculated that to keep the bridges operating would require a hundred thousand men working around the year. So after the third flood the government said, "Let them go. Who needs bridges?" And the dream road that was to have bound our nation together remained an aching monument to the folly of man.'

'What happened to the professor?' I asked.

'After the first flood he traveled from Kabul to Kandahar, refusing to believe what he saw. "I've built a hundred bridges over some of the greatest rivers in Europe," he shouted. He stood in the middle of one little stream two feet deep and wailed, "How could this little puddle wash out a bridge?" He refused, even then, to see the boulders which that little puddle had moved down from the mountain.'

'Did he leave the country?'

'No, he went back to Kabul and boasted to everyone who would listen that not a single one of his pillars had been destroyed. He made himself what the English call "quite a bore." He insisted upon explaining about the bridges. The German embassy finally called him in, and what they said we never found out, but that night he went to his room and blew his brains out.'

Nur shook his head sadly, still waiting for a truck to appear. 'You can't imagine the tragedy those bridges became. Whenever the government wanted to do some new thing the mullahs and the mountain chiefs would laugh: "Remember the German bridges!" You're an American and you may not like Germans since you fought them twice, but in Afghanistan they were wonderful people. Most of what we have that's good came from the Germans, but after the bridges even they were held in suspicion. Their effectiveness was chopped in half. Those damned bridges!'

He shook his head, then asked, 'By the way, you're meeting a German doctor in Kandahar, aren't you?'

'How did you know?' I asked.

As soon as I uttered the words I could have kicked myself. Perhaps it was the coldness of the river that had made me thoughtless, but the damage was done. Nur stammered, 'Well, I just know.'

It was a rule in Afghan-American relations that neither side would embarrass the other regarding spies like Nur Muhammad on their side and Richardson on ours. It's true that Nur had slipped when he let me know that somehow or other he had found out that one of my missions in Kandahar was to inspect Dr Otto Stiglitz; he should have kept his mouth shut. But once he did betray himself, I should never have challenged him. I had humiliated a good friend and an able spy. I was sorry.

He recovered by saying, 'In a few miles . . . if we ever get out of this river . . . you'll see a bridge that my father and Shah Khan built. You'll laugh at it, but it's stood for more than thirty years.'

A truck finally arrived and shouting men plunged into the river with ropes, which they attached to our front axle. With relative ease they pulled us free, then refused pay. We offered them cigarettes, which gratified them, and with much laughter they assured us that the rivers to the south would give no trouble. 'But in two more weeks. Whooo, whooo! Floods everywhere. Road washed out for six or seven days.'

When we resumed our journey Nur Muhammad said, 'So if I tell you, Miller Sahib, that we have an Afghan way of doing things, and it works, please don't think I'm being obstinate. It's just possible that it does work.'

'On the other hand,' I argued, 'if your country operates on unique solutions which no outsider can possibly understand, and if you use that as an excuse for doing nothing, then Russia will surely move in and make the changes for you.'

'That's the battle we're engaged in, you and I,' Nur agreed. 'May we complete the job before Russia takes over.'

'My government's policy is to help you,' I said.

'But do be reasonable on one thing, Miller Sahib. We'll soon be in Kandahar, and you'll be forming opinions about Nazrullah. Let me assure you, he's on our side. He understands these matters better than either of us. Don't antagonize him at the beginning. If we destroy men like him, Afghanistan is lost.'

'I don't want to destroy him,' I snapped. 'I want to find out where his wife is.'

'So do I,' Nur promised. 'But in the Afghan way.'

I was about to make an acid reply when Nur stopped our jeep at the bridge his father had built across one of the lesser streams, which the Germans had left for later. It was a silly affair that looked like a roller coaster at a run-down amusement park. It was built of wood and showed no evidence of European beauty, but it looked good for a hundred years. I thought: If a German professor-architect designed a bridge like this they'd hang him from the Brandenburger Tor.

'The secret,' Nur pointed out, 'is the big dips in the road before you reach the bridge itself. See how they work?'

'Not exactly,' I replied.

With his forefinger he drew in the dust on the jeep windshield a profile of the bridge, showing a level road which dipped sharply, rose again to cross the bridge, then dipped on the other side. Nur's diagram looked like a scraggly capital W. 'You might call it an Afghan bridge. It says to the river, "I want to cross you, but I know I mustn't pinch you in. So when you want to run wild, go down the dips in the road and leave me alone. The rest of the year I'll leave you alone." Silly, but it works.'

Hesitantly I asked, 'But during the flood you can't use the road?'

'Of course not,' Nur agreed. 'But if you allow the river its way, it closes the road only once or twice a year. Who needs a road all year? Maybe it's better to give it a rest.'

I thought of six good answers to this evasion, but I was constrained from using them by one overriding fact: while crossing rivers which the German had tried to conquer my bottom was wet, but while crossing on the tricky Afghan bridge my bottom was dry, and things had been this way for nearly fifty years. I kept my mouth shut.

We were about to resume our journey when a truck came down the road from Ghazni bearing a strange group of men who were dressed in vivid clothes of many colors and who wore their black hair long in the manner of ancient Greek page boys: thick bangs in front, elsewhere a shoulder-length bob. The faces of the men were aquiline and paler than those of the normal Afghan. All were handsome but there was one young man not yet in his twenties, I judged, who was positively beautiful. At first I wasn't sure he was a man and I must have pointed toward him as the truck crossed the bridge, for in Pashto he screamed a very filthy phrase, which caused his truckmates to cheer his insolence. In acknowledgment he made a pretty gesture like a girl, but he was startled when I shouted back in Pashto a phrase equally obscene. He laughed with gusto, moving his head so that his long hair flashed in the sunlight. Then he pointed at me with a languid, graceful arm and shouted, 'I know what the ferangi wants, but he can't have it.' Once more the men in the truck applauded their special member, and proceeded on their way to Kandahar.

'Who were they?' I asked.

'A dancing team,' Nur replied. 'They tour the country all year.'

'The long hair?'

'Traditional. Judging from their clothes they must be a pretty good team.'

We had completed most of the trip to Kandahar when we overtook a young man in his early twenties, conspicuous because he wore not only the customary baggy pants and long shirt, but also a tattered overcoat made originally for a woman. It must have been a beautiful coat, with long flaring panels and a tight waist, and looked as if it might have come from Paris. Wine-red in color, it still possessed an air of grace.

I asked Nur to stop and we invited the young fellow to join us and his eyes widened with pleasure. He climbed in the back and adjusted his coat carefully over the spare tires on which he had to crouch.

'Ever been in a car before?' I asked in Pashto.

'No. It's exciting.'

'Going to Kandahar?'

'Yes. To the spring festival.'

'Ever been before?'

'No,' he replied with a flashing smile. 'But I've heard of Kandahar. Who hasn't?'

'Where do you live?'

'In the hills. Badakshar.'

'I don't know it,' I said to Nur, who with four or five pinpoint questions developed that it was several hundred miles north.

'Must be a dump,' he said in English.

'Good place?' I asked in Pashto.

'Oh, yes!' the young man replied warmly. 'Last year we had a good crop. In the autumn I sold a horse to the Povindahs as they went south. So I am coming to Kandahar with some money, I can tell you.'

As soon as he said this he realized that his boasting might cost him his life, for he did not know who we were, and travelers were frequently murdered when it was known they had money. No doubt it had sometimes happened near Badakshar, and he looked at us fearfully.

'Shut your mouth, you fool,' Nur snapped. 'This time you're lucky. We're from the government.'

The young man sighed and fell silent, but I asked him, 'Where'd you get your coat?'

He was a congenial fellow who enjoyed talk, so he said quickly, 'It's been in my family for many years. My father wore it to Kabul once. I haven't been to Kabul, but my brother wore it to Herat, which is a large city, he says.'

'Where'd your father get the coat?'

The young man refused to answer and Nur Muhammad asked, 'He killed a man for it, didn't he?' The traveler said nothing and Nur continued. 'A stranger came through the mountains wearing this coat and your father got hungry for it. So he shot him, eh?'

I turned around to look at the young man, across whose face had come a beatific smile. He said, 'You government men know everything, don't you? How to raise sheep. How to pay taxes. What roads to build. But you don't know about this coat, do you?' He chuckled and in sheer pleasure wrapped his arms a little tighter about himself.

'Who killed who?' Nur pressed.

The young man laughed openly and wagged his finger at Nur. 'No, no, Mr Government! That's one thing you're not going to know. And before you ask any more questions stop the car and I'll walk.'

'Take it easy,' Nur said.

'All right,' the young man said gravely. 'But forget about the coat.'

We rode in silence for some miles, then heard a gasp from the rear of the jeep, for our rider had spotted some of the minarets of Kandahar. 'It's the city!' he cried.

At first I saw nothing, but gradually the outlines of Kandahar, much older than Kabul, stood out against the horizon, and as we approached the walls I could not say who was the more excited, the young man with the European coat or the man from the American embassy about to engage in his first diplomatic mission.

We dropped our passenger in the middle of the city, a sprawling, dirty, camel-train metropolis whose mud walls looked as they had in the time of Darius the Persian. Nur found us a place to stay, much better than the hole in Ghazni but without the Persian rugs, and when the jeep was under armed guard I said, 'Since you already know I'm here to see Dr Stiglitz, could you find where he lives?'

'Now?' Nur asked.

'Now,' I repeated, and he soon returned to lead me down a mean, narrow street where from one dirty mud wall projected the sign

DOKTOR

UNIVERSITY OF MUNICH

'Want me to stay with you?' Nur asked.

'No thanks.'

'Kandahar is rougher than Kabul,' Nur warned.

'I can handle myself,' I assured him and entered the doctor's quarters.

The waiting room startled me. It was a small, dirt-floored, misshapen room with one bench and two very old chairs, on which sat men in turbans. One rose to offer me his seat, but I said in Pashto, 'I'll stand,' and the bronzed faces stared at me. Finally one asked, 'Ferangi?' and I replied 'American.' The staring continued.

After some minutes the door leading to the doctor's office opened and a turbaned man departed. The next patient in line moved in to see the doctor and he must have said that there was a ferangi outside, for the door quickly burst open and a man of middle years and middle height rushed out, not to see me but to inspect me.

'Who are you?' he demanded in crisp, accented English. I gave my name and he drew back suspiciously. 'What do you want?'

I tried to say that I'd wait until he was through, but he interrupted, shouting in Pashto, 'These damned Americans come here demanding special privilege. They always do. Well, he must wait in line till all of you are finished . . . all of you.'

In Pashto I said, 'When you're through, Doctor.'

My use of the language did not impress him. He stepped back, eyed me closely and asked cautiously, 'What is it you want?'

'Did you ever treat the American wife of Nazrullah?'

He glared at me, drew a protective shell of some kind about himself, and returned to his office, slamming the crude wooden door. In a flash he was back in the waiting room shouting in Pashto, 'He must wait in line all of you . . . to the very end.' Once more he slammed the door.

By the time the last Afghan had seen the doctor, darkness had fallen and I was left alone in the shadowy waiting room. The wooden door creaked open and Dr Stiglitz said graciously, 'Now perhaps we can talk.'

He did not invite me to his office, but he did leave the door open so that some light from the single unshaded electric bulb entered our room. He was balding, with a blond-gray German crew cut, and he had a pipe. He looked more frightened than bellicose, and his forehead was deeply wrinkled. 'Yes, I treated Madame Nazrullah. Not quite a year ago. Sit down.' He invited me to take one of the rickety chairs while he sat wearily on the other. 'Be careful of the chair,' he warned. 'In Afghanistan wood is so scarce that any chair is a treasure. You can't imagine the trouble I had finding that door. I shouldn't have slammed it so, but visitors make me nervous.' He made a conscious effort to relax and asked with some show of generosity, 'Now what do you wish to know?'

Before I could speak, the door to the street opened and a thin Afghan in his fifties entered, followed by a chaderi. The woman stood obediently near the door while the man bowed and pleaded with the doctor. 'My wife is ill,' the man whispered.

'All right,' Stiglitz growled in what I thought was an offensive manner. 'She's late, but I'll help her.' With no enthusiasm he returned to his office, and I moved my chair aside to let the woman follow, but she was left standing in the outer room and it was the nervous husband who joined the doctor. Stiglitz, seeing my surprise, said, 'You'd better come in here. He wouldn't like you alone with his wife, and what happens may interest you.'

So the American visitor, the German doctor and the Afghan husband consulted in the inner room while the sick woman remained standing by the door of the waiting room. 'Tell her she can sit down,' the doctor began, and the husband went to his wife, who obediently sat on the floor.

While he was gone I had an opportunity to inspect the doctor's office. It was a dirty little mud-floored room with practically no medical equipment and one cupboard containing flyspecked bottles of pills. There was a desk made of packing crates and the swinging, glaring electric light bulb.

The husband returned and Stiglitz asked, 'Now what's wrong?'

'Pains in the stomach, Doctor.'

'Fever?'

'Yes.'

'High?'

'No, medium.'

'Does she vomit?'

'No.'

'Pregnant?'

'The midwife says no.'

'Is her period regular?'

'I don't know.'

'Find out,' Stiglitz ordered, and the husband dutifully returned to the other room, where he sat on the floor to consult with his veiled wife.

While he was gone I asked, 'Don't you examine her?'

'A wife? In chaderi? I'd be shot.'

The husband returned and said his wife's periods had been regular, so the examination proceeded. Six times the husband was ordered to ask his wife intimate questions regarding her health and six times he relayed his understanding of her answers to the doctor. Once, when the man was gone, Stiglitz confided, 'The real evil of this system comes when the husband thinks his wife's symptoms reflect discredit on him. He suppresses the information. And if the apothecary charges too much for the medicine I prescribe he simply doesn't buy it.'

'What happens to the woman?' I asked.

'She dies,' he replied without emotion. 'That is, she dies a little sooner than otherwise.'

The husband now decided that he had told Dr Stiglitz all that was relevant and he waited for the doctor's decision. 'It's an amazing thing,' Stiglitz said in English, 'but after a while you instinctively know what ails the woman and you probably do her as much good as if you'd taken her pulse and temperature.' In Pashto he instructed the husband what medication to buy for his wife and the man laid down a pitiful fee, which the doctor accepted. When the man went to inform his wife he left the door open and I could see him kneel beside her and console and reassure her, with obvious love etched on his face. His wife, who must have been seriously ill under the chaderi, breathed deeply two or three times, then rose and followed her husband out of the office.

'Now about Madame Nazrullah,' Dr Stiglitz began. 'Since you're interested in her you must be from the American embassy.'

'I am.'

'And you've been sent down here to spy on me?'

'No,' I lied.

'You're lying. Right this minute you're thinking, What's a man like Stiglitz doing in a hole like Kandahar? Go ahead and spy on me and I'll spy on you.'

Before I could reply, Stiglitz hopped up, ran to the door leading to the street, and barred it. When this was done he sat on one of the chairs, using it in reversed position so that its unsteady back formed a chin rest. 'Young man,' he said. 'Will you please bring me my pipe?' He was tired and he looked it.

I joined him in the waiting room and studied him as he lit his pipe. His hands were nervous, but I remembered that this was the end of a long day. His close-cropped head was a little larger than normal, and his hard blue eyes looked at all things with a blend of cynicism and challenge. He was inclined toward plumpness and was clearly no self-reliant German superman. I was disposed to like his quick honesty and felt intuitively that he ought to move to Kabul, where the various embassies could provide him with patients well able to pay. As he had foreseen, the major question in my mind as I studied him was, 'What's a man like this doing in a hole like Kandahar?'

'Nazrullah's wife lived in this region for a little more than a year,' he reported grudgingly. 'Why are you interested?'

'She's disappeared.'

'What?' he asked with real surprise.

'Yes. Her parents haven't heard from her in thirteen months.'

He began to laugh, not heartily but in disgust. 'You Americans! My parents haven't heard from me in four years but they don't go running to the German embassy.'

'With an American woman married to an Afghan the problem is somewhat different,' I said sharply.

'Any ferangi who marries an Afghan does so with her eyes alert,' Stiglitz replied impatiently. 'I treated Madame Nazrullah several times.'

'What for?' I asked.

Stiglitz looked at me coldly. 'She was a well-adjusted, likable young woman. Quite happy with her husband and he with her. I've grown to respect Nazrullah as one of the finest Afghans. Say, Herr Miller, are you hungry?'

'I am.'

'You eat pilau and nan?'

'At every chance.'

'Good. I'm starved.' Then, for the first time, I saw him hesitate, as if he were unsure of himself. 'Herr Miller, may I be very rude?'

'You may.'

'I wish that the invitation I just extended could mean what it would in Germany. That I was taking you to dinner. Frankly, Herr Miller . . . You saw the fee they pay here.'

'I'm taking you to dinner,' I assured him.

'No! My own dinner I can afford. But sometimes you ferangi eat like such pigs . . .'

He summoned a watchman, who appeared from a room in the back carrying a rifle and two daggers. Carefully Stiglitz locked the cupboard with its pitiful supply of drugs, then unbarred the door, which the watchman locked behind us as soon as we had left. Stiglitz led me to the public square, which contained an eating place of better than average appearance.

Cautiously he asked, 'Do you like beer?'

'Not particularly.'

'Good,' he sighed with real relief. 'I manage to find a few bottles each month and it makes life bearable. So if you don't mind I'll not offer you one. Why don't you have an orange?'

'I usually drink tea.'

'Better for you,' he laughed uneasily.

When our meal was served, the waiter produced from some well-protected corner a bottle of lukewarm German beer, which Dr Stiglitz attended to personally. With meticulous care he pried away the top, quickly pressing his mouth over the foaming bottle to catch each drop that would otherwise have been wasted. Next he took a long, slow, satisfying draught, closed his eyes, and placed the bottle reverently on the table close to his right hand.

'What would you have said,' I asked, 'if I had liked beer?'

He opened his eyes slowly and winked. 'I'd have said, "How unfortunate. In Kandahar the mullahs allow no alcohol," and right now we'd both be drinking tea. I won't try to explain, Herr Miller, but this is my only contact with Europe. It's so precious . . .'

'Would you have any guess as to why Nazrullah's wife disappeared?'

'I'm not satisfied she has.'

'Any rumours?'

'I give no credence to rumors.'

'That means you've heard some.'

'Herr Miller, I hadn't even heard she was missing.'

'You hadn't?'

'Why should I?' he asked impatiently. 'They left here last July to work at Qala Bist. Haven't seen them since.'

'Was she all right . . . when you knew her?'

'All right?' he asked angrily, licking his fingers. 'Who's all right? Maybe she was planning to murder her husband and have a baby by a camel. Who can you point to in Afghanistan and say, "That one's all right"? She was healthy, she laughed more than she cried, and she was well groomed.'

'How do you know about the crying?'

'I don't. Every time I saw her she was laughing.'

It was obvious that he intended the interrogation to end, but I could not resist one final question. 'Did you know her by her western name?'

Dr Stiglitz threw down the piece of nan he had been using as a fork and sputtered, 'No more! Eat!' He took a long swig of beer.

This relaxed him and he asked philosophically, 'Herr Miller, have you ever speculated as to why it was such a terrible punishment in these lands to cut off the hand of a thief? No? The awful part about it was that they always cut off the right hand. Look around this restaurant and see if that gives you an idea.'

There were perhaps fifteen eating areas in the dusty room and at each men were eating pilau, but I didn't see the connection. Stiglitz pointed out, 'They're all eating with their right hands. See!' He pointed to a rug on which five bearded Afghans were digging freely from a common bowl, and each used his right hand. The left never appeared in motion.

'I don't understand.'

'Only the right hand is allowed in the food bowl,' Stiglitz said ponderously, like a German professor, 'because when a man goes to the toilet he must always wipe himself with his left hand. In lands where there is little water, this is a prudent rule.' He took another drink of beer and reflected, 'It was a terrifying punishment, to cut off a man's right hand. Automatically it banished him from the food bowl.'

I was about to ask the point of this story when I saw two men rigging a string of lights across one corner of the square. 'What goes on over there?' I asked.

'That's for the dance,' he explained. 'Spring festival brings out the dancing boys, the dirty little monsters.'

I described the team I'd seen on the truck and he banged his empty beer bottle. 'That's the kind. They're all alike. Filthy animals.'

'The ones I saw looked fairly clean,' I protested.

'Clean? Yes. Even perfumed. But they're cruel little pederasts . . . sodomites. When they come to town they create a great evil.'

'You astonish me,' I gulped.

'I shouldn't. If you have a society where women are forbidden, men must volunteer for the female functions.'

'I was remarking on that the other day. But not in this context.'

'This is the context that counts,' Stiglitz snapped. 'Our handsome dancing boys are all dirty little whores. How could they otherwise afford the clothes they wear?'

The lights were now in position and a stage was being marked off, about which began to cluster several hundred men in turbans and a few in karakul caps. From an alley which was to serve as dressing room a man in his fifties, whom I recognised from the truck, appeared to make a speech.

'Let's go see the little monsters,' Stiglitz proposed, and we walked slowly across the square to join the crowd. We were in time to hear the speaker assure us that he had brought to Kandahar the finest troupe of dancers in Afghanistan, who had just finished a season in Kabul, where they had danced for the king. Five musicians came on stage, older men who played flutes, drums and a bucket-like fiddle containing at least twenty strings. The music had a standard Oriental, wailing quality, but also a fierce rhythm quite alien to countries like China and Japan. This was the throbbing music of the upland plateaus, a modification of Indian, Mongol and Greek strains. As sound it was attractive; as rhythm it was compelling.

'I've grown fond of the music,' Stiglitz said, 'and these men are good.' They played for some minutes and induced in the crowd a subtle change. Men stopped talking. Bodies began swaying, and a sense of excitement became almost tangible. Then, with a shout, two young men in candy-striped costumes leaped out of the alley and began a whirling dance in which their long hair stood out straight from their heads. They were unlike western dancers, more controlled in their torsos, but more abandoned in the way they used their extremities and their heads.

I whispered to Stiglitz, 'Do you deny they're artists?'

'It's their other skills I object to,' he snapped.

During the first half-hour the star of the troupe did not appear and the interval was filled with flying bodies and wild music. The audience seemed to grow impatient and it was clear they were waiting for the young man who had insùlted me on the bridge, and I too was waiting for him. The master of ceremonies knew this and took advantage of our anticipation by sending his musicians among the crowd to collect donations in their karakul fezzes.

'What do I give?' I asked the doctor.

'As little as possible,' he growled, and I saw him throw in a few small coins, which caused the musician to sneer at him as a ferangi. I contributed a bill and gained a professional, ingratiating smile.

The musicians reassembled and the master announced that we were now to see what we had been waiting for, the premier dancer of Afghanistan. The long thin drums, with goat leather at either end, began throbbing and flutes scurried up and down the register. The music halted and from the alley appeared, in the slowest of rhythmic steps, the young man who made such an impression on me that morning.

He was dressed in a tunic cut from some rare purple fabric threaded with gold. His trousers were gray whipcord that flowed about his legs as he danced, and his turban was of pale blue silk, its free end flying out from his left shoulder. At this stage of the dance his extraordinary hair was held in place by the turban, but at his shoulders it was free to twist and move in the flickering lights. He was a young man of extreme physical beauty, and I was repelled by him for the reason that he knew he was beautiful and intended using this beauty to create confusion.

The tempo of the music increased, but now the audience did not move and the solitary dancer began to shift his body and his feet more deftly. I noticed that he kept lagging behind the beat of the music, as if he were too languid to keep up, and this gave his dance a quality of sexual boredom and lethargy.

Then the musicians began to shout and hammer their drums in planned frenzy, giving the impression that the boy was being driven to dance more rapidly, and as he did so the end of his turban pulled loose and soon expanded into a flash of color and a hypnotic gyration that I had to admit was thrilling. No woman in a steamy hall, loosening her garments one by one ever generated more excitement than this young man did in twirling away his blue turban until his furious black hair was free to whirl out in great circles parallel to the earth. He now intensified his rhythm until he was beating the earth like a drum, his head twisting in ecstasy.

Dr Stiglitz, who refused to acknowledge his spell, growled, 'Probably his last year.'

'He's not twenty!' I protested. 'He could dance thirty more years.'

'You forget. His job isn't dancing. He's here to attract customers for a troupe of nasty little boys. When they grow too old to attract these swine,' he said, indicating the silent, panting watchers, 'they're through, and that sweet little man playing the fiddle finds himself ten more teen-age mountain boys who enjoy sodomy.'

I felt a little sick at this scientific appraisal of what I was seeing, but such thoughts were banished when I looked across the stage to see in the front row the young man from Badakshar, who stood mesmerized, swaying back and forth in his tattered European coat. I tried to attract his attention, but he was enchanted and could not take his eyes from the young dancer, who now entered the final portion of his performance.

Elbowing my way through the crowd to speak with the young mountaineer, I incurred bitter remarks from Afghans who were similarly bewitched by the exciting dancer, but I ignored them and came at last to the youth from Badakshar. 'He's good, eh?' I asked in Pashto.

He did not hear me. He was not aware that anyone had joined him, for he was captivated by the expert who now whirled about the stage in wide circles, his hair flashing in the night, his gold and purple costume rippling like crests and sand in a windswept desert.

I poked the young mountaineer, and he blinked his eyes. Finally he was able to focus on me, as if from a distance, and he muttered weakly, 'Without wings, he flies.' Having uttered this, he returned to his trance and watched as the dancer leaped and gyrated into a furious finale. Now even I had to pay attention, for I did not believe that a human body could move so fast and yet maintain control. The drums exploded and the flutes ran riot. There was a flash of hair and wild eyes and grinning mouth and golden cloth. The dance ended. At my side the young mountaineer gasped and said, 'In Badakshar we saw no dance like that.' I wished him good night, but I fear he heard no words.

7

When I awakened in the morning I saw Nur Muhammad perched on the spare tires, a mirror propped against a knee, a can of hot water at his side, shaving contentedly, for in the hotel at Kandahar there was no bathroom. After admiring his dexterity for some minutes I said in English, 'That dancing boy we met on the bridge put on a terrific performance.'

'The one who cursed you?' Nur asked.

'Stiglitz said they were all sodomites.'

'They are,' Nur said methodically. 'But the police watch them.'

I pondered my next question for some time, then asked, hesitantly, in Pashto, 'Nur, would you tell me what you know about Stiglitz?'

He continued shaving, inspected his chin as if today a good shave were important, then dried his face with ostentatious care. Apparently Nur had anticipated this question before we left Kabul and had consulted with government officials as to how he should answer. Carefully he replied, 'We first heard of Otto Stiglitz in February of last year. That's 1945. Without any warning he crossed the border from Persia. Had no valid papers and was arrested in Herat. Never been to Kabul. He did carry with him papers that claimed a doctor's degree in medicine from some German university.'

'His sign says Munich.'

'I believe it was. When the war ended we directed our ambassador in Paris to investigate the matter and he satisfied himself that Stiglitz was a legitimate doctor. His degree was authentic. As I recall, we received a copy of his university record. It was impressive.

'But it's so difficult to get permission to enter Afghanistan,' I pointed out. Since we were speaking in Pashto I automatically used the standard pronunciation, as if the word contained no *gh* sound at all. To us who worked or lived in the country, it was Afanistan. 'How could an ordinary man like Stiglitz just walk in?'

'You forget,' Nur pointed out. 'He wasn't an ordinary man. He was a doctor, and we need doctors. He was also a German, and we've always needed Germans. Forgetting the unhappy experience with the bridges, our nation has been built by Germans. We're sometimes called "The Germany of Asia," and we're not going to turn away German refugees now.'

'You believe he was a Nazi?'

'Weren't they all . . . legally?' Nur asked quietly, as he began to pack away his shaving gear and offer me the hot water.

'That's all you know?' I pressed.

'Obviously, he came to Kandahar and opened shop as a doctor. Local people advise us he's very good. At any rate, we're glad to have him and I suppose he'll stay here for many years.'

'Why do you say that?'

'For most Germans, Afghanistan is the end of their road. From here there are few places they can go.'

'Not even back to Germany?'

'There least of all.'

'How many German nationals have you in the country?' I asked, with a kind of morbid fascination, for although I was no professional German-hater I did have to acknowledge that had I been a citizen of that country in 1937 I would now be dead. And my relatives and many of my friends would also be dead. And since I'm a man who has always found joy in my association with relatives and friends, the thought of their being mutilated and starved and dead was not only morally repulsive. It scared the very devil out of me. Instinctively I feared Germans and always will.

I don't think this sprang from an unhealthy preoccupation with death. From early childhood I had been prepared by my parents to face the fact that people died, and I knew that one day I would; but Jews have a love of continuity–which accounted in part for the delight I took in the history of Afghanistan–and prior to World War II, whenever I thought of myself as dead, I thought of future Millers continuing. 'There'll always be some Miller who has tickets to Symphony Hall,' I assured myself, and if I weren't among them my absence would be regrettable but not tragic; but if Millers and Goldbergs and Sharps and Weinsteins were not there–if all were gone–it would be unbearable. Had my family not emigrated from Germany we would now all be dead, and I could not ignore that fact.

These personal reflections kept me from hearing all of Nur's reply, but I did catch the figure of more than six hundred Germans reaching Afghanistan, some with exalted credentials.

'All Nazis?'

'That's a matter of definition. Many were decent men and women who hated Hitler and who had scars on their backs and minds to prove it. I talked about this with Moheb Khan . . .' Again I lost what he was saying, for his phrase 'I talked about this with Moheb Khan' didn't jibe with my experience of the two men. Whenever I had been with Moheb in the presence of Nur, the former had treated Nur like a servant. Apparently there was much I didn't comprehend about Afghan espionage and I supposed that some day I would find that Nur was Moheb Khan's younger brother or nephew to the king.

'If Stiglitz is so good, why doesn't he come to Kabul?'

'An understanding we have with all refugees. They've got to settle in different parts of the country. Where they're needed. If he proves himself in Kandahar, he could be invited to Kabul.'

'Then he's not free to move around?'

'You aren't free to move around,' he pointed out. 'You had to get permission from Shah Khan.'

'I'm an outsider.'

'So's Stiglitz. Until he proves himself.'

'Is he doing so?'

'Yes.' Obviously, Nur wished to say no more on this subject.

But I asked, 'What's the average Afghan pay for a visit to a doctor?'

'Possibly eight cents.'

'So the refugees don't get rich?'

'Not in Kandahar.' Again he ended the conversation, then added with cool calculation, 'But if later on he could move to Kabul, then perhaps he'd be able to serve the diplomatic community. Perhaps even officially. And for that he'd receive good pay.'

'Do you suppose Dr Stiglitz would consider coming to Kabul?'

Nur looked straight at me as he filled my shaving mug with hot water. 'I should imagine that he dreams of nothing else.'

'Could you give me an opinion as to how long his apprenticeship in Kandahar will be?'

'That will be decided by our government . . . and yours, if you should be thinking of employing Stiglitz as embassy doctor.' I made no comment.

I was amused when Stiglitz and Nur met at lunch that day. The German was much more careful with Nur than he had been with me, for he quickly guessed that Nur might be an official with some power in Kabul. 'It's a pleasure to meet Your Excellency,' Stiglitz said ingratiatingly.

'I'm not an excellency, sad to confess,' Nur parried. 'I'm Miller Sahib's driver.'

Stiglitz looked carefully at Nur's western shoes, western suit and expensive karakul cap and decided not to fall into that trap. 'I must congratulate Herr Miller on having one of the finest drivers in Afghanistan. I wish I spoke English as well as you, Nur Sahib.'

'I wish I were a doctor with a fine degree from Munich,' Nur replied, and the pudgy German radiated gratification.

In succeeding days I saw a good deal of Stiglitz, and the more I saw the more assured I became that the embassies would be getting a good doctor if they got him, and I decided to help engineer his promotion to Kabul. We often ate together, he jealously guarding his bottle of beer, I asking questions by the score, and he was willing to permit this because I paid for the meals.

My questioning assured me of one thing: Stiglitz was no Nazi. He had a humanitarian attitude toward medicine and an understanding of what it could do to alleviate mental as well as physical suffering. He was hungry for philosophical discussion and each night dined with me on nan and pilau, then accompanied me to see the dances, after which we talked till midnight as he smoked his pipe.

One memory of Stiglitz persists when I recall those exciting days in Kandahar: his outspoken disgust over the dancing troupe and the lead dancer in particular. 'They're a blot on Afghanistan,' he railed, pronouncing the name of his new land like a native. 'They represent a deep malaise. By God, they ought to get the women out of chaderi and put this country on a normal psychological basis.'

One day at lunch we were discussing this with Nur and he laughed tolerantly. 'Every ferangi who comes here has some one thing that ought to be done right away. Dr Stiglitz says, "Get the women out of chaderi." The French ambassador says, "Educate two thousand more medical men." The American ambassador tells us, "Pipe water into the city from the hills." And the Russians say, "Pave your streets." Do you know really what we must do first?'

'What?' Stiglitz asked eagerly. This was the kind of conversation he liked.

'All of them,' Nur replied. 'Yes! Laugh! But we've got to move the entire nation ahead on all possible fronts. And that requires more brains and more courage than we have available. Pray for us when you go to sleep.'

'I've been praying that you'd take me to the house where Nazrullah lives when he's in Kandahar,' I said.

'I completed arrangements yesterday.' Nur bowed. 'Will you join us, Doctor?'

'I would be honored,' he said formally. He was about to dig into his pocket for some change when a pleasant thought struck him. 'Is the ferangi paying for this lunch?'

'I am,' I said. No refugees worried so constantly about money as the Germans. He sighed with relief when I produced the money, and I noticed that just before the bill was totaled he grabbed an extra piece of nan, which he munched as we hiked through the streets.

Nur led us to the typical walled house, where the inevitable gate watcher inspected us grudgingly, then allowed us to pass. The establishment contained no unusual feature: it had a garden, some fruit trees, mud walls, some Persian rugs, and a male servant. There was a big colored photograph of the king and on the table three very old copies of *Time*. The furniture was upholstered in a bilious pink mohair.

Then something quite different happened. From one of the doors appeared an apparently young woman in a pale blue silk chaderi. Dr Stiglitz showed amazement when he saw the shroud worn indoors, as did Nur Muhammad, who introduced me as the gentleman from the American embassy. In Pashto the shrouded figure said, 'I am proud to welcome you to Nazrullah's house.' Then she whispered to Nur, who nodded assent, and she called for a male servant, who appeared with two children, a girl four years old and a boy only a few months old.

'Nazrullah's children,' Nur said approvingly. 'The oldest is the age of my youngest.'

'How many children have you?' I asked Nur.

'Three,' he replied.

'Is your wife Afghan?'

'It's none of your business,' Dr Stiglitz snapped.

'She's from the north,' Nur said obligingly.

It was obvious that we were speaking among ourselves because the presence of the woman in chaderi embarrassed us. Normally any Afghan man advanced enough to bring a ferangi into his home for presentation to his wife would tell her, 'You can remove the chaderi, dear.' And Mrs Nazrullah must have wanted to do so. But she was restrained by the fact that Nur Muhammad was an official of the government and might be a man committed to retaining the chaderi. To protect her husband, she had to remain covered.

Nur, on the other hand, was known to be positively as an enlightened Afghan who wanted to see the chaderi go, and he was certainly inclined personally to say to Mrs Nazrullah, 'With us you can drop the chaderi,' but he was afraid that someone might report his action to Kabul, and he was not sufficiently well placed in government to establish his own rules.

So two people who knew the chaderi was doomed were thus locked into positions where pragmatically they defended it. I broke the impasse by asking, in English, for I had no idea how a man addressed a woman whom he couldn't see, 'Why didn't Mrs Nazrullah accompany her husband to Qala Bist?'

'Ask her,' Nur said, so I restated my question in Pashto.

'There were no quarters for us,' she replied softly. It was a curious sensation, hearing words issuing from a shroud.

'I understand,' I said, but at the same time I remarked to myself: Ellen Jaspar found quarters.

'Do be seated, gentlemen,' she said as the servant appeared with four glasses of orange drink. I wondered: How's she going to drink with a chaderi on?

'We'll be seeing your husband soon,' I said. 'Can we take him anything?'

'You're very thoughtful,' she replied in what I detected as embarrassment. Then she laughed charmingly, and I saw by the wall a box of things already waiting for us to take to Qala Bist.

'Nur's been here before me,' I said with what gallantry I could command.

'Yes,' she said easily. 'He arranged it yesterday, but I'm pleased you have the same idea. I wouldn't want Nur to exceed his prerogatives.' Her use of words was so precise that I had to readjust my concept of the Nazrullah triangle. His Afghan wife was no barefoot desert girl hurriedly acquired to have babies which would extend the family line.

'Can you speak other than Pashto?' I inquired.

'French.' Then slowly, and with pride, she added, 'And a little English.'

'Wisely so,' Stiglitz grunted. 'Some day she'll be an ambassador's wife.'

Mrs Nazrullah didn't hear this and Nur repeated the compliment in Pashto. The veiled figure laughed, then turned to the doctor and asked, 'Do you speak French?'

'Yes,' Stiglitz replied.

'Do you, Miller Sahib?'

'Yes, madame,' I nodded.

'Then why don't we all use that language?' she asked in good French. I looked at Nur, and Madame Nazrullah assured me, 'Oh, Nur speaks better French than I.'

I must have looked startled, for Nur explained, 'Where do you suppose I worked before I worked with you? French embassy.' I thought: When the Afghans get hold of a good man they see he gets a practical education.

Dr Stiglitz remarked, 'You come back in three years, Herr Miller. Your man Nur will be speaking Russian.'

'Well,' Madame Nazrullah said with that handsfolded, businesslike way women can adopt, 'I've been told why you're here, Miller Sahib, and I wish I could help you. But I haven't any idea where my husband's other wife has gone.'

'Isn't she with him?' I asked.

'I think not,' she said.

'And she's not here?'

Madame Nazrullah laughed pleasantly. 'No, we haven't had any ferangi wives walled up here in Kandahar for weeks and weeks.'

'Forgive me,' I said.

'But I suppose if you went back a few years, you might find an example or two. So your suspicions are excusable.'

'Thank you.'

'I do want to assure you of one thing, and please believe me as a friend who would do neither you nor Ellen harm. She never fought with me. I never humiliated her. During the short time we shared a house in Kabul we behaved like sisters. She used to sing to my daughter.'

'Had she been warned–a second wife, I mean?'

'Of course!' the shrouded figure laughed. 'On the day we met she kissed me and said, "You're Karima. Nazrullah told me all about you."'

'I can't believe it,' I said flatly. 'No American girl . . .'

Nur interrupted. 'Don't speak like that, Miller Sahib. Is what Karima says any more difficult to believe than other things we already know to be true?'

'No. I apologize.'

'I know how difficult it must be to understand my country,' Madame Nazrullah said softly. 'But in your report cling to this fact, Miller Sahib. In Nazrullah's home Ellen was treated with love and respect. She treated us in the same manner.'

'Does that include Nazrullah's mother . . . and sisters?'

'For two hours each afternoon Ellen took lessons in Pashto from Nazrullah's mother. She was an adorable girl and our family loved her . . . all of us.' She rose, bowed graciously and started to leave. Her orange drink remained untouched.

'One more question, please,' I pleaded. 'Have you any guess, no matter how bizarre . . .'

'As to what happened? No. But I will assure you of this. Whatever Ellen did was an act of intelligence. She willed it to occur just as it did occur, for she was in possession of all her faculties and they were extraordinary. She was a brilliant, wonderful person, and if evil has come to her I am bereft, because there is one other thing you must know.' She hesitated and I believe she was crying, for she put her right hand to her mouth, or so I judged, for the chaderi masked her motions. 'When Nazrullah brought her to Kandahar and left me behind in Kabul, it was Ellen who insisted that I rejoin them. When I arrived she met me and said, "I was so homesick for the little girl." Between us, Miller Sahib, there was only love.'

She left the room, then reconsidered and said from the door, 'Possibly she asked me to come to Kandahar because she knew I could have children and apparently she couldn't. Dr Stiglitz will confirm that.'

The lady in the shroud, whatever her complexion or beauty, bowed and we saw her no more. When she had gone I said, 'I expected a barefoot nomad from the Hindu Kush.'

'Her sister went to school in Bordeaux,' Nur observed.

I turned to Stiglitz and said, 'About the matter of having children . . .'

In disgust Stiglitz barked something in German which I did not understand. He turned to leave the house, then snapped in Pashto, 'Such matters are no concern of an embassy.' Abruptly he left us and stalked off, and I could see that he must have fled Germany for good reason. He was an honest, hard, opinionated man and for him life under the Nazis must have been hell.

Slyly Nur observed, 'His way of confirming what Karima said.'

'Think so?'

'Include it in your report,' Nur advised. 'You won't be far wrong.'

That evening Nur and I missed Dr Stiglitz at dinner, but after our nan and pilau we wandered across the square to watch the dancers and I told Nur, 'You could take this troupe to New York right now and they'd be a sensation.'

'Is that true?' he asked skeptically.

'Of course. That lead dancer could fit into any ensemble I ever saw. Do you realize how good he is?'

'Look!' Nur chuckled during one of the intermissions. 'Overcoat Sahib.' And there was the young man from Badakshar, still stupefied by the dancer who 'without wings, he flies.'

My comment about the troupe saddened Nur, in a way I could not have predicted. 'In many things we have great talent in Afghanistan. I've heard old men in the hills who could tell long stories better than most of the European novels I read. You say the dancers are good. Do you realize how miserable it is to grow up in a country where there's no outlet for talent?' I felt it best not to comment on this, but Nur asked, 'Is it true that in Russia they take dancing teams like this and sometimes give them medals and even send them to Paris?'

'Of course,' I replied. 'All countries do. In the middle of the war I was in China, where they fought the Japanese all day and went to Chinese opera at night. The Chinese were no better dancers than these men.'

'Is that true?' Nur mused. Again, the idea depressed him.

But next morning we received another view of the dancing team, for while I was seated on the spare tires, shaving, I heard my name called in the courtyard. One of the armed guards who had been sleeping in our jeep was announcing that a visitor had come to see me, so I wrapped a towel around my neck and went to the slit window. The visitor was Dr Stiglitz.

'Let him in!' I called in Pashto.

In a moment the German doctor joined us. 'Want to see something unique? Probably nowhere else in the world to see it.'

'What's up?'

'Didn't you hear the commotion . . . about four this morning?'

'Yes,' Nur replied. 'Fighting in the streets. I put it down as a brawl.'

'You were half right,' Stiglitz said. 'It started as a brawl.'

'What about?' Nur asked.

'The usual. Men got to fighting over the dancing boys. Particularly the one Herr Miller admired.'

'The one I said could succeed in New York,' I reminded Nur.

'He succeeded last night,' Stiglitz said wryly. 'Two men were fighting over him. It ended in murder.'

Nur Muhammad swore in Pashto. 'Another of those?'

'Yes,' Stiglitz replied in Pashto. 'I warned our American friend that this boy was evil . . . evil. You never understood, did you, Herr Miller?'

'I didn't anticipate murder,' I admitted in Pashto, and for the remainder of the terrifying incident in which we were to participate we continued to speak that language.

Nur Muhammad must have guessed what we were about to witness, but I didn't, for nothing in my reading about Afghanistan, nor even the grisly events in Ghazni, had prepared me for the public square in Kandahar that lovely spring morning. Dr Stiglitz, having witnessed such an event in Herat, knew what was afoot, and on our short walk to the square asked us to stop by his office, where the armed guard admitted us to a doubly locked trunk from which Stiglitz produced a Leica camera. Testing it by snapping Nur and me in his consulting room, he slung the camera over his shoulder and put on a karakul cap. Then he led us to the square.

Where the dancers had performed the night before, a large group of men had gathered, but now the string of lights was gone and the bare earth glistened rock-like in the sun. To one side stood an elderly man, the focus of all attention. He seemed not to be a distinguished citizen, for his sandals and shirt were tattered and his vest was nearly in shreds, but he commanded attention if only because of the noble manner in which he bore himself. He was surrounded by the mob, yet not part of it, and all who came close to him offered deference, which he accepted as hereditary right. He was obviously one of the causes why the mob had gathered.

When the sun was well up, there was a beating of drums, not intended as the passionate accompaniment to dancing, for they were somber and of a different timbre, intended to announce the arrival of eight uniformed policemen, grim and forbidding in appearance. In pairs they marched to compass points previously marked by piles of pebbles, and then I saw that each pair had a mallet and a short stake, which was driven into the ground, leaving about eight inches showing.

The drums throbbed again, and from the alley that had been used as a dressing room appeared two mullahs, small, roundish men with clean-shaven faces, quite unlike the gaunt beak-nosed mullahs of the hills. They signaled the drums to cease, whereupon they prayed, first one, then the other. I did not catch all their words, but they seemed to be cleansing the minds of those who were about to participate in a time-honored rite. They also prayed that each of us, seeing this thing, would henceforth respect the commands of God and the precepts of His chosen Prophet. When their prayers ended, the drums beat again and a shackled man, obviously a prisoner, was led forth.

'It's the young man with the coat!' I cried.

Nur said, 'From Badakshar!' Then he cautioned me to remain silent, while Dr Stiglitz busied himself taking photographs of the procession.

The young man from the hills was in a daze. I doubt that he understood what was happening or had happened. He had come to Kandahar with a year's savings and had been engulfed in a whirlpool beyond his comprehension. The guards moved him about as if he were merely an animal.

'Is he the murderer?' I whispered to Nur.

A man to the left explained, 'Last night, when the dancing ended, the prisoner tried to buy the dancing boy. But a policeman had already spoken for him. The mountain boy refused to understand that the dancer could not be his. In a blind fury he killed the policeman. Everyone saw him do it. There's no question of guilt. Only of punishment.'

'What's the punishment to be?' I asked.

'I wish you weren't going to see it,' Nur replied.

'Are you staying?'

'What happens . . . I must report,' he said with resignation.

The two mullahs went to the bedazed mountain man and said, 'You have committed murder.' The prisoner was unable to acknowledge the charge. I didn't know what to expect next.

The mullahs moved to a man whom I had not seen before, a fat fellow with a karakul cap, and asked, 'Does the government wish to assume control of this case?'

The fat official replied, 'This is a crime of passion. The government is not concerned in any way with this case.' He nodded to the mullahs and departed.

Next the mullahs moved to the elderly man in the badly torn vest and announced, 'Gul Majid, this prisoner has murdered your son. By the law of the Prophet, he is handed to you for punishment. Do you, Gul Majid, accept this responsibility?'

The old man stepped forward with great dignity, raised his eyes so that they stared directly at the young man, and announced in a clear voice, 'I accept the prisoner.'

The mullahs said a final prayer, beseeching justice and mercy, and we saw them no more.

The men who had been guarding the prisoner shoved him forward until he was almost touching the old man, and it was now a matter solely between the young murderer and the elderly father of the murdered man, a morality play conceived by desert people thousands of years ago and honored by them through countless generations. State and church alike had withdrawn. It was the guilty and the bereaved, standing face to face, and the crowd, which formed a significant part in this re-enactment of the passion play, remained tense and silent until the old man cried in a loud voice, 'Let the prisoner be tied!'

At this the crowd broke into a shout of wild approval, and I heard Nur whispering in Pashto, 'I wish to God that just once there could be mercy.' On this day there was to be vengeance, not mercy.

The young murderer was whisked to the stakes, stretched upon the ground face-up and lashed by ankles and wrists until he was spread-eagled in the manner of St Andrew at his crucifixion. No further attempt was made to keep this a religious ceremony; we were about to participate in retribution, sure and implacable.

When the young man was securely tied, the guards who had done the job stepped away, to be replaced by a cordon of police, brother officers to the murdered man. They stood at intervals about the prisoner, close enough together to prevent a riot but far enough apart to provide everyone with a clear view. The crowd grew silent and men elbowed their way forward to find good spots from which to view the spectacle.

The father of the dead policeman now stepped forward and stood at the feet of the staked-out prisoner. He mumbled a short prayer, then shouted boldly, 'Give me the scimitar.' I'm not sure you would translate his word as *scimitar*, but at least it wasn't the word for *sword*, and from his band of associates a man stepped forward with a rusty old nineteenth-century bayonet. In a clear voice the old man shouted, 'My grandfather captured this from the British at the siege of Kandahar.' The crowd cheered.

I looked down at the young man, who appeared not to comprehend what was happening, for his eyes were glassy and remained in the trance that he had entered at the time of the murder, when he was battling for the favors of the dancing boy. But when the old man's address to the public ended and he knelt beside the young man's head, the prisoner at last saw the rusty bayonet and began to scream.

It was a horrifying, animal scream that came from far back in the history of human development. It was, I thought, exactly the right kind of scream for such a scene, for it put us all solidly in the animal category. 'No! No!' screamed the staked-out young man, but we had passed the time for words.

The old man steadied himself, twisted his left hand in the victim's hair, and pulled his neck taut. With the rusty bayonet in his right hand he began sawing at the prisoner's throat, and with each awful passage of the bayonet, the boy's head twisted back and forth, while terrible screams emanated from the throat which had not yet been severed. I thought I would vomit.

Then, by the grace of God, a figure hurried out from the crowd and intervened with the old man. The insanity stopped. I breathed again.

The intruder was Dr Stiglitz, and he argued with the old man in Pashto, but the impassioned executioner failed to comprehend and looked at the German in bewilderment. Then I saw Stiglitz point to the camera and say in a clear voice which I and the others could hear, 'If you work from the other side, the light will be better.'

The old man shrugged his shoulders and Stiglitz asked harshly, 'You want your picture taken, don't you?' At last the executioner understood, and I watched aghast as he switched his position and started cutting from the other side. The sun was unobstructed.

With four powerful drags of the bayonet the old man slashed the victim's throat and silenced the horrible cries. Then he continued bearing down until the cartilage and bone were severed, whereupon with some awkwardness and fatigue from his exertion he rose, keeping his left hand twisted in the victim's hair, and marched triumphantly about the circle, showing each of us the death's head.

When the old man came to me, I had to look away and found myself looking directly at the sodomite dancer whose alluring performance had launched the tragedy. His face was enraptured as he followed the passage of the severed head. His clothes were as neat as ever and he smelled of perfume. When he caught me staring at him with loathing he flashed his most ingratiating smile and whispered in Pashto, 'It was horrible, wasn't it?'

'Herr Miller!' I heard a voice calling. Dr Stiglitz had seen the sybaritic dancer standing beside me and had come for a picture of us. He worked on the focus for a moment, while the dancer, accustomed to having his picture taken, assumed a dramatic pose and I looked astounded in my karakul cap. I still have the picture, and it serves to remind me that what I have described did happen.

Nur and I walked silently across the square to the restaurant, but I was too shocked to want food. Before long the doctor joined us and said, as if nothing had happened, 'I'll have a bottle of beer. Nur can't join me because he's Muslim and you don't like beer.' When another of the precious bottles was produced, Stiglitz observed, 'I'll have two good reasons to get to Kabul eventually. You don't have these public executions up there, but you do have German beer.'

'If the execution appalled you,' I asked weakly, 'why did you photograph it so carefully?'

'I believe we should have a record,' he replied. 'All historical processes should be recorded. In a few years what you saw today will vanish. Nur Muhammad will see to that.'

'But when you stopped the old man . . . Surely, you could have prevailed upon him.'

'Me?' Stiglitz cried. 'They'd have killed me.'

'They would have,' Nur agreed.

'But to ask him to switch sides. God, it's ghoulish.'

'I altered nothing,' he replied, carefully prying the cap off his bottle of beer.

I was choked with moral rage, and then I began laughing. Deep, gusty, cackling laughter overtook me, and although both Nur and Stiglitz tried to stop me, they couldn't, for I was pointing across the restaurant to the public square, where the old man who had conducted the execution was marching home. In his right hand he held the historic bayonet which had avenged family dishonor, while in his left he held the hand of the sodomite dancer, who walked along bowing to the approval of the crowd. It was not this incongruous mating which had caused me to burst into uncontrolled laughter. At the scene of the execution the old man had discarded his sorely tattered vest and he was now wearing the dead man's overcoat, that beautiful, torn and ravaged but still serviceable woman's coat from Paris. It fitted his spare body well, and he actually looked dapper in his new garment.

'Wait!' I called as he passed, and the old man stopped. 'Doctor!' I shouted. 'Get a picture of this, too,' and I struck a pose between the unlikely pair.

When I rejoined my table Nur Muhammad was so angry that he cast aside his role of polite government aide. 'Why did you do that?' he demanded bitterly.

'It was so goddamned ridiculous,' I said, suddenly ashamed of myself.

'You're using Mr Jaspar's word,' Nur said acidly.

'What's that? Who?' Stiglitz asked, carefully putting away his camera.

'A friend of Miller Sahib's. Every time he confronts something he doesn't understand he calls it ridiculous.'

'I'm sorry,' I said.

'Some years ago a Frenchman took a series of excellent photographs . . . in Alabama . . . of a lynching. Was that ridiculous?'

'I was laughing because my nerves were shot,' I explained lamely.

'Good. I think that now you may be ready to discuss your problem seriously.'

'What do you mean by that?' I asked angrily.

'You've seen the terror of my nation. Now let's talk about Ellen Jaspar.'

'I'm willing,' I said in some bewilderment.

'Let's have no more diversions. No more amusing yourself with old men in public.'

'I apologized,' I snapped.

'Good,' Nur said grudgingly. 'When you ridiculed the old fool and the evil young man I thought . . .'

'I think it was the coat . . . It rounded out the story.'

'I've forgotten the incident,' Nur said. 'Don't you remember it as the way we live in Afghanistan.'

'We can talk frankly, then?' I asked.

'You always could, with me,' Nur replied.

'The other day when I spoke with Shah Khan he confided that he had heard rumors that something extremely bizarre had happened to Ellen Jaspar . . . so bizarre, in fact, that he wouldn't even repeat the rumor.'

'What rumor?' Dr Stiglitz interrupted.

'The one I asked you about the first night.'

'I told you. I have no speculation,' he growled, returning to his beer.

'Have you?' I asked Nur.

'As I told you before, she's run away and perished.'

'You're honestly convinced that she didn't die at the hands of fanatical mullahs?'

Nur was plainly irritated. 'Miller Sahib,' he protested, 'you asked me that last week in Ghazni, and I swore it could not have happened. Don't you take my word for anything?'

'What we just saw,' I said quietly, pointing toward the headless corpse which would lie on the ground till sundown, 'permits a man to check answers, doesn't it?'

'Not when the answers have already been verified,' Nur replied.

'But the mullahs?' I repeated.

Nur laughed pleasantly. 'Those two mullahs happen to be among the finest men in our priesthood. They were acting in strict accordance with Afghan custom, but they know public executions like this can't continue indefinitely. And when it comes time for men like you and me to end them, they'll be on our side.'

'They will?' I asked incredulously.

'Of course. I've a brother who's a mullah and a lot better citizen than I am.'

'I'd like to meet him,' I said brusquely.

'When we get back to Kabul, you will. Miller, you miss the secret of Afghanistan if you think that Islam is a religion which condones what you've just seen.'

'It's a damned fine religion,' Dr Stiglitz interrupted in Pashto, where the oath was more colorful. 'Matter of fact, I became a Muslim last year.'

'You did?' I asked in undisguised surprise.

'Why not? This is my home from now on. It's an exciting country with a profound religion.'

'You've surrendered Christianity?' I asked with an abhorrence which I didn't try to mask.

'I repeat,' he began in Pashto. Then for some inexplicable reason he started speaking French. 'I repeat,' he said in French, 'why not?' A religion is not something eternal. It's got to function in a given time and a given place. If it doesn't function, it's no good and you'd better get another. Have you ever considered how your Christianity functioned in Germany? The total perversion of society it permitted? The mass executions? The horrible betrayal of humanity? I swore when I reached Herat, "If Christianity can't do any better than it did in Munich, I'll take whatever religion they use here. It can't be worse." Actually, it works out rather well.'

Nur added something that astounded me. 'I suppose you know that Ellen Jaspar also became a Muslim?'

Before I could speak, Dr Stiglitz said, 'Sensible girl. We talked about it the last time I saw her. She said she found great solace in her new faith. Called it "a desert faith." When I asked her what she meant by that, she said that Christianity had become a convenient ritual for those who overeat on Saturday, commit adultery on Saturday night, and play golf on Sunday.' Ellen's description, when delivered in French, sounded witty, ugly and profound. 'She said she needed a religion much closer to original sources. One thing she said impressed me. She pointed out that Islam, Christianity and Judaism all started in the desert, where God seems closer, and life and death are more mysterious. She said that we are all essentially desert animals and that life is meant to be harsh. When we live in an oasis like Philadelphia or Munich we become degenerate and lose touch with our origins.'

'Would you return to Munich . . . if you were free to do so?' I asked.

Dr Stiglitz looked at me with contempt. Nothing he had so far said implied that he was barred from returning to Germany, but his self-committal to a new world permitted only one conclusion, and I had publicly stated it. He was angry with me for having done so and replied in German, 'No, I would never return to Germany.' Then he translated into Pashto.

At this point the pilau was served, a rich, steaming dish with extra pine nuts and raisins, and although immediately after the beheading I had been repelled by the thought of food, with the passage of time I had grown hungry, and we three dug into it with our fingers, achieving a kind of hard brotherhood as we did. Dr Stiglitz was then forty, Nur Muhammad was thirty-two and I twenty-six, but because each of us had a certain integrity which he was willing to protect, we were growing to respect one another, and I was happy to be with them. Indeed, I was proud to be with them, eating in communion after a ritual execution.

'You must not think of Islam as a religion of the desert,' Nur warned. 'It has much vitality and the world has not yet heard the last of it.'

I was driven to ask an impertinent question. 'If a new state of Israel is fashioned out of the desert, will you Muslims be able to accept it?'

'You can trust the Jews to look after themselves,' Stiglitz said bluntly, and the brotherhood that had been burgeoning collapsed. I was shocked that a German refugee would make such a statement publicly, but what followed shocked me even more: 'And if they should need help, men like you and me would help them. They deserve a country of their own.' He returned to his beer.

'The Muslims won't like it,' Nur reflected, 'particularly the Arabs. I won't like it. I don't want Jews taking part of my homeland. But the alternatives I like even less. We Muslims will give the Jews a little . . . not much, but a little.'

After a while I remarked, 'We have no proof at the embassy that Ellen Jaspar became a Muslim.'

'Many ferangi wives do,' Nur replied. 'We see no reason for official comment one way or the other.'

'They do?' I asked.

'Of course. You Christians always think that conversion goes one way. Right here you see proof to the contrary. Dr Stiglitz from Germany and Ellen Jaspar from Philadelphia.'

I began to laugh again, this time non-hysterically. 'What about that beer?' I asked, pointing at the half-empty bottle.

'A German can be many things,' Stiglitz explained robustly. 'A Catholic, a Jew, a Lutheran, a Muslim. But always he's a beer drinker. I have a dispensation from the mullah . . . the one you saw today. He's an understanding liberal.'

8

Two substantial rivers ran through the part of Afghanistan in which I was traveling, the Helmand, which started in the Koh-i-Baba west of Kabul, and the Arghandab, which flowed down past Kandahar. It was at Qala Bist that they met to combine forces for a dash across the desert, and it was at this confluence, in the most ancient times, that a powerful civilization developed. From the way Shah Khan had described it, I would have wanted to see Qala Bist even had I not known that Nazrullah was working there and that Ellen Jaspar had vanished from that point.

The ruins lay only seventy miles west of Kandahar, but since many of those miles were across open desert, Nur Muhammad had our jeep packed before dawn and we drove out of Kandahar with the first rays of sun. We must have made an impressive one-jeep caravan, for we had now discarded western clothes and were dressed like desert Afghans, except that we kept our karakul caps. I was impressed by the road west, for it led through fruit groves and well-established farms, each protected by high mud walls with box-like structures at the corners.

'What are the boxes for?' I asked.

Nur laughed and said, 'Those are melon fields.'

'I still don't get the boxes.'

'They're for the lookouts,' he explained. 'Growing melons in Afghanistan is extremely difficult. During the entire month they're ripening the farmer has to station armed men at each field to shoot thieves.'

I must have looked as if I thought he was teasing, for he added gravely, 'My father raised melons, and at the age of nine I stood night watch with a shotgun. Otherwise every melon would have been stolen.'

'Why do you permit such thievery?' I asked.

'We're a brigand society,' Nur said. 'Our king doesn't rule in Kabul the way your president rules in Washington. In this country we murder kings.'

We had now reached the village of Girishk, where we were to leave the pleasant melon patches and turn south across the desert. For me this was a rare moment, for we were about to enter upon the great world-desert that sweeps from Central India across Arabia, through Egypt, over the Sahara and on to Morocco, where it is finally halted by the Atlantic Ocean. I had not previously seen this enormous desert, and now as the early sun showed me the windswept land and the burning rocks I knew I was entering a new world. This was the universe of shifting sand, the mournful camel chewing sideways, the men in dirty white. I remember with great clarity my first impression of this vast desert and my astonishment at its enormous vistas.

The segment which we had struck was in some ways an ideal introduction, for it was both smaller than the better-known deserts of Arabia, Egypt and Libya–less than two hundred miles on a side–and more savage. It had no oasis, no vegetation and no protective rocks. It was a bleak, barren waste across which the wind howled perpetually, and to be lost on it meant death, a fact which was amply proved each year, and it was from this remorseless character that the Afghan desert had obtained its lurid name, which I hesitate to repeat, since it sounds so exhibitionistic: The Dasht-i-Margo, the Desert of Death.

We had traversed the dangerous wastes for about two hours when we saw ahead a sight that I knew was coming but which nevertheless startled me. Rising from the desert, along the shores of the Helmand River, stood the arch of Qala Bist, an enormous clay-brick structure rising high in the air. A thousand years ago it had formed part of some Muslim edifice, but even the memory of the mosque was lost. Yet there the arch stood, so tall it seemed impossible that a desert people had built it. It was the more surprising because it was an unsupported arch, a lofty, soaring flight of brick composed in beautiful proportions, and when we stopped the car to admire it I told Nur, 'You had some architects in the old days.'

'Wait till you see over there,' Nur laughed, and as we approached the suspended arch I began to see the outline of a great deserted city: walls that crept up from the river and enclosed enormous areas, turrets of majestic size, and battlements that once accommodated thousands of soldiers.

'What is it?' I asked.

'Nobody knows.'

'You mean it's just there?'

'It's one of our smaller deserted cities,' Nur assured me. Pointing westward across the desert he said, 'On the other side, where the Helmand disappears, there's an empty city seventy miles long. No one knows who built it, either, but there it is.'

'What do you mean, where the Helmand disappears?'

'This river,' he said, indicating the powerful flow at our feet. 'Out in the desert it just disappears.'

'Into what?' I asked.

'Into air. The Desert of Death is so dry that the river runs into a lake that just dries up.' I looked at him suspiciously and realized he was not teasing, so I dropped the matter, but the city before me could not be casually dismissed.

'Who built this?' I probed.

'It's always been here,' Nur laughed.

'No name?'

'No. Qala Bist is our modern name for the arch.'

'It's a masterpiece. If we had something like this in America, we'd make it a national park.'

'You started about a thousand years too late to have something like this,' Nur laughed. 'We do have some ideas, of course. Possibly it was the winter capital of

Mahmud of Ghazni. He was rich enough to have built it. But I agree with the experts who argue that it must have been here for a long time before Mahmud's day.'

'And that's all that's known?'

'You see what I see,' Nur replied defensively. 'There was a great city in the desert, and now even its history is gone.'

The idea tantalized me and I was about to say, I'm going to find out what happened here, when I saw on the ramparts above me a young man in his late twenties, dressed in desert costume and turban. He was waving to us and Nur cried, 'It's Nazrullah,' and I saw that he wore a mustache and beard. On the city wall he made a fine figure and could have been a young captain of the guard a thousand years ago.

'Eh, Nazrullah!' Nur shouted. 'I've brought an American with me . . . from the embassy.' This news somewhat deflated the young man on the wall, for he ceased waving; but then his pleasure at seeing visitors overcame any hesitancy, and he scrambled down from the high wall and ran forward to greet us.

'Nur Muhammad!' he cried with real pleasure, and they embraced in a manner that satisfied me that my driver was no ordinary Afghan. Nazrullah then turned to me and said in English, smiling warmly, 'You are welcome to my humble abode, such as it is, four hundred rooms.'

We laughed and Nur said in Pashto, 'This one speaks our language. And he's come to spy you out for the evil fellow you are.' It was apparent that Nur desperately wanted us to get along.

Nazrullah extended his hand and said generously, 'You're most welcome! Drive this way. We've cut a breach in the wall and you can bring your jeep into the city.' And he led us to the opening.

There he climbed in with us, for his camp site was far inside the walls–three-quarters of a mile, I judged–and as we traveled I tried to study both Nazrullah and his extraordinary city. He was an attractive fellow, not so tall as I but more wiry and better co-ordinated. He had a mercurial brilliance, in both gesture and speech. His hair was rather long, possibly because barbers were rare in Qala Bist, but he was extremely clean, even though he was living under unusual conditions. He seemed a well-organized man and I could understand the high regard in which Moheb Khan, Nur Muhammad and Dr Stiglitz held him.

The deserted city was equally impressive. Stout walls many feet thick and sometimes twenty feet high swept over rolling ground for some eight or nine miles, enclosing an area which once contained substantial farmlands, water systems and separate villages for menials. The brick city itself was a confusion of palaces, minarets, fortresses and what must have been administrative centers. I can best describe it this way: By the time I had seen one complete set of related buildings I thought: This is the city. But it wasn't, for it was connected by ramparts and forts to a larger segment, and this was repeated six or seven times.

After a considerable drive we reached a large field contained within the walls, and here Nazrullah had pitched his tents, from which he was conducting surveys of the area that was to be irrigated by water taken from the Helmand River. He had at his disposal two jeeps, three engineers and four servants. No women were evident, but one tent, finer than the others, must have been the one in which Ellen Jaspar had lived when she came to Qala Bist nine months ago, and where possibly she still remained. I tried cautiously to study this tent without attracting attention, but I failed, for Nazrullah volunteered, 'That's where I live. Let's unload your gear.'

'Don't let us inconvenience you,' I apologized.

'You're my first guests from Kabul,' he replied expansively. 'Of course you'll stay with me.' He threw back the flaps of his tent and bade us enter. I remember two things: the floor was covered by an expensive Persian rug, and on the desk stood a portrait of Ellen Jaspar dressed in the surplice she wore when singing Beethoven's *Ninth* with the Philadelphia Orchestra. Nazrullah made no comment about the photograph.

He indicated where we were to sleep and sent his servants to fetch our gear, which they unpacked for stowing in cardboard trunks which Nazrullah had acquired in the bazaar, but as they worked I saw in another corner a trunk made of leather, stamped with the initials E.J. It was locked, so I could not tell whether it was empty or full, but it seemed to be waiting for its owner to return.

Nazrullah now took us to a tent some distance from the others, and here, seated on rugs, we had our inevitable lunch of nan and pilau, but this was different, because near the tent the cook was operating an oven that must have been more than a thousand years old, and for the first time I saw how nan was baked. A conical mound of clay, looking exactly like a beehive with the top cut off, rose above a shallow pit in which charcoal was kept burning. The opening of the beehive gave access to the inner sides, which sloped over the coals, and it was against these sloping sides that the raw dough was fixed, though why it did not fall onto the coals I never understood. I asked Nazrullah and he said, 'By trial and error the desert people developed this stove three or four thousand years ago. The dough is just sticky enough to cling to the sides and the fire is cool enough not to bake the bread too quickly. It's obviously impossible, but it works.' The hot bread was delicious.

After the meal, when our greasy fingers had been washed by servants, we returned to Nazrullah's tent, where he said reflectively, 'It's been my salvation, living here on the edge of the desert. After Germany and America, it's reminded me of what Afghanistan is. Do you know what it is?' he asked me directly.

'Until I saw the Desert of Death I thought I knew. A mountainous land marked by inhabitable valleys and plateaus.'

'Precisely. That's what I thought it was. But four-fifths of our nation looks like what you see outside these walls. Desert, cut by rivers. And wherever we can lead those rivers onto the desert, we're rewarded a thousandfold. Before you came here, Miller, did you realize that the Afghan is probably the world's best irrigation expert?'

I said I hadn't and he continued, 'We waste hardly a drop of water. The skill of our peasants is unbelievable. They take a little stream coming out of the mountains and lead it hundreds of yards to irrigate a field, then take it back to its main bed so that others can borrow it farther down the mountainside. One insignificant stream will be used many times.'

'I've never seen that,' I replied.

'My job is to do on a grand scale with the Helmand what the farmers do so well with little streams. We're going to build a gigantic dam up in the hills and capture all the water you see going to waste out there.'

The concept had inflamed his imagination, and with boundless vitality he rushed us out of the tent and over to the city, where we passed through silent streets that must once have been glorious with ribbons from India and furs from Russia. We climbed stairs that were almost as good now as when erected and came to a vast reception hall, its walls still marked with murals, then entered the battlements which troops could have used that night. Nazrullah moved quickly, for he was familiar with the ancient city, but I was tardy because I wanted to absorb the implied splendor of the place. It was incredible that men had ruled here whose dynasties were forgotten, that a city of this magnitude could have perished without leaving in the records even the name by which its enemies described it. As I caught up with Nazrullah on the battlement I said, 'Must give you an eerie feeling, living in a place like this.'

'It does. No matter how indifferent you are to history, when you live here you speculate.'

'Any conclusions?'

'None. I don't have to solve the past.' He pointed down to the river that ran along the foot of the wall on which we stood. 'My job is to get water out of that river.'

'What'll you do with it when you get it?'

He pointed beyond the river to the bleak desert, where wind was churning up the sand, and I supposed that he was going to say that farther out lay an arable district. Instead he replied, 'What looks like desert down there is potential farmland. Wherever we can lead the water, we can grow crops. When we're through, this land will be as valuable as it was when this city supported perhaps half a million people. They lived by irrigation.'

'You think so?'

'Look!' he cried with infectious enthusiasm, and he intended that I look upstream where old embankments proved that the Helmand has once before been tapped for irrigation purposes, but I saw instead a curious procession of tall mounds that led away from our city toward a group of small mountains some twenty miles to the east. The mounds had obviously been made by man, because they appeared at regular quarter-mile intervals, and since each was of considerable size, and there were eighty or more visible, I was looking at a project of magnitude, whatever it was.

'What are you staring at?' Nazrullah asked.

'That chain of mounds,' I replied.

Nazrullah thought for a moment, then banged his right fist enthusiastically into his left palm and cried, 'Miller, are you game for something exciting?'

'The ambassador told me to look around.'

'You'll be the only American who's ever done this.' He ran to a point from which he could call to Nur Muhammad: 'Nur, you want to go with us through the karez?' He pronounced the strange word in one syllable to rhyme with *breeze*, and it had an instant effect upon Nur.

'Not me! And if Miller Sahib has any sense, he won't go either.'

'He's already volunteered,' Nazrullah shouted enthusiastically, 'and if he goes, you'll be ashamed.'

'I stand before my ancestors shamed,' Nur laughed. 'You uphold the honor of Afghanistan. I'm a coward.'

We hurried through the deserted city and climbed into one of Nazrullah's jeeps, which he raced expertly through the breached wall and onto the desert. Soon we were pulled up beside one of the mounds, which was built of mud brick rising to a height of fifteen feet or more. A crude ladder led to the top.

When we had climbed it, I saw inside another ladder, much longer than the first, leading down to darkness. Nazrullah dropped a pebble, which splashed in water, far below us, and I realized that we were perched atop a shaft which led to an underground stream.

'Down we go!' Nazrullah cried like a college boy, and I watched his excited face, its beard covered with dust, disappear. I followed, and when I reached bottom found myself standing on a narrow edge of earth bordering a clear stream of water only faintly illuminated by sunlight seeping down the shaft.

'Is each of the mounds like this?' I asked.

'Yep,' Nazrullah replied, proud of his American colloquialism. 'It's an underground irrigation system bringing water down from the hills. You game to crawl through to the next mound?' He must have seen my apprehension, for he flashed on a light and added, 'We've cleaned it out for just such expeditions.'

I looked at the low ceiling of the tunnel and discovered that once we left the mound, which permitted us to stand, we would be walking in very stooped positions–duck-walking, we had called it as children–and I wasn't sure my legs would take it. 'You won't feel it . . . in a quarter of a mile,' Nazrullah assured me.

'Here we go,' I cried, more bravely than I felt, and bent over to creep duck-wise into the tunnel.

My back quickly began to ache and, as I feared, my leg muscles became numb, but lithe Nazrullah was pushing ahead with such enthusiasm that I had to follow. At midpoint we could begin to see slight indications of light from the next mound and this encouraged me to bear my pain; it also permitted me to see the construction of the tunnel. Its ceiling was protected in no way and was held in place merely by the cohesion of clay, and whenever I bumped it with my head, bits of earth splashed into the water. I thought: This thing could collapse at any moment, and I began to feel my throat constricting.

Fortunately, we reached the next mound and I was able to stand erect. My feet were soaking wet and my back creaked as I stretched it, but I was too stiff to want to climb the ladder immediately, so we stood in the small shaft of light and breathed the cool air.

'Now you understand why Nur refused the invitation,' Nazrullah laughed.

'I'm glad I came. Who invented the idea?'

'Maybe the Persians. More likely the Afghans. It's the best way known to transport water across a desert. If we tried to do it on the surface, the sun would evaporate it all.'

'How old is the tunnel?'

'Assuming that it was used by the city, which it probably was, the hole we're standing in could have been dug twelve or thirteen hundred years ago.'

'Let's get out of here!' I cried.

'Of course, it's been redug many times. The tunnels do collapse,' he said brightly.

'I wondered about that as we were crawling through,' I replied.

Nazrullah held the ladder by one hand and said, 'The karez system was very costly of human life. Water experts would go to the mountains and dig at likely points . . . sometimes seventy feet down, but because they were experts they usually found water. They would then calculate where that particular level would work itself to the surface, and they would dig these underground tunnels for ten to twenty miles, following the natural line of the water's flow.'

'Why didn't the ceilings fall in?' I asked.

'They did, frequently. The one we crawled under could collapse at any moment,' he said without emotion. 'In desert regions men who worked the karez formed a special caste. They lived under special laws, ate special food, had extra women. Mullahs and police were powerless to molest them, for generally they lived short lives and when they died, usually of suffocation, for they never shored up the ceilings and trusted to luck, their few possessions and their women passed along to the next karez man.'

I was beginning to feel the approach of claustrophobia and started up the ladder, increasing my speed when I saw how fragile the clay bricks were under which we had been standing. When I regained freedom I gasped deeply, then saw Nazrullah smiling, his beard gray with dust. 'Lucky I didn't tell you that when we were halfway through,' he apologized.

'That tunnel is going to fall on me every time I go to sleep for the next month.' I laughed thinly.

'I've thought of that myself,' Nazrullah confided. 'After a series of collapses they often had to beat the men with whips to drive them back into the karez. At the beginning of the system the kings ordained that any boy born to a karez man had to inherit the job. In some districts they were branded at birth.'

'You live in a rugged land,' I remarked, shivering in the hot sun.

Nazrullah climbed down the outside ladder and sat with me in the shadow of the mound. 'It is a cruel land,' he admitted. 'The existence of this karez reminds us how cruel. But even today in Afghanistan I could show you things that would shock you.'

'I've seen some of them,' I assured him.

'What?' he asked suspiciously.

'In Ghazni . . . a woman stoned to death. In Kandahar a young man committed murder over a dancing boy. They cut off his head . . . with a rusty bayonet.'

'You've been initiated,' Nazrullah said without inflection. He seemed wholly composed, but his inner tension was betrayed by quick gestures and the nervous movement of his beard. 'I force myself down to the karez occasionally so that I may remember the heritage of human suffering we're trying to eradicate. If I'd known you'd seen the executions I wouldn't have dragged you into the tunnel, but I find I can't talk with ferangi who haven't had some similar experience.'

'I've had three now,' I said. 'We can talk.'

'I think we can,' he agreed, 'and I'd like to say two things. It will require some words, but like your journey through the karez, it may be worth it.

'I went to Germany at the age of twenty. Before that I'd been educated by private tutors whose main job, it seems to me now, was to impress me with the moral depravity of Afghanistan and the timeless glory of Europe. I knew no better than to accept their indoctrination at face value and reported to Germany fully prepared to exhibit my tutors' prejudices. But when I reached Göttingen I found that the true barbarians were not the primitives who stone women in Ghazni–and we have some real primitives in this country–but the Germans. From 1938 through 1941 I remained as their guest, to witness the dreadful degeneration of a culture which might once have been what my tutors claimed but was now a garish travesty. Believe me, Miller, I learned more in Germany than you'll ever learn in Afghanistan.

'As you know, I went from Germany to Philadelphia, where half the people thought that I was a Negro. What I didn't learn in Germany, you taught me. Why do you suppose I wear this beard? Before I grew it I made a six-week experiment. I decided to be a Negro . . . lived in Negro hotels, ate in their restaurants, read their papers and dated Negro girls. It was an ugly, ugly life, being a Negro in your country ... maybe not so bad as being a Jew in Germany, but a lot worse than being an Afghan in Ghazni. To prove to Philadelphians I wasn't a Negro, I grew this beard and wore a turban, which I had never worn at home.

'My education was worth every penny my government paid for it, because after six years in Göttingen and Philadelphia I positively hungered to get home and go to work. Miller, we can build here just as good a society as the Germans or the Americans have built in their surroundings.'

I looked at his surroundings: a bleak desert, a muddy river, blazing empty hills, an abandoned city. Because I had seen Afghanistan, I appreciated the Herculean task he had set himself.

'The second thing I want to say is this,' he continued with fervor. 'Having made my transition from a boy who wanted to escape Afghanistan to a man who fought to get back, I find daily joy in being here. Imagine, at twenty-eight I can be appointed head of a project that will revolutionize this part of Asia. In Philadelphia a man at a cocktail party offered me the stirring job of helping to sell shoes. "You're enthusiastic," the man said. "Women will go for that beard." Miller, I'm here in the desert because I want to be here. I want to stir the earth like the karez men stirred theirs ... fundamentally ... in the bowels ... at the bottom of the ladder in a deep hole. And if the ceiling collapses on me, I don't give a damn.'

There was another moment of tension, then he laughed and said, 'We'd better drive back,' but when we tried to enter the jeep, the metal was so hot we could not touch it, for we were really in the desert, and if the ancient karez men had not dug their perilous tunnels, water could never have crossed this land and the city could not have existed.

In the days that followed, Nazrullah talked eagerly about all aspects of life in Afghanistan, but whenever I broached the subject of his wife, he was adept in putting me off. Ellen was not at Qala Bist, however; of that I was satisfied. If Nazrullah did not respond to my overtures on the subject, he did take every opportunity to let me see the kind of man he was, and as I watched him with the engineers and the workers I knew that I was observing a man who had matured far beyond his years.

He had an enviable capacity to elicit from others their best efforts. I understood why the shoe company in Philadelphia had wanted to hire him and why a German engineering firm, looking to the future, had recently written to ask if he would represent them in Asia. He had a quick smile, an infectious wit and a generosity of spirit that was engaging, and I could now understand his effect upon a junior at Bryn Mawr, bored by her native surroundings. It was reasonable that Ellen Jaspar had fallen in love with him, but it was not reasonable that she should now, because of him, be in serious trouble, if indeed she were alive.

In a way, I was sorry that I had interviewed Nazrullah's Afghan wife in Kandahar, for if that silken, shrouded voice had not convinced me that she and Ellen had been friends, it would now be easy to conclude that only the shock of discovering a previous marriage had unnerved Ellen. But if relationships were as placid as reported, and if Nazrullah were as congenial as he seemed, what dark force operating on this trio could have occasioned tragedy?

It was also interesting for me to compare Nazrullah with Nur. The former had been set free pyschologically by his travels abroad, while Nur was still uncertain of himself, because of an insular limitation which he was working desperately to correct. Nazrullah utilized a broad, frontal approach to problems and for an Afghan was markedly outspoken, partly because he was honest and partly because he lacked the ability to maneuver, whereas Nur was a master of manipulation. The big difference, however, lay in their concept of what process would lead to their country's salvation. Nur, the traditionalist, whose brother was an enlightened mullah, felt that Afghanistan would be saved through the rededication of the individual and the moral regeneration of Islam. Nazrullah, in our long talks in the tent, argued that what happened to the Muslim religion was no great concern of his. From having studied various religions at first hand, he suspected that any of the three great desert religions, Islam, Christianity or Judaism, was as good as any other but that Islam was rather better fitted for the social structure of Afghanistan. 'But what's going to save this nation is the creation of a contemporary world–a new economic system, a real representative form of government, dams, roads, farms . . . the things that we can create.'

As he said this he snapped his fingers and cried, 'Miller, to show you what I mean, I'm going to take you to the site of the new dam. How soon can you start?'

Nur protested that the location was too far away, but Nazrullah would not listen. 'You've got to go there anyway. Saddle up the jeeps!' He dashed about camp and within fifteen minutes had a major expedition assembled. 'You're going to see the future of Afghanistan!' he promised.

We roared out of the old walls in a caravan of three jeeps because Nazrullah felt that any penetration of the desert in machines was so inherently perilous that group protection was advisable, but on this day nothing happened. We reached the junction town of Girishk, from which we struck off across forbidding land on a trail that jeeps could barely negotiate. Finally we ground to a halt at a goat trail, where we left the jeeps under guard while we climbed on foot to a high elevation, from which we could see, far below us, the roaring Helmand River as it carried the spring thaw through a narrow cleft in the mountains.

'To build a dam, a great dam such as the American and German experts advise,' Nazrullah cried, pointing with a stick, 'requires two things, a gorge and a mountain close by. Down there you see the gorge, with steep, solid walls, and over there you see one hell of a mountain.'

'What's the relationship?' Nur asked.

'You build a road from the mountain to the gorge. Then you lead that road over a temporary bridge that crosses the gorge, high up in the air. Then you dynamite the mountain rock by rock and haul it in trucks to the bridge, where you drop the rocks into the river. And after you do this day and night for three or four years, you have a dam.'

He showed us where the road would be built and where the bridge would be slung, high above the rapids. 'For seven months trucks will dump rocks off that bridge and nothing will happen, because the river will wash our boulders downstream as if they were straw. But one day the rocks will begin to hold, and the river will start to back up–just a little. But on that day we have it strangled. Then we can do with it what we will.'

He called for his field glasses, which enabled me to see bench marks already cut into the cliff north of where the dam would be and other marks south, many feet above the present water level. 'Any idea what that's to be?' He asked, and when I admitted my ignorance he replied, 'That's the tunnel. While we're throwing in the rock, we're also digging that tunnel, and when the river starts to back up, it gradually rises to that level, and runs away through the tunnel. Then we move in hundreds of trucks and throw thousands of tons of rock into the ravine, pack them with earth and after some years concrete the exposed face and find ourselves with a dam.'

It was difficult to visualize the completed dam, it was of such magnitude, but Nazrullah had surveyed the ground so often that to him the gigantic structure already existed. Pointing to a mark hundreds of feet above the river he said, 'The water will rise to there. We'll collect the floods in the spring, when they aren't needed in the fields, and release them in the summer, when they are. And the beauty of this system is that every pound of water that drops through our tunnel will generate electricity which we'll send over the mountains to Kandahar.'

Remembering that primitive city I predicted, 'In Kandahar they won't be using much electricity.'

'Ah! That's where you're wrong!' Nazrullah cried. 'In Germany we made a study of fifteen primitive societies'—I liked his using the word *primitive*; our ambassador had forbidden us to do so, claiming it insulted the Afghans—'and we found that when irrigation dams were built in primitive areas, the financial experts always fought against wasting the money to add generators at the same time. They argued, "The people are so primitive they'll have no use for electricity." In every instance, within five years the original output of electricity, which the experts had called wasteful, was being utilized and further capacity was required. If we can get electricity to Kandahar, they'll find ways of using it. Progress creates its own dynamics.'

The concept was so new to me that I asked for an illustration of a primitive society where this had happened. 'I'll give you a classic,' he said instantly. 'The Tennessee Valley Authority.'

'I'd hardly call Tennessee primitive,' I argued with some asperity.

'I would,' he replied flatly. 'The hill region anyway. I made a study of it, on the spot, and in its way, compared to New York, it's as primitive as Girishk compared to Kabul. And the T.V.A. found it couldn't make electricity fast enough.'

I was not satisfied with his description of part of my country as primitive, having always reserved that word for other nations, but I was impressed by his excitement about his job and the poetic insights he brought to it. For example, he stared down at the river which now ran wild through the gorge and said softly, 'Isn't it a gripping idea, Miller, that on the day we drop our first load of rock into that turbulent river it'll have no idea of what's happening? Rocks like that have been falling off the cliffs for a million years, and it's washed them aside. But these rocks will be different. They'll be the beginning of something not even that river is strong enough to halt. And we will continue . . .' He hammered the air with his fist, visualizing the enormous aggregation of rock that would ultimately jam that gorge and tame the river.

He turned to Nur and me with dancing eyes. 'Each day we must throw similar rocks into the human river of Afghanistan. Here a school, there a road, down in the gorge a dam. So far our human river isn't aware that it's been touched. But we shall never halt until we've modified it completely.'

As I looked down at the turbulent Helmand, rushing freely between the cliffs, it seemed to symbolize the wild freedom of Afghanistan, and I said half to myself, 'It's rather a pity that such a river must be brought under control.'

Nazrullah grabbed me by the arm and whipped me about. 'What did you say?' he demanded.

'I said, It's a shame such a river has to be dammed.'

'That's incredible,' he muttered, not in surprise or anger or any other emotion that I could recognize. 'That's really incredible, Miller.' He snapped his fingers, tugged at his beard and stared at me as if trying to reassemble fragments. 'Those are the exact words Ellen said while standing here.' He bit his forefinger, then added with impatience, 'You damned Americans are so sentimental. You've organized your own land to the limit, but you criticize others who want to organize theirs.'

'I was speaking symbolically,' I protested.

'So was Ellen,' he snapped. 'What you both meant was, The more modern Tennessee becomes, the nicer it would be to keep Afghanistan a primitive place where we could come to observe the peasants. Well, Miller, we're going to change it . . . profoundly.'

'I want you to. Perhaps Ellen meant that old-fashioned ways are always better. A lot of Americans believe that nonsense. But I don't.'

'What do you believe?'

'That it's always sad to see freedom lost. As for change, that's why we have an American embassy in Kabul. To help you make the changes, yet stay free.'

'You'd better help,' he warned. 'Because if you try to hold us back, Russia will be eager to jump in and help us.'

'To what?' I asked, but he had turned away and now stamped angrily down the mountain trail. When he reached the jeeps he jumped into one and roared down the dangerous trail to Girishk, leaving Nur and me to ride with an assistant engineer, who drove us back to Qala Bist. But often as our jeeps passed and repassed on the desert I caught sight of Nazrullah, brooding in silence, the knuckles of his left fist pressed against his bearded chin.

9

Our caravan had barely come in sight of Qala Bist when we spotted a strange jeep speeding at us from the walled city, throwing a cloud of dust across the desert. It was Dr Stiglitz, driven by an Afghan military officer, coming out to intercept us as quickly as possible.

'Where's Nazrullah?' the German shouted as he drew close.

'He's back there,' I cried.

The four jeeps drew together in the desert and Stiglitz said in German, 'I bring you bad news.'

He and Nazrullah continued talking in German, but I caught the fact that something had happened to the American engineer Pritchard, who had crossed the Desert of Death some months before to measure the spring flow of the Helmand River. I waited impatiently while the two discussed the problem, and finally they took cognizance of me. 'Sorry, Herr Miller. My visit really concerns you.'

'How?'

'There's an official message for you,' Nazrullah replied, and he spoke to the Afghan officer, who handed me a paper containing directions which the American embassy had phoned down to Kandahar military headquarters that morning. It said:

Miller. Proceed immediately to The City, thence to Chahar, where Pritchard broke his leg three weeks ago. See if the German Dr Stiglitz can accompany you at our expense, but travel in at least two jeeps because earlier investigators dispatched by the Afghan government have not been heard from. Obtain fullest local advice before attempting journey.

It was signed by Verbruggen and I could imagine his rough, worried voice on the telephone. I asked Stiglitz, 'You know what's in this message?'

'Of course.'

'You'll go?'

'I'm here.'

'How much?' Before he could reply I led him away from the others, where he stood silent for some moments. I was certain he had guessed why I had called on him in Kandahar and I knew he wanted me to carry back a good report which might enable him to jump from Kandahar to Kabul, so he would be disposed to request a low fee in hopes of winning my favor; on the other hand he was a trained doctor and proud of his German degree, in addition to which the cost of German beer in Kandahar was not trivial, so that he had reasons for asking a substantial fee. It was a delicate problem, and the poor pudgy man was not equal to solving it. I grew ashamed of myself, especially since I was a Jew and he a German.

'I'm sorry, Doctor,' I said. 'I should've spoken first. Two hundred dollars plus twenty dollars for each day beyond five that we're out.'

Stiglitz breathed deeply, and I judged that my offer was more generous than he had dared to demand. 'I accept!' he said, continuing with profuse thanks which became almost embarrassing, 'You've no idea, Herr Miller, how those damned Afghans rob me for my beer.'

'Agreed.' Then I asked the Afghan soldier, 'Are you driving us?'

'He is not!' Nazrullah protested. 'I am.' He drew his staff about him and shot a series of questions: 'What's the state of the moon?' 'Which of our jeeps is in best condition?' 'Miller, will you turn over your K-rations to us?' 'Water, crowbars, tow ropes?' When he had satisfactory answers he looked at his watch and said, 'We'll leave Qala Bist in forty minutes. We're taking Miller's jeep and mine. Nur Muhammad to drive one. I'll drive the other. Stiglitz and Miller the only passengers. I want everything assembled in front of my tent at once. O.K.?'

He jumped in his jeep and sped for Qala Bist, leading us through the ponderous wall and across the fields to the camp. As he ran for his tent he shouted, 'Nur, stay with me,' and in the next minutes I watched two Afghan gentlemen assume command of an expedition that could turn out disastrously if anything went wrong. Nur, who understood jeeps, took care of matters in that area, while Nazrullah checked the logistics, then supervised the packing. 'Turbans for the ferangi!' Nazrullah shouted, and one of the engineers solved this by lifting two from the heads of the servants. 'You'll need it,' Nur assured me as I packed mine.

It was several hours before dark when we approached our loaded jeeps, where Nazrullah consulted for the last time with his staff and with the Afghan officer. Taking a map he drew a tentative line from Qala Bist across the desert to an extended area marked simply The City. There he turned his line south until it reached the remote village of Chahar. 'We'll be going this way,' he announced in Pashto, 'and if anything should happen, I promise I won't be far off this route.' He watched while Nur and the officer traced the route on their maps.

'Now,' Nazrullah asked sharply, 'where do you think the missing men could be?'

He stared at his staff, at Nur, at the officer. The latter spoke: 'Ten days ago we sent two men in a jeep . . .'

'One jeep?' Nazrullah asked, tugging his beard.

'Yes.'

'Great Jesus Christ!' Nazrullah snapped, uttering an oath quite inappropriate for a Muslim, something he had picked up at the Wharton School. 'One jeep?' He stabbed at the map. 'Driving across that?'

'Yes,' the officer replied, unruffled. 'They left Kandahar ten days ago, drove to Girishk, and started across the desert on this course.' On Nazrullah's map he drew a firm line which converged on our projected course about halfway across the desert.

Nazrullah reflected and said, 'With the lines running that way we might spot them anywhere during the second half.'

I added, 'If they're broken down, they'll probably have a flag waving that we can see.'

Nazrullah looked at me with compassion, then asked, 'Did they know the desert?'

'Yes.'

'They the type who follow instructions?'

'Best men we had.'

Nazrullah studied the map for some minutes. 'I want you to change my route just a little. We'll drop up here and take a look.' He drew a jog to the north, almost off the desert, and said, 'We'll never be far from this route. Salaam aleikum.' With that he spun his wheels in a tight circle and sped for the wall. In a few moments we were entering the desert, headed west for the setting sun, a simple caravan of two jeeps, each marked by high poles from which fluttered large squares of white cloth.

The Afghan Dasht-i-Margo was not a desert in the accustomed sense, for although it did contain vast unbroken stretches of sand, it was also an accumulation of shaly detritus laid down by deteriorating mountains which had eroded through millions of years, so that across the desert we found bands of this shale sometimes half a mile wide along which our jeeps could race at forty miles an hour, while we saw on either side the glorious sweep of traditional dunes that characterize the usual desert.

An additional feature marked this desert: When we were well into its heart we could not see a single thing growing nor any shred of human existence. There were no lichens on the rock, no seedlings in crevices, no shrubs, no birds, no gullies touched with a little water, no lizards, no eagles, no oases of any kind. There were no fence poles nor relics of forgotten homes nor even stones laid in a row. There was only the most blazing, heat-racked emptiness I had ever seen. I remember thinking once, when we were surrounded by dunes: In the polar regions they at least have frozen water and insects. Here there's nothing . . . except heat.

'How hot is it?' I asked Nur.

'Hundred and thirty, but it isn't the thermometer that worries us,' he said as he studied the desolate landscape. 'It's the wind.' He checked some drifting sand and said, 'Wind's thirty miles an hour. Later it'll grow to fifty. That's what kills you on the desert.'

I now began to appreciate the flags that Nazrullah had provided for our jeeps, for as our caravan moved across the desert we were frequently separated, since neither driver could be sure that what looked like a potential road would turn out to be so; and often it was the driver in second position who found the successful trail, whereas what had looked good to the first man had turned into a wall of impenetrable sand. When this happened, the unsuccessful driver would whirl about, look for his companion's flag, and set off in hot pursuit. Neither waited for the other, but each felt responsible for seeing that the separation did not become too great.

'Is it possible to work your way into a real dead end?' I asked.

'Sure. Probably what happened to the missing men. In this business you need that other flag.'

We had been on the road for well over an hour when Nazrullah, whose jeep was now in the lead, stopped abruptly and waited for us to join him. He signaled for silence, then pointed to a small herd of gazelles–not more than fifteen–that had penetrated these dreadful wastes where I had been unable to see a shred of forage but where they were acquainted with hidden areas that no man had yet identified.

At first I didn't understand why the gazelles fascinated me, but I sat spellbound watching the small, delicate animals standing gracefully on the face of the burning desert. What could they be doing? What did they signify? Afghanistan had untold valleys where an animal could find forage. Why were they here? And why was I so moved by seeing them?

One of their lookouts spotted us, and with a disembodied grace the small animals leaped, exploded in the dying sunlight, twisted, turned and fled like wraiths across the desert. I had never before seen such flawless motion, and as they sped away like the sound of retreating music, one female, small and without horns, ran toward us with a breathless poetry, then saw the jeeps and turned in mid-air, throwing her sharp hoofs to one side as she changed direction. As she did this marvellous thing, I was forced to cry out, for I saw that she was colored like the chaderi Moheb Khan's niece had worn, and she was not an animal at all, she was not a gazelle, but the embodiment of the hunger I felt. In this cruel land of recurring ugliness, where only men were seen, the gazelle reminded me of womanliness, of girls at a dance, of the mystery of half the world. I watched her go in matchless grace, darting this way and that until she vanished behind a distant dune, and there were tears in my eyes and I felt I could not tolerate the awful loneliness of the desert. I was lost in Asia. I was forsaken on the high roof of the world and the gazelles had been a sighing, drifting premonition.

Then I heard Nazrullah saying, 'They must have come down from the caravanserai,' and we took out our maps to discover that we were near the jog that Nazrullah had drawn to the north. 'There's a chance the other two might have made for the caravanserai.' And we turned north.

The sun was just setting when we reached the top of a dune from which we could look down upon one of the sights that has always inspired the traveler in Asia: a walled caravanserai looming out of the dusk at the end of a long journey. It remains unforgettable: a gaunt, square, mud-walled sanctuary built around a central open space where animals of the caravan were sheltered. One leg of the wall comprised a fort devoid of windows but well supplied in recent centuries with slit holes for rifle fire. Entrance was by a solitary gate, a handsome structure built in fine Arabic proportions. The serai had been erected hundreds of years ago, possibly even in the days of Muhammad, and through the centuries had served continuously, for it stood at the edge of the desert near the end of a little gully in which grass grew and stagnant water accumulated, and to it had come, as we now came, thousands of caravans needing protection for the night. It was a rule of the desert that whoever succeeded in entering a serai was safe for the night, no matter what antagonist he encountered inside, and there must have been many stirring tales of blood enemies who shared sanctuary here under unexpected circumstances.

As we approached the gate, Nazrullah halted the jeeps and he and Nur debarked to study, on hands and knees, all the surrounding sand, entering the walls to continue their search. After a while they reappeared and said, 'They didn't get this far.'

I hoped that this was a sign that we were to move on, for whereas I had found the ruins at Qala Bist so immense as to be commanding, I found this old deserted caravanserai a place of brooding quiet that was in a sense terrifying. Possibly I was still influenced by the gazelles, possibly by the haunting loneliness of a desert twilight, but the idea that a wayside inn had once flourished here but had now lost its reason for being was at the moment too gloomy for my acceptance.

'Are we leaving?' I asked hopefully.

'We'll eat here,' Nazrullah replied, and he took us to the fort, where he and the doctor began laying out blankets on the earthen floor. Nur lit two Coleman lamps, whose incandescent glow showed the high roof of the caravanserai to good effect, and if anything were calculated to make me feel gloomier than I already did, it was the way the flickering light threw enormous shadows on the mud walls. I thought: Genghis Khan could come through that door, and he'd be right at home.

Two-thirds of the way down the hall, a stout circular column about twelve feet in diameter rose from the floor and continued through the roof. It was built neither of wood nor of mud but of plaster, and our lights played upon its uneven surfaces in exciting patterns. 'That's a beautiful column,' I remarked. 'What's it used for?'

'Famous, too,' Nazrullah replied without looking.

'What for?'

'Manner of construction,' he replied.

'What's unusual, the plaster?'

'The insides.'

Dr Stiglitz interrupted. 'What's inside?' he asked and years later when I reconstructed that night I became convinced that somehow he knew what the answer was going to be.

'It's not pleasant,' Nazrullah cautioned. 'Want to hear it before dinner?' When I said yes, he continued, 'Some time around 1220, Genghis Khan . . .'

'I just thought of him!' I cried.

'How so?' Nur asked.

'I was looking at those shadows and thought, If Genghis Khan came in now, I wouldn't be surprised.'

'He was here,' Nazrullah laughed.

'What about the pillar?' Stiglitz asked.

'Genghis Khan destroyed Afghanistan. In one assault on The City he killed nearly a million people. That's not a poetic figure. It's fact. In Kandahar the slaughter was enormous. Some refugees fled to this caravanserai . . . this room. They were sure the Mongols wouldn't find them here, but they did.' His voice resumed its flatness.

'And the pillar?' Stiglitz pressed.

'First Genghis erected a pole right through the roof. Then the Mongols took their prisoners and tied their hands. Laid the first batch on the floor over there and lashed their feet to the pole. All around. That's why the pillar is twelve feet across.'

'Then what?' Stiglitz asked, perspiration standing on his forehead.

'They just kept on laying the prisoners down, one layer on top of the other until they reached the roof. They didn't kill a single person that day, the Mongols, but they kept soldiers stationed with sticks to push back the tongues when they protruded. And while the pillar of people was still living–those that hadn't been pressed to death–they called in masons to plaster over the whole affair. If you'd scrape away the plaster you'd find skulls. But the government takes a dim view of scraping. It's a kind of national monument. The Caravanserai of the Tongues.'

No one spoke. The meal was ready but no one seemed hungry, so finally Nazrullah said, 'I tell you these things only to explain the terrible burdens under which Afghanistan has labored. Our major cities have been destroyed so many times. Do you know what I expect . . . seriously? When a thousand men like me have rebuilt Kabul and made it as great as The City once was, either the Russians or the Americans will come with their airplanes and bomb it to rubble.'

'Wait a minute!' I protested.

'I'm not speaking against Americans . . . or Russians. You won't destroy us in anger. Genghis Khan wasn't angry at us when he destroyed The City. Neither was Tamerlane or Nadir Shah or Baber. And I'm not downcast because we're doomed to be destroyed again.' He shrugged his shoulders. 'It's inevitable. We go on building while we can.'

He laughed and inspected the cans that lay opened on the blankets. 'I for one love American K-rations. But please, gentlemen, you must see to it that Nur Muhammad and I get ones that contain no pork.'

'Tonight,' I said with some embarrassment, 'everyone has pork and beans.'

'Then Nur and I shall make a great show of picking out one shred of pork each and placing it upon your plate . . . thus. "Please take this pork from us, Miller Sahib, because we are Muslims." But the rest of the pork I shall jolly well keep on my plate, because I love it.' We ate as a family group, two Muslims, a renegade Christian and a Jew, and my sense of loneliness was erased, but when it came time to clean the dishes I noticed that Dr Stiglitz, who sat facing the pillar, had eaten little.

It was after our meal that I learned with pleasure that we would not stay in the serai but were pushing across the desert in the cooler night air. As I left the refuge I said, 'One nice thing about it. It's the only building I've seen that I can date. It was here in 1220.'

'Probably been rebuilt since then,' Nazrullah said without further comment.

We went into the night and for the first time in my life I saw the stars hanging low over the desert, for the atmosphere above us contained no moisture, no dust, no impediment of any kind. It was probably the cleanest air man knows and it displayed the stars as no other could. Not even at Qala Bist, which stood by the river, had air been so pure. The stars seemed enormous, but what surprised me most was the fact that they dropped right to the horizon, so that to the east some rose out of dunes while to the west others crept beneath piles of shale.

While I was staring at the unfamiliar stars, Nazrullah borrowed a light and wrote the following note on a scrap of paper in Persian, Pashto and English:

On the evening of April 11, 1946, we stopped here to seek evidence of the missing soldiers but found nothing.

Using a sharp piece of shale, he wedged the message into the door and we started up the gully to the desert.

Then I understood why Nazrullah had halted our caravan at the serai; while we were listening to the explanation of pillar the burning wind had abated and the moon had brightened and was nearly full. It now stood well above the horizon, a huge center of light which made our trip across the desert possible. It was an unworldly experience, with moonlight reflecting from the dunes as if it were day. I noticed that we now traveled at less than twenty-five miles an hour, and since the path looked just as good as it had in the afternoon when we did over forty, I asked why and Nur explained, 'At night we can't spot the gotch.'

'The what?' I asked.

'Gotch. A flaky white substance that comes in big patches. I think you call it gypsum.'

'That's worth something, gypsum. It occurs in piles?'

'Desert's full of it, always in patches. That's where Genghis Khan got his plaster for the pillar.'

'So that's what gypsum's used for,' I mused.

'Mixed with water it's useful,' Nur cautioned, 'but don't hit it when it's dry.'

At this point we heard a horn blowing insistently, and I looked about for Nazrullah's flag. It was stationary in a valley ahead and he was signaling us not to follow. 'He's trapped in gotch,' Nur said. 'In this light you can't see the stuff.'

'Did we pass some this afternoon?'

'Acres of it,' Nur assured me. 'But then it was no trouble.'

We parked our jeep and hiked ahead to where Nazrullah was stuck. 'Nothing serious,' he said. 'The wheels slow down . . . pooosh.'

I knelt to feel the gotch and found it a flaky powder, very soft to the fingers and providing no traction for a spinning wheel. 'Here's the rope,' Nazrullah cried. 'Give me a little tug.'

We edged our jeep carefully forward, attached the rope, and with no trouble pulled Nazrullah free. When he drew up beside us he warned, 'If you hit this stuff at more than twenty-five you may break a nose.'

'If we do hit,' Nur added, 'protect your face. We stop very suddenly.'

It was now our turn to lead, and we set forth upon one of the few flawless journeys a man can take: to be moving over the desert at night when the great stars are overhead and a white moon illuminates the ghostly world; to be rising suddenly from a depression and on the crest to see a great sweep of desert appearing like a cross between a blizzard of snow and a garden of white flowers in spring; to watch the rise and fall of dunes as they make their poetic march across the shadowy horizon. Most impressive was the silence, the absolute silence of the desert at night. No insects marred it, no night birds whispered, there was no echo of wind nor sound of distant thunder. If we stopped to reconnoiter, we could hear Nazrullah's jeep chattering unseen behind some hill, and I remember once when we had worked ourselves into a cul-de-sac of sweeping dunes how the sound of our engine echoed from each as we tried to fight our way to passages that did not exist. We were hemmed in by floating sand, but as we studied our position I caught sight of Nazrullah's flag whisking past us on the correct road.

We had proceeded thus some forty miles deeper into the desert when I thought I spied something unusual off to the north. I watched it for some minutes and at first took it to be a pile of shale. Then I drew Nur Muhammad's attention, but he had been concentrating so intently on gotch that at first he saw nothing. Finally his eyes adjusted and when they did so he said, 'It's a jeep!' And I saw that he was right.

We then faced the problem of how to flag down Nazrullah, who was well ahead of us. We could drive faster, but that might pitch us into gotch. We could blow our horn, but would they hear? I suggested, 'Let me get down and stand here, so that you can find the jeep when you come back.'

Nur looked at me in horror. 'In the desert?' he asked.

He flashed his headlights, whereupon Nazrullah's jeep promptly turned about, and when he had joined us, he asked, 'What's up?'

'Miller found the jeep,' Nur replied. Then he added, 'He suggested that he get down and wait here till I caught you.'

Nazrullah looked at me and groaned. 'My God!' Then he looked toward the ghostly jeep and said, 'I hate to go up there.'

Slowly we drove north and it soon became apparent that we were entering a huge concentration of gotch. Nazrullah called out, 'Drive back and plant your flag on the hard surface.' We did so and then reassembled our little caravan and moved cautiously forward.

Even from a distance we saw what we had hoped not to see: two men sitting in a jeep. They had bogged down in gotch, had tried to pile stones under the wheels, had probably burned out their clutch.

We hiked across the soft gypsum and reached the uncanny sight: two men fully dressed for desert travel, resting in their jeep, their eyes wide open but completely dried out. They had been dead for eight or nine days, but rarely had the hand of death been placed so gently upon two human beings, for the desiccating wind, blowing constantly through the day with a hundred and twenty or thirty degrees of heat, had completely mummified the bodies.

'We'll leave them here,' Nazrullah said finally. 'Nothing'll harm them now.'

I studied the bodies for clues, but there were none. The jeep contained ample food, some gasoline, but no water. Nazrullah said, 'Shift him over, Miller. I'll see if the clutch works.' With some apprehension I lifted the driver away from the wheel, while Nazrullah slipped in and started the car. The dead man weighed little. The engine choked, coughed, started. There was no clutch. 'Poor bastards,' Nazrullah said. 'Put him back.'

When we were back at our jeeps he said, 'They may have lived two days . . .

no more. Miller, if you leave a jeep even for twenty yards in this climate, you're dead.'

Nur asked in Pashto, 'I wonder who blamed the other?'

The idea was so unexpected that we all stared at Nur, but we were also forced to look back at the dead men, and whatever hideous recriminations may have passed between them were now silenced. The younger of the two had been driving.

When we stopped to recover our flag Nazrullah said with real sadness, 'Foolish, foolish men, to take one jeep across this desert. Miller, why don't you ride with me on this leg?'

After we had taken the lead I asked, 'Did you know them?'

'Fortunately no. I'd hate to think my friends were so idiotic.' We drove for some time, then he chuckled. 'It's rather fun riding with Stiglitz. He's so German.'

'Is it true that he's a Muslim? Or is he just kidding?'

'Why not? He has to live here the rest of his life.'

'How do you know that?' I asked.

'The minute he steps across our boundary, the English will arrest him, or the Russians.'

'Nazi crimes?'

'Naturally.'

'Guilty . . . or just charges?'

'We've seen the legal papers. That is, the government has.' He said carefully, 'I'd say the charges weren't hypothetical.'

I pondered this for some minutes and wondered to myself: If the Afghan government has the dossier, why hasn't it been shared with our ambassador, who's obviously looking Stiglitz over as a possible doctor? I didn't want to ask Nazrullah about this directly, but I did hit upon what I considered a neat alternative: 'Surely the British must know about him, if they've threatened to arrest him.'

'They do,' Nazrullah laughed, for he had guessed the purpose of my question. On his own he added, 'As a government, they know his record, and if they could catch him in India, they'd arrest him. But if he gets clearance for Kabul, which I'm sure he will, the embassy people as individuals would consult him medically.' Dryly he added, 'I'm sure your ambassador would behave in the same way–arrest him in New York but use him in Kabul.'

'You're probably right,' I said noncommittally.

We dropped the matter there, but later Nazrullah observed, 'You expressed surprise that Dr Stiglitz had become a Muslim. Surely, if I'd stayed permanently in Dorset, Pennsylvania, with Ellen's people I'd have become a Presbyterian.'

The fact that he had mentioned Ellen of his own volition startled me, but his casual attitude toward abandoning Islam seemed even more striking, for I was then in the days when I believed that Muslims, Christians and Jews were destined not to shift back and forth, so I argued, 'Could you really have become a Christian?'

'For six years in Germany and America I was a Christian in everything but formal conversion. Suppose you lived in Afghanistan permanently, wouldn't you pray as a Muslim?'

I thought: Wouldn't he be amused if he knew whom he was asking this question of. That conceit produced my next question: 'But if you were to work in Palestine with the British, could you become a Jew?'

'Why not? If the facts were known, probably half our Afghan heritage is Jewish. For hundreds of years we boasted of being one of the Lost Tribes of Israel. Then Hitler decreed us to be Aryans, which gave us certain advantages.'

'What's your own opinion?' I asked bluntly.

'I think we're a delightful hodgepodge. Have you heard our marvellous myth? In the valleys west of Kabul we have a concentration of the Harzara people. Know what we believe about them? We claim that every Mongol who ever settled in Afghanistan—and there must have been millions—settled in those particular valleys and never once intermarried with any of us. A thousand years of racial purity. If the truth were known, I'm probably descended from the bastards who plastered up that pillar.'

'You mean you could become a Jew?' I repeated seriously.

'I probably am a Jew,' he insisted. 'And a Mongol, and a Hindu, and a Tajik. but I'm also a hundred percent Aryan, because I have a certificate from Göttingen University to prove it.'

We lapsed again into the deep silence of the desert and the faint stirrings of a brotherhood that was developing between us. Then I asked what I know Nazrullah intended me to ask when he suggested that I ride in his jeep: 'Where's Ellen?'

'She ran away.'

'You know where?'

'Not exactly.'

'You think she's alive?'

'I know she is,' he said, clenching his hands on the steering wheel. 'I'm morally sure she is.' From his actions and manner of speech I had to conclude that he was still in love with his wife, hungrily, deeply; yet I found it almost comical that I should worry about a man, no matter how much I respected him, who was worried about his second wife when he had a perfectly good wife waiting for him in Kandahar. It all seemed so Muslim. I was then too young to know at first hand any of those average American men who deeply loved their wives but who could at the same time become agonized if something untoward happened to their mistresses. It was the same problem in two different guises, but at the time I didn't know it.

'She hasn't written to her parents in thirteen months,' I said.

With a certain grim humor he asked, 'Have you met her parents?'

'No, but I've read their reports.'

'Then you know.' He smiled as he recalled them, then added, 'They're like this, Miller. If they'd seen that pillar at the caravanserai they'd have cried, "Goodness, something ought to be done about that," but they'd never have understood if you replied, "About Genghis Khan you can't do anything."' He grew painfully intense and said, 'There wasn't a thing they could have done about Ellen. They were fated to lose her. I was fated to lose her. And there wasn't a goddamned thing that any of us could have done to prevent it.'

I waited till the signs of his bitterness vanished, then asked, 'Is she still in Afghanistan?'

I remember distinctly, and at the time I remarked upon it myself, that before Nazrullah answered he leaned out to look at the stars, both west and east, then said quietly, 'I'm sure she is. Yes, she's in Afghanistan.'

I wanted to pursue the matter further, but at this moment I saw to the west, where Nazrullah had peered in search of his wife, a star that seemed brighter than the others and pointed it out to my guide. 'Good,' he said, halting the jeep till the others could overtake us. When they did he pointed to the star and said, 'The City.'

I looked again at the star and none of us except Nazrullah knew it was a light and not a star. 'It's a light at The City,' Nazrullah said. 'We'll camp here.'

'If it's so close, why don't we finish the drive?'

'It's sixty miles away,' Nazrullah replied.

'Impossible,' I protested, but Nur supported his friend.

'When you first see something like this, you can't believe it. The light may well be sixty miles away.'

'It is,' Nazrullah assured us. 'Let's get out the sleeping bags.'

I looked for low ground that would give me some protection from the wind that was rising, but Nazrullah led us to the highest part of a small hill and when we were prepared for bed he explained, 'Tonight we saw two men who died in the desert from sun and heat. For everyone who dies that way, a hundred die from floods.'

Stiglitz and I looked at each other in the white moonlight and Nazrullah continued, 'Once every three or four years it rains over some part of this desert. In a way you never saw before. Terrible, shattering. A wall of water builds up thirty feet high and destroys everything before it. Moves whole dunes from one place to another, and anything caught in a low spot is crushed.'

We looked at the gullies with new respect as he finished, 'Probably hasn't been any water down there in five hundred years. But just south of here–due south, as a matter of fact–Alexander the Great was marching his troops home from their conquest of India. They camped in the desert and in four minutes a wall of water swept over them, killing two men in three. This is a tough country, Miller. Don't sleep in gullies.'

At dawn we rose and headed west, and when I saw the last sixty miles of terrain I appreciated why Nazrullah had left Qala Bist in a hurry, for we could not have traversed at night what now faced us, and if we had tried to drive through the heart of the desert at midday, the heat would have been unbearable. In these last sixty miles the sand had largely disappeared and we were forced to pick our way through heaps of shale which thundered the day's heat right back at us. The humidity was down to nearly zero and a strong wind dried us out as we moved across the blazing dasht. Nur Muhammad warned me, 'Be careful not to bump your nose. The mucus dries up into little needles which puncture the skin. Bad infection.' Warily I touched my nose, and he was right. The thirsty air had sucked away all moisture, and my nose was lined with needles.

At one period I thought I would collapse if we didn't stop for a drink, but Nazrullah fell back to warn us, 'We've plenty of water and cans of fruit juice, but we're not going to touch it until we're sure we'll reach The City today.' He must have seen my disappointment, for he added, 'You can discipline yourself, Miller.'

So we pressed on, parched with heat. In the States I had never known anything like this, a heat so forceful that it seemed to fight with you for all body moisture. I could feel water evaporating from my skin, and my thoughts constantly returned to the soldiers who had perished in the jeep: This damned wind sucked them dry as they sat there.

Slowly I began to exercise the discipline of which Nazrullah spoke, and I began to find ways to adjust. I wasn't as thirsty as I thought, nor as near dead as

I feared. I was on an ugly mission across inhospitable terrain that would kill me if I gave it a chance, but there were many ways to survive, and Nazrullah now taught us one. 'We'd better put on the turbans,' he suggested, and when we had done so he produced a canister of river water, not for drinking, and from it poured water directly onto the turbans until they were dripping down our necks. We then drove on.

The turban, about eight yards of cloth, held a lot of water and released it slowly, lowering the temperature of our heads as it evaporated. I thought: This is the way to lick the heat. But within twelve minutes the voracious wind had sucked all moisture from the cloth. So we stopped again and sloshed on more river water, and for a while we were cool, but after ten or twelve minutes the turbans were again dry.

At last we reached a narrow pass that dropped down between rocks, and having descended this canyon for about a mile, we reached a low plain and saw ahead of us trees and signs of life and a village, beyond which lay an ancient city and a large body of water. We cheered and blew our horns, for the transit of the desert was completed.

A few Afghans in dirty desert dress straggled out to greet us, but we did not stop. 'Tell the sharif we'll be back!' Nazrullah called, and we sped for the lake, where we quickly undressed and lay in the water, so that our bodies could absorb the liquid they had lost.

'Look at him!' Stiglitz said after a while, and I saw Nazrullah far out from shore, where the water came only to his knees. When I caught up with him he said, 'You can walk completely across, if you care to.'

It was here, in this vast shallow lake, that the great Helmand River ended, for the desert sun and wind evaporated the water as fast as the mountains near Kabul delivered it. The powerful Helmand simply flowed into the desert and died. I hadn't believed it when Nur told me, but here it was, the death of a river. In late summer even this lake might be gone.

When we dressed, the sharif joined us. His title was pronounced *sha-reef*, with the accent on the second syllable, and he brought us melons and fruit, which in their richness, dripped juice from our chins. He listened impassively as Nazrullah explained the location of the missing jeep, and said that he'd dispatch a scouting party. No one was much perturbed about the deaths; if men crossed the desert often enough, some were bound to die, and many from that area had done so.

Talk then turned to the American engineer Pritchard, and we were all brought into the conversation. The sharif reported that twenty-two days ago the American, who worked at Chahar, seventy miles to the south, had broken his leg while taking water levels. It was originally intended to haul him to this village on a stretcher for a trip across the desert, but the sharif at Chahar had felt that local practitioners could heal the leg, and no stretcher was dispatched. A week ago news came to the village that an infection had set in.

'Did the broken bones puncture the skin?' Dr Stiglitz asked.

'We were told so,' the sharif replied.

'And they tried to treat a case like that?'

'They've been doing it for three thousand years,' the sharif grunted. He sent a servant to fetch a man who hobbled in on a leg that had been broken three weeks ago. 'We fixed his.'

Dr Stiglitz examined the leg and said in Pashto, 'It's as good as I'd have done.'

Nazrullah asked, 'You'll send a guide with us?'

'Of course,' the sharif said, and he ordered servants to refill our water bottles. 'But I wouldn't travel in this heat.'

'We have to,' Nazrullah replied. And we were off.

I have said that when we dropped down off the desert we saw a city by the lake. What we actually saw was one of the marvels of Asia, The City, and we were about to explore a fair portion of its incredible length. For more than seventy miles this nameless metropolis stretched along the lake, the marshes and the river that formed the western boundary between Afghanistan and Persia. At the dawn of history it had been a stupendous settlement. In the age of Alexander it had been one of the world's major concentrations, and he had camped near its bazaars. For a millennium after his departure it flourished to become one of the prime targets of the Mongols, and Genghis Khan had once slaughtered most of the people in the area. Tamerlane . . . all the others had ravaged the treasure, and now it stood in majestic silence, mile after mile after mile.

I thought: We're probably in error, calling this a city. It must have been like Route One between New York and Richmond. At intersections there were towns, and some were sizable, but much of the distance must have been interurban, so that city merged into town and town into rural area, with always the roadway itself hemmed in by buildings of some sort. Here the roadway had been the Helmand River, and now as we traversed it we saw the relics of The City.

At times there would be walls of substantial height running for miles, broken by majestic gates and marked with niches in which, before the Muslims outlawed human statuary, depictions of local heroes had stood. At other times we saw municipal buildings which might have sent emissaries to Jerusalem a thousand years before the time of Herod. And everything we saw was withering in the dry air, an inch or two eroding every hundred years.

There were rugged forts, obviously built by the Muslims: against unorganized shepherds from Persia they must have been impressive; against the skilled troops of Genghis Khan they probably lasted a day or two, at most, after which all the defenders were slaughtered.

We drove along the entire length of The City, and I cannot recall many moments when we were out of sight of really noble monuments. The architecture was solid and secure, wholly fitted to the bleak terrain, and the impression was one of dignity and organization. Qala Bist, at the eastern edge of the Desert of Death, had stunned me with its magnificence. The City, on the western edge, left no such impression. It was so huge, so beyond normal comprehension, and yet so intimate—I felt that men had actually walked these streets and collected taxes in these buildings—that no reaction was required. There it was. Damn it all, there the stupendous thing was, abandoned in the desert the way Route One, two thousand years from now, might reach in shadowy grandeur from what used to be New York to what used to be Richmond.

If the early morning heat on the desert had been oppressive, the heat we experienced at noonday along The City was almost unbearable. Of it I will say only this: Whenever we came upon an irrigation ditch or an arm of the river, we jumped from our jeeps, held our watches and wallets over our heads, and plunged fully dressed into the water, soaking in the moisture through aching pores. We then took with us large cans of dirty water, which we poured over our turbans as we rode, but as before, any relief was temporary, for within a few minutes we were once more completely dry. At least ten times we jumped into the ditches, and if we had not been able to do so, we could not have continued our journey. We would have been forced to seek protection in one of the vast, vacant buildings and wait for nightfall.

After one such dunking Nazrullah again asked me to ride with him, but he would not speak of his marriage. He wished to discuss the old days, when The City flourished. 'It probably had trade with areas as far removed as Moscow, Peking, Delhi and Arabia. It was never the superb city that Balkh was, but it must have been impressive. What do you suppose killed it?'

'Genghis Khan,' I replied with confidence. 'In school I read about him, as a name, but never appreciated what a devastating force he was. He stood before your city and shouted, "Here I am!" and pretty soon there was no city.'

'No,' Nazrullah laughed, 'you give good old Genghis too much credit. Now Balkh, the best city we ever had . . . He did destroy that. But not this place. Nor Herat. He wiped out the population, but people are easy to replace and Herat still exists. He didn't wipe out The City. Something else did that.'

'Plague?' I hazarded, for my mind was not yet geared to Central Asia.

'Three hypotheses are predominant, not mutually exclusive,' he said slowly. This was the kind of talk he liked, arguing in Germanic patterns, like most learned Afghans.

I interrupted him, laughing. 'It just occurred to me, Nazrullah. I've been with you and Moheb Khan and Nur Muhammad for some time now, and none of you ever says, "By the beard of the Prophet," or "By the blood of the infidel," or "Allah shall be revenged." I don't believe you're real Muslims.'

'I have the same complaint against you,' he replied seriously. 'Not once do you or the ambassador say "By cracky" or "Gee whillikens." We're living in a denatured age.'

'Proceed, Son of the Prophet.'

'That reminds me of something amusing,' he said. 'For a while I dated a Penn coed whose sole knowledge of Asia was that fine ballad "Abdul Abulbul Amir." Funny thing was, she made about as much sense as any of the others.'

'What did wreck The City?'

'First, this used to be the world's foremost example of irrigation. I think Alexander commented on that. You can see relics of the old system everywhere. Over there, for example. Probably a reservoir. But people got lazy. They didn't keep working on it. They felt that what had worked for a hundred years was good enough for the next hundred years. They stopped cleaning the ditches . . . built no new dams. They guessed right. For a hundred years, no trouble. But the death warrant had been signed. Genghis Khan can't be blamed for that. The people had grown fat and lazy.

'Second, and I place much emphasis on this, there was salt. If you irrigate a piece of land long enough, the constant flow of water must deposit salt, so that each year you raise a crop, you deteriorate the land that made the crop possible. Therefore I don't blame the lazy people entirely. Maybe the salt was just too big a problem to handle. In some future century, perhaps, all of Colorado and Utah will be useless because the men of this century were such good farmers. Your salt levels are rising ominously. Behold, Denver, Colorado!' And he pointed to the ruins.

'The third reason is the most tantalizing of all. Goats. Those damned goats are the curse of Asia. God gave us a fertile land, covered with magnificent trees and soil rich enough to feed all men. But the Devil got even by giving us just one thing. Goats. And they took care of the forests. Ate all the young trees. And the rich fields. Ate the cover off and turned them to deserts. Probably the most destructive animal ever created. Much more dangerous than the cobra.'

'But how would goats affect The City?' I asked.

'When this was a metropolis,' Nazrullah explained, 'the hills you see must have been covered with trees. Brisk business in timber and charcoal. Excessive cutting killed some forests, but goats took care of the rest. So today in Afghanistan we have almost no forests. Do you suppose we live in mud houses on purpose? They're miserable, but we have no wood. All the time I was in America I wondered, "What is the goat in America?" I found out. It's the man who destroys your forests.' He paused, then observed, 'You defeated Germany in this war, but in the future Germany's bound to win. Because Germans plant trees.'

I tried to lead the conversation back to Ellen Jaspar but was forestalled when our guide, perched on the spare tires behind my ear, sang out that we were approaching Chadar, where Pritchard lay. We looked for a ditch and plunged in to refresh ourselves, then stood on the bank as the monstrous wind sucked us dry, and when our turbans were no longer wet we replaced them with karakul caps. We straightened our clothes to make ourselves as presentable as possible, and while we were doing this I asked, 'Why all the falderal?'

Nazrullah replied, 'Down here you impress the sharif, or you get nothing.' As we drove into the village he added, 'We're so far from Kabul that government doesn't actually exist, except in the person of this brigand who rules as he wishes. Who's going to drive across that desert to correct him?'

It was an attractive village with an oversized caravanserai and cool pomegranate trees whose blossoms sent me an unfamiliar fragrance. The sharif came out to greet us, a huge fellow well over six feet in height, and I thought: How often we choose tall men to govern us.

And this sharif governed, that was obvious. As absolute monarch of a tiny kingdom, he had his own army, his own judges, his own treasury. Since he lived so close to Persia and so far from Kabul, his little kingdom used mainly Persian coins and Persian stamps. 'Dozens of these principalities remain in Afghanistan,' Nazrullah explained, and I understood why, in Chahar, the evacuation of an American with a broken leg was impossible. When you got sick here, the local medicine man cured you, or you died.

The sharif led us to a low, stifling hut tucked away in a corner of the caravanserai, and there on a straw mattress laid over a rope bed we found the gaunt, gray-faced American engineer John Pritchard, a wiry man in his late forties. Nazrullah held out his hand and said, 'Hello, Professor. The American embassy's sent a man to get you out of here.'

'I'm willing to go . . . right now,' the sick man replied. The sharif's servants had kept him clean, fed and shaved, but he was in pitiful shape and I sensed at once that he was close to dying, for his left leg, exposed to dry air to speed the healing, had been punctured by two fractures and was now clearly gangrenous. The skin was taut and greenish.

Dr Stiglitz hurried to the bed and studied the leg for some minutes, smelling his fingers as he did so. He then probed the man's groin and armpits. When he was done he placed his right hand on Pritchard's shoulder and said quietly, 'Herr Professor Pritchard, the leg must come off.' The engineer groaned and his face went even whiter than it had been.

Stiglitz continued, as if to convince the rest of us, 'In my opinion there's no chance on earth to save this leg. I'm positive other doctors would agree. I'm sorry, Herr Professor, but you must know.' Pritchard made no further sound; he must have expected such a decision.

Stiglitz added in a dispassionate professional voice, 'We face a difficult choice, for which we are all responsible–Pritchard, Nazrullah, Miller. I can take the leg off here, but where would you recuperate? Tell me that. Or I can medicate the leg now, then rush you back to Kandahar, where the operation could be performed much better and where you could recuperate at ease. In that case the question is, Could you stand the trip across the desert?'

Each waited for the other to speak, then Pritchard said firmly, 'If I stay here, I will surely die.'

Stiglitz asked, 'Then you want to go back to Kandahar?'

'Yes! Yes!' Pritchard cried.

'What do you think, Nazrullah Sahib?' Stiglitz continued.

'I'd like to ask one question,' Nazrullah countered. 'Professor Pritchard, you remember what the desert was like. Do you feel strong enough to cross it now?'

'Yes!' Pritchard repeated. 'If I stay here I'll die.'

'We'll take you to Kandahar,' Nazrullah said firmly, and when the decision was reached he became once more his efficient self. Looking at his watch, he said crisply, 'We must get back to The City before darkness. We'll sleep there. Start across the desert at dawn. You fellows up to it?' Nur and Stiglitz said they were. Then he addressed Pritchard directly: 'This is the last chance. You're sure you can cross the desert?'

'Right now,' the engineer replied.

'We go,' Nazrullah announced.

But I was appalled, both at the decision itself and at the hasty manner in which it had been reached. 'Wait a minute!' I protested. 'Dr Stiglitz, is Professor Pritchard qualified to make a decision like this?'

'I am,' Pritchard interrupted. 'I've waited here too damned long. If I stay here, I'm going to die.'

'Have you ever crossed the desert?' I asked, betraying my nervousness at intervening in such a matter, for I was the youngest present.

'I'm here, aren't I?' Pritchard asked contemptuously.

'You remember the heat?'

'Look, Miller, I refuse to stay here. Let's get going.'

'The heat?' I shouted. 'Have you ever crossed in daytime?'

'Yes!' the sick man shouted back. 'I can take it.'

I appealed to Dr Stiglitz. 'You know very well, Doctor, that intense heat and movement will increase the danger from that leg.' The German was silent and I shouted, 'Don't you?'

'Yes,' Stiglitz grudgingly assented. 'And every minute we don't operate increases the risk.'

'That's what I thought,' I said weakly. I felt as if I were going to burst into tears. Very quietly I said, 'We'll operate here–right now.'

Stiglitz spoke solemnly: 'But the risk to his life is just as great here, Herr Miller.'

'For God's sake!' I cried. 'Give me an answer, yes or no.'

'There is no answer, yes or no,' the German replied stubbornly. 'There is risk. There is risk here and risk there. I cannot decide.' He turned to Pritchard and asked gently, 'You know you're in grave danger, don't you Herr Professor?'

'Three days ago I thought I was dead,' Pritchard said. 'I'm not afraid any longer. In your opinion, Doctor, which way gives me the best mathematical chance?'

'That I cannot answer,' Stiglitz insisted. 'You and your American adviser must decide.'

The sick man looked up at me, and I almost had to turn away, death seemed so close. 'Young fellow,' he said quietly, 'I calculate my own chances as being best if we go to Kandahar.'

I was so certain that once we got that leg on the desert it would insure his death, pumping poison constantly throughout his body, that I could not accept either his answer, or Nazrullah's assent, or the doctor's impartiality. I knew we must take the leg off at once. In my anguish I looked at Nazrullah and said, 'Could we walk in the garden a moment?'

'You're wasting time,' Nazrullah warned me.

'I need your advice,' I said.

'You have my advice . . . Kandahar.'

'Please,' I begged.

Against his will I led him out beneath the pomegranate trees, sweet in the spring, where I had a chance to confront the hard quality of his mind. 'You're the American in charge,' he said harshly. 'You must decide . . . in fifteen minutes.'

'But, Nazrullah, you're a scientist. You know that a leg like that is pumping poison right through that man's blood. He can't possibly get to Kandahar.'

'The doctor thinks he can. I think he can. We should leave.'

'But if we do decide to operate here, will you arrange things for us?'

'Absolutely, Miller. I'll stay here a month if necessary. You make the decision and I'll abide by it. But make the decision.'

'Help me do what's best,' I pleaded. 'There's a man dying in there.'

'I can't do your job for you,' he said coldly.

'Could I see the doctor again? For just a minute?'

'Stiglitz? He's incapable of a moral decision. He said clearly: The facts are these. You decide.'

'What did he say the facts were?' I asked, sweating nervously. 'I want to hear them from him again before we decide.'

'No!' Nazrullah cried. 'You can't evade your responsibility.'

'Please, review with me what he said. I don't have it clear.'

'He said,' Nazrullah repeated impatiently, 'that Pritchard would probably die, whether we amputated his leg here or hauled him across the desert to do it.'

'He never said that!' I protested in real confusion.

'He implied it. He believes it. And if that's true, which I'm sure it is, the problem becomes simple. What's best for your country and mine?'

'That's a hell of a way to talk about a man who may be dying.'

'Miller, he is dying. What's best for you and me to do? Speak up or we're leaving.'

'Wait a minute. Let me think,' I pleaded. 'Nazrullah, we know he wants to get out of here. How much weight should I put on that fact?'

'The whole weight, Miller. If he stays here he knows he'll die.'

I hesitated, then said firmly, 'All right. We take him to Kandahar.'

'That's your decision?'

'Yes. Let's get started. Right now.'

'Please put it in writing.'

'What are you trying to do?' I cried.

'Things like this often end badly,' Nazrullah said cautiously. 'Americans like to blame Afghans . . . make us look stupid. If a stupid decision is being made you'll make it, and you'll put it in writing.'

'I'm not afraid,' I said bravely, feeling much older than twenty-six. 'But in that case I've got to talk with Stiglitz and Pritchard.'

'You have ten minutes,' Nazrullah said. 'After that we stay here . . . for many weeks.'

We returned to the sick room and I asked Dr Stiglitz to join me in the garden. He protested but Nazrullah said in German, 'Go ahead.'

'Your honest judgment, Stiglitz, and you can't evade now. What's best for this man?'

'This is a decision I cannot make,' Stiglitz insisted stubbornly.

'That's a hell of a position for a doctor to take.'

'It's the only one under the circumstances,' he said defensively.

'What are the circumstances?' I shouted, losing control of my patience under the hammering I was undergoing.

'Pritchard is going to die,' he replied bluntly.

'I say that if we take the leg off right now he'd have a chance.'

'You're right.'

'And if you haul him through the desert death is almost inevitable.'

'You're right.'

'Then for God's sake, let's go in there and operate.'

'I warned you, Herr Miller, that this is not a decision I can make. Pritchard is convinced that if he stays here any longer he will die. His spirit is worn out . . . can you understand that at your age? Worn out. It might be wiser for him to risk the journey to Kandahar if it restores his hope.'

'Who can decide this?'

'Pritchard.'

I returned to the room and told Nazrullah, 'I'll write out the order in five minutes.'

'You'd better,' he said.

I went to the sickbed and before I spoke to Pritchard I looked at the bleak walls of the caravanserai and smelled the stale, baked air. I would not have wanted to live in that room, even in health. But to have laid in that stifling heat for three weeks while local practitioners ruined my leg, to have watched it swell and grow green, would have been intolerable, and now to face the prospect of six more weeks would kill my spirit.

I sat on the bed and told Pritchard, 'I guess it's up to you and me. Here or Kandahar?'

'I know I'm in bad shape. But if I stay here . . . what'd you say your name was?'

'Miller. I'm from the embassy.' Then I had an idea. 'You know, Professor Pritchard, the ambassador himself sent me here. He's deeply worried about you.'

'I didn't know anybody gave a damn.' He turned his head, unable to control his tears. 'Jesus, Miller, this is the end of the world.'

'I can see that,' I agreed.

'How the hell did I get here?' he mumbled. 'Making a water study for a nation that just don't give a damn.'

'Don't say that. You wrote to us about Nazrullah. He's a fine engineer.'

'The guy with the beard?'

'Trained in Germany,' I assured him.

'Some of the best come from Germany,' he said in the approving manner of practical men who recognize excellence wherever developed.

'You're determined to make the run to Kandahar?'

'If I stay here I'll die.'

'You appreciate the risk?'

His spirit cracked. Rising on one elbow he shouted 'If you're afraid of your lousy job, I'll put it in writing. I want to get the hell out of here.'

'I'll do the writing,' I said, feeling miserable, for I knew I was condemning him to death. I call Nur Muhammad to bring my brief case, and on official paper I wrote:

> Chahar, Afghanistan
> April 12, 1946
> I have this day ordered the American irrigation engineer John Pritchard to be transported to the hospital in Kandahar, so that medical attention unavailable here may be given his badly infected left leg.
>
> Mark Miller
> United States Embassy
> Kabul, Afghanistan

Feeling sick at what I had done, I handed Nazrullah the directive. He read it twice, showed it to Stiglitz and Nur Muhammad, and folded it carefully. 'We'll leave in ten minutes, sleep at the edge of the desert and start our crossing as soon as we can negotiate that bad approach.'

He had overlooked one fact. John Pritchard refused to leave his post until his water-level records were collected. 'That's why I came here,' he said. 'If they want to build that dam, they'll need these records.' To my surprise, Dr Stiglitz supported him.

'A scientist should keep records,' the German said.

So I was led by a guide to a spot two miles down the Helmand, where John Pritchard had been collecting the data on which Nazrullah would build his dam. More significantly, perhaps, Pritchard's word would form the basis for riparian treaties between Afghanistan and Persia, who had threatened war over the river. We found a small shed, boiling hot, some water gauges, a sheaf of irreplaceable records. The guide warned me in Pashto to watch the steps leading to the shed, for it was here that Pritchard had broken his leg; and as I stood in this lonely shack, this veritable end of the world where the temperature was daily above a hundred and thirty, I thought of all the careless speeches made in Congress about the cookie-pushers of the State Department, those striped-pants boys who haunt afternoon teas, and I wished that some of the arrogant speakers could have seen the work that John Pritchard had accomplished for our nation and for Afghanistan.

'Was Pritchard a good man?' I asked the guide. It was a kind of judgment he had not previously been asked to make, and he was confused. Finally he said brightly, 'Yes, he could handle a gun with skill.'

I was to ride with Nazrullah in his jeep, while Nur and Stiglitz supervised loading Pritchard in the back of theirs. As they did so the German said heartily, 'If I ever saw a man with a good chance to get across the desert, it's this one.'

'We'll make it!' the engineer called as we set forth, and it became my duty when we stopped to pour as much water as possible over the stricken man, thus keeping his temperature down, but before we had traveled far he became partially delirious and asked that I ride with him, as he wished to speak of America.

Thus we rode past the brooding, empty buildings of The City, and in the cooler evening his fever abated and we talked. He was from Fort Collins, Colorado, and had spent each autumn hunting in the Rockies. He was, he admitted, a fairly good rifle shot and had bagged elk, bear and mountain goats. He had a low opinion of the latter and felt they did more harm than good. He was optimistic about one thing: said he knew a one-legged man in Loveland who had no trouble hunting.

'I'm that kind of man,' he said, 'who won't give up till I learn how to walk with a wooden leg.' But at the next stop Dr Stiglitz decided to give Pritchard a knock-out pill, and the engineer fell asleep.

10

As soon as morning light permitted, we negotiated the canyon, and when the sun was well ablaze we were on the desert, stopping frequently to pour water on our turbans. At first I rode with Nur and the sick man, keeping his body under wet compresses, but he grew constantly worse, and at one of the water stops Stiglitz insisted upon changing places with me so that he might supervise the invalid. The more drastic steps he took to keep Pritchard alive worked. At the start of our trip I had given the engineer no chance to live, but apparently I was going to be proved wrong.

I now rode with Nazrullah, and after we had discussed Pritchard's leg, he asked me bluntly, 'What else do you need to know about my wife?'

The question startled me, for I had been devising stratagems whereby I could trick him into comment, and for a moment I could not think clearly, so I repeated lamely, 'She ran away?'

'Yes. Last September.'

'That's eight months ago,' I stammered.

'Seems longer,' he reflected, rubbing his beard. In his soggy, formless turban he looked quite Asiatic.

'Why did she run away?'

'You wouldn't understand,' he replied with a nervous laugh. He wanted to be helpful, but the facts were so preposterous that he was unable to evaluate them, so he kept silent, reminding me of the worried Afghan husband who had hustled back and forth between his sick wife and Dr Stiglitz: he would report only what he himself understood.

I appreciated his effort at good will, for the conditions under which we rode made conversation difficult. The desert was intolerably hot and we were both gasping for air. 'This must be hell on Pritchard,' he observed.

'It's what I was worried about yesterday,' I reminded him.

'We've been through that!' he cautioned. 'I have your order, in writing.'

'Did you warn Ellen Jaspar that . . .'

'That I was married? Yes.'

'The other day in Kandahar I met your wife, your Afghan wife, that is.'

'I know. Karima told me about it in her letter.'

'How could she send a letter?' I asked, like a movie detective trapping a suspect. 'I saw her only a short time before I left.'

'The messenger who brought Dr Stiglitz also brought her letter,' he explained, and I had to laugh at my own suspicions.

'I'm sorry,' I apologized. 'This whole thing seems so shadowy.'

'To me it's even more so,' he confessed.

'Then what Karima said was true? You did tell Ellen?'

'Whatever Karima says is apt to be true.'

'Is she a beautiful girl?' I asked for no obvious reason.

'Very. It was stupid of her to wear the chaderi. I don't require it.'

'I suspect she was afraid of Nur Muhammad.'

Inappropriately, Nazrullah began to laugh and I must have looked at him with censure, for he said, 'I'm sorry, but when you mentioned the chaderi I remembered something which explains Ellen rather better than anything else I could tell you. I sympathize with your suspicions. You're sure that I mistreated her and that my family kept her prisoner and that she's walled up somewhere pining for freedom. Miller, when she arrived in Kabul, all of us . . . everybody . . . tried to make her feel at ease. You know what she did? On the morning after the marriage she came down to breakfast wearing a chaderi.'

'What?'

'Yes, at breakfast. A very expensive silk chaderi which she had asked a dressmaker in London to make from a picture in a book. She was going to be more Afghan than the Afghans. My family tried not to laugh, and I had tears in my eyes to think that she was such a good sport. We explained that you don't wear a chaderi at breakfast. But I had one hell of a time keeping her from wearing it on the street.'

He laughed in memory of that bizarre event as a father laughs during a business lunch when he recollects his child's mistakes. 'You may have heard that one day in Kandahar the mullahs spat at her. When it was all over, she started to cry, not at the mullahs but at me. "If you'd let me wear the chaderi," she whimpered, "this wouldn't have happened."'

'I don't understand.'

'None of you Americans understand what an extraordinary woman Ellen is. Obviously her parents didn't. Nor her professors. Don't call her a girl any more. She is a woman. I doubt that she was ever a girl. She is a rare human being who sees through to the essence of God. I suppose you know that on one of our first dates she told me all about the atomic bomb.'

'You met her in 1944,' I checked. 'At that time there wasn't such a bomb.'

'She invented it,' he said cryptically.

I looked at him askance and he was about to elaborate when the rear jeep signaled us to stop, and in the moments we waited for them to overtake us he added, 'Ellen foresaw that if the nations continued their madness, they would be forced to invent some super-terrible weapon. She even described it rather accurately. "It's the age of air, so they'll deliver it by air, and it'll wipe out whole cities." She added that there was no way to prevent it and probably no way to escape. She said, "I hope I can get to Afghanistan before they destroy us all." At first I thought she was using us as a refuge . . . because we would be the last place bombed, but that wasn't her idea. She told me, "There isn't going to be any refuge, and if I'm to die, I want to die in Afghanistan, which is as far away from our pitiful civilization as any place I know. Let's live and die close to primitive things." I suppose that's what she had in mind when she protested my building the dam.'

Dr Stiglitz walked gloomily to our jeep and said frankly, 'He won't make it, Nazrullah. He wants Miller to ride with him.'

But I was so close to probing Nazrullah's secret that I protested, selfishly: 'I want to talk with Nazrullah . . . just a little longer.'

Stiglitz said without expression, 'Pritchard wants to talk, too. To an American.'

'Forgive me,' I said, and when I took my seat, close to the engineer's fevered head, I started applying towels, but he merely gasped and rolled his eyes at me. He was very close to death.

Finally he whispered, 'I can't breathe.' Nur was weeping.

'I can't breathe either,' I assured the dying man. 'This heat.'

'With you the cause is different,' he replied lucidly. 'You don't carry a leg that's beating like a drum. I can feel it pumping poison.'

I bit my tongue to keep from reminding him that he was repeating my words. I said, 'We're better than halfway through the desert.'

'I want you to give my wife a message,' he said with painful effort. 'She lives in Fort Collins. Damned good woman. Tell her . . .' He winced, as an almost visible pain streaked across his face, driving him to incoherency.

I soaked his turban and applied wet rags to his leg. The river water was used up and I proposed to Nur, 'We've got to use some of our drinking water.' Nur looked at me in dismay, studied the desert ahead, then listened to Pritchard moan. I saw tears start down his cheek and dry to salt in the desperate air.

'If he needs water, give it to him,' he said in Pashto.

I poured some of the drinking water over Pritchard's head and he regained consciousness long enough to dictate jumbled phrases to his wife. She was to consult with a Mr Forgraves in Denver. The kids must graduate from college, both of them. Then, for some reason I didn't understand, he went into a long discourse about a new kind of paint he had seen described in a technical journal. It would cure their cellar problems once and for all. Be worth two hundred dollars but he thought she might get it for less.

'Pritchard,' I broke in after the paint monologue, 'I think I'd better get Dr Stiglitz.'

'Don't. If I'm gonna die, let me die with my kind, not some goddamned Nazi.' He stated shivering. Then a dreadful sweat broke out across his face and little rivulets of perspiration accumulated, to be evaporated instantly in the swirling heat.

'I'm burning up!' he shouted. Nur Muhammad, who heard the conversation, began to cry openly and finally stopped the jeep.

'I will not drive a man to meet death,' he sobbed as he stood bareheaded in the sun. 'If death wants this man, death must come . . . here.'

In a kind of frenzy I saw the jeep ahead pulling away, so I blew the horn repeatedly. 'Knock off the noise, you kids,' Pritchard cried.

Nazrullah caught my signal and whirled about on the blazing dasht. 'What the hell's the matter with you?' he stormed at Nur.

'I will not drive a man to meet death,' Nur stubbornly repeated. Taking a small rug from his gear, he spread it on the sand and, kneeling westward to Mecca, prayed.

'He looks awful,' Nazrullah said, and Dr Stiglitz hurried over to check the delirious engineer.

A strange, desert prayer came to my lips, silently: 'Oh, God, spare my countryman.' At the mumbling of these words, John Pritchard died.

I looked distractedly at Nazrullah, who shrugged his shoulders and said, 'It was a chance. Nobody thought it was a good chance.' The callousness of this remark made me want to storm at the incompetents who had permitted this disgraceful suicide, but that obligation was taken from me by Nur Muhammad, who wept, 'You're all criminals. Bringing this doomed man onto the desert.'

This was too much. I shouted, 'If you thought that, why didn't you say so?'

'Nobody asked me,' he sobbed, and it occurred to me that if he had once supported my argument, we never would have left Chahar and Pritchard would now be alive. But I knew why he had remained silent: he had been afraid to contradict his social superior, Nazrullah, so now we were on the desert with a dead body to deliver . . . remorselessly assaulted by the noonday heat.

Nur Muhammad was quite incapable of driving, so I took charge of the second jeep, the one with the corpse, and we headed for Kandahar, but when we reached about forty miles an hour on the shale I suddenly saw looming ahead a field of gotch, which I swerved sharply to avoid, recalling the soldiers who were dead for not having done so, and I threw the jeep against a series of jolting rocks which snapped the front axle.

Nur Muhammad went to pieces, berating himself for the fact that he was not at the wheel in this difficult terrain and cursing fate because the corpse had been thrown out of the jeep and now lay in horrible contortion on the dasht. Nazrullah, in contrast, was superb. He quieted Nur, absolved me of blame, and helped Dr Stiglitz load the corpse into the workable jeep. He then quietly studied his map and informed us, 'The Caravanserai of the Tongues must be a little distance to the north. We'll tow the broken jeep there and decide what to do.'

But while we were attaching two ropes Dr Stiglitz said, 'Why don't we drive back and take the front axle from the jeep of the two soldiers?'

Nazrullah stopped sharp, dropped the ropes and stood in the blazing sun considering the alternatives the German had suggested. Clutching his beard he mumbled, 'Why didn't I think of that? Stupid. Stupid.' He walked away from us, positioning his opened hands as if they were two jeeps. For a long time he strode back and forth across the desert, then returned to us.

'For three reasons we must go directly to the caravanserai,' he said. 'First, I'm not sure we could find the other jeep if we wanted to.'

'It's right back there.' I pointed.

'It's more than forty miles,' he corrected, 'and sometimes you can't find things a second time in the desert. Second, we don't have enough water to double back and forth. But most important, suppose the sharif's scouting party has already been there? Suppose we go back and find that the jeep is gone?'

Saying no more, he completed tying the ropes, then hauled us up to the Caravanserai of the Tongues, into which we limped at four that afternoon. His note was still fastened to the door.

We pushed the jeep into one of the honeycomb rooms, then held a council in which Nazrullah explored the alternatives available to us. We decided that two men in the good jeep must try to get back to Qala Bist, taking Pritchard's body along. It was no use risking four lives. The other two men, with what food could be spared, must remain at the caravanserai with the damaged jeep until such time as a rescue party could return. 'There's only one question,' Nazrullah concluded. 'How shall we pair up?'

Learning from the past, I responded quickly: 'I'll write an order and accept full responsibility. Stiglitz and Nur will stay here. Nazrullah and I will drive to Qala Bist.'

'Reasonable,' Stiglitz grunted.

Nur Muhammad, still shaken, wrecked that plan. He sniffled, 'It's my duty to stay with Miller Sahib.'

'Your duty is discharged,' I replied in Pashto.

'No! You are in my care,' Nur insisted.

'The whole argument's irrelevant,' Nazrullah said. 'If anyone must cross the desert it's got to be the Afghans. Miller and Stiglitz, stay here. Nur, jump in the jeep.' Nur started to voice some new objection, but Nazrullah shouted a phrase remembered from his American education. 'For Christ sake, scram!' When Nur was settled, Nazrullah and I hiked with the water jugs to the stagnant pool that provided a meager supply for the caravanserai. 'Can you live on this stuff for three or four days?' he asked.

'You get back here before then,' I joked, but I remembered the terror that Nazrullah felt about being on the desert with only one jeep, so I took all the jugs of sweet water and gave them to him. As I did so I said. 'Keep this crate away from the gotch.'

As he drove off he assured me, 'When I come back to get you, Miller, I'll answer all your questions about Ellen. That's a promise.' He headed the jeep back toward the desert he dreaded, and I last saw him speeding eastward, his lone flag whipping in the furnace-like air.

At dusk Dr Stiglitz and I ate a frugal meal and drank a little of the brackish water. We could exist on it, but the prospect was not attractive. We then went out to watch the blazing sun sink behind the dunes and sat together in the refreshing coolness until the great stars appeared, and the white moon. We were about to retire when Stiglitz whispered, 'What's that?' And we heard a soft sound, as if a human being were creeping upon us.

We remained very silent, and then saw moving into the moonlight a small group of gazelles, more graceful now, perhaps, than they had been in sunlight. They had been feeding somewhere to the north and were returning to the safety of the desert, where none of their predators could surprise them. They formed such a contrast to the ugly death we had witnessed, that both Stiglitz and I watched them for many minutes. Then, with an unexpected clap of his hands, he startled the little beasts and they leaped and spun in the moonlight, vanishing at last over the dunes.

'Exquisite,' Stiglitz whispered, and for the first time I felt some kind of identification with the German. I still wanted to know why he had made the incredible decision of hauling Pritchard onto the desert, and I was about to question him on this when he said, 'It's after nine. Let's get ready for bed.' We entered the vast caravanserai and lit our Coleman lamp, studiously avoiding the ghostly pillar at the far end of the fort. But it was there.

I said, 'You surprised me at Chahar when you refused to make a medical decision . . . when the facts were so clear. Once Pritchard carried that leg into the desert . . . he was doomed. Why didn't you support me?'

'Was he doomed?' Stiglitz asked cautiously.

'Of course he was. Even I saw that.' Something in the way I spoke shattered the empathy we had felt while watching the gazelles. Perhaps Stiglitz suspected that when I returned to Kabul I would use Pritchard as an excuse for not recommending him to our ambassador.

A darkness came over his face and he asked contemptuously, 'So even you could make that diagnosis, eh? Well, let me tell you, my young friend, I couldn't make it. And I've been a doctor damned near as long as you've been alive. There are many diagnoses you're not qualified to make, Herr Miller.'

Without warning he rose and stamped off to the pillar, taking with him our only carving knife, which he scraped vigorously against the plaster, as if driven by some harsh compulsion.

'Nazrullah said it's a national monument,' I warned from the opposite end of the room.

'It's a universal monument,' he corrected me, 'and I'm going to see what's inside.' He spoke with determination, then called, 'Come here, Miller. It's a human skull.'

Against my better judgment I walked slowly down the room, lugging the Coleman lamp, which Dr Stiglitz grabbed from my hand to hold against the pillar. Behind the inch of plaster I could see a rounded bone. 'Is that a skull?' I asked.

'Yes. How many bodies would you estimate are in this pillar?' Before I could answer he did a most ghoulish thing. He planted the lantern in the middle of an open space and said, 'This will be the central pole.' Then he lay flat on the earth, his toes near the lantern, and commanded me: 'Mark where my shoulders come.' When the scratches were in the earth, he shifted his body so that I could mark off a new shoulder, and so on around the imaginary pillar.

'Well,' he concluded with some satisfaction, 'that makes thirty bodies jammed into one layer. Now how many layers?' He stepped back to calculate the number of tiers required to reach the roof. 'Perhaps forty-five layers.' He paused and a slow look of horror crossed his face. 'My God! There's over thirteen hundred people in that pillar.'

We sat on the floor, surveying the grisly monument, and I was struck by the grip it had on Stiglitz. Finally I asked, 'When Pritchard died, did I see you crossing yourself?'

'Yes.'

'You were a Catholic?'

'In Munich, yes.'

'Yet you turned apostate?'

'Of course. Since I'm to live here the rest of my life.'

'Why?' I asked bluntly.

'Surely you've been told, Herr Miller,' he said with contempt. 'That's why this pillar fascinates me. Gives me hope.'

'What do you mean by that?' I asked.

'It proves what I've always suspected. The things we did in Germany . . . the really dreadful things, are what men have always done.' Before I could express my disgust at excusing the civilized man Adolf Hitler by citing the barbarian Genghis Khan, he added, 'In each civilization some men run wild. If we're lucky, we control them early. If not . . .' He pointed to the pillar.

We spent the hours before midnight discussing this theory, and he marshaled strong support for his idea that what he had seen in Germany was a recurring sickness which might strike any nation at any time. I argued against this theory of inevitability, but he was adamant in extending it.

'To be specific,' he said, 'I haven't been to America but I've seen your films and read your books. I'm positive that in your country there would be no difficulty in finding S.S. volunteers for the job of collecting Negroes and throwing them into concentration camps.'

'Wait a minute!' I cried, condescendingly.

'Herr Miller!' he replied, pulling my face close to his. 'Don't you know in your heart that you could do to the Negroes what we did to the Jews?'

I said quietly, 'Don't judge us by the fact that we have a few sick people.'

'You have an endless supply,' he assured me. 'We turned ours loose on Jews. Some day you'll turn yours loose on Negroes.'

'But never Buchenwald,' I resisted.

'In the beginning, never,' he agreed. 'Your sensibilities would not permit it. Your Bill of Rights . . . But after two or three years of total propaganda . . . the president, churches, newspapers, cinema, labor unions . . . don't you understand that you would find many Americans eager to shoot down Negroes with machine guns?'

'No,' I announced confidently.

'Herr Miller, you're an idiot,' he stormed. To my surprise he leaped to his feet and rushed to the pillar, which he banged with his fist. 'Do you think that Genghis Khan started with this pillar? No. He marched step by step until this pillar was nothing. I could find in any American city you care to mention men who would be glad—joyous, shall we say—to be led step by step until they were building this pillar with living bodies. Do you think we Germans started out one day by building pillars? No, Herr Miller, no! Do you think I started with this?' He beat the pillar until I expected his knuckles to come away bleeding.

Breathing hard, he came and sat beside me. It was now past midnight and we were both worn by the tragic day on the desert, but the pillar kept us awake, and Stiglitz said softly, 'Do you really think, Herr Miller, that the reports the Allied governments have on me started with a pillar like that grisly thing? Oh, no! I was a fine, respectable doctor in Munich, married to the daughter of an important businessman . . . a member of the church. My wife and I saw certain promotions available through the Nazi party and we joined. Many prudent men and women did. It was easy at first. The Jews, whom we all despised'—he told me this in a confidential voice, as if I would appreciate why any reasonable man would despise Jews; indeed, as if our hating them together made us brothers—'were merely to be sequestered. That was all, sequestered.

'One day they asked me to check the health of the Jews they rounded up, and I did so, very carefully. Believe me, Herr Miller, if I found a Jew who needed an expensive medicine, I said so, and there are many Jews alive today solely because I prescribed expensive medicine for them.' He nodded in confirmation of his own plea, and I judged that he had often conducted this dialogue with himself. There were Jews living today because of what Dr Stiglitz had done for them, of that I was sure.

'If I were ever brought to trial,' he assured me with great confidence, 'the health records of the City of Munich would show case after case where I saved the lives of Jews. It's all there . . . in the reports.'

He looked at me beseechingly, a tired, pudgy man with turbaned head, wrinkled brow and worried eyes. I thought, perhaps, that he was perspiring, but he was sitting with his back to the lantern, and all I could see was shadow. Persuasively, cautiously, his words resumed: 'Unexpectedly other problems arose. A Jew was to be certified mentally deficient so he could be sterilized. The government wanted me to designate a complete stranger as three-quarters

Jewish so his property could be confiscated. I'd never seen him before, but he was obviously Jewish . . . you can always tell a Jew. So step by step my soul was corrupted.'

He was driven by some deep hatred back to the pillar, which he hammered with his open hands. 'Miller,' he cried in a hoarse shout, 'do you suppose that the man who applied this plaster over living, breathing mouths started with this job? Do you believe that you're immune?'

'To killing Jews, yes!'

'Ah, but the Negro is your Jew. Are you immune there?'

'Of course!' I shouted in disgust.

'Herr Miller, you're a liar! You're a self-deceiving liar!' He beat the pillar again. 'This is your pillar, too. This is the pillar of Americans and Englishmen and Germans alike. I couldn't have built this alone, you know.'

To my embarrassment his voice began to choke, as if he were going to burst into tears of confession. Then, thank heavens, he gained control of himself and rejoined me on the floor. It was now about two in the morning and in the flickering light of our Coleman lamp I could see his drawn face, weary yet driven to further revelation, and in some strange way he looked as he had that night in the square at Kandahar when he was condemning the dancers. I could hear his voice speaking the words but this time applying them somehow to his own history: *They're cruel little sodomites. When they come to town they create a great evil.* What ugly passage in his own life among the Nazis did that repeated phrase illuminate?

Toward four he got to the heart of his chronicle: 'Finally, when we were winning the war on all fronts—it was 1941—they came to me and said, "We're looking for a director of research. Military problems of the gravest significance. Involved is the final destruction of England." What could I say? I was flattered.

'They gave me a fine laboratory in Munich. I could live at home.' He seemed to savor, here in the Afghan desert, those bright visions of a happy German home life in Munich. 'I could live at home,' he explained persuasively, as if eager to convince me. 'I had to take the job, you can see that. At first it was routine experiments on colds . . . very sensible, very productive. I believe they're selling in America now a cold remedy that came from my researches. I convinced myself that I was helping win the war.

'I enjoyed other successes and then one day in 1943 they asked me to explore a purely theoretical question: How much can a human being tolerate? Now that's a nice question. A very important one, militarily speaking.' He paused a long time to stare at the pillar, then laughed in a high-pitched giggle. 'Without my knowing it, we were about to conduct pragmatic experiments on the same subject . . . at Stalingrad.' He laughed openly. Undoubtedly he had used the joke before.

'A fascinating medical question, Herr Miller,' he said reflectively. 'How much cold can a human being tolerate? Yesterday, for example. You were very hot . . . thought you couldn't take any more. But Nazrullah said, "You can discipline yourself," and the thermometer rose fourteen degrees and you did discipline yourself. How much heat could you have stood? That's a nice question. How much cold . . . I remember the exact phrasing because I wrote it down the day they posed it. You see, Herr Miller, I have a love for keeping records. Yesterday I could sympathize with John Pritchard when he said, "I must have the records." Because it is only from careful records that science can . . .' His voice broke and he dropped his head in his hands. His turban fell off and I could see the gray hairs on his stubby head; I could see his shoulders moving up and down, silently. Finally he put his hand on my knee and said, 'The English captured my records. I was meticulous. I was meticulous.'

For some minutes we said nothing, then he rose, overcome by a terrible emotion which I did not try to specify, and walked about the pillar several times, his mouth moving as if he were making a speech. The flickering light–the Coleman lamp gives a very white light and throws facial shadows in deep relief–made him look old. Suddenly he leaned against the pillar and issued a flood of words: 'In the cage there was this Jew. About fifty years old, a fine human being. His name . . . you can check this in the records . . . was Sem Levin. I had tried all sorts of experiments and had proved what required to be proved, but I had not applied my findings to an average, healthy man like the older soldiers in our army. So I chose Sem Levin. I chose him right from a nondescript group in the cage. I told my aide, "That's the man! Now we'll see what's what."'

He hesitated. He could look from the pillar to where I sat and he must have seen the horror and revulsion rising in my face, but he could not silence himself. 'Each morning we put Sem Levin completely naked into a room whose temperature could be exactly controlled. We dropped it lower and lower. After eight hours' exposure we discharged him and he returned to the cage filled with nondescript Jews. At first he merely dressed and talked with them. Later, when he joined them blue with cold, two fat middle-aged Jewish women began caring for him. They took his frozen body and held it between them, as if he were a baby. Everyone in the cage who had clothes to spare piled them over the three Jews, the two fat women and shivering Sem Levin.

'I grew to hate this tough little Jew, because each time he entered that room he announced quietly, "I am still alive." And when he said this, the Jews cheered, no matter what we had done to them that day. "I am still alive." Now it became with them a matter of honor to keep him alive. They saved food for him. Massaged him. Stole medicine for him. And from their resolve he too became determined not to die.

'No man could have withstood what he withstood. He'd come back to the cage with his dirty little penis shriveled up and blue, and he's say, "I am still alive." And the fat women, remembering their husbands dead somewhere in Germany, would take him in their arms.

'It was at this point, when pneumonia was about to begin, that he started greeting me each morning with the same statement. Very polite. "Good morning, Herr Professor. I am still alive."'

Stiglitz leaned against the pillar, weak with horror. Then he said in a ghost-like voice well suited to the silent room, 'And all the time my filthy wife was going to bed with anyone who had a little authority.' He looked at me with the beseeching face a man uses when he is beyond personal salvation and asks help of a priest or a rabbi. In a kind of wail he protested, 'But I was honest about the experiment. I could have killed Sem Levin any time I wished, and silenced that speech: "I am still alive." No, I held rigorously to the schedule as planned. We lowered the degrees day by day. My records will show that . . . exactly as planned.

'Much later than anyone would have dared predict, this dirty little Jew'–ten minutes ago he had been a *fine human being*–'contracted pneumonia. He should have died. By all human precedent he should have died. But those fat women somehow infused life into him. All that I took away they gave back. On the last three days he could scarcely make his voice heard, but he rasped, "Good morning, Herr Professor. I am still alive."

'Finally we broke him. Would you believe it, Miller, he spent three days stark naked in a room two degrees above zero, your system.'

Neither of us spoke. Then, in a wild rage, he shouted, 'That's why, you stupid American, I could not make the decision yesterday. John Pritchard would have refused to live if we had left him there. If Sem Levin could refuse to die, why couldn't Pritchard refuse to live? Tell me that, Mr Know-it-all.'

'What happened?' I asked in unconcealed horror.

'He died. Two full weeks after we had predicted ... fourteen days ... he died. The man in charge was so infuriated with the fat women that he sent the whole cage full of Jews away.'

'Away?' I shouted. 'Say it. Where?'

'Away,' he repeated dully. Then quickly: 'I don't know where he sent them. He signed the order ... the other man.'

'Stiglitz,' I said quietly, trying to keep control of myself, 'you're lying.'

'No, no, Herr Miller. It was he who signed the order.'

'You're lying,' I repeated, not moving.

'No, before God, he signed the order. For Sem Levin I was responsible. That I admit. The records will prove my guilt regarding him. But the others ...'

'Stiglitz!' I screamed, driven to my feet by an impulse outside me. 'I am a Jew!'

He stared at me in awful disbelief, then drew back against the pillar. He tried to laugh, as if I were joking. He moved his mouth to speak but could say nothing, and failing, ran behind the pillar for protection. 'Herr Miller ...' he gasped weakly.

'I'm going to kill you,' I threatened, making a lunge at him, but he used the pillar adroitly to protect himself, and I did not touch him.

In the large room there was no furniture, no weapon of any kind except the knife he had used for scraping away the plaster. It had been left lying on the earth near where I stood, but I didn't see it. To my surprise, Stiglitz left the protection of the pillar and made a lunge at me. I felt I could handle him, although he was heavier than I, and I got set to tackle him head on, but my preparation was useless, because he had no interest in me. With a swoop, he fell on the knife and leaped to his feet, jubilant.

'I'm going to kill you,' I repeated slowly. 'For Sem Levin and the others in the cage.' He grinned at me, holding the knife awkwardly with both hands before his chest, and I made a strong feint to the right, then a drive to the left, aiming a kick at his groin. I caught him well and sent him down in a screaming heap, with the useless knife still held before his chest. Had there been a chair in the room, I would have killed him then, beating him to death, but since I had only my hands, I refrained from leaping on him. Instead, I started kicking at him savagely as he lay huddled on the floor. Then, with a second feint at his head, I drove in with a powerful kick at his stomach, straightening him out and sending the knife softly into the dust. I made a football lunge at him and caught his throat in my hands.

I was about to strangle him when the great door of the serai creaked open, admitting daylight and a tall Afghan. With a deep voice he asked in Pashto, 'Who would fight in a serai?' I looked up and saw above me a dark-faced man with mustaches and a flowing turban. Across his chest were bandoleers and in his belt a silver-handled dagger.

'Who would fight in a serai?' he repeated.

'There was no reason,' I replied in Pashto, scrambling to my feet.

'Good,' he cried, and with a deft kick of his booted foot spun our knife against the wall, where it fell quietly to earth. Recovering it, he jammed it into his belt beside his own and said, 'The knife I well keep.'

As he spoke, other men began filing into the fort and finally a woman, tall and stalwart, with bangles in her nose and no chaderi. Then I recognized who the intruders were: the Povindahs I had seen at Ghazni, and this tall man with the two daggers was the one whom Nur and I had met that day on horseback.

He seemed to recognize me too, for he turned away and strode to the door, where he issued commands which I could not hear. When he returned, additional men appeared bearing bits of wood and utensils, which they carried to the center of the room, where a substantial fire was started.

When it was well ablaze, with smoke drifting out a hole in the ceiling, three Povindah women marched in with that wild, matchless gait I had admired in Ghazni. They were dressed in good gray blouses and black skirts, and since they passed close to me and wore chaderies, I stared at them and found them handsome . . . not beautiful in any way but handsome.

After they had taken their places about the fire another Povindah entered, and she was not only handsome; she was betwitching, a saucy pigtailed girl of seventeen or eighteen, dressed in red skirt and pink blouse. We looked at each other, and I recognized her as the girl chasing the goat at Ghazni, and I saw that in her nose she wore no bangles and that her face was extremely clean and sensitive. She kept looking at me as she moved toward the fire and seemed to smile, as if she recognized me, and the grace of her movement reminded me of the gazelles, who could twist and turn at any moment, and so we stared at each other until the man with the bandoleers cried roughly, 'Mira!' And the girl went to him for instructions which I did not hear.

She either did not understand what the leader directed or she thought his words unwise, for she stood perplexed, whereupon he gave her a shove and cried, 'Mira, do as I say.' He propelled her from the serai and I had to assume that he was angry with her for having paraded before me, but I was wrong.

For soon she appeared at the door bringing with her a most beautiful young woman with blond hair, fair complexion and sparkling blue eyes. She was obviously not a Povindah, even though she was dressed as one in black skirt and bracelets. It had to be Ellen Jaspar–tanned from long hours of marching in the sun, slim, vibrant, more challenging even than her photographs.

I can't recall now what I had expected Ellen to look like: vaguely, I had supposed she would be brittle, or obviously neurotic, or reticent with an overt fear of sex, or generally odd-ball like the typical college girl who reacts negatively to the world. She was none of these. Not a single cliché of the sterile revolutionary was visible in this unmarked, wonderful face, and I could hear Richardson of Intelligence saying in the embassy: *I'd date that one. She's stunning.*

Then I understood why her husband, when I had asked him on the desert if she were in Afghanistan, had looked first to the eastern and western stars, judging from them that it was the season when his wife would return to this country with the march of the nomads. Any man who had ever known Ellen Jaspar would keep in his mind a schedule of her movements. It was to this band of Povindahs that she had run away, and I stepped forward to introduce myself and to tell her that I had come to rescue her. But before I could speak, she nodded slightly, as if she already knew who I was, and hurried past me to where Dr Stiglitz remained in a dazed condition on the ground.

I remember clearly that her lips started to form a word, then stopped. On her second attempt she cried, 'Dr Stiglitz!' He looked up, saw who it was, and more or less collapsed, hiding his face from what he could scarcely believe.

She knelt beside him, took his hands and gently pulled him from the ground. 'Are you all right?' she asked.

'Madame Nazrullah, I can't believe . . .'

Having restored him to his feet, she left him abruptly and came to me, her blond hair peeking from beneath an embroidered Asian cap. Standing before me she said graciously, 'I'm Ellen Jaspar, and you must be Mark Miller from the American embassy.'

'How did you know?' I asked in some confusion.

'Our people followed you at the execution in Ghazni,' she explained.

In some strange way her composure made me feel out of place, and I didn't know what to say. 'I'm glad to find you alive,' I fumbled.

She suppressed a smile and said, 'The savages have treated me rather well.' Then she moved to the side of the tall leader and linked her arm with his in one of those automatic gestures which cannot be explained but which betray everything . . . only a woman who is living with a man ever makes that particular movement. Ellen Jaspar had run off with the leader of a nomad caravan, and it must have been this improbable rumor that had reached Shah Khan in Kabul. Little wonder that he had refused to repeat it or have it attributed to him in our embassy records.

'This is Zulfiqar,' Ellen announced.

'Is the feud ended?' the big nomad asked Stiglitz and me. When we nodded he cried, 'Then let us eat!' And I had my first meal with the nomads.

I I

We had not finished breakfast when two Povindah boys with darting eyes and quick gestures–the kind who steal you blind in a bazaar–came yelling that a jeep was hidden in one of the rooms. The Povindahs piled out to see the vehicle and Zulfiqar demanded, 'Whose is it?'

'Mine,' I said.

'Why is it here?'

I pointed to the broken axle and explained, 'I hit rocks on the dasht.'

'What were you doing on the dasht?'

The Povindahs gathered round, and since Dr Stiglitz was still unnerved by the unforeseen consequences of the pillar, I had to explain Pritchard's death in Pashto. Having done so, I began translating into English for Ellen, but she interrupted, in good Pashto, 'I learned the language.'

When we returned to our breakfast, Zulfiqar surprised me by inquiring bluntly, 'Now what do you want to ask us about Ellen?' He pronounced her name gently, in two syllables: *El-len.*

I turned to Ellen and asked, 'When you first saw me . . . how did you know who I was?'

Zulfiqar replied. 'They told us in Ghazni.'

'No one in Ghazni knew what I was doing,' I protested.

At this Zulfiqar laughed and indicated with his thumb that Ellen was to speak. She brushed back her blond hair and chuckled. 'Two minutes after you arrived in Ghazni, Mira saw you in the bazaar.'

'There were no women in the bazaar at Ghazni.'

'Mira is everywhere.'

'Is that true of all Povindahs?'

The indulgent smile on Zulfiqar's face disappeared and he banged his extended fingertips onto the rug from which we were eating. 'We're not Povindahs!' he exploded. 'That's an ugly name given us by the British. It means that we're permitted'—his voice assumed much scorn—'permitted, if you will, to cross their lands. We are the Kochis, the Wanderers, and we ask no nation's permission to cross boundaries. It was we who established the boundaries, centuries ago!' He subsided, but warned me quietly, 'We are the Kochis.'

Ellen resumed: 'Mira saw you in the bazaar and sprinted back to camp to warn us that a ferangi was in town. She already knew that you were from the embassy, had a jeep, traveled with an Afghan driver who worked for the government, and that you were headed for Kandahar. Don't ask me how she knew.'

I looked at Mira, whose dark eyes were flashing satisfaction. She smiled, but said nothing.

'When you attended the stoning of the woman, three of our men were spying on you. Later they talked with your armed guards. They found you were headed for Qala Bist, and when you hiked out to our camp at the edge of Ghazni, I watched you from the tents.'

Zulfiqar smiled again and said, 'She wanted to speak then, but I argued, "No. Don't spoil his fun. He's a young man. Let him go to Qala Bist. Find out for himself. Let him follow us across the desert. He'll talk about it the rest of his life."'

I was struck by his shrewdness and recalled the things I would have missed: Kandahar, the arch at Qala Bist, The City, and this caravanserai. In some way I must have betrayed my thoughts, for with a twist of his hand he imitated a man fighting with a knife and observed, 'A caravanserai at dawn . . . who would steal this from a young man?'

I looked at Zulfiqar with new respect and reminded him, 'You offered to answer my questions. Why is Miss Jaspar here?'

With no resentment he explained. 'Last September we camped for three days at Qala Bist. On our way to winter quarters at Jhelum. And this American woman came out from the fort to visit with our children . . . with our women. She spoke some Pashto and our people talked. She asked them where we were going, and they said, the Jhelum. She asked by what route, and they told her Spin Baldak, Dera Ismail Khan, Bannu, Nowshera, Rawalpindi. As we were leaving she came to me and said, " I'd like to travel with your caravan!" I asked her why, and she replied . . .'

'I said,' Ellen interrupted in Pashto, 'That I would like to march with the free people.'

I turned to Ellen and asked in English, 'Is he married?'

In Pashto she replied, so that all the nomads could hear, 'It seems I can love only married men.' Then she pointed to one of the handsome older women and said, 'That's Racha, Mira's mother.' It was thus made obvious to all what my English question had been, and thus I began my acquaintance with Ellen Jaspar in irritation and embarrassment.

The older woman, with a golden bangle in her nose, bowed gracefully, and I felt like a reproved child. I thought: I'm two years older than Ellen Jaspar, but she makes me feel like an infant. I remember that as I finished this thought, I happened to look across the rug and saw that Mira was smiling at my confusion.

When we finished eating, Zulfiqar asked Ellen in Pashto, 'Is the fat one a doctor?' Ellen replied that he was, and Zulfiqar said, 'Ask him if he'd look at some of our people.' Ellen said, 'Ask him yourself. He speaks Pashto.'

'I'd be happy to help,' Stiglitz volunteered, eager to re-establish himself after the fight at the pillar.

Zulfiqar announced, 'The doctor will look at your sores,' and the Kochis lined up to show him torn fingers, scarred legs and teeth that should have been yanked earlier. As I watched Stiglitz work, I was again impressed by his skill in handling sick people and I was torn between admiring him as a doctor and hating him for what he had once done as a doctor; while on his part he began to revive his hope that in spite of last night I might still recommend his employment by our embassy. Once he looked at me with a half-smile and asked in English, 'For a people without doctors, the Kochis are quite healthy, aren't they? They get along very well without doctors.'

I felt it unnecessary for me to put him completely at ease, so I ignored the question and had started toward the door when I was met by a travesty of a nomad, one of the funniest-looking men I ever saw. He was about five feet three, scrawny, unshaved, dirty, and clothed in the grimiest rags imaginable. He wore his filthy turban with one end almost to his knees and grinned through broken teeth and a left eye that had a scar dropping three inches from the corner to his jawbone. He shuffled along in sandals that almost fell from his feet and nodded obsequiously to all.

He had been bitten by something, and showed his left arm to Dr Stiglitz, who asked, 'What happened?'

'That damned camel!' the man railed, spitting between his black teeth.

'Looks like you've been chewed,' Stiglitz mused, looking at the ugly, extended wound.

'This is Maftoon,' Ellen explained. 'He tends the camels. What happened, Maftoon?'

'That damned camel!' the little man repeated.

'He has great trouble with the beasts,' Ellen laughed. She spoke rapidly with Maftoon and he nodded. 'One of the camels gummed his arm,' she said.

'Don't you mean bit?' I asked.

'No, I mean gummed. Camels have no upper teeth, you know. At least not in front. When they get mad at you, and Maftoon's are always mad at him, they gum you.'

'What are you talking about?' I asked.

'Come along,' she volunteered, and she took me out to the camels, where she threw bits of nan at them, so that they opened their mouths wide to catch the food and I could see that she was right. In front the beasts had strong lower teeth but no uppers, only a broad plate of hard gum against which they bit to chew off grass or other fodder. In back, of course, they had grinding teeth.

'I never heard of this,' I said, looking for a baby camel that I could inspect more closely.

'Try this one,' Ellen suggested, and she called an enormous brute some nine feet tall at the hump, the female with a bad disposition who had attacked Maftoon and sent him to the doctor. 'This old devil hates Maftoon but gets along well with me. Hey, hey!' she called, and the huge beast came close, lowered her head, and muzzled Ellen for a piece of nan. The split upper lip opened and Ellen pressed her thumb against the hard flat gum, then threw a chunk of nan, which the camel caught. 'You try it,' she said, and I took the nan and got the old camel to open her mouth. The plate against which her lower teeth hit was hard as bone.

'Extraordinary,' I said as the big beast ambled away, but as she did so she caught sight of little Maftoon coming from the doctor, and she began to make noises, showing her irritation. I say 'make noises' but I'm sure that isn't the right phrase: the camel uttered a sound that was a combination groan, growl, gurgle and grunt. And it was clear that whereas Ellen and I could inspect her teeth, Maftoon had better stand clear.

'Watch!' Ellen whispered, as the little camel driver took off his turban and threw it on the ground. He took off his long shirt, his tattered pants, his sandals, everything until he stood quite naked. Then he moved back and waited while the embittered camel shuffled up, smelled the clothes and began kicking them violently. She bit them, stamped on them, spit at them and then pushed them about the sand with her head. When she had vented her spleen she stalked majestically away, gurgling and grunting.

When she was gone, Maftoon recovered his clothes, dressed and went in pursuit of the placated camel. When he reached her head he scratched her neck, she gurgled amiably, and the two walked off toward the meager pasture.

'What's it all about?' I asked.

'The old camel drivers believe . . . and it seems to work . . . that a camel bears terrible grudges. Maftoon and the old lady had a fight, and even though she gummed his arm, she'd attack him again and again unless he allowed her to fight his clothes. She's satisfied and tomorrow he'll be able to load her again.'

We followed the little man and his camel for some distance, then sat on the rocks to watch the animals graze over land where I could see nothing. Ellen said, 'I never tire of watching camels. I suppose it goes back to my Sunday school in Dorset, Pennsylvania. At Christmas we traced camels on the wall. Goodness, that seems years ago.'

My interrogation of Nazrullah had been so constantly postponed that I was determined to learn as much as possible in my one day with the Kochis, so I launched right in: 'Why won't you write to your parents?'

She was expecting some opening attack like this and replied easily, 'What could I tell them?' She looked at me pleasantly as the bright sun illuminated her well-scrubbed face. 'If they couldn't understand a simple problem like Nazrullah, how could they possibly understand this?' She pointed to Maftoon, the camels and the caravanserai.

'Perhaps I could understand.'

'Not likely.' She spoke with a contempt which erased the pleasantness I had observed before.

'Nazrullah is still very much in love with you. What happened?'

'He's very kind. He's very tedious,' she replied.

I was irritated by her assumed superiority and was about to comment on it when I saw at the caravanserai gate the tall figure of Zulfiqar, spying on us, but after a while I had to conclude that he was not spying, for he seemed neither jealous nor suspicious; he looked as if he were glad that Ellen had found a chance to talk with an American. I thought: Wonder what they talk about when they're alone. Aloud I asked, 'Can Zulfiqar read and write?'

'Books, no. Figures . . . better than either of us.'

She said this in a bored manner implying that no further comment from me would be welcomed, so I observed, 'Nazrullah seemed one of the ablest men in the country.'

'He is,' she said with equal finality and equal boredom. Then with a show of real warmth she added, 'His wife Karima's even better.'

'I met her . . . in chaderi.'

'Karima! She never wears chaderi if she can help it.'

'I had a government official with me.'

'That's how it works,' she observed, reverting to a monotone. 'Karima observes the custom to protect Nazrullah, and he assures the government that he approves in order to protect Karima.'

It was a neatly phrased summary, but I remembered what Nazrullah had said on the desert: *On the morning after the marriage Ellen came to breakfast wearing a chaderi.* Probably I should have kept my mouth shut, but she had gone out of her way to irritate and embarrass me, so I remarked, 'Nazrullah told me that when you first came to Afghanistan you wore the chaderi.'

She blushed angrily, blood coursing across her beautiful face. 'Nazrullah talks a lot,' she said.

'Karima talked a lot, too,' I continued. 'She told me that while you were still in America you learned that Nazrullah already had a wife.'

She laughed uneasily. 'Why are you American men so preoccupied with such trivialities? Of course I knew he was married. This proves, Mr Miller, why you could never understand my reasons for leaving Dorset, Pennsylvania.'

'Any chance of my understanding why you left Nazrullah?'

She looked at me steadily, almost insultingly, with deep blue eyes, then laughed. 'No one who works for the American embassy could possibly understand.'

That did it. 'If you were a man,' I said coldly, 'I'd bust you in the nose. Why don't you have the decency to tell your parents where you are?'

My bluntness shocked her and she bit her knuckles, then toyed nervously with the embroidery on her blouse. 'Your question is a sensible one, Mr Miller, and it hurts. My parents are good, decent people and I'm sure they mean well. But what can I possibly write to them?' She looked at me with the first compassion I had seen since we started talking, but it quickly faded. 'Would you suggest something like this?' she asked brightly, as she began reciting an imaginary letter.

'Dear Mumsy and Dadsy,

I have run away from Mr Nazrullah because he's one of the most boring men on earth, and I'm sure his other wife thinks so too. He could move right into Dorset without causing a ripple, because he believes like you, Mumsy-wumsy, that God wants men to have big cars, that electricity makes people happy, and that if you sell enough canned goods, tensions will cease. You were deadly afraid of him, Dadsy-wadsy, but you shouldn't have been. He's your twin brother and if you'd recognized a good thing when you saw it, you'd have fought to keep him, not me. Because he could sell insurance ten times better than you ever did.

Your loving daughter,
Ellen
Bryn Mawr 1945, busted out

P.S. I am now living with a man who has no home, no nation and no responsibility except ninety-one camels. His wife made me the most adorable gray blouse you ever saw in your life, and I'm wearing it as I hike over the Lower Himalayas. I'll write to you next from Jhelum when we get there eleven months from now.

Your Ellie'

She looked at me bitterly and said, 'If you think that would put them at ease, send it to them. Frankly, I haven't the guts.'

I was disgusted with her. She sounded like a freshman I knew at Mount Holyoke, except for two things: the other girl's father sold stocks and bonds in Omaha, and in her sophomore year she got some sense. This Jaspar girl was irritating, and I said something which must have made me sound foolish: 'When the years pass, you'll be old. What will you do in a Kochi caravan then?'

'What will Senator Vandenberg do? He'll be old. And you . . . what's your first name, Miller?'

'Mark. Groton and Yale.'

'That's just dandy. If there's anyone I like to meet in the middle of the Afghan desert it's a Yale man. Tell me, do you honestly believe that in my home town of Dorset, Pennsylvania, there's a basic good, while here in Afghanistan there's a basic evil?'

'I believe that anyone does best when he clings to his own nation, his own people . . . and his own religion. I understand you gave yours up.'

'Presbyterianism is not difficult to give up,' she replied.

'A moment ago I said to myself, She sounds like a Mount Holyoke freshman. I put you about four years too high. You sound like a high-school freshman.'

'Damn you!' she snapped. 'I'm sitting here among the camels thinking: That poor dear boy, Mark Miller. Groton and Yale. The years will pass and he'll be stuck in some pothole like the embassy in Brussels. And he'll be old. And he'll have missed the whole meaning . . . the whole goddamned meaning.' She looked at me sadly and said, 'You're a young jerk and you're already prematurely middle-aged and I'm terribly sorry for you.'

I stared at her. I said nothing for at least four minutes, just stared at her. Finally she shrugged her shoulders and said, 'I surrender. Get me some paper. I'll write the letter.'

I asked her if she would come inside, but she replied, 'I never get enough of this free air,' and as I entered the caravanserai to get some paper from my brief case I met Zulfiqar and told him, 'She's going to write to her parents,' and he replied, 'I asked her to, months ago.'

I handed her the paper and she sat scrunched up on the rocks, biting my pen. Then, as she started writing freely and easily, I had a second chance to study her. If I hadn't just heard her bitter comments, I would have sworn that she was exactly what I had guessed when I first saw her in the caravanserai: a lovelier, more beautiful, more delightful person than we had seen in the embassy photographs. She simply did not look like a disgruntled post-adolescent. She was a mature, sensible-looking woman with a plenitude of charm, and if I could have erased her recent conversation I could easily have agreed with her enthusiastic roommate, whose report I now recalled so clearly:

Ellen Jaspar was a dear, sweet kid. She was loyal, responsive, and trustworthy. It sounded like the Girl Scout oath, but now Ellen came to a difficult part of her letter and a scowl crossed her face—a harsh, belligerent scowl—and I could not possibly kid myself into thinking that I was dealing with any Girl Scout.

'Will that do?' she asked, thrusting the finished letter at me. I took it, turned away from the bright sunlight, and read:

Dear Folks,

I'm terribly sorry I haven't written sooner, but some rather dramatic things have been happening and frankly, I found it almost impossible to explain them to you in a letter. Let me say quickly that they leave me happier than I have ever been, in better spirits, secure in all things. I love you very much.

My marriage to Nazrullah didn't work out too well, but it was not because of his unkindness. He was an even better man than I told you, and I am terribly sorry to have hurt him, but there was no escape. I am now with some wonderful people whom you would like, and I'll tell you all about them later.

To show you how crazy this world can be, I am now sitting with a herd of camels on the edge of the desert talking to a perfectly delightful Yale man, Mark Miller, who will send you a fuller letter of his own explaining all that has happened. He will tell you that I am happy, healthy and alive.

Your loving daughter . . .

Thinking of my own close-knit family in Boston, I could have wept at her inability to communicate with her people. I returned the letter and said, 'Sign it, and I'll airmail it from Kandahar.'

But before writing her signature she let the pen hang idly and mused, 'God knows, Miller, I told them the truth. I am happy, healthy and alive. And if I were to grow old as pleasantly as Racha has done, I'd be content.'

She signed the letter, addressed the envelope carefully, then bit the pen for some moments. Extending the sealed letter provocatively toward me, she waved it twice, then studiously tore it into minute bits, which she scattered among the camels. 'I cannot send such evasions,' she said hoarsely.

We stared at each other for some time and I saw in her eyes hatred, bitterness and confusion. But as I continued to look at her, these ugly attributes vanished and I saw merely the appealing gaze of an attractive, perplexed young woman. I said, 'I'll write to them.'

'Please do,' she replied.

I returned to the caravanserai, where I faced one of the more difficult decisions of my mission: on the one hand I was dead tired from the long, tragic day on the desert followed by the sleepless night at the pillar, so that my whole autonomic system demanded that I fall asleep; but on the other I awaited the momentary arrival of a rescue mission led by either Nazrullah or troops from Kandahar, so that before the rescue party took me away I wanted to see as much of Kochi life as possible. I forced myself to stay awake, watching the children and the older women working at their jobs. I thought constantly: I'm probably the only person from the American embassy who ever saw the Kochis close-up. I can sleep tomorrow.

But when I looked at Dr Stiglitz, spread out on the floor by the pillar, it became impossible to fight sleep any longer. I dropped on the hard-packed earth and almost immediately lost consciousness. My last memory was of Racha throwing a shawl over me.

I awoke in darkness and my first thought was: Good! If the rescue party hasn't made it by now, they won't come till tomorrow. I can stay with the Kochis tonight. The big room was filled with the smell of cooking, for Zulfiqar had ordered a substantial fire, around which many were working. Then I became aware of someone sitting beside me, and it was Mira in her red skirt, and when I stirred she said in Pashto, 'Zulfiqar told me to keep the children away.' Then in broken English she said, 'Ellen tell me English few words.' She spoke in a lilting, pleasant voice that sounded as if it belonged to a younger girl, and she had a gamin smile. When I reached out to inspect her attractive pigtails, which no other Kochis wore, she smiled with pride and explained, 'Ellen fix my hair American way.' She pronounced Ellen's name as her father did, in two gentle syllables.

In Pashto I asked, 'Does Ellen work in the camp?'

'All work,' she replied in English, followed by Pashto: 'Have you come to take Ellen away?'

'I wanted to, but she won't come.'

'I am so glad.'

'Who told you I was going to take her away?'

'We've always known she would leave some day,' Mira replied. 'Look how she works.'

Ellen, not knowing that I was awake, was busy at the fire, the antagonisms of her letter lost in work. Zulfiqar had killed a sheep in honor of the ferangi and it was roasting, with Ellen in charge to see that it didn't burn. From time to time she stuck a long fork into the flanks and tasted it, smacking her lips as she did so. Children stayed close to the fire, begging her for stray pieces of mutton, as if she were their mother, while against the wall lounged Kochi men, waiting silently for the unscheduled feast. Other women were preparing pilau in stone vessels, while Dr Stiglitz and Zulfiqar were opening K-rations, whose tops were promptly licked clean by other children. Except for the American cans, it was a scene that dated back to the beginning of man on the plains of Central Asia.

'We eat!' Zulfiqar announced, and it was exciting to watch Ellen, relaxed and motherly, standing by the roasted sheep and passing out portions as if she had done so all her life. From time to time, with greasy hands, she brushed her blond hair back from her moist face, appearing as feminine as any woman I had ever seen, and I recalled her words from the destroyed letter: *I am happy, healthy and alive.* Clearly she was, and when it came time to serve me she smiled as she gave me a chunk of well-browned meat.

'Be sure to try the nan,' she advised, as I helped myself to pilau.

Mira led me to a rug where the leaders were sitting, and I found a place across from Dr Stiglitz, beside whom Ellen would sit. Later, when I tasted the nan Ellen asked, 'Delicious, eh?' I replied that it had a nut-like flavor and she explained in English that it had been baked directly over dried camel dung. 'Can't you taste it?' she pressed, and I could. In Pashto she said, 'It is of the earth. It is of our life.'

Zulfiqar nodded and said, 'The sheep you're eating . . . we raised.'

Later I told Zulfiqar, 'Ellen wrote the letter to her parents, but tore it up.' Ellen added 'Zulfiqar understands. I can't explain Dorset to him, nor him to Dorset.'

The big Kochi chieftain said, 'You write, Mil-lair.'

'I will . . . tomorrow.'

My mention of this word evoked a sadness, and at our rug nothing was said; each looked at the other with a sense of strangeness. Mira broke the spell: 'What will you tell her parents?'

'What should I tell them?' I asked the group, and to my surprise it was Racha who spoke.

'Tell them,' Zulfiqar's wife said, 'that now we head for the Oxus and in the winter back to the Jhelum. We live between the rivers.'

'But don't call it the Oxus in your letter,' Ellen warned. 'They'll go crazy looking for it on their maps. Correct name's the Amu Darya . . . about a thousand miles from the Jhelum . . . and we make the round trip each year.'

'Two thousand miles?'

'Each year.'

'You ride the camels?' I asked.

This occasioned great laughter and Ellen explained, 'Only the babies ride camels. The rest of us . . . we walk.' She indicated Zulfiqar: 'He has a horse, of course, but he must ride back and forth watching the animals.'

'Do you mind the walking?' I asked.

Ellen indicated her legs tucked beneath the black skirt. 'They get very strong,' she assured me.

'How long has your clan been making this trip to the Jhelum?' I asked, and Ellen consulted Zulfiqar.

'There is no memory,' he replied.

'Where exactly is the Jhelum?' I asked.

'Far over the border in India,' was Zulfiqar's answer, which caused me to burst into laughter.

The big Kochi looked at me quizzically and I explained, 'At a meeting in the American embassy we were trying to guess where she might be.' I indicated Ellen, who said in English, 'I'll bet you were.' Quickly she translated the joke into Pashto, and the group laughed.

'And this important officer said' – I imitated Richardson's pipe-puffing, self-assured style – '"The chances of an American girl's entering India without being noticed are just not measurable."'

Zulfiqar chuckled. 'The British! A million of us pass back and forth each year and no one knows where we go or how we feed ourselves.'

Ellen added, 'We're the wanderers who make fools of petty nations.'

'Where are you headed now?' I asked.

'Musa Darul, Daulat Deh . . . in twenty-five days, Kabul. Bamian, Qabir . . .' Then he added a name that excited my imagination, for I had known it from boyhood days: Balkh, in ages past the greatest name in Central Asia.

'Balkh!' I said, and for a moment I daydreamed of how it would be to visit Balkh, but my fantasy was broken by Ellen, whose unpredictable behaviour I was about to witness for the first time. Because our argument over the letter had become acrimonious, I expected her to be resentful, but to my surprise, and for reasons I could not decipher, she said quietly, 'We go right to Kabul.' Zulfiqar nodded, and from something in the way he acted or from some nuance in Ellen's speech, I received the impression that I might be welcomed on the march to Kabul. I leaned forward to broach the matter and Mira did the same, as if she were anticipating hopefully my reaction to one of the most tenuous invitations ever extended.

'You go right to Kabul?' I repeated. No one spoke.

Then Zulfiqar said quietly, 'You're young. They'll send soldiers to fetch the broken jeep.'

I turned to consult Dr Stiglitz, whom I had continued to rebuff, and he said in English, hoping to win back my approval, 'He's right, Herr Miller. You should see the mountain passes. I'll stay with the jeep.'

Ellen contradicted: 'You must come too, Doctor. We could use you in the caravan.'

Zulfiqar leaned back and surveyed the ceiling, then asked Racha, 'Could we use such a doctor at Qabir?' Racha studied the German and nodded, whereupon Zulfiqar warned, 'We won't reach Qabir for many weeks. Will you join us?'

Dr Stiglitz licked his lips and replied weakly, 'Yes.'

At this, Zulfiqar ended consultation with the women. 'You two,' he demanded of the ferangi, 'how much money can you share with us?' I had two hundred dollars Afghan and Stiglitz much less, but he pointed out, 'The Americans owe me money. When you pass Kandahar on the way back this autumn . . .' Zulfiqar reached out and gripped the doctor's hand.

But before the agreement was sealed I felt, for some reason I could not have explained, that it was my duty to warn Stiglitz of the risk he was taking. I led him away from the table and said, 'With me it's simple. If Verbruggen gets mad, I'm sent home. I'll gamble, because from something he said I think he'll understand. But with you, Doctor, if you antagonize the Afghan government . . .'

'I'm a sick man, Herr Miller,' he said weakly. 'You know how sick I am. Unless I can find a rebirth . . .'

'You could be thrown out of the country,' I warned. 'You know what that could mean.'

'Unless I can purify myself . . .'

'You're placing a great burden on the Kochis,' I pointed out.

'Zulfiqar knows that,' he argued. 'He will use me as I will use him.'

'I wonder what he meant, Could we use him at Qabir?'

'I don't know,' the German replied. 'But I must make this trip. It will be my salvation.' And we rejoined the others.

As we did so, Mira came to me and said, in the dying light of the fire, 'The Kochis would like you to join us, Miller.' Then in English she added, 'I like it too.'

'I'm going to,' I said.

We sat as a group by the embers and I repeated the story of the pillar, to which Ellen responded, 'That's no surprise. One more outrage in a long series.' Zulfiqar inspected the exposed skull and others satisfied themselves that bodies were immured in the pillar, but no one seemed perturbed.

At bedtime I had my first doubts: Suppose Nazrullah arrives with the rescue party? I'd have to go with them. Suppose the ambassador blows his stack when he gets back from Hong Kong? This could finish me with the State Department. Suppose Shah Khan makes an official protest? I'd be packed out like the two Marines. Then I heard Zulfiqar's powerful voice announcing, 'We will move forward at four in the morning.' Somehow this set my mind at rest. Nazrullah was not going to intercept me, and once I started north with the Kochis, it didn't matter what the ambassador and Shah Khan thought. They couldn't do a damned thing about it till I reached Kabul.

I was awakened by the fearful clatter of Kochis preparing to launch their caravan for another day. Protesting camels were loaded with trade stuffs. Black tents were struck and folded. Animals in the courtyard were herded onto the trail, and children were assigned tasks to which they attended promptly to avoid stout blows from Zulfiqar. If I had ever thought of nomads as lazy, such ideas were dispelled that morning.

As we were about to leave the serai I recalled how careful Nazrullah had been to post messages which would explain to others where he had been and what he had accomplished, and it occurred to me that I ought to extend him the same courtesy, so I scribbled a brief note stating simply that I had found his wife in good health and that I was hiking to Kabul with a caravan of Kochis. Would he advise our ambassador? 'That'll give the old man something to chew on when he gets back,' I chuckled, but when I told Zulfiqar what I was about to do he went suddenly pale–I mean he turned almost white–and ordered me to stay where I was while he went to consult the leaders. Sometime later he returned, badly shaken, and asked me to redraft the note omitting any reference to Kochis. I did so, and he asked Ellen to read it, but she could scarcely keep from laughing. She said cryptically, 'It's accomplished its purpose,' but he asked for further minor changes and at last I carried it with a bit of string to the jeep, where I tied it to the steering wheel.

In darkness we started our journey north, an ageless caravan heading across an ageless land. In the lead, with checkered vest and French overcoat, rode Zulfiqar on his brown horse, complete with dagger, German rifle and leather bandoleer. On the camels rode several infants and one sick woman in her late fifties. The rest walked, slowly, comfortably, tending the sheep or keeping the ninety-one camels in line. Donkeys burdened with panniers chugged along, and behind them marched Ellen Jaspar, wearing stout army-type shoes, and Mira, in sandals.

The busiest person in line was jagged-eyed Maftoon, flapping back and forth along his string of camels, checking the ugly beasts to be sure their burdens were riding properly. I was to discover that during each day's hike, some one of the camels was outraged at Maftoon and made his frenzied life miserable: the ugly beast would not rise, would not lie down, would stray from the caravan, would fight and gurgle in protest. It was amusing to watch Maftoon as he tried to keep his camels in line.

At dawn the sun made Ellen's blond hair shine like gold, and she knew she was a beauty among the dark Kochis, for she carried herself with dignity. She had developed a healthy stride and her broad shoulders swung in the morning sunlight; but she was not alone in her beauty, for beside her with matching stride and jet-black hair hiked Mira, daughter of the chief and a notable person in her own right. She sensed instinctively when I watched her, and this pleased her, for occasionally I would catch her whispering to Ellen and pointing at me.

A day's trip was about fourteen miles. Except in the desert, where all travel had to be at night, we walked from pre-dawn till about noon, stopping at predetermined spots to which the Kochis had been returning for years, and this pitching and striking of tents became the dominant beat of the day's rhythm. I volunteered to help with the camels, for the preposterous brown beasts continued to fascinate me, and I often sat for hours watching them chew, with flopping jaws that seemed to lack all terminal attachments.

Once, when I was observing the frowsy old female who had attacked Maftoon, it occurred to me that the forlorn beast with the droopy eyes looked exactly like my Aunt Rebecca in Boston. I could hear her whining as I left for Afghanistan, 'Mark, be careful. Find yourself a nice Jewish girl.' Like the camel, Aunt Rebecca uncovered an endless supply of things to complain about, her eyes were jaundiced, and she chewed sideways. If she had had a coat of hair, I'm sure it would have been as bedraggled as the camel's. It was uncanny how much alike they were, and I was fond of them both. I started calling the camel 'Aunt Becky,' and she responded in a way that infuriated Maftoon. She would nip at him, bump him, cry bitterly when he approached her, then turn to me and be as docile as an indulgent old woman. I made her my special charge and often hiked beside her during the long marches.

My legs grew strong. I acquired a good tan and my sleep was unbroken. My appetite was unbelievable and I had never felt better. I thought: No wonder Ellen joined the Kochis.

But any illusions I had about the nomads as noble savages were dispelled on the sixth day, when we reached the outskirts of the little bazaar town of Musa Dural, for as soon as we struck camp six Kochis and four camels, including Aunt Becky, headed for town and in due course returned with an unprecedented supply of melons, meats, shoes and other necessities. That day we had a choice lunch and all would have been well, except that in mid-afternoon Dr Stiglitz approached me while I was talking with Mira, and pleaded in a begging manner: 'I'm hungry for tobacco. This empty pipe drives me crazy. When you mail your report to Kabul, could you get me a little at the bazaar? I have no money.' I replied that after my nap I would see what could be done.

I mailed my report to the embassy, then wandered through the bazaar, seeking parcels of tobacco, and an old Afghan said, 'I know I had some right here, but I must have misplaced it,' and I was about to leave empty-handed when I was overtaken by a thin, ingratiating Afghan who spoke a little English.

'Sahib, you got car?'

In Pashto I replied that I did not, whereupon the salesman assured me, 'I have a bargain you can't resist, sahib. You owe it to yourself.'

'What is it?'

'Wait till you see,' he whispered, taking my arm and leading me to the stall of an accomplice. There, amid karakul caps and fabrics from India, were six relatively new automobile tires. 'Quite something, eh?' he asked admiringly.

I was startled by the tires. How could they have reached Musa Darul? Then off to one side I spotted a jeep carburetor, an oil filter, a jack, a complete set of tools and practically everything else that could be removed from a jeep frame. There was even a steering wheel, to which was attached my letter to Nazrullah.

'Where'd you get these?' I asked.

'Just came in this afternoon,' he said happily. 'From Russia.'

'You've got a bargain here,' I assured him, as I ticked off some twenty separate items which I knew were going to be charged against my salary in Kabul. 'But you may have to wait some time for a customer,' I warned him.

He laughed and said, 'Five weeks, six weeks. If nobody wants them, we'll ship it all to Kabul.' I winced as I thought of myself wandering through that bazaar, buying back these useful items.

'You send them to Kabul,' I said with resignation. 'Somebody'll be sure to need them.'

I stormed back to camp and the first person I met was Ellen Jaspar. 'These damned crooks!' I bellowed. 'They invited me on this trip solely to steal my jeep . . . piece by piece.'

Ellen tried to control her laughter but couldn't. 'What did you think they wanted, your charm?' she chided.

'Did you know what they were up to?' I asked in outrage.

'Didn't you?' she countered. 'Remember the panic you caused when you said you were tying the note to the steering wheel? Didn't you see me laughing at Zulfiqar, who tricked you to stay inside? Miller, when you started for the jeep, the steering wheel was already packed . . . on Aunt Becky.'

I felt humiliated. 'You mean they stole my jeep and hid it on my own camel?'

'Miller, you should have seen those Kochis unpacking the wheels off Aunt Becky and propping them back onto the jeep until you tied the letter to the wheel.'

'It's going to cost me a month's salary,' I said ruefully.

'That's cheap, for a trip like this. And don't protest to Zulfiqar. Strictly speaking, what he did was a breach of honor and he's ashamed. No man should be robbed in a caravanserai.'

I was about to raise hell when Mira came in to hand me something. It was three packs of smoking tobacco. 'I got them at the bazaar . . . for doctor.'

I looked at Ellen and asked, 'How did she get them at the bazaar? She has no money.'

Ellen replied, 'Mira is very quick.'

12

I was deflated by my discovery that the Kochis had invited me to Kabul merely to steal the wheels off my jeep, but I soon forgot my irritation. For one thing, after Musa Darul the terrain became more interesting, since we were heading up the Helmand valley, which would untimately deposit us near Kabul, a valley that few foreigners had seen. It lay west of the barren plains of Ghazni and east of the towering Koh-i-Baba mountains. No roads traversed it and for days we saw no villages and often only the barest of trails.

As we hiked, I grew to appreciate Nazrullah's complaint about the goats of Asia, for weeks passed and we saw not a single tree in what seemed otherwise almost virgin territory. Once great forests had covered these hills; there were historical records of that fact; but slowly the goats and the greed of men had denuded even the remote plateaus, leaving only rocky bleakness. I often wondered how our sheep existed as they plodded from one barren pasture to the next, but like the hungry camels, they usually found something.

In our caravan there were about two hundred Kochis, and on the march we were strung out over several miles, with camels and sheep predominant, so it was Zulfiqar's responsibility, as inheritor of this clan, to ride constantly back and forth, supervising our progress. He offered a striking appearance: tall and dark, with heavy mustaches, and a rifle to maintain his authority. On the trail he wore a white turban, but his conspicuous traits were his taciturnity and his smile. He smiled because he knew that keeping his people contented was half the battle; he kept his mouth shut to cultivate the legend that he knew more than his followers.

When the Kochis had served me roast sheep at the caravanserai, I did not appreciate how special the meal was, for the nomads ate poorly. At breakfast we had hot tea and a slab of nan, on which we hiked for twelve or fourteen miles, after which we had a meager helping of pilau lacking meat. In the evening we had curds and a little nan with some shreds of meat, if any was available. We lived close to the poverty level and seemed to thrive on it, but the children were perpetually hungry. I worried about this until Ellen pointed out, 'They don't have protruding bellies. They're wonderful specimens,' and I had to agree that what little they got nourished them, but I also noticed they were starved for fat and would avidly lick up any scraps, even if they had fallen to the ground.

Three aspects of nomad life distressed me: the Kochis were dirty; they were unkempt; and they made no attempt to develop intellectual interests. The wild free life of the wanderer left much to be desired.

The baggy trousers and flapping white shirts of the Kochi men were rarely clean, while the felt skirts of the women were apt to be streaked with dirt and tangled with briars, which they ignored. They washed infrequently, but I must admit that the extreme dryness of the air prevented offensive odors from accumulating. In my own case, with the humidity at two or three I could wear a shirt for more than a week because nothing could happen to it except a downright accident: there was no soot to soil the cloth and it was anatomically impossible for perspiration to collect. the minute it appeared it evaporated. I suspected that many Kochi garments were worn for months at a time without washing; only thus could they have become as dirty as they did.

The slovenliness of the Kochis was principally shown in the way they managed their hair. Women rarely combed theirs and men wore shoulder-length bobs which flapped with any vigorous movement. Their heads, men's and women's alike, were actually matted and probably worse. I often thought how much fun it would be to run the whole clan through a barber shop some afternoon to see what surprises would turn up.

As for the life of the mind, the speculation about good and evil, the judgment of past and future, there was none. Since they could neither read nor write, and since there was no radio, conversation was limited to the chance events of the caravan: the birth of sheep, the straying of a camel, the long march, outwitting the border guards and who stole what at the last bazaar. Days sped into months and months into years without any extension of the group intellect. It may be that the Kochis were supremely happy in their rough adaptation to nature; I often found them boring, and I had the ungenerous suspicion that Ellen Jaspar found comfort in the caravan partly because against their illiteracy she could stand out as a person with desirable skills. In any event, I noticed how often she came to Stiglitz or me to escape the dullness of the Kochis and to talk philosophically with an educated person.

There were two exceptions to this tradition of dirtiness, slovenliness and apathy: Zulfiqar and his daughter Mira were alert mentally and far above average in cleanliness, largely due to Ellen, who cut Zulfiqar's hair and tended his clothes. As to Mira, she kept herself well groomed partly because Ellen gave her instruction and partly because she mimicked whatever Ellen did in the way of cleanliness or personal adornment.

She owned several changes of costume: red dress, blue dress, gray felt dress; blue, red, white, green blouses; filmy gray, brown and white turbans; and an extra pair of sandals that she wore only when heading for some village bazaar off the caravan trail. Best of all, she had acquired a stout comb with which she managed her black hair and a washrag which she applied to her clear and even skin. Her face was brown and she wore no makeup, but her eyes and brows were so black that in comparison her face looked more creamy white than brown.

On the trail I often walked with Mira, whose job it was to help mind the sheep, which represented a large proportion of the Kochi wealth, and to swing along beside her as she chattered in Pashto or broken English was delightful. I tried repeatedly to fathom her narrow world and soon discovered that she knew nothing of history or other school subjects and had no desire to learn. But she did not share the apathy of the other Kochis, for she knew much about Central Asia and in all matters affecting the Kochis was an expert. Skilled in trading, witty in negotiation, and a master in the care of animals, she confessed a major sorrow: her clan had but one horse, and it was assigned to Zulfiqar.

'A man like you should not walk with the rest of us,' she told me. 'In your own country you would be a chief.' I asked her not to feel sorry for me and reminded her that I did have a jeep, which in some ways was better than a horse. She considered this for a moment, then concluded, 'Where we go a horse is better.'

'Don't worry. I like to walk.'

'A chief ought to have his own horse. Look at my father! Would he be so powerful without a horse?'

But if there were disappointments in nomad life there were also congenial surprises and none was more appealing than Maftoon, the cockeyed cameleer. We had marched five days toward Musa Darul when I happened to see a camel halted for no reason that I could ascertain. I therefore started across the meadowland to retrieve the beast when I saw, crouched down between her hind legs, Maftoon, with turban awry, mouth open, and on his face an expression of almost heavenly bliss. With his right hand on the camel's teat, he was squirting a flow of milk directly from the udder into his mouth, drinking at the rate of about a quart a minute.

'What the hell are you doing, Maftoon?' I shouted.

'Hungry,' he said, halting the flow of milk and looking at me with his good eye.

'Get up! That milk's for the babies.' He made no effort to leave his lunch, so I added, 'And by the way, Maftoon, I've found out why Aunt Becky tries to bite you so much. You abuse her.'

The little man stayed crouched between the camel's legs and looked at me with an expression of sorrow and disgust. 'I abuse that beast?' he stammered.

'Yes!' I insisted. 'I've listened to you the last three mornings. It's a wonder she didn't gum your arm again.'

'You listened . . . to what?'

'To Aunt Becky, complaining of the way you overload her, mistreat her. Damn it all, Maftoon, get away from that camel and listen to me.'

Reluctantly the little Kochi left his meal, stood up with his turban reaching his knees, and to my surprise laughed at me. 'Tomorrow,' he said, 'you'll load Aunt Becky.' With that he left.

Next morning I was routed out of bed by the little cameleer and taken to where his beasts were being loaded. Aunt Becky, one of the largest animals we had, still rested on the thick callus built up on her chest, her pedestal it was called, and she was loath to leave it, but when she saw that I was to load her, and not her enemy Maftoon, she seemed as happy as a mournful, droopy-eyed, coat-shedding camel could; but as soon as I placed the first blanket on her–it must have weighed about three-quarters of a pound–she let out a sob that would have broken the heart of Nero. It was almost human, a wail of protest against the harshness of the world. I slapped her muzzle, and placed on the blanket a few items that she could hardly have felt, and her groans increased to the point of despair. She really sounded like my own Aunt Becky back in Boston, complaining of the Irish politicians, the Italian grocers, the Jewish merchants, and the ingratitude of her family. 'How can I possibly bear this awful burden?' Becky the camel sobbed. No matter what I put on her back, the groans increased, and when she was burdened much more lightly than she had been when running over the desert with my jeep, she struggled to her ungainly feet as if this were her last day on earth; for me she would make that extra little effort and then collapse in a heap before my eyes. I gave her a slap and felt more kindly toward Maftoon. At eleven that morning Aunt Becky was striding along the trail with as much joy as a camel ever exhibits and gave me a pleasant nuzzle as I went past.

The next morning Maftoon summoned me again, and this time as soon as I approached Aunt Becky she became apprehensive that I was about to torture her once more, so I placed on her broad, hairy back a handkerchief. It had barely touched her when she began to rage in protest: 'Oh, this is more than a poor camel can bear!' she seemed to say. A stranger listening from a distance would have sworn that I was pushing hot swords into her great bulk, and this kept up all during the loading; so on the third morning I said to Maftoon, 'Let's see how much this ugly beast can carry.' And this day we loaded her down with well over eight hundred pounds. Her protests were exactly the same; her reluctance to rise identical; and her loping, carefree performance on the trail no different from before. In fact, once we got her started, it was hard to stop her. She loved the heft of the burden and again nuzzled me as I went by. After this indoctrination I decided to leave the camels to Maftoon, and it was well that I did, for when it came time to unload Aunt Becky her dim brain remembered that today she had been mistreated, and she started mauling Maftoon. Luckily he escaped, but soon I saw him naked before the camel while she attacked his clothes. When he was dressed he warned me, 'Miller Sahib! You better undress!'

I laughed at the suggestion, but as I approached the huge camel she started for me. Maftoon interceded and, since he had made his peace, saved me. Prudently I undressed and stood by while Aunt Becky kicked the very devil out of my clothes. She bit them, spat on them, and even urinated a little. The next morning we were friends again.

Caravan life provided moments of pride and arrogance: as dawn was breaking we would reach some rise in the trail from which we could look down upon a sleeping village, where dogs would spot us and begin to bark. A few men would appear to see what had agitated the dogs and, seeing the Kochis coming to town, would signal their neighbors, whereupon the villagers would rush about in a frenzy, moving indoors anything that might be stolen. Women in their chaderies would dash out to grab their children lest they be kidnapped, and families would remain cautiously by doorways as women stared through veils waiting for the approaching nomads. An excited hush would fall over the village, at whose outskirts the first Kochi camels were already sniffing.

At such entries Zulfiqar rode at the head of the column, a handsome figure with his rifle slung insolently across his pommel. He affected not to see the frightened families and ignored the pestilent dogs. Behind him came the lumbering camels, with Aunt Becky thrusting her big, inquisitive face from side to side, followed by a large group of Kochi men; then the sheep and most of the women; finally the donkeys, the children, and the rear guard of armed men. It was an impressive caravan when seen in the close confines of a village street, but what outraged the villagers, men and women alike, was the brazen manner in which our women marched handsomely forward with no chaderi.

When Zulfiqar's clan moved through a village we had with us three additional elements for arousing suspicion and disgust: there was Ellen Jaspar, obviously not a Kochi; there was Dr Stiglitz, and what was he doing in such a motley group; and there was the young American who marched with the beautiful nomad girl in the red dress.

Several times infuriated mountain mullahs dashed among us to spit at Ellen as they had done at Kandahar, but she had since learned to ward them off indulgently. She understood the moral and mental pressures these fanatics were experiencing in a changing world and she wished to do nothing that would exasperate them, but if Zulfiqar saw them coming, he patiently cut them off with his horse, whereupon the long-robed mullahs would back against some mud-walled house and curse our passing.

When the villagers tried to abuse Stiglitz or me they got a sharp surprise: we swore at them in Pashto, claimed to be light-skinned Kochis, and warned them to mind their own business. Sometimes they stopped dead and stared at us, whereupon we laughed and they laughed. Braver men among them would run beside us, asking if we were ferangi, and at such times we would confess that we were German and American, and the animosity would vanish. Occasionally some young man in the village who wanted to comprehend his world would march with us for miles, even to our camp, asking a hundred questions. Such men became our friends, and even if I had not mailed my report to Kabul, these inquisitive men would have got the message to our ambassador, by word of mouth from one village to the next until it crossed Afghanistan. It was such a rumor that had reached Shah Khan in Kabul: 'Traveling with the Kochis is a blond ferangi.'

We had reached the halfway spot on our march to Kabul when we came upon an especially pathetic village, where I had a chance to see for myself the gentler side of Ellen Jaspar's honest concern with human problems. It was not yet dawn as we moved down the main street, glaring back at frightened faces which peered at us through darkness, and Ellen whispered, 'It does my heart good to compare these suspicious villagers with our free nomads.'

'I agree. I get a positive bang out of marching through a village like this.'

'Just think!' she cried with real intellectual excitement. 'In a few years Afghanistan will destroy prisons like this'–she indicated the tight-barred houses–'and the country will go back to the ancient freedom of the caravan.'

I should have allowed the subject to drop, but I was struck by a fundamental contradiction in her thinking: the idea that freedom could be preserved only by turning back the clock. I could hear her arguing with Nazrullah at the site of the future dam: *It's a shame that the river must lose its freedom,* refusing to realize that only when the river was harnessed and used could Afghanistan know the real freedom of release from poverty. Therefore I said, 'I'm afraid you have it backwards, Ellen. Afghanistan will never gain a single freedom by reverting to the caravan. It will save itself by generating true freedom in the villages.'

'How?' she asked with some contempt.

'Roads, books, Nazrullah's electricity.'

'Oh, Miller!' she cried passionately. 'You misunderstand history and the nature of man. We are born free, like the nomads. But step by step we insist upon crawling into little prisons on little streets in mean little villages. We must destroy these prisons and restore the nomad spirit.'

'I'm sorry, Ellen. What you want is impossible. What we must do is go into the villages and rebuild them on a basis of freedom. We must go forward. We can't go back.'

'But in Pennsylvania, my father is the village. In Afghanistan these surly people are the village. Will books and electricity cure my father . . . or these clods?'

'Only books and electricity can do it.'

She stopped in the middle of the road, pressed her right hand to her mouth, and weighed my arguments. Light from one of the houses, reflecting on her bracelets, flashed across her lovely face. 'Miller,' she whispered generously, 'in part you're right, but you forget that men like my father . . .'

I was not allowed to hear her rebuttal, for out of the shadows darted a pretty little girl of nine or ten, less fearful than her elders. Running through the darkness, she caught Ellen's hand and cried in Pashto, 'Your bracelets are beautiful.' With a gesture of instinctive warmth, Ellen caught the child, swung her in the air, kissed her, and held her in her left arm while she took off one of her bracelets to give the child.

It was a moment I cannot forget. There in an alien street, beset by enmity, Ellen cradled the child in timeless pose: a lovely young mother holding in the darkness a child who intuitively trusted her; and I was forced to recall Karima as she said: *Ellen knew that I could have children and apparently she couldn't. Dr Stiglitz will confirm that.* I wondered if this were true, and if so, did it account for her essential barrenness of spirit?

My reflections were shattered by the agonizing shriek of the child's mother, who burst upon us screaming, 'The Kochis have stolen my child!'

This was a signal for villagers, long trained to repulse such thefts, to rush at us from many sides, and there were fighting. But what stunned me was the arrival of six or eight determined women in chaderies, moving swiftly through the darkness like avenging furies. Their shadowy forms engulfed Ellen as they tore at her hair, her clothes, her face. One thin figure in a gray chaderi swept in like a ferret and grabbed the child. Seeing that the little girl held a contaminated bracelet, the thin figure tore it from the child's hands and threw it back at Ellen.

'Don't steal our children!' a voice of passion warned. The avengers withdrew, but from the shadows came a gaunt, bearded man rushing belatedly to the brawl and hissing hatred.

'Whores! Whores!' he shouted, maneuvering like a robed ghost in his efforts to spit at Ellen.

Zulfiqar had seen the mullah coming and had deftly swung his horse across the man's trajectory to drive him away. The mullah followed at a distance, screaming impotently; and thus we left the frightened villagers, who remained in excited groups, congratulating each other on having once more thwarted the Kochi kidnapers.

Zulfiqar, concerned over Ellen's welfare, dismounted to assure himself that all was well, and she buried her head in his shoulder, sniffling, 'All I wanted to do was give the little girl a bracelet.'

'How did it start?' the big Kochi asked indulgently.

'Miller and I were having a peaceful argument . . .'

'About what?'

'I claimed that originally Afghanistan knew the freedom of the caravan, but that willfully the people put themselves in these village prisons under the rule of mullahs.'

'You're right about the past.'

'Miller claimed that we can never go back to the caravan. That we will know freedom only when the villages have books and roads and electricity.'

'He's right about the future,' and before Ellen could protest the decision, he leaped upon his horse to lead our caravan from the niggardly village, but then he galloped back to us and cried, 'Some day all of us will live in villages like this. But they will be better villages.' And he was gone.

The very next morning I had poetic confirmation that Zulfiqar's vision of the future was more likely than Ellen's, for in the early hours when light was just beginning to break across the peaks of the Koh-i-Baba, we sighted a village where dogs were silent, and we crept upon it unawares and were well inside the confines before we were discovered–great camels lumbering down the main road, peering into windows as the villagers were rising–and at one corner I saw a house lit with candles, and it seemed, there in the shadow of the mountains, like all the warm, homely refuges of the world. It was a small segment of space, walled in against the wandering nomads and the camels. It was one man's home. Not even the soaring freedom of the Kochi tents, pitched beside torrents in the mountain passes, could equal the security of that chance home we saw in the half-darkness of dawn. The village people knew something the nomads would never know, a kind of spiritual freedom, and if they were forced to pay a terrible price for it, perhaps that was their choice.

To my surprise, as I brooded on these matters I looked up to see Zulfiqar, on his brown horse, staring at me and the house, and I think he was remembering our discussion of the morning before, and deciding anew that he and I were right; but a dog began barking, the villagers poured out, and the old antagonism between nomad and villager was resumed.

At first I hadn't realized why the villagers were so apprehensive about locking things up as our caravan approached, but after I had seen flashing Mira at work I understood their antagonism. Whenever we made camp after transiting a village I found that she had acquired some new piece of clothing, or a farm tool, or a kitchen utensil. Ellen once said, 'The only thing that child hasn't stolen is a bed. You watch! If somebody leaves a door open some day . . .'

At one camp I caught Mira with a new saw and asked her, 'Why do you steal from the villagers?'

'When we march through,' she replied, 'they look at me with hate and I look right back at them the same way.' Then she added, 'But do you notice how the men follow me so hungrily with their eyes? They'd like to join the Kochis . . . for one night. I could spit at them!'

Our clan had ten large black tents, but many of the Kochis preferred sleeping on blankets in the open. Zulfiqar, his wife Racha, Ellen and Mira occupied one of the smaller tents, notable because it had an awning held up by two additional poles forming a kind of porch where rugs were thrown and where the camp's social life took place. In the late afternoons, when the animals were at ease, Zulfiqar would sit cross-legged between Racha and Ellen, discussing matters with his people. I often joined them and thus formed the foundation for the friendship which developed between the Kochi leader and me.

He asked me many questions, but I learned more than I taught. The Kochis were Muslims who ignored the tyranny of the mullahs but who held Mecca in as deep regard as any Suuni. As we discussed Islam, with its strong reliance upon nature and a powerful God who motivated all natural things, I better understood how Ellen and Dr Stiglitz had been able to embrace this religion.

One afternoon as we sat under the awning, Ellen said, 'I could never explain my apostasy to my parents, and that's the real reason why I can't write to them. You see, I was raised to believe that God personally hovered like an unseen helicopter just above the steeple of the Presbyterian Church on Adams Street in Dorset, Pennsylvania'—I had remarked earlier how she loved to reel off that rubric, as if names alone symbolized the focus of her rebellion—'and although He was free to keep a weather eye on the Lutheran church down the street, His real responsibility was our congregation. We were the true religion. All else was delusion. I think that if my parents had only once, while I was growing up, intimated that God might also be personally worried about the Jews, I would still be in Dorset. For that would have made sense.'

At the end of this rather protracted speech Zulfiqar asked, 'Do all American women talk so much?' I said yes and he shrugged his shoulders the way scar-eyed Maftoon did when he couldn't comprehend the behaviour of a camel.

The figure of speech Ellen had used disturbed me. Had she spoken with spurious concern for the Jews because Stiglitz had warned her that I was one? In English I asked, 'Did Stiglitz tell you I was a Jew?'

'You are?' she shouted in real delight. 'Zulfiqar! Miller is a Jew!'

The big leader, his bandoleer and rifle beside him on the rug, leaned forward to inspect me. 'You Jewish?' I nodded and he burst into laughter.

Ellen said in Pashto, 'You should hear what this big fool believes about Jews!'

Again Zulfiqar laughed, attracting other nomads, who gathered to see what was happening. He stood beside me and compared his large Semitic nose to my small Nordic one. 'I'm the real Jew!' he shouted, and other Kochis stepped up to compare their faces with mine. A long discussion followed, at the end of which Zulfiqar asked, 'Millair, are Jews really as avaricious as we say?'

I thought a moment, smiled at Ellen and replied, 'Let me put it this way. Zulfiqar, if you parked your jeep near a bunch of Jews . . . they'd steal the tires while you weren't looking.'

It took some moments for the boldness of my reply to sink in, and some of the lesser Kochis caught on before Zulfiqar. They were loath to react until he had set the pattern, but they obviously relished my gall. Then he exploded in rollicking laughter and imitated a steering wheel. 'Millair,' he laughed, 'you scared us when you started for the jeep. We had most of it packed on camels.' Then he stopped laughing and looked suspiciously at Ellen. 'How did you know about the jeep?'

'In the bazaar at Musa Darul . . . they tried to sell it back to me.' My discovery of their duplicity pleased the Kochis, and from that moment Miller the Jew became blood brother to the Aryan nomads.

But to one obligatory aspect of Kochi life I never did become adjusted. As we marched week after week through the treeless valleys a detail of four women worked at the rear of the caravan, moving back and forth across the landscape, and it was their duty to gather the fresh droppings of the camels, the sheep and the donkeys and with their bare hands to mold the manure into briquettes which were carefully hoarded in the panniers carried by the donkeys; for in a land where there were few trees other fuel had to be found, and dried dung was excellent. It burned slowly, like punk, had a pleasing odor which imparted flavor to food cooked over it, and was light in transportation.

The Kochi children delighted in coming upon dried dung which the sharp-eyed women of some former caravan had overlooked, and it was a kind of game for them to see who would spot the next camel dropping. One day Mira and I were following Aunt Becky, who as usual was straying, when the camel dropped a large deposit which the women would probably miss; so I gritted my teeth, turned my nose away, and scooped up the precious stuff, running it to the panniers, where the women tending the caravan cheered. I was blushing when I returned to Mira, who, when she satisfied herself that no one was spying, threw her arms about me and kissed me for the first time. 'You're a real Kochi!' she teased, and thereafter when I went to her father's awning-porch it was to see her and not to talk with him; and we took long walks among the deserted hills.

Two days after our first kiss, we were hiking up a narrow valley where flowers were in bloom and I thought: The Kochis know only two seasons, the best of spring and the best of autumn. I looked at Mira and asked, 'You never know winter, do you?'

She surprised me by pointing to the mountains overhead and saying, 'It's always ready to pounce on us.' And there it hung, the snowline of the Koh-i-Baba, an ominous threat which reminded me of our impending arrival at Kabul, when I would have to leave the caravan.

I think Mira must have sensed my sadness, for she kissed me ardently, but the moment was spoiled by the sharp voice of Ellen, who said, 'You'd better join the others, Mira.'

When the little nomad left the valley, Ellen said with some asperity, 'You be careful what you do with that girl. One day in India a camel attacked her and in rage she nearly killed it. She takes nothing lightly, and remember . . . she is the chieftain's daughter.' Then she added, 'She's also much smarter than most of the girls I knew in college.'

'Why don't you teach her to read?'

'You be careful what you teach her,' she warned.

It was after this intrusion that I first began to notice that Ellen was also becoming involved in matters which could lead to dangerous conclusions, and that when she warned me about Mira she was perhaps thinking not of me but of herself. For example, on the trail she most often walked with Dr Stiglitz, ahead of the camels; and under the canopy, when we gathered in the afternoons, she took her seat beside him. One of the reasons why Ellen sought out Stiglitz was that at Bryn Mawr she had studied German and French and could thus converse with him in four different languages, and they maintained long discussions on philosophical matters.

I wondered if Zulfiqar took umbrage at this, for I had read in many books that men of the desert were subject to ungovernable passions where their women were concerned, and certainly in normal Afghan life the chaderi and the high wall topped by broken glass proved that the books were right; and I began to fear that my affection for Mira might get me involved in these nomad rages; but the more I watched Zulfiqar the more confused I became, for he certainly did not act like the vengeful, romanticized sheik of fiction. On the contrary, when Ellen and Stiglitz were hiking together, Zulfiqar often rode by on his brown horse, kicking its ribs expertly, and he would occasionally stop to talk but more often he continued past, according them his professional smile, and I got the clear impression that instead of being jealous of Stiglitz, he was somewhat relieved to have in the caravan a man who had spare time for arguing with his second woman.

With me the problem was somewhat different, for Mira was his daughter. I was sure that once or twice he had seen us kissing, and he must have noticed how we always sat together at the tent or at meals, yet he treated Mira and me much as he did the others: infrequent conversation, inevitable smile.

On the night before we reached Kabul, the Kochis prepared a farewell feast for me. Maftoon impressed some men who formed a noisy orchestra for nomad dancing and songs from many trails in Asia. I tried to keep away from Mira, for leaving her was proving to be extremely difficult, and several times I caught myself staring at Stiglitz and Ellen, thinking: They're the lucky ones. Together all the way to Balkh.

That night as I crept into my sleeping bag I asked Stiglitz, 'Have you told Ellen what you told me . . . at the pillar?'

'I've told her I can't leave Afghanistan.'

'Have you told her why?'

'Sooner or later everyone knows everything,' he replied. 'The timetable of discovery is not significant.'

'That's not true. When I discovered your history . . . in the caravanserai . . . I might have killed you.'

'It would have been of no consequence,' he said fatalistically.

'How do you feel about me now . . . as a Jew?' I asked.

He considered this for some minutes, while the camels moved about behind us, and at first I thought he had fallen asleep. Then he replied in evasive fashion, 'I've given up my home, my family . . .'

'You called her your filthy wife,' I reminded him.

'I was speaking of my children,' he corrected. 'They were different. I surrendered everything . . . profession, opera, a city I loved . . . so in a sense, Herr Miller, I'm a dead man, and dead men have no further responsibility for passing judgments.'

I made no comment to this and he continued, 'To the Jews I did terrible things. You're a Jew. Believe it or not, Herr Miller, the two facts are completely unrelated. Toward you as a Jew I have no feeling whatsoever. Toward you as a man . . . I'd like to be your friend, Herr Miller.'

'Would you stop calling me Herr Miller?' I asked.

'I'm very thoughtless,' he said, reaching out from his sleeping bag to grasp my arm. 'Please forgive me,' he begged, and a cesspool of bitterness began to drain away.

After a long silence he asked, 'Do you remember how our discussion at the pillar started? No, I thought not. You were berating me for not having amputated Pritchard's leg at Chahar. I tried to tell you that there are factors in life which go beyond medical comprehension, and I equated Pritchard's determination to die with Sem Levin's determination to live. The point is this, I'm sick with shame and grief over what I did to Sem Levin, because I acted against his will, but I haven't the slightest regret over the case of John Pritchard, because I acted in furtherance of his will. One way or other he had commanded himself to die.'

'I'm beginning to see what you're talking about,' I admitted.

'With me it's the same way,' he added. 'I'm dead. If the Russians hang me it's no matter. They're hanging a dead man. But if I'm allowed to live, I have willed myself to be reborn. When you saw me in Kandahar I was a walking corpse, concerned only with my bottle of beer. Now I shall be a human being.'

I asked, 'Has Ellen accomplished this?'

'Yes,' he confessed. 'But don't forget, Miller, when you leave us in Kabul you'll be a living man too.' He allowed this to sink in, then asked, 'Have you ever made love to a woman?'

'Certainly,' I lied, counting some frenzied moments in war as qualifiers.

'Well, leaving this nomad girl is going to be a different experience from what you imagine. I am wondering what you will do after Mira vanishes. What will you do, Miller?'

'I'll go back to the embassy,' I said brashly. 'Pick up where I left off.'

'With the smell of camels haunting you? Don't be stupid.' He turned over and went to sleep.

From the caravanserai to Kabul had been a distance of some three hundred and fifty miles, which required twenty-five days of marching, but since we occasionally held camp for two or three days at sites with adequate forage, it was not until the middle of May that we came over a pass and saw below us the sprawling capital whose center was filled by the low mountain. I stood with Mira and explained, 'My house is over there . . . to the north of that mountain. Tomorrow I'll be sleeping there.'

The nomad girl rejected my prediction and took my face in her hands. She kissed me warmly and whispered, 'Oh, no, Miller! Tomorrow night you won't be sleeping there.'

Few Kochi caravans ever entered Kabul with the advance excitement caused by ours, and as soon as we pitched our black tents in the traditional nomad area some miles west and south of the British embassy, we were visited by three important emissaries. First Moheb Khan, trim and polished in a new Chevrolet, drove out to investigate my report that Ellen Jaspar was traveling with the Kochis, and he consulted lengthily with Zulfiqar and Ellen while Mira and I lingered outside the tent trying to eavesdrop. I remember her asking me, 'Who is this Moheb Khan?' I explained that he was an important official who would do her father much harm if he was made angry and she agreed: 'He does look very important.'

I avoided seeing Moheb, because I did not want to talk with him at that moment, dressed as I was in Afghan clothes; but after he had gone, a lesser official reported to see Dr Stiglitz, and they sat in a corner of our tent conversing in German, so I did not understand what they were saying, but the upshot was that Stiglitz was not to be arrested or sent back to Kandahar.

Now came my turn, for Richardson of Intelligence drove out after lunch at the British embassy, lit his pipe with infuriating care, stroked his mustache and said in his deep voice, 'Miller, I'm afraid there's hell to pay over that jeep.' He watched the effect on me and added, 'Going to cost you . . . say . . . six hundred dollars. Miller, they stole everything but the name in front. Nazrullah had to make two trips across that desert.'

I threw myself on his mercy: 'It was stupid, and I know it. But I did feel that Verbruggen would understand.'

'The ambassador is raising hell,' Richardson confided, and I could feel the boom being lowered.

'What's the bad word?' I asked.

'Well, you saved your neck by that report from Musa Darul. We notified Washington and at least the senator from Pennsylvania's mollified. But the girl's parents! Why doesn't she write to them?'

'She has written . . . several times. I sat over her while she did the last one. But there's so much to explain she tears the letters up. I've drafted this letter, which we can send them, and this complete report.'

'Good, and I don't think you need worry too much about the ambassador. Washington's rather pleased that you rescued Miss Jaspar.'

'Rescued her? She's never been happier in her life.'

'You mean she's staying with the Kochis?' Richardson gasped.

I thought: If I try to explain everything . . . Zulfiqar, Stiglitz, Islam . . . he'll get all balled up. So I said. 'I didn't rescue her. She rescued me.'

'Now what the hell do you mean by that?' he asked huffily, drawing on his pipe.

'I'll explain in the office tomorrow.'

'Now wait a minute,' he protested. Then he changed his mind and asked quietly, 'Could we take a walk?'

'Why not? I've just walked three hundred and fifty miles.'

'Don't you ride the camels?' he asked, and I looked at him with scorn.

When we were far from the tents he said, 'Maybe you won't be in the office tomorrow.'

'They sending me home?' I asked with a sort of sick feeling.

'No. Washington's come up with a peculiar idea.' He paused to let the drama sink in, then sucked his pipe and studied me. 'You ever heard of Qabir?'

'No.' Then I reflected. Where had I heard that name? I corrected myself: 'I've heard the name but I forget where.'

'It's an important meeting place of the nomads,' he said. 'Somewhere in the Hindu Kush.'

'Where?'

'Doesn't show on the map.'

'Did you ask the British? They know these areas.'

'They know it only as a name,' he said. 'Qabir. Qabir. Does it mean anything at all to you?'

Then I remembered. 'One night the chief was ticking off the route of the caravan. Musa Dural, Balkh. And he said he'd be able to use Dr Stiglitz at Qabir.'

'In what capacity?'

'He didn't say.'

Richardson walked away from me and kicked pebbles for some time. Then he asked bluntly, 'Miller, could you manage some way to stay with the Kochis till they get to Qabir?'

'Why?'

'It's damned important that our side have someone who's been there. We've no information about it except that every summer the nomads gather there, and we think that Russians, Chinese, Tajiks, Uzbeks . . . the lot . . .'

'Supposing I could get there, what do you want me to do?'

'Just look. Find out who the Russians send and how they get across the Oxus.'

'I'd stand out like a sore thumb,' I protested.

'That may be an advantage,' he said. 'Think you can arrange to stay with the caravan?'

'Possibly,' I evaded, trying not to show the joy I felt at the reprieve.

'If you could,' he said cautiously, 'I think we'd forget about the jeep.'

I said, 'I'm not keen on Qabir. Sounds dull. But I've always wanted to see Balkh. Can I come in tonight for some fresh gear?'

'No. We don't want you around the embassy. Tell me what you need and I'll get it.'

'Some money, a few vitamin pills, some nose drops . . . boy, your nose dries out . . . and some note pads.'

'Don't take any notes on Qabir,' he warned.

'I haven't said I could get there,' I cautioned. 'If there is such a place.'

Late that afternoon, while Mira was scrounging the Kabul bazaars, Richardson returned with my gear and a batch of mail, and in a gesture unprecedented for him shook my hand warmly and said with feeling, 'Miller, do you even dimly comprehend the opportunity you have? For seven years we've been trying to get to Qabir. So have the British. For God's sake, keep your eyes open.'

'What did the ambassador say?'

'He said, "Imagine such a job going to such a squirt."' Richardson left, and I swore to myself: Somehow or other, I'm getting to Qabir.

I sat at the edge of my tent in the twilight and wondered what trick I could use for staying with the Kochis, and as I pondered the problem I realized that I wasn't much interested in Richardson's Russians but I was keenly concerned about continuing with Mira. With no plans at all, I felt: Something's bound to work out.

I turned to my mail. Girls had replied to my letters, but now I couldn't even remember their faces. A letter from my father sounded as if Mr Jaspar were arguing incomprehensibly with Ellen, and provincial Boston matters which had once been of significance were now tedious. How could a group of Kochi women gathering camel dung seem more important than my aunts in Boston? How could my adventures with a gang of nomads and a mixed-up girl from Pennsylvania pre-occupy my thoughts? More particularly, how could I manage to stay with Mira?

My problem was unexpectedly solved by Zulfiqar. Accompanied by Dr Stiglitz he came to my tent and said half apologetically, 'The doctor has official permission to stay with us. He's coming to Qabir.'

'Where's that?' I asked, trying to appear nonchalant.

'Where the nomads meet each summer. In the Hindu Kush.'

'Hope you have a good trip,' I said to Stiglitz. 'Sounds a long way off.'

'It is,' the German agreed. 'But what we wanted to discuss with you . . . we need a lot of medicine.'

I put on a serious face and said, 'I suppose you could buy what you need in the bazaar.'

'Yes . . .' Zulfiqar said, 'if we had the money.'

'This time I have no jeep,' I reminded him.

'But the American officer . . . when he came, did he give you any money?'

'Yes,' I replied, and waited.

'We were wondering,' Stiglitz proposed. 'Would you buy us the medicine if . . .'

'If what?' I asked cautiously.

'If we took you to Balkh with us?' Zulfiqar suggested.

I wasted time so that it would look as if I were judging the proposal, then asked suspiciously, 'How much money would you need?'

'About two hundred dollars,' Zulfiqar replied.

'I have a hundred and fifty,' I offered, unable to control my excitement at having tricked him into doing what I wanted.

'Good!' he cried, and four hours later he and Stiglitz returned to camp with a cache of drugs and medical implements that would have done justice to a small pharmacy. They had been blackmarketed from as far away as Paris and Manila, and in the areas where we would be heading they'd be worth a fortune. 'You got a lot with my dollars,' I observed.

'For what we want to do we'll need a lot,' Zulfiqar said briefly. He advised us to get to sleep promptly, for we were off to the high mountains next morning at four.

Stiglitz, tired from the bargaining at the bazaar, followed his advice, but apparently Zulfiqar himself did not, for before I could fall asleep I heard the clatter of horses' hoofs, and since no one was permitted to ride the brown horse but the leader of the clan, it must have been Zulfiqar. There came a scratching at my tent and a boy of eight or nine slipped in to advise me that I was wanted. Throwing a shawl about me, I went out expecting to meet the Kochi but saw instead the stars and a beautiful white horse that Mira was holding for me.

'It isn't right that you should walk, Miller,' she said.

'Where'd you get this?' I asked, dumbfounded.

'In Kabul,' she said softly. 'My present to you.'

'But, Mira! Where'd you find the money?'

'I was afraid that if you had to walk all the way to Balkh you might leave us,' she whispered. 'You require a horse, Miller. An important man like you deserves one.'

I was about to protest her extravagance when I looked at the right flank of the beast, and there emblazoned deep was the letter W. I was being handed a white horse branded with a memento of the Wharton School in Philadelphia, and when Moheb Khan discovered the theft I could be arrested. I started to upbraid her for having the horse, but I was halted by a powerful doubt as to just how she might have acquired it. I recalled her keen interest in Moheb Khan. Weakly I asked, 'How did you know I was staying with the caravan?'

She replied gently, 'For days my father and I have been trying to think of some trick that would keep you with us. Last night he told me, "Go to sleep, Mira. I'll think of something."'

I thought of my lost hundred and fifty dollars and asked, 'You mean that Zulfiqar was trying to get me to stay with the caravan?'

'Yes,' she whispered. 'How did he manage it?'

'In a very interesting way,' I replied.

Slowly, gently she took my hand and told the little boy that it was now time for him to leave us, and she led me and the white horse far from camp to a spot where that afternoon she had cached a blanket and I noticed for the first time that from somewhere–probably the bazaar in Kabul–she had stolen a bottle of perfume, and in a wild embrace we found each other. For each of us, I discovered, it was the introduction to love, under a full moon on the high plateau of Asia; so that when toward four the next morning we headed back toward camp, I had the most persuasive reason in the world for accompanying the Kochis to Balkh.

13

For many centuries there had been a circuitous highway leading from Kabul to the historic Vale of Bamain, where Buddhism had flourished centuries before the birth of Muhammad, and gifted travelers from the age of Alexander to the present had described the rugged beauties of this road; but Kochis avoided it, for they knew a caravan route which climbed directly into the Koh-i-Baba, a route so spectacular, passing as it did through gorges and along cliffs, that its grandeur was reserved for those who traveled in the ancient caravan manner. So far as I know, this road has never been described in books, because only Kochis used it, and they did not write.

The mountains were fifteen and sixteen thousand feet high, forbidding bulwarks whose peaks no man had climbed, and wherever we looked they dominated the view; it seemed unlikely that anyone could penetrate them, let alone a caravan of camels. But under Zulfiqar's experienced guidance we headed for one apparently solid wall after another and somehow each barrier provided us with one lucky escape: sometimes a gorge, sometimes a green valley that opened dramatically to the north.

Now the animals grew fat on abundant grass and on some days even the camels modified their grumbling. I spent hours watching our fat-tailed sheep, those preposterous beasts that looked not like sheep but like small-headed beetles stuck onto very long legs. They derived their name from an enormous tail, perhaps two feet across and shaped like a thick country frying pan covered with wool and rich with accumulated lanolin. The tail bumped up and down when the sheep walked, a grotesque afterpiece that served the same function as a camel's hump: in good times it stored food which in bad times it fed back to the animal. I was told that the lanolin was not solid but could be moved about with the hands; certainly it could be eaten, as we proved in our pilaus, but now that the tails were at their maximum they made the ugly sheep seem like something an ungifted schoolboy had scratched on a tablet, and as I sat watching the huge bustles bounce up and down I used to speculate on how the beasts managed to copulate. To this day I don't know.

Our fat-tails were made to look even more farcical by the fact that we occasionally overtook the caravan of some mountain tribe with a flock of karakul sheep, those superbly built patricians with long necks, expressive faces, deep-set eyes and soft ears. They were the finest animals in Afghanistan and were extremely valuable, since karakul skins were a major item in the nation's trade with the outside world. Whenever one examined the fortunes of men like Shah Khan in Kabul, it was usually found that their wealth derived in some way from karakul. The wool of the older animals was not impressive and had, so far as I know, no particular value, but newborn lambs were covered with the silky, close-matted, curly fur that is treasured in all countries; and to compare these aristocratic sheep with the ungainly fat-tailed clowns of our caravan was

all to our disadvantage. I asked Zulfiqar why we had no karakuls and he
explained, 'I'd like to, but the desert marches would kill them.'

Because the mountains of the Koh-i-Baba grew increasingly difficult for the
caravan—camels growled at rocky areas—we made shorter journeys than before
and were inclined, when we found good pasture, to halt for three or four days.
It was in these periods of rest, these peaceful days in the high mountains, that
Mira and I had our good times. We would leave my white horse in camp for the
children to ride and with a chunk of nan would hike to some higher plateau
where we would lie in the cold sun, talk and make love.

To be with Mira was a primitive joy. By now I was able to share her concern
with matters of the caravan: 'Where should we stop?' 'When will the ewes
throw their lambs?' 'Could you live in a village like the one we saw yesterday?'
It was her opinion that six weeks of village life beneath a chaderi would kill her,
a judgment that I was prepared to accept.

She was like an elf, old enough to be married but young enough to run after a
herd of camels with a stick. She had shown no inclination to accept any of the
nomad men as her mate, nor did she think of me as a potential solution. On the
fifth day north of Kabul she said, 'It would be pleasant if you could ride with us
forever, Miller. On the trail you're a strong man.'

When I asked her how Kochis organized their marriages she said, 'We don't
usually consult mullahs. A young man goes to an older man like my father and
says, "I want your daughter Mira. How many sheep do I get if I take her?" Or
he may demand some camels. Of course, if they do get married he stays with the
clan. That way the animals don't leave. Neither does the daughter.'

'Is there a feast?' I asked, still uncertain as to what the ceremony consisted of.

'Drums, flutes, a roasted sheep. The children get colored candies and the
bride two new sets of clothing. When I marry I'll get a black skirt.'

'Ellen wears a black skirt. Is she married to your father?'

'Oh, no! He didn't give her the black skirt. Racha did, out of kindness,
because Ellen's were wearing out.'

'Did Racha give her the bracelets, too?' I asked idly as we lay looking at the
white clouds seeping over the edge of the Koh-i-Baba as its peaks watched us
from the north. Mira explained that Zulfiqar had given Ellen the bracelets, but
I did not hear her full reply, for I was thinking: I've been with them eight weeks
and not a moment of rain. Not even a cloud. What an amazing world, drifting
along like this year after year. Then an irritating thought oppressed me: What's
so amazing about it? They probably have the same kind of days in Arizona. But
I found consolation in one fact: In Arizona they don't have Mira.

As I ended my soliloquy, she ended her explanation of the bracelets, then
asked pertly, 'If somebody asks you, "How did you join the Kochis, Miller?"
what will you say?'

'I'll say, "For the first part of the trip, I had to join because somebody stole
my jeep."'

'Did you know that I helped take off the wheels? When we sold them at Musa
Darul I got some of the money.'

'For the second part of the trip . . . that's more difficult to explain. Maybe I'll
say, "A beautiful Kochi girl bought me with a white horse."'

Mira kissed me and ran to a brook to catch a drink of fresh mountain water,
bringing me some in her felt cap. 'How did you get that horse?' I asked, with a
nagging memory of Moheb Khan and the possessive way he had taken the arm
of the Swedish girl Ingrid.

'With the money I got from stealing the jeep, I bought the horse. Isn't that fair? Lose a jeep, find a horse?'

My recollection of Moheb Khan reminded me of Nazrullah and I asked, 'Did you ever meet Ellen's husband, Nazrullah?'

'I saw him. He has a beard.'

'Did your father meet him?'

'Why should he? As my father told you in the caravanserai, we made a three-day camp at Qala Bist . . . because of the desert ahead. At the end of the three days Ellen asked Zulfiqar if she could come with us. Up to then she had never spoken to him, so he had nothing to do with her running away. It was us she loved, the caravan and the camels and the children. It was much later that he allowed her to sleep in his tent.'

'Was Racha angry?'

'Why should she be? He allowed her to stay in the tent, too.'

'Are Ellen and your father . . .' I didn't know the Kochi words and started again. 'Is she his woman?'

'Of course,' Mira laughed, using the vulgar Kochi gesture for sexual intercourse. 'But not like you and me. Not for great fun under the stars.'

'Does she love your father?' I persisted.

'Everybody loves my father,' she said simply. 'In some clans men try to kill each other. Not in ours. But she doesn't love him the way I love you, Miller.' To demonstrate the difference, she grabbed me and we ended up rolling on the ground, then seeking a protected crevice in the rocky walls.

It was tacitly understood that Mira and I would not embarrass Zulfiqar by sleeping together in the camp, since he chose to ignore his daughter's misalliance. We were therefore driven to sleep in the open and it became customary for Mira to make a show of going to bed in Zulfiqar's tent, while I did the same in mine, and then later for her to throw pebbles against the black felt, whereupon I would drag out my sleeping gear and lug it beyond the camels, where we would sleep till just before the break of camp.

Strangely, it was in daylight on the trail that I experienced my deepest sense of love for Mira, and I find it difficult to explain why; but when I was riding the white horse, moving up and down the column like Zulfiqar, I would occasionally overtake Mira when she did not see me, and for some minutes I would watch her, swinging along the road in her loose sandals, her shawl falling across her shoulders and her black pigtails bobbing in the sun, and I would recognize her as the freest human being I would ever know. She envied no one, loved whom she wished, took what she needed, concerned herself only with the immediate problems at hand, and lived on the high plateaus where nature was superb or on the edges of the desert where life was as clearly outlined as man ever sees it. The she would hear me, and she would look over her shoulder at her man on the horse she had acquired for him, and in her look was both equality and pride, and it was sharing that look which made me feel so much a man I had survived the war as a courageous boy; on the caravan trails, riding through the Koh-i-Baba on a white horse, I discovered what it was to be a man.

We had been traveling like this for five or six days when I began to detect a marked change in Dr Stiglitz. The apprehension I had noticed in Kandahar and Musa Darul, when he worried about his tobacco and his beer, had left him, and the strong sense of guilt that had characterized him at the caravanserai was gone. He strode briskly along the trail without turban or karakul, his steel-gray hair close-cropped for sun and wind to play upon. At times he looked even happy, in a studied Germanic manner, and made overtures to extend the mutual respect which had begun to develop on that last night before we reached Kabul.

One day he left his position at the head of the camels and fell back to talk with me. Ignoring Mira in his German manner, he said, 'A man could march on like this forever.'

I suggested, 'Maybe it's because your health is better . . . the open air.'

'I place no great reliance on exercise,' he assured me professionally. 'In Munich I lived perfectly happily walking a few blocks from my home to my office.' He lost himself in contemplation of those good, gone days before the war, then added significantly, 'I think what accounts for the difference is the confession I made to you at the caravanserai. To be able to tell those things to a Jew . . .'

'You feel you've purged yourself?' I asked coldly.

'No, Miller! Remember, when we spoke I didn't know you were a Jew. Of what I did I can never purge myself. But I can learn to live with history . . . to accept its full burden. That I'm doing.'

'Why was the release deferred until this trip? The evil occurred years ago.'

'Ah, so!' he agreed. 'But always before I was preoccupied with myself. Could I get out of Germany? Could I enter Persia? Would I be caught and hanged?' He shuddered. 'I was pathetic, involved only with myself and my tobacco and my beer.'

I asked him what specifically had led him beyond himself, and he said, 'Fighting with you in the serai. For years Sem Levin had been a ghost hanging upon my throat. But fighting with you by the pillar made Jews real again . . . quit them from being ghosts. I killed a man . . . a living man, but I've paid the penalty. The caravan moves on.'

I said bluntly, 'I hate to think I enabled you to exorcize your ghosts.'

'You did. The caravan moves on. Germany moves on. In a few years America will be begging Germany for friendship. Strange, isn't it?'

'You think this erases the past? A fist fight with a Jew?'

'In a sense, yes. We can bear terror only so long. Then it goes away, either because one fights with a Jew, or because one makes a trip with Kochis, or because the calendar reads 1946 instead of 1943. The pillar remains standing in the serai, with the bodies sealed inside, but in the sunlight the nomads graze their flocks.' He looked at me in triumph as he cried to the encroaching mountain, 'The terror goes away.'

Then, still ignoring Mira, he stopped on the rocky trail and asked, 'Miller, as a final act of contrition, may I kiss the hand of Sam Levin?'

I was repelled, but when I saw how much he needed this act of absolution, I had to say, 'Yes.' As the animals moved past us he knelt on the rocks and kissed my hand. When he rose I clasped his shoulder and said, 'What you say is true, Dr Stiglitz. The terror does go away. I no longer look at you as a depraved animal. You're one of us . . . one of us.'

He nodded and walked on to resume his customary place with Maftoon and the camels; but when he was gone, shrewd Mira, to whom he had not once spoken, said in Pashto, 'He talks a lot, but his real trouble is . . . he's in love with Ellen. Pretty soon . . .' and she made the Kochi sign for sex.

I asked, 'What will happen if they do?'

'You mean?' and she made the sign again.

'Yes.'

'Maybe my father kill him,' she said without emotion. She told me of the time Maftoon's wife had fallen in love with a bazaar man in the Indian town of Rawalpindi, and Zulfiqar had beaten her savagely, so that she had crawled away from the caravan and gone to hide with the townsman. But Maftoon had followed her and knifed the bazaar man to death. 'That's his wife over there,' Mira said placidly, and I looked at one of the four women gathering camel dung, a woman somewhat older than Racha, vibrant, laughing, handsome, with a gold medallion piercing the right side of her nose. She suspected that Mira was speaking of her and she came to us in great peasant strides.

'What's that one telling you?' she demanded.

'That Maftoon killed a man . . . for you.'

'He did,' she laughed. 'He broke off this tooth, too,' and she showed me the stump. 'I'd never have been happy in the city.' Then she winked at me and warned, 'You go away from Mira, Mira kill you, too.'

When she returned to the camel droppings Mira laughed and said, 'I'm not so foolish. When the time comes, you go. When the time comes, I go.'

For two days I studied Stiglitz and Ellen as carefully as possible, and I had to admit that Mira was right. They were in love and Zulfiqar knew it. So far he had kept the German from the tent and of course Ellen was not free to leave her bed at night as Mira did, but I looked for an opportunity to warn her of the danger she was inviting, for in spite of his seeming acquiescence I was convinced that Zulfiqar would kill Stiglitz if honor required.

I had never seen Ellen looking so radiant. We were now in cold country, well above ten thousand feet, with snow only a short distance above us and occasionally in some high pass actually nipping at our ears, and Ellen had acquired a long gray burnoose like those worn by Tajik mountaineers. It was made of raw wool and reached to her ankles; so that even in very cold weather it was comfortable. Into its attached hood Racha had worked gold and silver threads, showing Ellen's lovely blond head to good advantage, and when she rode my white horse, as she sometimes did when I wished to walk with Mira, she created the image of a fair young goddess leading her Aryans to some mountain fortress. I understood why Dr Stiglitz had fallen in love with her.

Well before dawn on the ninth day out of Kabul I was lugging my sleeping gear back to the camels for loading when I saw that Ellen was standing in the darkness, watching for a chance to talk with me, so I wandered over to her and asked, 'You need some help?'

'Not in packing,' she replied. 'But could we talk?'

I threw my gear to Maftoon and told him, 'You can ride the white horse,' whereupon Ellen and I started down the trail.

It was a matchless time for the discussion of ideas, since we were about to enter one of the noblest areas of Asia, the great Vale of Bamian. Because we were approaching it in darkness from the west, we would be hiking toward the sunrise, and the silvery cliffs on the north would loom out of the shadowy world just as our bodies and our incorporate thoughts came into being from their own universe of shadow. But it was the vale itself that lured us on: a lush, irrigated valley of historic richness from which Buddhism had spread to China and Japan, a vale crowded with trees and cool brooks and pasture lands. It was lined with poplars like a formal Italian garden, and to come upon it in the darkness, when each step revealed new beauties, when the approach of the still-distant sun brought more and more illumination both to the vale and to the problems we carried to it, was an experience not to be forgotten.

In the darkness Ellen cried, 'Miller, I've fallen in love!' and the anguish of her cry, the honest perplexity it echoed, had to be respected.

'Mira told me . . . some time ago.'

'We've tried to keep it secret . . . even from ourselves.'

'Mira says you could invite great danger,' I warned.

'I'm not concerned with danger,' she said boldly. 'I left Bryn Mawr seeking something like this. I left Qala Bist for the same reason. Now that I've found it . . .'

We hiked in darkness, with now and then a fugitive ray of light streaking across the sky like a scout sent forward by some Mongol army. In the gloom Ellen cried, 'Miller! What shall I do?'

The pleading in her voice enlisted my sympathy and I tried to be as helpful as possible. 'Let me ask your question another way,' I suggested. 'What are you already doing . . . hiking along a caravan trail at four-thirty in the morning in Central Asia? Ellen, what are you doing?'

She became defensive and countered, 'I might ask you the same question.'

'With me it's easy. I was sent here. By the government. To find you.'

In the darkness she laughed. 'Oh, no! The government didn't send you here. It sent you to Qala Bist, but you came here on your own account.' Something of the gentleness that had marked her beginning observations now vanished and she added with some asperity, 'You're here because for the first time in your circumscribed little life you're sleeping with a wonderful girl, and I don't blame you a bit. But please don't try to convince Aunt Ellen that the United States government told you, "Go out and sleep under the stars."'

'That takes care of me. Now what about you?'

Her gentleness returned, and as new streaks of light appeared in the east she explained, 'I was driven here. It wasn't Nazrullah, who was a most considerate husband, and it wasn't Zulfiqar, whom any girl could admire. It had nothing to do with love or men. I suppose I was driven here by what I saw happening in the world . . . I was driven by something I was powerless to fight.'

I listened, tried to understand, walked for some time in silence, then said, 'Ellen, I've done my damnedest to analyze your behavior, and I've failed. When we were in Kabul I turned in my official report, so this discussion concerns only you and me. Can you please explain in simple words?'

'I don't think so,' she replied thoughtfully. 'Either the words I've already used trigger your intellect or they don't. Either you intuitively feel that America is making terrible mistakes, or you don't.'

'Well, I don't feel it. America's doing a damned good job.'

'I'm talking to an idiot,' she groaned in the darkness. 'Dear God! I need help so desperately, and You send me an idiot.'

'Try it again,' I said with resignation. 'In the simplest words you can muster.'

'I will,' she said softly. 'Miller, don't you see that we're bound to build bigger bombs and then bigger bombs and finally bombs so big that we can destroy the whole world?'

'What you say could be true, but I take consolation in the fact that America is building those bombs and not somebody else.'

'Miller!' she screamed. 'Do you think no one else can build them?'

'Of course they can't. Russia? China? They'll never have the technical skill.'

'Miller!' she shouted. 'Don't be an idiot! We're talking about your soul and mine. Don't you see that . . .'

'Who's been feeding you this line? Stiglitz?'

'Yes, he says . . .'

'Does he also say that he was a Nazi . . . in charge of killing Jews?'

'Yes,' she replied softly. 'And that's why I must live with him . . . the rest of my life.'

I was so infuriated with her garbled nonsense that I raised my hand to slap her, but in the half-light she saw it and drew back. 'Talk sense,' I growled.

The sun, as if eager to provide an illumination which we could not find for ourselves, crept toward the eastern horizon and sent shafts of light high across the heavens. Ellen, happy that the night was ending, shook the gold and silver cowl from her head and allowed the twilight to play upon her shimmering hair. Looking at me in deep confusion of spirit she said, 'I am talking sense. Promise me that no matter what I say in the next few minutes . . . no matter how I outrage your logic, you'll listen and try to understand.'

'Out of sheer curiosity, I will.'

'Let's say I was a girl growing up in a normal family, in a normal church, with a normal group of friends. Boys liked me, and teachers too. I went to dances, gave parties, did well in college. But one day when I was about fifteen . . . long before the war . . . I saw that everything my family did was irrelevant. We were keeping score . . . I can't call it anything else . . . in a game that simply didn't exist except in our imagination. Did that idea ever occur to you?'

'No.'

'I'm sure it didn't,' she replied, without rancor. 'Well, World War II came and I listened to such nonsense as men rarely display in public. I kept my mouth shut, primarily because Father took it so seriously. He was home safe . . . too old to fight. So he could be pretty heroic. As chairman of the draft board he gave a rousing speech to all the young men he sent away. It would have moved you deeply, Miller. Some of the boys my age told me, "Your old man makes you want to march right out and do your job . . . and his." Some of my classmates weren't so dumb.'

'Some of my classmates weren't so dumb either,' I snapped. 'I remember a philosophy major named Krakowitz. He said, "There's only one thing worse than winning a war. That's losing it." It was his opinion that when you were fighting Hitler, Mussolini and Tojo it might be true that nobody could win, but it was also true that if you lost, it could be real hell. Krakowitz. He died at Iwo Jima.'

'I'm deeply touched,' she said, bowing in the morning twilight. 'So in college I met this gang of kept professors. What else can you call them? Their moral responsibility was to dissect the world, but they were paid to defend it. I suppose they had a job to do . . . learn, earn; pray, stay; live, give. They had one hell of a system going for them, those professors.

'But there was one who used to drop hints that he knew the world needed dissecting, and he caught on to me very fast. Taught music and wrote to my parents that I was rejecting the world. Boy, was he right! Father bullied him in his best draft-board manner and pointed out that I was doing all right in my "real" classes. Reminded me of the passage in Plato where citizens looked so long in the mirror they confused image with reality. It never occurred to Father that this befuddled music master was looking at the real world while the others were marking me on attributes that would never matter . . . not even when Gabriel blows his horn.'

She paused, leaving me space to confute her if I wished, but I was so befuddled by her succession of comment—as compared to the ease with which Mira accepted the life of the caravan, and to hell with what was bothering London or Tokyo—that I refrained from entering the argument. I had asked for an explanation, and I was getting it, whether I understood it or not. She continued, 'When the worst part of the war arrived, my vision was confirmed. I don't know why I wanted to marry Nazrullah. For one thing, in those days I hadn't discovered that he was exactly like my father. Dear Nazrullah! He'll have paved roads in Afghanistan yet. I suppose I came here because Afghanistan was as far from American values as I could get.' She paused, then added a curious comment: 'The fact that Nazrullah already had a wife made the decision easier. Do you follow me?'

'I'm lost,' I confessed.

'What I mean is, my father described anything out of the ordinary as ridiculous, and I wanted to outrage his whole petty scale of judgment. What was the most ridiculous thing I could do? Run off with an Afghan who had a turban and another wife.' She laughed a little, then added, 'Do you know what started my disillusionment with Nazrullah? That turban. He wore it in Philadelphia for show. He'd never think of wearing it in Kabul.'

'I still don't understand,' I replied.

'Lots of young people in America will,' she assured me. 'They're beginning to reject any society built by men like my father.'

'Then God help America,' I said bitterly.

'It's the young people like me who will save America,' she responded. 'They'll understand what's happening, and they'll change things.'

I was pondering this chicanery of mind and thinking: I have to respect the passion of her thought and the sincerity with which she advances it, but I certainly distrust the logic—when the sun burst above the horizon and poured some much-needed light into the Vale of Bamian, illuminating the series of white limestone cliffs that rimmed the northern boundary. They rose high above the vale and were deeply eroded, so that shadows played across them in fascinating variety. The green poplars that grew so plentifully elsewhere stopped at the cliffs, alowing them to stand forth in sharp relief. Then, as the sun grew brighter, Ellen called, 'Miller! Look!'

At first I did not see what had startled her, since I was looking for some ordinary thing. Then, looming from a gigantic niche cut in the face of the tallest cliff, appeared a towering statue of a man, many scores of feet high, wonderfully carved from the living rock. It was apparently a religious figure of heroic proportions, but what gave it an eerie quality was the fact that its enormous face had been chopped away: lips and chin remained, big as human beings themselves, but all above was a flat expanse of limestone.

While we stood in awe before the towering statue, the rest of the caravan drew up, permitting Zulfiqar to point with his gun at the faceless figure and announce, laconically, 'Buddha.'

The caravan moved on to its accustomed tenting space, but Ellen and I remained staring at the hypnotic figure. I asked her to stand for comparison by the mammoth feet while I stood back to calculate how tall the statue was: my rough guesswork yielded about a hundred and fifty feet. Who had carved it here in the heart of a Muslim country? Who had chopped away the benign face?

I was not to find an answer to these questions, but as we studied the gigantic statue I became aware that the cliff beside it was honeycombed with caves, whose windows were literally peppered across the limestone. 'What are they?' I asked, and Ellen suggested this might at one time have been a monastery. We looked some more and found an opening which seemed to lead to the caves, and Ellen indicated that she would like to explore them.

We entered a dark shaft that led upward through solid rock and after much climbing and skirting of precipitous ledges came to a small wooden bridge that carried us to the top of Buddha's head. We were now far above the earth and a fall would have been disastrous, but we perched safetly on the god's head, surveying the vale that opened out before us. In the distance, in bright sunlight, we could see our tents going up.

From the head we found another passageway leading eastward to an interlocking nest of larger caves, which in the old days must have been lecture halls seating hundreds of monks. We found one especially lovely room whose windows, a hundred feet above the earth, framed a view of the Koh-i-Baba, and it was here that Ellen sat cross-legged on the rocky floor, her burnoose covering her body, as she resumed her argument with me.

'When you see the world for the pathetic thing it is'–at the moment I was at the window, inspecting one of the most glorious views in Asia–'my mother used to tremble with gratification when we bought a bigger car than the one before or a college missing the whole point of education but congratulating itself on a million-dollar dormitory . . .' She was trapped in a sentence from which there was no escape and laughed nervously. 'You decide to turn your back on the whole thing and find some simpler base. I thought Nazrullah was simpler than Dorset. Zulfiqar was simpler than Nazrullah. And now Otto Stiglitz is simpler than all.'

'How can you say that? The man's an M.D. from a good university.'

'He's simpler because he's a non-man. In Munich he descended into hell. He's carried the memory of it halfway around the world. He's fought free of the world and its burden. He's a non-man . . . the thing from which we begin all over.'

'Do you really believe this nonsense?' I pleaded.

'You're the way I used to be, Miller,' she said condescendingly. 'You honestly think that someone up there is keeping score on your life. If you learn fifteen new birds, you get a merit badge. If you study calculus, you make the junior honor role. If you keep your nose clean in the navy, the old man signs a favorable letter. If you obey the ambassador, he may sign another favorable letter. All these little credits are entered in a big book by what some sportswriter called the Divine Scorekeeper. It's a comforting theory . . . made my father very happy. He built up points and got a bigger car. Because he had the big car he was entitled to a bigger house. He won the house, so he was voted into the country club. And because he was in the country club his daughter was welcomed at Bryn Mawr. See where it leads? If his daughter does well at Bryn Mawr she's entitled to marry Mark Miller, who by the same series of tricks earned the points to enter Yale. Now see what happens? His daughter and Mark Miller have got to start collecting their points, and if they don't, the old folks will be scared stiff.

'No, Miller, you're betting on the wrong game. There's no scorekeeper. Nobody really gave a damn whether or not you kept your nose clean in the navy. And when we reach Balkh and you walk out on Mira, the Divine Scorekeeper ought to kick the living bejeezus out of you and set your score back to zero for having been such a swine. But He won't. Because the Scorekeeper, supposing there is one, will be laughing at what's happened and observing to

His cronies, "That boy Miller's a damned sight better kid than when he joined the caravan." And at Balkh, when you leave Mira, I too shall leave . . . but I'll go with Otto Stiglitz.'

I looked at the old lecture hall in which we sat; from here wisdom had been poured to the ends of the nations, as they then existed, and I felt morally certain that every lesson propounded in this classroom, this curious cell in the beehive of the monastery where men spent years surrounded by rock, out of touch with the earth until their passions were burned away and their vision clarified–almost every lesson had refuted what Ellen was saying. The wisdom of the world, whether Buddhist, Muslim, Christian or Jewish, insisted that there were desirable ends, that society was worth preserving no matter how badly scarred at a given moment in time, and that there was a Divine Scorekeeper, man himself perhaps, who did judge some deeds as better than others. To the ancient lessons which came to us from this lecture hall in the cliffs of Bamian I was committed, and if Ellen Jaspar was not, the more pity I felt for her.

'Have you slept with Stiglitz?' I asked bluntly.

'No, but I shall when he asks me.'

'I suppose you know that Mira's afraid Zulfiqar might kill Stiglitz . . . or you.'

'That's of no consequence to either of us.'

'It is to me,' I countered.

'But you tried to kill Stiglitz yourself.'

'I've grown beyond that.'

'Miller! That's what I mean. That's the first sensible thing you've said on this trip. Now can you understand me when I say that Stiglitz and I have grown beyond your prejudices? We have, Miller. We are cleansed of this world, and whether Zulfiqar kills us or not is of no significance.'

'Might it be of significance to Zulfiqar?' I asked.

Ellen grew grave and said, 'That's a difficult question. I had no moral right to intrude on Nazrullah, but I excused myself by remembering that he had a wife and a daughter.'

'He now has a son, too.'

'Oh, Karima must be so happy!' she cried spontaneously. 'He wanted a son so much. Well, I also admit I had no right to intrude on Zulfiqar, but he can stand it. He has a good family and a caravan which couldn't exist without him. But Otto Stiglitz has nothing . . . hardly even a job. It's through his regeneration and mine that the world has a fighting chance. Frankly, Miller, with men like you and Nazrullah and Zulfiqar the world neither gains nor loses. You're of no moral significance whatever.'

I asked, 'You know that Stiglitz could be extradited . . . and hanged?'

'Yes. For that very reason he needs me most. But one of the good aspects of living in a non-nation like Afghanistan is they they don't extradite non-men who have already died.'

'At Balkh we're only a few miles from Russia. He could be kidnapped.'

'Civilized nations don't kidnap,' she argued, and I thought it indicative that she rejected civilization when it suited her philosophy to do so, but fled to it for protection of her desires.

'You forget–or did he tell you?–that he kept day-by-day records of his experiments. "I'm a real scientist," he boasted, "I keep records." The English have those records, you know. He's a prime war criminal.'

'You've stated my case for me, Miller. He's already convicted and dead. I've rejected all the lives I've known, so I'm dead too. I can live only at the bottom . . . at the bottom dregs of an insane world. Where hope is being reborn. Does this at last make sense?'

'No,' I said.

'It's strange you're so obtuse,' she reflected sorrowfully. She rose and went to the far end of the cave, drawing her burnoose about her as if it were an academic robe. 'Every honest teacher who stood on this spot lecturing to his students is listening now to what I'm saying. They're applauding. They know that society becomes corrupt and that men must reject it if they are to remain free. They know that life, to replenish itself, must sometimes return to the dregs, to the primitive slime. The men who stood here know that I am right, even if I can't make you listen.'

As she left the cave, she waved to the unseen docents who had instructed generations of Buddhist monks in this rock-girt university, those savants who were already dead and buried centuries before America and Dorset, Pennsylvania, were known. 'They'll understand,' she whispered, and smiling left them.

14

On the second day north of Bamian I had finished checking the caravan on my white horse and had ridden off casually to explore the lateral valley, when I saw two figures climbing over the rocks above me. I was about to hail them but stopped, for when I rode closer I saw that they were Ellen Jaspar and Dr Stiglitz, and I sensed intuitively that this day they did not wish either companionship or surveillance. I became sure of this when they turned a corner which would hide them from the caravan and ran to each other in hungry embrace. In a moment the German started undressing Ellen, and I withdrew unseen.

I would have returned to the caravan, except that as I rode away a pebble fell from the rocks and struck me, and then another, and I realized that someone perched on the high ledges overlooking the lovers was trying to signal me. I reined in the horse, scanned the rocks above me, and spotted a figure in red dress and pigtails. It was Mira, who, having anticipated the intentions of the lovers, had gone into the valley before them to sequester herself at a vantage point from which she would observe the proceedings.

I waved to her angrily: Get off that ledge! But she pressed her fingers against her lips, cautioning silence; then, after watching the lovers for some minutes, she raised her hands triumphantly above her head and made the Kochi sign for successful sexual intercouse. And so the four of us remained gripped in the mountains, Ellen and Stiglitz in their long-delayed passion, Mira spying on them from the overhanging ledge, and I watching her gestures from the valley below. It was one of the most erotic moments I had ever known, but it was colored by a sense of tragedy, for I was convinced that if Zulfiqar discovered their passion, Ellen and her German doctor were self-committed to disaster.

After the lovers rejoined the caravan, I signaled Mira to scramble down from her ledge and join me on the white horse. 'You mustn't mention this to the others,' I warned.

'They know,' she laughed, gripping me about the waist as we galloped back to the caravan.

'How could they know unless you tell them?' I demanded.

'Anybody can look at those two and know,' she insisted.

And she was right. By noon, when Zulfiqar halted the caravan, it was known throughout the clan that the long-predicted encounter had taken place and we awaited the consequences. Since Zulfiqar was much larger than Dr Stiglitz and could presumably strangle him if he wished–I thought it incredible that any woman should trade in the great Kochi for the insignificant German–I supposed there would be a savage beating if not a murder, but to my surprise nothing happened. In the succeeding days Ellen became an increasingly beautiful woman, lovelier even than her high-school photographs or my first sight of her in the caravanserai. Her smile grew more warm. Her freedom of movement was enhanced. Even the manner in which she wore her long gray burnoose became more feminine and alluring, but I remember best the way her blue eyes sparkled during the long uphill hikes.

When Zulfiqar failed to react to their affair, the lovers grew more bold. They began sleeping in the doctor's gear under the stars, along the edge of the camp, and in the afternoons Stiglitz no longer went to sit with Zulfiqar and Racha beneath the tent awning. The effect of this upon the German was profound and with one exception was good. He was no longer so obviously preoccupied with himself, and often when he fumbled with matches while lighting his pipe, he smiled. His nervousness disappeared and he would sometimes lean against the pole in our tent and actually relax.

The only ill effect occurred on the march, for whenever Zulfiqar rode by on his brown horse, Stiglitz tensed himself in case the big Kochi should leap upon him with dagger unsheathed. No amount of inner glow could halt this involuntary reflex, and I thought: They started this mountain-top love affair as non-people indifferent to Zulfiqar, but the deeper they fall in love, the more scared they become.

The march from Bamian to Qabir required eleven days along the most spectacular portion of the caravan route: we were penetrating the heart of the Hindu Kush, and while there were taller mountains in Asia–indeed, the Pamirs, the Karakorams and the Himalayas were all higher–none surpassed these mountains of Afghanistan for their combination of rocky grandeur and valley charm. Sometimes we would swing around the end of a ridge and see before us ten or fifteen miles of green valley without a single indication that men had ever been there before. At other times the trail would narrow to an ugly defile down which a river tumbled, and the trail would halt abruptly against the face of a cliff, but a rickety bridge built years ago by nomads would carry it across the river and send it onto higher land. It was exciting, fresh, magnificent.

One aspect of the Hindu Kush reminded me of the desert. On the fifth day north of Bamian we rounded a corner on the trail to see before us a valley of some magnitude. At the far end, say four miles, rose a striking mountain, and I thought: We'll probably camp under that mountain at noon. But when noon came, the near-at-hand mountain was a few miles away. On the next day we resumed march and at noon the elusive peak was still a few miles distant. So on the following day we plugged along until the mountain was almost near enough to touch, but when another day arrived, the damned mountain was still ahead of us! It finally took us four full days and fifty miles of marching to reach a spot which at first had looked as if he would overrun it before lunch.

During the days when we were trying to reach the mountain I saw little of Ellen Jaspar, for she and Stiglitz were so preoccupied with their burgeoning affair that I had no wish to intrude, and we spoke only occasionally when we met lugging our sleeping gear to and from the tents. Then on the day we finally reached the mountain, Ellen came to me as we were unpacking and made the comment which first set me wondering about her basic sincerity. She said, half in earnest, half in jest, something which I could have taken as an honest concern in my future but which for some reason, I didn't: 'Miller, this caravan is bound to end one day. Don't injure yourself by taking Mira too seriously.' This seemed a most inappropriate comment from a girl whose own love affair with Stiglitz was so intemperate that it could incur even murder, and most contradictory to the things she had said about Mira and me during the trip to Bamian. I was about to question her on these incongruities when Mira came to help me, and Ellen moved on.

'I think Ellen likes you,' Mira observed casually, but I was so captivated with Mira herself that I forgot her words.

It was no wonder. For each night we slept under the stars in a series of the most spectacular boudoirs two lovers had ever known: the mountains hovered aloft to protect us, the rivers brought us music, the moon was our night lamp, while not far away the sounds of the caravan reassured us. When we finally went to bed beneath the elusive mountain, Mira was especially adorable, a crazy, elfin thing with an unpredictable insight into human affairs, and the majesty of our surroundings and the knowledge that soon we would leave the Hindu Kush and perhaps the loveliest weeks of our lives forced me to consider what might happen to both of us at the end of the caravan trail. I say forced me to consider because a young man who lives with a girl like Mira slips unconsciously, day by day, from first rapture to deepening realization to the gnawing suspicion that she has become an inescapable part of his life, not to be dismissed easily nor forgotten ever, and he does not willingly explore the future. To my surprise, Mira was willing to do so and with frightening accuracy anticipated each problem that disturbed me. The nimble fingers of her thought ransacked my mind to uncover my most sensitive apprehensions.

When I asked what Zulfiqar might do to her when I left: 'He can't do anything. Who would inherit his camels?'

When I asked if she would be able to find a husband within the caravan since all the men knew of her love for me: 'If I have the camels, I have a husband.'

When I asked what might happen if she had a baby: 'What happened to those children over there? Some mothers are dead. Some fathers are unknown.'

When I asked what she wanted in life: 'In winter Jhelum. In summer Hindu Kush. Any better in America?'

And when I asked her if she loved me: 'I bought you a white horse, didn't I?' She kissed me and added, 'Go to sleep. It is the woman's job to worry about these matters. After all, we have the babies, not you.'

But it was when I had asked no question that I sometimes learned most about this delectable young nomad: I was hiking with Mira, having turned the horse over to Maftoon, who galloped up and down the file like a Kazak, when without preparation she observed, 'Ellen is the prettiest woman I've ever seen. I would like to look like Ellen. But I would like to be like Racha.' When I asked why, she replied, 'All the people Racha touches are made stronger. That is not so with Ellen.'

I objected and pointed to Dr Stiglitz, whom Ellen had transformed. At this Mira chuckled: 'He was a dying man. Any woman with a good pair of legs could have saved him. I don't count Dr Stiglitz at all.'

'What's going to happen to him . . . when Zulfiqar gets mad, I mean?'

'My father may kill him,' she speculated as before. 'On the other hand, my father may be grateful that Ellen has been taken off his hands.'

'That's an astonishing thing to say,' I exploded.

She ignored my question by saying of Racha, 'She helps women in childbirth, and handles the camels well, and knows how to care for sick sheep. You know, Miller, Racha is the only one able to argue with my father in the councils, and he trusts her to put the caravan money in the bank at Jhelum.' She paused, thinking of her mother, and added, 'Racha wears gold in her nose and does not comb her hair, but she is the heart of our caravan, and Zulfiqar would be stupid to trade her for Ellen. He knows that.'

'Did he ever love Ellen?' I asked.

Again she evaded my question. 'If you stayed with us, Miller,' she promised, 'I would be like Racha for you.' At this point Maftoon rode up on the white horse and asked, 'Would the sahib like to have it back?' and Mira snapped, 'Yes, you dirty loafer. It's improper for you to ride while he walks.' She cupped her hands to make a stirrup for me, and with a quick heft of her tiny body tossed me onto the horse.

As I left Mira, Zulfiqar rode up flashing excitement. 'Follow me, Millair!' he cried, and for several miles I trailed him until he reached the crest of the ridge, where he reined in his brown horse to wait for me.

Pointing to an extensive plateau unfolding below us, he said, 'That's Qabir.'

Richardson had told me that this was a place of much importance, but even so I had not guessed its magnitude. Across the great plain two rivers came from different ranges of the Hindu Kush and met to form a stately Y. As far as I could see, along both the tributaries and the main river, nomads had erected clusters of black tents. Estimating roughly, I judged there were at least four hundred caravans like ours, which at two hundred persons per caravan meant . . .

Startled by my own figures, I asked, 'How many people?'

'Who cares?' he asked in boyish excitement. 'Sixty thousand? Maybe more.'

It was difficult to believe that for more than a thousand years the nomads had been convening in this remote spot at the confluence of rivers and that no national government was yet sure where the meeting place was, nor who attended, nor how the camp was composed. Now that the war was over, airplanes would soon penetrate the secret, but for the time being this was the last outpost of free men.

'Here we go!' Zulfiqar shouted, and he spurred his horse into a gallop that carried him down onto the plateau and among the gathering caravans. I followed as boldly as I dared, but it was some time before I caught up with my Kochi. When I did, I found him hurrying from one caravan to the next, shouting to old friends, reporting on his winter in India and making plans for trading sessions. It was obvious that he was one of the unifying forces of the encampment.

Finally he remembered that I was with him and crying, 'Millair! Follow me!'

he galloped along the left bank of the nearest tributary until he found an attractive area as yet unoccupied. 'We'll camp here,' he shouted. 'You wait and tell the others.' With this he dug his heels into his horse and sped off to new greetings, but he had gone only a short distance when he reared his horse handsomely, spun him around and came dashing back to me: 'As soon as they arrive, tell Maftoon to roast four fat sheep.' The horse reared again and he was gone.

It would be an hour before the Kochis could reach us, and the waiting became one of the most poignant times of my life, for around me swirled the enigmatic caravans from the heartland of Asia. I saw beside me men and women from tribes I had never known existed, camels that had crossed the Oxus from areas a thousand miles away, children with round red faces, and women wearing fur boots and wonderful tanned smiles derived from months spent in sunlight. In the distance, at some caravan up the river, a man played a flute and it was like an evocation of the Arabian Nights or the music of Borodin that I had heard at the symphony in Boston. As a stranger on a white horse I attracted attention, and some of the nomads even tried to speak to me in strange tongues, but to all I made it clear that this choice spot by the river was reserved for Zulfiqar and I found that people respected his name.

The poignancy grew more intense when I happened to look toward the Hindu Kush and saw the Kochis coming out of the mountains on their way to the camp ground, and for the first time I saw our caravan in its entirety and realized what an impressive aggregation it was: two hundred people, nearly a hundred camels laden with costly goods, several score of donkeys, some goats and more than five hundred choice sheep. This was my caravan, these were my people; and when I remembered the warm family life I had enjoyed in Boston, I felt grateful that I had been allowed to know this larger family.

And then I saw, marching together, dark little Mira in her red skirt and pigtails and shining Ellen, the hood of her burnoose thrown back, so that her beauty flashed in sunlight, and I was unable to move or think or speak. I merely sat on the white horse and looked at these two persons as they came toward me, the nomad whom I loved so much and the strange, fair woman whom I wanted to help and whom I found so difficult to understand, and as I looked at them the thought came from outside me: They are your life, the essence of your caravan.

In a kind of repose–quiet and unfathomed and undisturbed by the men of Asia moving around me–I watched as the Kochis approached, until three of our men spotted me and shouted, 'Here we are!'

'This is the place,' I called back, and with a whip of the bridle I sent the white horse speeding toward the caravan, where I leaped to the ground, kissed Mira in front of everyone and whispered, 'I was afraid . . .'

'Of what?' she asked quietly.

'That . . . well, that you might not come.'

She did not laugh, nor did Ellen, but she plunged her quick hand into my pocket and asked, 'Miller, you got any afghanis?'

I came up with a few local coins and when I handed them to her she smiled like a little child, and rounded up all the youngsters of our caravan and led them across the plateau toward the sound of music. I followed my pigtailed Pied Piper until she brought her charges to a traditional spot where some Russian Uzbeks had erected a primitive merry-go-round: a wooden socket had been sunk in the ground and into it was fitted a strong, upright pillar, from whose top branched out ten arms. At the end of each arm hung a free-swinging iron pole, which ended in a rudely carved wooden horse. In half a dozen different languages the Uzbeks shouted, 'The wildest rearing horses in the world!'

'Give them all a ride,' Mira told the Uzbeks, and our Kochi children were piled on the rough horses, quivering with apprehension and joy. Then two burly Uzbeks, pressing their chests against poles that projected from the pillar, began moving slowly in a tight circle, which made the pillar and the horses revolve, and everything was so neatly balanced that soon the Uzbeks had their contraption spinning smoothly, whereupon they ran faster and faster until at last they had to spend little effort, while the squealing children on the horses spun at great speed, their little bodies almost parallel to earth.

'These horses are the first exciting thing I can remember,' Mira shouted, as children from scores of different tribes cheered the flying Kochis. 'When I was young, Zulfiqar always gave me a ride.' Her face was radiant, as if she were again one of the wild and happy children. Then without warning, she turned and pressed her head against my shoulder and whispered, 'Oh, Miller! I am again so happy.'

It was in this manner—from Mira's spontaneous turning to me while mothers from many caravans watched—that the nomads of Qabir discovered that we were in love, and if there was any one thing that made my mission at the encampment easier it was this fact: as a strange American set down on the high plateau I was bound to be conspicuous and ineffective; but as a young man in love with a spirited Kochi girl I was so obvious that the nomads felt sorry for me and I was accorded freedoms that no other stranger would have been permitted.

Then, as the Uzbeks halted their merry-go-round and Mira recovered her children, I saw that on the other side of the circle Ellen had gathered a group of nondescript children whose mothers were not present with coins, and she brought these round-faced youngsters to the Uzbeks and there was some haggling in Pashto. Finally Ellen took off two of her bracelets and gave them to the Uzbek, who tried to bend them in his fingers. He accepted them, and Ellen's children were placed on the horses and again the burly Uzbeks groaned against the poles to get the pillar spinning; and as the children rose higher and higher, speeding through the air, Ellen stood in the afternoon sunlight, biting her knuckles and watching.

At dusk, when the four sheep were well roasted and Ellen had taken her accustomed place to serve the portions, we heard a shout at the edge of our caravan and Zulfiqar appeared, bringing with him some thirty leaders of other caravans plus an orchestra of Tajik musicians, who found a place by the fire and started banging their drums. 'Ellen!' Zulfiqar shouted. 'Leave the cooking!' And with a sweep of his arm he brought the American girl into the center of the crowd and danced with her vigorously. The visitors watched, then reached out for Kochi women and launched a hilarious celebration. Soon Zulfiqar passed Ellen along to one of the Russians and came to me, out of breath. 'Millair,' he laughed, 'I want you to meet one of the leaders,' and he took me through the gyrating dancers to where a tall, heavy, baldheaded man in his late forties stood in fur boots, rough wool jacket and brass-studded belt. His big face was round and clean-shaven, while the slant of his eyes indicated Mongolian ancestry. Grasping him by the shoulder, Zulfiqar said, 'This is Shakkur the Kirghiz. He smuggles guns and sells most of the German rifles on the high plateau. He sold me mine.'

The big Kirghiz nodded pleasantly, showing large white teeth with a prominent space in the middle. 'You English?' he asked in broken Pashto.

'American,' I replied.

He burst into a generous laugh and made a machine gun with his arms. 'Ah-ah-ah-ah-ah, Chicago!' he cried. 'I see cinema.'

I respected the man's vitality, but was irritated by his view of Americans, and on the spur of the moment I dropped so that I was sitting on my ankles, and with my arms folded I did a poor imitation of a Russian dance. 'I see cinema too,' I laughed.

'No!' he protested boisterously. He shouted at the Tajik musicians and they began a new selection to which he danced a passage of real Kirghiz violence. Here there was no mock clicking of the heels but rather the heavy-booted stamp and whirl of the steppes. Seeing Ellen standing near the roast sheep, he leaped at her, grabbed her by the waist, and swung her into a sweeping, dipping step which made her burnoose swirl over the earth. They were a handsome couple, and although she could not follow the intricate steps, the Kirghiz kept her moving so easily that it looked as if she were indeed dancing with him. The Tajik orchestra brought its music to a climax and the big dancer swept his partner high in the air, turned her about, and put her down gently beside the waiting sheep.

'Time to eat!' he shouted, and Ellen started handing out chunks of mutton to the hungry visitors.

When the feasting ended, Zulfiqar asked Dr Stiglitz to stand beside him while he announced, 'This is a German doctor. He has many medicines.' Turning toward one of the tents he shouted, 'Maftoon! Bring the box of medicine,' and when the impressive collection was displayed Zulfiqar said, 'If you have any sick, bring them here tomorrow.'

'What charge?' Shakkur the Kirghiz asked.

'No charge,' Zulfiqar assured him, and next morning outside our tent a line of men and women, dressed in many different tribal costumes, sought aid. In caring for them Stiglitz was assisted by Ellen, who acted as his nurse, and once while she talked with patients in Pashto the doctor wandered over to me to observe, 'You've no idea, Miller, how refreshing it is to treat a woman patient who takes off her clothes and says, "It hurts here." Believe me, if I ever get to Kabul the men will turn their wives over to me and leave. No more chaderies in my office.'

I had not been at the sick line long when Zulfiqar appeared, leading my white horse. After noticing the patients approvingly, he said, 'Come along,' and we rode to the other end of the encampment, where he began a systematic visit to all caravans. At each he did two things; he advised the traders in that caravan how to earn more profit from their goods, and he invited each group to send its sick to his German doctor.

I was impressed with Zulfiqar as he moved among the caravans: a smile, a joke, a reference to me . . . It all made commercial bargaining something more than a mere business occupation. I found that I was in the presence of a real political talent, a man who knew that his simple smile and transparent honesty could win him rewards that another might miss. He was politicking like mad, but I didn't know what for.

Thus I made my way into the yurts of the north, those brown hide-walled circular tents where men with Oriental eyes laughed easily while the buxom wives served yak cheese and roast mutton. Casually I shared hospitality with nomads who had come from all parts of Central Asia and I learned how they made their pilgrimages, what goods they traded, the condition of life in their valleys. I was satisfied that no Russian soldiers accompanied the nomads and probably no political commissars, but of this latter I could not be certain. The great gathering at Qabir seemed to be just that: one of the largest commercial fairs in the world, rivaling Nizhni Novgorod and Leipzig. But there was one thing I was not allowed to learn, perhaps the most important of all, and my defeat on this score was a disappointment. I never did find out where these Russian migrants crossed the Oxus.

Richardson had ordered me to take notes, but at night I memorized the various tribes and subdivisions I had been with that day. From India came the true Povindahs, the Baluchis, and the stocky men from the kingdoms of Chitral, Dir and Swat.

From southern Afghanistan came the Pashtuns, the Brahuis and the Kochis.

From central Afghanistan came the Durani tribe of the Pashtuns, who now ruled the kingdom, the Ghilzais, who used to rule it, and the curious Kizilbash, a Persian tribe of gifted traders.

From northern Afghanistan came the Tajiks, Uzbeks and Kirghizes, all of whom had related tribes north of the Oxus in Russia, the Karakalpaks, the Nuristanis, who were supposed to be of Greek origin, and the Hazaras, who were descendants of Genghis Khan's troops.

From western Afghanistan came the Jamshedis, the Firuzkuhis, the Taimuris and the Arabs.

From Persia came the nomads of Meshed and Nishapur, the Sakars, the Salors, and additional tribes of Kizilbash.

From Russia came its segments of the Tajik, Uzbek, Sart and Kirghiz tribes, plus the Kazaks and traders from the old market city of Samarkand.

From remote areas came the nameless tribes of the Pamirs, the Chinese from Kashgar and Yarkand, and the handsome mountaineers of Gilgit and Hunza.

And from everywhere–Persia, Afghanistan, Russia, China–came members of that mysterious and omnipresent group, the Turkomans, a people not clearly defined but brave and canny traders.

When I had spent some time in the tents and yurts of all these tribes, I began to feel a certain smugness that I, of all the foreigners in Afghanistan, should have been the one to penetrate Qabir, but so far I had seen only the externals. On the fifth day Zulfiqar saddled up the horses and said, 'Today you will see Qabir,' and he led me to the confluence of the rivers where an area had been marked inside of which only men were allowed, and only the leaders of the men. We pulled up before a large Russian-style yurt, whose primitive sides were made of skins and whose spacious interior was decorated with guns, daggers, sabers and three handsome red-and-blue Persian rugs. This was the centre from which the encampment was governed.

At the far end a small, low table stood on a white rug brought down from Samarkand, and on this rug, cross-legged, were seated the two sharifs who controlled Qabir. The first was Shakkur, the Kirghiz gunrunner who had danced at our feast, and as he sat in the place of honor he was impressive indeed, a big hulk of man with shining head and penetrating eyes. The humor that had marked him at our feast was gone, for ruling this large encampment was a serious business.

The other sharif was an elderly Hazara, a man whose Mongol ancestry would have placed him beneath contempt in Kabul, but who had built a substantial trade in karakul, so that a fair portion of the skins bartered that year at Qabir would come under his jurisdiction. He wore the tattered clothes of a peasant and often listened to argument with his eyes closed, but he was known as a shrewd trader. 'He was sharif when my father first brought me here,' Zulfiqar explained, and I asked if I might speak with the old man.

He spoke good Pashto and told me, 'You're the first westerner ever to see this yurt.' I asked him if Russians from Moscow had attended the camp and he smiled indulgently, saying, 'No Communists.' Then he added, 'This year we have a special event which will make the bazaar exciting for you.' I replied that it already was.

Almost every man I met in that yurt was an authentic epic, but my favourite was an old Mongol in his seventies wearing a Gilgit cap. He had come from far beyond the Karakorams with two donkeys and a horse. Of the men who frequented the yurt he wore the filthiest clothes, yet his white beard and toothless mouth were constantly flapping in negotiation. He had been alone on the highest road in the world for eight weeks, starting as soon as snow melted in the high passes, and he carried a considerable quantity of gold, one of the few nomads who did. He told me, 'I've been traveling this route sixty-six years. Everyone knows me as the old man with the gold.'

'Ever run into any trouble?'

'Never shot a bandit in my life.'

Later Zulfiqar told me, 'He's telling the truth. All he shot were honest people. For the first forty years on the trail he was a robber in the Karakorams.'

Toward the end of the fourth week a Tajik was caught stealing goods from an Uzbek and the culprit was dragged to the big yurt, where the two sharifs were discussing other business. The Tajik had no defense. Witnesses had apprehended him with the goods and he had to confess.

We gathered about the white rug as the two sharifs discussed the matter, and I realized that no nation exercised any sovereignty over this congregation of seventy or eighty thousand people. By consent these two sharifs, one a gunrunner and the other an outcast, enjoyed absolute control. If they now decided to execute the trembling Tajik, they could, but after a short consultation Shakkur the Kirghiz announced the verdict: the right hand to be cut off.

I gasped at the severity of the judgment and impulsively stepped forward. In Pashto I offered to pay the value of the goods stolen, but the old Hazara pointed out that my gesture made no sense. 'The goods have already been recovered. What we try to accomplish is not punishment of this poor thief but prevention of further stealing. Carry out the order.'

The Tajik began to whimper, but attendants whom I had often seen in the yurt and had taken as mere loungers grabbed the thief and whisked him outside. There was a pitiful scream, after which an Uzbek returned with a red dagger and the man's right hand.

The Hazara sharif, seeing that I was shaken to the point of sickness, took me aside and said, 'We must be harsh. I've been sharif here for many years and this is the last cruel judgment I shall make. Don't think unkindly of me.'

'Are you retiring?' I asked.

'Tomorrow,' he replied with no regrets, 'and there are many who think that your friend Zulfiqar should be the next sharif.'

Then it became clear! Zulfiqar, having shrewdly guessed the old Hazara's intention to step down, had been conniving for twelve months to be his successor. He had used Ellen, Stiglitz and me exactly as he would have used us had he been bucking for a promotion at the General Motors office in Pontiac, Michigan. In a perverse way I was delighted with my discovery of Zulfiqar's frailty, for it proved that my view of the world was correct and not Ellen Jaspar's. Men everywhere behaved pretty much like her father in Pennsylvania; they had the same banal ambitions, which they expressed in the same banal phrases. But no sooner had I reached this conclusion than a chilling thought possessed me: This isn't Pennsylvania, and there are differences. If Zulfiqar tolerated Ellen's common-law adultery only because he wanted to achieve a goal here in Qabir, what will he do to Ellen and Stiglitz when he's through using them? Then an even more disturbing thought: For that matter, what will he do to me? Because as sharif of the camp he could order anyone destroyed, and who would halt him?

In this gloomy frame of mind I returned to our tents and hurried to see Dr Stiglitz. 'A dreadful thing happened at the yurt,' I began, but my news was unnecessary, for in the glow of a lamp Ellen stood holding the right arm of the Tajik thief while Dr Stiglitz cauterized the wound.

'How did this occur?' Stiglitz asked.

'In this camp two sharifs hold absolute power. Half an hour ago this Tajik was caught stealing; his trial took about four minutes. This is the clean-cut primitive life you wanted, Ellen.'

The sight of the bloody stump, plus my news of how the camp was run, became too much for Ellen, and she started to faint, but the Tajik, sensing that she was about to fall, tried instinctively to catch her, and his bloody right arm tore across her burnoose, lacerating the nerve ends so that he screamed with pain. His cries brought Ellen to her senses and she gripped the table. The sight of her ashen face dispelled any sense of triumph I might have had. Afghanistan was much different from Pennsylvania and I wondered how this beautiful woman was going to extricate herself from the complications into which she had so willingly marched.

The next day Zulfiqar shaved with special care and asked me to accompany him to the yurt, where I entered a formal meeting in time to hear the old Hazara karakul merchant announce that he wished to relinquish his duty as sharif. He said, 'You must choose a younger man, who can be depended upon to serve you for many years.'

I never knew whether Zulfiqar had the meeting rigged or not, but as soon as the old Hazara sat down, a young Kirghiz who had frequented our tent rose and said, 'Since one of our sharifs is my clansman Shakkur from north of the Oxus, I think it proper that the new man come from the south.' I considered this a rather nice tactic, for the retiring Hazara did not come from the south; as a matter of fact, he came from about as far north in Afghanistan as one could and still remain in the country.

But the trick worked, and an Uzbek who had frequently shared our hospitality asked, 'Why should we not select the Kochi, Zulfiqar? He's reliable.'

There were no cheers, but there was quiet discussion, and by a process which I did not understand, my caravan leader Zulfiqar was elected sharif of the great encampment. It was a moment of triumph. Those who could speak Pashto told me, 'We supported your friend because we were impressed with the way he shared his medical services ... free.' When I left, Zulfiqar was surrounded by the leaders he had been so assiduously wooing in the preceding weeks.

I rode out to camp and broke in upon Stiglitz and Ellen. 'Heard the news?' I cried.

'What?' the German asked, as he tended an elderly Uzbek woman.

'Zulfiqar's been elected sharif of the encampment.'

'What does it mean?' Ellen asked.

'You saw the Tajik thief . . . no right hand. It means power.' She blanched.

It was Stiglitz who first acknowledged the implications of this election. Slowly he pieced together his conclusions: 'Zulfiqar's been plotting this for months . . . must have guessed there'd be an election . . . knew he could impress the caravans with me as doctor . . . Ellen for entertaining . . . Miller for the money. Damn! He used every one of us.'

Ellen protested. 'You're making it sound too pat.'

Stiglitz continued, 'So as long as he needed us for the election . . .' He looked at me and I nodded approval of his analysis.

'I'd leave camp,' I added. 'Right now.'

'No!' Ellen cried. 'Miller, you must not spread panic. We will not run away. Otto and I believe what I told you in the caves at Bamian. If this is the way it's to end, it's better than anything I ever anticipated.'

She kissed Stiglitz and the two lovers renewed their determination to act as planned. I should have been impressed by Ellen's noble sentiment, but I wasn't; for in recent weeks whenever she had made one of her high-sounding speeches I had remembered my conclusion on the road to Bamian: *I have to respect Ellen's sincerity, but not her logic.* Now, for some subtle reason which I could not explain–perhaps because of her casual dismissal of Mira or her willingness to hurt Nazrullah and Zulfiqar–I was beginning to doubt not only her logic but also her sincerity.

In the days that followed, Zulfiqar treated me as a son-in-law. I cannot believe that he knew I had been commissioned by our embassy to spy out Qabir, but he could not have been more helpful had he been my assistant. He said, 'In the camp we hear many rumors that this is the last year the Russians will permit their nomads to cross the Oxus, and that was one reason why I wanted the job of sharif. If next year Shakkur the Kirghiz cannot return . . .'

Thus he exposed his final tactic. He suspected that Shakkur might have to relinquish his job as sharif, which would leave him, Zulfiqar, as leading sharif if not the only one. I asked him why the Russians were threatening to close the border and he replied, 'When India becomes a free nation, she'll close her borders, too. The day is coming when Kochis will have to stay home.'

'What will you do then?' I asked.

'That's why Racha banks our money in Jhelum,' he confided. 'We're collecting what funds we can and in a few years we'll buy land.' He hesitated, then spoke to me as he would have to a son: 'I was discussing this with Moheb Khan when we met in Kabul. When the new irrigation dam is built, there will be much new land available at the edge of the desert.'

'And you applied for some–to settle down?'

'A winter base,' he replied. 'We'll go to India no longer. In the spring, of course, we'll bring our goods to Qabir, but only a few of us. The rest will stay home to tend the fields.'

'Do the others know?'

'They wouldn't believe it,' he laughed, 'but Racha and I have about decided. Soon it will happen.'

It was a moment when the sweep of time stood exposed, and I thought of the arguments Ellen and I had conducted on this very problem. 'Remember the morning when the villagers thought we were kidnappers?' I asked. 'Ellen argued that Afghanistan must go back to the caravan and I argued that the caravan must go forward to the village?' I stopped. It was a hollow triumph. 'God,' I cried, 'how exciting it was to march through those dreary villages at your side. Will your village be any better?'

'When you have known freedom,' Zulfiqar said, 'there's always a chance.'

'Why are you stopping now?' I asked.

'Because the old freedom is slipping away from us. They're sending troops to check us at the borders . . . tax collectors. Next they'll inspect our tents. Qabir . . . how many more years will we assemble here?'

I looked at the sprawling tents where I had been so happy and said, 'They'll be here when you and I are forgotten.'

'No,' he corrected. 'The black tents are doomed.'

'Does Ellen know you think this way?'

'She may have guessed. Perhaps that's why . . .' He didn't finish his sentence. Instead he gave me his professional laugh and said, 'People like Ellen always have fixed ideas about how nomads should live . . . and think. We aren't like that, and I'm sorry if we are disappointing.'

'But you worked so hard to become sharif. If the black tents are doomed, why did you do it?'

'The tents will go, but the trade will continue.'

'And you want to become a trader? An important man like the old Hazara?'

'In ten years few of the tents we see today will be here. Just a handful of men like me and the Hazara and Shakkur . . . bringing camels and a few servants to load them. We'll trade twice the goods—five times as much. It's clear, Millair, that four-fifths of this camp is unnecessary. The women and children accomplish nothing.'

'Do the others agree?'

'All of us in the big yurt . . . especially the Russians.' Then he surprised me by using the phrase that Stiglitz had spoken: 'The caravans move on. They move to a distant horizon.'

The time had now come for disbanding the camp and I discovered that this event was traditionally marked by a game of Afghan polo. Early one morning Zulfiqar sent Maftoon to find me and the cameleer asked, 'You like to play polo?'

I said, 'Tell Zulfiqar I know nothing about polo,' but Mira clapped her hands and cried, 'Tell Zulfiqar he'll play.' But when I saddled up she checked the lashings and warned, 'Better tie everything twice. This game can get rough.'

I joined Zulfiqar and we rode to a field east of the confluence, where children waited, chattering with excitement, and the women of the camp, who made a place for Ellen and Mira. The field was crowded with horsemen clustering about the old Hazara, who was trying to establish some rough-and-ready rules. He did not ride his horse well, for under his left arm he held a white goat who struggled to get free, but the old man did succeed in showing us the two goal lines, about two hundred yards apart. Then he cried, 'Shakkur, have your men pass out the arm bands,' and the big Kirghiz gave the signal.

Shakkur gave me a white arm band and said, 'Fight well.'

It was to be south-of-the-Oxus versus north-of-the-Oxus, for Shakkur kept on his team the Uzbeks, Tajiks, Kazaks and Kirghizes, while Zulfiqar had riders from Afghanistan, India, China and Persia. There were about forty to a side, but for reasons which became apparent to me later on, no one bothered to insure that we were evenly matched.

Zulfiqar's White team lined up to defend the eastern goal and the Russians opposed us. In the center the old Hazara held aloft the goat by his rear legs while an Uzbek whipped out a knife and cut off the animal's head. With a savage cry the umpire threw the goat's body high in the air and left the field, not to interfere again. Before the goat, spurting blood, could land, a Tajik horseman swept in, caught the animal and raised it over his head in a mad gallop toward our goal line. He had covered only a few yards when he was hit from three sides by our riders, who tackled, grabbed, gouged and beat him. Finally one of our Turkomans leaped almost clear of his horse, grabbed the goat and wrenched it away from the battered Tajik, who was now bleeding from the mouth.

Our Turkoman set off boldly for the Russian goal, but a force of shouting Uzbeks and Kirghizes slammed into him and not only stole the goat but also knocked down his horse, so that he catapulted across the rocky playing field. No one stopped to see if he was hurt, and after a while he recovered his horse and rejoined the game. Meanwhile, one of our Afghans drew even with the Uzbek who had captured the goat and literally threw himself at his opponent, knocking the Russian rider right out of the saddle, but before the goat touched earth, Shakkur the Kirghiz sped in, caught it by one leg and fought his way through the mob to find himself with a clear path to our goal. The polo game was over, for no White rider could possibly catch him.

At this point the essential feature of Afghan polo was made clear. When the victorious Russian team saw that their captain was about to score they regretted that the game was ending, so one of their own men, a fiery Uzbek, set forth in hot pursuit and just as the baldheaded sharif was about to cross our line, this Uzbek teammate came up from behind, gave him a wallop across the back of his neck, grabbed the goat and brought it back into play. Both sides applauded, and the game continued. Thereafter, when any player threatened to score, his own teammates slugged him, gouged him and tried to knock him from his horse. It was always one rider fighting forty of the enemy plus thirty-nine of his friends, and sometimes it was the latter who did the worst damage.

For nearly sixty bruising minutes we played without my distinguishing myself–it seemed that half the other riders were bleeding from the mouth–when I happened to gallop past the children of our caravan and heard them shout, 'Get in the game,' I saw Ellen, and she looked a bit stunned by the brutality of the sport, but little Mira was furious. 'Why did I get you the horse?' she shouted, 'Do something!'

So I dashed into the middle of the fracas, where I accomplished nothing until a north-of-the-Oxus Kazak broke loose with what was left of the goat and headed in my general direction. It was apparent that unless I stopped him, the game was over, so I tried to turn him back into the mob, but the Russian decided that he could scare me into yielding ground, so he drove directly at me, and so far as I was concerned his strategy would have worked, for I was willing to withdraw, but Moheb's horse had been trained for just this kind of challenge and, ignoring my reins, leaped ahead seeking contact. We struck the Kazak with stunning force, spun him around and caused him to drop the goat, which to my surprise I caught.

But before I got started for the Russian goal, I caught a glimpse of Shakkur bearing down on me and in order to escape him tried evasive action. He anticipated my move and with his left arm clubbed me across the back so violently that I nearly pitched over my horse's head. In attempting to regain control I exposed the goat, which Shakkur grabbed, literally tearing it from me. He rode off with the body; I was left with one leg.

Dazed from his blow, I started in pursuit, but the chase was fruitless, for Shakkur had a clear run for the goal, and even though one of his own Kazaks tried to knock him from his horse, the big sharif defended himself by clubbing the Kazak in the face with the bloody goat. Thus ended our game of polo, the sport of gentlemen.

Of the eighty players, more than half had substantial contusions and cuts, and of these, twenty-two were injured seriously enough to require help from Dr Stiglitz, who set broken bones, pulled broken teeth and applied antiseptic to several square yards of flesh from which the skin had been abraded in sliding falls across the rocky field. This year, however, there had been no deaths.

As we finished treating the last of the cripples and listened to the sounds of festivity in the tents, where the game was being celebrated, I could not resist observing to Ellen, 'Sort of like Saturday night after the Yale-Harvard game, isn't it? Or the country club in Dorset after a golf-match?'

She had a good answer for this, I'm sure, but she was prevented from giving it by the arrival of the old Hazara, who had come by to congratulate me: 'Your play was a credit to Zulfiqar and he should be pleased. A year ago I warned him, "In 1946 I shall retire. If you act wisely you could be my successor." Well, everything he's done this year has been correct and your presence and the young lady's'—he smiled at Ellen approvingly—'has helped him very much.' He bade me farewell and rode back to the yurt.

When he was gone I saw that Ellen was trembling, partly from outrage, partly from apprehension. 'He's been plotting this for a whole year,' she muttered, her composure gone. 'He's used us most shamefully. I wonder what he'll do now?'

I should have been sympathetic with her, but for some reason I wasn't, and an irreverent thought possessed me, which I ungallantly shared: 'Rather neat trick he pulled, picking you up at Qala Bist and keeping you on ice for ten months.'

She glared at me, but ignored the joke. 'What do you think he'll do?' she asked nervously.

Toward me, at least, his friendship increased. The day after the polo we rode to see the Russians dismantling the administration yurt and watched as a colorful procession of Uzbek, Tajik and Hunza caravans wound slowly to the east, heading for the crevices of the Hindu Kush. A visible sadness seized the Kochi leader and he turned on his horse to say, 'If they do die, these caravans . . .' He paused, then said quietly, 'Who could believe Qabir if he had not seen it? Son'—he had never called me this before—'I wanted you to see this plain with four hundred caravans. I saw it when I was a boy . . . no, when I was an infant too young to see anything. This is how men should live.'

But each day we became more lonely. The Nuristanis next to us had departed and so had the Tajiks to the west, and a very real sense of doom enveloped our camp. I was constantly expecting retribution to overtake Ellen and Dr Stiglitz, and I am sure they were too. In fact, I became so jittery that I began spotting where the guns were, and the knives, in case I was myself attacked, for it seemed to me that the brooding figure of Zulfiqar was everywhere.

Finally even Shakkur the Kirghiz departed with his eighty camels, and our caravan was alone on the high plateau. I overheard little Maftoon complaining to the other cameleers, 'If we don't start soon for Balkh, on the return trip the snows will trap us.'

'Zulfiqar will tell us when to move,' they assured him.

'He's not thinking of the snows,' Maftoon lamented.

The next morning I heard a shouting at Zulfiqar's tent and I rushed over to find him standing with dagger in hand, towering over Dr Stiglitz, who was unarmed and terrified. In his baggy Afghan trousers and dirty turban Stiglitz made a pitiful contrast to the powerful Kochi.

'Give him a dagger,' Zulfiqar commanded, and when there was hesitation he shouted at Maftoon, 'Give him yours. It killed a man in Rawalpindi.'

Fumbling, Maftoon placed his dagger into the trembling hands of the doctor, who knew no more how to use it now than he had that morning in the caravanserai: he held it in both hands, pointed out from his chest.

I fought my way to the front of the circle and shouted, 'Zulfiqar! No!'

'You be still!' the huge Kochi roared, and men grabbed my arms.

At the doorway to the tent Racha and some women held Ellen Jaspar, and I looked beseechingly at Mira, who refused to look back at me. Then Ellen screamed and I saw Zulfiqar, with a quick lunge, dive at Stiglitz, who, in a response born of despair, managed to escape the flashing blade but took no steps to attack his adversary.

Zulfiqar whirled expertly and drove at Stiglitz from the opposite direction, but again Ellen screamed and the doctor jumped aside just in time. He was terrified and was obviously about to be killed, except that Ellen, who had convinced him that death was of no consequence, now shouted, 'Otto! Protect yourself!' And with this cry the insignificant man wanted to live. He became wary.

What followed occurred with dreadful swiftness, but each motion was etched on my mind. I shall never forget. I thought: I hope Stiglitz wins. I despised him, both for what he had done and for what he represented, but now that he was close to death at the very moment he had found Ellen Jaspar to restore his life, I wanted him to survive. Dear God, I prayed, let the German live.

A roar went up as Zulfiqar made a savage lunge at Stiglitz, who drew himself in so that the Kochi dagger missed, then stabbed at Zulfiqar as the latter flashed by. Stiglitz had drawn blood and the crowd murmured in astonishment.

I never knew whether Zulfiqar realized he was hit or not, but with a roaring leap he struck his opponent with both boots and knocked him to the ground. Like a cat he pounced upon him and wrenched away his dagger. Applying his knees to the doctor's arms, he stared down at the terrified face.

Ellen screamed as Zulfiqar's dagger flashed in the air and I was caught with horror as I watched it speed downward. I heard the crowd sigh. Then I heard voices.

Zulfiqar had driven his dagger into the soft earth, less than an inch from the pudgy doctor's neck. The powerful Kochi left it there as he pushed himself up, loomed over the fallen man and carefully spat in his face.

'Leave the caravan!' he cried in a terrifying voice.

He then stalked to the doorway of his tent and grabbed Ellen away from the women. With a cruel swipe of his hand he knocked her off her feet. Contemptuously he spat in her face and repeated his order: 'Leave the caravan!'

Then he stepped across the two stupefied westerners and grabbed me by the throat with his left hand. With his right he gave me a blow that sent me staggering backward in the dust. 'Get out!' he roared. 'Get out!'

Finally he grabbed little Maftoon and lifted him off the ground. 'They're your friends,' he shouted scornfully. 'Take them to Balkh. Now! Now!'

In a storming rage he tore into his tent and began throwing out all the possessions that Ellen had accumulated. This done, he rushed to my tent, where he did the same with everything belonging to Stiglitz and me. The doctor's bag landed on one corner and popped open, spilling medicine which the silent Kochis began greedily grabbing.

'Put it back!' Zulfiqar shouted. 'We want nothing of theirs.'

In this manner he continued, with blood reddening his back, until he saw us packed, the white horse saddled, and Maftoon ready with the camel Becky, who carried a tent for us, and a donkey whose panniers contained some food.

'Get out!' he bellowed, and as we crept away down the river trail toward the confluence where he had gained glory in the yurt, I saw him rip off his shirt to inspect his wound. It was not deep and he yelled for Racha to wash it. That was the last I ever saw of Zulfiqar or his wife Racha.

15

We formed a pathetic caravan as we moved out of the Hindu Kush. Stiglitz, shaken by his approach to death, was allowed to ride the white horse, which he did in silence. Ellen was in a state of unbelief: her jaw was sore and her vanity abused. Confusion was increased by the effect of her gray burnoose, which made her look soft and feminine while her words made her harsh and unlovely.

'How dare he strike me?' she asked several times. 'And spit at me? He's no better than an ignorant mullah. I should have killed him myself.' She was shaken with anger at the memory of her humiliation, and as I studied these bedraggled lovers I was willing to concede that they had converted themselves into non-people, those rejected dregs on which the world rebuilds, and I was sure they felt confirmed in this claim.

Little Maftoon was equally disturbed, because when he got rid of us at Balkh there was no escape: he would have to rejoin the caravan, and it had been his knife that had wounded Zulfiqar, his friendship for me that accounted for his being with us. The scar-eyed camaleer found no pleasure in this caravan, nor did his enemy Aunt Becky, who like all camels protested any trail that descended, since it threw unaccustomed burdens on her awkward front legs. She growled and gurgled so much that pretty soon somebody in the caravan had better undress and let her fight his clothes or there would be serious trouble.

Nor was I exempt from the sense of melancholy which had been closing in on me for days. I had lost Mira, the elfin spirit of the caravan, and I could imagine her trapped in the mountains by her father's hatred of me. In my loneliness I was forced to admit, for the first time, that I loved her without reservation. On the high plateaus she had laughed and teased her way into my heart, and she would remain a part of me as long as I lived. To have lost her without even a farewell was intolerable. But I had also been abused by her father, who during the preceding weeks had been treating me as his predilected son, sharing with me thoughts he would not confide to others. He had gone out of his way to help me with my mission, introducing me to the Kirghiz sharif, and from watching him at work I had grown to admire his cool calculations and mastery of politics; yet our friendship had ended with his knocking me down, cursing me and throwing me out of his camp. Frankly, I couldn't understand what had happened.

In fact, if one considered the entire complement of our cut-rate caravan, the only member not spiritually wounded was the donkey. He plodded along with panniers banging his sides, content to know that if he didn't work for us, on this trail, he would have to work for someone else, on some other trail.

We had proceeded thus for two silent hours when I heard Maftoon cry, 'Miller Sahib! Look!'

I turned to see what new misfortune had befallen us, half expecting to find that Aunt Becky had broken a leg, but instead I saw Maftoon pointing back along the trail we had traveled, and there came Mira, in red skirt and pink blouse, running to overtake us.

'Her father will kill her,' Maftoon lamented.

She was more than a mile away, a marvelous little hummingbird skipping across the meadowland, and I started running back to meet her. 'Take the horse,' Stiglitz offered, but I was already on my way.

Out of breath we met on the trail and rushed into a long kiss, which convinced me of how desperately I needed her, how ashamed I had been at being forced to leave the caravan without speaking to her. I think that as we finished our embrace she was weeping, but I do not know, for in these matters she was proud and she buried her face in my shoulder as I lifted her and carried her along the trail.

The others came back to meet us, all except Aunt Becky, who, when she started downhill, turned back for nothing. We looked at her gaunt brown figure plopping across rocks and began to laugh. It was so joyful to be with Mira, and cockeyed Maftoon, and the lovers and the beat-up old camel.

As I put Mira down, Ellen ran to embrace her as if they were schoolgirl roommates, and the affection between the girls was real, for to Ellen Mira owed her dress, her manner of doing her hair and her few English sentences; and it was obvious that she was pleased to be with the American girl again.

But Maftoon warned in a doom-laden voice, 'You should not have done this, Mira. Your father will kill you.'

To our astonishment Mira replied, 'He told me to come.'

'He what?'

'Of course. I told him, "I'd like to go to Balkh with Miller," and he said, "Why not?"'

'You mean that Zulfiqar . . .'

'He's not mad at anybody,' Mira assured us, expressing surprise that we should think so.

'He knocked me down,' Ellen protested. 'He spat at me.'

Again Mira embraced her friend. 'He had to do that, Ellen. The others were looking, waiting–the whole caravan.'

'He almost killed me,' Stiglitz added, rubbing his neck.

Mira looked almost condescendingly at the German and asked proudly, 'If my father had been truly angry, do you think he would have missed with his dagger? His honor demanded that he do something about you, Doctor. But he wasn't angry. It was only make-believe . . . in front of the others.'

I caught Mira by the shoulders and shook her: 'Are you telling the truth?'

She laughed at me as she broke free. 'Miller! When my father said good-bye just now he was chuckling. He told me, "Tell that damned German he put up a good fight." And he sent you this, Dr Stiglitz.' From her pink blouse she produced the Damascus dagger Zulfiqar had used in the duel. Handing the silver sheath gravely to the German, she said, 'His wedding present to you. My father said, "It will remind the wife that her husband was once willing to fight for her . . . with daggers."'

Then she took me aside and explained softly, 'When you left, Miller, my father went to our tent and threw himself on the rugs. Again and again he said, "He was like my son. He was my son. Why did I strike him?" For a while at Qabir I think he hoped that by some miracle you would stay with us and help him run the caravan.' There was a moment of intense silence, broken by her sharp cry, 'There goes Becky!'

The willful old camel had spotted, off to one side of the trail, some grass that she fancied and, having eaten it, now continued straight ahead in the new direction even though it was taking her into dangerous rocky areas. Nothing would stop her, dumb beast that she was, for she would continue plodding ahead until she destroyed herself, unless some human teased her into running to the trail. By those who knew them best, camels are considered the stupidest of animals, and Aunt Becky was to prove her claim to the title, but she was forestalled by Mira, who dashed after the lumbering beast, cursing her madly, and we fell to laughing as the determined little nomad pursued the huge camel, scrambling over rock and shale until she had maneuvered Aunt Becky back to safety.

This was the tonic our bedraggled group needed, and without fully appreciating what I was doing or its consequences I took Ellen by the hands and teased her in a schoolboy's way. 'Ellen and her men!' I chanted, waving her arms up and down. 'She wants to reject the world, so she runs off with Nazrullah, whose only ambition is to build a big dam. So she drops him for wild free Zulfiqar, who wants to settle down beside the dam. Then she chooses Dr Stiglitz. Look at him up there grinning on that horse. He's planning to build a hospital on Zulfiqar's land beside Nazrullah's dam.'

'Ring-around-a-rosy,' Ellen cried, joining in the joke. And with a sudden lilt of her body she began dancing me over the trail, her gray burnoose swinging free in haunting beauty. Then I felt the pulsating throb of life in her hands as they gripped mine and realized that this was the first time I had touched Ellen. She was vibrant and her eyes flashed, making her irresistible and quite different from the troubled young college girl we had discussed that wintry day at the American embassy in Kabul. I was caught by an embarrassment which sprang from reasons I did not then fully comprehend, and I let her hands fall, so that the force of her dancing spun her away in lovely gyrations until she collapsed in laughter on a grassy bank.

Dr Stiglitz leaped from his horse to lift her to her feet, but Mira reached her first and asked with real concern, 'Are you hurt, Ellen?'

'I could dance right out of the mountains,' she told the little nomad. Then she reached up and kissed Dr Stiglitz as he helped her back onto the trail.

In this manner we re-formed our little caravan and, with Mira restoring the levity we had lost, began one of the loveliest journeys any of us would ever know. From Qabir to Balkh was only eighty miles, which we should have covered in about five days, but we were in no hurry and our patient progress through the mountains became an extended joy. It had been one thing to carry on a light love affair with a bright-eyed nomad girl, built of hasty meetings in rocky enclaves; it was quite another to live with that girl twenty-four hours a day, helping her prepare pilau, watching her as she loaded the donkey and sharing her life as if we intended never to part. Once she said, 'We should find mountains where it never snows and get us a flock of karakuls,' and she laughed when Ellen teased, 'Can't you imagine Mark Miller herding karakul sheep on Boston Common?' But her easy laughter did not hide the fact that we were falling deeper and deeper in love, so that our final parting was bound to be a matter of anguish.

At the same time I had a chance to observe Ellen and her doctor as they started their new life freed from the presence of Zulfiqar, and as I watched them I had to admit that there was some substance to Ellen's confused thesis about the non-people. She and Stiglitz worried about nothing. For them there was no past, no future, no responsibility. The days came and went, and the two lovers existed. They were non-people who on a high plateau in Afghanistan had found each other after a series of improbable adventures, and the days of their rebirth from nothingness were brilliant to watch.

Yet as soon as I have said this, I must confess that it was also now that I became aware for the first time of a dark presence when they were with us in the tent, an element of strangeness, almost of tangible foreboding. It was Mira who pointed this out to me. For us, love had been a relaxed and easily accepted experience. To be sure, the little nomad girl reveled in an exquisite passion, which she found joy in sharing, and I, although I am no expert in these matters, felt sure at the time that my response was adequate. But on the first night out of Qabir, when the bunks were made and all four of us had gone to bed in the black tent, Mira and I were astonished at the sounds which came from the opposite side of our quarters. It was as if those other lovers feared that nights were numbered and that at Balkh some tragedy would envelop them. Mira whispered, 'We better leave the tent for them,' but as we crept away I had the curious feeling that this extraordinary performance in the other bed had somehow been directed at me.

Mira and I walked in the gray light of the full moon, passing the nook where Maftoon slept with the animals, while the white horse, that symbol of leadership and manliness that Mira had brought me, grazed on the hillside. In Pashto Mira said, 'I am convinced now that my father was relieved when Ellen started sleeping with Dr Stiglitz.'

'That's still an astonishing thing to say.'

'I think he'd had enough of lovemaking,' she suggested.

'With a girl like Ellen? You must be crazy.'

'Do you remember that first morning?' she asked. 'At the caravanserai? My father found you fighting and ran out to warn us, "Hide Ellen. The American is here looking for her." So we hid her in one of the little rooms. But only a few minutes later he ordered me to bring her before you.'

I tried to recall the scene. Zulfiqar had taken our knife and the Kochis had entered, including Mira, whose saucy pigtails I could still see. Yes, Mira was right. Zulfiqar had sent her out specifically to fetch Ellen, and had he not done so, we need never have known that she was with the Kochis. He had intended me to find her.

Mira and I walked for some hours through the great mountains of Afghanistan, then crept quietly back to the tent where Ellen and Stiglitz were asleep, but on the second night the performance in the other bed was repeated and again Mira suggested that we leave, and in this manner my ambivalent feeling toward the other couple developed: in the day they were persons of feeling and judgment with whom I found an increasing sense of identification; but at night they became something strange. One curious facet of this ambivalence concerned Dr Stiglitz, for I had gradually been forced to concede that he had transformed himself from a Nazi criminal into a man determined to serve humanity. My hatred for what he had done to the Jews in Munich was exorcized; our weeks together, our long discussions, had made him like a brother. I therefore had to conclude that whatever uneasiness I felt about the couple must stem not from Stiglitz but from Ellen.

For example, on the third evening out we pitched our camp in a rocky gorge that would lead us out of the Hindu Kush, and at the end of day Maftoon spread his little prayer rug on the rocks. Estimating where Mecca stood, he knelt to pray, but he had uttered only a few words when Dr Stiglitz, impressed by the gravity of the mountains at dusk, joined him, and they knelt as the Koran directed, shoulder to shoulder in that brotherhood which Islam fosters and which is unknown to most other religions.

Women were not allowed to pray with men, so well to the rear Mira knelt and after a while Ellen joined her and I was left standing alone within the circle of rocks, wondering how there could be any connection between that spot and Mecca. I respected Islam, but I had never felt either a part of it or capable of ever becoming a part; but at this moment I remembered Nazrullah's question: *If you lived in Afghanistan permanently, wouldn't you pray as a Muslim?* Impulsively I knelt beside Dr Stiglitz and felt his shoulder touching mine, and for some minutes the five of us prayed and I heard illiterate Maftoon chanting, 'God is great. God is great. I am witness that there is no God but the one God, and I am His servant. For God is great. God is great.' At that moment of fellowship I could believe that this strange religion, so difficult for a Jew like me to comprehend, had been specially ordained for deserts and high plateaus, and it had been sent by God Himself to make men in these lonely areas act as brothers. At that moment I experienced an intense sensation of Otto Stiglitz as my brother.

'God is great. God is good. We are the servants of God,' Maftoon chanted, and it occurred to me: In all the Muslim prayers I have actually heard recited as compared to those one reads in books, I've heard only of God, never of Muhammad. Maftoon, as if he had overheard my thoughts, ended his prayer, 'God is great, and I am witness that Muhammad is His Prophet.' When we rose I looked back at the girls, and there was dark little Mira in pigtails still kneeling beside blond Ellen, whose burnoose fell about her stately figure like the robes of some saint in prayer, and there was a sense of beauty hovering above the worshipers so harmonious with the setting that for a long time we stayed in the shadow of the mountains saying little.

On the next day we penetrated the last range of hills separating the Hindu Kush from the arid plains leading to Balkh, and as Aunt Becky stumbled out of the mountains and saw flat ground again, she gave a series of joyful gurgles and started loping across the dusty fields, as if here at last was the true Afghanistan.

The heat became considerable, for this was mid-July, and we had to exercise caution in our use of water. We also reverted to the desert practice of traveling at night, but since the moon was nearly full this added to the beauty of our trip. During the day we slept, Stiglitz and Ellen in the tent, Maftoon with the camel, and Mira and I wherever we could find shade.

'I thought Ellen was your dearest friend,' I chided Mira as we hiked through the heat looking for a place to sleep.

'She is,' the little nomad replied, 'but it will be safer if you sleep away from her.'

'Why do you say a thing like that?' I demanded.

At first she refused to speak, then added simply, 'It was while she was sleeping with my father that I discovered she was in love with Dr Stiglitz.'

'How could anybody know a thing like that?' I asked with some irritation, for we were finding no shade.

'I told you at the time, didn't I?' she reminded me.

'How did you know?' I snapped.

'I knew, that's all.'

Toward midnight of our fourth day on the plains I was riding the white horse at the head of the caravan when I spotted, in the silvery moonlight ahead, an extensive area denuded of trees but marked by solitary mounds on which grass seemed to be growing in scanty spots. In the semidarkness it looked like a burial ground for giants, but when Maftoon overtook me in the moonlight he said, 'That is Balkh,' and I rode on to inspect the meaningless sweep of empty earth.

So this was Balkh, mother of cities, fair Balkh where Alexander had married Roxane, the learned city at the crossroads of the world, the leading metropolis of Central Asia! As a boy I had been fascinated by this city, ancient and famous even before the days of Darius. All the remembered travelers of Asia had recorded their impressions of this dazzling treasure house: Ibn Batuta, Hsuan Tsang, Genghis, Marco Polo, Tamerlane, Baber. Its history was resplendent. Its memory was obscured. And now even its outlines were destroyed.

Could this be Balkh, this empty field of arid mounds where herd boys tended goats and wandering Kochis came to camp? This expanse of buried rubble with no plaques, no banners, not even a line of brick indicating where the great libraries had once stood . . . could this be the end of the city?

I felt inconsolably lonely, as if I were lost in the paralyzing sweep of history, a shard left by time. I felt like crying out in protest, and when I saw our faltering caravan approaching–one camel, one donkey, for Balkh–I could not find solace even in the thought that Mira would soon be with me.

At Rome the imperial ruins had also depressed me, but only for a moment, because it required no great imagination to believe that something of that grandeur persisted. But in Afghanistan my depression not only affected me; it also permeated the land and the culture and the people. It was difficult to believe that civilization had ever graced this arid waste or that it could return. At miserable Ghazni, at silent Qala Bist, at The City, at faceless Bamian and here at Balkh nothing remained. Were the generations indifferent to history, allowing their finest monuments to disappear while Rome retained hers? Or was it simply that Asia was different, its conquerors so terrible that western man could not visualize their cargoes of horror?

Many times I had crossed the path of Genghis Khan, merely one of the scourges and not necessarily the worst, and each time I had stood where he had erased a population. Perhaps a society cannot absorb such repeated punishments. Perhaps the scourging does something to the minds of men, converting citizens into frightened nomads who feel safe only when carrying their goods with them under their own surveillance. Perhaps it was Genghis Khan who explained why the Kochis and the Kizilbash and the Tajiks remained wanderers with no fixed civilization to sustain them.

Brooding in the moonlight at Balkh, I found increased respect for men like Moheb Khan, Nazrullah, and my preceptor Zulfiqar, who were determined to build a new Afghanistan that would conserve the memories of Ghazni and Balkh yet built upon the newer ideas of Russia and America. Had I been an Afghan, I would have allied myself to these impatient men.

As I reached this conclusion Maftoon brought his little caravan to the ruins, where for the past centuries the Kochis had camped, and while he and Stiglitz unrolled the tent Ellen came to me in the moonlight and said generously, 'I'm sorry, Miller, that we quarreled so much on this trip. I've been struggling to find understanding.'

'Found any?'

'Some. When it looked as if Otto might die in the duel, I did learn one important fact. That life of itself is good. I found myself praying that he would live.'

'It's lucky he did,' I replied. 'You and he are bound to accomplish some great thing in Afghanistan.'

'The non-people don't accomplish,' she corrected gently. 'They exist, and from them the world takes hope.'

'One thing makes me feel better, Ellen. At last I have a glimmer of what you're talking about. But I'm like Nazrullah . . . committed to working for the civilization I'm caught in.'

She smiled warmly and grasped my hands, and the effect was as electrifying as before. 'How adorable of you, Miller, how predictable! To say a thing like that at Balkh.'

'Why Balkh?' I asked.

'Don't you know that at the apex of their history the people here talked just like you? The mullahs proclaimed, "Allah has this city in His special care. No harm can befall it." And the generals boasted, "Our forts are impregnable. No enemy can reach us." And the bankers were especially reassuring: "Last year our gross city product rose four percent. We can all afford two slaves in every kitchen." And here is Balkh. And here is New York.'

'Do you honestly believe that the same thing will happen to New York?' I asked, and immediately I was irritated with myself, for I had to recall my own thoughts when traveling down the ruins of The City: *This is Route One between New York and Richmond.*

'I believe that this is the future,' Ellen replied. 'But you mustn't. Because you're young. You're destined to go back to Boston and work there the way Nazrullah will work in Kandahar. I shall pray for you both, but I will never believe in what you're doing. It's really of no consequence . . . none whatever.'

I told her, 'I'll try to explain to your parents,' and she was on the verge of speaking about them contemptuously when she changed her mind and kissed me, not politely on the cheeks but full on the lips with that abundance of love which had marked her life, and for a moment I comprehended the passion which had carried her so chaotically to Balkh. The impact of her kiss was like the touch of her hand at the dancing: it conveyed the sense of a woman with tremendous vital power and against my better judgment I was driven to wonder: What might have happened had I met her in the States? In reply I heard the Haverford College boy telling the F.B.I. agent: *I always felt that somebody else might have kept Ellen on the track. But I will admit this. I wasn't the man to do it.*

I was about to break away when, to my surprise, she gripped my shoulders and kissed me again, desperately. 'I wish I'd met you in America. After you'd learned what you have in Afghanistan.' She brushed the hair from her forehead and looked at the ruins of Balkh. 'No, I'd have been horrid for you. These ruins were in my bones.' Laughing nervously she added, 'Besides, you're so young and hopeful. And I've always been so very old.'

As she said this the moonlight played upon her lovely face. Her body swayed backward in the gray blouse that Racha had embroidered, and her bare legs showed beneath the black skirt of the Kochis. Her ankles were caught by thongs from her sandals and she was beyond comparison the most vital and attractive woman I had ever seen. This time it was I who kissed her, and with a violence of consent she pressed her beauty into my arms and against my face and through my being. I was astonished by the overwhelming power of her response and betrayed my fear that the others might see us, but with a practiced eye she calculated that the men would be occupied for some time with the tent while Mira would remain engaged in unloading the camel.

'They won't miss us,' she assured me as she sought a hiding place among the mounds. She found one and beckoned.

'What are you doing?' I asked in astonishment.

She had kicked off her sandals and was untying the cord that held her skirt. 'Didn't we just agree that life of itself was good? Let's enjoy it.' When I hesitated she argued, 'What difference would it make if they did find us?'

The idea stunned me and I remained where I was. 'Mira would make the difference,' I stammered.

'Don't you want to?' she asked provocatively, as the skirt fell about her ankles.

'You know I do.'

'Then come on,' and with ravishing grace she stepped from the fallen garment.

I knew that any man who hesitated at such a moment was bound to look pathetic, both to the girl and to himself, and I longed to join those slim, inviting legs. Instead I heard myself making the most improbable reply: 'You shouldn't do this to Stiglitz.'

With a kind of disgust—whether at me or Stiglitz or Mira I did not know—she recovered her skirt and refastened the cord. 'I've done everything for Stiglitz I could,' she said. Barefooted she came to me and whispered, 'Besides, sooner or later the Russians are bound to get him.'

Her callousness seemed as bleak as the desert and now I was glad that I had not followed her deeper into the dunes. 'What happened to your idealism about Stiglitz?' I asked. 'A few minutes ago you said you had prayed for him to live.'

'He lived.'

I thought: I'll bet she used the same kind of argument with Stiglitz when she was inviting him to move in on Zulfiqar. *But Otto, Zulfiqar's busy with other things. He won't care.* And she had been right. 'Your flowery ideas about the non-people?' I asked. 'You give them up? For a couple of days back there you had me convinced.'

'Ideas come and go,' she replied. Recovering her sandals, she said, 'You know very well what we ought to do. Get us a sleeping bag and leave that tent right now.'

'With Mira there?'

'I warned you on the trail that you were taking Mira too seriously. Besides, in a couple of days she'll be back with her father.'

I drew away, appalled. 'At Bamian you made fun of men who play what you called the point game. Right now I appreciate how important that game is. I honestly believe that if I treat Mira decently I get a point in my favor. And whether you like it or not, if you kick Stiglitz around, you lose points.'

'With whom?' she asked contemptuously. 'The Divine Scorekeeper?'

'No, damn it all. With me.' She started to laugh and I got angry. 'You reject religion. I don't. Millions of Jews are dead because they took religion seriously. So do I.'

'Miller!' she cried, almost loud enough for the others to hear. 'You don't take being a Jew seriously, do you?'

'Skip it,' I said impatiently, sorry that I had raised the subject. 'But the way you reject religion—what were you, Presbyterian?' She laughed and I added, 'You know, Ellen, if you took Islam seriously . . .'

'I might be saved?' she asked mockingly.

'It wouldn't take much to save you. The more I hear you bleat about Dorset, Pennsylvania, the more convinced I become that it must be a pretty fair place. You ought to try it some time.'

She laughed again and I became embarrassed with my prosaic philosophy and inept performance as a lover. I started back to camp but had moved only a few steps when she overtook me and grasped my arm. Again I could feel the lovely urgency of her body as she made an honest effort to conciliate our quarrel. Without rancor she asked, 'Seriously, Miller, doesn't it make you self-conscious? Sentimental speeches like this . . . at Balkh, of all places?'

Her words were forceful and they made me stop. I looked at the undulating graveyard of the great city and saw, in my imagination, the rise and fall of Balkh—Balkh of the Flying Pennants it had been called, as if the city were proud to advertise its accomplishments, temporary though they proved to be—and I sensed some of the meaning behind my mission. I said, 'I don't accept your view of Balkh. Cities crumble and civilizations vanish, but people go on. And damn it all, they eat and make love and go to war and die according to certain hopeful rules. I accept those rules.'

'The rules?' she asked quietly. 'They don't permit you to make love?' She moved close to me and I saw her in the moonlight, as beautiful a girl as I would ever know, more provocative a dozen times than Mira. 'The rules won't permit you?' she repeated.

'Not with Mira over there,' I fumbled.

'In the morning? Won't you feel like an idiot?'

'How do you suppose I feel now.' I grasped her hands and said, 'You're marvelously beautiful, Ellen.'

She was pleased that I had done this, and returned to her former imaginings. 'Why didn't we meet two years ago?' she asked softly. Then, more desperately, she cried, 'Miller! Why didn't you come to Bryn Mawr that spring? In your clean white uniform? With your courage and your hopes?' she dropped my hands and asked quietly, 'Why weren't you there?'

I left her and dodged among the mounds until I could present myself casually among the others. Improbably, they had not missed us and soon Ellen slipped inconspicuously back into the group she had been prepared to abuse. Once I caught sight of her unpacking the donkey, and as the night wind tugged at her hair she looked as if she had always been a part of these harsh, impersonal steppes.

It was now about three in the morning, and we made a little tea and pilau before going to bed, and as we sat about the fire Ellen said, through either accident or perversity, 'Only a few miles up there is Russia.'

A visible chill came over Stiglitz, but no one remarked upon his fear, so Ellen added, 'Wouldn't you love to see what Samarkand looks like? They say its public square is the most exciting in the world.' No one responded to this, so after a while she said languidly, 'I think I'll go to bed,' and Stiglitz dutifully followed her.

To share the tent with her that night would have been impossible, so I dragged out my sleeping gear and Mira lugged along a pillow, but before we had left the camp Maftoon took me aside and like a conspirator slipped me his dagger: 'You must keep this, Miller.'

'Why?'

'Because the German . . .'

'What about him?'

'When you and Ellen were in the dunes, he crept over to listen.' The little cameleer sucked his teeth, then added, 'And remember, he has Zulfiqar's dagger.'

I felt dizzy. 'Does Mira know?' I asked.

'It was she who asked me to give you my dagger,' he explained. 'She watched Stiglitz following you.' And he was off.

When I rejoined Mira she said nothing, but ran her hands across my clothes till she felt Maftoon's dagger. 'It's safer,' she said.

There was nothing I could reply, so we looked for a sleeping place and after a while she observed quietly, 'You and Ellen are the best friends I have. All I know about being pretty she taught me. She's a wonderful girl . . . like a sister. I told you, Miller, that she was hungry to sleep with you, but you laughed. After I go back with my father, why don't you and Ellen . . .'

I took her brown hands and kissed them. 'I'm here because it's you I love,' and I told her of the discovery I made while being expelled from the Hindu Kush without her: 'You will be part of my life forever.'

'Go to sleep,' she said. 'We have not many more nights.'

The sun was well up when scraggly-bearded Maftoon hurried to where we slept and warned me. 'Important government car from Kabul. Man to see you, Miller!'

I assumed this must be Richardson of Intelligence, so I dressed hastily in order that he should not see me with Mira, but when I reached the tent area I found that it was Moheb Khan looking very official in a tan sharkskin suit and silver karakul cap. He was patting his stolen white horse, behind which, to my surprise, I saw Nazrullah, come north to reclaim his lawful wife. Instinctively I felt sorry for him, and because I had not seen him since his forced trip across the Dasht-i-Margo I hurried first to him, embraced him warmly and asked, 'How was the desert?'

'As always, hateful.'

'We kept our fingers crossed.'

Now Moheb Khan interrupted, speaking with severity: 'How'd you get my horse?'

I couldn't tell whether he was truly angry or merely joking, so I temporized: 'Mira bought him in Kabul.'

Moheb brushed dust from his suit and asked, 'You certainly knew it was mine. Didn't you guess it was stolen?'

'Was it?' I bluffed.

Moheb was unable to continue the pose and began laughing. 'You know how it is. You find a pretty girl. You roll over thinking, "This is going to be a night of passion." And you find that your white horse has been stolen.'

'Don't punish her.'

'Did she steal it for you?'

'Yes.'

'Then it's you I curse. For eight weeks you ride and I walk.'

I replied, 'You know how it is. Roll over again. There's your white horse, well fed and cared for.'

Now Mira appeared on one of the mounds lugging our sleeping gear, which told its own story, and when she saw Moheb Khan, from whom she had stolen the horse, she dropped the bedclothes and started running for the tent, but I caught her by the wrist.

'Little thief!' Moheb snarled.

Mira was like me. She didn't know whether Moheb was joking or not, but her irrepressible nature asserted itself—or perhaps she remembered Moheb in some earlier pose—for she broke out laughing and pointed with derision at the handsome Afghan. Making involved gestures, which could only be interpreted as the pantomime of her escape through a bedroom window to steal the white horse, she soon had Moheb laughing with her.

But then Mira saw Nazrullah and recognized him by his beard. 'You're Ellen's husband!' she cried in dismay, and the involuntary manner in which she moved protectively before the tent proved that Nazrullah's wife must be inside. Slowly, step by step, Mira retreated, bowed ceremoniously and ducked into the tent.

'Is Ellen there?' the engineer asked me.

'Yes.'

He started for the tent but I stopped him. 'Is the big Kochi with her?' he asked suspiciously.

And suddenly I realized that whole new cycles of adventure had engulfed his wife, none of which I fully understood but some of which I was myself involved in. At any rate, I couldn't explain these new developments to Nazrullah, so I stammered, 'Look, this is going to be difficult to get into focus. But that big Kochi . . .'

I was spared by the appearance of Ellen and Stiglitz. What kind of hateful truce they had patched up during the night I couldn't guess, but in the morning sunlight Ellen Jaspar was dazzling, and if her husband was still determined to win her back, I could sympathize, for when I saw her in daylight I had to say, against my own conscience: It's you she wants to leave with, you idiot. Move in. Move in fast.

Nazrullah was bewildered by the facts before him and refused to accept their implications. As if nothing had happened, he stepped forward to greet his wife. 'I've come to fetch you,' he said. 'You remember Moheb Khan. Moheb, this is Dr Otto Stiglitz.'

The tall diplomat bowed gracefully and shook hands. 'We'll drive you back to Qala Bist,' he said to Ellen with a studied air which seemed to say: We're going to give you one chance. Don't mess it up.

'I'm not going,' she said firmly, whereupon Moheb Khan shrugged his shoulders and withdrew from the conversation. He had made a conciliatory offer and it had been rejected.

It was Nazrullah who took over. 'Please, Ellen. We have the car waiting.'

Stiglitz gave the answer: 'She's to stay with me. I'm sorry, Nazrullah.'

The engineer was determined not to surrender his wife and appealed to Moheb for support, but the diplomat ignored him and asked me, 'Is this what happened? Stiglitz?' My nod triggered a dramatic barrage of decisions announced by Moheb.

First he blew a whistle, which was answered by a group of soldiers who had followed him in a truck. 'I want that horse taken back to Kabul,' he ordered. 'This man,' he snapped, indicating Stiglitz, 'is to be kept here under arrest. The American woman is not to leave this tent. You, Miller, get in the car. I want to interrogate you at headquarters in Mazar-i-Sharif. Nazrullah, come along.' And while the soldiers moved quickly in response to his commands, he led Nazrullah and me to the car.

We sped toward Mazar-i-Sharif, which lay some twenty miles east of Balkh, but as we reached the city our car was impeded by an extensive camel caravan which was setting forth to central Russia, and we had to wait while some eighty lumbering beasts went by, poking their ungainly heads toward our car and grunting at us as they adjusted to the heavy burdens which they were to carry north. The camel drivers, an unusually dirty and unkempt gang, stared at us like their camels and Moheb remarked with some irritation, 'Of all the people you meet in our country, ninety-four percent are illiterate, Are we crazy, trying to build a modern state from such rabble?'

I looked at the camel drivers, barely out of the bronze age, and said to the two impatient men beside me, 'If I were an Afghan, I'd certainly make the effort.'

'I wish we had a million Afghans like you,' Moheb replied, as the last camel went by, leering at us. And then I saw, riding a sturdy black horse, the master of this nondescript caravan and I understood why his cameleers had looked so filthy. Their owner had wanted them to look that way lest his camels give the impression of carrying some unusual wealth which might attract brigands.

For this was the caravan of Shakkur, the Kirghiz gunrunner from Russia. He had loaded his camels at Mazar-i-Sharif, and was now on his way to cross the Oxus and the great Pamirs and the steppes of Central Asia. Since his was the most dangerous route followed by any of the major caravans attending Qabir—perhaps this was the last time a caravan of such magnitude would make the trip—he sought to avoid attention.

As he rode by I called to him and he remembered me from the encampment. Stopping his horse near our car, he poked his huge bald head our way and, after studying Moheb with suspicion, asked, 'Government man?' When I nodded, he said, 'So you were a government spy? I warned Zulfiqar.'

'No,' Moheb laughed. 'We've just arrested him.'

The big Kirghiz put his left hand over his forehead and cried, 'My sympathy to all prisoners,' and he spurred his horse so that he might overtake his eighty camels.

At the government offices Moheb ordered tea and biscuits with honey, reminding me of how primitively we had been eating for the past seventeen weeks; but I was dragged back to the present problems when he summoned a secretary—a man, of course—and started arranging papers as he asked, 'Now what shall the official report state regarding that horse?'

'Is this for the record?'

'That's why I'm here. The horse and the American woman . . . both stolen.'

'Mira told me she bought the horse.'

'Where would a Kochi girl get the money?'

'She said she got it from the jeep they stole.'

'Jeep?' Moheb repeated.

'Could I strike that from the record?'

'You'd better,' Moheb nodded to the secretary.

Nazrullah interrupted. 'What did happen to that jeep?'

'Can I speak confidentially?'

'Of course,' Moheb agreed, nodding again to the secretary.

'While I stood not twenty feet away, those damned Kochis stole every movable part.'

Abruptly Moheb asked, 'Who exactly is Mira?'

'Daughter of Zulfiqar,' I explained.

'The same Zulfiqar?' he asked, indicating Nazrullah.

'Yes.'

'Now as to the new developments regarding Ellen Jaspar.'

'It's difficult to explain,' I fumbled.

'We have plenty of time,' Moheb assured me, pouring some more tea.

'Well as you know, she ran away from Qala Bist last September. It wasn't love. It wasn't sex. Nazrullah wasn't at fault. Neither was Zulfiqar. When she joined the caravan she didn't even know who Zulfiqar was.'

'Is that what you're going to say in your report to the American government?'

'I've already said it.'

'Where did she spend the winter?'

'Jhelum.'

'All the way to Jhelum? On foot?' Apparently Moheb knew less about some of his country's customs than I did.

'Was she ever in love with the big Kochi?' Nazrullah asked.

'Never.'

'Miller,' Moheb asked carefully, 'if this secretary has to record one simple reason for Ellen's behaviour, what shall he write?'

I pondered this question for some minutes, reviewing Ellen Jaspar's motivation as I understood it. It wasn't sex, because her behaviour with Nazrullah, Zulfiqar and Stiglitz had an almost sexless quality; she was neither driven by desire nor faithful to anyone who fulfilled it. I wondered if she might be suffering from some kind of schizophrenia, but I could find no evidence that she was; no one was persecuting her; she persecuted herself. At one point I had thought she might be a victim of nostalgia for a past age, but she would have been the same in Renaissance Florence or Victorian England; history was replete with people like her, and although she despised this age, no other would have satisfied her better. It was true that like many sentimentalists she indulged in an infantile primitivism; if bread was baked over camel dung it was automatically better than bread baked in a General Electric range, but many people were afflicted with this heresy and they didn't wind up in a caravan at Balkh. There remained the possibility that she suffered from pure jaundice of the spirit, a vision which perverted reality and made it unpalatable; but with Ellen this was not the case. She saw reality rather clearly, I thought. It was her reaction to it that was faulty. And then I heard the dry, emotionless voice of Nexler reading from the music professor's report: *I saw her as a girl of good intention who was determined to disaffiliate herself from our society.* This didn't explain why she acted as she did, but it certainly described what her actions were. I looked at Moheb and suggested, 'Put it down as rejection.'

'Name one man she ever rejected,' he demanded.

I preferred to ignore his condemnation and replied, 'She rejected the forms and structures of our society . . . yours as well as mine.'

'It's about time somebody rejected her,' Moheb snapped, 'And I'm the man to do it.'

'Don't abuse her,' Nazrullah pleaded.

'Would you still take her back?' Moheb asked incredulously.

'Yes,' Nazrullah replied. 'She's my wife.'

'He's right,' I told Moheb. 'You'd both better get used to Ellen Jaspar,' I warned. 'Because once you let your women out of chaderi, Afghanistan's going to have a lot of girls like her.'

Moheb groaned. 'Do you believe that?'

'It's inevitable,' I assured him. Then to protect Ellen, who in so many ways merited help, I added, 'Give her the benefit of one thing, Moheb. She loves your country. In fact, she plans to live here the rest of her life.'

'With Stiglitz?'

I started to say yes, but hesitated, and from the way Moheb Khan looked at me I knew he suspected something between Ellen and me. I was another of the men she had not rejected, but Nazrullah, still fighting to get her back, missed the interplay, so I finished my sentence. 'Yes, she's staying with Stiglitz.'

'Tell me about him,' Moheb said.

'She knew him in Kandahar, but I'm sure nothing romantic happened.' Then I was forced again to pause, for I saw before me the caravanserai and my first meeting with Ellen Jaspar, and she was sweeping past me on her way to greet Stiglitz. I heard her clear voice crying, *Dr Stiglitz! Are you all right?* Now what had really happened became clear to me. When she unexpectedly saw Stiglitz against the wall that morning her lips had begun to form a word, which she suppressed instantly. The discarded word was *Otto*, and I could now see it on her lips. Had they known each other that well in Kandahar? Had her blond, Germanic beauty so deeply affected him there at the edge of the desert?

'Something romantic did happen?' Moheb pressed.

'No,' I said firmly. 'Now about Stiglitz. On our trip north . . .'

'Who suggested that he come north?'

I had not previously considered this matter, but now I tried to reconstruct additional events from that first day with the nomads, and after a long pause I had to say, 'I think it was her idea. I think she planned it all . . . that evening.'

'I thought so, too,' Moheb replied.

'At any rate, on the trip north they fell in love. At Qabir there was a dagger fight. Stiglitz handled himself capably and even wounded Zulfiqar. After which we were all thrown out.'

'Is she determined to live with him?' Nazrullah asked quietly.

'Absolutely,' I lied, as Moheb smiled.

'Could I possibly win her back?' Nazrullah pleaded.

'Never,' I said with some assurance.

'Suppose we deported Stiglitz?' Moheb suggested.

I thought I was listening to Ellen's insidious suggestion: *Sooner or later the Russians are bound to get him.* I hesitated, and Moheb continued, 'When Stiglitz left Kandahar for this . . . this stupid caravan, he broke our law. We've the right to throw him out. Shall we?' The two Afghans leaned forward to catch my reply.

I hesitated. Here, in a strange room in a drowsy provincial capital, my whole mission in Afghanistan was coming to focus. To calm myself I took a drink of tea and thought: These men want me to recommend his deportation. If I really wanted revenge on Stiglitz, I could get it now. The possibilities were gruesomely fascinating, particularly if I recalled the cage full of Jews he had destroyed; but I could feel against my shoulder, as if it were a real force in that room, the pressure of the German's body against mine as we prayed at evening, and I heard myself diverting Moheb with the question, 'Does your intelligence report on me cover the fact that I'm a Jew?'

'It does not,' Moheb replied, masking any surprise he might have felt.

'I am. That night at the caravanserai, Stiglitz betrayed the horrible things he had done in Munich. More than a thousand Jews sent to death.'

'We know,' Moheb observed, indicating his papers.

'I tried to kill him. Would have done it, but Zulfiqar arrived with his caravan. I despise Stiglitz. He's a criminal and he ought to hang. But on this trip I've come to know him. He'll serve your country well, Moheb. You just said you needed men like me. He's much stronger than I would ever be. Don't deport him.'

'Why not?' Moheb asked cynically. 'His going would solve Nazrullah's problem.'

'Don't do it!' I warned.

'Why not?' he repeated.

'Because it would be wrong . . . morally wrong.'

Nazrullah broke in: 'Is there nothing I can do to bring her back?'

'Nothing,' I said with great finality. 'Even if you were to hang Stiglitz, you'll never get her back.'

The force of my words struck the bearded engineer, and to my surprise he dropped into a chair and buried his head in his arms. For some moments his shoulders twitched while we watched in embarrassment. Then Moheb coughed and said, 'Dear friend, Miller's right. You've lost her and there's nothing to do about it.'

I remember thinking: It's really ridiculous, carrying on like this over a second wife, but then I recalled Ellen as she had been among the ruins, as she was in bed with Stiglitz in the black tent, and I admitted to myself: He's no fool. No wonder he wants to keep her.

Moheb took my arm and said, 'Leave him alone,' and he led me to another room, where he dismissed the two government clerks and checked doors to be sure no one was listening. When all was secure he moved close and stared into my eyes. 'What did you discover at Qabir?' he asked.

'Nothing,' I replied with as much simplicity as I could muster.

'Don't lie to me,' he snapped. 'Don't you suppose I know why you were sent north?'

'I don't know what you're talking about,' I bluffed.

'Miller, for heaven's sake! Richardson drove out to the Kochi camp in Kabul and personally handed you orders: Go to Qabir and see what the Russians are up to.'

'He did not!'

'Damn it all, we know he did. How else do you suppose he got Shah Khan's permission?'

The reasoning was logical and I was almost ready to come clean when I thought: What if he's bluffing? I replied with some impatience, 'If that's what he was supposed to tell me, he certainly forgot. All he did was raise hell about that stolen jeep.'

He had been bluffing. 'What'd he say about the jeep?' he asked lamely.

'That they were docking my pay six hundred dollars.'

Seeking to catch me off guard, Moheb whipped his long forefinger into my face and shouted, 'Miller! You know damned well the American embassy would never let you wander off to Qabir without orders. What were they?'

'Richardson didn't give me orders. I asked to go.'

'Why?'

'Because I'd fallen in love with Mira.'

'You mean that you told the American ambassador you wanted leave for ten weeks because,' and here his voice dripped with contempt, 'you'd fallen in love with a little nomad girl?'

'I didn't tell Richardson about her.'

'What did you tell him?'

'I reminded him that Washington wanted me to stay on the Ellen Jaspar case until it was settled.'

Moheb dropped his truculence and asked casually, 'So what did happen at Qabir?'

'Like I said. Zulfiqar damned near killed Stiglitz.'

He slammed his fist on the table. 'The Russians?'

'I don't know anything about the Russians,' I protested. Then I changed my voice. 'I did discover one thing. That big Kirghiz we just saw was the leading sharif at the camp.'

'How does he get into Afghanistan?'

'I wouldn't know about that.'

'What the hell do you know about?'

'That the other sharif was this old Hazara who trades in karakul.'

'We know about him.'

'But this year he retired.'

'He did?'

'And to take his place they elected Zulfiqar.'

'Indeed?'

'And since Zulfiqar is eager to settle down on some of that new irrigated land near Qala Bist, you might do a good thing for Afghanistan if you settled his clan on five or six thousand acres.'

Moheb tried to mask his irritation over the fact that I knew of this confidential matter and asked quietly, 'Miller, if we offered Zulfiqar the land, would he take it . . . and stay put?'

'Positively.'

'How can you be so sure?'

'We discussed it.'

'Why would he confide in a ferangi? On such a matter?'

I wanted to say something that would help Zulfiqar, so I lied, 'One day I mentioned that I knew you, and he said, "Moheb has power of life and death over those lands." He didn't ask me to intercede, but I know he hoped that I would.'

'Well, at least you found out something.'

'Then you'll give him the land?'

'We have many applications,' he evaded.

'But none like Zulfiqar. He's a man like you and Nazrullah. He needs the land and you need him.'

Moheb looked at me with compassion and said, 'Why are you Americans so hopelessly stupid? I'll bet there were a dozen Russian agents in that camp, but you saw nothing except a nomad girl.'

'I wasn't worrying about Russians,' I laughed. He shook his head in amiable disgust and we returned to where Nazrullah was staring at the wall.

'What must I do?' the engineer asked us, no further in his solutions than when we left.

'I know what I must do,' Moheb replied briskly. He summoned the secretary and asked, 'Did you check my portfolio to be sure the alternative papers are in order? Good . . . Nazrullah, Miller, come along.'

'To do what?' Nazrullah asked.

'To find three white pebbles.'

'No!' Nazrullah cried. 'I won't.'

'Then I will,' Moheb replied matter-of-factly. Then he stopped, reflected and said, 'There is another way out for you.'

'What?' Nazrullah asked eagerly.

'We'll turn your wife over to a bunch of mountain mullahs. A woman taken in adultery.' He laughed at his grisly joke, then added gently, 'Old friend, take my advice. Find the white pebbles.'

As we left the office the secretary stopped us: 'Don't forget your call to the British Embassy.'

'Of course!' Moheb agreed, sending us ahead, and before we left the building we could hear him shouting into the fragile Afghan telephone, 'Hello, hello, hello! Is that you, Your Excellency? Here is Moheb Khan. Your Excellency, I want the British government to be alerted . . .' We did not hear the rest.

On our trip back to the barren fields of Balkh, Moheb consoled Nazrullah by reciting verses from the Persian poets, but when the car stopped at our capsule caravan it was Moheb who started hunting for the three white pebbles. When they had satisfied themselves, Nazrullah walked boldly to the black tent and called, 'Ellen.'

The soldiers brought her forth dressed in black skirt with gray blouse and three gold bracelets on her left wrist. Her tanned face was radiant in the sunlight, her marvelous blond hair framing it in windblown lines. As her legal husband approached, she looked solemnly at him and waited for his question: 'Wife, will you come back with me to Qala Bist?'

'No,' she replied in an icy voice, whereupon he raised his right hand and threw one of the pebbles to the ground.

'I divorce thee,' he announced. Again he looked at her, beseeching her to rejoin him, but again he had to raise his arm and throw a second pebble to the ground.

'I divorce thee,' he announced as Ellen listened without emotion. For the third time he pleaded with her, and for the third time she rejected him. Looking at her with eyes that had filled with tears, he hesitated in hopes she might reconsider, but she remained impassive, and he dropped the last pebble.

'I divorce thee,' he said in a ghostly whisper. Unable to look further at the beautiful woman he had wooed in a strange land, he turned and walked with dignity to the car.

As he went, I watched Ellen Jaspar, now legally divorced, standing immobile by the tent. A smile of quiet satisfaction marked her lips, for now she was free, and from the right side of her body she lifted her hand ever so slightly so that she could form with her thumb and forefinger a circle, which she flashed at me, signifying: 'All's well.'

'Bring out Stiglitz,' Moheb ordered, and the German was led forth, blinking in the sunlight. He must have guessed that Ellen intended to desert him, for he ignored her and looked only at Moheb.

'Otto Stiglitz,' Moheb began, 'we've informed the British government that you're being surrendered to them at Peshawar, in India. You're a criminal of war, and we have no place for you in Afghanistan.' He blew his whistle and other soldiers appeared. 'Take him to Peshawar,' he announced, and an officer started clapping handcuffs about the German's wrists.

But this was to be no easy arrest, for Stiglitz broke loose and threw himself at me. 'Jew! Jew!' he screamed. 'You've done this to me.' He scratched at my face until one of the soldiers tore him away.

Then he lunged at Moheb Khan, pleading, 'Excellency, don't believe him. He's a filthy Jew and he told you lies. Why did he lie to you? Because he wants the girl himself. Yes! Yes!'

The commotion brought Nazrullah back in time to hear Stiglitz cry, 'Yes, Excellency! Last night this Jew took the girl over there. They committed indecencies. And while they were doing it they plotted my death.'

He left Moheb and threw himself at Ellen, who drew back in disgust. 'This one made love with the Jew behind that mound. And she told him, Hand the German over to the Russians, they'll hang him. Excellency, the Jew has poisoned your mind.'

Moheb ordered the soldiers to pinion the doctor's arms, and when this was done he stood before the German and said, 'The Jew you condemn has just spent an hour with us, pleading for your life. At your trial, I'm sure he'll testify for you.'

Snapping his fingers, Moheb ordered the soldiers to drag the prisoner off, but as he went he tried to grab my arm. 'You will tell the judges what I said at the pillar? There are many Jews in Munich alive today because . . . You will testify for me?'

'I will,' I said, and he was dragged away. The truck engine sputtered. The wheels spun in the sand, and the soldiers were gone.

'Take the girl to the car,' Moheb ordered Maftoon, and the unshaved cameleer led Ellen away. Since I had assumed that I was to remain in Balkh until Zulfiqar arrived, I supposed that this was the last time I would see Ellen Jaspar, and it was with real confusion that I saw her go. Her fair head was as provocative as ever, her lithe body beneath the gray blouse and black skirt as exciting, and her long legs ending in the leather sandals were as alluring. The clever rationalizations I had given at the interrogation seemed irrelevant when confronted by the girl herself.

I broke the spell by turning away and going to Mira, but I was unexpectedly halted by Moheb, who grabbed my arm and said, 'You, too, Miller. We start for Kabul . . . now.'

'I'm not leaving.'

'Shah Khan's orders.'

'I've got to say good-bye,' I protested, bringing Mira to my side.

'Say it. In five minutes we go.'

'What about my gear?'

'You,' he shouted at Maftoon, 'pack his stuff. Hers too.'

I led Mira away from the tent to one of the mounds of Balkh, from which we could see the foothills of the Hindu Kush, where we had been so happy. 'I hoped we'd be here for a week,' I began.

'You will look after Ellen,' she replied. 'She talks strong but she needs help.' She was about to speak further when her nomad boisterousness took command and she cried, 'Look at that crazy camel.'

We left the mound and walked to where Aunt Becky was searching for grass. Her droopy eyes, ungainly feet and preposterous lower jaw kept her a comedian, even at this painful moment, and in gratitude for her having brought us so far I reached out to pat her in farewell, but she was not one to be tricked by sentiment. She interpreted my gesture only as a preamble to being loaded with burdens and withdrew uttering loud protests, and we were left alone.

'Mira, Mira,' was all I could say, for in these last precious minutes there was so much we should have said and so little capacity for speech. Our parting had come so suddenly and was accompanied by so much ugliness that any chance for a decent farewell had been destroyed.

'Qabir, Bamian, Musa Darul,' she recited. 'When we are at those places . . .' She looked at me, deeply ashamed of the tears forming in her eyes. She blinked them away, laughed, and said, 'Without you the caravan will be a marching of ghosts. You were very handsome on your white horse.'

At the car Moheb was blowing the horn.

Then I remembered the warning which Stiglitz had sounded in the black tent: *Leaving this nomad girl is going to be a different experience from what you imagine.* But to leave her in this manner . . . a part of my conscience, of my growing up, was being torn away.

'Inshallah,' I mumbled.

'Inshallah,' she replied.

Unable to look back, I hurried to the car where Moheb sat at the wheel with Ellen beside him and Nazrullah in the rear. The engineer, ignoring his former wife, sat gazing through field glasses at the foothills of the Hindu Kush.

'It's uncanny,' he mused. 'How could she have seen such a distance?'

He handed me the glasses and I saw that Mira had left the ruins and was striding purposefully toward the mountains, out of which her father's caravan had appeared, following those ancient trails which soon the nomads would travel no more.

On the drive back to Mazar-i-Sharif no one spoke. Ellen's presence, following the charges against her that Stiglitz had broadcast, was more than we could cope with at the moment. Besides, I was affected by real suspense concerning her future, for I could not guess Moheb's plans, and he drove in imperious silence, his firm jaw locked in self-counsel. I supposed that when we reached Mazar we would deposit her at the government building, but we did not.

To my surprise we drove straight through the city and picked up an ancient road, thousands of years old, leading to the northeast. Along it plodded a camel caravan, insensitive to our intrusion, and as I looked ahead I saw on his black horse Shakkur, the Kirghiz gunrunner.

'Ho, sharif!' Moheb called from the car, and the Russian galloped up and dismounted.

He saw me sitting gloomily in the rear seat and asked seriously, in broken Pashto, 'You taking the criminal out to shoot him?'

'No,' Moheb laughed. 'We have a passenger for your caravan.'

Now the big Kirghiz saw Ellen, with whom he had danced that night at Qabir, and intuitively he grasped the situation. 'This one?' he asked.

'Yes.'

'She have papers?'

'Yes.' From his portfolio Moheb took Ellen's green passport and handed it to the sharif. In Arabic, Cyrillic and Roman writing, signed jointly by Shah Khan and the Russian ambassador, it was stated that the bearer had permission to transit Russia on her way home to America. On a special page, for me to see, was the official notice that Ellen Jaspar, having been legally divorced from her Afghan husband, was free to exit the country. Ceremoniously Moheb Khan handed Ellen the precious document and announced, 'Madam, you are being kicked out of Afghanistan.'

To the Kirghiz he explained these matters, handing him a substantial number of Afghan gold coins. 'This will pay her passage to Moscow. We'll cable her parents, and they'll have the rest waiting there.'

'Christ Almighty,' I exploded, jumping from the car. 'You can't do this.'

'I'm not doing it,' Moheb protested. 'She's doing it herself.'

'What do you mean?'

'I came to Balkh with two sets of papers for this girl. One would have restored everything as it was. The other set kicks her out of the country. I gave her the choice. She made it.'

'She didn't know what was involved!' I protested, trying to get Ellen to appeal for a second chance.

The tall Afghan turned his back on us and explained to Shakkur, 'The poor boy's in love with her.'

The big Kirghiz smiled indulgently, then asked with caution, 'Does my friend Zulfiqar know of this?'

'He kicked her out of the caravan,' Moheb reported. 'We're doing the same.'

Apparently the young leaders of Afghanistan were not afraid of making difficult decisions, but in the case of Ellen Jaspar their decisions were wrong, so I went to Moheb and warned him in rapid French, 'This could cause serious trouble between our governments. How do you know what will happen to this girl?'

At that moment Moheb was helping Ellen from the car and he replied thoughtfully, 'This girl? Nothing will ever happen to this girl.' And he escorted her graciously to the Kirghiz, to whom he also delivered her pitifully small bundle of clothes.

At this point I had to interrupt. I took Ellen and Shakkur away from the others and asked, 'Ellen, do you appreciate what's happening?'

With infuriating equanimity she ignored me and asked the sharif, 'Where are we going?'

Pointing northeast he replied, 'We cross the Oxus at Rushan, cut through the Pamirs, then Garm, Samarkand, Tashkent.' It was a trip I would have given a year to take, and Ellen appreciated this, for when Samarkand was mentioned she smiled at me with deep satisfaction.

'Will we get there safely?' she asked.

'That's my job,' the sharif replied, and I reflected: For ten weeks I tried every trick in the book to find out how the Russian nomads cross the Oxus.

Now the top man tells me.

I said, 'Ellen, I could force the Afghan government . . .'

'I'm not afraid,' she answered, and she looked at me as if she were free and I the prisoner.

I summoned the others and announced, 'I want everyone to hear that in the name of the United States government I do protest most vigorously this incredible act.'

Ellen laughed and replied, 'You heard him, gentlemen. If he catches hell, we'll all have to testify for him.' She held out her hands, took mine and kissed me. 'I do wish we'd met in America,' she said.

With this speech she intended to leave, but decency would not permit her to go without acknowledging Nazrullah, so at last she stepped before him and said, 'Dear friend, I am most sorry.' They looked at each other without moving and I thought again of how, on the desert, he had consulted the stars before assuring me that Ellen was safe once more in Afghanistan. Now he would follow those same stars till he knew that she was safe in America.

Finally she turned away and swung easily into the rhythm of her new caravan, as if she had been traveling with it for many months. I watched as the big Kirghiz galloped back to the head of his camels, spurring them on; for this caravan, excused from the encumbrance of either sheep or families, did not intend to cover a mere fourteen miles a day. It was headed for towering passes that must be cleared before the fall of snow, and for these travelers to Russia there would be no restful halting at noon.

The last camel passed us and we stood alone on the ancient road, watching the caravan as it lost itself in dust. I last saw Ellen Jaspar with her blond hair and black skirt swirling among the camels, marching east toward the greatest of the mountains.

'It's barbaric,' I protested weakly, and Nazrullah agreed.

'She would have destroyed you both,' Moheb Khan replied.

NOTE TO THE READER

The scene of this novel is the Kingdom of Afghanistan in 1946. Conditions are described as they existed in that year and as truthfully as research and memory will permit.

The reader may be curious about what has been happening in the intervening seventeen years, and a brief note covering recent developments may prove helpful.

Few nations have experienced a more spectacular growth and change during this period than Afghanistan. Kabul has paved streets (Russian money). Kandahar has an airport (American money). The city of Kabul has a fine public bakery (Russian). And many towns have good schools (American).

Foreigners have been visiting the country with ease and frequency. President Eisenhower was there in 1959, and many Russian leaders arrived both before and after that date. The vigorous struggle between America and Russia for Afghanistan's affection, referred to in this novel, goes on unceasingly with ultimate victory uncertain. An overriding fact is this: Russia abuts on the northern border for nearly seven hundred unguarded miles, while the United States is nearly eight thousand miles away. Under these circumstances it is remarkable that our side has done as well as it has.

Our victories have been the result of selfless work by dedicated men and women like John Pritchard, the fictional engineer of Chapters Nine and Ten. Apparently, when our country needs such men, there is an endless supply, but we rarely call upon them or find a worthy place for them when they are called.

The battle between old and new which is a feature of this novel has produced some interesting skirmishes. In 1959 women were allowed, even encouraged, to dispense with the chaderi in public. A few did; many preferred the isolation and protection of the shroud ... or more likely, their husbands did. Symptomatic of the future, however, was the plebiscite held in neighboring Iran in 1963 on similar matters of civil freedom and relaxation of mullah rule. In Iran, which is about fifty years ahead of Afghanistan in social change, the vote was on the order of 4,000 to 1 in favor of modernism. Young women, wearing no chaderi stormed the streets on election, begging people to go to the polls. Old-fashioned mullahs interpreted the vote as the end of organized religion, which of course it was not.

The bright young men represented in this novel by foreign-trained Moheb Khan and Nazrullah and by locally trained Nur Muhammad have brought their nation improved administration. They have by no means achieved victory, but they have won a position from which victory is possible. Many such young men find themselves inclining toward Russia; others, thank heavens, see promise in continued links with the West.

The patterns of social life depicted in the novel have changed radically in the past seventeen years. Kabul now has a good hotel, newspapers, radio, a public cinema to which westerners can go, stores other than bazaars, and several restaurants. Amenities in the cities like Kandahar and Mazar-i-Sharif are also better, but Ghazni remains pretty much as described.

The public punishments described in the novel are no longer common. Since the reader may wonder, I witnessed the first execution, but not in Ghazni; as for the second, I arrived in Kandahar only a few days after it occurred and was given a series of photographs taken by an enterprising man who told me that he had prevailed upon the father to work from the other side because the sunlight was better. Afghan polo, properly called buzkashi (goat dragging), still flourishes and is both rougher and more fun than I describe.

The great dam on whose preliminaries Nazrullah worked in 1946 is in being–one of the marvels of Asia–and its electricity is eagerly sought. The land opposite Qala Bist which was to have been irrigated was found, alas, to be too full of residual salts to be productive. In a sense, this failure of one aspect of the Helmand Project had unfortunate overtones not dissimilar to those that grew out of the German bridges: Afghans looked at the mighty dam, at the cost, at the partial failure and asked, 'Why bother?' The German bridges, when I traveled the road from Kabul to Kandahar, were exactly as described; but the Afghan bridge built by Shah Khan and Nazrullah's father stood on a different road.

As for the Kochis, restrictions have been placed on them at every turn. They cannot enter Russia. Traders from China can no longer penetrate the Pamirs with goods. Pakistan, the western portion of old India, conducts a running fight with Afghanistan over the nationality of Pashtuns and halts many of the nomads at that arbitrary border. The tents are still black; the women are still superb in their freedom; the fat-tailed sheep are still among the most preposterous of animals; and the camels still protest at everything.

The reader may also wish to check my credentials for writing this novel. My first acquaintance with Afghanistan came in 1952, when I was living in the Khyber Pass and had a chance to scout the Afghan border for many miles north and south of that historic area. It was then that I conceived my determination to visit Afghanistan. It was then also that I came to know several Kochi tribes fairly well–Povindahs, we called them, for I did not hear the name Kochi until later–and decided that one day I might try to write about them.

In 1955 I was able to enter Afghanistan itself and made these journeys: First, Khyber Pass to Kabul; second, Kabul to Qala Bist; third, across the Dasht-i-Margo to the Chakhansur, called in this novel The City, which is perhaps a more appropriate name; fourth, down to Chahar Burjak, one of the worst trips I have ever made; fifth, up to Herat and back down to Girishk; sixth, Kabul to Istalif and the lower Koh-i-Baba; seventh, Kabul to Bamian and on to Balkh; eighth, Kandahar to Spin Baldak and Quetta. And there was a ninth trip, perhaps the most memorable I have ever taken, from Qala Bist along the untraveled left bank of the Helmand River to Rudbar. This took us across the Registan desert in a caravan that camped at night in sand dunes with little water and less food. It was from the experiences on this trip, not referred to in this novel, that I developed my love of desert life.

On one of these trips I was visited by friends of a European woman who sought my help. Some years before she had married an Afghan and had passed into the limbo described in parts of this novel. I asked to see her and was taken to a pathetic hovel where I talked with her for the better part of an hour, but I was unable to help. Later I heard of similar cases and met with people actively concerned in liberating wives of foreign origin. However, in fairness I must add that I also met several European women married to enlightened Afghans, and these wives led normal, happy lives; they wore no chaderi, visited Europe when they wished, and were pleased that they had come to live in Afghanistan. Today, of course, quite a few American girls have been marrying Afghans without encountering difficulties with citizenship or the right to travel.

Qabir is an invented name, but the facts associated with it are not. The massive nomad convocation met at no regular place, and where it did meet bore no proper name, for the land is unbelievably wild, empty and unknown. It was called merely The Abul Camp and was probably larger than I suggest. Also, the subsidiary camps for attendant families seem to have been farther from the trading center than I have indicated. The Abul Camp was for men only. Until 1954 no known outsider had ever visited the camp, so that events depicted in this novel are anachronistic by eight years. As for a foreign woman's visiting the camp, there is no record of its having happened.

The archaeological sites referred to—Qala Bist, The City, Bamian, Balkh—are faithfully described. Bamian remains one of the compelling sights of Asia. My notes, penciled hurriedly as we approached from the east, tell the story:

Bamian: at eastern approach the Red City (name Zak?) high on hill and cliffs several hundred feet high. Note little castles guarding trail all the way up. City 4 main levels. It was here Genghis Khan lost his son. Destruction of Bamian followed. Red City on right bank of Bamian River. City at Bamian named Ghulghulah and stood back of present hostel. KOCHI is Farsi word (those who move).

Cliffs 350 feet high, reddish tan. Probably over 500 cave entrances visible, each leading to 4 or 5 rooms. Some caves 300 feet high, sheer drop. Magnificent corridors. Frescoes. All faces routed out. Located foot of soaring sepia and purple-brown mountains facing Koh-i-Baba.

From one room in the highest level of caves I counted 61 snow-covered peaks in midsummer, all over 15,000 feet high.

The Caravanserai of the Tongues, its location and its pillar are inventions, but each is true to the spirit of Afghanistan. I camped in many of these deserted caravanserais, great lonely structures scattered over the land, and never failed to be impressed with their mood and their function. It was at one that I met my first Kochis in Afghanistan and jotted down the outline of a novel much different from this one. As for the pillar, I forget where I heard about an event of similar import; possibly it was at Herat, where Genghis Khan is reliably reported to have slain a million people. One contemporary authority wrote that it was a million and a half.

My contacts with Islam have been consistent and varied: Indonesia, Borneo, Malaya, Pakistan, Afghanistan, the Near East, Turkey. I have written favorably of the religion, have known many of its leaders, and hold it in both respect and affection. My experiences, as the reader may guess, place me in opposition to the rural mullahs.

Practically every Afghan word, when transliterated into the Roman alphabet can be spelled in alternate ways (Kabul, Caboul; Helmand, Helmund) and consistency in orthography seems at this point impossible. The editors of this book and I drew up lists of many variant spellings. We consulted numerous experts, some with rather exalted credentials, and in the end found ourselves repeating the lament of Omar, the poet from nearby Persia:

> Myself when young did eagerly frequent
> Doctor and Saint, and heard great argument
> About it and about: but evermore
> Came out by the same door wherein I went.

It will be some years before the Roman spelling of essential Afghan words is standardized. Those which offered the most interesting variants include:

> chaderi, choudhry, shaddry, chadhri, charderi
> ferangi, farangi, faranji, ferengi, feringhee
> Tajik, Tadjik, Tadzhik
> Pashtun, Pushtun, Pushtoon, Pakhtoon, Pathan
> Kandahar, Qandahar
> Koran, Qur'an
> Bamian, Bamyan, Bamiyan
> Kochi, Kuchi
> Pashto, Pushto, Pushtu, Pukhto
> Povindan, Powindeh

I must make it clear that our decision to spell a given word in a given way was never taken without extensive study, but I must confess that the final decision was usually arbitrary and that consistency from one decision to the next did not seem possible in view of the conflicts existing among the experts.

For two usages I am alone responsible. In 1946 in this part of the world Iran was known as Persia, the Amu Darya river as the Oxus. If I were writing about today, I would of course use the contemporary forms.

In recent years whenever I have been asked which of the countries I have seen I would most prefer to visit again, I have invariably said Afghanistan. I remember it as an exciting, violent, provocative place. Almost every American or European who worked there in the old days says the same. It was, in the years I knew it, what Mark Miller says: 'One of the world's great cauldrons.'

·SAYONARA·

JAMES·A·MICHENER

On April 4, 1952, I shot down my sixth and seventh MIGs. It happened up
near the Yalu River and when I returned to base at J-10 I was excited. The Air
Force doctor took one look at me and said, 'Gruver, you've had it.'

Boy, they were sweet words. They meant I was through flying for a while.
But since I'm a West Point man I felt obligated to appear eager before the flight
surgeon who had been called back from civilian life, potbelly and all. So I
frowned and said, 'Nothing wrong with me, Doc. A bottle of beer'll fix me up.'

'That's right,' the doc agreed.

He had taken my eagerness seriously and for a minute I felt a little sick inside.
I didn't want to fly any more. Not just then. I wanted to appear rough and ready
but I also wanted some solid chairborne duty.

But the doc was smart. He laughed and said, 'Don't turn pale, Gruver. I was
only kidding. I never take this hero stuff seriously.'

I relaxed and said, 'Thanks. I could use some Korean sleep.'

'It's even better than that,' Doc said, putting away his stethoscope. 'You're
going back to Japan!'

From the way he said this you knew he thought Japan was paradise, but I'd
been through the place and it never impressed me much. Dirty streets, little
paper houses, squat men and fat round women. I had never understood why
some Air Force people got so steamed up about Japan.

I said, 'If you go for Japan, I suppose it's good news. I'd just as soon rest up
right here at J-10.'

Doc said, 'You mean you never tangled with any of those beautiful Japanese
dolls at Tachikawa?'

I said, 'I'm a four-star general's son. I don't tangle with Japanese dolls,
beautiful or not.'

Doc looked at me sorrowfully and said, 'Chum, you're sicker than I thought.'

I hadn't meant to sound stuffy, but when you know your outfit sort of has you
ticketed for fast promotion right through to colonel and maybe one-star
general by the time you're thirty-five, a lot of the ordinary razzle-dazzle
connected with military life doesn't impress you. On the other hand, I had
always tried not to act superior to reserve officers just because they were
civilians at heart.

I said, 'I'll think of you, Doc, when I hit those clean Tokyo sheets and that
good Tokyo beer.'

He shook his head with a tricky little leer and said, 'For you, Chum, it ain't
gonna be Tokyo. For you . . . special orders.'

Like a warning flash and without my actually thinking the word I blurted,
'Kobe?'

'Yep, Chum! You made it.'

Instinctively I put my left hand on my hip and felt for my wallet. I said,

'About these special orders? Were they from General Webster?'

'Yep, Chum! You're in.' He gripped his hands in a tight little ball and winked at me. 'Why wouldn't one general look after another general's son?'

I had always known the doc to be a second-class sort of guy and I refused to be drawn into an argument. I played his game and said, 'It's what they call the West Point spirit.'

'That's what I mean,' the doc said. 'Kelly has your orders.'

'I'll go see Kelly,' I said, glad to get away from this know-it-all civilian.

But as I left the medical tent and started down the gravel path to squadron headquarters where Kelly worked, another civilian called me: 'Gruver, could I speak with you?'

I turned and saw the chaplain and since he almost never spoke to anyone except about trouble I stopped short and asked, 'Kelly again?'

'Yes,' he said almost sorrowfully. 'Kelly.'

I waited on the gravel path while he picked his way across the brown Korean mud. J-10 was almost all mud. When he joined me I asked, 'What's he been up to now, Padre?'

'This time it's serious,' he said sorrowfully. He led me to his tent, a beat-up affair with Bibles, crucifixes and the special silver gadgets for conducting Jewish ceremonies.

'Kelly face another court-martial?' I asked.

'Worse. He's appealed to his Congressman.'

I'd always been disgusted with enlisted men who write letters to Congressmen. The Air Force had a sensible and just way to handle any problem. Congressmen weren't needed. So I asked, 'Why don't you advise the colonel to throw this guy out of the service?'

'Under the new rules . . .'

The new rules! I was always forgetting the new rules. Starting in 1945 a lot of soft-headed do-gooders in Washington had revised the basic rules for military conduct and as a result you now saw enlisted men writing to Congressmen. I had always agreed with my father. Knock such stoops on the head and throw them in jail. Then the do-gooders could really sob.

'So under the new rules, what happens?' I asked.

'So Kelly gets his way. He goes back to Japan.'

'Ridiculous,' I said. 'The Air Force is becoming a kindergarten.'

'And when he gets back to Japan, he marries the girl.'

This was too much. I sat down in one of the padre's rickety chairs and asked, 'You mean that in spite of all you and the colonel have said to this kid he still gets permission to marry the girl?'

'That's right.'

'Why doesn't somebody bust him in the head?'

'That's no solution. I want you to talk with him.'

'Nothing more I can say.'

'Does the boy realize that if he marries this Japanese girl he can't possibly take her back to America?' the padre asked.

'Sure he knows. I made him sign the paper proving that he knows. He signed and told me what I could do with it.'

'You must talk with him once more, Gruver. He's a misguided boy.'

'He's a dead-end criminal, Father, and you know it.'

'Not a criminal! A tough boy who's had trouble in the Air Force. He's just hot-headed.'

'That's not where the heat is, Padre.'

He laughed and said, 'You're right. That's why we mustn't let him make a fool of himself.'

I was tired from flying and said bluntly, 'Look, Padre. Kelly belongs to your church. You're the guy who's got to save him.'

Chaplain Feeney became very serious and took my hands in his. It was a trick he used when he wanted to make a point and it accounted for much of his success with the squadron. He was never afraid to plead with a man. 'You must believe me when I say I'm not trying to save Kelly for my church. I'm trying to save him for himself. If he marries this Japanese girl it can lead only to tragedy. In ordinary times such a marriage would be unwise, but under the new law . . . when he can't even take her with him to America . . . What's to happen, Gruver?'

He spoke so passionately that I had to give in. 'All right. What do you want me to do?'

He was embarrassed at what he was about to suggest and hesitated a moment. Then he said, apologetically, 'You're engaged to a fine, good-looking American girl. You showed me her picture one night.' He smiled as I automatically reached with my left hand for my wallet pocket. 'When you're flying and things begin to get rough you pat that picture for good luck, don't you?'

I said I did. It was a gimmick I had picked up when I shifted from propeller planes to jets. Like most pilots, I was scared of the jets at first so whenever it looked like trouble I would pat my wallet for luck, because Eileen Webster had been good news for me ever since that special week-end I met her in San Antonio.

Chaplain Feeney said, 'If the opportunity presents itself, show Kelly your girl's picture. Let him remember what a fine American girl looks like.'

I said, 'I'm not selling anything.'

The padre was a smart man. 'Who asked you to?' he said. 'When he says he's determined to get married tell him you understand. Tell him you've seen some really wonderful Japanese girls.'

'Trouble is, Padre, I haven't. They're all so dumpy and round-faced. How can our men–good average guys–how can they marry these yellow girls? In '45 I was fighting the Japs. Now my men are marrying them.'

'I've never understood it. Such marriages are doomed and it's my job to prevent them.'

'I agree.'

'Then you'll speak to Kelly?'

'Wouldn't it be simpler for the colonel just to order him not to get married?' I asked.

Chaplain Feeney laughed. 'Some things can't be handled that way. We've investigated the girl Kelly wants to marry. She's not a prostitute. She's not subversive. As a matter of fact, she got a good recommendation from our investigators. Used to work in a library. Kelly has a right to marry her.'

The word *marry* caught me strangely and I was swept back four years to a spring week-end in Texas when a gang of us left Randolph Field for a big time in San Antonio. We were walking down some stone steps to an open-air theater by the river that runs through the middle of San Antonio, when suddenly I saw this beautiful girl coming up. I did a double take and cried, 'Aren't you General Webster's daughter?' And she gave me a dazzling smile and said she was and I stood right there staring at her and asking, 'Why didn't you look like this when you lived across from me in Fort Bragg?' and she said she'd looked like this but I had been too busy going away to the Point to notice. I tried to recall but couldn't even remember her clearly from those days so I said, 'You must have been a long-legged kid of eleven when we were at Fort Bragg.' Then she said something which stopped me cold. She ignored the other Air Force men standing beside me and said, 'I'm still a long-legged kid.' And she was right and eighteen days later we sort of made up our minds to get married. But Eileen's mother and Korea took care of that.

So I brought myself back to Korea and told Chaplain Feeney, 'I'll do what I can.'

'Thanks, Gruver.' As I started to go he asked, 'Mind if I speak to the colonel about you?'

'What for?'

'You're as tense as a watch spring, son. I'm going to tell the old man you ought to be grounded.'

I laughed and said, 'The doc beat you to it. I'm on my way to Japan.'

'Wonderful,' he said. 'Tokyo?'

'No, Kobe. My girl's father is general down there.'

'That's fortunate.'

'It has its drawbacks.'

'I mean Kelly is going to Kobe, too. You can keep an eye on him.'

I was disgusted. 'You mean you're flying him back to where the girl is?'

'His Congressman insists on it.'

I started to say what I thought of Congressmen who butt into military affairs like this but the padre said, 'You might save the boy.'

I thought of mean, sawed-off Joe Kelly and said as I left, 'Nothing could save that bum.'

JOE KELLY: 'G.I.'s married to Jap girls always
look as if they knew a big important secret.'

It was a curious day in Korea. Our air base at J-10 wasn't what you'd call warm, but there was a shot of spring in the air and the ground was beginning to thaw and even Korea felt pretty much the way any part of the world feels in spring. I took a couple of good deep lungfuls of air and walked down headquarters street, a dismal drag even with spring nibbling at its edges, and I said to myself, 'Skip Kelly. Let him take care of himself.'

I headed for my bunk, where there would be some beer and a poker game, but then I realized that Kelly had the hot dope on my orders, so I went into the squadron tent where I found this mutt sitting behind a hand-painted sign big enough for a general: AIRMAN KELLY.

He was a runty kid in his teens. I was twenty-eight and everybody younger than that seemed immature, but Kelly really was. He'd never been to school but had a quick animal intelligence and a sort of gutter know-how. He'd come up through a tough section of Chicago and had sandy hair and an up-with-your-dukes Irish face. He was against the world and against all officers in particular. He had the weird record of having been promoted to corporal four times—and busted back each time. He was bitter and always in trouble and the last man in our outfit you would expect to get involved seriously with any girl.

He shoved my orders at me and said, 'Pays to have friends.'

I had been responsible for one of Kelly's court-martials, but he had astonished me on the second by requesting me as his counsel. He respected no one, but he did like men who flew the jets. When he jammed the papers at me I was going to haul him up again, but he grinned and said, 'Hear you bagged two more today.'

'Boom, boom.'

'How was it up there, Ace?'

'Never gets easier.'

'You know what's in your orders?' he asked in a snide way that a gangster might use in asking about a pay-off.

'Kobe,' I said, picking them up.

'Yeah, but I mean how you happened to get them?'

'I've never discussed things like orders with enlisted men,' I said, turning for the door.

Kelly was different. He said, 'What I mean is, did you know about General Webster writin' to the colonel?'

It was infuriating. I wanted to bust this little twerp in the face but he kept me on the hook. I hesitated and said, 'They're friends.'

'Sure, but these letters were about you.'

'Me?'

'Yeah, General Webster started all his orders, "Of course I don't intend to intrude on your handlin' of the squadron but . . ." He always got the *but* in.'

'But what?'

'But he would sure like to have Major Lloyd Gruver come right the hell down to Kobe.'

I stuffed the papers into my pocket and said, 'I didn't ask for orders like that.'

Kelly laughed in an ugly way and said, 'You ain't heard nothin' yet, Ace.' He seemed to despise me for being an officer yet to tolerate me because I was a working pilot. He said, 'General Webster's had you assigned to the Interservice Aviation Board, which means you sit on your parachute all day long and do nothin'.' Then he grinned and added, 'But oh them nights.'

'What nights?'

Kelly poked his blunt little head in one direction then the other and asked, 'Ace, can you keep a secret?'

I had always been careful never to discuss military secrets with anyone and I said, 'I'd rather not hear about it.'

Kelly threw me a nasty salute and said, 'This ain't Air Force secret. It's Ace Gruver secret.'

'What do you mean?'

'Why do you suppose you're gettin' orders to Kobe? And a cushy job? And a priority flight?'

I sensed that I was getting in too deep with Kelly and changed the subject. 'Chaplain tells me you're heading for Kobe, too.'

'Yep.'

'I hear your Congressman arranged it.'

'Yep. Chaplain said no. Colonel said no. You said no. But the Congressman said yes.'

I let him know by my manner that I was disgusted with such procedures and asked with some irony, 'And I hear you're getting married.'

'Yep.'

His insolence killed any intention I might have had to help Chaplain Feeney by arguing with this low-grade character. I signed the receipt for my orders and headed for the door. But Kelly stopped me short by saying, 'I hear you're gettin' married too.'

'What do you mean?' I asked.

'The general's daughter is arrivin' in Kobe. Tomorrow.'

Kelly stared up at me with a nasty grin and when I asked if this was true he said, 'Yep. General Webster arranges it so you can marry his daughter. My Congressman arranges it for me. Generals for the officers. Congressmen for the peasants.'

Kelly and I looked at each other in one of those odd moments when you seem to see life in absolutely clear cold light. You see another human being without uniform, without degrees, without past or future. There he is, with his own problems and ambitions that are miles apart from yours but which at the same time are part of yours. The Secretary of War once told me that my father's great success in the Army sprang from his ability to see each man he had to work with dangling in free space, suspended by a string leading to the hand of God. I could respect Kelly. He was trying to get my goat and he was an evil little twerp, but I could respect him.

I took out my wallet and asked, 'Have I ever shown you a picture of the general's daughter?' I think Kelly must have been looking at me in that same cold clear light for he leaned forward like a human being and said no.

But I got mixed up–I'd never before bagged two MIGs in one day–and the picture I grabbed was not my prize shot but one of Eileen and her mother. Kelly studied the picture and asked, 'Is the battle-axe your mother-in-law?'

I recovered the picture and said, 'This is the one I meant to show you.'

Kelly whistled and said, 'Wow! She sure fills a bathing suit.'

I said, 'She intended to.'

Kelly said, 'She's a dish. Even for a general's daughter, she's a dish.'

I said, 'It's pretty exciting to think of a girl like that waiting for you in Kobe. Thanks for the good news, Kelly.'

He said, 'You ever seen Katsumi?'

'Where's Katsumi?' I asked.

'The girl I'm marryin'.'

'I'm sorry. I don't know Japanese names.'

'Think nothin' of it,' he said brashly.

He produced a small P.X. picture of his girl. I was embarrassed because this Katsumi was certainly no Madame Butterfly. She had a big round face, prominent cheeks and what looked like oil-black hair. If you'd never been in Japan you'd probably have taken her for an Indian or an Eskimo maybe. But if you've ever seen Tokyo you'd recognize Katsumi at once. She was one of the millions of girls who could never be pretty, who did all the heavy work and who dressed as if the only clothes in Japan were made from old flour sacks.

I had to say something and by the grace of God I remembered about her working in a library. I said, 'She sure looks intelligent.'

Kelly said, 'She's a lot brighter than me.'

I was about to leave when I recalled my promise to the padre. I asked, 'Aren't you taking a big risk?'

'Risks don't scare me any more,' Kelly said defiantly.

'I mean about not being able to take her home?'

'That's what don't scare me,' he said.

'How old are you, Kelly?'

'Nineteen.'

'You're only a kid. Why don't you think this over?'

'I have. The Army and the Air Force and the State Department have ganged up to keep me from gettin' married. Only makes me more determined.'

'What do you mean, ganged up?' I don't like people who feel sorry for themselves.

'When my Kobe skipper saw I was really gettin' serious about Katsumi he gave me the bum's rush to Korea. Then the doubledomes in Washington set a deadline. "If you marry a Jap girl after then," they said, "we won't let you bring her back Stateside." So I drew a court-martial for demandin' that I be sent back to Japan to marry the girl before the new law. I never made it. And now each week Father Feeney hands me a pamphlet provin' how stupid I am even to be thinkin' about such a thing.'

He ripped open a drawer and slammed down some mimeographed sheets widely used in our area to bring young kids to their senses. The one on top was titled, 'But Will Your Family Accept Her?'' Kelly grabbed it in his hairy hand, crumpled it up and pitched it into the basket.

'They've tried everything to stop us, but do you know what I'm gonna do, Ace?'

'Something stupid, I'm sure.'

'That's right. I'm stupid enough to be in love. It happens that I love this girl. And if I have to give up my American citizenship to marry her, that's O.K. with me.' He was trembling mad and put his girl's picture back in his desk.

I was outraged to think that any American man would dare to talk like that. Give up his citizenship! I wanted to grab the young idiot and knock some sense into him, tell him that anyone who even thought of surrendering his American citizenship for a Japanese girl ought . . . He turned his back on me and started on some paper work, as if to dismiss me.

I don't take that from anyone. I got sore. I reached out, grabbed him by the shirt and spun him around. 'Who in hell do you think you are?' I cried.

To my amazement he cocked his fist and threatened me. 'I'll let you have it, Ace.'

For one brief moment I wanted to mix with this squirt and pin his ears back, but I realized that would be murder. I could have massacred him any day in the week. So I dropped my hand and said, pretty well shaken up, 'You get to be a hophead with these damn jet planes.'

Kelly was completely at ease. He laughed and said, 'We could use some more men like you.'

I said, 'Excuse me, Joe. But you sounded crazy when you said you'd give up your citizenship—for a girl.'

'I am crazy,' he said. 'I'm in love—crazy.'

I felt a little dizzy and said, 'Let's go over to my bunk and split a beer.'

'Wonderful!' he cried, slamming his desk shut. As we walked through the late afternoon sunshine with the hint of spring warmth about us he said, 'You know, Ace, back there I wasn't afraid to sock you. Because I know that if I did you'd knock my block off fair and square and you wouldn't yell for a cheap court-martial.'

'Oh, brother! How wrong can you be? I just finished arguing with the chaplain that you ought to be court-martialed for having written to your Congressman.'

'I mean, you wouldn't turn me in over a personal grudge.'

I thought a minute and said, 'I guess you're right.'

'That's what I mean,' he said.

We went into my bunk and promoted a fifth of Suntory. I said to Joe, 'The Japs must make this out of farmer's socks.' But Joe took a murderous gulp and cried approvingly, 'Wow, that's man's stuff.'

It was obvious that he wanted to talk with someone. He asked, 'You really do think I'm nuts, don't you? The guys at the mess hall do too. That is . . .' He paused, looked at me carefully and said, 'That is, some of them do. But you know a strange thing, Ace? In the bunks at night you never hear one man who married a Japanese wife complain. You hear a lot of other guys complain about their women. But not the ones who got hitched in Japan.'

This seemed so unlikely that I took a long pull at the bottle and asked, 'How come?'

'Sounds old-fashioned, Ace, but it must be love. If a white man with good Air Force pay goes ahead and marries a yellow girl, it must be love.'

'That's ridiculous!' I felt the old yearning coming back to knock some sense into this kid but he was dragging on the bottle again, so I said, 'I'm in love. Half the men around here I know love some girl back in the States. What's so special about loving a Japanese girl?'

He said, 'You ever been in the bunks at night? Men with wives back in the States talk about Junior's braces and country-club dances and what kind of car their wife bought. But the men with Japanese wives tell you one thing only. What wonderful wives they have. They're in love. It's that simple.'

This flustered me because he might have been talking about my own family. My father was a four-star general with a tremendous reputation as a result of what he accomplished in Guadalcanal and the Philippines, and my mother had written a couple of stories that had appeared in the *Atlantic Monthly*. They were excellent people, they were exciting people, but they had never been in love. In his bunk at night I think my father must have talked about my braces and the kind of car my mother drove. I'm sure he never talked about love.

I said, 'There's a better explanation. The guys with Japanese wives are younger. They don't have kids to talk about.'

Joe thought that one over, took another swig, and said, 'You could be right, Ace. But I ain't takin' no chance. Because when I see Katsumi I see a dame who could fill my heart for the rest of my life.' He looked down the tent as if pondering his next comment, then went ahead and made it. 'Tell me, Ace, do you feel that way about your girl?'

He had me again because I was a professional soldier. My future was all cut out and I knew that I would never find any one girl whose presence filled my heart forever and ever. Among the young officers in my gang love wasn't like that. You looked the field over and found a good-looking solid citizen who could stomach you for the rest of your life and if she came from a military family, like Eileen, so much the better. I couldn't explain to Kelly that Eileen would be the finest wife an Air Force officer could have and yet not be the way he was describing.

I said, 'You come see me in ten years and you'll see a happy citizen!'

Joe took a final slug and cried, 'I believe you, Ace. Boy, Ace, you're one in a million. Ace, you're one officer in a million I could talk to.' He shook my hand clumsily and banged his way out into the dusty company street. Then he looked back and cried, 'Boy, Ace! We got it made! We're gonna get married!' and he staggered off to the mess hall.

MRS WEBSTER: 'I don't mean the Japanese are inferior, but I do mean we ought to remember who won the war.'

On Monday Pvt. Kelly and I flew over to Japan on the same plane and as I watched him strap himself into his bucket seat with real joy at the idea of getting home to his girl I thought how different our two journeys were. He was heading for dumpy, round Katsumi and a future that no one could guess, while I was heading for the big surprise that General Webster had arranged for me: a safe desk job, marriage to his beautiful daughter Eileen, and before too many years a promotion surely to colonel and maybe to general.

I didn't talk with Kelly on the trip over because there were some colonels aboard and it seemed wiser for me to sit up front with them and exchange ideas about the Russian pilots we were meeting over Korea. But when we reached Japan the medics came aboard to disinfect the plane, and while I was standing in the aisle Kelly whispered, 'Ace, you're the only friend I know here, and you bein' with the squadron . . .' I thought he was going to touch me for some cash and I prepared to hand him a fin, but he said, 'I was wonderin' if you'd be my best man. Saturday?'

The colonels started moving out and I couldn't stand there arguing. My whole inclination–everything I had ever been taught, all I had experienced–led me to say no, but I blurted out, 'O.K.'

'Thanks,' he said, and as he trudged across the field, bowlegged and with a gangster slouch, I thought that this square-headed, sandy-haired kid was not the kind you read about in books when they describe the great lovers. Somehow you didn't think of Pvt. Joe Kelly fighting through the walls of flame to win the princess. You thought of him as the tough kid at the filling station who whistles through his teeth at bobby soxers going past in jalopies. But he was off to marry an Asiatic girl in a strange land and I had to admit that he had guts.

I was watching him when General Webster called my name and when I looked his way there stood Mrs Webster, too. I shouted, 'Surprise! When did you get here?'

Mrs Webster was a handsome woman–the kind who appear in ads wearing tailored suits and white hair and telling the young bride why one cleaner is better than the other–and it was widely understood in Army circles that Mark Webster owed most of his success to this brilliant and energetic woman. I once heard my father say, when some of his classmates from '22 were visiting, 'Mark Webster at the Point was an inevitable colonel. Absolutely impossible for him to go further. But a first-class wife came along and made him a general.' There was no scorn in his voice when he said this–and no envy.

When Mrs Webster saw me she hurried forward to kiss me on the cheek. I had to make believe I didn't know where Eileen was so I asked, 'What's the news from Eileen?'

The conspirators looked at each other archly. 'She's still at work in the oil company,' Mrs Webster said. 'But she finds Tulsa dull without you around.'

'Boy, did I find Korea dull without her!'

General Webster said, 'I hope you didn't mind my dragging you away from the Russians.'

'Frankly, sir, I approved. I was getting a bit jittery.'

'Well, we'll drive you in to Kobe and let you see what the setup is. You're on the Interservice Aviation Board, you know, but you don't start work for a week.'

'I'll get some sleep,' I said, and the Websters snickered to themselves.

He led me to a black Cadillac with one bright red star on the license plate. He had always been something of a dandy, ten pounds underweight, extra-sharp uniforms and a smart headquarters company to make him look good. He was what enlisted men call chicken because he demanded all the military courtesies, straight caps, shined shoes. He himself moved with an exaggerated stride and cultivated a straight-from-the-heart look. Having known my own father well and having discovered in him a real general who cut right through the nonsense to the hard core of every problem, leaving glossy shoes and snappy salutes to others, I often suspected that Mark Webster was merely playing at being a general. Once I remarked on this to my father, who grew very angry. He said, 'Look, Know-it-all! The Army needs many different kinds of generals. Mark Webster can do a dozen things I can't do.' Then he scowled and said, 'Not that I would want to do them. But don't underestimate the men who keep the organization running.' About three days later we were dining in a restaurant that featured a lot of swank and father said, 'I always admire headwaiters who appear unflustered yet keep the organization running.' I put my hand over my mouth and mumbled, 'That's what you said the other day about General Webster.' He looked up sharply, considered for a moment and said, 'I guess that's what I meant—if I said it.'

But on this ride in from the airport General Webster was way off stride. He wasn't his urbane self at all. In fact, he was downright uncomfortable, but it wasn't until we neared the center of Kobe that I found out what was eating him. Mrs Webster was riding herd again.

We were passing a corner at which half a dozen enlisted men—we had orders not to call them G.I.'s any more—were loafing. They were in Kobe for Rest and Recuperation from the front in Korea. Like most soldiers, they were recuperating with streetwalkers. Five chunky Japanese girls were standing with them and as we drove by, one of the soldiers slapped a girl on the bottom. She squealed.

'That's what I mean,' Mrs Webster said.

'Kobe's a recreation center,' the general said grimly. 'I can't change it.'

'It's disgraceful.'

'I know it is,' the general snorted.

'Furthermore, it degrades the military uniform.'

'There seem to be no rules against it,' General Webster mumbled, leaning back in a disgruntled slouch.

Mrs Webster, seeing she could get no further with the general, asked me, 'What do you think about it, Lloyd?'

'Don't try to make me argue against a general,' I pleaded.

General Webster sat up. 'Seriously, Gruver, what do you younger officers think?'

I had just started to say, 'I've never understood how any self-respecting officer can go with a Japanese girl' when I stopped sharp. For straight ahead of our Cadillac was a tall Marine lieutenant coming out of a nylon-underwear shop accompanied by the first beautiful Japanese girl I had ever seen. She was slim and black haired and her eyes didn't slant. And she laughed. But this extraordinarily beautiful girl laughed and tucked her parcel of nylon underwear beneath her left arm. Then, like any American wife at a busy corner, she grasped her Marine's hand warmly and smiled up at him.

'It's a disgrace,' the general snorted.

Mrs Webster leaned forward to watch the Marine and his girl. 'Why, he's a handsome young man,' she gasped. 'Probably from a very good family. What's he doing with a Japanese girl?'

I had a smart-aleck reply to that question but stifled it and then caught the general's eye and saw clearly that he had thought of the same reply and had killed his, too, for the same reason that I had killed mine. Mrs Webster looked at us and asked, 'Is it true, Mark, that some of our young men have actually married such girls?'

'About 10,000 of them,' he replied gruffly.

'I simply can't believe it! Yellow girls as mothers of an American home! Even the poor fellows who married French girls last time . . . Remember those awful Farringdons at Camp Polk?'

General Webster asked, 'Any of your outfit married to Japanese girls?'

I said, 'I spent all afternoon last Friday arguing with a kid who's determined to marry one of them.'

'How deplorable!' Mrs Webster sighed. She spoke with real compassion, and it was apparent that she honestly felt sorry for any nineteen-year-old boy who, far from home, had got himself mixed up with a Japanese girl.

At that moment a fat Army major, obviously a civilian, came ambling down the street, window-shopping as he might have done in San Francisco, and on his arm, window-shopping too, was a Japanese girl. Some fellow officers wandered by and the fat major stopped them to introduce his girl just as if she had been a girl he was dating at home. The girl chatted with the other officers for a moment and then led her major on down the street.

'You must do something about such behavior,' Mrs Webster said grimly. 'At least on the officer level.'

Our Cadillac stopped at Camp Kobe and General Webster bounded out of the car and said, 'I have one disagreeable job to do. Nancy, you go on back to the club. Lloyd and I'll meet you there soon.'

Mrs Webster smiled at me archly and said, 'They're having a special luncheon for us today. I might almost say an extraordinary one.'

The general showed me a davenport in his outer office–paneled in Japanese pine and very handsome–and told his aide, 'All right, I'll see him now.' A colonel with highly polished boots disappeared into an inner room and said crisply, 'General Webster will see you now.'

Through the door came sawed-off Airman Kelly. Playing the Air Force game, he never acknowledged he knew me but stared straight ahead, following the spruced-up colonel, but as he disappeared through the door leading to General Webster's inner office, he shrugged his shoulders.

I studied the maps in the general's waiting room and browsed through his copy of the *Infantry Journal*, but my reading was disrupted by the general shouting, 'Why in hell do you want to marry her, anyway?'

Then I heard the colonel argue more persuasively, 'But, Private Kelly, if you do marry her you can't take her back to the States.'

Kelly's response was muffled but judging from what happened next the kid must have said, 'I don't want to go back to the States,' because the general shouted, 'By God, I'll send you back whether you want to go or not. Colonel, send this young whippersnapper home. Tonight!'

That was when I first heard Kelly's voice. He said, 'I won't go.'

The general exploded. 'You won't go!'

Kelly said, 'That's right, because Congressman Shimmark has arranged it for me to get married.'

I have found that no matter where you are in the military–Army, Air Force, Navy, it doesn't matter–things quiet down when somebody mentions Congress. I remember hearing about the time my father was stuck in the Philippines without supplies. It was during the battle when he got his fourth star and MacArthur could drop dead and Nimitz was a bum and he would bust Roosevelt in the nose. But a five-foot-four-inch Congressman appeared and Father became as smooth as butter. Because he knew that Congressmen run the military. They approve the budget.

So General Webster retreated before the name of Congressman Shimmark. 'All right,' he blustered, 'go ahead and ruin your life. I've done my duty. I've tried to stop you.' Then he apparently turned to the colonel, for he snapped, 'Arrange the young fool's wedding. Next we'll be running a nursery.'

The colonel was grim-lipped as he led Kelly back into the waiting room. 'Who do you think you are,' he muttered savagely, 'speaking to a general that way?'

Kelly said with great finality, 'I ain't takin' no more pushin' around. I'm gettin' married.'

The colonel showed him to the door and said, 'You'll regret it as long as you live.'

Kelly looked at the colonel and laughed. Then he saw me and shrugged his shoulders again. 'Saturday,' he said through the corner of his mouth.

When he had gone the general appeared. He was red in the face and mumbling. 'By God, in the old days we'd have thrown an insolent moron like that into the stockade. Now it's the new Army, and every young pup writes to his Congressman. Damn, I wish all Congressmen would drop dead.' Quickly he looked about the room to see if anyone had heard this remark.

The colonel tried to make a joke and said, 'You can't stop men from marrying women!'

The general looked at him as if he had gone off his rocker and growled, 'But you can keep officers of the United States Army from making utter fools of themselves in public. And by God I will.'

Then he saw me and, taking me by the arm, said, 'Lloyd, I certainly do wish the imbeciles I have under me were sensible like you. But then you've been reared in a tradition of service to the nation. You understand what a uniform means.' He looked for his Cadillac, which hadn't yet returned, and called for a Buick instead. As soon as we got inside he said, 'Speaking of Eileen, let's eat.'

'I wasn't speaking of Eileen.' I laughed.

'I was,' he said. 'Because . . . I mean . . . it's inconceivable that these officers you see parading Japanese girls could ever have known clean, decent American girls like Eileen . . .'

He turned abruptly and his voice sputtered like a volcano gasping for air. Across the street stood the fat major and his window-shopping Japanese girl.

They were looking at dresses, holding hands in the spring sunshine. The general leaned forward and asked his driver, 'Isn't that Major Bartlett?'

'Yes, sir.'

'A shoe salesman in civilian life,' the general snorted. 'What can you expect?' The driver corrected him. 'Major Bartlett's the one who owns the chain of filling stations, sir.'

General Webster relaxed, 'God, what an army!' he sighed.

We drove up to the de luxe Japanese hotel which housed the officers club and I could sense the general becoming excited at the prospect of surprising me with Eileen. As a matter of fact, I got pretty steamed up myself because I hadn't seen Eileen for more than a year. Nervously I slapped my wallet for good luck and started up the marble steps.

A Japanese bellhop greeted the general. A Japanese bell captain handed him some papers. A Japanese elevator operator took us briskly up to the general's suite and a Japanese chambermaid hurried down the hall ahead of us. A Japanese butler opened the door for us, grinning happily, and a Japanese housemaid bowed almost to the floor, honoring the general.

I stood at attention, waiting for the tall library doors to open, and I remember saying to myself, 'Now look, squarehead, you've got to act surprised.' But I didn't need the coaching, for Eileen appeared unexpectedly from the hallway and she was twice as lovely as I had remembered. 'Wow!' I cried, hurrying to her, and I noticed that she was more what you might call curved, more lovely when she smiled.

She hurried to meet me and we kissed and I said, 'Wow! what a wonderful way to bring a man back from Korea!' and she said, 'I wanted to cable you the minute the Army said I could come, but Mother said, "We'll surprise him."'

Mrs Webster interrupted, 'We didn't want to take your mind off your flying,' she said.

Eileen asked, 'Was it pretty rough this time?'

'They've got the first team playing.'

I held her two hands tightly and stepped back to study her. 'Hair fixed differently, eh? Oh, that beautiful blonde hair when everyone out here has black. And your dress . . . It seems to go in and out a lot–nice.'

'It's meant to go in and out.' Eileen laughed. 'I go in and out.'

General Webster coughed and I said, 'You're much prettier than any photograph you sent me–except maybe that special one in the bathing suit. Boy, did that one go in and out!'

Eileen said, 'That one was all out. I weighed eight pounds more that summer!'

General Webster said, 'Do you suppose we could go down and eat?'

But Mrs Webster was enjoying the romantic scene she had arranged and said, 'First we'll drink to the young lovers.' She produced a set of shimmering wine glasses and explained, 'From the P.X. The little Japanese sales-clerk said they were made right here in Kobe.'

General Webster poured the sherry and declaimed dramatically, 'To the lovers!' Then he looked at his wife and complained, 'What an ugly phrase! Aren't lovers French people who live in an attic and never get married?'

'No!' Eileen cried. 'Lovers are people in an English movie who live in a grass cottage and the vicar's wife condemns them.'

'Very unpleasant word, anyway.' He poured fresh sherry and said, 'To Major Lloyd Gruver and Eileen Webster, United States Air Force. That sounds a damned sight more American and a damned sight more healthy.'

Mrs Webster laughed. 'You're right, Mark, but *lovers* has another perfectly good meaning too. Average American people whatever their ages who love each other–even when they've been married twenty-six years.' She went over and kissed the general warmly.

My own father and mother had never gotten along together too well and from about ten on I realized that no matter what great advancements my father received and no matter how ordinary Mark Webster's career turned out, my parents envied the Websters because Mark and Nancy were in love while my father and mother were not. Sometimes Father would betray his contempt for Mark Webster's willingness to be pushed around by his wife, and my mother, who came from a famous German family in Lancaster, Pennsylvania, usually stayed there with her circle of friends and spoke sadly of Nancy Webster, 'chasing about the world like a camp follower.'

At this moment in Kobe, when the senior Websters were kissing, I shared my parents' feelings and for the first time I realized with a certain degree of shock that when I married their daughter Eileen I would more likely resemble my father than become a second Mark Webster. There would always be some restraint upon me; yet standing there before Eileen and seeing her so radiantly lovely I concluded that I was deeply in love–in my way and my father's way, and I thought in that hesitating moment that my partial love, as you might term it, could lead to the creation of a solid family like Father's, to my promotion in the Air Force like his promotion in the Army, and to a substantial position in society like the one my mother enjoyed in Lancaster. I said to myself, 'This is a soldier's way of loving.'

But I think Mrs Webster, who knew my parents well, must have sensed my thoughts, for she cried, over her husband's shoulder, 'Kiss the girl, Lloyd.'

I did and the general begged, 'Now can we eat?'

We went down to the dining room, where the Japanese headwaiter had arranged a pretty dazzling table with flowers and a church carved out of ice. Three Japanese waiters held our chairs and a three-piece Japanese orchestra hammered out a jive version of 'Here Comes the Bride.' The officers at nearby tables rose and applauded, but the luncheon was spoiled because right next to our table sat the Marine lieutenant with his beautiful Japanese girl, while next to the orchestra were the fat major and his window-shopping girl.

Mrs Webster fidgeted with her napkin and said, 'If I knew it wouldn't humiliate you I'd leave. Who won the war, anyway?'

Eileen grasped her mother's arm and whispered, 'They're fine girls. Please don't create a scene.' Mrs Webster subsided and started to splash her spoon in her cup but soon stopped.

'I simply have no appetite,' she said firmly.

The luncheon was a calamity and as soon as he could decently do so General Webster dragged me back to his office where he shouted at his aide, 'Go out and haul in Major Bartlett.' Then he called his secretary and dictated a sharp note: 'Effective immediately no Japanese nationals shall participate in any functions of the Kobe Officers Club, including specifically but not exclusively eating in the Club dining room.'

'Post it conspicuously!' he said, and as the secretary started to leave the general boomed out, 'Be especially sure there's one in every elevator.'

When Major Bartlett appeared the general really ate him out. The fat major, one of those particularly exasperating civilians who won't take military life seriously, didn't even bother to snap to attention.

'Your behavior is a disgrace.'

'I understand.'

'You can't understand, or you wouldn't go lollygagging down a public street holding hands with a Japanese girl.'

'I understand.'

'Damn it all, these people were our enemies a short time ago.'

'Not mine. I fought in Germany.'

'Well, your country's. You ought to respect your nation's responsibilities.'

'I understand,' the major droned in an unusually offensive way.

'You understand that you're not to bring that girl into the Club again?'

'I understand.'

This infuriated the general, who said sharply, 'And you're not to be seen on the public streets with her.'

The major looked at me, raised his eyebrows and said, 'I understand.'

This was too much for the general. He said sharply, 'Major Bartlett, I've been ordered to send a levy to Korea. You'd better go along.'

'Certainly.'

Now I'd had enough. I cried, 'Certainly, *sir*. You know there's such a charge as insolence through manner.'

'Certainly, sir,' the fat man said to me, nodding slightly.

'Stay out of this, Gruver,' the general commanded. 'Bartlett, the levy moves out tomorrow.'

'Certainly, sir!' he said with the greatest military precision, throwing us each an extra-snappy salute.

When he had left the general said, 'The perpetual civilian. Well, there's no use court-martialing a man like that. Maybe Korea'll knock some sense into him.'

'I wish you'd let me handle him,' I said.

'You'll learn that the Army gains more in the long run by taking civilian nonsense. But, by God, you don't have to take it at meals.'

That evening when we returned to the Club and entered the elevator, the general noted with satisfaction that his memorandum had been posted, but when he read to the bottom of the typed sheet he turned a bright purple, for someone had scrawled in pencil, 'Signed, Mrs Mark Webster.'

'Who did that?' the general shouted.

The Japanese girl who ran the elevator could not read English and had no idea of what the general was enraged about. He pointed at the penciled signature and demanded, 'Who do this?'

'Me no see,' she whispered, cowering in the corner.

In her confusion the elevator stormed past the general's floor and by the time the frightened little girl could get it back under control, General Webster had ripped down the announcement. Then he dragged the girl into his suite and rang furiously for the hotel manager, who established the fact that Major Bartlett had ridden in the elevator that afternoon. But it was impossible to prove anything and by mealtime every officer in the hotel knew about the incident, for civilian officers are like schoolboys—always giggling with delight when something embarrasses the headmaster.

Dinner that evening was a chilly affair. Eileen and I sat in silence and absorbed the hateful stares of the officers who normally brought Japanese girls in to dinner. Major Bartlett appeared, bowed my way and sat right where the general would have to see him, chatting happily with some cronies and telling dirty stories. But the principal target of the icy stares that night was Mrs Webster, who didn't seem to mind at all. She had been through many Army crises with her husband–some, like this, which she had precipitated–and she had never wilted under criticism. My father did not approve of her meddling in Army life but once said, 'If you ever get into trouble, Lloyd, be like Nancy Webster. Stick your chin out and take it.'

Now she brazenly pointed at a table where three American schoolteachers were dining with some civilian men employed by the Army to run the gasoline-supply system. In a voice just loud enough to be heard by eaves-droppers she said, 'Isn't it charming to see those pretty American girls at that table?'

Somebody had to say something, so I offered, 'After you've been in Korea, it's wonderful to see an American girl.'

I realized immediately that this sounded pretty awful, and I was sure of it when Major Bartlett suddenly picked up his spoon and started polishing it like mad. I glared at him but he simply looked at the spoon, breathed on it the way you do when you're polishing apples and polished some more.

Any trouble between me and the fat major was averted by the appearance of the young Marine lieutenant and his lovely Japanese girl. He had apparently not seen the notice, for he headed toward a vacant table and everyone in the room looked up to see what would happen.

The headwaiter pounced on the couple, explained the situation to the girl in rifle-hot Japanese and the obviously well-bred girl turned away in an agony of embarrassment. The Marine wouldn't take this. Calmly he grabbed his beautiful girl by the hand and led her against her will to the table. The headwaiter was furious. He hissed instructions at the girl and he had the bad luck to use some words which the Marine understood, for the American let go the chair he was holding for the girl, hauled his fist back and launched a haymaker.

Another Marine anticipated this and deftly caught his friend's hand. Then he explained the new rule and joshed the troublemaker into leaving, but the first Marine now realized that General Webster and his party were in the room. He was aghast. Quickly he shooed the slim Japanese girl out the door and came over to our table and said briskly, 'I'm extremely sorry, sir. I thought they were kidding me.'

'It's all right,' the general laughed.

'I'm extremely sorry, Mrs Webster.'

She was most gracious and the general felt good. He said, 'Lieutenant Bailey, may I introduce Major Gruver. He joins your board next week.'

The Marine said, 'We've heard about you. Seven MIGs?'

I winked and he said, 'We could use you.' He bowed and left and the general said, 'Somehow or other you've got to respect the Marines. They're publicity hounds but they know what discipline means.'

Mrs Webster said, 'It's not that I dislike Japanese. Goodness, they're wonderful people. So clever and all that. Even in the short time I've been here they've shown me unusual courtesies. But a conquering army must retain its dignity.'

'I agree,' the general said, 'but those yokels in Washington say we've got to woo them now. Nancy, you ought to read the directives I get!'

'I approve one hundred per cent!' Mrs Webster insisted. 'Japan is now a free country. We must woo them to our side but we must also remember our position. And be firm.' Ignoring the fat major, she proceeded to eat her dinner with relish.

EILEEN WEBSTER: 'I could never consent to live
the barren life your mother did.'

On Friday Mrs Webster gave striking proof that she really did like the Japanese – if they kept their place. She and Eileen called for me about noon and drove me a short distance out into the country in the black Cadillac. Mrs Webster said, 'I have a real treat for you, Lloyd. We're going to Takarazuka.'
'Where?' I asked.
'Takarazuka,' she repeated slowly.
'What's that?'
'For one thing it's a village with a delightful zoo. But it's also something especially Japanese.'
'For instance?'
'You'll be amazed!'
In a few minutes we entered the Japanese village of Takarazuka. At the head of an extremely narrow lane we got out and walked into a kind of fairyland. For it was now mid-April and the path ahead of us was lined with cherry trees and I had never seen such trees before. The blossoms were extraordinarily profuse, a kind of grayish, sandy purple, rich and delicate. Laden branches dipped down over us and the blue sky of spring showed through. The walk was filled with people hurrying beneath the blossoms to some destination I couldn't see. There were women in kimonos, young girls in bobbysocks, old men in black, babies in bright clothes and half a dozen brilliantly beautiful girls in a kind of green dress that swirled about their ankles as they walked.
'Who are they?' I gasped.
'Those are the Takarazuka girls,' Mrs Webster explained.
'What's that mean?'
'The most famous collection of girls in Japan.'
'What do they do?'
'That's the big surprise.'
But I wasn't to find out for some time because she led us down the flowered lane past scores of little shops that sold mementoes of the village, past old trees that offered shade and past minute restaurants at whose doors women stood offering cheap food. We were in the heart of Japan and Mrs Webster was enjoying herself as much as any Japanese.
We had gone only a short distance when a thin young man in black joined us and bowed very low, drawing breath in through his teeth. 'Many, many pardons,' he said. 'I was waiting for you at the main office.' He took us to the zoo, where there were beautiful lakes and flower beds and charming benches on which you could sit beneath the cherry blossoms and watch children play.
The young man asked in good English, 'Are you the pilot who shot down seven MIGs?' He was impressed and said, 'I used to be a flier. Now I work here.'

'What is this place?' I asked in a low whisper.

'You don't know?'

'Never heard of it.'

Mrs Webster saw us talking and cried, 'Oh, Lloyd! Don't spoil the fun!'

'I hate mysteries,' I said.

'All right, we'll go.'

She and the thin young man took us out of the zoo and up to an enormous building which looked like an armory in Kansas City. It was a theater. We went to our special seats in the very first row and there we faced one of the largest stages in the world on which was enacted the most amazing performance I had ever seen.

I can't say I understood the play. It was called, the young man said, *Sarutobi Sasuke*, meaning *Little Monkey Sasuke*, and Sasuke is a boy's name. It dealt with some children who accidentally conjure up a wizard who helps them save a castle from the enemy. Who the enemy was or what the castle I never understood because at Takarazuka it wasn't the story that counted. It was the overwhelming effect of size.

The play started at one and ran till six. It had thirty-four different scenes, each the biggest and most lavish you could imagine. I never saw a Ziegfeld show, but Mrs Webster said that any Takarazuka scene outdid the best Ziegfeld ever put on. There was music, there was dancing, there were songs. In fact, there was everything. In this one show there were two gorillas, a jeep, two live pigs, a wizard, three different trios singing three different kinds of songs, a ballet, a football game, a live goat, a motion-picture sequence showing the wizard at work, a passage from an opera and a cave whose trees moved about. But most of all there were girls.

There were more than a hundred girls on stage, and they were all real dazzlers. I thought to myself, 'And you were the guy who said he'd never seen a good-looking Japanese girl! Wow!' But at the same time there was something ridiculous about this excess of beauty, for there were no men actors. The most striking girls played men's roles, and I whispered to Eileen, 'This show could use a few Clark Gables.'

Mrs Webster heard me and laughed. 'In Tokyo there's another theater which has no women. There men play all the parts.'

'Doesn't sound sensible,' I said.

'It's Japanese,' she explained.

I soon tired of the show—one enormous set after another and beautiful girls making believe they were men. I said I was willing to leave whenever the others had had enough. Eileen said, 'I'm ready,' and as we walked up the darkened aisle I began to appreciate the enormous size of this theater. It must have seated more than 3,000 people. I asked our guide, 'Is it always filled this way?' for there wasn't a vacant seat. He sucked his breath in proudly and said, 'Every day in the year. Twice on Saturday and Sunday.' I didn't tell him so, but I figured there must be something in a Takarazuka show no American could understand because I was bored by this one and so were Eileen and her mother. But the Japanese loved it. They sat on the edges of their seats, their round faces transfixed with intense pleasure.

We started to return to our car but the guide stopped us and said, 'The Supervisor has invited you to attend a special rehearsal of our next month's show.'

'Have you two companies?' Eileen asked, a bit bedazzled by the 115 girls she had just seen.

'We have four,' the guide said proudly. 'One plays here, one in Tokyo, one tours, and one is in rehearsal.'

He led us to a huge empty stage where some young girls in green skirts were walking through an intricate dance, while a man at the piano hammered out a tune that sounded like Schubert. In another empty room another man played a song that sounded like Gershwin for a trio of young girls, also in green skirts. 'They wear the Takarazuka costume,' the guide explained.

Then suddenly he came to attention and the girls at the piano stopped singing. Everyone looked at the door where an elderly man with a white beard stood for a moment, discovered Mrs Webster and hastened toward her, bowing very low and saying, 'Mrs General Webster! It is a superb honor.' He waved his hand deprecatingly and said, 'Rehearsal only.'

As he turned he disclosed behind him a most lovely slender actress in a plaid skirt, brown vest, and cocky green tam o'shanter set saucily over one eye. I did a sort of double take and whispered to Eileen, 'That's the girl who was with the Marine lieutenant.' Eileen studied her and said, 'Of course it is.'

The Supervisor saw us staring at the remarkable girl and said, 'Mrs General Webster and honored guests, may I present Fumiko-san, one of our finest actresses?' Although I am certain the girl recognized us, she did not betray that fact but stepped sedately forward and bowed low before Mrs Webster. When she reached me I held out my hand, but she started to bow again, whereupon I withdrew my hand and saw that she was looking up at me with immense gratitude for my not having recognized her in front of the Supervisor. Eileen saw this too and had the presence of mind to say, 'We did not see you on stage, did we?' The girl replied in a soft voice, 'I not play this week. I . . . Moon . . . Troupe.'

Hastily the guide explained, 'The four troupes each have a name. Moon, Star, Snow and Flower. You would say that Miss Fumiko is one of the best stars of the Moon Troupe.' I was about to say that I had already seen Miss Fumiko when a distinct glance from her begged me to remain silent.

With extraordinary grace Miss Fumiko walked over to a piano, but I didn't hear her sing, for just as she began we left for the flower path leading back to our Cadillac. As we walked beneath the swaying cherry blossoms I noticed that each of the shops we had seen earlier had on display large glossy photographs of the principal Takarazuka actresses. As we passed slowly along, the pictures of the beautiful girls, half of them dressed as men, had a mesmerizing effect, but while I was studying them Eileen discovered one of the real phenomena of Japan. 'Oh, look!' she cried.

The play *Sarutobi Sasuke* had ended and from the dressing-room doors the Takarazuka girls were entering the flower walk. The youngest were dressed in formal green skirts and about them pressed an adoring crush of people trying to touch them, trying to lay hands on the green skirts or press a letter or a gift upon the actresses. When a particularly famous girl appeared the crowd would utter a little cry and fall back and the actress would move on in a kind of courtly grandeur.

The Takarazuka girls passed along the flower walk, their green skirts swaying softly beneath the cherry blossoms and I could hear a sigh go up from the crowd as the girls turned the corner, entered upon a bridge and crossed the river to the other side, where I was told they lived like nuns in a secluded dormitory. When they were gone the crowd at the dressing-room doors looked about idly as if now there was nothing to do, and for the first time I realized that every person in the milling mob was a young girl. There were no Stage-door Johnnies. They were all Stage-door Jills.

Mrs Webster said, 'The young girls of Japan idolize these actresses.'

Eileen said, 'No wonder! The actresses are so beautiful.'

'And the girls outside are so ugly,' Mrs Webster said. 'Have you ever seen so many round, red faces? Such dumpy little creatures?'

'I don't know,' Eileen said. 'America has its share. When I was thirteen I would stare in the mirror and pray God that I might grow up to look like Myrna Loy.'

'Ah, but you were never a square-beamed little urchin! Lloyd, this child was always beautiful.' Then she played her trump card. 'I'm having dinner with the Supervisor–that sweet old man with the beard. He's very important. You two drive along home.'

And she looked at me with that perfectly frank stare as if to say, 'You're twenty-eight, Lloyd. You should have married Eileen four years ago. Grow up.' And she was, as always, 100 per cent right. Even though she herself had prevented the marriage that first year–she hadn't been aware of the fact–and even though I could use the Korean war as an added excuse, I had never been able to explain to myself honestly why Eileen and I were not married. We had fallen completely in love, she had risked a lot of public trouble by riding a bus down to a remote Texas air base for a crazy week with me, but we both knew that whenever the big moment of actually getting married approached, I shied away. With jet airplanes I was comfortable. With women I wasn't. I guess that watching Mrs Webster and my mother had made me gun-shy.

One night I heard one of our medical doctors talking in a bar. He'd been a big shot in civilian life and he was saying, 'We find that if a man comes from a broken home he's apt not to marry early. It's as if he had to be introduced to love. If he doesn't meet love in his own family he could, conceivably, go through an entire life without ever meeting it. Of course,' he had added, 'at any time almost any girl could provide the introduction if she wanted to take the trouble. But spoiled men who don't marry before they're forty–the men who have never been introduced to love–are hardly worth any girl's trouble. So we can say that some men actually do pass through an entire lifetime without ever meeting so simple a thing as love. No one bothered to introduce them.' I often recalled the doctor's words but I was satisfied I wasn't like that, not in all respects. True, my parents had failed to introduce me either to their own love or to the idea of having a home with some girl's love as the central pillar. I think that explains why I was twenty-eight and vaguely in love with Eileen and unmarried. And I think Mrs Webster knew it and now she was pushing us together.

'I'll see you in the hotel,' she cried and left us, towering a good four inches over the little Japanese man who was leading her back to the Supervisor.

I had been hoping for a chance to talk with Eileen alone and as soon as Mrs Webster left I pulled her into a corner of the Cadillac and gave her a big kiss. She said, 'All the way out on the plane I dreamed of meeting you in a romantic spot like this.' She pointed out of the car to where we were passing little rice fields pressed close to the road and tiny houses set back among the trees. There was a sweet heaviness of spring in the air and as we watched the little workmen of Japan trudging along the footpaths at dusk we felt very much a part of this strange country.

Eileen whispered, 'I didn't want to leave America. The idea of . . .' she hesitated, then added, 'getting married in a foreign land didn't appeal. But now . . .'

I pretended not to have heard her remark about marriage and said, 'I was proud of you today.'

'About what?'

'That girl.'

'The actress?'

'Yes. You knew she was the one your father threw out of the dining room. But you didn't embarrass her.'

'Why should I? She came to the Club as a guest and she seemed a very pleasant girl.'

'But your mother . . .'

'Mother's all right. She just has to feel that she's running everything.'

I asked, 'Would she be frightfully sore if we didn't show up at the Club dinner?'

'She knows we're courting.'

'What a quaint word for a Vassar girl!'

'I'm not always a Vassar girl. Don't let the tag fool you. Pardner, I been a-livin' in Tulsa, where folks go a-courtin'.'

'Let's court.'

'What had you in mind?'

'A Japanese night club.'

She thought a moment, then smiled and said, 'Let's court!'

The driver reluctantly dropped us at a corner and even more reluctantly indicated how we could go halfway up an alley and find the Fuji Nights, which turned out to be a tiny room specializing in beer and fried fish. A geisha girl, her face white with cornstarch, came and sat with us and showed us how to order. Soon four other white-faced geishas came up to admire Eileen's blonde hair. One who could speak English placed a strand of Eileen's against her own jet black hair and sighed, 'How beautifur!'

Eileen said, 'Isn't it fascinating, the way they can't say *l*.'

I asked the geisha, 'How do you say *lovely lady?*'

She laughed and said, 'You tease.'

'Please!' I begged.

She put her slim fingers under Eileen's chin and said, 'You have one ruvrey radie.'

Eileen clapped her hands and said, 'Your kimono is lovely too.' The girls talked for a while and then the radio was turned on and we danced. The geisha who could speak English said to Eileen, 'May I dance with your officer? Very important we know American dancing.' Eileen said, 'Sure,' and for the first time in my life I danced with a foreign girl.

It was pretty dull. The geisha had something sticky on her hair and so much cloth about her middle that I couldn't hold onto her anywhere. She had apparently run into this problem before, for she took my hand and slipped it securely under a particularly huge bundle of cloth and in that way we danced. I asked her why geishas wore so many clothes and she said shyly, 'I not real geisha. I only après-guerre geisha.' I thought she had used a Japanese phrase and asked her what it meant. 'Après-guerre,' she said. 'Maybe French. After-the-war geisha.' I still didn't catch on and asked if that were some special kind. In real embarrassment she looked away and said, 'In here we only make-believe geisha. (She pronounced it *onry make-berieve*.) To be real geisha need many year study. Many kimonos. We poor girls. We buy one kimono, make believe for Americans. We got to make money.'

When she led me back to the table two of the other make-believe geishas started talking in a real jabber and finally one of them ran to the back. It was amusing to see her move, for such girls walk extremely pin-toed, which gives them a peculiar sing-song motion. In a moment she appeared with a Japanese newspaper and there, about the size of an American penny, was my picture. This excited the five geishas and they made me stand up so they could inspect my uniform. One held up seven fingers and I nodded, whereupon the girls gasped and the first geisha said to Eileen, 'You must be very proud.'

'I am,' Eileen said, and later that night, as we drove home she kissed me warmly and whispered, 'I like courtin' with you.'

I remember that I thought to myself: 'This is it, squarehead. Either you get this woman problem settled now or quit for good.' So I took the plunge and said, 'Where I come from, Podner, courtin' means marryin'. When?'

Eileen smiled gently, as if something very right had happened, and said, 'I want to get married .. if . . .'

I had dived in and the water wasn't as frightening as I had expected so I struck out and said something pretty polished for me, 'I've been flying where seconds mean hours of ordinary time. I don't want to wait a single day.'

She laughed nervously and said, 'Can't a girl be jittery over her first proposal?'

I was eager to play the determined lover–I was beginning to like the role–and said, 'You've known all along I could live with no wife but you.'

It was then that I first saw she actually was perplexed. She was honestly in doubt. She fumbled a moment and said, 'It's difficult for me to explain, but several times here in Japan I've wondered whether you would ever make a better husband than your father.'

'What do you mean?' I gasped.

'You know. Everybody knows your father lives for one thing. The Army.'

'Is that bad?'

She ignored my question and said, 'I've had a weak and terrible feeling, Lloyd, that the day would come when you would think of me as your father thinks of your mother.'

Suddenly the water I had dived into was bitter cold and I asked, 'You think there's something wrong with my father?'

'Frankly, I do,' she replied. 'The way he's content to leave your mother walled up within a circle of a few close friends, there in Lancaster, while he plunges off to the wars. That isn't good enough for me.'

I said, 'We'd better get our feet on the ground and get some things organized.'

She accepted my suggestion. She opened the car door and stepped into the street. 'Good idea,' she said.

We dismissed the chauffeur and wandered aimlessly along the streets of Kobe until we reached the waterfront where the great Inland Sea of Japan has from the most ancient times provided an anchorage for roving ships and their rich cargoes. Eileen studied one of the dark vessels and said, 'I came to Japan because I wanted our marriage to start right. I'm younger than you are, Lloyd, but I'm just as smart. And I think I'm just as brave. I want to be with you . . . in all kinds of weather.'

'I don't get what you're talking about,' I pleaded.

'About us. No, I'll be honest. About you.'

'What's about me?'

'I've never told you this, Lloyd, but nine months ago I visited your mother. I was driving through Pennsylvania and stopped off. I was appalled at the loneliness in which she lives . . . in which she's always lived.'

I felt weak. I knew what Eileen was saying was true but nevertheless I protested. 'Mother wants to live that way.'

'Nonsense! No woman wants to live any way but body and soul with the man she loves. Your mother may be a fine sport about the way she has to live, since she has no other choice . . . Lloyd, tell me this. That time I followed you down to the air base in West Texas . . . Why were you so scared?'

'I was worried about you.'

'What about me?'

'Well . . .'

'You mean . . . my reputation?'

'Well, yes.'

'Rubbish, Lloyd! The reason you were scared stiff was that you discovered you had on your hands a girl who would insist upon sharing your full life. Well, you were right. You could never tuck me away in a corner of Lancaster.'

I felt blood rising into my throat and said dizzily, 'I think I'd better take you back to the hotel.'

There was an ugly moment of silence–which I now know I should have broken with a rousing kiss–and when I did nothing Eileen said dully, 'I guess you're right. Which way is the officers' club?' We walked in gloomy silence for a few minutes. Then she said, 'Lloyd, dear. Don't get little-boy sorehead about this. It's of absolutely fundamental importance. Please think about it.'

'About what?' I shouted.

'Don't lose your temper. About the fact that half a marriage isn't good enough for either you or me. I've got to have a man who loves me with his whole heart. Go ahead and become the greatest general in Air Force history. But love me too.'

'Damn it, I do love you,' I protested as the lights of the hotel appeared around the corner.

'Sure you do, in a cold, partial little way. Let's think about this for a few days.'

Suddenly I was fighting to get married and I said, 'I thought you came to Japan for a wedding.'

'I did, but I've got to marry a complete man. Not just the shreds that are left over after he's led the important part of his life somewhere else.'

I was infuriated, not because of what she had said, but because she had seen so clearly the kind of man my father and mother had made me. Rationally my father had decided it would be good for him to marry a general's daughter who had a ready-made family life in Lancaster. She wouldn't be an encumbrance and she might prove to be a help. Now I was reasoning the same way. Marry Eileen because she was from a military family and would understand Air Force ropes without a lot of civilian argument. She was beautiful and, as she had proved tonight, plenty smart and courageous. She would be a catch for any man and I wanted her, but she was right when she said that I did not come to her with a whole heart. I knew what she was talking about, for I knew that I had never loved her in the absorbing way that sawed-off Joe Kelly loved his Japanese girl.

But this was the big point: I wanted to learn. In my heart I knew that my parents' way wasn't good enough and I wanted Eileen to help me find something better.

So I took her in my arms and gave her what we called 'The Unconditional Surrender,' a kiss so long she had to beat on my arms for air. When I put her down she laughed that wonderful golden grin of hers and said softly, 'For the first time I have the feeling we'll work this thing out.' Then she kissed me in the ear and whispered, 'You act a lot better than you talk.' And I do believe everything would have turned out all right if it hadn't been for what happened the very next morning.

THE BIG GIRL: 'It's no fun to be a Stateside reject watching cute Japanese girls getting all the American men.'

Before I got out of bed Private Joe Kelly called me and said, 'Well, Ace, this is Saturday!'

'What about it?' I asked drowsily.

'Ace, I'm gettin' married!'

I couldn't focus for a minute. Then I said, 'Well, congratulations.'

'Ace,' the little gangster shouted. 'Don't you remember? You're gonna be my best man.'

I started to say, 'Gee, Kelly, I have an appointment . . .' but he was on my team. Wreck that he was, he belonged to my squadron. So I said. 'I'll break the appointment, Kelly. Where's the big event take place?'

I walked down to the grubby building in which our consul had his offices and was amazed to find four G.I.-Japanese couples waiting to be married. Any man under such circumstances instinctively looks at the girls to see if there are any he would take for his wife, and believe me there was none I would care for. Katsumi, Joe's girl, looked exactly like her picture: big round face, high cheeks, thick black hair and small eyes. When she smiled during the introductions I saw that like most Japanese girls she had in front a big gold tooth.

'We're gettin' that changed,' Joe said with some embarrassment.

Katsumi was uncertain whether she should offer to shake my hand or not, so when I extended mine she collapsed in agonizing giggles and popped her left fist over her mouth. Her knuckles were bright red from chapping, and as I studied these girls I wondered why it was that our G.I.'s—even though we'd been ordered not to use that word, it crept in—always seemed to marry the ugliest girls and never the pretty ones we saw at Takarazuka.

It was a dismal morning. Since Joe's marriage was third in line I watched with mounting disgust the spectacle of American soldiers marrying whatever girls they had been able to pick up. I was ashamed at having been drawn into this sordid spectacle and was looking down at my fingernails when a bright voice called, 'Are you Major Ace Gruver?' I looked up and breathed relief, for it was an American girl. She was oversize, but I was glad to know there were some American girls still alive.

She whispered, 'I'm a secretary here.'

'Interesting job, I bet.'

She shook her head. 'One marriage after another.'

'Don't they know they can't take the girls home?'

'Sure they know. But what I wanted to see you about is that I have a kid brother who is crazy about airplanes. He told me if I ever meet a real jet pilot, to get his ottograft. I want your ottograft!'

She led me into her inner office where she gave me a sheet of paper to sign then added another. 'Maybe the kid'll be able to sell this one at a fancy price–like a baseball glove.'

'What I don't get,' I said, 'is why the Government allows these marriages in the first place.'

'The Government is smart. Public pressure back home insists the men be permitted to marry, so the Government does permit it, then washes its hands of the whole affair.' She showed me a form which each G.I. had to sign, on top of all the others, and it was about the frankest and most brutal I had ever seen. Kelly, for example, acknowledged that he was outside the law, waived his legal rights, said he would look after the girl on his own account and stated in writing that the Air Force was in no way responsible for his wife. At the bottom he swore that he was in right mind and that he had signed before witnesses.

'But these guys go right on?'

'Day after day.'

'Why?'

'That's not a fair question to ask me,' she said somewhat sharply.

'You work here.'

'All right!' she said. 'Would you call me pretty? No, nobody would call me pretty. I'm a plain Jane who couldn't get married in America so I came out here where there were plenty of men.' She laughed at herself in a delightful, horsy sort of way and said bitterly, 'They stamp us "Stateside rejects"! Sure, there were lots of men when I got here. But the damned Japanese girls had them all.'

'I still don't get it.'

'Like a soldier told me,' she explained. 'He kept saying, "You American girls wouldn't understand."'

'Understand what?' I asked.

'The men all say these Japanese girls do something for them.'

'Like sex?'

'Not sex. I'm not bitter any more so I don't charge it up to sex. Didn't you notice?'

She showed me a wedding ring and said, 'The man I finally got had been in love with a Japanese girl for two years. Said frankly he knew I'd never be half the wife she would have been.'

'Then why did he marry you?'

'Said I'd fit in better in Denver.'

She went to her purse and pulled out a wrinkled photograph. 'My rival!' she said in obvious amazement. Before looking at the picture I could guess that the girl probably looked a lot like Katsumi. Red face, round features. The American secretary stared at the picture and said, 'To me she looks absolutely ugly. I stole this picture when my husband burned the others. I keep it as a reminder that I must be a good wife.'

'Where's the girl now?'

'She committed suicide.' She placed the damaged photograph back among her junk and assured me, 'It all happened before I met Gus. I had nothing to do with the suicide.'

The door opened and the consul hurried through. 'We'll be ready for the next one in a couple of minutes,' he said. 'You the witness, Major? Go on in.'

The girl led me into the office from which he had come. It was bleak with a writing table, a Bible, a portrait of President Truman and a coat rack. 'This is where the foul deed takes place.' She laughed. 'I'm always one of the witnesses and it's beginning to tear me apart because every G.I. who comes into this room has the same look in his face that my husband gets when he speaks of his Japanese girl.' She hammered the table and cried, 'Damn them all! They all have the same secret.'

'What?'

'They make their men feel important. I try to build my husband up–as a wife should. But with me it's a game. With these ugly little round-faced girls it isn't a game. It's life.'

The door opened and Katsumi came in, followed by Joe Kelly. They expected to see the consul ready to marry them and Joe shrugged his shoulders at me and asked, 'They figure out some new way to louse me up?'

The secretary asked, 'How long they been messing around with you, soldier?'

'Please, lady! Not soldier! Air Force.'

The secretary said, 'If the body's warm it's a soldier.'

The consul came in and started arranging papers. He was a young man with balding hair, a strained look and very big feet. His hands were awkward with the papers and he was irritated when he saw Katsumi. 'You must wait outside,' he said sharply.

Obediently, Katsumi left. Joe started after her but the consul told him to stay, so Joe said to me, 'Ace, don't leave her alone at a time like this.'

I went and sat with the little girl while we heard Joe shout at the consul, 'Yes, damn it all, I've read the papers. Yes, I understand I'm forfeitin' all rights. Yes. Yes. Let's get the thing movin'.'

'I'm only asking you as the law demands,' the consul said.

'And I'm only tellin' you that Congressman Shimmark told me I could go ahead and get married.'

I hadn't known it before, but apparently State Department men are just as scared of Congressmen as generals are, because right away the door opened and the consul said brusquely, 'Come in, Miss.'

He lined the couple up before the desk, had them sign still some more papers, then conducted a brief ceremony. He was mad at Pvt. Kelly, dismayed by Katsumi and fed up with the whole affair. It was an ugly ceremony performed with grudging spirit and I was ashamed at having been witness to it.

But as I looked up from my embarrassment, I happened to see Kelly's face as he bent down to kiss Katsumi and in that instant the ugliness in the room vanished and I had to bite my lip. The horsy American secretary wrote something in a book and wiped her eyes, while the consul said to Kelly, 'You understand that you have surrendered numerous rights in this matter?'

Kelly couldn't take any more. He looked at the consul and his nose twitched. 'You son . . .' he began and I knew that the consul was about to get the full Kelly treatment, which is about as profane as anyone can get. But Katsumi, already the wife, quietly took her husband's hand and said, 'We go now, Joe.'

Joe collapsed like a ruptured balloon. He looked at me and said, 'It's hell to be married. Take it from me, Ace.' Then he asked, 'Ain't you gonna kiss the bride?'

I was unprepared for this and must have betrayed some shock for I could see

Joe cringe with bitter humiliation when he realized that I had absolutely no desire to kiss that big mouth with the bright gold tooth. I, in turn, wanted to drop through the floor for having insulted a member of my own squadron at such a time. Mine was the last in a long line of insults administered by his nation, his commanding officers, his consul and even his religion. In my defense it had never occurred to me that anyone would actually want to kiss a yellow-skinned Japanese girl. You fought the Japs on Guadalcanal. You organized their country for them in Kobe. You defended them in Korea. But it had never crossed my mind that you kissed them.

I took Katsumi's big face in my hands and said, 'The secretary told me Japanese girls make wonderful wives. You be a good wife to Joe.' Then I kissed her. It was repugnant, but at the same time I felt that I had in some trivial way helped one of my men marry the girl he loved.

'Good luck, kids,' I said.

'Thanks, Ace,' Joe replied.

When they left the consul said, 'Such marriages are dreadful mistakes. We do our best to prevent them.'

'Do you succeed–very often?'

'You'd be surprised. We make the paper work so cumbersome a good many of the young hotheads lose steam. Actually we've helped forestall some inevitable tragedies.'

'You didn't have much success with Joe.'

'We see everything here. Fights, tears. But if a boy's had the gumption to write his Congressman we know he's determined to go ahead. Now all Joe has to do is get his Congressman to pass a special bill and he'll get Mrs Joe into the States. Frankly, between you and me, I hope he succeeds. But it's my job to paint a gloomy picture.'

The secretary stepped out of the room to call the next couple and the consul whispered, 'Take that girl you just saw, my secretary. She's married to a G.I. with whom I had some luck. He was going to marry an extremely ordinary Japanese girl, but our paper work and delays brought him to his senses.'

''What did you say to him?' I asked.

'As I remember, he was from Denver and I simply asked, "If you take this girl back to Denver will she fit in?"'

'What happened to the girl?'

'You saw her. She works here. My secretary.'

'I meant–what happened to the Japanese girl?' I wanted to hear his explanation.

Before he could reply the secretary brought the fourth couple into the office and the consul droned, 'You understand what you've signed?'

The young man, a sailor, stood on one foot then the other and replied with studied patience, 'Yes, sir. Yes, sir.'

The girl was just as ugly as Katsumi and I started to leave, but the consul called me back and said to the sailor, 'How would you like to have Ace Gruver be your witness?'

'You Ace Gruver?' the boy asked.

'That's right.'

'I'd be proud,' the boy said. He turned to his girl and spoke to her in rapid Japanese, using his hands to indicate airplanes in combat. The girl looked at me, giggled furiously and clapped her hand over her gold-crowned teeth.

It was this same well-meaning consul who got me into my big trouble, for when he turned in his weekly report on G.I. marriages to General Webster he must have mentioned his surprise at seeing me as Joe's witness. At any rate the general called me into his office and stormed, 'I'm astounded that you should lend yourself to such a thing–especially since you know Mrs Webster's and my objection to fraternization.'

'This wasn't fraternization, sir. It was marriage,' I said.

'To a Japanese,' he stormed, spitting the words out.

'The kid's from my outfit in Korea, sir.'

'All the more reason you should have tried to save him from such folly.'

'I did try, sir.'

'Carstairs tells me you even kissed the girl!'

'I did. He asked me to.'

'Who, Carstairs?'

'No, Kelly.'

The general was outraged. He banged out of his chair and stood looking at a map. Finally he exploded. 'I'm damned if I can understand how a man like you, brought up in the best traditions of the service, can outrage military propriety in this way. Such marriages are sordid, disgraceful things. We have to tolerate them because Washington says so, but we don't have to polish our buttons and go down to kiss the bride!'

'I . . .'

'Nauseating. The whole thing's nauseating, but it's especially sickening to have a member of your own staff–you might say your own immediate family . . .'

The bawling out I got from the general was nothing compared to the one I took from his wife. She was sweet as butter during dinner but after the general and Eileen had left on prearranged signals she said bluntly, 'Do I understand, Lloyd, that you actually encouraged a Japanese marriage this morning?'

'One of the men from my outfit.'

'But you surely didn't attend–not officially?'

'He asked me to help him out.'

'And you went to the consulate, before other Japanese who might know you . . .'

'Look, Mrs Webster, it was a guy from our outfit.'

'It wasn't just a guy, Lloyd. It was humiliation to the service and a direct slap in General Webster's face.'

'I didn't approve of it, Mrs Webster. I argued against it for days.'

'But your very presence signified approval. In this dining room right now half the officers are laughing at me.'

So that was it. She wasn't really concerned about the welfare of the service nor the standing of her husband. She was angry that something which she had started–non-fraternization–should have backfired and brought ridicule upon her. She was especially angry that the instrument of this ridicule should have been, in General Webster's words, a member of her own family.

I asked, 'How could I have refused to attend the wedding . . .'

'Don't call it a wedding! It was a mean little surreptitious ceremony on the most sordid level. It was permitted only because some lily-livered idiots in Washington have no courage to face facts.'

'I agree with you, Mrs Webster.'

She didn't want agreement. She wanted to knock me into shape, once and for all. When I saw her closing in on me, trying to make me apologize for what I had done in good faith, I sensed pretty clearly that she saw herself fighting her daughter's marriage battle. Years before she had taken on young Mark Webster in just such a fight and she had been victorious and the entire Army knew she had won and from that time forth she had molded and marched Mark Webster into a one-star generalship that he could never have attained by himself. Now she was going to teach her daughter how to march me into four or five stars.

She frowned and said, 'If you expect to make a name for yourself in service, Lloyd, you can't offend the proprieties. You can't insult generals.'

I got mad and said, 'I've made a pretty good name for myself so far. Shooting down MIGs, not worrying about social life.'

She gasped and put her hand to her mouth as if she had been slapped. With profound rage she cried, 'You're an insolent little upstart.' Immediately she was ashamed of herself and tried to recover by saying something halfway sensible but fury was upon her and she stormed ahead, 'You're like your insufferable father.' I knew that Mark Webster was afraid of my father–he was deathly afraid of anyone who had more stars than he–and I was surprised that Mrs Webster should have launched an assault on someone who might be in a position to affect her husband's career, but she was trembling mad and didn't care what she said. She added, 'You ought to be careful you don't grow up to be a second Harry Gruver.'

She sounded exactly like her daughter and I recalled with a sense of shock that almost every time I had seen Eileen's picture in the society columns of towns where she had lived, she was invariably with her mother. They were like sisters, shoulder to shoulder against the world.

My father had commented on this once and had said he knew there were two kinds of Army marriages, his where the wife stayed home and Mark Webster's where the wife tagged along. He told me he would honestly have preferred the latter, but he observed that it usually did hard things to the wife. 'She's always on the move and her children are always on the move. So the women folk band together in tough little cliques. I can honestly say I never feared the Japanese or the Germans but I do fear such cliques of Army women.'

I heard Mrs Webster saying bitterly, 'I should think Eileen would be ashamed and disgusted.'

I didn't say anything. I didn't even say that I was sure she would see to it that Eileen became disgusted. Instead I looked at her very carefully and when I saw her clean, handsome, hard face with not a wrinkle out of place I thought of Joe Kelly's Japanese girl whom I had kissed that morning, and all at once I caught a glimmering of what the American secretary must have meant when she said, 'These damned Japanese girls have a secret.' I had an intimation of their secret: they loved somebody–just simply loved him. They weren't going to make him a four-star general or they weren't going to humiliate him over some trivial affair for which he had already apologized. They just got hold of a man and they loved him.

I had now seen two American marriages at close hand: my parents' where people got along together in a respectful truce, and the Websters' where there was an early surrender followed by a peace treaty without vengeance. But I had never witnessed a marriage where two people loved each other on an equal basis where the man ran his job on the outside and the woman ran her job at home and where these responsibilities were not permitted to interfere with the fundamental love that existed when such things as outside jobs and inside housekeeping were forgotten.

Mrs Webster said acidly, 'Eileen asked me to tell you she'd be at the hairdresser's.'

I thanked her, held her chair as she rose and showed her to the elevator. I think she knew that she had presented a dismal picture during our talk, for she said, 'I do hope you won't embarrass the general again.' I promised her that I wouldn't irritate the general and refrained from pointing out that we had been talking about something quite different: my irritating her.

I went down to a lower floor of the hotel where there was a hairdresser for the American girls who worked with our Army in Japan, and there I saw Eileen coming out more brilliant and lovely than I had ever seen her before. She had what *Life* magazine once called the well-scrubbed look and was absolutely adorable with the fresh bright charm that only American girls ever seem to have. I was disgusted with myself for having quarreled with her the night before and suggested that we sit in a corner of the elegant lounge, where a Japanese boy in bright blue bar-boy's uniform served us drinks.

I said, 'If you looked so adoráble all the time no one would ever be able to fight with you.'

'We weren't fighting last night,' she teased.

'I'm glad,' I said, 'because I've got to keep in the good graces of at least one of the Websters.'

She frowned and asked, 'Mum give you a bad time at lunch?'

'Very bad,' I said.

'Mother's a special case, Lloyd. The Army's her whole life. She watches over Father like a mother hen and she's been very good for him. Therefore he's got to trust her and if she says she doesn't like to see American officers with Japanese girls . . . Frankly, I don't think Father approves of all the orders he's had to issue because traditionally the Army is pretty adult about men and women getting together–any women. But he's learned that in the long run Mother is usually right.'

'Is she?'

'Yes.'

'Now it's my turn to be scared.'

'What do you mean?'

'You're afraid I'll be like my father. I'm really scared you'll be like your mother.'

'What's so bad with that?' she asked.

'I can't stand being pushed around.'

Eileen lifted her glass and made circles on the marble table. She said slowly, 'I don't think I'd be bossy the way Mother is because you're much stronger than Father ever was. But mostly I wouldn't hurt you because I love you so much.'

That was what I wanted to hear and I said, 'I'm twenty-eight now and I've been going around with too many airplanes. What I want now is a wife and family.' She sneaked in a kiss and I said, 'Whenever I've thought about a family it's with someone like you–a girl with an Army background like my own . . .'

She became gently irritated and protested, 'That's just what I mean. Why do you say, "a girl like me"? I'm not a type. I'm me. Damn it all, Lloyd, haven't you ever wanted to just grab me and haul me away to a shack somewhere?'

Now it was my turn to get on edge and I said, 'When you're an officer you meet endless problems of enlisted men who just grabbed something and hauled it away. It doesn't appeal to me.'

She said, 'Lloyd, a man has to surrender himself sometimes. You're not so important you have to defend yourself like a fort.'

From the manner in which Eileen spoke I could tell that she was just as tense as I was and it occurred to me that if I married Eileen we would always be a little bit afraid of each other, a little bit on edge always to be ahead of the other person. Mrs Webster, frankly, had scared the devil out of me and now I could see the same marital tendencies in her daughter. I could see her organizing my life for me solely on the grounds that she loved me, but the definition of what was love would always be her definition; and I thought of Joe Kelly and the girl he had found. Their fight was with the outside world—the Army and State Department and General Webster—but with themselves they were at peace.

Now Eileen had me scared exactly the way her mother had a little while before. I've learned to admit it when I'm scared because it takes courage to know when you ought to be afraid. I remember when I was fighting three Russians up at the Yalu. I didn't see my wingman get shot down, but all of a sudden I thought the world had gotten awful quiet and I got scared as the devil. I started to run like hell and just as the MIGs were closing in for the kill four of our planes turned up in the distance. I didn't care how bad I looked because I was scared. Point is, if I hadn't been frightened silly I wouldn't have started running and my four rescuers would never have reached me in time.

I said, 'What you said last night turned up a lot of new ideas.'

'You make it sound very unpleasant.'

'Didn't you intend it that way? Your mother sure intends it when she gives a man hell.'

She got out of her chair and said, 'I don't think you want to take me to the dance tonight.'

I didn't want to answer this so I said, 'Some of the things you said last night made sense. We ought to think things out.'

'That's fine with me. I suppose you want to do your thinking—tonight—alone?'

I said, 'O.K. by me,' and she started walking across the lounge. It was late in the afternoon and the place was empty, so I ran after her and said, 'Eileen, what are we fighting about?'

And she replied, 'The next fifty years,' and she looked so cold and so much like her mother that I turned and walked away and caught a ride out to Itami air field, where I astonished everybody by reporting for duty two days early.

MIKE BAILEY: 'As a Marine I have certain theories which explain everything.'

You could say that Itami is right in the heart of Japan, for it stands in the triangle formed by the three great cities of the south: Kobe, Osaka and Kyoto. Actually the three are one big city, for you can travel all the way from Kobe to Osaka without ever being in the country but for some reason they've been kept apart: Osaka criss-crossed with hundreds of canals, Kobe with its big docks, and Kyoto with endless museums and temples. From Itami you can get to any of these places in a few minutes, so that a man stationed there has right at his elbow all aspects of Japanese life, if he were interested.

As soon as I got to Itami that Saturday night I felt better. I was home. Planes, neat air strips, men I knew. My work there was a dead cinch. General Webster had arranged it as a kind of present to his daughter, so I could be with her. The board I was on met a couple of times a week but the three senior members did all the work and had a bunch of us pilots in from Korea for consultation, if needed.

One of these was Lt. Bailey, the Marine who had brought the Japanese actress into the Kobe Officers Club that day. He was a real hot-shot jet man, and since we agreed on most problems the older officers were quite satisfied if we missed meetings because they never liked what we had to say. So Mike Bailey and I really had things squared away and at the end of the first week he said, 'We ought to see something of Japan. I finagled it so you can move into the Marine hotel. Proved it was necessary for our consultations. And I promoted a Chevrolet.' He loaded my gear into it and we set out for his quarters.

'We live six miles from the air base.' he explained. 'Extra advantage is that we're not hooked into the Itami phones. They don't bother us much, Son, I got us really fixed up.'

He drove so fast that it seemed only a couple of minutes before we came to an interesting town with narrow streets and hundreds of people wandering about. We inched our way down an alley and up a small hill to a big rambling four-story hotel.

'Marine Barracks,' he said proudly. 'Look at that Jap kid come to attention.' A bellhop tossed Mike a snappy salute and whispered, 'Seven o'clock, Makino's.' Mike gave the kid 100 yen and said to me, 'Finest people in the world, the Japanese.'

I said, 'I thought you told me you fought them at Tarawa.'

'Who bears a grudge?' He told the boy to show me the room vacated by the Air Force major who had preceded me on the Board and when I got there I found I had an excellent view of the town. Below me was a wide and rocky river which cut the place in half. Up our side of the river came a railroad from Osaka but right below us it cut across to the other side and stopped at the edge of a beautiful park. There were some very large buildings facing me and, as I watched, huge crowds of people left them and started hiking toward the train.

But as I studied these people pressing toward the station I saw another crowd gathering at the rear of the buildings and into this crowd plunged a dozen young girls, arm in arm, each wearing a long green skirt that swished about her ankles.

'Hey, Bailey!' I cried. 'What's this town called?'

'Takarazuka,' he yelled.

'These girls in green . . .'

Mike rushed into my room and looked across the river. He grabbed me by the arm and shouted, 'My God! We're missing the show.'

He shoved me out the door and down the steps onto a narrow street along which we hurried to a large and handsome stone bridge bearing the sign in England, MUKO RIVER. CARE PEDESTRIANS. With a long finger Mike pointed across the bridge and said with drooling relish, 'Here they come, the pedestrians.'

Then I saw them, the Takarazuka girls coming home to their dormitory after the day's performance. First came the beginning students whose job it was to crowd the back of the stage in big numbers. They were the fifteen- and sixteen-year-olds, and they walked proudly in their long green skirts and cork zori. Already they considered themselves to be Takarazuka girls. Baily nudged me as they passed and asked, 'Ever see more beautiful kids in your life?'

I had already seen these dazzling children at the rehearsal and I knew they were beautiful but as I watched them disappear into the evening twilight they seemed to drift away from me with extraordinary grace. They walked in a curious way, one foot set carefully before the other so that their long green skirts swayed noiselessly above the dusty streets. They had now passed so far from me that they were becoming haunting ghosts when Mike nudged me and said, 'Watch this one! Imagine General Webster tossing her out of the Officers Club that day.'

I looked across the bridge and there came the exquisite girl I had met during my visit to Takarazuka. She was accompanied by two other actresses and they formed such a gracious trio that townspeople who were attending the procession drew back against the sides of the bridge to watch them go by. As they approached us, Mike's girl kept her dark eyes straight ahead.

I asked Bailey, 'Aren't you going to say hello?'

'In public?' he cried. 'A Takarazuka girl! You must be nuts.'

The three girls were now abreast of us and Bailey's girl, without actually turning her head, gave him ever so slight a nod, which Bailey pretended not to have seen. Then, like green shadows over some field at the end of day, the girls passed down the narrow street.

Now came a lively burst of fifteen or more, all chattering happily among themselves, all making believe they were unaware of the crowds who watched them. They were young, they were pretty, they were graceful. They wore little makeup, spoke in soft voices and kept their eyes straight ahead when the American Marines on the bridge stared at them. They were true Takarazuka girls, probably the most curious and lovely group of women in the world, and as I watched them pass in the strangely warm April twilight I was captivated by the poetic swaying of their long green skirts and the lithe, hidden movements of their beautiful bodies as they passed into darkness.

At last the principal actresses appeared, the ones famous throughout Japan, tall, stately girls whose distinguished and memorable faces advertised all kinds of products in the magazines. They moved with special authority and were besieged by mobs of young girls seeking autographs. Among these actresses I noticed several who took men's roles on stage and who now dressed like men in public. That is, they wore slacks and sweaters and berets, yet in doing so they managed to look enticingly feminine. They were subjected to special crowding and sometimes grown women would press in upon them demanding a signature across the face of a photograph purchased that day.

The formal procession of the Takarazuka goddesses was ended, but on the far end of the bridge appeared one last girl in a soft white stole, gray kimono and rippling green skirt. She had been delayed and was hurrying to overtake her friends. Her green zori tapped out a gentle rhythm as she hastened pin-toed toward us, her body leaning forward in unstated urgency. Her face was flushed and extraordinarily beautiful. She seemed more like a country girl than the others, less sophisticated in her precious green uniform and when she passed she looked at me in surprise and smiled. I saw that her face was unusually animated and that her teeth were dazzling white and even. I never saw this girl again; I never even discovered her name. She may have been only a beginner of no consequence, but as I watched her soft disappearance into the spring night I felt as if I had been brushed across the eyes by some terrible essence of beauty, something of whose existence I had never before been aware. I desired to run after that strange, lovely girl but she was gone forever.

Mike Bailey tugged at my arm and said, 'Well, let's get down to the restaurant.'

'What restaurant?' I asked.

'Makino's,' he said, and he led me through a jungle of thin and winding streets and I felt that I had never before really seen a Japanese town: the crowded life, the tiny shops, the paper doors with small lights shining through, the people in all kinds of costumes from spectacular kimonos to drab business suits, the varying faces, the multitudes of children, and the police boxes on the corner. At times I felt like a whale swimming upstream against a flood of minnows for I towered over the people and no matter how far or how fast we walked the same number of Japanese seemed to press in upon us.

We came at last to an extremely narrow alley and ducked into a restaurant doorway hung with red and white streamers that brushed our faces as we passed. Inside were many Japanese crowded at small tables eating fish, which I have never liked. A Japanese woman greeted us with three low bows, a little maid fell to her knees and took our shoes and two powdered make-believe geishas showed us up a flight of narrow stairs.

We entered onto a top floor where three couples sat quietly at small tables. I keep using the words *little* and *tiny* because it's a pretty powerful experience for a fellow six-foot-two to travel in Japan. For one thing, you're always ducking your head to keep from bashing your brains in on door jambs and everything you see seems to have been constructed for midgets.

In a corner, imprisoned by a quarter-circle of a rounded table, stood a fine-looking chunky Japanese man of sixty, watching over a charcoal stove on which bubbled a large deep pan of fat, into which he tossed chunks of fish, swishing them around with long metal chopsticks. This was Makino-san. The après-guerre geishas told us that we were to sit on the floor at the quarter-circle table that cut Makino off from the rest of the room.

Mike said, 'This is the best tempura restaurant in Japan.'

'What's tempura?' I asked.

'Look.' He pointed to a menu painted on the wall in Japanese and English. Makino-san had twenty-nine varieties of fish from lobster to eel, including squid, octopus, shrimp, sardines and the excellent Japanese fish, tai. He also served about the same number of vegetables, especially ginko nuts, Japanese beans and shallots.

'This is living, son,' Bailey cried, putting his arm about one of the make-believe geishas, who laughed and called him 'Mike-san.' The other geisha started to arrange my dishes for the meal but Mike said, 'All right, girls, beat it.' They nodded obediently and went downstairs. I must have looked disappointed, for he said, 'It's silly to keep geishas at your table when you have a girl joining you.'

'I didn't know a girl was eating with us.'

'Didn't you see Fumiko-san say she'd be here?'

'The girl on the bridge?'

'Yeah. Fumiko-san. She gave me the high sign as she passed on the Bitchi-bashi.'

'What's this Bitchi-bashi?'

'*"Bashi's* Japanese for bridge. We call the one where the girls pass the Bitchi-bashi because there is so much lovely stuff there and you can't touch the merchandise.'

'Look, Mike,' I said. 'I don't get this special approach. You know the girl. Why don't you just go up and ask her for a date?'

Bailey's jaw fell and he said, 'A Takarazuka girl isn't allowed to have dates.'

'Why not?'

'Well, in the old days theaters had a lousy reputation in Japan, so the railroad decided to keep Takarazuka what you might call impeccable.'

'What railroad?' I asked.

'This whole resort grew up as a place for excursion trains from Osaka and Kyoto and Kobe. Started with a hot springs, then a zoo and finally some genius thought up these girl shows.'

'You mean a railroad still runs this?'

'Sure. They don't make a nickel on the town or the theater, but they do a fabulous business on the railroad. Everybody comes out to see the show. Fifty lavish scenes, a hundred beautiful girls–gorgeous, gorgeous, gorgeous.'

'And none of those girls has dates?'

'Immediate dismissal. The railroad combs Japan for these kids, spends a lot of dough training them. They've got to behave.'

I considered this for a moment and asked, 'But if the girls can't have dates, how come you're dating one of them?'

'Like I told President Truman, "Harry, you was wrong when you sold the Marines short."' He started to jab me with his long finger when he stopped suddenly, scrambled to his feet and hurried to the door. 'Fumiko!' he cried with real emotion.

The delicate actress seemed entirely changed from when we had seen her shortly before on the Bitchi-bashi. Now she wore a kimono and hurried toward Mike in little running pin-toed steps that made her exquisitely charming. Her kimono was a powdery blue and at her neck at least five undergarments showed, each folded meticulously upon the next so as to form a handsome frame for her golden face. Her hair was not fixed in the antique Japanese manner but hung nearly to her shoulder, thus forming the rest of the frame for her slender and expressive face. She wore white tabi socks, white cork zori instead of shoes and an enormous sash tied in a flowing knot in back. When I rose and extended my hand she barely touched it with her own, which seemed impossibly gently and I was amazed at how graceful she seemed, how young.

Mike Bailey had passed the point of amazement. He was drooling and arranged her cushions and plates as if he were a French headwaiter. Then he pinched her ivory-colored cheek and said, 'It's murder trying to see you, baby.' She laughed at this and her voice was high and tinkling like that of a child playing with dolls.

When she sat with us the tiny restaurant seemed to thrust back its walls, our talk grew more expansive and Makino, tucked away in his corner, started to fry the fish. Mike said generously. 'This American is Ace Gruver, Seven MIGs.' He showed her how jets fight and when she started to admire me perhaps a little too much he tried to change the subject, but she said, 'I meet Gruver-san already.'

Mike did a double take and Fumiko-san laughed again. 'How you like me in *Swing Butterfly?*' she asked him.

'You were wonderful!' he cried. 'But I'll bet if you'd put that show on while MacArthur was here he'd have thrown you all in jail.'

I asked why and Fumiko said–I can't explain how she talked or exactly what she did with English and Japanese gestures, but she made me understand–'*Swing Butterfly* make fun of American sailors who falling in love with Japanese girls. But Butterfly not commit hara-kiri.' Here she grabbed a butter knife and performed the ritual. 'If you like laugh, if you not too proud, you enjoy *Swing Butterfly*, I think.'

'Did you like it?' I asked Mike.

'Anything this babe's in, I like,' he drooled.

'What's she play?'

'I geisha,' Fumiko explained. 'I fight off whole shipload American sailors.'

With a deft twist of her shoulders she demonstrated how she played the role and Makino and two men in the restaurant roared and suddenly I didn't like being in that little upstairs room. I didn't appreciate having a fat cook laugh at Americans. I didn't like being hidden away in a corner with a Japanese girl, no matter how pretty, who ridiculed our men. In fact, I didn't like anything I'd seen happening in Japan since General MacArthur left and I didn't want to be a part of it. I found to my surprise that I was pretty much on the side of Mrs Webster. After all, who did win the war, anyway? I said to Mike, 'You probably want to be alone. I'll blow.'

He got very excited and cried, 'Hey, you can't, Ace.'

I stumbled awkwardly to my feet but he pulled me back down. 'Ace,' he said. 'If any Takarazuka snoopers broke in here and caught Fumiko alone with me. Much trouble.'

'What good do I do?' I grumbled.

'You are in the way,' Mike admitted, 'but it would be a lot easier on Fumiko if it looked like an innocent dinner for three, wouldn't it, lady?' I turned to see if Fumiko agreed and saw to my astonishment that she had turned pale and was trembling.

For at the entrance to the room stood three Takarazuka girls, tall and shatteringly beautiful. Two of them wore the Takarazuka green-skirted costume but the girl in the middle did not. She wore gray slacks, a blue-gray sweater, white shirt and tie and slate-gray cap. She was obviously disgusted at catching Fumiko-san seated with two Americans.

In three decisive steps she stood over us and spoke harshly to Fumiko-san who scrambled away in disgrace. I remember looking up at the strong face of this intruder. She was extraordinarily beautiful, yet strangely cold. I felt curiously insulted by her and cried, 'Are you the boss of this outfit?' but she spoke no English and snapped at me in Japanese. Then brusquely she turned away and led Fumiko-san to a table where the four actresses ignored us.

I started to get up but Makino, the cook, grabbed my arm and translated, 'She not angry. Only she say very dangerous Fumiko-san walk with Americans.'

'She wasn't walking,' I cried. 'She was sitting here.'

'Please!' Makino protested. 'I not speak good. Trouble too much.'

Now Mike started to join the Takarazuka girls but Makino pleaded with him, 'Soon you leave Japan, Mike-san. I got to stay. Please, no trouble.' He whisked away the dishes from which Fumiko-san had been eating and Mike and I sat glumly staring at our mess of tempura. It galled me to be sitting on the floor, Japanese style, while the Takarazuka girls, by whom we had been rebuked, sat at a table, American style. I said, 'Let's get out of here,' but before we could leave, the leader of the girls–the one in slacks–came over, looked me gently in the eye and spoke softly.

Makino translated, 'She have no English. She most sorry but Fumiko-san young girl from famous family in Japan. Suppose she get fired Takarazuka, everybody lose face.'

The lovely actress looked at me beseechingly and said, in Makino's interpretation, 'Very difficult to be Takarazuka girl. We got to protect one another.'

She smiled at me, bowed graciously and returned to her table. I felt lots better but now Mike began to boil. 'What in hell am I?' he demanded. 'A man or a mouse?' He pushed Makino's restraining hand away, strode over to the table, reached down, grabbed Fumiko-san by the chin and kissed her until she had to struggle for breath. Then he bowed politely to the girl in slacks and said, 'I'm mighty sorry, too. But us boys also have to protect one another.'

Then we left, but at the door we looked back to see the four Takarazuka girls sitting primly on the chairs, staring at their plates.

When we got back to the barracks Mike said, 'I don't blame the girls. They're under strict rules. If they get caught with an American soldier they're fired. But that snippy babe in slacks sort of got my goat.'

I asked, 'Why do you bother with them, if you can't date them?'

He put down his towel and looked at me in amazement. 'Since when does a man have to have reasons for chasing a pretty girl?'

'But you can't even talk with her!'

'Son!' Mike cried. 'Didn't you read when you was young? Didn't you stumble upon them there fairy tales? Where the prince fights his way through the wall of fire? The more rules they put up against you the more fun it is.'

'But she's a Japanese girl.'

'Drop the adjective, son. She's a girl.'

'When you kissed her . . . It looked as if you could really go for her.'

'Son, when I come to any country I want to do three things. Eat the food of that country, in this case sukiyaki which is horrible. Drink the liquor which is also horrible. And make love to the girls, which in the case of Fumiko-san would be delirious.'

'Even though there's no chance?'

'I hate to be stuffy about this, son, but you Air Force men wouldn't understand. When you're a Marine there's always a chance.'

'Even with those girls?'

'Son, when I was in New Zealand in the last war, waiting to hit Tarawa, there was a pretty barmaid in town and all the boys tried to make her. I didn't bother because there was also a very wealthy and famous gal who lived on a hill and you'll find as you grow older and wiser in the ways of the world that they're the gals to go for. Because they got everything: power, position, the mad acclaim of the world . . .' He dragged his hand back through his hair. 'But there's one thing they ain't got–l'amour.'

I started to ask why he was so sure they were lacking l'amour but he interrupted me and said, 'Same with the Takarazuka girls. They got fame, wealth, their name in the bright lights . . .' He started to sob and concluded, 'But it's all like ashes because they ain't got l'amour. And you watch, son! Takarazuka girls ain't none different from that there gal in old New Zealand. And I'm the guy who can bring l'amour into even the drabbest life.'

We went down to the shower room and while Mike was yammering away I had the stifling premonition that I ought to get out of Japan. When we returned to the hall Mike headed for his own room but I said, 'Come on in a second,' and we talked for a long time. I said, 'I had the strangest feeling just now. I wanted to get out of Japan. I was scared, I think.' I started to tell him about my bad luck with Eileen and he interrupted.

'Don't tell me! The general's wife started to throw her hooks into you. I sized her up when she tossed a girl like Fumiko-san out of her third-rate club . . .' He shook my hand warmly and said, 'Son, when you escaped Mrs General Webster, you escaped horrors worse than death.'

'But I didn't want to escape,' I said. 'I wanted to marry Eileen and have a wife I could be proud of and a home somewhere and a good life in the Air Force. Everything was arranged and I liked it all.'

'So now what?'

'I had the craziest feeling, Mike, that I was back in St Leonard's.'

'Where's that?'

'Prep school. I went to St Leonard's. I was all set to take the exams for West Point, but there was a teacher there who loved English literature and he got me a part in the school play. It was by a Hungarian called Molnar, and all of a sudden I didn't want to go to West Point. I didn't want any part of it and my mother, who's written a couple of dammed fine stories for the *Atlantic,* came to school and said, 'We've always expected you would go to the Point, like your father and his father.'' I said, ''Suddenly I feel as if I'd had a vision of a completely different world.'' At that she started to cry and talked pretty incoherently, but what I got was that if you ever once experienced that vision don't let anything stop you. She wouldn't come right out and say I shouldn't go to the Point, because her own father went there and became a pretty famous general. But I could see that that's what she meant.

'For the next two weeks I went through hell. Everybody at the school was just swell. They didn't rave at me and say I was ruining my life if I gave up the appointment to West Point, and the English teacher wouldn't say that if I did go to the Point I was selling out. But then Father flew up from Texas and he was like a breath of sea air in a Kansas drought.'

'He put you straight, eh?'

'No. Father never rants.'

'He's a general isn't he? Then he rants.'

'You Marines get the wrong idea sometimes. Just because a couple of generals fouled up Koje-do, you take it for granted all Army generals are horses' necks.'

'Right animal, wrong anatomy.'

'If you ever meet my father you'll meet the man who justifies having generals. He looked at me that day and said, ''If you don't want to go to the Point, Lloyd, don't. Unhappiest men I know are those who've been forced into something they have no inner aptitude for.'''

'That was a noble start,' Mike said, 'but what did he use for the clincher?'

'What do you mean?'

'How did he apply the screws? How did he force you to go to the Point?'

'He didn't. We just talked and he flew back to Texas and I went on to the Point. And up to this very night I've never once been sorry. But tonight that old sick feeling came over me and I had the distinct impression that maybe I didn't want to stay in the Air Force and buck for a star. Maybe I didn't want to marry Eileen and mess around with her silly old man and cantankerous mother.' I put my hand against my forehead and said, 'Maybe I felt my whole world crumbling under me.'

Mike grew serious and said, 'Boy, do I know! I watched my old man go through the depression. I watched a world really crumble. That's why I don't put much stock in the permanent security of worlds–of any kind. But what hit you? You don't just decide a thing like that for the hell of it.'

'Well . . . I'm almost ashamed to tell you what hit me.'

Mike had a very quick mind and he said loudly, 'Fumiko-san! You took a good look at Fumiko-san close up. Well, son, she'd put anyone off his rocker–anyone, that is, but an old hand at l'amour like me.'

I laughed and said, 'I wish it were so simple. I could duel you for Fumiko-san in F-86's at 40,000 feet. But the other day I was best man at a marriage between a G.I. and a Japanese girl. Boy, she was no Fumiko-san, but she impressed me powerfully. Like a chunk of earth in the middle of a cheese soufflé. And tonight, seeing that other part of Japan I wondered . . .' Suddenly I clammed up and couldn't say it.

'You wondered what?' Mike asked. 'You certainly don't want to snatch the enlisted man's wife.'

'This sounds silly but I flew down here ready to marry Eileen. When she and I started to hesitate about that, I started to wonder about everything else–even about staying in the Air Force. I know it's ridiculous but that G.I. and his dumpy Japanese girl . . .'

Mike stared at me in slack-jawed horror and asked in a hushed voice, 'You mean you're ponderin' life?' He mussed his hair down over his eyes and sobbed, 'Oh, what does it all mean–the eternal struggle–sex–the New York Yankees!'

'All right, louse it up. But suddenly I felt as if I were in a world of swirling darkness where the only reality was this earth–this earth of Japan.'

'My God!' Mike cried, clutching his head. 'A new Sigmund Freud!'

I had to laugh, and while Mike phoned down for some cold beer I asked, 'Don't you ever get crazy ideas like that?'

'A million of 'em. They never hurt anybody.'

'But to have an idea like that suddenly bust open your whole world . . . I thought I was back in prep school again.'

'I think it's easy to explain,' Mike said after his second bottle of beer, which gave him added authority. 'You've been fighting like crazy up in Korea and you get this big idea about comin' down to Japan and getting married . . .'

'She didn't even tell me she was coming to Japan.'

'Don't let details mess up my theory. Then when you see the battle-axe her mother is . . .'

'She's not really a battle-axe.'

'Who threw me out of the Club with Fumiko-san?' The question awakened all of Mike's animosities and launched him into a tirade against generals' wives and he never did finish his explanation.

But next night we were at the Bitchi-bashi watching the stately procession of Takarazuk girls as they approached us through the evening dusk to vanish into the deep shadows. I was deeply moved by the passage of these quiet figures and they appeared to me as members of a military group dedicated to their rituals and promotions the way I was tied to mine. They lived and acted with a sense of their military responsibility while I was conditioned by the rules of my army. They were not free and I was not free, for I believe that no man who flies a plane against the enemy or steers a ship into enemy waters is a free man. He is bound by certain convictions and restraints that other men never know.

I was pondering this when Fumiko-san came by. She was accompanied by the actress in men's clothes who had reprimanded us the night before and when the bobby soxers on the Bitchi-bashi saw this tall girl they made a wild dash to surround her and demand autographs. The actress cooly shoved them away but other little girls took their places.

I said to Mike, 'She must be somebody.'

He asked a Japanese girl who the actress was and the girl broke into horribly confused giggles. She did, however, summon another girl–she couldn't have been more than fourteen–who spoke English and this child said, 'She–is–Hana-ogi-san. Number one girl!'

I repeated the name and some children near me, giggling furiously, began to chant 'Hana-ogi-san!' and the beautiful actress stopped for a moment on the bridge and looked our way. Mike bowed very low and blew a kiss off his thumb to Fumiko-san but both actresses ignored him and resumed their way into the night shadows.

KATSUMI-SAN: 'Japanese like gold teeth but I get white one for Joe.'

I had to miss the Monday night procession at the Bitchi-bashi because General Webster sent a message ordering me in to Kobe to report on how my work was going. I knew what he really wanted was to ask me why I hadn't been around the Club. No doubt Mrs Webster had commanded him to find out and I wondered what I would tell him. It was difficult for me to explain even to myself.

It had something to do with the fun of living with a gang of men that you can never explain. The relaxation, the freedom of running down the hall in your shorts, the common interests in a common problem. I remember how my father used to glow when he came in from a six-day exercise with his foot troops. I was a kid then but there was something enormously real and rugged about my father on those occasions. True, he was a fine man about the house–I think a good many other families, mothers and kids alike, would have been glad to have a father like mine–but there were times when he insisted upon living in a man's world and I think that much of his resolute determination to follow the camp fires rather than the bridge parties had been deeply ingrained in me. I had always liked aviation meetings like the ones at Itami. I liked evenings in Bachelor Officers' Quarters. I liked going with Mike to the little fish restaurant. And I liked getting a gang together on the spur of the moment, racing through the dark Japanese night and winding up at some American movie in Osaka or Kyoto. Most of all I enjoyed working at the air strip when somebody I knew in Korea boomed in with the latest hot scoop.

For example, one day a big Swede who flew an Air Force C-47 as a taxicab from one Korean air base to the next arrived in Itami and we had a long night of laughing about some of our experiences in that dismal country. I especially remembered the time he was ferrying a bunch of us into Seoul on a rainy day. The cloud cover was broken and there were only about five holes through which you could descend to the island in the middle of the river where the air strip was. We got tied up behind a Marine pilot who had never flown into Seoul before and he was being extra cautious. He missed the first hole through the clouds, he missed the second and damned if he didn't miss the third. The Swede piloting our plane began to get irritated and he shouted to the tower, 'For Christ sake, tell junior to land that kite.' When we landed the Marine was waiting for us and demanded to know who had called him junior. We looked among us to see who was tallest and a six-foot-four Air Force man stepped forward and said, 'I called you junior. You were screwing up the procession.' The Marine looked up at the big man and said, 'I'm new around here. I was looking for the island.' The real big man said, 'I'm glad you found it cause we damned near ran out of gas.' I started to laugh and for a minute it looked like a fight and all the rest of the time we were in Korea whenever we saw a Marine plane some wise guy would yell, 'There goes junior.' I told Mike Bailey about this but he didn't think it funny. Living with these pilots again I honestly did not want to go into Kobe and sit around a fancy officers club and try to explain to Mrs Webster why I wasn't courting her daughter.

But that's what I had to do. In his office the general asked me a lot of trivial questions he couldn't possibly have been interested in and then led me down to the Cadillac. At dinner I looked for Eileen but he said she was in Kyoto visiting a museum and wouldn't be able to join us. I looked at Mrs Webster eating her shrimp cocktail and lost my appetite.

It was a chilly meal and after dessert the general excused himself to do some paper work and I observed silently, 'If my father ever becomes Chief-of-Staff I'll warn him not to put Mark Webster in charge of intelligence, because he sure telegraphs his hand.'

Mrs Webster didn't bother to telegraph hers. When we got to her apartment she asked bluntly, 'What's wrong between you and Eileen?'

'I'm sure she must have told you.'

Lloyd, don't be evasive. You haven't seen her in more than a week.'

It was obvious that this was one time when I'd better stick to the truth. I said, 'We had a quarrel. She told me . . .'

'A quarrel? Whatever about?'

I gulped and said, 'She's afraid I'm too much like my father.' Mrs Webster started at my honesty but made no move to stop me so I finished. 'And I think she's–too bossy.' There was something in the inflection of this sentence that betrayed clearly the fact that I thought Eileen was too damned much like her mother. But Mrs Webster never batted an eye.

So I added, 'And then I've been working.'

'Ridiculous,' she snapped. 'Mark found you this job because there wasn't any work attached to it.'

'If that's why I got it . . .' I began with standard dignity.

'. . . you'd sooner be back in Korea?' she concluded.

'Yes.'

'Lloyd, don't be silly. It's obvious to everyone in Kobe that you are an extremely brave young man whom General Webster brought back to Japan so that you could be with Eileen. There's nothing dishonest about that–if you plan to get married.'

'We planned that for a long time–sort of.'

'How do people get married–sort of?' She was sitting on an expensive lounge purchased in Paris and she leaned forward, repeating the offensive words: 'Sort of?'

'I mean there's nothing definite. Has Eileen said there was anything definite?'

'Of course she hasn't. She hasn't talked with me about this but I can see how humiliating it is for her. The whole hotel . . .'

I knew Eileen pretty well and I was sure she didn't give a hoot what the hotel thought. But Mrs Webster did because if we didn't get married it would make her look ridiculous. I said, 'We wonder if we're the right people for each other.'

'At this stage? Why, you've known Eileen for years. Same backgrounds. I don't see . . .'

'But that's what Eileen said when she started this fight . . .'

'A fight! Lloyd, this is just a lovers' quarrel and it has no more significance than that.'

'Maybe it didn't at the start but Eileen's questions and some of the thinking I've done made me wonder if perhaps my whole idea of life isn't wrong.'

Now I had struck something serious and Mrs Webster accepted it so. She spoke very deliberately and at the same time fidgeted nervously with a lace handkerchief. She said, 'If an Army man ever questions the big idea of military service he's lost. Believe me, Lloyd, I've seen it many times and it's the worst thing that can happen to you. From your baby days you were cut out for the service. You've never known anything else.'

I could have contradicted her and said that for two weeks—a long time ago—I had imagined another way of life but that would have raised too many questions which I couldn't have answered. It was one thing to confide such a secret to an easy-going mind like Mike Bailey's. It was quite different to give the idea away to Mrs Webster. In three questions she'd have you undressed and you'd stand there naked to the world, just as stupid and silly as you were back at St Leonard's.

I said, 'Wouldn't it be better all around if your husband sent me back to my outfit?'

'In Korea?'

'Yes. That would settle my doubts.'

To my surprise, she agreed. 'It does seem better now. But it would be wrong for two reasons. It would make Eileen seem ridiculous. Couldn't hold her man. And it would be the cowardly thing for you to do.'

'Eileen doesn't need me,' I said.

'You're absolutely right, Lloyd. She's asked to parties every night. But not by Army men. By civilians in Army suits. Suppose she falls in love with one of these civilians? She'll settle down as a druggist's wife in Chicago and that's not for Eileen, believe me.'

I found Mrs Webster a lot too tough for an airman twenty-eight years old to handle. I said, 'I'll drop in and say goodnight to the general.'

But this woman kept hold of you like a steel trap. She said, 'And there's a third reason why going back to Korea would be wrong. Because you would be running away from your fundamental problem.'

I wanted to shout, 'What I want to run away from is you. I'm running away from your daughter because she's so much like you.' But a man can shoot down Russians and still be afraid to shoot down his commanding officer's wife. I said, 'I'll call Eileen tomorrow.'

She said, 'Good. I know Eileen and I know she wants to marry you. Don't let lovers' quarrels keep you apart. That would be foolish.' She tucked the handkerchief into her sleeve and added with powerful emphasis, 'And don't let a temporary uncertainty tease you into thinking you've made a mistake on your whole life. You're an Army man, Lloyd. You were bred to it.'

I found General Webster in a workroom lined with books. He indicated them with a wide sweep of his hand and said, 'The colonel who had this suite three years ago got these books together. Practically any subject you might be interested in.'

I said, 'I suppose you know what Mrs Webster and I were talking about. I think it would be better all around if you sent me back to Korea.'

The general drummed his fingers and said, 'Better, maybe, but it would be so damned obvious. That's what's wrong with military life. Every move can be so easily interpreted by the enemy. But damn it all, Lloyd, what's wrong between you and Eileen?'

'Nothing's wrong, sir. It's just that we both feel uncertain about our getting along—ultimately.'

'Very sensible.' He poured me a stiff drink and said, 'Your're not much of a man unless you're scared silly by the prospect of marriage. Take me. Night before my wedding your father had to get me blind drunk to keep me from sending a Western Union messenger to my wife's house.... Father was Colonel Keller—got into that serious scrape with the Persian Ambassador. They called it Persia then.'

He related in his rambling way the case histories of half a dozen military marriages and of how all the men at some time before the wedding or after had wanted to funk out on the deal. 'But in the long run,' he assured me, 'marriage is the best thing for any man. It was the making of me. And j'your father ever tell you about his classic wedding? He was engaged to your mother, Lieutenant-General Himmelwright's daughter, and two days before the wedding he fell in love with another girl. Just about went mad from indecision. But suppose he had gone off his rocker and said he wasn't cut out to be a general. By God, twenty years later America might of lost Guadalcanal.'

He poured us a couple of more drinks and said, 'Look at it this way, Lloyd. What the hell were you put in this world for? Be one of those washed-up old fuddies with no home of his own, sitting in a club somewhere yakkity-yakking about China?'

I guess the whiskey made me brave, for I said, 'Ask Eileen if she'll have dinner with me tomorrow.'

'Good boy!' the general cried, whamming me on the back. 'I ordered my wife not to speak to you on such a subject. Humiliating to Eileen and all that. But Nancy said there came a time in every girl's love life . . . Isn't that a horrible word?'

'I'll call Eileen about twelve,' I said.

General Webster tossed off an extra one and said, 'I feel ten years younger. If you have children, Lloyd, have boys.'

As I went down in the elevator I saw a new sign which read, 'Officers of this command will not appear on the streets of Kobe walking with girls of the indigenous personnel. This order also applies to officers when on the streets of Osaka and Kyoto. Signed, Mark Webster, Commanding.' I thought, 'Oh, boy! The general's wife is really determined to clean up all Japan,' and then I got to laughing because here the American Army was forbidding its men to be seen with Japanese girls, while the Takarazuka army was forbidding its girls to be seen with American men.

I was still chuckling when the elevator doors opened and I heard my name. It was Pvt. Joe Kelly, wearing a service revolver as big as a cannon. He yelled, 'At last the Air Force gave me a break. Transferred me to the Joint Message Center. I got the best job in Osaka.' He waited for an officer to sign a receipt for important mail, then joined me. His Ford was at the curb.

'Where can I drop you?' he asked, unstrapping his artillery.

'Look, I work at Itami.'

'So what's the difference to me. The Army pays for the gasoline.'

'And I live at Takarazuka.'

'I'll go that way.'

We piled in and he reported on how things were going with him and Katsumi. 'We found a nice house . . . Say, Ace! It's early. Why not drive into Osaka and visit with us?'

He was so energetic and I was so interested in him in the way I had explained to Mike that I agreed. He barreled the Ford along the Kobe-Osaka road and I tried to observe exactly what this ancient and historic Japanese road was like. I saw the little paper-windowed houses stretching mile after mile, with never a sign of countryside. I saw the open-front stores that did business all night and the thousands of people moving along the road in the twilight and of how a single lamp lit in any of the houses seemed to light up the whole section of road near it.

But pretty soon I stopped thinking about Japan and asked, 'How fast you driving, Joe?'

'Sixty-eight,' he reported.

'Don't the M.P.'s ever pinch you for flying so low?'

'They all know me.'

'I'll bet they do.'

'First thing I did was invite 'em over to the house and Katsumi fed 'em special grub.' He waited till a prowl car came along. Then he leaned way out and shouted some Japanese insults at the M.P. and everybody roared and Joe said, 'Great bunch.'

As we entered Osaka he bore to the south until we came to a road which dropped down beside one of the numerous canals. Soon it petered out and four Japanese kids assumed guard over the Ford while we hiked up a narrow alley down which two men trudged with wicker baskets of enormous size. As they passed each house light from the paper doors shone on them for a moment creating an impression of deep warmth.

At the far end of the alley stood an inconspicuous one-storied shack made of wood long since weatherstained to a blackish gray. The porch was outlined by concrete blocks which confined the center of packed earth. The roof was of orange tile, laid in Chinese fashion with a slight swoop upward at each end. In the States we would not have called this a house at all. With its sliding paper doors it would have been a shed, and cows or farm tools would have been kept there, but when Joe slid his doors back, there was Katsumi in a kimono, cooking the evening meal. Promptly she took my shoes and offered me a cup of bitter green tea and said in lovely, stilted English, 'It is fine to see you among us tonight.'

'She's been takin' English lessons,' Joe said proudly, 'and I study a little Japanese.' He rattled off a few phrases and Katsumi beamed at him as if he had written an encyclopedia.

'It's nice here, Ace,' Joe said expansively. 'Two rooms, the canal down there, a good job and good food. Ace, I'm livin'. For the first time in my life I feel like a human bein'.'

He showed me where to put my shoes and how to prop myself up with pillows as we sat on the tatami mats. He said, 'I grew up in an orphanage but I was sort of adopted by a family. They found me disappointin' and deserted me–not that I blame 'em, I was a stinker–so I went back to the orphanage and then to reform school. I tried to enlist in the Army for the last war but they trapped me into tellin' my real age and I wound up in Chicago and then the Air Force. Now I'm a family man.' He looked at Katsumi with glowing approval and asked, 'Notice the big change, Ace?'

'I like the kimono,' I said, for Katsumi was one of those ordinary Japanese girls who in flowing kimonos become almost attractive.

'It ain't the kimono, Ace. Watch her smile!' In Japanese he commanded his wife to smile but when she did so I still didn't catch on, so Joe cried, 'The tooth, Ace! The tooth!' Then I saw. The big gold tooth had been removed and in its place some Army dentist had fitted a trim porcelain crown. Katsumi really did look attractive in kimono and tooth.

'It's a reformation,' I said.

'It's a miracle,' Joe sighed. 'And she don't giggle no more, do you, Babe?' He dragged Katsumi toward him and kissed her on the cheek. 'Because I told her that if she ever giggled again and stuffed her fist in her mouth I'd break her arm off at the wrist.' He gave Katsumi a solid wallop on the bottom and she giggled like mad, stuffing her hand into her mouth.

'Sometimes she forgets, Ace, but this is livin'.'

He explained to his wife that I bunked at Takarazuka and she spoke in rapid Japanese which he interpreted for me: 'A hell of a fine idea, Ace. We're goin' to Takarazuka tomorrow to see the new show. Join us.'

'I'd like to, but I have a dinner date in Kobe.'

'So what! Show's over by six and I'll race you right in to Kobe, no stops.' He pulled an imaginary cord and made like a train whistle. 'It's a deal, Ace, because with Katsumi you'll really enjoy it. She knows all the actresses and can tell you what's goin' on.'

He gave Katsumi a command in Japanese and she went to a chest where she kept her prized possessions, appearing shortly with a magazine in bright covers. It started at the back, the way Jap books do, and she showed me the photograph of a dazzling stage set. I asked what the magazine was.

'Fan magazine for the Takarazuka shows,' Joe explained. 'She subscribes to three of them.' He shuffled a pile of colorful magazines and I could tell from the devoted way in which Katsumi put them back in order that she had once been one of the enchanted girls who stood each night by the bridge to watch the great stars pass. Now she had become the typical housewife who still treasured autographs of the leading actresses.

'I suppose she belongs to a fan club,' I joked.

'Don't kid!' He spoke in Japanese again and Katsumi returned to the chest from which she handed me a stack of photographs. Apparently they went far back in time to when Katsumi had been a child. I asked, 'Does she have the pictures of the girls who were in last month's show?'

Katsumi immediately shuffled through the pictures and assembled the entire cast of principals and explained what each did. She even sang two of the songs and I asked, 'Does she know all the shows as well as this one?'

Joe patted her arm affectionately and said, 'She never misses one. Hasn't for years.'

'Then it's a date for tomorrow. But you promise to get me back to Kobe for dinner.'

He didn't have to because when I called Eileen next day she played hard-to-get and told me abruptly. 'I'm having dinner with a Marine.' I said, 'That's too bad, how about Friday?' and she said Friday was booked too, so I said, 'Boy, I'm playing in tough luck. I'll call you later.' But neither of us would have bet much money on when that later would be.

FUMIKO-SAN: 'When Japan know America win, my father kill himself–honorable–Japanese style.'

Actually, when I went to the theater that afternoon I was rather relieved. It seemed to me that Eileen and I were pretty well washed up and I didn't have to worry any more about Mrs Webster. I said to Joe, 'I'm sort of steamed up to see this show,' but I was hardly prepared for what Takarazuka did to *Madame Butterfly*. At any moment they might run in a scene unconnected with anything that had gone before or would come after. There were old Japanese dances to please the classical fans, jitterbugging to represent 1890 America, wrestling, microphones, a dance hall sequence, mutiny aboard an American ship, twenty stupid Japanese cops and a fire.

But running through this burlesque of a great opera there was one solid thread: ridicule of American military men. I have to admit that Mike Bailey's girl, Fumiko-san, was terrific as a ravishing geisha holding the American fleet at bay. Her fine long face and expressive movements made her hilarious when wrestling with a drunk G.I. on leave in Tokyo. There was nothing really offensive with her pantomime but you felt that all the Japanese in the audience were egging her on because they had had a bellyful of Americans.

But the star's performance was quite different. The girl in slacks who had reprimanded us in the restaurant played this part and her Lieutenant Pinkerton was blatantly ridiculous. He was arrogant, ignorant and ill-mannered. Yet at the same time the actress herself seemed more essentially feminine than any of the other girls on stage and it was this that made her version of Pinkerton so devastating. She was all Japanese women making fun of all American men.

One act of such petty nonsense was enough for me. I didn't think I was stuffy, but I couldn't tolerate people making cheap fun of men in uniform, and when the people doing the burlesque were Japanese I drew the line. When the Act I curtain fell I got up to go, but Katsumi put her hand on mine and said, 'No, no! Now is the best!'

From a side entrance the star appeared dressed in old-style samurai costume, pursued by two villains. They attacked her, and in the highly ritualistic dance which followed I for the first time fell under the spell of Japanese art.

I cannot tell you what there was about this dance that captivated me. It might have been the haunting music, for now the Western instruments like violins and oboes were silent and in their place were three horribly weird sounds: the hammering of a slack-headed drum, the clicking of wooden blocks thumped together, and the piercing wail of an Asiatic flute. Or it might have been the dazzling curtain before which she danced, a vast gold-and-blue-and-red affair with eight gigantic embroidered irises standing in solemn Oriental perfection. But mostly it was this remarkable woman I had seen in the restaurant, this Hana-ogi. She wore no shoes, only white tabi drawn tightly about her feet and it was principally her feet that impressed me. She used them as a very great athlete might and slowly I became aware that I was watching one of the greatest dancers in the world. Silently, in the Japanese manner, she wove back and forth between her assailants. Instead of a sword she used the traditional symbol, her right hand held vividly upright, and as I watched this hand it traced a wonderful pattern against the gold curtain. I had never before seen a dancer like this, one who could fill an entire stage with her authority.

The scene came to a frenzied close with Hana-ogi stamping an unforgettable rhythm and weaving that bright hand through the darkness. The crowd burst into applause and I whispered to Kelly, 'Tell Katsumi I'd like to meet that girl.'

To my surprise Kelly said, 'That's easy. Katsumi knows 'em all.' But when he spoke to his wife she became grave and Joe reported, 'Katsumi says that your particular girl wouldn't speak to an American.'

'Why not?'

'We hung her brother as a war criminal. Killed her father with our bombs.'

I sat back in my seat and, strange as it may seem, felt exactly the same kind of relief I did when I heard that Eileen couldn't have dinner with me. I had the distinct sensation that I was back in St Leonard's engulfed in important decisions that I simply couldn't make. At that moment I desperately wanted to be in a jet plane rousting about up around the Yalu. Up there I felt safe and here in Japan I felt dreadfully loused up. As if I were coming back to earth from another world I looked at Joe and thought, 'Jesus! What am I doing? Lloyd Gruver, West Point '44, propositioning an enlisted man to arrange a date with a Japanese girl?' I said to Joe, 'Let's get some air.'

Joe said, 'Why not? We'll blow and Katsumi can come home by train.'

Right there I could have avoided all that followed, but I cried, 'No! I didn't mean that. I want to see the rest.' Then I asked, 'How does Katsumi happen to know an actress like that?'

Joe laughed and grabbed his wife's handbag, rummaging through it till he found half a dozen pictures. They were all of the dancer, showing her in some of her famous roles. She was a Spanish bullfighter, Venetian gondolier, a Broadway playboy and a Japanese samurai. She was always the man and she always looked devastatingly feminine.

Joe exaplained, 'Katsumi organized a fan club. Osaka girls who idolized Hana-ogi.'

'What's her last name?'

Joe asked Katsumi and said, 'Just Hana-ogi. It's a stage name. My wife is crazy about her. Until Katsumi married me she was a real moron. Used to stand in the rain to see her goddess.'

'But why?'

'Look, Ace. Suppose you were fat and dumpy and had to work like a slave all day. Then there's this tall, slim, beautiful girl who's famous all over the country and makes a lot of dough. One actress like Hana-ogi proves what a girl can become. If you ever break into our house you steal the pots and pans but don't steal these photographs. Katsumi worships them.'

Katsumi understood our conversation but said nothing. Quietly she recovered the photographs, restored them to some preferred order and replaced them in her bag. Then she explained in broken English the story of Act II, which she read from one of the magazines which Takarazuka mailed out to its faithful patrons. It contained a large picture section, which I leafed through. I saw some sixty excellent photographs of the Takarazuka girls off stage. They were knitting, or skiing, or promenading, or going to a symphony concert, or strolling. Gradually I began to notice a curious pattern. Always the girls were in pairs or larger groups. Never were they alone and never with men. The photographs portrayed a rich and successful and celibate world and I recalled Mike's insistence that a wise man always looks for love in that kind of world, because, as Mike so eloquently pointed out, such women have everything but l'amour. I felt this especially when I saw the three photographs of Mike's Fumiko-san. She was perhaps the most striking of the Takarazuka girls, for she wore her clothes with dazzling effect and her pictures were additionally interesting to me because in each of her photographs she was standing with Hana-ogi, the star of today's performance, and Hana-ogi invariably wore men's clothing—yet it was Hana-ogi who looked the more feminine and desirable.

Act II was an amazing experience, for Hana-ogi proved that she was much more than a mere dancer. She had a fine clear singing voice, striking power for dramatic scenes and a wanton comic sense. I leaned across Katsumi and asked, 'Joe? Do you think this girl could get by in New York?' He whispered back, 'I never been to New York.'

But Katsumi heard my question and she realized even before I did that I was determined to meet Hana-ogi that day, so in the darkness she touched my hand and said, 'After, we go on flower walk. I speak you to Hana-ogi-san.'

When the final curtain fell on *Butterfly* I started to leave but again Katsumi whispered, 'No, Ace-san. Now everybody so beautiful.' Quickly the curtain opened and there was the entire cast of 120 standing in glorious kimonos, singing a farewell song. A runway reached out into the audience and the stars came down and posed right above us. Our seats were such that Hana-ogi stood very near me and for the first time I saw her in woman's clothes. She was adorable. True, she was also proud and combative, nervously excited at the end of an extremely long performance. But above all else she was adorable in her triumphant moment. Her kimono, I remember, was green and white.

Katsumi now led me through the crowd and we came to the flower walk and the tiny little gate through which the Takarazuka girls passed on their way to the Bitchi-bashi. A large crowd had assembled to applaud them as they appeared and dozens of round-faced little girls pressed tight against the gate, hoping to touch the great actresses, and as I looked at the girls it seemed incredible that any of these pudgy figures might one day grow up to replace Fumiko-san or Hana-ogi.

Now the lesser Takarazuka girls appeared, then Fumiko-san and the dancers in green skirts and leather zori. At last the leading actresses came through the gate as the crowd pressed in upon them and above the clamoring heads I saw cool Hana-ogi. We looked at each other cautiously, as if testing to see if either had been offended, then slowly she moved toward me through the great press of people and I think my mouth fell open slightly, for on this day, fresh from triumph, she was a glorious woman.

Katsumi broke the spell by catching Hana-ogi's hands and gabbling away in Japanese. Finally she said to me, 'Hana-ogi-san hope you like her play.' The tall actress looked at me over Katsumi's shoulder and I replied quietly, 'I liked the play but not the American sailors.'

Katsumi reported this and Hana-ogi blushed and said something which Katsumi was reluctant to translate. 'Go ahead!' Joe insisted.

'Hana-ogi-san say Americans to be funny. Not bad.' She pressed her hands into her stomach and indicated laughter.

'It wasn't funny,' I said. Hana-ogi caught my meaning and frowned, so I added quickly, 'But Hana-ogi-san's dancing was wonderful.' I imitated her fight with the villains and she smiled.

Hana-ogi's other fans now pressed in upon us and I said awkwardly, 'Why don't we four have dinner?' But when Katsumi translated this, Hana-ogi grew very angry, said something harsh and passed abruptly down the flower walk.

I now entered upon a week of dream sequences. The Korean fighting must have exhausted me more that I knew, for my sudden relaxation on the make-believe job at Itami permitted my nerves to find their own level. It wasn't high and I felt as I had once at the Point when we were about to play Navy and I was certain I would louse up the works. At other times I imagined I was back in St Leonard's totally confused about whether or not I wanted to attend the Point.

Sometimes at night I would wake with a start and believe myself to be in a falling jet fighter up at the Yalu River, and I would struggle to regain control both of the plane and of myself. Then, as I lay in the dark Japanese night I would see hurrying across my midnight wall that lone, exquisitely lovely Takarazuka girl I had seen on the Bitchi-bashi that first day and I would try to hurry after her and find her name.

But in all these imaginings I was kidding myself and I knew it. For inevitably I would think of Hana-ogi-san and I would see her dancing and I would follow the subtle curves of her adorable body and I would see her oval face smiling at me, ever so small a Japanese smile, and I would wonder how a man could be so tossed about by the mere idea of a girl. I had not really spoken to her. I knew nothing of her character or her personality, but almost willingly I was hypnotizing myself over this strange girl. Much later I would recognize that I was creating for myself the image of love and that without this image a man could well live an entire and empty life.

So each evening I fed my delirium by standing at the Bitchi-bashi to watch Hana-ogi pass by and if, during the preceding hours, I had by chance begun to question whether she really was as lovely as I imagined, one sight of her dispelled that heresy. She was even more desirable. On Friday I returned to see *Swing Butterfly* and at the final promenade I applauded so loudly that Hana-ogi had to look at me, but she betrayed nothing and looked quickly away. Saturday night I was really jittery and Mike Bailey dragged me along on another secret date he had with Fumiko-san and I spent most of the evening questioning her about the Takarazuka girls, hoping that she would speak of Hana-ogi.

Fumiko-san said, 'My father famous man but he kill himself when Japanese surrender. No money no hope for me. I read in paper Takarazuka seek new girls. I brush my hair each night, study dance, shout with my voice. I chosen and one year I work ten hours each day and think this my one chance. Supervisor like me and I go Moon Troupe with Hana-ogi-san. She kind to me and I act parts good. I live dormitory with other girls but best time when Moon Troupe go Tokyo.'

I said, 'You in love with someone in Tokyo?'

'Love? How I love someone?'

'Aren't you going to get married?'

She looked at me quizzically. 'I Takarazuka girl. What else could I want be?'

Her answer so amazed me that I did an impulsive thing which astonished me as much as it did Fumiko-san. I took her hands in mine and said quietly, 'Tonight, when you go back to the dormitory you must speak with Hana-ogi-san. Tell her that I am in love with her and must see her.'

Fumiko-san withdrew her hands and said in dismay, 'Never hoppen! Hana-ogi-san never speak men. And with American! Never hoppen!'

'You tell her,' I repeated, for I was convinced that no one could dance as passionately as Hana-ogi without knowing the outlines and purpose of love. I knew that she could not refuse to see me.

The next afternoon Joe Kelly drove out to Itami and said abruptly, 'Wife says you're to be at our house for supper at seven.'

'I can't make . . .'

'Be there, Ace,' the sawed-off squirt said ominously.

'I've already . . .'

'Be there, Bub. Hana-ogi's comin'.'

THE WOODCARRIER: 'Japanese girls nice to kiss—yes?'

I cannot remember how, exactly, I got to Joe Kelly's house that night, but when I finally turned up the alley from the canal, when at last I saw the little wooden building and the sliding paper doors my heart was hammering like thunder. I slammed the doors aside and rushed in expecting to see Hana-ogi standing there. Instead Joe and Katsumi were horsing around and cooking food. They told me to sit on the floor and from that position I watched this couple in love and it occurred to me that I myself had never lived in a house where love was. My parents loved each other in the required way and I am quite sure that General and Mrs Webster loved each other, but it was always love for some ultimate purpose: army advancement, social position in Lancaster, children. Here I was visiting the house of love itself.

'Joe,' I asked as we waited for Hana-ogi, 'what was it you told me in Korea? American husbands talk about country clubs and getting junior's teeth fixed?'

'Yeah, but if they're married to Japanese girls they talk about love.'

'Suppose you went back to the front now . . .'

'God fabbid.'

'What would you talk about?'

Joe held Katsumi off at arm's length and said, 'Topic for tonight. Ace, I fought to get this baby and I'm satisfied with what I got.' Then he spoke to her in Japanese and she burst into an uncontrolled giggle. She started to jam her hand into her mouth but Joe gave it a terrific belt and said, 'Honest to God, Ace, it's easier to train a dog.'

As he said this the door opened and Hana-ogi entered. Softly and with infinite grace she slid the doors closed behind her and slipped out of her zori. She was dressed in a gray-blue kimono and her hair was rumpled. She stood so silently that Joe and Katsumi did not realize she was there; so while their backs were still turned I stumbled awkwardly to my knees and started toward her, finally gaining my feet. She laughed at my discomfort and the sound of her voice was so gentle that I was compelled to reach down and take her hands to my lips and try to kiss them, but as I did so she instinctively pulled them away and I noticed with indescribable emotion that they were a decided ivory. I stood aside to let her pass and said, 'I am so glad you came.' She did not understand my words but even so she nodded in acknowledgment and I thought that she was less irritated than she had been when I tried to kiss her hand–and for my part I knew that she was twice as beautiful as I had ever seen her on the stage when she was dressed in men's clothes.

Katsumi now hurried forward and embraced the actress while Joe greeted her in broken Japanese, at which she laughed heartily, and I got the distinct impression that she was not at all the remote glamorous girl I had stared at on the Bitchi-bashi, for her gentle good humor was exactly what you would expect from a good, happy country girl working in the city.

But I had seen only two aspects of Hana-ogi and she was infinite, for when I asked Katsumi what her last name was and when Katsumi blushed and said she wouldn't dare ask that question I insisted, and when Hana-ogi heard Katsumi translate she grew extremely angry. I couldn't understand what was happening but Katsumi, blushing a fiery red which showed through her yellow cheeks, said, 'Takarazuka girl never tell her real name.'

'What do you mean, her real name?'

'Her name not Hana-ogi. Only stage name.'

'What is her real name?' I insisted.

Katsumi spoke to the actress and the only word I understood was America and Hana-ogi grew very solemn and spoke harshly, after which Katsumi said, 'She will not say her name. Even I don't know that.'

Joe interrupted and said, 'That's the way with all professional girls in Japan–geishas–whores . . .'

'Wait a minute!' I cried. 'This girl . . .' I reached out to take her hand, but she drew away from me and Katsumi said, 'More better we eat.'

It was a pretty formal meal. I asked a half dozen questions, none of which Hana-ogi really answered and it was not until Katsumi produced an album of Hana-ogi's pictures that there was any real animation. Then the two girls spoke in rapid Japanese, laughed a lot and sang bits of songs from the famous shows Hana-ogi had starred in. Finally the ice thawed a bit and I learned that Hana-ogi came from the north of Japan, where a woman in a nearby village had once seen a Takarazuka show in Tokyo. This woman had suggested that Hana-ogi apply for the examinations. Her father had been killed in the B-29 raids on Tokyo. Her brother had been hung for what he did to American soldiers in a prisoner-of-war camp.

Hana-ogi's willingness to tell of her family encouraged me to speak and I said I had a good start in the Air Force and with my background I surely ought to become a colonel and from there on it was the roll of the dice. I said that if I did become a general I hoped I would be as good a one as my father. She asked his name and when I said Hot Shot Harry Gruver she grew silent and Katsumi said, 'All Japanese know Gruver-san–Guadalcanal.' The evening grew formal again.

Hana-ogi rose and indicated that she must go. I was deeply agitated at having seen her, having talked with her–even though it was in translation–and I did not want to have her go. I said, 'Katsumi, please ask her to stay.'

Hana-ogi replied something sharp which Katsumi refused to translate. When I insisted she stood stubbornly silent, so I appealed to Hana-ogi, who looked at me in a quiet, submissive Japanese way which betrayed no emotion, but which dared me to budge her one inch. Softly, as if she were a child of seven, she said, 'America . . . no!' I could sense in her gentle reply a finality of hatred and steel, but she bowed slightly, smiled with an infuriating complacency, and looked back at me from the sliding doors. 'America . . . no!' she repeated softly, but long after she had gone I recalled the graceful way she bent down by the doors to put on her zori, the rare delicacy with which she arranged her kimono, so in spite of persistent apprehension that I was headed for trouble, I determined that no matter what she thought of Americans, no matter what orders Camp Kobe handed down regarding Japanese girls, I was going to see her again.

For the next two nights nothing happened. I posted myself at the Bitchi-bashi to watch the procession of girls and when I saw Hana-ogi, her hair in the wind, step upon the bridge at the opposite end, my heart actually hammered like one of those riveting machines you fix airplane wings with. God, she was like a medieval princess walking out from the palace. She was so straight and proud and sure of herself. And her black eyes shining out like fires from her golden face . . .

'Son, you got it bad!' Mike Bailey warned me on the second night.

'I'm going to see that girl. Tomorrow.'

'Son, are you taking this seriously?'

I turned to look at Mike and he seemed to be a complete stranger. 'Don't you take Fumiko seriously?' I asked. 'Who started this, anyway?'

'Fumi-chan?' he laughed. 'Son, a Marine has to be involved with a pretty girl or he isn't a Marine. But who could get serious over a Takarazuka girl? They got sawdust for hearts.'

'What is this?' I asked. 'A little while ago you were telling me . . .'

Mike scratched his head and said, 'I had a cousin once who came to stay with me right before a big high-school basketball game. I looked at the ugly little squirt and said, "Hell, he can't be gettin' measles." But he was and I was quarantined. Son, I think you're gettin' measles.'

I said, 'Tomorrow night I'm going to storm that Bitchi-bashi and I'm going to have a date with that girl.'

'Son,' Mike said, 'you can't have measles but, by God, there are red spots!'

Prudently he stayed away from the bridge on that third night and as the first Takarazuka girls crossed I felt my heart hammering again and soon there was Hana-ogi, accompanied by three other stars, and I stepped right into the middle of them and took Hana-ogi's hand and brought its yellow knuckles right up to my lips and kissed it. Then I said, 'I have got to see you,' but none of the girls spoke English and Hana-ogi drew her hand away and started to leave, but I no longer gave a damn so I grabbed her by the shoulder and swung her around and kissed her on the lips. We kept our eyes open and I remember that in this crazy moment I could not tell whether her eyes were slanted or not, but they were very black, like the sky at night.

She pushed me away and crossed the bridge and I heard behind me the muttering of Japanese men and I thought, 'Oh, damn, a public mess and I'll be courtmartialed,' but when I turned there was no animosity. The men were laughing and one old fellow with a load of wood pointed at some more Takarazuka girls approaching on the bridge and made motions encouraging me to kiss them too, but I hurried back to the Marine Barracks, where Mike Bailey greeted me with a pair of field glasses and the crack, 'It looked good, son. The subtle approach. Grrrrr.'

I said, 'I promised to see her tonight. I did.'

He said, 'Ace, don't let this thing get you. If you want to make a play for a pretty actress–O.K. But don't let it get you. Frankly, you looked silly as hell down thereon the bridge.'

In a few minutes a Japanese boy appeared with a message for Mike and he said, 'Fumi-chan wants to see me in the restaurant. She wants you to come along.'

When we got there Makino-san, the cook, had already heard of my behavior and he gave me hell. 'Very important in Japan these girls. You do much wrong, Ace-san.'

'What did I do?' I demanded. 'I kissed a girl.'

'A Takarazuka girl,' he said with reverence. Before he could argue further Fumiko-san appeared, extremely beautiful and very feminine. She did not cry but she did plead with me and said that something like that could ruin a Takarazuka girl and that if Hana-ogi ever lost her job her mother and her younger sisters . . . 'She very poor, Hana-ogi,' Fumiko told me.

'What do you mean?' I asked.

'You Americans not know what poor is. Hana-ogi never tasted meat until she came Takarazuka. Never had one nice clothes. Ace-san, you not speak her again–please?'

She told me that Hana-ogi's only chance in life–her one opportunity to escape from terrible poverty–was Takarazuka. 'I know this girl,' she said solemnly. 'Before she come for examination not eat for three days to get . . . How you . . .' She indicated a permanent wave.

She said there was already a likelihood that Hana-ogi might become one of the rare lucky ones–kept on at Takarazuka forever 'as teacher of the dancing' when her days as an actress were over. 'Here is good life for Hana-ogi-san. There is no other.'

I asked Fumiko why she risked seeking Mike Bailey and she laughed. 'I not great success. I not poor girl. My family making lots of money again.'

Then she pleaded, 'Do not come to the bridge again, Ace-san. Please?'

I wanted to see Hana-ogi, I wanted to see her eyes close to mine and her golden face pressed against my lips, but I said, 'I promise.' To my surprise Fumiko-san kissed me, her beautiful Japanese face leaning across the table, and she said, 'American men so good. Even when Hana-ogi-san come home tonight and say "American men no good," I speak her they all right.'

But although I kept my promise not to haunt the bridge it meant nothing, for the very next morning Joe Kelly wheeled up to Itami Air Field and said with real joy, 'Dinner again tonight, Ace!'

My heart must have bled out through my eyes, for he laughed and said, 'Yep. Hana-ogi came into Osaka late last night and talked with Katsumi for three hours.'

'What did she say?'

'How should I know?' And he rattled off a jumble of Japanese.

I wish that throughout the rest of my life I could occasionally know the excitement that captured me that night. I shaved at Itami, polished my shoes and set out for Osaka. I went nearly crazy in a tiny Japanese taxicab. The driver was all smiles and said yes, he understood just where I wanted to go, but we wound up in hell, I think, and in desperation I had to get a little boy to lead us back to the main station and I went to Joe's house on foot. I thrust back the sliding doors and cried, 'Hana-ogi, I . . .' But she was not there. Katsumi was alone, singing to herself as she prepared dinner. I sat on the floor and watched her time-christened movements over the charcoal stoves that Japanese women have used for centuries. For them there were no can openers, no frozen foods. Each item was laboriously prepared by hand and as Katsumi did this ancient work she hummed old songs and it seemed to me that she grew lovelier each day–but how truly lovely I was to learn in a few minutes.

For little Joe Kelly came busting into the house trembling with anger. He threw a package on the floor and cried, 'This son-of-a-bitch of a colonel!'

I had heard Joe sound off against officers before and I tried to tone him down, but this time he had real cause. 'This bastard, Colonel Calhoun Craford! He rides me. Every damned day he rides me.'

I happened to be watching Katsumi at the brazier. She never looked up, but I could see a terrible tenseness come over her entire body. Her ankles, in their white tabi socks, trembled slightly and I knew she was desperately afraid for her man.

For I had heard of this Calhoun Craford, a tough guy who hated colored people. Joe said, 'Every guy in that outfit who's married to a Japanese girl goes through hell with this bastard Craford.'

Katsumi, aware that Joe's trouble had been caused by her, now left the charcoal brazier and came into the middle of the room. She pushed Joe down onto a pillow and took off his shoes. 'You not to come on tatami with shoes, Joe,' she said softly. She brought him a tiny cup of hot sake wine and when he had drunk this she led him into the other room where there was a Japanese bath and soon I could hear tensed up little Joe Kelly, the dead-end kid, sloshing about in the tub while his patient wife soused him with cold water and rubbed his back. After a while they joined me and Joe scratched himself under the dark blue kimono Katsumi had made him. He said, 'To hell with Colonel Craford. Look what I got!' And he produced a bottle of Italian wine which Katsumi took.

Then, as we heard the soft click of zori on the alley stones, we all fell silent and I think Joe and Katsumi were as excited as I, although their hearts couldn't have been pounding as hard. The paper doors slid back and there was Hana-ogi in a green-and-gold kimono, her lips slightly parted in a smile, her brilliant eyes glowing from her night walk and her jet black hair mussed by the wind that blew along the canal. She started to speak but I caught her in my arms and kissed her. This time we closed our eyes, but when we finally drew apart–for she was kissing me too–she passed the back of her hand across her forehead and I think she knew then that for a girl dedicated to Takarazuka and a man dedicated to American military life love could result only in tragedy, and she pushed my hand away from hers and gently removed her zori and sat down on the tatami and spoke quietly to Katsumi, who spoke to Joe in Japanese, and all three of them fumbled around, not knowing how to translate what Hana-ogi had said, so she held out her hand to me and invited me to sit upon the mats beside her, and finally Katsumi said, 'She not mad no more.'

After dinner Katsumi said, 'Joe, we take walk.' Hana-ogi did not protest and as soon as the fragile doors slid shut I took her in my arms.

We sat upon the mats unable to say a word. I put my finger on her wonderful face and said, 'Nice,' but she could not understand. She gave me some instructions in Japanese but all I could do was shrug my shoulders, so she laughed and grabbed my big toe and pulled my cramped legs out straight and patted my knees, indicating that I must be stiff from sitting Japanese style. Then she made a pillow for my head in her lap and in that way we continued our meaningless conversation on the tatamis.

It was apparent to each of us that we would meet many times, but that when she passed me on the Bitchi-bashi she would look straight ahead and it was also apparent that she intended us to be lovers–but not on this first quiet night–and that as the days went by we would postpone one decision after another until finally some external force, say Takarazuka or General Webster, intervened to make the climactic decisions for us, but as she looked down at me with calm eyes, as her wonderful hands held my face and as her slim, graceful legs stretched out at last beside mine on the tatami mats, one question at least was answered. I had often wondered how a self-respecting American could get excited about a Japanese girl. Now I knew.

When it came time to leave, Hana-ogi refused to be seen with me on the street and caught a train back to Takarazuka. Joe drove me over to Itami, where I took the bus to Takarazuka, but something must have delayed Hana-ogi's train, because when I got to my room and looked out at the Bitchi-bashi, there was Hana-ogi crossing it in the April moonlight. I rushed down to speak with her but she passed proudly by, her cream-colored zori going pin-toed along the railroad track to her dormitory.

I didn't sleep much that night because when I got back to my room I found a letter which had been delivered by special messenger. It contained a routine reminder of recent orders issued by Camp Kobe and along the foot in capital letters I read: ANY PUBLIC DISPLAY WHATEVER OF AFFECTION FOR A JAPANESE NATIONAL BY A MEMBER OF THIS COMMAND IS FORBIDDEN. OFFICERS SHOULD NOT EVEN APPEAR ON PUBLIC STREETS ACCOMPANIED BY WOMEN OF THE INDIGENOUS PERSONNEL.

I knew that I was entangled in a ridiculous situation, for I could not walk with Hana-ogi in the city and she could not walk with me in town. If General Webster caught me dating a Japanese girl I would be disciplined and if the Takarazuka people heard of Hana-ogi dating an American she would be fired from the Moon Troupe. It seemed like something borrowed from the play I was in at St Leonard's. Then I was a prince trying to prevent my niece from marrying a penniless schoolteacher. The kid who played the schoolteacher was a miserable drip in real life and I remember that on-stage I became pretty outraged, but now it was happening to me, and Mrs Webster riding herd on me and the Takarazuka railroad company protecting their investment in Hana-ogi were going to be a lot tougher than a Ruritanian prince played by seventeen-year-old Lloyd Gruver.

For about two hours that morning as I lay awake–from three to five–I decided the whole affair was too damned silly, but toward dawn I began to see Hana-ogi dancing along the wall of my room and her classical postures, the stamping of her feet and the gestures of her right hand allured me so that I could think only of her tight and disciplined body. My thoughts were filled with the grace of her movement and as the sun rose I fell asleep knowing that somewhere within the triangle of the three cities we would meet.

OLD FARMER: 'Each drop of fertilizer I place
against the stalk of the plant by hand—not to
waste any.'

It came unexpectedly. On a warm day in May I waited for Hana-ogi at the Bitchi-bashi but she did not appear and disconsolately I wandered down to the railroad station to purchase a ticket back to Itami, but as I approached the cage I saw Hana-ogi standing off to one side, holding a ticket in her hand and impulsively, even though we were in the heart of Takarazuka, she came to me and we went to the ticket cage together and we bought two tickets for a small town at the end of the line, and on this lovely day we walked for the first time through the ancient Japanese countryside.

Hana-ogi, unable to speak a phrase of English, and I quite as dumb in Japanese, walked along the rice fields and across the little ridges that ran like miniature footpaths beside the irrigation ditches. We nodded to old women working the fields, laughed at children, and watched the white birds flying. Hana-ogi wore her green and white kimono and her cream zori and she was a bird herself, the May wind catching at her loose garments and the branches of trees tousling her delicate hair.

Wherever we went the land was crowded. Where in Texas there would be one farmer here there were forty. Where the footpaths in New Hampshire might be crowded with three people, here it was overwhelmed with fifty. There were no vacant fields, no woodlots, no mossy banks beside the wandering streams. On every foot of land were people and no matter how far we walked into the countryside there were always more people. More than any day I ever lived in my life I treasure this day because I discovered not only Hana-ogi's enormous love but I also discovered her land, the tragic, doomed land of Japan, and from it I learned the fundamental secret of her country: too many people.

In Korea we used to joke about enlisted men who bought Japanese girls of sixteen or seventeen—a man could buy a young girl anywhere in Japan—and we thought it a horrible reflection on Japan, but today I saw that it would always be possible to find some Japanese farmer who would be eager to sell his daughter to a kind man, for if she stayed at home and had to fight for her share of the skimpy rice in the family bowl she could never do as well as if she went off with a man who could buy rice for her. All the problems we used to laugh about as being so strange—so unlike America—I saw explained this afternoon. The Japanese were no different from us. Their farmers loved their daughters exactly as Iowa farmers love theirs. But there was not enough land. There was never enough food.

I thank God for that May evening walking among the rice fields while the crickets droned at us, for if I had not seen this one particular old man tending his field I am sure that when I finally learned the terrifying truth about Hana-ogi I could no longer have loved her; but having seen this old man and his particles of soil I loved her the more.

He stood where a trail turned off from the main road, leaving in the joint a thin sliver of useless land that in America would have been allowed to grow up in burdock. In Japan this tragic triangle was a man's field, the sustenance of one man's large family. On this May night he was bent over the field, digging it to a depth of fourteen inches. The dug soil he placed reverently to one side until his tiny field was excavated. Then, as we watched, he took each handful of soil and gently pulverized it, allowing it to return to its bed. Pebbles he tossed aside and sticks and foreign things, and in the two days that followed this man would finger each item of his soil. Not for him a plow or a harrow, but the gnarled fingers and the bending back.

It is difficult for me to report these things, for I cannot explain how Hana-ogi explained them to me. By pointing, by gesturing, by little pantomimes with the old man she explained that he was like her father except that her father's field—before the American bombs killed him—was slightly bigger. But her father had nine children.

It was breathlessly apparent to us as the sun sank below the distant hills that in terribly crowded Japan Hana-ogi and I were seeking a place in which to make love. There was now no thought of Japanese or American. We were timeless human beings without nation or speech or different color. I now understood the answer to the second question that had perplexed me in Korea: 'How can an American who fought the Japs actually go to bed with a Jap girl?' The answer was so simple. Nearly a half million of our men had found the simple answer. You find a girl as lovely as Hana-ogi—and she is not Japanese and you are not American.

As we walked into the twilight we drew closer together. She took my hand and also took my heart and as dusk fell over us we searched more urgently from side to side. We were no more looking at the white birds or the old men bending over their fields. We were looking for a refuge—any kind of refuge—for we were desperately in love.

I remember that once I thought I saw a grove of trees, but they were houses, for random trees were not allowed to grow in Japan. Again Hana-ogi pointed to a barn, but it was occupied. In Japan there was not even spare land for love.

But at last we came to a structure that was familiar to me, two inclined massive poles with two more set across them at the top like an enormous capital A, flat at the point. It was the timeless symbol of a Shinto shrine and here there were trees, but as always there were people too. We watched them come through the towering A, stand silently before the shrine, clap their hands three times, bow and depart, the torn white paper and the rice ropes of their religion fluttering quietly in the wind above them.

Hana-ogi took my hand and led me past the shrine until we came to a grassy bank partially protected by four trees. Villagers passed ten feet from us and dogs barked nearby. Across the mound we could see the dim lights of houses, for there was no empty countryside as I had known it in America. There was no place where there were not people. But at last we had to ignore them and it seemed to me as I sank beside Hana-ogi in the May twilight that we were being watched by the million eyes of Japan.

I remember vividly two things that happened. I had no conception of a kimono and thought it a kind of wrap-around dress but when we embraced and it was clear that Hana-ogi intended that we love completely, I tried to undo this gossamer dress, but it led to another and then another and to still more and although we could not speak we fell to laughing at my astonishment. Then suddenly we laughed no more, for I was faced with the second vast occurrence of the day, for when in the fading light I at last saw Hana-ogi's exquisite body I realized with shock–even though I was prepared to accept it–that I was with a girl of Asia. I was with a girl whose complete body was golden and not white and there was a terrible moment of fear and I think Hana-ogi shared this fear, for she caught my white arm and held it across her golden breasts and studied it and looked away and then as quickly caught me to her whole heart and accepted the white man from America.

We returned at last to Takarazuka and as we approached that lovely place we went into separate cars and I waited long till Hana-ogi had disappeared across the Bitchi-bashi before I appeared on the streets, heading for the Marine Barracks. Mike Bailey was in the shower and when he heard me go by he yelled and brought me back to military life with a fearful bang.

He said, 'Mrs Webster saw me in Kobe today and asked me a lot of questions.'

'About you and Fumi-chan?' I asked, nonchalantly.

'Don't play coy, son. About you and Eileen.'

'What'd'j tell her?'

'It isn't so much what I told her as what she asked.' He waited for me to press the point, but I called downstairs for some cold beer and he said, 'She asked me if you were going with a Japanese girl.'

I sort of gulped on my beer and Mike said promptly, 'Of course I said no. You aren't, are you?'

I took another drink of beer and pondered a long time what I ought to say. Then the pressing desire to talk with someone overcame me and I said, 'I've been walking with Hana-ogi. We must have walked for five miles and I'm so deep in love . . .'

Mike was a fine character to talk with at a time like this. He laughed and said, 'I feel like a traitor, Ace, getting you into this. Hell, I'm the one who's supposed to be in love.'

I said, 'It hit me like a propeller zinging around when you aren't looking. Jesus, Mike, I tell you the truth, I'm desperate.'

Mike laughed again and said, 'No need for a guy to be desperate in Japan. If you can't cuddle up to Hana-ogi because she's an actress, there's always the Tiger of Takarazuka. Better men than you . . .'

I started to say boldly, 'But we . . .' My voice trailed off and I ended lamely, 'The stars came right down and knocked me out.'

Mike looked at me quizzically, then said without joking, 'Look, Ace, I know better than most men around here how sweet a Japanese girl can be. But don't get involved. For the love of God, Ace, don't get involved.'

'I am involved.'

'Mrs Webster said the M.P.'s have instructions to pick up officers seen holding hands with indigenous personnel. That's a lovely phrase, isn't it?'

'I just don't give a damn, Mike. To hell with the M.P.'s and to hell with Mrs Webster.'

'I agree with you, Ace. But while I was talking with the general's main tank division her daughter came up and I got a good look. For Christ sake, Ace, that girl's a ravin' beauty. Why do you have to mess around with a Japanese actress if this Eileen is on tap?'

I put the beer down and stared at the floor. That was the question I had not wanted Mike to ask. I saw Eileen as I had known her at Vassar, bright, eager, a wonderful sport. I saw her that winter in Texas when her father was a colonel at

San Antonio and I was at Randolph Field. Why hadn't I married her then? Why had she turned down the other young officers and insisted upon waiting for me? I felt like the announcer who asks the burning questions at the end of each radio program about breaking hearts, but I knew that you could turn my radio on the next day and still not get the answers.

I looked up at Mike and said, 'I don't know.'

He asked me directly, 'Are you afraid of American women?'

I said, 'I hadn't thought of it.'

He said, 'I've been over here a long time, what with one thing and another. I've watched lots of our men go for these Japanese girls . . . Hell, I won't be superior about it. I do myself. Frankly and all kidding aside, Ace, I'd a damned sight rather marry Fumiko-san than Eileen. But I just wondered why you felt that way?'

'I don't feel that way. At least if I do I don't know about it. But why do you?'

'With me it's very clear. One thing explains it all. You ever had your back scrubbed by a Japanese girl? Not a bath attendant mind you. That's simple. But a girl who really loved you?'

'What's back scrubbing got to do with it?'

'Ace, either you understand or you don't.'

'What are you driving at?'

'I'm trying to say there are hundreds of ways for men and women to get along together. Some of the ways work in Turkey, some work in China. In America we've constructed our own ways. What I'm saying is that of them all I prefer the Japanese way.' He laughed and saw that I didn't entirely understand, so he banged his beer down and shouted, 'All right! One easy question! Can you imagine Eileen Webster scrubbing your back?'

It was a crazy question, a truly hellish shot in the dark, but I could immediately visualize fat little Katsumi Kelly the other night, taking her sore and defeated husband into the bath and knocking the back of his neck and getting him his kimono and quietly reassuring him that her love was more important than whatever Lt. Col. Calhoun Craford had done to him, and I saw runty, sawed-off Joe Kelly coming back to life as a complete man and I had great fear–like Mike Bailey–that Eileen Webster would not be able or willing to do that for her man. Oh, she would be glad to storm in and fight it out with Lt. Col. Craford, or she would take a job and help me earn enough so that I could tell Lt. Col. Craford to go to hell, or she could do a million other capable things; but I did not think she could take a wounded man and make him whole, for my mother in thirty years of married life had never once, so far as I knew, done for my father the simple healing act that Katsumi Kelly had done for her man the other night.

Mike said it for me. He laughed and said, 'There are all kinds of things wrong with Japan. But Japanese women aren't one of them and their view of love suits me fine.' Then he added, 'But I hate to see you be the one to take it all seriously. Because the Air Force would never let you marry a Japanese girl . . .'

'What would the Air Force have to do about it?'

'You'd see. You're one of their bright young men and they'd bring all sorts of pressures to bear . . .'

'Who's talking about marriage?'

Mike sighed. 'That's better. The way you started, you were talking about marriage.'

'I said I was confused.'

'I'd be confused too if I was involved with two women like Eileen and Hana-ogi.' He grew thoughtful and added, 'It's very strange. I'd never have picked Hana-ogi. She's always so mannish. Come to think of it, I've never seen her in girl's clothes. Have you?'

I thought of her rare charm and started to speak reverently but this scared Mike and he said, 'Ace, I know damn well you're thinking about marriage and it's going to be tough. Son, it's going to be tough.'

I insisted that I didn't know what I was thinking about, but my problem was solved for me in an unforeseen manner. Katsumi and Joe dropped by the air base the next afternoon and Katsumi took care of everything. Haltingly she said, 'We have find house for you, Ace.'

'A house!' I drew her toward a wall where no one could listen.

'Yes, one small house.'

'What do I want with a house?'

'Where else you and Hana-ogi-san stay?'

'Wait a . . .'

'You not love Hana-ogi?'

'Sure I love her, but . . .' I appealed to Joe, who grinned and said, 'When a Japanese girl loves you, Ace, it's solid. How you suppose I got my house?'

I said to them, 'Hana-ogi could get into trouble . . .'

Katsumi looked at me incredulously and said, 'When Hana-ogi come our house to see you it mean she love you. When she walk to Shinto shrine it mean same thing. Where you two make love? Here at Itami? I don't think so. (She pronounced it, 'I don' sink so.') Officers Club Kobe? I don't think so. Takarazuka? No!'

I was about to call the whole affair off when Katsumi handed me a map showing that the house was not far from hers. Then she said, gravely, 'Today Hana-ogi-san number one girl at Takarazuka. She work very hard for this. You be good man not tell anyone you love Hana-ogi. She make very dangerous come Osaka for you.'

'If it's so dangerous . . .'

'But she tell me all time she work hard she think some day she meet . . .' Katsumi blushed and could not continue, so I waited until she gained courage, whereupon she whispered, 'Hana-ogi tall girl. Not little fat girl same me. Long time she dream she meet tall man—same you.'

I must have shown my disappointment at being chosen because I was six-feet-two, so Katsumi said, 'She meet many tall men but no one brave like you—no one brave to stand at bridge many times to see her.' That was Katsumi's speech and as she left she said, 'Hana-ogi come your new house tonight seven o'clock.'

I was now overboard in the slipstream where things happen so fast you never get your parachute open. I was tumbling about and all thought of General Webster's orders, my promotion in service and my early ideas about the Japanese enemy were swirling in confusion. But of one thing I was determined. I would go to that house in Osaka early in the afternoon and I would clean it and I would stock the shelves with food and I would make it a home.

But at three-thirty I was called into an urgent meeting and it was nearly seven when I reached Osaka. I hurried up the main street to where my canal ran off to the right and I passed along the narrow footpath until I came to a little store, where I bought an armful of things to eat. Then I took a deep breath and walked out into the May twilight.

As I approached my house I saw that the sliding doors were open and from them came a bright light and a sight I shall never forget: a tiny cloud of dust followed by the merest flick of a broom. Hana-ogi had hurried to the new house to clean it for my arrival.

I dashed into the room, threw the food on the floor and took her in my arms. I kissed her wildly and pressed her golden cheek next to mine, but instead of the flood of kisses I anticipated she pushed me away, pointed to my shoes and cried, 'Oh, Rroyd-san!' For a moment I was bewildered and then she knelt down and started to untie my offending shoes. Quickly I prevented her from doing this, so she picked up the food I had dropped and when she placed it on the shelf I saw that with her own money she had already stocked the kitchen.

There was a pot cooking over the brazier and I looked in, then turned quickly to find Hana-ogi cleaning my shoes and placing them in the corner. I took three steps, lifted her away from my shoes and carried her into the middle of the room, where I stood looking about me helplessly till Hana-ogi laughed and with her expressive head indicated a closet which I kicked open, releasing the bed roll. I spread it as well as I could with my feet and gently placed Hana-ogi upon it. She closed her slanted eyes for a moment, then looked up and smiled, pulling me down beside her.

EASY LESSONS IN ENGLISH, 1879: 'Ever your devoted and humble servant.'

In the days that followed I often recalled the stories I had read about American and English sailors who had fallen in love with island girls and of how idyllic it was. But these damnable stories invariably ended with the big kiss and it had not occurred to me that after the big kiss these island lovers must have had things they wanted to talk about. But how did they talk without any language? How in hell did they talk?

I do not think that those who have always stayed at home can understand how terrible a thing language is, how dependent we are upon it. During the tremendous weeks that followed when May flowers bloomed along our canal there were times when I almost tore at my throat trying to find some way to express an emotion to Hana-ogi. It's all right to gesture at a girl's eyes and indicate that they are lovely but if you feel your heart expand at the very sound of her quiet approach along the canal—if you feel the earth tremble at night when she brings your soft pillow to the bed roll while beside it she places her canvas pillow filled with rice bran—then you feel that you must speak to her or perish.

I knew exactly four Japanese phrases. *Ichi ban* meant *number one* and I used this interminably. When I first saw Hana-ogi undressed I gasped at her amazing beauty and cried, 'Ichi ban!' When she cooked a good meal it was 'Ichi ban.' When she saw President Truman's picture in the paper I said, 'America ichi ban.' And once when she suggested that her breasts were too small I protested, 'Ichi ban! Ichi ban!'

I also knew *Domo arigato gozaimasu*, which meant *thank you.* I used it all the time and it was curious how this phrase of courtesy came to mean so much to us.

We were deeply indebted to each other, for we had undertaken unusual risks, so there was an extra tenderness about all we did. When I spread the bed roll I would say, 'Dom' arigato' but more often I used the full phrase. I was in a land of courtesy where great courtesy had been extended me.

Of course I knew the universal Japanese words *takusan* and *sukoshi* for *much* and *little.* Every American in Japan used these words as his final comment upon an infinity of subjects. The words look strange to me as I write them, for in Japanese the letter *u* is not pronounced in connection with *k* and it was taksan this and skoshi that just as it was Ta-ka-raz-ka and skiyaki rather than sukiyaki. I remember once when I was moved to great depths by something Hana-ogi had done and I pointed to my heart, put her golden hand above it and cried, 'Takusan, takusan!' And I indicated that it was for her that it had become takusan after having been sukoshi for so many years.

And finally I knew that strangest of Japanese phrases, *Ah, so desu-ka!* It was usually abbreviated *Ah, so!* and meant exactly what it would mean in English. It was also shortened to *Soka, Soda,* and *Deska* and I used it for everything. Often I would hear Hana-ogi and Katsumi talking and one of them would be narrating something and the other would repeat over and over in the most mournful way, 'Ah, so desu-ka! Ah, so desu-ka!' We all laughed hilariously when Joe found an American newspaper item in which a famous woman journalist from New York said that even the Empress of Japan was becoming Americanized because she spoke a little English. 'All the time I talked with the Empress she nodded her head and whenever she agreed with me she said clearly, "Ah, so!"'

Hana-ogi, on her part, had acquired just about as much English. Like all Japanese girls her favorite phrase was *Never hoppen!* She could say this with the most ravishing wit and effectively kill any high-blown idea I might be trying to make, but once when I said that some day she would see New York she said with great finality, 'Never hoppen.'

A second phrase she used a great deal was one she picked up from Katsumi and it too was common all over Japan: *I don't think so.* Hana-ogi had trouble with *th* and this phrase of classic doubt usually came out, 'I don' sink so.'

But if Hana-ogi had difficulty with *th,* her conflict with *l*'s and *v*'s and *f*'s was unending. She had acquired, from her Takarazuka shows, a few American phrases which she loved to use on me at unexpected moments, but they were so mangled because of the limited alphabet of sound in the Japanese tongue that I often had to think twice to detect her meaning. Once, at the end of a long night when we stayed up to clean our tiny house she caught me in her arms and cried, 'Oh Rroyd, I rub you berry sweet.' I was unprepared both for her emotion and her pronunciation and for one dreadful moment I almost laughed and then I looked down at her dear sweet slanted eyes and saw that they were filled with tears and we sat down on the tatami as morning broke and she told me in signs and kisses and strange half-words that she had never thought that she, Hana-ogi—dedicated to Takarazuka and knowing nothing else—would ever discover what it was to . . . She stopped and we had no words to finish the thought. Then she jumped up and cried, 'I make you cawhee.' And she took down the coffee pot.

It was true that not being able to talk made our physical love, there on the tatami mats, more powerful, but when that was past, when you lay there on the dark floor and heard feet along the canal path, you yearned desperately to talk of ordinary things, and once I thought of what Joe had said and I wished to God that I might be able to talk with Hana-ogi about the country club or the braces on junior's teeth or anything trivial at all–like the news that Katsumi-san was going to have a baby. I wanted to talk about that baby, what it would be like, would its eyes be Japanese, would it live well in America, but all I could do was to place my hand on Hana-ogi's hard flat stomach and whisper, 'Katsumi-san takusan–takusan.' And she kept my hand there and said back, 'Maybe some time Hana-ogi takusan' and we looked at each other and I think we both prayed that some day Hana-ogi would be takusan.

The matter of praying gave us some trouble, as it did Joe and Katsumi. Joe, being a good Catholic, was repelled when Katsumi established in their home a Shinto shrine, complete with symbols to be prayed to. There were some heated words and the shrine came down, but I don't think Hana-ogi would have agreed to surrendering her Shinto faith, for one day I came home and found that she had erected in our home three separate shrines: Shinto, Buddhist and Catholic. I tried to explain that I wasn't any of the three, but she said she was willing to be all of them for me. I asked her why she honored both Shinto and Buddhism and she said that many Japanese were both and that some Christians as well, and she found nothing curious in tending the three shrines faithfully and I noticed that she paid just as fair attention to my one as she did to her two.

It became so imperative that we converse with each other that we looked forward with sheer delight to the visits of Joe and Katsumi and I was glad whenever Katsumi sneaked away from Joe's surveillance and came to our house to pray to her Shinto gods for her baby to be a boy and strong. Whenever she appeared Hana-ogi and I would unleash an accumulation of questions about the most trivial things. I would say, 'Tell Hana-ogi I like more salt in all my vegetables.' Imagine, I had been unable to convey that simple idea accurately. And Katsumi would reply, 'Hana-ogi want know, you ever eat octopus?' and I would cry, 'Is that what she was trying to ask?' and I would repeat the word *octopus* and Hana-ogi would tell me what it was in Japanese and thus we would possess one more word to share.

But the hoard of meanings grew so slowly that I used to look with envy upon the G.I.'s I saw who had mastered the language. Once buying groceries I met a tough Texas boy with his Japanese girl and they were having an argument over some apples. Finally he asked in disgust, 'Hey, whatsamatta you?'

The little Japanese girl caught her breath, grew trembling mad and slapped the Texas G.I. right across the face. Then, hands on hips, she demanded, 'Whatsamatta you, you whatsammata me? I whatsamatta you first!'

The G.I. laughed and picked up a box of candy, saying with a bow, 'You my gal friendo ichi ban. I presento you.' The little girl put her arm in his, cocked her head on one side and asked him if he thought her pretty: 'Steky-ne?' He kissed her and cried, 'You're steky-goddamned-ne, baby.'

I envied the couple, for they had created a language of their own and it permitted them to convey their affection accurately. Like young children who refuse to be bothered by language, they ignored both Japanese and English and inhabited a delightful world of their own.

I returned with my purchases and asked, 'Hana-ogi, what *steky-ne?*' She thought for a moment then put my finger on an especially attractive design on her kimono and said, 'Steky-ne.' I thought she was referring to the needlework and I pointed to another part of the kimono and asked, 'Steky-ne?' but she shook her head.

I was perplexed, so she thought and took my finger and outlined her wonderful oval face, leaving my hand at her chin, asking, 'You think–steky-ne?' And then I realized what the word meant and I kissed her warmly and whispered, 'Steky-takusan-takusan-ne.'

But as the days passed and as we fell more hopelessly in love we discovered that it was impossible to exist as passionately as we insisted without better communication of ideas, so I started to learn a little Japanese and Hana-ogi–who despised Americans and what they had done to Japan–reluctantly joined an English class. She bought a little conversation book which she studied each day on the train back and forth to Takarazuka and one night she volunteered her first complete sentence in English. Screwing up her courage like a schoolgirl reciting Milton, she swallowed, smiled at me and declaimed, 'Lo, the postillion has been struck by lightning.'

The shock of these words was so great that I burst into uncontrolled laughter and I saw Hana-ogi slowly freeze with hatred. I had laughed at her best intentions. I too was an American.

I rose quickly from the floor to apologize, but when she saw me move toward her she ran away. Grabbing her English book she tore it to pieces and threw them at me. Those pages which fell at her feet she trampled upon and screamed in Japanese as she did so.

Finally I caught her hands and kissed her. I held her head to mine and when she started to sob I could have torn my tongue out. This cruel inability to speak was killing us and we were becoming lost people in a void of ideas . . . We were lovers who could not love and when Hana-ogi had sought to bridge this gap–humiliating herself and surrendering her hatred of the enemy–I had laughed at her.

I realized then that words must no longer be permitted to keep us apart. I lifted Hana-ogi to the bed roll and placing her beautiful legs toward the fire, I held her head close to my heart and burst into my own words, whether she could understand them or not. That night I said, 'Hana-ogi, Hana-ogi! I love you with all the heart and mind within me. I've been a barren desert . . . I've been a man flying a lost plane far in the sky and I have never before known a human being. Now I've come to an alien land among people I once hated and I've met you and taken you away from these people and brought you to a tiny house and you have made a shred of heaven here. Hana-ogi, if I've hurt you through my ignorance you ought to lash me through the streets of Osaka, for my heart is in your care and if I were to hurt you I would be destroying myself. Whether you understand or not, these words are for you.' And I kissed her.

I believe she comprehended what I said, for with her face now pressed to mine she spoke softly in Japanese and I think she unburdened herself of the accumulated passions that had been tormenting her word-stricken heart. I closed my eyes and listened to the wonderful sound of her voice as she uttered the strange, angular syllables of her native language. She said one word which sounded like *hoshimashita* and I looked up and said it and she laughed and kissed my lips to keep them still while she completed her statement. She did not use one word I understood, but the meaning of her thoughts somehow seeped through and we knew that we were more deeply in love than ever before.

From that night on Hana-ogi and I talked with each other a great deal and we discovered that in love what is said is far less important to the person spoken to than the one who speaks. If I wanted to tell her that the days were growing longer and that I first noticed this during the year when I was a young boy on an Army base in Montana, I said just that, and it was marvelous for me, for then I remembered how I felt as a boy–the great cleanness of life and the bigness–and I had a larger heart with which to love. And Hana-ogi spoke to me of her childhood and of how she dreamed of going to Tokyo and of how, when she got there, it seemed so much smaller than she had imagined. I understood only a little of what she intended, but one thing I understood with amazing clarity: when she had talked of these things for a long time she was lovelier than I had ever imagined a woman could be. In those long nights of talking, there in the bed roll on the tatami mats, I think we came closer to sharing with complete finality two human lives than will ever be possible for me again. Forbidden the use of words, we drove our hearts to understanding, and we understood.

In the morning after Hana-ogi tore up the English book I gathered the mutilated pages to burn them, but in doing so I noticed that her book had been published in 1879 by a brilliant Japanese scholar who had apparently been bowled over by English during those first wonderful days when Japan was opening her gates to Western learning. This gentleman's first sentence 'for young ladies to use when starting a conversation in public' was Hana-ogi's epic 'Lo, the postillion has been struck by lightning,' and although I am sure the ancient scholar never intended it so, that sentence became the gag line of an American-Japanese home. Whenever trouble appeared in any form Hana-ogi would declaim, 'Lo, the postillion!'

I became intrigued by the book and smoothed out some of the other pages which yielded gems like 'The portmanteau of my father is in the room of my mother,' Hana-ogi asked me what this meant and I tried to explain, but the more I endeavored the sillier it all became until we were convulsed with laughter and I remember thinking, while Hana-ogi tickled me in the ribs, of the G.I. booklet on Japan which said: 'The Japanese have no sense of humor.'

But the phrase that quite captivated me was the very first one for use at a formal tea 'where the participants are not well acquainted.' The professor advised loosing this bombshell. 'The camel is often called the ship of the desert.' It seemed to me that this sentence was the essence of Japan: few Japanese had ever seen a camel and no one could care less what a camel was like than young ladies at tea, but the stubborn fact remained that the camel had sometimes been called the ship of the desert, so the sentence was judged to be just as good an opening salvo as any other. I tried to explain to Hana-ogi how ridiculous the whole thing was but she went to great pains to explain, with gestures, how the camel strides over the sand and seems to be a rolling ship and how the beast can go for many days without water and how there are two kinds of camels, one with one hump and the other with two. I tried to stop this flood of information, but she grabbed me by the hand and ran me down the alley to Katsumi's, where the two girls fairly exploded Japanese and Katsumi brought out her treasure chest and Hana-ogi ran through the magazines till she found one with her picture on the cover and on the inside were half dozen pictures of her as a noble Arabian bandit in a desert extravaganza called *The Silver Sheik.* Then she commanded Katsumi to translate and Katsumi said, 'But the camel really is called the ship of the desert.' I bit my lip and pointed to a picture of Hana-ogi in flowing robes and said, 'Ichi ban, ichi ban,' but Hana-ogi studied it and shook her head no. She pointed to another and said, 'Very nice,' ('Berry nice,' she called it) and this one showed her in better profile.

From time to time during this long spring of the year I used to reconsider Mike Bailey's question: Did I love Hana-ogi because I was afraid of American women? At first the question had seemed ridiculous. True, I was afraid of the incessant domination of a mother-in-law like the general's wife, but I was certainly not afraid of Eileen, except when she imitated her mother, and so far as I knew I had never been afraid of American women in general. In fact, I had always liked them very much and so far as I can remember there was never a dance at the Point or at any of the Air Force bases that I didn't attend–and almost always with my own date. I decided that American women didn't scare me. But then came the problem of the weekies and I was never again so sure.

I had noticed that for some days Katsumi-san had been trying to speak with me alone and I guessed that she was hoping I might know some special way whereby she could get into the United States. Since I could give her no help I tried to avoid discussing the doleful question, but finally she caught me and asked, 'Major, you my friendo ichi ban?'

'Yes.'

'Then maybe you buy me weekies?'

'What are weekies?'

'You go P.X. Pleeze, Ace, I not able to buy weekies.'

'Why not?' I demanded. 'All wives get P.X. cards.'

I remember that Katsumi held back, as if not wanting to report Joe's troubles, but under my questioning she said, 'Colonel Craford not give me pass. Not give any Japanese wife pass. He hate us. He hate Joe for marrying Japanese.'

This made me sore, so I started out for the big avenue where the Osaka P.X. was but I stopped short and returned to the alley. 'Katsumi,' I yelled, 'what in hell are weekies?'

She slid back the paper doors and tried to explain but she was promptly overcome with embarrassment and said only, 'Pleeze, Gruver-san. I want to be same like American girl. I want to make Joe takusan happy.' So I set out.

At the P.X. two tall guards shrugged their shoulders when I asked what weekies were and I would have given up the job except that I was disgusted to have a gentle person like Katsumi pushed around. So I found one of those super-efficient Japanese officials who sit at desks and always seem to know everything. When I consulted him he frowned noticeably and said, 'Fifth floor, frame four.' He spoke slowly, wrestling with each difficult letter so that his reply sounded; 'Hihth hroor, hrame hore.'

I took the elevator to the fifth floor and found to my uneasiness that it contained women's wear. On the whole floor there were only three men, enlisted soldiers buying things for their girls. But there were nearly a hundred American wives and when they saw me in this department they were unanimously outraged. I was obviously another American man shacked up with some cheap Japanese girl and I had come here to buy her nylons or a dress or some other gift as part of my purchase price. I started to blush as stares of disgust followed me and mumbled to myself, 'You're out of your depth, squarehead.' But that was before I knew what weekies were.

I stepped up to the stocking counter and a pert Japanese girl said briskly, 'You are not allowed to buy nylons, Major, unless you have your wife's card.' There were a half dozen officers' wives at the counter and they smiled indulgently. I said quietly, 'I didn't want nylons. I wondered if you could tell me where the weekies are.'

The American women started to laugh outright and I was grateful when the Japanese clerk said, with exaggerated politeness, 'Over there, Major.' She pointed to the frame containing silk underwear while the women behind me laughed again.

It would have been simpler, I suppose, if I had cut my throat right then. Certainly the stores couldn't have been any tougher or my confusion greater. But I walked as inconspicuously as I could to the lacy counter where, as if by prearrangement, the clerks waited on everybody else first. So as I stood there, trying to look at some indefinite spot on the wall but always hitting brassieres or girdles, I became aware of the conversation around me. It was intended for me to hear.

The first officer's wife said, 'I suppose many of our men get trapped by these girls.'

The second said, 'I never see them fighting very hard to stay free.'

The first replied, 'I can understand enlisted men and Japanese girls. Probably never knew any decent girls in America.' You could tell from the emphasis that unquestionably the speaker was decent.

The second agreed, 'But what is impossible to understand is how an officer can degrade his uniform.'

Fortunately a clerk appeared and I said, 'I'd like some weekies.'

The American wives broke into laughter and the clerk said, in the sing-song professional voice used by Japanese girls, 'Small, medium or large?'

I gulped and asked, 'What are weekies?' This caused a real flurry of laughter in which the Japanese girl joined.

She reached under the counter and produced an open carton containing a bunch of pink nylon panties. Grabbing one she dangled it in the air and asked, 'Small, medium or large?'

Now more women gathered about the counter and there was an outburst of uncontrolled hilarity. I figured that nothing else could happen so I said, 'I'll take that one.'

At this there was hysterical laughter and the Japanese girl popped her hand over her mouth for a moment, then showed me the band of the panty she was holding. 'Major, weekies are one for every day of the week.' And she showed me the embroidered word Thursday.

Frantically I indicated the entire pile and said, 'I'll take them all.'

But the clerk said, 'These sample only. Small, medium or large?'

In despair I tried to think of how Katsumi looked. My mind was an aching blank and I pointed blindly at another Japanese clerk and said, 'Her size, I guess.'

Behind me one of the women whispered sweetly, 'He doesn't remember how big she is!'

I looked around me at the faces of my countrywomen. They were hard and angular. They were the faces of women driven by outside forces. They looked like my successful and unhappy mother, or like powerful Mrs Webster, or like the hurried, bereft faces you see on a city street anywhere in America at four-thirty any afternoon. They were efficient faces, faces well made up, faces showing determination, faces filled with a great unhappiness. They were the faces of women whose men had disappointed them. Possibly these harsh faces in the Osaka P.X. bore an unusual burden, for they were surrounded each day with cruel evidence that many American men preferred the softer, more human face of some Japanese girl like Katsumi Kelly.

As I paid the clerk I overheard the first officer's wife say, 'All little Jap girls who live with G.I.'s are crazy for anything that will make them seem more American.' The second turned to watch me go and added, 'Including American men.' But as I left these tough, bitter women and walked through their circle of bleak and unforgiving faces I saw near the elevator an American girl who could have been Eileen Webster. She was beautiful and fresh and perfect and I almost cried aloud with pain to think that something had happened in American life to drive men like Mike Bailey and me away from such delectable girls.

BUDDHIST MONK, 1794: 'This bell we received as a
gift from the girls of Yoshiwara.'

Since I now knew that the secret of love is communication, I wish I could tell you exactly how Hana-ogi and I learned to talk in those exquisite days of early love, but I cannot recall how it was done. I do remember the evening when I tried to ask Hana-ogi what her name meant. I was barefooted and wearing the cheap blue-and-white kimono so common in Japan. I sat with my back against the fragile wall, my feet awkwardly out upon the tatami. I tried to convey the idea: 'What does Hana-ogi mean?' but I did not succeed for the only two words she understood were *what* and her own name and she naturally suspected that I wanted to know what she wanted. So with tiny gestures and much pointing she indicated our small house of great love and said that all she wanted was to be here with me, that she wanted to hear me splashing in the tub, that she wanted to cook our meals over the glowing fire and that when she slid the paper doors shut in the evening she wanted to lock us in and the world out.

Quietly I sat against the wall and tucked my kimono tighter about me, relishing the delicate thoughts she had expressed for both of us. But then I tried again and this time she cried, 'Ah, so desu-ka! The other Hana-ogi! Yes, Rroyd-san. I tell.'

It is here that I wish I could explain, but I can't. Knowing almost nothing of my language this extraordinary girl nevertheless told me the following story, while I scrunched against the wall, my knees against my chin. Some of the passages she danced, some of them she pantomimed, and some she spoke in such expressive Japanese that I could fairly guess their meaning. And this is the story she told me:

Once upon a time in a small village near Tokyo there was a girl of great beauty. No one knows her name, but she was to become Hana-ogi, the most renowned prostitute in the entire history of Japan. As a child she lived with her widowed mother but it soon became apparent that her only possible future lay in the green houses of Yoshiwara, the ancient walled quarter by the marshes of Tokyo, where the unwanted young girls of farmer families were trained to become glowing and cultivated courtesans.

The old mother sold Hana-ogi when the rare child was seven, and for eight years this girl, always more beautiful, waited on the established courtesans of Ogi-ya, the green house which she would later make the most famous in all Japan. While she still wore her obi tied behind with its long ends signifying that she was virgin, the older girls taught her the skills of their trade and on her fifteenth birthday Hana-ogi discarded forever her real name, tied her obi in front, and took her first customer.

He was a young man from Odawara and he fell so desperately in love with Hana-ogi that he used to haunt the steps of Ogi-ya even when he had not the money to come inside. In perplexity he watched Hana-ogi become the most prized woman in Yoshiwara, and there were more than four thousand there at the time. She became famous for her poems, exquisite sighings of the heart and delicate memories of farm life when the early dew was on the rice fields. Priests in the temples sometimes told the worshippers of this saintly girl who took no thought of buying her own freedom from the green houses but who sent all her money home to her old mother. On holy days Hana-ogi went to a Buddhist temple that was known as the silent temple because it had no bell to record the great days and one evening Hana-ogi led a procession of thousands from the Yoshiwara bearing a bronze bell for this silent temple. It was her gift to the priests who were poorer than she.

Her fame became so great that visitors from China came to see this glory of Nihon. (My Hana-ogi rarely called her country Japan, never Nippon.) Poets wrote famous songs about her. Men close to the Shogun came to talk with her, and above all the painters of the passing world, the wood-block artists who lived along the edge of the Yoshiwara, made many portraits of her. Today, in the museum at Kyoto, you can see maybe three dozen famous paintings of Hana-ogi. When I see them, said my Hana-ogi, I think that this immortal woman is speaking to me across the years and I take courage.

Now all the time that the great men of the Shogun's palace and the world-famous painters were with Hana-ogi, the young lover from Odawara was watching, too, and one spring as the cherry blossoms were about to bloom he abducted Hana-ogi from the green houses. Where they hid themselves, these two happy people, no one knows. Whether they had children of their love no one can say. The years passed and bad luck fell on the house of Ogi-ya. No more did the rich men and the painters come there and no more did the priests of the nearby temples receive gifts from Hana-ogi. The portraits of this unforgettable girl were sold in great quantity, for everyone wished some memento of the loveliest woman Japan had ever produced.

Then one day there was a burst of glory. (Here the real Hana-ogi, my living grace, assumed a kind of cathedral beauty as she simulated an incredible procession.) Hana-ogi had come back to the green houses. She was thirty-four years old, more beautiful than she had ever been, more stately. Young girls walked before her, bearing flowers. A minister of state walked proudly behind her. Two men held umbrellas over her head, and she was dressed in an exquisite blue kimono with rich flowing robes of purple and the geta upon her feet were eleven inches high. Within five days the greatest artists of Japan had issued magnificent pictures of her joyous return, and we can see them still, the stately procession, the rare, wonderful woman coming back to her strange world.

It was the golden age! In those days there was singing and long talks and beautiful pictures and fine women and Nihon was never so joyous. And queen of the golden age was this country girl, Hana-ogi. She never explained her absence, she never told what had happened to her lover, but people guessed that like all Japanese men he had grown tired of her and had abused her. She lived at the Ogi-ya for many years and when she was too old to serve the visitors any longer she disappeared one day and no one ever again heard of Hana-ogi.

My living Hana-ogi folded her hands and sank upon the floor.

I was aghast at such an ending to so powerful a story and I cried, jumping to my feet, 'No! No! What happened to Hana-ogi?'

It took some time for me to explain myself and then my beautiful Japanese narrator stared up at me in surprise and said, 'In Nihon many girls. Every time new girls in Ogi-ya.'

I shouted that I knew that, but what had become of Hana-ogi? My adorable oval-face on the floor looked up in confusion and said, 'Hana-ogi become old girl.' (She pulled down the lines of her face and indicated that a tooth was missing.) 'She old, she go.'

'But where? Where did she go?'

My living Hana-ogi shrugged her shoulders. Then, sensing my disappointment, she formed the sign of a Buddhist temple and made believe to ring the bell which the ancient Hana-ogi had bought with her few coins and she indicated that no doubt this most glorious woman of Japanese history had been thrown out of the Ogi-ya when her teeth were broken and that she had possibly taken a position near the steps of the temple to beg alms.

There was an overwhelming ache upon my heart and I knelt upon the floor beside my Hana-ogi, who had fled her prison for her lover and whose future was as uncertain as her predecessor's. There was an enormous bond of tenderness between us and that was the definable beginning of my determination never to surrender this rare woman, this tender and gracious miracle.

The consequences of such a determination I did not then foresee, but they were explained to me in part by an event which occurred three nights later. Like any husband and wife we ultimately felt even our perfect home confining and we wanted to go to a movie, but this was no easy trick. Hana-ogi knew that I might be arrested if I appeared on the streets with her and I knew that she would get into serious trouble if she were seen with me, so she left our paper doors first and in five minutes I followed and we met inside the darkened theater and held hands like any beginning lovers, congratulating ourselves on having evaded the chaperones. But our luck didn't hold because this movie concerned the French Foreign Legion attacking a desert outpost and across the screen lumbered a long convoy of camels and Hana-ogi whispered, 'Ships of the desert!' and I fell to laughing so hard that finally she clapped her hand over my mouth and cried, 'Rroyd-san. Somebody see us.'

She was right. People did stare and two women recognized Hana-ogi as the great star at Takarazuka, so that when the lights went up these women choked the aisle and begged an autograph and soon Hana-ogi was surrounded by young girls.

We hurried out a side door and she fled alone down a back street and I ambled up the main street and when I got home I found her sitting dumb on the floor, her head bowed. She told me that she had always known that some time we would be found out and that she was not frightened. She would have to leave Takarazuka but she might find a job in pictures. Or there were certain theaters in Tokyo which might offer her work. She said, 'I not scare. But Takarazuka I like very very much.' (She said, 'I rike berry berry much.')

I suggested at once that perhaps she should leave me and return to Takarazuka dormitory and endanger no longer a brilliant career but she kept staring at the floor and said quietly words which meant this: 'I always planned to act till I was past forty, for I shall grow old slowly, and when my days as an actress were over I intended to take the place of Teruko-san, who was the greatest dancer Takarazuka ever had and who now teaches us the classical steps. But when I came here, Rroyd-san, I knew the danger I ran and if tomorrow were yesterday I would come here again.'

I think that's what she intended to say and I was deeply troubled by the responsibility I had undertaken and by the resolve I had made never to desert her, but when she saw my silent fears she put her soft hand upon my face and said, 'This time only time I be in love. I not stop our love one day before . . .' She made a great explosion with her hands as if the world had fallen in. She embraced me and we fell back upon the bed roll and I undressed her and her slim yellow body shone in the moonlight like a strand of gold that had fallen across my pillow, and she started to whimper and said, 'I not speak true. Oh, Rroyd-san, I afraid. I not want to leave Takarazuka. I not want to sit by temple – begging – old woman – teeth broken away. But if I go you now, I never find courage to come back. I never love nobody no more. Never, never. (She pronounced it, 'I nebber rub nobody, nebber, nebber.') I not want to be alone. I want to sleep here, with you.' Beside my head she placed her hard, tiny pillow stuffed with rice bran and we talked no more, for we were finding, as so many people must, that the ways of love are often terrifying when the day is done and one can no longer avoid studying the prospects of the future.

But next day she gave me proof of the courage she said she did not have. We were eating cold fish and rice when our doors slid back and disclosed beautiful Fumiko-san. A curious change came over Hana-ogi and it seemed that she was no longer in our little house but back on the stage at Takarazuka and I appreciated how desperately a part of her that theater was. Fumiko had come, she said, to warn us. An Osaka newspaperman had seen us at the movies and had informed the Supervisor, who had not reprimanded Hana-ogi that afternoon because he hoped she would come to her senses before he was forced to take official action. Fumiko-san implied that he had asked her to speak with the brilliant star who had so much to lose if she persisted in her indiscretion.

Hana-ogi was deeply disturbed by this news and I became aware that these two girls had long ago formed a team of mutual protection and that they had always stood together as a team against the difficulties and defeats of their profession. Earlier Fumiko had found an American who had imperiled her career by kissing her in public and Hana-ogi had protested. Now it was Fumiko's turn to sound the warning. The two exquisite girls talked for a long time in Japanese and I judged they were assessing the various risks in the situation but Fumiko's arguments did not prevail and she left with tears in her eyes. When she had closed the doors Hana-ogi said simply, 'I stay.'

I discussed with her the possible results of this choice, even at times coming close to arguing on Fumiko's side, so that Hana-ogi stopped short, stood facing me, and demanded, 'More better I go?' When I cried no and kissed her, she closed the discussion by saying, 'I stay.'

There was a firmness about her mouth when she said this and I was surprised, for I had come to look upon her as the radiant symbol of all that was best in the Japanese woman: the patient accepter, the tender companion, the rich lover, but when Hana-ogi displayed her iron will I reflected that throughout the generations of Japanese women there had also been endlessly upon them this necessity to be firm, not to cry, not to show pain. They had to do a man's work, they had to bear cruel privations, yet they remained the most feminine women in the world. Now that I knew them, these strange Japanese women, I saw the contradiction everywhere. Katsumi was having a baby when she hadn't the slightest idea how it would be cared for or under what flag, yet it was she who bolstered up the spirits of her family. Hana-ogi had placed her career in jeopardy for a few months in a tiny house along a canal with a man who could never marry her. The young girls I saw with their American soldiers, the little women bent double carrying bricks and mortar to the ninth story of a new building, the old women in rags who pulled plows better than horses, and the young wives with three children, one at breast, one strapped on the back, one toddling at her heels. I concluded that no man could comprehend women until he had known the women of Japan with their unbelievable combination of unremitting work, endless suffering and boundless warmth—just as I could never have known even the outlines of love had I not lived in a little house where I sometimes drew back the covers of my bed upon the floor to see there the slim golden body of the perpetual woman. I now understood why ten thousand American soldiers had braved the fury of their commanders and their country to marry such women. I understood why there were supposed to be many thousands of American-Japanese babies in the islands. I understood why perhaps a half million American men had wandered down the narrow alleys to find the little houses and the great love.

LT. COL. CALHOUN CRAFOD: 'You goddamned nigger-lover.'

On this night I could not sleep. I was agitated by Hana-ogi's problem although as events turned out, I should have been concerned about my own. I was aware that I had found that one woman whose mere presence beside me in the dark night made me both complete and courageous. Toward four in the morning I hammered my pillow in confusion and Hana-ogi wakened and felt my forehead and said, 'Rroyd-san, you sick!' And she leaped up from our bed and tended me as if I were a child and I hadn't the fortitude to tell her that I was in a trembling fever because her picture of an old woman huddling beside a Buddhist temple had made me nightmarish.

She cooled my head and wrapped dry sheets about us and I went to sleep assured that somehow we would escape from the inevitable consequences of our acts. But when I woke I was shivering again, not from fever but from outrage. For Lt. Col. Calhoun Craford, a paunchy red-faced man who hated every human being in the world except certain Methodists from his corner of a hill county in Georgia, stood over our bed. His round florid face looked like a decaying pumpkin as he stared down at us.

'Well,' he drawled infuriatingly. 'You doin' mighty fine down there, Major.' He kicked at the bed roll and Hana-ogi drew a sheet about her neck. Then Lt. Col. Craford got purple in the face and shouted, 'You get to hell up here, Major Gruver. The Giniral's gonna hear about this.' He muscled his way about our tiny room, knocking things over, and I leaped from bed, but before I could do anything he threw my pants in my face and grunted, 'Fine spectacle you are. A giniral's son, shackin' up with a nigger.'

With an almost premonitory sense I recalled Joe Kelly's violent threat one night when he had come home beat: 'Some day I'll kill that fat bastard.' I felt that if Lt. Col. Craford said one more thing in that room I'd beat Kelly to the job. I think the colonel sensed this, for he looked contemptuously at Hana-ogi huddled beneath the sheet and stalked through the paper doors. They trembled as he passed.

When Lt. Col. Craford showed me in to General Webster's office in Kobe the old man minced no words. 'What in hell does this mean, Lloyd!' He was much more profane than I can repeat and he had all the details. 'A fine, clean, upstanding man like you! The son of a general in the United States Army. Shacking up with some cheap . . .'

I stood there and took it. He never mentioned Eileen, but it was obvious that he was bawling me out on her behalf. She had been held up to public ridicule. His wife had been made to look silly. And I had outraged the military decencies.

He shouted, 'Did you sign that paper we sent you acknowledging my order about public displays of affection with indigenous personnel?'

'Yes, sir.'

'Then you know what's in the order?'

'Yes, sir.'

'But you defied the order?'

'No, sir.'

He exploded. 'What in hell do you mean, no sir?'

'I've never been guilty of public affection with a Japanese girl.'

Lt. Col. Craford stepped forward and said, 'One of my men saw them in the movies the other night. He followed them along the back streets. They were holding hands,' he added contemptuously.

'You're a liar!' I shouted.

General Webster rapped on the desk. 'You be still, Gruver. This is serious business. Now Craford, what actually happened?'

The repugnant colonel coughed, pointed at me with disgust and said, 'He flagrantly broke the order, Giniral. Made love on the streets with a Jap girl. Set up house-keepin' with her. We've checked her record. A cheap whore.'

'You . . .' I sprang from my position at attention and rushed at Craford. General Webster astonished me by reaching out and shoving me back.

'So you say you weren't seen with her?'

'That's what I do say, General Webster,' I cried.

He became quite angry and asked in a low voice, 'What do you call living together? Don't you call flagrant cohabitation a public display of affection?'

'No, sir,' I said. 'Not in terms of your order. We were never seen on the streets.'

The general lost his composure and said, harshly, 'I'm going to court-martial you, young man. You've broken every law of decency. You're under house arrest. Understand what that means?'

'Yes, sir.'

'Watch him, Craford. If he does anything, throw him in the stockade.'

'I will, sir,' Craford wheezed.

'Furthermore,' the general said, 'I've cabled your father.'

I gulped and he saw that that one had hurt, so I recovered by saying, 'All right, sir, but I wish you hadn't.'

'I wish you hadn't made an ass of yourself. Craford, take him under guard to his quarters.'

Lt. Col. Craford enjoyed humiliating me, especially since I was the son of a four-star general, and he made quite a flourish of depositing me in my informal prison. He marched me into the lobby of the Marine Barracks, up the short flight of steps leading to the elevators, and down the hall past all the open doors. 'This is it, nigger-lover,' he growled.

As soon as he was gone I called the motor pool to see if I could get hold of Joe Kelly. After the fifth call I made contact and he whispered, 'Can't talk, Ace, I'll be over.' He arrived around noon that morning and slumped into a chair, 'Jeez, Ace, the fat's in the fire.'

'What happened?'

'Old Blubber-gut sent a bunch of strong-arm boys to search your house. They photographed everything. I hope you didn't have any Air Force papers you shouldn't have. Anyway, they wrecked the joint and boarded it up for good.'

'What happened to Hana-ogi?'

'The neighbors say she slipped out right after you were arrested. Katsumi watched Blubber-gut's men tear up the house. Then she hurried out to Takarazuka with the news but Hana-ogi never batted an eye.'

'How can people take things so calmly?' I cried.

'You learn,' Joe explained. 'When you're a Japanese woman or an enlisted man, you learn.'

It was that evening that my real torment began, for when the performance of *Swing Butterfly* ended I looked down from my prison and saw graceful Hana-ogi, moving like a goddess down the flower walk and across the Bitchi-bashi and through the vegetable stalls and onto the path that led to the dormitory and long after she had disappeared I could see the image of that slim and graceful girl disappearing into the shadows—and I became more determined than ever that I must not lose her.

On the third evening after my house arrest began, I was sitting before the dismal meal of Marine food brought to my room by the waiter, when Mike Bailey opened my door softly, cased the joint like a detective, then motioned down the hall. In men's clothes, looking like a would-be janitor, Hana-ogi slipped in to see me. Mike made a hasty sign of benediction and tiptoed out.

I cannot describe how joyous it was to see Hana-ogi in my room. Not only had I been tortured by my longing to have her beside me in the bed roll but—as I realized now—I was even more hungry to hear her soft voice chattering of the day's events and I believe my heart actually grew bigger as she told me of the little things: 'Fumiko-san say I crazy. When Colonel Craford smash house two kimonos rost.'

'What do you mean, *rost?*'

'Men take. I no find.'

I became so incensed over the lost kimonos that I realized that I had reached a new meaning of the word *love*. I was engaged in a heavenly contest with Hana-ogi to see which of us could give most to the other and this experience of surrendering my desires to another human being was new to me and frightening in its implications. I was already thinking vaguely about the future and a perplexing problem popped out as a blunt question: 'Hana-ogi, how old are you?'

She counted thirty on her fingers and I felt as if a basket of icicles had been dumped over me, for a woman of thirty and a man twenty-eight seemed abnormal. I had known several officers married to women older than they and it always turned out badly. I was suddenly glum till I remembered that a Japanese girl is considered to be one year old at birth so we figured it out that Hana-ogi was really only twenty-nine and that furthermore during eight months of each year we would be the same age. It was extraordinary how much more beautiful she seemed at twenty-nine than she had been at thirty.

Toward morning she dressed and left my room, asking, 'You have dinner tonight – Makino's?'

I explained what house arrest meant and said that I had pledged my honor as an officer. She said simply, 'I have pledge my honor too. I have pledge the honor of my mother and the food of my two sisters.' Then she kissed me and left.

So that night I put my honour way down in the bottom drawer among my socks and crept through the alleys to Makino's and as I climbed the stairs to the little room where I had first seen Hana-ogi my heart beat like the throbbing of an airplane engine and I thought, 'God, that I should have become so involved,' but when I got there Hana-ogi in green skirt and brown blouse was waiting for me. Old Makino made us tempura and to my surprise I found I was getting to enjoy Japanese food. We talked of many things and Hana-ogi said that soon *Swing Butterfly* (she always called it *Butterfry*) would close in Takarazuka. Maybe it would go to Tokyo. The news was terrifying and I hadn't the courage to discuss what it might mean to us but she said, 'I no go Tokyo. I stay here and wait for you.'

It was incredible to me that she would give up Takarazuka and I said, 'Hana-ogi, you can't.'

Before she could reply Makino came running in and cried, 'M.P.'s!' Ashamed of myself I crowded into a cupboard and heard the heavy tread of Lt. Col. Craford's polished boots and in that moment I understood what an ugly thing fear was and why we had fought the last war against the Germans: we were fighting the tread of heavy boots. And then like the wind on a stormy day I completely changed and felt disgusted with myself, an Air Force officer breaking my word, hiding in a closet with a Japanese girl who should have hated me. It was the low spot of my life and when Lt. Col. Craford stamped down the stairs I stepped out of the closet and said, 'Hana-ogi, I've got to go back.'

She looked at me closely and asked, 'When M.P. come . . .' She pointed at the closet and asked, 'You sorry?' She could not find the right word for *ashamed* but she did bring a blush to her cheeks and she did act out my shame.

'Yes,' I said. 'I gave my word.' But as I turned to go a flood of terrible longing overtook me and I grasped her face in my hands and cried, 'Don't go to Tokyo, Hana-ogi. Wait here. I cannot let you go.'

Her slim, straight body grew limp and she whispered to me in Japanese, something which meant, 'Not Takarazuka or my mother could take me away.'

I kissed her hands as I done that first night. There were a hundred things I wanted to say, but I was choked with confusion. I walked boldly down the stairs, marched openly along the street to the Marine Barracks. Hana-ogi, aware of the deep shame I had felt in the closet and sharing it with me, marched just as brazenly beside me in her distinctive Takarazuka costume and kissed me goodbye at the barracks. 'Rroyd-san,' she said softy, 'I love you takusan much.'

GENERAL GRUVER: 'Say, do you think the Japanese can be trusted after we go home?'

When I entered the barracks, my father and General Webster were waiting. My father looked down the street at Hana-ogi walking bravely back to the dormitory and said, 'Pretty girl. Almost pretty enough to justify an officer's breaking his word.'

General Webster started to bluster but Father cut him short. He took us into the manager's office and let me have it.

My father is no puling one-star general ordered about by his wife. He said, 'You idiot. You poor, bewildered idiot.'

I have never heard my father swear. He chews gum when he's mad and makes the muscles in his jaw stand out and right now he looked as if he could beat me up. I stood at attention and looked straight ahead.

'What are you gonna do?' he asked contemptuously. 'Dishonor your uniform, humiliate your friends?' He walked around me then snorted. 'Some officer!'

General Webster said, 'You've broken your word of honor and you're going to be court-martialed.'

Father cut in and asked, 'Well, what are you gonna do?'

I said firmly, 'As soon as I get out of here I'm finding another house.'

General Webster gasped and Father stormed. 'That you won't do! There's a night plane to Korea. Get on it. I had some orders cut. Take them and get out.'

I said, 'All right, and when I come back it'll be to Hana-ogi.'

The effect of this strange name on my father was startling. Apparently he was unable to accept the fact that Japanese girls actually had names and that American officers might love those alien names and the curious creatures to whom they belonged. He shouted, 'Ruin yourself over some common whore!'

I had taken a lot these last few days and I'd had enough. I hauled back my right fist and let my father have one below the left ear. He staggered back, got his footing and came at me, but General Webster separated us. We were all trembling and furious but Webster spoke first: 'By God, you've struck a . . .'

'Get out of here, Webster,' my father snapped. 'I'll handle this.'

Frightened and dismayed, General Webster retreated and while we watched him go, I had a moment to steel myself for the brawl I knew must follow. Four times in my father's career he had dragged colleagues into a boxing ring where in the anonymity of shorts he had massacred them. Before our fight began I thought in a flash of how strange it was that I had belted my father for saying far less than what Lt. Col. Craford had said and I experienced a dizzy sensation that when he turned back to face me I would see my enemy and my friend.

I shook the dizziness away and cocked my fists, but when he turned he was grinning and chomping his gum. 'I take it she's not a prostitute,' he laughed.

I started to say, 'Sir, this girl . . .' but he interrupted me and pulled me into a chair beside him and asked, 'Son, what's this all about?'

Again I started to explain but he said, 'I flew out here from the Presidio to knock some sense into you. But you're not in the market for sense, are you?'

I said, 'I don't want any lectures.'

He laughed and chewed his gum and said, 'Son, I wouldn't respect you if you hadn't swung on me. She seemed right pretty and you say she isn't a tramp?'

I told him who she was and he said, 'By heavens, Mark Webster must have dropped his drawers when he heard about you having a house. He drove me in to see it. Say, they don't build very big houses in Japan, do they? Say, tell me how you promoted a house?'

I started to tell him about Katsumi and Joe but he said, 'Lord knows, son, I hoped you would marry Eileen Webster. Good family, staunch military background. Mother's a bit of a bore but in service you can always get away from her. Say, have you heard the news that really galls Webster? His daughter's serious about a real-estate salesman from Seattle. Major, I think. Webster's furious and is rotating the fellow back to the States.'

He sized me up carefully, chewing his gum, and said, 'Y'know, son, if you still wanted Eileen you could have her. Wait a minute! Don't underestimate that kind of marriage. Right now you're all boiled up about sex, but a man lives a long life after that fire goes down. Then you appreciate having a woman you can talk to, some one who knows military life. What do you and Madame Butterfly talk about?'

He waited for me to speak but as soon as I started he said, 'Let's get back to Eileen. You ever know any officers married to women who disliked the military? Sad lot. Sad business. Your mother and I haven't been what you might call romantic lovers . . .' He slapped his leg and burst into real laughter. 'Could you imagine your mother in a shack along a canal! But anyway we've always been able to talk. We want the same things. We want the same things for you, Lloyd.'

He paused and I thought I was back in St Leonard's on another occasion like this. My father was saying, 'Your mother and I want the same things for you, Lloyd,' but even then I knew for a certainty that Mother had never wanted those things for me and I had the strange feeling that if she were in Japan right now–and if she knew the whole story–she would be on my side and not Father's.

He said, 'I suppose you've figured what your present course would mean to things like life plans.'

'What do you mean, present course?'

'Well, getting married to a Japanese girl.'

'Married!'

'Sure, married.' He chewed his gum real fast and then said, 'You mean you haven't thought about marriage? You mean you think you're the smartest guy on earth. Can shack up with a girl, have children even, and never think of marriage.'

'I wasn't thinking of marriage,' I said weakly.

'I know you weren't,' he roared. From the other room General Webster stuck his head through the door and asked nervously, 'Everything all right?'

'Get out of here,' my father commanded, and I thought how rarely men like him could respect men like Webster or men like the one I seemed on the verge of becoming. 'Squaw man,' the Army would have called me in the old days. He walked up and down the room flexing his head muscles and then turned sharply, speaking in machine-gunlike tones.

'Don't you see what's gonna happen, son? You're gonna work yourself into a box. You'll be unable to find a solution. So suddenly you hit on marriage! You'll marry the girl and that'll make everything just dandy. Good God, son! You're twenty-eight years old. Why didn't you marry Eileen that summer in San Antonio?'

Softly, with the mention of Eileen's name, that first dreamy summer flooded back to me here in Kobe and I said, 'I never really understood, Father. I guess it must have been that bachelor party.'

'What party?' he asked suspiciously. 'What'ja do?'

'Not what you mean. Remember when General Hayward's son was marrying Della Crane?'

'You mean Harry Crane's girl?'

'Yes. Her father had been killed at the Bulge . . .'

'Damned brave man. We could use a few men like Harry Crane in Korea.'

'So Mark Webster's wife was more or less arranging the wedding. Very formal. But the night before a gang of us younger officers took Charley Hayward out and got him so drunk he was fifteen minutes late for the wedding. Everybody thought it was very funny except Mrs Webster. After the wedding she gave us a terrible tongue-lashing. It wasn't that we'd spoiled Della and Charley's wedding. It was that we'd spoiled her plans. I've always been afraid of Eileen since then.'

'Afraid?'

'Well, sort of. After the ceremony the four of us who had gotten Harry drunk drove out to Randolph Field. Nobody said anything and we drove very fast and once when a Ford truck almost socked us one of the men said, "That would be the second truck that mowed us down today," and we all laughed and got drunk again and for the rest of that summer I never really seriously thought about marrying Eileen. Then Korea came along.'

'But you have thought about marrying Madame Butterfly?'

'No,' I said.

'A son doesn't bust his father, Lloyd, unless he's thinking pretty deeply about something. Look, son. Suppose you do marry this yellow girl. I'm on the selection board and your name comes up. I'd pass you by and if I wasn't on the board I'd advise the others to pass you by. We don't want officers with yellow wives. And where would you live in America? None of our friends will want you hanging around with a yellow wife. What about your children? Y'can't send half-Jap boys to the Point.'

I thought it was very like my father to assume that all his grandchildren would be boys who would naturally attend the Point. I was going to say something about this, but he kept talking.

'Son, Mark Webster was blustering. I've talked him into forgetting your court-martial. When I was sore I asked him to cut orders sending you back to Korea. Even yet it's a great temptation for me to approve those orders and tell you to get back there and fight this thing out. But you've had Korea. Say, how are those Russian jets?'

I said they were good and he asked, 'Y'think that Russian pilots man those planes?'

I said I thought so but we hadn't captured any.

'Those Russian are bastards,' he said. 'Real bastards.'

I said, 'We've been able to handle them so far.'

He banged the chair and said, 'Son, don't take sex too seriously.'

I said, 'What should you take seriously?'

He said, 'A whole life.' He chewed his gum furiously and said, 'A whole, well-rounded life.'

I said, 'Promotions and place in society and things like that?'

He looked at me quizzically and said, 'You pulling my leg, son?'

I said, 'Like the way you married a general's daughter?'

He said very calmly, 'I ought to clout you. I just don't understand you sometimes. In ten years you'll be fighting the Japs again.'

'Maybe. But I won't be fighting Hana-ogi.'

'How can an officer get mixed up with a Japanese girl and take it seriously?'

I said, 'Look Pop. This gag worked once. This man-to-man . . .'

He looked half amused and asked, 'What do you mean?'

I said, 'Remember St Leonard's when I thought I wanted to skip the Point and study English or something like that?'

'Long time ago, I'd forgotten.'

'No you didn't, Pop. All the way out here from the Presidio you tried to remember what trick it was that convinced me then to do what you wanted me to do.'

He blustered a moment and said, 'Son, let's not obscure the facts. I'm here because you're my son and I'm very proud of you. Believe it or not I'm even proud that you had the guts to ignore Mark Webster's stupid order and find yourself a house in Osaka. But I don't want to see a decent American kid like you waste his life. Son, I've watched our men marry German girls and French girls and even Russian girls. Invariably, if you know the man, it's a sign of weakness. They're all panty-waists. Strong men have the guts to marry the girls who grew up next door. Such marriages fit into the community. They make the nation strong. In your case and mine such marriages fit into military service. Leave it to the poets and painters and people who turn their back on America because they're afraid of it to go chasing after foreign girls.'

He chomped his gum and said, much more slowly, 'I ever tell you about Charley Scales? Resigned his commission and joined General Motors. Said he'd make a lot of money and he did. Some years later he came to proposition me about joining him. Lloyd, that was in 1933 when the Army was the garbage can of democracy but I didn't even think twice. I've been tempted in my life but never by Charley Scales. Right now!' He snapped his fingers and said, 'Who'd you rather be, Charley Scales or me?'

It was a childish trick but it had a great effect on me. In my mind's eye I could see Charley Scales, a big, happy man of some distinction in Detroit and the world. But to compare him with my father was ridiculous.

Father said, 'You talk this over with your Madame Butterfly. You'll find she agrees with me.'

I said, 'I will.'

He said, 'By the way, where'd she learn English?'

I said she didn't speak English and he cried, 'You mean you've learned Japanese?'

I said, 'No.'

He stopped chewing his gum and looked at me. 'You mean—you have no common language? French, maybe?'

I said, 'Well, you see . . .'

'You mean you can't talk together?'

'Well on a really intricate problem she . . .' I was going to explain that she danced the words for me, but I felt that Father wouldn't understand. But he surprised me.

When he realized that we shared no language he became unusually gentle. I cannot recall his ever having been quite as he was at that moment. He put his arm about my shoulder and said reassuringly, 'Son, you'll work this thing out.'

He called for General Webster and said gruffly, 'Mark, I was wrong. I'm tearing up these orders for Korea. This kid doesn't need Korea. His problem is right here.'

General Webster said, 'That's what I told him and look how . . .'

'Mark, don't blow your top at this kid.'

'Why not? Disobeying an order, breaking his word, striking a superior . . .'

Father laughed and said, 'Now you and I know, Mark, that it was completely silly to issue such an order to a bunch of healthy young men surrounded by pretty girls. But that's beside the point. Don't get sore at Lloyd.'

'Why not?'

'Because he's going to be your son-in-law.'

'He's what?'

'He doesn't know it yet, and Eileen doesn't know it yet but if you want to do something constructive, keep real-estate salesmen away from your daughter. Because sooner or later she's going to be my daughter, too.'

The two generals stamped out of the barracks and in three hours my father was on his way back to the Presidio.

WATANABE-SAN: 'You pull this level and the steel ball shoots up there and falls back down.'

If Father thought that the tricks which had defeated me in prep school would still work he was misled, for now I knew my mind. I had met a delectable woman, one whom I could love forever, and I simply wasn't worried about fathers and generals and Air Force rules. Here on this earth I had found Hana-ogi and by the time my father arrived back in California she and I had things worked out. We made a deal with Joe and Katsumi whereby we took one corner of their house and here we established a life as warm and loving as two human beings have ever known.

I would come home from the airfield to find Joe and Katsumi preparing the evening meal. They would tell me what had happened that day and I would exchange military gossip with Joe, but it would be a nervous time, for I would be watching the door and finally we would hear Hana-ogi's soft steps coming up the alley and Katsumi and Joe would slip away for a moment to gather wood or buy things at the store. The door would open and there would be Hana-ogi, a glimmer of perspiration on her soft golden cheeks. Like all Japanese she carried her books and bundles wrapped in a bright silk shawl tied cross cornered, and when I think of her at the sliding door of that little house I see her kick off her saddle shoes, drop the silken bundle, run her hand through her hair and hurry across the tatami to kiss me. At such times I would catch her in my arms, swing her into the air and drop her behind the screen that cut off our portion of the room. There she would swiftly slip off her Western clothes and slowly fold herself into a brocaded kimono. She was lovely; beyond words she was lovely.

But I must not imply that the warmth and wonder of that house came solely from Hana-ogi, beautiful and complete as she was, for I think that I have never seen a more satisfactory wife than Katsumi Kelly. She organized her house to perfection and kept it immaculate, even though Hana-ogi and I were apt to be careless. She could cook, she could sew, she could talk on many subjects and as her pregnancy advanced she gave promise of being an even finer mother than she was a wife.

Sometimes I used to watch her and I recalled with embarrassment that once in the consul's office I had almost refused to kiss her because she seemed so clodden and repugnant with her giggling and her big gold tooth. Now she seemed to me one of the most perfect women I had ever known, for she had obviously studied her man and had worked out every item of the day's work so that the end result would be a happy husband and a peaceful home. I asked Joe about this once and he said, 'Ten years from now in America there'll be a club. Us fellows who married Japanese girls. Our password will be a suppressed giggle. Because we won't want them them other lugs down the street to discover what gold mines we got.'

I asked, 'Are all Japanese wives as good as Katsumi?'

He said, 'I admit I got somethin' special. But you don't hear the other boys kickin'.' We wrapped our kimonos around our legs and sat back to enjoy one of the sweetest moments of the day. The girls were preparing supper and we listened to them talking Japanese. Katsumi spoke rapidly—the day's gossip, no doubt—and Hana-ogi, washing our rice, said over and over at least two dozen times, 'Hai! Hai!' The phrase shot out of her mouth with such force it seemed to have come from the very bottom of her stomach, a cry of primeval terror. Actually it was merely the Japanese way of saying *yes.* But in addition to this machine-gun *hai* she kept nodding her head and chanting mournfully, 'Ah, so desu-ka! Ah, so desu-ka!' To hear the girls in any trivial conversation would convince you that some sublime tragedy had overtaken us all.

Joe finally asked, 'What are you sayin'?'

Katsumi looked up startled and explained, 'I speak Hanako-san about a fish my father catch one day.'

I started to laugh but Joe said quietly, 'Was it a big fish?'

'More big than this one,' Katsumi said proudly. 'Hanako-san say she never see such a fish.' I liked Katsumi's name for Hana-ogi. Japanese girls often take their names from feminine or poetic words to which they generally add -ko or -yo. Thus at Takarazuka most girls had names like 'Misty Snow' or 'Spring Blossom' or 'Starry Night'. And their names usually ended in -ko. For myself, I preferred the other form, Hanayo, and once Hana-ogi told me, 'Hanako more Japanese but Hanayo more sweet.'

The longer I lived with Joe Kelly, reared in an orphanage and rejected by his foster parents, the most astonished I was that he could adjust so perfectly to married life. He was a considerate husband, a happy clown around the house and the kind of relaxed and happy family man you see in the advertisements of the *Saturday Evening Post*.

Speaking of the *Post*, it helped me understand a little better what married life is. On May 30th the girls were all whispers and at dinner they sprang the big surprise! It was an American holiday, so they had pumpkin pie. Where they had finagled the pumpkin we never knew, but the pie was something out of this world, for they had used the pumpkin as you would apples or cherries and had baked it just as it came out of the can and it was really dreadful. I took one look at it and started to say, 'What . . .' but Joe cut me short and tasted his piece.

'It's good,' he said laconically.

The girls bit into their pieces and you could see them sort of look at each other as if to say, 'Americans must be crazy. To eat something like this on holidays.' We finished the disgusting dessert in silence and four days later Katsumi leafing through an old copy of the *Post* saw a picture of a real pumpkin pie. She waited till I got home and surreptitiously asked me if that was pumpkin pie. I said yes and she asked me how it stayed so thick and so soft and I told her how you made pumpkin custard and she started to cry and when Joe came home she hugged him and kissed him and told him how ashamed she was and since Hana-ogi wasn't home yet I sat glumly in my corner and thought about the time I had laughed at Hana-ogi for her sentence, 'Lo, the postillion has been struck by lightning,' and I concluded that Joe's way was better and I wondered how a kid from an orphanage could understand a problem like that while I hadn't had the slightest glimmer.

However, I must not imply that all Japanese women are perfect wives. A trip along our alley would convince anyone that Japanese homes contained every problem to be found in American homes; plus some very special ones. In the narrow house next to us lived the Shibatas. He was a minor business official who received practically no pay but had an enviable expense account from which he drew on most nights of the week for expensive geisha parties. He siphoned off part of the expense account to support one of the pretty young geishas on the side. It was rumored that he kept her in a second home near the center of Osaka and traditionally his wife should have accepted such an arrangement with philosophical indifference, but Mrs Shibata was not traditional. She was modern and tried to stab her husband with a knife. At three in the morning when black-coated little Shibata-san came creeping home we could catch a moment of silence as the door to his house opened, followed by an explosion from his wife who used to chase him with a club. She was notoriously shrewish, and Katsumi and Hana-ogi apologized for her. 'Japanese wife expected to understand men like geisha.' they said.

Nor were most Japanese wives the patient silent creatures I had been told. When Sato-san, a railroad employee, took his wife shopping she trailed a respectful three feet behind him and never spoke a word unless spoken to by her immediate friends. But at home she was a tyrant and rebuked Sato-san contemptuously for not earning more money. As I came to know the wives of Japan I had to conclude that they were exactly like the wives of America: some were gentle mothers, some were curtain dictators and some few were lucky charms who brought their men one good thing after another. I decided that which kind a man found for himself was pretty much a matter of chance, but whenever I looked at Hana-ogi I had an increasingly sure feeling that I had stumbled upon one of the real lucky charms.

Across the alley lived the widow Fukada and her twenty-year-old daughter Masako, who had had a G.I. baby without being married. Sometimes at night we could hear the grandmother screaming at Masako that she was a slut, and other women in the alley agreed. The American baby was not wanted and was not allowed to play with pure Japanese babies, and although everyone in the alley loved Joe Kelly and Katsumi and although they were proud to have a great Takarazuka actress living among them with her American flier, there was deep resentment against Masako Fukada, who had disgraced the blood of Japan.

Down the alley were the hilarious Watanabes. His wife was almost as broad as he was tall. They got along together fine except that Watanabe-san had a mistress even more compelling than a geisha: he was mad-crazy to play pachinko. He spent all his money at pachinko and all his spare hours at the pachinko parlor. When the police closed the parlor each night at eleven he would reluctantly come home and we would hear fat Mrs Watanabe shouting derisively, 'Here comes Pachinko-san! Dead broke!'

The pachinko parlor stood in the corner nearest the canal, an amazing single room lined with upright pinball games. For a few yen Watanabe-san would be handed seven steel balls, which he would shoot up to the top of the pinball machine and watch agonizingly as they fell down to the bottom, almost always missing the holes which paid the big prizes. The pachinko parlor on our alley was filled from morning till night and everyone was bitten by the pachinko bug, including Hana-ogi and me, and it was a curious fact that my friendship with the pachinko players in that crowded parlor would later save my life.

Across the alley from the pachinko room was the flower shop. You would have thought there could not be in that entire alley one rusty yen for flowers, but almost everyone who lived along our narrow gutters stopped into the flower shop for some solitary spray of blooms which was carried reverently home for the alcove where the gods lived. I cannot recall a moment when there were not flowers in our alcove and I–who had never known a violet from a daisy–came to love them.

The next shop is difficult to describe. In fact, it is impossible because in all the rest of the world there are no shops quite like these in Japan. It was a sex shop where husbands and wives could purchase tricky devices with which to overcome nature's mistakes and short changings. To satisfy our curiosity Katsumi-san took Joe and me there one day. The shy owner listened as we laughed at his amazing collection of sex machines. Then he said in Japanese, 'Go ahead, laugh. Young Japanese men laugh, too. But when they're married and reach forty they come to me for help.' Katsumi translated and then broke into an uncontrolled giggle. I asked her what she had said and she explained, 'I tell him Joe no need help.' The shy owner smiled nervously and replied, 'At twenty nobody needs help.'

But the true wonders of our alley were the children. I could neither count them nor forget them. They had round faces, very red cheeks, straight black bangs, fat little legs and boundless joy. I don't think I ever heard a Japanese child cry. Certainly I never saw one struck and I came to believe that the most delectable children I had ever seen were these noisy, hilarious children. Whenever they crowded around me as I came up the alley I loved Hana-ogi more.

Each house in our alley was desperately packed, so that one tiny room often became the equivalent of a full-sized American home and these teeming masses of people lived and worked and had babies and argued politics just like all people across the world. But there was this difference. Not a shred of anything was wasted, not even the human manure which was so patiently gathered each morning and from which sprang the flowers and the food. I recall certain evenings that spring when I entered this narrow alley at close of day and the front of every house would be open and dozens of children would run, black-bobbed, to greet me and from every open room facing the alley and the people of Japan would speak with me and I shared a warmth and goodness that I had never known in Lancaster or the camps where I grew up. I was one of the people—one of the millions of people who cling to whatever shred of hope and property they can grab hold of, and from this alley with the myriad children and the brawling and the flowers and the unwanted American-Japanese baby and the pachinko games and the sake drinking I borrowed a strength I had never had before.

CONSULAR REPORT: 'Eskivan, Peter. Mother says, "No damned good." '

It expressed itself in an unforeseen way. I was in my office at Itami Air Base when a sergeant appeared to tell me that Lt. Col. Calhoun Craford was outside. The florid colonel stepped in and got right down to business. 'You think you're smart' (he said it: *Yawll thank yore smaht*) 'gettin' a four-star giniral to come out and save your neck. You accustomed to hidin' behind your pappy's back?' Then he let me have it. 'My men been trailin' you, Gruver. We know you and that tramp are holed up in enlisted man's quarters. But we can't touch you because of your pappy. So we're doin' something better. We're sendin' Joe Kelly back to the States.'

'But what'll happen to Katsumi?'

The fat colonel looked at me with disgust. 'Who's Kats-what's-his-name?'

'Kelly's wife.'

'The Jap girl. Not up to us to worry what happens to her.'

'You're not breaking up this family?'

'Don't call it a family. The girl's a cheap Jap tramp.'

I said that Katsumi was a decent girl, that she was studying to become a Catholic, like her husband, but apparently Lt. Col. Craford hated Catholics worse than he hated colored people, for he said, 'And when we finish with Kelly we'll figure out some way to handle you. Father or no father.'

He left me and I sat for a long time staring at my desk, contemplating the mess I had made of things. I had proved myself a shoddy officer. I had loused up the life of an enlisted man. I had made Eileen look ridiculous and I hadn't done much better with Hana-ogi. Then I began to weigh what I had accomplished in Japan and things looked brighter. I had come to know what a home meant, an unpretentious home where love was. I had found a beautiful girl filled with tenderness and grace and wit. I had learned at last to share my heart with another human being. And most of all I had discovered the tremendous passion of turning down the bed roll at night and seeing the slim, perfect body of Hana-ogi. I jumped up and cried, 'Gruver-san, if you lose that girl you're nuts. Marry her, stupid. Marry her.'

But as soon as I had said the words I began to sweat and I remembered all the predictions my father had made that night in the Marine Barracks. My career gone, my wings and their promise lost, my place in my American world vanished and I with an Asiatic wife. It was then that my new-found courage asserted itself.

I recognized the trick my father had played on me. He had planted those poisonous seeds so that they could flourish at just such a moment, and I decided that it was against such tricks that I was revolting. I did not want to become a general like my father, with his cold cut-offness from the world. I didn't want to be a second General Webster, ruled by Eileen. And I certainly didn't ever want to become a Lt. Col. Craford. I wanted to be one man, standing by myself, sharing whatever world I could make with the woman who had helped me to discover that world. In my moment of resolution and light I knew that I would never waver from my purpose. I was going to marry Hana-ogi.

I called Joe Kelly and asked him to meet me at a tiny bar we knew in Osaka where M.P.'s never came. It's impossible to describe such Japanese bars to Americans. How can you explain a bar so small that it has space for only four customers and two hostesses?

'Joe,' I said in greeting, 'can you keep a secret?'

'Sure, Ace.'

'I mean two secrets. Big ones?'

'Hanako havin' a baby?'

'Joe, Blubber-gut is laying for you. He's going to ship you home first chance he gets.'

'That's no secret. He threatened me openly two days ago. I didn't tell anybody. Didn't want to worry you. But he shouted, "All you nigger-lovers are goin' home. Soon."'

'Joe, I want you to promise me you won't do anything stupid.'

'Me? I should be stupid like him?'

'Look. One night I heard you tell Katsumi you were going to shoot Blubber-gut.'

'Me? I'm no rod man. What's your other secret?'

I ordered another beer and took a big gulp. 'Exactly what papers do you have to sign to marry a Japanese girl?'

Joe whistled and said, 'Look, Ace. This ain't for you. Suppose Hanako is beggin' you to marry her! It ain't for you.'

'Joe, don't jump to conclusions. I haven't told her yet. But so help me God, I'm going to marry that girl. What are the steps?' He repeated his earlier warning and I asked, 'You mean you're sorry you married Katsumi?'

A big grin broke on Joe's face and he said, 'One night I told you that bein' married to that Buddha-head was livin'. It ain't. It's somethin' much finer than livin'. It's like you was dead and all the stress and strain was over and all that was left was the very best—and it's the best because it's all wrapped up in her. It ain't livin', Ace. I used to live in Chicago. This is way beyond that.'

I sat with my hands over my face and didn't look up for a moment. Then I said, 'I feel exactly that way about Hanayo.'

Joe ignored this and said, 'Ace, I don't believe you could take the bad time they give you.'

'What do you mean?'

'They wear you down. Enlisted men get used to bein' worn down but you ain't had the experience of diggin' your heels in real stubborn and resistin'.'

'How do you mean?'

'They give you so many papers. The chaplain prays over you. And everything they do they do with crazy smiles, like you was off your rocker and only they could save you. And what's worse, they ask the girl so many heart-burning questions. Hana-ogi won't tell you but some night when you kiss her she'll break down and cry for an hour. I don't think you could take it.'

I said, 'Tomorrow morning I'm starting the paper work.'

He said, 'Ace, you're a big man. It would make them look silly to lose you to a Japanese girl. So they'll hit you with big stuff.'

'I'm ready.'

'Ace, they'll hit you with generals and admirals and men who knew your father. The only way you can swing it is to get the help of your Congressman. Who is he?'

'I don't know.'

'Where do you live?'

'I don't have . . .'

'Well, where do you vote?'

'I've never voted.' For the first time I realized that I was completely a military man. The Air Force was my home. I cast my vote with the talking end of an F-86.

Joe studied this and said, 'Don't worry. Practically any Congressman would love to fight your battle. You want me to take it up with Shimmark? He loves to get his name in the paper.'

I thanked Joe and said I'd work it out somehow, but that very night they started to throw the big reasons at me, even before I had told Hana-ogi that I was going to give up the Air Force and marry her. It happened a long way off, in Texas, for that night I heard a radio program explaining why the Democrats of Texas were going to support Dwight Eisenhower for President. I had known the general at several different bases and had played with his son. Suddenly, there in the dark streets of Osaka, Eisenhower became the symbol of what a major in the Air Force might become: a man ready for many different kinds of action if his country needed him. For one hellish hour I walked the streets weighing what I was doing and then I found myself at the entrance to my alley, and skinny Watanabe-san had struck it rich at pachinko and ran out in the street to offer me a beer and I got a rosy glow on, and about eleven Hana-ogi came down to take me home, but I did not tell her then of the great decision I had made.

In the morning I sneaked into Kobe, for I did not want either General Webster or Lt. Col. Craford to see me, and I went to the American consulate. Luck was with me, for Mr Carstairs, the fuddy consul, was not yet in and I could talk privately with his secretary, the horse-faced girl who had married a G.I.

She recognized me at once and said, 'You made my kid brother the hero of his whole block.'

'How do you mean?'

'Your autograph. The kids take Korea seriously, even if grownups don't.'

Although she said this with a smile I noticed that she was eyeing me suspiciously and after I had made a few awkward starts at conversation she put her two hands firmly on her desk and said, 'Major Gruver, did you come here to find out about marrying a Japanese girl?'

I gulped and must have blushed, for she added immediately, 'I can spot you guys a mile off. What are you ashamed of?'

I asked her what she meant by that and she laughed. 'You all think there's some tricky way to get around the red tape. And you're all ashamed to speak to your superior officers.' She looked up at me with such infectious amusement that I had to laugh, whereupon she said, 'But you, Ace Gruver. I never thought you'd tumble for a Buddha-head.'

I fumbled a bit and asked, 'Just what are the paper requirements?'

'I can't tell you a thing, Major.'

'You work here.'

'Forbidden. You military heroes have to clear everything through you chain of command.'

'You mean it's as tough as that?'

'It's tougher, Major. We don't want men like you marrying Japanese girls. We make it extra tough for men like you.'

'I was only asking,' I said.

'Sure! There hasn't ever been a soldier in here who really intended to get married. They were all only asking!'

'Then you won't help!'

The big girl looked out the door to see if Mr Carstairs had arrived yet. Satisfying herself on that point she said, 'Old Droopy Drawers lives by the book. He'd fire me if he saw me talking with you about legal matters. But I figure if a man can shoot down seven MIG's he's entitled to some help.'

She showed me a completed file on a sailor who had married a Japanese girl. I had heard of the paper work. I had even seen some of it during Joe Kelly's marriage. But I had not comprehended how repetitious and degrading it was. I began to understand what Joe meant when he said that only an enlisted man, conditioned to standing in line and taking guff, could see a Japanese wedding through.

I said, 'Isn't this a pretty tough obstacle course?'

The girl laughed and said, 'If I had my way, we'd make it tougher. Men like you oughtn't to grab Jap girls just because they're available.'

'I don't want a lecture,' I protested.

'Look, Major. I'm your big sister. Remember? We just made a study of which Americans were marrying Japanese girls. The findings aren't pleasant.' She riffled some papers and read off the dismal case histories: 'Wyskanski, Noel. Orphaned. No education. Had a fist fight with the Catholic priest. Reform school.' 'Merchant, Nicholas. Ran away from home. Been in guard house regularly since being drafted. Two court-martials. Threatened the Japanese social worker who proved that the first girl he wanted to marry was a notorious prostitute.' 'Kelly, Joe. Your friend. Worst record in the Air Force in Korea. Constant discipline problem. Accused of murdering a drunk in Chicago but case thrown out of court on technicality. Always on the verge of criminal prosecution. Recommended twice for dismissal from the Air Force.' She tossed Kelly's paper aside and asked bluntly, 'How'd you get mixed up with a dead-end mutt like him?'

'He was in my unit.'

'Did you meet your Japanese girl through Kelly?' I hesitated a moment trying to frame an answer but the smart girl understood. She put aside the file and said patiently, 'Major Gruver, you're simply not the type. These men—these perpetual failures . . .' She hammered the file and turned away to blow her nose. At that moment the front door opened and in came prim Mr Carstairs. In one instantaneous glance he saw me and the marriage file and his secretary wiping her eyes. He stepped precisely into the middle of the doorway and said, 'My goodness, Major Gruver isn't thinking of getting married to a Japanese girl, is he?'

The secretary looked up and sniffed. 'Yes, damn it all, he is. And I've been telling him he's a complete fool.'

'You are,' Mr Carstairs said. He passed through our room and said sharply as he left, 'But there's nothing to worry about. The Air Force wouldn't let such a stupid thing happen.'

When he was gone the secretary asked, 'Has your Jap girl started her part of the paper work?'

I said, 'Well . . . I haven't . . .'

With great relief the big girl started to laugh. 'I understand! You haven't asked her, have you? Thank God!'

I blushed and said, 'Look, we're getting married.'

She ignored this and said, 'I feel so much better. Ace, dozens of you men come in here to ask about getting married. But most of you haven't proposed yet. Then I breathe easy because everything is all right.'

'You have some special way of stopping it?'

'No,' she said surprised. 'It's just that first-class Japanese girls won't marry American men. They prefer Japan. Ace, believe me, it's ten-to-one that the girl you deserve won't marry you, and the kind you can get, you wouldn't want.'

I looked at the shabby office and at the pile of marriage reports. Grimly I said, 'You can start a new file. 'Gruver, Lloyd. Well educated. Never in trouble. Best man the Air Force had in Korea. Clean-cut American type. Married a Japanese girl because he loved her.' Show it to your Mr Carstairs every day.'

In real anger I went over to the village of Takarazuka, where I waited in a vegetable stall near the Bitchi-bashi and toward noon I saw the first Takarazuka girls go by in their swaying green skirts. Then Fumiko-san passed me and I hid in the back of the store until she had disappeared. Finally I saw Hana-ogi approaching and I had that rare experience that a man sometimes knows when he sees the girl he loves picking her way along a crowded lane unaware that he is watching, and at such times—when the girls are not on their good behaviour, you might say—they are extraordinarily lovely and ratify doubly all thoughts and decisions of preceding days. Hana-ogi was like that. She wore a gray kimono flecked with silver and gold, and it encased her lovingly, and her feet in light gray zori threaded an intricate pattern through the crowds of noonday shoppers, and as she drew near my vegetable stall I was fluttering like a broken propeller but at last I knew what I wanted. I reached out, grabbed her arm, and drew her in beside me. The man who ran the stall smiled and moved out onto the pavement as if accustomed to having his shop invaded in that manner every day.

'Hanayo!' I cried with a passion I had never before experienced. 'I've made up my mind, and I've started the paper work. We're going to be married.'

Apparently she didn't understand for she said, 'What do you say?'

'I'm going to marry you. Take you back to America.'

I remember that the shop was filled along one wall with enormous white Japanese radishes, four feet long and thick as a man. Hana-ogi drew back against them and held her hand to her cheek, where in the Japanese style short hair grew down in sideburns. She looked at me for a moment and tears came into her dark eyes.

'We no speak of marriage, Rroyd-san. No. No.'

'I know it's a surprise,' I said. 'But I've thought it all out and I'm willing to give up the Air Force and find some other job.'

'But Rroyd, I no go America.'

'We'll work that out, too,' I said. 'Some time they'll change this crazy law so a man can take his wife home.'

'You no understand, Rroyd-san. I no want to go.'

I stepped away from the giant radishes and stared at Hana-ogi. It was incomprehensible to me that any Japanese girl, living in that cramped little land with no conveniences and no future, would refuse America. What was it the officer's wife in the Osaka P.X. had said: 'The damned little Jap girls lay in wait at street corners with lassos and rope the American soldiers in.' I said, 'I'll explain it all to you tonight.'

But she replied most strangely, 'Some day you leave Japan, Rroyd-san. Before you go I like you see pictures of real Hana-ogi. In Kyoto.'

'I don't want to see any pictures!' I cried. 'Damn it, I came here to tell you we're getting married.'

'You get auto tomorrow morning—early.' She moved quickly toward the door of the shop, then turned to kiss me passionately on the lips. 'When you go back America,' she said, 'I want you remember great beauty of Hana-ogi.'

THE CURATOR: 'It is unlikely that even one foreigner in all our history has truly understood Japan.'

Early next morning we left Osaka in Lt. Bailey's Chevvy and drove along the side of a river which for untold centuries had carried water to the rice fields of this region. It lay far below the level of the road, hemmed in by strong dikes built many generations ago and upon all the land there was the mark of much toil and the footprints of many people. Wherever we looked women were at work hauling and lifting.

Our entrance to Kyoto was memorable, for we saw in the distance the soaring towers of great Buddhist temples, their tiers built with corners upswept in the Chinese style. And along one street we caught a glimpse of the famed Heian Shinto shrine, a glorious vermilion thing with enormous blood-red torri guarding it.

But today we were not interested in shrines or temples. We went along a side street burdened with age-old pines, where underneath a canopy of evergreen we stopped to enter a museum. It was built like a temple, with nearly a hundred statues of stone and wood, as if the old heroes of Japan had gathered to greet us, frozen forever in their stiff ceremonial attitudes. The curator hurried up to us and when he learned that I could speak no Japanese he summoned a striking young man. He was in his thirties, I judged, and wore heavy glasses. He had excellent teeth, a frank smile and a rare command of English.

'I studied at Oxford,' he explained, 'and served for some years in our store on Fifth Avenue and for two years in our store in Boston. What did you wish to see?' It was clear that he did not know Hana-ogi and that he supposed her to be merely some attractive street girl I had picked up for the day. He was therefore somewhat distressed when she spoke to him in Japanese, so I interrupted and said, 'I understand you have an unusual collection of prints of Hana-ogi, of Ogi-ya.'

Immediately he withdrew deep inside himself and studied me carefully. Then he looked at Hana-ogi and bowed very low. 'You are Hana-ogi-san of Takarazuka,' he said in precise English. 'You are very beautiful. And you, Major, are Lloyd Gruver. Yes, yes. Even in Kyoto we have heard of you.' I did not know whether he meant that he had heard of me as a flier or that he had heard of Hana-ogi and me, but he nodded formally and said, 'I can truly appreciate your desire to see the famous prints of the other Hana-ogi.'

He led us upstairs, past the frowning Japanese heroes, and I felt that I was in hostile land. In this strange building I at last got the feeling of being an invader, surrounded by an alien religion and a strange art many centuries older than my own native land. I experienced the feeling even more deeply when I sat on the floor in front of an easel while the young curator went to a locked cabinet. Hana-ogi must have sensed my uneasy thoughts, for she put her hand in mine and whispered, 'Now you see greatest beauty.'

I was totally unprepared for what I saw. I had developed a mental impression of the ancient Hana-ogi. She must have looked, I thought, something like my Hana-ogi: exraordinarily beautiful, yet with a distinctive oriental cast. I believed the pictures of her would look something like Botticellis.

I shall never forget the extreme shock of that first print. The young curator held it from me for a moment and said in reverence, 'The first one is of Hana-ogi as a young girl, just come to Ogi-ya. It is by one of our finest artists, Shuncho.' Then, bursting with pride and affection, he displayed the picture.

It was disgusting. The girl's face was pasty and flat. Her hair was a mass of yellow combs. She was swathed in seven kimonos that gaped at the neck. But worst of all, her eyes were caricatures, mere slants, and her teeth were a horrid black. In this portrait of dead beauty I could not find one shred of loveliness.

I must have betrayed my disappointment for both Hana-ogi and the curator tried to explain that the design was controlled by Japanese artistic tradition, the way a portrait of a woman by Picasso does not appear really beautiful. I remember trying real hard to remember who Picasso was, but before I could get it they took away the first picture and brought in another by an artist whose name I didn't catch, but my dismay was greater than before. The famous courtesan had the same pasty face, slit eyes and funereal teeth, but this time her head was twisted into such an angle that I remember thinking, 'If she doesn't straighten up she'll strangle.' In her left hand she held one of the endless combs which she was jabbing into her mass of oil hair, and in her right she grasped a black ebony fan which made the whole picture look stupid. Even the half dozen kimonos were poorly painted and in odd colors.

It was the third picture which caused the argument. I took down the name of the artist, Masayoshi, for he showed Hana-ogi returning to the House of Ogi-ya after her elopement. She was dressed in many kimonos covered by a purple robe and followed by two barefoot servants carrying an umbrella and a massive bouquet of flowers. I studied the picture with dismay, for I recognized it immediately as one that Hana-ogi had described for me that night when she danced the story of her predecessor, but what she had not told me was that this picture of Hana-ogi showed a remarkably ugly woman with a big nose, dirt smears over her eyebrows and paunchy cheeks. 'Why she's ugly!' I cried. I felt defrauded.

My Hana-ogi withdrew as if she had been struck and the young man pulled the print away. 'I am afraid,' he said in clipped syllables, 'that you have no appreciation of our art.'

'I was told that this Hana-ogi was the most beautiful woman in Japanese history.'

'She was,' the young man insisted.

'But these pictures . . .'

'It's our style of art,' he explained.

'But look at Hana-ogi here. This one. She's really beautiful.'

The young man did not look at Hana-ogi-san. Instead he took the portrait of the ancient Hana-ogi back to the cabinet and returned with another. Quietly he said, 'I am afraid you are blind to the problem, Major. But would you like me to explain in a few words?'

'Indeed I would,' I said.

'You'll forgive me if they're very simple words?'

'I will. I've heard so much of this Hana-ogi I don't want to go home disappointed.'

'If you have a free mind,' he assured me, 'you will go home elated. The picture I'm about to show you is by one of Japan's supreme artists, Utamaro. Have you heard of him?'

'No.'

'No bother, but will you believe me when I say his work is prized all over the world? Good. You are going to see one of his loveliest creations. When you look at it don't think of Hana-ogi. Think only of his heavenly yellow.'

He flashed the picture before me and the yellow was indeed like a fine sunlight. He continued his narration, pointing out the perfect proportions of the design, the exquisite line, the subdued color harmonies and the suggested textures. I followed him carefully and agreed with what he said. Then brusquely he said, 'As for the face of Hana-ogi we Japanese think it was sent down from heaven.'

The intensity of his comment caught me unaware and from some distant corner of my brain came the affirmation, 'The men who knew this woman thought she was beautiful.' And immediately there came another terrible memory–of a time when some of us young officers were attending a wedding and we saw the bride and there was a moment of awful silence and somebody behind me whispered, 'Well, every man thinks the girl he's marrying is pretty,' and I could see myself back in America, about to introduce my Hana-ogi to strangers who had never known her and I could feel them cringing away from my Japanese girl–unlovely to them–as I now cringed away from the long-dead Hana-ogi. I looked again at the treasured face, at the curious slanted eyes and the black teeth and from my own humility and the vanished green houses of the Yoshiwara came the assurance that she was beautiful. I said, 'I think I understand.'

The young man started to take the Utamaro away but I said, 'Let me study it some more.' I pointed to the colorful printing in the upper corner and asked what it was. During the remarkable discussion that followed the young curator stood crisply at attention with his left hand upon the easel. I have only to close my eyes to see him standing there with his faded echo of the great Hana-ogi.

'It's impossible to say what this printing means, Major. It's a poem, written by some unimportant man who visited Hana-ogi. These symbols are his name: The man from the other side of Yanagiwara. That's all we know about him, a stranger who came from a distant village and saw the great woman once. But his poem will live among us forever.'

'What did he write?'

'I'm sorry but I cannot tell you the meaning.'

'You can't translate the symbols?'

'Oh, yes!' he assured me proudly. 'I was translator to our Foreign Office during the peace treaty at San Francisco. But the Japanese language like Japanese beauty and Japanese life can never be truly translated. For example, the name Hana-ogi means *flower* and *fan,* and its symbols are woven into the poem, but what they are intended to mean in this particular poem no one can say. The stranger from Yanagiwara himself did not know.'

'What do you mean, he didn't know?'

'In Japan a man sees a beautiful woman and he expresses words, but they have no specific meaning.'

'How can words have no specific meaning? There's the symbol. Right there. Why can't you read it?'

'Ah, but I can, Major. Trouble is, I can read it in so many ways. According to one way the stranger from Yanagiwara is saying, "Even a mere glimpse in autumn of that night-blooming flower, Hana-ogi, floods my soul with summer."'

'That's clear enough,' I said.

'But it isn't clear, because I'm only guessing that that's what the stranger meant, for the words can also be read, "Hana-ogi is more beautiful than that evening flower I once laid on a fan for a love of old days and brings no chill of autumn to my heart."'

I was confused. 'You mean those same symbols can mean such different things?'

'They can also mean many other things, Major. Our life in Japan is one of implied meanings, hidden significances. For example, they say that you have fallen in love with Hana-ogi-san. Which Hana-ogi?'

At the mention of her name Hanayo-chan put her hand around mine and I said, 'Which one? This one. The living one.'

'But which of the living ones?'

'This one. Here!'

The young man, who must have hated Americans for taking his art galleries in Boston and London and New York, stood bitterly erect by the easel and said softly, 'But there are many Hana-ogi-sans with us today. She is famous in Japan, this girl, and deeply loved. There is the peasant girl who is good to her mother and her six sisters. There is the young courtesan who was in training to be a geisha. Didn't you know that her father had sold her to a green house? There is the famous beauty who was rescued by one of the rich Matsudaira men. The one who committed suicide. His daughter, Fumiko-san, is at Takarazuka now. Or the gracious actress Hana-ogi who always used to be seen with Fumiko-san. Or the ascetic young woman who aspired to be Japan's greatest dancer. Or the reckless girl who ran away with an American flier. You see, we are a very subtle people. Our words mean many things.'

I think that Hana-ogi had some intimation of what the young man was saying, for she kept her hand close about mine and when he was finished she rose and pulled me to my feet. Staring purposefully at the young man she said quietly, 'I never tie my obi so.' and she pointed to the picture of long-dead Hana-ogi, the rare, the wonderful courtesan whose memory still burned and she indicated Hana-ogi's obi, tied in front the way professional prostitutes did to advertise.

I wanted to maul the young curator for having told me these things but suddenly he smiled at me and said, 'I must show you one more portrait, Major. In some ways it is the loveliest of all.' He brought us a delicate thing, all gold and yellow and faded blue. From it a young Hana-ogi looked back across her shoulder at us, sweet and beautiful as I had wanted her to be. She seemed to tantalize the mind and in a lower corner of the picture appeared one of her youthful attendants, a child of nine playing with battledore and shuttlecock. Lovingly the curator indicated the child and said, 'This was Tatsuta. Even the names of the children who attended our immortal Hana-ogi are recorded.' Then quite unexpectedly he placed his hand tenderly on my Hana-ogi's head and rumpled her hair. 'This one was a Tatsuta, too. See, the obi tied in back.'

I thought for a moment that he had told me of my Hana-ogi's history because he was in love with her and jealous of me; but as we left the treasure room I turned and saw him jealously storing the forty-one portraits of the famous girl who long ago had graced the green houses of Yoshiwara and I realized that he was indeed in love with Hana-ogi, but not with my Hana-ogi.

On the drive home we were silent until we came to a part of the river bank where three women were tilling a rice field. Then suddenly Hana-ogi took my hand and kissed it and whispered, 'We very poor. My father no want to sell to geisha house. Japanese fathers love their daughters. Same like in America. But . . .' We never said another word about it, not about the Matsudaira man who had bought her nor about his daughter Fumiko-san for whom Hana-ogi now felt responsible. For a few minutes after leaving the museum I had feared that knowing my Hana-ogi's history might make it impossible for me to marry her, but one mention of her father ended such doubts, for I recalled the old Japanese farmer we had watched on the first night we had slept together. That was poverty, when a man sifted each grain of soil by hand to make it yield a little more rice. I knew that if Hana-ogi's father had sold her it was because he had no human alternative. I said with new dedication, 'Now we'll get married,' but she merely drew closer to me and I believe that she had taken me to Kyoto so that I might know of her childhood and that if the curator had not told me, she would have done so when we studied the pictures. With my right arm I drew her tousled head to mine and drove the car quite slowly beside the ancient, turbulent river.

I was disturbed, however, that she had not yet actually said that she would come with me to America. I judged that she was hesitating in order to provide me with an escape from my rash promise to leave the Air Force. Then, in a dramatic way, I learned that perhaps she really was determined not to marry me, for an elderly woman showed me Hana-ogi's reasons for staying in Japan.

This gentle mask-faced Japanese woman came to the Marine Barracks in Takarazuka accompanied by a smart young woman who spoke good English and they explained that they wished me to accompany them on a matter of greatest importance. I followed them to the Bitchi-bashi, then through the vegetable stalls and onto the footpath leading to the girls' dormitories.

This was the first time I had been on this path and as I approached the building where Hana-ogi had lived before she met me I grew quite excited but then I saw the dormitory itself and it was forbidding: a plain wooden building covered with bamboo matting and protected by a row of cryptomeria trees planted to make a high hedge. The house was like a fortress and I was pleased at the prospect of invading it.

But my guide didn't stop there. Instead, she led me down a narrow path past the cryptomeria trees and up to a small hill that overlooked the river. There she stopped at a curious gate that looked like the miniature entrance to a temple and after opening this she took me into a beautiful garden which surrounded a superior Japanese house made of highly polished wood. It was guarded by an enormous flat stone upon which sat nine young girls wearing the green skirts of the Takarazuka uniform. The girls jumped to their feet and bowed very low until the elderly woman had passed.

She led me to a room covered with exquisite white tatami and containing at one end a raised platform of matched cypress planks of a polished golden brown. It was obvious that this was the room of a dancing teacher.

The woman introduced herself as Teruko-san, one of the first great Takarazuka stars. She had been, in her day, a legend and now she handed the legend down to the young girls waiting for her on the rock. They came to her five days a week and submitted themselves to the tyranny of her masklike face which now drew close to mine.

Teruko-san sat with me on the floor, arranging her kimono with precision, and I saw that her garments were five shades of gray matched in delicate harmony and accented by a single thin line of blue showing about the neck. Her tabi were white and accentuated the outlines of beautiful and powerful feet. They reminded me of Hana-ogi's superb feet and Teruko-san must have intended this, for she said promptly, 'Major Gruver, if you cause Hana-ogi to leave us it is not only the great stage she will lose. It is also this.' With a slow motion of her hand, as if she were participating in a dance, she indicated the perfect room, stopping with her finger pointed at a frame containing a massive motto written in strong characters by a great Japanese novelist.

She said, 'Our motto: "Be pure. Be right. Be beautiful."'

Then she said, 'When I die Hana-ogi is to follow me, for she is our finest dancer. I believe she is to be even greater than I, for when I danced I was alone and stood out like Fuji-san. But today there are many good dancers and

Hana-ogi dominates them all. And do you know why they are good?'

I bowed deferentially toward her and she said, 'Yes, they are excellent because I teach them as a famous old man taught me. In this way we keep alive the art of Japan.'

As Teruko-san droned on I could hear Hana-ogi's bright voice with its sometimes-hoarse edge cutting at my heart, I could see the meticulous manner in which she folded the edges of her kimono to outline her wonderfully strong neck, and I could see the classic manner in which she danced. I could believe that these things had come in part from this room. Teruko-san said, 'If you persist, Hana-ogi will never return to this room.'

Then she pulled a clever trick. She said, 'You must sit here, Major Gruver, for I am to give a lesson,' and the interpreter went to fetch the nine young girls. They came in quietly, practiced little steps on the tatami then deftly dropped away their green skirts and climbed onto the low stage in bright dancing tights.

Teruko-san was transformed. Instead of a gracious elderly lady she became a vigorous, stage-stamping dancer much better than even her best pupil. She led them through one single step for a long time and I detected one or two girls who looked as if they might honestly become dancers and I realized that Teruko-san had intended that I see in these struggling children–they were fifteen I judged–the Hana-ogi of some years back and as I looked at these lovely faces now perspiring as Hana-ogi did when she had run through the alleys to our home, I could imagine the days and years she had studied.

When the girls left, Teruko-san said, 'I have wanted you to understand exactly what you are doing.' She led me to the gate and to my surprise dismissed the interpreter and walked with me back to the dormitory, which was deserted in the late afternoon. She nodded to the guard and took me to a small room, pushed aside the paper door and told me to enter saying, 'Hana-ogi.'

The room was as beautiful as the girl I loved. Along one wall were the lacquered drawers and trays and chests in which she kept her belongings. The rest of the room was bare and clean and glittering. There were eight creamy white tatami, so it was not a big room, and six bright cushions around a very old brazier of gold and green ceramic in which charcoal rested on a pile of gleaming white sand. A low table and four jet-black bowls for food completed the furniture except for one shelf which held copies of the plays Hana-ogi had acted in. The only ornamentation was a single Japanese print in excellent colors of a bridge suspended in the moonlight over a rocky gorge with a crescent moon low in the sky. I felt that I was growing to understand Japanese prints, and the more I understood them the more I liked them.

But this time Teruko-san had been too clever, for it had been her intention that I see this room and lament that I was taking Hana-ogi from it; but it had quite the opposite effect. The room cried out in the late afternoon shadows that I should go ahead and marry its owner. No woman so vital as Hana-ogi could be destined for so narrow a prison. The wood of the room was beautiful, but Hana-ogi was more so. The tatami were neat, the books were important and the Japanese print no doubt represented one of the peaks of art–but so did Hana-ogi, and in addition she was a glorious woman, one who delighted in hurrying through the dark alleys of Osaka to join the man she loved.

But if her room gave me permission to love her, what I saw next gave me a direct order to do so, for as Teruko-san and I passed down the hall from Hana-ogi's room I happened to look through sliding doors that were ajar and saw the room next to Hana-ogi's.

It was remarkable in that it was also of only eight tatami, but it was crowded with dolls and fluffy brown bears and pillows edged with pink and blue lace streamers and tables with birds out of glass and corners filled with delightful odds and ends. It was the room of a young girl who enjoyed all aspects of life and it abounded in that happy clutter so loved by people who don't have to make up their minds. I looked at Teruko-san and she said, 'Fumiko-san.' Then she pointed to the table, low and exquisitely carved in the ornate Chinese style, and with no English at her command told me that that was the table Fumiko-san's father used when he committed hara-kiri in the debacle of August, 1945. The room frightened me and I wanted to get out of it.

At the entrance to the dormitory I bowed very low and said, 'Domo arigato gozaimasu, Teruko-san.' She was pleased that I spoke even that trivial Japanese, so she bowed equally low and said, 'Do itashi mash:te, dozo,' and I hurried to the train that would take me back to Osaka just as fast as possible.

How can I recall the journey of a young man desperately in love as he moves across the picture-book landscape of Japan to a city of canals where he will meet his beloved? My train crossed the Muko River and I could see the Bitchi-bashi, where I had often waited for Hana-ogi and where young girls now passed swirling their green skirts. For a few seconds I followed the footpath that led to the dormitory and here four of the great stars walked arm in arm. At the dormitory itself I saw Fumiko-san entering the dark and towering wall of cryptomerias.

Now I was in the countryside and I could see the rice fields crowding right up to the last inch of railroad tie. Beyond were the trim clean villages with roofs of red tile and temple roofs of golden tile. In the fields were old men pulling harrows and women digging, while along the village streets children laughed and played loud jumping games.

There was a momentary thrill as the train pulled into the junction town of Nishinomiya, for I knew that when I looked across the station platform I would see a gigantic poster for *Swing Butterfly* with a huge picture of Hana-ogi in the middle. I spent my time waiting for the through express, wondering what the people on the platform would think if they could have known that in a few endless minutes I would be with Hana-ogi and she would be slipping into a gray and blue kimono so that she could sit upon the floor with me for a bowl of cold fish and vinegar rice?

The express from Kobe roared in and I avoided the coach where the officers of General Webster's command sat very formally in freshly pressed uniforms. Instead I sought out a back car from which I caught glimpses of the Inland Sea and soon we came to where the river emptied into the sea through great concrete culverts, and promptly we entered Osaka itself, where the train plunged through a canyon of ugly houses hung with laundry and into a tunnel which brought me to the noisy, crowded station. As I approached the canal I was alive with excitement. I was young and I was coming to the end of a journey that I wished I might make each day of my life: from Takarazuka to Osaka, where Hana-ogi was waiting.

And when I reached home the wonder of my journey was increased, for there was Hana-ogi waiting for me with the news that Joe had driven a colonel to Tokyo and Katsumi would be gone for two days on business of her own. Once more we had a home to ourselves. I slipped into my blue-and-white cotton kimono and shared cold fish and rice with her. When the meal was over I said, 'Teruko-san came to see me today. She showed me her dancing school. The one that could be yours some day. Now I know why you want to stay at Takarazuka.'

She sighed and said she was glad that I understood why she could not come with me to America, but I added, 'And I also saw your little room. With the lovely print.' I made my hands fall like the gorge in her solitary picture. At this she blushed and held her hand against the stray-hair sideburns along her cheek. I said, 'And when I saw that bare room which holds you like a prisoner–no life–no one to love . . .'

I caught her in my arms and a tremendous surge of love attacked us and later when I lay upon the tatami watching her select her clothes for tomorrow I said, 'So we'll be married as soon as possible. You'll love New York. You can see hundreds of shows, some like Takarazuka, but none of the actresses will be beautiful like you.'

I was imagining her in New York, so I rose and showed her how she could pull the wanton hair that crept upon her cheeks up into place. She did so and studied herself in a mirror. 'Now you look like an American girl,' I said. She pulled the hair back down and said, 'Japanese way more better.' But I convinced her that if she wanted to she could look almost American, so she tucked her hair in and the Japanese sideburns were gone. This sounds strange, but I believe that on a New York street few would recognize that she was from Japan.

PHARMACIST'S MATE: 'In Kobe there's this guy who can straighten her eyes for eight bucks.'

In the morning I begged her to stay with me to the last minute, but she insisted upon leaving early and asked me to call a taxi. I recall the language we had finally invented for ourselves:

Hana-ogi: Rroyd-san, you takushi preeze. (Please get a taxi.)

I: Daijobu, I takushi, get, ne? (All right, I'll get one.)

Hana-ogi: I rike stay with you. Keredomo I train go, honto. (But I must catch the train, really.)

I: More sukoshi, stay, kudasai. (Stay a little longer, please.)

Hana-ogi: Dekinai, Rroyd-san. No can stay. (I'm sorry. I can't stay.)

I: Do shi'te, whatsahurry? (Hey, why hurry?)

Hana-ogi: Anone! Takarazuka, my job-u, ne? I job-u go, ne? (Listen, I have a job.)

I: Chotto, chotto goddamn matte! Takarazuka ichi-ji start now. Ima only 10 o'clock, ne? (Wait a minute!)

Hana-ogi: Anone! Rroyd-san, you mess my hair, ne? I beauty saron go, make nice, desho? (Desho is the sweet meaningless word which makes the sentences of Japanese girls musical and tender.)

I: No, no, no. Anone! You takusan steky now. (Listen! You're plenty pretty now.)

But she left, nevertheless, and my last warning was that she must have her hair done American style. Toward evening Joe blew in with some Suntory, the Japanese whisky we had both come to like so much, and we had a quiet celebration while we waited for the girls and pretty soon Hana-ogi arrived in her new hair-do. It was a transformation. 'Wow!' I cried. 'She could walk down Fifth Avenue and knock them all dead.' She blushed nervously and I believe she would have been pleased with her American look except that Katsumi arrived and ruined everything.

She had bandages over her eyes and peered out through slits. Joe immediately guessed that she had been in an accident but I remember looking with a certain agony at Hana-ogi and muttering to myself, 'Oh, damn it to hell! She's gone and had that lousy operation!'

And I was right. Dear, good Katsumi wanted more than anything else to look like an American. Then Joe would be proud when he took her home; so on the first day he had left her alone she had sneaked over to the quack doctor in Kobe. For eight dollars he had slashed her upper lids to make the Mongolian fold fall back into place. He had performed this operation over a thousand times and sometimes his remodeling enabled girls to lose their Japanese look completely.

Proudly Katsumi stood before us and dropped away her bandages. Joe cried, 'What have you done?'

Even more proudly the little girl opened her eyes slowly, one by one. 'Now I have good eyes,' she said.

The result was horrible. I gasped and Hana-ogi looked away. But Joe just stood there. He was about six feet from her when she turned to face him and he could see that what had been a glorious and typical Japanese face was now a conglomeration. I was watching Joe but no one could ever guess what he thought just then. Once he started to speak but stopped. Then he went over and kissed his wife and said, 'By damn, Katsumi, you look more like an American than I do.'

'I so proud,' she said, dropping her new face against his arms.

There was a moment of silent intensity in the room and then Hana-ogi said, 'Rroyd-san, we walk take, ne?' Joe looked at me and asked belligerently, 'Whatsamatta, anythin' wrong?' and I replied, 'Nothing at all. I think Katsumi looks swell.'

But as soon as Hana-ogi and I reached the canal she cried, 'Why she do that? She not proud to be Japanese?' Deftly she thrust her two forefingers onto her upper lids and pulled them up into mere slits, crying, 'I like Japanese eye. I like!' Then she started to sob and I tried to comfort her, but she pushed me away and with strong fingers clawed down the strands of hair that I had tucked up and they fell upon her cheeks in the Japanese style. As she did this her fingernails caught in her flesh and a thin stream of blood trickled down to her chin. I tried to wipe it away but she cried, 'I proud to be Japanese. I not want to be American. I like Tokyo, not New York.'

I had to stand there in the cool night and watch her slapping at her face until the blood stopped. Then she turned to me defiantly and said, 'You no like Japanese girl, eh? You ashamed Japanese face. You want me cut my eyes, too?'

I put my arm about her and kissed the torn skin. I said, 'When you pulled your eyes far up you looked like the Utamaro print. You were beautiful. But that day in Kyoto I wasn't prepared for such beauty.'

I was about to say more when she clutched my arm and whispered, 'Ssssh!' pointing to a group of young street-walkers lounging by the canal. They were the unlucky ones who had not been able to grab onto a G.I. for the night. Osaka was a leave city for our troops in Korea and had accumulated more streetwalkers than any other city in the world, so that any one girl's chances were slim. They recognized Hana-ogi and gathered about her.

'Is it true,' they asked, 'that you are marrying an American?'

When she said she didn't know they were depressed, for to them the highest dream they could envisage was to trap a G.I. who might take them to the States, but they knew there was little chance, for American chaplains and Japanese secret police investigated all girls, and prostitutes were weeded out. Unemployed for the night, they pressed in on Hana-ogi and asked, 'Have you a picture?' She had none, so they produced strips of paper on which she printed her name in the Chinese characters used for all names. One of the girls studied her signature and asked, 'What's your real name, Hana-ogi?'

At first the actress refused to say, then, feeling deep in the Japanese mood, she said softly, 'My name was Kaji.' Immediately the girl touched Hana-ogi on the wrist and cried, 'You are kaji, kaji!' Then she twisted her hands high into the air.

I asked what this meant and Hana-ogi said, 'In Japanese my real name means fire.'

One of the girls who knew English struck a lighter some G.I. had given her and cried, 'Fire, fire!'

Another girl quickly called, 'Cigaretto, Major?' I passed a package around and in the night I could see a ring of little flames, and later Hana-ogi said defiantly, 'I am proud to be an actress for such girls—for all the girls in Nihon.'

When the streetwalkers had departed I resumed my argument and asked, 'What did you mean when you said you didn't know if you were marrying an American?'

She made a sign with her hands, like a flame falling through night air, and said, 'The fire goes out.'

'No!' I cried. 'There are some fires that never go out.'

She leaned against a tree growing near the canal and said, 'Long ago Teruko-san loved the Supervisor. They were very happy and were going to commit suicide at Kegon Falls. But they didn't and now he's a famous man and she's a famous woman and they meet sometimes and have tea. She speak me today.'

'But the flame didn't go out—or she'd have forgotten. Believe me, the flame was still there.'

Then she said an astonishing thing. 'You'll go home and marry Eileen . . .'

'Eileen?' I cried. 'Where did you hear . . .' I had never spoken her name.

'Yes,' she said. 'You marry Eileen (she pronounced it *Eireen*) your father tell me.'

'My father?'

'Yes. General Hot Shot Harry. He come see me late one night.'

Bitterly I kicked the earth, for I could feel my father ordering things again. 'Did he talk you into this?' I demanded.

'No! He say if I want to marry you O.K., but he know I never do it.'

'What did he tell you?'

'He very nice, very kind man. He speak you marry Eileen. I think so too.'

I pleaded, 'Don't believe what he said. Years ago he dragged me into a life . . . I've done all right but it was never my decision.'

She touched the insignia on my blouse and asked, 'You no happy? Air Force?'

I cried, 'It's been one life . . . I've liked it . . . But there could be others.'

She grasped my hand tightly and said, 'Sometimes I have been afraid of you because you are in uniform. My brother was in uniform and he became cruel. Your army hang him. I am afraid of uniforms.' Then she put her head on my shoulder and said, 'But you–your father–good men.'

I was deeply agitated and struggled desperately to get down–for once in my life–to the hard bed rock of living. I said, 'Hanayo, you are the hope of my life. If you leave me all the things . . .'

She said in Japanese, 'I know, Rroyd. For me you are also the key. With you I could become a woman and a mother and we could travel in London. I could love you and help you . . .'

She became exquisitely tender and I knew then that with her as my wife I could find the solid basis for existence that had so far escaped me; and I was aware that for her, too, I was the only escape she could ever know. If she rejected me now she could become only the glorious outline of a woman, imprisoned in little rooms or on mammoth stages–loved only by other women.

I lifted her in the air and cried, 'Then we'll be married?'

She stared at me and said 'No.'

I dropped her gently to the bank and kissed her impassive, golden face, thinking bitterly of the stories I had read about white men in strange lands. Always the yellow girl tried to seduce these clean-cut men away from their decent white sweethearts, for everyone knew that yellow girls plotted evil ways to lure white men. And if the yellow girls succeeded the white men sank lower and lower toward barbarism. 'Damn it,' I cried, 'this story's all loused up!' When Hana-ogi looked up in surprise I said, 'I'm a West Point honor man. In the story you're supposed to beg me to marry you. Hanayo-chan, please beg me.'

She started to laugh at my comic plea, but then I think she glimpsed the empty years that faced her, for she took my hands and held them to her face, confessing in a tone of Japanese doom, 'I don't want to become the lonely old woman who teaches dancing.' (I recall her words: 'I not grad be woman old in house dance teach no man come.')

Her lament burned my heart and I cried, 'Then marry me.'

This time she answered in a lower voice, still freighted with that inevitable sense of tragedy that seems to haunt the Japanese, 'I never intended marrying you, Rroyd-san. Japanese-American marriages are no good. We read about Japanese girls in America–what happened in Cedar Rapids.'

'Then why did you come to live with me?' I demanded in anguish.

She pressed her lovely head against mine and said softly in Japanese: 'I know it was wrong. But for me it was my only chance in life to love a man. No Japanese man would marry me–what the man in museum told you. Oh, maybe a fish-catch boy or a rice-plant boy, maybe such a man would have me. But Japanese men are very cruel to wives like me. Rroyd-san, in all the world you were the only man I dare love.'

She started to cry, the bitter lament for a section of her life coming to an end at age twenty-nine. It was hellish to be there with her, to hear her committing herself to the inverted world of the Takarazuka girls and the green, flowing skirts and me to airplanes and the management of war. I grasped her hands and cried, 'Hanayo-chan! Please! It's our lives you're speaking of. Marry me!'

Limply and in despair she drew her hands away. Then, raising her arms as if to embrace the entire sleeping city of Osaka she said with tragic finality, 'I Japanese. I always Japanese. I never be happy nowhere.' (As she said it: 'I nebber be grad.') Then the misery of her heart overcame her and she started to cry again. Looking down, to keep her tears from me, she saw one of the crumpled Kodak envelopes used by the P.X.'s in Japan. One of the prostitutes, photographed by some soldier lover, had discarded it. Delicately Hana-ogi stooped for the orange paper and pressed it out. Then with an achingly beautiful hand she pointed to the trademark used by Kodak in Japan: that tremendous and sacred statue of Buddha at Kamakura, the ancient capital. Its vast, impassive face was enshrined as a symbol of the Japanese nation and slowly Hana-ogi's hand left it and indicated her own symbolic face with its beautiful Japanese eyes and classic mouth. 'One poet say my face same like this face of Kamakura. I very proud.' Then in a tender, forgiving gesture she pointed to our dark alley and asked sadly, 'Katsumi-san marry American boy, ne? What happen to her, desho?'

The answer to that one arrived next day in the form of a special Fourth of July present for Joe Kelly, our overseas hero. We had celebrated the holiday by sneaking out into the country with a couple of picnic baskets. In the distance we had heard fireworks going off in some village near Kyoto and Katsumi had said, 'Japanese love to celebrate. Even American holidays we enjoy.' But when we got back to Osaka, Joe found the fateful letter tucked under the door. We had all known it must arrive soon but even so we were unprepared. Joe's hands trembled as he read the bad news.

'They sending you home?' I asked.

'Yep,' he said weakly.

He showed me the sheet of paper which I at once recognized as one not intended for enlisted men to see, and my West Point training welled up. 'How'd you get hold of this?'

'A friend of a friend,' he said.

I read the impersonal phrases which two months before would have meant nothing to me. 'American military personnel married to Japanese wives will be rotated home immediately lest their allegiance to the United States be eroded.' Farther down it said, 'This applies especially to personnel whose marriages have occurred since April 1, 1952.' Then there was the usual baloney passage about commanders providing every assistance to men who must make unusual arrangements for wives forced to remain in Japan.

Joe asked bitterly, 'What do they mean by unusual arrangements? Getting her a job in a good whore house?'

'Joe, take it easy!'

'It ain't easy to take.'

'Joe, I've seen hundreds of orders like this. They all peter out.'

'I think they mean it this time, Ace. Should I write to my Congressman?'

In spite of my original feelings on this point I now said, 'Take it clear to the President, Joe,' I turned and kissed blackened-eyes Katsumi on the cheek and said, 'I wish we had a million gals like you back home.'

Joe said, 'This is important to you, Ace, because one of these days you may be tryin' to bring Hanayo into the States.'

'I'm already trying,' I said. Then desperately I added, 'Hanayo can't make up her mind but I started the paper work this morning. Just in case.' I noticed that Hana-ogi gasped at this and was about to protest, but Joe interrupted by pointing to the corners of the wood-and-paper house.

'I had it good here,' he said grimly. 'Wonderful wife, baby comin', friends, a home. Well, that's the way the ball bounces.' As he surveyed the impending ruin he took refuge in the phrase which our men across Korea had adopted as their reaction to the dismal tricks of war: 'That's the way the ball bounces.'

For Joe the ball took an evil twist. An implementing letter arrived next day with a cold, hard list of the men who were to be sent home and under the K's Joe found his name. He took the list immediately to Lt. Col. Craford, who said, 'I told you you were goin' home. I got four men on that list. Everyone of 'em's been in to cry the blues.'

'But my wife is havin' a baby.'

'All wives have babies. That's what wives are for.'

'Can I be transferred back to Korea?'

The colonel grunted, 'You're the fourth guy who would rather go back to war in Korea than go home to the States. You really prefer Korea?'

Joe saw a chance to remain in the area and cried eagerly, 'Yes!'

Lt. Col. Craford turned away in disgust and said, 'It's disgraceful when a man prefers Japan to America, but when he'd rather go back to Korea it's insanity.'

'Then I can go?' Joe begged.

'No!' Craford shouted. 'You get to hell home. All of you Jap-lovers, get home where you belong.' He looked at Joe's papers and asked, 'Where is your home?'

Joe said, 'Osaka.'

Craford flushed and said, 'I mean your real home.'

'Osaka,' Joe repeated doggedly.

Craford banged the desk and shouted, 'You get out of here. I oughta court-martial you.'

Without thinking Joe caught him up on it. 'Would that mean I could stay in Japan?'

Craford became apoplectic and sputtered, 'All right, wise guy. All right. When the shipping list comes out you won't have to look. Because your name is gonna be first.'

When Joe reported all this I got sore. I've watched my father deal with hundreds of human problems and although he's as tough a general as they come, he always puts men first. In France there was a saying in his outfit: 'If your wife is dying, don't bother with the colonel. He'll say no. See General Gruver. He'll say yes.' So I told Joe, 'You hate the military, kid, but this isn't standard. I'll fight this all the way to General Webster.'

I caught the train to Kobe and when we stopped at Nishinomiya there was the poster of Hana-ogi smiling down at me.

General Webster didn't smile. For the first three minutes he never gave me a chance to get a word in. 'Who in hell do you think was just in here?' he concluded. 'The Supervisor of the Keihanshin Kyuko Railroad!' He waited for this to take effect, but I didn't comprehend, so he said in disgust, 'The railroad that runs the theater where you've distinguished yourself—beyond the call of duty.'

I waited for the explosion but there was none. General Webster smiled pleasantly and said, 'It's all been settled. The Japanese-American scandal has been solved by the Webster-Ishikawa negotiations.' He bowed and said, 'His name was Ishikawa.'

Mimicking a diplomat he continued, 'The terms of the Webster-Ishiwaka treaty are these.' He handed me a sheaf of stapled papers and said, 'You fly back to Randolph Field. The actress girl goes to Tokyo.'

'When?' I cried.

'Both of you exit these parts on July 10—five days.'

Then, to my amazement, he insisted that I have lunch with him, and when we got to the Officers Club Mrs Webster and Eileen were waiting. We conducted ourselves with the punctilious indifference you give a man who has returned from a leprosarium, but Mrs Webster was too old a veteran of the social battlefields to play such a game for long. Her opening salvo was, 'Have you seen this month's show at Takarazuka? The girl who plays the lead is lovely.'

I was still sore about the way Joe Kelly was being treated, so I said to myself, 'If all bets are off, here goes,' and I said aloud, 'I know the girl and she's very talented, but I came to Kobe to try to argue your husband into letting Private Kelly remain in Japan.'

'Who's Private Kelly?' Mrs Webster asked.

'His Japanese wife is having a baby and he's being sent home–without her.'

The general grew red in the face and tried to change the subject but Eileen jumped in on my side, 'Rotten trick, I'd say.'

Her father said, 'Don't scowl at me. It's an area order.'

'What happens to the baby?' Eileen asked.

The general laid down his napkin and said, 'I argued with Kelly for half an hour, warning him not to marry a Japanese girl.'

This did not satisfy Eileen who asked, 'Does the Army force them to desert their wives? Aren't they legally married?'

'Yes, they're legally married,' snapped the general. 'We have to allow them to get married and then we have to leave the wife stranded.'

'This is serious,' Eileen protested. 'Doesn't anyone try to prevent such inhuman foolishness?'

General Webster addressed Eileen directly, 'I argued with this boy. Lloyd argued with him. Where'd it get us?'

But Eileen said, 'I'm not talking about what has happened. I'm talking about the injustice of what's going to happen.'

Mrs Webster interrupted and asked, 'How are you involved in this, Lloyd?'

I took a deep breath and said, 'Kelly's from my outfit in Korea.' (From the corner of my eye I saw the general sigh with relief that I had not embarrassed him by mentioning Hana-ogi, but I had no intention of avoiding the issue.) 'And it also happens that I'm planning to marry a Japanese girl myself.'

I had dropped my napalm. The general gulped. Mrs Webster blushed an absolute scarlet and Eileen put her hand on mine and said, 'I always knew you had guts.'

I said, 'Thanks, I guess I'd better go now.'

Mrs Webster asked weakly, 'The actress?'

'Yes.'

The general said, 'Lloyd's not marrying any actress. He's being sent home on Thursday.'

I started to leave but Eileen insisted upon walking to the door with me, as if I were the girl and she the escort. 'I'm proud of you, Lloyd,' she said. 'I wish you all the luck in the world.' We shook hands and I thought of a dozen things to say but none of them made much sense, so I said, 'I'm sorry we got things loused up,' and she said, 'It was mostly my fault,' and then as I was leaving she laughed and said, 'Remember the time I asked you if you ever felt like just grabbing me and hauling me off to some shack?'

We both smiled awkwardly at this and she said, 'That's just about what you did, wasn't it? But with somebody else.' She kissed me on the cheek and said good-naturedly, 'Well, I'm glad you turned out to be a man and not a mouse.'

When I got back home I found Joe and Katsumi alone in a kind of dull panic.

'I been all over it with everybody,' he said. 'Even went to see the consul, but everyone flashes the marriage papers at you and says, "You signed 'em. You knew you couldn't take her to America." As if that made everything just dandy.'

Since I already knew that his name was at the head of the list I hadn't the courage to ask him what the latest hot dope was, but he came out with it, 'I'm first on the first draft.'

Katsumi, saying nothing, prepared the meal while I watched the door for Hana-ogi. She arrived about seven and I could tell that she had already been ordered to Tokyo. She had a nervousness about her that I had not seen before and I wondered if she was aware that I was being flown home. We looked at each other for a moment as she kicked off her zori and then neither of us could continue the duplicity. She ran weeping across the tatami and cried, 'Rroyd, Rroyd! I Tokyo go five days!'

I caught her in my arms and hugged her as if I intended to crush her so that she could never escape. 'I fly back to Texas right away.'

She pushed me away and cried, 'You leave Japan?' I nodded and she burst into sobs, calling to Katsumi in Japanese. The two girls stood in the middle of the room and looked at Joe and me and for the four of us the world slowly fell apart.

HANA-OGI: 'Not soap in tub, Rroyd-san. Outside soap, please.'

There is one Japanese custom I had grown to love and Hana-ogi fled to this as relief from the tension of our crumbling home. She went to the bath corner and started a charcoal fire raging under the huge square wooden tub. When the water was hot she called, 'Come on, Rroyd-san. I scrub your back.'

I went into the little room where steam enveloped me and washed down with soap, rinsing myself off before I climbed into the tub. The water was almost scalding and Hana-ogi took a kind of soft bark and scrubbed my back for twenty minutes while we talked of that day's decisions.

When my heartache had been soaked away she soaped herself down, rinsed off and took my place while I scrubbed her back. As soon as we exited Joe and Katsumi took over and at nine we were all sitting cross-legged about the sukiyaki bowl while Katsumi served us an excellent meal. Hana-ogi said, 'We never forget this time,' and the warmth of the bath, the vigor of the scrubbing and the good friendship of our home made us ignore for a while the penalties that hung over our heads. I think we all knew that never again in our lifetimes would we know quite the same intense friendship and love that we shared that night and Joe said glumly, 'I hate to think of livin' in some Chicago roomin' house–waitin'.'

Toward midnight the inescapable gloom of our position settled firmly upon our little house so that Hana-ogi and I felt we had to break free and walk in the cool night air. The stars over Osaka were the same that had shone upon America seven hours earlier: Vega and Arcturus and Altair. They recognized no national barriers and I found myself–an officer sworn to protect the United

States–thinking that some day we might catch up with the stars.

But as so often is the case, no sooner had I entertained this fleeting thought than I willingly became more of an American than I had ever been before. For at the head of our alley appeared a large gang of toughs, screaming, 'Americans go home! America go to hell! Go home!'

They swarmed down the alley in frenzy. When they reached the house of Masako Fukada, the girl with the G.I. baby, they knocked the door in and dragged her into the street, screaming, 'Kill the American bastard.'

Before I could do anything, Hana-ogi dashed toward the center of the infuriated mob. Although she was risking her life at Takarazuka, and more besides, she dived for Masako, who was being kicked in the stomach, and threw herself across the girl's body.

This enraged the hoodlums, who waved their torches and shouted in high-pitched voices that Hana-ogi should be killed for going with an American. I started for them but Hana-ogi cried a warning to stay away. This caused the mob to turn toward me and in the lurid light of their flickering torches these fanatical faces looked exactly like the cartoons of the Japanese barbarians we had kept posted in our ready rooms during the war years. I remember one horrible face rushing at me. It was distorted, evil, brutal, and inhuman.

'You're for me, you Japanese bastard!' I cried and launched a dive at his belly. Another Japanese swung a club upward at the same moment and I thought my head had been knocked away, but my momentum carried me on and I crashed into the ring leader and felt the wonderful impact of my body against his and the thudding fall onto the ground with him uttering a shaken grunt. I started to smash at his distorted and hateful face. At the same time I had sense enough to shout, 'Hey, Joe!'

The little tough burst right through his own paper doors brandishing a rifle butt. He flailed a path to me and we tried to defend ourselves, but I was bleeding from the face, and started to faint.

'For Christ sake,' the little gangster cried. 'Not now! We got 'em runnin'.'

The next second he collapsed under three Japanese clubs and I fainted. Later I learned that the anti-American mob would have killed us except for the pachinko players. They were at the canal end of the alley, sitting gloomily in the dark after the closing of the pinball parlor and one of them to whom I used to speak in English when I played pachinko heard Joe shout my name. They realized we were in trouble and they knew we were their friends.

Little Watanabe-san and the man who was keeping two geishas and the man whose wife beat him and the man who beat his wife and the man who had been in the penitentiary rushed up the alley. I am told there was a violent battle, but I knew nothing of it. The last thing I saw was a Japanese face–not one of the evil masks, but Hana-ogi's oval and yellow beauty as she lay fearful and with her eyes closed across the body of unconscious Masako Fukada.

When they brought me to I heard little Joe repeating quietly, 'No, no! Don't send for an Army doctor. Get a Jap doctor.' He was explaining to one of the pachinko players, 'I learned it in Chicago. Never call a cop. Cops never help anybody.' When I awakened, with a touchy streak of bruised face, I saw Hana-ogi again. She said, 'I not hurt.' Immediately I felt better and as the night progressed I began to feel absolutely good, for our little house was crowded with alley people. They stood about in kimonos or sat cross-legged on the floor, sucking in their breath and sipping the green tea that Katsumi-san served them. They said, all of them and with repeated emphasis, 'The hoodlums who attacked you–they were not Japanese. They were Korean communists. We are Japanese. We are your friends.' I remember one young man, a tough, capable laborer who still wore the peaked cap of the Japanese army. I had played pachinko with him and had given his four children presents. He spoke in mumbled tones and knew no English but he said, 'They weren't all Koreans. Many Japanese hate you Americans. But I fought against you in Guadalcanal.' (I thought: 'In those days you'd have beheaded me.') 'And you have behaved much better in Japan that I expected. Now I am your friend. Those in the street, they were communists.'

All the same, next day Masako-san and her American baby left our alley and we never heard of them again. Masako's mother stood in the roadway cursing the girl for having caused the riot and the other women of the alley looked away.

That was Sunday. On Monday the Air Force officially notified Joe that he would be flown back to America on Wednesday. To Joe it was the sentence of torture. I found him sitting cross-legged on the floor studying the notice with dull resignation. He looked up grimly and asked, 'Why should I be punished? Why should I have to go back to the States?'

Automatically I replied, 'The way the ball bounces.'

'No!' he shouted. 'What's there for me in America?'

I assured him, 'You'll get out of the Air Force and find a job and pretty soon Katumi'll follow you.'

He looked at me sadly and said, 'I wish it was goin' to be so simple.'

I recall every incident of that powerful and uneventful day. I drifted out to Itami to wind up my paper work and have lunch with Mike Bailey who told me, 'My affair with Fumiko-san is washed up cleaner than a sergeant's shirt on inspection. She said she was afraid something bad would happen. Suicide, broken life, unwanted baby. She said such things occurred in her family because they were aristocrats and took life awful hard. She said Hana-ogi was the kind of girl to be. Strong and brave.'

I went over to Takarazuka for my mail and found a letter from my father which said, 'I follow the war news more intelligently since my talk with you. No doubt your attractive little Butterfly has told you I called on her that night. You're lucky to have known such a fine girl. I have hopes Mother and I shall see you in Lancaster one day soon. Until then, I am profoundly proud of a son who can bag seven enemy planes. Harry.'

In mid-afternoon I caught the train into Osaka and once more experienced an overpowering sense of identification with this strange land. The fields I saw could have been fields that Hana-ogi and I were working. The old people were her parents and the fat young babies were ours. The endless struggle for life was our struggle.

Once when Joe Kelly had cried, 'I don't want to go back to America,' I was on the point of knocking him down as an unpatriotic moron. Now, on the Takarazuka train, I knew that a man can have many homes and one of them must be that place on earth, however foreign, where he first perceives that he and some woman could happily become part of the immortal passage of human beings over the face of the earth: the childbearers, the field tillers, the builders, the fighters and eventually the ones who die and go back to the earth.

I had discovered this passionate emotion in Hana-ogi's country and for me–a United States officer bred in patriotism–the crowded fields between Takarazuka and Osaka, the insignificant canals, the tiny house, the tatami mats and the bed roll unfurled at night would be forever one of my homes.

This haunting sensation stayed with me as I walked through Osaka that sunny afternoon for on passing a print shop I saw in the window an old wood-block portrait of some classic beauty of Japan. She had a mountain of black hair with big yellow combs stuck through, and she reminded me of that day in the Kyoto museum. Instinctively, I stepped inside the tiny shop and bowed to the proprietor. 'Do you happen to have a wood-block print of Hana-ogi?' I asked. I wanted to take her with me when I left Japan. The proprietor grew quite mournful and indicated that he had no English, but in a whisk he was out in the street shouting and soon the inevitable girl who had learned the language from sleeping with American soldiers appeared.

'What you want, Major?' she asked.

'I'd like a picture of Hana-ogi.'

'Ah, so desu-ka!' The man hurried back to a case and soon appeared with six of the glossy photographs sold at Takarazuka. They showed my Hana-ogi as a sheik, a Venetian gondolier, a Chinese prince and as three other handsome young men. I bowed very low and said, 'I did not mean that Hana-ogi. I meant . . .' and I pointed to the picture in the window.

'Soda!' cried the man.

'Ah, soka, soka!' cried the girl, and they indicated by their manner that if I were interested in such a picture I was one of them. Two hangers-on in the store joined us as the man shuffled through a stack of prints. Finally he produced one, a brilliant thing with iridescent black background showing Hana-ogi upon the day of her return to the green cages of Yoshiwara: glorious with amber needles through her hair and many kimonos. Her eyes were notably slanted and tinged with blue, her teeth were jet black and the hair around her ear down in sideburns. She was timeless and she was Japan.

The little street girl said, 'This picture not real. Only copy. But very old. Maybe one hunner years.' The men watching sucked in their breath and complimented me as I carried away the living memory of Hana-ogi.

THE NOODLE VENDOR: 'Soba, soba, soba.'

It seems strange, but I can remember each of the trivial things that filled this lovely Japanese day. When I entered our alley I passed the pachinko parlor and stuck my head in to thank the men who had helped me in my brawl with the communists, but most of them were so engrossed in their pinball games that they scarcely looked up. I then crossed the alley to the flower shop and indicated that I wanted a bouquet for our house. The little man—I keep using that word because these men were really so very small—started a cascade of Japanese, then went to the street and shouted till a boy came. Always, in Japan, there is someone who knows English. This boy explained that since I must soon go back to America, the flower man wanted to give me three most special flowers. When the shopkeeper handed them to me they looked like the ordinary flowers that American girls wear to football games. I had often bought them for Eileen Webster but now the boy said, sucking in his breath in astonishment, 'Very unusual, chrysanthemum blooming in July.' He added that this was the national flower of Japan and looked with absolute covetousness as I took them from the flower man.

Thinking little of the gift I carried the flowers to our house, but as soon as the girls saw them they sucked in their breath just as the boy had done, and Katsumi ran into the street to announce that we had chrysanthemums in July. Soon our little room was filled with neighbors who sat upon their ankles staring at the three wonderful blooms. From time to time new men would arrive, bow to Hana-ogi, sit upon the floor and contemplate this miraculous accomplishment. Even Watanabe-san left his pachinko to see. The boy who had been my translator joined us and explained this strange thing: 'On the road to Kobe a florist has a big glass house in which he grows these flowers. In one section there are cloth blinds to keep out the sun. With an almanac to guide him, this clever man causes the sun to set earlier each day so that within the space of three weeks it seems to run the course of four months. The flowers are fooled. They think that autumn is upon them and they bloom.' The men sucked in their breath in admiration.

Now Katsumi suddenly felt the first life in her womb and fell slightly forward. Hana-ogi washed her forehead in cold water and Joe, faced by the necessity of leaving his pregnant wife behind in Japan said loudly, 'I hope just one thing. I hope Colonel Craford goes home and buys himself a new Buick, light blue, and I hope he's drivin' it down the avenue when I'm comin' up the other way with a Mack truck.'

I was about to caution Joe against taking a pass at Craford when I looked up to see Hana-ogi arranging her kimono. It was blue and white, very soft for summer wear. With it she wore two undergarments of thinnest cloth; pink silk and white cotton. I thought I had never seen her so lovely. Unmindful of me she experimented with the sheer lines of her garments until she brought them into a pattern which made her more beautiful than the picture I had bought. I was about to share this with her when she raised both hands and combed down the hair about her face so that it rested in the Japanese style. Studying herself in the mirror, she nodded approval. Then she heard me laugh and quickly knelt beside me. 'Rroyd-san,' she said. 'I got to be this way. I Japanese.' I think she expected me to be hurt, but I unrolled the print and as soon as she saw the bold characters in the upper corner she cried, 'Hana-ogi! Rroyd-san, you buy?' When we had studied the picture for a moment she went to Katsumi's trunk and returned with a drawing brush and an ink stone. Using the firm Chinese characters long ago adopted for Japanese writing, she added a fresh column of print at the picture's side: 'Hana-ogi of Takarazuka-za loved an American.' I caught her in my arms and kissed her but in so doing I destroyed the arrangement of color and cloth at her throat so she stood and fixed the kimonos once more.

For women in love there could be no garment more entrancing than the kimono. As I watched Hana-ogi I knew that in the future, when even the memory of our occupation has grown dim, a quarter of a million American men will love all women more for having tenderly watched some golden-skinned girl fold herself into the shimmering beauty of a kimono. In memory of her feminine grace all women will forever seem more feminine.

When Hana-ogi was finally dressed, she and Katsumi sprang their surprise! They were taking Joe and me to see the puppets of Osaka. Boldly, for we no longer cared who saw us upon the streets, we walked through the lovely summer's dusk to an ancient theater, small and off to one side, where for many generations the famous puppets of Japan had been exhibited. The girls, resplendent in their kimonos, bought our tickets for a few yen and ushered us proudly into cramped seats, where we witnessed a remarkable performance.

The stage was small and peopled with many men dressed in black. In their hands they carried four-foot puppets of strangely human quality who acted out one of Japan's classical tragedies. At first it was impossible for me to accept the illusion, for it took three grown men to operate each puppet and the men were constantly and completely visible. If the heroine were to walk across the stage, one of the towering black men openly manipulated the puppet's kimono to simulate walking, another worked her left arm and kept her clothing arranged, while a distinguished old man, dressed in a shimmering kimono and formal winglike jacket operated the puppet's head and right arm. It seemed ridiculous to have six human arms so busy in vitalizing one doll, but before I was aware of the change, I had completely accepted the convention. Curiously, the towering black men did indeed become invisible, like spirits from another world organizing human life, and I became truly engrossed in the tragedy of these dolls.

We were watching one of the many classical plays in which two lovers commit suicide. In this one a married man fell in love with a beautiful Yoshiwara girl, whom Hana-ogi identified for me in the dark as 'just like old-time Hana-ogi.' I don't imagine any American has ever really understood the ins and outs of a Japanese tragedy but I did get the impression of two people caught in an increasingly unbearable set of pressures. Just what these pressures were I never grasped but Hana-ogi and Katsumi wept softly and when I asked what about they said, 'It's so sad. People talking about this man.'

But what I did understand was the musicians. For the mysterious men in black never spoke. The dialogue was sung by an amazing man accompanied by four musicians playing samisens. Maybe *sung* isn't the right word, for I have never heard more eerie sounds. The singer was a fat, bald-headed man in his late sixties who sat on his haunches, and as tragedy on the puppet stage deepened he would lean forward and scream in unbelievable fury until his round face became purple and the veins stood out in his neck. During love passages he would narrate the scene in a quivering feminine wail and as the remorseless pressure of society bore down on the lovers he would make his voice rough and horrible like a broken saw against a rusted nail. To hear this man was a terrifying experience for I had not known the human voice to be capable of such overpowering emotion. I would defy anyone not to be unnerved by that stupefying voice.

Now, as the hounded lovers approached the historic scene at Amijima where they would commit suicide together, the mysterious black figures on the stage whirled about in what seemed like a confusion of fates, the wooden dolls marched stiffly to their doom and the inspired story-teller shrieked in positive terror while the muted samisens played doleful music. There was another sound in this remarkable tragedy, but this I wasn't aware of until the curtain had closed: all the women near me were weeping and as I looked away from the epileptic singer, his face at last relaxed as if he had gone suddenly dead, I saw lovely Hana-ogi sitting with her hands folded in her kimono sobbing desperately. She was so bereft that tears might have come to my eyes, too, but when I turned her face toward mine I saw that she was in no way unhappy. A look of ecstasy had captured her wonderful face and her eyes glowed. I was astonished and whispered, 'What's the matter, Hanayo-chan?'

'It was so beautiful,' she said.

'What? The singing?'

'No,' she replied softly, taking my hand. 'The double suicide. It was so tender.'

'What do you mean?' I asked.

The women around me were rising now and on each face I saw this same look of ecstatic satisfaction. Apparently the double suicide had inspired them even more than it had Hana-ogi. I was not surprised, therefore, when she made no attempt to explain this mystery, but when I looked at Katsumi and saw on her tear-stained face the same look of rapture I had to acknowledge that for the Japanese audience this double suicide had provided a vitally satisfying experience.

'What's it all about?' I asked Katsumi, indicating the weeping women.

'The lovers,' she said quietly, pointing to the now barren stage. 'At last they found happiness.'

'They're dead,' Joe said.

As we walked through the broad, clean streets of Osaka back to our canal I became hurtingly aware that there would always be many parts of Japan that Joe Kelly and I could never penetrate. 'What happened back there?' I asked Joe. 'All I saw was a bunch of dolls and a man shouting.'

The little guy laughed as if he hadn't anything to worry about and said, 'Every three weeks Katsumi-san breaks down into sobbin' fits. You'd think her heart had broken. Used to scare me sick. Then I found out what was cooking'. First time it was an ex-army general who shot himself because he was charged with stealin' government money. Katsumi said it was so beautiful she had to cry. Next time it was a geisha from Kyoto. Cut her throat. That was especially lovely.'

Hana-ogi heard me laugh and turned sharply. I expected her to upbraid me but instead she took my hand and sniffled, 'You not understand,' she said. 'To have courage. To have honor. Is very beautiful.'

As we entered the pathway leading to our canal, conversation was broken by a substantial commotion. We heard voices crying and hurried to our own alley in time to see the launching of a magnificent display of fireworks. 'Ah!' Hana-ogi whispered. 'I forget. Tanabata!' And long after the fireworks had ceased the people of our alley stood staring up at the stars. In Japanese Hana-ogi explained: 'Vega, the princess star, fell in love with Altair, the herdboy star. Unlike American fairy stories, the herdboy married the princess without any trouble; then like our stories, he loved his wife so much that he allowed his sheep to stray so that the king threw him onto the other side of the Milky Way river. Once each year in July he swims the river and makes love with his princess. For the people of Japan this Tanabata is the night of love.'

But Hana-ogi and I as we spread our bed roll reasoned that we had two more nights to spend together, so we left the love-making to the princess and her shepherd while we lay side by side listening to the exquisite sounds of the Japanese night. The old blind man who massaged sore muscles and burned moxa powder on nerves to make them well passed along our alley, sounding his melancholy flute and tapping with his gnarled cane. For a while there was silence. Then we could hear Watanabe-san coming home from his pachinko game with his wife snapping at his heels. Hana-ogi snuggled close to me and said, 'All time we never fight,' but I touched the trivial scar beneath her sideburns and asked, 'What about the time I wanted you to become American?'

Then she grew somber and said, 'Because I know you, now I better Japanese. You better American.' Then I almost broke down. I wanted to lose myself in her love and confess, 'I can't live without you, Hanayo-chan. God, I cannot face the lonely world without your tenderness.' But I knew that we had two more nights to spend together and I was afraid that if I allowed myself full sorrow now the next nights might be unbearable. I choked once and buried my face against hers, feeling her Japanese eyes against my lips, her black Japanese hair against my face. 'Oh, darling,' I whispered, 'why can't you marry me?' She clasped her arms about me as she had done that first night in the woods by the Shinto shrine and said, 'Some people never love anyone.' (She said it: 'Rots peopre nebber rub nobody.') 'Oh, Rroyd-san, I love you till my feet are old for dancing–till my teeth break off same like Hana-ogi's.'

I thought I could not bear this but then came the sweetest night sound I have ever heard, the soft passage of the noodle vendor, pushing his belled cart while he played a rhythmic melody upon his flute. All through the night the noodle men passed through the streets of Osaka sounding their lovely melody. Some used five running notes ending in a faint call. Others played a minor tune. Some played random notes and a few, whom you came to remember and cherish, played songs that might have been termed love songs, for they seemed always to come by when you were sleeping with the girl who shared your bed roll on the tatami.

For the rest of this night, as I recall, Hana-ogi didn't even place her arm across my body and although it seems ridiculous this is what we said. I asked, 'Don't you think we ought to take Joe and Katsumi to dinner tomorrow?'

She replied, 'No, I think we should.'

'Damn it, Hanayo, will you explain once more why you say, "No, we should," and "Yes, we shouldn't."'

Patiently she went over it again. 'In Japanese polite to say that way. If you speak no to me, I say no to agree with you.'

'I still don't get it.'

'Ask me a question.'

'Don't you want to marry me?'

'Yes, I not marry you.'

'But what I asked was, "Don't you want to?"'

The game stopped for she whispered, 'No, no, Royd-san. I do want to.'

I grumbled, 'I can't understand either your grammar or your heart.'

She placed my hand upon her heart and the delicate golden warmth of her slim body swept over me and she said, 'My heart for you takusan, takusan. Remember when you say me that?'

I remembered, as as the sweet song of the noodle vendor echoed down our alley we fell asleep.

If Monday was peaceful, Tuesday was not. Hana-ogi and I woke about eight-thirty to find that Joe had left for one last appeal to Lt. Col. Craford. Katsumi, sensing that we would want to be alone, went out to lament with friends, so I started a fire and Hana-ogi, wrapped in a sheet, tried to get breakfast, but I kept pulling the sheet away until she finally surrendered it altogether, whereupon we propped a chair against the sliding doors and let the fire go out.

At eleven Hana-ogi dressed for Takarazuka. I tied her obi for her and she insisted that I leave the ends dangling almost to the floor. Taking a few mincing steps she cried, 'I maiko girl!' Then deftly she swept the ends together in a bow, symbol of older girls, and said, 'I virgin no more. I married woman.' So far as I can remember those were the last words she said that morning. I watched her go down the alley and all the women in the open-front stores and houses called out to her on that summer morning.

She was gone only a few minutes when Joe came back. He was licked. He threw his cap on the floor and asked in final despair, 'Ace, what can I do?'

'Take a deep breath,' I said. 'Stick it out. They'll have to change the law.'

'In Washington they got fifty senators like Craford. You think they're gonna change the law?' He looked wild-eyed.

'Joe! Ease up.'

'How can I? Ace, I'm a no-good punk. If I go home without Katsumi it's pool halls and hamburger joints. I couldn't take it.'

'For a while you have to.'

He sat down cross-legged on the tatami and said grimly, 'In Chicago, I killed a man. A mixed-up affair—not all my fault. They couldn't pin anything on me. I'm not apologizin', because it could just as well have been my fault. Because I was no damn good. And if I lose Katsumi I'll be no damn good again.'

I knew there was something I ought to say, some standard word of courage, but I couldn't think of any. Joe said, 'A guy like you, from a good home—you wouldn't understand. For the first time in my life I'm livin'. At night when I hear Katsumi come up the alley shufflin' her wooden shoes—later when she puts that crazy hard, little pillow next to mine—when I see the plain goddamn goodness that girl . . .' He looked down at the tatami and I guessed that he had tears in his throat. I wanted to say that I knew but I was tied up.

'Joe, promise me you won't get into trouble with Col. Craford.'

He looked up at me as if Craford were already dead. 'Him?' he sniffed. 'The only time I believe in God is when I think of that fat slob. God must be keepin' score on bastards like that. Otherwise nothin' makes sense.'

I said, 'Remember, Joe. You promised you'd make no trouble with that . . .' I searched for a name and suddenly the total misery of Joe's problem rose in my mouth like bile. I grew purple and cursed Craford for several minutes. I cursed my father and General Webster and Mrs Webster and every convention that made it impossible for Hana-ogi and me to marry. Then I stopped, but I was still quivering with accumulated fury.

Joe looked up at me and said, 'Thanks, Major. I thought you felt that way.'

I was still shaking. I said, 'Even so I believe things'll work out.'

He said, 'I don't.'

There was nothing to add. He knew how I felt. He knew I was with him. Maybe I had steered him away from some hot-brained mistake. That's the best I could hope, so I went over to Itami to clear out my desk and borrow Mike Bailey's car, but as I left the air base for the theater, where I was to see the last performance of *Swing Butterfly*, I had a disgusting experience which even at the time seemed to me a premonition of tragedy. Outside the main gate of the air base at Itami a broad road stretched for more than half a mile. It was filled with cheap dance halls, beer joints, razzle-dazzle dives and plain whore houses. In front of each establishment lounged gangs of young girls and the stretch was known as 'The 1,000 Yard Dash.' It was claimed that any American in uniform who could negotiate this honky-tonk strip and keep his pants on would receive a prize of $1,000 for heroism beyond the call of duty.

As I drove out of the air base for the last time I saw the frowsy halls: 'Village Bar,' 'Club Little Man,' 'The Flying Bull,' and 'Air Force Heaven.' Then, to my disgust, my car stalled and three girls promptly surrounded it. One climbed in and said, 'O.K. General. Where we off to?' Immediately an M.P. appeared and hauled the girl back onto the strip and gave me some brotherly warning. 'Watch out for her, Major. She's no good.' He saluted and pointed to a saloon up the stretch, 'If you want something real nice, Major, you can trust the girls at the "Silver Dollar."'

When I got my car started I saw with dismay that from the other direction had come a Packard from Toneyama Heights, the nearby residential district where the big brass lived, and in it were two colonels' wives who knew me. They watched with disgust as the three persistent little street girls started to climb back into my car as soon as the M.P. had left. As I chucked them out I thought that some day in the future I would recall Hana-ogi and I would have to speak her name to someone and if he had been at Itami he would remember 'The 1,000 Yard Dash' and the brassy prostitutes and he would wink at me and say, 'Boy, do I know those Jap girls?' But he wouldn't know, and nothing I could ever tell anyone who had seen Itami would explain Hana-ogi. I shivered at the wheel of my car and mumbled, 'All this should have happened fifty years from now. Then maybe there would have been a chance. In my day there was no chance for such a marriage.' I saw myself in years to come. Junior officers would boast, 'You can say that General Gruver looks tough and formal but did you know that when he served in Japan he ran off with a geisha girl? Yep, took her right out of a house.' But they would never know.

However, the distaste of this experience along the strip was expelled by Hana-ogi's exquisite performance. When I had first seen her I had been insulted by her burlesque of Americans and I had been unable to appreciate her ability. Now my reaction was different, for I discovered that even against my will I had to laugh at her lampoon of Americans. The reason was simple. She had studied with intimate care my mannerisms and now reproduced them in burlesque form. When she lit a cigarette she mimicked me, when she propositioned Madame Butterfly it was me trying to kiss her on the Bitchi-bashi. This time I, more than anyone else in the audience, enjoyed her burlesque of Americans.

As her big dance number approached I became apprehensive, for I suspected that her aping of Americanisms would dull her Japanese touch, but I was wrong, for in her samurai there was now a freedom and swagger that no maiko girl, as Hana-ogi termed the virgin dancers, could have created. Hana-ogi was the artist. Even more than mistress or wife, she was an artist, and if her American jitterbugging was more hilarious for having studied an American at close hand, her Japanese classical dance was stronger for having known that American not as a subject for study but as a lover—as one who cried eagerly to marry her. I understood what she had said the night before. She was now a better Japanese.

When intermission came I wanted to rush backstage and embrace her and tell her that no matter if she lived a million years cooped up at Takarazuka, I would be with her every time she danced—but I was not to see her, for I could not get into the dressing-rooms.

CPL SHARKEY: 'You damned Buddha-heads, you gotta stand back from the door.'

So the rapture was lost. The great deep rapture I felt when watching Hana-ogi perform was never reported to her, for as I took my seat at the beginning of Act II an M.P. came up to me and asked, 'Major Gruver?'

'Yes.'

'You'll have to come with us.'

The curtain had not yet risen, so Hana-ogi did not see me leave and I was grateful for that, for I was trembling. I thought that Lt. Col. Craford was shipping me home early, but when I got outside and I saw two other M.P.'s with guns I asked, 'What's up?'

'Airman Kelly,' they said.

'Joe?'

'Yep. Deserted.'

'Impossible. I saw him this morning.'

'We know. We thought you might tell us . . .'

Another M.P. broke in and said, 'He was called special at 1300. He was scheduled to fly out tomorrow but a special plane came through and Col. Craford said, "Get him on it."'

The first M.P. said, 'I checked him in at the airport at 1250 but before the plane took off he beat it.'

'We figured you might know where he is.'

'No! Last time I saw Kelly . . .'

'When was the last time?'

'About 0815. No! It was 1120.'

'You know where he lives?'

'Sure.'

I had a dry ugly taste in my mouth as the siren wailed into Osaka. At Itami I asked, 'Did the plane take off?'

'Yep. It's desertion.'

I began to sweat. Now Joe Kelly was really done for. Insubordination and desertion would be the charge and he might never get Katsumi into the States, so I asked, 'Jesus, are you sure he deserted?'

'I checked him in. Sharkey saw him leave.'

We stopped at the canal and I led the way to the alley, where two M.P.'s tried the door. It seemed to be barred, so they were going to break the freshly mended paper, but at that moment it seemed like my house and I didn't want the paper broken, so I said, 'Maybe a chair's against it. I'll use the window.'

One M.P. came with me to the back of the house while I forced open a window and started to crawl in. While my leg was still suspended I saw Joe. He was on the floor with his head blown apart by a .45. Across him, obviously having died later, lay Katsumi with a kitchen knife plunged completely through her neck.

For a moment I didn't call out anything. All I could do was look at the floor—at the two lovers who had needed each other so much. The M.P. came up and looked over my shoulder. Then he called loudly, 'You better break the door down, Sharkey.'

I watched the frail doors bend and break. I heard the clatter of wood and the tearing of paper and the doors through which Hana-ogi had so often come at dusk, dropping her silken packages on the floor, were gone. Sharkey took one look and said, 'Get the camera. You wanna catch this just as it happened.'

Sharkey barked to the man at my shoulder, 'Eddie, you inform the Jap police.' Then he saw me and said, 'We'll need you here, Major.'

I got down out of the window and walked around to the front of the house where a crowd had gathered and where children were screaming the tragedy across the canal to other children. An old man pried his way in through the broken doors and came out to report accurately upon the double suicide.

I was numb with helpless anger. Of all the people in the world, Joe and Katsumi Kelly should have been protected and kept alive. I thought of them laughing and helping each other and I got all sick inside, but then I thought of Hana-ogi, who would be coming home soon and I grew panicky for her because the photographers had arrived and were taking pictures like mad.

And then I saw, on the outskirts of the crowd, two of the little prostitutes Hana-ogi and I had met the other night. They were already working the main streets and had stopped by to witness the tragedy. I said to them, 'You remember Hana-ogi?'

'Sure, Major.'

'You watch up there. Tell her to go back. Please.'

'Sure, Major. You got cigaretto?'

The other girl pointed to the house and jabbed herself in the stomach as if with a knife. 'They kill?'

I nodded and they stared at the house with grim fascination. 'Japanese girl and G.I.?'

I said yes and the little girls moved toward the head of the canal where they could intercept Hana-ogi while the reporters swarmed at me. They were bright young men, most of whom spoke English, and I had enough sense to keep my mouth shut, for if I had said anything at all I would have blurted out, 'They wanted to ship him back to America but he insisted upon staying in Japan.' Finally I composed myself and said, 'He was with my outfit in Korea. This is a complete shock.'

The reporters saw somebody else and swarmed away but one stayed and asked, 'Aren't you Ace Gruver?'

I nodded.

'You the one living with Hana-ogi?'

I wanted to shoot him dead but everything had collapsed now, so I nodded grimly and he pointed up the canal.

There at last she was, Hana-ogi. Late afternoon sun played upon her tousled black hair and illuminated the fall of her kimono. With eager pin-toed steps she hurried along the canal, coming so close that I could see the slant of her adorable eyes and that sweet mouth always ready with a teasing smile.

The two prostitutes stopped her, informed her of the suicides and tried to prevent her from joining the crowd. She ignored them and started coming toward me down the canal bank but the newspaperman who was standing with me broke away, ran toward her and spoke rapidly. She peered across the crowd searching for me, and when she failed to find me she broke away from the guardian prostitutes and the warning newspaperman to fight her way resolutely toward the very spot where the police waited.

In that moment I could see the reckless collapse of her world and instinctively a shout rose to my lips. I called in panic, 'Lo, the postillion!'

She stopped. The smile that had crept upon the edge of her lips vanished and her lovely face once more became an impersonal mask. Standing on tiptoe, she peered across the crowd, still seeking me, but I hid myself so that she would have to go back. After a moment she turned away from the crowds that shoved toward the suicide house and I last saw her moving with extraordinary grace back to the main street. The summer breeze, drifting down the canal, tugged at her kimono and twilight rested on her hair. I can still see the folds of cloth meticulous about her neck. Then she moved behind a pillar and I never saw her again.

For just as I started to run after her, Lt. Col. Craford waddled up and he seemed almost to relish the tragedy. It proved he was right and that guys like Kelly were no damned good. He saw me and lurched over to repeat his warning that he was shipping me . . .

'You bastard!' I cried. 'You stinking bastard!'

He jumped back as if I had kicked him and began to bluster but I couldn't take any more. 'You swine! Kelly told me what you said to him, you bastard! You killed this kid!'

He was astonished at my outbursts and suddenly became aware that if I was really outraged I might carry the fight to my father, so he tried to pacify me, but I said, 'Don't be afraid of me, you dirty bastard. I'm not going to squeal on you—but you murdered this kid.'

He withdrew and a Japanese police official said, 'You come with me,' and for three hours while I ached to seek out Hana-ogi I had to answer questions and fill out reports as to the death of Katsumi-san. It was after ten o'clock when I was released and I caught a cab whose driver gasped when I said Takarazuka, but he drove me there and at eleven that Sunday night I hurried past the cryptomerias and into the dormitory where Hana-ogi lived.

Apparently I was expected, for old Teruko-san and her grim-faced interpreter were waiting for me. 'Hana-ogi-san is not here,' they said firmly.

'I know she's here!' I cried.

'Hana-ogi-san is on her way to Tokyo.'

'She can't be! I saw her!'

'Please, Major Gruver. Hana-ogi-san is not here.'

Unthinkingly, I forced my way past the two women and along the corridor on which Hana-ogi lived. The Takarazuka girls peered at me as I stormed past, then sighed when I reached Hana-ogi's empty room. It was so empty. The little things that made it hers were gone.

From the next room Fumiko-san appeared and said, weeping, 'Hana-ogi-san really go, Major.'

I turned around like a madman. It couldn't end this way—across a canal, over the heads of a hundred people at the scene of a suicide and Hana-ogi departs forever. 'She's here!' I insisted.

I stood helpless and then saw in one corner of her room a zori that she had forgotten. I stepped across the tatami on tiptoe as if she were still there, reproving me for not having removed my shoes, and I lifted the zori and it seemed as if her powerful, inspired foot were there in my hand, with the big toe clinging to the zori strap and the Japanese music beginning and the samurai dance about to start and Hana-ogi . . . oh, Hana-ogi . . .

'Hanayo-chan!' I shouted. 'Hanayo-chan! Where are you?' From their doors the beautiful Takarazuka girls stared at me impassively. The world seemed to grow dark and I screamed, 'Hana-ogi, don't leave me.' Then I felt Fumiko-san put her hand on my shoulder. 'You go now, Rroyd-san. Is no more.' And she led me to the roadway.

GENERAL WEBSTER: 'Whatever makes you a better man makes you a better husband.'

General Webster called me in to Kobe next day and said, 'That was a dreadful affair last night in Osaka.' He asked me if I had heard any rumors that Lt. Col. Craford had handled the affair badly. I wanted to put a blast on the fat blubber-gut who had murdered Kelly, but something old and powerful inside me argued, 'Why start a military mess?' and I kept my mouth shut. Then I shrugged my shoulders and said, 'I guess Craford handled it O.K.'

But immediately I knew that I was reverting to the man I had been when I first argued with Kelly against marrying a Japanese girl. I was defending the Army against the man and I felt ashamed of myself. I must have shivered, for General Webster said gruffly, 'Lloyd, don't take this so bitterly. Kelly's dead. Nobody can do anything about it. You told me yourself he was a dead-end punk—beyond saving.'

I looked at the general. A man under his command had committed suicide rather than return to the United States and he was shrugging it off. I asked, 'What about that colonel in Tokyo who shot himself rather than leave his Japanese girl? Or the major in Yokohama? Were they punks?'

'Yes! They were second-class men. I've seen reports on seven such suicides and they were all shoddy material. First-class men sometimes fall in love with native girls, of course they do. But they get over it. They forget the girls and they go home. They go back to work.'

'Damn it!' I shouted. 'Why do men like you and my father call them native girls? Can't you believe . . .'

General Webster was remarkably patient. He stopped me by thrusting a yellow paper into my hand. 'I suppose a young man's no good if he doesn't have the guts to fight for what he thinks is right,' he said. 'You've had the courage to fight for Joe Kelly and his native girl. It was gallant, Lloyd, but it wasn't necessary. Read it.'

The yellow paper was from Washington and it said a law was being passed to permit men like Joe Kelly to bring their Japanese wives into the States. 'Now they do it!' I cried.

'They were doing it all along,' Webster said. 'Everyone knew the old law was bad.'

I thought of Joe and Katsumi lying in blood and I felt sick. I had to see Hana-ogi. In all the world she was the only person who could help me now. My heart and my mind cried out for her. 'Sir,' I blurted, 'I've got to get to Tokyo.'

'It's forbidden, Lloyd. You're flying home.'

'I don't care what happens. I've got to see Hana-ogi.'

The general winced as I used the strange name, then said calmly, 'If you disobey another order . . .'

'All right, I'll leave the Air Force. I'll get a . . .'

I expected General Webster to hit the roof, but when he's away from his wife he isn't so bad. He said, 'Sit down, Lloyd. I'm not going to throw my weight at you. You're being a stupid idiot and we both know it, but you come by it naturally.'

'What do you mean?'

'This seems like 1924.'

'I don't understand,' I said dully.

'Your father was mixed up with a girl–the one I told you about. There was one member of our class you've never met. Chap named Charley Scales. He had a chance in '24 to drop out of service and take a good job with General Motors. So your father decided to marry the girl and chuck the Army and go along with Charley, but some of us saner fellows talked him out of it. Must run in your family.'

'My father was going to leave the Army?'

'Yep. He was all broken up.' General Webster laughed and scratched his chin. 'I remember that we were quite sorry for him. We thought he was pretty weak to be broken up like that over a waitress. Look at him now.'

I said, 'I think he made a mistake in 1924.'

General Webster breathed a sigh of relief and said, 'So do I, but I guess any man has a right to get mixed up with a waitress once . . .'

'I don't mean that. I mean he probably should have married the waitress.'

'Lloyd! Your father a Chevrolet salesman!'

'I mean he should never have married my mother. They've never been happy.'

'Happy? What's happy? He's a great general.'

'I think he's made a mess of his life.'

General Webster got mad. 'You think! Who in hell are you to think? Only a few men in any generation can be great generals. Don't you forget it!'

I said, 'I still want to marry this girl.'

'Son,' General Webster said, 'the Supervisor of Takarazuka and I stayed up late last night figuring how to keep his outfit and mine free of bad publicity over the suicides. We protected ourselves and we can't let you ruin things.'

'At least give me a chance to say good-bye to her!'

'No, she herself wanted it this way.'

'She didn't!'

'I saw her. She said to send you back to America.'

I said, 'I don't believe that.' So he handed me a letter which had been written two days before. I knew because Hana-ogi had written it on my stationery and as I read it I could hear her gentle voice groping its way through my language:

Darring,

Pretty soon *(That was a phrase I used a lot . . .)* our rast night. I Tokyo go. You America go. *(A passage was scratched out, then . . .)* I not think fire die. Frame not go out. I think you many times. *(Then she added a passage from her phrase book . . .)*

Ever your devoted and humble servant,

and the letter was signed with the Chinese characters representing her name. How strange they were, those characters, how beautiful, how deeply hidden from me behind the wall of Asia!

I wanted to fling myself upon the floor and weep as Hana-ogi might have wept had we been at home, but instead there came to me that sad and final Japanese word which she had refused to teach me: 'Sayonara, Hana-ogi. Sayonara, you beautiful dancer. You've chosen the tough way. I hope your gods give you the courage to follow it. Sayonara, Katsumi, little mother. Forgive me that I once thought you too ugly to kiss. You can't know it now but I fought my way through four M.P.'s to kiss you good-bye and fat Col. Craford shuddered. Oh, Katsumi, sayonara. And Goddamn it, Sukoshi Joe, you died too soon. They're passing a law right now to let guys like you bring your wives home. It was a good fight that night until I fainted. Sayonara, Sukoshi Joe. You did it too soon. To the alley and the canal and the little houses and the pachinko parlor and to the flutes at night—sayonara. And you, Japan, you crowded islands, you tragic land—sayonara, you enemy, you friend.'

But even as I said these words I knew that I had to put them out of mind, for I was forced to acknowledge that I lived in an age when the only honorable profession was soldiering, when the only acceptable attitude toward strange lands and people of another color must be not love but fear.

Like the voice of my own conscience I heard, as from a great distance, General Webster saying, 'Pull yourself together, son. Whatever makes you a better man makes you a better officer.'

I looked up and said, 'What?'

'I oughtn't to tell you this, Lloyd, because it isn't official yet. But as soon as you get back to Randolph Field they're making you a lieutenant-colonel.'

Instinctively I saluted.

The general said, 'We'd better move along. Eileen wants to drive us to the airport.'